oll

SACAJAWEA

a

SACAJAWEA

ANNA LEE WALDO

AVON BOOKS ◆ NEW YORK

SACAJAWEA is an original publication of Avon Books.

AVON BOOKS
A division of
The Hearst Corporation
1350 Avenue of the Americas
New York, New York 10019

Copyright © 1978, 1984 by Anna Lee Waldo
Published by arrangement with the author
Library of Congress Catalog Card Number: 78-61446
ISBN: 0-380-84293-9

First Avon Printing: April 1979
First Avon Mass Market Printing: May 1980

AVON TRADEMARK REG. U.S. PAT. OFF. AND IN OTHER COUNTRIES, MARCA
REGISTRADA, HECHO EN U.S.A.

Printed in the U. S. A.

K-R 10 9 8 7

In memory of my father,
Lee William Van Artsdale

Acknowledgments

To the people in libraries and historical societies in the states of California, Idaho, Illinois, Iowa, Kansas, Missouri, Montana, Nebraska, New York, North and South Dakota, Oklahoma, Oregon, Utah, Washington, and Wyoming, and in the cities of Montreal, Canada, and Stuttgart, Germany, I wish to acknowledge my indebtedness. Your patient letters and guidance made possible the proper research for this book. In particular I thank the late Edna McElhinney Olsen, of the Historical Society of Missouri in Saint Charles, Missouri, who gave enthusiasm to the work, and also Martha Mann, of the Kirkwood Library, Kirkwood, Missouri, who sent for innumerable books, manuscripts, and pamphlets through interlibrary loan, giving me invaluable sources of information.

I am grateful to my husband, Bill, who thrice toured the Lewis and Clark Trail and the West with me and argued out most of the book, especially geography, critically read the manuscript, and saved me from making a good many errors I certainly would have made except for him.

If any of our five children, Skookumchuck, A Polliwog, Williwaw, Kloochman, or Hee Hee Tum Tum, read this book I have so insistently talked about with them, they will probably feel shock and relief that it is actually finished. I acknowledge that I could not possibly have written the book if they had not criticized my ideas, walked over Lemhi Pass, or had not been quiet while I "worked," which was beyond the responsibility of usual siblings and offspring.

I thank Carol Sturm Smith and John Burnett Payne for assistance with the manuscript. I thank Jan De-

Vries and Jim Harrison for their kind assistance with the revised manuscript and Candace Finkelston and the Library Services staff at St. Louis Community College at Meramec for their excellent information system.

Like any creation based on literature searches and oral traditions, there are many individuals who have gone before me to whom I owe a large debt of gratitude and thanks for their time and effort. Historians, keepers of diaries or journals, and keepers of legends, which we call folklore, supplied ideas and facts for the basis of this novel. Without these dedicated people, much of early American history would be long forgotten and lost. I am most grateful to the Lewis and Clark party for keeping journals and writing what is still considered the best historical account of Sacajawea's life, though these accounts cover a period of barely three years.

I am grateful to all those others who wrote about the early Shoshonis, Mandans, and other Missouri River tribes, the river Indians of the Northwest, the Pacific Coast tribes, the Comanches and Arapahos, etc. I am grateful for the historians who believe and show in writing that Sacajawea died at Fort Manuel Lisa when she was only twenty-five. I am equally grateful for those historians who wrote or told me of the persistent oral-tradition stories among the Comanche and Shoshoni that Sacajawea lived a long life. Their controversies make her story elusive, mysterious, intriguing, and speculative.

I do not know if Sacajawea died in 1812 or 1884, but as a novelist I prefer the long-life story. I hope that my readers will be thankful for a story that begins with a child wondering about the origin of the ancient medicine circle and ends with an old woman sensing the termination of a free, nomadic culture.

I am thankful that I grew up in northwestern Montana, where Sacajawea is and always has been a heroine for Native and all other Americans alike.

ANNA LEE WALDO

Contents

The tropical emotion that has created a legendary Sacajawea awaits study by some connoisseur of American Sentiments. —More statues have been erected to her than to any other American woman. Few others have had so much sentimental fantasy expended on them. —And she has received what in the United States counts as canonization if not deification: she has become an object of state pride and interstate rivalry.

Bernard DeVoto, *The Course of Empire*.
New York: Houghton Mifflin Co.,
1952, p. 618.

SACAJAWEA

A MAP OF
UNITED STATES IN 1804
Also showing places connected with
SACAJAWEA
The Bird Woman and her family

Lewis and Clark's Route to the Pacific
Lewis and Clark's Return Route

British Possessions

MAINE

VT.
N.H.
MASS. Boston
NEW YORK R.I.
CONN.
N.J.
INDIANA
PENNSYLVANIA
MD. DEL.
TERRITORY
OHIO
Washington
D.C.
ouncil Bluff
United VIRGINIA
St. Louis
KENTUCKY
NORTH CAROLINA
hase
TENNESSEE
SOUTH
CAROLINA ATLANTIC
OCEAN
States
MISSISSIPPI
TERRITORY
GEORGIA
Spanish Florida

GULF OF MEXICO

N

Book One
IN THE BEGINNING

A mysterious relic in the Big Horn Mountains west of Sheridan, Wyoming, in Shoshoni country, is an elaborate circular pattern traced out in stone on a flat shoulder near the top of a 10,000 foot remote peak. The Medicine Wheel has a circumference of two hundred forty-five feet, with twenty-eight spokes and six stone cairns spaced unevenly around its rim, and a seventh about fifteen feet from the wheel. These shelters are very low with a slab of rock across the top. Two of the cairns zero in on the rising sun of the first day of summer—summer solstice—when the sun reaches its northernmost rising point on the horizon. Two of the cairns zero in on the summer solstice sunset. Alignments of others point to the rising points of three bright stars, Aldebaran, Rigel, and Sirius. West of Armstead, Montana, now Hap Hawkins' Lake, near U.S. 91, south of Dillon, Montana, is another wheel-shaped pattern of stones. These undoubtedly predate the Shoshoni nation as we know it.

Montana, A State Guide Book, compiled and written by the Federal Writers' Project of the WPA for the State of Montana. New York: The Viking Press, 1939, pp. 32, 292.
JOHN A. EDDY, "Probing the Mystery of the Medicine Wheels," *National Geographic*, 151 (January, 1977), p. 140.

1

Old Grandmother

The history of the Shoshoni, most northerly of the great Shoshonean tribes, which all belong to the extensive Uto-Aztecan linguistic stock, is full of paradox. They occupied western Wyoming, central and southern Idaho, southwestern Montana, northeastern Nevada, and northeastern Utah. The Snake River country in Idaho was their stronghold, but their expeditions sometimes reached the Columbia. Holding somewhat in contempt their less vigorous cousins to the south—Ute, Hopi, and Paiute—they themselves seem to have been almost equally despised by the Plains tribes. The northern and eastern Shoshoni were riding and buffalo-hunting Indians. Their traditions are full of references to a period when they had no horses, when small game took the place of the buffalo, and when they had no skin tepees in which to live. None of the Shoshoni were ever known to be agriculturists, but in the Wind River of central Wyoming, huge pestles have been discovered, about five feet in length, consisting of a ball eight or nine inches in diameter and a stem tapering to about four inches. They were found by Shoshoni Indians who suggest they were used for grinding grain, grass seeds, and dry berries, by some early tribe.

Wyoming, A Guide to Its History, Highways and People, compiled by Workers of the Writers' Program of the WPA in the State of Wyoming. New York: Oxford University Press, 1941, pp. 52–7.

It was early morning in the Agaidüka, the Salmon Eaters encampment, and struggling puffs of cooking-fire smoke reached into the chilly dawn air. Everywhere in this Shoshoni camp there was the pungent smell of burning pine. Moving silently, robe-covered women fed each fire and cooked the first meal of the day. Inside the tepees children came half-awake; small babies felt hunger pangs and began their crying.

Near the center of the encampment was the tepee of the head chief, Chief No Retreat. This morning he rose from his pine-bough sleeping couch early, disturbed by thoughts in his mind of things he did not understand. Ages ago, beyond the time of counting, there had been a tribe living here, in the Big Horn Mountains, different from the people he knew.

The day before, Chief No Retreat and his younger daughter, Boinaiv, Grass Child, had wandered onto a great circle of stones. To him it seemed larger than the circle of the sun. He had seen the similar but smaller circle of stones to the north, but never had he dreamed there was another and of such imposing size. He was certain it had been built before the light came to the Agaidüka Shoshonis, his people.

The old man had looked at the great circle then in awe and spoken to his child about the Tukadükas, the Sheep Eaters, who had built stone game blinds and bighorn sheep pens with stone fences. He had seen them often. "The Sheep Eaters were once many tribes and lived in caves and mountain canyons to avoid their enemies. They had dogs to help them hunt. Now they are gone. Their time is over."[1]

"Were they happy?" asked Grass Child.

"*Ai*, they felt as we, sometimes sad, sometimes angry, and sometimes happy. They lived. Now we live."

"Did they paint the buffalo in the caves?"

"*Ai*, they painted the animals they were going to hunt. This is the way they breathed life into herds so that there was always food for their people. They drew the buffalo as if he were alive. In their firelight his eyes glistened, his muscles seemed to tense beneath the hide,

4

and his tail to lash to and fro in excitement—like the beasts grazing on the grassy hillsides."

"Did they color him with the same paints we use to paint bodies before the hunt?" asked the curious child.

"*Ai*, the same. They took the best ocher and bear's fat and mixed it carefully and put it on the picture with tiny sticks dipped in the paints. They used charcoal or the black earth for contours and shadows to give the beast depth or life. They used vermilion to fill in the glowing eyes."

"I would like to do that," exclaimed the child.

"Women are never painters of stones. They paint only clothing and their faces," laughed her father.

"I could do that, though. Did the people of the sun-circle paint?"

Chief No Retreat was deep with his own wondering. Were the people who built the smaller circle in the north and then this larger one of the same nation? He wondered how long ago these people had gone away from here. Who were their enemies?

As he gazed at the large circle of stones, Grass Child pointed to the center cairn, about as high as the chief's waist. "What is there?"

"You ask more than a girl-child should," he admonished his inquisitive offspring. "Women need know only cooking, sewing, and keeping a neat tepee and a contented man."

"Maybe it is Father Sun," she said. "In the middle is the sun, and on the outside are the stars, and this one way over here, the moon." She laughed at her analogy. Then she counted the "spokes" radiating from the "hub." "Five hands and three fingers," she said.

The chief counted, then said, "That is the number of suns from one full moon to the next."

Grass Child began to examine the six low shelters, peering under the slab roofs.

"Grass Child! Keep your head out of there!" The chief quickly stood the child on her feet. "See, that flat stone is tipping. The pine logs are old and rotting. They no longer can hold it up. The spirits of this nation may be near. Do not disturb their sacred place. Now, watch where you step! Do not step on the stones."

On the stone slab of the center structure rested a

bleached buffalo skull, placed so that it looked toward
the rising sun. Chief No Retreat, trying to picture in
his mind the people who had used this sacred place,
gently placed his hand on the white skull, but it was
old and some of the bone crumbled under his hand. He
tried to repair the skull, but it crumbled more. He
jumped like a small boy caught doing something forbidden.

"Do not keep your eyes long nor too close to these
ancient stones," his child said.[2]

He took the small hand of Grass Child in his large
brown weathered one and quickly retreated. "You must
not talk out so much. Even your brothers do not talk
when it is not their turn. Your sister, Rain Girl, does
not ask questions or speak her mind to me—perhaps
to her mother or grandmother, yes, but not to me, her
father. Women must keep their tongue inside when
they are among men."

Grass Child hung her head for a few moments, then
softly she said, "Father, what was the buffalo skull?"

"An ancient thing. I do not know what it represents.
My mind cannot tell me."

"What were the little lodges?"

"Grass Child, I do not know. Maybe some chiefs lay
there to pay respect to the Great Spirit or to Father
Sun."

"What was one little lodge so far away from the others for—was it the moon as I said?"

Chief No Retreat was sorry he could not answer the
questions. It had always been his policy to give his sons
correct answers as far as he knew. This youngest girl-
child had accepted that policy but could not understand
why he should treat the girls differently from the boys.
There were so many things for each to learn, and their
father, to her, knew everything that was worth knowing.

Later, while Chief No Retreat sat with his women
beside the evening cooking fire, he was silent, wrapped
in thoughts of those ancients who built the old medicine
circles. He knew that an ancient people lived ages ago
in nearby mountain caves. He had seen the caves with
their sooty walls, bone and stone tools hidden in rock
recesses, discarded meat bones strewn near the long-

deserted, black clay fire pits. His own grandfather had told him winter tales about people living in the high, rocky mountain country, who rolled huge stones down on their enemies. The chief reasoned that the ancients lived in caves to avoid contact with hostile people or the large, hungry animals, like the mountain lion. If anyone knew the name of these ancients, it could not be spoken because the Shoshoni code forbade saying the name of the dead aloud.

Chief No Retreat thought those ancients had probably never seen a horse. Maybe that early man would call the horse "an elk that had lost its horns," or "a big dog."

Chief No Retreat's tribe was rich in horses, long ago having acquired them from their cousins, the Comanches, or from the Utes in the south. Sometimes the Agaidüka ate a horse because their bows were not adequate for game larger than a badger. The Agaidüka were always in a near starving condition by the time spring arrived.

The chief began to think of the names of the many tribes in the Shoshoni nation. He counted them on his fingers of both hands. He wondered why all these people were called Shoshoni. The real meaning of the word was lost with time. Some nations called them Snakes, or Rattlesnakes, because their tribal sign was made with a wiggling motion of the hands. The motion was also similar to the in-and-out motion used in weaving grass for making their temporary summer shelters. He knew no nation actually thought of Shoshonis as snake-like or slithering away from anything, not even the Arapaho, their lifelong enemies.

The chief was of average height, and was bowlegged from much horseback riding. He had powerful shoulders and was lean for want of food. Like all Agaidüka men, he had no beard. If facial hair appeared, it was pulled out by a favorite woman or sister with two sharp-edged stones. The chief rarely smiled, but when he did, his fierce, dark eyes softened. He was constantly anxious for the welfare of his family. His woman, Fragrant Herbs, was his greatest love.

No Retreat was chosen chief partially because of his special cleverness and partially because he had boasted

truthfully of his accomplishments in battle. The headband of his warbonnet showed eight holes above the
forehead, two for each successful exploit.

He felt much concern for the members of his tribe.
He tried to make the Agaidükas' life easier, more pleasant, by locating the summer or winter camp in a place
that gave pleasure to the eyes or was close to colored
rocks so the women could make beautiful paints to decorate their clothing. He had taught his people to harvest
their winter supply of meat after the freeze-up, when
it could be hung high in a tree, kept, and used like fresh
meat. Of course, some of the meat was dried on a rack
above a low fire in the usual manner of the Shoshoni
and stored as pemmican in gut containers.

Chief No Retreat was respected for his bravery and
intelligent, agile mind. He was the undisputed leader
of the Agaidüka Shoshoni. The Shoshoni tribal government was a pure democracy with each warrior his own
master. The chief was looked to for advice rather than
orders.[3]

As in most Indian tribes, the women performed most
of the camp chores, while the men captured and trained
horses, made weapons, hunted, and protected their tribe.
The children scampered around the tepees doing generally as they pleased, for their elders thought too much
discipline would break their spirit.

Chief No Retreat's woman always served him and
was his constant companion. Fragrant Herbs had not
desired another squaw in the tepee to make her work
easier. She had not wanted to share her man with another squaw, no matter how quiet or industrious she
might be. Her mother lived with them and had been a
great help to Fragrant Herbs until this spring. Old
Grandmother was now approaching the time when she
must die. It was increasingly hard for her to move around
the camp, collect wood, and cook and sew.

It was the hope of Chief No Retreat that Cameâhwait, Never Walks, his eldest son, would in time take
his place among the People, as the Salmon Eaters called
themselves. This was because they were certain their
tribe was the favorite of the Great Spirit, and the greatest, most powerful, and most pleasing tribe on earth.
Spotted Bear, the second oldest child, had a lively taste

for hunting. The chief's daughter, Rain Girl, was about twelve summers (the Shoshoni kept no track of ages according to years), and Grass Child was three or four summers younger. The girls had been betrothed as infants to the sons of Red Buck by a present of six large bay horses. Rain Girl was curious about her future man, but Grass Child, not yet having reached puberty, did not bother thinking of something so far in the future as a secure womanhood.

After the chief had eaten the food prepared by Fragrant Herbs and smoked a pipeful of dried willow bark and kinnikinnick, he took a bow that needed new wrappings and a handful of thin buckskin to the edge of the encampment where twelve men squatted on their heels conversing. The chief fell into the mood that was new for him. He began to talk of the stone circle. He repeated what he had told his child about the various parts. Someone mentioned the picture writing they had seen many seasons back on the high white cliffs, and the red pictures found in a cave of a doe and fawn. No Retreat recalled the huge pestles, the length of a man, with a ball the size of two fists on the end of the stem.

"The people of these drawings and the huge grinding stones have not been seen for many seasons. Where did they go? Who were they?" asked Chief No Retreat.

The men shook their heads and huddled closer together. It was not a usual experience for them to wonder about others who had lived on their land. Nor did they care to know. The Agaidükas were wary about anything unknown, because too much curiosity might unleash unwanted powers from the tribal medicine man. The medicine man could hide a black stone in some tepee and cause much misery in camp. Interpreting dreams and visions, foretelling success or defeat in hunts and warfare was the duty of the medicine man. He gave much thought to explanations for unusual events, such as an eclipse of the sun or moon. He tried to keep his information on a mundane, familiar level. He predicted the movement of enemy camps, changes in weather, and cured most disease with the knowledge that given time a body heals itself, if it gets plenty of plant material and good meat to eat.

They ate fish and roots because they fared badly in wars with the Blackfeet, who lived in buffalo country. Sometimes the People joined forces with the Flatheads, finding strength in numbers, and invaded the buffalo country for meat and skins. Occasionally their bone-pointed arrows sank into antelope, deer, mountain sheep, or goat. They planned only two annual buffalo hunts, spring and winter. There was great feasting when the hunters brought home fresh meat. After their forays, they retired again to their meager life in the mountains.

Now Chief No Retreat moved from the customary squatting position and sat cross-legged. "We could build long sticks and beat the wild grain ourselves as those ancient people might have. We could collect it in large, soft hides. It would fill our empty bellies in the Moon of the Howling Winds."

Again the men huddled close. This was a new thought. Several women, who had gathered in a circle behind the men, placed hands over their mouths in astonishment as they heard the words of their chief.

Finally an old man spoke. "If the grass had wanted us to keep its seeds in such larger quantities, it would have grown closer together," he said.

Chief No Retreat's son Spotted Bear had come up to the circle in time to hear the old man, and he answered him.

"Grandfather, the buffalo does not run to us. We must chase it. Perhaps if we harvest the seeds we come upon, out emptiness in the winter will not be so sharp. Perhaps our women can learn to give the men something new to taste." He looked intently at the women standing behind the circle of men.

"*Ai, ai*, perhaps so," answered a few, including his mother, Fragrant Herbs.

Early the next morning, Chief No Retreat tied his spears in a bundle and put his newly made arrowheads into a skin bag. He left his tepee, shrugging a wordless greeting to Fragrant Herbs, who was adding pine pitch to make her fire hotter, and looked around his quiet village, then up to the tall trees, and to the hills. He breathed deeply. "The air smells as if the Season for Gathering Nuts is almost over. We should strike the tepees within three suns and move toward buffalo country and more safety for the winter."

Fragrant Herbs stirred the fire to a fresh blaze. "I had hoped we could stay here long enough to gather the grass seeds," she said without looking up. "Our son's thought was good."

"Oh, woman, sometimes men and boys have thoughts that do not fit a hunter of meat. The People need the buffalo hunts to keep them together. Plucking tiny grass seeds will do nothing but stick in our teeth."

"I was thinking," Fragrant Herbs said, looking at the face of her man, "that if our food supply could be increased a little, our people would not grow so weak during the winter. Then there would be no end to our abilities to repel the Blackfeet or even the Sioux that come for our horses early in spring. Instead of being weak like our Ute cousins, our braves will retrieve the horses and bring distinction to themselves."

"A woman is not made for thinking so much," shrugged Chief No Retreat.

Fragrant Herbs had no sooner uttered her words than she became aware of a disturbing thought. With the assurance of food all year, what would be the impact upon the People? They knew the balance between life and death. An unending supply of food would disturb this balance. There would be more old ones to help with the lodge work. Then they would have more time to tend to the babies, or for cooking or sewing or sitting in the sun doing nothing but visiting. Fragrant Herbs thought a shift in the balance toward a life of ease and laughter would be something good. "Perhaps we could have more feasts, with dancing and games. The winter cold would be more bearable. We could laugh at the howling winds if there were no belly growlings."

Chief No Retreat looked closer into the face of his woman. "Oh, most loved woman, your words run deep, deep." Confused that a woman could have such thoughts, he ducked back into the skin tepee and rumpled the matted heads of his children, waking them to the brightness of the sunshine, before he ducked out the flap back to the side of his squaw. He watched her broad smile. She was a delicate woman with long black hair combed into two smooth braids. She was also a woman

with strong character and outspoken opinion. So he was
not surprised when she asked, "Why is too much ease
a bad thing?" But it was a new thought to him and he
was not prepared to answer right away.

Flustered, he stared at the fire a moment. "If enough
grass seed can be collected to ease the hurt of winter's
hunger, that cannot be bad for the People. It will make
them laugh at the blizzards. That is good. But so much
seed is needed. You cannot collect enough. It will be
like trying to store water in a torn buffalo bladder—
never enough to go around. You know how it is with
meat. The more we have, the more is eaten. The People
would grow soft and fat and lazy." Even as he spoke he
wondered what had really made the people of the circle
of stones disappear. Their life had been altered by some
force unknown to him. Perhaps the people of the stone
circle made life too easy for themselves and in their
softness were slaughtered by their enemies. Perhaps
they were forced to move on by their greed for more
food. He thought of his own father and his father before
him doing what was expected to keep the People together. To visualize fathers farther back in time was
difficult. Who were the ancient ones of the stone circle?
Did their blood run with his blood? At this moment he
changed a little, he was humbled. And when his woman
gave him a flat, hard biscuit made from freshly pounded
grass seed, he wondered if living and keeping a tribe
together was as simple a thing as he had thought. Once
or twice in the past he had suspected that his people
would not of themselves survive, but there was some
mysterious force, something from the Great Spirit that
allied itself with them to conquer their fear of the
weather, or starvation and sickness, and even the great
mystery of death.

"How do you like it?" asked his woman, handing him
another biscuit made from the grass-seed flour, water,
and bear grease.

"It is crisp and good to the taste and deserves a gift
in return." He pulled something from inside the waiststring of his trousers, hoping to distract her profound
thoughts with something gay. "A smooth blue stone. I
have been keeping it for some special time, for this day.
I took it from a Blackfoot after he and a companion

skulked around our best ponies at sundown during the Month of No Rain. His companion will be getting back to his camp about now—if he went all the distance on foot as I last saw him."

"My Chief, the color is like the spring sky, cool and fresh! Pound a small hole here so that I can put a thin thong through and wear it around my neck."

"A woman requires things of beauty as a man requires food," mumbled the chief, not daring to look at his woman's radiant face. He was not afraid of the emotion deep inside his belly; he wished only to keep it under control in front of his children. "Uuuugh." He cleared his throat and watched the four youngsters emerge from the tepee ready for their first meal of the day.

Fragrant Herbs hid her feelings only in the presence of strangers. "Each sunrise my feeling for you grows. This feeling is greater now than when you first came to my mother's tepee."

"Is it not strange," asked the chief, "that the birds and animals decorate their bucks, while we decorate our squaws?"

"Would you have me decorate you with quills and shells and bright flowers in your hair?" Her eyes snapped.

"Would you have the men laugh behind my back and the women giggle behind their hands?"

"I feel like a young girl in love, beautiful," she smiled.

Chief No Retreat coughed and turned to see his boys scuffle over a smooth stick. Grass Child spotted the whiteness of it. "That is mine," she cried shrilly. "I have gathered yellow grass to make a tunic and wide sash for the stick. It is to be my papoose."

Rain Girl ran between the boys. "Give the baby her stick-papoose. You can make another with a cutting stone. Give it to her so she won't scream."

Fragrant Herbs quickly pushed tightly woven willow bowls into the hands of each child. "Eat, and enjoy the fall air," she said gently. "Perhaps your father will take the boys hunting before we strike camp. Rain Girl and Grass Child, try to finish your sewing before we break camp in three suns."

Rain Girl took a bowl of meat broth to Old Grandmother inside the tepee. "We want to sew today," she said. "In three days we leave."

Old Grandmother's eyes were as bright as wet black stones. Her hair was sparse and matted in the back, with a few black wisps showing over her forehead. Her brown face was like a shriveled, dried plum. She had taught both her granddaughters to sew, to tan hides, and to make pemmican. While she taught with her hands, she sang songs for happiness, songs for sadness, and songs of praise to the Great Spirit. Her songs used a range of only five notes, but they were from the depth of her soul's memory. They were songs from the memory of her own grandmother. Near the end of each winter, she retold the legend of the origin of the Shoshoni to her grandchildren.

"Once," Old Grandmother would say, "a great flood covered the land. A water bird swam about the surface with tufts of grass in its bill. The Great Spirit breathed life into the tufts, which became people, white as the fresh-fallen snow. After several children were born to them, the women ate some chokecherries given them by Coyote the Trickster. When the fruit made their mouth draw up, they induced their family to try it. The more they ate, the darker their flesh became, until it was a nice rich brown."[4]

Today a friend, Willow Bud, about twelve summers like Rain Girl, came to listen to Old Grandmother's stories as she worked on a pair of moccasins for her father.

"Teach me to sew on quills, Old Grandmother. I wish to surprise my father so he will have moccasins to wear when we move to winter camp. See the long tops I made for them and the tiny fringe drag at the heels?" Willow Bud held the high-top moccasins up proudly.

Old Grandmother sat on her bed of buffalo hides and crooned to herself as she picked out red- and yellow-dyed porcupine quills from a small leather pouch. Her hands shook as she arranged them in a design on the earth.

"Turkey tracks," squealed Willow Bud with delight as she recognized the design.

"Old Grandmother, tell us a story while we sew," begged Grass Child.

"Oh, *ai*," cried Rain Girl.

Old Grandmother's hands shook in her lap like bone rattles. She sat very still, staring at her hands. Her eyes took on a fresh luster, and she began softly, "I have told you of the Great Mystery of birth, and now I tell you another mystery is death. It comes to all those that live." She stopped, closed her eyes, and scratched at a fly on the back of her neck with a long, yellowed fingernail. "It is soon time for me to go to the Great Spirit. The journey is not long," she announced in a whisper, her eyes remaining closed as if to see the trail to the place where there was no hunger, no pain, no sadness, only sunshine, clear streams with many fish, and grassy meadows with much game.

"No, no!" exclaimed all three girls.

"We need you," said Willow Bud.

"Our mother needs you," said Rain Girl.

"I can never learn all the things I must know to be a woman without you," said Grass Child, tears welling.

"You are foolish. You think of yourselves," scolded Old Grandmother. Her voice was raspy and stayed in her throat. "I am lonely for the people I used to know. Those who have already taken the long journey to the Land of Everfeasting. I have the stiffness in my joints and can hardly walk. My hands spill the soup before it reaches my mouth."

"But we love you," sobbed Grass Child.

"*Ai*, I love you, too, but this is my time now. Do not grieve. Look ahead."

"What is there ahead?" said Rain Girl, her head bowed as a tear slid from her cheek to the soft tanned skin on her lap.

Old Grandmother bent unsteadily and clasped her thin fingers around Rain Girl's hand. "I have had a feeling. A strange omen has been pushing at my thoughts. My granddaughter, you will never feel the joy of being an old grandmother. *Aiieee!* That is sadness."

Rain Girl looked into the pinched face of Old Grandmother. She smiled and remembered that Old Grandmother had always told of omens. She could even smell the weather.

"Do not be sad about that, Old Grandmother. It is

perhaps because my children will not marry. I am betrothed to Heavy Runner, son of Red Buck, remember?"

Old Grandmother shrugged and pulled a robe over
her thin knees. "I do not know more."

Grass Child moved closer to Old Grandmother, forgetting about her sewing. "What about Willow Bud?
Have you had a feeling about her?"

"*Ai*," smiled Old Grandmother. "She will make a
good wife and mother, and her sewing will improve each
season." She shuddered and opened her mouth. Her
bottom teeth were gone, so that nothing held back the
saliva. She wiped her mouth with the back of a shaking
hand. "You will go on a long journey into an unknown
land. Soon."

Willow Bud laughed. "I know; we are going to winter
camp. That's a long journey and is coming soon."

"What do you know of me?" asked Grass Child, eager
to have something strange and mysterious revealed to
her, also.

Old Grandmother was resting, her eyes shut tight.
The girls waited. Soon her eyes glittered, and the restlessness of the girls told her they were waiting for an
answer.

"*Ai*, for a long while I have wanted to tell you. Your
mother has forbidden it."

Grass Girl peeked out the doorway. "She is gone."

"Now is the time. All of you listen so that you may
know I told you true what I feel."

Shivers ran down Grass Child's back. She strained
her ears not to miss a word. "Tell me. What is it?" she
asked.

"You, Grass Child, are a chosen one. You will have
many names. You will be a leader. Something like a
chief to bring full bellies and happy faces to the People."
Old Grandmother's face became flushed, and her eyes
snapped. "You will be known in legends many old men
from now, and loved by other nations. You will die
young, yet you will live to a very old age." Her voice
became a whisper. "Lately I have had this strange notion that the beginning of this is near, like Willow Bud's
journey." Old Grandmother coughed and wheezed and
lay herself back on the robes.

Rain Girl burst into fits of laughter. "Oh, this little papoose a chief? A squaw, a chief?"

"Rain Girl," Old Grandmother said from her couch, "hush. I have more." The girls sat in silence, waiting. "I have had more than one dream of Willow Bud as a slim young woman weeping and running nearly out of her moccasins to embrace Grass Child. And Grass Child does not at first recognize her. There are many men, braves, standing around with their pale eyes big with disbelief. It is a strange dream. I do not understand it." She shook her head and covered her eyes with her trembling fingers.

Willow Bud sat waiting for more revelations. Then Grass Child broke the silence by scrambling around, untangling herself from sinew and tunic so she could put her hand into Old Grandmother's. She bent her head and whispered near the sallow, wrinkled face, "I shall not forget this day." The child placed the knotted hands of Old Grandmother over her heart, signifying love between them.

The following morning the sun was still strong, but the wind had a chill that warned of colder times. Fragrant Herbs was busy packing clothing and the little food that was left so that when the time came for striking the tepee her work would not take too long. Willow Bud came to see if Rain Girl and Grass Child could take their baskets to the edge of camp and gather some of the fall asters to make flower chains.

The girls ran in the dry grass and began picking long-stemmed purple asters. Soon they were thirsty and hurried over to the water hole. Then Grass Child saw a windfall across the game trail leading from the water hole. Its freshly upturned roots were still covered with moss and earth. The branches, upon which it had fallen, lay torn and broken on the rocks.

"It's a tamarack," said Rain Girl, "we can go right through. The needles are soft."

They were careful not to walk on the slivered branches as they pushed aside the boughs in front of them and climbed along the huge rough trunk in follow-the-leader fashion.

Grass Child straightened—she heard a hiss and the

sound of scrambling. She searched through the boughs,
holding one to keep her balance. On the other side of
the tree she saw a little black bear cub hitching himself
up another tamarack, scattering bark and black deer
moss with every push of his short legs. She started to
laugh and point to him, when directly in front of her
the mother bear rose on hind legs and let out a fierce
roar as she pawed the air, long claws gleaming in the
sun. Another cub came up beside the mother.

The girls froze, too frightened to move, then Rain
Girl whispered, "Don't move too quickly. She'll chase
us."

"I'm not going to stay," Willow Bud replied. Feeling
the solid trunk of the tamarack through her moccasins,
she slunk slowly back into the protective branches. Rain
Girl followed her example, letting boughs fall slowly
into place between them and the mother bear. Grass
Child moved cautiously.

As soon as they were clear of the windfall, they turned
in unspoken agreement and leaped from rock to rock
with a strength and speed they would not previously
have believed they possessed. Panting and gasping for
breath, they slumped to the ground and were aware
that the hideous roars had grown faint. The bears did
not come through the tree.

"She thinks we are still there," Grass Child found
breath to say. As the girls grew calm, they looked at
one another.

"It is good that the wind has stopped," said Willow
Bud seriously. "It is known that bears can smell and
seek out girls during the flowing time. They attack and
kill. The smell makes them crazy."

Rain Girl gasped. "Have you come to the time of
being a woman?"

"*Ai*, four suns ago for the first time," said Willow
Bud proudly.

"The she-bear was only interested in protecting her
babies. She did not care that you are now a woman,"
snorted Grass Child.[5]

"Then it was our looks, not your smell, that made
her roar," laughed Rain Girl. They burst into gales of
laughter as they walked into the security of camp. They

offered their baskets of asters to Old Grandmother, who was on a pallet of hides in the warm sun.

Grass Child wove some of the purple blossoms into the thin gray-black hair of Old Grandmother.

"You are beautiful," said Grass Child, noticing for the first time that the old woman smelled unclean.

Old Grandmother searched through her robes until she found a piece of licorice rootstalk, which she gave to Rain Girl to break into three pieces. She listened with half-closed eyes as the girls chewed on the root and told her of the encounter with the she-bear.

After a fit of coughing, Old Grandmother slowly began to laugh in a high cackle. Tears ran down her wrinkled face. "That old bear will roar at you until sundown. She'll think you are still in the tamarack windfall; she will smell you there. Oh, that dumb bear." And she cackled again. She rummaged through her robes and found a small piece of suet near the foot of her pallet. "Come here," she said to Grass Child. She rubbed the suet over the scratches on her legs, then motioned for each of the other girls to come to her. She coughed. When she could speak again, she said, "The brush cuts when you run through it heedlessly and fast. Suet will help the healing." Then, slowly, Old Grandmother began telling them the healing powers of various roots she could recall. Wild geranium was good for healing stomach ulcers, skullcap for mild heart trouble, crushed violet leaves for lung infection, seeds of the morning glory and jimsonweed for serenity of thought, and peyote for relaxing the crowded mind.

Old Grandmother knew a great deal of anatomy, as did most Indians. She once could massage movement into a stiff leg in an hour. She knew the healing power of the sweat house; and she could sew together deep skin gashes with hair from the victim's head, and the wound would heal clean, free from infection. Now, when Old Grandmother coughed, which was frequent, she noticed specks of blood. Talking to the children tired her.

After taking her cup of medicinal herbs that evening, Old Grandmother spoke to Chief No Retreat. "Leave me here. I am very old. I was the woman of a great chief. I can no longer chew the skins to soften them, and sew them with sinew. I cannot cook with my shaking hands. I cannot shake out my robes. I cannot relieve myself outside the tepee; I no longer have control. This season I have done nothing to earn the meat that you cut up for me to swallow. I cough, and that makes me tired. I have been a burden on my people. Now, unless you leave me here, I will cause you to be caught by the enemy or caught in the blowing snow on your way to the winter camp. The winter white robe will be thick, and there will be little food before it is all melted off the land. I, no longer any good, will be the cause of good ones dying, good ones that I love. To leave me is all I ask. In the morning, darken my eyes so I cannot see; then I will not lie trembling and alone. That way, you will pay me for the milk I gave my babies and all else I gave." Old Grandmother coughed, and when it subsided, she lay exhausted.

Chief No Retreat quickly rose and turned the back of his hand over his eyes. Fragrant Herbs went to him, held him close to her warm body, then resumed her place at the head of Old Grandmother's pallet. Chief No Retreat stayed at the foot of her sleeping couch all that night.

Grass Child's heart was heavy. She sat close to Old Grandmother and held her dry, withered hands. Willow Bud came in and watched the slow rhythmic breathing of the old woman and left soon.

Rain Girl and her mother gathered two small parfleche boxes of dry grass seed and pounded it fine between two stones. "This can be extra food for Old Grandmother," said Fragrant Herbs. Spotted Bear and Never Walks brought in some rabbits so that a small, soft robe could be made for Old Grandmother to rest her head on. The boys were unusually quiet and subdued around the tepee.

"Daughters," announced Fragrant Herbs, "it is time to build the winter tepee for Old Grandmother." She could not speak further, but busied herself with unrolling hides.

Old Grandmother's black eyes were without luster as she stared straight ahead, watching every move Fragrant Herbs made. She did not criticize when her robes fell to the dirt floor and no one hurried to pick them up.

A crude lean-to was made from willow branches with strong cottonwood poles at the corners. Several antelope hides were spread over the top to keep out rain, and one at the sides to keep out the wind. Grass Child helped make the sleeping couch soft with pine boughs and then laid Old Grandmother's buffalo hide over the top. A tear slipped down her chin into the thick, curly brown fur.

A pile of *yampa*, wild carrots, was left close to the couch, along with thistle taproots and balsam roots. Fragrant Herbs brought several armloads of firewood and laid them out in the center of the lean-to so that a cooking fire or one for warmth could be built. Several leather pouches of bread made from a mixture of wild grass seeds, lamb's quarter, and serviceberries pounded together were left, with a little jerky and a buffalo bladder filled with fresh water. Enough food for perhaps one moon.

The others of the village were beginning to leave for the winter camp. Chief No Retreat sat on his pony watching the young boys round up the horses as the camp dogs yapped at their heels. Fine horses were the greatest wealth of the People. Largely of Arabian stock, these animals had been traded for or stolen from the Spaniards in the south. Some bore Spanish brands, and a few of the Indians sported Spanish saddles and bits. The People, mindful that their horses were their point of superiority over other tribes, carefully and expertly bred them.

Chief No Retreat had already bidden Old Grandmother farewell and darkened her eyes with a soft band of doeskin. Now, content that all was well with the horses, but heavy in his heart, he called for his family to hurry.

Rain Girl and Grass Child clung to Old Grandmother, tears streaming down their faces. Fragrant Herbs admonished them gently, "A girl of the People does not cry about things that must be done for the good of the tribe. Come along now."

Grass Child saw her mother's eyes moisten while her fingers fumbled the thin knotted thong from around her neck. Threaded on the leather lacing was the sky-blue, polished stone. Grass Child knew her mother cherished this recent gift from her father. Fragrant Herbs bent over Old Grandmother and placed the necklace in the cracked, parchmented hands, saying softly, "The stone is as clear as a summer sky, and to look at it will make you feel young. I leave a piece of my heart with you." Fragrant Herbs's eyes misted, and she turned to test the strength of the hides tied to the inner frame of the lean-to.

Old Grandmother's eyes crinkled into deep creases. Her tongue seemed to push her lips into a smile. Grass Child could no longer control herself. She rushed to Old Grandmother and fell beside her. "I'll come back to see you," she promised between sobs. "You'll be waiting for me. I'll bring you fresh meat to keep you through the Month of Howling Winds."

Old Grandmother motioned. No, no, this is the way it has always been, it must be. She could not speak for fear of betraying her own emotion and deep love for the child who carried her own girlhood name, because they had both loved to watch the wind make gentle waves in the grassy meadows.

After several days of slow travel, the horses dragging travois, the chief found a place sheltered from the wind, so that the tribe could camp a few days and hunt game to add to the meager food supply for the winter.

While the men were hunting, the women sewed and cut strips of fresh meat to dry on racks for jerky. Fragrant Herbs and her daughters beat the wild grasses and sunflowers for all the seeds they would yield and caught them in skin robes. Some of the women were inclined to laugh at the wife of their chief for her labor, but refrained because of her reputation as a fine cook. That evening, the hunters brought in several antelope and many rabbits. The women prepared a feast, and there was a dance of thanksgiving to the Great Spirit for sending his people to such a fine place with plentiful game. The old men told stories and smoked dried kinnikinnick. The boys played buffalo hunt. The child who was "it" bellowed like a bull, while the other children tried to catch him. The girls kept the pots of meat and vegetables hot so that when anyone felt hungry, he might eat.

It was a glowing time of red and yellow falling leaves. On the third day, Never Walks and Spotted Bear went on the hunt with the men. Rain Girl and Fragrant Herbs went from their temporary grass shelter to beat more tiny seeds into the old hide. Grass Child visited with Willow Bud and her family.

On the pretext of getting some sewing, she slipped away and took two skinned rabbits from her mother's supply under a pile of fresh leaves and stones. She wrapped them in an old buckskin. She took a small bag to collect fall berries and quickly started on her way back to the abandoned summer camp on the Little Big Horn, the lean-to of Old Grandmother. She was no papoose, she told herself, and could come and go as she pleased. It was easy to find the way because the travois marks were still plain and the horse tracks were everywhere. Nights she curled herself up in a warm pile of leaves like a bird in a nest.

When Grass Child came in sight of Old Grandmother's lean-to, the small bag was full of huckleberries, large and dusky blue. Her hands, face, and tongue were stained blue. She was not hungry. She was content and happy to be close to her beloved Old Grandmother. She had not thought of being afraid. The outdoors was her home, and most of the animals were friendly. The squirrels chattered at her, and the blue jays scolded as she walked past. If she met a moose or bear, she could quickly climb a tree.

The child was not prepared for the sight in front of her. Fresh blood was on the ground. Old Grandmother's body lay still, slashed to death, partially devoured by wolves. Grass Child tried to let out a high shriek, but her throat was so constricted that no sound came. She sat on the sleeping couch where the top robe had been pulled off and left lying in the doorway. The rabbitskin pillow was shredded and flung against the back of the lean-to. The pouches of bread had been gnawed open and the contents spilled. She stared at the hideous mess for a long time, suddenly aware of the putrefying stench. Then she noticed her teeth were clenched so tightly her jaws ached.

Finally she rose, picked up the buffalo robe, and spread it on some clean grass. She dragged her grandmother's mangled body outside and dropped it on the hide, then rolled the hide around the torn flesh quickly and tightly. She wiped her hands on the grass to rid them of the foul smell.

She looked at the round bundle and visualized her grandmother peacefully sleeping. "I was too late!" Grass Child cried. "Why didn't I come sooner?"

From the far side of the hill came a growling. "Why couldn't she just have fallen asleep forever? Why did the wolf have to interfere?" Grass Child tore at her tunic in anguish.

She thought of the circle of stones on the top of the mountain not far away. It had offered no protection. And she wondered why she had left too late to save this beloved person. Why was the sun hiding? Could it not look upon this terrible Mother Earth? Where was the Great Spirit when this happened? Deep in the forest, the child stood over the body of her grandmother and wondered. She felt only the absence of the Great Spirit, and the need for something to fill the emptiness.

Instinct told her that the wolf would be back again this night to finish what he had started. She searched the lean-to, found her grandmother's firestones, and rubbed them together over a few dry leaves. The sparks caught quickly; she added a few small twigs. When they caught, she added some larger ones, and finally she pushed some dry, dead windfall into the fire. Then she added all the tanned skins from the lean-to. She kicked up the dirt over the dark paths of dried blood, and pushed the food supply, including the two fresh rabbits and bag of huckleberries, into the fire. The skins made a great smoke and stench.

She looked around for something to cut off her long black hair, but her mind began to function, telling her it was dark and she'd better not move too far from the fire. She sat with her back against a tree, facing out into the dark forest. She thought she heard coyotes call in the distance. She pushed the dry sticks further into the fire. Sparks flew up around her. Soon there was the point of fire and vague outlines moving beyond, swimming in its flicker, and close about her the wall of darkness. Grass Child pushed back against the tree and put her head on her arms. She heard the cracking of the fire, heard the wind high in the trees, heard an owl hoot. The earth swung with her.

Grass Child awakened shivering with cold in the first flush of the morning. She sat up slowly. The fire was a gray ash. The breeze brought a tuft of wolf fur across it. She tasted her mouth and made a face and brought her finger to her eyes to rub the film away. She looked around. The buffalo robe was still on the ground in a large, round ball. A rotten stench enveloped her. She began breathing through her mouth so as to block off the smell. Her head ached, and her eyelids felt like crusty sand. A slow restoration of nerve and duty came. And she knew she had an obligation to honor her grandmother's memory by following the Shoshoni custom of cutting off the first joint of a finger. This ancient custom of her people accompanied the mourning of a loved one seen in death.

She could not find a sharp stone, so she rubbed a stick on a flat rock until it was fairly sharp across the end. She kicked the ashes at the edge of the fire, found the firestones, rubbed them together over a handful of dry leaves, and added dry brush when they caught fire. The blood seemed to drain away from her head, and she felt faint. She sucked in great gulps of air, bent with her head low, and laid her left hand on the flat rock, palm down. Cold sweat ran down her back. She pushed with all her strength on the knifelike stick against the first joint of the little finger of her left hand. The rock was smooth, cold, and hard. The flesh tore open, and blood oozed out. The rock was warm and wet. The pain was great. The earth tilted and fell back and tilted again, and she bent closer over her hand on the rock. She pounded the stick into the joint, trying to snap it off. The rock became red; the stick and her tunic became red with her blood. The cartilage was elastic and stubborn. With a final thrust, the end of her little finger lay on the rock, alone. It was no longer a part of her. It was gone forever. Her grandmother was gone from her forever. Grass Child's eyes stared at the flow of blood from the stump. Her brain seared with the pain.

She forced herself to move slowly to the small fire and to bend over it.

She became aware of the heat on her hand, and still Grass Child could not nerve herself for the final ritual. She turned her face toward the sky. She heard a sound from there, a sound that she knew. The glossy black carrion crows were flying around and around, watching her every move. She moved further over the fire, and with her right hand she pushed her little finger against a glowing stick to stanch the flow of blood. The fire became a small pinpoint of orange, and the darkness fell around her. The cawing of the crows ceased.

When Grass Child awoke, the fire was cold. She got up too quickly, put her hands to her head, and closed her eyes to steady herself. She went to the water hole and lay down and drank, feeling the cool touch of the water at the pit of her stomach. She got up slowly, keeping her uneasy balance with Mother Earth, and suddenly her stomach tightened like a squeezed water bladder. Holding to a sapling, she hung over it and vomited. Her eyes watered, and she rubbed the tears out. Then she saw a glint of blue in the dry grass. She pulled the familiar smooth stone from the tangled growth. The attached thong swung beneath her throbbing hand. At the edge of the dead fire lay her small leather bag. She wiped at the huckleberry stain inside the bag with the bottom fringe on her tunic. She dropped the sky-blue stone into the bag, picked off the yellow spears of grass entangled with the thin thong, and when it was clean, she stuffed it into the little bag. She tied the drawstring of the bag to the drawstring at the neck of her tunic. She pushed the bag inside the tunic for safekeeping. She could feel the pouch press against her skin. Tears flowed over her face. She took a deep breath and looked to the tops of the mountains that hid the morning sun. It seemed to Grass Child that the tops of the mountains pressed back the fingers of the sun. She shivered. While her face was damp she rubbed cold ashes on her cheeks to indicate that she was in mourning. She looked at her left hand. The small stump was not swollen but the end was black and beginning to scab over with a thick yellow ooze. She picked at a small blister on a balsam pine, and when the pitch ran out, she gently put the stump in it. She stripped off some alder leaves and pressed them around the wound. It throbbed. For a moment she sat with her eyes shut. Then, gradually, her mind began to clear, and she realized there was still work unfinished.

She pulled at the loose, thick leather thongs that held the lean-to together. Then she pulled at the corner cottonwood poles. Dragging them from the sagging shelter, she pushed one up across a tree branch barely within her reach. She had a vague picture in mind of a wooden platform on which to place the body of her grandmother, out of reach of the wolves. A decent burial place for one so beloved. She climbed the tree, heedless of scratches, and pulled the pole over to a branch of a neighboring tree of about the same height. Without resting, she did the same with another pole. She used the long thong to tie the robe around her grandmother's body into a secure bundle. It was awkward work for the girl; she could not count on her left hand. When, finally, she was done, she threw the free end of the thong up into the branches. It took several tries, but finally it rested above the poles. She scrambled up the tree again and pulled the thong down further over the branch. Carefully, slowly, she pulled the bundle off the ground.

"Oh, Great Spirit, do not let the thong snap," she prayed. Twice it dropped, and she was sure she would have to give up. Her arms ached, and her head throbbed. Then, with a final exhausting heave, the bundle rested on top of the poles. She sat a moment, watching the morning mists rise, holding up her left hand to ease the pain. Above the mountains to the east, the sun appeared, but there was little warmth this time of the year in the morning sun. She was sweating, however, and her hands were wet as she wrapped the long thong around the poles and tree branches, and once again around the bundle, and tied it securely. She felt the stirring of triumph within her aching body. The wolves would not get Old Grandmother now. Old Grandmother was safe.

Grass Child slid down the tree and started down the hill toward the northwest without once looking back.

She followed the same route she had taken with her family nearly half a moon before.

Grass Child did not stop. Childhood seemed to be gone, but a feeling of gratefulness came to her.

"Thank you, Great Spirit, for looking after me during the night. You were there, and I did not know. Look after Old Grandmother on her journey to the Land of Everfeasting."

Timidly she picked a dried rose hip and placed it in her mouth. It was dry and mealy. She picked more. She made a face with the unpleasant taste. Her mother would be wondering about her, she thought. Maybe grieving, thinking that she had been carried off by enemies or some animal—a wolf. Her father would not think too much about her—a girl-child was not as valuable as a boy. Yet deep inside she knew her father had some feeling for her—that was why he answered her questions and chided her when they went on walks together, saying, "Keep your mouth closed, your eyes and ears open, and your head up. Walk into life bravely like an Agaidüka Shoshoni."

A weakness came on her again, taking her strength. There was no use trying to be a small child anymore. She had no one to share her wonderment for Mother Earth, no one to make clover chains for, no one to take the time to listen to her stories, or to tell her stories. She loved her mother, but mothers were always busy with cooking, tanning hides, mending moccasins, and talking with the other women. Grass Child straightened, her head pounding to her step, her eyes following the horse and travois tracks on the trail. Her bare arms prickled with the chill of the wind; she quickened her pace.

Ahead, near the trail, she saw a patch of ripe buffaloberries. The bitterness of the berries gagged her. Fresh meat would taste better. She replaced the alder leaves on her finger with buffaloberry. Her little finger had turned black and blue, but it was not swollen, a good sign it would heal quickly. She picked up a pinecone and pulled it apart to find the nuts at the base of each hard petal. She left a trail behind her of broken cones. For a fleeting moment she wished she had taken her grandmother's firestones so she could make a small warm fire, and later at the edge of an aspen grove, she lay down wishing she had kept one antelope skin as a robe. Sleep closed in upon her.

Morning came, wet and dismal. Grass Child's left hand throbbed. She sat up, squirmed the cramps from her muscles, and pushed her tangled hair back. Her long black hair was unkempt, for she thought no more of caring for it than the horses her people rode cared about their manes. She liked it best when she ran in the wind and it fanned out behind. She looked at her scratched and bruised legs. She crumpled the yellowed grass with sage leaves and rubbed the juice on the cuts. Then she set out, hunched against the rain. She was wet to the skin, but soon became warm from moving. She walked quickly; already she had a well-developed pigeon-toed gait, making it easier to go uphill or downhill. She hoped to reach her camp by nightfall. After all, she could travel faster alone than with a travois and squalling babies trailing after it, who had to be fed four or five times a day.

She ate more berries. Chokecherries made her mouth pucker and did not satisfy her insides—besides, they brought to mind the story of the Shoshonis' origin, and Old Grandmother. She found wild carrots and munched on them as she walked.

She began to wonder if Rain Girl and Willow Bud would notice she was no longer a papoose, or would they scold and tease her for running off? Would they remain at the temporary camp or move on? Even her father would not stay for one girl-child when it was time to move. To a man's way of thinking, she was not worth much. She was aware that boys were worth more because they could defend the camp and hunt. But were not women useful? They kept the camp together and made warm tepees for the men and boys to come home to. They cooked and made clothing. They had the babies. *Ai*, she decided, she was worth something, if only a nebulous thing in the back of her mind. She thought maybe she could find the right time to talk to her father about it. Maybe she ought to talk with Willow Bud first to see how she felt.

It was still early when she caught sight of smoke

and stopped to consider. It could not be her camp yet. If she circled it, she would lose time and might lose the trail. She pulled away from the thought of entering the ravine, of being caught by an unfriendly tribe. She ate a few huckleberries she had saved by making a pouch of her tunic, holding the skirt sides together in front with one hand. Her stomach made an uneasy turning; the ache in her hand seemed to be fading. She turned from the trail and struck an arc around the thin line of smoke below.

Beyond it, the tracks were harder to find because of the rain. No longer could she feel sure that it was the right trail, because the travois marks were washed out. The horse tracks might have come from other horses, not the People's.

She traveled all day, walking even-timed, thinking about her mother and father, her sister and brothers, her friends, and always about her grandmother. Grass Child could no longer speak her name out loud. Old Grandmother was dead, and the dead were not spoken of. The living must go on, keeping life for themselves, leaving the dead behind with silence.

The day darkened. Grass Child kept walking. When she could no longer see the trail, she burrowed under the heavy, wet grass to where it was warm and dry. She piled more dry grass around her legs to keep the wind out. Soon her shivering stopped and sleep came.

Grass Child was awake before dawn. She flopped on her belly and poked a stick into the reddish-brown earth and thought how really hungry she was. There was no stream nearby for a drink to take the night taste from her mouth. She sat up and found more rose hips. Then she thanked the Great Spirit for leaving these bushes near her by throwing several berries into the grass, then some at the four corners of the earth and some at the sky.

She started on her way, made a turn on the path, and suddenly there was Willow Bud riding toward her. "Willow Bud!"

True to her word, Willow Bud had found Grass Child. It was just as she had told Grass Child's grieving mother.

Grass Child had gone back to comfort her dying grand-mother.

"Did you find Old Grandmother?" asked Willow Bud, dismounting and letting the horse rest and feed on the grass.

"*Ai*, do not speak her name," said Grass Child. With tears running down the faces of both girls, Grass Child told her friend the story of her grandmother's camp, carefully avoiding the name Old Grandmother.

Willow Bud looked at Grass Child's little finger and shook her head in approval. "You are true Agaidüka," she said, looking away.

"How did you find me?" Grass Child asked.

"Before sunup I left the camp and came this way for you. Only your brother Never Walks knows I have gone. He tried to stop me, saying I was just throwing myself after someone already gone on the same journey as the old woman. So I threatened to tell your father that Never Walks spends time with Yellow Eagle's daughter in the willow grove," said Willow Bud with a wide grin on her broad face.

Grass Child giggled. "Never Walks is older than I thought!"

The horse stopped munching the long, wet grass and stood still for the girls to mount. Willow Bud had spread a deerskin over the back of the horse and fastened it on with leather tongs tied under his belly. Willow Bud guided the horse with leather cords tied in the fashion of reins.

Grass Child pointed back up the trail. "There's a camp, maybe a day's ride."

"Our braves are still out hunting. It is their camp, I suppose. I hope they found a large deer or two. I want a new winter robe."

"I need a new tunic," said Grass Child, looking down at her soiled and torn one.

Overhead, the sky stretched blue and immense. Here and there a little pearl-white cloud sailed high and majestically. A fresh wind blew over the land, stirring the short, dry grease grass into ripples like those on a gentle sea. The dry leaves crunched under the hooves of their pony. Gradually the shadows of the trees grew longer, and the flies and yellow-jackets that had plagued

the girls all day gave way to the stronger wind that
came from the north.

Then they heard the happy shout of Spotted Bear as
he informed the People that Grass Child was riding
behind Willow Bud.

CHAPTER

2

Captured

Lewis's Journal[1]

From the Lewis and Clark Expedition, Saint Louis to the Pacific, 1804–1806.

Sunday July 28th 1805

Our present camp is precisely on the spot that the Snake Indians were encamped at the time the Minnetares of the knive R. first came in sight of them five years since. from hence they retreated about three miles up Jeffersons river and concealed themselves in the woods, the Minnetares pursued, attacked them, killed 4 men, 4 women a number of boys, and mad[e] prisoners of all the femals and four boys, Sah-cah-gar-we-ah o[u]r Indian woman was one of the female prisoners taken at that time; tho' I cannot discover that she shews any immotion of sorrow in recollecting this event, or of joy in being restored to her native country; if she has enough to eat and a few trinkets to wear I believe she would be perfectly content anywhere.

BERNARD DEVOTO, ed., *The Journals of Lewis and Clark*. New York: Houghton Mifflin Co., 1953, p. 171.

The days grew shorter, but the winter held off. The pleasant haze of a belated Indian summer persisted through half of the Agaidükas' journey into a warm winter camp.

The band remained no place for long. The life of the Agaidüka Shoshonis was migratory. The People were profound realists. They hunted as they moved. Often the men brought in a deer or several antelope or a fat bear. The women cut the meat in strips and dried it over hot coals during the day camp. There were no fires at night to attract raiders. Many times now they moved only at night, heading into the foothills of the Shining Mountains for protection from the Blackfeet and Sioux.

One night Grass Child felt the piercing loneliness more than ever. Her thoughts were back on the Big Horn. She wondered if the spirit of Old Grandmother made this great show of northern lights spreading in shimmering waves over the dome of the sky. Sometimes it formed bands of pale green and rose; sometimes there were great beams slowly climbing upward.

"Far in the north it will talk," said Fragrant Herbs that evening. "It crackles and hisses. Our people do not go that far these days. There, winds do not stop howling, the snow blows, and the fires go out. The People leave that land to the Blackfeet."

"Where will we stop for our encampment?" asked Grass Child.

"We will cross the ridge to the waters of the Big Muddy, then slowly we will go on to the place where the river divides into three forks," answered her mother.

"Will the Blackfeet be there?"

"Oh, Grass Child, you ask so many questions. It is really not fitting for a young girl-child. Wait and see. Look and listen. You will find you can teach yourself."

"Well? Will they be there?"

"No, the People have never yet found the Blackfeet at this retreat."

"What if this time they are there?"

"It will be too cold to fight or raid horses. They will not be there."

Grass Child tried to imagine what it would be like, however, if the enemy were at their winter retreat. She could feel their savage eyes, but what they looked like and what they would do was a mystery.

The warmth of the next morning's sun had chilled by midforenoon, and the temperature began to drop so fast that ice was forming on the horses' nostrils by noon. Several times Chief No Retreat stopped and had the men clean off the horses' faces before going farther. The women would take that time to rearrange the travois loads or let the children who were riding on top of the household goods walk a bit, then snuggle down again inside a buffalo robe to keep out the fingers of cold. The sticks on the drags were checked, and the leather that bound them to the horses was checked and repaired if worn thin. The gale whipping out of the darkening northwest gave promise of the winter's first blizzard.

Several days later, it was too cold to skin the hunters' catch of several deer without risking frostbite. The squaws built a rough lean-to with a fire in the front and skinned the animals there. The small children sat around the fire for warmth and chewed small, succulent pieces of raw flesh that were handed them once in a while.

When they were on the trail again, thankful the wind was at their backs, the first stinging pellets of snow began flying. As they walked along the low gullies, their leggings became encased with ice from the knees down. They were half-frozen as they plodded along, always keeping sight of the river. Finally they dropped down into the welcome, comparative shelter of a cedar grove. This became their winter encampment.

That winter on the Three Forks was hard. They had set camp near water and good grass for the horses, in a place sheltered from the north wind, but the People had not killed enough meat during the summer to last the winter, and that which they had taken in the fall was soon gone. There was great concern, but thoughts of cold and weariness fled when a scout came to the village one afternoon shouting, "Buffalo, buffalo! There are many in a small canyon to the south!"

To the People, the welfare of the tribe came first. No Indian hunter practiced "free enterprise," attacking and alarming a herd of buffalo alone in winter. Under the stringent laws of the winter hunt, he would have been put to death before he could climb down from his pony. The winter chase was communal, and the kill divided equally among all of the tribe. Soon the hunters were organized and riding to the south with bows and lances ready.

Chief No Retreat brought his hunting party back in a blizzard. The wind had struck in from the north in the afternoon, blowing sleet, and the People at the camp had taken to the shelter of their warm tepees. An old woman had been gathering buffalo chips against the cold, and she had not returned. Her family found her frozen body half-buried in the snow the next morning. Spotted Bear, son of No Retreat, brother of Grass Child, returned with his group just after the old woman was found. He raced his pony ahead of the rest and ran through the camp yelling, "Our group is back. More hunters are back!" The People spilled out of their tepees to greet the hunters in spite of the fierce wind, for they were returning heroes, and seemed saviors to those who had remained behind and were out of meat.

They brought eight fat buffalo; with the ten of Chief No Retreat's party, each lodge was entitled to half a carcass.

Two weeks later, Chief No Retreat hunkered over the fire in his big tepee. "How much meat do we have now?" he asked Fragrant Herbs.

"We have only the bones of the half buffalo."

"Were the scouts out while we hunted?"

"They have done their best, but the other herds went away."

"Are you hungry?"

"No, we have the grass seeds."

She put several flat, crisp biscuits before him. He mused as he munched the food. "Some laughed as you gathered the seed, but I hold with you. This will keep us from starving. We will divide what we have with the other lodges. They ought to be glad we saved the seeds."

The chief portioned out the fine seeds carefully, cautioning the People about spilling them. They buckled down to the task of living on little, and they wasted nothing. The women could not dig for roots in the frozen ground. Children squabbled with the dogs for a warm place by the tepee fire. Babies cried. The grass seed was used sparingly—making it last.

Grass Child missed the storytelling of Old Grandmother—with it she could have lost for a time the gnawing hunger pangs in her stomach as Old Grandmother carried her to another place and another time where wonderful things happened. She remembered one and told the story to Rain Girl.

"About as long ago as it takes three men to live, a large tribe of Shoshonis stayed behind in the land of the Shining Mountains to be safe from the Blackfeet. There was a storm, and all the warmth went from Mother Earth. The Shoshonis died, and there were no signs of life. The snow made a robe as tall as the tallest man. The buffalo were gone."

"This is a terrible story," said Rain Girl.

"It is true, though," continued Grass Child. "Snow covered the land and did not melt. It hung heavy on the great pine boughs. When the time for melting snow came, there was so much snow that there was a great flood over all the land. Everything was covered with water except the very top of one mountain peak. On top of that peak one Shoshoni man and his woman rested in a canoe. When the water dried, they were the only ones left. There were no great animals, only small ones and lots of birds. Their lodges had to be made from small rabbit skins and feathers. That is why we still weave some feathers in our summer lodges. Then the birds can see how beautiful they look and know that we are still grateful to them for helping our old brother and sister so many winters ago."

"I think you just made that up," sniffed Rain Girl.

Grass Child, Rain Girl, and their friend Willow Bud worked up and down the river with the women, cutting cottonwood sprouts and dragging them in the snow to the small herd of horses near camp.

Some of the men spent the winter days hunting small game. They ran rabbits into hollow logs, one end of which had been tightly sealed with mud or hard-packed

snow; then they plugged the other end with sagebrush
and set it on fire and fanned the smoke into the log. As
soon as the rabbit stopped squealing, they pulled out
the smoking brush and grabbed the animal. Others built
snares for snowshoe rabbits by hanging a noose of tough
bark from a tree, baiting it with the tender inner bark
of cottonwood sprouts.

One day, Grass Child stood still and listened. There
seemed to be a faint sound everywhere—the murmur
of waters, snow falling off tree limbs, and, barely audible, maybe imagined, a knocking sound far away up
the river. With progressive speed and gathering power,
day by day now, the sun wore away and tore apart the
river ice. More and more water flowed as it melted on
the surface and close to the banks. The Chinook winds
hurried the melting, leaving the snow honeycombed
with pockets of air. Soon the last support broke free on
the river, the cracks became crevices, the whole ice
moved, fragments and floes grinding and heaving, ice
cakes tilted endwise, and the Big Muddy was true to
her name, too thick to drink and too thin for yellow
paint.

The Agaidükas lost only one old grandfather during
the time of the snowy moon and freezing winds and
considered themselves fortunate. The winter had been
cold and long. Several horses were dead and good only
for buzzard bait. The warm Chinook winds were a signal that the winter storytelling period was over. The
women could go out now and dig roots in the thawed,
soft mud and the men could hunt, easily following animal tracks in the soft earth.

By the time spring's first signs appeared it was forbidden by social tradition to continue telling winter
tales because of the belief that it would displease the
old trickster, Coyote. During the long winter months
the older members of the tribe had often gathered
around someone's center fire, smoked a mixture of kinnikinnick, willow bark, and buffalo dung, in an atmosphere
of leisurely storytelling. The people's memories were
refreshed with the most important tribal records in this
way. But the winter tales always ended with the coming
of spring, letting the younger women hunt roots and
the younger men hunt game for the stew kettle.[2] How-

ever, once a story was started it had to continue until the end. Therefore, Grass Child continued making up dramatic events with her friend, Willow Bud. Each girl added a new thought as it occurred in order to lengthen the enjoyment of the story.

Grass Child was lying on her back near a smoldering center fire, looking through the smoke hole, inventing ideas to prolong a story she and Willow Bud had been telling for days. "And so, during the time there was water all over the land, Coyote paddled around until he found some geese."

Willow Bud hitched her bare legs under the skirt of her tunic, took a deep breath and added, "Coyote asked those geese for feathers so that instead of paddling he could join them flying. The geese flew off to the nearest mountaintop for a powwow."

Grass Child sat up, brushed a sleepy spring fly off her nose, and said, "Those geese decided to wash the whole earth and Coyote would have drowned but he pulled a white buffalo robe over the hole that lets water leak from the sky."

Willow Bud laughed. "If we aren't careful, we'll finish our story and not be able to tell another until the snows begin again."

Grass Child stood up. "Let's look for something to eat. My belly cramps for want of food. I'd like to stuff myself and not have to share with anyone."

Just then Fragrant Herbs poked her head in the tepee. "Girls, your daydreams are real! Come, listen."

Grass Child and Willow Bud hurried to follow Fragrant Herbs outside. She put her hand over her mouth and they all listened. The camp crier was out, calling among the tepees on the other side of camp. "The scouts have sighted buffalo!" He continued to call as he came closer and closer to their side of the camp. "Everyone get ready!" By now everyone in camp was outside in the crisp spring air. There was happy chattering and questions. "When do we go?" "How many buffalo?" "Where are they located?"

The crier began his second round of the camp. "Hunters and strong women! Leave tomorrow morning! Due west to the high cliff! East of the Three Forks!"

Grass Child knew the spot exactly. There were a few

aspens, and the high ground was buff-colored and punctured with rock. At the bottom of the cliff, where the
Old Muddy was joined by three wide, fast-moving
branches, there were flat gravel beaches with wild
strawberry patches sheltered by thick willows. Grass
Child's mouth watered. She was ready to go.

The scouts kept their horses at the spot they'd picked
for the hunting camp and kept a watchful eye on the
buffalo grazing on the brittle yellow grass left over from
the previous season. Next morning more men on horseback and the strongest of the women and children, carrying cutting knives carved from animal bones and
bundles of willow sticks wrapped with thin hides for
temporary shelters, left the main camp.

Despite the still-chilly weather the men wore only
breechclouts and moccasins and carried their bows and
a quiver of arrows. A thin leather thong attached to
the underjaw of the hunting horse served as a bridle.
When the women arrived, they quickly set up camp at
the junction of the eastern and middle fork. Looking
from the crest of the hill overshadowing the main river,
Grass Child could see how the Old Muddy broadened
out on the untimbered valley plain. The eastern fork
was more rapid, but not as deep nor as wide as the
others.[3]

The men now motioned the women to leave the temporary camp and follow a little behind them up the
northern bank and along the western fork. Then the
men all moved out and forded the river, signaling for
the women to wait there. The buffalo herd was close;
the smell was rank and sharp. The Agaidüka hunting
party was now about four miles up the western fork.
The women remained quiet with their own thoughts.
The few children who had been allowed to come stayed
in little bunches, bragging to one another about the
prowess of a father, brother, uncle, or grandfather.

The blue sky and scattering of white clouds were
reflected in the pools of clear river water near the banks.

Willow Bud poked her elbow in Grass Child's side.
"My father will get most."

Grass Child countered, "Mine will give away most."

Rain Girl said, "Maybe our brother, Never Walks,

will get a buffalo. Did you see how he rides a horse more gracefully than he walks on his own two feet? He's meant to be on horseback."

"I pity his woman—if he ever gets one," giggled Willow Bud.

Fragrant Herbs scowled fiercely at the three noisy girls. "Hush! No one will get near a buffalo if you chatter like sparrows and giggle like loons," she whispered loudly.

When it was quiet the girls could hear the snorting and bellowing of the buffalo being surrounded by hunters.

Grass Child spotted a wild strawberry blossom, then a trillium and a springbeauty. She hitched her way down to the springbeauty and her little fingers dug into the soft earth, feeling for the tiny bulb. She wiped it on her tunic and popped it into her mouth while her other hand looked for another delicious bit to eat. She ate another and another and stretched herself out in reach of one more. She heard something and looked up, holding her body tense, her eyes narrowed. Those were not buffalo chased by hunters coming around the crest and up the narrow river valley. Those were horses carrying riders she had never seen before.

Someone blew a shrill signal on a wing-bone whistle, and the intruders swarmed down into the valley and splashed across the river. Continuously they yelled, "*Kiyi!*"

The women screamed a warning for everyone to hide themselves. Grass Child looked around frantically; then ran to her sister and Willow Bud.

The ominous newcomers—black-and-yellow stripes painted down their chest—jumped down and advanced toward the women. Grass Child and Willow Bud ran behind some older children, with Fragrant Herbs and Rain Girl in the lead, heedless of the slippery grass on the ridge. Grass Child fell. A terrible cry burst upon her ears, louder, closer. A shot rang out, then another. This was the first time she had heard a flintlock, but she knew instantly it was the firestick the Agaidüka warriors spoke of. They had wanted to trade for them in the south with the Spanish, but the Spanish would not trade their precious firesticks, not even for a fine Shoshoni horse.

Grass Child's breath felt hot in her throat. She rose to her knees and looked toward the river. Willow Bud was on the bank. Grass Child looked up the embankment for her mother, who was dodging a black-and-yellow figure running with a war club raised ready to bring it down on her head.

"No!" yelled Grass Child as she ran up the hill.

As long as she lived, Grass Child never forgot the sound of that club. It reminded her of the squashing noise of a buffalo bladder full of water flung against a flat stone.

Quickly the attacker cut and pulled off the scalp with one powerful sweep. The face of Fragrant Herbs was red with blood; one leg twitched with unnatural rapidity. He had cut the scalp lock above one ear, and there was a single bloody braid dangling from his waiststring when Grass Child reached him.

With a cry she slashed the murderer's face with her fingernails, scarifying it with three deep, red furrows. She saw a face with a big nose that was long and hooked like the beak of a buzzard. Evil, it looked grisly in the deepening shadows of late afternoon. Her scalp tingled. Another stranger rode his horse between Grass Child and Willow Bud, separating them. Grass Child found herself standing alone, staring at the strange rider. She turned and raced as hard as she could toward the riverbank where she had last seen Willow Bud. Her feet flew, and she did not feel the stones under them. Her lungs felt scorched. At the river's edge she did not see Willow Bud; her feet slid in the mud. She slipped quietly into the cold water. She was a good swimmer, but never had she swum so frightened before. She could not breathe; water flooded her lungs; she choked. Finally, she let the current carry her downstream, where she bumped a sawyer just under the muddy water. She was sure she saw something move in the thicket of willows, so she clung to the sawyer and kept her head under as long as possible. She heard the splashing of water over the wild thumping of her heart, and before she could get the mud cleared from her eyes, she felt a blow on the back of her head and for a brief moment felt herself sinking into the cold, watery darkness.

Grass Child opened her eyes. Her head hurt miserably. The sky was fading to a gray tinged with a few streaks of pink. She was bound facedown with thick thongs to the back of a scrawny pony, and, slowly moving her head and opening her eyes to a squint, she saw beside her one of the bays from her father's stock. Her mind reeled, and plainly she heard her father speaking to Never Walks, his eldest: "A horse is a tool. Do not let him go dull. Some men break their beast until he has no will, only a sweating horror at their approach. These men know how to make a horse kill himself, how to make him do an added mile at top speed after he is ready to quit."

Slowly she came up from the darkness that had surrounded her to the reality that she had imagined her father's voice, and she smelled acrid smoke from the burning of hides and green willow. Her eyes watered as she looked at long plumes curling from the direction of the People's hunting camp. Four yellow-and-black striped figures emerged at the top of a small bluff, each carrying a child. Grass Child dropped her head to the horse's rump; her eyes closed, pushing out the sting with hot tears. She had recognized the children. Drummer, just learning to walk, and Blue Feather, a summer older. Both sons of Water Woman and Yellow Rope. Water Woman was somehow related to Grass Child's mother. She remembered the women called each other sister. Small Man was kicking at his captor. He was the son of Red Eagle, who had been so full of thanksgiving at the boy's birth that he had celebrated for more than a week, giving away all his belongings to members of the village. Last, there was Something Good, little son of the old Medicine Man and his youngest wife, Gall.

The sickening knowledge exploded inside Grass Child that the People were raided for ponies and children. These strangers had also been looking for the buffalo, but had found something better.

Taking horses from an enemy was not considered stealing, but an accepted practice of daring and wits.

All tribes initiated their young boys in the endless craft of stealing horses; how to study a herd to ascertain the leader, how to hold the rest together through him. But the taking of children and women to be used as slaves left a terrible debt unpaid.

Grass Child's head ached cruelly, and she could feel blood oozing down the inside of her tunic from the wound. She had lost her moccasins. A strange, fierce-looking man reached for the leather thongs bound around the horse's neck and led Grass Child to the group milling around at the bottom of the bluff. The man grinned from ear to ear as he lifted his hand in pretense of slapping her if she cried out. He had a puckered white scar across his forehead. The four naked boys had been tied on horses. Grass Child recognized the horses as coming from the People's herd.

She moved her head to the other side, then let it drop to ease the pain, then opened her eyes. In front of her were some Agaidüka women tied to scrawny beasts, the mistreated horses of their captors. She was about to shout to them when a quirt across her back stopped her. It felt like fire. Gradually the pain subsided. Someone tied her feet around the horse's belly with a long piece of rawhide. It dawned on her that she would be going with these strange people. She tried to kick out at the man tying her feet. She could not see him. She could hear his low belly laugh. Two others came and stood close to her face; one was Buzzard Beak, who pointed to the three slashes on his face. The men laughed and talked as if teasing Grass Child for fighting them.

Then they mounted their shy, scrawny horses. Some led prisoners on horseback; others led only the beautiful Agaidüka horses. As they trotted down the valley, Grass Child twisted, trying to look back. The effort agitated the welt across her back, and she cried out. Someone slapped her on the side of the face, opening the head wound. It was the ugly-looking fellow with the white scar across his forehead, and he lifted his hand in pretense of slapping her again if she called out. She felt blood ooze down her neck. Scar Face mounted a horse and took up the reins of one behind that seemed too weary to put one foot in front of the other. Grass Child blinked in disbelief. Willow Bud was sitting upright on this tired old horse. The eyes of the girls met, but they dared not speak. Again, hot tears stung Grass Child's eyes. Her head throbbed in time to the throbbing in her back. She sobbed quietly. In her grief she could not even sing the shrill mourning song of the People. Her mind refused to go over the day's events.

They rode all night, never stopping. Grass Child began to wonder if her father and some of the other warriors were on their trail, following. Surely he would come with her brothers if he could find the trail. Was Rain Girl with them, she wondered, or was Rain Girl— Her mind could go no farther. Only the sound of that watery thud came clear and sharp in her mind, and the sight of her mother's limp, bloody form lying in a crumpled heap in the dust.

It took all of her strength to stay out of the dark, endless pit that pulled her downward. She was determined not to give in to that sinking feeling where the blackness rushed over the top of her head. In the early-morning light she looked, trying to find Willow Bud or Rain Girl among the semi-naked riders.

Soon the sun's rays shone warm and the birds were singing. Grass Child saw that they were traveling northeast along the Big Muddy. She wanted to tell this discovery to Willow Bud. Finally she could no longer fight, and she slept without wanting to. In the warmth of the sun the deep cut across her back began to smart and swell. She felt it throb with each stride of the horse. When the sun was overhead they stopped by a stream. Her mother's murderer, Buzzard Beak, removed her bonds and pulled the tunic down from her shoulders, loosening it from the back wound. He left it tied at her waist. When he lifted her down, she could hardly stand on her sore legs for the first few moments. He took jerky from a pouch and offered her some. She turned away. He pushed her toward the stream. He motioned for her to kneel down in the fashion of squaws and drink. The water tasted good. She scooped some and let it splash her face and the back of her head where her hair was matted with dried blood, but when it touched her back below her shoulders the hurt was too much. Willow Bud had knelt beside her. Grass Child wanted to put her arms around her friend. "Don't touch me," warned Willow Bud, "he will strike us. He comes from a large village in the east," she added softly, "called Minnetaree."

"How do you know this?" asked Grass Child.

"Hush, not so loud. The old Agaidüka, Moon Woman, is riding near me, and she said it in the night. She recognized their hunting paint and several words."

"Where is Rain Girl?"

"I last saw her behind a juniper with some little children."

"Dig your knees deep so as to leave some sign that women drank here," said Grass Child, turning some stones so that their heavy sides leaned against one another, a call for aid. "I think my father will come after us."

Farther up the stream, Scar Face pulled his hands from the water. He drank so as to leave no sign but the tips of his moccasins, and then blurred these. He sauntered toward the girls and kicked hard against the side of Willow Bud, knocking her to the ground, blurring her knee sign. He motioned for her to get back up on the horse that was grazing. She tried to tell him he didn't have to kick, she would go. But he jerked her up and made some guttural sounds as if scolding her. Grass Child found her horse; she could not mount him, for her back hurt too much. Buzzard Beak threw her belly-first, on the horse. Somehow she managed to get one leg over, and rode sitting up. They rode with the sun striking at their backs.

Soon, Grass Child wanted another drink. Her legs ached worse than ever, and the throbbing in her thin back continued on and off like dull waves. She tried to look at her captors. She tried to think about where they lived. She could tell they were not very good horsemen. She felt sorry for the Agaidüka horses because these men had no regard for the physical welfare of the animals, running them at full speed over the stony ground and making no halts to breathe them. Even an Agaidüka papoose like Drummer knew enough to treat a horse well so that he would treat his rider well. The captors' horses had not been brushed to make their hides shine. Their hides were matted with sticks from the low brush. Most of the captors looked younger than Grass Child's father. They all had muddy red circles painted around their eyes, making them look alike and hideous. The only two Grass Child could distinguish were Buzzard Beak and Scar Face.

That night they camped in a copse of white birch. Grass Child felt herself pushed and then pulled off the horse. She could not stand at first. The ground floated closer and closer to her face. She placed one small bare foot beneath her and managed to stand straddle-legged. Her body throbbed.

Buzzard Beak lifted her and sat her on the ground beside some rocks. Willow Bud, the four little boys, and four Agaidüka squaws were there. How good it was to see them. Her head cleared, and Grass Child began to pour out words of hope for their early rescue.

Moon Woman, tall, almost gaunt for an Agaidüka, with angular features, shook her head, her eyes focused on the firelight. She cringed and drew into herself, going rigid. To lighten the moment, Grass Child said, "This will be the last night with them. Even now, No Retreat and Yellow Rope, Red Eagle, and Medicine Man are following our trail." Moon Woman had not heard her. "Moon Woman—"

But Moon Woman's black eyes were glazed, turned toward the captors' fire, seeing neither the fire nor the men around it, but some specter Grass Child could not glimpse. She sat there ill at ease, not knowing what to say. She could feel tears of exhaustion just under the surface. She kept them in check.

Blue Feather and Drummer clung to their mother, Water Woman, a buxom woman whose abundant black hair looked as if it had not been combed in a long while. Her eyes were a fathomless brown in which were traces of fatigue. She looked calmly, unblinking, at Grass Child for a long minute. Depths of quietness, wells of thoughts seemed to lie behind those eyes. Still she said nothing.

"I'm not staying with these skunks," said Willow Bud. "I can follow the Big Muddy back to our camp. I can."

"Anyone with feeling would say the same." Water Woman's voice was matter-of-fact. "Maybe this was bound to happen," she went on. "Now is as good a time

as any to decide whether we'll escape or not—provided
we make our decisions based on truth."

"What do you mean—truth?" asked Willow Bud.

"The way life really is."

"Not all life can be as bad as what we saw yesterday."
Willow Bud's words had rebellion in them.

"*Ai*, every bit of life, every one of us has a dark side,"
Water Woman hurled back. "When we decided to hunt
the buffalo, we were venturing out of our hiding place
in the mountains. Moon Woman knows. She lived in a
secret place, too. Her people were confident they could
not be found by their enemies. Yet she was found drinking at the water hole one day by an Arikara. She got
her first good look at the way life really is, and she ran
back to shelter in a hurry."

"She? Was she a captive once before?"

Water Woman's reply was a chuckle so soft that it
was almost a sigh. "She? *Ai*. And she loved the young
Arikara man. But she was not yet ready for living with
any man. She was a child, and the idea of a man had
not entered her mind, except as in the manner of a
father. After that, she never wanted a man. And ever
since, she has thought of nothing but her Arikara."

"Pah," spat Fish Woman, "a child like Willow Bud
would die or be eaten alive by wolves—or worse, tortured by Blackfeet—before she reached the river of
three forks. The only road to survival is for all of us to
hide again in the mountains."

Small Man and Something Good sat close to Fish
Woman. In profile she had a rugged face, as if her features had been chiseled out of rough stone and the final
smoothing and polishing had never quite been finished.
When she looked at Willow Bud, her eyes were intuitive, perceptive; their corners were crisscrossed with
smile lines. She had a sensitive mouth, as if the sculptor
had given special attention to that. Her hair was neatly
chopped off at the ends and fell into her face. This gave
her a girlish look.

"Those evil devils," said Pine Woman, pointing with
a broken fingernail in the direction of the resting Minnetarees. "They would slash your throat if you tried to
creep away." Her dark eyes blazed in her wrinkled face.
She folded her hands across her stomach. "Grass Child

is right. We must wait until our own braves come for us. We must wait and see what happens next. In the meantime, we might see if we can get some sleep, and think of making trail signs every chance we get. We must keep our minds occupied with good thoughts."

Water Woman looked at her curiously. "*Ai*, that is good to say, but no man will come." She seemed to be seeing into the past. She took a deep breath, plunged on; nothing could stop her. "Remember, I said to look at life the way it really is now? So you've got to take your hands away from your eyes before you can do anything about changing our course. Grass Child, no one can mention the name of our chief again. His name is gone from our lips."

The words poured over Grass Child. "They killed him?" Her horror showed in the half-light from the campfire. But Water Woman took no notice.

"I was in the ravine running to my man, who was down. I saw an enemy horse trample him. I was wild with fear. My heart was in my throat. I could not get to him; I saw his face and could not recognize it—it was nothing, pulp. The men were regrouping and riding toward the camp, but I noticed some of the women running up the river, pushing the children ahead of them. I ran to them to help pull the little ones along. But before I reached them I saw a horse running in circles and pitching up on its hind legs, trying to shake the rider off. The man was hanging over the front of the horse. A loud crack came from the front of me, and the man slid from the horse. An enemy horse ran over him, the rider screeching to heaven. Out from a grove of aspen rode a man waving a firestick. I knew it must be something from the firestick that had knocked the man from the horse. The man was our chief. I must have kept running. I do not remember. Finally, when I thought my chest would burst, I stopped and hid in the woods by the river. I had each of my boys near me. I had not noticed them before. I saw Rain Girl, and Something Good, and several other children lying under a juniper. The horse fell, the one carrying our chief; I remember red bubbles coming from his nostrils as he lay still beside his master." Water Woman stopped and looked around at the listeners; her pause was long.

Grass Child held her hands to her face. She made no sound.

Pine Woman asked, "Did you hide or stand in the open gawking so these dirty skunks could find you?"

Water Woman soothed the sleeping children on her lap. "I do not know any more. That is all I remember. When my eyes opened, I was on a rawboned horse and my two papooses were bound together next to me." She nodded, smiled with her eyes at her two sons, saying nothing more.

Around and behind each one's thoughts stood the question: Could anyone escape? Would they try?

"So what does that have to do with me following the Big Muddy back to the People?" Willow Bud dared to ask.

"Everything to do with it. Who are we?" answered Moon Woman, slapping her thigh for emphasis.

"I wish I knew," said Grass Child feverishly, half-asleep.

"But you can know. Each of us is important. No one can fill our place." She hesitated with this new thought. "If you don't do the work that is given you to do, that work may never be done. Why are we here?" She folded her arms and legs into a comfortable position and began snoring, as though her thoughts had been deep and taken much out of her. No one answered her question. The question was to sleep on.

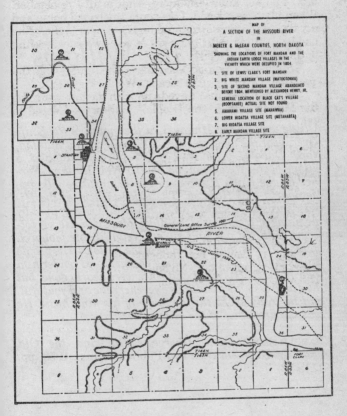

Permission to reproduce this map was given by James E. Sperry, superintendent of the State Historical Society of North Dakota, January 28th, 1970. Taken from *Sakakawea*, by Russel Reid, State Historical Society, North Dakota, *30*, No. 2–3, 1963, p. 110–11.

3

People of the Willows

A little way up the Missouri, at the mouth of the Knife River, near the modern cities of Washburn and Stanton, North Dakota, to the west of U.S. 83, was Mahaha, a village of the Wetersoon, or Soulier Noir Indians. Farther up the Knife River were two Minnetaree villages, Metaharta and Hidatsa. The chief sachem of the Hidatsas was an ancient and patriarchial looking man by the name of Omsehara, the Black Moccasin. He sat tottering with old age and silently reigned sole monarch of this little community, People of the Willows. His people dropped in to cheer his sinking energies and render him their homage. His sight and voice were nearly gone, but the gestures of his hands were yet energetic and youthful, and he freely spoke the language of his kind heart. He was the first chief of the Minnetarees.

HAROLD MCCRACKEN, *George Catlin and the Old Frontier*. New York: Crown Publishers Inc., 1959, pp. 111–12.

The next morning, two men passed jerky and parched corn among the captives for their morning meal. Grass Child had never seen parched corn before. She pushed it around in her hand.

"These people plant the seeds, and it grows for them on sticks," Moon Woman explained.

"Oh, I would like to see that!" laughed Willow Bud, unbelieving.

Grass Child's back and legs were stiff, but the raw places were scabbed over, and even though they looked ugly, she knew they were healing underneath. She chewed on the corn, wondering why anyone thought it tasted good.

Buzzard Beak walked over and surveyed the group. Suddenly he pointed his flintlock directly at Pine Woman's belly.[1] His lip curled into a sneer. Grass Child noticed scars on his chest and arms. She stared unabashedly for some time, thinking that he must be a great warrior among his people. He must respect bravery in others. The flintlock was not lowered, but it moved slowly to point at the forehead of Grass Child. She sucked in her breath fearfully. She wanted to step backward, but she did not dare. She stared him in the eye, and, with no thought other than "How fierce he thinks he is," she moved her hand upward little by little and lowered it just as slowly, taking the flintlock barrel with her, pushing it to one side. He spoke to her in his strange tongue. He pushed her forward as if he wished her to go somewhere with him, then suddenly his foot was in her path. When she fell to the ground, he guffawed loudly and walked away.

Grass Child fainted. When she came to, she was aware of blood in her mouth, and she was surprised by the saltiness of the taste. She did not want to sit up. She tried to push her mind deep into some inner sanctuary where nothing could hurt her. She thought this might be dying, this sinking into darkness slowly, slowly.

A long time later, it seemed, Grass Child felt herself moving hesitantly outward toward consciousness of the shell that was her own body. This sensation was re-

peated again and again. Each time she was rebuffed by
the wave of violent pain and slipped back thankfully
into the comfort of that inner oblivion.

It was midafternoon when she came out of it far
enough to realize that she was lying naked on a clean
blanket and that somebody was rubbing her with bear's
oil. It did not seem surprising that it was Buzzard Beak
who was doing the rubbing. He had shown them what
would happen if they tried to escape. Now he was sorry
that he had hurt her. He felt her pulse. Several other
strangers were standing around. Their faces and bodies
had been washed, and they looked more friendly. Buzzard Beak nodded and laid her head gently on the blanket. She felt the softness. It was not a fur robe; she
noticed the color—dark blue, like the sky on a cold
starlit night. This was something different, something
unfamiliar. She moved her hand against the blanket
once more. Buzzard Beak began to feel her sides as if
to locate broken ribs. Rolling her gently, he pointed to
the swollen quirt mark on her back and the bump on
her head under the blood-matted hair. He chuckled deep
inside himself as he rubbed ample bear's oil over them.
She could hear his words, but she had no idea of their
meaning. She continued to feel drowsy inside, with a
fear wrapped lightly around the outside. The strangers
all around her and the strange blue robe gave her no
security. They wrapped her gently in the blanket and
left her to sleep more.

Finally, at midmorning of the fifth day, they again
started eastward along the river. Grass Child felt somewhat better, but her head still ached with the motion
of the horse. When they stopped for water, she let herself be pulled from the horse and pushed beside the
small stream. She lay in the cool leaves, rubbing some
of them on her hot, swollen face, remembering the medicinal quality of crushed buffaloberry leaves. These
cool leaves served just as well, her distant mind told
her. She managed a few sips of the cooling water, then
was placed roughly upon the horse again. There was
no time to talk with Willow Bud.

A week passed, more slowly than Grass Child had
believed time could pass. Her condition went from unbearable discomfort to outright agony. The leaves she

had reveled in at the spring were the low-growing three-leaved ivy. She itched and burned and longed to scratch arms and legs, and most of all, her swollen, parched face and lips. Buzzard Beak had tied her hands behind her back and placed her on the same horse with himself. There was no position she could assume in which his body behind her was not torment. Yet she had enough sense to know she could not have ridden a horse alone, sitting with her hands tied behind her back.

The midafternoon sun made the ivy-caused blisters on her legs and arms break and water. Once she thought she felt perspiration from the horse, but she was not sure. When the horse began to founder, Buzzard Beak used his quirt vigorously and the animal went a little faster. The horse made a sudden lurch and fell on its side, frightening Grass Child so that she cried out. Buzzard Beak leaped nimbly to the ground, pulling her with him. Holding the thong reins and Grass Child with one hand, he began to strike the horse. He kicked and pounded it over the head with the butt of the quirt. The horse tottered to its feet. Carrying Grass Child, Buzzard Beak leaped astride, and they galloped farther eastward.

Water Woman, nursing Blue Feather, with Drummer held tight in her other arm, sang to Grass Child in the night when she could not sleep. The captives were permitted to huddle around the fire now for warmth. Each day Water Woman soothingly told of the great improvement in Grass Child's condition. Willow Bud tried to describe the land they rode over, sometimes rocky and hilly, other times flat and grassy with small gurgling streams. Grass Child's eyes were swollen shut.

Only the day that her eyes opened did Grass Child feel she was improving. That day the grass looked greener than it had ever seemed and the trees taller and straighter, her friends' smiles broader.

"Tomorrow," Water Woman encouraged, "you will be strong enough to ride alone. You can ride with us. No more sitting with Buzzard Beak." That night she and Willow Bud pretended to gather wood, but stood on a small hill to see if they could see any sign of the rescuing Agaidükas.

"We are as ants in the field," Pine Woman sighed, smoothing her dirty tunic over her stomach.

"But if they travel along the river, sooner or later they will stumble on us," said Willow Bud. "We will watch for them while we remember landmarks each day, like putting beads on a string. Today there was the big cottonwood broken by lightning. Yesterday there was the spring water coming out of the dark earth. It took us half a morning to get through that muck. Before that, there was the tall stone with vines on one side and—"

Fish Woman placed a blue-veined hand over Willow Bud's and spoke as if to one of her own children. "Poor girl! Your head is swollen with knowledge of the trail we've followed, and still you want to push more into it. Don't shove so much in that it pushes on the trail back to the People and lets some spill out, or don't let these skunks beat it out of you."

Moon Woman sighed—and shut her eyes. They were closed so long that everyone was beginning to think she had fallen asleep when suddenly she began to speak. Her eyes were still closed, but her voice had changed: it was soft, almost caressing, with a smile in it. "I was about as many summers and as skinny as Grass Child when the Arikara warrior carried me away. I was young enough so that I never knew that women were carried off for slaves. I just never thought about it. I lived in his lodge with two other woman. They made me fetch water, push down weeds between the mounds of corn and beans, make the stew, and sew. My sewing was bad. I was not old enough to be able to make good trousers. At night they beat me. When he came home he scolded them and fed me thin hot soup to stop my wailing. Then he sent me out for firewood. I could scarcely find a stick around those lodges, and then he would beat me." Her eyelids fluttered open. "I'll tell you about them. They are called Arikaras. I was their captive once, as I have told you."

Willow Bud nodded, then everyone nodded, not knowing what to expect.

"The Arikara village is downriver a short trail from the Westersoon. Once I heard the Wetersoon eat worms.

Farther up are villages of the People of the Willows, our captors, the Minnetarees."

"And they probably eat dogs," said Willow Bud, making a distasteful face.

"The Arikaras' lodges are heaped up like an anthill, made of wood and mud outside." She made a face. "Ugh. But inside, like something from a medicine dream. Big, space to put many things, even a horse in cold weather. And warm, no wind could get in, even the smoke hole fixed so the wind would not go down. The sleeping places not on the ground, but up on logs and soft branches. And pots for cooking, not clay or willow, but black and hard, heavy; never break. Houses inside of the lodge made with skins. People in one house and people in another. No one to get in someone's way. Tunics laid across branches to keep them clean. These houses are not moved. These people do not move. I worked hard sewing, cleaning, keeping out of the way of those two women. My man sometimes smiled on me, and sometimes I was too tired to do as he asked and he beat me. That was proper for him. Inside, I felt myself fading. Once I fell against the ground and stayed there quiet, feeling the strength of Mother Earth before I pushed and pulled on more weeds in his garden. But the fading never stopped. I was starving to death, even though I was eating. I didn't know what to do. Then one day I was cutting a tunic and something came to me: I could find my way to the People. It was simple. I could remember every step of the way. From that time on, I smiled a little more and stopped fading.

"I could feel my thoughts racing toward the People. In the spring when the land was green, I put some seeds in a pouch and hid jerky inside my tunic on a string around my waist. I went out to push the weeds down. I never stopped walking—I went through the saplings across the ditch that surrounded that village and, with one foot ahead of the other, headed in the direction of the People. It was not long before the seeds and jerky were gone, but I found roots and berries and skinned a rabbit with a sharp stone. I found the People. But they did not celebrate my coming home. They did not know who I was for a long time. I could not talk to tell them. I was sick and tired and only wanted to sleep for many suns. I could not remember my name. Then I found that my family had been killed in a raid and I had no close relatives to look after me. No one to hunt meat or get hides for me. I took what was left over or what was thrown my way. I closed my heart and mind to the People. In my mind I lived with *him*. And I do not even remember *his* name. Now I am old, and I am going back near *his* village. I do not fight it; I do not look forward to it. They will not know that I was there among them once. So now it is time for me to wake up and use my knowledge to help my friends. This is my work."

She looked at her friends with blazing eyes. Her hands reached out to them as a benediction.

"Oh, Moon Woman," cried Fish Woman, jumping to her feet and reaching out toward her friend. "If we'd only known. But you never said a thing. I can't remember any stories about you. Only that you were always so shy and quiet and never laughed with the others. You made your own tepee, and I never wondered much why, I was always so busy with my own man and my work." Fish Woman babbled on and on quietly beside Moon Woman. Moon Woman smiled kindly at her.

Willow Bud edged over beside Grass Child. "I'm going to get back to the People." She whispered so no one might hear. "Eat and become strong and you go with with me, maybe tonight."

"*Ai*, but I cannot make it," whispered Grass Child. Still, she began to nibble slowly at a heat-dried rib with stringy meat.

"That is a horse that would no longer walk," said Willow Bud. "It will give you strength."

"*Aaagch*," replied Grass Child, but she continued to gnaw.

"We will wait until the skunks sleep. We will take two horses and ride back to our village."

Grass Child felt calmer. This was a good decision. If Moon Woman could walk back, surely they could ride faster. And even nonrecognition among the People was better than the unknown agony that lay ahead.

Because there were no robes and the blue blanket had been taken away, they all lay close together for warmth. Grass Child was always made to lie beside Buzzard Beak. On the other side of her was Willow Bud,

then another Minnetaree, then Water Woman with
Drummer and Blue Feather, then a Minnetaree, and
so on.

Buzzard Beak smelled of horse sweat and body filth,
so Grass Child tried to pull away and lie closer to Willow Bud, but he only pulled her closer to him. She felt
nauseated but held it down because it was warm inside
the encircled arms of her mother's murderer.

Sleepily she wondered where they had tethered the
horses. A quarter moon rose over the meadow, giving
very little light. That was in their favor, she thought,
and snuggled further into the strong arms of Buzzard
Beak, who breathed deeply through his mouth, making
a *swish-swash* sound like trees scraping together in a
strong wind.

Grass Child remembered hearing that "Men who
snore on the warpath can never go far with other braves,
nor a man who sneezes unexpectedly." Such men were
in the class of horses that stumble. Maybe Buzzard Beak
was not so much respected among his people after all.

Grass Child awakened to a kick on her behind. It
was not yet dawn, but the Minnetarees were up and
preparing for the day's march. She had slept too long.
Willow Bud had not wakened her. While the Minnetarees were eating raw horse meat, Grass Child looked
for Willow Bud. Had she gone alone? Had she actually
escaped? No one seemed aware of anyone absent. Where
was Willow Bud? An acute loneliness engulfed Grass
Child.

All morning she rode, staring at the sweating brown
back of Buzzard Beak as he led her horse. The spring
sun seemed like midsummer to Grass Child. She began
to think of the Ninambea, who were known to the
Shoshonis as elfin people with an evil disposition. These
miniature men lurked in the dark recesses of mountains and looked eagerly for a chance to shoot arrows
of misfortune at the Shoshonis who displeased them.
She recalled all the times she might have displeased
the Ninambea. The only way to be safe from these little
men at night was to be in tepees, which the little men
could not enter. Maybe the Ninambea had shot all of
them full of arrows of misfortune. This miserable bobbing up and down on a frothing, perspiring horse, head-

ing for the village of a strange people, and Willow Bud
gone, was surely misfortune. To add to her predicament,
she was afraid to speak to any of the Agaidüka women
about Willow Bud, even though she knew for certain
that their captors would not understand. She longed for
the self-confidence Willow Bud always managed. She
longed to talk with her at the end of this long day's
ride.

At last the Minnetarees stopped for camp, and Grass
Child waited for an opportunity to ask about Willow
Bud. No one had mentioned her name. Scar Face suddenly stood before Grass Child. Rage ignited his face.
Poising his quirt above Grass Child's head, he brought
it down so hard that she fell to the ground. Again and
again he raised new welts across her thin, aching back.

The Agaidüka women and small boys huddled closer
and closer together, no one daring to cry out or come
to Grass Child's rescue. At last Scar Face seized her by
the arm and talked with signs. He wanted to know
where the other girl-child and his spotted horse were,
or she would get more beating. Would she like that?
Grass Child cowed to the earth and shook her head no.
He indicated that he wished her to make signs to tell
what she knew. Her hands shook as she raised herself
and explained that she did not know anything about
his horse. Two riders came quickly into the camp, dismounting near Scar Face and waving their hands back
and forth in front of them, indicating: all gone, disappeared. These two had been sent out to find the run-
away. But the girl was nowhere—gone. Willow Bud
had escaped, and there was no way to know if she would
find the People and tell them where the Minnetarees
were headed so rescuers would come, or if the wolves
would find her first. With that thought, Grass Child
gave in to her pain. She was little comforted by Pine
Woman's sudden, long, deep-throated death howl; it
climbed to a shrill crescendo. Fish Woman joined her
in the wailing song of Agaidüka women mourning for
a loved friend.

A lump grew large in Grass Child's throat, and she
could not swallow, nor could she spit it up. The wailing
of the mourning song pounded with deadening anguish
inside her head.

"All right," Water Woman said. "Shut your mouths. Dry your eyes. Our captors now believe we think the child is dead. Let us not speak her name again. Let us pray to the Great Spirit that she arrives in the village of the People in good health. There is something to be done here. We must put balsam pitch and bear's oil on those welts of Grass Child's." Her voice, calm as ever, was heavy with sudden fatigue. Now they could all think of Willow Bud going home to the People, with no fear that the captors would send out more scouts to hunt for her. Grass Child felt an overwhelming gratitude toward Fish Woman and Pine Woman. From the quietness around her, something emerged through her fear, an impulse like love for these women.

Two days later, in a misty rain, they angled down a long slope aiming to the right, toward the river. There was a wide trail worn by wandering buffalo, and the avenue of elk and other hoofed creatures. Grass Child no longer cared where they were, or that Scar Face continued to torment her, even though Buzzard Beak had given her water and protected her at night, wrapping her in the blue blanket. She was dizzy from pain and loss of blood, and she seemed to be riding through cold mist. She was nauseous. Nothing seemed real.

"Grass Child, are you sick?" The voice sounded a great way off. It was Water Woman. Grass Child nodded. There was no use denying it.

"Hold tight to your insides. Open your eyes and look way down there by the river. See! Held in a large cage of tall sticks are mounds, like large anthills."

Grass Child opened her eyes and fought down the nausea. Surely, she thought, no anthills are that large. "What is it?"

"The village of the Minnetarees," said Moon Woman.

Buzzard Beak rode up to them and grinned before he nudged his horse with his quirt and galloped faster and faster down the slope.

On a barren undulation the riders let their horses rest. They sat in their sweat, their breath blowing white, as they gazed through the cold mist to the flat, gray-green prairie sloping to the east ahead of them.

A rising breeze came from the northwest; the low

gray clouds of the early spring afternoon moved with
it. Even in the wind's raw breath there was some
warmth, and the women began to feel an impending
excitement.

The men sent a young warrior ahead to inform the
village that they were coming in, and the captives
watched in fascination as they prepared for their return
home. The men smeared their faces and bodies with the
black-and-yellow stripes of paint. They rubbed the horses
with bunches of dried grasses and polished their lances
and rusty flintlocks. Buzzard Beak circled the three
long furrows Grass Child had clawed into his face with
vermilion paint, as though he were proud of his wounds.

Then the Minnetarees cried out to each other and
broke into long yells and whoops that rang over the
prairie. They dug their heels into the flanks of their
tired horses and hurried them toward the village.

The huge village consisted of hundreds of rounded
earth huts standing close together in a circular pattern.
In the dim light of the gray afternoon they looked dark
and depressing. Smoke hung in pallid clouds over the
flat rooftops, forming a low-hanging cloud over the entire village. Beyond the encampment, outside the closely
placed skinned posts that formed a sort of fence around
the village, horses grazed in large herds, speckling the
gray prairie. Just inside the fence, near a small creek,
lay a meadow and several thickets of willows. This
meadow was not like any Grass Child had seen. Fresh
green leaves were growing in it everywhere; some
seemed a lighter shade of green than others, and these
grew in patterns of straight lines, row after row. She
paused to look, but Scar Face flew by, striking Grass
Child's mount across the hind legs, and the child was
almost unhorsed as the beast lunged down the slope
after the others.

As they rode closer, Grass Child saw brush arbors
and fires and tied horses and many women and children
among the earth huts. The smaller children, up to the
size of Grass Child, wore nothing. Their skin was smooth
and deep brown.

Some of the women began singing, a chant of the
strangest nature Grass Child had ever heard. They were
not singing the same song. Each seemed to be rejoicing

in her own manner at the return of the men. They pulled open the huge picketed gate and let it swing wide as the horses rode through.

Grass Child thought the women hideous. They wore dark deerskins with fringes along the sides of their short skirts, and elk's teeth and pink shells dangled from their ears and on their tunics. Some of the women were bare down to a short fringed skirt, with beads around their throat. Their coarse, straight black hair was chopped and uncombed. The insides of their ears were filled with vermilion paint. They looked as if they never used the river for bathing, and smelled like it, too. But the joy on their broad faces was unmistakable.

Grass Child was pushed from her horse, and she fell to the ground on hands and knees. Buzzard Beak had pushed her. She was taken to stand with the other captives. The Minnetaree women were shouting things she did not understand. One naked Minnetaree child picked up a handful of dust and flung it into the face of little Blue Feather. He coughed and clung to his mother.

"Stop that!" Grass Child told them. "He didn't do anything to you. He's only a papoose."

They laughed, and one of the larger boys took the little boy into the crowd of *kiyi*-ing women.

"Stop him," called Water Woman. "He's my baby." They only yelled and screamed back.

Too weak to resist, the captives were pushed into the center of the encampment. They were between lodges that were elbow-to-elbow, and the spaces between were not clean. Animal and vegetable refuse in every state of putrefaction was scattered about. Grass Child thought of her own clean village, kept all the cleaner by moving to a new camp each winter and summer. She held her nose to show her distaste of the smell and to keep out the slow black smoke that breathed out of the smoke holes and bit her lungs.

The Minnetaree squaws led the horses, grunting and jabbering and pointing. Water Woman carried Drummer and grabbed for the hand of Grass Child as she stumbled into one of the trenches that were dug around the outside of each lodge to guide off the rain. "Keep your head on," she whispered. "I can see Blue Feather being carried by a young squaw. She is gentle with him."

Grass Child noticed that the doors on the lodges were made of rough wooden planks tied together and painted blue, red, or yellow.

The smell of spoiled meat was everywhere. Ferocious-looking dogs came out from behind the huts to look at them. Their long red tongues dripped saliva upon the hard, damp ground. They barked and slunk away when the party came near them. It came to Grass Child that these animals lived only to devour the offal tossed behind the lodges. They were not pets.

More squaws and naked children ran to join them, yelling and laughing. Big boys scooped up fresh horse droppings and pelted Grass Child and the Agaidüka women. Girls ran toward them. Grass Child felt the wetness of their spittle on her bare face and arms. They crowded and quarreled to get a closer look or to touch her, then fell away laughing.

Grass Child felt their behavior unbearable, and she began to withdraw inside. This feeling she had experienced several times lately. She said to herself, "I am one of the People. I am an Agaidüka." She walked proudly and pretended to ignore them and their uncouth actions.

Somehow she became separated from Water Woman, but she kept going with the crowd. There was no way to stop. A woman with a baby at her bare breast jabbed a finger into the side of Grass Child and shouted vituperations down at her face.

The procession was now in the heart of the encampment, where there was a huge flat area with a Council Lodge at one side facing the rising sun. Grass Child had never seen so many people at one time. The people nearest her shouted wordy abuse and shook their fists threateningly. She continued to ignore them, but she was filled with apprehension. What were they going to do? What more could happen to her?

She shivered as the northwest wind grew keener. It seemed to forget spring, and to speak only of imagined fall and the onrush of winter. The small boys of the village had put on fringed leggings; the women had drawn robes over their shoulders. The horses swung their tails in the wind, waiting patiently, subdued, with bowed heads.

Suddenly Scar Face lined himself between her and the last remnants of daylight that seeped in through the crowd. He stood there, maybe two man-lengths away, silent for a moment. Then he laughed deep in his throat and began to talk. Grass Child could see his even, white teeth. She could not understand what he was saying. He began to use his hands to make signs. A circle with his index finger and thumb, then the other index finger pointing at the circle, then moving inside it.

"Do not answer," said Fish Woman, coming out of the crowd.

Grass Child thought he was indicating something about eating. She had been without much food too many days. She did not feel hunger, only pain and weakness and a desire to sleep.

The men were forming a circle around the fire. Several women brought sticks and laid them in the shallow pit where the fire glowed. Grass Child and the women were pushed roughly to one side. Their wrists and ankles were bound. Scar Face bound her hands so tightly her fingers went numb.

People ambled past to stare at them, then leave. Something Good nuzzled Moon Woman and sobbed quietly. Grass Child's mouth began to water. There was a wonderful smell in the air. Over the fire hung an iron kettle, and choice pieces of meat were being roasted, filling the air with a fragrance she had almost forgotten. She breathed deeply. The men seated in the circle passed the pipe, as in a council meeting. But they ate instead of talking, digging their fingers into the kettle and making many slurping sounds. Even so, Grass Child's mouth watered.

When the men were done, the Minnetaree women ate, crowding around the kettle, pushing and shoving. Another kettle filled with food was brought, then another, and another, so that they all might be fed.

A short woman with fat legs came through the crowd, and the villagers moved aside to let her pass. She stopped in front of the prisoners with a broad wooden plate heaped high with chunks of steaming meat and fat yellow seeds. Grass Child fell to the business of eating as

noisily as her captors. She bent over the plate on the
ground—the bindings on her hands did not stop her
from using her mouth. She finally looked up. The four
Agaidüka women were staring at her. Then Water
Woman laughed, knelt down, and began to shove the
plate down toward her boys with her chin. The boys
sucked up the stringy hunks. Suddenly Blue Feather
was lifted up. A young woman was holding him close
and nuzzling his neck while making soothing sounds.
The strange young woman then plunked the baby down
in the lap of Water Woman and untied her wrist bindings. She whispered something Water Woman could not
understand. Water Woman rubbed the warmth back
into her hands. The stranger broke off hunks of meat
for Drummer and the other two boys, indicating that
Water Woman should nurse the baby, Blue Feather.
She spoke again and slipped away.

When Blue Feather was asleep in his mother's arms,
Grass Child moved beside Water Woman, who loosened
her tight wrist bindings. She loosened the bindings on
Moon Woman so she could help Small Man and Something Good eat more of the warm, sweet yellow seeds.

Grass Child wondered at the seeds. They were so
good, so different from the parched corn used by the
men on the trail. Soon her stomach felt full, nearly
bursting. All the women ate the yellow seeds and remarked at their goodness.

"The People should have these," said Fish Woman,
her mouth full. "They would taste fine with the wind
howling outside the tepee."

Suddenly Grass Child felt as though she were being
swallowed by her own stomach. Her hands and face
were cold and clammy. The tightness at the pit of her
stomach grew to a swollen ball that suffocated her. She
was afraid to open her mouth for fear her insides would
break apart. She could think only one thought: Nothing
could be the same. The Agaidükas had lost their great
chief. Grass Child could not say the name of her mother
or father aloud to anyone. She was now no one. The
captors did not know she was the daughter of a great
chief; they did not even know her name.

Suddenly, involuntarily, her mouth flew open and
she heaved. The half-chewed yellow seeds lay sour on

the ground. As the heaving subsided, she felt anger and fear of these kidnappers who spoke words that made little sense. She crawled to the other side of her group. Water Woman clicked her tongue and impassively pushed dirt and pebbles over the fermenting discharge, all the while holding her breath.

Grass Child's sadness returned, but it was mixed with the pride of being Shoshoni. She vowed to conduct herself in a manner befitting the daughter of a great Agaidüka chief.

Grass Child raised her loosely manacled wrists and dropped her arms around little Blue Feather and hugged him. Then she leaned toward Drummer and gently nudged him with her chin and nose. His eyes opened wide, and he smiled when he saw it was Grass Child.

In the cold darkness a guard forced the Agaidükas to their feet and led them beside the great council fire. The warmth slowly edged through their stiff bodies.

Directly in front of the huge fire sat the chief sachem, titular head of all the Minnetarees, and his family. He was very old, his face as wrinkled as a dried apple, his graying hair piled in a spiral on his head. The Minnetaree women chanted one word, "Omsehara, Omsehara."

Moon Woman whispered, "That is Black Moccasin. He is chief of all the Minnetarees. His word is law. People jump when he speaks. Not like the People, who can rule themselves. These people have someone tell them when to plant seeds, when to hunt, when to sing. This chief makes a fence around his people."

Swaying to the chant, Black Moccasin stood. He spoke slowly so that all his people might hear and understand. His voice was strong and confident. It came from deep within his chest, and it seemed that he was kept alive by his heart that refused to grow old. He spoke two names. Moon Woman again whispered, "They are warriors who did not return from the hunt. They were killed in the Agaidüka raid."

The women of the two warriors immediately mourned them in high, shrieking cries that could be heard throughout the entire village. The warriors' names would not be mentioned again by anyone, since it was also taboo for the Minnetarees to speak of those an-

nounced dead. Yet their women and families might
mourn them for many years.

Black Moccasin then brought his people good news.
There were many new, beautiful horses in their herd.
The fine horses of the Agaidüka Shoshonis. And besides
that, there were four Agaidüka boys to replace the two
warriors. There were five women; he showed them by
holding up the fingers of his right hand. In time, these
women might be taken by men of the People of the
Willows and bring good warriors into the tribe.

Moon Woman whispered her translation as best as
she could remember the language. Water Woman kept
shaking her head up and down to indicate she understood perfectly well what he was saying if Moon Woman
would keep up her explanations.

The Minnetarees shouted their full agreement with
their tribal leader with *"Ai!"*

The fire showed in his face as old Black Moccasin
called out the names of those who would care for the
little Agaidüka boys. His choice was made carefully.
He gave Something Good to a couple who had lost two
boys with winter sickness. Something Good held his
little back straight and his chin high, just as Grass
Child had told him, when his new family came to take
him to their lodge. Little Man clutched tightly to Moon
Woman's fingers as he was pointed to by the old chief.
A middle-aged warrior with many scars running down
his neck grabbed Little Man by the arms and swung
him high for the crowd to see. Finally he had a son.
Before this there were only girls in his lodge.

Suddenly the chief pointed to Drummer. Water
Woman whispered something to her elder son and
pushed him toward the old man. The boy did not whimper, but held his face straight and fixed his eyes on the
old man. Back at the center fire, with Drummer at his
side, the chief began a speech.

"Speak up. What is he saying?" asked Water Woman.

"I cannot be sure. I think he wants Drummer for
himself," answered Moon Woman.

"Why would he want a papoose like mine? Should I
claw his eyes out?"

"Be still. If your mouth keeps barking, I cannot hear

what he is saying. I think he wants your other son, also."

"You do not tell it straight! He cannot want two babies. You are a wart-faced toad!" Water Woman was beside herself with fear of the unknown thing to happen to her babies.

Slowly, Drummer was walking back to the prisoners. The crowd became silent. The boy put his hand on his little brother and pulled him to his feet; then, part dragging him, part toddling, he brought him also beside the chief. The four Agaidüka women huddled together in fear of what was to come next. Grass Child could not control her shivering.

Black Moccasin called out a name. The people became alert, and every eye was on the young woman who stood beside the chief, cradling little Blue Feather in her arms.

"That is the same vulture that had the boy in her arms earlier," hissed Pine Woman.

"Shut your mouth," snapped Moon Woman. "I want to hear what they say."

The chief had moved to one side so that all the people could see the young woman with the baby in her arms. A deep "*Ooooooo*" went through the crowd. They approved. The woman held the child up for all to see that she now had a son of her own. Two sons of her own. She pushed Drummer in front of her. Her face reflected her joy.

"That is the old chief's youngest and favorite wife," translated Moon Woman. "Her name is Sunflower. It is known that he is beyond the age of giving life to children. It would be considered a great shame upon this chief if any of his wives bore a child fathered by anyone but himself. But these people recognize it as a great thing if an old man and his young wife adopt a child, two children."

Water Woman sobbed quietly, her arms around Grass Child. Pine Woman and Fish Woman sat with their heads bowed, moaning softly.

"The young wife is whispering something to her husband," said Moon Woman with surprise. "I cannot remember that women are allowed so much freedom here. She does not have good manners at all. The chief is

smiling at what she has said and nodding his head. You
don't suppose he takes orders from her? *Pagh*, what a
weak old man. Not really fit to be chief, I'd say." Then
Moon Woman stopped. She stood on her tiptoes. "It is
strange," she continued. "The people around the chief
look displeased at something. Not at what the woman
said, but at something the chief said."

Soon all the Minnetarees were chanting, "*Eeeech,
eeeech, aaaagch*," in disapproval.

"What is he saying now?" ventured Grass Child.

"He is explaining that he does not need another
woman as long as he has the young one, Sunflower, and
his other women to keep his lodge neat and cook his
meals. He is shaking his head no. He is glaring at the
young woman, Sunflower. He says his word is law and
final in this matter."

"That's how it should be," snorted Pine Woman.

"Wait," continued Moon Woman. "He raises his hand
for silence. The woman called Sunflower is smiling; she
holds Blue Feather gently so he can see the chief. The
chief is now holding Blue Feather."

"That's enough to make that baby cry," sniffed Fish
Woman.

"He cradles the baby and sways to and fro. He is
talking. He says he wants a woman. No, it is not he,
but the baby who needs a woman. His woman, Sunflower, is not able to nurse her new baby, and so in
order to please this Sunflower and his new son, he wants
to take in his tepee the mother of the baby."

"Me be one of his women!" Water Woman stood up.
"Oh, no! I'd rather have death."

A warrior motioned for Water Woman to follow him
to the chief. She went, cowed. Not another word was
heard from her lips as she stood beside the chief, her
face still as stone.

The young wife, Sunflower, smiled as she placed Blue
Feather in Water Woman's arms and pushed Drummer
close beside his own mother.

A cheer went up from the crowd.

"She is to be a slave in his household, taking care of
all the children," said Moon Woman. "I think she will
soon find her darkest moment to be her brightest."

Another cheer went up from the crowd. They could

understand that. A slave to take care of the children. Yes, their chief had good use for that now.

"A slave!" sobbed Pine Woman. "How horrible!"

"Wonderful," said Moon Woman, with tears spilling down her cheeks. "She will not mind being a slave when she can raise her own children. Her work has just begun. These people do not like to see young children separated from their mother. A child needs his own mother's milk to make him strong." Quickly she wiped her face dry with her fingers and stared stoically into the flames.

"Their own mother to care for them," Grass Child repeated.

CHAPTER

4

Bird Woman

The five river villages, two Mandan, two Minnetaree
(Hidatsa), and one Wetersoon (Amahami) at the head
of the Missouri River used a round boat, built like a tub,
of raw hide stretched under a frame of willow. Women
carried the boats on their head from the lodge or storage
place to the water and back again. They stood in front
and propelled the tub by dipping a paddle forward and
drawing it to them instead of paddling by the side.

This is exactly the technique employed by the men in
Wales today who use a small round boat, called a coracle, made in the same manner, for fishing. The paddle
made by the American Indians of the river villages had
a claw at the top of its loom, which was identical with
the type of paddle used on the River Teifi in Wales today.

With this sort of navigation, both men and women of
the upper Missouri were very expert. In summer they
killed buffalo, made round boats of the hide, put the
meat inside and paddled their boats home. Fifty, sixty,
or a hundred tubs could be seen, all loaded, each manned
by a single paddler, plying its way, even in a high wind,
against the rapid, dangerous current of the Missouri.

RICHARD DEACON, *Madoc and the Discovery of America*.
New York: George Braziller, 1966, pp. 224–26.

It was evening in the Minnetaree big Hidatsa village. Moon Woman, Pine Woman, and Fish Woman had each stood before the old chief and then been led off to an empty lodge that had once belonged to a family that had all died of dysentery. The women had not been given to any specific family, but would serve as general servants to the entire village. They would remain this way for the rest of their lives unless traded to another tribe or chosen by a brave to take a place among the other women in his lodge and become like them, no better, no worse.

Grass Child's pinched, worried face had lost its scowl. She was more relaxed. Surely her fate would be the same as the women's, a general slave in the big Hidatsa village. That could be endured. So, to make certain the nearsighted chief thought she was truly a woman, the child grabbed handfuls of dried grass and turned from the firelight to stuff the wads down the front of her loose-fitting tunic. It was her turn to approach the ceremonial fire.

The old chief shifted his feet and stared with his near-sightless eyes from his great moon-shaped face, all furrowed with folds of dry skin. The chief's hands were energetic as he called for one of his braves. Grass Child was startled to see Buzzard Beak step forward. He proudly held his flintlock and lance above his head. Grass Child tried not to look at the neat black braid that swung in the firelight from the stock of the flintlock with two other tiny tufts of shiny black hair. The story of the raid was retold. The crowd listened with a kind of quiet frenzy. Their eyes flashed and their fists clenched as Buzzard Beak relived the battle again.

As another bronzed brave took up the story, Buzzard Beak moved away; and someone pushed Grass Child forward, so that she stood facing the old chief. The bronzed brave pushed up his flintlock for all to see the scalp lock dangling at the butt. A red feather was twisted in the long hair. Only one man that Grass Child knew had worn such a red feather in that twisted manner—

73

Chief No Retreat. She felt her insides rise to her throat, and the darkness enveloped her.

The young squaw, Sunflower, lifted her up and tried to comfort her. At that moment there was no one who could offer comfort. A large hole had been torn inside Grass Child. Was anyone left of her blanket? Had her two brothers and older sister shared the same fate?

Buzzard Beak grabbed at Grass Child's shoulders and spoke sharply to her. She shivered uncontrollably: urine slid unchecked down her legs. Seeing her father's scalp lock had been too much; her head swam. Chief Black Moccasin beckoned, and she regained some composure. She remembered the grass wads inside her tunic and held her chest out tight against them. "I am woman of the Agaidüka," Grass Child said in Shoshoni, fighting down her fear, trying to keep her voice relaxed and even.

"Umph," said the chief as his hands began their slow descent over her skinny body, over her chest. Her heart skipped, but the grass did not slip. It was almost over, she thought. Now they would take her to the lodge. Chief Black Moccasin was making an announcement to the crowd and they were yelling in approval. Grass Child began to understand. She was not to go with the other captives. She was to be a gift from the old chief to one of his honored warriors, Buzzard Beak.

The chief began to pass Grass Child over to Buzzard Beak, then stopped and gave her a fast, sharp slap in the belly. Her stomach and chest caved. She vomited the meat and corn she had eaten earlier in front of her feet, spattering the wads of grass that fell from her tunic. After retching, she hung her head in shame.

The old chief smiled, and the folds of flesh around his chin quivered. His laugh was deep and hearty. Buzzard Beak whooped and jumped up and down. The Hidatsas slapped each other on the back and guffawed. It was a great joke. She was now fully accepted as a member of the Minnetaree tribe, of the big Hidatsa village, of the People of the Willows.

· It was smoky in Buzzard Beak's lodge. He pulled his horse inside first, then came back and led Grass Child past the horse that stood in the narrow entry passage, about the length of two grown men. She was shivering, although the round earth lodge was overheated. A sharp gust of wind blew smoke back down the smoke hole. Her eyes stung. She could no longer stand on her shaky legs, so she fell onto the dirt floor. She was aware that her hair was matted with dirt and sweat. Her body was covered with scars, scabs, and half-healed welts from the quirt lashings. Her tunic and body smelled strongly of urine. She was feverish and thirsty. She was unable to focus her eyes on the people moving in and out of the faint light of the fire.

In the morning she was awakened by shouting. It was one of Buzzard Beak's women, called Talking Goose, a short woman with fat legs, a fine cook, but possessed of a tongue that made everyone quake. She was stirring the fire with a peeled willow stick and yelling for the other woman Buzzard Beak supported, Antelope, to put on the iron pot of stew. Antelope, the younger woman, good to look at, skilled with her hands, sat on the dirt beside Grass Child. Her cool hand was on the child's feverish cheeks.

Slowly Grass Child looked around the lodge at the curtained compartments against the walls of the big room. These were for sleeping. On pegs were finely tanned and decorated skin garments, weapons of war and hunting, and a medicine bag. On posts fixed in the ground in the small space between two sleeping compartments was an elaborate headdress made from the woolly black head and horns of a buffalo. Grass Child did not know the significance of all the things she saw. Drowsily, she felt a huge curiosity about her captors. Antelope dipped her fingers in a nearby clay pot of water and wiped them across Grass Child's parched lips, cheeks, and forehead.

Grass Child awakened suddenly from a sharp slap on her bottom. She cringed, blinking her eyes. The sky was blue, and the sun shone through the smoke hole. Catches Two—the tribe called Buzzard Beak by the name of Catches Two because he had two women—pulled her from the sleeping compartment and pushed his flintlock against her chest. Grass Child wondered if he were going to shoot her, but her body did not stiffen in fear; she could not muster up any emotion so strong.

She wished he would shoot quickly; she was so tired; her legs ached and folded involuntarily. Catches Two lowered the gun, chuckled, and kicked Grass Child so that she lay sprawled on the dirt floor. She was curious about him but unable to move or ask what he planned for her. Exhaustion was overpowering, and she was beyond doing. Catches Two placed the charge in the barrel. Grass Child watched steadily as he poured powder into the muzzle, dropped a lead ball in, and forced even more powder down with a ramrod. He grunted and put the cold barrel against Grass Child's hot forehead and fingered the trigger. Her eyes closed and she thought of cool spring water. The trigger snapped. The cock, pushed by a spring, moved forward in a tiny arc. The flint, held fast in the cock, glanced against the blue steel, and a shower of sparks dropped into the priming pan. But there was insufficient priming powder and the flash did not penetrate to the powder in the barrel. The gun did not fire, and Catches Two tossed the weapon aside disgustedly.

Aware that the child was really sick, he gave another grunt and, slinging the numb Grass Child over his shoulder, took her past the horse in the narrow entry passage and out into the morning air. Antelope was nearing the entrance with water in a turtle shell. She pressed it against Grass Child's lips as Catches Two held her upright. Her throat was swollen and sore; to swallow was agony. Antelope indicated that Catches Two should put her back in the sleeping compartment, that Grass Child was not well enough to be in the damp morning drafts. Mumbling, he slung Grass Child over his shoulder, and took her back inside the lodge. Antelope placed hot, wet skins on the child's head. Over and over she did this. She put bear's oil on the festering lacerations, combed the child's tangled hair with a dried buffalo tongue, washed her stinking tunic, bathed her scrawny body, and coaxed her dry, cracked lips open to let water trickle over her tongue and down her throat. Grass Child slept.

Day after day she stayed on the sleeping couch, too tired and too weak to move except to be taken by Antelope to the toilet place behind the lodge. Antelope watched her with compassion and brought bits of meat

and the fat yellow corn seeds, which she pushed between her lips. Grass Child felt a growing thankfulness
toward this strange woman who showed kindness. One
day she thought of all the things her family had done
for her. She had not thought these attentions unusual,
but as part of her due. Now she began to appreciate
their devotion. Surreptitiously she felt along the drawstring of her tunic for the little leather bag. She felt
the bag to make certain she still carried her totem. The
sky-blue stone on the thin thong had come to represent
the family she no longer had. Now, thinking especially
of her mother, who had given the blue stone to Old
Grandmother, she thought that the greatest kindness
must be that for which the giver gets no reward.

Soon, Antelope and Talking Goose began to give her
small jobs. There was much to do. In addition to Catches
Two and the women, there was Talking Goose's baby
girl, Little Rabbit, her old mother, who walked with an
unexpected, hip-swaying gait, and her old grandfather,
who kept his mouth shut and did very little talking.
Grass Child pounded corn, carried wood and water, and
gradually began to help the women scrape the flesh
from pegged-out buffalo hides. As the summer pro-
gressed, her strength returned, but she did not laugh
and found it hard to be amused by anything. Nothing
seemed right. Her body was too thin and seemed more
awkward than it had ever been before. Her thoughts
were shallow—never of yesterday and barely of tomorrow. She felt constantly tired.

Antelope tried to dispel her depression by teaching
her a few Minnetaree phrases. It was difficult for Grass
Child to adjust her tongue and mouth to the new sounds
and to make the correct accents on nasalized vowels,
although soon she understood enough to know that she
was in the big Hidatsa village, and lower down the
river, called Knife, was another Minnetaree village
called Metaharta.

One morning when she was coming back from the
water hole, Grass Child was stopped by old Black Moccasin. He took her by the arm, peered into her face,
then asked, "Do you like it here?"

She was afraid to answer him. A chief never took
time to speak to a slave, especially a female slave. "It

is not a bad place," he said, touching her head with his knobby fingers.

Antelope had watched this and noted that he had made a sign above the girl's head. The sign of something valuable and worth having, like a prize. Antelope was puzzled because men did not go out of their way to praise women. The old one is getting childish, she thought. But as the days wore on, she noticed that Grass Child had eyes as sharp as the hawk's, and ears as long as the rabbit's.

"Her spirit is as strong as the grizzly," said Talking Goose. "If only we can persuade it back into her face— so we can see it in her eyes."

"Her spirit is gone," contradicted Antelope. "She moves as one in sleep—seeing, hearing, but not planning."

"She is not well yet," said Talking Goose. "When she has more flesh on her bones, you will see someone who will make even the eyes of our man turn. *Pagh!* I will not like her then! Remember how our man said her people were strong-willed and fought hard to keep the hunting grounds for themselves. Our braves could not shoot the buffalo until they had shot some of her people. They were clever at dodging and hiding and knew how to use a bow and arrow with talent. Remember we had two warriors killed that day, and their men shooed the buffalo away so that neither nation could have them. It was a hard fight to capture their horses and a few slaves. Ah, she is strong."

"I have an idea," Antelope said.

Early in the morning, while Grass Child was pounding dried strips of lean meat into a crystalline powder to mix with fat or suet for pemmican, Talking Goose and Old Mother came out to show her the iron cooking pots that Catches Two had traded for hides with an itinerant British Northwester. Grass Child had never seen anything so black and heavy. Antelope was right behind, showing off two large Sheffield steel knives Catches Two had bartered for. Grass Child had never seen anything so sharp. Old Mother went back to the lodge and brought out several fresh-looking elk hides. Chuckling, she pointed out that Catches Two hadn't found these while he was trading, so now they were hers. She put them in the iron pots and poured water over them, placing them in the sun so that during the day the water and hides would become quite warm. Grass Child wondered if they meant for her to work the hides and make pemmican at the same time.

The next morning the women were up before Grass Child. They staked out the hides, flesh side up, on level ground, pounding little wooden stakes through them into the ground every foot or so. The three women fleshed the hides using an elk leg bone that was set in a wooden handle wrapped with rawhide. By the time Grass Child came out to pound meat, most of the fat and tissue was scraped off. The women gossiped and smiled at Grass Child as they washed the smooth hides with soapweed, then rinsed them clean with several pots of water and left them staked in the sun to bleach and dry.

The following morning Antelope had Grass Child help her pull up the stakes and turn the hides over in order to take the hair off with a scraper made of elk antler. It seemed ages ago that Grass Child had used a similar scraper, helping her mother dehair a hide. Grass Child placed both hands on the scraper and pulled in a sidewise movement. Antelope was amazed at the dexterity shown by Grass Child. Even Old Mother and Talking Goose smiled with approval when they brought out the stone hammer.

Talking Goose worked with the hammer first, using short, glancing blows with the back of the stone head. The blows overlapped each other so that every bit of the yellow, horny hide was pounded. Whenever Talking Goose, whose face shone with perspiration, felt her arms would drop off, she made a grimace and handed the hammer to Old Mother.

When finished, the hides were beautifully white. Grass Child ran one hand across their softness and nodded in admiration. Antelope motioned for her to step onto the hide, smiling that it was all right. Grass Child thought that it would make a fine floor covering and wondered if anyone would paint designs on the rugs. Would they go over their bright designs with the juice of a prickly pear whose spines were sliced off, as her mother had done? She could almost see her mother patting the surface with a half cactus, leaving a light protective coating over the painted designs.

Old Mother, whose teeth were missing and whose hair hung in wisps, began to use one of the Sheffield knives to cut the hide around the dusty outline of Grass Child's footprints. Before the sun set the three women and Grass Child each had a new pair of moccasins. They had no special decorations nor drags, but they were snug and comfortable.

Old Grandfather sat in the shade with his back against a pine tree. He watched the women as he chipped small bird points from several large pieces of red chert.

On an impulse Antelope darted toward the lodge. She was back in a few minutes, bringing a clean but well-worn tunic. She held it to Grass Child's shoulders and clicked her tongue over how much of the skirt lay on the ground. Using one of the sharp knives, she cut a wide strip from the bottom of the tunic. Talking Goose grabbed the leftover piece, cut it into several same-width strips, and told Old Mother to braid the pieces together. Finally, Antelope yanked Grass Child's old, dirty tunic off and, before she could object, pulled the clean, shortened one over her head, tying it at the middle with the newly braided belt.

Quickly Grass Child took the leather from her old tunic, opened it, and pulled out the blue stone. She tied it around her neck so that it lay in the middle of the front yoke. Antelope looked pleased.

"Such a pretty thing should not be hidden," said Antelope, feeling the smooth blue stone. "*Ai*, that is something beautiful."

Talking Goose gathered the scraps of skin, all the time planning how each piece would be used in a tunic for Little Rabbit. Old Mother took Grass Child's tattered, outgrown tunic to the back of the lodge and left it on top of the refuse heap. Old Grandfather had left a small mound of wafer-thin chert discards. He carried a handful of bird points and walked silently around Grass Child as though examining the new tunic. His eyes were bright beneath his coarse, shaggy gray eyebrows.

At first she felt strange wearing these clothes, but the tunic was comfortable and slit at the sides, permitting her to take long walking strides. The tunic was longer than her short Shoshoni tunic, and no trousers were made to go with it. Old Mother walked around her, pulling here and there, chattering, smacking her gums together. "Well done, well done," she said. "Good girl. Now work hard."

"I would like to wash now," Grass Child said.

Old Mother sucked in her breath and cackled as though it were some kind of joke. Talking Goose, always sharp of tongue, said, "Time to work, and she wants to bathe. If we let her go, she'll want not only a bath but to sit in the sun and talk to other women as well." Then she managed a smile and pulled Little Rabbit from the skin robe slung around her back as a carrier. She stood the naked girl-child on the ground. "Little Rabbit needs a wash." She squeezed her nose with thumb and forefinger and with the other hand pretended to push away the foul odor of her papoose. Grass Child did not hesitate, but grabbed Little Rabbit's hand and pulled her toward the river.

Little Rabbit was almost two and a half years old, nursed by her mother day or night, whenever she fussed. She was handed soft bits of meat and vegetables any time from the cooking pot, which she ate with relish. Antelope called after the two, "I'm coming! The rest of the sewing will wait for tomorrow!" Talking Goose turned to Old Mother and said something about lazy Hidatsa squaws washing the sweat off before it was there. Grass Child was never referred to as a Shoshoni. She was now a Hidatsa.

There were no palisades on the river side of the village. At the shoreline floated many bull boats, which were used for fishing and crossing the river. Many more of the round, tublike boats were turned upside down on the beach sand. Nearly every lodge had one stored on the top of its mud roof. A row of ball-tipped paddles leaned against a bleached piece of driftwood. Antelope pulled off her clothing and dropped it in a heap, then pulled one of the boats into the water and motioned Grass Child to climb into another. Grass Child sat Little Rabbit beside some bits of sticks and colored pebbles and pushed them around so that the child would play alone for a few moments. Quickly she left her dress and moccasins behind and stepped inside a tub, wobbling back and forth with the circular motion of its spinning on the water. The body of the boat was made of willow bent round in the form of a basket and tied to a hoop three or four feet in diameter at the top. Green buffalo hide was stretched under the frame, the hair outside. The hide was dried and smeared with tallow.

Antelope half stood, half squatted in her boat and made pawing motions in the water with her paddle directly under the boat, which turned half around, then half around the opposite way with the alternate strokes. Grass Child tried pawing the water. The boat spun. She placed the rounded tip on the river bottom and poled the craft. Still it spun. Little Rabbit laughed from the shore. Grass Child began to laugh. The harder she pawed, the faster she spun.[1]

Antelope sprang out of her boat and swam toward Grass Child, dragging her lightweight boat behind. Grass Child laughed and leaped from her boat. The boat was almost impossible to climb into from the water. Grass Child was still laughing as she brought her boat to the shore. She then realized it was the first time she had really enjoyed herself or laughed since she had come to live with these people. Little Rabbit splashed the cool water. Grass Child shivered and ducked into the water again to keep the breeze off. The Knife River was still cold, but not as muddy as it had been before the spring rains had ceased.

Antelope stood in the shallows and marveled at Grass Child's swimming ability. The Minnetarees thought no one else could swim as well as they. Grass Child dived to the bottom and brought up a large clam shell for Little Rabbit. The papoose chattered and rolled in the sand. Antelope told Grass Child the shell's name. Grass Child knew many words now, and could make herself understood in the lodge of Catches Two.

"Tell me what your own people called you," said Antelope as Grass Child sat dripping in the warm sand with Little Rabbit on her lap. "You must have a suitable name. I am tired of calling you Girl."

Grass Child shook her head, scowling. It was taboo for an Agaidüka Shoshoni to say one's own name. A name was something special, unique, and given because of some deed or because it was characteristic of the bearer. If the bearer spoke his or her own name, the goodness or power of the name would be lessened a little. Finally the name would be nothing if the bearer said it many times. So the Agaidüka never said their own names.

Antelope's eyebrows shot up as Grass Child explained she could not tell her name. Then she said, "When you pushed out in the boat, I wanted to call you Boat Launcher. You looked like you knew exactly what you were doing. But when you began spinning around and around and just stood there giggling, I knew that was not right for you."

"A name is something one has for a long time. It is important."

"Well, so, I know that," said Antelope. "My name came when I was older than Little Rabbit. One day I climbed a grassy hill and began running back down. I had not walked in the presence of my mother before. She said I looked just like an antelope loping over the ground with its behind waving in the air. And because of that name I do not walk slowly today, but with hurried, skipping steps."

Grass Child nodded, knowing that a name could affect one's whole life. She told Antelope about a man called Coyote who always played tricks on his friends. "That is because Coyote is known as the trickster among all the animals."

"Now, was he named Coyote because he played tricks, or did he play tricks because he was named Coyote?" asked Antelope.

Grass Child shrugged her shoulders and smiled.

Antelope looked at the girl and wondered how she could give her a fitting name. She was learning there was a whole world of difference between them. She did not really know how this girl had been reared. It took a thing or two now and then, like her wanting to bathe after receiving a new dress, and her swimming with great poise, to bring to mind that this girl had been brought up with favor among her tribe. Antelope had never heard this girl utter one word of complaint at the conditions of her life now. She ate what there was to eat, worked as hard as the other grown women, got

dirty and smelled as high as any of them, picked lice
off her sleeping couch, and kept, mostly, a good heart.
She was ignorant about the Hidatsa ways and didn't
pretend she wasn't. She didn't put on airs about her
learning in other matters, though she had let slip once
that she could sew beautiful patterns with elk's teeth
and quills. She listened, in these present circumstances,
to women who were her betters, but she learned so
quickly she never made the same mistake twice. There
were plenty of girls and women on the prairies who
were slaves with the old grit in them, but they had not
all been beaten and punished, and they took to the life
of a slave without strain. Antelope had to grant courage
to this girl. She didn't know if she could have done as
well. This girl seemed to fly through the day and still
have time for a cheerful song in the evening, much the
same as a bird in the forest.

"That's it!" cried Antelope. "Bird! You ought to be
called Bird."

"Well, what kind of name is that?" asked Grass Child.
"Bird what? What kind of bird? One that chatters or
scolds, or one with beautiful, graceful wings?" And Grass
Child got up from the sand and raised her arms in the
air and ran. "Do you see me running about like this?"
she laughed. Then she dived into the water and pretended she was the long-legged water bird diving for
fish, graceful and sleek.

"Ah, that is it—*Sac-a-ja-we-a*! Bird Woman! You do
look like a bird diving into the water. Sacajawea, that
is your name!" Antelope danced around Grass Child.
Then she turned to Little Rabbit and told her to say
Sac-a-ja-we-a two or three times to hear how it sounded
so Little Rabbit would not forget. Little Rabbit toddled
around and around the two, calling, "Sacajawea, Sacajawea, Sacajawea."[2]

Grass Child felt pleased. She smiled and thanked
Antelope for the gift of the name. It was melodious.
More than that, it was good to have a name to be known
by, rather than just Girl. Sacajawea was not the name
her grandmother had left her, but it was right to have
a new name, for now she was with different people.
This was a more grown-up name. She recalled that many
people changed names as they grew older, depending

upon the deeds they did or what befell them in life. There was Yellow Eagle, who had previously been called Afraid of His Horse until he had shot the great pale eagle and brought the feathers back to decorate war bonnets.

Sacajawea began to rub sand in her hair to take out the rancid grease and soot. She shook it in the water and smoothed it back from her brown face. She sun-dried it to a glossy blue-black. Then she dressed.

More Hidatsa women were coming to the bathing place. They all swam in the bold and graceful manner of the Minnetarees, as confidently as so many otters, their long black hair streaming behind, while their faces glowed with jokes and fun. The evening sun was creeping lower in the sky and the dew was forming on the grasses when Sacajawea, Little Rabbit, and Antelope returned to the lodge.

As it grew dark, Catches Two came from the prairie, where he had played games with some other braves. They had ridden their horses as fast as they could, passing a stick among them. The rider finishing at the designated stopping place with the stick in his hand was left out of the game next time.

"I'm hungry as a bear in early spring," he said.

"No food," announced Talking Goose with a hiss and a dark look toward Sacajawea.

"You lazy squaw. There is plenty of food. Take the winter squash from storage. It is time to use it before it spoils." Catches Two looked from one face to another. The women stared back, their faces blank. "Didn't any of you do anything today?" Again he looked at the women.

"She took a bath," said Talking Goose, pointing to Sacajawea.

"A bath!" He jerked Sacajawea toward him. "And a new dress! You get the squash and boil it fast," he snapped.

Sacajawea looked about frantically. She did not know where the squash was stored.

"She went for a bath, also," said Old Mother, pointing a sharp, ragged fingernail at Antelope. Her mouth bunched. "She knows the grease keeps her warm, but she scrubbed it off today. And she gave a name to our

slave girl. She is now to be called Sacajawea." Her voice
became high-pitched and singsong. "Soon she'll think
she is too good even to fetch water. Her head will be in
the clouds with her namesakes, the birds." Then,
quickly, she turned to Catches Two. "And you—you
played games. You did not go after meat." She began
to scold everyone.

Catches Two flushed and swung about, letting go of
Sacajawea. He snorted, "I am waiting now to be fed."
He sat himself cross-legged by the fire. "If you take
much longer, the squash will sprout mold!"

A shift of wind gusting down the smoke hole blew
up the ashes and made the fire in the pit smoke. Old
Mother scolded the wind for its bad manners, scolded
the fire for waywardness, made the fire tidy, set the
pot of water more firmly, and went back calmly to measuring bits of hide for moccasins for Little Rabbit.

"You are expected to get the squash and prepare it,"
whispered Antelope, her chin indicating the boiling pot.

"But I do not know where." Sacajawea felt the old
fear coming to her throat, making it squeezed up and
tight. "Where do I find squash?" Her voice squeaked.

Talking Goose turned her back on Sacajawea to show
her displeasure, and squatted, her well-padded backside spread on her heels.

Antelope led Sacajawea to the far side of the lodge
next to the sleeping compartment of Old Mother. She
pulled off large hunks of packed dirt and river sand.
Underneath were poles and hides over a hollow space
that had skins around the sides. Antelope pushed the
poles aside so that anyone as skinny as Sacajawea could
squeeze through. Into the darkness she went and blinked
to accustom her eyes to the lack of light. Soon she saw
the huge rounded squash stacked neatly on the ground
of this cache. She pulled out two and, climbing out, felt
their smooth, firm sides. They were orange as the summer sun. Sacajawea replaced the poles and skins, and
Antelope helped push the dirt and sand in place. Talking Goose clucked. She gave Sacajawea a kick just as
she bent to get the squash off the floor. This sent the
child flying, and the squash broke. Again, Talking Goose
scolded.

The broken squash was slippery and hard to handle.

Sacajawea wiped the dirt-soiled pieces on the edge of her skirt, smearing her new dress, and put the squash in the pot.

"You don't put the seeds in the cooking pot, you dumb Bird," snorted Catches Two. "Save those to plant. Dry them in the sun."

Sacajawea reached into the iron cooking kettle to fish out the seeds. She cried out that the water was too hot and burned her fingers.

Little Rabbit began dancing around the cooking pot singing, "Bird Woman, Bird Woman, Bird Woman, Bird, Bird, Bird, Sacajawea."

Catches Two looked up at Sacajawea, who was now seven or eight years older than the toddler, Little Rabbit, and laughed, his strong blunted teeth white against the dark of his face. "The clumsy girl burns her fingers," he said. "You are careless. You are nearly a woman; you should act more like one."

"*Ai*, it is hard to please so many," whispered Sacajawea.

Antelope brought a horn dipper and a leather pouch. "Put the rest of the seeds here. Dried, they are good to eat. Save some for planting, and some for eating."

Old Grandfather snored, and Old Mother reached over his head for the buffalo paunch. One eye of Old Grandfather opened, and he whacked Old Mother and laughed. She thrust his hand away and laughed with him, shoving the paunch into Sacajawea's hands. "More water for the cooking pot."

First Sacajawea stirred the boiling squash with the dipper, then she started for the water hole. Old Grandfather grinned as she walked past him and shot his foot out, bowling her over. She crawled up and scrambled for the paunch. Old Grandfather pinned her arms back. Catches Two let out a long, wild "*Yeeeeiiii, kiyi*." Talking Goose mumbled something, and Antelope slunk off to her sleeping couch, not daring to interfere with the men as they continued to tease Sacajawea. After all, it was up to any slave girl to do the master's bidding.

Old Grandfather heaved chestily and crawled over Sacajawea. She felt her hands sweat and her throat go dry. He pulled down his breechclout. Her scream of horrified disbelief attracted attention, which turned at

once into a general roar of laughter. The next minute
Catches Two imitated Old Grandfather and pulled down
his breechclout and tumbled Sacajawea over in his robes,
wanting her intensely, suddenly. Old Grandfather
pushed him to the floor. Sacajawea whacked the old
man's chest, pummeling him angrily but again he caught
her hands and held her helpless. Her back and legs
hurt; her hands felt squeezed between two stones. Old
Grandfather was heavy against her, and he pushed the
wind from her lungs. Her thighs ached, and a searing
pain went to the pit of her stomach. Then, feeling the
blood warmth in his old bones, Old Grandfather shoved
her away and stood, arranging his clout. Catches Two
heaved himself on her. Her breath came in gasps, and
she felt his hot, piercing fire, the pain spreading through
her buttocks. In another instant she was certain her
breath would be gone; then, suddenly, her breath came
back in small gasps and a great spasm shook the body
of Catches Two.

Talking Goose began to laugh hysterically. It was a
sight to see these grown men entertained on such a
skinny little girl. Sacajawea was resigned to the certainty that she herself would not live through the night.
Catches Two snatched a stick from the fire and began
to run about the room, waving the blazing end and
crying "*Kiyi!*" Old Grandfather at once took it away
from him and threw it back in the fire. Sacajawea inched
her legs up and pushed down her skirt. Her legs moved,
she turned on her side, and slowly, on hands and knees,
she crawled to her couch while the others smacked their
lips over a meal of soft, boiled squash.

There crept over Sacajawea a colder apprehension
than she had felt when she had taken it for granted
that she was soon to die. The threat that now appeared
was more real because it was more familiar.

The Shoshonis did not practice incest—not because
they understood the genetic principles of the inheri-
tance of recessive defects, but because it prevented alliances gained through marrying-out. There was no
advantage in marrying a granddaughter, since a man
would be marrying into a kin group with whom, because
of his previous marriage to the grandmother, he already
maintained good relations. If a man married his own

sister, he gave up all possibility of obtaining aid in the form of brothers-in-law. But if he married some other man's sister, and yet another man married his own sister, he then gained two brothers-in-law to hunt with or to avenge his death in a quarrel. The Shoshonis looked upon incest as something more threatening than repulsive. Incest established no new bonds between unrelated groups; it was an absurd denial of every man's right to increase the number of people whom he could trust. Marriages in the Shoshoni society were alliances between families rather than romantic arrangements between individuals. The alliances between families were maintained during the very long periods in which the families never saw each other. Each family spent approximately 90 percent of its time isolated from other families as it wandered about in small groups or tribes in quest of food. Yet when families or tribes did meet, marriage alliances served to make interfamily relations less haphazard, for kin cooperated with kin whenever possible.

The Minnetarees did not have an aversion to incest. They were not a people that had to range for food, and their camp was permanent, which gave them much security. Incest did not appear to have caused them any deleterious effects from inbreeding. Their people were strong, healthy, and intelligent, and they had survived many generations of sexual contact between mother and son, father and daughter, brother and sister.

Sacajawea could not remember a time when she had wanted a man, although she had heard other girls speak of the desire. But this attack of Old Grandfather and Catches Two was an abomination—she had not been ready, she had not thought of it, and it was as a punishment, a vile hurt. They would come again and again merely because she was not to be considered—she was a slave among these people, and her feelings were of no importance.

By the time the lodge fire was dead, the hurt in her loins had quieted to a dull throb. Sacajawea eased herself from the couch and hunted for the buffalo paunch Old Mother had shoved into her hands as she ordered, "More water for the cooking pot." She found the paunch and crept outside. Her whole body felt bruised.

An animal about the size of a wolf or large coyote skulked in the brush. Sacajawea hurried past the slinking animal, swinging her water paunch. The crackling brush became quiet. She heard a whine or whimper, then the animal was in front of her on the trail. She stopped. It looked like one of the camp dogs, but Sacajawea instinctively knew it was not used to human contact. It cautiously sniffed the ground. She could not move, her thoughts came in slow motion. She saw its eyes—deep amber in the moonlight. Its coat was a grizzled yellow to buff. The tail was dark-tipped.[3]

The paunch slipped from her stiff fingers and rolled on the ground. The dog slowly pounced on it and growled deep down in its throat as it gnawed the rawhide wrapped around the water container's neck. Then its head lifted and its ears twitched nervously. One ear looked as though something had chewed it. There were pinkish patches of bare skin on one shoulder. The dog barked, leaving the paunch, and stood in the center of the dusty trail, moving its head as though catching a sound or smell.

Sacajawea forced herself consciously to breath. She moved her eyes to the side of the trail, looking for a stick or stone to throw at the troublesome wild dog. "Go, Dog!" she whispered.

She breathed deeper and caught the rancid, rank odor of bear. The dog again growled—a low, vibrating rumble. The woods crackled with snapping twigs. With the gracefulness of a huge boulder rolling down a mountainside, a young bear with massive, humped shoulders bolted down the trail in front of them, crashed into the other side of the woods, and sniffed. The sniffing was as noisy as a glacial waterfall whooshing down a long rock embankment. There was a scraping on bark and both Sacajawea's and the dog's eyes widened as the bear stood on its hind legs and raked long, straight, yellow claws two or three times down a fir tree that was black in the waning moonlight. The bear dropped on all fours and loudly sucked something from the chunks of bark. With ease, two golden, half-grown cubs charged through the brush to join their mother in eating the insect delicacy in the peeled bark. In another moment the female and cubs moved away with a light gallop, cracking and popping dead twigs and branches underfoot.

The wild dog began to bark furiously, like a warrior *kiyi*-ing to unnerve an enemy. Then it stopped, sniffed the ground and the fallen water paunch, lifted its leg, and trotted quietly off in the opposite direction from the grizzlies. It never looked back.

Coming to her senses, Sacajawea realized the wild dog had saved her from a deadly mauling. She had been between the female and her cubs, and if that grizzly had moved downwind she would have smelled more than insects in a rotting tree. The wild dog kept Sacajawea from moving. She was grateful. She had a secret helper, a friend. The thought pleased her.

She returned to the creek, filled the paunch, and sloshed cold water over her naked loins to numb the ache. The coldness made her shiver. She noticed blood on the inside of her legs and washed it off.

Refilling the paunch, she took it to the lodge and poured the cold water into the stew pot. She had no appetite for the leftover squash. She blew on the fire and started it crackling, then eased herself back into her robes, exhausted, but waiting for the morning light to come. During these last several weeks she had become an intense and stoic adult, at the precocious age of only ten or eleven summers.

That summer, Sacajawea was given a rake made from reeds curved at the end, separated from each other by interlaced rods, and with the handle bound with leather thongs. Antelope taught her to use a hoe made of the deer's shoulder blade. She learned what "garden" meant. Catches Two had an acre plot of corn, beans, and squash that his women cultivated. Also on the plot the kinnikinnick was allowed to grow wild. This was the sacred tobacco used in the pipes of men, and women were not allowed to touch it.

The plot of each lodge was separated from the others by brush and rocks and pole fences. At times Sacajawea was able to talk with Moon Woman, Pine Woman, and Fish Woman, who worked for those who needed them. They were still public slaves. Seldom did they see Water Woman, except at the women's bathing place. Water

Woman seemed happy enough, and her boys were plump
and laughing. Moon Woman never said a lot, but Fish
Woman and Pine Woman complained about the large
lodge they had to keep clean and the hard work they
had to do each day.

Other women who had been captured also worked
as slaves for their families in the fields. Besides the
Shoshonis, there were Blackfeet, Crows, and Utes. Each
Hidatsa family had from half to one and a half acres
to cultivate.

Sacajawea watched the corn grow from the first two
slender blades. The stalks seldom exceeded two or three
feet in height, and two ears formed near the surface of
the ground. The grain was small and hard, and Antelope told her it was covered with a thicker shell than
the corn raised in warmer climates. They would harvest
about twenty bushels from the acre. When it was still
green, a portion would be pulled, slightly boiled, then
dried, shelled, and laid by in the cellar beneath the
lodge floor. The Hidatsas called this sweet corn. It could
be preserved indefinitely, and if boiled with a little
water, it did not taste much different from that taken
from the stalk.

The squashes grew on large, strong vines. The Hidatsas either boiled these, ate them when green, or
sliced and dried them for winter use. The unbroken
squash could be kept in the cold for several months
before molding. If dried, they were strung and became
very hard—these required an age to cook and were not
Sacajawea's favorite dish.

Sacajawea thought it strange that these people had
to plant seeds in the spring, tend them through the hot
summer, and at last harvest the crops. She thought of
the many plants that grew wild whose roots had been
food for her people. Her people did not plant and tend,
they simply harvested. They harvested what nature
planted and tended for them. They dug roots and picked
berries. But they did not think of planting seeds or
caring for the growing plants. Why should they go to
all that trouble when so much grew wild, thought Sacajawea. Yet these people had food for the winter and
her people never had enough.

Sacajawea hated the back-breaking slavery of gardening. The eternal, brain-numbing monotony made her draw farther into herself for some time. She crawled out of bed at dawn to water the horses, hoe the interminable rows of corn and beans, grub up alders and roots for a fresh field, transport rocks from the fields to the long gray walls around them, pull the sunflowers from the squash patches, rub bear's grease on the tethers of the horses so they would be soft, strong, and pliable, and perform all the chores women were expected to do, or be punished by the elder wife of her owner, Catches Two.

She hated to sit down to her meals, drenched with sweat, too tired to say anything except "More soup." She hated the waves of weariness that swept over her each night. As soon as she had served the men their stew and the women had eaten, she was glad to stumble into her sleeping couch. She hated the nights that Old Grandfather grunted and groaned on top of her, or Catches Two spread her legs and lay between them, playing with her small breast buds, pushing his large erect penis deep within her belly. She endured this and accepted it as something that could be sustained, such as the hot enclosure of the lodge in summer and the leaden slumber that brought surcease from her labors, but no rest.

Some days she had no time to look at and feel the things around her, although they kindled sparks of curiosity within her all day long—the broad, quiet water of the river, running slowly toward the fast white rapids at the river bend, then moving on—where? She wondered about the round bull boats that the men and boys took fishing; the round, clay-covered lodges with rooftops so strong that people could sit on them in the coolness of the evening; the flat prairie with few trees but much fragrant blue sage, whose pungent odor was a constant reminder of her own mother; the clear blue skies and the shadows of morning, noon, and evening. Soon her child's brown hands were so callused and her fingers so stiffened that she doubted they would ever again hold a needle for stitching.

Only one thing made the hatred of this drudgery bearable—the wild dog.

As Sacajawea hoed the beans at the edge of the field

one hot afternoon, she became aware that the mangy
yellow dog was watching her about fifty man-lengths
away. It simply stood there, staring at her. Across the
fence, Moon Woman looked up and threw a well-aimed
dirt clod, which struck the dog's side and drove it howling into the willow brake.

Moon Woman waddled to the fence. "Did it frighten
you?" she asked. But Sacajawea presented her with a
long, direct look, coldly erasing all feelings from her
eyes and face.

"It is an outcast and more lonely than I," murmured
Sacajawea, looking steadily ahead.

Moon Woman dropped her eyes and walked away.
Then, from across the field, she yelled in Shoshoni, "Do
you think it will be a friend to you like the dogs in the
camp of the People?" She jerked her head at the willows.
"Don't get chewed by that scavenger," she warned. "It's
more coyote than dog."

Sacajawea secretly saved scraps of meat and the large
pieces of flesh from hide-scraping to leave at the wood's
edge for the dog. After she had fed it several weeks,
she moved cautiously close to pet it, but it moved away.

Some days she could not get meat to feed the dog,
but it stayed at the edge of the field and watched her
work, anyway. One day as she wearily left the field for
her lodge, the dog seemed disappointed and followed
her, keeping a good distance behind, until she reached
the lodge.

Then, day after day, the dog could be seen following
her at a distance as she went to work and when she
returned from the field. She sometimes spoke softly to
it. "Come, Dog. Come. I have brought you meat." The
dog's tail moved vigorously as it acknowledged her
friendship. Moon Woman kept a heavy stick tucked
inside the bosom of her dress in case the beast reverted
to its savage nature. She never quite trusted the dog.

No one else really noticed Sacajawea in the field,
except to see that she worked. Antelope and Talking
Goose and Old Mother kept the lodge neat and made
the meals and sewed. The two young women looked
after Little Rabbit. Old Grandfather sat by the fire or
in the sunshine, smoking his pipe most of the day, never
saying very much.

The nights began to cool. The cottonwood leaves yellowed and dropped. The days were chilly. The dog still followed Sacajawea as she made her way to work in the field. It stood patiently watching her most of the day. Sometimes it would sneak off into the willows, then reappear when it was time for her to go back to the lodge. One day it lay at the edge of the cornfield and watched her. Its ears were straight up and its eyes were wide open. She was harvesting the small ears, putting them into a deep willow basket.

Suddenly she looked up. Scar Face stood in front of her, a sneer on his lips. "You are finished in the field of Catches Two, and you are to come to my field and pull squashes."

"I do not understand," said Sacajawea. "You are not my master."

"No, but I captured a girl to work in my field and you helped her escape!" he cried, irritated with explanations.

"Then she is not dead?" asked Sacajawea. "Willow Bud is not dead?"

"How do I know?" he asked, moving closer.

"She will bring the People here to find us," she said, looking him in the eye.

"No, too far to come. The Shoshonis never come here. You work now in my field."

She was uncertain what to do. Catches Two had not told her she was to work for the lodge of Scar Face. Surely Antelope would have said something about this.

"I can't go," she said.

Scar Face's broad, flat hand flew through the air. Sacajawea found herself on the ground with the side of her head throbbing. Several of the women, including Moon Woman, who was working nearby, saw what happened next: the dog, looking like nothing more than a flash of yellow, bounded from its resting place and leaped at Scar Face, sinking its teeth deep into the man's leg with an angry snarl. Scar Face fell to the ground, beating at the dog with his fists, but the animal would not release its grip. The women rushed forward and went after the dog with their bone hoes and willow rakes. Moon Woman, using her heavy stick, finally forced the dog to let go. They took Scar Face to the Medicine Man's lodge, where, amidst loud chants and the clanging of gourd rattles, the bleeding was stopped with the fur of a beaver tail, and the wound held together with a sticky wad of spider's web.

Several days afterward in the council Black Moccasin announced that the dog should live. He declared that the dog was the protector of the rights of Catches Two; even though this was an unusual situation, the dog should be left alone.

Scar Face, whose Hidatsa name was Bull Face, left the council with his head down and his face scowling. He was the loser.

One morning when it was too rainy to work in the field, Old Grandfather began to question Sacajawea. She ignored his questions and continued to tend a pot of boiling stew, but she realized how little she really knew about Old Grandfather besides his stale body smell when he was close to her, and his foul, panting breath. Perhaps he was thinking the same thing because he laid his pipe carefully beside his leg and asked, "Did your people have such fine iron cooking pots?" She made no reply, did not even look up. She just went on stirring.

Old Grandfather looked at her squatted down near the cooking fire. He shrugged and let it go. It didn't matter to him. But he wondered at the girl's displeasure. Why was she so angry? What did it matter? Was she angry because he found she brought some excitement to his blood? Sexual activity did not hurt a slave at any age. There were other slaves to be had. There was hardly a big man who did not have two or three, even a dozen in his lifetime. If a man took a female child as a slave, surely it was to be expected. Nobody gave it a second thought. It was nothing. Look at Kakoakis, grand chief of all the Minnetarees; he had many female slaves. And he did many things with his slaves—yelped, laughed, joked, pinched them, whipped them, tied them, gashed them, bit them, licked them—and these women readily worked in his fields without fuss. It was a strange strain in this female to be displeased about what he did in the sleeping couch with her for his pleasure.

"I suppose," Old Grandfather said, "you will want to

learn to make some clay cooking pots and to work the glass ovens."

Sacajawea finished with the stew and threw the wooden ladle carelessly on the ground. It went skidding through the dirt, collecting a mess on its wet sides. Sacajawea pushed up and rubbed her eyes with the backs of her hands. "Why?"

"Well," Old Grandfather began uncertainly. It was obvious. She was worn out from working in the fields. She needed to rest. He said, "You can learn. I'll show you."

"My people made watertight pots from willows and reeds and the long pine needles covered with pitch. They filled these with water and added red-hot stones to boil the water for cooking meat or roots or making herb tea," she said, spilling out the pride of her tribe. Then she thought she had said too much because Old Grandfather did not reply.

But within a few days she was learning to make clay vessels by shaping wet riverbank clay into basketry forms and baking them in the hot fire. Mortars for pounding corn were also made. These pots and mortars were gray-colored and stood fire very well. "If they were painted," suggested Sacajawea, "they would look much nicer." Again, Old Grandfather did not reply.

The dog watched from an alder grove.

On another day, Sacajawea went with both Old Grandfather and Antelope to find fine, clean river sand and to climb the limestone cliff and scrape the special stones from the wall into a basket. The chalky stones were pulverized with a pounding stone, and the powder was mixed with the sand. The mixture was divided evenly among the holes in an oblong clay form. The form was put in a clay oven that soon shimmered with hotness as skin bellows were used to make the fire white-hot. Old Grandfather puffed as loudly as the bellows as he pumped air onto the charcoal flame. Finally Antelope motioned for him to rest. The oven was opened so that the molten glass would cool. The clay mold was broken, and translucent glass beads rolled out. Antelope pointed out that they could be used for game-playing. Sacajawea soon learned to add bits of colored clay to the molten glass and to insert a roll of clay in the center in order to make colored beads. These beads were smooth and brick red, mustard yellow, gray-green, or a dirty blue.[4]

"This is something to take pride in," said Old Grandfather one day. "This is a thing that the other tribes come to us to trade for. We can get the good chalky stone, and if the Utes bring us white sand, the beads are nearly clear. They are something wonderful."

"Blue is my favorite," said Sacajawea.

Old Grandfather looked at her and cleared his throat. "That is a chief's color because it is like the sky with no clouds and like the rivers that run calm and deep." He grunted, then continued, "Like your own blue stone. The one you hide but secretly look at and fondle." His eyes became two pinpoints of fire. "Was your father's tepee in the center of the village?"

Sacajawea was stunned by the blunt question and his knowledge of her precious blue stone, which once belonged to her mother and grandmother. She averted her eyes, keeping her head lowered. She knew he meant "Was your father the chief?"

She ignored his question. "See, the stones I made here are red, but not clear like your paints or the paintbrush flowers. See, there is a bird in them, raised up from the surface. I think it is trying to fly out." She laughed quietly, staring at the two glass stones, which were about the size of hickory nuts. "I would like to make the deep-blue beads. A clear blue would be the most beautiful."

Old Grandfather would not be put off. "Your stone was found among rocks. One like that cannot be made by us. That was left in the rocks many ages past by the Great Spirit, who declared that they were to be used only by great chiefs. Those sky-stones come from a land far south from us." It was the longest speech she had ever heard him make.

Sacajawea found that many of the Hidatsa women made ornaments in the white-hot ovens on the side of the hill. These ornaments were used as beads, earrings, hair and dress decorations. On the way back to the lodge she asked if the rusty red were considered a chief's color also.

"Of course not," laughed Old Grandfather. "Anything you can make at the ovens is not considered bright enough for such a thing. You can wear anything you can make. But never wear your other stone in the open. That bright, clean sky-blue would be a blasphemy to our chief. Your life would be cut off faster than I could cut the head off a river trout."

Sacajawea put one of the red stones inside the pouch with her precious blue stone, and she took the other one to Antelope. "It is because you gave me my name," she explained, her face crinkling a bit around her dark eyes. "See the flying bird rising up out of the glass?"

Antelope was very much surprised. It was not the custom for a slave to give gifts or feel generous about anything.

"It was leftover bits, ready to be dumped on the ground," explained Sacajawea. "I used no one's good sand or paints."

"Get the vegetables well done tonight and put the eating boards in place," ordered Antelope, holding the treasure tightly in one hand. "Talking Goose will be pleased if things are ready when she comes in from visiting her relatives on the other side of the village. Keep your moccasins flying!" Antelope was pleased, yet embarrassed, not quite ready to admit that she would take a gift in friendship from a slave. To cover her confusion, she gave Sacajawea orders all evening.

Old Grandfather watched. "Close up your mouth, my daughter," he said. "Sacajawea does the chores before you have ordered them. She knows you are pleased. To hide it is bad. Accepting a gift cannot be that hard." He did not say more. But something was taking place in his mind. Something had pushed aside a shadow for an instant as if a ghost had walked, a strange wind had blown, a tongue had spoken, and he did not know the language. A young slave girl knew it. It would take him years to learn it. Only those who moved up and above wild animal instincts could ever learn it.

The feeling was as elemental as the gray rocks of the mountain, as the wild water of the canyons, but something more than the animals that haunted the wild places knew. It was an understanding, a giving with no thought of reciprocation, a kindness. It was love. This feeling Old Grandfather experienced did not negate sexual attraction, as that would go against his long, bred-in-the-bone training as a Hidatsa, but it went beyond that. He was left with a deep, intimate, father–daughter attachment to the girl. From that time on he could not treat Sacajawea merely as a sex object.

Old Grandfather could not bring himself to exploit sexually a person he had taught and worked with at the glass-making ovens. Sacajawea was a person he had come to respect and see as an individual. She had a new identity for him now. Through this interaction between himself and the slave girl, he found a companion.

5

The Wild Dog

There is a grave commemorating the legendary dog, Gelert, in the village of Beddgelert, Wales. In 1794 David Prichard, the first landlord of the Royal Goat Hotel (which is still in use), and two friends placed the large stone that now marks this grave on the bank of the Glaslyn River. The marker tells the story:

Gelert's Grave

In the 13th century, Llewelyn, Prince of North Wales, had a palace at Beddgelert. One day he went hunting without Gelert, "the faithful hound," who was unaccountably absent on Llewelyn's return. The truant, stained and smeared with blood, joyfully sprang to meet his master. The prince, alarmed, hastened to find his son and saw the infant's cot empty, the bedclothes and floor covered with blood. The frantic father plunged his sword into the hound's side, thinking it had killed his heir. The dog's dying yell was answered by a child's cry. Llewelyn searched and discovered his boy unharmed, but nearby lay the body of a mighty wolf, which Gelert had slain. The prince, filled with remorse, is said never to have smiled again. He buried Gelert here. The spot is called Beddgelert.

This dog story, also told in Persian, Hebrew, Irish, Hindu, and Buddhist mythology, is a version of an ancient Indian folktale found in the Sanskrit *Panchatan-*

tra, according to the Encyclopedia Britannica (Vol. 10, 1965, p. 55). It is one of those old legends that is moving enough to be told, retold, written and rewritten. At present, no one knows why the North American Mandan Indians had such a tale, which was closely related to the late Welsh version.

While living among the Mandans, Sacajawea no doubt heard the tale. Maybe she repeated it. The dog story in the following chapter makes use of this Welsh theme. It is an interesting tale to use in a historical novel as part of the legend of the unusual Mandans.

Most historians today do not believe the "Welsh Indian" myth—that the Mandans were descendants from the Welshman, Madoc, and his followers. They believe that the Mandans were descended from a branch of the early Sioux. Mandan prehistory is only dimly known and today there are no full-blood Mandans.

The anthropologist Dr. Edward M. Bruner writes that there were nine thousand Mandans in 1750, but after the small pox epidemic of 1837 there were only twenty-three male survivors. The descendants of these people are scattered in mixed Hidatsa and Arikara communities on the Fort Berthold Indian Reservation.

SHOWELL STYLES, *What to See in Beddgelert and How to See It*. Caernarvonshire, Wales: William H. Eastwood, 1973, pp. 9–12, 19–22.

EDWARD H. SPICER, ed., *Perspectives in American Indian Culture Change*, "Mandan," by Edward M. Bruner. Chicago: University of Chicago Press, 1969, pp. 187–277.

Winter was not far off. During the night, the marsh froze hard. For days the sun had fought against the ice. Sacajawea had kept the hope that the Agaidükas would come. Now she listened to the rattle of dry stalks, empty scabbards with summer drawn out of them. Chickadees slid down the stems, and her hope flowed away as the days grew shorter.

One morning she was aware that her lodge was preparing for some big event. Knives and hatchets were being honed on sandstone. Catches Two squatted over the fire, heating, bending, and straightening his arrows. Sacajawea wondered if he were preparing for battle and moved close to Talking Goose, who was nursing Little Rabbit.

"What is he doing?" She pointed to Catches Two, who was sighting along his arrows one by one.

"Going fishing," said Talking Goose. "The bass are in groups now. We will smoke and dry them for trading with the Sioux in the Moon of Storing Squash."

"Trading?" Sacajawea asked.

"*Ai*, you ask so many things. They come and trade buffalo robes, skins, and meat for our vegetables and the fish. It is a time of feasting and merriment. We will have some fun."

That night there was a dance in the middle of the village, with drummers and singers. Sacajawea watched from behind the old people and children. The people were dressed in their regular clothes, and two men came out and danced like fish swimming upstream. A few children imitated them, and the old ones patted hands and nodded to the drums. Sacajawea noticed that not all the village came out to dance for the fish. Only ten or twelve families were going on this trip. She walked back to the lodge and did not see the dog, which followed at the edge of the village. She slept to the monotonous beat of the drums.

The next morning, Old Grandfather said she was to go with them. Only Old Mother was staying behind to care for Little Rabbit. Antelope carried willow nets,

Talking Goose carried spears, and Sacajawea carried
the bows and arrows. At the river embankment they
laid the gear near Catches Two's bull boats. Old Grandfather sat in the sun to smoke his pipe. The other families had also risen before sunrise and trooped out of
the village to the riverbank. Frost made the short grass
slick where it melted in the first rays of the sun.

Catches Two assigned his boats, and, like the other
Hidatsas, they each clambered inside one and began
twirling downriver. Sacajawea stayed close behind Antelope so that she could imitate her actions with the
long pole. The first two craft to reach the bend in the
river hesitated, and their occupants yelled back to the
others to take care, there was white water. The others
held back until the first two had gone down around the
bend and out of sight; then they began fishing. Antelope
instructed Sacajawea to stretch her net over between
their boats, and they rode with it dragging in the water
for some distance. Some of the Hidatsas had already
caught fish in their nets. Talking Goose and Catches
Two had more than a dozen. Old Grandfather had several bass flopping around his feet in the bottom of his
boat.

Sacajawea tensed as her boat rounded the bend and
began to bob down in a stretch of rapids. Some of the
Hidatsa men and women had already leaped from their
boats to swim to shore, dragging the bull boats behind.

Antelope waited until she was close beside Sacajawea's fast-moving, twirling boat, then she flung a rawhide rope to Sacajawea and frantically poled toward
shore. Antelope held tightly to one end of the rope, then
her bull boat suddenly was pulled into a riffle. The little
round boat lurched and overturned. Antelope was
thrown into the water, which was waist-deep; she still
held the rope. She looked around and saw her small
craft right itself in the rapids and bob like a milkweed
pod until it reached a deep, quiet pool and gently float
to the riverbank. Antelope waded ashore against the
pull of the swift water, the rawhide rope digging into
her palm. She again looked back to the middle of the
river where Sacajawea was trying to keep her eggshell-
like craft upright as Antelope pulled it against the current.

At that moment, and without warning, Sacajawea's boat smashed against a boulder that lay hidden just under the water's surface and Sacajawea was thrown into the water. Fragments of the boat floated downriver. Sacajawea came up sputtering, gasping for air, fighting the rapids, trying to find something to wedge her body against, to put her feet against, or to put her hands around. She still had the rope in her hand and it cut into the flesh.

Antelope tried to maneuver Sacajawea out of the swift water, to get her closer to the riverside into a quiet pool she saw that was overhung with graceful willows. Antelope's arms ached, her shoulders throbbed, and her hands hurt from the pull of the rope. Her eyes watered as she ran from rock to rock along the shore.

Catches Two yelled at Antelope to let go the rope. "She is lost!" he yelled. "Don't fight the fast water." Then he turned to Old Grandfather, who was white as bleached bone. "She is only a female, a Shoshoni at that, not worth much."

"Oh," cried Old Grandfather, "Great Spirit, stretch your hand to the child. Help her!"

"Are you dizzy-sick?" asked Catches Two, staring at Old Grandfather. "She is only a slave. *Pagh*, young females are nothing. Come, let us get this other net untangled and catch more fish."

Old Grandfather grunted and turned the bull boat upright in the sunshine to dry. Catches Two twisted the rawhide from Antelope's hand and flung it far out in the water. It floated momentarily, then disappeared. Old Grandfather sighed and seemed to shrink as his shoulders hunched downward.

Sacajawea felt the tension go out of the rope and she felt herself again being carried along by the strong current. To ease the pain in her hand, she tried to loosen the rope a bit, but her movements were clumsy and an unexpected eddy flushed the rope from her fingers. She grabbed. Too late, she saw the rope disappear.

Suddenly the mangy yellow dog, looking more than ever like a half-starved coyote, came from nowhere, jumped into the water, and began paddling. Its head ducked and came up with the rawhide in its mouth; its front paws moved frantically. It seemed to be trying to get to Sacajawea, but both girl and dog were being carried relentlessly downstream and were still far apart. Antelope ran along the gravelly bank shouting for Sacajawea to get to the dog—and the rope.

The shouting was fruitless. Sacajawea stretched her legs downward, trying to find a foothold—a rock, a log, anything. She bruised her knee on a slippery, algae-coated rock that was smooth from years of water charging against it, but she was chilled and the bruise did not hurt much.

The dog was closer now. Its head bobbed in time to the churning of its front paws. She saw the dark rawhide dangling from its mouth.

Antelope's eyes followed the rope upstream and discovered the loose end floating near the willow overhang. She ran to the water's edge, reached through the scratchy brush and branches, hung on to a thick limb, and grabbed for the line as it trailed through the water. All the time she yelled instructions to Sacajawea, but she couldn't make herself heard above the churning of the fast water.

Sacajawea managed to propel herself closer to the dog. Finally she gave several extra-strong kicks, reached out, and with a cold, stiff hand grabbed the short wet fur and loose skin and hung on with white knuckles. The dog opened its mouth and the line slacked and fell out. Sacajawea caught it before it hit the water. The dog blinked. Its head bobbed as it turned and headed for shore. The current pulled faster than the dog could paddle and it rested, letting the current have its way.

The Hidatsas, clearly enjoying this sport, shouted for the dog to resume swimming. Old Grandfather cupped his hands around his mouth and called for Sacajawea to pull herself up the line, to fasten it around a log or rock. The others watched the dog compete against the force of the rushing water, and they made bets about the exact place the animal would come ashore—if it made it to shore at all. The men believed the girl could not hold out, and they made bets about how long she could keep her head above the rapids. The women clicked their tongues, hid their eyes, not wishing to see the moment when the girl slipped under the froth, never to be seen again.

Old Grandfather took the rawhide line from Antelope's right arm where she had wrapped it. He wound it four times around his hand and felt the strength of the pull. Antelope rubbed her arm, which was ringed with deep indentations, to bring the circulation and feeling back and to relieve the tingling. She heard a group of women call out encouragement to the dog, and she watched Sacajawea work painfully and slowly toward shore, moving hand over hand along the rawhide line.

Old Grandfather yelled for someone to help him, and a broad-faced brave with clamshell earrings ran over and also grabbed the rope. Both men now began pulling, and Sacajawea found herself moving so fast through the water that she could not keep her head in the air. She choked and gasped. A shin banged the sharp end of a submerged log, but she was barely aware of any pain. The men's pulling made her feel as though her arms were being pulled from their sockets. She tried to signal them not to pull so fast, but she couldn't raise an arm from the water. Her hands and arms were numb with cold. She tried rolling over on her back, but the water washed over her face; she could not breathe. I am going to drown, she thought. It can't matter if I let go the line. Clumsily she worked to twist the rawhide from her wrist, and finally it slipped off her hand.

Her knees sank and she lowered her feet with no thought anymore of finding footing. It was her knees that touched the gravel bottom. Her head came up and she could breathe. The breaths were shallow, and her lungs felt scorched when she inhaled. Her throat felt raw and sore. It was the *kiyi*-ing barks of the dog that caused her eyes to seek the shore. The dog was standing alone on a sandbank.

A group of men, Catches Two in the center, were below the dog making good their bets. The dog had come ashore at the big red rock. Antelope ran back and forth along the shore motioning for Sacajawea to stand up and walk. Sacajawea raised her aching right arm in answer. She got to her feet, but she was dizzy and her legs were like wilted cornstalks. She put her hands down in the cold water and crawled. At the shore she lay on her back, staring at the clear sky, her chest heaving with hard breathing. Antelope sat down beside her.

"What can I do?" asked Antelope.

"Bring me two, three fish," whispered Sacajawea.

"You want food?"

Sacajawea pointed toward the scrawny, silent dog.

Antelope hissed, "For that?"

"*Ai*," Sacajawea said, closing her eyes.

Antelope came back with two good-sized fish from Old Grandfather.

Sacajawea pushed herself up stiffly and walked on aching legs to the sandbank. She tossed both fish to the dog. It began to tear and chew chunks of fish hungrily.

Some of the Hidatsa shook fingers at Sacajawea, showing disapproval for wasting good food on the mongrel.

Later, Old Grandfather carried Antelope's bull boat over his head until they moved far enough upstream to be out of the white water. Then he put the boat in the water and let Sacajawea curl up in the bottom. He poled upstream along with the others, homeward to the big Hidatsa village. Not once did he complain about his aching arms. Nor did he scold because he could hardly move his feet in the little boat. When he saw that Sacajawea could not control her shivering, he told her to remove the wet tunic, and he took off his dry shirt and wrapped her snugly in it. He never once mentioned the bows and arrows she had lost in the water, nor the fish net, nor the boat she smashed to pieces.

Soon the weasels became whiter and a growth of frost flowers decorated the marsh edge. A small band of Sioux came to trade, their travois loaded with meat and hides. They stayed three days and promised to come back later during the time of the big spring trading fair. The women in Catches Two's lodge worked as they saw fit, going often to visit and gossip with the women in the Sioux camp. Sacajawea went out with the women, but when the dog followed, she felt many eyes on her. When she was sent to return a horse to the herd or to catch another to keep hobbled near the lodge, the dog stayed close by her. From the field, as she harvested the ripening squash, Sacajawea watched the games and horse racing between the Hidatsa and Sioux boys. They rode their horses flattened out like lizards. The older Sioux boys could ride a horse and fire arrows at the "enemy" at breakneck speed, miraculously clearing a series of small rocky gullies without mishap.

The Hidatsas had traded with the Sioux for much meat. Trees, bushes, and meat racks were covered with flat strings of it, drying, turning dark. The lodge of Catches Two had four skins from the Sioux; the hair on them was long, dark brown, shiny. The wind whistled out of the north, and the Sioux left for their winter camp before the first snow fell.

The dog often moved closer beside Sacajawea now. Although he was not allowed in the lodge, he seemed to live most of the time right outside the door, waiting for Sacajawea to come out. She continued to feed him, without Talking Goose's discovering. She had learned to take the food she wanted without asking.

At night when Catches Two came to her sleeping couch, she feigned sleep, and often he moved away to the bed of Talking Goose or Antelope. But one night when he came to her he said that she created a flame in his belly that burned like a prairie fire. His hands ran slowly over her thighs as he said, "I may catch you by the river or the water hole, and you will lay for me each time I ask. You will think about it and feel the same fire."

Sacajawea felt a sickening at the pit of her stomach.

"You are not fat like Talking Goose, or growing with child like Antelope, or old like Old Mother. You should look into the clear water. There you would see what I like—a young girl, barely a woman."

Sacajawea lay very still, afraid to push and kick him, for he would beat her until she lay limp.

"You have an obligation to me, for I captured you and saved you from the white water in the river," he breathed in her ear.

She shrugged and turned away so that he could not see her face in the firelight.

"It was the dog," she whispered.

She felt his hard-surfaced flesh. Every movement he made had the easy gracefulness of an animal, seemingly unhurried, yet lithe and quick. But she could think only of the dirt-clogged pores covering his nose, and the rank odor about him. His hands moved over her body— her shoulders, her back, her hips, her breasts. It was difficult for her to breathe as he lost himself in her; then nothing remained but the blaze and flash of sensation, and a thousand images, half-formed and swift, confused and fantastic, thronging like scurrying clouds heavy-laden with rain.

Then he slid from her bed and stood with his arms hanging at his sides. In the pale light from the lodge fire she could see his brown-yellow eyes, hard and uncompromising, watching her steadily. There was no doubt he meant every word he said.

"You will always be my slave."

She was careful not to go down to the river alone, or to the woods by herself. At night she would relax her tired body, then stiffen at the thought that Catches Two might come again. She felt uncomfortable when he was in the lodge. His eyes were like burning coals. She did not want her friend Antelope to know of his desire. Soon Antelope was going to have her first papoose.

Sacajawea began letting the dog in the lodge at night. She kept him in the entrance, and early in the morning she would let him out before the others awoke.

Ice thickened in the upland streams. In a brief thaw a trickle of water slid into the marsh. It resealed caverns; desperate fish gulped and choked and suffocated; and wise crows waited for the bodies to emerge through the ice.

There was much food in the storage cellars, and at no time did anyone know true hunger cramps in their belly. But about midwinter there was a great hunger in the soul for the green shoots of grass and the warmth of a spring sun. Snow smothered the grasses, and the horses were fed corn by the Hidatsa women. Sacajawea learned the merit in crop planting and storing for the long winter. Dimly she recalled the wild grass seeds her mother had wanted to store for the winter. That would have been good for trading with a friendly tribe for their oversupply of meat and warm hides.

In the warmth of the lodge, Catches Two made a new war shield and several long spears to be used for elk hunting. Old Grandfather left for several days at a time and returned with field mice and thin squirrels to add to the vegetable soup. The women made clothing and mended moccasins.

Almost daily, Sacajawea made a trip to the cache of vegetables in the field. She learned that she must keep busy to avoid the eyes of Catches Two. Sometimes she not only filled the leather pouch from the lodge with corn or hard, dry beans, but she stuffed some of the beans inside her tunic and shared jerky she found, hanging on bundles along the cellar walls, with the dog. She chewed the filched beans as she sewed and cooked.

That spring the Chinook struck the western country, and water flowed down the Big Muddy and Knife rivers in submarine arteries, then across the top of the rotting ice. Water streamed from shrinking snow and roared down gullies from the drifted prairie. The river ice cracked with reports sharper than an Indian trade flintlock, and broke into vast white blocks that began to move, crushing, grinding, piling up, and pushing in dirty banks and windows out over the flooded bottoms. Suddenly entire families, tired of the dank, smoke-filled lodges, went hunting. The Hidatsas often hunted with the other Minnetaree village, Metaharta, or their cousins, the Wetersoon, at the mouth of the Knife River.

When the first winter storms had come sweeping over the plains, buffalos and other large animals had begun their great migration toward the Yellowstone and Missouri rivers, seeking protection in the bluffs, the brush, and the timber. Often buffalo were drawn out upon weak ice, pushed on by the moving mass behind. Thousands might break through and be swept away, drowned, and then frozen. In the spring, the huge bodies were washed out and scattered along the riverbanks for hundreds of miles, the flesh greenish under the hide and ready to come alive on the first day of warm sun with flies and a horrible stench that only the buzzards, the Minnetarees, and their friends, the Mandans, could endure. When the sun woke the flies from their winter's nap, the meat was so tender it almost fell apart. It was ripe for those with a taste for that sort of

thing, as the Minnetarees had. Perhaps that taste had
been cultivated in the days before the horse, when large
supplies of meat were welcomed under almost any cir-
cumstance.[1]

The Minnetarees took to the river, the young men
leaping from one ice cake to the next, falling between,
to bob up elsewhere, towing buffalo carcasses to the
bank. The women slipped out of their doeskin dresses
and plunged naked into the icy water, too, collecting
driftwood for fuel, which was always scarce on the prairie. There was no shyness about the naked body among
the two Minnetaree tribes. The floating wood was important, and the ripened meat, like the hung game of
the British, the hung beef of some Americans, was a
great delicacy.

Everyone, except the very old and very young, was
armed with a horn spoon and butcher knife. Some carried leather bags to bring meat home; some carried
huge hunks of bark to use as sleds across the soft snow.
Overnight the hills began weeping freshets, and there
was the soft sucking *chug* of collapsing snowbanks. The
children laughed and the women sang. The air felt good
in the sunlight, where the eyes did not have to shut
against the sting of the warm smoke of the lodge.

Sacajawea threw a handful of soft snow at Antelope
and ran, laughing. Antelope ran to catch her. "Do not
make me run. This papoose inside is heavy as a large
stone."

"Does your stone have jumping-frog legs?" asked
Sacajawea, squinting through the sunlight.

"*Ai*—he will be the fastest runner in the village."

"*Pagh*," laughed Sacajawea. "He will be the fastest
dressmaker."

"When will you take a man?" asked Antelope suddenly.

Sacajawea's heart sank to the snow beneath her feet.
"I do not wish to become anyone's woman," she said,
her head bowed.

"You will be a woman soon, anyway, and then maybe
Catches Two will make you his woman," Antelope said,
teasing the young girl. "It is not all bad. Catches Two
is a good man. Good compared to Kakoakis, the chief
of the Metaharta. There's a man who is a beast. If you

talked back to him or refused his commands, he would beat you with water-soaked thongs and make you submit to all his subchiefs. He would tame you."

Sacajawea said, "I have been promised to the younger son of Red Buck."

"I suppose he lives in the Shoshoni camp, and I think he now has some woman who waddles more than she walks and he cannot remember whom he had promised to him."

"I don't want a man." Sacajawea coldly blanked all feeling out of her eyes and kept it off her face.

"I want you to be the woman of Catches Two," said Antelope, her eyes searching Sacajawea's face. "I want you to stay in our lodge. Old Mother says you are the best worker in the village and fast to catch on. You make our work light and bring happiness to Old Grandfather. He still tells the story of the dog and you in the river. He talks more now than he has in years and takes an interest in things outside the lodge, like the hunting and fishing and beadmaking."

"I do not want to be a slave squaw forever."

"But squaws do not ask for more. They are happy to serve their man and have his children."

Sacajawea raised her eyes. "I cannot live like a caged bird always."

"Your ideas are strange. Catches Two could beat you for them."

Sacajawea shuddered more from the air impregnated with the odor of putrefied flesh than from fear. She held her nose and moved in to watch the Minnetarees devour the soft meat greedily, thrusting their spoons into the meat that would scarcely stick together. Even the children crammed it down and seemed to suffer no inconvenience.

Suddenly she felt sickened by this sight and the stench of rotting animals. She moved away from Antelope and edged her way toward the women collecting driftwood. Slipping out of her dress, she plunged into the icy water to wash away the odor in her nostrils and to help Talking Goose attach a buckskin thong to a floating tree and haul it in. When they had collected a great deal of wood, Sacajawea slipped her dress on and headed back to the warmth of the smoky lodge.

She felt someone near, then an arm around her waist. Beside her was Bull Face. His leg was badly scarred where the dog had sunk its teeth. The skin was shiny pink, almost transparent along the long red scar.

"Come. We will find warmth together in my lodge." Bull Face laughed deeply, meaningfully into her ear. Then he put his hands around her back and moved them down to her buttocks, pulling her close.

She pulled away, sickened. His stench was that of the rotting carcasses. It was on his breath and in his hair—nauseating. She felt as though she were breathing underwater in a rotting swamp.

From somewhere nearby came a throaty growl. It was the dog.

"You skunk! You little yellow-livered skunk!" His whole style had changed. He spat the words out. "That beast hangs like a burr in my hair!" He cuffed Sacajawea and sent her sprawling. She rolled over and sat up, scuttling crabwise out of his reach and letting out a loud yowl.

"The dog is a friend," she said, reaching out toward the animal.

Bull Face caught her and clapped a hand over her mouth; the other he used to pinch her nostrils shut. She clawed and fought, but as her breath ebbed, she had to stop.

"Come with me," he ordered Sacajawea, "and I'll give you something to howl about."

The dog growled again, closer now. Bull Face turned and saw him coming with his white teeth bared, amber eyes never wavering in their intense regard, his whole body taut with concentration; and like an arrow Bull Face hightailed it in the direction of the stinking, rotting, dead buffalo, running, running as fast as his moccasins could go over the soft snow.

The dog stayed with Sacajawea.

From then on, the dog followed at her heels each time she left the lodge until she entered it again. Sometimes she spoke to him when no one was around. The village whispered behind their hands about the dog and the slave girl.

Even though the dog was near, Sacajawea found herself constantly on the alert, watching for Bull Face—

who had now been shamed twice by the dog—or her master, Catches Two. She knew that if Catches Two found her with Bull Face she'd be whipped; on the other end of the stick, if she refused Catches Two's desires, she'd also be whipped. This punishment was common practice among the Minnetarees, but for a Shoshoni, beating or whipping was the most degrading thing that could happen, even to a slave girl.

She kept to herself, sewing moccasins and leggings for the people of the lodge. She washed their garments in the cold river, cut the dried squash, and dropped the hard strips of jerky into the stew. In her heart was a tocsin of fierce unrest. She had learned long ago to keep her face impassive, no matter what she felt. She could keep her tears bottled up inside so they would not slide down her nose. She managed to live above the fear she felt when Catches Two came inside the lodge. The dog was her only solace, a thing of faithfulness and devotion, yet he was completely wild.

The dog trotted behind Sacajawea as she went to the water hole, but behind it were the spirits of coyotes. These ancestral ghosts dictated the dog's moods, so that often it turned away from Sacajawea, grabbing the meat she brought and darting into the brush to devour it alone, unseen. But it would return.

One morning Sacajawea carried Antelope's newborn boy to the bathing place. The dog, whose bare patches of pink skin were almost invisible now, hidden with new brownish yellow fur, followed behind them. When Sacajawea turned to look, it ran with its bushy tail pointing to the ground and hid behind the sagebrush. Then it trotted alongside, seemingly to have a look at the Hidatsa papoose. Sacajawea took the baby from the cradleboard and unwrapped the soft doeskin. The baby made soft whimpering noises. The dog stood off, watching, its yellow eyes glinting in the early morning sunlight. The dog growled deep from within its chest. Sacajawea turned her back on him and bathed the baby gently in some shallow water. The baby thrashed his legs about and waved his arms, howling about the cold water that was poured on him. She laid the baby on the doeskin and wrapped it tightly so that his arms and legs could not move. Certain that he could not roll down the embankment, Sacajawea set about cleaning the soiled cattail-down from the cradleboard. Then she pushed fresh down against the back and sides of the cradle. She adjusted the wrapping of the doeskin on the baby and placed him in the cradleboard. It was now arranged so that he could water without being taken out each time.

Sacajawea carried the baby, who had eyes like a bird, on her back up the trail, where she met Catches Two at the edge of the village. "I will have payment on the debt you owe me." His ruttish eyes leered, and he reached his hand toward the fork between her bare legs; swiftly he pulled the cradleboard from her shoulders and hung it over a dead limb protruding low from a single cottonwood that grew near the trail. The baby was asleep. Catches Two held Sacajawea by the arm and pulled her off the trail, down a sharp gully, away from the watchful eyes of any guards at the women's bathing place or anyone coming along the trail to or from the village. His breechclout was down, but in the next instant the dog stood between Catches Two and Sacajawea. The dog's growl was still deep within its throat, but much louder than it had been before. Its mouth, half-open, was dripping saliva. In a split second, Catches Two spun on his heels and disappeared. He did not return to the lodge until sundown. He was sullen and would not eat.

Another time Sacajawea took the papoose to a small mound of hard-packed earth outside the lodge so that Antelope might rest. Sacajawea hummed and rocked the papoose and half dozed herself. It was several moments before she saw the dog, its belly fur gleaming white in the sun. It carried a small deer mouse in its mouth. The dog walked up close, dropped the mouse in Sacajawea's lap close to the baby's face, and then trotted off. In a few minutes it was back with another dead mouse. The dead mice themselves did not bother Sacajawea—she knew they were a delicacy for the dog— but the lice-laden, furry body next to the baby's face was too much. Sacajawea said angrily, "Scram, Dog! Go!"

She brushed her skirt furiously, tossing the dead mice to one side and causing the baby to awaken and cry.

The dog turned, walked a short distance, then reared up on its hind legs and pounced, pinning its prey to the ground. The dog crushed the tiny mouse's head, then trotted back to place this new prize in Sacajawea's lap. She stood, brushing unseen lice from the frightened baby's face. She placed the baby on the ground, and kicked the mouse toward the dog. She found a piece of dead wood and threw it at the dog.

"Go away!" she yelled. "Or next time I'll beat your head in!"

The dog hunched himself and slunk down the trail and off into the woods without turning back to look at Sacajawea. She was panting with anger when she scooped up the screaming papoose, stepped over the dead mice and went back to sit against the outside wall of the lodge.

For several weeks the dog did not return. Sacajawea felt glad, yet sad at the same time. Old Grandfather reported that the dog was living in the willow brake and that it had mated. "The female and five pups live in an abandoned rabbit burrow, which the dog enlarged."

Catches Two smirked and brought out his dark thoughts on how to get rid of the wild dog.

Sacajawea said, "Good riddance." But in her heart she wanted to see it again. Antelope said she hoped it was gone for good. She didn't feel her babies were safe around it.

"That dog would not hurt anyone," defended Sacajawea. "It only looks for friendship. It brought dead mice to me as a gift, and I did not like my gifts crawling with lice. That does not mean the dog is a monster. The dog never touched the papoose. Forget it. It is gone and I do not care if it ever returns."

"It had better never touch my papoose! That coyote!" Antelope shut her eyes and shuddered.

Finally the dog did come back. It came to the edge of the bathing place one morning. Sacajawea saw it, and it seemed sullen, its brilliant, amber eyes seeming to question whether it would be welcomed. Sacajawea dumped a full buffalo paunch of water over its head. When it did not move, only shook violently until its fur was dry, she laid her hand on its head, then rubbed behind each ear. It licked her arm, then began to lick her bare feet, enjoying the salty taste. Sacajawea laughed at the feel of the rough tongue.

The spring air was warm, and the women sat outside and sewed. Antelope had hung the cradleboard from a low branch of a nearby tree. The dog stood some distance away, watching. Then, slowly and silently, it approached and sniffed the cradleboard. The women watched it and it ran, with its black-tipped tail almost touching the ground, into the trash heap behind the lodge. There it sniffed around and found an old elk bone. With the bone clenched in its teeth it trotted off toward the willow brake.

Antelope announced that it was probably taking the bone to its family. Sacajawea said it was going to charm its wife into having more pups.

So Antelope's distrust faded, and she let the papoose hang from a tree in his cradleboard when the dog lay lazily stretched on the ground—if someone were working nearby.

Then came the fateful day Talking Goose and Little Rabbit were planting corn and beans; Old Mother was sunning herself, half-asleep, near Sacajawea; the dog lay in the shade of the cottonwood. Antelope had set the baby in its cradleboard against the tree, intending to hang it up when she came back from the lodge with her sewing. That reminded Sacajawea of the elk skins she was tanning on the far side of the lodge, so she went to see if they needed more soaking, or to be turned over in the sunshine.

Sacajawea heard the scream and came running. Her throat tightened, and Antelope's keening sounded louder.

Catches Two came running from the lodge with a handful of feathers that he had been putting in the butt end of some fresh arrows. Antelope, her face the color of pale squash, ran sobbing to him, wild with hysterical fear, her arms flogging at his chest. Between sobs and crying she made it clear that a coyote or wolf had snatched her baby out of his cradleboard and eaten him alive.

"That's nonsense!" said Sacajawea. "No coyote or prairie wolf could have come near with the dog on guard.

But Antelope was staring hard at the dog, and when Sacajawea turned and looked, she saw that its muzzle, chest, and right shoulder were plastered with blood. The left shoulder was once again bare of fur and showed pink skin. The dog gave a low whine and pawed the ground, just as Antelope kicked at it. It growled deep down in its chest as if it had been wakened from sleep.

"I'll kill you!" Catches Two yelled at the dog, who was now standing and looking around from one face to the other with yellow, luminous eyes. Then it turned and started to slink slowly away.

Sacajawea looked incredulously from Antelope to Catches Two. She called out a warning and moved toward the dog. But Catches Two was quicker and reached the animal first, plunging his steel knife into the already bloody chest. With a grunt, he twisted the knife as he dragged it down toward the white belly fur.

The dog lay where Catches Two had knocked it down. The lustrous amber eyes blinked, then remained open. The head fell back and the mouth was filled with frothing blood. Its dark yellow legs twitched and the air was saturated with a vile smell released from the dark scent gland at the base of its tail.

In the sudden silence, a low whimpering sound drew everyone's attention from the dead dog. Their eyes caught something unfamiliar. Antelope began to sob loudly once again and point with her finger. A dead female coyote lay in a puddle of blood just beyond the place where the cradleboard had stood against the cottonwood. Near the tree lay a bull boat, bottom up. The whimpering came from under the old, discarded boat.

Still sniffling, Antelope ran to investigate. The papoose was out of the cradleboard, on his hands and knees under the lightweight boat. He was dirty and bedraggled and crying now because he was hungry— but he was unharmed.

"The dog saved him," breathed Sacajawea, pointing to the broken straps on the cradleboard. The straps and lacing looked like something had chewed on them.

Antelope picked up her papoose, cooing and soothing and cuddling him; but this sweet moment of relief was short. Without warning, Sacajawea leaped at Catches Two and began beating him about the face and chest.

Old Mother felt a slow fear dawn in her heart, and her eyes became dark and glassy. Her lips were stiff as she took a deep breath. "What will happen?" she asked Antelope.

"It is up to Catches Two," said Antelope, looking at Sacajawea, who had stopped hitting Catches Two, although her fists were still balled in rage. She could say no more, but gave a sickish laugh when Sacajawea rushed to the dog and threw herself on its back, embracing its scrawny head with the lifeless, amber eyes. Something great was gone.

Catches Two was bewildered by Sacajawea's behavior. "It is unforgivable," he said to Old Mother, "for a slave to beat her master and defile his lodge with a wild dog." And then Sacajawea pulled her good sleeping robe out of the lodge and pushed the hulk of the dog onto it. Catches Two sat on the earth and began to laugh softly, unregenerate laughter. He was unstrung after his encounter with the dog and the pounding he had taken from Sacajawea.

Sacajawea promptly restrung him with a sharp, dark look. "I'll lodgepole you," she warned, "if you or anyone makes another sound."

His laughter broke off and he glared at her. "No woman talks to a Hidatsa brave that way," he said, but then fell silent.

Carefully she tied the robe together with thongs found in the lodge. Then she dragged the huge parcel across the cultivated field, toward the willow brake. She tugged and heaved until it was firmly caught in the lower branches of an old sycamore. She tore at her hair until it fell loose. She tore her face with her fingernails until it streamed blood. She tore her tunic. She scooped up dirt and spread it on her head and face. The riverbank was filled with her high animal howl.

"We must get rid of her," said Catches Two. "She cannot stay here."

"Where can she go?" asked Antelope.

"I think the old chief Black Moccasin would take her," said Old Grandfather, pointing his pipe to the four corners of the earth and offering a prayer in behalf of the spirit of the dead dog.

"He has many slaves," said Old Mother.

"Give her to Bull Face. He is shriveling up for want of a slave girl," snickered Talking Goose.

"It is the Moon of the Trading Fair," Catches Two said. He sounded worried. "There is much to do, and it will not be good if the girl continues to mourn. It will not look good to the village. If she does not come to her senses, we must end her comings and goings."

"It is up to you," said Old Mother, looking closely at Catches Two. "You are the one who brought her to us." Her mouth bunched up and she scratched in the earth with the heel of her moccasin. Sacajawea's howls were still to be heard as Old Mother began pushing dust over the pools of dried blood left by the dog.

Antelope clutched her baby son. "Will the wild beast's spirit kill us because we did not believe in him?" she said.

It was a new thought. "*Ai*," said Talking Goose. "What do you think about that, Old Mother?"

"I do not know," she answered. "But perhaps the forces that made the dog react the way he did will be angry because the dog has been killed. We will offer an especially rich gift to the dog's spirit to show that the members of our lodge feel some remorse and will never again harm a wild dog."

Everyone supported her except Old Grandfather. He said, "I am not so sure this is necessary."

Old Mother ignored him. She said, "If we place many animal bones together under the tree in the willow brake where the girl took the body of the dog, the sun and the moon, and the trees and living animals, will see, and they will know that we wish the spirit of the dog well."

"Just how will they know this?" asked Old Grandfather.

"They will know," said Old Mother.

And so the women of Catches Two's lodge built a pile of bones as high as the branches that held the last earthly remains of the dog, and left a fresh hunk of bear meat on the top of the bone monument so that the spirit of the dog would not go hungry.

In the morning, Sacajawea was found sitting between the rows of new-planted corn, making believe the dog sat watching on his side of the brake. The meat

that Antelope had left was gone, and there were wild
dog or wolf tracks around the huge stack of bones.

"Those are the tracks of the dog's spirit," said Old
Mother positively.

The story of the bone monument was long recounted
in the big Hidatsa village, and each spring new bones
were added to the heap by the descendants of Catches
Two.

CHAPTER

6

The Trading Fair

If the Indians are right they went east to the great fur fair of Montreal in the late 1630's and returned with white-man goods. Gradually, visiting tribes brought meat and furs to the upper villages of the Missouri River, trading them for corn, beans, and squash. In spite of the competition and the growing wars among the crowded tribes, the Hidatsas managed to keep a hand on the good share of the trade through their favored upper-river position. For years now, the goods had been brought right through their gates by the British, enlarging the importance of the villages as a marketing place, rivaling the early fur-trading posts of Lake Superior, Rainy Lake, Lake of the Woods, etc. Thus it became a sort of Grand Portage at rendezvous time, but operated by Indians.

From *The Beaver Men*. Copyright 1964 by Marie San-doz, Hasting House, Publishers, Inc., pp. 15–21.

Before sunup the next morning, the *tum-tum* of hide drums was heard coming from the center of the village. The Moon of the Trading Fair, June, had begun. During the night the Hidatsa scouts discovered the Yankton Sioux setting up a camp close by. As soon as their presence was announced, others hurried out to welcome them back and to offer hospitality during their stay. Within the next few days a large group of Oglala Sioux came. The Hidatsa women began preparing meats and fresh cactus with the spines cut off and young, succulent thistle leaves for the thousands of visitors who were on their way to the enormous trade fair gathering in the area of the five villages of the Upper Missouri. The Hidatsa men prepared flat prairie area for various games of skill and chance and a wide, long track for horse racing.

For years, tribes from as far away as northern Canada and the southern plains had come to these sedentary villages to trade. The French-Canadians from around Hudson's Bay came on horseback, trailing ponies loaded with wool blankets, capotes, and long colored sashes. Ojibwas came with axes and awls of bone and arrowheads of copper and baskets of wild rice. The Kiowas brought bone knives and mallets, along with baskets of yucca pods. The Utes brought beautifully cured skins of mountain goats and goat horns filled with white quartz for beadmaking. The Crees' horses were loaded with rice, snowshoes, and packs of marten and mountain lion fur. The Teton Sioux brought skins of mountain sheep. The Apaches came with leather sacks of obsidian for spear points. Others brought seashells and walrus ivory from trade centers west of the Rocky Mountains. Some came with red pipestone, reindeer horn, and caribou skins. Many had leather boxes and woven containers filled with herbs: sassafras, peyote, cascara, foxglove, bergamot, sage, thorn apple, pokeroot, mullein, wild cherry bark, anise seeds, and coneflower root.

After bartering, these tribes took home dried corn, beans, squash, pumpkins, gourds, tobacco, dried currants, rosehips, skunkberries, glass beads, and deer-skins and buffalo robes embroidered with dyed porcupine quills.[1]

The visiting young boys were full of pranks, often stealing meat from the women's drying racks, then dashing off for a good laugh and a feast together.

All loved the games of chance. A Ute gambled away all of his property, even his wife. However, she told her husband she would not go anywhere, and sat on the ground refusing to budge; he was disgraced because she would not honor the gamble. In the end she hit him in the stomach with a heavy leather bag and he sprawled in the dirt, discredited. The winner, an Apache, took a good look at the couple and decided he would be better off leaving them together. He gave the humiliated Ute a kick in the back and stalked away, saying, "This bet is off!"

A group of laughing women played the game of hands with a pair of small sticks. One stick was marked with a string around the middle and the guesser had to point to the opponent's hand that held the unmarked stick. Some Yankton women were playing shinny against some Teton women with a buckskin ball, throwing it against a goal indicated by blankets on the ground. The Crow introduced their favorite hoop-and-pole game. Two players rolled a hoop on a level course and threw darts at it, and the way the darts struck the hoop determined the count. The French-Canadian traders held foot races while the Ojibwas and Kiowas held archery and horse racing contests. Often there were heated discussions and fistfights over who won these games. It was a time to collect and store memories of fresh stories to be told and savored during the coming snowy months.

Before sunrise on the morning of the fifth day after the death of the dog, Old Grandfather wakened Saca-jawea. She was still wearing mourning ashes on her face, and although she had resumed her chores, she would not speak to Catches Two, and had been seen at night near the willow brake—looking for the spirit of the dog, some neighbors said.

"Fix your hair in two braids. Put the red stripe down your center part and put red inside your ears. Wash your face, paint yellow rings under your eyes, and join me at the front of the council lodge," Old Grandfather told her. "If you have any valuables or trinkets you treasure, put them in a bag and hide them in your tunic. You are going to the fair with me." He nodded his head toward her sleeping couch as if knowing where she kept her most treasured possession, the sky-blue stone of her ancestors.

While Sacajawea readied herself, Old Grandfather lay himself down with his head in Antelope's lap. With great rapidity she picked off the vermin that resided in his hair. She smashed the enormous crawlers with her teeth, keeping them in her mouth until there were enough to spit out in the shape of a ball as large as a walnut. Then she stuck his hair together in tufts with pine gum and plastered the whole arrangement with white clay and grease and streaks of red paint.

Sacajawea was glad Old Grandfather had selected her to carry the trade goods back to the lodge. Perhaps the fair would help lighten her heavy heart. But she wondered why he was taking such pains to look handsome and why he had ordered her to look her best and to bring her treasures.

She cautiously took the small pouch from under her sleeping couch. Inside was the blue stone on the thin thong. The rusty red round stone, and a dark feather from a Canada goose she had found by the river last fall. It shone green in the sunlight. She had imagined that the goose had been south of the sunset where her People lived. Perhaps he had even seen the village of the People.

Sacajawea followed Old Grandfather across the camp, heading for the trading ground set up on the prairie. Not too far from the lodge, a quail whistled in the grass, so close to Old Grandfather that it startled them both; a cool whiff of wind rustled through the dew-laden buffalo grass beside them, and then died down. A scattering of gray clouds scudded in from the north. Slowly the lower sky faded into pearl gray; still lower, a faint area of clear, lake-deep green; and below that, a little line of mustard yellow right at the horizon. As she watched the sunrise, Sacajawea was overcome by the tranquillity of the dawn.

All the fevers of the last few days—death, murder, fear—seemed unreal. She felt suspended in a world without trouble or conflict. The breeze cooled her face; a scent of sage in the air refreshed her; the subdued sounds of the prairie soothed her with their familiarity and at the same time had a new and unaccustomed timbre as the traders began assembling for the day. Chippewas trundled sacks of rice; in every direction Indians carried bundles. And now she could hear shouts of instruction or warning: "Make way!" "Watch the ground!" "Throw out your grain!"—shouts of the counters, shouts of recognition, banter between nations. There were swarms of big-eyed, barefooted children standing about—torrents of laughter—excited eyes gleaming—white teeth in brown faces—lithe brown bodies naked to the waist—wind-tousled hair—movement, energy, hubbub, gaiety.

Sacajawea walked behind Old Grandfather, following him at the correct distance, until he stopped near a circle of braves who were already set up for trading. Sacajawea moved closer then so she could see inside the circle and watch what interesting things were being exchanged. Old Grandfather inspected the braves, then moved to the side of an Ahnahaway who had a rough face and unkempt hair that was smeared with red clay and tallows. The British called these Ahnahaways, cousins to the Minnetarees, Wetersoons, and the French called them Soulier Noir Indians. Old Grandfather tugged at the Ahnahaway's shirt and, when he had his attention, pointed to Sacajawea, making suggestive motions with his hands. Sacajawea went numb. The Ahnahaway's face brightened. He appraised Sacajawea for a moment, then said, "Come, I have something you will like."

From a pile of elk skins, the Ahnahaway produced a tightly woven willow cage. Inside was a black crow that rasped *"Haw!"* in a coarse, jeering way when the Ahnahaway's finger probed his side.

There was a sort of wicked gleam in the bird's canny eye and a world of wile in the sly cant of its head. The Ahnahaway fed the bird bits of dried meat and sunflower seed. Rising voices from the other traders could be heard. Sacajawea turned then, as if to move away, but Old Grandfather took her wrist in his hand.

"Crows live to be a man's age," said the Ahnahaway, looking at the girl. "Can you guess the age of this one?"

"Seems he is old enough to resign from hunting his own food," said Old Grandfather. "Will he fly off with his kind in the fall?"

"Not this bird. He knows a good thing. And besides, he has grown lazy."

"Haw!" jeered the captured crow.

Old Grandfather was pleased with the bird. "My youngest grandson will carry him on his shoulder and be known as Black Crow by his tribe. Perhaps he will teach the crow to talk. This is a day to remember."

"Ai, he is a wise bird and could easily learn to speak," said the Ahnahaway.

"It is a bargain, then," said Old Grandfather. "This Shoshoni slave girl is yours, and the bird is mine."

"I cannot go with this brave," Sacajawea said, trembling. "I live in your lodge. What will Catches Two say?"

Old Grandfather looked like a dog that had been whipped. "He and Old Mother will say plenty."

Sacajawea regarded him impassively for a moment. "What about Antelope and Talking Goose?"

"They will get along. You must go with him."

"Are you displeased with my work?"

"No, it is not that. Old Mother made the decision. Catches Two was to carry it out by evening today. One who mourns the death of a wild dog as if it were a relative is taboo. There is too much talk in the village. It is final. If you return with me today to the lodge of Catches Two, you will sleep forever beside your dog." With an explicit gesture he sliced his finger across his throat.

For a long moment Sacajawea did not reply. Her legs felt weak. "All I know about the Ahnahaways is that they eat worms."

"Not like Hidatsas, who eat each other," said Old Grandfather. Sacajawea suddenly noticed the dark circles of sleeplessness under his eyes, and his reddened lids.

"I will expect her to treat me with respect," said the Ahnahaway.

"Ah, she is not criticizing you," replied Old Grandfather, looking down his nose and grunting. "You'd better get her out of here before I change my mind about the trade." He picked up the bird in the cage, and without another word he turned around and trotted off.

Sacajawea watched as he was swallowed by the crowd.

"Come along," said the Ahnahaway.

"Are you taking me to your village?"

"*Ai*, but not now. I came here for a good time. I want to try some games. There is plenty of time for talking. Get the elk skins and follow me."

"Where are we going?" she asked.

He scowled and pinched his lips, indicating there should be no more talking.

Soon they were watching a game of arrows. A small tingle of excitement crept through her as she watched men shoot arrows as fast as they could into the air, seeing who put the most skyward before the first fell to the ground. Frequently as many as five arrows were up before the first struck the earth.

The Ahnahaway yelled, "Ho! Ho!" several times to show his approval of the contestants.

Sacajawea cried, "Oooo, good!"

The Ahnahaway frowned at her.

Someone yelled, "Winner take all," and four prize arrows were put into a ring marked out in the dirt. When an Ojibwa brave placed a parfleche of kinnikinnick mixed with tallow, his tobacco, and a gleaming, long-bladed copper knife inside the ring, the Ahnahaway could not contain himself.

"Put the skins in the ring," he said.

"All of them?" asked Sacajawea.

"*Ai*, and sit on the pile," he said.

"Why? It will not walk away," she said.

"You talk more than any woman I have ever met," he said. "I like women who open their mouth only for eating, and then not too wide."

There were boisterous cheers from the players and onlookers when Sacajawea did as she was told. The Ahnahaway swaggered around a bit, then quickly he took the bow and put seven arrows into the air with a fast whirring. It was the best performance. He let the other contestants gather the arrows. He put the knife in his belt, and the four beautiful arrows in his leather quiver, and he told Sacajawea to come along with the remainder of his loot.

"Are we leaving for your village now?" she asked.

"Ho! A moment!" called a man with great hollows under his eyes and loose skin in the dark planes of his face. The newcomer placed two prize weasel tails in the center ring and told the Ahnahaway to replace the wicked-looking copper knife and the skins with the girl. The game was not over. The newcomer picked up the bow, feeling the tautness of its string several times. He carried ten arrows in a quiver on his back. Then he placed his feet slightly apart and flexed his knees. The crowd became quiet as, faster almost than the eye could see, he released the arrows—one, two, three, four, five, six, seven, eight, nine—and then *plew*! the first hit the ground. The newcomer looked around for anyone to take the bow from him and top his record. No one moved. The man with hollows under his eyes picked up his weasel tails and lifted them high to the heavens then down to the earth and slowly to the east, west, north, and south. Then he laughed and the hollows in his cheeks seemed to fill.

This man was the new owner of Sacajawea.

He seemed to like the copper knife, and put it in the leather thong that held up his leggings. He put the parfleche of tobacco in the center of a buffalo hide with the four metal-tipped arrows, and all that in the center of the elk skins. Making a large, neat roll, he handed the bundle to Sacajawea.

The Ahnahaway watched while this was being done. "I heard her Hidatsa owner call her by the name of Sacajawea. And it is a fitting name—she chatters like a bird, a magpie. I wish you health." Then he disappeared.

Sacajawea followed her new owner through the groups of traders, past the games of chance, where someone called, "Fast Arrow, come show us how this is done." He waved his arm but did not stop. They walked past the camp of the Assiniboin and the larger one of the Oglala Sioux. At the next village they stopped to drink at a spring before continuing to walk on soft earth.

Sacajawea's face remained expressionless, but her

thoughts tumbled upon one another and she was bothered by the flies. They did not seem to bother the Metaharta. Maybe he had a good coat of bear's grease on him. She would miss Antelope and the children and Talking Goose, who scolded about things but didn't mean it so much, and Old Mother and Old Grandfather, and even Catches Two. She wondered if the Agaidüka women would hear that she had been traded for a crow, then won by a Metaharta at a game of arrows. Probably not—who was there to tell who knew? Suddenly she realized she was getting farther away from the hope of any rescue by the People. Fast Arrow nudged her, and she awoke from her thoughts.

The sun was in the middle of the sky when Sacajawea spotted a group of horses staked out beside a village of round earth lodges, similar to those she had just left. There was a pole fence around this village also. Fast Arrow led her through the gate and down a labyrinth of narrow paths between the earth mounds, and then inside a lodge.

The circular room was dim compared to the outdoor brightness. Three women were working near the little buffalo-chip fire in the center of the floor. There were an old man and several children there, too. The lodge was arranged in the familiar manner, with sleeping couches forming the outer circle around the room against the smoke-stained walls. Each bed was marked by a high post topped with an antelope, deer, or buffalo head. Sacajawea put Fast Arrow's bundle of winnings down beside him as he took his seat, an elevated one, made from short logs covered with an elk skin.

The small children ceased their noisemaking, and the adults sat cross-legged around the fire looking toward Fast Arrow. He stood, bared his blue-tattooed chest, made by rubbing ashes into tiny cuts, and puffed on a pipe decorated with many eagle feathers. His smile was boastful, but not cruel or lustful.

"My mother and great father, my sister, and my woman and children," he began, "this warrior"—pointing to himself—"has brought home a new knife with which my woman can skin the buffalo more easily. I have a robe from a very young buffalo. It is for Sucks His Thumb." A boy of about three years pulled his head

from his mother's lap, stopped sucking his thumb, and
toddled to Fast Arrow. The boy carried the robe back
to his mother's lap. "Here is a bag of tobacco. This is
for my mother." A middle-aged squaw reached up with
competent, work-hardened hands to catch the bag. One
hand stayed on that of her son for a single moment;
then she grinned broadly into his face. Her flattened
nose, full mouth, and low forehead were pure Metaharta, but her skin was lightened from dead brown by
a copper warmth. White blood ran in her. Many of the
Mandan Nation and some Minnetarees had the strain
from the seed of French traders, and perhaps from long
ago when the Welsh had come to settle.

"Four arrows with fine metal tips I will keep myself.
For shooting nine arrows into the air before the first
struck the ground, I have more. These elk skins I give
to my sister, who can make moccasins and a dress for
herself. And see this girl, who is not of our nation but
who is said to be called Sacajawea? I give her to my old
father so that she may bring some light into his life.
When he has no need of her, she may be shared by my
woman, who has much trouble keeping her children at
her side."

Someone snickered. It was the sister, with her hands
covering her face, her body rocking slowly from side to
side. Sacajawea looked from the swaying girl to the
father, who wiggled in satisfaction and looked toward
Sacajawea with an interested stare. She felt dizzy; a
sickness in the pit of her belly spread throughout her
body.

"*Ai*, she shall bathe me each morning and rub sweet
grasses on my back and feet. She shall bring my pipe
and keep my old bones warm. Ha! She will be better
than a buffalo robe in the Season of Cold Winds." He
laughed a high-pitched wail. "*Yeeewooo*, we may fly on
that wind!"

Sacajawea trembled, then caught herself. Anger rose
hot inside her. She would never warm that old one!
Tears were close to the surface. She stood very still.
She tried hard to make herself feel resignation at her
fate. The feeling would not come.

Softly the young wife, called Rosebud, said, "He is
teasing. Come hold the baby." Her face crinkled at the

sides and looked friendly. Sacajawea stared a moment, then slowly moved among the children and cradled the black-haired papoose, who stopped whimpering when she placed the small head in the hollow of her neck and rocked back and forth. It was some time before she relaxed and noticed that the baby had curled his hand around one of her fingers. Sacajawea looked up at the young mother, who was happily making a chain from joint grass, which she fitted around the waist of a little girl to hold in her small tunic. Everyone seemed to have gone about their business, and Fast Arrow had gone outside the lodge. The mother stirred the contents of the huge clay pot on the fire. Rosebud shifted another little girl on her knee and whispered to Sacajawea that the old mother's name was Grasshopper. The old father, Grasshopper's man and Rosebud's father, was Redpipe. Redpipe was tormented.

Sacajawea asked, "Tormented by whom?"

"By spirits. He is cursed." She pointed to her head. "He does not always know what he does. Our people have a high regard for him. He speaks with the spirit world. Therefore he is revered because he does not speak with his own mind. Treat him well."

Sacajawea looked again at the wizened old fellow.

"He speaks to the spirits in anger, so that he raves and lashes out at those near him," Rosebud went on. "But it is the spirits doing this, not Redpipe. Then for many days he will not speak with spirits, but will be himself."

"Here, child, take this to Redpipe," said Grasshopper, offering a dried pumpkin half-filled with soup to Sacajawea. She took it gingerly and stepped to the corner where the old man, who looked faded and shrunken, as though he had sat in the hot sun too long, sat sucking on his pipe. Her heart beat loudly as he looked up with eyes that were completely rimmed with white and seemed almost popping from his head.

Sacajawea served soup in pumpkin bowls to Rosebud and her children, and the sister, Sweet Clover, who continued to rock from side to side, and Grasshopper. The women ate after the man was finished. Then Sacajawea was handed a bowl. Sacajawea noticed that Grasshopper was a good-looking woman, dressed in a

tunic embroidered with colored beads and porcupine
quills, and on her wrists were bracelets of woven reed
stained bright colors.

Sacajawea thought she had no appetite, but as she
lifted the wooden spoon to her mouth, the smell was
overwhelming, sweet and savory. With a few quick
spoonfuls she emptied the bowl. She knew this time
that upon eating the corn soup she was to be considered
one of the members of the village.

"Would you like more soup?" asked Grasshopper. "I
think you have had a full day. It would be well to rest.
This bed is not used, and Sweet Clover has an extra
robe."

In a moment the couch was fixed and Grasshopper
had removed Sacajawea's moccasins. This unexpected
kindness left Sacajawea staring out of the corner of her
eye at the woman.

"You are such a little thing," said Grasshopper, who
patted her own broad behind, indicating she ate too
much, she was growing fat. "Those men had no heart.
You were starving, and they thought only of games.
I'm glad you are here. Just look at those callused hands.
Did you work in the fields for the Ahnahaways?"

"For the Hidatsas."

Grasshopper clicked her tongue and patted Sacajawea's face. "They are all savages, every one. We'll be
easier on you. Now sleep."

CHAPTER

7

Toussaint Charbonneau

Toussaint Charbonneau was born in Canada about 1758.[1] His mother was a Sioux and his father a French Canadian. He and his brother were traders and fur trappers from Lake Ontario to Lake Superior and the James Bay region. Charbonneau was mentioned as an engagé of the Northwest Fur Company in 1793, when he was about thirty-five years old. He worked as a trader at Fort Pine on the Assiniboine River.[2] In 1795 Charbonneau left from the Lake of the Woods area, moved down the Red River of the North and went west to the Upper Missouri where he lived, as a trader, among the Minnetaree in their Metaharta village on the Knife River. According to Hebard, a year later he was the only white man in the area and was living with the nearby Mandans. For a time he worked for the American Fur Company and in 1803–4 he was a co-factor at Fort Pembina with Alexander Henry.[3] Sometime before the Lewis and Clark men built Fort Mandan with the heaviest local timber available,[4] Charbonneau was back in the Metaharta village as an independent trader, bartering furs for supplies with the English in Canadian territory. During the latter part of 1804 until August 17, 1806 he was an interpreter for the Lewis and Clark Expedition.

The fur trader John MacDonnell knew Charbonneau during the ten years they worked in and out of the Winnipeg and Upper Missouri area and also during the five years Charbonneau lived in the Metaharta village. In

135

his journal, MacDonnell wrote that Charbonneau was one of three men who went "to court the Foutreau's daughter, a great beauty."⁵ A few months later an old squaw caught Charbonneau "in the act of committing a Rape upon her Daughter," wrote MacDonnell. The squaw pounded Charbonneau so hard with a canoe paddle that he could scarcely walk back to his own canoe. Mac-Donnell finished the story by writing that this was "a fate he highly deserved for his brutality."⁶

John Bakeless also wrote that Toussaint Charbonneau was "deep in aboriginal love affairs" during the years he lived in Indian country.⁷ The natives of the lower Minnetaree village knew Charbonneau's character and gave him at least half a dozen names, none of them overly respectful. They were "The Chief of the Little Village," "The Man Who Possesses Many Gourds," "The Great Horse That Came from Afar," "The Horse from Abroad," "Forest Bear." Another name, which Bakeless describes as "not very refined," may be translated to "Squaw's Man" or even more literally as "One Whose Man-Part Is Never Limp."⁸

In August, 1807, Charbonneau, his two sons, and two Indian wives arrived at St. Louis. He left the women and children and took a fur company trapping job in the southwest. Three years later he was back in St. Louis. He bought a piece of farm land in the St. Ferdinand Township near the Missouri River from Clark, who was Indian agent for the Louisiana Territory. On March 26, 1811, he sold the land back to Clark for $100.⁹

It is well known that Charbonneau and one of his wives accompanied Henry M. Brackenridge on an expedition up the Missouri in April, 1811.¹⁰ In July, 1816, Charbonneau was hired by Julius DeMun for Auguste P. Chouteau and Company to go from St. Louis up and down the Arkansas and Platte rivers trading for a year with the Indians. Three years later he was on the payroll of Captain Clark, Superintendent of Indian Affairs, as an interpreter at "$200 from July 17 to December 31, 1819."¹¹

In 1825, General Henry Atkinson referred to Charbonneau living at the Mandan villages with a wife and her brother. In the journal of Major Stephen Kearny for August 11 of the same year is a note about a Charbon-

neau Creek named for "a Frenchman, who accompanied Lewis and Clark across the mountains."[12]

Agent John F. A. Sanford, stationed on the Upper Missouri, paid "Tassant Charboneau," for work as an interpreter for the Mandans and Minnetarees on February 29, 1828. Other payments were recorded at the subagency to Toussaint Charbonneau, acting as an interpreter, from November 30, 1828 until September 30, 1834, for a total of $2,437.32.[13]

According to account books kept at Fort Clark, on the Missouri River across from the Mandan villages, Duke Paul of Würtemberg bought supplies that were delivered to James Kipp, the chief factor at the fort, to be sent on to Charbonneau at the Minnetaree village. Duke Paul purchased supplies on May 5 and May 30, 1830, with gunpowder and tobacco especially for Charbonneau. Two weeks later Duke Paul was at Fort Union, farther up the Missouri River—near Williston, North Dakota, today—where he bought more supplies for the "interpreter, Charbonneau."[14]

The famous German traveler, Maximilian, Prince of Wied, hired Toussaint Charbonneau as his interpreter in 1833 while he spent the winter at Fort Clark and later when he visited the Mandan villages. In June of the same year some Mandans tried to force the unwilling Maximilian to trade his compass for a horse. "It was only by the assistance of old Charbonneau that I escaped a disagreeable and, perhaps, violent scene," wrote Maximilian in his journal.[15]

Charbonneau always seemed to be involved in escapades with young women. In 1833 he had two wives, but one ran away. In his Fort Clark Journal, Francis A. Chardon wrote on October 22, 1834, that he was aware of Charbonneau's "two lively wives. Poor old man."[16]

At eighty Charbonneau married a fourteen-year-old Assiniboine girl and the celebration included "a splendid Chárivéree, the Drums, pans, Kittles and Beating; guns fireing etc."[17] Afterward "the old rascal offered his bride to the rest of the men in camp."[18]

In many respects the Charbonneau of Lewis and Clark fame was a feckless character. For example, in an emergency he seemed to be a coward, he abused his Indian women, and always seemed to manage to have only young

*girls in his lodge. Dr. Elliott Coues referred to him as
clumsy and boorish. John C. Luttig suggested that he
ought to be hung, and William Laidlow, of the Columbia
Fur Company in charge of Fort Pierre, referred to him
as "the knave."[19]*

*In August, 1839, Joshua Pilcher, Clark's successor
as Superintendent of Indian Affairs, wrote in a letter
that Charbonneau came to St. Louis "tottering under the
infirmities of 80 winters, without a dollar to Support
him."[20]*

*A promissory note written on August 14, 1843, by
Francis Pensoneau stated that he would pay J. B. Charbonneau $320 as soon as some land, claimed by J. B.
Charbonneau as coming from the estate of his deceased
father, Toussaint Charbonneau, was disposed of. This
note implies that old Charbonneau died sometime before
August 14, 1843.[21]*

*Grace Hebard wrote, "The exact date of the death of
Charbonneau has not been ascertained, and even his
burial place is unknown. Vague rumors persist . . . that
Charbonneau married a Ute woman and eventually died
and was buried . . . in Utah."[22]*

*The Antiquarian Society of Montreal states that it is
impossible to trace anyone with the name Charbonneau
or even Toussaint Charbonneau who lived from the late
1700s to mid-1800s. That French-Canadian name was
as common as John Smith is in the United States.[23]*

*It is interesting to note that Bakeless wrote that Tous-
saint Charbonneau was born in Montreal about 1759.[24]
This is a year after Hebard wrote that he was born. Roy
Appleman wrote for the National Park Service that the
old French-Canadian was forty-four years old in 1804.[25]
This would make his birthdate 1760.*

*In 1979, ninety-year-old Irene DeClue Haltermann
Coyle, born in the DeSoto, Missouri, area, but living in
Missoula, Montana, said that her family always claimed
that Toussaint Charbonneau, of the Lewis and Clark
Expedition, was her great-grandfather. Apparently, her
family records show that this Charbonneau was born in
Montreal on March 1, 1771. Mrs. Coyle said her grandfather, Louis Charboneau, a son of old Toussaint, was
born on October 16, 1812, in St. Louis.[26]*

In the small, Missouri community of Richwoods, close

to DeSoto and about sixty miles from St. Louis, there is an interesting white marble grave marker in St. Stephen's Catholic Cemetery on which are carved these words:

Toussaint Charboneau, Mar. 1, 1781–Feb. 19, 1866

Beside that marker is another similar one with these words:

*Marie LaViolette, Wife of T. Charboneau
Died Sept. 23, 1869, aged 86 years*

The Charboneaus in this area claim this is the Toussaint Charbonneau of the Lewis and Clark Expedition. In the cemetery are half a dozen other Charboneaus, all born in the mid or late 1800s. In the John Horine Private Cemetery, also in Richwoods, are at least four Charboneau grave markers, showing these people were born in the late 1800s and all used only one n in the spelling of their name.

From the few things that are known of the character of the Charbonneau of the Lewis and Clark Expedition, it is doubtful that the man would marry a woman seven years his senior as was Marie LaViolette to her T. Charboneau. Old Charboneau liked his women young. Bakeless said he was a squawman "who had a special weakness for very young Indian girls."[27]

The Coyle and Richwoods Charboneaus are both too young to have been on the Lewis and Clark Expedition because he was one of the oldest men in the group. If he had been twenty-four, he would have been in the same league with Shannon, who was the youngest member of the expedition. If he had been thirty-four, he would have been about the age of Lewis and Clark who, in 1804, were thirty and thirty-four, respectively.

Toussaint Charbonneau became a famous member of the Lewis and Clark Expedition because of his Shoshoni woman, Sacajawea. It appears that his birth and death dates and burial site are as elusive as hers.

Sacajawea was allowed to rest until her body felt completely restored. Until midday she lay dreamily inside the robe in Fast Arrow's lodge and then, prompted by an evanescent sixth sense that flickers on in the wiser among us, realized that things might not be too bad. She had examined and evaluated her new surroundings. The lodge was clean. Fresh river sand lay on the floor. Clothing was hung neatly on pegs placed in the four wooden supports holding the roof of the lodge. There were no stale vegetables or yesterday's meat lying around the cooking fire. Everyone worked, except the grown girl, Sweet Clover, who swayed and stared vacantly.

Sweet Clover's eyes were similar to the old father's, rimmed with white and ready to pop from her head. Her movements were slow and sometimes without direction, her mind elsewhere, her ears not hearing what went on near her. She laughed at nothing.

In the early afternoon the mother, Grasshopper, came to Sacajawea carrying a board with dried meat and cooked squash. She said, "Eat, you are one of us now."

Sacajawea rolled over, found her tunic, put it on, and ate. Sweet Clover came and sat on her sleeping couch. She drooled and picked at some of Sacajawea's meat. She grinned and stared at Sacajawea. With hand signs she indicated that Sacajawea was pretty.

"Shoo, outside!" said Grasshopper. "Play with the children." Sweet Clover made a face, but she understood and left. The children, Sucks His Thumb, Half Moon, Hungry Horse, and Chickadee, followed. Chickadee, the baby, crawled more than walked.

"That is my baby," said Grasshopper, pointing a stubby forefinger toward the door through which the grown girl, Sweet Clover, had just left. "She will never grow up."

"Is she cursed?" asked Sacajawea.

"*Ai*, but her torment did not come with age, as did Redpipe's." Grasshopper brushed her hand across her moist eyes. "Stay clear from the sight of Kakoakis, our one-eyed chief."

"One eye? Why?"

"I think maybe one of his women pushed his eye out." She put her short forefinger in her mouth and pulled it out with a pop. Over Grasshopper's simple broad face grew a smile, stretching her mouth from ear to ear. "I wish to call you daughter," she said impetuously. "What do you say? Are you pleased?" It was love the child hungered for, yet she was suspicious and held herself rigid. Then Grasshopper took the food board away. She motioned Sacajawea to sit close to her, and she cradled the child, who was now eleven summers old, against her ample bosom.

"This lodge is a good place to live, my daughter—except for one thing, one being. Listen and remember. The stinking Kakoakis came against this lodge. He is a chief, and thought by some to be wise. He is full of health and energy. One day he came here and asked for our youngest child to visit with his young wife. She was lonely, he said. With kindness in our hearts and gratitude to the chief for showing us special favor, we dressed Sweet Clover in her best and let her go with him. She was filled with fear when she found that his tongue was split. He had several white men and the Wolf Chief of the Mandans at his lodge. His wife was not lonesome. There were other young women in his lodge. It was Kakoakis who was the only man in his lodge without a woman that day. He then chose Sweet Clover. He had tricked us." Grasshopper paused, smacking her lips.

"Sweet Clover used her wits and looked about her for a weapon. She had not taken her skinning knife. She struck Kakoakis with his own war club. She stood tall and strong. Never was such a blow struck!" Her mouth became round, and she drew in air. "It would have been one of many great blows, except that one of the white men stopped her and tied her hands and feet. That is all she can remember to tell us, but we did not see her for three suns."

"So—if Kakoakis is more brutal than a handful of Blackfeet, why don't the people of your village choose another leader?"

Grasshopper looked down at Sacajawea and laughed, her strong blunted teeth white against the darkness of her face. "He is friendly with the white traders from the north, and he puts fear into the Hidatsas and the Mandans. Even the Sioux, Assiniboins and Chippewas fear to cross him, so that he is a protection to our village. Others will live longer because of him."

"And so—Sweet Clover?"

"*Ai*, she became an investment so that our village might be strong. She kept our chief happy for a time, and now he pays his debt with gifts to us from time to time. But I do not wish to make another investment. I will not!" She spat at the fire and listened for the sizzle. She clucked and went on about the badness of the chief. "He favors pretty women and keeps many in his lodge, giving them to white traders for the evil crazy-water the white men bring. Kakoakis has a deep thirst for this water and an insatiable hunger for young women. I believe his blood always boils, never cools."

"And the white traders?"

Grasshopper shrugged. "They do not know better. They believe Kakoakis is a mighty chief, and they do not turn aside his hospitality, especially when the chief will furnish them with the furs and hides they come after. But I am not trying to hold back secrets. And I do not try to frighten, but to warn you, my daughter. Everyone knows the time Kakoakis entered an Assiniboin village alone, by night, with no disguise except a blanket drawn over his head. Catching a young squaw alone in a lodge, he silently forced himself inside her, and while he was doing that, he killed her and scalped her. Then he withdrew safely and told of his exploit with a pleasant sense of duty done.[28] It was an enemy; but what if the Assiniboins start doing the same? This man makes sport of young women. He plays games with them. I know he made my Sweet Clover drink crazy-water and he played animal with her while she was bound. When her front side was worn out, he forced himself many times on her back side. Then he invited the white men to take their turns. Sweet Clover's mind slipped away from her body, and the spirits came in its place. They have never left."

A tear slid down Grasshopper's chin. She was silent, still rocking Sacajawea in her lap. Sacajawea's mind went over the tragedy of Sweet Clover. She looked carefully around the warm, clean lodge.

"Sweet Clover is my sister," she said in a voice barely audible. "I will show her kindness."

"The Great Spirit has favored us. If anyone asks who you are, say you are the youngest daughter of Grasshopper. I am your mother. I will make you a new dress with elk's teeth on the yoke and dainty shells on your moccasins and a fringed drag. Come," she said, releasing Sacajawea from her arms. "I will feed you."

"So—I have already eaten."

Soon Sacajawea was working with the other Metaharta women. She went with the berry-pickers and herb-gatherers and garden-hoers. She was pleased with her new clothes and her new home in Fast Arrow's lodge. She liked the embroidery work on her tunics, and the shells on her moccasins, like tiny bells, and the fringes dragging along behind them. Evenings she joined the water-carriers, shy with the boys and young men who seemed so ordinary during the day and so strange in the twilight. In no time at all, she was known in the village as the inquisitive daughter of Grasshopper and Redpipe. She asked questions incessantly.

She asked the small children to show her how to shoot their small bows. She asked why a woman always carried the small skinning knife in her belt. Soon she could hit her mark with an arrow, and she carried a woman's skinning knife in her belt, ready for digging roots or for defense if it were needed against enemies or any who would molest her.

Among the people of the Upper Missouri any woman who was not a slave had the duty of defending herself at all costs against attack, against any who would violate the chastity rope of soft doeskin she always wore when away from the lodge. Such violations were very rare before the whiskey days. Even after those days, the guilty man never made another attempt, for the stab with the skinning knife was automatic in a woman from earliest childhood. When this happened, the man was not driven out of the village, but he lived alone in a hut outside the lodge circle, with none to speak to him.

However, if Chief Kakoakis asked a maiden to honor him in his lodge, none could refuse, for there would be

certain death for her or a member of her family. That
grand chief was all-powerful and very cruel.

It was not many weeks before Sacajawea discovered
it was her time to go to the women's retreating lodge;
thereafter, she would go periodically to be separated
from the men for seven suns. When she returned from
her first visit, a crier went around the village calling
everybody to a feast for the one who had now become
a woman.

Grasshopper loved this little Shoshoni girl as her
own child. She called her friends to help with the fine
garments and the preparation of food. This was the time
to show off a daughter in handsome new clothes and
moccasins, long shell bands hanging from her hair, a
demure beauty in the paint of a woman.

While Sacajawea was at the women's retreating
lodge, she listened to the gossip of the other women.
They spoke of the bearded ones—the white men—who
lived at the edge of their village. They spoke of the fine
presents these men brought their women after a trip
to the north—blankets, combs, hard candy. One man,
whom the men called Chief of the Little Village, had
come from Assiniboin country recently, bringing his
Mandan woman a beaded leather belt and another
woman to help around the lodge. The other woman was
no more than a child. She had been bought from sickly
Blackfeet who had starved during the winter and were
glad to be rid of her. She was not of their nation, but
a Shoshoni.[29] They made the sign of weaving in and
out, like the weaving of a Shoshoni grass summer hut.

"Does this Shoshoni woman come to the retreating
lodge?" asked Sacajawea, very curious.

The women giggled. The Shoshoni squaw was only
a papoose, a child, hardly old enough to come to the
women's retreating lodge.

Sacajawea asked more questions, but she could find
out no more. No one seemed to know much about the
bearded one called Chief of the Little Village.

Grasshopper sang over the tunic being prepared for
Sacajawea. The symbol for the water bird, for which
Sacajawea was named, was set in the center of the outer
tunic and made of colored quills, mostly yellow. Under

the bird there was a white bank made of shells. The
edge of the skirt had buckskin whangs, which were
painted yellow, the color of pollen, for fertility.

When Sacajawea returned from the women's retreating lodge, she was bathed by Grasshopper's squaw
friends. They clucked and waved their hands and
smiled as they dressed her and seated her in the honored place of the lodge they had set up. This day of the
ceremony, Sacajawea presented Grasshopper with a
single white eagle feather. From this time on, Sacajawea would call Grasshopper *"Umbea,* mother," and
Grasshopper would call her "daughter." They would be
close to each other throughout their lives.

The chief Shaman came in an intricately feathered
bonnet and deerskin robe richly decorated with quillwork. He showed much pomp, knowing that only he,
with the highest religious authority, could conduct this
rite. He had a method of self-induced trance in which
he claimed to have direct communication with the
Great Spirit, from whom he relayed words of wisdom
to the Girl Who Had Become a Woman. His chant began, "It is the beginning of this young girl's flow that
marks her as entering womanhood. This is the beginning of her good life. This woman has wandering moccasins. She will live long. She will see much. What she
sees is unbelievable. I do not have words to tell."

The Shaman moved into the lodge, indicating that
the well-wishers could follow him inside. Sacajawea
moved with the well-wishers, receiving congratula-
tions, gifts, and songs of praise and promise. There was
an elaborate oration from Redpipe, who outlined the
duties of a woman of the Metaharta. First he harangued
them concerning the greatness of the village and then
about his family and Sacajawea's duties toward the
members of his family. "The honor of the people lies in
the moccasin tracks of the women. Walk the good road,
daughter, and the buffalo herds, wide and dark as cloud
shadows moving over the prairie, will follow you. The
spring will be full of the yellow calves, the fall earth
shaking with the coming of the fat ones, their robes
thick and warm as the sun on the lodge door. Be dutiful,
respectful, gentle, and modest, my daughter. And proud
walking. If the pride and the virtue of the women are

lost, the spring will come, but the buffalo trails will
turn to grass. Be strong with the arm, strong heart of
the earth. No people goes down until their women are
weak and dishonored, or dead upon the ground. Be
strong and sing the strength of the Great Spirit within
you and all around you."

Then Sacajawea did as instructed. She went out and
faced the sun. She lifted her arms to the heavens, to
the earth, and toward its four corners. To the observers,
she was quite lovely, as most young girls are at that
age.

Her face was shaped like the moon, painted soft white
with yellow circles under each eye. Her black hair, which
fell below her shoulders, moved in the sunlight with
blue-black glints. Her ears were red inside. Her lips
were full, the corners turned up. Her eyes were dark,
widely spaced, her nose straight, her cheekbones high,
and her skin silken. Her long bare legs broke through
her garments. Her voice was soft and filled with re-
straint, and her movements were unhurried. None could
see the scars that still remained white on her back from
the quirt of her former master.

"You are beautiful, my daughter," Grasshopper said
in a low voice. "Your body is straight and strong. What
comes to you from now until the ceremony is ended will
be the measure of your life. The things that you feel
now in your heart will mark your feelings henceforth.
What you like now, you will like until the end of your
days. If you eat well now, you will always have plenty
to eat. Watch carefully and study yourself, for this is
your opportunity to know yourself and what lies within
you, in your body and in your heart."

Sacajawea held her hands together; her lips quivered. "*Ai*, my mother," she whispered.

"You must not speak overly much because then you
will always have a long tongue. You must not laugh
because then your face will become old and wrinkled
before its time."

"*Ai*, my mother."

"You must listen to what the singer tells you and
believe him. If you do not believe in your heart what
he says, it will be of no benefit. You must not become

angry or use bad language, for if you do, such will be your nature for the rest of your life."

Grasshopper placed her hands upon the girl's head and said, "Now I must ask you this. No man has entered you and made you unchaste?"

"Mother," replied Sacajawea, trembling, "I did not know you would ask me that."

"Has any man of the Metaharta tribe touched you?"

Sacajawea's knees became water, then froze again. She felt she was now to be a disgrace, not only to her new family but to herself in front of all of Grasshopper's friends. "No, no one from this tribal village, but I was a captured slave of the—"

"You are ready, then," Grasshopper said quickly, so that Sacajawea need not go on with the whole truth, and took her to sit on a skin in front of the lodge to the south of where the Shaman supervised the raising of the ceremonial wickiup, singing with the singer as the poles were placed so the tips inclined until they met in a point at the top. "Plant a thought, harvest an act," they sang. "Plant an act, harvest a habit; plant a habit, harvest a character; plant a character, harvest a destiny."[30]

From the cooking wickiup nearby, women emerged with clay trays lined with arrowhead leaves and watercress, with fresh chokeberries, wild plums, and grapes. There was a kettle of soup with horn spoons, hump and rib roasts on wooden platters, and bowls of corn, squash, and pumpkin. All were welcome to come to eat, while the father, Redpipe, and his friends sat in a little circle smoking—as they would for birth, for death, for a son returning from his dreaming, so they did for the daughter today.

"So—here you are!" a voice shouted from a group of strange bearded ones who suddenly appeared at the festivities. Sacajawea had never seen these men in the village, yet she was sure they were the white traders that the women had spoken about in the retreating lodge. Her heart jumped to her mouth—maybe one of these men had the Shoshoni girl!

The man who had spoken was not a white trader. He glared with one yellowish brown eye as he moved to the food trays. The guests silently moved around him.

Sacajawea thought him the most violent-looking person she had ever seen. He was more than six feet tall, with a head that seemed large even for his gigantic body and a nose that hooked inward like an eagle's beak. His face was pitted with smallpox scars and the right eye was covered with a white opaque membrane, half-concealed by a drooping eyelid. A vivid scarlet scar ran from that drooping eyelid across his cheekbone to his earlobe. The earlobe on both ears had been slashed so that he could run a yellow strip of rawhide through, knotted in the back, with copper wire wound around the dangling rawhide in front. He stood slightly bent forward so that his neck seemed to be placed more toward the chest than back. His elbows and knees were flexed, and he looked as if he would attack anyone who disagreed with him.

Suddenly the huge man left the food and came close to Sacajawea. He wore only a breechclout, and around his bare neck was a circlet of black-tipped weasel tails.

"I wish to make a gift to the daughter of Redpipe." His voice boomed.

Before Sacajawea could respond, Rosebud stepped up. "I will take your gift on behalf of Redpipe and his daughter," she said, her face almost as white as the white pigment decoration circling her eyes.

"No, no, the young daughter of Redpipe must accept this," he said. "You are not the one. Where is the other? Where?" he demanded.

"Ho, Le Borgne knows where to pick the pretty flowers!" shouted one of the bearded men in broken Minnetaree.

"Hey, Chief, you think they'll come entertain us?" called another, stamping his feet and swinging his arms.

"Quiet," the huge man said, and his anger seemed to rise and boil within him. "You, then, take this to the one called Sweet Clover." Rosebud gasped as he handed her the weasel collar from around his neck. "Tell the one called Sweet Clover that Chief Kakoakis sends this gift."

Grasshopper drew in her breath.

Chief Kakoakis turned toward Grasshopper and blinked his one good eye at her. "I was not aware of this youngest daughter of yours. I see she is now ripe enough to be a woman. Send her to my lodge, and you will have a grand present. You do like presents, Old Mother?"

"There are enough gifts this day to satisfy the heart," spat out Grasshopper, moving to block Kakoakis from both Sacajawea and Rosebud.

"Some of my friends wish to dance," Kakoakis said, pointing to the bearded men. "I will tell them that you make them welcome." He turned to leave and was swallowed by the crowd that seemed to surge in behind him.

Grasshopper's face was ashen. "Kakoakis!" she spat, her voice shaking. Her mouth bunched up, and she rubbed her hands down her hips. "Give me the weasel tips." She grabbed them from Rosebud and stepped silently toward the refuse heap. She never took her eyes from Sacajawea as she wadded the fur necklace and threw it on the pile of bones and scraps. No one seemed to look at her, nor did they say anything for fear of bringing on the wrath of their chief.

When the sun began to set and the men who were to serve as masked dancers had donned their ritual shirts and moccasins, the Shaman rolled a leaf of mild tobacco, puffed smoke to the four directions, and asked the dancers to begin.

With the drums throbbing, they moved out to the center of the village to the council fire, moving forward and back, then circling. The people talked and joked, and soon the young people joined in, the girls keeping a watchful eye for a hand, perhaps a certain hand, to beckon them into the dancing and song, then to fall back to another, as was proper.

Sacajawea knew that she was expected to join the dancers, but the sight of Kakoakis and the white men sitting near Redpipe on the far side of the fire filled her with fear, and she watched the activities sitting safely on a blanket.[31] At last the festivities were over.

The return to the lodges from the dance was casual. The young people walked together in small groups, the old women a few steps behind, complaining among themselves about the late hour and the chill of the night.

When Sacajawea came through the lodge entrance, Grasshopper asked, "Did you enjoy your festivities?"

"*Ai*, thank you. It was nice." She showed Grasshopper her presents: paints, a belt with beaded shells, a scraping knife, a metal awl, several yellowed elk's teeth.

"I am relieved Chief Kakoakis did not bother us at the dancing," sighed Rosebud, "but you did not dance with anyone! You just sat there staring at the fire and the other dancers! You did not dance!"

"Shhh! My daughter did not wish to dance. She had a moment of bad experience," said Grasshopper, waddling over to sit beside Sacajawea.

"Is she my daughter or still a slave girl?" asked Redpipe, moving his skinny legs into bed. "It was embarrassing for me to have her sit. Chief Kakoakis asked me about her. When we could not find her dancing, he made a joke, 'Oh, oh, she is out in the brush with a man already. So—she is aware of the effect she has on men!' And he slapped me on the back so that I almost coughed up my buffalo steak."

"And then you pointed to where she was sitting?" snapped Grasshopper.

"I did not! One of the bearded white men did that. They had been watching her. These white men are slaves to urges that seem about to consume them. But they did not go near our new daughter. After a time they went home with the women loaned to them by Kakoakis. I think they imagined you beside our daughter and feared your long tongue."

Grasshopper whispered, "Great Spirit, help us!" Then in a louder voice she said, "I have noticed that about the whites. They are eaten by the thoughts of one thing—wanting our women. Nobody has taught them to be continent or restrained like our men, by fasting and controlling the body for what it must endure in war or in hunting and trapping."

"Mother," interrupted Rosebud, "the white traders in our village are not so bad. They have lived here for as many as five summers." She held up the fingers of one hand. "Their women do not complain about them. The women have many presents and do not have to work in the fields. Their men are able to trade for the vegetables from us. It is our chief, Kakoakis, I think, who spreads evil in our village."

Redpipe rolled over in his bed. "Women! Hush! Never

must you speak out loud of your dissatisfaction with our chief. He can bring disaster upon this household anytime he wishes."

Instantly Grasshopper remembered the discarded weasel collar and looked about the room thinking who might have seen her put it in the refuse pile and wondering if any would dare tell on her. On an impulse, she left Sacajawea's side and walked to the back of the lodge where the refuse had been thrown. She stopped, aghast. A squaw was hunting through the pile. It was possible her family did not supply her with enough to keep her sides from rubbing, and Grasshopper called to her, "Come, I will fix you some broth!"

Before Grasshopper could get a good look at her, the woman, who was not old, but young and agile, ducked and dodged past. Something was rolled inside the front of her tunic. Her hands pushed it securely to her breast as she ran across to the next lodge and then out of sight. Grasshopper called after her and ran to the edge of the next lodge, but the young woman had gone. Grasshopper's mind ran in circles. She gazed at the clouds in the sky and tried to think, to remember the features of the young woman. Was she familiar? Grasshopper wiped her hands on her tunic; they were wet with perspiration.

"That woman took the weasel-tail collar," said both Sacajawea and Rosebud together. They had followed Grasshopper from the lodge, and now they put their hands to their mouths. It was a sign of thinking another's thoughts to speak the same thing at the same time. "Why would she take that?" they asked together. Then, afraid to speak again, they looked to Grasshopper.

"She could be a woman of Kakoakis," Grasshopper said slowly. "But I don't think so. His women are well-dressed and good-looking. I did not see her face, but she was not clean." Grasshopper's decision was made. "Do not think on this. It is something we can do nothing about. Probably we will not hear of it again. The weasel collar is gone, and I say good riddance!" She clucked and pulled the wisps of hair from her face and returned to the lodge.

"I hope Grasshopper is right and there will be nothing more heard of the collar," said Rosebud.

"*Ai*," answered Sacajawea. "I do not want Chief Kakoakis coming around. He could give the small children bad dreams."

That night, Sacajawea slept little. She was a woman now, but vacillated between the impossible thought of running away and the other thought of quietly marrying one of the Metaharta braves. "Why not?" she asked herself. "My own people did not come to look for me."

Then there was that round, hard thing that came and stayed in her throat—the thing was the forgetting of the old Agaidüka habits. Several times she told herself, "I am an Agaidüka. I must throw off my Minnetaree ways and keep those of my own people. They cannot make me be a Minnetaree!" She thought of following the Big Muddy River back across the prairie, into the mountains—but if she were caught, she would be made sport of by Kakoakis, then she would be killed or sold to some other tribe. Grasshopper was kind, and life was not hard here as it had been in the big Hidatsa village. Maybe she should, after all, wash her mind of the past.

She lay quite still until the dawn light showed through the smoke hole and she could see the dark forms of her new family lying around the sides of the circular room. She rose quietly and went outside, pulling a woven grass sash tightly around her waist to hold in the sides of her tunic. No sound came from anywhere in the village. All was cool and still. She walked quietly down to the edge of the bathing place in the river and along the shore. She watched the killdeers swooping out over the river, catching insects on the wing, emitting thin cries as they rose from the river and flew out across the grassy plain. She watched until they were only a group of mingling, weaving specks, then nothing. She washed the paint from yesterday's ceremony from her body. She felt refreshed, and her mind was clear.

Sacajawea went back across the grassy rise and along the dusty path toward the village. On an impulse she wandered close to the sapling-picketed walls of the village along the bank of a little stream. She thought of the wild dog and wondered if there were others in the sagebrush out there, waiting to be friendly. She began roaming the woods. She had known little of childhood, but Mother Earth was her friend. The growing things that changed every day, the rocks that never changed at all—these were things she could count on. She thought, I always know what to expect of the things of Mother Earth. Sometimes they are cruel, but it is hard, clean cruelty. They don't torture you with their own weakness. She wondered then about Old Mother, Old Grandfather, and Catches Two, Antelope, and Talking Goose. Then her mind turned to her new family—the tormented Redpipe, and Sweet Clover, and the hideous chief of this village. Kakoakis could change people's lives without so much as thinking about what he was doing. You cannot count on people, she thought, and the corner of her mouth flickered with a grim little smile.

Alone this morning, she let herself go back to the fantasies her childhood had never completed. She entered into the magic realm that her new family would not have credited even if she could have told them of it. Grown-ups managed to forget all such things with maturity and could not visualize one who had been a slave for several years behaving with such abandonment and pure childish joy. She smiled secretly for delight, a child, forgetful of all yesterdays.

For several hours she wandered, playing in her own way, back into her nearly forgotten childhood, vying with the chipmunks in search of nuts, with the chickadees in the seeking out of secret places, and with the big green frogs in plumbing the depths of the woodland pools. She had smelled scents, seen colors, heard sounds, and felt joys so seldom in the summer air. Her fingers, no longer callused, were sensitive to the dryness of the rocks and the pleasurable contrast between the soft moss and the rough sand, all at one and the same time, in the instinctive way of young birds and animals.

About midafternoon, she came to the banks of a wide stream. She made boats of rolled bark, peeling it thin with her knife and sending boatloads of frightened people down the rushing stream to the far-off water. Her people were pinecones, and she sang to them with each launching in the old, monotonous, five-note songs of the

Agaidükas. Her songs were not remembered, but instantly invented to fit the freedom of her situation.

Presently a disturbing sensation that she was not alone began to steal over her—a sense that unfriendly eyes were close by. She hardly heeded it at first, but it persisted. Finally she stood up and strove to penetrate the blue-black shadows.

Then her heart gave a violent surge and she wished she had taken heed of those semiconscious warnings earlier. Something subtle as a shifting cloud had caused her to glance backward, and there, framed in a tangle of windfall, she saw a bushy black head with a furry face and dark eyes, and although there were no braids like the braves wore, and the face was not smooth and brown, she knew this was a man—a bearded white stranger. This was one of the white trappers from the village!

He'd been there a long time, fixing his beaver traps and watching Sacajawea at play. This was not the first time he had followed this same girl lecherously. He had seen her in the big Hidatsa village, and discovered her here more than a moon before. He had taken to watching her in the gardens, knowing well that he could not touch her without being obliterated with a fast stroke of her skinning knife. Each time he had shadowed this child, who was clear-featured and slim, exquisitely made, beautiful by the standards of whites and Indians alike, the one part of frenzied daring had come a bit closer to prevailing over the nine parts of sheer cowardice that composed his French nature. But an instinctive awe of very young females continued to hold him from success.

Today, in this lonely spot, he had aroused himself to the point of action. And like the blood lust of the prairie wolf, the bodily appetite of this half-white, half-Indian man, fully aroused, was not to be turned aside. Imagination had worked upon him until lurid flames burned in his raisinlike eyes and he could fairly smell the pleasure of the tender flesh of his prey.

Abruptly the shaggy black head withdrew for an instant, only to reappear at another spot several feet closer. As Sacajawea glimpsed his short, broad body, the strength of his shoulders, she felt a shaft of cold fear at the purpose she sensed in his sinister movements.

Breaking the spell of his evil watching eyes, Sacajawea turned and fled along the bank of the stream. Glancing backward, she saw the man crashing through the thickets, closing the distance between them. Her knife lay on a shell of birchbark, glinting in the sun.

Emboldened by the sight of the girl running away, the bearded man covered the ground in short bounds, keeping to the undergrowth. Now Sacajawea ran with frank abandon and with all the strength she had. She had never before known fear of a man's two eyes, but she was terrified at what she saw in their depths, fearing at each moment to be struck down. But her woods sense did not leave her; she knew just where she was— the stream led back to the gates of the village, and toward those she turned in her flight, knowing there would be refuge there.

The man was fascinated by the ancient game of chasing a desperate quarry. He came on, always keeping to cover, never getting closer, yet never falling behind. This was all that delayed the girl's capture in those first vital minutes.

Redpipe, as it happened, was rummaging disconsolately about the deserted clearing in front of the village gates, looking for spent arrows and old flint chips. He raised his head at the sound of a human cry that came floating to him from somewhere out at the edge of the woods. He peered with his myopic, hyperthyroid eyes and saw Sacajawea.

Sacajawea had reached the clearing in front of the gate in the very nick of time—the white man was at the clearing also, but an instinct for keeping to cover made him utilize every possible clump of undergrowth in his path.

Her breath coming in desperate sobs, Sacajawea spurted across to the gate with the last of her strength, the bearded one now only a couple of man-lengths behind. Mercifully, the gate was open. But then there came a fresh shaft of terror at the apparition of Redpipe's thin form as he made straight for her, walking with short, unsteady steps. She plunged in through the open gate just as the bearded one straightened, literally

beside himself with lust, and came lancing through the
air to land upon the feet and legs of Redpipe.

In the middle of the afternoon, Fast Arrow, rounding
the village after a desultory hunt, came upon the flat-
footed, moccasined tracks of the white man, toes outward, in the damp earth on the bank of the little stream.
He looked at the sunken beaver trap and knew the
owner by the wad of beaver-castoreum-soaked cloth on
a stick above the trap. As he had done before, out of
curiosity about the bearded one's ways, he turned to
follow the moccasin tracks. They looked less than a hour
old. Fast Arrow worked out the trail, which ran along
the bank, noting that the man had squatted at intervals
to watch and wait. What had the man been stalking,
he wondered.

He puzzled over the tracks where they finally left
the stream bank, and then he was startled to find mingled with them the footprints of a Minnetaree squaw.
It could be that the bearded one had come after a run-
away woman. Yet the squaw did not go back peaceably;
she ran, digging in with her toes.

Fast Arrow hurried forward now, his quick eye reading signs as he went. He came upon deepened toe marks
and saw that the squaw was in full flight. She was
small; her tracks did not sink far into the earth. The
bearded one followed with long strides—he was not
heavy-laden, yet he brought his heel down first and
then rocked forward to his toes. Fast Arrow's heart
began to pound; he was running, too, soundless in his
moccasins.

Stumbling through thickets, he sped toward the
clearing in front of the gates by the shortest possible
route. He was in time to witness the unscrambling of
his father-in-law, Redpipe, and the bearded one.

Ordinarily, Redpipe and this bearded one avoided
one another in their comings and goings, through mu-
tual and well-warranted disrespect. But in this instance
all such inhibitions were swept aside. When old Redpipe
suddenly appeared in the clearing, it seemed to the
bearded one a direct attempt to rob him of the pleasure
he had so patiently stalked—an unforgivable action.
Instantly he sprang forward to annihilate this blun-

dering redskin; the distrust between red and white men was not new by this year, 1802, in the history of the American plains.

Redpipe was flung forward on his nose as the two hundred pounds of bulk landed on him. Immediately the slow, deathly rage of his phlegmatic spirit was lashed to flames. In his nostrils was the beaver-castoreum scent of his attacker, the Squawman, Toussaint Charbonneau.

Redpipe's mind exploded with this knowledge. Rearing upward with a bawl of rage, he flung all his frail strength into the struggle, mouth open in the savage caricature of a grin. Suddenly he fell backward, gasping for breath, his bulging eyes rolling up into his head, in an epileptoid fit.

Fast Arrow saw Sacajawea make the entrance to his lodge and knew that she was safe from her attacker.

It was a minute or so before Toussaint Charbonneau realized that Redpipe was having a seizure; Redpipe's affliction was well known. Charbonneau's fury abated; he fell back to examine his arm, which was deeply scratched from elbow to wrist. Then, seeing Fast Arrow standing near, he abruptly rose and ambled forward in sudden friendliness.

"*Mon dieu*, that old Redpipe is still a warrior," he said in halting Minnetaree mixed with French phrases. "He tripped me as I came for the gate." Charbonneau's breath came in fast, shallow gulps, and the upper part of his face, which was not whiskered, was as red as his neck.

"Squawman," said Fast Arrow, his face dark, "you were running after my small sister?"

Before Charbonneau could think of an appropriate answer, Fast Arrow had bent to tend to Redpipe. Perspiration laced spidery channels through the crusting dust covering his body. He shook and slavered like a trapped wolf.

"*La jolie femme?*" Charbonneau said. "She is your sister?"

"My sister since the Moon of the Trading Fair," Fast Arrow indicated with hand signs.

"Was that her ceremony in the village yesterday?"

"*Ai*, and you chased her as if she were a village slave."

"Slave—*oui*. It is known you won her from an Ahnahaway. She is known in the big Hidatsa village as the Girl Who Loved a Dog." Charbonneau began to laugh and hold his sides. "That is a nice picture for you. A girl making love to a dog! What a *diable* she must be!"

Fast Arrow straightened and looked directly at Charbonneau, who was now wiping the tears from his eyes as he laughed harder.

"That girl is known as Sacajawea, and she is the daughter of my mother, Grasshopper; she is no man's woman. You lie about her and some mangy dog."

"Woman! She cannot even keep hold of her skinning knife for protection, and she plays in the water like a small child. *Aagh*, that papoose, she did not even dance at her own puberty ceremony. I saw! The Hidatsas threw her away. Why did you pick her up? She is really still a child, a nothing, a female child of no importance, something to give away. I'll take her. I'll give you an ax for her. Then you will not have so many mouths to feed in your lodge. You will thank me and call me your friend."

Fast Arrow's eyes narrowed as Charbonneau continued to speak in his halting Minnetaree, begging for the young girl who appealed to him.

Finally Fast Arrow had heard enough. "If you are lucky, you will stop an arrow before the new moon."

Charbonneau sneered back; then his shoulders sagged and he spat on the ground before heading toward the village gate. *"Zut! Diable!"* he shouted back at Fast Arrow.

8

The Mandans

There are some who believe that a Welshman, named Madoc, discovered the new continent of America prior to Columbus' famous voyage. They find old Welsh and English records to prove that Madoc and his men came to America in 1170 and anchored nine or ten ships in the Bay of Mobile. These Welshmen retreated from the coast to find security from attacking Indians and eventually reached the mountains of east Tennessee. No one knows how many months or years passed before they were forced to move from their fortified villages because of the greater number of attacking Cherokee Indians. The legend takes the white men back to the Mississippi River where they slowly migrated upriver toward the northwest to the Missouri River country. These people built fortifications around their sedentary, earthen hut villages. Their skin clothing was not made in the same fashion as that of the Upper Missouri tribes. Some of these people supposedly spoke and understood the Welsh language. They carried skin-wrapped parchments, which they could not read. The legendary Welshmen in early America made a primitive kind of harp for music on special occasions. Early explorers said these Welsh Indians recalled their ancestors coming a long way to reach the Upper Missouri, even traveling a long time on a great expanse of water. The explorer Verendrye first mentioned blue-eyed, light-haired people called Mandans, *who had non-Indian fortifications and lived in the Missouri River valley.*[1]

   Mandan mythology explicitly tells that the first ancestor of these people was a white man who, in the mists of antiquity, came to the country in a canoe. Long before the first missionaries reached the Mandan they are alleged to have known of a gentle, kindly god who was born of a virgin and died a death of expiation; they told of a miracle having close affinities with the feeding of the five thousand; they related the story of the first mother of mankind and her fall, of the ark and of the dove with a green twig in his beak; they believed in a personal devil who sought to win over and subjugate to himself the world of men. The clear traces of European blood which the Mandan exhibited in the middle 1700's cannot have been the outcome of a relatively fleeting contact with white men; they must have sprung from some much more profound intermingling. What great adventure lies behind this strange and now vanished tribe? We do not know.[2]

   Many explorers after Verendrye wrote about the white Indians. This word white seemed to lead them into being a mythical kind of Indian. Their hair was light, sometimes red, eventually turning gray; their eyes were blue or hazel. Ethnologists offer a normal, genetic explanation. The white Indians were albinos. The nearby tribes of Hidatsa, Arikara, and Crow showed less frequent—but similar—albino traits. The Welsh historian Williams says that "as legends go, it is genial, human, and humane. It appeals to everyone."[3]

For several days the Minnetaree village of Metaharta had been making preparations. It was soon the time for braves from the neighboring Mandans to be coming. These Mandans were the buffalo scouters, and they traditionally invited the Metaharta to help in their annual spring and summer hunts.

Sacajawea was sitting on her sleeping couch with the skin curtains pulled aside, lazily combing her hair, when she heard a great commotion outside.

Exclaiming, "Rooptahee Mandans!" Grasshopper ran out the door.

Sacajawea dressed as fast as she could. She was eager to see the men from the Mandans who had hair white as snow and eyes the color of summer sky. Rosebud had told her so.

The council area was full of people, waving and shouting to the riders, and dodging the horses. Some of the horses were loaded with buffalo-hide packs, and others were being unloaded. Men herded the unloaded horses into open spaces on the slopes above the village.

Some of the men were Minnetarees; and some must have been Mandan, for their hair was streaked with silver or gray and some was the color of dried grass. Their bodies were copper-colored in the sunlight. Their faces were streaked with paint, eyes outlined in white, with horizontal white bars across their cheeks. Sacajawea could not tell if the men were grinning at each other or baring their teeth. They looked terrible. They wore torn, dirty shirts and trousers that flapped as they rode. Their knee-high moccasins were fuzzy with gray prairie dust, and they carried murderous-looking lances. Sacajawea noticed that two or three of the men had straw-colored beards on their faces. They were shouting—at the horses, at each other, at the people in the council area—and they were flexing their great muscles and leaning from their horses to grab the hands of pretty girls. Some of these men had blue or gray eyes. Some were singing, and though they were so dirty and so terrible-looking, they were radiant with triumph, and whatever they were shouting or singing, it all

161

sounded like one great splendid hurrah: *"Ni-effi coe-dig!"* "We are hunters!" "The buffalo are near and plentiful!" *"Buch! Buch! Buch!"*

Pressing against the wall of a lodge to keep out of their way, Sacajawea felt the little tingles that rippled through her whenever something really thrilling took place. These men, riding horses loaded with meat and hides, gave her a feeling deep down inside that she could not have expressed. It was a feeling that these men were strong and right and splendid, the sort who rode proudly over the earth and made villages strong. Today she felt proud to be a Minnetaree.

She caught sight of Rosebud, not far away in the crowd. Rosebud was holding a robe over her hair to keep the dust out. Sacajawea edged her way along the wall and spoke to her.

"What a morning!" said Rosebud. "Isn't this like a fair?"

They heard a string of angry Mandan, *"Nehi! Ake-e-vee!"* as one of the riders shouted to a Minnetaree on foot who was in the path of his horse. Sacajawea smiled. "They are frightening, aren't they?"

"Frightening? I never saw such a bunch of horrors in my life. Maybe they'll look human when they've washed and dressed for the Buffalo Dance." Rosebud looked pleased. "That is much fun to watch. We'll go on horseback with Fast Arrow and Redpipe. They know some of the important men in the Rooptahee village."

Suddenly Sacajawea grabbed Rosebud's arm. "Do you think the black-bearded one will be there?"

"No, he's probably gone looking after his beaver traps. The white traders don't often come to the Buffalo Dance." Then Rosebud scraped her moccasins in the dirt. Looking down, she said, "It is best that you know our chief will be there. He will be the guest of the Mandan chiefs. But we can stay out of his sight, and besides, Fast Arrow will be with us."

The next morning, Sweet Clover brought four horses from the pasture. Fast Arrow and Redpipe would each ride one. Sacajawea and Rosebud would ride together, leading the spare, which would be used for carrying meat and hides.

"Redpipe—he should not become tired because it might lead to another long illness," Grasshopper whispered. "Encourage him to stay and visit his old friend Four Bears instead of going on the hunt with the younger men."

"I can suggest it," answered Rosebud, "but he is stiff in opinions."

"Stubborn," said Grasshopper. "Only Redpipe knows what is right. He will tell you so himself," she said sarcastically.

"I will try to see that he rests frequently, my mother," said Sacajawea. "If Rosebud and I become thirsty and must stop for a drink at a stream, he will have to wait for us, or get a drink for himself. We will drink often."

It was a long but easy ride to the village of the Rooptahee once they passed the edge of the Knife River. From there they rode on sandy ground to the Big Muddy River. They forded the river and soon passed an old abandoned village. The weeds grew waist-high in it. The girls, who had fallen back to ride with the other Minnetaree women, followed the men through the center of the old village. The mud huts were falling apart. The wooden doors on many were gone or swinging with the wind.

"Where are these people?" Sacajawea asked Rosebud. "Why did they leave their homes?"

"The coughing sickness came on the back of the north wind," said Rosebud. "Half the village died. Those who were left did what they could, and with heavy hearts moved across the river to the Mahawha village where their cousins the Ahnahaways live."

"But their medicine men? Where were they when the sickness came?"

"*Ai*, the people were told to make use of the sweat lodges, then to run directly to the river to cool off their hot bodies. Many never came out of the river."

"So—was it the sweat lodges of the medicine men or the river that killed them?" asked Sacajawea.

"You forget the coughing sickness."

"Did they take it to the Ahnahaways?"

"*Ai*, they did. But they had a great fear about staying in the same lodges where so many had died, and so they had to move."

"But they did not fear crossing the river where so many had died? And you do not fear riding through their old village?"

"You ask puzzling thoughts," said Rosebud.

Eighteen-foot-high timbers formed a stockade around the round mud huts of the Rooptahee village. Rosebud pointed out to Sacajawea where some of the timbers were spaced apart to permit firesticks or arrows to be fired between them. There were great shouts of greeting, and the village gates were opened to them. The Minnetaree men dismounted and let the old women of the Rooptahee take the reins of their horses and lead them away.

"They will be kept in the grazing ground, and we will find them again," Rosebud assured Sacajawea.

Close against the inside of the stockade ran a three-foot ditch, which, Rosebud explained, further screened warriors from the view and weapons of attacking enemies.

Then a tall man, naked except for a loincloth, his broad, heavy chest covered with the symbol of the sun in red and with the sign of lightning in yellow, his arms hidden from his wrists to his elbows with bands of woven grass and leather, pushed his way through the crowd.

"That is the Wolf Chief," said Rosebud. "He is a friend of Chief Kakoakis and chief of all the Mandans. See, over there, they talk now." She pointed to where the two men, Kakoakis and the Wolf Chief, were standing encircled by men from the two villages, Metaharta and Rooptahee.[4]

The people were hushed so they could hear the two leaders speaking with one another.

"What makes you think you will leave here alive?" asked the Wolf Chief, looking directly into the forbidding face of Kakoakis.

Sacajawea felt herself breathe in and out six times before Kakoakis replied, "It is known that the head chief of the Mandans is the greatest leader of all time. It is known that he respects truth and bravery. It is known that he commands respect and is a crooked-tongued snake in the grass."

The last words might not have been spoken. There

was not a flicker in the eyes of the titular head of all
Mandans to indicate he had heard or understood. Kakoakis waited quietly.

"You are a brave man to come to one of my villages,"
the Wolf Chief said, his face straight. "I am honored.
But what are you doing outside your own village without guards?"

"I do not need protection when I am among people
who are soft as prairie chickens. With one twist of the
neck by my one hand, the head of any one of your braves
would drop off. The men in my village stay strong the
whole year. The men of your village remain weak, like
women, until it is hunting time. Then they pretend they
are strong by showing how loud they can make their
voices. They are like barking dogs who are afraid to
bite."

The Wolf Chief was a haughty and overbearing man,
more feared than loved by his people. He had inherited
his high office from his father, and he had managed to
hold on to his authority in spite of his shortcomings as
a governor and warrior. He and Chief Kakoakis enjoyed
pretending each was an object of misery almost beyond
belief. The Wolf Chief knew and encouraged his people
in the knowledge that the moment Kakoakis was replaced by a weaker, less cruel man, the Mandans would
extend their totalitarian rule to the Minnetarees.

Now the Wolf Chief turned and inspected Chief Kakoakis with an air of pity. "I'd almost forgotten what
an ugly old dog you are. It is always a shock."

"Ha-na-ta-nu-mauk," said Chief Kakoakis. "What
has happened to your beautiful yellow hair? It is becoming red like the sunset."

"Well, so, it is better red with paint than black with
soot and vermin as is yours. Have you forgotten the
way to the river for a wash? Your smell is worse than
ten horses kept in a tight enclosure for ten suns."

"My smell is of the earth itself. I would not have my
woman fix me like a dandy with crushed mint in my
mouth and sage rubbed over my body so I smelled as
you, which is more like a roasting duck with herbs."

"And so," said the Wolf Chief, smelling his under-
arm, "now that you have found my village, have your

people put their temporary skin tepees in the usual place."

The lodges of the Mandans were similar to those of the Minnetarees, yet more elegant. The streets were wider and much cleaner. It was obvious to Sacajawea that the Mandans were the leaders of this type of culture. Somewhere in forgotten history, the Minnetarees had moved in and copied the ways of the Mandans. Some said the Minnetarees were once a band of frightened Sioux fleeing from the Blackfeet. The stockade-type village was built to keep out these deadly fighters.

When they reached the campsite, Sacajawea and Rosebud undid the packs and strung up a temporary skin lean-to, a type that did not need heavy lodgepoles. Other women did the same with the gear they had brought. While they worked, Rosebud told Sacajawea what she knew about the Mandans, and about the Wolf Chief, who practically never said exactly what he meant, and never told the entire truth about a subject if there was an opportunity to make up a better story.

Redpipe, sitting a few feet away, added information to what Rosebud told her, and now he took a long drag on his pipe, spat upon the ground, and said, "That is the way the Wolf Chief gets his amusement."

Fast Arrow, who was pretending to be asleep in the shade of a low sagebrush, said in a hushed voice, "He is a first-rate storyteller at heart; he is a mockingbird wasting his song on the wind, generally." Then he, too, began to speak of the Mandans.

His friend Four Bears, a well-loved subchief of this village of Rooptahee, still remembered the words of his old father, Ddraig Goch, Red Beast.[5] He had told Four Bears years ago that his name was very old and that it was in some way related to the several sacred gold disks kept in the large sacred ark. The markings on those disks were as foreign to him as the scratchings found on a few flat stones on the prairie. He said that they were the last remnants of ancestors who had pale eyes and pale skin. Now there was only one golden disk or ancient coin left. No one knew what had become of the others. The Mandans, the People of the Pheasants, were descendants of a man ages ago called Madoc.[6] This was something to be kept safe and not talked about. Four Bears's fathers said they had not always lived at the headwaters of the Big Muddy; they had lived farther to the south, but enemy tribes had pushed them north until finally they had settled here in several villages. More villages had been in this area then, and they were all well fortified in a manner remembered from some remote, enigmatic land called Cambria, from which these ancient ancestors had come. They had traveled in large canoes, the number of which was indicated by the fingers on both hands, to the land in the south by the huge salt waters. After many ages of men, they had come to this place, near the Big Muddy and Knife rivers, to live.

But there came a time when the people became tired and lost their strength, and the young did not follow in all the ways of the old. The young made sport of the old ideas and invented new ones. Ideas such as not planting as many crops and depending upon the spring fairs for meat and animal skins, instead of hunting both in spring and fall. Hunting kept a man's eyes sharp, but now the young ones did not believe that. Hunting was a waste of time to them if someone else would do it for them. The young braves of the Mandans had become soft and lazy, willing to let the women work in the fields and harvest crops while they raced their horses or played games of chance. Even hunting had become a game for them. They raced to see who could ride the best-decorated pony or shout the loudest on the way to the hunt.

Sacajawea listened as she began smashing dried corn in a bowl. Rosebud had started a fire in front of their lean-to, keeping pace with the other women who were doing the same. Sacajawea was excited and wanted to explore the village. She noticed a small girl with pale eyes and yellow hair skip past them, then climb a ladder made from saplings and leather bindings to the top of a lodge where several old women were gossiping in the sun. The women had snow-white hair. Sacajawea pointed at them.

"You will see more," said Rosebud, "and some of the men have pale skin and much face hair."

Sacajawea laughed. "Do they wish to look like the white men?"

"That is hard to believe," agreed Rosebud. "Each nation believes it is best. We think we are better than the Mandans. And they think they are better than us. They think having hair on the face is something grand."

"Do the white men believe they are better?" asked Sacajawea, laughing. "We know we are better than they. Come, I would like to go to the council area for a look." She helped Rosebud fill a clay pot with the ground corn, and they left it soaking on a low fire. Redpipe was still enjoying his pipe with half-closed eyes, and Fast Arrow was asleep.

All of the lodge doors of the village opened toward a large arena in the center, at least thirty man-lengths in diameter, in the middle of which stood a large structure made of hand-hewn planks and hoops, almost two man-lengths high. There was a hole in one side where sacred objects could be removed or replaced. Fast Arrow had said the structure represented an ark or canoe used by the First Men when waters covered the earth. It contained the nation's most precious medicine—buffalo skulls, bat-wing bones, eagle feathers, and the gold disk, which was smooth and worn from generations of handling, but still visible on one side was the distinct tail of a fish and some lettered characters. On the obverse side was an image of an instrument not too different in appearance from the gut-string and bent wood harp played today by Mandan musicians. There was also a flat quartzite stone inscribed on both sides with unknown characters, something saved from antiquity.

The Mandans told of forebears once finding some of the same inscribed characters fixed on a stone on top of a rock cairn, which they believed had been standing in the hills since time began for their people. Once in a great while on a buffalo or elk round, a young Mandan brave would still come back to tell of seeing one or more of these pillars, or walls formed of several pillars stacked on their sides. Now these walls were used as a blind to hide behind while stalking game. The Mandans could not remember who had been the first people to place these great pillars of stone in the woods and on the plains. But they were certain that they had been the

First Men, and they had a word for them that was
remembered but not spoken. It was a taboo word, something to be guarded, a word that in certain circumstances would be used for safe conduct or an expression
of trust.

Rosebud circled the medicine structure from a good
distance, not daring to go too close. Sacajawea endured
her curiosity as long as possible, but soon she was bending far over in the dark hole to see inside this huge
landlocked canoe, smelling the musty smell of things
dead for many seasons.

Rosebud called to her to come away quickly. A woman
was never permitted so near such a sacred place, but
Sacajawea did not hear. Rosebud moved to the shadow
of the Council Lodge, not wanting to be part of something considered unwomanly, something never done.

Sacajawea's mind went back to the time she had
stood in the medicine circle with her father. It now
seemed merely a dream as she thought on these things
left by others who had lived in some distant age. These
others had once been young and laughing in the sunshine, then old and sad in the cold of winter.

"Woman, why do you keep your eyes on the relics of
the People of the Pheasants?" someone asked sharply,
but with formal courtesy.

Sacajawea spun around and saw a stranger dressed
in leggings rich with elk's teeth and shells. He wore no
shirt. His shoulders were splendid in the sun. On his
bronze chest was a vermilion handprint with wide yellow streaks going around to his back, meeting in jagged
lines, like lightning, on the rough scars there.

Sacajawea took time to gather her wits. She noticed
that his moccasins were of fine white leather with dark
blue whangs on the front, each with a white shell tied
at the end. She raised her eyes, noticing he wore an
eagle feather headdress, with the soft breath feathers
framing his forehead.

"You are too bold for a woman. Your manners are
disgraceful."

"*Ai*, you are right. I was carried away. I am a visitor
in your village. I will go to my camp now." Her voice
was steady, but her knees felt like thin gruel.

He stood in her path. "The day is good." He did not move to let her pass.

Sacajawea fell back one or two steps. He was standing with his back to the light, but she could see that his hair grew to a point on his forehead, that he had a long face, narrowing at the temples. His mouth was straight, almost grim, and he did not smile as he spoke. He did not look as if he ever smiled very much.

Sacajawea's mind went looking for words to tell him she had only been curious, that she had meant no disrespect.

The man said, "You are not a Minnetaree."

Sacajawea hesitated a moment, looking about for Rosebud. "I am a Metaharta, daughter of Redpipe. We have come for the Buffalo Dance. I am sorry; for a moment I forgot I was a woman. My mind flew away on bird's wings. I now know and have regained my manners." She tried to move past, thinking she had apologized sufficiently to let the matter drop.

A frown appeared between the man's black eyebrows. "You! No! A daughter of Redpipe?" he asked.

"Ai!" she exclaimed, glad to find that he spoke Minnetaree now, not the strange sounds of Mandan.

"You will forgive me," he said with grave courtesy. "I can see you are *prydfa*, beautiful." He seemed embarrassed. "I mistook you for one of the *akeevee*, the disgusting women of your chief, Kakoakis. You spoke not a clear tongue of Minnetaree, and I assumed you were a captured slave."

"*Ai*, and so I will go now," Sacajawea said, pushing past the man.

"Redpipe is here?" he asked.

She had taken a step to one side to give herself room to pass him. He turned toward her, so that now the sun fell full on his face as he added, "I am Four Bears, old friend of Redpipe."

"And," Sacajawea said, looking up at him, her knees no longer soft gruel, "Fast Arrow is here, too."

Then she felt embarrassed, wondering if she had said too much. He did not move, but looked down at her with a stern face. She had not noticed how tall he was, a good deal taller than most Mandans, and very lean and hard. Now that the sun shone on his face, she saw that it had a very light coloring, and she saw, too, that though his hair was dark, his eyes were a light blue-green, the color of ice on a winter lake, and just as cold. He had a granite grimness, and she tried not to let her thoughts get into her voice; she wanted now only to leave this place.

"I have not lived with Redpipe and Grasshopper for long."

His green eyes narrowed involuntarily. His thin lips parted in astonishment. "Then you are a slave?" He said it again, as though to make sure he had really heard her. "They have taken you as a slave?"

Now she was sure her tongue was wagging at both ends. She had talked more than had been called for. She wet her lips. "No, they adopted me. Grasshopper had the Becoming a Woman Ceremony. I am her daughter."

"But where did you come from?"

It was unusual for a man to take so much time speaking with a woman he did not know, she thought. Why was he asking all these questions? Still, she could not keep her tongue quiet; he seemed to be somebody important, and so maybe had a right to stand and ask a woman questions.

"I came from the land of the Shining Mountains. I am of the People, the Shoshoni."

"Oh, I want to know where you came from after that," he asked, his face grave and rather forbidding.

Sacajawea felt a twinge of puzzled irritation. She had thought she was going to like the Mandans, but she did not like this one. She tried to be polite because he was a friend of Redpipe's.

"I belonged to a Minnetaree from the big Hidatsa village. I was sold and traded at the spring fair."

"And," said Four Bears, "you know the story from that village about the Girl Who Loved a Dog?"

"*Ai.*"

His lips parted in what she supposed she would have to consider a smile. It was not a friendly smile, nor even an unfriendly one; it was simply the courteous movement of the lips that a man might make if he were amused by a child.

Sacajawea felt her irritation rising. Now that he

thought he knew she was the Girl Who Loved a Dog, he was not going to trust her. She tried to hold on to her temper, but she could not help showing her annoyance. "Who were the people who belonged to the stone with the strange markings?" she asked rudely.

"You will be punished severely if you touch those things. I will not allow you to take the stone to some white trader who believes he can trade it for many beaver pelts in the north."

"But I—" Sacajawea was startled, and her tongue now would not move. She could not imagine anyone bartering with these ancient tokens like vegetables and hides. To her they were valuable because they resided in the ark, reminding the villagers that they were not the first to live upon this land. She could not imagine why he had spoken in that manner to her.

"You are foolish this day," he said. "Do not be foolish tonight, and enjoy the Buffalo Dance." He turned to the open area.

Sacajawea bit her lip. She did not like Redpipe's friend. She walked past him, hurrying when she saw Rosebud come through a crowd of people.

"Sacajawea! I saw you talking with Four Bears," Rosebud said cheerfully. "I'm glad you are acquainted, although he looked as if one of his women had fed him bugbane for the morning meal."

The girls began walking back to their lean-to.

"Is he always like that?" Sacajawea asked suddenly.

"Like what? You mean judging people before he knows them well? *Ai*, he is like that. That is what makes him a good chief. He is not surprised by anything. He already has guessed what his enemy will do. But he can be jolly. He is always kind to women and does not treat them as though they were only to wait upon him or other men."

"I cannot believe that. Not the way he just acted here."

"Well, I'll tell you a story that Grasshopper tells about him. One day Four Bears lifted me high on his shoulder and gave me a braid for each hand. I was only a little girl then. He said *'Tchtch,'* the sound that starts horses, and he pranced. I felt shy and clutched him about the head with my arms, and everybody laughed.

Grasshopper came, and he stopped so she could reach me. She told me that my fingers had to be pried from the reins, his strong black braids!" She giggled. "A girl clinging shamelessly to the hair of a neighboring chief!"

"Does he remember?" asked Sacajawea.

"No, probably not. Girls are not so much to be remembered, or even talked about later. But my father, Redpipe, said that it showed Four Bears had a special bond for girls and his children would probably all be girls."

"And so—"

"He has seven women and many papooses. They are all girls."

Just before nightfall, Rosebud and Sacajawea followed at the correct distance behind Redpipe and Fast Arrow to the council area, where the tom-toms were already beating and the harps were twanging in anticipation of the Buffalo Dance.

"See that child's hair—like milkweed fluff. It is unbelievable," said Sacajawea, pointing to a towheaded girl running barefoot through the dust.

"And so, we told you to watch for such things here," said Rosebud, smiling.

Sacajawea noticed that most of the men of the village were stripped down to breechclouts because of the heat. Each carried his bow and bag of arrows and a knife. Their women carried their buffalo headdresses. Many were moving toward the Medicine Lodge, on the right of the Council Lodge, where they would prepare themselves for the dance. Some other women pointed. Sacajawea followed their fingers and saw a pair of Mandans dancing alone. A sand devil rose up from the flat, open space, gathered a whirling cascade of sparks from the ashes of the fire, and showered them over the two dancers and their beautiful unsoiled tunics. They brushed at their dresses and stamped on the sparks with big, bare, bony feet. The feet were men's feet.

Sacajawea asked, "Are they women?"

"*Ai*," said Rosebud. "And then, no."

Sacajawea said, "She looks like a man, and so does she."

Then Rosebud said, "They are dandies. The Mandans

call them *ber-da-shes*.⁷ Don't you know anything at all?"

"I know a man, and I know a woman."

"So, he's a woman of this village and so is the other one," said Rosebud.

Sacajawea said, "I never knew there were people who could be both."

"There are never many of them," said Rosebud.

Sacajawea watched, fascinated, as the dandies mounted dappled ponies and waved to their friends with fans made of turkey tail feathers. On the wrist of one was a whip and flybrush. They rode on saddles ornamented with porcupine quills and ermine tails. Their dresses were decorated with swansdown and quills from ducks.

"Would they rather be women?" asked Sacajawea.

"You do ask a lot of questions—just like Four Bears," said Rosebud. She poked her foot into the dust. "I might as well tell you all I know because you will ask until I do. The boy is a dandy from the time he has his first dream. When he comes to the age for dreaming in the hills, he still dreams he wears a dress. His mother calls in four dandies if there are the sacred number of four in the village at the time; otherwise, she calls in enough old women who know the singing to make up the four. They sing all night over the boy while his mother or grandmother makes his tunic. In the morning he wears the tunic, dances the sacred number of times—four— around the fire of his lodge, then dances outside the door. He is now forever a dandy."

"Strange," said Sacajawea.

"To tell the truth now," said Rosebud, "I think it is the mother who makes the dandy—a mother who has only one son, or a youngest son she might want to keep around camp. She can keep him from going to war or going to live with some girl. She starts on him when he is young, lets him sit like a woman beyond the time when he should be taught to sit like a man, teaches him to play with dolls and to think like a woman. She can teach him to talk like a woman and to dread things that men do—like hunting and war. Then the boy dreams he is a dandy. *Ai!* The mother can work on him until he can't dream a man's dream at all. Then all he can do is stay at the village and take care of the women and children and worry about his beauty, smoking a pipe while he fans himself to sleep dreaming of beautiful tunics."

Sacajawea was silent, thinking on all this.

Suddenly the flames of the center fire shot high and Mahtoheha, Old Bear, principal Shaman of the Rooptahee, began wailing in a fast, high crescendo that rapidly decreased until his voice died away.

A group of men who had gathered together in a close huddle moved off toward the Medicine Lodge.

"They are getting ready to start!" cried Rosebud.

"I can see," said Sacajawea. They squatted down among the women, directly behind the men's circle, where they could watch everything.

The Shaman came out of the Medicine Lodge with a buffalo head on his shoulders. The last rays of the sun were filtering over the arena, and Sacajawea caught Rosebud's hand when twelve men, each wearing a buffalo head and carrying a favorite hunting bow or spear, began to dance. The drum became louder, the harpists twanged more strongly, and the rattle shakers began.

Because neither the Mandans nor the Minnetarees traveled long distances from their fortified villages for a buffalo hunt, they frequently resorted to this medicine to bring the migrating herds close to them. More warriors and more women and children came from the village to watch. Men stood around, wearing their headdresses, weapons in hand, ready to take the places of those who became too exhausted to continue. When a dancer reached the end of his endurance, he began bending his body lower and lower. Then one of the others would draw his bow and hit him with a blunt arrow. The man would fall to the ground like a wounded buffalo. Then he would be dragged out of the way by the bystanders, who would go through a pantomine of skinning and cutting him up just as a dead buffalo was handled. That dancer's place would be taken by a new dancer.

Far into the night the dance would continue, to the sounds of the drums and the harp and the Shaman chanting, *"Madoc Paho Paneta am byd dyawf buch,"*

"Great Spirit, forever thank you for bringing the buffalo."

The sky had turned dark and the watchers on the high lodges had lit torches so the hunting scouts could see them when Redpipe left the dance and made his way to the lodge of Four Bears. His friend had insisted they eat together this night.

On a pole by the lodge entrance were whitened shields, quivers, scalps of warriors exposed as evidence of warlike deeds, and a medicine bag. Redpipe knocked loudly. A young woman came to the door and led Redpipe to the inside, where he was seated upon a handsome robe. Four Bears nodded to his friend; he was seated on another robe close by. Another woman with a light tan, round face and merry gray eyes brought in woven rush mats, on which she placed a large clay bowl of roast buffalo ribs, a bowl of wild turnip flour pudding flavored with dried currants, and a clay tray heaped with pemmican and marrow fat. Beside the feast was laid a handsome pipe and a tobacco pouch filled with kinnikinnick.

Four Bears lit his pipe and after a few puffs presented it to Redpipe. No word had yet been spoken. With his knife Four Bears cut a small piece of meat and cast it into the fire, giving his thanks to the Great Spirit for food. Redpipe then drew out his own knife and began eating. The guest ate first, while the host sat by at the guest's service, ready to wait upon him. Four Bears and Redpipe sat cross-legged. Four Bears cleaned the pipe, preparing it for another smoke. After it was filled he took out a dried beaver castoreum, the bitter, orange-brown substance from the animal's perineal glands, and shaved off very thin pieces to add flavor to the tobacco. Then he sprinkled a pinch of powdered buffalo dung on top. Four Bears sat patiently with the prepared pipe in his lap, waiting for the right time to light it. His women were seated in silence around the sides of the lodge, waiting for their man's orders. The small children were kept very quiet.

Redpipe finished his meal and reminisced with Four Bears while the latter ate. They continued amid clouds of smoke after the meal. Then Redpipe rose to leave, asking if Four Bears would come back with him to watch the remainder of the Buffalo Dance.

"Do not leave just yet," said Four Bears. "I wish to make you a present of the pipe and the buffalo robe you are sitting on."

Redpipe, his face expressionless, bowed his thanks and sat again upon the robe.

"We do not lie to each other," said Four Bears.

"No."

"Then I am glad I have the scar in my side where the Sioux arrow rested instead of going into your back. That was some battle, huh?"

"You have said that before. I have said before I am glad you saved my life," said Redpipe. "You have something else on your mind, and it is hard to speak of, my friend."

"You have a new daughter."

"Ohhh. *Ai*, I have a new daughter. You think I would have been wiser to adopt a son? *Ai*. I suppose that is true. Women are not so valuable. They shed tears; they ask questions; they nag."

"Your daughter is a former slave of the Hidatsas."

"That is right. She is not Minnetaree, though; she is from the northern nation of Shoshonis." Redpipe peered at his old friend, who only stared back, waiting for Redpipe to say more about his new child. "She has curiosity about things around her."

"*Ai!*" agreed Four Bears. "Much for a woman. She is not restrained."

"She is a joy to have around the lodge. She sings and learns quickly. Grasshopper, my woman, bestows much love on her. The child seems to need the love. She was not well when she came to us. The Hidatsas must have been heartless with her."

"You speak with a straight tongue." There was a glint of firelight in the blue-green eyes of the subchief.

"Why would I do otherwise with you, my friend?" asked Redpipe, puzzled by the conversation of Four Bears. He did not understand why his friend was interested in Sacajawea. She was just one more woman, and that was all Four Bears had in his lodge. He ought to be nearly surfeited by women by this time.

"I have met your daughter. I have spoken to her. She

is not shy. She speaks back. She looked into the sacred
ark and asked me about the ancient stone resting there."

"*Ai*, I can believe that. She wants to know about all
things."

"There is a strange story going around about a young
slave girl from the Hidatsas."

Redpipe started, then he relaxed, waiting to hear
what Four Bears had to say.

"The girl loved a dog more than her captors. The dog
also loved her. He was like a guardian and saved her
life on several occasions. It is said she could talk the
wild dog's tongue, like an animal. When the dog was
killed, she mourned it as she would a relative. The spirit
of the animal stood over the lodge she lived in, and to
appease that spirit a shrine was built to honor it, a
shrine of cast-off bones and meat, an actual rubbish
heap!" There seemed to be an amused upturn to the
mouth of Four Bears.

Redpipe listened carefully, wondering what this story
had to do with him or his new daughter.

"The girl was a curse to her captors. They feared her
power with the wild dogs. They thought she walked
with spirits. She was to have been killed, but one who
had befriended her sold her instead to an Ahnahaway
in exchange for a caged crow. The Ahnahaway did not
know how fortunate he was when he lost the girl to a
Metaharta in a game of arrows."

Redpipe was unable to speak. He had not heard the
story before. "You speak with a straight tongue? This
story is not some made-up thing?"

"There is no fork in my tongue," Four Bears said.

"The story is unbelievable. Yet as I think slowly on
it, I see that the daughter I have could have made friends
with a wild beast. She is gentle and does not push herself with small children or even adults. She is straight-
forward and firm also. She is not devious. Yes, she is
devious! She has put herself around my heart as if I
had raised her from a small cub!"

The green-blue ice of Four Bears's eyes were full of
yellow sparks, and his mouth was curved upward. A
chuckle came from deep in his belly. "Two grown men
we are, sitting here discussing the behavior of a daughter. This is either for women to discuss, or to dismiss.

But we have been doing the talking—about a woman who is as nothing, really, not much use, except to keep one of our young men happy." Again, Four Bears seemed to be laughing deep inside his belly.

"There is more on my mind," said Redpipe, handing the pipe to Four Bears to refill.

"Let us sit, then, and smoke your pipe awhile," suggested Four Bears.

"I know as you know that it is wrong for grown men to worry about women. They are of no consequence." Redpipe paused, glancing at the seven women of Four Bears sitting at the far side of the lodge.

"We are like women to talk or worry about even one of them," agreed Four Bears. "But I have no man-child to think about in my lodge, so I do not find it unusual to worry or speak of a daughter."

Redpipe felt easier and he went on. "I had the fainting sickness. I went on a journey of not waking, and there learned that this new daughter of mine would go to a white man."

"And so—I believe she will be able to protect herself more than you think," answered Four Bears after a moment of meditation.

Redpipe stood up and walked a little. "I have a feeling that this daughter will someday link us with the white men. She will be a go-between. Do we want this?"

"Now you speak strange thoughts." Four Bears gazed at him in bewilderment. "The white man is arrogant and makes his own laws, even in our land. Do you think this daughter would go to live with that?"

"Not of her own will. But she has been shuffled from one village to another, enough to know that she has no say about her destiny. The Great Spirit guides us all. But I am frightened for her now. I do not deny it. If the Hidatsas knew the Girl Who Loved a Dog was here— It makes a man shake."

"Speak for yourself."

"I am. But I am speaking as well for the members of my family who love this woman."

"Times have changed," Four Bears said. "For every Hidatsa who would harm her, there are many more who want nothing but to be left in peace and not be bothered about a shrine of stinking bones."

"Aa-agh!" Redpipe agreed. "But now we go in circles, like a tethered dog."

"A dog"—Four Bears said it softly—"is not the only thing that might go in circles on a tether. Have you ever seen the body of a man who has done that, around a Hidatsa stake, with his own guts ripped out and tied to the post to tether him? Well, I have. *Ai*, you are right in being frightened."

Four Bear's cheeks sucked in against his teeth, and his lips went flat and whitened. "My skin crawls. We must pledge not to speak of this to anyone outside our families. Women gossip. The Hidatsas can have their sacred pile of bones and you can have your beloved daughter and we will both live in peace. We will not tell what lies secretly in our hearts."

"But what if my daughter ever tells her story?" Redpipe asked.

"She will not tell, and if others mention it, you will deny it and make your shoulders shrug as though it is something that has nothing to do with your family. You will clean your mind of the event now, wash it out."

"*Ai*, you have given me much to work over this night."

"I do not hear the drums," said Four Bears. "The young men have gone on the hunt. Your son has gone, too. Will you rest here for the remainder of the night?"

"I find it good here."

"Then we will rest until the sun is in the sky. The night has walked its way across the sky already. And I have another thing for you to sleep on. Listen now. I would like you to come to our Okeepa Ceremony, in another moon. I would like you to bring your son, Fast Arrow, with you. Let him put himself in the Bull Dance as my son. With only women in this lodge, I need someone to smoke with once in a while. I would like someone to make arrows for. I am asking that you share your son with me."

Redpipe sat up. "You honor me! The man of my daughter, Rosebud, my son, Fast Arrow, who came to us from Black Cat's lodge, will be honored to become your foster son. There is nothing to sleep on. It is a matter settled. You shall have my son for your son. We are friends. We share."

A smile crept up to soften Four Bears's mouth.

"Would you like another daughter? I have one or two I can share."

"Now you are making sport," said Redpipe, puffing on the pipe, his eyes twinkling.

"I must be completely truthful. The name Black Cat has brought something else to the front of my mind. Many seasons past, Chief Black Cat was friendly with a white man called John Evans. They talked many nights through about the beginnings of our nation and the significance of the few things left to us from our old, old grandfathers. Evans knew how valuable these things are to us. He told other white men. We have been warned that a woman of one of the white traders will try to take our sacred relics so that this man can trade for them. When I saw her looking into the medicine ark, I thought your daughter was the woman who was friendly with the white traders and had been instructed by them to take our sacred relics."

"You must judge more carefully," scolded Redpipe. "Perhaps there is a woman in your own village who is friendly with the white traders and could do such a despicable thing. Sacajawea would take nothing she did not feel was rightly hers. Somewhere in her training she was taught by good people. You can be sure it was not the Hidatsas!" Redpipe spat the last word out as if it were spoiled, bitter gall.

The Buffalo Dance had been a success. By the middle of the next afternoon, the hunters were back, leading loaded horses. Their hands and arms were dirty with dried blood. Sacajawea and Rosebud helped unload and open the great furry bundles brought by Fast Arrow. Rosebud was proud of her man. She thought she had never seen so much meat in her whole life. Every horse that had been ridden away had come back loaded. There were great hams, broad rib slabs, juicy hump steaks, rolls of thin meat, kidneys, livers, tongues, and great white chunks of fat. The air was filled with a strong, sweet blood smell.

The men did not work, but lounged around smoking and talking in the arena of the village. Rosebud and Sacajawea took their horse out to pack the remainder of Fast Arrow's kill. When they returned they were

covered with blood, their arms and legs caked. Sacajawea laughed at the sight of Rosebud. Rosebud scowled
at her with dark eyes, but her mouth smiled. Then both
looked up as Redpipe's voice called to Fast Arrow, who
was lounging in the shade.

"Ho there, my son, you did find the buffalo plentiful?"
Redpipe stopped and examined the buffalo hides. Fast
Arrow made a quick jab with his knife, as though stop-
ping a buffalo in its tracks.

"We missed you," said Rosebud, hurrying to the side
of Redpipe. "Where did you go last night, father?"

"I had a long talk with my old friend, Four Bears."
He turned away from her to smile proudly at Fast Ar-
row. "Four Bears has invited you to take part in the
Okeepa. You are to make yourself strong for the Bull
Dance."

Fast Arrow scowled at him. Redpipe scowled back—
fiercely. Fast Arrow laughed. He bent, pawing the earth
with his hands in the fashion of a charging bull buffalo,
then pointed sternly and proudly to his bronze, blood-
caked chest. He was ready. Redpipe saw and gave a
grunt of grateful assent. They would return in a month
for the ceremony. The two men went to join other men
so that Fast Arrow could tell of his prowess at killing
his buffalo.

Rosebud and Sacajawea went about the task of roasting some of the meat. The liver and heart were cut and
wrapped in a long piece of gut around and around a
willow branch and then tied in place. Rosebud held the
branch in the outdoor fire until the meat browned and
the juices sputtered. Sacajawea sliced off thin lengths
of meat and hung them on drying racks of willow she
had bound together with rawhide. Flies swarmed everywhere around the makeshift Metaharta camp. Sacajawea was careful to throw away the pieces of meat where
small piles of white eggs had been laid. The flies made
it hard to get the meat cut. They found the bare flesh
of the women's arms and faces and legs. Bright blood
welled up from the shallow incisions left by the flies.
Rosebud put some decaying leaves in the fire to make
smoke and eliminate some of the flies; Sacajawea
wrapped a huge green skin around her waist so that it

covered her legs. They worked hard, talking to one another, sometimes eating bits of raw meat.

Finally Rosebud could no longer tolerate the flies. "I am going to the riverbank for wet leaves. The smoke will be thick and roll around us."

"*Ai*, but we'll have watery eyes!" Sacajawea said.

A young woman who had been working several tepees to the left came slowly toward Redpipe's camp as Rosebud walked away. The gaunt, hot-eyed creature had two small children with dirty tunics and dried blood on their faces. Their hair seemed fine and showed glints of red in the shaft of sunlight.

"You are being careful," she said. "You will not have maggots in the meat." The young woman wiped her hands on the dirty skirt she wore. Her blouse was loose at the neck and the sleeves were fringed, but there were no other decorations. Her hair was long and black and piled on top of her head. It was held in place by sticks and thorns and daubs of mud. The insides of her ears were red, and she had a red line between her eyebrows, making her look as if the top of her head had been finely cut away from the bottom half. "My man would beat me if our meat spoiled."

"Beat you?" said Sacajawea. "But if it was not your fault, why would he beat you?"

"*Ai*," cried the woman, dropping the neck of her blouse over her shoulder so that unhealed burns between her shoulders were visible.

"He hit me with a smoldering chunk of wood only this morning when I had not built up the morning fire." She swayed and grinned at Sacajawea. "My man is very important in the other village. He can speak the language of the Metaharta, and Mandan, and two tongues of the white men." She held up two greasy fingers, her eyes snapping with pride.

"Did your man go on the hunt?" asked Sacajawea, wondering why the woman had not put melted buffalo fat on the burns.

"No, my man has gone north to trade with other white men. I am preparing the meat of some of his friends."

"Your man is white?" asked Sacajawea, unbelieving.

"*Ai*, Jussome, a Frenchman." The woman grinned.

"My man is bearded—on his face, on his chest and back, and on his arms and legs." She laughed.

"What is French?" asked Sacajawea.

The woman shrugged her shoulders and sat down near the smoking fire. Sacajawea wondered why this woman had come to talk with her, why she was not working.

"Recently there was a Becoming a Woman Ceremony," the woman said unexpectedly.

"*Ai.* I was honored by my mother, Grasshopper," said Sacajawea with a hint of bragging in her voice.

The woman got to her feet and danced to the right and to the left. "*Hih-hih-hih.* I knew it. The food was good there."

"I will tell Grasshopper. She will be pleased with your comment."

"Will she also be pleased to know that I found the weasel collar she left in the trash heap?" the woman said. "Kakoakis would not like to know his present was so poorly treated."

Sacajawea felt her forehead crinkling in a frown, and her eyes pulling together as though she were trying to see through the smoke. This was the woman Grasshopper saw running from the refuse heap! Who was this woman? Why was she here?"

"Why would you tell Kakoakis?"

"You are not very smart," said the woman, tapping a finger to her head. "My man is friends with all the chiefs, and especially Kakoakis and the Wolf Chief. They are three important men. *Hih-hih!* Jussome is a go-between for the white traders and the Mandans." She stuck her grubby right hand inside the front of her blouse and, pulling the weasel collar out, placed it around her neck and paraded in front of Sacajawea.

Sacajawea felt no compassion at all for the woman and her burned shoulders anymore. She felt blind anger. "You had better take that off," she said, trembling. She searched for Rosebud for help, but Rosebud had not yet returned from the riverbank with the wet leaves.

"I will take it off and maybe let you have it if you will tell me what is in the bottom of the sacred medicine ark."

"I will tell you these things are very old and belong

to this village! They do not concern you. They were left by the first Mandans who lived here, ages before us."
Sacajawea reached out her hand for the collar.

"I'm wearing it while I eat at the lodge of the Wolf Chief in the company of Chief Kakoakis," said the woman with a sharpness to her tongue that cut deep into Sacajawea.

"But you said—"

"I wanted to know why you were looking in there yesterday. My man has asked me to get a talking stone from there. He said he could be a rich man if he had that. Will you get it for me?"

"No! It belongs here. It is of no use to anyone personally. It is a village thing. It is something from their past. Only the Great Spirit remembers the significance of it. For you it would be a bad token."

"Something bad?"

"*Ai*, something that would make your man soft and your children find an early death. Like the root of the mayapple when held tightly over a deep wound. Perhaps by morning you would be dead."

The woman gaped wide-eyed at Sacajawea. "Dead? You are making a mistake."

"Grasshopper made a mistake with the gift Kakoakis gave to Sweet Clover, and I will take the collar as you said."

"Grasshopper's mistake! *Hiiaaa!*" The woman stepped closer to Sacajawea, her children on either side of her. "I know your sister. I was there when she became sick. It was only in fun, but she was soft, a weak one. I played the man-and-woman games, too, and it did not make me crazy in the head. *Ai*, look what it got me." She pointed a dirty finger at her boy and girl. Then she made an obscene gesture with her hands and hips toward Sacajawea, and broke into a barking, staccato laugh. Controlling herself, she added, "Handsome, aren't they?"

"What is Jussome that he would want the sacred relics in the medicine ark?" Sacajawea said.

"*Yiiii*," the woman burst out mockingly. "What is Jussome? What is French? That is the language of my man. He calls it *français*. You take a lot of time asking questions. You do not know much!"

"I am finding out," said Sacajawea, disliking the woman more and more. "Your man is from the nation of Jussome, and he speaks *français*."

"I ought to give you a good pounding for talking smart, but instead I am going to wear this collar and not give it back to you." She rubbed her grimy hand on it and smoothed the white fur. "Kakoakis owes me a gift, anyway, and I have wanted this for moons. He knew it, too—the filthy skunk."

"Does Kakoakis owe you a present? What for?" asked Sacajawea, once again holding out her hand for the weasel-tail collar.

"Why, I ought to—I ought—that just shows how dumb you are! Kakoakis likes the roundness of my body and my hard breasts thrust against his bare chest. It is the sight of them that holds his one glittering eye and makes the saliva drip from his loose-lipped mouth. He owes me a lot!"

Sacajawea took a step backward in surprise. The woman looked wild and disheveled, primordial, pagan. Her hands were filthy, and her clothes smeared with grease and blood. Her hair had loosened and was coming down about her shoulders in uneven lengths. The way she looked, it did not seem possible that anyone would like her. The woman had caught her breath and started again. "And my man likes the presents he gets from the Wolf Chief and Chief Kakoakis, so he sells me for a night or two."

"Sells you? Trades for you?" asked Sacajawea, low-voiced. "And you do not mind?"

"What can I do?" the woman asked. "I have nothing to say about it." She wrung her hands in helpless resignation. "But I do not care. They play games I enjoy. My man is nothing compared to the excitement those chiefs can bring to me. *Eeeeiii*—they make me wild with urges, and I will do anything for them. They are devils. Like the devil of Okeepa." She looked toward the heavens and pushed her full breasts together, squeezing tightly.

"Why did you come to talk with me?" asked Sacajawea. "You talk longer than an old squaw. What is truly on your mind?"

"Do you think I did not observe Kakoakis's foolish

looks at you during your ceremony? And you danced with no man. That made others swing their glances in your direction. They forgot about me. Kakoakis is still hot for you. Then I found you here, talking to Four Bears. I want you to think of those sweet small breasts under your chin that Kakoakis finds so exciting, even though he has not seen them. How would you like one of them cut off?" She made a slash with her hand toward Sacajawea.

Sacajawea stepped quickly backward. She felt the blood leave her head, and her feet felt heavy. Then her anger returned, and she reached out and snatched the weasel-tail collar from the woman's neck.

"Give that back to me!"

"I will not! And if you do not leave, I will tell Four Bears that you plan to steal the relics from the ark."

"You would not!"

"*Ai*! I would."

The woman turned and walked away, with her two children following. Her backside moved with each step as though she were put together with extra loose sinews. "Kakoakis is becoming completely blind!" yelled the woman.

Rosebud came back, flushed of face, with a great skirt full of wet, soggy leaves, which she dumped near the fire.

"Do you know her?" Sacajawea asked, pointing toward the swaying hips.

Rosebud began an angry guttural discourse. "She is Flower Who Awaits the Bee, woman of a white trader. She is also known as Squaw of Any Man. She has another name that will stay with her for a long time. The Mandans call her Broken Tooth, because one time her man hit her on the mouth with the end of his firestick after she sneaked out to Kakoakis's lodge without his permission. Everyone knows about her and her white man, who has strange laws. If he gives his permission for her to go, it is all right. If he does not tell her to go, she must not. But everyone knows she goes to Kakoakis when she wants."

"She is the woman Grasshopper found at the refuse heap. She had the weasel collar," said Sacajawea. "I took it away from her. She talked of many strange things."

"So—it was Broken Tooth! I am not surprised. She thinks she is the answer to all men's desires, and she does not like anyone who has things prettier than she."

Then Sacajawea asked, "What are we going to do about the collar?"

"That is easy," said Rosebud. "We will bring it back to Grasshopper and tell her what happened. What is not easy is how we are to finish our work! We must be ready to return home with Fast Arrow and Redpipe in the morning." She began stuffing the wet leaves into the meat-smoking fire, and soon Sacajawea was too busy cutting buffalo meat to worry further about Broken Tooth and the weasel collar, which she had tucked into a pouch for safekeeping.

In the morning they prepared to leave the village of the Mandans. It had been a successful buffalo hunt, and Sacajawea and Rosebud were pleased that they would return with Redpipe and Fast Arrow in one month, for the ceremony of the Okeepa.

CHAPTER

9

The Okeepa

All the mysticism, religious devotion, and endeavor to be in the good graces of the Great Spirit, found its ultimate expression in what the Mandans called O-keepa. Among the rituals of the peoples of the earth it would be difficult to find any practice of self-imposed penance more excruciating. Sacrifice was an important part of the Plains Indians' religion. It was widely practiced and took many forms, from the simple offering of a bit of meat cast into the fire before eating, or the burning of the first ear of corn before the harvest, to the inflicting of pain approaching the brink of death. But nothing equaled the ordeal of the O-kee-pa.[1]

HAROLD MC CRACKEN, *George Catlin and the Old Frontier*. New York: Crown Publishers Inc., 1959, p. 101.

The women of Redpipe's lodge chatted excitedly as they erected a small buffalo-hide tent. They were preparing for Fast Arrow's steam bath, which was part of the formalities to be undergone before offering oneself to the Mandan chiefs for the Okeepa Ceremony. Grasshopper waddled off to the Council Lodge of her village for the wicker bathtub that was used for the men's steam baths. Rosebud had pushed several large stones into the center of a hot fire near the hide tent. Sacajawea gathered sticks for the fire. Redpipe sat nearby smoking and letting his grandchildren climb in and out of his arms. Several villagers walked past, but using the steam bath was a common thing—they did not stop to talk.

Naked, Fast Arrow solemnly climbed into the tub and sat on fresh-crushed sage leaves with his arms wrapped around his knees. Rosebud rolled the hot stones by means of a long stick into the tent, and Sacajawea sprinkled more crushed sage and other medicinal leaves on the hot stones, at the same time dousing them with cold water. Thick clouds of steam rose, extracting the exhilarating aromatics from the sage and feathery green anise shoots. The women left while Fast Arrow inhaled deeply into his lungs, purifying his body so that he would be ready to take his part in the upcoming Pohkhong rites, the torture of the Okeepa. Fast Arrow thought of his great honor in becoming the adopted son of Chief Four Bears.

Before the steam cooled down and completely condensed, he dashed out and plunged into the cold water of the Knife River. Rosebud followed Fast Arrow with a buffalo robe and wrapped him in it for warmth on the way back to the lodge. A few curious eyes watched from the doors of the lodges, but no one was so curious as to come out and ask why he was using the steam bath this particular day. Rosebud rubbed him vigorously with bear grease, while Sacajawea and Grasshopper served him a meal of simmered anise and hard-boiled duck eggs.

After a pleasant nap, Fast Arrow dressed in his finest

garments and paraded himself around the village, stopping once in a while to gossip with passersby.

The following day, Grasshopper fussed over Fast Arrow as though he were her own son, instead of the man of her daughter. She took great care in painting his face and shoulders. "My son should be the finest-looking brave at the Okeepa," she said, drawing up her mouth and studying the designs she'd just finished painting on his chest. "My daughters will tell me everything, so that I will not miss a thing by staying home with the babies."

"*Ai*," agreed Sacajawea, climbing over Sucks His Thumb as she hunted her moccasins for the trip. The little boy pulled out his clean thumb from his mouth and offered it to his father. Fast Arrow swatted the child and sent him scampering and laughing to the other side of the lodge.

"You are not afraid, are you?" whispered Grasshopper to Fast Arrow.

He looked at her in disbelief, shaking his head no. Certainly Fast Arrow was not frightened—this was going to be the greatest experience he had ever had or expected to have. Attending the Mandan Okeepa Festival and then actually taking part in the holy torture rites was what every brave dreamed of to show his strength and prove he was worthy of being a member of the nation.

They were seated on the ponies, Fast Arrow and Redpipe each on their own and Rosebud and Sacajawea together on a little tricolor, when Grasshopper thought of something she had forgotten.

"Take my good wishes to the wives of Four Bears," she called, "especially to the one with the silver hair, Sahkoka, the Mint, and the youngest, Sun Woman. Tell them that your sister Sweet Clover is in good health and my grandchildren drive me crazy as a loon. Let's see how well you can remember to give my greeting."

They were soon out of sight, and Grasshopper shooed the children back into the lodge and ordered them to sit quietly around the fire.

Chickadee, who was too small to keep her legs tucked under, extended them out front at full length and smiled at Grasshopper, who was now busy sprinkling cornmeal

at the edge of the lodge fire. Sweet Clover came shyly
to the fire to sit with the little ones. She smiled and sat
with her legs crossed, not understanding why she did
this.

Grasshopper mumbled a prayer to the Great Spirit.
Her mind was joyous, yet there was something held
back as she thought of Fast Arrow going through the
torture rite. It was a ceremony, a ritual to show a man's
bravery to everyone. It had been used for ages beyond
remembering. But a man's spirit came close to that of
the Great Spirit at that time, and afterward he was
different, never the same as before. Grasshopper pondered this thought: A man comes home wiser, more
understanding, if he is fortunate, but a man can become
haughty and cruel, then everyone suffers from his
change. Good men die. Brave men die. No one will stop
the torture, so it must go on each year until one day in
the unknown dawn it will wear itself out. Sacred things
wear out, just like a pair of leggings that have been
worn overlong and seen much abuse.

That wayward something in her mind continued the
argument: That is what the Great Spirit is—a faith in
something unseen, as a tent peg under the earth. But
it is ceremonies and rituals also. That is why men offered smoke in six directions for a successful hunt, or
a woman set out a prayer stick for the recovery of a
sick child. That is why she was now dancing a prayer
into the earth for the safe return of Fast Arrow's soul.
It depended on what was believed.

She shuffled around the fire. The terror that possessed her now was immeasurably greater than that
which she had felt as, smiling, she had sent her beloved
ones toward the Mandans asking if Fast Arrow was
afraid. That night, it was she, not Fast Arrow, who had
a monster to wrestle with. The monster was her inborn
mother-love that needed to protect her family from any
harm or unpleasantness.

It was midmorning on the way to the Rooptahee village when the sign appeared to them. And according
to the nature of such events, it came while everything
seemed safe and serene and the thought of such a thing
was far away.

Engrossed in talk, the little party did not see the squall line come up over the hill ahead of them. The wind began to blow and the rain beat in their faces. The four of them climbed from the horses and stood beneath a tall pine until the rain stopped. Wet sage filled their noses, and they felt an anticipation of excitement as they mounted to cross the river. The sun was not yet out from behind the clouds, but the sky was pink. Suddenly Sacajawea pointed in awe to the rainbow hanging in the sky. It was suspended with neither foot touching Mother Earth, and the center was filled with crimson-colored clouds.

"My people believed that to be a symbol of strength and peace," said Sacajawea, breaking the silence.

"You have no people but us," said Redpipe sharply. "Look, my daughter, this is not usual. The colors do not touch the earth. The Great Spirit cannot touch his feet to the ground when he rides in such a canoe." Now his face wore a forbidding look and his voice became hard as flint. "It is a sign to us."

"The sky shows that one of us will rise to great heights," offered Fast Arrow in a hushed, confidential tone.

"Ai"—Redpipe's words sounded cold and distant— "that must be the meaning, and it must be you, my son. You are beginning your rise to power with the Okeepa Ceremony. My life is going downhill; it surely is not I." He deliberately did not mention the women, as they were of no concern in such great events as a sign from the heavens. However, he thought of his friend Four Bears and then remembered how they had agreed that his adopted daughter was unusual. And now this omen. Was it all something that should be put together, connected?

The suspended rainbow began fading. The horses shuffled their feet, anxious to be moving. "Come," said Fast Arrow. "We can think on this sign another day. We must get to Rooptahee before the sun is under the earth."

Toward midafternoon they reached the village of Rooptahee. They saw two men dressed only in breechclouts come plodding up a hill with a log between them

on their shoulders. Then two more men brought up
another the same size. They disappeared into the Medicine Lodge. Sacajawea heard thumps as the logs were
dropped, and then the *chuk* of bone axes and the noise
of digging. She saw in front of the Medicine Lodge three
sacrifices offered in behalf of the village for the Okeepa
Ceremony. There were long swathes of blue and black
cloth, each purchased by the white man, Jussome. The
cloth had been folded to resemble human figures, with
eagle feathers on their heads and masks on their faces.
According to Four Bears, this was the first time Jussome had made any contribution to the ceremony, although he had lived among them for many winters. "I
think he is after something," said Four Bears to Redpipe.

Hanging beside these figures, which had been erected
about thirty feet over the door of the Medicine Lodge,
was the skin of a white buffalo. It was the first white
buffalo Sacajawea had ever seen. She stood quite still,
looking at it.

"The white buffalo is extremely valuable. In all the
herds there is maybe one in five million," Four Bears
explained to her, making the count by sifting earth
through his fingers to show thousands upon thousands.
"The hide is so scarce that it is possessed only as tribal
medicine."

Nothing seemed to absorb the Mandans' interest so
deeply as the legendry of the past, which was inter-
woven with the Okeepa rites.

No one but the medicine man knew the exact date
when the ceremony was to commence. It was the day
when the willow leaves became full-grown, for according to tradition, the twig that the bird brought in across
the Great Flood was a willow bough and it had full-
grown leaves upon it. In the Mandans' version of the
story of the Great Flood, the bird was the mourning
dove, and this bird was never disturbed or harmed in
any way by these people.

The four of them slept in the lodge of Four Bears.
The women rose at dawn to work. Sacajawea took an
immediate liking to Sahkoka, the Mint, who was short
and stocky with gray eyes and graying hair, and Sun

Woman, mother of the papoose Earth Woman, whom she was holding.

"She is named so that as she grows she will remember to see the rocks and trees and mountains and flowers and plains," Sun Woman said.

"We should let her see the Okeepa for something to remember," said the Mint with a twinkle in her eye. "Four Bears gives all of his attention to this small one, pretending she is a son."

On the other side of the lodge, amid the smoke from his pipe, Four Bears gave a loud chuckle. His hands were long and slender. The skin was burned a rich brown, and his hands looked very strong.

His voice came easily to the women's side of the lodge. "The rocks you can count on to be the same. You can always count on the things of the earth. You know what to expect of them. You can count on the wild dogs. But people are not the same. You can't count on them." He glanced up, and the corner of his mouth flickered with a grim little smile as he added, "I went to visit the Hidatsa monument built of bones to honor the spirit of a dog."

Sacajawea felt one hand closing on the clay floor. Her other hand clasped the cooing papoose more tightly.

"I know what you are talking about!" said Fast Arrow, recalling something the man Charbonneau had said to him about a girl and a dog.

Four Bears stood and smoothed over his breechclout front and back, then stepped up beside Sacajawea. "We all know—but it will not go beyond this lodge door."

Sacajawea pulled at the soft doeskin blanket that wrapped Earth Woman's feet. She said in a low voice, "I think I should be angry. You were checking into something that did not concern you."

"It did concern me," said Four Bears. "You did not act in the manner that women do. You peered into the sacred ark and asked what the objects were. No woman is that curious. No woman questions a chief, even a subchief. I supposed that day that you had used the name of my old friend Redpipe in some kind of spell, for the story being told is that the Dog Girl is some kind of Shaman."

"Oh, no!" said Sacajawea, aghast.

"It was something of a joke on me when I found you
the true daughter of Redpipe, and only an ordinary
woman." He spread his hand to indicate his lodge. "With
women I am at ease."

Sacajawea was moved by his words.

Fast Arrow addressed himself to Four Bears. "The
white trader called Charbonneau suspects my sister is
the Dog Girl. I told him his words were like birds chirping in the wind. But it is true?"

"True."

"Well, so. That is gone now, and she is one of us. He
cannot bother her. He is only one of those poor white
traders. My woman treats her like a sister. She works
hard in our lodge. She was unhappy and sickly when
she came to us. Now she is singing and her arms are
plump. *Ai*, if I am ever asked, I will not know anything
about a Dog Girl." Fast Arrow's face puckered in concern.

Sacajawea shut her eyes and covered them with her
hands. She did not wish either man to see the emotion
there. The feeling ran deep.

The Mint came to fuss with Earth Woman while
Sacajawea composed herself. She was smiling and not
at all embarrassed by the display of emotion.

Sacajawea raised her eyes to meet Four Bears's. To
her surprise she found she could speak steadily.

"What did you find when you visited the Hidatsas?"

"No one knows what has become of the girl. She has
disappeared into the air." His powerful hands swirled
about him, and he chuckled. "They would kill her if she
came back because she is more valuable as something
to talk about. They have forgotten she was like themselves. They speak mostly of the spirit of the great dog.
It is remarkable. So—you can't foretell the ways of
people." Four Bears's still face lighted; unsmiling, it
seemed to smile.

Sacajawea thought she had never seen a man who
gave out such a feeling of quiet strength. He put his
arm around the oiled shoulder of Fast Arrow. "Now we
shall never refer to this matter again unless one of your
family tells me they want to talk about it. It is washed
away. That is all." He smiled briefly at Sacajawea and
said as he turned to go with Fast Arrow, "I have respect

for you, but men do not show that they think about women more than they think about a piece of property. So, this talk is ended. That Hidatsa girl is gone."

Sacajawea sat still. She looked around at the seven wives of Four Bears, busy with their girl-children and smoothing out the sleeping couches, preparing for a new day. She pulled off her headband, made from grasses with a raven's feather woven into it for good fortune, and tied the headband to Earth Woman's cradleboard.

Sun Woman's eyes shone. "Thank you. It is baby boys who are given gifts. Now I can see why Redpipe's family has such a strong feeling about you. Earth Woman is greatly honored."

Early the next morning, the sound of a single drum came from the council area.

"So, this is the day," announced Four Bears. "Are you ready, my son?"

"*Ai.*" Fast Arrow's hand poked out and caught Rosebud by the elbow. "Please make my face paint bright today," he said.

By afternoon the Mandans had assembled at the Council Lodge, their hair combed neatly, their clothing elegant.

Redpipe and Fast Arrow sat next to Four Bears in the council circle, each painted and dressed magnificently. They were next to Chief Black Cat, who was elegant in his beaded shirt and leggings and headdress of snow-white eagle feathers. Fast Arrow was the son of Black Cat. When Fast Arrow took the woman Rosebud, he left his own family to live with the mother and father of his woman. This was the custom. His woman's parents were now his parents.

Rosebud and Sacajawea sat in the women's circle with Sun Woman and the Mint. Suddenly someone yelled, and all eyes were turned to the prairies in the west, where a lone figure made his way toward the village. Sacajawea joined in the excitement, waving her arms and pointing. Along the clear shoulder of the hill, the lone figure climbed the lower slopes, coming toward them now with swift, purposeful strides. Soon all were standing, gazing at the figure and expressing a pretended great alarm. The men strung their bows and

tested their elasticity. Horses were caught by the young
boys and run into the village. Warriors were blackening
their faces, and every preparation was being made, as
if for a fight. During all this confusion the lone figure
came on. His long legs moved with their knees bent,
with the smooth, slouching glide of a woods-runner used
to husbanding his strength. He moved as if his legs
were circles, and his body rode on them erectly. Easily,
effortlessly, his body held itself as straight as a young
sapling. His shoulders had a squareness to them, a lean
confidence, that gave an air of grace to his loose-fitting
white wolfskin robe. In his left hand was a long-stemmed
clay pipe, the long diagonal rising behind his head,
covered with raven's wings.

His features were still unclear, but his face was white,
almost the color of birchbark, and painted with river
clay. The crowd parted as he came into the council circle
and touched the hands of the chiefs and men of importance.

"That is really Old Bear, the Medicine Man," whispered the Mint.

Again the crowd parted. The runner went to the Medicine Lodge and officially opened the door. His robe of
four white wolfskins was dropped on the ground; his
entire body was a glistening white.

"The First Man, Mumohk-muckanah, Madoc,"
chanted the Mandans.

The First Man designated four men to enter and
clean the Medicine Lodge. Willow boughs were brought
to place on the floor, and wild sage was scattered over
the boughs. Buffalo and human skulls and the articles
used in the torture rites were positioned. The First Man
stood silently, overseeing the work, his body harsh in
its whiteness.

After a time, the First Man began to move through
the crowd, screeching until all were listening. Then he
related the catastrophe that had happened on earth
when the waters of the rivers overflowed, saying that
he was the only person saved from the calamity. He
had landed his big canoe on a high mountain in the
west, and had come down to open the Medicine Lodge.
For this he demanded a present from each lodge of some

sharp cutting instrument as a sacrifice so that the water of the Great Flood would not come again.[2]

Sacajawea leaned toward Rosebud and the Mint. "The Shoshonis have a story of the waters overflowing," she whispered. "It was the mightiest buffalo who was saved from the waters, and he was instructed by the Great Spirit to make all the other animals from mud and sticks and give them names. He made two of each and gave them names, and he made the Shoshonis and called them brothers, so that the People and the buffalo have helped each other ever since."

Rosebud was delighted with the story. "So, our stories are similar. We are indeed sisters."

The Mandans had shifted their gaze to the Medicine Lodge for the next event, the Bellohck-nahpick, or Bull Dance. This was more elaborate than the Buffalo Dance and was repeated the sacred number of times this day, four.

The next day the Bull Dance was repeated eight times, then twelve times on the third day, and sixteen times on the fourth and final day of the ceremony. Twelve men, the village's bravest, danced around the sacred wooden ark. For this ritual the ark was called the Big Canoe and represented the boat used to float in the Great Flood. The dancers wore buffalo skins with horns, hooves, and tail. They imitated the movements of the animal, twisting and contorting their bodies.

Their bodies were nearly naked, and painted black, red, and white. Each man carried a gourd rattle and long white staff. On each man's back was a large bunch of green willow boughs. The men were grouped in pairs, occupying the four cardinal points around the wooden ark. The pair toward the south represented Mother Earth. Separating the pairs were single dancers, naked except for a large headdress and an apron of eagle's feathers, and carrying a rattle and staff. Two of these men were painted black with pounded charcoal and grease to represent the night; white spots of oiled clay were the stars. The other men were painted vermilion to represent the day, and were streaked with white ghosts, which the rays of the sun were chasing away. During intervals between dances, the men went into the Medicine Lodge to rest and repaint for the next performance.

Each day the villagers came back dressed and painted in their finest for this celebration. Some brought strips of dried meat and passed them among their friends; others brought small hard cakes of corn-meal. There was much shrieking as the performing fig-ures catapulted themselves in gigantic leaps, the clatter of their rattles making weird sounds.

Sacajawea responded easily to the mass hypnotism of this final night of preparatory chanting and frenetic dancing. Her blood beat with the drums. She shuddered in the violence of the assault on her rationality, the gyrations and weird intermingling of light and dark shadows, of noise and silence, of grace and violence.

When the First Man appeared carrying the hatchets and knives he had collected, the sudden, complete si-lence fell upon her like a blow. He deposited the collection in the Medicine Lodge; then this strong, ghostly white First Man slipped away to hide through the night. When the dancers, too, had disappeared into the blackness, the people of the audience quietly strolled back to their lodges. There was to be no more talking until the First Man reappeared at sunrise.

Sacajawea and Rosebud slept late into the morning. Redpipe and Four Bears were up talking and smoking when they awoke. Fast Arrow was meditating.

"My son is preparing himself for the severe ordeal he will pass through," said Four Bears. His long hands tapped nervously on the pipesteam. "I do not feel hun-gry, but my guests shall eat well before going to the council this day."

His women had prepared a feast. Parched corn had been pounded in a mortar and made into rolls, which were not cooked, but pleasant to taste. The Mint, flushed from blowing on the lodge fire coals, brought Redpipe a kind of hominy made of corn bruised in a mortar and soaked in warm water. The tastiest dish was roast goose. Three geese had been smeared with thick coats of mud. Then the birds were put into a hot fire and covered with live coals. When the clay cover-ings became red hot, they were cooled gradually until the fire died out. The shells were cracked with an ax, and the feathers and skin came off with the clay, leaving the flesh of the birds clean and well done. The women and children ate after Redpipe.

Rosebud was unable to eat, and left the lodge. A peculiar mood had drifted over her. It seemed to float on the morning breeze, to issue out of the heart of the untamed nature around her. It lurked in the very vastness of the prairie surrounding the village on every hand; it even seemed to rise like an impalpable mist out of the ground on which she now sat in the women's circle. Other women had also begun to gather. The mood was difficult to interpret, but all knew that anything might happen during the Pohkhong, the torturing rites. A shiver passed over her, as if she were having a child.

Four Bears walked to the edge of the arena and picked up a large stone with a broad end in which a groove had been filed. The stone was round. When he returned to his place in the council circle, his eyes were burning. He turned to survey the people of his village; then he spoke. His words had an emphasis that seemed like the beating of a drum.

"We are small. Lost in time. What we do is of as much importance as what two fleas do. How many men have gone through this rite, and now what is left of them, their good, and their thoughts? Each man has his limit. He can go no farther than his own manhood. But in new experiences and feelings and exchanging of ideas with another, a man may go a step beyond himself to gain strength and wisdom. That is a great step upward for man—but not much in the face of the strength and wisdom of the stone I hold." He raised the stone for all to see.

"A man moves toward his death each dawn. This stone has looked upon many men. The life of a man must be less to a stone than the life of a flea to us. Each man believes that lesser things are of lesser importance, and things of long ago are less important than things now or things in the future. But men do not reach the final wisdom of rocks. A rock knows nothing of time, whether of long ago or yesterday or whether the sun will rise again. All things are equally meaningful and meaningless."

His voice took on fire. "There is nothing we do ourselves. We are each driven. Man is like an arrow. The string is pulled and at a certain instant it is released and the arrow goes in the direction it is pointed. The arrow, which so shortly before has been flying through the air like a bird, falls to the ground and is lifeless." Four Bears leaned forward, his face sober, earnest, his arms flung out in a sort of benediction, his hands gripped together. Then he sat, his arms folded across his legs, which were folded underneath him.

The crowd turned to the white figure of the First Man, who now beckoned the candidates for the rites to enter the Medicine Lodge and be prepared.

Rosebud sucked in her breath and held it when Fast Arrow reappeared. On his left arm was his war shield and his bow and arrows, with a quiver slung on his back. He was covered with red, blue, and yellow clay paint mixed with bear's oil, and he carried his personal medicine bag in his right hand. His face was sober, with a look of strength and determination on it that told of an inward resolve to keep full control of himself during the Okeepa Ceremony.

The candidates paraded around the arena, the sun glistening on their oiled skin. Rosebud drew a half breath, keeping her eyes on Fast Arrow. He moved with noiseless and gliding quickness, like an animal or a ghost. Then the young men moved back inside the Medicine Lodge. Four Bears, Redpipe, and the other chiefs and subchiefs of the village followed the candidates into the Medicine Lodge. All had gone through this same ordeal in their youth. This day, they were witnesses.

The women were forgotten. None was permitted inside the lodge. Some of the women began to moan and wail.

"Why do they do that?" asked Sacajawea.

"They know what is to take place inside," answered Rosebud, her face graying with each woman's cry.

The First Man lit and smoked his pipe and then delivered a short speech to the candidates, who were seated beneath wall pegs on which they had hung their weapons. He encouraged them to trust in the Great Spirit for protection during the ordeal they were about to undergo, and then passed authority in the form of a special medicine pipe to Okeeae Kaase-kah, the Conductor, an aged Medicine Man who would continue the ceremony. The First Man then shook hands with the Conductor and performed his ritual departure for the mountains in west, whence he had come to begin the Okeepa.

The Conductor, whose body was painted yellow, lay down by the blazing center fire and began crying out to the Great Spirit. He held his pipe toward the heavens. From this moment, the candidates were permitted communication with no one, and were to abstain from food, drink, and sleep until the end of the four-day ritual.

Fast Arrow's eyes wandered from the arrangement of buffalo and human skulls on the floor to examine the scaffold. Tree trunks had been set into the ground. The dirt was scuffed in around the butts and tramped on until the posts stood as solidly as the upright corner posts of a Mandan mud lodge. On top of the posts were slabs set in notches, wedged tight with wood chips. On one of the slabs, not more than a man's length and a half above the ground, rested his small medicine bag. He forced himself to look away.

The Conductor had moved under the scaffold to place a scalping knife beside a bundle of bone splints or skewers that rested on the center of the ring of skulls. He had brushed past the stout rawhide cords that hung from the top of the scaffolding, and set them in motion. Fast Arrow shuddered, once, twice, before he took firm control of himself.

Outside the Medicine Lodge, the women kept a staggered vigil, punctuated by shrieks and screams, accompanied by the barks and howls of the dogs. Rosebud and Sacajawea spent time in Four Bears's lodge, helping the other women with the meals and caring for the children. As the evening shadows deepened each night, they joined the people gathered around the fires in the arena.

On the second night, Sacajawea and Rosebud unexpectedly met Broken Tooth and her children. None of the women was pleased by the meeting. On Broken

Tooth's face there was open animosity; her greeting was
curt, and she walked hurriedly past, swinging her hips.
She was followed by a young woman who seemed quite
unsure of herself, as if unable to understand the meaning of the words Broken Tooth spoke to hurry her along.
In her anxiety to be gone from Sacajawea, Broken Tooth
pushed through the crowd, and the timid girl, whose
eyes had been on the ground, looked up to find herself
abandoned. She was not more than eleven or twelve
summers old. She was wrapped in red cotton trade cloth,
and she looked frightened, like a doe. Her face was
round and her legs short and stocky.

On an impulse, Sacajawea spoke a greeting in Shoshoni. The young woman looked startled, then a smile
crept to her lips and she responded. Breathlessly, Sacajawea translated for Rosebud. "This woman once lived
with the People, the Shoshonis! Hear her tongue!"

Rosebud looked at the round-faced woman. "Who is
she with? Broken Tooth?"

Sacajawea repeated the question in Shoshoni.

"The Blackfeet were paid a good price for me three
moons back—a beautiful shining knife. I am now the
woman of Charbonneau."

"Charbonneau!" gasped the two women.

"Ai," the stranger said. "He does not scold too much
and does not often hit with a piece of firewood, like
Jussome and his woman. He leaves me with them when
he goes. He is gone much and brings back plenty of
food."

"But you are not old enough to be a man's woman,"
said Rosebud.

"Ai, my man likes them very young. He prefers me
to his other woman, Corn Woman, who is older now."
She shrugged. "It is not bad."

"What are you called?" asked Sacajawea.

"Otter—Otter Woman," said the stranger. "Charbonneau gave me that name. The Blackfeet only called
me Squaw."

"And this Jussome, he beats you? Why?"

"Every day, almost, he hits me, because I do not
speak his tongue."

"And so, Broken Tooth beats you also, because you
cannot understand her talk?"

"Sometimes I do not know why she beats me." Otter Woman felt for the welts on her back, and fear crawled across her face. "If she catches me, she'll do it again." She looked longingly at Sacajawea, and then she edged away. "I am glad to find one who understands my tongue," she said.

Broken Tooth returned just in time to hear this. "You talk crazy like her!" she screeched at Sacajawea, and she gave Otter Woman a vicious look.

Otter Woman did not look again at Sacajawea, but followed Broken Tooth sadly, her eyes downcast.

Rosebud grabbed Sacajawea's arm. "That man Charbonneau has two women, and still he chased you in the woods," she said. "I see that you would help Otter Woman; but if you follow, it will only anger Broken Tooth, it will not help her."

"For a moment it was like finding a relative, someone of my own blanket," admitted Sacajawea. "She is of the Sheep Eater Shoshonis. I can tell by her talk. Maybe I will see her again."

The final day of the Bull Dance began with the coming of the sun's rays.

The whole village, their faces painted, red lines down their center hair parts, gathered in the arena or on the crowded dome tops of the lodges nearest the large Medicine Lodge. Suddenly a terrible scream burst above the shouting and singing, and a strange character appeared. He was running across the open prairie, darting about like a boy chasing a butterfly, heading for the entrance to the village stockade. His body was painted black, with white rings here and there. He had large white markings, like canine teeth, drawn on his face. The hideous creature uttered frightful shrieks as he dashed toward the crowd, and now it could be seen that an artificial penis of colossal dimensions, carved in wood, descended from the buffalo hair covering his pelvis. The penis moved as he ran, extending below his knees. It was painted as jet black as his body, with the exception of the glans, which was a glaring vermilion. Women and children screamed and ran for protection, dodging from his path. If a woman was not fast enough, he waved a wand over her hands, and as he did so, the penis rose.

"That is Okeeheede, the Devil, the Satanic majesty of the Evil Spirit!" shouted Rosebud. "To be caught by him is worse, much worse, than being caught by the white man!"

When the bizarre character entered the arena of the dancers, Sacajawea saw that he had a small thong encircling his waist, and a buffalo's tail behind.

The Conductor of the Bull Dance thrust his pipe before the eyes of the Devil, and its charm held him temporarily motionless. The women and children took this opportunity to retreat a safe distance. Seeing that he had lost the women, the Devil placed himself in the attitude of a buffalo bull in the rutting season, and approached the dancers. One by one, he mounted four of the dancers as the crowd shrieked in high amusement. When the Devil finally appeared fatigued, the women and children slowly surrounded him, no longer afraid, coming closer and closer until someone broke his wand. Then he was driven away. A huge crowd of women followed, pelting him with clods of dirt, until he was in the prairie and the frightful appendage was wrested from his black body.[3]

The triumphant captor, none other than Broken Tooth, brought the huge penis proudly into the arena. She was lifted onto the scaffolding on the front of the Medicine Lodge, directly over the door. She harangued the people about the evils of this powerful counterpart of the Great Spirit. Her voice was high-pitched and raspy.

"I see clearly now," whispered Rosebud, "why it was that the white trader, Jussome, contributed the trade cloth to the ceremony. His woman is the one to capture the Devil and thus be an important person in this village."

"Ai." Sacajawea nodded.

From the east side of the arena came a steady beating of drums and rattling of gourds, but Broken Tooth continued to talk, pushing her stringy hair over her eyes, telling how the Evil Spirit can come into anyone if he is not suspecting and watchful at all times. Then she did a fantastic thing. She positioned the black penis upward and spread her legs to straddle it. Slowly she sat down until the thing disappeared, her eyes blazing.

And even as the watchers roared and clapped and made coarse jokes and obscene signs with their hands, laughing and screeching in fever-pitched voices, the solemnity of the Okeepa came to claim the village.

Calling through a thin-walled wild goat horn, the Conductor of the Bull Dance ordered the dancers to halt. The official witnesses entered the Medicine Lodge to judge the bravery of the candidates.

Fast Arrow noticed the Wolf Chief and Chief Black Cat come into the lodge. He felt he was in great danger, but he could not rouse himself to stand on his feet. He was shaking so badly that he could not move. He had suffered hallucinations for some time now, the result of the strict four-day fast and no sleep. Brightly colored images, larger than life, floated past his eyes. He wondered if he had truly seen others enter the lodge. He was lying on his back on a robe. The leather thongs hanging from the top of the scaffolding became long, black bull snakes, writhing. He could not concentrate on the reasons for his fear. He seemed to turn to water inside himself. He had never felt this way before. Finally, with great effort, he turned his head from side to side and saw other candidates lying upon robes. Some seemed asleep. But that could not be. They were watched by seated officials.

Attendants singing a song about bravery worked under the scaffold. One worked on the scalping knife with a stone grinder. Another was sorting the bone splints into separate small piles. Now names were being called.

Fast Arrow managed to stand when it was his turn to go forward, although it did not seem that his bones were stiff enough to support his body. He swayed from side to side, and he felt as if he would fall down. Then a circlet of thorns, prickly pear spines, was jammed onto his head by the Conductor, as one had been placed on each man called before him. He felt a trickle of blood seep over his forehead as the thorns tore into his skin. He imagined the blood oozed onto the dirt floor and inundated his bare feet. From far away the Conductor was speaking about bravery, and of a man many sea-

sons before who had worn thorns upon his head and
hung high above the crowd.

Fast Arrow did not understand; he could not gather
his thoughts enough to make sense of the story. He was
frightened and could hardly control himself. He felt as
if he must run away, but he was not able to do so. An
attendant placed his hand upon Fast Arrow's shoulder
and handed him his medicine bag, directing him to hold
it tight no matter what he felt or thought. The man
spoke in a low voice. He explained that the center poles
from which the rawhide cords hung were set deep into
the ground and great stones had been put on the earth
around them so that the poles would be held firmly,
but Fast Arrow did not hear. He saw only the yellow-
and-white diagonal stripes decorating the man's chest.
The stripes wove in and out like small worms crawling
over his oiled body.

The man placed the scalping knife under Fast Arrow's nose so that he could see it. Then he held it up
to the sun coming into the lodge from the smoke hole,
and he prayed to the spirits of the air. He prayed to the
spirits of the earth, and to the spirits of the water. Then
he took hold of the skin on Fast Arrow's right breast,
pinched it up, and passed the knife through it. The knife
was not sharp; it had been hacked and notched with
the stones to produce as much pain as possible. Fast
Arrow gritted his teeth and spread his feet to steady
himself.

An attendant forced one of the wide bone splints
through the wound underneath the breast muscles to
keep it from being torn out. A rawhide cord was lowered
from the top of the scaffold and fastened to the splint.
In the same way, the attendants fastened a cord to Fast
Arrow's left breast. The pain was deep and caused his
whole body to throb. Fast Arrow kept his eyes open,
but his mind seemed outside somewhere, seeing but not
fully believing that this was taking place on his own
body.

The knife and additional splints were passed through
the flesh on each arm below the shoulder, below each
elbow, on each thigh, and below each knee. Fast Arrow
could not perceive all this happening. He could hear a
candidate groan, and another go *"Ai-ii-iee, ai-ii-iiee"*

nearly as fast as he could breathe. He was determined to remain silent. He felt himself falling into a deep pit that was as black as the night. His mind could not bring him out of the pit into the light. His mouth was dry.

The rawhide cords were pulled, and he was suspended just off the ground, blood streaming down his body. His shield, bow, and quiver hung on the splints below his shoulder, elbow, and thigh. A single buffalo skull was hung to the splints below one knee. When the weights were hung on the splints, his mind came back to life. His cheeks pulled up as if trying to lift him out of the pain. His breath sucked into him in little gasps that got louder and louder as his weights bore down. The weights swung clear of the ground.[4]

Fast Arrow's head swung forward on his breast, but some of the young men's heads were thrown backward by the suspension. One young man suspended thus was already dead. His soul was carried away by the beat of the death drums. The warmth of his body left as the blood coagulated on his arms and legs and no longer dripped to the ground. The shrill wailing of women outside could be heard as the death drums beat.

"*Yo-hay.*" The ominous phrase of ending rolled around the circle of witnesses. There was silence, broken by an outcry from the father of the young man. It was drowned by the heavy, ruthless beat of the death drums. There was no more to be done for that one. His body was pulled down and laid on a clean robe in front of the fire. He was lean and angular. His thin brown arms were laid straight beside him, and his hair freshly greased. On his face was still the echo of horror and agony; they had not been able to shut his eyes. The tireless, heart-shaking monotony of the drums went on. The young man's face was painted as if for a feast.

Outside in the open arena, the waiting women took up the death chant, each one mourning as though it were her relative that had started his journey to the Land Beyond Sunset. A shell containing the black paint for mourning was passed. Rosebud and Sacajawea painted their faces and loosened their hair. Rosebud ripped her tunic to the waist and, with naked breasts and shoulders, moved quietly to the swaying beat. The arena fire was built higher, lest the soul not know its way home.

The death drums beat on; they beat in the women's blood. Sacajawea heard not the singing of the women, only the drums leap and change their rhythm. The women began their circling dance; voices began to chant to the rhythm of the drums. The arena fire gave heat. Even so, Rosebud pulled her tunic up and fastened it with a small stick. She pulled Sacajawea along to the swaying beat. Now they were rising, stealthily, slowly. They were crouching and rising and stepping behind the others, their high voices rising and falling in the terrifying cries of the chant. Swept by the vibrancy, by the pulling of Rosebud, Sacajawea leaped into the circling dance. She was deeply one with the drums and cries; she was singing as she moved in the repeated rhythms. She forgot all but the sound of her own voice, crying with the others, "We shall also follow!" as her arms flung up and her feet stamped with other feet.

The dance slackened, then swept on.

The fortitude with which the finest young men of the Mandans bore the final torture of the Okeepa surpassed credulity. They were completely suspended from wounds in their flesh, and now the attendants turned each around with a pole, gently at first, and then faster and faster until the candidate could control the agony no longer and burst out crying to the Great Spirit to support him.

If death should come to me, Fast Arrow thought, let it be quick.

The attendant and the witnesses now watched each candidate intently, until he hung as if dead, and his medicine bag, which he clung to, dropped to the ground. Then the signal was given and the young man was lowered to the floor of the Medicine Lodge. The cords by which he was suspended were pulled out, leaving the weights hanging to the splints.

No assistance was allowed to be given any man in any way, for each now trusted his life to the keeping of the Great Spirit.

Little by little, the strips of skin and muscle on Fast Arrow's breast, legs, and arms stretched out longer and longer. His legs jerked involuntarily under him. He knew that if he had not fasted he would have been incontinent, unable to control the bowel spasms that shook him; if his bladder had been full, that would have emptied without his will long ago.

The drums beat on. Fast Arrow sensed that one candidate was crawling on the ground, screaming, past the witnesses. The witnesses spoke low among themselves; he could not know what they said.

There was silence as the attendants lowered another candidate to the ground and loosened his bindings.

Fast Arrow's mind wondered if the last man's skin had broken or if he had dropped his medicine bag. Horrified, he noticed that his hand no longer squeezed hard on the soft leather pouch that held his own medicine collection. He pushed his finger against his palm; there was no feeling. He could not tell if he held the bag, although his fingers seemed circled stiffly around something. He dared open his fingers a little. Nothing; there was nothing! Just as he had thought at first! An attendant suddenly was lowering him to the floor. The dark pit rushed past his ears and swallowed him up. The blessed darkness.

Fast Arrow did not know how long he had been on the ground. He did not care. He felt the vibrations of the drums, and the rhythm of the dancers' feet pounding on the earth. He gathered the strength and courage to get up on his hands and knees. He knew he could never stand. He crawled to where Redpipe and Four Bears sat by a dusty buffalo skull. He collapsed in front of them, his eyes shut; then he sensed that he was surrounded by light. His ears were sharply aware of a mounting chant and exultant shrieks inside the Medicine Lodge, and the drums—the drums. Finally he opened his eyes. It was too bright! He puzzled over it and squinted his eyes down for a better look. His eyes burned, and he thought he had his face in the fire. But when he tried to see why the fire was in his face, all he could see was a long ray of the afternoon sun coming in through the smoke hole.

Four Bears leaned down and looked at him. He held a sharp hatchet. Fast Arrow did not understand. Had he been a coward?

Four Bears grunted and placed the little finger of
Fast Arrow's left hand on the earth, spread away from
his other fingers. Then Four Bears prayed, saying, "Listen, Great Spirit, this is the sacrifice that my son is
now making to you. You have heard how he cried to
you for help in his deepest agony. Now hear this last
prayer." The hatchet was raised and down before Fast
Arrow could wake up his mind. His little finger had
been chopped off at the first joint as a sacrifice of
thanksgiving to the Great Spirit for sparing his life and
permitting him to be the adopted son of Four Bears.

Rosebud and Sacajawea both screamed as the first
candidates were led outside the Medicine Lodge. All
the weights still dragged from their mutilated bodies.
Fast Arrow was among these first men. Rosebud tried
to go to him, but she was restrained. The Ehkenah-
kanahpick, the Last Race, was yet to be endured—and
endured within public view.

Each man was taken in charge by two attendants.
Rawhide straps were wrapped around his wrist, and
these straps were used by the attendants to race him
furiously around the sacred ark in the center of the
arena. The men struggled to remain on their feet as
long as possible. The skulls and other weights dragged
behind.

When his endurance could carry him no farther, Fast
Arrow fell like a dead man on the ground. His face was
blotched green and white, like a peeled sycamore.

He had survived the Last Race of the Okeepa.

Fast Arrow was left to lie where he fell until he could
get to his feet without aid. Then, staggering like a drunk,
he made his way to Four Bears's lodge. The crowd opened
silently to let him through.

Redpipe, waiting in the lodge of Four Bears, was
exultant. His mighty son-in-law had passed the ordeal
with bravery and was now considered the Mandan son
of Chief Four Bears. He danced, sang, smoked, and
danced again.

Fast Arrow crawled through the lodge door that had
been left wide open. He could go no farther. The darkness enveloped him again.

Redpipe roused him with water from a buffalo paunch.

What little he was able to drink came back up. "Now, my son," he said, "you shall sleep in this lodge until your legs once again hold your body up." Redpipe placed the shield, medicine bag, bow, quiver, and arrows near the couch to which the women carried Fast Arrow. "If you are spoken to in your sleep, remember carefully what is said to you," he said.

But Fast Arrow was asleep and did not hear the prayers that were said for him.

Sacajawea felt a great nausea engulf her at the sight of Fast Arrow's mutilated body. She moved out of the lodge and vomited. She felt pride for Fast Arrow, who, Redpipe said, had taken the ordeal without an outburst of protest, but a single thought stayed in the front of her mind. Was this ceremony necessary to prove bravery? This torture that took a man so close to death— why did they do it? Fast Arrow would bear permanent scars. She prayed to the Great Spirit that his muscles would heal properly so that he would not limp and that his arms would not remain so defective they could not be raised past his ears for the rest of his life. Her pride was not filled with elation for Fast Arrow, but with grief. She looked at the silhouetted lodges in the moonlight and felt as though she were passing into another time. The great rocks on the plains and the juniper and sage jutted arrogantly against the pale prairie and were at once older than now. She felt the passing of time within herself, as though it had a demanding quality. It seemed to her that she had lived many lives already; in each one she had done nothing but wander and wander, always straying farther from the People that had been so dear to her.

Inside the lodge, the women of Four Bears brought out leather boxes of healing salves. They helped Rosebud untie the weights, pull out the splints, and bathe Fast Arrow's wounds.

Redpipe and Four Bears were showing their old torture scars, laughing and slapping each other across the knees. Rosebud sat limply beside her man's couch. Fast Arrow slept deeply, with his mouth open. He snorted loudly. His tongue was swollen and his lips cracked from lack of water. Rosebud bent over him and mois-

tened his lips with her tongue. He did not know they
celebrated his victory over death.

Gently Rosebud began to stroke Fast Arrow's forehead with a soft, damp leather cloth. She talked to him
on and on, in a voice as soft as drifting feathers. Again
and again she bent and moistened his lips with her
tongue, letting a little of the saliva trickle down his
parched throat.

CHAPTER 10

The Game of Hands

Traded from one warrior to another, Sacajawea was finally put up on a blanket by her current owner and gambled away to Toussaint Charbonneau, a squawman from Montreal, who had a special weakness for very young Indian girls.

Excerpt from p. 155 in *Lewis and Clark: Partners in Discovery* by John Bakeless. Copyright 1947 by John Bakeless. By permission of William Morrow and Company.

Sun Woman and Sacajawea put fresh red paint down the middle of their hair parts and on the insides of their ears. They put fresh paint on the front of their moccasins and scrubbed the grease and dirt spots from their tunics. They were to go with Four Bears and Redpipe to the council area. Refreshed and rested after eating, and relieved that the Okeepa had been completed with honor this night, Four Bears and Redpipe would come to sit around the arena fire to tell, with pride in their voices, of the bravery of Fast Arrow. The telling of the stories of each candidate would be mingled with social dancing and the playing of gambling games.

It was dark now. Only the arena fire gave light. Other young people were slipping from their lodges, heading for the firelight. It was not far, but there in the chill dark, with the red light ahead, the black shadows, the soft *lum-lum-lalum* of the drummers, and the distant keening of the village mourners, it seemed very long.

Sun Woman, plump and smooth-faced, guided Sacajawea behind the men's circle, and with their backs to the ring of men and their arms intertwined with other women, they danced to the drummers' rhythm, moving toward and away from the men. Following the rules of this dance, the men pretended to ignore the women, whose dancing gradually became more and more animated, and who began to sing as they danced. Soon the harp musicians came to add their music to the drums. The women broke their circle and darted suddenly through the circle of seated men. The men began to sing, with an elaborate pretense that nothing was happening.

Sacajawea picked up the mood of the dance and let her pent-up emotions loose; she leaped, swaggered, and cavorted in incredible gyrations, following the movements of the Mandan women as they danced the history of their culture, from the warrior and fertility dances to the dance-dramas about love, nature, and the ancient pale-faced fathers of their people. Sacajawea became flushed and her eyes twinkled as she laughed and tried

216

to keep up with the singing. She was in turn feverish, then seductive, then haunting. She did not even mind that Broken Tooth was in the circle.

The drums, drums, drums pulsated insistently. The women tapped men lightly on their shoulders, then returned to their original places and reformed their circle, leaving space this time for the chosen men to fill in.

It was now a test for the men, for each one had to know who it was who had tapped him. Each man rose and joined the circle, going to the woman whose finger had brushed his shoulders. If he failed to go to the right woman, it was considered a grievous insult. The men began dancing with high-leaping athletic prowess, looking carefully at each woman, some of whom were now bare-breasted.

Redpipe and Four Bears were finely dressed. Four Bears's leggings were fringed with scalp locks, and Redpipe's were trimmed with porcupine quills painted yellow and blue. They wore no shirts; their chests and backs were painted with yellowish daubs to resemble the sun's rays. Around Four Bears's neck was a long string of elk's teeth. Around Redpipe's neck was a white leather collar adorned with small pearly shells. The women of the lodge had worked hard this night to make the men look so handsome.

Chief Black Cat, his face painted with dots and triangles, seated himself next to Four Bears. He seemed in a cheerful mood, perhaps relieved that the torture rites were over for one more year.

Then the Wolf Chief appeared with the huge, ugly Chief Kakoakis and two men with long, black, bristly beards. Sun Woman pointed them out to Sacajawea. "The Wolf Chief has visitors for this festive night," she said, clicking her teeth. "Look, they take off their shirts and come to join the dance."

A chill swept over Sacajawea. She pulled Sun Woman into the shadows, out of the firelight around the dancers.

"Are you tired of dancing?" asked Sun Woman.

"No. I was enjoying myself," confessed Sacajawea, "but I do not want to dance with the white men. The bearded one next to Kakoakis is the white trader called Charbonneau."

"The other bearded one is the man of Brooken Tooth," said Sun Woman. "See, the one with the squinted eyes and the black cloth tied around his neck? That is the man they call René Jussome. The white men do not look like men, much, but like animals, with such thick hair on their bodies and faces. I would call that one Big Bear!" She giggled.

They watched the three men approach the men's circle for dancing. Kakoakis, who wore a beaver tail to the front and back of his breechclout and an elaborate neckpiece of bear claws, knotted thongs, and painted eagle feathers, made a beeline for Broken Tooth, who was wearing a tunic with an elaborately decorated yoke of brightly painted shells and quills. He laughed loudly as he moved into the open space at her right and took her hand.

Charbonneau wore soft leather boots, baggy pants, and a red kerchief at his throat. He weighed about two hundred pounds and was not tall. His eyes were nearly black, and his face bore the large nose and high cheekbones of the French-Canadian métis, or half-breed. He looked around the circle of giggling girls, then with an awkward imitation of the Mandan leap, he entered the men's circle. The dance began again.

Jussome, who had placed a cloth cap with an eagle feather jauntily fastened to the side on his head, stood on the far side of the circle watching his woman, Broken Tooth, dance with the tall, repulsive, one-eyed Kakoakis. The dance went on until the dancemaster, who was the Medicine Man of the Bull Dance, signaled the drummers to stop and said, "Let no one walk out into the brush," as a warning to the young couples who had made love pacts.

There were braves stationed at strategic places on the outer rim of the arena to see that no one wandered out to the brush, but not all the lovers were kept within bounds. Kakoakis, chief of the Metaharta village, moved furtively out into the darkness with the giggling, loose-hipped Broken Tooth.

Charbonneau moved toward Jussome, who was now talking in loud guffaws with Four Bears. "How about a little game of hands? I bring five quarts of rum from

Fort Pine last time I visit." He repeated his offer in Mandan to Four Bears.

Jussome made signs indicating to Four Bears that it was good crazy-water and would warm his innards.

"Have you ever watched men at this game called hands?" asked Sun Woman. She had read the signs the men exchanged.

Sacajawea nodded no. She had never seen men play the game, but she had played it with Rosebud's children many times.

"They will play the game a long time before they go to the lodges. Let us go watch awhile. Sometimes they play for knives, or arrows, or beads, or shells. Four Bears might win something for me."

Jussome, in a row with the Wolf Chief, Black Cat, Four Bears, and Redpipe, faced a row of men including Charbonneau. Seven men were facing only six, and Charbonneau was passing firewater and complaining because his row was short a man, delaying the start of the game. The Mandan Charbonneau spoke was heavily accented with French and English, and it was hard for Sacajawea to understand him.

Finally, Chief Kakoakis was sighted coming across the flat ground behind the Medicine Lodge. Broken Tooth came a few paces behind, the top of her tunic pushed around her waist as it had been during the dancing. Her breasts bounced as she walked along the hard ground. Charbonneau, who was seated cross-legged, watched her dangling breasts and broke into a lecherous grin. He took a pull from the rum jug.

"*Jésus*, what a woman," breathed Charbonneau, his roundish face pushed out low from the hunched thrust of his shoulders. His voice came from deep down in his throat.

Jussome glared at Charbonneau. "You have forgotten one thing," he said in his French-Canadian patois. "That is my woman, and if you want her you pay me in worthwhile goods, the same as Kakoakis does."

Kakoakis took his place in Charbonneau's line, opposite Redpipe, and now seven men faced another row of seven. They were spaced about three feet apart. A ring was drawn in the earth between the rows. The Wolf Chief began a low chant that was picked up by

Redpipe and then Kakoakis. The rum jug passed between the players and the game began, accompanied
by yells of encouragement or hisses at opponents by the
onlookers.[1]

The hands game was played with small bones that
could be concealed in a man's hand. One of the bones
was carved with lines and dots around the center; the
other was polished, but left plain. The object was to fool
an opponent into picking the hand that contained the
unmarked bone. Markers, in the form of sticks, twelve
on each side of the ring, kept the score.

Kakoakis kept time to the low, monotonous singing,
moving his hands about in front, to the side and behind
his back, under his leg, over his head and under his
arm. He moved his hands slowly and flashed the bones
so that Redpipe, whose face was flushed with rum, could
plainly see them. Then he moved them quickly high in
the air keeping the backs of his hands toward Redpipe
as his hands came together and apart, seeming not to
open, keeping time to the beat. Suddenly, swaying to
and fro, Kakoakis brought his hands toward Redpipe.
Redpipe pointed to the right clenched hand.

Kakoakis opened his hand to show the marked bone.

Redpipe had won the point.

Kakoakis placed one of the twelve sticks lying on
his side of the ring beside the twelve sticks on the side
of the ring closest to Redpipe.

"You cover those sticks like they were a woman—
with experience," guffawed a man near Kakoakis.

"I cover a woman different, old warrior!" Kakoakis
chuckled.

Sacajawea caught a glimpse of Broken Tooth skulking back from a trip to relieve herself in the woods. She
moved around the two rows of men, then slid down
petulantly next to Kakoakis. She looked up into his
face and made a little pouting mouth.

Sacajawea looked at Jussome and thought, That man
does not even care if his woman is moon-eyed in front
of all these others! She looked from him to Charbonneau. The more closely she examined the faces of the
white men, the more difficult it was to tell them apart.
White men all look alike, she thought.

Redpipe now held the deal and moved the sticks here

and there. Under one leg, then the other, and back and forth in front of his opponent. Finally he held them out. Jussome spoke up fast.

"I bet the favors of my woman for a look at your left hand."

There was much laughter, for this bet of Jussome's would liven up the game. Redpipe was sitting very erectly, not wishing to offend the white trader, but at the same time not wishing to collect any favors from Jussome's woman, Broken Tooth. He shrugged and opened his left hand.

There was much shouting, for Jussome had guessed wrong. He motioned to Broken Tooth, who went over and sat next to Redpipe, giggling and heaving her breasts to and fro.

Kakoakis took another swig of rum and bent to Redpipe. "Put up as a prize this woman of Jussome," he said.

Redpipe blinked. His face remained blank. Inside he felt a great relief. The idea came to him to lose quickly and get rid of the brazen young Broken Tooth, who meant nothing but trouble.

Redpipe, however, won his round, and Kakoakis passed his turn to Charbonneau.

The rum bottle was brought out, and again the chanting began. At the same time, several men got up and voided, seeing who could wet earth the farthest.

Sacajawea felt herself wilting. The day had been strenuous and long. It had been filled with experiences she had never had before, emotions and excitement that would live in her memory for a long time. Her eyes closed with sleep.

"Come along," said Sun Woman, "we have stayed too long." She helped Sacajawea to her feet. "Our men will be along toward morning. Let us sleep."

Charbonneau turned at that moment and saw the women rise. He pointed a finger at them.

"He looks to us," gasped Sacajawea.

"It is nothing," said Sun Woman, unconcerned. "It was a gesture meaning nothing to us." But Sun Woman was wrong.

"Bring that *femme* to me!" Charbonneau called.

"Redpipe, I wish you to place that daughter of yours as a bet instead of Broken Tooth."

"Leave the child out of it," Four Bears said to him before Redpipe could answer. He rose and walked to the women. "Go to our lodge," he told them.

Charbonneau was complaining violently. He threatened to quit the game and take the firewater with him when he saw Sacajawea and Sun Woman begin to walk away.

"Stop!" bellowed Chief Kakoakis. "Come forward! I will have a look at these two."

Even Four Bears dared not disobey this grotesque man.

"Chief Kakoakis," Four Bears said. "This daughter of Redpipe is a guest in my lodge. I have told her to take my woman there." He pointed to Sun Woman's full breasts. "Her papoose needs feeding."

"So," Kakoakis said. He looked thoughtful, and took a drink of rum. "All right," he said. "We will wait on this matter. Your woman may go, but the girl stays here." He reached out for Sacajawea and pulled her beside him. "You should be honored. You are a fair one. You would be even fairer wearing a weasel collar." He laughed, and his long, bony fingers ran around her neck. She shivered, afraid to speak. Sun Woman was gone. She and Broken Tooth were the only women at the men's game.

Four Bears indicated that Sacajawea should sit to the side of Redpipe; then he turned to Charbonneau. Four Bears's hands doubled into fists. He raised them in front of Charbonneau and then let them flop down. "I do not want any trouble." He emphasized his words again with hand signs.

Charbonneau eyed Sacajawea, then looked at the hussy, Broken Tooth.

Redpipe spoke up at last. "*Ai*, the bet has already been made. It is for the lithesome child, Broken Tooth."

Charbonneau sighed heavily, testing the feel of the bones. "The bet has been made," he said, passing Redpipe the jug. "Put more rum in your belly. You have the guess." Charbonneau poured some rum down his own throat, then handed the jug to Black Cat, who passed it to Kakoakis. Kakoakis drank, licked his lips, and began the chant. The game of hands resumed.

Sacajawea sat hunched, trying not to look at the drooping eyelid that half concealed the milk-white film on Kakoakis's blind eye, nor the two beady eyes under the bushy black eyebrows of Charbonneau, who was now moving the sticks. Her eyes flicked to Four Bears and Redpipe. Their faces told her nothing. She kept her eyes on Charbonneau's hands.

Four Bears rose to put more sticks on the fire; then he leaned toward Sacajawea.

"You," he whispered, "keep your shirt on."

"I have no shirt, only a tunic!"

"That's it! Good," he said approvingly. "You have good nerves. As long as you can joke, you are all right."

She had not meant it for a joke. She did not feel like joking.

Charbonneau celebrated the winning of his bet by placing his cupped hand on the bare breast of Broken Tooth. He looked at Redpipe, who celebrated his loss of Broken Tooth by putting his hand out for the jug.

"This one is nice," Charbonneau said, passing Redpipe the rum, "but she is too far from a virgin. It is *that* one I want"—he pointed to Sacajawea—"the young one."

"She was not the bet," Redpipe said.

"Well, I *want* her to be the bet!" Charbonneau yelled.

"Wanting is not enough," Four Bears said.

"Wanting is not enough!" Charbonneau mimicked, pronouncing the Mandan words very badly. "Wanting is not enough!" He rose to face Four Bears, who stood also. "And what business is it of yours? She is just a squaw, so wanting *is* enough."

And then, faster than Sacajawea could comprehend, Jussome and Black Cat were standing near Charbonneau, who had raised his skinning knife and jammed the point of it into Four Bears's ribs. It was no light blow. Four Bears' mouth came open. He stepped backward, and the point followed him.

"All right, Big Tess," Jussome said in French. "Let him be. Sit and play the game properly. Your head runs too hot."

"No," Charbonneau said. "I say for Redpipe to put

up his daughter for your line, and I will put up Jussome's squaw for mine."

At that moment Charbonneau's head turned in search of Broken Tooth. She was not in the vicinity of the game. She had slipped past the arguing players, past the onlookers, and stealthily moved to the center of the arena. With furtive glances now and again back toward the noisy crowd, she groped inside the ancient medicine ark. Then her hand felt the round coolness of the golden coin. There was no mistake—this was something valuable, and her man, Jussome, could trade or sell it for many goods. She thought of the riches and the power it would bring. She was filled with vainglory as she caressed the coin.

Moving fast, Four Bears nearly knocked Chief Black Cat over as he spotted Broken Tooth with her hands clutching something to her breasts. He sucked his cheeks in between his teeth as he went forward shouting, "Stop!" It was abrupt and clear.

Broken Tooth stopped as if stung. Her eyes flashed, and her mood changed into savagery like a stirred snake's. She flung the coin at Jussome, who moved slowly with the crowd up behind Four Bears. It struck him in the breast, but if it hurt, he gave no sign. He covered the coin with both hands for a moment, then let it drop like a hot stone. He turned away from the face of his woman to stare into the icy eyes of Four Bears. "I think she, my woman, she was looking—ah— looking for another jug of rum. *Zut! Stupide femme!*"

Four Bears's eyes were like bits of ice. "It was not rum she looked for. You know that." He took a step toward Broken Tooth.

Her face twitched, and she felt her legs shake. She ducked from his grasp, picked up the coin, and dropped it with a thud back through the dark, dank hole of the ark.

"So, it was you who planned this raid on our sacred artifacts. You who thought of nothing but the riches they would bring. You did not take time to think that things from a past age could be wiped out, so that one day there would be no one left to recall them. You are less than a pack rat. I could slash your throat!"

Broken Tooth shrank back. She could not go far with

the crowd packed in around her now. Four Bears lunged for her neck. Sacajawea drew in her breath as she saw Jussome's hand rise up until his hunting knife appeared above the back of Four Bears like a spear. Then the crowd swarmed in front of Sacajawea's eyes, and hands from everywhere took hold of Broken Tooth and slapped and pounded. They pulled and pushed. The crowd was made up of faces with mouths wide open, yelling, and arms flaying and punching.

Four Bears stood now like a man turned to stone as the crowd heaved back and forth, almost the way trees sway back and forth in a strong wind. Charbonneau elbowed his way in with the jug under his arm. He offered it to Four Bears, who, trancelike, drank huge drafts. Then Charbonneau offered the jug to Redpipe.

"No," sputtered Redpipe, staggering to the far edge of the crowd. His face was red and getting redder. His head dropped a little forward. His thick shoulders dropped, too—not sagging, but hunching solidly. His head and shoulders swayed a little as his eyes stared along the edge of the crowd.

"Oh, by *Jésus*!" Jussome said, throwing his hat on the ground.

Sacajawea looked from Broken Tooth to Redpipe. She wondered if he were drunk or having one of his falling spells. She was feeling detached, past the point of fear.

"Go back and sit down!" yelled Chief Kakoakis to the crowd. "Women—they are the curse of man. I will show you how to handle the situation." Chief Kakoakis rose to his full height, pulled a knife from under his breechclout, and pointed it to the starlit heavens, giving a big shout. Then Kakoakis reached down with his powerful hand and pulled Sacajawea to him by one braid of hair. All hands were still, and all eyes were on Chief Kakoakis. All this was so unexpected that Sacajawea could hardly make her legs hold her up. Her heart beat like hummingbird wings. Kakoakis slashed the knife across his own wrist, across the right wrist of Sacajawea, and then he held their wounds tightly together. Blood ran down to Sacajawea's elbow and dripped to the ground. She was so surprised by this sudden happening that her wrist did not seem to hurt at all. With the two wrists together, Kakoakis said in his loud voice, "See, here, this girl is the blood daughter of Kakoakis."

Redpipe gave a funny, choked laugh.

Kakoakis went on, "Let us forget this unfinished theft. It will not happen again. You have my word. Remember the game. I say for Jussome to put up his squaw for his side and I will put up my new blood daughter for my side." He laughed, enjoying the look on the faces of Redpipe and Four Bears.

Mostly the men roared approval of Kokoakis's solution, although there were a few mutterings and one loud *"Na-aah!"* from Four Bears, who shifted his weight as he felt the probe of Charbonneau's knife, which was once again against his ribs.

Kakoakis bowed and returned to his place. "Two women are better than one," he said. "It is settled. If my new blood daughter is won in a fair game, let her go as the woman of my old friend Charbonneau, whose man part never hangs limp!"

Jussome slapped Charbonneau on the back as Charbonneau gave a mighty shout and pawed the earth in the manner of a bull buffalo.

Broken Tooth's volatile mood changed again, and she showed delight with Sacajawea's discomfort. She gestured to Jussome. With glittering black eyes and guttural gloatings of relief that her neck was intact, she suggested that his buffalo robe be placed in the center of the players and that the two prizes sit on the robe. Jussome was eager to comply with the frivolity and beamed at his woman for such a splendid suggestion.

Sacajawea began to inch backward toward the woods. An instinct for survival had been touched in her. Her breathing was hard, and her chest hurt. Jussome saw her, gave a low laugh, and spun around, scooping her up in his arms and returning her to the group of laughing men. "This child thinks she can slip away from the mighty Bear of the Forest. She shakes like a frightened meadow mouse." He placed her beside Charbonneau. She looked away, toward Redpipe. She screamed.

The men were startled. Four Bears recovered first and looked toward Redpipe, whose head had fallen and who was making bubbling noises. Four Bears pushed Redpipe's head up, he saw his pale face twitch, his eyes roll, and his head, body, and limbs begin to jerk about as his hands opened and closed.

"The falling sickness!" Four Bears exclaimed. He ran to Redpipe. Foam had gathered at the corners of Redpipe's mouth, bloodstained from his tongue, which was caught between his teeth and was deeply bitten.

Four Bears could not pull Redpipe's mouth open; his jaws were snapped together like a sprung beaver's trap. The men shrank back. Redpipe's breathing became shallow. Four Bears called for help to carry Redpipe to his lodge.

Jussome's knife flashed in the firelight toward Four Bears's chest. "He will not move away. Leave him here. We are still in the game," said Jussome.

Like the other Mandan men, Four Bears had come in good faith, unarmed. Now he could do nothing for Redpipe, but must sit quietly between Jussome and Charbonneau, two of the three armed men in the game.

Sacajawea saw only one thing to do. She stood on her feet. She did not attempt to run away, but stood very still. Her head ached, and her hands were damp. She could feel a little river of sweat beginning to flow down the center of her back. She sucked in a deep breath of air to steady herself. To speak was an unheard-of thing, she knew that. Women never spoke up in front of a group of men. But if she did speak, if she were able to say anything, surely Charbonneau would see how completely undesirable she was. For a Shoshoni woman, or any woman of nearly thirteen summers, this was a brave and bold step. She would try this shameful thing. She would be scorned for a time, but in the lodge of Redpipe and Grasshopper there would be understanding and solace.

Her first sound was barely audible, and her knees shook; then a shrill roar from deep within her chest came with such a shattering explosion that the men sat with their eyes popping out as she found her voice.

"My father, Redpipe, is ill. Are you cowards? My father's friend, Chief Four Bears, is held down. Are you no braver than weak squaws crawling in the sage, or dying coyotes with their heads in holes? It takes no bravery to give me to a man who is the winner in a game of hands. You are no more than rabbits, a nation of magpies with broken wings. If the fur-faced one wants a woman, why don't you let him find one for himself—one who is willing to sleep with a furry buffalo."

There was some sniggering, and Charbonneau sat stock-still, his mouth open, listening to the Minnetaree words of this bold young girl. If someone had told him that an Indian female had that many words in her head, he would not have believed it.

"Since a child, I was promised to a great Shoshoni warrior with no hair to speak of, except on his head, where the Great Spirit intended man's hair should be. This great warrior gave many horses for me. The man who takes me as his woman should pay much to my Minnetaree family. I cook, sew, and clean, and keep a neat lodge. I do not speak out much."

Most of the men roared and guffawed and slapped each other on the back, as though she had told some great joke.

"God almighty!" Charbonneau said in disbelief; he had lowered his knife.

Kakoakis's face was contorted with anger, but Sacajawea saw that she had aroused some of the men to her side; Four Bears and the Wolf Chief were now talking with three other men close to the place where Redpipe rested in a pool of his own urine. His fine leggings were stained and the paint on his chest smeared. No one stopped Sacajawea as she moved toward Redpipe. His words were incoherent. He was speaking in the world of spirits. His breathing was stertorous. Someone had placed a heavy buffalo paunch filled with water nearby.

"I will get him out of here," Four Bears said. The men made a move to help.

"No!" said the Wolf Chief. "This man who speaks with spirits could bring us a message—perhaps the spirits will tell what should be done with the overbold young squaw."

"It is settled!" Charbonneau said. "What should be done is to start the game."

"It is not settled," Sacajawea said. "Perhaps the spirits will be angered by the thought of men arguing about a woman when the worthy Redpipe is left to lie on the ground!"

Jussome snorted. "She is the right age for you, but her tongue is like a knife," he said to Charbonneau.

"She is full of fire. She is what I want. I am going to be the man to tame the Girl That Loved a Dog."

Jussome perked up. "Are you saying that she is the Dog Girl?"

"Yes, that is her, right there. I saw her with the Hidatsas."

"When did you see her with the Hidatsas? Where?" Jussome asked.

"I saw her in the spring gathering rotten buffalo. I saw her with the dog."

"You mean *she* is the Dog Girl?" the Wolf Chief exclaimed.

"She is."

"Mon dieu!" Jussome swung himself around. "You hear, Kakoakis? If we had known, we could have taken her without any game of hands. That settles things."

"It settles nothing," Four Bears said. "It does not change the facts."

"I will give you rings for your ears, and metal rings like those you find in the north!" Charbonneau said suddenly to Sacajawea. "And a long string of colored beads! The rings and beads will make you feel like a woman. I will teach you passion, and you shall learn desire."

Jussome laughed out loud.

"A bargain?" Charbonneau asked eagerly.

"No." Four Bears's monosyllable was abrupt and clear.

Charbonneau started as if burned. His eyes flashed, and his mood became untamed and wild, like a caged mountain lion's. The rum had destroyed his caution and inflamed him. His hand went for his knife. Just as suddenly, Four Bears's hand slapped across Jussome's back and slipped deftly downward to the knife in the leather sheath at Jussome's side.

He had the knife, but Jussome tripped him. Charbonneau's hunting knife hung above the nape of Four Bears's neck like an ax.

Sacajawea's stomach churned. The frozen feeling that had come upon her broke suddenly, like spring water gushing through a covering of ice. She did not think.

There was no time. It seemed the churning boil inside her lifted and moved her. She lifted the full, heavy water paunch from the ground and swung it backward, back behind her hipbone. A shudder that she could not stop went through her, but she heaved the paunch, harder than she'd heaved one at the dog long ago, and her aim was good. The shudder had not come in time to spoil it. All the water in the paunch struck Charbonneau in the face. His knife slashed down, but it missed Four Bears's neck. It grazed him on the thick meat of his left shoulder, and Four Bears squirmed around and got hold of the knife with his left hand, driving the point upward into Charbonneau's right shoulder. Charbonneau let go and put his fists up to his eyes to dig the water out.

Four Bears took two steps backward, toward the circle drawn in the earth for the game of hands. He had both Jussome's and Charbonneau's knives. He leveled both, waist-high, the butts clamped against his body and his hands tucked around the hilts.

The whole thing had not taken half a minute. The men still sitting in the rows had not moved. They had had no time to, and although they were close enough to see what had happened, they looked as if they were not sure they had seen it.

Charbonneau sat on the ground. Blood seeped through the cut in his leather shirt. He felt it and winced at the blood on his fingers. He looked at Four Bears pointing the knives.

"I do not want trouble," he said. "I would not like it if someone got hurt." He shook his head.

"*Jésus*," Jussome said. "Here you are bleeding and causing trouble and you say 'I do not want trouble.'" He said it the same way Charbonneau had said it.

Chief Black Cat laughed. Grins broke out on the clustered faces. It was good to have the tension gone.

Kakoakis walked over to Charbonneau and ripped off his leather shirt in one fast, sweeping motion. He threw the shredded shirt to Sacajawea. "Tie the shoulder," he said.

But Sacajawea was past the point of caring. All caution was gone. She was being treated as if the matter had been decided, as if she were, in fact, already the woman of Charbonneau.

"No," she said. "He is not my man. I will tend to my father, Redpipe."

"He *is* your man," Kakoakis said in a rage. "I gave you to him. Forget the old man. His blood is cold."

"You cannot do that," Four Bears said. "She is to be wagered in the hands game."

Then Kakoakis laughed, an evil laugh, and he said, "Good. The matter is settled. Let us play."

In all the sky there was nothing but coolness; the air was washed and fresh. The rays of the sun shot far out from under a cloud, the last vestige of the roaring thunderheads that had come with the end of the night, floating like a tuft of sage on the clearest of water. The mist lifted, revealing lone hackberry trees, cottonwoods, and above the river course, miles of flat prairie.

"You will pull the moccasins from your man's feet, Sacajawea," said Charbonneau, taking her hand to pull her across a spring with a bottom of black muck.

Sacajawea thought back to the time when she had taken off Redpipe's moccasins and washed his old, wrinkled feet, rubbing them with sage and sweet-smelling grasses. She thought of Grasshopper and Fast Arrow and Rosebud. Her heart was in her moccasins. She thought that one of the most terrifying things about nature was its complete disinterest in a human's fate. She wondered if Grasshopper would mourn for her, if Sweet Clover would miss her. And as she followed Charbonneau walking toward the sun, like a wing fluttering open, Sacajawea could no longer keep her anguish buried. A long cry broke from her throat, a long, shuddering, keening cry.

Charbonneau turned his head to look at her, her cry penetrating some dim inner consciousness. Her head was thrown back; she was tearing her hair over her face, and her mouth was twisted. She drew in a sobbing breath and cried again, clawing at her face. It was a high, horrible animal sound, tremulous, concerted, thin as birchbark but piercing as a high-pitched bone whistle.

Charbonneau flew into a rage at the woman. He

cuffed Sacajawea, sending her sprawling. "Son of a bitch,
shut up! Shut up that crazy yowling! Shut it up, now.
You hear?"

Sacajawea rolled over and sat up, clutching at her
heart; she scooted out of his reach, with no pause in
her ululating howl. Charbonneau caught her and
clapped a hand over her mouth, pinching her nostrils
shut with the fingers of his other hand. She clawed and
fought.

"I'll lodgepole you!" he warned. "That is no way to
sound on your wedding day!"

She did not understand all of his broken Minnetaree,
but her crying had softened. She would bury her life as
the daughter of Redpipe and Grasshopper in her own
way, with her imaginings and memories.

When white traders lived with Indians, they adopted
many Indian ways. They stopped, for instance, having
any set time for eating. Among the Indians, food was
always cooking and ready to eat, and each person ate
when he was hungry or when it suited him. There was
no gathering together for meals, except when there
were visitors to be honored. So, late that morning, as
if they had expected a new woman, Corn Woman and
Otter Woman had built up the fire in Charbonneau's
lodge and filled a bowl for him and one for Sacajawea.
Then they waited to see what would happen. Corn
Woman returned Charbonneau's grunts with bawdy
and ribald remarks. Otter Woman brought his bowl of
stew.

When he finished eating, Charbonneau made a flat,
downward, cutting-off motion with his hand.

"Today there is just me and the little Bird Woman,"
Charbonneau said bluntly. "You are in the way. Go out!
Go find some willow and weave a basket," he said.

Behind him, Sacajawea's eyes were round and frightened. But she would not cry out before the others. She
would accept this, absorb it, and sink quickly into her
role. She would not disgrace Grasshopper by being a
bad squaw. Charbonneau had won the game fairly, and
he had paid trade goods to Redpipe's lodge in addition.

"Bring me water, Sacajawea."

She found the drinking water and brought some to

him in the tin mug. He made a motion, and she tugged
at his moccasins until they fell to the floor. Then she
rubbed his feet gently with warm water and crushed
sage. The lodge was set straight. It was dry, warm, and
good-smelling. There was plenty of wood and meat here.

She sat for a long time watching Charbonneau blow
smoke from his pipe. Then he came to her slowly, and
pulled her tunic over her head. His eyes assayed her
body, the white scars on her straight back, her small,
brown breast points. He did not touch her, but dropped
a robe around her shoulders.

She drew the robe close around herself. She was
tired. At times rage and despair swept over her. She
knew she was beginning another life. She sat waiting,
silent, an immobile figure inside the fur robe, watching
the curling blue pipe smoke.

When the pipe was dead, he carried her to his couch.
She lay beside him, her hands touching the robe over
them, trembling, withdrawing not so much from Charbonneau as from life itself pressing toward her.

"You don't really like me," he said. "Do you?"

"*Ai*, maybe," Sacajawea answered, "maybe I do,
some."

She could have moved closer to the wall, but she only
glanced up at him with a scared smile. She was perhaps
thirteen years old. Charbonneau was forty-three.

He pressed her tightly against the couch. "Maybe
I've liked you for a long time."

She struggled against him then, but his left arm was
an iron cage, and his heart pounded against hers. He
nuzzled his face into her neck. His right shoulder, which
Four Bears had stabbed, was stiff and hurt him. He
fingered her neck and shoulders, and soon, without understanding how, he found himself kissing her, blindly,
smotheringly, like a man sinking underwater. He
kissed her neck, her shoulders, her throat, her chin, her
mouth, sucking at her lips. His hands did the duty im-
posed on them by a million years of human lovemaking.
His hands moved to her just-obvious breast swellings,
and then on down, stroking closely, past her thin, flat
belly, her hips, and her thighs. His hard, work-firm
palms were startled at the smoothness and softness of
her legs, and paused awhile to speculate on the wonder

of femininity. Then his hands moved up to her hips again, where one came to rest on the warmth between her legs and the other went up and around her back to her shoulders. He wet her small breasts with his tongue and fumbled stupidly with the knot in his belt as if it were some horrible mechanism too complex for his fingers to understand. When it was loose at last, and the eternal pain pushed toward refuge, she sighed and moved and put her hands hard on his breast.

"Do not hurt me!" she cried.

He answered, shivering, "*Oui, un moment* we become *un deux-dos cheval*." Fiercely he pinned her arms beneath his and brutally buried his face in her breasts, writhing in helpless ecstasy. When release came at last, he pushed her aside and drew on his trousers, leaving off his shirt because his shoulder throbbed. He was hot, and there was perspiration on his narrow forehead.

Book Two
RETURN
TO THE PEOPLE

*Washington
June 19th 1803*

To William Clark:

Herewith inclosed you will receive the papers belonging to your brother Genl. (George Rogers) Clark, which sometime since you requested me to procure and forward to you....

From the long and uninterrupted friendship and confidence which has subsisted between us I feel no hesitation in making to you the following communication under the fulest impression that it will be held by you inviolably secret....

During the last session of Congress a law was passed in conformity to a private message of the President of the United States, intitled "An Act making an appropriation for extending the external commerce of the United States." The object of this Act as understood by its framers was to give the sanction of the government to exploreing the interior of the continent of North America, or that part of it bordering on the Missourie, and Columbia Rivers....I am armed with the authority of the Government of the U. States for my protection, so far as its authority or influence extends; in addition to which, the further aid has been given me of liberal pasports from the Ministers both of France and England....I shall embark at Pittsburgh with a party of recruits eight or nine in number, intended only to manage the boat and are not calculated on as a permanent part of my detatchment; when descending the Ohio it shall be my duty by enquiry to find out and engage some good hunt-

235

ers, stout, healthy, unmarried men, accustomed to the woods, and capable of bearing bodily fatigue in a pretty considerable degree; should any young men answering this description be found in your neighborhood I would thank you to give information of them on my arivall at the falls of the Ohio.... The present season being already so far advanced, I do not calculate on getting further than two or three hundred miles up the Missourie before the commencement of the ensuing winter.... You must know in the first place that very sanguine expectations are at this time formed by our Government that the whole of that immense country wartered by the Mississippi and it's tributary streams, Missourie inclusive, will be the property of the U. States in less than 12 Months from this date; but here let me again impress you with the necessity of keeping this matter a perfect secret....

Thus my friend you have so far as leasure will at this time permit me to give it you, a summary view of the plan, the means and the objects of this expedition, if therefore there is anything under those circumstances, in this enterprise, which would induce you to participate with me in it's fatiegues, it's dangers and it's honors, believe me there is no man on earth with whom I should feel equal pleasure in sharing them as with yourself; I make this communication to you with the privity of the President, who expresses an anxious wish that you would consent to join me in this enterprise; he has authorized me to say that in the event of your accepting this proposition he will grant you a Captain's commission which of course will intitle you to the pay and emoluments attached to that office and will equally with myself intitle you to such portion of land as was granted to [officers] of similar rank for their Revolutionary services; the commission with which he proposes to furnish you is not to be considered temporary but permanent if you wish it; your situation if joined with me in this mission will in all respects be precisely such as my own. Pray write to me on this subject as early as possible and direct to me at Pittsburgh....

With sincere and affectionate regard Your Friend and Humbl sevt.

Meriweather Lewis

REUBEN GOLD THWAITES, ed., *The Original Journals of the Lewis and Clark Expedition, 1804–1806,* vol. 7. New York: Dodd, Mead and Co., 1904–5. Reprinted by Arno Press, 1969, pp. 226–30.

CHAPTER

11

Lewis and Clark

Clark's Journal:
Mandans.—   *27th of October Satturday 1804,*

*we met with a frenchman by the name of Jessomme
which we imploy as an interpreter. This man has a wife
and Children in the village. Great numbers on both Sides
flocked down to the bank to view us as we passed. we
Sent three twists of Tobacco by three young men, to the
villages above inviting them to come Down and Council
with us tomorrow. many Indians came to view as Some
stayed all night in the Camp of our party. We procured
some information of Mr. Jessomme of the Chiefs of the
Different Nations.*

4th November Sunday 1804

*we continued to cut Down trees and raise our houses,
a Mr. Chaubonie, interpeter for the Gross Ventre nation
Came to See us, and informed that [he] came Down with
Several Indians from a hunting expedition up the river,
to here what we had told the Indians in Council. This
man wished to hire as an interpiter*

BERNARD DEVOTO, ed., *The Journals of Lewis and Clark.*
New York: Houghton Mifflin Co., 1953, pp. 58–9, 63.

At the first light of dawn over the Five River Villages, Sacajawea was up with the others, Otter Woman and Corn Woman. She wore a shapeless, dirty red blanket and scuffed moccasins, but she wore the polished sky-blue stone on a thong close to her thoat. She built up the cooking fire with pieces of dry, seasoned wood that were within reach of her bed; they burned with a practically smokeless fire.

Otter Woman wore a leather tunic and calf-high moccasins that were baggy and dirty. She sat on her hide-covered bed and nursed a boy of two summers who lay naked in her lap on a mound of black deer moss.

"I was sick in the mornings when I carried this one," Otter Woman said in her native Shoshoni. "You are lucky."

"*Ai*," Sacajawea said.

Corn Woman, still in her teens, was the eldest woman of Charbonneau. She sat on a pallet of cornhusks, motionless, silent, head bent, wrapped in a gray wool blanket, staring at her hands. Stuck into a well-worn animal hide hanging from a wooden beam behind her bed were her needles for sewing skins. Bits of sinew, pieces of leather, and skins lay about within easy reach. At the foot of her pallet were wire rabbit snares and a few rusted traps. Some animal skins were drying on the stretchers leaning against the side wall. In one grand motion she gestured toward the fire and rummaged among the leather and skins to find her vintage felt hat, which she pulled down over her wisps of coal-black hair.

Sacajawea saw the gesture and stirred the contents of the stew pot on a cooking crane over the fire. She laid the stirring bone on a piece of bark. What had gone into the stew she could not recall. It had started early in the fall with meat, barley, beans, and sliced pumpkin. As time went by, whatever was handy was tossed in—headless and footless, uneviscerated bodies of rabbits, a fish or two, some dried corn, a wild parsnip, some meat. The stew pot would be cleaned in the spring when Charbonneau moved his camp to a creek nearer his trap lines. Then the stew pot would simmer its way until fall when they moved back to the permanent earthen lodge in the village of the Mandans.

Charbonneau pushed aside the wooden door, stamped his calked boots, and brushed off his baggy pants. He tossed a felt hat aside; his black hair was matted to his head. As he tossed a leather pouch near Sacajawea's feet, he said, "Here's that tea I got from the feller McCracken. She go in hot water. A little bit." He dug around in his pants pocket and pulled out a wad of cigarette papers and a nearly empty pack of shag tobacco. "Come on, we have a good feed and a pot of tea."

Corn Woman, glad he spoke the familiar Minnetaree she could understand, smiled and picked up the leather pouch. She put several pinches of tea leaves in a small iron kettle, poured water from a clay pot and replaced the stew pot with the teakettle.

As he sealed his cigarette, Charbonneau thought how he did not much mind being called Squawman. He did not mind if it meant this—being warm and well fed by women who did as he commanded. They were chattel. He was the boss. For a few trinkets and bits of foofaraw, the women were always there to make him feel like the Emperor Napoleon. Even if he left for a hunt or trapping for the Company for three or four months, the women would be waiting for him and his kill with freshly made trousers, jackets, and moccasins.

He found a stick and lit it in the fire, inclined his head, and got his cigarette going. "Pour that tea slow!" he yelled at Corn Woman, who was pouring the hot, bitter tea into a tin cup. "I want to drink, not chew this." His nostrils distended as they took in the aroma. He pulled off his boots, sitting on the earthen floor, which was so hardened from use by bare and moccasined feet and swept so clean that it had almost a polished appearance. He wiped the back of his hand across his mustache and smoked again. Then he sipped the tea.

Sacajawea picked up the stirring bone and wiped the bark bowl clean with the edge of her blanket. With an elk horn she dipped out some thick stew. Charbonneau poured the stew into his mouth. The first swallow made him twist his face as the thick gruel burned his innards.

With his fingers he picked up strings of meat and hunks
of soft pumpkin. "By gar, I get lots of fur. Make plenty
of money this winter. Charbonneau is damn good man!"
His look almost dared the women to question his statement. Then his face softened. He smiled and pushed
the child off Otter Woman's lap. Charbonneau had given
his son his own name, Toussaint, but usually called the
baby Little Tess.

"Little Tess, he be feller like his papa. He grow smart.
He should work for Company, but he no bum like Jussome. That Jussome is a bum, anyway." He picked up
the child and bounced him across his knees. He thought
of René Jussome. He did not like Jussome. He did not
trust him. But Jussome was the only one Charbonneau
could think of now to team up with for the winter. His
friend Baptiste LePage had left. He was starting late;
he did not like to travel alone in winter when the loose-
blowing snow held no moccasin tracks. Charbonneau
did not wish to be found gray and lifeless beside a snowbank crusted as hard as glass. It was better for traders
and trappers to work in twos, he thought—besides, he
had heard that Jussome was getting a pack of huskies
and a sled for hauling from the Assiniboins. That fellow
McCracken had told him he was going to ride them
back for Jussome. Charbonneau wished his own brother
were here, camped with the Mandans, instead of in the
Canadian Rockies somewhere, hunting the mountain
goats.

Charbonneau scratched his whiskers, gave Little Tess
back to Otter Woman, tied a red kerchief around his
neck, found his felt hat, and swung the blue capote over
his shoulders.

"I go to see Jussome," he said.

"Why don't you hunt so we will have enough meat
to fix a proper stew for the morning meal?" Corn Woman
said.

"Shut that mouth. You got nothing to do, maybe you
go hunt. *Femme, paugh!*" He was gone.

Silently the women tidied the lodge. Otter Woman
put fresh deer moss in the cradleboard before placing
her child inside the warm nest. She had rubbed bear's
oil on the child's soft skin. He had grown so that he

was not always happy confined inside the cradleboard all day.

Soon Charbonneau was back. "I cannot find Jussome, I go on the hunt with some Mandan fellers. They go right now. Get me jerky and corn and the horse." He rummaged around and found his royal-blue three-point blanket and his flintlock.[1]

Several days later, Broken Tooth came to the lodge in midafternoon. Jussome had sent her for Charbonneau. "Did you hear?" she asked. "There is a lodge on water with many men in it. And two canoes coming along behind. One of the men is black as a burned stick and tall as a lodgepole."

"Is it true?" asked Sacajawea, skeptical that anything Broken Tooth had heard was to be believed. Perhaps it was something for amusement. Then they heard shouting from the village as children and adults streamed out of their lodges and raced for the river.

"Let's see, too," said Corn Woman, heading toward the front wood flap.

"Probably the men coming in from the antelope surround," said Otter Woman, but she laced Little Tess in the cradleboard and found a robe to wrap around herself against the cold. Sacajawea was already outside.

Looking into the wind, they saw something they could not believe. Moving up the river was a huge boat with a sail. It resembled a lodge floating upon the water with a soft gray cloud fluttering beside it. There were men at the sides pulling on long poles, moving the boat slowly upriver. Following the great boat were two smaller boats. They were canoes being pushed upriver. Who were these people? More and more curious Indians were crowding along the riverbank to watch.

"*Taiva-vone*! White skin!" Otter Woman shouted excitedly in Shoshoni. The onlookers moved closer. Some of the Indians were impatient with watching from shore and got into the tub-shaped bull boats and paddled downstream to see better.

The wind went through to their very bones as they watched the canoelike boats, the pirogues, go past their village upriver toward the other Mandan village. One pirogue was red, the other white.

Sacajawea hoped that Charbonneau was standing on

the embankment somewhere watching these boats, because if he did not see them himself, he would never
believe her own description. He would curse her, saying
she talked with a crooked tongue just to confuse him.
He might beat her with firewood. And he would be too
vain to ask anyone about her story. He could not admit
there was something he did not know about.

The next several days were full of excitement in the
villages along the Missouri, an excitement enhanced
by severe and unexpected winds. Although these Indians were used to having white men among them,[2]
never had they seen as many together as there were
on this expedition headed by Captains Meriwether
Lewis and William Clark. The party numbered close to
forty-five men and one dog.

Through the Indian grapevine Sacajawea learned
that Kakoakis was suspicious of these pale eyes who
said they had come to make peace. And she learned
that the council of chiefs, called to meet at the white
men's camp downriver, had been delayed because of the
cold, violent winds that made it impossible for Chief
Shotaharrora, or Coal, from the lower Mandan village,
Matootonha, to cross the Missouri to attend, although
Coal's subchiefs Kagohami, or Little Raven, and Sheheke, or Coyote, managed to get across in a round bull
boat. Sheheke was immediately called Big White by
the Americans because of his light complexion. Sheheke explained to his people that the white chiefs
wanted to talk of a Great White Father who lived far
off and would send white traders to bring the villages
useful things if there was no war among the nations.[3]

"When the wind dies, we will all go across the river
for a smoke with these pale eyes. They want us to make
peace with the Sioux and Assiniboins, but how can we
make peace unless the Sioux and Assiniboins know our
intentions?" With cool logic, Shotaharrora repeated
these words over and over among other chiefs and subchiefs.

Sacajawea wished more and more that Charbonneau
had not gone off hunting with the Mandans so quickly.
The white men had been delighted to find an experienced English-speaking French-Canadian interpreter

for the Hudson's Bay and North West companies in the big Hidatsa village—Jussome had learned to speak English from the Canadian explorer David Thompson. Then, too, Sacajawea had seen the flat stone that reflected the face of Broken Tooth the same way as a deep, still pool of water did. It was a gift to her from the white chiefs. Jussome had some wonderful gifts also—a knife, a tin plate, and a new red handkerchief.

The wary mind of Chief Kakoakis was set on edge by the white strangers. He knew that only a constant state of preparedness would ensure the Minnatarees' continuing liberty and well-being. In years past, when his people had moved into the security of a fenced village, they had learned a grim lesson that was passed from one generation to another. If a people had nothing and lived in a poor land, they could preach peace and be known everywhere as friendly; but if the same people acquired possessions, such as horses, plenty of vegetables, or guns, and became prosperous and strong in their rich village, they would be called hostile and dangerous, a bad people, enemies and makers of war.

Chief Kakoakis sat on his horse watching the camp of the white men from a bluff upriver. He saw that the men worked continuously. He noticed their rifles and the brass cannon on the white-winged boat. He saw the discipline of the crew and watched them fire their weapons at small and distant targets upon orders from a chief in charge. He saw that the targets were hit regularly.[4]

Chief Kakoakis was uneasy. "These men are not traders," he said to the Wolf Chief. "They speak of peace but bring guns."

"I see that," said the Wolf Chief. "They clean and shine the guns to preserve them. They bring gifts but take nothing. What kind of people gives without taking something in return?"

"A bad kind," said Chief Kakoakis.

"It is puzzling," said the Wolf Chief, "but the white chief, the red-haired one, seems friendly. I do not feel afraid of him. He smiles and shakes hands as a sign of his friendship. Jussome speaks for him."

Chief Kakoakis put his hand on the Wolf Chief's

shoulder. "That is how the enemy works. He is wise. He gets close to us and seems friendly. What if he decides not to go west in the spring, but to stay here with us? To hunt our buffalo? Eat our corn? Take our women? Now I begin to feel fear."

"I do not know," said the Wolf Chief.

"Their pale eyes and pale skin tell me to stay away. They seem friendly, but they will destroy my people."

"No," said the Wolf Chief. "I would hear what they say."

"Do not forget my warning," said Chief Kakoakis, turning his back.

On the afternoon that the wind died down, it was learned that the council was meeting in the Matootonha village. Otter Woman brought the news. Otter Woman pulled the cradleboard from its place against the side of the lodge and pushed Little Tess against the flat board backing; then she deftly pulled the flaps of soft buckskin and laced them together. She checked the semicircular guard of bent willow fastened to the upper part of the board, designed to protect the papoose's face in case the board were hung in a tree and somehow tumbled down. She pulled the leather tumpline across her forehead and was ready to go to see what was happening with all the white men nearby. Sacajawea and Corn Woman could not stand to be left behind. Hurriedly they pulled warm fur robes over their shoulders and closed the wooden slab on their empty lodge. There was a light skiff of snow upon the ground.

The council had been meeting many hours when they arrived, but the sun had not left the sky and everyone was in the center of the village watching and listening to the white chiefs, the chiefs of the Mandan and Hidatsa villages and the two Arikara chiefs who had come to make peace with the Mandans. The women and children stood in a circle behind the men of the village. Sacajawea stood on tiptoe to see the pale strangers and hear what they said. She could not understand the sounds these pale eyes made, but one of them, the red-haired chief, used hand signs well, so that she could follow some of what they talked about.

Otter Woman lifted her cradleboard from her fore-

"This is great medicine. You can see your own face in it," said Sacajawea.

"If it is learned that Kakoakis means to have you punished, I will send you this stone to keep you from harm. Then you must find a way to escape to the Shoshonis, your own people, that day," said Sun Woman. Her eyes were wide and serious.

"You are a friend. But it is foolish. I have thought of it many times. I could not find the People now. It is nearly winter, and I have been gone too long. To take that trail would pull my heart out and leave it on the ground to be picked at by the crows and hawks, and risk the papoose I carry. If Kakoakis comes for me and Charbonneau is not here, I must take the punishment I surely deserve."

"If your nose is cut off, I will not bar our lodge door to you. You will always be welcome to visit at the lodge of Four Bears."

Earth Woman began to cry. Sun Woman pulled the cradleboard from her back, untied the child, then began to nurse her. Sacajawea helped straighten the empty board and pulled the old buffalo robe around her friend and the papoose. Sun Woman was still young, but already her face had the lines that come from hard work in the hot sun and cold snow. Her clothing was plain, with very little beadwork, and her only jewelry was white shells hanging from her ears. Her tunic was bleached from the weather, and her knee-high moccasins were patched. When there are seven wives and many children, there are not so many things to go around, Sacajawea thought.

When Earth Woman finished nursing, Sacajawea helped her friend arrange the child on her back. Then Sun Woman took the warm silver medal from Sacajawea and dropped it safely into the cradleboard.

Reluctantly, Sacajawea found Otter Woman and Corn Woman and set her moccasins in the direction of their lodge. Her mind flew over the trails of memory to the time she was not called Sacajawea and not known as the youngest woman of the white Squawman who traded pelts to Indians and other white men from the north. Her name had been Boinaiv, Grass Child. She wondered why. She tried to recall. Her memory pushed back into

the past. She smelled the pungent burning pine of the
Shoshoni morning cooking fires. She promised herself
to talk to Otter Woman in their Shoshoni tongue more
often.

Charbonneau had been gone for nearly half a moon,
and so much had happened that Sacajawea no longer
worried that he would not believe. The presence of the
white men of the Lewis and Clark Expedition had become a reality of day-to-day life, for they would stay
until the spring. The Mandans told the white chiefs
that there was no longer fun in killing the Arikaras—
they had killed so many—and agreed to make peace.
The news that the white men would build a camp of
wood and that fifty lodges of Assiniboins would winter
in peace with the Minnetarees spread through the village like a prairie fire. They brought many parfleches
of wild rice to exchange for dried pumpkin and squash.
Crees and Ojibwas from the north began to appear about
the villages. They had all heard of the white men and
were curious.

Winter was coming fast. The wind blew colder, and
the snow became thicker. Sacajawea and Otter Woman
put extra clay around the sides of their lodge to keep
it warm during the time of the Snow Moon. Sacajawea
listened to the honkings of Canada geese moving south.
She rubbed her fingers over the blue stone dangling
from the thong around her neck. She had thrown off
her fear of punishment by Kakoakis and spent what
free time she had watching the strange activities of the
white men who were using the Indian's land, his trees,
his river, and his game. Mandan men came and squatted over their pipes along the new walls in the afternoon
sunshine. Women with children on their backs came
and worked rawhide or sinew or beading. Sometimes
several men played a little game of chance, shaking a
gourd bowl with marked stones or plum pits while they
kept an eye on all that was going on. Sometimes Sacajawea watched, but never if they played a game of
hands. When mess call came, the Indians expected to
eat, too, for they were guests.

One clear night, long, brilliant tongues of cold flame
licked over the Indian villages and the white men's

camp. The northern lights had returned to stream and shimmer over the plains, and in the morning Charbonneau returned.

"*Sacré diable!* Is it true the Americans are here? People get gifts? About these fellers—they build huts with cottonwood for winter?" Charbonneau came bursting into the lodge.

"*Ai*," said Sacajawea.

Otter Woman and Corn Woman were busy at the cooking kettle. "She can tell you about it," said Corn Woman. "She heard them talk with the chiefs."

Sacajawea scowled at Corn Woman and flushed, fearing she would tell how she had loosened her tongue at Chief Kakoakis.

"*Je ne sais pas!*" Charbonneau said. "There's talk; talk everywhere. Big boats there; I don't happen to see. Jussome is not home. Can anyone tell me?"

Speaking with hand signs and much Minnetaree, Sacajawea tried to explain. "The pale eyes are downriver by the village of Chief Black Cat making their own village from great logs. I have never seen anything like it. I heard they asked Jussome to tell them what the Minnetarees and Mandans say, so Jussome works for the pale eyes now."

Both Otter Woman and Corn Woman nodded in agreement. Sacajawea had told him the truth.

"That sneaking cheat, that mean, dirty louse, that pissant! I stop to visit, and he goes off to the strangers to take work with them. *Zut!*"

"It is also said that Jussome and his squaw and children will live the winter with the pale eyes in their camp," said Sacajawea, hoping that by now the day of the council of the chiefs had been forgotten and Charbonneau would never learn how outspoken she had been. Maybe Corn Woman and Otter Woman would keep their mouths shut and not hint about her humiliation and the tongue she had wagged at Chief Kakoakis.

"Our Chief Kakoakis does not trust the white men or Chief Red Hair," said Otter Woman, shooting a sidelong glance at Sacajawea.

"*Rouge?*"

"*Ai*, it is true, hair as bright as red war paint. And the greatest wonder of all—they have a man who is

black all over, with hair like burned prairie grass."
Otter Woman felt important with her information, and
a certain loyalty made her give it all to her man.

"Charred wood used as paint," sniffed Corn Woman,
who had seen the man but could not believe her eyes.

"No, I heard that Four Bears rubbed his arm and
face. The black did not come off, even when he licked
it with his wet tongue," announced Otter Woman, significantly licking the back of her hand.

"*Oui*, the *noire* people, called Negro. I have seen them.
They can do the work of three men. These fellers, they
are like the giant. By dang, these fellers make a trading
post here?"

"I hear they come to make peace between enemy
nations so that they can all live as one family under
the hand of a white chief who lives far down the river
in a place called Washington," said Otter Woman.

Sacajawea and Corn Woman had heard this also, and
had laughed behind their hands. Imagine all the nations living under the leadership of one chief! Otter
Woman scowled at them.

"One family?" Charbonneau threw back his shaggy
black head and laughed so that his yellow teeth showed.
"There is always somebody who wants to be the chief.
No tribe lives peaceably forever. There is always chief
somewhere who wants to get even with some enemy."
He kicked off his boots and held out his feet for Sacajawea to put on his moccasins. "They come to get ideas
from Hudson's Bay and the Northwesters and get the
Indians' help. They think what they hear is the thing.
Zut! I got plenty know-how. I go visit those men in the
morning. I will take four packhorses loaded with pelts
and meat to trade. I will show Jussome! I can interpret
for them, too. Now, feed Charbonneau! He is hungry."

Next morning, Corn Woman rose early to take extra
hay out to the four packhorses. Otter Woman rolled the
pelts and called Sacajawea to pack the meat to carry
on the horses.

"Can we all go?" asked Sacajawea, curious to see the
inside of the pale eye's camp.

"*Ai*. Otter, carry these buffalo robes, then help Sacajawea with the meat. Her load is getting plenty large!"
he added, extending his arms suggestively around his

belly. "Corn, stay and take care of Charbonneau's lodge
and my son." He bent in front of his boy. "Little Tess,
shake hands with your papa."

The boy hung back against Corn Woman's skirt.
"Mother," the child called, looking pleadingly at Corn
Woman. He felt as secure with Corn Woman and Sacajawea as he did with Otter Woman, for Indian children were raised so that any of the women in the lodge
where the child lived would act as the mother.

"Mon dieu! L'enfant believes his own papa is actually
the Bear of the Forest. I put a scare in him!" His head
rolled back and he laughed. "He knows his papa is boss."
Charbonneau grabbed the little boy's hand and shook
it wildly. "That's *au revoir.*"

"Do I ride?" asked Sacajawea. "Horses walk faster
than I with all this to carry."

"Bonne nuit!" said Charbonneau. "Squaws, they are
lazy." Finally he relented. Charbonneau, Sacajawea,
and Otter Woman rode to where the big sandbar showed
itself in the middle of the river. There they forded, letting the horses swim in the cold water until they could
touch bottom again. Crossing the sandbar, they had
only a few yards to ford and the water was not deep.

The white men's camp was being built in the form
of a triangle. Stout log cabins formed two sides, opening
inward. The base of the triangle was closed by a semicircular stockade of large pickets. The cabins were not
finished. Everywhere men were working—sawing,
hammering, fitting logs.

Sacajawea deliberately slowed her walk after dismounting and tending the horses. She looked and listened. One man called Pat seemed to be the chief in
charge of raising the strange wooden lodges. This was
Patrick Gass, the head carpenter. Among the enlisted
men of the Lewis and Clark Expedition, Gass was out-
standing. He was a barrel-chested Irishman from Pennsylvania. Ruddy-faced like so many Irishmen, he hid
the fact behind a bushy beard. As a civilian he had
helped build a house for the father of the future President James Buchanan. Although uneducated, having
had only nineteen days of formal schooling, he was
nevertheless intelligent and an experienced Indian
fighter. While stationed at Kaskaskia, Illinois, he had

applied for Lewis's expedition, but his commander—not wanting to lose his best carpenter—had refused. Gass had then gone directly to Lewis, who had persuaded Captain Russell Bissell to let him go west.

There were other Indians standing off in little groups watching. They had never seen such industry before. Sacajawea tried not to miss a thing. Once in a while she would pull at Otter Woman to show her something, such as the men drying strips of meat and working pelts and skins into leather for clothing. "These men have no squaws?" asked Otter Woman.

"White man, he can do anything," boasted Charbonneau.

"Squaws' work?" questioned Otter Woman. "Men cannot be happy if they must stay in camp for cooking and sewing like soft women. Men should hunt and fish."

"*Oui*," answered Charbonneau. "These men, they hunt and fish, too."

Sacajawea shook her head. It was hard to understand. Then she pulled on the arm of Otter Woman again, showing her a lodge that held large round pots with covers.

"Those canisters of ammunition are for guns," said Charbonneau. "She would be enough for two, three wars between us and the Sioux. *Pow! Pow!*"

Sacajawea had never seen so many guns. Charbonneau's gun was the only one she had really ever seen. The Agaidükas did not have guns. How powerful these white men must be, thought Sacajawea. The People would be better fed and more secure if they had all these guns.

"Your people could shoot off the Blackfeet with those guns," said Charbonneau, seeming to read Sacajawea's thoughts.

"*Ai*, hunt much better," she answered, misunderstanding Charbonneau, for the point of fighting between Indians was usually not to kill opponents but only to embarrass them, to steal horses or dogs or women. It was only once in a while that raiding got out of hand and Indians killed each other.

Otter Woman pointed to some large cooking kettles made of metal like the guns, not copper like those which the northern tribes had brought in. And they saw that the spoons were not made of horn or bone, but a shiny metal. The women's eyes grew large in wonderment at all they saw.

Charbonneau tugged at the women and urged them to follow him. Otter Woman was carrying two of the buffalo robes, and Sacajawea carried the other two. The meat packs had been left on the horses. Charbonneau stopped to ask a white man if he could speak to the *patron*, the chief, the headman.

"You want Captain Lewis or Captain Clark?" asked the man working on a door to one of the cabins. He was George Shannon, a blue-eyed Pennsylvanian of only seventeen years, the youngest man in the party. He was a likable young Irishman, handsome, clean-shaven in a hirsute age, intelligent, and well educated for his youth. "I think both of them are in that tent over there."

"*Oui*, that's him, Capitaine Clark. I come to work for him," said Charbonneau.

The women followed behind Charbonneau. He motioned for them to wait while he went inside. They squatted against the outer tent wall. Sacajawea moved her bundle of robes so that she could watch the men talking. Charbonneau soon motioned for them to bring in the robes. He nodded and smiled as they handed the captains the fine hides. The white men seemed pleased. The red-haired one, Captain Clark, tall, rawboned, and powerful, put one across his knees and felt the fine thick fur. Sacajawea said nothing as the keen eyes of both captains studied Charbonneau, Otter Woman, and then herself. Then the captains exchanged glances and Captain Lewis came around a table and shook hands with Charbonneau. This man was younger than the red-haired one, and he did not smile. There was rock in him. Sacajawea sensed at once the force he possessed. She would never want to make this sandy-haired, blue-eyed man angry. His face was oval, like the egg of an owl. Small of mouth and long and slender of nose, he was neither handsome nor attractive.

"Capitaine, these robes were made by the hands of my two *femmes*. This is Otter Woman, and this is Sacajawea, Bird Woman. They wish for a small trinket in return. Not much, but something they can show off."

"York," said Lewis, "will you find two looking glasses for these young ladies, please?"

Ben York, whose mother, Rose, had worked for the Clark family as long as she could remember, had been Clark's body servant since boyhood. He had been standing out of the line of Sacajawea's vision, and now Sacajawea felt a strange excitement as she glimpsed the huge dark man for the first time close up.

Otter Woman sat down on the floor at the sight of him. Captain Clark laughed, which effected an amazing transformation in his personality. Unlike Captain Lewis, in Clark it was the softer side of his nature that remained hidden. He motioned for Sacajawea to sit down on some packing crates.

"*Assieds-toi*," ordered Charbonneau.

Neither woman had ever sat on anything but the ground or a log or a hide couch in a lodge. Gingerly, Sacajawea sat on the box. It was strange. She looked down—her feet just touched the ground.

York handed something to Charbonneau, who grunted his thanks. "Here," he said, giving a small square looking glass to each woman. "This is a mirror like the white women use in Capitaine Red Hair's village, Saint Louis. Perhaps it is so. Who knows these things?"

Sacajawea took the pewter looking glass, aware instantly that she saw her own image in it. She had never before held such a thing in her hand. It seemed alive. It danced in a light of its own, like a hard bit of smooth water hole.

Sacajawea could not understand what the white chiefs were saying to her man. Then Charbonneau spoke in Minnetaree. "They want to ask you questions," he said. "They will ask me, and I will ask you and then tell them what you say. Tell them about your people and where they live."

At first Sacajawea did not understand. "My people are the Minnetaree, and they live here in the village. I belong to the big Hidatsa village."

"*Sacré coeur!*" said Charbonneau. "They want to know about them Shoshoni. The Snakes." He made a wiggling motion with his hands. "Tell them about your *maman* and *papa*, where they lived, what they did, how many horses they have in camp." Turning to Captain Lewis, he explained, "They give me plenty trouble, them *filles*. It's exasperate to me!"

Again she looked at her man, puzzled. She could not talk about her mother and father; they were dead. Then she looked at Chief Red Hair. He was smoking, and, to her relief, he smiled. She looked at the other chief, and he was smiling, too. It was not that they were amused by Charbonneau's exasperation; rather, they were completely warmed by Sacajawea's round, childlike face, her huge, intelligent eyes, her graceful hands as she made signs while speaking, and the incongruity of her obvious pregnancy at the age of only twelve or thirteen.

"Tell them, *femme*. Tell them about the land of your birth. She is one big shining *montagne, oui*?"

"No, many mountains, with cool green valleys in summer, and·tall pines that sing in the wind."

"*Merci beaucoup*," said Charbonneau, wiping his brow with his red kerchief and telling the captains in his halting English-trader patois what his woman had just said in Minnetaree.

She went on, "In winter the People move to warmer valleys in the south, but the food is scarce and enemy raiders are thick. We lose many horses."

"Could you find your way back?"

"Back?" Back to the People? She was sure she could find them if no enemy interfered, but it would be many days from here and there were raiding parties along the trail and it was winter now—she had told Sun Woman it was a foolish time for travel. The people had not come to find her, but she could find them if she had good horses and much food.

Both captains watched as she spoke, using her slim hands for emphasis. They were sure she remembered her home in the mountains.

"Do you remember landmarks on the trail? If you say you don't, I'll beat you plenty when we get home."

She looked at her man and could not answer.

"Come on. You speak out plenty when Chief Kakoakis is talking. Why you quiet now?"

Fear ran up her spine, and she put her hands over her face to hide her nose. He had heard, after all!

In fact, Otter Woman had told Charbonneau. But Charbonneau had thought it rather amusing that his

woman had been bold enough to speak out once again
against that chief. Now Charbonneau let out an explosive sigh. "Tell about the signs on the trail! Can you
remember?"

"My nose can stay?" she asked softly.

"*Oui*! You think I want a woman with an ugly face?
Not Charbonneau!"

"*Ai*," she sighed, looking at Otter Woman, who was
half-asleep against the wall. She looked at the captains,
who had not understood. Then she said, "Much poison
three-leaf creeper. I was a small child. I can remember
only little. A beaver-head stone and three forks in the
river. Those are on the land of the People. You will not
punish me?"

"She remembers! She remembers many landmarks,"
Charbonneau translated. "There is a large rock shaped
like a beaver; and the river goes three ways at one place.
And the poison ivy everywhere." Charbonneau folded
his hands across his stomach and grinned at the captain. "She has a quick memory, which I, Charbonneau,
have trained. My other squaw, she is also Shoshoni.
Her papoose, my son, named for me, he is almost ready
to talk many ways. I teach him myself."

Captain Lewis then asked to talk with Otter Woman,
and Charbonneau sent Sacajawea to fetch the horses.
She was reluctant to leave, but dared not disobey.

When she returned and they were preparing to leave,
Sacajawea took Otter Woman's hand and asked what
she had told the men. Sacajawea spoke in the soft, deep
tones of their native tongue. Otter Woman stared, wondering at this outburst of long-pent-up Shoshoni words.
Sacajawea did not often speak their native tongue, despite the promise to herself to do so. This questioning
had aroused a great longing in her. "I told them the
Shoshoni had many horses, but if the winter is bad,
there will be few horses by spring, but at least the
People had meat," said Sacajawea.

Otter Woman said, "Chief Red Hair asked if my people went through the mountains by canoe or on horse.
I said no canoes could go through the mountains. Imagine a squaw telling a grown man canoes do not travel
on mountains." Sacajawea put her hand over her mouth
and laughed with Otter Woman. "They asked if the

Shoshoni would trade for horses. So I said for food and guns, *ai*."

"Speak Minnetaree," scolded Charbonneau. "Keep that Shoshoni gibberish for when you reach that *montagne* land of yours."

For an instant Sacajawea looked at Charbonneau. His words sank deep within her: *when you reach that* montagne *land of yours*. Did that mean he was going to take her and Otter Woman there someday?

Captain Clark had one more question. He wanted to know if the Shoshonis had ever seen white men before. Otter Woman shook her head; she did not know. Truthfully, she could not remember her own people.

Sacajawea said to Charbonneau in the Minnetaree he understood, "No, not in the villages, but the People have gone south to the Spanish trying to trade for their firesticks. The Spanish would not let the Shoshonis trade for these shooting sticks, but pointed them at the men who asked for them. The men came back tired and disappointed, for they could not hunt as well with their spears and bows and arrows. I was young, but I remember the talk about those men. They were called 'senor,'" she said, to the amazement of all.[5]

In the days that followed the visit to the white men, Sacajawea worked at jobs that demanded all her attention and engaged even the deep parts of her mind, so that she forgot to think of those words her man had spoken: *when you reach that* montagne *land of yours*. She would sometimes forget her reason for being a good worker and lose herself in the satisfaction of her work, saying silently, "It is going well." It was that way when she was making bead designs on moccasins and, caught up in the humming of Corn Woman, hummed one of the Mandan songs with her. Suddenly she saw herself clearly, and a feeling of guilt flooded over her. How could she have forgotten? She felt that she had been unfaithful to those who had loved her so many winters ago, those who lived in some snug little valley, with little food in the winter. She had asked Otter Woman what she thought of the words of their man, and she had replied, "Nothing. The words were said to make us speak in the language of this village. We are fed here,

and we have good clothing. I do not wish to leave now.
I do not remember any of my people, and I am forgetting
the Blackfeet captors I served. This is the life for me.
I have a strong, healthy child; why should I want to go
away to some poor, thin nation that I do not even know?"

A bold pounding came from the outside of the slab
door. Corn Woman went to see what it meant. She
screamed and ran back into the lodge, clutching at Sacajawea, who was rubbing bear's oil on Charbonneau's
winter moccasins.

The women looked toward the door. Bending his huge
body almost double was Ben York, and he was calling
Charbonneau's name. "Monsieur Charbonneau, is you
here?"

"Devil, Okeeheede!" screeched Corn Woman, looking
at the jolly obsidian giant.

"I'se only York, the manservant of Captain Clark,
ma'am. I'se come to ask Monsieur Charbonneau to come
with me to see the captains."

Otter Woman and Sacajawea were speechless.

Sacajawea reached for Otter Woman's hand and
started slowly toward the huge black man. York smiled
down at them, his teeth flashing in the firelight. "I don't
bite," he said.

Sacajawea could not understand his words, but she
looked at his face and could not help smiling. He held
out his hand. She did not know what to do with the
proffered hand. She touched his fingers shyly and said,
to hide her confusion, "Would you like to rest and eat
some stew?" She indicated the bubbling pot.

"Hey there," called Charbonneau, coming into the
lodge, "she's mine! I won her in a fair game of hands."

"Monsieur Charbonneau, I scarcely understand her
palavering. I think she is the one called Sacajawea,
though. Captain Clark, he say I would know because
her eyes shine. And the other, with longer braids, that
is Otter. Captain Clark did not say you have three
women—you're quite a rascal, living out here among
the Indians." York grinned broadly.

Charbonneau shrugged.

"Captains are waiting," said York, pointing to the
doorway. "They will talk to you about interpreting."
Then both men left.

"Oooooo!" cried Corn Woman. "He is big and strong."

"Something different," said Sacajawea. "Something good."

"Didn't you see how the palm of his hand was white," asked Corn Woman, still shaking, "and how red his tongue was? And the whites of his eyes, and his teeth— like *yampa* flour. Great medicine."

Little Tess cooed, and the women crowded around him, each wondering if he had seen the big black man. "That is something you can tell your children about," said Otter Woman.

"He'll forget," laughed Sacajawea. "He is too young to remember the importance."

"I'll keep telling him," said Otter Woman.

"Why did he want our man?" asked Corn Woman suspiciously.

They were still chattering when Charbonneau returned. "By gar, I'm to be interpreter for them this winter, same as Jussome. I find why they come to this river country, by dang!"

CHAPTER

12

Birth of Jean Baptiste Charbonneau

February 11th

We sent down a party with sleds, to relieve the horses from their loads; the weather fair and cold, with a N.W. wind. About five o'clock one of the wives of Chaboneau was delivered of a boy; this being her first child she was suffering considerably, when Mr. Jessaume told Captain Lewis that he had frequently administered to persons in her situation a small dose of the rattle of the rattlesnake, which had never failed to hasten the delivery. Having some of the rattle, Captain Lewis gave it to Mr. Jessaume, who crumbled two of the rings of it between his fingers, and mixing it with a small quantity of water gave it to her. What effect it may really have had it might be difficult to determine, but Captain Lewis was informed that she had not taken it more than ten minutes before the delivery took place.

ELLIOTT COUES, ed., *The History of the Lewis and Clark Expedition*, Vol. I. New York: Dover Publications, 1965, p. 232.

Sacajawea straightened slowly and pressed her two hands to her back to ease the ache. "Little Tess, stay close. Do not wet your moccasins." She sighed while she looked enviously after the papoose's mother, Otter Woman. Otter Woman was slim and agile. She trotted upriver to find a quiet place where she could break the ice and dip her stained tunic in and out of the water. Other squaws were washing skin tunics in the icy water. Sacajawea dipped a huge clay pot into the clearest water she could find. She knew that if the water were warmed the grime and grease would come out more easily. She longed for the slippery yellow soaproot that her mother had used to make a milky, frothed water that left skins clean and soft.

Washing was a chore in the winter, when water had to be warmed in the lodge. For Sacajawea, washing was even more of a chore now—her arms did not have the strength for wringing that they used to have, and her breathing was not deep and satisfying, but shallow, coming in little gulps as the air pushed against her distended diaphragm. She could not bend easily, and her legs tired quickly. She cupped her free hand over her swollen belly as a small foot pushed against the womb's confining wall. Then her hand dropped to catch Little Tess's chubby fingers. With the thick wire handle of the water pot adjusted in her other hand, they walked slowly to the lodge.

Her thoughts hovered over the morning's activities. Charbonneau had surprised them. Unexpectedly he had said, "This day we move to the pale eyes' camp. How you like that? The white chiefs, they want Charbonneau close to where he work."

"Move? In winter?" asked Otter Woman. "Our man has strange orders."

Charbonneau had threatened her with a stick of firewood over her backside if she did not hurry with his stewed meat and flour-and-water cakes. He had pushed her and had held a glowing stick near her feet to get them moving faster.

Now our tunics will be clean when we move to the

village of the pale eyes, Sacajawea thought. And we will be able to see that huge black man, who looks burned, more often. She smiled to herself.

Coming to the mud lodge, Sacajawea hurried and pulled Little Tess after her. "*Aiee!*" called Corn Woman, who was still sitting in the sun, not moving a muscle, "you drag along that big papoose outside and a big papoose inside." She chuckled to herself. "Pale eyes will not look two times." She then stirred enough to point a broken, dirty fingernail toward the river. "Where is Otter Woman?"

"She is coming. I took this jackrabbit home with me because when she turned her back to peg her tunic down to dry, he stepped into the water. Otter Woman cannot watch him all the time."

"*Heee*— when I was a papoose no one thought about me walking into the river. They deliberately pushed me, and I learned to swim. We learned to take care of ourselves in those days. This boy will have soft white muscles, like flour dough. *Pagh!* What kind of men will women make these days? Soft like dead fish, lazy as fat cats, pale as dusty bones—that is not men, that is shadow."

"*Chit, chit,*" answered Sacajawea. "Gather your belongings, and while the water is heating I will gather those of our man so that we can move this day." Sacajawea pushed the lodge door open and nudged Little Tess ahead into the dark passageway. There was much work to be done.

Sacajawea was pleased that they were moving to the fort, except that they would pitch their tent next to Jussome's. She did not like the idea of being so close to Broken Tooth, who did not wish to be referred to as Broken Tooth anymore, but by her newest name, Madame Jussome. Otter Woman had told her this, and Sacajawea had asked what it meant. Charbonneau had explained that it was correct French for Jussome to refer to his woman as madame.

Now Corn Woman asked, "Could you call me Madame Charbonneau?"

Charbonneau threw back his head and exposed his yellow teeth, laughing uproariously. "*Magnifique!* My own *mère,* she was called that. *Yi!* She hated it. She preferred her own name, *Tchandee*, Tobacco. That was a fine Sioux *femme*. She left my papa when he called her Madame Charbonneau once too often. *Femme*! *Mon dieu*! Who knows what *la jeune fille* wants?"

Charbonneau then became more serious. "Baptiste LePage, my old trapper, is back with many beaver pelts—fat, sleek ones. He has sold the pelts to the pale eyes and has joined up with them for the long journey we take in the spring."

Sacajawea lifted the robes from Charbonneau's sleeping couch and folded them in a pile by the door. "Good, we like LePage," she said. The trapper had visited with them in the early fall.

"*Ai*, there will be someone we can recognize. The men in the fort all look alike to me," said Corn Woman, grunting and puffing as she carried clay cooking pots to the door. "Except the one that was painted by the night wind." They all laughed, thinking of Ben York.

By that afternoon, they had moved into the fort, and with the help of the tall, skinny youth, Shannon, Sacajawea and Otter Woman had pitched their leather tepee beside Jussome's.

All the men of the Corps of Discovery liked George Shannon, even though he was not well versed in woodcraft—several times on the upriver trip he had got lost while hunting. But he was eager, whistling and scampering with Captain Lewis's big black Newfoundland dog, and he took his teasing well. Charbonneau had explained to the boy that his squaws would take care of everything—that was the reason for having many *femmes*, after all. But this puny pale eye had actually done squaw's work and hauled in the rolls of hide and clay pots. The women had giggled as their man made signs with the boy. No man, however young, would do a squaw's work. Still, while Sacajawea giggled, she was glad of the help, and Shannon and Otter Woman had taken an immediate liking to one other. By the end of the afternoon, they were exchanging Minnetaree and English words.

The first hard blizzard of the winter hit. The temperature fell below zero. From the vantage point of the tepee, Sacajawea could see the white men leaning into

the blasts of driving snow as they crossed the frozen
stream just outside the fort and returned to stack the
logs they had dragged in from the woods. They seemed
to take no account of the weather; besides, the snow on
the ground eased the task of dragging the logs for firewood.

That first blizzard was succeeded by another and,
after a week of intermittent heavy snow, by a third.
When the last one ceased to howl, it left in its wake
the stillness of intense cold. The timbers of the building
groaned, and limbs snapped from the trees. The snow
creaked underfoot. Encircled by their newly finished
stockade and assured by the existence of the storeroom
of an ample food supply until spring, the men settled
by their firesides for a pleasant respite until it was time
for the guards to change at the gate and in the tower.

"Whilst there's snow on the ground, we got no call
to fret about Injuns. They never like to hunt for trouble
nowhere's that's way off from where they belong, account ye cain't go nowheres in the snow without yer
leavin' tracks." Young Shannon was repeating the facts
of wilderness winter life he had learned from Otter
Woman to Captain Clark. "It goes agin' the grain with
an Injun if'n other folks see where he's been. Injuns
ain't a-goin' to bother us none till the snow goes off in
the spring."

"I hope I can count on that," said Clark, puffing on
his pipe.

Nevertheless, the captains insisted on the regular
guard.

Dark days followed, the noons as dim as twilight.
Having banished the sun and the stars, the leaden overcast seemed to have obscured the distinction between
minutes and hours and days. Each day centered about
the morning and evening meals. The men went hunting
in groups of two or three. Charbonneau, Jussome, and
the two Fields brothers, Reuben and Joseph, who were
excellent woodsmen, went out early one morning and
returned with an enormous bull moose. A neck shot
from Reuben had dropped him.

The Indians soon discovered that in addition to food
and trinkets, the white men had strong medicine, and
the Mandans began bringing their sick to the fort. The

captains found themselves thawing frozen feet, amputating frozen toes, and treating pleurisy. They knew that those who were relieved of pain would know the Americans meant to help them. It was good for the women of Charbonneau's lodge, also, for seeing friends made them feel less isolated.

One crisp, cold morning Sacajawea awoke to a volley of rifles and a loud salute from the swivel gun. Charbonneau was already awake, trying to rouse Corn Woman to add wood to the fire and boil water for his tea. Corn Woman scratched her head and tucked a few of the hair wisps beneath her felt hat before she inspected the fire.

"What are you? Big lazy turtle? She is cold in here. Add more sticks to the fire. She day of medicine for Americans. She Christmas. Holy Mother! I want to see how they celebrate day of Holy Infant's birth." Charbonneau crossed himself and spat toward the smoldering fire.

Now the three women dressed quickly, chattering softly. Otter Woman dressed Tess in his best leggings and shirt. They, too, were eager to see a white man's celebration. This was something new.

Charbonneau was one of the first in line for his ration of brandy, with Jussome following close behind. Broken Tooth did not show herself. Captain Clark had stopped her from soliciting gifts from his men in return for favors from some Mandan squaws she had recruited, and he had threatened her. She did not want another scolding.

Some of the men cleared the mess room and began dancing to a tune Cruzatte was playing on his violin. Pierre Cruzatte, a private, was chief waterman. He was a wiry, one-eyed Creole whom the irreverent soldiers of the expedition had nicknamed Saint Peter. An ex-trader with the Chouteaus, he spoke the Omaha language and was well liked by the detachment, particularly for his fiddling. With only one eye—and that one nearsighted—he could guide boats through the worst rapids or shoals better than many watermen blessed with two eyes.

Some of the men tooted on the trumpets, or tin horns, Lewis had bought in Saint Louis. Warmed by the brandy,

Charbonneau played a French horn, or mouth organ; then Jussome joined him in singing "*Mon Canot d'E-corce.*" The voyageurs then sang something of their own composition, "*La Sauvagesse.*"

When Ben York came in, the audience gasped. On his back, bare to the waist, the image of the sun gleamed in white paint. His kinky hair was brushed out like a wild man's, and around the eyes that he rolled from side to side were huge circles of grayish white clay. White also circled his red lips.

"Good Lord!" exclaimed Captain Lewis.

"Is that a necessity on Christmas?" asked Captain Clark, astounded.

"*Ai,* the Devil of the Mandan celebration, the Okee-heede," cried Corn Woman gleefully, giving Sacajawea a poke in the side. The Indian women doubled over with laughter.

Dinner was a feast of roast turkey, deer, elk, and buffalo. There was flour thickening in the dried apples, which were baked with cinnamon. The corn had been seasoned with salt and pepper, making it taste like some rare dish. And there was hot tea with plenty of sugar.

Sacajawea casually rubbed some buffalo fat from her dinner into her braids to make them shine in the firelight, and thought how wonderful it was to have plenty to eat.

Shortly after Christmas, just days before the thermometer at the fort fell to thirty-eight degrees below zero, the weather-wise buffalos sought the Upper Missouri, where the snow blew off the rises and there were bluffs to protect them. Many of the men, unused to the deceptively dry cold, were frostbitten, York among them. It became a great joke, particularly when the news spread to the Indians. A Sioux, a recent captive of the Mandans, called this year the Winter the Black Man Froze His Man Part.

New Year's Day was as festive as Christmas. Sacajawea wrapped herself in a gray wool Army blanket given her by the captains. She sat against the wall of the mess hall. Otter Woman paraded in her new blanket before Madame Jussome. Little Tess paraded with his father. Two shots were fired from the swivel, and a round of small arms was shot off early in the morning, followed by a round of rum. Cruzatte brought out his violin again, and George Shannon appeared with a tambourine. About midmorning, half the men left, saying they had invitations to the Mandan village "to dance." Cruzatte, Shannon, and George Drouillard (with a tin trumpet) went with the men.

Drouillard had responsibility second only to that shared by the commanders. He was Lewis's scout, interpreter, and chief hunter. His mother was a Shawnee; his father, Pierre, a friend of Clark's brother. Lewis exempted him from guard duty, promised him extra pay upon the completion of the expedition—and got it for him. His accuracy with a rifle was uncanny. He was tall and ramrod-straight. He had inherited his mother's stoicism and reserve as well as her jet black hair and dark brown eyes. He was second only to Reuben Fields as a strong, fast runner, and his proficiency at woodcraft, or plainscraft, made even such men as Colter and the Fields brothers look like rank amateurs. Unlike many of his full-blooded French colleagues, Drouillard could write tolerably well, and he was fluent in Indian sign language, which Lewis knew was the lingua franca of the plains and Rockies. To Lewis, obtaining the services of Drouillard as nimrod, dragoman, and dactylologist at twenty-five dollars per month was just about the best bargain he had ever made.

Lewis and Clark watched the men leave, then returned to their cabin.

"Good Lord," Lewis said as he was going through the storeroom, "they've been in here. A marvel that Indians just being in a room should leave so strong a smell."

"It's the bear grease they use." Clark groped in after Lewis and closed the door. He felt his way along the piles of goods, took a candle from the shelf, and lighted it from one of Dr. Saugrain's matches on the shelf alongside the candles. These matches were phosphorous sealed in glass tubes. The phosphorus was ignited by breaking off the end of the tube. As he straightened, he heard Lewis gasp. He spun around, holding up the candle. Motionless as a statue against the wall, his eyes catching and reflecting the dim glow of the candle, was the dark, bulky, fur-shrouded figure of an Indian.

"Who is on guard?" Lewis asked, taking care to keep his voice steady and calm.

"I don't know," Clark said.

"Fran'," said the Indian. He tapped his chest and grinned. His face was not painted, and he was not armed with bow and arrows. Lewis glanced down, and only then did he notice that the Indian had his fingers tightly closed over the snout of the dog Scannon, to keep him from barking. "Fran'—Fran'," the Indian was chanting loudly while pointing in vigorous and alternate succession at Lewis and Clark.

"Friend," agreed Lewis.

The Indian snatched a pipe tomahawk from a shelf beside him and extended the hand that still held closed the snout of Lewis's dog. The dog shuffled and tried to pry loose. "Swap? Swap?"

Lewis looked around, giving himself time to think, apprehensive lest he make some useless but provocative gesture of belligerence. He should not have feared. Clark, his arms laden with calico shirts, shoved them under the Indian's nose. Scannon was released and began to bark loudly. Clark opened the door and feigned smoking on the pipe. The Indian laughed merrily and by cheerful gestures indicated that he still had something to give the captains, as was right and proper among such good friends. Behind him, out of range of the candlelight, stood a woman dressed in a fresh white deerskin tunic decorated with blue beads and held around her waist by a belt of blue beads. She had on leggings and white moccasins decorated with the same kind of blue beads. Her head was bowed, but every now and again her eyes looked up to see the wonders on the shelves. Obviously this was the Indian's most favored woman.

"He wants you to have his woman, I think," said Clark with an amused look.

"Oh, Lordamercy, we'd better straighten this out in an amicable way," said Lewis. He sent York for an interpreter. While they waited, the Indian petted and patted Scannon and offered him a bit of jerky, which he pulled from somewhere in the folds of his fur robe. Scannon lay contentedly at the Indian's feet.

Unexpectedly, York returned with Sacajawea and Otter Woman. Both Jussome and Charbonneau had left the fort, probably on a hunting trip, he explained. Otter Woman now knew a good many English words taught to her by Shannon, but she would not come to the officers' quarters alone.

The Indian took one look at the two women who were to interpret his hand signs and refused to talk. But then Captain Clark asked a question and Sacajawea pointed a slim brown finger toward the Indian. "Le Loup," she said softly, imitating her man's French.

The Wolf Chief nodded and emitted a guttural laugh, recognizing Sacajawea. This was not squaws' business, but if the white men let squaws repeat their words, then he would do the same.

The captains felt the charge in the air. "You two know each other?" asked Clark, looking from Sacajawea to the Wolf Chief.

"*Ai*," indicated Otter Woman shyly, trying hard to be helpful but feeling much out of place, still not sure how she had come to be here telling the white chiefs that the Wolf Chief was head of all the Mandans. Too much had happened too suddenly for her.

Sacajawea, by far the more intelligent, talked to her, making signs and clucking noises.

After Otter Woman's first panic had subsided, she began to speak slowly. Sacajawea helped with the important hand signs. "This Wolf Chief played in the game of hands with Charbonneau when Sacajawea became Charbonneau's squaw. Sacajawea sat upon the blanket," added Otter Woman slowly, her face flushed.

The Wolf Chief threw the women a haughty look.

Half a lifetime of cowering before men had taught Sacajawea that there was no more certain road to approval than obedience. She sat on the floor and bowed her head.

"Now what is the matter?" asked Lewis. "I thought this was the young woman who had all the spunk. Just look at her now!"

Otter Woman, finished with her story, squatted in

a corner, her arms wrapped around her knees. No thoughts showed on her face.

Clark surveyed the situation, then with a slow movement of his hands turned from Otter Woman to Sacajawea. "Why does this man cause you to bow your head? Did you not want to become Charbonneau's squaw?"

Sacajawea could not answer. For her there was no question of wanting or not wanting, one only did as one was told. She could not understand that she could have had a choice. For captured Indian women, there was never a choice. She looked into the face of Clark. His blue eyes were searching for something in her face. She wanted to say something, to tell him anything to make him happy. Her mind stirred. "You healed the frostbitten fingers of Le Loup's first born son. He is so grateful that he has brought his most beautiful pale-skinned woman so that both American chiefs can use her for the night as a gift from him." Her hands rested limply in her lap, her eyes still on the captain's face. She waited patiently for his answer. If he refused, he would offend the Wolf Chief, and that would be a rude thing.

Otter Woman, in the meantime, had grown inquisitive about the pretty clothes on the young squaw and was fingering the beads and looking at her moccasins and beautifully worked leggings. The tenseness in the small room grew. Otter Woman could not be enticed or cajoled to come back to talk with the American chiefs. She was completely preoccupied with the garments on the prized squaw. Sacajawea watched the room with bright, sharp eyes. Suddenly she felt something new to her; she did not want Chief Red Hair to accept the offer of the Wolf Chief's young squaw for the night.

Lewis began to talk softly to Clark. The Indians listened quietly as if they understood, but the Americans knew that they did not comprehend one word, and if Otter Woman heard a familiar word or two, she did not indicate it.

"Don't fool yourself that Indians aren't smart. They play every angle. You saw how he grabbed Scannon and used him as hostage to get the pipe tomahawk?" Clark nodded, sucking intently on his own pipe. "We know Indians are natural traders. All they have ever had in their existence is what they've traded for. Now"—

Lewis pointed the stem of his pipe at Clark to emphasize what he was saying—"here's the thinking of an Indian in a trade. You'll never get the better of him. Here's his logic." He paused for a puff or two, then went on. "He'll never give up anything he wants or for which he has the slightest use. He wants something you have. So he'll give you something that is worthless to *him* in trade for something he wants. So you're getting nothing for something. So, you see, he's always got you beat."

"It looks that way," said Clark thoughtfully, making little sucking sounds on the stem of his pipe.

Finally he turned to Sacajawea, his hands still moving slowly, and at the same time using English words. "Say to the chief we thank him very much for this great honor. His young woman is very attractive." Sacajawea had him repeat the words so she could get the thought across to the Wolf Chief. "Tell him he would please us more by giving us information in regard to the westward country and the mountains. Is there a water passage through those mountains?"

Sacajawea stared at Captain Clark. Didn't he already know there was no water passage? Her mind moved swiftly. She thought Chief Red Hair asked questions only to divert the Wolf Chief and make him feel important.

She pulled up a box in front of the Wolf Chief and talked to him in his language, elaborating on the beauty of the young woman and on his fine judgment of women. The captains watched, seeing the brightness of Sacajawea's eyes as she talked with the Wolf Chief, and noting that Otter Woman, who knew more English words, was not much interested in using them, but interested only in clothing and trinkets. Sacajawea sat on a box in the manner of the white men, not on the floor as Otter Woman continued to do.

"Fran'," the Wolf Chief repeated, almost genial again. He patted the tomahawk and settled it more snugly under his arm. He motioned that he was willing to tell what he knew of the west. He slipped the fur robe to the floor and then took his deerskin shirt off and smoothed it down in front of the fireplace.

Captain Clark understood. He brought out an elk hide and a piece of white chalky stone. "I want him to

make the best picture he can of the Big Muddy," he
said.

Little by little, amid much groaning and clucking,
the Wolf Chief made the marks of the western course
of the Missouri, showing the Little Missouri and the
river called Rochejaune by the French, coming in from
the south. Sacajawea did her best to interpret his motioned words. He drew a big stream and made it very
white—the Milk River, which emptied into the Missouri from the north. Then, smiling, pleased that he
could draw so well, he showed where the Missouri dipped
to the south and then cascaded into a series of large
falls: "a creation of the Great Spirit!" Sacajawea pointed
to parts of the picture and spoke with the Wolf Chief,
who shook his head yes.

Captain Clark was excited with his good fortune this
night. "You know some of this trail?"

"*Ai.*" Sacajawea looked up at him. "I was a child, but
I can remember the way to the People. With no enemies
on the trail, I could go back. It is not an unheard-of
thing to the People."

Sacajawea's eyes flashed as the Wolf Chief spoke
rapidly. She moved from one moccasin to the other.

Surprised at her agitation, Clark asked, "What did
he say?"

Slowly, with trembling hands, she replied, "He will
make war on the Shoshonis when the snow goes. He
likes their horses and women."

"Tell him it is wrong to make war." Captain Clark
spoke in a very stern voice. "He must keep peace with
his neighbors. He can get horses in peaceful trading."

"Peace." The Wolf Chief shook his head doubtfully,
and Sacajawea emphasized the hand signs he made.
"The braves who steal a horse count coup, take a prisoner and be a hero, kill an enemy and not only count
coup but rise toward the high office of chief. War is the
measure of tribal valor. White chiefs would make sons
soft with this strange talk."

Sacajawea shifted her weight; this philosophy was
difficult to put across in hand signs.

Captain Clark said, "The tribes and nations who do
not keep peace and do not open their ears to the counsel
of the white men will lose the protection of the Great

White Father. Sooner or later you will have to listen. War cannot continue."

"I will wait," promised the Wolf Chief, "but if other nations do not keep peace, *aaahoooooooo!*" He let out a bloodcurdling war whoop.

While the Wolf Chief was smoking with Clark, Lewis rummaged around on a shelf and found tortoiseshell combs for the women. Then he went outside and motioned for the guard to let them out. He was surprised at the depth of emotion he felt toward Sacajawea. Clark was absolutely right; she was very intelligent.

When the Wolf Chief left, Clark stared at the map so long that when he finally spoke, Lewis was startled.

"A mother with a child climbing the warm foothills with a handful of grasses and flowers," mused Captain Clark. "It might work in a wonderful way to appease the Indians. When spring comes and we can smell the tree buds, and we count heads for our journey west, I believe a woman of the Shoshoni Nation ought to be included."

Lewis looked at Clark with amazement and disbelief in his deep-set blue eyes. "Clark, is this meant to be a joke? A woman and a baby—on a military expedition?"

"Well, I was thinking along those lines," said Clark, taking a deep draw on his pipe. "It might not be as silly as it sounds at first. I'm trying to think like the Indians we'll meet. They resent being called Indians, you know. That is a paleface name to them. They want to be known by the name of their particular tribe. They have a pride in the nation they belong to and want to be known as an individual from a certain group. I guess we have pride like that, too—we want to be known as men from the United States, representatives of the American government. We are proud to be from the state of Virginia or Missouri or Kentucky. If you saw a contingent of Sioux with a woman and child, would you think that they were on a raiding mission or some war party?"

"No, I'd like to believe they were maybe hunting or looking for a new spot for a camp," said Lewis, glaring at Clark. "Why do you ask this non-sequitur question?"

"Oh, but it does follow logically. If we take a squaw with a child, no Sioux, Blackfoot, or Crow will figure we are at war, but they will immediately know we are peaceable. And if the squaw is a Shoshoni, then that tribe will welcome us as friends."

"So, we can be friends with the Shoshonis. That's fine, but I can't see what that has to do with us getting on to the west."

"The Shoshonis have horses. What if they are willing to trade for some of our trinkets or ground corn? Wouldn't that help get us west?"

"But we are going to go by water all the way to the Pacific! This is a northwest waterway we are going to explore." Lewis shook his head as he looked at Clark.

"I was just thinking that in case there is no water passage through the mountains, or if we have to portage for any distance, it would be much easier to have horses to carry our supplies. And I'm in favor of riding whenever I can, instead of walking."

"All right, that *does* make sense, but I thought you were going to get sentimental and go on about how a pretty squaw would be something enjoyable for the men to have around on the rest of the journey. Or how she'd give you all her family secrets about how her 'Aunt Pokeberry' or 'Granny Gingerseed' made tea and tonic with mustard flowers or lupins and buttercups. Instead, you're mercenary. You want to trade friendship for horses. You want a reward for friendship."

"Hire horses, yes. I told you I was thinking in a straight line. I'm serious. And there *will* be wild plants— ferns, and mushrooms, roots, bark, and leaves—that have medicinal uses. A squaw *does* know about these things, and that could be helpful to us. Just suppose you and the medicine boxes go overboard because a pirogue overturns? We'd be in a hell of a fix without those drugs and medical supplies that Doc Saugrain and Ben Rush packed for us in Saint Louis."

"What about me? Clark, I swear you're impossible this morning."

Both men laughed and walked together outside to look at the thermometer on the side of their quarters. The morning was clear and the sun shone bright; the snow crunched underfoot. The thermometer stood at twenty degrees below zero.

Lewis jogged around to keep warm. "Clark, are you wearing my extra woolen socks? They're not in my foot locker where I laid them last." Lewis led the way back inside their quarters. Their breath made vapor puffs in the cold air.

Clark sat on a packing crate and pulled at his pipe; the tobacco was cold. "Look, at the very least it is up to me to decide whether we want that old rascal Jussome or the Squawman, Charbonneau, with us as interpreter. I've thought some, and I say Charbonneau. He's not as bright as Jussome, but he's not as scheming, either, and I like the looks of his young wife."

Lewis looked out of the corner of one eye at Clark. "You're not—surely not! You're not really thinking of taking that Frenchman's woman! Who ever heard of any military expedition going into unknown land, into a foreign country, up an uncharted river, guided by a female—a pregnant squaw! Lord, that's ridiculous. We'd never be able to hold up our heads in front of President Jefferson!"

Clark filled his pipe with fresh tobacco and lit it with a stick from the fireplace in the room. "We'll do this with our eyes open. Nothing to be ashamed of. By spring the child will be here. You can record in your journals the plants she gathers and what she uses them for—mullein for cough syrup; crabapple bark for asthma and sneezing. She'll be helping in a scientific way."

Lewis bent down to look at the woolen socks Clark was wearing. "Those are mine. And those remedies aren't new. Your grandmother knew all that. So did mine, and I've had my fill of each. We can find out from the various tribes we meet what they do with this grass or that twig, and I'll write the information down for the President. I've already got enough information on the Mandans and Minnetarees for a book."

"Lewis, I'll give you back your socks if you'll hear me out. That young squaw of Charbonneau's is brighter than the usual. Look at the way she helped us today. What would you do if your dog, Scannon, had a snakebite? I'll bet you she'd know how to save him. You wouldn't want Scannon to die, would you?"

"Of course I wouldn't. I'd be willing to let her advise me on what to do. But what do you think Jefferson would say to such a plan?"

Pulling off his moccasins, Clark took the outer pair

of gray woolen socks from his feet and threw them at
Lewis. "It's a wonder I haven't been frostbitten. Wish
my moccasins were fur-lined. I bet those mountain folks,
the Shoshonis, know how to keep the cold out. They
haven't seen many white men. Even the British are
afraid of a Shoshoni brave, and those savages don't even
have guns. Our men would be at their mercy in the
mountains. They are masters with a bow and arrow.
An arrow could whang itself into your chest before you
even knew they were around. You know that Charbonneau's young squaw is a Shoshoni, don't you?"

"Oh, Lordy, how could I forget when you keep mentioning it?"

"You saw how her eyes lit up when she spoke of her
mountain home. She could help us restore our supplies,
and if her people do have horses, we could make a deal."

"The baby—what do we do with a baby on this expedition?"

Clark looked at Lewis in astonishment. "You've got
to put your moccasins on right and think Indian. A
papoose is no trouble. The squaw stuffs him in the cradleboard and shifts it to her back. Indian women are
strong creatures, and they can fend for themselves. They
are never ill, and they don't complain. They are cheerful
about taking orders and never talk back. You know
how they behave."

"Lord, you're actually serious about this."

Clark paused to relight his pipe. "Out here, among
a different kind of people and a different way of living,
values are not the same. Look—in an office in Washington or Saint Louis, this would be funny. I'd be the
first to admit it, the first to laugh. But right now, here,
it is the most logical thing in the world."

"You want us—me—to hire a pregnant squaw to be
counted in our expedition?"

Clark thought a moment. "I could give you half a
dozen situations where a military operation has not
always gone by the book. You know as well as I that
sometimes it is impossible."

"Maybe we could take Charbonneau's older woman."

"That's the way! At least now you're thinking, Lewis!
But we want someone with spirit, not just a follower.
Someone to follow orders cheerfully, but to be a bit

creative and more than just a slave; someone useful as well as helpful. That other one won't do, but Sacajawea has spunk. She is not afraid to speak out. Her people would be friends, and we could trade for supplies. She could speak to them for us. We might even leave her with her people until we return from the Pacific. Then we wouldn't have a woman and child along for the whole expedition."

Lewis looked at Clark in consternation, as if he wanted to argue but didn't dare. Clark's words had hit home. He thought, Maybe this young woman has some knowledge of the northern territory that would lead to the Saskatchewan territory from her homeland in the mountains. Jefferson had privately directed Lewis to solve this problem. Then he thought of trade with the Shoshonis in the mountains. A trading post in the heart of the Rockies was not a bad idea—or, better yet, a post in the Saskatchewan territory.

"This young woman will be a token of friendship. The tribes will not mistake our motives and always know we come in peace," continued Clark.

"If we could develop trading posts, maybe at first east of the Continental Divide, in American Louisiana, perhaps her people would come down to them. Later we could set one up in the mountains for them, and then still later, when the system has grown in strength, posts could be established west of the Divide, in the home country of other tribes that would be our customers."

Clark rose to his feet and stretched his big frame. "Lewis," he said, "you're a realist, and you know that that country isn't American yet—you old son of a gun."

"And you're a sentimentalist! A broad-shouldered, red-haired, emotional sentimentalist."

"And we both have to be smart, like the Indians. They have a way of thinking that pushes all trifles aside. From them comes a wisdom that we often overlook. So, that's settled—we'll take Toussaint Charbonneau as our interpreter and his young squaw to interpret in the homeland of her own people, the Shoshonis. Her papoose could be our talisman."

"A baby for a good-luck charm? I see I was only half-right—you *are* sentimental, but you are also superstitious," said Lewis with a twinkle in his eyes. "All right," he said then, giving in, "I'll talk to Charbonneau."

Charbonneau entered the tepee, tossed his cap on the floor, and assumed a swaggering air. "I am going with the Americans in the spring. We plan the trip together. I am their chief interpreter." He was pleased with the sound of these words.

The three women looked at him, their work interrupted.

"I will miss you," sighed Corn Woman barely audibly.

Sacajawea looked at her bulging belly and thought, So, this is the way it will be. I will have a papoose but no man. There was nothing else to think about.

Otter Woman sprang to her feet, letting the nursing Little Tess slide to the floor. "You go to the land of the Shoshonis? Maybe I go, too?"

"Les capitaines disent non. I tell them I take you—you are the best squaw, I say—but it is they who say *non."* It was this part of the arrangement with Lewis and Clark that he did not like. It hurt him to think of leaving Otter Woman behind. "I must take the other one," he said.

"So, then they want me to keep you fed and comfortable?" said Corn Woman, all smiles now.

"Non, not you, and not anyone but Sacajawea. They make it clear."

"So, you take the one big as a cow buffalo?" snapped Otter Woman. "The white men would not want her!"

Sacajawea looked up. She felt her child give a push inside her. It was a good sign. He was eager to begin his new life.

Otter Woman directed a couple of spitting shots at Sacajawea, but when she and Charbonneau seemed to ignore her, she spit again.

He leaped to his feet. *"Diable!* Why do that? I am not to blame, it is *les capitaines."*

"But they called for me to interpret for them," shouted Otter Woman.

"And now they call for me and Sacajawea to come live in a wood hut," Charbonneau said.

Otter Woman's jealous rage mounted. She upset the

stew kettle and tore Sacajawea's bed, tossing the soft cornhusks here and there, like a gopher pushing the dirt high in the air so he can get into his burrow.

That evening, Sacajawea left the leather tepee and returned to the old earthen lodge. She built herself a fire to keep off the chill and lay near it on a buffalo robe. She wanted to think, to plan and dream. She knew she had won the contest, but she did not think about the cost. She owed thanks to the Great Spirit, yet she kept seeing the face with the summer-sky eyes and red hair. She was going back to the People, back to the Shining Mountains. She was dizzy with her championship.

February was a cold month. Men went hunting and came in with frozen fingers and toes. The northwest wind howled around the fort and kept the men busy chopping wood for the fireplaces.

Sacajawea stayed close to the fireplace in the room given to her and her man for sleeping quarters. She softened thin deerskin for a warm, soft robe for her coming papoose. York brought her stewed fruits and tea with plenty of sugar cubes. Women were never treated thus by the Indians. At first she was shy, but soon she began to like the attention.

Then one morning, she sat up, sobered. There was something oddly out of key. Instead of being famished, she felt dull and depressed. Her back ached, and she bent in the middle with a cramp. She looked for Charbonneau, then for Clark, but both men had gone on a hunting trip with Sergeant Gass and another man.

Patrick Gass was an old Army Regular who had fought Indians, had known Daniel Boone, and had become acquainted with the Clark family as early as 1793. He was a little man, standing only five feet seven, but broad-chested and sturdy. He was a good soldier and an experienced carpenter and had built the ladder to the loft with extra-wide rungs so that Sacajawea could go up to her sleeping couch more easily. However, he was quite resentful toward the captains for taking a woman on a trip with military men. But his sense of fairness won out when he saw the thick mat of dried grasses and hay under Charbonneau's sleeping robe

and nothing under Sacajawea's. With a burst of spunk
he pulled out much of the soft matting and arranged it
under Sacajawea's sleeping robe.

Sacajawea tried to lift the kettle from the fire, but
had to set it back and bend over to ease the pain. York
came in with an armload of wood for the fireplace.

"Oho, missy, I'm going to get Captain Lewis if it's
the last act—if your time has come." The huge dark
fellow helped her climb to the loft and to her buffalo
robe. He spoke softly to her, saying that he would return
right away. She answered with a spasm that spread to
her face, and her body writhed under the robe. When
the spasm passed, her small brown face seemed loose
and tired. Sacajawea opened her eyes, and in that instant, in that second of knowing, Ben York saw not a
little Indian squaw; he saw his mother and his sister,
he saw Mrs. Clark, mother of the captain, the mothers
of all the men on the expedition. He saw womankind.
Then he saw himself and knew her look was the humble, hurtful, anxious look that was hope and bone-deep
in all of mankind.

York climbed down, meeting Lewis coming in. York
pulled the big kettle off the wall hook, filled it with
snow, and hung it over the fire. "Always heat the water
to boiling." He smiled at Lewis. "I'se seen birth an'
dying long before either was a shock, so I reckon I'm
going to help with this here birthing. Biemby I 'spect
I'll have to sing lullabies."

They sat near the door wondering if they should get
some Indian woman to help, but Lewis reasoned that
Indian women can take care of these things by themselves. They heard Sacajawea calling, her voice low and
indistinct at first, then rising in shrill terror. She was
afraid to be alone. Her own body frightened her. It had
turned and set itself against her. It gripped her with
such a building up of one agony on top of another that
she was afraid to trust herself with it alone, as if its
system of torturing her was something secretive and
intimate that the presence of somebody else could hold
back.

York suggested they make a couch by the fireplace
and bring her down from the loft. "Too hard going up
and down that ladder," he said.

York dipped cloths in boiling water and laid them on Sacajawea's distended abdomen. Once, for a breath, he dared look into her eyes again, and again he knew that she was kin to him and to all other men—red, black, or white, it did not matter. Their entrance into this world was the same.

The pain did not seem to increase much, but the sudden blasts of it stiffened her body for two or three minutes at a time, leaving her weak. The sun moved up and down the roofs on the fort. Toward evening, she felt the sharp spasms closer together, one almost on top of the other. The constant pushing—the pushing she could not stop—was doing no good; the papoose did not come. York wiped her face with a cool cloth, then her hands and arms. Lewis smoked his pipe wishing that Clark were here—maybe he could think of something to do to help.

Suddenly there was a yipping and a loud "Whoa there," and Jussome came bursting into the cabin, letting in the frosty air. His sled dogs yipped and growled, then quieted.

"*Dieu,* I looked everywhere for you," he said to Lewis. "I wanted to ask if we could keep that grinding machine here after you leave in the spring. We could get a lot of cornmeal from it."

"Ssshhh! Cain't you see this little squaw is having a monstrous time?" hushed York. "Don't you know some native potion hereabouts that hastens this here business?" he asked anxiously.

"Monsieur York, you have asked the right man. Snake rattles. Make a powder of them, and *le bébé,* he will come within *un moment.* Make a tea from rattles. Have her drink it. The Assiniboins and Arikaras use it."

"Rattles! That sounds like voodoo," said York sarcastically.

"Try it," urged Jussome, taking off his blanket coat and stomping his boots on the hearth.

Lewis remembered some huge rattles he had collected a little way out of Saint Charles. He went to his cabin to look among the bottles and jars and boxes. He found them wrapped in some writing paper.

Jussome took two rings, put them in a tin cup, and

with his fingers broke them into little pieces. He put
hot water into the cup and stirred. York held Sacajawea's head up so that she could drink the concoction.
Jussome explained to her what it was supposed to do.
Sacajawea's hands grabbed for York. Lewis looked out
the door at the sinking sun and wondered how long this
could go on.[1]

Sacajawea knew that this was the time she must
make the push count. She was beyond calling out or
speaking. Her thoughts were her own, but she was one
of a million women before her, and a sister to every
woman who had been along this path. Her feelings were
as primitive and as civilized as any woman's. There
was no distinction between primitive and civilized in
the event of birth. This was an involuntary thing. It
possessed her. She was not in control. She felt herself
sinking into a black void; then, from far off, she heard
York's excited voice.

"I can see! It is a boy! His face is as round as his
belly. He is just as lively as a cricket in the embers."

When she opened her eyes, Lewis was holding the
baby awkwardly as York washed him in warm water.
The baby was yowling like a little coyote. York wrapped
him in the soft skin robe she'd made. His eyes closed,
and his fist came up beside his mouth.

"Black hair—no red," she sighed.

"What?" asked York. But she was asleep, secure and
safe, hardly stirring with the afterbirth. She dreamed
of her child bronze and shining with golden-red hair,
playing happily at the foot of snow-topped mountains.
She dreamed of the many trails that had brought her
here to the white men's village.

In the morning Charbonneau came in with the other
hunters, to learn the news of his new papoose. The men
were tired from tramping through knee-deep snow and
carried in two antelope and one buffalo.

Looking deep among the robes around Sacajawea, he
found his son and put a big hand near the baby's face.
"Oooom, she is nice. I call her Jeannette."

York laughed, showing white teeth. "When she asks
you why and craves to raise Cain 'cause of her name,
don't come crying to me. This here ain't no little gal."

"She is a boy?" asked Charbonneau, his face falling. "I already have a boy."

"Give him a good name," suggested Lewis. "One he can handle when he's a man. One that spells easily, like—Jean."

"*Oui*, I call him Jean Baptiste," said Charbonneau, looking up and grinning so that his yellow teeth caught the firelight. "That is a good French name. My brother and LePage, they have this name. My squaw will like him. She will like the name I give papoose. *Mon dieu!*" He slapped his knee, and the tiredness seemed to drain away. "Jean Baptiste Charbonneau! *Yiii!* I can see this *enfant* refused his milk before his eyes were open, and called out for the bottle of red-eye! That's my papoose! Talk about grinning the bark off a tree—that ain't nothing! One squint of mine at a buffalo bull's heel right now would blister it!"

CHAPTER

13

Farewell

Clark's Journal:

March 12th 1805

Our Interpeter Shabonah, deturmins on not proceeding with us as an interpeter under the terms mentioned yesterday, he will not agree to work let our Situation be what it may nor Stand a guard, and if miffed with any man he wishes to return when he pleases, also have the disposal of as much provisions as he Chuses to Carry in admissable and we Suffer him to be off the engagement which was only virbal

1805, 17th of March Sunday—

Mr. Charbonah Sent a frenchman of our party [to say] that he was Sorry for the foolish part he had acted and if we pleased he would accompany us agreeabley to the terms we had perposed and doe every thing we wished him to doe etc. etc. he had requested me Some thro our French inturpeter two days ago to excuse his Simplicity and take him into the cirvice, after he had taken his things across the River we called him in and Spoke to him on the Subject, he agreed to our tirms and we agreed that he might go on with us etc. etc.

BERNARD DEVOTO, ed., *The Journals of Lewis and Clark.* New York: Houghton Mifflin Co., 1953, p. 85.

Capitaine," said Charbonneau. "You are a man in authority, and there can be no scalping between us. So tell me, will that man-child I begot turn into a log-leg or leather-breeches like me? Will he be a green-shirt or blanket-coat, land-trotter or river-roller, or a man for a massacre?" Then, giving himself a twirl on his foot, he proceeded to other antic demonstrations of joy. "Ain't he a ring-tailed squealer?"

Clark had come with Charbonneau to have a look at Sacajawea's papoose. "I'll just have to see for myself," he said.

The door to the cabin had been left ajar. Probably York had forgotten to pull it tight. It was still not light, but the sky was graying near the horizon. Scannon plodded up and, ignoring the two men, sniffed at the door. Just inside the threshold he halted. Up went his splendid head.

"Shhhh," said Clark. "That old dog wants to have a look at your papoose. See there, how he goes gently?"

"*Oui*—that *femme*, she like dogs to keep her feet warm when the nights get cold, but I don't like dogs— small dogs or large dogs." Charbonneau stopped at the door and watched with Captain Clark to see what the big Newfoundland would do.

Scannon's eyes sought out the sleeping figures before the dim fireplace. For a second or more, Scannon stood. Then he began to creep toward Sacajawea—hesitantly, one slow step at a time. The cold air blew from the opened door, and Sacajawea was roused from her sleep enough to pull the robes more tightly about herself and her papoose.

Clark stepped quietly inside. Charbonneau motioned frantically at the huge dog. He did not want the dog sniffing at his newborn child. "Shhh!" said Clark. "He will not harm either mother or child—watch."

The dog was large inside the small room, with his black coat shining in the firelight. His deep-set dark eyes seemed to have a soul behind them. The tip of his tail twitched uncontrollably. Then all at once he began to lick the outstretched hand of Sacajawea. He lay down

beside her pallet and put his huge head beside her hand.
Half-asleep, she stroked his head and called him Dog
in the Hidatsa tongue.

Charbonneau moved, but Clark pushed him back
against the wall. Sacajawea rose up on her elbow, but
she saw only the dog. Her eyes took in the whole color
and shape and hide of the dog; she studied his massive
shoulders and powerful legs, his drooping ears and intense eyes. The dog sneezed. She looked at him with
curiosity and slowly crawled from the robes to close the
door, stepping across Scannon's legs and waving tail.
Her hair was neatly plaited, and her tight braids hung
over her shoulders. The linsey nightgown she was bundled in would have held two of her. It was the one
nightshirt Lewis had brought. He had insisted she wear
it. She was lost in the fullness of the floor-length garment. It fit her like a circus tent; she could hardly walk
without stepping on the hem. A second step checked
her so quickly that she fell head first on the hard dirt
floor.

"That *femme* don't much like a night-dress on,"
Charbonneau told Clark.

He did not have to point that out, because Sacajawea
had slipped her arms out of the wide flapping sleeves
and pulled the fluttering material up over her head.
Her head was out of sight. The more she pushed and
pulled upward, the faster she kicked her slim, brown
legs. She twisted from side to side in the manner of a
squiggling, hatching butterfly shedding its soft, fibrous
case. Getting on hands and knees, she wiggled away
from the yards of flannel, at the same time muttering
some incomprehensible Minnetaree gutturals.

Charbonneau said, "If that ain't a tent-moth hatching out a cocoon, I ain't a proud papa." Charbonneau
began to titter. Clark chuckled. Then the two men broke
out in loud guffaws, clutched each other, and laughed
until their sides ached. Charbonneau pulled away and
put his hands on his belly as if to save the lacing on
his shirt. He moaned and tears ran down his cheeks.
Clark wiped his eyes.

The young mother sat on the voluminous nightshirt
contentiously, as if to prevent it from engulfing her or
smothering her in its wide folds. She clamped her lips

together, sat up straight, and shook both her fists at
the laughing men.

The door banged open, and Ben York peered into the
dim room. "Hey, Master Clark, you got here before you
have breakfas'!" Then he looked at Sacajawea, and his
eyes moved from the heap of linsey to the two men.
They shook. Their laughter would not stop. Charbonneau's hands slipped helplessly to his thighs and beat
upon them.

The young mother turned to the new voice. With a
small, scurrying rush, she flung herself upon York's leg
and clung to it. With a wide sweep he scooped up the
nightgown and dropped it over her head.

York scowled at the two men. "She's not used to
wearing clothes in bed."

The men sobered and nodded.

"Lend me your whittle, Charb," York said.

Charbonneau's forehead puckered as he drew his
knife.

"You can trust me," said York. He thrust the blade
into the twisted thong that held up his trousers. "Got
more here than I needs," he said as he hacked off a strip
of the leather and held it up. "We'll make a sash of
this." He pulled it around Sacajawea's waist and tied
it in back as he turned her around. "There, it'll be comfortable and warm and let you walk. Go on back to bed."

Her black eyes glittered. She tucked herself among
the robes, letting Scannon smell at her and nose gently
at her papoose. She was upset by the laughter.

"That papoose, he has hands and feet in the right
place. 'Magine me playing nursemaid to an Injun and
her papoose," laughed York, shooing the two men off
toward the door. "Too many in here. Let the little mother
rest."

"You're enjoying your nursemaid role," Clark joked
as Lewis unexpectedly pushed open the door, letting in
another draft of cold air. The morning sky was now
light gray.

"Oh, Lord, that damn dog is here!" whispered Lewis
rather loudly. "Scannon, you have no good business
here. Lord, who let him in?" The other three men stared
blankly at one another as Lewis sent the dog bounding
out the cabin door. "Now there is more room to admire

that papoose," he said, kneeling beside the pallet of furs and hides. "So now, little mother, may we see your fine son?" His hands moved as he explained to her that he wanted to admire her child.

Soon Clark was bent on the other side of the pallet, his big, rawboned hand feeling the smooth skin on the face of the papoose.

Sacajawea tried to scowl fiercely; she did not like to be laughed at. But she knew she had been a funny sight squirming out of a tunic as large as a tepee. She continued to frown as she gathered the wide open neck of the nightshirt close around her neck. She was cold. She looked from Charbonneau to Clark. Calmer now, she realized they were not ridiculing her, but were interested in her welfare and the newborn child. She smiled and handed the tiny papoose to Clark for inspection. The papoose was swaddled in a soft white doeskin with much absorbent cattail fluff stuffed in the bottom half of the wrapping cover.

"Pompy," she said.

"What? Is that his name?" asked Clark, taking the swaddled baby like a rare porcelain doll and holding him to the firelight. Clark sat on his haunches and looked at the tiny brown hands and long, silky black hair. "Perfect," he said, then asked again, "What name did you give him?"

Charbonneau answered eagerly, "He is called Jean Baptiste."

"No, I mean what the little mother calls him. Maybe some nickname."

Charbonneau spoke a few phrases in Hidatsa.

Reluctantly, Sacajawea took her eyes from the child. "Pompy," she said with a hint of pride. She lay back to rest a moment.

"That Pompy is firstborn in the tongue of her people, I think," explained Charbonneau. "He's known by me as Jean Baptiste. A good French name." He crossed himself and spit into the fire, making it hiss. "That's same name as LePage. And it is my brother's name, and my papa's name, also."

"LePage will be pleased to have a namesake," said Clark, his hands under the baby's head and back as he pushed him under the robes toward his mother. Sacajawea pulled down the top of the nightgown and put the baby to her breast before he began to whimper.

"I like that Pomp name best." York grinned.

"Looks like the papa, eh?" asked Charbonneau, coming over to the pallet.

"I had thought he looked like his mother, sweet and innocent," said Clark, laughing.

Sacajawea began to crawl out of the robes, her feeling of being laughed at making her uncomfortable.

"I'm not making fun of you," said Clark anxiously. "I'm not laughing at you. Please." His blue eyes pleaded with her to understand that he had not meant to torment her. He could never hurt any living thing.

It was curious how his look affected her. She gazed into his eyes and saw at the same time the yellow glints of firelight dancing off his shock of red hair. Her mind began to rest easy, and she knew she could trust him. She had learned politeness from Grasshopper, and it tied her tongue. She could not hurt Chief Red Hair's feelings.

"You, mama, stay put. I'se going to make hot tea for you. And you men want some?" York asked as he watched Sacajawea crawl back into the fur robes.

The men nodded.

"With sugar," added Charbonneau, tugging at his capote.

It was comforting to lie there with the soft robes around and the fire warming her side. It reminded Sacajawea of nights when she'd slept on a pile of robes with Grasshopper crooning nearby. She thought how comforting Grasshopper had been. That had been the best time she could remember in her whole life. York had the same comforting qualities. He had the same wise mixing of authority and tenderness so that she had not been frightened to have her papoose among the paleface men. She was relaxed with York around. She did not understand how he managed to give her peace of mind, but she trusted him completely. Now she sat up and drank the hot, sweet tea, enjoying the hushed tones of the men as they talked of the day's work ahead of them. She had a drowsy sense that the whole world was filled with blue sky and sunshine, and York merged with the big black Newfoundland dog, Scannon, who had sneaked back inside the cabin to sleep at her side.

When she woke up, she was cold. The men had gone, and the fire was low. It was daylight, and the camp was in a hubbub, like a village on trading fair day, with moccasined feet pounding on the hard-packed dirt and people calling out names and men bawling back at them.

Then she noticed that the room had been put in order, and a handsome carved and woven cradleboard stood at one side of the fireplace so that she could easily see it. The weaving was familiar to her, and she knew at once that her adopted Metaharta mother, Grasshopper, had done the work.

The Minnetaree grapevine had worked quickly to bring news of Sacajawea's firstborn to Grasshopper. She wondered if Charbonneau had spread the news or if Otter Woman had gone to visit Grasshopper.

She lay on her back and looked at the split cottonwood log ceiling. She felt good. She stretched herself lazily, her arms flat against the hides and all her fingers spraddled. She curled one arm around the sleeping baby, scratching her belly with the other and, at the same time, pulling up the linsey nightgown that was itself scratchy. It was then she noticed that she wore a woman's belt packed thickly with cattail down. She remembered a pile of it heaped in one corner of the cabin. Not since being with Grasshopper had she been treated with such consideration. York came in with more sweetened tea. "You better get between them covers. Gather your strength afore you gad about, little mama," he scolded gently. Noticing her wistful expression, he whistled softly. Scannon padded in, right to the edge of her pallet, sniffing, then curling himself as small as possible between her and the fire. York nodded in approval, knowing he was taken by this guileless little squaw.

"Dog," she said in English, surprising York. "Nice dog, nice York."

York's smile spread across his face. "Thank you, little mama." York stepped forward. "Captain Clark, he told me to tell you about this here Injun squaw that came early this afternoon. She was decked out in some fine garb—yes, ma'am! Her hair was daubed with mud

and wound around her head like a crown, and her ears
was red painted inside. She made Captain Clark promise you got the papoose board. She was all for coming
in to see you, but the captain, he made her understand
you need rest. That there lady waddled off singing to
herself. She was that happy you had a buck papoose.
You know anybody like that?" His hands worked as he
talked so that Sacajawea could read his hand signs.

"*Ai*, Grasshopper!" she cried, sitting among the robes.
"She did come!"

That afternoon, Charbonneau brought in the large
hind quarter of an antelope and some of its entrails.
He lounged around, smoking and talking and broiling
the meat. He said that Otter Woman and Corn Woman
had the rest of the animal. He wrapped a long piece of
the small gut, which contained the marrow, around a
stick and tied it. Then he held it to the fire until it
sputtered and browned and the juice dripped. He ate it
as he talked with Sacajawea and York about hunting
with the Americans.

The weather became warm in the middle of the
month, but by the end of February the men were again
wearing their fur robes and Mackinaw coats. Sacajawea
had moved back to the skin tent with Charbonneau.
She sliced the meat he brought in and spread it out on
drying racks in the sun—it froze before the moisture
evaporated. But the meat dried because the water
seemed to sublime rather than evaporate out in the
subzero weather. She scraped the hides inside the tent
where the center fire was warm.

One morning Charbonneau was called inside the fort
because the Mandan subchiefs, Sheheke, the Coyote,
and Kagohami, Little Raven, had come to see Captain
Clark. Charbonneau took his older son, Little Tess, with
him. The two chiefs shuffled their moccasins in a dance
when they saw the three-year-old son of Charbonneau.
Little Tess walked behind them, imitating their dancing. This made Sheheke laugh, and he pulled the child
up on his shoulders while he danced. After their frol-
icking they motioned for Charbonneau to come sit with
them on the floor of the officers' cabin. Sheheke produced a pipe, and they smoked. Clark waited patiently

for Charbonneau to translate why these subchiefs had
come.

They wished to consult their Medicine Stone, about
three days' march to the southwest, and wanted Clark
to go with them. Each spring, and sometimes in the
summer, they visited the stone. They built a fire and
let the smoke roll across the porous face of the rock,
which was about twenty feet in circumference. Then
they slept. In the morning the stone had certain shiny
white markings that represented peace or war for their
village. Sometimes other things could be read from the
markings as well.

"Tell them," said Clark, "that I would like very much
to go with them, but I have promised my men working
on the canoes that I would bring them more scraping
knives for hollowing out the insides of the dugouts. I
cannot go back on my word to my men."

Sheheke smiled. "Chief Red Hair speaks true. He is
a man to be trusted. He will not wage war with us unless
he tells us first. Some other day he will come to our
Medicine Stone."

When they left, Charbonneau became owlish and
rude. "They asked a favor. To them the Medicine Stone
is great. They think you are impolite."

Clark looked at Charbonneau. "I could see by Little
Raven's smile and the handshake that the Coyote gave
that they thought I was right in keeping a promise I
made first to my men. They are leaders and they understand that one's own men must come first. That will
hold for you, also, on our trip. You will follow orders,
as the others do."

Not looking Clark in the face, Charbonneau said,
"By *Jésus*, on that trip I will not stand guard. I am an
interpreter. I am not a soldier. I will go maybe as far
as the big falls the Indians talk about. Then I wish to
return here. This place, she is not so bad when I work
for the Northwesters and Hudson's Bay. I join hands
with them. If I join with you, I want my share of rations—as much as I can carry. My squaw, she is sickly,
see? She need plenty of good food, and sugar in her tea."
Charbonneau straightened Little Tess's shirt, then drew
himself up importantly. "I am interpreter for many
years, I am somebody important here. I think I am

important man, and I do not have to do the same things your soldiers do. I would not have to do that if I continued to work for the Northwesters."

Clark was at a loss to know what to say in response to Charbonneau's arrogance. After a long silence he answered, "Think it over for a couple of days. If the weather clears, we'll be pulling out in three or four weeks. Maybe we can make an agreement so that you'll take the responsibility we first spoke of. If not, I promise we'll see if Monsieur Jussome will go with us."

Charbonneau had not thought Captain Clark would let him go like that. He had expected an argument, but he thought the captain would give in to his demands and he would go with the expedition. Captain Clark was a hardheaded man, Charbonneau decided. He reached for his cap and sash and had stomped out the door before Clark could refill his pipe. Little Tess scampered behind his father, who shooed him back to the tepee alone.

Charbonneau did not return until dusk, drunk on trader's rum.

"Do you wish your meal now?" asked Otter Woman.

"Shut up," he answered in a surly tone. He had not liked the way that the American captain had spoken to him that afternoon, and he had decided that he ought to live on the other side of the river where the British trappers, MacKenzie and Larocque, had their camp. He was going to take his wives and two sons with him. He would live in a big skin tent and have many important guests and powwows in his lodge. He held his head to see if the fog inside it would clear. It settled deeper, making it hard for him to focus his eyes.

Leaning against a pile of furs, he gave orders to pack and get the gear by the water's edge by nightfall, including the leather tepee they were in.

Otter Woman and Corn Woman, who hadn't liked the idea of Charbonneau's leaving them behind, immediately began preparing for the move while Sacajawea listened to Charbonneau with a growing horror. If they moved across the river, she would not be going back to the People. And she would never again see the black, laughing face of York or smell the warm, panting dog, Scannon, or see the stern face of owl-eyed Captain

Lewis, or hear the deep voice of Chief Red Hair, or see the boyish grin of Shannon when he tried to teach Otter Woman his words.

"No!" Sacajawea said. "I won't go!"

"When are you going to learn to keep your damn mouth shut?" barked Charbonneau. "You take orders from me with no back talk. Follow Corn—she takes orders like a squaw should."

Corn Woman had already taken a load of furs outside, but Sacajawea could not stop. "I hate your ways." She made furious signs with her quick hands. "If you leave the Americans, I will run away with my papoose where I can think and not be pushed down." She trembled, surprised that she had actually said those bold words herself.

Angered, Charbonneau grabbed her arm, squeezing it until it was white, and hit her across the mouth, cutting deep into her lower lip. Now she said nothing, only wiped the bright red stain on the back of her hand. This physical pain did not hurt as much as the mental anguish that she felt with her hopes of going back to the People destroyed because she had a weak, foolish man.

Someone coughed and cleared his throat outside the tepee. It was their friend Baptiste LePage kicking the ice and snow from his boots. Sacajawea greeted the husky brown-eyed Frenchman with a half smile. LePage could pass for a Shoshoni, she thought. He had the same barrel chest with prominent sternum and clavicle, and the same long-stringed muscles in his thighs and legs. His wrist and hand bones, and his ankles were small. His hair was black and straight, without sheen, and he wore it banged, with a red band to keep it from falling in his eyes. He rarely wore a head covering. He had joined the Northwest Company long after Charbonneau, but he had stayed longer because the discipline appealed to his sense of getting a job well done. Charbonneau could never stay long with one outfit before he went off by himself as an independent trader or changed his mind unexpectedly, on a whim, as he had done now. LePage glanced around the tepee, then squatted beside Charbonneau and handed him his tobacco pouch. The two men talked in French while the women finished the packing. Little Tess, dressed for helping the women outside, grew warm and had to be unbundled. Sacajawea decided that no longer did she need a blanket on her papoose. She removed the robe and hung the cradleboard on a large peg on one of the lodgepoles.

"So, that's my namesake?" said LePage. "That's why I came in. Captain Clark told me the papoose had been named after me. The news made me feel good. *Magnifique*! I'll teach him some songs." And he began to sing. The women laughed.

Charbonneau became uneasy. He wondered what else Captain Clark had told LePage.

LePage took the baby, cradleboard and all, and began to dance. Then he unlaced the coverings and peered at the baby, who lay naked in the fine, soft, creamy robe Sacajawea had prepared.

Charbonneau crowded up and hunkered over his shoulder. "*Zut*, Baptiste!" he said. "Ain't he a fine boy, an' fat? Fat as a little possum."

The papoose was a métis like his father, part Indian and part French-Canadian. He was a pinkish brown, not as dark as his mother. He was under two feet long and so fat he looked almost like a soft ball. His wrists and ankles were ringed with chubby fat and his neck was nearly hidden by his chin. There was a thatch of dark hair on his head, the hair fine as a nursling beaver's coat. There was no untoward blemish anywhere. His deeply colored eyes were tightly shut and he sucked with faint wet noises on a fist as his fat legs, bent at the knees, kicked out at the air.

LePage reached for one little smooth foot. It was swallowed up in his hand. His stomach felt queer, as if he had a sudden spasm of hunger. He grabbed a tiny copper fist and held it beside the foot thinking that he'd never seen anything human so small and so beautiful. What would the future bring to this infant? Would he be just another half-breed? He could be a British free trader like his old man, or he could be a squawman, trapping and living with whatever tribe was near. What would his old man do for him? For that matter, what could he, LePage, do for his tiny namesake? He touched the short, flat nose. Then he noticed the other child,

Little Tess. I don't know, he thought, I guess you brothers—half brothers—will have to find your own way,
like the rest of us dumb bastards.

The baby opened his eyes and looked directly at
LePage. The fist fell from his mouth, his face pushed
together, and he began kiyi-ing loudly, stopping only
to take a deep breath.

"*Mon dieu*," LePage said admiringly, "he's sure got
a good set of lungs, ain't he?"

Charbonneau laughed. "And a temper, looks to me.
Like his mama."

For a while, Sacajawea watched proudly while the
baby howled; then she gathered him up and cradled
him, soothing him to sleep.

"Say, get your French harp out, Big Tess, and we'll
sing some more."

"We have to go," Charbonneau said. "We are going
to move to new quarters across the river."

"I don't believe it," said LePage. "You aren't! Not
after all the Americans have done for you. They took
your advice and gave me a job. They took care of your
woman, gave you rations and ammunition. What is in
your mind? Can't you see beyond the nose on your face?
This is the chance of a lifetime—to see this country
west where no white man has gone. You'll discover
valleys that are more beautiful than your mind can
imagine—in the spring, mallards skimming across the
water, bear stepping along and snuffing. That bear will
be your pillow at night. At your sides and scattered all
around will be deer and wild turkeys, and a stack of
beaver plews as high as your shoulder. You can bet *I*
will not miss all this."

"You don't understand," Charbonneau whined, trying
to justify his decision to leave the Americans. "The
Northwesters; they go west, too, and if I ask Larocque,
he will let me take the three squaws with me, and I
don't have to act like an Army soldier. I can be big man.
I can be interpreter, explorer, voyageur—three in one.
Do the Americans have other interpreters? *Oui.* So I
will not be so important, and they let me take only one
squaw. They choose which one. I would have chosen
Otter Woman—she does not speak out so much. She

minds only me, her man." He pointed a finger at Otter Woman.

LePage began to speak in French. "Both the American captains believe that your youngest squaw is the most intelligent, the smartest, the one who will help most when they come to the land of the Shoshonis. But you said something—something about Larocque."

"*Oui.* I hear he offers good rations, with taffee, trader's rum, each evening." Charbonneau patted his expanding belly. "Larocque has orders from the British to go west and keep ahead of the Americans."

"West? What for?" LePage was sure that the American captains did not know this news—that the Northwest Company was rushing to expand its trade facilities or trapping area.

Charbonneau kept his voice low, in a whisper, as though he were telling a secret. "He explores the territory for the crown. For England, to make Canada big."

So it was a race. A race between countries for that unknown land beyond the Rocky Mountains. LePage gulped in his surprise and puffed hard on his pipe. "My friend, I am surprised that you would make such a grave mistake, a smart man like you. One who is called Chief of the Little Village must be wise in something. Don't you want to be on the winning side?"

"Winning side? *Oui,* of course." Charbonneau always wanted to be with the winning team. He tried hard to think if maybe he was making a mistake. LePage was his good friend, and he knew the Northwesters as well or better than the Americans. His judgment was worth something in a case like this.

LePage, feeling he was beginning to get through to this thick métis, went on, "You are smart. You know who owns the land we are sitting on?"

"*Oui,* the Americans," Charbonneau said.

"You are right. They own the land to the foothills of the Rockies, too. Soon they will be kicking the British traders out of here—and the trappers and the French-Canadians, too. Then where will you be? Where?"

Charbonneau blinked and shook his head.

"You're damn right again. Out—with them. But if you go with the Americans, as you promised in the first place, you will be secure for many years. Maybe for the rest of your life. You can have plenty of red-flannel shirts. You'll be a big man, and rich, with as many squaws as you wish when you return. They will wash your aching feet and fill your belly with roast buffalo humps and squash and keep your bed warm."

Charbonneau's face glowed, then became dark again.

Baby Pomp cried for his milk. Little Tess was jumping on his father's sleeping couch and laughing. Otter Woman had removed her fur robe and was putting more sticks on the cooking fire.

Sacajawea was listening, trying to catch a few French words along with the English she knew, to put things together. It was hard. She knew that LePage was trying to persuade her man to be more friendly with the Americans. Was he persuading him not to move across the river with the Northwesters? She fervently hoped so. She wondered if Corn Woman already had the furs on the other side of the river. How long would she have to wait across the river for the rest of them to come over? Sacajawea listened some more.

"I will do something for you," offered LePage. "I will go to the American captains and tell them that you are sorry and that you realize you made a foolish mistake. But now you are wiser and will go with them on the expedition on their terms. *Bien*?"

Charbonneau thought things through slowly. LePage continued, "It ought to be the winning side for a smart man like you. Let me try to make the captains understand you now wish to go with them. If they won't take you back, then you can go with Larocque and MacKenzie. But those Canucks won't get far." LePage drew on his pipe and shrugged his shoulders.[1]

Charbonneau scrambled to his feet, knocking LePage's pipe to the ground. "*Merci*, go to the Americans," he said impulsively. "Go tell *les capitaines* I am sorry for the way I acted. Tell them I can work like a horse and I can do what they say—and tell them I cook. *Oui*, can I cook!"

Sacajawea handed LePage his pipe. He put his hand on her shoulder. "Get *le bébé* ready for a long canoe trip, *ma beauté*," he said, winking.

"I better send someone after Corn Woman. That *femme* will sit on the Northwester side of the river until it freezes again. *Presse je suis!*" Charbonneau grabbed his blue wool capote and hunched down and out of the tepee.

Toward the end of March, the two pirogues that had so surprised the Indians in the fall, and the six pirogues that had been built from huge cottonwoods during the winter, were safely in the river. The snow was melting fast, and the ice had broken away from the water's edge. Captain Clark oversaw the loading and lashing on of the cargo while Captain Lewis worked with Corporal Warfington and the crew that were to take the keelboat, *Discovery*, back to Saint Louis.

Nine boxes were packed with specimens of plants and animals and curios for President Jefferson. There were animal horns, Indian gear, skeletons of small animals and botanical specimens in small jars, and mineral samples. Lewis had them labeled and dated. With great care, Lewis also oversaw the arrangements for transporting to the President his live specimens: a prairie dog, four magpies, and a prairie chicken. "The American Philosophical Society ought to have some of these things," Lewis wrote in his letter to the President.

There was a song in the heart of Sacajawea as she stood beside Charbonneau watching the keelboat sail downriver. She had on a clean tunic trimmed with fringes and held in at the waist with a woven reed belt painted red and yellow. Captain Clark had told her that she would be regarded as one of the crew on the expedition, not just as the woman of Charbonneau. She could help Ben York with the cooking, and she would be called upon to interpret when they reached the mountains and the home of her people.

This morning, April 7, 1805, she had wakened early to say good-bye to Corn Woman and Otter Woman, who were busy moving back into Charbonneau's mud lodge in the village of Metaharta. There they would wait for him; arrangements had been made with Jussome to make sure that they would have food and other necessities while he was away.

Sacajawea had bathed her papoose, cleaned his cradleboard, and now checked for the tenth time to make sure there was enough cattail down in her pack to last

a good while. Her own hair had been washed and combed
into neat braids.

The Mandans and Minnetarees were still shouting
farewells after the keelboat, but their eyes were fastened on the eight remaining boats lining the bank of
the river.

While saying good-bye, Otter Woman had held Sacajawea back. "I fear I shall never see any of you again.
I will be here alone. It is a trick!" There·were tears in
her eyes.

"Get hold of yourself or our man will surely whip
you," said Sacajawea. "It is no trick, and we·will all
return with many things to tell about."

"You would tell him to beat me?" sobbed Otter
Woman.

"Oh, no," said Sacajawea, gasping. "Never!" She patted Little Tess on the shoulder. "You are my Shoshoni
family here. You are my sister." She looked at Otter
Woman, who found parting so hard.

"I will never be your sister again. You have come
between my man and our child. You are a dirty schemer,
a mountain cat. This is good riddance!" Otter Woman
sobbed louder.

Tears overflowed. Sacajawea could scarcely see as
she walked with her toed-in stride, learned as a child
in order not to lose balance, instead of slipping and
sliding with no dignity down the path to the loaded
pirogues. She could not believe that Otter Woman actually meant what she had said.

Suddenly out of the crowd came the Coyote and Little
Raven to wave good-bye with both arms. There were
the women of Four Bears, too, including Sun Woman
holding out her arms. "A great thing," she said, "you
going with the palefaces!" Grasshopper had come also.
She pushed a small leather bag into Sacajawea's hands.
"Give it to your man," said Grasshopper. "That is the
best use of the greasy weasel collar." Her hand clung
to Sacajawea's. "My daughter," she began, but her voice
broke and she crossed her arms over her breast in the
sign for love. Tears streamed down her face, but her
mouth smiled.

Silently the women fell into single file; others came
to walk before Sacajawea and to follow. Last week they

would have told her to shut up, or maybe pushed her into the water while walking this close to the river. To her surprise Sacajawea found she was not too sure she liked her new status.

"Yesterday I was an ordinary squaw, cleaning out my tepee and packing to go on a journey with my man," she said to Grasshopper. "Now I walk in the middle of all of you like a venerated grandmother, and you look at me out of the corners of your eyes."

Grasshopper, her face lined and weather-worn, gave Sacajawea a nod. "There on the meadow of yellow flowers we walked—how long ago we walked in that pleasant way." There were tears still in her eyes.

"Here, it is for you," said a shy voice from behind Sacajawea. Sun Woman slipped a small leather pouch with a round quill design on both sides into Pomp's cradleboard. "It is the shining stone of the Americans. It is for good fortune."

Sacajawea blinked back a flood of tears and found her voice. "My heart stays with you." She pressed her face against the cradleboard so that Sun Woman might not notice the tears spilling down her face, and said a final farewell. Charbonneau, who was already on board, motioned her to join him.

A shot from the swivel gun on the keelboat's deck was heard. The Minnetarees and Mandans became quiet as Captain Lewis, looking smart in his blue Army uniform, wearing the tricornered hat, raised his hands to indicate he had something left to say.

"Good-bye, our friends. We thank you for your kindnesses and hospitality. We will return to see all of you once more before we go back to our Great White Father and tell him of your peaceful and kind manners."

Sacajawea saw Jussome and Broken Tooth on the bank; she then spotted Water Woman. Everyone was waving and milling about and cheering.

"Yiiiii, eeeee! Hooooklaaaa!"

Sacajawea gasped. Old Black Moccasin was being led forward by his woman, Sunflower. He stood in front of Captain Lewis and raised his hands in friendship to the natives, and then to the Americans. There was now dead silence because this old man no longer came before any kind of gathering very often. He could not walk easily and he did not see well, but his voice was still powerful. Sacajawea recalled its vitality when she had first encountered him nearly six summers before.

"Palefaces, our Great Spirit will watch over you. We trust you. Our hearts are bigger because we have seen you. We wait for you to return in peace."

Black Moccasin's veined hand clasped the peace medal he wore proudly around his neck.

The hushed silence was shattered with the crowd's roar. Never again would Black Moccasin appear at such a large public gathering. Everyone seemed to sense this and already to feel the loss. The crowd surged as one person around the old chief.

The Coyote moved through the crowd to stand before Captain Lewis. He was wrapped in a United States flag, with fifteen stripes and fifteen stars. He stood out in bright red, white, and blue contrast to the dull fur robes of the others. He made his hand signs high so that everyone might see them. "I will always be a loyal friend to the Americans."

Suddenly the crowd seemed to stop and stumble uncertainly. Chief Kakoakis in his war paint and regalia dashed through the people to the shoreline on a raven black horse. He surveyed the pirogues with his protruding one eye as they pushed off from the shore. He noted the mounted swivel gun on the prow of one of the pirogues, and his cruel, dissipated face broke into a ghastly grin.

Sacajawea, sitting in the white pirogue, with Captain Clark, Drouillard, Cruzatte, and Charbonneau, trembled at the sight of Kakoakis and the abrupt change in mood he brought to the people. They shuffled after him to the center of the nearest village. The Coyote and Little Raven stood off by themselves. Black Moccasin moved his arm slowly, and a few of the people obeyed and shuffled off toward their own lodges. Then some came close to the shore to shout their farewells. Sacajawea noticed that soon there were not too many left to follow Kakoakis like sheep and stand around in a circle waiting for him to speak. She imagined she could hear him say, "They will not get far. The Sioux or Blackfeet will massacre the whole bunch."

And she imagined he spat upon the ground as his handful of followers shouted, "*Ai!*"

The six canoes and two pirogues poled up the river that late afternoon as far as the Mandan village of Matootonha, where the Coyote lived. They camped for the night on the south side of the river. Both captains, Drouillard, Charbonneau, Sacajawea, and Pomp slept in the skin tent Charbonneau had brought along.

Sacajawea breathed deeply of the cool spring air, and exhaled just as fully as though to get rid of the foul, smoked-filled air of the Minnetaree villages. Where would she go now? She found her mind full of thoughts. She knew well where she had been. She thought about the first time she had learned that Otter Woman was also a Shoshoni. Her thoughts took her back over the years, highlighting the events that had led to her being taken to the lodge of Toussaint Charbonneau as his woman.

14

A Sudden Squall

Lewis's Journal:

Tuesday May 14th 1805.

...*I cannot recollect but with the utmost trepidation and horror; this is the upsetting and narrow escape of the white perogue. It happened unfortunately for us this evening that Charbono was at the helm of this Perogue, in stead of Drewyer,[1] who had previously steered her; Charbono cannot swim and is perhaps the most timid waterman in the world.... the Perogue was under sail when a sudon squawl of wind struck her obliquely, and turned her considerably, the steersman allarmed, in stead of puting, her before the wind, lufted her up into it, the wind was so violent that it drew the brace of the squarsail out of the hand of the man who was attending it, and instantly upset the perogue and would have turned her completely tosaturva, had it not have been from the resistance mad by the oarning [awning] against the water.*

Thursday May 16th

...*the ballance of our losses consisted of some gardin seeds, a small quantity of gunpowder, and a few culinary articles which fell overboard and sunk. the Indian woman to whom I ascribe equal fortitude and resolution, with any person onboard at the time of the accedent, caught and preserved most of the light articles which were washed overboard.*

BERNARD DEVOTO, ed., *The Journals of Lewis and Clark.* New York: Houghton Mifflin Co., 1953, pp. 109, 111.

Charbonneau shivered, pushed the perspiration off his forehead with his red neckerchief, then wound it just above his eyebrows so that it would sop the wetness and keep it from stinging his eyes. Poling his canoe was work. Friendly shouts rang out from canoe to canoe as the expedition searched for a suitable camping site.

The spring days were chilly with squalls. The air was sharp, and the water froze on the oars in the early morning. Now and then a flurry of snow came to whiten the April green. When the wind was kind, the sails were spread and tired arms rested. Cruzatte and Drouillard, and sometimes Lewis, took turns steering the pirogues. The captain's old tricorn, jogging on his head, looked like a live, stubby-winged bird on a small perch, which was looking into the water; it took little swoops, as a bird would.

The expedition passed a high bluff that seemed to be on fire, throwing out great puffs of smoke. The party choked and coughed on the sulfurous fumes.

"*Le sacré diable* of the river!" called Charbonneau to the men on shore pulling the cordelles—the two ropes attached to the canoes—so that they moved off the sandbars and stayed out of the fast water with its hidden logs.

Someone yelled back, "It's a volcano!"

"That is burning lignite," corrected Captain Clark.

Scannon rose from the bottom of the canoe and coughed. He looked as gigantic as a grizzly bear. Charbonneau moved a little out of the way of his tail, which was as big around as Charbonneau's arm.

Sacajawea called the dog to come sit beside her. As she did, Patrick Gass frowned. She wondered why Gass did not care for her. She had no way of knowing that he felt a woman had no business on a military expedition. She lay her hand on Scannon's head as he wrapped himself around her feet in the bottom of the pirogue.

By midafternoon the pirogues were beached in front of a meadow rounded into a hollow of a hill and rimmed about with black oaks.

"I show you how to make Indian cakes in the ashes, eh?" Charbonneau suggested to Ben York as he brought out the brass kettles.

"Ashes, eh? It grits my teeth just thinking about it. Why not on a hot stone?"

"With good oak bark in the fire, the cake is clean." Charbonneau had never thanked the captains for taking him back, and for him there was really no way—except that he could help York with the meals. He could make good corn cakes. He pulled one of the kettles aside, lifted the leather bag of cornmeal, and stood holding it, taken aback at his own brashness. He had no right to make free with York's things. He began to apologize.

"Go to it!" said York. "You've my leave, and more. If you can eat your cooking, I can."

While York got out the tin plates and spoons, Charbonneau took a swing through the woods and found a black oak with a hole in it. It was mostly dead where the hole was. Charbonneau stuck the handle of his ax underneath the bark and pried; the thick shags peeled off easily. He came back to the meadow with his shirt pulled up in front of him like an apron, full of bark, and made a small fire using one of Dr. Saugrain's matches.

York had given him a match and told him to break it over a bunch of dry buffalo grass. Charbonneau had never seen such an easy way to make a fire. Then York told Charbonneau exactly what Captain Clark had told him—that Dr. Antoine François Saugrain, a physician to the Spanish garrison at Saint Louis, had made them with phosphorous and sulfur tips. He had brought all the latest scientific lore from France. When all the world depended on flint and steel to make a fire, Paris and Dr. Saugrain made matches. They weren't magic; they were only a chemical invention, but very handy.[2]

The fire was going briskly when York came back with a kettle of clear water. The rest of the outfit was settling the gear for the night and turning the canoes over, backside up, on the beach.

Charbonneau looked for a large piece of bark for a mixing board but could find none that suited him, so he pulled off his leather shirt and smoothed it on the ground. The back side looked clean enough. He poured the meal there from a tin cup in the bag. He found the small clay pot of drippings from the antelope ration they had had the night before, and he placed the pot near the fire until the drippings melted. He poured the grease into the meal, kneading as he poured, until the grainy stuff was wadded into a large, stiff ball. He dipped the pot into the water kettle. He could hear Captain Clark's ax going *whkk, whkk* across the meadow, slashing saplings for the camp. When the ax strokes changed to a *tssh, tssh* sound, he knew that the captain had finished cutting and was trimming boughs off the young trees to make their beds more comfortable. He also knew that his woman was there helping the captain bring the boughs into camp.

His knuckles worked the water into the big lump of meal until it felt about right. He portioned the lump into about three dozen pieces, setting them on a clean rise of green moss after he had patted each of them into a round cake the width of his hands and thicker than his thumb. The oak bark had burned down by then into a pile of gray ash with red underneath. He raked a hollow in the ashes with a stick and laid a dozen cakes wrapped in leaves into it, just so, with a deep layer of ash brushed over them. He built a wall of fresh bark all around them.

"That sure do look like a little council house with a smoke vent all along the roof," said York, smiling. The fire began to creep up through its walls.

"By damn, it is too small," said Charbonneau, putting on his shirt. The captain was coming out of the woods, his arms full of dry sticks. Sacajawea came trailing a few paces behind, her arms loaded high with the brush boughs.

"We'll be eating directly," said York. It was getting dark fast in the glade. Charbonneau put another dozen cakes in the coals, carefully pushing aside the first batch.

Then Charbonneau started gnawing at the hole in the oak trunk with an ax again. Long slabs came away—good dry stuff that had seasoned while the tree was dying. He'd come back and fell that tree after supper; it would keep them in wood all night. When he gathered up an armload of the splintery slabs and headed for the

swale, he saw that Sacajawea was coming in again with
more boughs to make the ground soft under the men's
blankets. "Hey, *femme*, don't you forget my bed!" he
yelled. He put the last batch of cakes in the red coals
and piled more ash over them, then a layer of fresh
bark, keeping the other cakes warm at the side.

While he sat with his back against a tree, Clark
munched his cake and looked over the large medicine
box, taking a rough inventory. When Sacajawea was
finished, she came to sit quietly and watch. Lewis
brought his cake over and sat down counting out vials
and boxes with Clark.

"Say, Bill, look at this!" exclaimed Lewis, holding
up a tiny vial. "I'd almost forgotten about these." He
took out five more small, thin glass bottles. "That roy-
alist Saugrain gave them to me with explicit instructions on how to vaccinate. It's something new from Paris,
but I think Saugrain said it was first used last year—
no, the year before, in London. Anyway, it is new, and
according to the doc everybody is talking about it."

"I've not heard of it until now. What is it?" teased
Clark.

"It is something that might—will—change medicine."

"Aw, Lewis, Saugrain is enthusiastic about the sim-
plest remedies. What is this? Some of his 'electrified
water'?"

"Bill, it's something we should have used before. Already it could have lost its virtue. It's cowpox serum."[3]

"Cowpox? And who wants that?" But with intense
interest Clark watched Lewis break the top of the fragile vial and motion to Sacajawea to hold out her leg.
Just above the knee he made a tiny scratch with the
broken glass. She pulled her leg back, making a face.

"No, no—not yet," said Lewis. Carefully he put a
drop of the serum from the vial on the scratch and
scratched over that again.

Sacajawea frowned.

"You're hurting her, Lewis," said Clark.

"Good Lord, what's a little hurt now if it keeps her
face from getting deep scars. This will keep her from
having smallpox."

Clark used hand signs to tell Sacajawea that the tiny

scratch would keep her from having the dreaded smallpox and her face would always be smooth, not marked.
Sacajawea put her hands on her face. It was impossible
that a scratch could be so powerful as to stop such a
killing sickness.

"You should have used it on those Omahas who died
like cattle in that plague of smallpox," Clark continued.

"I know I should have used this stuff before. Loses
strength if it sits around. Hey, you want some? I ought
to give it to the men just in case we run into an Indian
camp that is infested."

"I'll let you try it on me, but I'm not sure it works.
Why don't you use it on our boy Pomp?"

"You hold Pomp firmly, and Lewis will make a scratch
on him," said Clark. Slowly Sacajawea nodded agreement, holding out the baby's leg. Pomp's eyes grew large
and watery, but he did not whimper.

"In a few days there will be a hard scab over the
scratch," explained Lewis. "Do not touch it. It will heal,
and that will be a sign you will never have the pox."

For a long time Sacajawea stared at the scratch above
her knee.

Lewis took the handful of vials and went out after
the men who had not had smallpox.

"Hey," called Clark after him, "hadn't you better
vaccinate yourself first?"

"If there's any left, I will!" yelled Lewis. "Lord, I'm
glad I found this stuff before it spoiled."

The days became milder and the sun warmer. Hunters were sent ahead, who picked out campsites next to
a spring or clump of trees. It never took long for the
brass kettles to swing across gypsy poles, nor for Charbonneau to twist the dry buffalo grass into a round pile
so that he could light it with a match.

When the hunters dressed a buffalo they had killed
one morning, Charbonneau, now acting as cook, called,
"Keep all the guts! Two bobs and a flirt in the muddy
Missouri and she is ready for stuffing and the fine meal."

Charbonneau held fast to one end of the six-foot-long
piece of large gut with his right hand, while the thumb
and forefinger of his left hand compressed to discharge,
as he explained, "That which we'd choke on." He stuffed

the gut with fillets and kidney suet, salt, pepper, and flour, calling it "*Bon pour manger.*" Then he tied both ends of the gut, boiled it, and fried it to a golden brown in bear's oil over a fire of buffalo chips.

Sacajawea licked her fingers when she had finished her sausage, then wiped her fingers in her hair to make it shine from the bear's oil.

One evening Lewis set himself up as cook and made a suet dumpling for each man. But generally he was off in the hills with Clark, taking a look at the country, finding plant and mineral specimens, or recording the temperatures and wind directions and measuring the terrain, noting the information later on his maps.

Sacajawea often brought in cress and other greens for an evening salad. She studied the ground, searching for things that were edible. In sunny spots the white stars of the bunchberry were already opening, and bluebeard lily buds swelled at the tops of their tall stems. Wild strawberry blooms hid under sprouting ferns and grasses like bits of leftover snow. She saw brown toads blink in the damp shade and brightly spotted green frogs hop away from her. Once a tiny chipmunk fled with a squeak and watched her from the top of a stump that was garlanded with trailing strands of dark green, soon to be covered with paired, pale pink twinflower bells. She stopped at some driftwood and saw the holes that field mice had made. She poked into the holes and then dug deeply as she found the clean white artichoke roots the mice had stored. She made several piles of the wild roots, then ran to find Clark.

"Eat." She indicated they should be boiled and eaten.

"It seems to me," Clark said, "if they are good, we should have them for dinner." He helped her take them back to the camp.

York and Charbonneau served the boiled roots on the tin mess plates with roast venison.

"Hey," said Pat Gass, "these here wild potatoes ain't bad."

"That's a treat from Sacajawea, here," said Clark.

Gass glanced quickly in her direction and spat on the dirt.

Drouillard laughed. "Once she gets to your belly, you'll think the woman is wonderful."

Some of the men guffawed and slapped their knees.
"Never!" snapped Gass. "It is not my idea of a military outfit to let a squaw gather its food."

Around the evening fire the captains brought out
stub quill pens and inkhorns so that they and the others
could record the day's adventures. Ben York sang a
spiritual, soft and low, and Scannon howled at the night
sky.

Sacajawea, who was never idle, bathed Pomp with
warm water from the cooking fire, and filled his cradleboard with clean moss. Then she mended several of
the men's moccasins, fortifying the shoes with hard,
dried buffalo skin so that the sharp stones and prickly
pear thorns would not so easily penetrate them.

Shannon sat shyly beside her. Using hand signs and
the words of Minnetaree he had learned from Otter
Woman, he told Sacajawea the words in York's songs.
Then he began to talk of Otter Woman. "She is quiet
and not bossy like the white girls back home." Sacajawea smiled, understanding that the boy felt a tenderness toward the sad-eyed Shoshoni girl. She put her
hand over her mouth so that Shannon would not talk
more, for Charbonneau had come to sit close by. His
jealous nature would not permit another man to admire
his women.

"Hey, this soldier is still hungry!" yelled LePage,
who was sitting beside the cradleboard, contentedly
watching his namesake make sucking noises in his sleep.

"He be mostly belly!" yelled Charbonneau back at
him.

Sacajawea reached for the baby to put him to her
breast.

The men gradually rolled up cocoonlike in their
Mackinaw blankets, with their feet to the fires, while
one man stood guard, listening to the melancholy wail
of coyotes and humming insects. Sacajawea, with Pomp,
the two captains, Drouillard, and Charbonneau, slept
on the soft boughs in the skin tent. The wind rose off
the prairie grass and roared among the cottonwoods.

On two sides of the expedition's camp lay camps of
the Sioux, each one's presence unknown to the other.
This tribe had gone to attack the expedition's camp at
Fort Mandan because they thought the white men were

bad medicine. They had missed them and were now going home. Chief Black Cat of the Mandans had disapproved of this Sioux scheme so strongly that he had not let his people trade or give food to them. By Indian standards this was the sharpest rebuff possible. Black Cat knew this band was warlike and wanted mainly the guns and ammunition the white men carried.

The Missouri River was beginning to look something like a swamp. The bed was shallow, and the men with the cordelles were sometimes out all day pulling and hauling the canoes. Sometimes the banks were steep and the men had to wade up to their armpits in the cold river; other times they climbed and scrambled over the sharp rocks and prickly pear along the shore. At times the banks were slippery with mud that clung to their moccasins, so they were forced to go barefoot. Dirt and stones showered these men from the crumbling cliffs.

One afternoon during a heavy rain, the expedition was forced to stop. A fire was laid on high ground in the center of the skin tepee, and as many as could gathered inside to keep dry. The others built small lean-tos that were not completely watertight but much better than sitting in the open or even under a tree.

Gathering sticks and saplings for the lean-tos, Gass noticed hoofprints. Drouillard and Cruzatte came to investigate. They reported to Clark that a Sioux war party traveling with many horses had been in this same spot only twenty-four hours before. No one wanted to meet these Sioux. The men began to speak of Corporal Warfington's party going downriver to Saint Louis in the keelboat. Would they miss the attacking Sioux? Fortunately both parties had traveled sooner and much faster than the warring Sioux had reasoned they would. The Pirogues and canoes averaged about twenty miles a day going upstream.

Alkali dust rose, blown into clouds, and sifted into Clark's double-cased watch until the wheels refused to move more than a few minutes at a time. The riverbank was perfectly white, and the river itself became milky white. Lewis remarked, "The Missouri looks to me like a cup of tea my grandmother used to make, with a tablespoon of milk stirred in it."[4]

The game became so tame that the men had to drive the elk and deer from the cordellers' path with sticks and stones. Sometimes the yellow cougar watched from some rock ledge. When a rock was thrown in its direction, the animal would growl and slink away. The expedition ate beaver, elk, prairie hens, turkeys, and ducks.

Little meadows were radiant with shooting stars, honeysuckle, morning glories, trillium, dogtooth violets, spring beauties, and buttercups. Wild cherry and plum blossoms perfumed the air. For two days they traveled past second-growth fir. The original timber had been burned off a generation before. The undergrowth was filled with vine-maple, or Virginia creeper. The captains investigated a clone of aspen, genetically identical, which had grown from one root.

Toward the end of April, Lewis studied the map drawn by the Wolf Chief and led a small party ahead to the mouth of the Rochejaune, or Yellowstone River. This had been named on a map drawn by James Mackay ten years earlier. Lewis had a copy of that map for study also, and he decided that the junction would make an ideal location for a future trading post. Pat Gass suggested the post be made of local limestone. Charbonneau suggested starting trading fairs, such as the Mandans and Minnetarees held.

Lewis and Drouillard wandered about, studying the terrain. There were a couple of square miles of open ground, walled on three sides by a stand of black fir timber that looked solid until the men got within two yards of it; on the fourth side was a growth of mountain-ash saplings fencing the river. The open ground was a swale of yellow snapdragons and lavender-flowering wild pea vine. Silently, out of the timber, loped two grizzlies.

Instantly Lewis recalled the awe and terror with which the Mandans had described these "yellow bears," the king of western beasts. Never did they go out to meet the grizzly without war paint and all the solemn rites of battle. As with the cave bear of ancient legend, no weapon of theirs was adequate to meet this dreaded beast. In parties of six or eight they went, with bows and arrows or, in recent years, the smoking-sticks of the French-Canadian traders. To kill one grizzly was equivalent to killing two enemies.

With these things swirling in their minds, Lewis and Drouillard faced the snarling animals. Each man fired his rifle; each wounded his bear. One beast ran back into the dense copse. The other turned and chased Lewis. A lucky third shot from Drouillard laid the bear low. He was only a cub, but the men estimated his weight at close to five hundred pounds, larger than any bear in the Atlantic states.

No wonder Indians who slew the grizzly were respected and in line to become chiefs. No wonder the bear's claws became a badge of honor, an emblem of unflinching valor, and the skin a chief's robe. There must be no enemy so fierce as an enraged and famished grizzly, thought Drouillard.

They pulled the huge animal to the shore for butchering, and its fleece and skin made a load that two men could scarcely carry. York rendered several gallons of oil from the bear. Charbonneau was so pleased with this much bear butter for his cooking that he volunteered to steer the white pirogue that afternoon.

No one, except perhaps Lewis, quite realized that Charbonneau was the worst steersman of the party. Both the captains were on shore at the time, which was very unusual. Almost always, one of them remained with the pirogue.

Charbonneau began to sing, "I'm a riverman. I'm half alligator and half horse, with the rest of me crooked snags and the red-hot snapping turtle. Cock-a-doodle-do!" He stopped, amazed at his own powerful voice. He was going to steer the pirogue and show those rogues he was more than just a cook with this outfit.

Scannon barked. Charbonneau turned and grinned, "By gar, you growl at me again and I'll scream through my nose. I'm all bull 'gator. If I set my teeth in your ear—"

He became silent; a puff of wind came up, then another, stronger one. Instead of putting the pirogue before the wind as he had been told, he luffed her into the wind; then he gloated about his seamanship, never giving another thought to luffing. A sudden squall struck

the pirogue obliquely. The wind came in such a strong
gust that it drew the brace of the square sail out of
Drouillard's hand. Sacajawea looked about, then toward the shore. Lewis had fired his gun to attract Charbonneau's attention, gesturing him to cut the halyards
and take in sail.

"Let Drouillard steer!" called Sacajawea.

The craven Charbonneau stood paralyzed with fear.
His knees were jelly, his mind water. He squawked,
"Shut up, squaw, we are going to drown." Then he
dropped the tiller and crossed himself, saying, "*Jésus,
l'enfant,* save us."

Charbonneau had turned pale and was staggering.

"Take hold of the helm, or I'll shoot you on the spot!"
yelled Cruzatte, enraged at Charbonneau's cowardice.

Charbonneau was conscious of a tremendous weight
upon him and the feeling that he would burst open.
Instinct alone made him cling to the bottom of the boat.

Looking three hundred yards across the river, the
two captains saw the pirogue heel over, then lie for an
agonzing half minute on her side. Finally the sail was
pulled in and the pirogue righted, but she was filled
with water to within an inch of the gunwales. Lewis
began unbuttoning his coat to swim out, but then realized how hopeless that would be. "Lord help that
Frenchman!" he exploded.

Gradually Charbonneau came to and began to spit
out muddy water and gasp for breath. Cruzatte hauled
him out of the water in the bottom of the pirogue, and
Charbonneau slumped against the gunwale in a half-
conscious condition. His hands were numb, and he kicked
a cask of water, deciding that was the weight that had
been on top of him as he lay half-submerged in the
bottom of the pirogue. If his life had depended on his
doing something, he would have been lost.

Sacajawea, with her baby tied to her back in the
cradleboard, began swimming after papers and articles
that had floated off the deck. Beside her was Scannon,
who had rushed into the water the moment she did.
Drouillard frantically bailed as Cruzatte rowed the pirogue to shore.

There was nothing to do but stop the expedition for
the rest of the day and unload the dripping, muddy

cargo. Sacajawea paddled to the shore. Her arms were filled with papers from Lewis's journal and his botanical notes. Hitched under one arm she carried Cruzatte's violin in its dripping case, and the sextant. Slumping down on the moss-covered bank, she pulled the tumpline from her forehead and slipped out of the cradleboard. She was spreading the baby's clothes, which she carried in the foot of the cradleboard, on stones to dry as Lewis ran up.

"Man," he said to Charbonneau, "if the pirogue had capsized while you were steering, it would have cost us dearly."

Scannon shook himself, spraying water over the two men, then barked loudly.

Charbonneau cringed. He dried his face with his shirtsleeve, but it stayed wet.

"You realize," Captain Lewis went on angrily, "we have valuable instruments, papers, medicine, and presents for natives on board, to say nothing about the people here, including your own woman and child. Clumsiness cannot be tolerated on this trip!"

Charbonneau hung his head and mumbled, "Go to the devil!" And he mumbled something about a changing wind. He looked at Scannon and shook his head. What good was the dog, anyway, he thought.

Scannon growled and showed his teeth.

Charbonneau stared at the dog. "Holy saints, that dog's mouth looks like a crater, and his bark can shake the canoe worse than the river rapids. It was that dog that caused the pirogue to shift. I'll shoot him if he tries to bite me!"

"He won't bite," Lewis said, then softened his reproach of the dejected Charbonneau. "Lord, you gave us a scare today. But the damage to the pirogue is less than it might have been. Let's have a drink."

Charbonneau slowly relaxed.

Lewis had York break out a ration of spirits all around while they inspected the pirogue's cargo. Some of the small medicine vials were ruined, but others could still be used and they were set out to dry. Only a few articles had rolled off the deck and sunk. The rest of the equipment could be salvaged.

Cruzatte examined his violin. "Dry in the prairie air

and she be good as new. Many thanks." He bowed to
Sacajawea. "I'll show you how to make music. You show
me how to dance—sometime soon?" Sacajawea nodded
and put her fingers on the sagging strings. "Oh, after
I tighten a few things," said Cruzatte.

Sacajawea went to help Lewis place the wet pages
from his journal and his loose botanical notes on a clean,
sandy place, with small stones on the corners of the
papers to keep them from blowing into the river again.

When she finally sat down beside Pomp, she was
exhausted. She picked up the baby and nursed him,
half dozing herself. Something wet bumped against her
arm. She looked quickly. It was Scannon, who lay with
his head on his front paws beside her. She put a hand
on his head, and it felt solid and strong. She passed
down his neck, his back and flanks. He seemed to quiver
and leaned his huge body against her. Then he bowed
his head and licked her wet moccasins.

She began to talk. She told Scannon about the People, the family of Catches Two, Redpipe, and Charbonneau. Scannon listened, his eyes half-closed.

Charbonneau came over to tell her that York had
food ready and she ought to dry her clothes out.

"Why you talk with that beast?"

"He does not talk back," she said.

"*Zut!*" spat Charbonneau.

Lewis did full justice that evening to Sacajawea. "She
showed equal fortitude and resolution with any person
on board," he said to the men. Clark clapped his hands,
and the others followed. Sacajawea lowered her head.
Never had she had such great praise.

"*Mon dieu*," said Charbonneau. "I'll never be able to
do anything with that squaw if you make her something
special and give her compliments."

Sergeant Gass looked darkly at Charbonneau. "She
didn't ask for anything, but a little praise goes a long
way. It is harmless."

Sacajawea looked up. What had Gass said? She had
understood only part of it. Was he defending her against
her man?

"You have to thrash women once a week, maybe
more if you treat them too nice," answered Charbon-

neau. "I guess you don't know women like I do." He laughed from deep within his throat.

"You ought to be hanged and have it prove a warning to you," snapped Gass. "Maybe we could call the lass our mascot. Soldiers often have mascots, you know."

The men clapped. Sacajawea sensed he had said a good word for her, and was pleased.

"Hey, Frenchy!" called John Ordway, "what were you thinking of out there this afternoon?"

Charbonneau looked up, shaken. "I—I did what I could." He became quite pale.

"What does that mean?" asked one of the men.

"I can't swim," said Charbonneau with an awful grimace of embarrassment.

"My dear friend," said Pat Gass, "you made the princely and self-sacrificing gesture of steering the pirogue when you were a stranger to water? We are two or three thousand miles from anywhere. With less men and equipment, the captains would have had to turn back."

"*Oui*," admitted Charbonneau, his liver doing flip-flops.

"Your behavior is intolerable in a military outfit," said Gass.

"I'm mortal sorry," said Charbonneau. "The dog growled and jumped at me, and I must have blacked out for a moment. *Oui*, that is it—I blacked out for a moment. Fainted."

Sacajawea looked from her man to the others. It would not be the last time she would see him go to pieces under stress, but this night she did not know this and excused him, thinking he was frightened by the dog and had miscalculated the strength of the wind in the sails.

CHAPTER

15

Beaver Bite

Clark's Journal:

May 19th Sunday 1805

Capt Lewis's dog was badly bitten by a wounded beaver and was near bleading to death.

BERNARD DEVOTO, ed., *The Journals of Lewis and Clark.*
New York: Houghton Mifflin Co., 1953, p. 113.

The game was still abundant and tame. One fat, complacent wolf was killed with nothing more than an espontoon—a spear and ax combined—which was part of each officer's equipment.

Not all the game was equally submissive. Scannon made the mistake of catching a beaver, probably the first he'd ever seen. He was bitten so severely that he nearly bled to death. Sacajawea showed Lewis how to stitch the wound together with some of the longer hairs from the dog's tail. Three days later, the paw was swollen to double its size and infected. Scannon was listless and lay in the bottom of the pirogue. Sacajawea stared down at his face. The dog was suffering terrible pain; his features were distorted in agony. She placed her blanket so the sun was shielded from his eyes. Lewis could not help; he was busy on shore collecting rocks and leaves.

After the evening meal, she examined his foot, felt it, turned it over, clicked her teeth, and said "Ahhh," as if she had done nothing else all the days of her life but tend such cases. The paw was as hard to the touch as a piece of firewood. She went to the cooking fire for the kettle of hot water. York thought she was going to bathe Pomp, but the papoose would go without his bath this night.

The sick dog kept his eyes fixed intently on her. Several of the men had come to see what she was doing with this huge Newfoundland, which was nearly as large as she. A close circle formed around the two. The captains also joined. Her face was sober, but all the while she kept talking in fast Minnetaree syllables.

"I think it is blood poisoning, sure as the Lord's watching," said Lewis.

"Let's give him a bit of laudanum so he will be still while she works on him," suggested Clark, going after one of the medicine boxes.

"Ought we to let that squaw work on my dog?" asked Lewis.

The dog pulled away from Clark and had to be forced

323

to drink the water with the alcohol-opium mixture. He refused to be moved from Sacajawea's side.

"Can you do something with that swollen foot?" asked Lewis, looking doubtfully at Sacajawea.

"*Ai*. Bad spirits inside!" She dipped her hands in the hot water and rubbed them several times on the swollen paw. Slowly she dipped the paw in the water. Finally the dog permitted her to hold his paw in the hot water for several minutes. She drew on the great store of knowledge she had gathered as a child from her grandmother. First, she massaged the flesh around the wound for a long time, then moved upward to the dog's ankle. She rubbed with the palm of her hand, making circular motions, gently for a while, then more strongly, and firmly. By then, the dog was sleeping.

She looked up and said something to Charbonneau. "She wants a drink of rum!" he spluttered.

"Well, she shall have it, then," said Clark, sending York for a tin cup.

"My Lord!" exploded Lewis. "The nerve of her!"

Clark handed her the cup of spirits. They all expected her to drink it. Instead, she drew the sleeping dog's paw from the warm water and poured the rum directly into the now soft, oozing wound. Her face was flushed, and her eyes shone in the firelight.

She made motions of wrapping the great paw. Lewis pulled some strips of white linen from the medicine box and swathed the paw. The dog gasped and whined and moaned as the opium wore off, but he did not try to stand. All night he lay beside the little fire. Sacajawea was certain from the dog's face that the pain was growing no worse. He even slept off and on.[1]

The whole camp was asleep now. Sacajawea felt tired and drowsy. Both captains had gone to sleep, and Drouillard was snoring. Pomp was asleep in the cradleboard, and she could see York with his feet close to the fire in the center of the skin tent. The dog slept. She lay on her robe, half-asleep. Suddenly she lay very still, listening. In another instant she was wide-awake. She had heard steps off to one side, steps that seemed to be hesitating as if in fear. They came on cautiously, drawing closer and closer; then they stopped, as if the person were listening. Sacajawea glanced around. The dog was still sleeping; the fire was low and did not give much light. The others seemed asleep. She got up quickly and squatted close to the fire, looking for a large piece of firewood to use in case she needed some protection. The steps were now approaching firmly. The next moment her man, Charbonneau, stood within the circle of the campfire's glow, looking at her silently, the partially empty cup of rum shaking unsteadily in his hand. His yellowed teeth flashed as he raised the cup to his lips.

Sacajawea whirled like a flash and caught hold of his arm; she grasped it firmly and gave it a violent twist. A howl of pain echoed through the camp.

"What are you doing?" cried Charbonneau in Minnetaree as she wrenched loose the cup with her other hand.

"That is medicine for my friend. Do not touch it." She spoke in broken English, looking so fiercely at him that he slunk off to his robes.

"That woman needs no help," whispered Clark, sitting up in his blankets. He yawned and lay back down. There was a gentle chuckle among the others.

"She spoke of the dog as her friend," said Lewis. "She actually spoke of Scannon as though he had a human soul. Lord, she sends a chill through me."

In the morning, Sacajawea was up, her eyes on the dog, whose breathing was shallow. She remained silent as the men prepared for the day. Tears hung in her eyes; her heart fell. She pushed a tin plate of water near the dog. His eyes opened, and he drank a little. Then his nose gently nudged her hand, which held two breakfast biscuits York had brought to her from the cooking fire. He ate one, then the other; then he lay back. He was panting, and she pushed more toward him. He whacked his tail against the ground.

"I am happy to see my friend once more. I have not forgotten how you ran through the tall weeds to chase a rabbit. You made my papoose laugh. I have not forgotten how you barked at a bear cub in a tree, or howled when York sang. You made us all laugh."

When Scannon fully recovered, Lewis knew he had to give Sacajawea some gift to show his appreciation of what she had done for his dog. He fetched out a silk handkerchief that was in the stores he had bought in

Saint Louis more than a year before. It was checkered
all over with bright colors, and the silk had a glossy
surface that set those colors off to great advantage.

To Sacajawea that silk handkerchief was a more than
satisfactory return for cleansing and massaging Scannon's painful paw, and noticing his weakness and hunger, and making him strong with her biscuits. The
intrinsic value of an article had no meaning in the mind
of Sacajawea. She cared only that her effort was appreciated, but the gift tickled her fancy.

Soon Scannon was distinguishing himself again by
his skill at catching wild geese and bringing them ashore
for the expedition's dinner.

One evening past the middle of May, when camp had
been made near the river named the Musselshell by
the Mandans, and clearly drawn on the Wolf Chief's
map, Pat Gass stood up after supper to announce that
there was a river, about fifty yards wide, that discharged itself into the Musselshell River about five miles
from its mouth. "I propose that the captains name it
Bird Woman's River after our Shoshoni woman. We can
make a note of it in our writing this evening."

"Hey, I thought you didn't like squaws!" yelled Bob
Frazier.

"Well, that is generally so, but this here one saved
old Scannon from blood poisoning, didn't she? And she
dug and brought us these here vegetables for supper.
They taste fine, like carrots. She ain't so bad. She ain't
complained once. Which is more than you can say for
some of us."

Sacajawea felt greatly honored, and her problem of
what to do for Pat Gass in return was solved a couple
of days later when Drouillard and Gass killed two Rocky
Mountain sheep. Sacajawea was wide-eyed when they
were brought into camp. Rocky Mountain sheep were
highly prized by the Shoshonis for their meat, skin, and
horns which bent backwards and were encircled with
a succession of wavy rings.

She fingered the horn of one animal, then with deft
hand signs told Pat Gass she would like a small section
of the horn. He laughed at her childish request and
chopped one side up for her. She grabbed two pieces
and ran down to the gravel bed by the mouth of the

river. There she spent several hours chipping and forming a small, semitranslucent bowl for Gass. She explained that her people made cups, small plates, and spoons from the big horns.

Gass was so taken with the gift that he showed the crude bowl to Clark.

"Say, Pat," said Clark, "I can imagine that our white women would like this elegant material made into hair combs."

"Sure," agreed Gass. "Even Janey"—which was their nickname for Sacajawea—"might like that. She combs her head with a pear thorn or her greased-up fingers."

Everything living responded to the increase in the warmth and length of the days. The deer, which were still plentiful, had changed to their reddish summer coats, and the does were accompanied everywhere by their fawns. Wood duck cruised with their fleets of ducklings on the small tributaries of muddy water that foamed on either side of the Missouri.

Several huge cedars had toppled because their roots were shallow in the marshlike soil. Large gaps of light, where the trees had once been, formed windows in the forest roof. Sacajawea could see the crossed branches of giant trees. It seemed like a battle of arm wrestling. The limbs pushed and pulled at one another under the influence of wind until one of them fell. Lewis, Drouillard and Sacajawea, with Pomp on her back, walked along the bank, enjoying the sunshine after the damp, foggy days. The air was filled with the smell of honeysuckle blossoms and the buzz of bees, mosquitoes, and metallic, blue-colored flies.

Lewis found an old moccasin under a large windfall. A tongue had been sewn in the front of the single piece of buckskin, which was cut square across the heel end and curved around the toe. A T-shaped cut had been made in the upper leather piece, with the stem of the T starting at the back. The tongue was attached to the cross of the T, and the two halves of the back of the moccasin were joined in a vertical seam. The cuff of the moccasin stood straight up. The rawhide sole was cut larger than the foot and sewn to the upper a little above ground level. "Here, does this belong to any people you know?" he asked Sacajawea, who walked a little way behind him.

She looked and turned it over, peering closely at the stitching and outline of the sole, then shook her head. "No, not Shoshoni—see, no heal drag, and shaped to fit left foot, not identical for both feet. Blackfoot moccasin." She pointed to the north, from which the Blackfeet came down on their horses ready for hunting or horse stealing, whichever came their way. She looked around and sniffed audibly.

Lewis thought to himself, There is something animallike about the manner in which she always looks and reports what is near. What is it she smells in the air now?

"The Blackfeet have gone for buffalo," she announced, looking upstream. "Not far from here."

"Enough walking," said Captain Lewis. "Let's get back in the pirogue. I do not want to surprise a troop of Blackfeet hunters."

Before long, everyone was aware of a horrible stench, and then the expedition passed by the remains of nearly a hundred mangled buffalo carcasses, which were lying at the bottom of a precipice of about a hundred and twenty feet.

Sacajawea, sitting near the dignified Captain Lewis, turned, pointed, and then indicated that she had smelled this earlier. "Blackfeet here."

"How did it happen, do you suppose?" asked Captain Lewis, restraining himself from holding his nose altogether.

Slowly, to make herself understood, Sacajawea described how the Blackfeet selected a fleet young man and disguised him in a robe of buffalo skin with the animal's head worn like a cap. All the mountain tribes did this, she explained. The man disguised as a buffalo would find a place between the herd and the precipice. The hunters would surround the herd and start them moving toward their companion and the cliff. The buffalo, seeing the disguised man, would think it was the lead animal and follow him right over the edge of the cliff. The decoy must be quick and agile to hide himself in a cranny in the cliff.

"The decoy is one of the bravest men," explained Sacajawea. "If he is not fast, the buffalo will crush him to death or drive him over the precipice, and he will be killed with them."

"Good Lord, what a way to hunt!" exclaimed Captain Lewis.

"My people sometimes get their winter meat supply this way," she said, "because they have no guns. Arrows do not kill enough in a short time. The women must work quickly, too, because it may take a week or more at a place like this, cutting and packing meat and returning to the winter village. Meat and robes must be taken before the wolves come. There is always a good feast at these places." She smiled broadly, her white teeth flashing in the sun.

"Primitive," replied Captain Lewis. "A shameful waste."

Mosquitoes appeared in the afternoon warmth on the river. Clouds of them rose from the edges of the water, whining, singing about the heads of the party. With every breath they inhaled them into their throats, and coughed and spat mosquitoes. The men on the cordelle ropes were sweaty; they splashed themselves with water and mud; some rubbed the mud on thickly to protect themselves from the mosquitoes. Sacajawea rubbed buffalo grease on herself and on the face and hands and arms of Pomp as protection. She offered her grease to the captains. Captain Clark was glad to use it profusely, even though the smell was strong and rank, and even Captain Lewis dubiously rubbed some on his arms.

A misty rain fell from low, gray clouds all afternoon. The vegetation grew thick along the river, but the animals seemed to have abandoned the ground for food and light up above. Cockroaches, crickets, centipedes, ants, and mice scurried along mossy tree limbs. The bald eagles soared high. Sacajawea saw ospreys, gulls, pelicans, and trumpeter swans. Huge limbs stretched out horizontally to interlock with crowns of neighboring trees. Honeysuckle vines wove among the trees, forming a green lace roof. Each plant fought for its share of sunlight under that roof; the sword fern grew as tall as a man. The ground near the water's edge was like a cave with a deep bed of springy leaf mold and dying bracken. The temperature stayed constant, as did the oppressing humidity.

Toward late afternoon one day, the fog lifted and clear sky appeared. Captain Clark stared at an extremely clear, sparkling river that emptied on the left of the Missouri, and his thoughts returned to his home in Virginia. He thought of his girl, Judy (Julia) Hancock, and he imagined he heard her clear, sparkling laughter. She was barely sixteen when he last saw her rosy face framed in soft brown curls.

"This is the Judith River," he said aloud, deciding the river must be named after her.

"What did you say, Chief Red Hair?" asked Sacajawea, who had followed Clark about two and a half miles up the shore of the river. He turned, scarlet. Sacajawea was looking into his face. He was confused for a moment, and then brought sharply back from the dream of the girl he would marry soon after the expedition returned to the States.

"A beautiful river. It should be named for a beautiful woman. See how it rushes proudly and defiantly—like a thoroughbred horse."

"*Ai*," she agreed. "The water is clear and pure like rivers in the mountains. No salt in them to upset your belly." She referred to the last couple of weeks on the Missouri when the water was saturated with mineral salts.

"I'm naming this river after a girl—about your same age. A winsome creature with laughing eyes."

"A paleface?" Sacajawea's heart beat unevenly against her ribs.

"Yes. She is called Judy."

"Judy? What does that mean?"

"It really means nothing—it's just a name," laughed Captain Clark. "Just as I call you Janey. It means nothing, just *you*."

Sacajawea was puzzled at the way white men had names. Her people were named for some deed or physical aspect or special happening. She drew in her breath. Chief Red Hair had a woman! She was called Judy. Then her logic told her: Why not? Her man, Charbonneau, had three women. Chief Four Bears had seven, and Chief Kakoakis had so many there was no counting them. She stood for a while without saying anything; she seemed like a squaw whose strength was giving out, trying to climb a steep hill. All at once she went closer to the bank and stood looking at the clear water. Captain Clark followed.

"She is your woman?" Sacajawea asked timidly.

"She is a friend, Janey. I have no woman."

Sacajawea looked at him. "That is true? You mean that?"

"Of course I mean it! Most of the men, except Charbonneau, are single. They have friends back home, but not women—which we call wives."

"So the white men are still boys?" To her this was an incredible thing. All men had a woman or two when they were grown. Underneath she had a feeling of joy that pushed the jealousy aside when she found that Chief Red Hair was single. She was afraid to examine this joyful feeling too closely.

"My dear Janey, have you worried about that?"

"*Ai*—among my people and the Minnetarees, the men take a woman before they are the age of your man that whistles, Shannon."

"There is nothing so unusual about this, except that my men have been too busy to look for a woman to keep them tied in one place."

Sacajawea gazed at Captain Clark. Slowly, her shyness receded. With a deep breath, she pulled her body straight. "So it is true that white men do not take their women from place to place as our men do?"

"Oh, that is true. But there comes a day when they settle with a woman whom they choose."

"Choose—what is that?"

"Well, our men find their own women—no one helps them much. Then there is a big celebration—like a big feast—called a wedding. Maybe I'll choose Judy to be my woman." Captain Clark was deeply moved that his feeling for Judy Hancock could be so strong out here in the prairie land so far from Virginia.

But his words stunned Sacajawea. She felt a hurt like a cruel blow. This feeling crushed her insides so that she could scarcely breathe. She had to get away to hide the feeling. Quickly she turned and left him;

then she began to run faster and faster, as a small,
vulnerable animal would run from danger.

Captain Clark gazed after her, slightly amused,
shaking his head. Whatever could have happened? Had
her keen ears heard something he had not? Indian
women acted strange at times. This one—so young, yet
so responsible and capable and, yes, intelligent—was
burdened with a baby and a loud, outspoken braggart
already. She might have been better off with some bright
brave, he thought, instead of Charbonneau with his
irritating arrogance. Captain Clark's heart was wrung
with pity and compassion for the little Shoshoni woman.
He looked once again at the beautiful Judith River and
slowly returned to the camp.

Sacajawea sat hidden among the weeds for a time.
She tried to consider her feelings and what to do about
them. First she tried to picture the white squaw, Judy,
spending much time walking by Chief Red Hair's side,
then sitting close against him in a pirogue. Could she
pick up the paddle and help spell him so that his arms
would not ache? Had she sewn moccasins for his feet
or rubbed them when they were sore and tired, noticing
how the tiny red hairs glinted in the firelight? Had she
taken care of his belongings and put up his tepee for
him? No—the white man's ways were different; she
already knew that from what Charbonneau had told
her. She sat up straight and shifted the cradleboard on
her shoulders. She could hear the baby making soft,
gurgling sounds. One day at a time she should live. So
now she would not think about something she knew
nothing about. Her thoughts moved more slowly and
in an orderly manner. Chief Red Hair and Chief Lewis
had allowed her man to take her on this long trail so
that she might see her own people. Now she could think
only of that. Surely the Great Spirit would not bring
her this far and then not let her complete the entire
journey. So she would look after Chief Red Hair and
the other white men. Beyond that she would not try to
imagine—it would be an alien village until she got
there. In the far corner of her mind a thought fluttered,
saying there was more to her life than being with these
white men, something even her intuition could not fore-

see. But it was too deep, and she calmed the flutterings
and would not think on it. She broke off the stems of
the purple fireweed. Here was something she could give
to Chief Red Hair to flatten and dry in one of his big
books.

16

Sacajawea's Illness

The most serious medical problem was Sacagawea, who had been taken ill at the mouth of Maria's River. Clark bled her on two successive days, the approved treatment at the time, though the wonder is it did not kill her. When she grew worse, he tried "a dose of salts," which did no good at all. Charbonneau, though he had been warned about her diet, foolishly allowed her to gorge on "white apples" and raw fish, after which she became alarmingly ill. Her pulse could hardly be felt; her arm and fingers twitched, she began to refuse medicine. Only Charbonneau could get her to take it, and even he could do so only when she was delirious. Without much hope, Clark tried cataplasms of bark and laudanum. "If she dies it will be the fault of her husband as I am now convinced," Clark wrote in his journal on June 16, 1805, gloomily, for he liked the little squaw.

On that same day Lewis wrote, "I believe that her disorder originated principally from an abstraction of the mensis in consequence of taking could."

Both captains knew that if Sacagawea died, the expedition would find itself left with a four-months-old baby, which would have to be carried across the continent and back with no available milk supply—a unique problem for a military expedition, which even Lewis had never foreseen.

Excerpt from pp. 212–13 in *Lewis and Clark: Partners in Discovery* by John Bakeless. Copyright 1947 by John Bakeless. By permission of William Morrow and Company.

On the third of June the expedition made camp on a point formed by the junction of two rivers of equal size. The north branch, which looked sluggish with a bed of mud and gravel, also looked as if it flowed a long way through flat plains. The south branch was clearer and swifter, with a bed of round, smooth stones, and it looked as if it flowed directly from the mountains not too far in the distance.

"The only sure way to settle this question is to make a more complete reconnaissance," said Captain Lewis, and after much debate the captains decided to separate, splitting the expedition. Sacajawea sat silent, listening, and making out some pieces of conversation. Soon she stood and waited to speak.

"White men talk and talk. Smell now," she said.

Captain Clark sniffed. "Well—I smell smoke from our fires," he said.

"The big falls are there," she said, pointing.

Captain Lewis saw her eyes look as if they knew what was in that direction. It is that animallike something about her, he thought. She seems to know when we have gone a proper distance and when to make a proper turning. Maybe, he thought, she has some instinct whites do not have—some sense of the sort that infallibly brings a dog home, no matter how winding the trackless course he follows. But Captain Lewis could not trust a woman, especially an Indian squaw, to guide his expedition in the correct direction. He had to make certain himself.

He took Sergeant Nat Pryor, George Drouillard, and four others up the North Fork. Captain Clark took Pat Gass, Ben York, and three others up the South Fork. The rest stayed in the base camp, tanning hide for shirts and trousers, mending moccasins with double-ply soles. The ground had been cut by buffalo hooves when wet, and the sun had baked it into sharp ridges, which, along with prickly-pear spines, cut into nearly all the tough leather they had used.

Sacajawea wanted to follow Captain Clark. She knew he was on the correct river. But she had taken cold during the days of drizzle and squally rain. She felt quite miserable. She did not tell the captains she felt ill; she was ashamed of showing any weakness. She would not tell Charbonneau, either. He would not know what to do for her. He would accuse her of giving the sniffles to him or his son. But by the time the men returned, she was feeling feverish.

Pierre Cruzatte argued with Captain Lewis, saying the North Fork was the river for the expedition to follow.

Captain Clark's party had gone forty miles up the South Fork, and found snow-covered mountains to the north and south—more evidence that the South Fork led directly to the Continental Divide. Captain Lewis's party had gone upstream sixty miles on the northern branch, which he named Maria's River, after his cousin in Albemarle, Maria Wood. He reckoned if Clark and Gass could name rivers for girls, he, Lewis, could do the same.

The captains were in complete agreement that the South Fork was the correct branch to follow, but Cruzatte stoutly maintained they ought to take the North Fork. He had great skill as a waterman, but he had no knowledge of topography. The other men, knowing nothing of the problems, agreed with Cruzatte. Suddenly Captain Lewis had an idea. He brought Sacajawea into the circle of men and asked Captain Clark to find the elk hide that the Wolf Chief had made for them. The hide pictured the Missouri dipping south of the sunset where there was a series of falls. "A creation of the Great Spirit, this river scolds all other rivers," the Wolf Chief had told Captain Clark.

The men crowded around the painted hide. "Now, where are those waterfalls?" asked Bill Bratton.

"Up the South Fork," replied Sacajawea, standing on the outside of the men's circle. "Long ago my relatives roamed around the falls. My people tell stories of them."

"Have you seen them?" asked Cruzatte skeptically.

"No, I never went there with my people," she said. "But the falls are there. Put your knife in the ground and put your ear on the handle."

"I can't hear a damn thing!" shouted Cruzatte. "I guess there are too many big feet tramping around."

"Smell," Sacajawea suggested, pointing her nose southward.[1]

Charbonneau laughed, pointing toward his woman. "She thinks she tell a bunch of men where to go! Ha! That squaw got some skeeters in her head buzzing around. That's what she hears."

Sacajawea felt fever in her body that evening, and she asked Charbonneau to feed Pomp. "I am worn out from nursing him."

Charbonneau looked at her. "I know that papoose, he is all mouth, but you are getting lazy. I don't know nothing how to feed the *enfant*. He is too little for me. Besides I got no titties."

She walked a short distance away and sat upon a bunch of soft grass, too weary to go farther. "Bring a bowl of thin soup from the cooking meat and a spoon. I will feed him."

"You not nurse him?" asked Charbonneau, not believing she would suggest feeding his son soup.

Her sickness had started in an ordinary enough manner. With the rain and dampness she had caught cold and the chills. Her body ached. Then out of contrariness she had eaten several clusters of wild red currants, even though the berries were barely colored. That night she had tossed under her robe, and by morning she had had abdominal cramps, which she had not admitted to until now with Charbonneau. She sat up and told him it was nothing but underripe currants.

"*Non*, it cannot be," he said. "Currants do not cause such cramping. I have ate them myself."

"What is it, then?" she asked, afraid of the griping that built up in her body as though it had turned on her.

"Charbonneau knows! You are with another *enfant!*" he exploded. "You let yourself be mauled by one of these men. Now I know—it is *le capitaine*. You are always gathering the flowers in the woods for that Red Hair. What else do you do in the brush? I, Charbonneau, am no fool! I can figure that one out. It is the nature of Indian women to lie in the brush, like a bitch."

"Oh, no!" she screamed. "You have a mind of scum

and think men and women do only one thing. It is not true. Go talk with Chief Red Hair." The pain became worse, and she doubled over. She cried, at first low and indistinctly; then her cry rose shrilly.

There was nothing Charbonneau could think of to do about her. He could move her farther toward the spring and away from the camp so that the men would not hear her cries. He did that, and she slept some until he woke her up and muttered fiercely about her self-ishness, callousness, cowardice, clutching her desper-ately so she would not leave him alone with a small child. He talked out of spite and hatred of her. It was hard for her to understand. There was nothing she wanted him to do except to see that the baby was taken care of.

"It is like a squaw to get a fellow in a spot. The men will tease me—Holy Mother, they will tease when she becomes large with another man's child. Damn fugging Indians!" He kicked at the grass she was sitting on, and she fell forward in a faint. When he pulled her up, he realized that her arm was unnaturally warm. He laid her out on the grass and tried to think. With the heel of his hand he pounded his shaggy head.

He looked over at the swamp grown up with reeds and red willows, then up at an eagle coasting alone over him. His eyes lowered to the cream-colored lilies clustered in the undergrowth like grass heads in a hay-field. He remembered seeing Sacajawea walking through the lilies to gather the wild currants and gooseberries, which were not ripe, and he also remembered her with an armful of wild roses. Their pink blossoms with large yellow stamens and sticky stems covered the hillsides. Captain Clark would gather his own roses! The sky got red and then dark. Charbonneau could see the campfire and hear the men joking and singing. He remembered something else. Chief Kakoakis had said something about getting rid of things early. What exactly had he said? Was it the beaver castoreum? Beaver castoreum was good for nearly everything else. Maybe that was it. It was worth a try. He got up.

"No use keeping on with this," he said. "I'm going for soup to feed the *enfant*." That was not honest, but he patted the sleeping squaw and left to find where his son was perched in the cradleboard. When he found him he said, "He is too large for that bed. My son grow big!"

Sacajawea stirred and awakened. She was ashamed of her weakness and wished desperately she had not eaten the berries. She began to wonder if she would die. People left alone and helpless have been known to drift on to the Land of the Shadows. She was afraid to fall asleep. Her head seemed hot and her mouth dry. Her throat hurt if she swallowed, and her bones ached.

Charbonneau was back with a leather pouch. "Dried beaver castoreum ought to work the trick," he said, taking out two or three round stones and pounding them on a flat rock.

"Where is Pomp? Did he get soup?"

"Oh, well, he is sleeping now. This is the important job."

"What is it for?" she asked, smelling the strong odor of beaver.

"Lie back, *ma chérie*. This is what your smart Charbonneau remembers from Kakoakis. He know many papooses not good for the squaw."

"I am not having a papoose. You know that. I do not talk with a split tongue. Take that smelly stuff away!"

"I will not be the laughingstock of these men. The men are jealous of Charbonneau already because I have a squaw and they do not. I don't boast about our sleeping arrangements. It was not I who violated the Indian custom of no cohabitation for one year after a birth. I did not tell you to refuse to keep my bed warm. They would find out you kept another warm. Spread your legs, damn you. Don't fight with your man!"

He sat on her legs to hold them apart.

The blood pumped audibly in her ears, and she closed her eyes.

He jabbed and pushed his long forefinger with a gob of beaver castoreum mixed with buffalo fat up, up as far as he could go. He held her. His fingernail cut into soft tissue.

She stifled her scream and tried to twist from his grasp. He placed his fat leg higher and jabbed once more, thrusting his finger up and down. She caught her breath and gave a loud sob.

·"Shut up. Charbonneau fix you. See, your man know where to poke, eh? I not forget. Tomorrow the blood, she rush out along with what is left of *l'enfant* that has now got hold of your insides. We knock him out!" He thumped on her belly, pummeled her to and fro, and Sacajawea gave up attempting to hold on to her courage. The fact that he was responsible for new pain seemed to release her from any obligation to stand it, and she turned on him, crying and accusing.

"You are a beast. You torture me. You leave your child uncared for. Take the child to York or to LePage. They will care for him." She sobbed and could not talk further.

Charbonneau got up, wiped his hands on his leggings, and slowly picked up the cradleboard. "*Mon petit*," he said to the sleeping child. "Your *maman* not make eyes at anyone but me. I fix her. Your *papa*, he's a smart one."

Sacajawea was engulfed in a stupor. She remained in the same position until the campfire was low. Then her senses slowly began to revive; she realized she was lying on the ground, that no one knew where she was except her man, and that Charbonneau had pushed the evil-smelling castoreum inside her.

In the night silence, she could hear the gurgling of the spring. It was difficult to move, but she was determined to clean herself. She started toward the spring, then looked back at the campfire on top of the hill; it began to swim, dip, and sway off center. Her legs trembled, and she hung on to a small juniper with clammy hands. She found her way to the water. It was cool. Slowly she removed her moccasins and put them to one side.

"No, better put them in my lap before I lose them." Next moment, she forgot all about them. She took off her tunic and laid it next to a stone. She was shaking violently from head to foot; she had to lean back against the damp earth.

She got up and squatted near the water, scrubbing all over with sand. She did not want any of the greasy beaver castoreum left on her. Something warm ran down the inside of one leg. She scrubbed. What had her man done? She was bleeding. Bright red blood streamed down

her leg. She felt weak and sat down. It was not time
for this ! Big beads of sweat stood on her forehead. She
pulled herself out of the cold water and felt her inner
heat. The outer cold made her head light. She fumbled
with her tunic; finally she had it over her shoulders
and fastened at the waist. She found her moccasins
floating near the bank of the spring and slipped into
them, pushing the water out with her feet. She swayed
toward the base of a willow.

"—Come on, Sacajawea, help me a bit. Put your head
forward—that's a girl. Can you make it up the hill?
Say something!"

She put her face down, crying silently; she had clasped
her hands together with a grip of iron, but soon she had
to break the grip to wipe the tears away. She lay thus
until the paroxysm had passed and she felt she could
master herself. The inner heat had solidified into a
strong pressure on the back of her neck.

"There's a warm fire up yonder. Capitaine Clark sent
me looking for you. *Sacre*, you can't stay here all night.
This is your friend, LePage. Big Tess said you were not
well and went for a walk. It's not like you to be so
foolish."

Whenever she tried to speak, her throat closed. When
she opened her eyes, she felt she was staring at the
ground miles below, between two sloping hills. Then
she saw that the hills were her legs, and her head was
being pushed between them. In the process, her middle
was doubled up. It felt as if somebody were squashing
it between two flat stones covered with the spines of
the prickly pear.

"Haaaiii!" she gasped, trying to straighten up, trying
to relieve the intolerable pressure inside her body. "Let
me up!" she whispered hoarsely.

The weight on her neck instantly lifted, and she
straightened her back. Crouched beside her, Baptiste
LePage looked anxiously into her face. The darkness
by the river made his hair seem to be hanging in long
strands from under a fur cap. She was sure he did not
wear a cap.

"You must have fainted!" he exclaimed in awe.
"Luckily I came looking along here. Whatever happened? Did Big Tess give you a drop too much rum? He

came into camp asking for a dram. Capitaine Clark gave it to him, believing it was for you. He said you had a chill."

Sitting up had done nothing to relieve the cramping agony inside her. She clasped her forearms over the pain and bit her lips. It was deep inside her belly, agonizing.

"You feel hot!" LePage cried. "Come on, you can't stay here in the night dampness."

Fright began to take hold of her again. She felt she had to tell him something. It was the first time for her bleeding after the child was born, and it was a great hemorrhage. Having him know that much made her feel able to stand it.

"Maybe in a few days, when all this clears up, you will be all right," comforted LePage. "I'll tell one of *les capitaines*. They know what to do for most every kind of bellyache." He knew not a thing about female problems, but he was aware the Indians viewed these things with no greater propriety than talking about how to fashion a new moccasin. They were not stuffy or Victorian in their explanations or discussions of sickness and sex.

"It's not far. On your feet. That's a good girl." Coaxing and hauling, he managed to get her upright. She clung to LePage and tried to keep her nails from digging into his arm. With the other hand she pressed her belly. It made the pain worse, but she kept hugging it, holding it. With LePage urging her, she put one foot ahead of the other and started to move. She talked herself into so much courage that the pain died down for a moment, and she relaxed her hold. Then it came again like a whiplash.

Without protest she sat by the fire drinking cup after cup of strong willow-bark tea.

"She fainted," explained LePage to Captain Lewis; then quietly he told him about the loss of blood she was suffering. "Someone ought to get packings of cattail fluff for her."

When Sacajawea found it impossible to swallow another drop of the hot tea, she insisted she felt fine and went to the skin tent to lie down. She rummaged through the leather boxes until she found the down she had collected for Pomp's cradleboard. She packed herself as another spasm came and went. Never would she tell these men the truth of what her man had done. A recurring cramp forced her to sit. The world began to drift again, but she remembered and got her head down quickly. With her cheek resting on the ground, things came back into focus almost at once. She was learning to fool the dizziness. She pulled herself to her buffalo robe and found Pomp sound asleep there. The effort of getting out of her tunic and moccasins muddled her; she was not sure any longer where she was—she seemed to know only that she had to get under the robe and hold her baby safe.

Captain Clark came inside and gently raised her hand and felt her pulse. She seemed weak, and there was no color in her lips. He consulted with Captain Lewis and came back with a dose of salts. She took the bitter medicine and hardly realized what she had done. He tucked a woolen blanket around her, saying if she would only take a good sweat, this cold would soon pass off. Sacajawea obeyed like a docile child while he took a rag, dipped it in lukewarm water, and wiped her face.

"In the morning I may decide to bleed you before we load the canoes." He patted her head. "This is just a cold. Captain Lewis is getting over the same thing. Nothing to be ashamed of. Here, let me take Pomp to York for the night. You get some rest. York loves kids." Captain Clark gently took the baby and called for Ben York.

"Yes, sir," said York, looking down at Sacajawea. "That there child look peaked all right."

"Take care of the baby. See that he has some warm soup if he wakens, and do not bother his mother."

York looked again at Sacajawea. "I knew it was a-coming. You gonna make a mammy out of me."

"It's fine practice," Clark said, smiling. "You might have to do this sometime to your own young'uns. Might as well start now."

"Aw, Master Clark, sir," York said, thinking of his Kentucky sweetheart, "Cindy Lou sure does want a passel of children, that's the truth." He lifted the fat papoose out of Clark's arms, found a blanket from his bed to wrap around him, and hung the four-month-old boy over his shoulder like a sack of flour.

"Come on, Pomp, you got to listen to them songs around the fire tonight."

Sacajawea was asleep. Captain Clark felt her pulse again and heaved a sigh of relief. It was fuller and more regular.

In the morning Cruzatte took half a dozen men to a dry place on high ground and showed them how to make a cache. They cut the heavy prairie sod from a twenty-inch circle and laid it aside, then dug down to enlarge the hole underneath. The earth they removed was carried to the river and dumped in, so that there would be nothing to give wandering Indians any hint that anything might be buried nearby. When the excavation was six feet deep, the bottom was hollowed out to receive any water that might seep in, and dry sticks were used to keep the contents from touching the moist earth. When the hole was nearly filled with the things they were to leave behind—Captain Lewis's writing desk, the forge, tools, reserve rations, salt, ammunition, tin cups, steel traps, skins, and specimens—the cache was covered with leather hides, and earth rammed in between this covering and the surface. A few days after the original twenty-inch circle of sod had been replaced, the grass had grown enough to conceal the hiding place completely. This was an Indian scheme.

The captains decided at this time to get rid of the red pirogue that Lewis and six others had been paddling upstream. They hauled it to the middle of a small island in the North Fork and tied it with leather strips, face down, with bungs out but tucked safely inside, to several low-growing juniper bushes. The bushes completely hid the pirogue, which lay snugly on the ground. The men made deep, jagged cuts in four nearby trees to mark the place where the pirogue was hidden in order to find it easily on their return trip. Also, wandering Indians would not touch anything that had been marked in such a manner.

Sacajawea slept that entire day, but during the night she woke bent over with cramps. Captain Clark gave her a dose of opium in hot water to reduce the cramps and put her back to sleep. In the morning, when she seemed no better, he bled her with his penknife, which he sterilized over an alcohol flame. She wanted to tell him that she was already bleeding profusely, but she could not find the words. He also gave her a full cup of mineral water laced with opium to drink.

"York has your man, Charbonneau, out looking for cattails for your son's cradleboard," he said, trying to reassure her that the child was well taken care of.

The following morning Captain Lewis, who had developed a cold and was feeling weak, with aching joints, took Scannon, George Gibson, the Fields brothers, Si Goodrich, and Drouillard up the South Fork to study the river and look for signs of Indians in that region. The others were to follow the next morning if Sacajawea was able to travel.

Captain Lewis's party had not gone far when he realized he was really ill. By midday he had violent intestinal cramps, and as the pain increased, so did his temperature. "You and the little squaw have the same bugs eatin' on your innards," explained Gibson.

"Take the leaves off the chokecherry twigs there and boil the twigs in a little water. We'll pull the canoes in here," Captain Lewis ordered, then twisted about as another spasm of pain hit his middle.

The bitter black concoction puckered his mouth, but he drank a pint and in an hour repeated the dose.

"I wouldn't take any more," suggested Gibson. "Your teeth might dissolve."

By that evening Captain Lewis was free of pain and fever. He had a good night's rest and was ready to start out in the morning, quite revived. He recalled his mother, Lucy's saying that an ounce of prevention is worth a pound of cure, and so he drank another pint of the vile astringent liquid. At noon he was able to eat several perch that Goodrich had caught.

Sacajawea insisted that she was well enough to travel, but she was fretful in the bottom of the pirogue, and she seemed delirious at times. Captain Clark tried to make her comfortable, and regretted he knew so little about relieving her ailment.

Charbonneau sat at the back of the pirogue, not looking at his woman, wishing she would not create so much attention, and praying to the Holy Mother that his "medicine" had caused her to abort, if by chance she were pregnant. He had asked permission to take her back to the Minnetarees and their Medicine Man, but Clark had refused. Charbonneau could not have managed the trip by himself, and there were no men to spare.

York held Pomp propped between his knees as he sat at the bow and paddled.

"You are a sweet-looking mother," Charbonneau kidded him clumsily.

"Well, I don't hear you asking to bounce your son on your knee." York scowled. "Besides, if you did, I wouldn't say yes. This here child is too much fun. I'se going to teach him to fish and shoot himself a bear."

"I'd like to teach him to read and write," added Captain Clark.

For days the canoes made their way slowly upstream on the South Fork of the river. Sacajawea was hardly aware of their progress, conscious only that Captain Clark tended to her needs and plied her with medicines. These days were hard on the men, who kept a sharp eye out for grizzlies, which were more and more numerous. The men with the tow ropes tried to keep the canoes from shipping too much water and their feet were cut and bruised on the sharp stones and spines of the prickly pears. They slipped in the rattlesnake-infested mud trying to pull the canoes past sawyers, dead trees bobbing underwater. To make matters worse, several others fell ill with the intestinal cramps, two men had toothaches, two had large boils, and another had a carbuncle plus a slight fever. Private Whitehouse had the cramps, too, but he kept quiet about them, only writing about his griping pains in his journal when the expedition camped for the night.

One morning Sacajawea was well enough to walk to the spring beside which they had camped. She gave thanks to the Great Spirit for showing Chief Red Hair the medicines to bring her health back. Soon she was examining the pink moccasin flowers, and then her eyes found the wild crabapples in most of the trees around her. She tasted one, then another. Their tartness was good. Charbonneau sauntered to the spring and gath-

ered a few apples, telling her that if they tasted good
they certainly wouldn't hurt her.

"Hey, don't let Janey eat too many of those green
apples," warned Captain Clark.

Still hungry, she went to Ben York and asked if he
had some perch left in the pan from the morning meal.
York was so delighted to see her up and feeling better
that he gave her several raw fish and pointed to the
frying pan. Then he chided Charbonneau, who snatched
the pan away, saying, "Squaws like raw fish best. Just
look how she gulps them fish down."

"You should take better care of your missus. Raw
fish don't seem like fitting food to me."

When the party turned in for the night, Sacajawea
awoke moaning with pain. Her fingers were clammy,
and her stomach ached. She refused all medication, not
wishing to cause more trouble, but became delirious.
Captain Clark continued to nurse her, for Charbonneau
had turned surly and refused to tend to her. When she
seemed hardly able to breathe at all, Captain Clark
cried out to Charbonneau.

"If she dies, it will be your fault, Charbonneau. You
don't take good care of her, you lily-livered coward. I
admit once in a while I was amused by your bragging,
but now I am fed up—up to here." He put his hand on
top of his head.

Ben York calmed his master down, knowing that he
was worn out from nursing the little squaw. York knew
also that if Sacajawea died he would have the four-
month-old child to carry across the continent and back,
spoon-feeding him with soup and gruel the best he could
manage. "I guess we'd better use God and pray for this
squaw," he said.

And then, on the evening of June 14, Joe Fields came
with a note from Captain Lewis, who was proceeding
slowly up the river, to say that the forward base camp
was only ten miles from the falls that Sacajawea had
told them about. They would be in Shoshoni country
any day now.

Captain Clark was more than happy. The news would
perk up Sacajawea, and he had dreaded retracing his
steps if they were on the wrong river branch. Clark
went to see Sacajawea, who was bedded down in a lean-

to made with the skin tent. She was much worse and looked like skin and bones. Captain Clark sat on the ground beside her. "You must get well now," he said.

"I am sorry to be trouble."

"No, no, we are sorry we cannot help you. All the men depend on you. We need you. We are coming to your people's land. Your son needs you. And your man needs you. Without you he is nothing."

My people, she thought. My people are near. We have reached the River That Scolds at All Rivers. Her eyes filled with tears.

"There, don't get upset," soothed Captain Clark. "Rest and get well." York was squatting near the entrance.

"Watch over her," said Captain Clark to York. "I'm going to send someone to bring some water from the sulfur spring we passed about six or eight miles back. I should have thought of it then."

Several of the men volunteered, but Shannon was the one who took a pail and hurried off. When he returned, Captain Clark forced Sacajawea to drink almost a pint of the foul-smelling sulfur water, and then gave her a mixture of quinine, opium, and oil of vitriol. He spent the night nearby, with a great deal of anxiety, as she slept.

By morning she was perspiring, and her pulse was fuller and more regular. The crisis had passed.

Cloudburst

Clark's Journal:

June 29th Satturday 1805

...the rain fell like one voley of water falling from the heavens and gave us time only to get out of the way of a torrent of water which was Poreing down the hill in the River with emence force tareing everything before it takeing with it large rocks and mud, I took my gun and shot pouch in my left hand, and with the right scrambled up the hill pushing the Interpreters wife (who had a child in her arms) before me, the Interpreter himself makeing attempts to pull up his wife by the hand much scared and nearly without motion, we at length reached the top of the hill safe where I found my servent in serch of us greatly agitated, for our wellfar, before I got out of the bottom of the reveen which was a flat dry rock when I entered it, the water was up to my waste and wet my watch, I scercely got out before it raised 10 feet deep with a torrent which [was] turrouble to behold, and by the time I reached the top of the hill, at least 15 feet water ...

BERNARD DEVOTO, ed., *The Journals of Lewis and Clark.* New York: Houghton Mifflin Co., 1953, p. 152.

When the expedition reached the falls, they were faced with the unhappy prospect of an eighteen-mile portage. A hole for another cache was dug, and the white pirogue was hauled to the bank, the bungs removed, and the whole thing covered with leaves and branches after being tied to trees in the same manner as the larger red pirogue they had already hidden. The other canoes were brought as close to the falls as possible, to shorten the portage.

Eighteen miles around the falls was a long way to carry supplies, with the sultry wind and no trees to give shelter or firewood for cooking. But there would be plenty to eat. Thousands of buffalo, in one herd, went down to the falls to drink as Captain Clark watched. Elk, deer, and antelope roamed about, and there were rainbow trout, pike, cutthroats, bluebacks, and chub, all easy to catch from the river.

A base camp was set up at a place they called Portage Creek, and Sacajawea stayed there with Captain Clark, Charbonneau, York, Goodrich, and Ordway, so that she might benefit from the nearby sulfur spring. The portage began on June 20, 1805, the day Sacajawea was really on her feet once again.

It took thirteen days for the expedition to transport itself from the camp on Portage Creek. Each day meant hardship. Sacajawea spent time repairing moccasins, which were constantly torn by rocks and prickly pears, and wondering how other men, coming after these, could possibly find her people for trade. Three moons had already passed since they had left Fort Mandan, and still the expedition was not in the land of the Shoshonis. They had seen only deserted campfires and scattered, abandoned tepee frames, all belonging to the Blackfeet. Captain Clark had said there would be trading posts for her people. How?

And then came the day Sacajawea had waited for. With Captain Clark and the rest of the men who had manned the base camp, she paced off the final miles that would lead her to the boundary of the land of the Shoshonis.

The rush and roar of the falls became louder, the mist of the spray heavier, until at last they stood still, enchanted by the sight of the cascade eighty-seven feet high, fully two hundred feet across, forming a sheet of white beaten foam, hissing, flashing, sparkling. They watched, fascinated, as the water dashed against a huge abutment of rock, then rose again in great billows and vanished. The Great Falls of the Missouri was a gigantic wildlife rendezvous. Thousands of impatient buffaloes pushed each other along the steep, rocky paths to the water. Hundreds went over the cataract to feed the buzzards and wolves below.

Sacajawea raised her eyes in search of the eagle's nest that her people spoke about, built high beyond reach of any man or beast. Then she noticed the ominous black sky. A storm from the west would soon be upon them. She touched Chief Red Hair's hand and pointed. "When the rain comes, this will be a bad place."

Surprised, he gave a quick start, then said reassuringly, "Well, we are prepared. I have brought along the tomahawk with the umbrella attached to the top, a present from my brother when I started on this trip. I thought it was funny, but it may well come in handy."

He shifted the rest of his load so that he could put up the umbrella. Sacajawea laughed at such a funny contraption, like a huge leaf to keep the rain off one's head.

"We've got to find shelter," said Captain Clark. It was getting black-dark now, and the wind was gusting. He looked in both directions and then pointed. "The rocks in that deep ravine—they'll give some protection. We'd better run for it." A bunch of sagebrush ripped away from a dying clump and came sailing over their heads with a great *swoosh!*

"My feet hurt," complained Charbonneau.

A chain of lightning dissolved with a teeth-rattling, ear-splitting crash.

Captain Clark pulled Pomp's cradleboard from Sacajawea and tucked the child and board under his arm. He gave Sacajawea the umbrella to carry. The other things he carried over his shoulder in a leather sack.

Charbonneau, carrying nothing but his gun, sprinted

toward the ravine. Captain Clark and Sacajawea followed.

The wind became fierce; the lightning flashed; the rain was coming. The ravine would be a dangerous place to be in case of a flash flood, but there was no other shelter. Captain Clark jumped toward the shelving rocks just ahead and felt the first big drops of rain strike his face. Charbonneau clambered up the rocks. Sacajawea stumbled, almost fell. Captain Clark gave her the leather sack and pulled her along. They passed Charbonneau.

"If I'd my eyes on the outside of my head, I'd never have come down into this rat trap!" Charbonneau yelled through the wind. Then he called for them to wait so he could catch his damned breath. But they went on, stumbling and gasping, the wind rising and whipping away their breath.

They reached the projecting rocks and leaned, breathless, against the side walls. Sacajawea sniffed the air. It was still warm, but there was a new smell to it. "*Ai*—the rain will be hard."

Her mind was easier standing on this safe ledge, but her body was tired.

"Blow like *le diable*," said Charbonneau, climbing up to them, gasping. "I never like the plains now with no trees to hide under."

"Right!" agreed Captain Clark, putting down the cradleboard and unlacing it enough to remove the baby. He sighed, "That cradleboard is heavy."

"So—it is packed with Pomp's clothes," said Sacajawea, putting down the leather sack and umbrella.

"Caw! No wonder he has outgrown the board. There is no place to put his feet!" screamed Charbonneau.

Then nobody spoke, and the darkness crashed down with the thunder. The blackness covered them. During a flash of lightning Sacajawea saw Charbonneau's eyes contract and a shadow of terror cross his face.

The gusts of wind came in increasing frequency and from every direction. Some passed overhead with a whooping rush and scattered gravel. Some pelted their backs with the gravel and tore the sand from under their feet and threw it into their faces.

"If the wind does not come out of the west, we are safe," said Sacajawea.

"What was that?" asked Charbonneau. And as the message was passed on, some of the words were high and clear in a moment of silence, some were strained and distorted through a rush of wind, and the final words were blanked out entirely by thunder and the rolling echoes that came after.

Captain Clark had opened up the umbrella to keep the rain off the baby. "The men on the plains will get soaked along with the equipment. No help for that, though."

Charbonneau complained that the blinding flashes and sudden blackouts hurt his eyes.

The color of the clouds had changed from ashen to a sickly yellow, full of wind and hail. The lightning flashed blue, and then the wind came out of the west, very suddenly and with devastating force, bringing rain mixed with sand and snatching the umbrella from Captain Clark's hand, sending it sailing around like a bull boat floating in the muddy Missouri.

Then a fine mist, sucked into a partial vacuum under a curtain of wind-driven rain, felt like an early-morning mountain fog on Sacajawea's face. It was cold. She thought, this should feel good after such a hot morning, but it is too cold.

Captain Clark screamed with the wind, "It's a cloudburst for sure!" The rain shot directly off the top of the rocks in a hissing sheet, carrying loose gravel whistling over their heads to strike the opposite side of the ravine with such force as to dump a flood of mud and rock into the churning water that was already filling the wash below.

"Lie down so we won't get blown off when the wind changes!" shouted Charbonneau. He lay down. He had a gnawing, sickening, uneasy feeling. At the next bright flash he looked over into the wash where they had stood only minutes before. The stream, boiling along twenty feet below, was undercutting the bank.

Sacajawea moved closer to Captain Clark, and his arm tightened on Pomp, who kicked his bare feet. Clark put his free arm protectively around her waist and drew her closer, unaware of the danger they were in.

Another rat's hole, thought Charbonneau, I got to tell the captain. He bent forward, dragging his flintlock; he had gone hardly ten feet when the wind changed and drove the full, suffocating force of the rain right into his face. A vivid flash of lightning showed a boulder half the size of a flour barrel set in the bank four or five feet above him. Slowly he climbed up to it, realizing that he was badly spent. He slid his body over onto the rock and found it was still warm from the blazing sun and he felt amazingly comfortable.

The beginning of terror came during a lull in the wind when Sacajawea heard the rumbling below them. She pulled away to look, and saw a wall of water come thundering down the hill, tearing away huge rocks and mud and sweeping everything before it. She pointed to the raging torrent coming straight toward them.

"Good God!" shouted Clark. "Let's get out of here!" He grabbed for his gun and pouch and reached for Sacajawea. She was kneeling behind a large stone. Pomp began to cry. When the next roll of thunder died away, the captain heard Sacajawea singing, her words rising over the rush of wind and the wash of rain. She was singing about the First Times and the Big Flood. It was a death song. The tone and cadence carried her mood, a strange, discordant jumble of sound that beat against the roar of water and the wail of wind, pulsating as did the lightning with the crash and fall of the thunder. She was throwing away her dream because the trail had caved in above and below. Death was near, and there was no use fighting against it.

"Up this way—up the bluff!" yelled Clark. Sacajawea looked up and saw Charbonneau clinging like a bear to the rock; she felt Clark's tug as he pulled her; she heard the baby crying as Clark hitched him up more tightly under his arm. She was dragged by her hand upward to the safety of that huge rock. She fought her fear and tried to force the Shoshoni fatalism into the back of her mind whence her terror came. The wind lashed her hair about her streaming face.

Charbonneau, thinking about the Minnetarees and his young Otter Woman, and the dry, warm Dakota plains where he had lived in ease and plenty, was jerked back to the present by Clark's yelling. "Charbonneau, you fool, take the baby! Here! Help your squaw now! Pull her up! Come on, man!"

He knelt over the ledge and slowly put his trembling hand over the edge. He pulled the screaming, flailing baby up, hanging on to one arm.

Sacajawea waited for his hand. There was nothing more from above.

"Come on! Reach down again, you heathen!" Captain Clark called. Finally a weak, shaky hand extended over the rock. But Sacajawea found no more help from it than from a dead branch. She could not get to the top.

"Pull! Charbonneau, pull! Up, up!" yelled Clark. "Dammit, man, what's the matter with you? I'll wring your neck if you don't extend a hand!" Then, pulling himself up with every inch of his six feet, Clark shoved Sacajawea until she was able to grasp a projecting root and climb over the rock.

For a moment she rested, trembling from exertion and fright. Then she looked over the edge to help Chief Red Hair. She put her hand down and gasped, horrified. He was scrambling for a foothold as the river of mud and stone surged down upon him. She shrieked a warning. "Quick!" Terror-stricken, she watched as he lost his foothold and missed her outstretched hand.

Unconsciously, Sacajawea keened the death cry; final and horrible, it was a natural thing. Hearing her, Charbonneau began to scream with the baby. Sacajawea stopped and stared at her man. Her fear was forced out and brushed aside by a torrent of words that came out and raced screaming toward her cowardly man. "You cry like a pregnant woman, while Chief Red Hair gives up his life for us!"

She leaned over again, expecting to see Chief Red Hair's body being swirled away with the tremendous current. She gave a shriek. He had gained a foothold; he had a chance. The water was closing in; he must not slip. "Slow, come now," she called softly, placing her body flat on the rock ledge, her words swept away by the gusts of wind. Carefully, step by step, Clark secured himself, the race with the torrent more and more difficult. He felt the water surge in around him, deeper and deeper. It came past his feet and legs. The water streamed down his face, blinding him. He pulled up one step and then another, feeling with his feet for a tiny foothold. He felt the water swirl about his waist, pulling at him. He looked up. It was only a few more feet to the small brown hand outstretched strong and firm toward him. Could he make it? Another step up. Still another. "Come, come to me," she called.

Gratefully he took her hand, and with a final tug and gigantic effort he was up and safe. Over all the other noise he heard his own voice cry, "Oh, my God! Thanks! Janey, thanks! I'll do something fine for you! I thought I was a goner!" And the wind died then, as though it had never been.

For a few moments all of them sat huddled together, dazed, trembling, soaked to the skin. Finally Clark stirred. Below, where he had stood only moments ago, there was nothing but water—almost fifteen feet of water. "Thanks, Janey!" he mumbled again.

"Let's get out of here," said Charbonneau. He needed no pushing—on he went, up to the top, leaving Sacajawea with the baby in her lap, and Captain Clark.

No one spoke for some time. Then Sacajawea said, "I'm hungry." She patted her stomach and took off the pouch that hung around her waist. It contained her traveler's rations. She counted each grain of corn and each pumpkin seed and gave exactly half of them to Chief Red Hair. They chewed excessively, as though those kernels were the last food in the world.

Sacajawea smiled at Captain Clark. "Once I hit my finger with a grinding stone. It hurt terrible. The storm was like that. Then, when my finger quit hurting, it felt awfully good and warm all at once. I feel all over like my finger felt then."

Captain Clark smiled and tugged at her arm, at the same time boosting the baby up to his shoulder. "That was not the place to be during a thunderstorm—not down there!" He looked cautiously over the edge once more. "We have some traveling to do. Come."

At the top of the bluff they walked through the new, clean, wonderful world, with all the dust washed away and each gravel pebble bright with its own true color— as bright as the vermilion paint, yellow clay, purple sandstone, and red-brown of the distant mountains—

but Sacajawea saw none of it. Her mind was working
on a puzzle.

Why had Chief Red Hair risked his life to save hers—
the life of a squaw, another man's woman? And the life
of her child? The child had no usefulness yet. Her man
would have let her and the child drown to save his own
life. The life of a grown man was more important. A
man is the hunter, the warrior, the protector; his life
is valuable. Why was it that Chief Red Hair valued all
life, even the lowliest—from that of the helpless papoose to the keening squaw?

Sacajawea looked up at Chief Red Hair, and his eyes
met hers. For a brief moment their walking stopped.
The baby gurgled and smiled. Slowly Clark put his free
arm about her waist and drew her to him; and then, to
Sacajawea's amazement and delight, he kissed her
lightly on the tip of her nose, letting her go quickly.

Never before had she experienced such a thing. Her
heart patted against her tunic so that she was afraid
he would hear it. She felt the glow of happiness. She
remembered this moment a million times over in her
long life.

After a while her voice came back and she was able
to say with much shyness, "I have great feelings for
you. You gave me back my life, my dream."

"Oh, my dear Janey," said Clark huskily, "you are
so tiny, so young, and you've this boy to care for. I did
what any self-respecting man would do."

"Any man?" she asked. "Not my man."

"Well, Charbonneau is not quite like any man," said
Captain Clark carefully. "You see, he has lived with
the Minnetarees so long that he is not sure what he is.
When we get to your people," he went on, trying desperately to change the subject, "you'll be the most valuable person in this whole outfit."

The warm glow inside her grew in spite of her shivering and her feeling of being dog-tired. She stood by
herself soaking up the sunshine and watching Captain
Clark trot with her son across the buffalo grass to meet
York, who was grinning and swinging his arms in welcome.

"Lordy, what a soaking storm that there one was!
Yes, sir, I'se fairly wet through. And you two look no

better than a couple of drowned rats. You nursemaiding for now, Master Clark?" York grinned at the sleeping infant on his shoulder. "I sent Charbonneau high-tailing it back to camp to get a pot of tea boiling. And if he uses his head, he'll start up a hot stew."

They walked into camp shivering in their wet clothing. York took the baby, who was now whimpering from hunger and cold, and wrapped him in one of his old woolen shirts. Then he fed him some pot liquor from the buffalo stew simmering.

Charbonneau had lost his flintlock. The baby had lost his cradleboard and the clothing in the bottom. Captain Clark had lost his compass, the only large one the expedition had, his umbrella, his rifle, shot pouch, powder horn, and extra moccasins, but he was alive, and he knew what was needed to restore their spirits and give them warmth. He gave each of the men a dram of rum, then passed the tin cup to Sacajawea. She gulped her portion of rum and felt the warmth spread through her body.

A bobwhite called until another answered, then through the breeze came the sound of Cruzatte's violin, and suddenly everyone had tales to tell of the hail and rain they had experienced during the sudden storm. Many were battered and bruised from the large hailstones, but none had found themselves in such a bad spot as the ravine Captain Clark and his party had climbed out of.[1]

Next day, a search party found the all-important compass and fished it out of thick red mud. None of the other lost items was ever found. The ravine was filled with rocks, washed down by the flood of water, each one large enough to have crushed Clark's whole party to death.

CHAPTER
18

Tab-ba-bone

Drouillard came to a stop. So did the Indian. In fact, the Indian turned his horse as if to wait for them, casting his eyes from Drouillard to the captain and then to Shields, who, however, on his part, was continuing to advance as before.

The captain, too, kept striding forward. He held high the trinkets for the Indian to see. He stripped his shirt sleeve to show the color of his skin. He called, at the top of his lungs the ringing words, "Tab-ba-bone! Tab-ba-bone! White man! White man!" Proceeding in this manner he was able to get, finally, to within one hundred paces of the Indian, when the latter gave whip to his horse, and disappeared behind some willows on the other side of the creek.

Reprinted by permission of the publishers, The Arthur H. Clark Company, from *George Drouillard* by M. O. Skarsten, 1964, p. 101.

On Monday, July 15, 1805, the canoes were launched above the Great Falls. Captain Clark followed by land along an old native trail. The contour of the country changed from level plains to hills and hummocks, and great rocks jutted from the earth. In some places cliffs rose from the water's edge to over twelve hundred feet.

Captain Lewis was enthusiastic about the sights. "Never have I seen such a magnificent masterpiece of nature!" he exclaimed. He looked up at the canyon walls—vast columns of rock, beautiful overlapping precipices, clear gushing springs. He took a deep breath of the clear fresh air. "This will be called 'the Gates of the Mountains.' The entrance to the Rocky Mountains. I can almost see the sun glitter on the snow way up yonder."

Sacajawea could not take her eyes off the mountains that lay ahead with their tops covered white as though clouds rested there during all the seasons. Unexpectedly she pointed to the southwest and cried, "My people! My people! Smoke in the hills!"

Captain Clark saw the smoke signals, clear evidence that natives had detected their approach and were spreading the news. Suspecting that they might get behind him and follow on his trail, Clark left bits of clothing, strips of paper and trinkets at intervals, with signs indicating that his party were white men and friends. York helped Clark make a lop stick, a common trail sign. A tall tree was found and its branches lopped off so it created an unusual mark in the landscape. This was used as a portage sign or sign that the main trail was here. Sacajawea showed York how to make designs in the earth with a sharp stick to indicate that they were friendly. They tied the grass in three bunches to indicate that their trail went "this way."

The party traveling overland found the going so rough that they decided to stop by the shoreline until Captain Lewis and the canoes appeared, and for the next few days they proceeded by water, watching for signs of the Shoshonis, killing game for food, and tending to blis-

tered feet. But none of the men had eyes as sharp as
Sacajawea's.

Coming upstream in Captain Lewis's canoe, with
Pomp sitting in her lap and waving his chubby arms,
Sacajawea suddenly pulled at York's shirt. "Look!" she
said. Long before he spotted them, she had pointed to
several deserted brush wickiups and traces of old fires.
She read him their story. "They were hungry and moved
to find more game. They followed deer." She pointed to
the small cloven hoof tracks and told him a deer could
easily be followed in the tall grass because it has a scent
gland between its hooves and a larger gland on each
hind leg that exudes a strong odor as the animal wanders through the brush.

She laughed like a carefree child, pointing to the
bank where the rock was red, a source of vermilion for
the People. Suddenly she was aware that she must not
make a spectacle of herself before these men, especially
Captain Lewis, who remained dignified and aloof much
of the time. She did not want him to see her letting go
and acting like a small child. Surely he would frown;
after all, she was grown and had a child of her own.
And so, she thought, what will the People say about
this beautiful fat baby? Will they nod their approval?
Will the old women click their teeth and smile, stretching out their arms to hold him?

Lewis put his hand on his mouth, indicating no more
talk for a time. The canoes were facing a rapid current
and everyone had to be at full attention. The oars were
useless. The men poled and the poles would not grip
the smooth, flat stones of the river bottom. Captain
Lewis, however, rose to the situation and put fishing
gigs on the ends of the poles. The gigs gripped the bottom or wedged between rocks much better.

"Hey, hey! Capitaine, sir, you push a tolerable good
pole there!" called LePage to Captain Lewis, who was
poling his canoe himself. Captain Lewis nodded, knowing that if he let go even with one hand to wave at the
canoe opposite him, his pole might slip.

During the long afternoon Sacajawea watched the
overhanging, gray granite walls pass by the canoes. She
nursed her baby and hummed softly, but her eyes were
on the passing shoreline. The walls she remembered as

if it were yesterday when she was captured by the Minnetarees. She could almost feel the terror she had felt then; her hands tightened on her child. A constriction in her chest made it hard to breathe. She looked at the tops of the hills, anticipating an enemy riding there bedecked in hunting paints and feathers. Her outer countenance showed nothing. She hated this spot. Right here it was that she and Willow Bud had been tied to the horses.

Toward sundown her tension eased, and she told the men the story of her capture. "Tell that again," urged Captain Lewis. "I'd like to keep that spot in our permanent records. I'll write your story in my journal when we are in tonight's camp."

"My story? In your marking-book?" she asked, unbelieving. "A woman cannot be important enough to go down in those tiny markings. In that book the men mark about trees, flowers, birds, rocks, wind, and rain, but no marks about the babblings of a woman."

"Yes, of course," said Captain Lewis, "everyone on this trail is important."

This was nearly incomprehensible to her, but she shrugged and told her story again.

Watching her, Captain Lewis thought she showed absolutely no emotion or sorrow in recollecting the event of her capture. He also thought she showed no joy in being restored to her native country. But Lewis had not listened closely to her words, nor had he watched her hands. Lewis, philosophic, introspective, and moody, did not share the fondness and interest in Sacajawea and her baby that Clark showed. Yet he was disturbed by this girl. Once when Clark had remarked, "She's a good soldier," Lewis had said, "Yes, a pity she's redskinned."

The men camped at the Three Forks of the Missouri to refresh themselves for a few days. The men who had gone overland were suffering from badly cut feet, the result of the yellow prickly pear, which was beautiful and in full bloom, but a great annoyance, and the men who had poled the canoes were exhausted from the strenuous work. Lewis and Clark were excited by the prospects of a trading post at the spot.

"See," said Lewis, "the rushes in the bottom, high as a man's chest and thick as wheat. This would be a perfect winter-pasture for cows and horses. And we could have the post built of stone or brick, much cheaper than wood, and all the materials are right here on the spot. The sandbars are near with pure white sand, and the earth on that bank—over there—looks as if it would make good bricks."

Clark bent to pull a blade of grass to pick at his teeth and chew on. When he stretched, the heel of his hand struck the ground. It sank deep into the soil. He stood up to look out at the valleys of perennial green. He looked back at the print his hand had made. It was filling with water.

"This loam's sponge," he said. He felt excited. He felt good this morning. He looked at the blue jays, cedar waxwings, and meadowlarks. He thought of the beaver, otter, and muskrat cavorting in the river—this was a trapper's paradise. There were sunflowers, wild rye, purple clover, sweet clover, buffalo peas, and Indian paintbrush. He looked about. All the trails seemed to converge at this point.

"This is it," said Lewis. "This is where the squaw said the Blackfeet come on raids against the Shoshonis."

"I'll go find her," Clark said.

Sacajawea was bathing herself. Her feet sank deep into comfortable mud. Wading out was like stepping into rabbit robes in a snug mud hut, pulling the robes up slowly, feeling the warm fur sleek against the skin. It was like that except that the water in this little backwash was softer than the fur. It curled in around her thighs. She treaded water, and paddled with her arms, helping out her legs. When Clark came to the bank for her, he turned his back. She came out, the tips of her toes touching silt. Coming up out of the river was like falling headlong into icy water. The wind cold, scorched her wet skin. She felt good. She pulled on her tunic and slipped into her moccasins, wrung her hair on the sand and pushed it behind her ears. It was early. Directly westward were the mountains, not dark, but blazing redly in the new sun.

Lewis asked her to tell them again about what lay

northwestward, across the valley space and beyond the foothills. His right arm was sweeping back and forth. His body bent forward, as if he were trying, unconsciously, to gather all details of the great scene about him.

"The Shoshonis go back and forth here in annual hunts to the Yellowstone," she said, sitting a little apart from the two men. "The Nez Percés and Flatheads come here for robes and meat. Big Bellies come from the north for good hunting."

"She means the Gros Ventres from Saskatchewan, I bet," said Clark.

"No tribe lives here permanently, but the roads are deep, like trenches, worn by trailing their lodgepoles and travois. This is common hunting ground," said Lewis, his imagination spinning.

"This land would feed thousands of cattle and feed 'em fat!" said Clark. "And it is sure enough wheat country."

"Lordy, wheat!" said Lewis. "That's it. Wheat would be up as thick as the hair on a dog's back inside of two weeks after the last spring snow!"

"There!" exclaimed Clark. "We'll come back here and farm. Wouldn't Judy like it out here?"

"Judy Hancock, here? She'd have none but Indians to ask to her cotillion!" laughed Lewis.

Could either man but have known his words were prescient of the day when this would be the heart of the Montana wheat and cattle country, their thoughts would not have been so lighthearted.

Now there was a problem of more immediacy: which fork of the river to take? Patrols were sent out to explore while the hunters went for game and equipment checks were made. Their stay at the Three Forks was a long one, for it was vital to choose the correct fork, and although Sacajawea had been right before and now told them to take the fork leading west, Captain Lewis waited for the men to scout before reaching the same decision.

Lewis named the southeast fork, which he explored, the Gallatin, in honor of the Secretary of the Treasury. The middle fork became the Madison, after the Secretary of State, and the northwest fork was named the Jefferson, after the President of the United States. Cap-

tain Clark provided the first basic survey of the Three
Forks area. He added it to his manuscript maps.

The canoes were reloaded, and the expedition began
to ascend the Jefferson on July 30 to its head in the
Bitterroot Mountains, and to continue their search for
the Shoshonis.

"You'll never find them in the open," explained Sacajawea. "They lived once on the plains, but they have
been driven from them by enemies."

Captain Lewis was worried. The expedition must get
across the Rockies before the early autumn snow came
down in their upper reaches because it would block all
passes. Lewis was afraid a few more weeks' delay might
be too late, and he wanted to abandon the search for
the Shoshonis, but the captains had no reliable information about the mountains or the passes through them
and only the vaguest idea of the distance between navigable canoe water on the upper Missouri and upper
Columbia. Captain Clark thought it important to find
the Shoshonis, for through Sacajawea they would be
able to converse easily and buy horses for the overland
trip. This had been the chief reason for bringing her on
the expedition, and this was to be her real service.

Sacajawea did her best to explain that her people
had taken refuge in the most inaccessible uplands so
that it was not worth a war party's time to follow them
far into the mountains, so little was the plunder to be
gained when they reached their camps. There was little
food, and their robes were thin and worn. The people
had learned to accept semistarvation in order to escape
being massacred.

She was certain the People had watched their party
and probably heard the hunters' rifles. She had seen
the thin line of smoke wisps for several days, low on
the horizon, filtering above the silvery bulk of snow-
covered mountains, like far-off clouds. In her mind's
eye she could see the People's hunting parties coming
back to the hills, recalled because of the approaching
strangers.

They traveled at a steady pace, day after day. The
river in this place was filled with beaver dams, strong
currents, and shallows. Towing was torture, but had to
be done. Sacajawea felt she could not sit in a canoe and

have the men pull her. She got out to lighten the load and trudged with her son hung on her back in a two-point wool blanket. Captain Clark and York also usually walked. Occasionally they found old signs of the Shoshonis, and once moccasin tracks made during the night by a single buck were found when camp was broken in the morning.

Often Lewis or Clark paused to scan the terrain with the glass, but they found only the uplifts of hills and few trees; once Clark picked up some elk, and another time he saw antelope—only those things, and occasionally smoke signals, which became gradually fainter.

The country became less rugged. They emerged onto the floor of a wide valley that waved away in small lakes of yellow and white boulders in a slope toward the north. The entire earth seemed to have been tilted in that direction. Against the sky ahead rose a high range of timbered hills.

"Sixteen days," sighed Captain Lewis. "Sixteen days today, since we left the forks."

The expedition ran into antelope and had plenty of food. On one of the meadows the antelope were frantic. Their curiosity exceeded the bounds of their instincts at times, bringing them close to the river's edge. They ran along the bank as if racing one another, stopped, and gazed at the party in amazement and wonder. They pivoted suddenly and bounded away on springlike legs, only to whirl about and stare again. They stood in groups on knoll tops as if chatting with one another, and for no visible reason suddenly scattered in all directions as if a noiseless explosion had occurred in their midst.

On August 8, Sacajawea pointed to a steep, rocky cliff shaped a little like a beaver's head, one hundred and fifty feet above the water, an Indian landmark from the beginning of time.

"The Beaver Head," she said, pointing, "is not far from the summer camp of my people. We will meet them soon, on this river or the river beyond, west of the source of the Big Muddy. Not far now." She settled herself in the bottom of the canoe, Pomp in her arms, her knees to one side. She rocked the baby when the water was still, and hummed to him. When he fussed or cried, she nursed him until he fell asleep.

That evening Sacajawea listened intently to the conversation around the cook fire, grasping much of its meaning. She stood holding Pomp over one shoulder as he pulled at her braid and put the end of it into his mouth. She stepped forward just a little. "My people's cheeks are painted with vermilion. Red on the cheeks is a sign of peace between men. See, I have been wearing a red line in the part of my hair and some on my face so that the People might notice."

"Balls of fire!" said Captain Lewis. He had tied his hair back with a rawhide string, but the ends stuck out unevenly, like oddments of old straw hanging down his neck. The queue looked like a badly made sheaf gleaned from the yellow stubble on his face. "I wondered why you wore that gaudy stuff!"

"They are near, but they are scared."

"Then we have to flush them out like a covey of grouse. Tomorrow I'll take a couple of men and scout out around the river. I want you to stay in camp with Captain Clark. You and York see that he stays off that foot. It's nasty-looking tonight. If we meet with any kind of tribe, we'll wait for you to come upriver and then you talk with them." He turned and strode away to speak with Captain Clark.

Sacajawea followed and looked anxiously at Chief Red Hair. A carbuncle on his ankle had become so large that he could barely walk. She let out her breath with a sigh. "Have you been walking?" she scolded him.

Captain Clark grinned as if he knew he'd played a joke on her. "Nobody's offered to wait on me—yet."

Captain Lewis noticed the expression on Sacajawea's face as she looked at Clark. He suddenly thought, Why that little savage loves Bill Clark. She loves him as deeply as any white girl could. And I do believe that Bill enjoys her attentions. Good Lord! I hope that man of hers does not find out! Lewis hunched his back against a tree and stared at the sky. He thought he could understand the relationship between Sacajawea and Bill Clark, the man who was his equal in rank and authority and whom he respected as men of great intellect respect one another. His silence was without strain. The day lost itself, and he slept.

When the sun lighted the east side of the camp, he roused Drouillard, who knew the Indian hand signs nearly as well as he knew English, John Shields, who was not overly bright but could follow orders very well, and Hugh McNeal, a good hunter and reader of trail signs, and prepared to track the elusive Shoshonis. Clark and the rest of the men would rest for a few days, and then follow with the canoes.

Sacajawea applied hot mud poultices to Captain Clark's ankle and brought him the tenderest meat from Charbonneau's cook fire. During the next few days in camp, she made clothes for her baby and herself. She wanted to look nice when she went to the People. She put little blue beads on her baby's moccasins and on the yoke of his small shirt.

"Hey, Janey, bring me some of those beads," called Captain Clark. "I have to do something, and I'm tired of writing, drawing pictures, and sorting seeds. Maybe I can make something pretty."

She looked questioningly at Chief Red Hair and chuckled to herself. Did he really want her to go in the stores and get out some beads? York had been the one to bring the beads to her, along with a fine metal needle and linen thread.

"Sure, it's all right," he said. "You bring me the color beads you like best, a good needle, some strong thread, and a long piece of tanned, soft hide."

On August 13, the expedition moved forward, with Captain Clark sitting in a canoe, letting Cruzatte pole, while he sewed blue beads on the strip of leather. Most of the men were towing supplies in the canoes, but Clark insisted that those with large blisters and boils on their feet ride as he did.

Sacajawea collected the sticky ooze from balsam blisters at each stop and told the men to keep their sore feet covered with it. She brought armloads of thimbleberry leaves to wrap their feet at night. This herbal treatment and the strong constitutions of the men kept the infections at a minimum and hastened healing. Clark's ankle improved each day now.

* * *

Captain Lewis, with Drouillard, Shields, and Mc-
Neal, had scouted around the river, hunted a suitable
portage, and followed several well-traveled game and
native trails. There was plenty of low brush, but few
tall trees. Captain Lewis stopped frequently to look at
the hills with his spyglass. They were several days ahead
of Clark when Lewis looked ahead at the plains and
saw a man on horseback. The man saw him and watched
silently.

"Look, he is different from any of the natives we have
so far met," Captain Lewis said, handing the spyglass
to McNeal.

"He may be as nearabouts to a Shoshoni as any we've
seen," said McNeal.

"I'm thinking the same," said Captain Lewis. "See,
he carries a bow and a bag of arrows on his back. The
horse is elegantly painted but has no saddle and only
a thin bit of braided horsehair going under the jaw for
a bridle. Just the way Janey described the Shoshoni
horse."

Captain Lewis, about half a mile from the strange
horseman, loosened his blanket from his pack and held
it by two corners, throwing it up in the air higher than
his head, then bringing it down to the ground as if to
spread it out. He did this three times. It was the Shoshoni sign of hospitality taught him by Sacajawea. It
meant, "Come, sit on the robe with me in peace."

Still the stranger kept his position, looking on with
suspicion. Signaling the other men to halt, Captain
Lewis walked slowly toward the man on horseback,
holding several trinkets, beads, and some ribbon in his
outstretched hand. *"Tab-ba-bone, tab-ba-bone!"* he
called, believing the word to mean "white man" in
Shoshoni, and stripping up the sleeve of one arm to
show the white color of his skin.[1]

The Indian kept his eyes on Drouillard and Shields,
who continued to move forward, not realizing that when
Captain Lewis was negotiating with the Indian they
should stand still. Lewis now risked a signal to halt.
Drouillard obeyed, but Shields failed to see the signal.

The Indian paused, looking from Drouillard to the
advancing Shields and then to Captain Lewis, who went

slowly forward for another fifty paces. Shields, rifle in hand, foolishly moved ahead so that he would soon be in the Indian's rear. From the Indian's point of view, it looked like a trap.

As Captain Lewis came forward shouting, the suspicious Shoshoni fled like a frightened deer. No amount of calling or motions could bring him back.

Captain Lewis picked up his three men and tried to follow the horse tracks, hoping to be led to the man's village. They passed places that looked as though the women had dug roots that day. Lewis fixed a pole with several strings of colored beads, moccasin awls, and some little tin boxes of paints and a looking glass attached to one end. He planted the other end in the ground beside their old campfire, hoping that some Indians would come by and see that the white men were friendly. Only friends would scatter such valuable goods about. McNeal carried the small American flag with fifteen stars tied to a pole, and whenever the men stopped he planted it in the ground.[2]

On the morning of August 12, Captain Lewis and his three men traveled along the foot of the mountains on a wide, well-traveled trail. A sudden shower wiped out any tracks, but Lewis was confident if they continued on the trail they would find the Shoshonis soon. By late afternoon they had made no contact with any Indians. They traveled beside a small stream, which all four men regarded as the headwater of the Missouri River.

McNeal thought of the long struggle up the muddy Missouri to this small stream they followed in the foothills. Exultantly he put his feet on opposite banks of the clear stream and shouted, "Thank God that I have lived to bestride the mighty and almost endless Missouri!"

The men drank from the stream, which they were convinced was the headwater of the Missouri. Captain Lewis himself, however, believed this small stream to be the headwater of the mighty Columbia River.[3] The four men went on to the top of the dividing ridge. There they could see tall mountain ranges in front of them, their tops partially covered with snow. Lewis went down the other side of the ridge and found it much steeper.

Next morning the men were up early, going slowly down a long descending valley, when all of a sudden they saw on a flat, broad stone in front of them two women, a man, and some dogs. These natives watched them for some moments, then disappeared.

It was an annoying situation to be so near an Indian encampment but fail to find it or even speak with the inhabitants. Yet Captain Lewis and his men were certain that Indians watched every move they made. This was a hopeful thing. Lewis continued to walk along the wide, dusty trail with his three men walking behind him in single file. The size of the trail told them that the camp must be nearby and fairly large. A village of any size was not easy to hide, yet these people had kept their encampment well concealed. They walked on in the summer heat another dusty mile; then, around a mountain-ash thicket, they surprised three squaws. The approach of each group was hidden from the other by a series of small ravines. A young woman ran away. The older woman, with a little girl who was perhaps two or three years younger than Sacajawea, sat down and bowed her head, as if expecting instant death.

Slowly and gently, Captain Lewis approached the old woman. He stripped up his sleeve.

The old woman's eyes widened. She was barefoot, to save her moccasins for more important times, when the weather would be cold. Her tunic was stiff with grease, old, and cracked. The child was also barefoot. Her tunic was short and not so old, but black-wet and plastered to her body from the heat of the day. Her hair, in two braids, was bound with leather strips. They were amazed at the sight of Lewis. He was the first white man they had ever seen. Then Drouillard, McNeal, and Shields came up the ravine, wiping perspiration from their foreheads. Lewis gave the old woman and child beads, moccasin awls, mirrors, and vermilion paint in small tin boxes. While they examined these splendid things, Captain Lewis told Drouillard about the squaw who had run away.

"It naturally jars a man to find out that the people he finds don't know that they're being looked for," laughed Drouillard. He made hand signs, telling the old woman to call back her younger companion. She did so, and quickly the young woman came back, out of breath, her face shiny with perspiration, but her hands outstretched. Lewis gave her trinkets also.

The child was looking first at Lewis and then at Drouillard and then back again. Lewis slowly painted the child's forehead with vermilion. Then he did the same to the young woman and the old woman to show that he came as a friend, in peace. Chuckling to herself, the old woman stood beside Lewis and wiped her hand across her forehead and then put the paint on Lewis's cheek slowly, shyly. He, too, was now smeared with the red mercuric sulfide pigment mixed with bear's grease.

Drouillard motioned to the old woman and then extended his hands to her. He stood silent until she touched him; then he made a quick series of signs. He let her follow his hands with her sharp, clear eyes, his gestures sweeping, each curving into the next with few angular or abrupt motions. When he finished, she smiled and motioned with a sweep of her right arm, "Come on." The young woman, in a bleached-out deerskin tunic that had seen much washing and much sunning, led the four white men down the trail about two miles.

Then Captain Lewis's laugh burst like a war whoop. In an open area milled a party of sixty warriors armed with bows and arrows. Some of the men had a feather or two in their hair. Others had thongs twisted around the sides of their long black hair. Their horses were large and fine-looking. They had been alerted by the man Captain Lewis had seen earlier with the two women and many dogs on the large flat rock.

The old woman stepped back to Drouillard, and her hands moved in front of him, nimble, swift, hardly seeming to touch one another or be encumbered by the gifts under her left arm. Her face was not twisted and frightened now, but suffused with interest and curiosity. She told Drouillard that the warriors thought they were meeting a Blackfeet war party who had defeated them in a fight not long ago.

Leaving his rifle behind with Drouillard, Captain Lewis went toward the chief and two others who were a little ahead of the main party. He carried the small American flag tied to a pole. Lewis's three men and the three women followed him.

The chief, still on his horse, spoke quietly to the three women, who proudly showed him their gifts and red-painted foreheads. He was reassured—no war party ever went about giving presents to women.

Two important men of the tribe dropped from their horse and one after another threw their left arm over Captain Lewis's shoulder, pressing their greasy painted cheeks against his, saying, "*Ah-hi-ee, ah-hi-ee!*" Their bodies had been rubbed with grease, making their flesh glisten. They had drawn designs on their faces, chests, and backs with red, yellow, and white paints. Their personal war medicines were bound in their hair or tied around their necks. Brightly painted shields caught the light. From time to time a man would dash up and hug the captain, repeating, "*Ah-hi-ee, ah-hi-ee!*"

"I believe that means 'We are delighted with you,'" said Drouillard after a very large fellow had just given him the national hug.

Then the chief dismounted. Captain Lewis put a little vermilion paint on his forehead, and this started the hugging all over again. Lewis was caressed and smeared with grease and paint and soon was heartily tired of this Shoshoni hug.

Slowly he motioned for his sack and brought out his long calumet of red pipestone. He filled it with tobacco and lighted it, instructed McNeal to plant the pole with the flag, and suddenly the Indians were seated in a circle around the pole and had pulled off their moccasins. Drouillard leaned toward Lewis and whispered, "Take your moccasins off. These birds are waiting for us to finalize their sacred act. This here indicates their wish that if they are ever treacherous or insincere with their friends, they might ever after go barefoot."

After the men had passed the pipe around the circle several times, Captain Lewis passed out more presents. They liked the blue beads and vermilion paint best.

Then the chief lit his pipe at the fire and gave a short speech, pointing the long stem to the four cardinal points of the heavens, beginning at the east and ending at the north. His pipe was made in an oval shape from the transparent green jade of the Bannock Mountains, highly polished. After he smoked, he passed the pipe to Captain Lewis and then to each of the white men.

When this smoking was finished, Lewis gave the remainder of his gifts to the women and children who sat outside the men's circle.

The chief, called Cameâhwait, had eyes sharp and black as a hawk's and lank jaws. He told the white men by hand signs that his people had very little food, but the newcomers were welcome to what they had. That evening's meal was cakes of serviceberries and chokecherries that had been dried in the sun. While eating, Lewis looked at the chief and thought perhaps he was twenty-five; then he thought, maybe even forty-five— it was hard to tell. There was a timeless, enduring quality about him, as of old, long-used leather. His face was bony, high-bridged, beginning to wrinkle around his eyes where the skin was loose. His nose was thin and straight, and his eyes deep-set. His expression was unchanging, neither harsh nor pleasant. Lewis could read nothing in his face, and yet he perceived—without knowing how—an unshakable pride, similar to that possessed by Sacajawea.

Chief Cameâhwait wore a vest decorated with dried porcupine quills, and leggings that were once whitened buckskin but now shiny with grease on the knees and legs. His moccasins were old and decorated with yellow quills, molded roughly to the bones of his feet. His hair was in two long strands, the right wrapped with strips of thin leather, the left decorated with a band of four eagle feathers dangling down in front, and a hoop wound with rawhide held one red feather near his ear. He had beside him a lance, some nine feet long, worked with white puma claws. It was tipped with a long point of the moss-green jade found high in the mountains, and tailed with the wing feather of a hawk. As Lewis watched, the chief turned suddenly from the business of eating and extended his hands to Drouillard, the interpreter. Pausing until Drouillard put down the serviceberry cake, he made a quick series of signs.

"Captain, the chief wants you to go with his friend to a lodge where you will be presented with something more for your hearty appetite," interpreted Drouillard.

Lewis did not hesitate, but followed an old man who had the habit of leaning with the wind as he walked. Inside the old man's tepee Lewis was given a small bit of boiled antelope meat and a piece of fresh-roasted salmon. He ate both and wiped his hands on his trousers; then he untied the rawhide string in the back of his hair and combed his fingers through several times before tying his hair back in a queue. This latter show of gratitude for the meat pleased his host so much that Lewis was given another piece of salmon. This was the first salmon Lewis had seen, and he was convinced now that he was at the headwaters of the Pacific Ocean.

The Shoshonis danced most of the night in celebration of the white men's presence among them. The next morning, Captain Lewis asked Chief Cameâhwait about the geography of his land. The chief drew rivers on the ground and built mountains with mounds of dust. He told Lewis that the mountains so closely hemmed in the river, which was white with froth, that there was no way to cross. None of his people had been over the mountains, but there was an old man, a day's march from where they were, who might give Captain Lewis more information about the country to the northwest.

"Are there any of your men who would go with me tomorrow to the forks in the river to help carry the baggage of another white chief up here to your village?" asked Captain Lewis.

By signs the chief indicated that his men would do that for these friends.

"We will stay for some time with you and trade some of our goods for some of your horses and then make ready to go on to the ocean," said Lewis. "We're headed as far west as we can go!"

19

The People

Saturday August 17th, 1805

On setting out at seven o'clock, Captain Clarke with Charbonneau and his wife walked on shore, but they had not gone more than a mile before Clarke saw Sacajawea, who was with her husband 100 yards ahead, began to dance and show every mark of the most extravagant joy, turning around him and pointing to several Indians, whom he now saw advancing on horseback, sucking her fingers at the same time to indicate that they were of her native tribe [they had eaten together]. As they advanced, Captain Clarke discovered among them Drewyer [Drouillard] dressed like an Indian, from whom he learnt the situation of the party. While the boats were performing the circuit, he went towards the forks with the Indians, who as they went along, sang aloud with the greatest appearance of delight.

The party soon drew near to the camp, and just as they approached it a woman made her way through the crowd towards Sacajawea, and recognizing each other, they embraced with the most tender affection. The meeting of these two young women had in it something peculiarly touching, not only in the ardent manner in which their feelings were expressed, but from the real interest of their situation. They had been companions in childhood, in the war with the Minnetarees they had both been taken prisoners in the same battle, they had shared

*and softened the rigours of their captivity, till one of
them had escaped from the Minnetarees, with scarce a
hope of ever seeing her friend relieved from the hands
of her enemies. While Sacajawea was renewing among
the women the friendships of former days, Captain Clarke
went on, and was received by Captain Lewis and the
chief, who after the first embraces and salutations were
over, conducted him to a sort of circular tent or shade
of willows. Here he was seated on a white robe; and the
chief immediately tied in his hair six small shells resembling pearls, an ornament highly valued by these
people, who procure them in the course of trade from the
sea-coast. The moccasins of the whole party were then
taken off, and after much ceremony the smoking began.
After this the conference was to be opened, and glad of
an opportunity of being able to converse more intelli-
gibly, Sacajawea was sent for; she came into the tent,
sat down, and was beginning to interpret, when in the
person of Cameâhwait, the chief, she recognized her
brother. She instantly jumped up, and ran and embraced him, throwing over him her blanket and weeping
profusely. The chief was himself moved, though not in
the same degree. After some conversation between them
she resumed her seat, and attempted to interpret for us,
but her new situation seemed to overpower her, and she
was frequently interrupted by tears. After the council
was finished the unfortunate woman learnt that all her
family were dead except two brothers, one of who was
absent, and a son of her eldest sister, a small boy, who
was immediately adopted by her.*

NICHOLAS BIDDLE, ed., *History of the Expedition Under
the Command of Captains Lewis and Clarke*, Vol. I.
Philadelphia: Bradford and Inskeep, 1814, pp. 381–83.

On August 16, Captain Clark rose early. He hoped to find Lewis soon. His ankle was nearly healed, and he walked easily. He spotted Sacajawea coming from a backwash in the river where she had bathed and washed her hair. The neat braids were still wet and shining.

"I'm hungry this new day," she said, smiling. "I will get the fire going, and surely the other men will be up soon."

"First," said Clark, holding her with his eyes, "I have something for you." He reached into his trouser pocket and slowly pulled out the blue-beaded belt he had been working on as he recuperated from his carbuncle. The design was lines and crosses made of dark- and light-blue beads; in the center back of the belt were dark-blue flowers with a row of green leaves on either side. Leather thongs at the ends were made for tying the belt around the waist. "See if it fits."

"It is for me?" she said, unbelieving. "Chief beads?"

"Well, sure, who else would wear a belt as fancy as all that? Now put it on. I want to see how it looks after all that sewing I did on it."

"Ai, it is the most beautiful color." For a moment Sacajawea wanted to touch him, but she could not. She must not show her pleasure where people could see. She must have pride. She flushed with happiness.

Slowly she put the belt on and turned so that Chief Red Hair could see how well it fit around her tunic. She could not believe that he had made this beautiful gift for her. Her heart jumped up and down like a frightened rabbit. She dropped her eyes. "I, the woman called Janey by the Chief Red Hair, is full of thanks," she said, confused.

Clark gently put his hand under her chin and smiled into her large brown eyes. Then he let go and looked down. "It is my gift to you because—because a pretty woman ought to have pretty things."

Sacajawea looked at him, puzzled. It was incomprehensible to her that a man such as Captain Clark, Chief Red Hair, might think her attractive. Often enough

Charbonneau had lamented her lack of flesh, and the want of keeping her mouth closed.

And then a sudden premonition came to her. This would be the day. This day they would find her people, the Agaidüka Shoshoni.

While the men loaded the canoes, she bathed Pomp and put on the new shirt she had made for him. In the canoe, she placed the blanket she now used to replace the lost cradleboard at her feet. The morning air was warm.

All morning she watched the horizon for signs, and when she finally saw movement along the shore, she could not move, could not speak. She could only point westward. Two horsemen were galloping toward them. Captain Clark pulled the canoe to the rocky bank. Then he, along with Francis Labiche, another man good with hand signs, Charbonneau, and Sacajawea, with Pomp swung in the blanket on her back, walked toward the riders.

"People I have eaten with. They are! They are!" Sacajawea sucked on the fingers of her right hand.

"Janey, I hope so!" Clark exclaimed. "I sure as hell hope so!"

"See, Shoshoni dress, Shoshoni horses! *Ai, ai, ah-hi-ee!*"

Then, suddenly, one of the riders pulled in his horse and galloped right back toward the west. Sacajawea's heart dropped to her moccasins.

Captain Clark waved wildly to the approaching lone horseman and was saluted with a non-Shoshoni, "Hulloo, strangers!"

"Drouillard!" cried Clark, his face dark. "You're dressed like a Shoshoni? If so, that's a poor joke to play on us!"

"No joke, Captain," said Drouillard, adjusting the white ermine-skin cape of the Shoshonis and pointing to the vermilion on his face and down his hair part. About his neck was a necklace of bear's claws. "We have found 'em!"

"You camp with the People?" asked Sacajawea.

"Oh, you bet, and they dance for us and sing, and invite us to dinner."

Questions poured from Sacajawea and then from

Captain Clark, so that Drouillard could not answer coherently.

Charbonneau contemptuously fingered the blue belt at her waist. "Like a white woman," he said scornfully. "I've never heard a woman speak up so much as you. Even the white woman keeps her mouth shut once in a while."

Sacajawea trembled. "I am coming to my land," she said.

"Captain Lewis is coming with more than sixty Shoshoni men," said Drouillard, his horse's hooves clicking on the rocks. "They will help us."

"Ride back and give the others the news," Captain Clark ordered Drouillard. "Tell them Labiche, Charbonneau, Janey and I are on our way to meet Lewis. We're walking."

With a wild Shoshoni whoop, the half-Shawnee, half-French Drouillard galloped toward the canoes.

This cannot be a dream, thought Sacajawea. I am with these white men, and they are not in the spirit world. What if these people are not the Agaidüka Shoshoni, but some other tribe? The Agaidükas may be farther back in the mountains. I cannot get my hope too high. My heart beats as though it would fly out.

It was then that memory rose up before her to merge with the familiar landscape: far below, near the river, a great circular enclosure at the foot of a bluff, and above, a fan of gray stones spreading back from the bluff's edge like wings over the green, undulating hills. The picture spread vividly before her, overlaying the short pines ahead, and she became a girl on a painted horse, looking down from a high hill. White clouds bloomed and grew towering against the sky edge of the world, casting shadows below, islands in the green sea. A band of sheep, a moving cloud shadow, circled, flashing as white as foam on each turn, a promise to the People of warmth and contentment.

From the white circle of lodges in a green valley, a thread of people on horses moved toward the enclosure, buckskin bright with quillwork, and paint bright on the horses. They stayed silent at the base of the bluff, then went on, upward, separating into lines that moved out along the wings. Beyond the last stones a herd of bighorn sheep grazed, gray-white on the green grass; among them birds rose and circled and dropped. She saw the caller of the sheep in his brown skin robe dancing near the animals to catch their attention; the herd moved toward her, gathering to a white stream, flowing between the converging wings toward the bluff. The leader plunged wildly over, and the stream was solid, flesh of the earth sliding, a fall of meat and robes—life for the People. Dust rose in the stone enclosure, and the vision was gone, fading to the silver forks in the river ahead, the grass changing to dust made by galloping horsemen coming toward them. The dust rose shadowy against the sky. The riders had bright-painted faces; their horses were strong and beautiful, spotted and decorated with handprints of red, yellow, and white. Bird feathers were tied to their manes and tails.

The riders were singing as they approached. The song rang in Sacajawea's ears, feral as the cry of a hunted animal. She caught her breath and recognized the Greeting Song of the Shoshonis.

Sacajawea scanned each face eagerly, her heart thumping with excitement. One after another passed, but there was not one whom she recognized. She stood still a moment, her head bowed, uncertain, her baby heavy on her back, her heart as heavy as stone. These Shoshonis were all strangers, not her tribe, not the Agaidüka.

The horsemen wheeled and pranced around her, Captain Clark, Labiche, and Charbonneau. Labiche smiled and *kiyi*-ed with them. Charbonneau sputtered, "*Jésus*, them Snakes think we have lots of meat to give them."

Sacajawea had a shadowy, unclear feeling of a dream begun, not ended; she was at the edge of awakening. She began to wish she had not put the red circles on her cheeks nor the vermilion down her center hair part.

The horsemen were leading them to a larger group of Shoshonis. There was a sudden movement among the mass of people, and Sacajawea recognized Captain Lewis through the crowd, with red paint smeared on his face and on the straw-colored wisps of hair that poked wildly from his queue.

A squaw stared, watching Sacajawea curiously. Her

hair was in strings at the sides of her face, and her
tunic was unwashed. A tear at the bottom had been
mended with thick buckskin. Her straight hair hung
as if to hide her sunken cheeks. This unkempt woman
began making the sucking motion with her fingers and
crying words that came from long ago, a scrap of a
familiar song.

Sacajawea caught the smell of these people, the living earth smell—leather, woodsmoke, mulch odor. The
squaw was pressing her way through the crowd, coming
toward her. Sacajawea instinctively stepped back, but
the squaw was at her side, moving her hands firmly
and lightly over her arms, then over the face of Pomp,
then over Sacajawea's face. The woman gave a quick
little cry, and then her arms were about Sacajawea;
tears were warm on Sacajawea's cheeks, then cool.

"Boinaiv, Grass Child, you have come home to the
People."

Sacajawea's arms closed convulsively about the
woman, and she could not keep her tears back. "Willow
Bud, it is you!" Between tears she laughed and no longer
noticed the others around her. "So—these are the People, my people?"

"*Ai.* The scouts have been watching the white men.
None said you were with them. It is hard to believe.
And a baby, too. Where is his father?"

Sacajawea pointed to Charbonneau, who had a wide
grin on his face as he watched the Shoshonis dance for
these newcomers.

"A white man! *Hai-hai-ee!* And your papoose, he is
beautiful."

Questions tumbled out, but there was no pause for
them to be answered. Sacajawea put her finger on her
lips for the sign of silence, and both women laughed
and clung to each other again; then Willow Bud took
Pomp and walked to a spot that was shaded by tall
pines and sat cross-legged, holding the baby close to
her heart. Pomp tried to free himself as she smelled
him and ran her hands over his face and plump body.
She rocked him gently back and forth as a tear slipped
down her chin.

"The papoose that was mine did not live through the
Month of Howling Wind. She was so tiny. Her mouth

opened like a baby bird's, and I had no milk for her.
There was no other nursing woman who could spare
extra milk. Food was scarce. Stomach cramps were
everywhere. She lived eight moons. We laid her tiny
body behind the white rocks by the gurgling stream.
My man sat there with no food, only the icy water, for
one moon. He said the morning sun makes the white
rocks glisten like water going over a high falls, so we
shall always know where our papoose sleeps—in the
glistening stones. He put many stones over her body
before he came back to the tepee. It will always be
hidden from wolves or buzzards."

Inpulsively Sacajawea slipped her blue-beaded moccasins from her feet and pressed them toward Willow
Bud, thinking of them not as a possession, or gift, but
as a word, a phrase of sympathy spoken by the gesture.
The meaning was clear and understood. For the moment there were only the two of them with the child
between, an awareness of each other, a communication
felt as palpably as a touch of the hand.

Sacajawea slipped her feet into the worn moccasins
cast aside by Willow Bud. She looked back over the
years and saw Willow Bud, a beautiful, self-reliant child,
with fat, brown cheeks and a straight, sturdy body. Now
she was hollow-eyed, slightly bent, thin and haggard,
her toes turned in even more than most squaws'. She
was probably about fifteen or sixteen summers old, but
her thin face looked much older. Winters of near-star-
vation had done that.

Willow Bud hunched herself to her feet. "Come along.
We will go to my tepee and do nothing but talk. Yellow
Neck, the one who is my man, is with his brother. They
have gone to see the white men you have brought to
our village."

Inside the summer lodge a smell of leather and sage
enveloped them. Sacajawea's sight cleared to the darkness, and she stepped closer to the small center fire. It
was hot inside, and the air was thick with the smell of
musty roots simmering in a tightly woven grass container. The walls were hung with bows, arrows, quilled
bags, painted rawhide parfleches, herbs, dried roots.
The floor was hard-packed, clean-swept clay.

For a moment Sacajawea could not speak. Her mind

took her back to a day when dawn came in a mirroring of light, a springing wash of color. The cottonwoods, aspens, and willows flared from the mist and darkness along the creek, leaves bright green against pale trunks. The whole camp was astir as children swirled among the tepees, shouting, waving their arms, dogs barked, women worked by the fires or brought wood and water to their tepees. Near the camp she imagined she saw the horse herd, red, yellow, black, white—pinto, piebald, spotted—bright flares against the green short grass. The camp was preparing to move to a summer home in the cool shade of the mountains. She could see her grandmother and her mother packing the household goods. Her father sat before the lodge, dignified, smoking in the sun. The day brightened and she was brought from her reverie when the tent flap was pushed aside by women.

Sacajawea searched their faces as they crowded inside the hot tepee. They had come out of curiosity and respect to see and make welcome this member of their tribe who, by some magic, had led many friendly white men to the Agaidüka camp. One old squaw remarked it was like seeing a person come back from the dead to see this grown woman who had left them as a child. They were curious about the baby, made by a white man. They passed Pomp back and forth, examining him more thoroughly than a white man's doctor. Pomp did not cry out; he seemed to enjoy the attention and squealed with laughter when they looked at his fat feet and counted his toes. Sacajawea smiled at them as they fingered his clothes and nodded approval at the way she had made them soft and white from thin doeskin.

The old squaw fingered the mosquito netting that was folded in his blanket. Sacajawea explained that the white men used this to keep the biting insects off.

"Is it better than bear's oil?"

"*Ai*, better," she answered, and they crowded closer, eager to hear stories of the white men. Some left and returned with food so that they could stay longer and listen to Sacajawea tell about the round mud lodges, food that was planted in spring and harvested in fall, metal horns, men who did women's work, a scratch that would keep away the smallpox.

"Unlikely. Her tongue is crooked," laughed an old woman feeling the blue-beaded belt at Sacajawea's waist. Then she looked at Willow Bud's new moccasins with the beads on top. These women had never before seen glass beads. Their bone needles could never pierce the tiny holes; nor could their cordage—even the finest made from the fibers of the false nettle—go through the tiny beads.

Sacajawea showed them the pewter mirror that Chief Red Hair had given her.

"Like carrying a part of a water pool in your pocket," said an old squaw who made delightful faces in the mirror and smiled a wide, toothless grin and grabbed Sacajawea by the arm.

"My daughter," she said. "I clearly remember your family. You are the true shadow of your mother. We are pleased to have her image back among us." Again she smiled, and then she was gone. In a moment she returned with a small quilled fawnskin robe, which she held out silently. Sacajawea accepted it and waited until the old woman was ready to explain.

"The mother of this woman," she whispered almost inaudibly, choked with emotion, "made the robe for my firstborn son. I thought it too beautiful to use. Later I thought it was a mistake not to have used it, but now I know why it had to be kept. For the son of the woman we call Boinaiv."

There were many wet eyes in the tepee. Sacajawea moved back, making room where she could spread out the blanket for all to see. The designs around the edge were beautifully intricate, intimate circles, suns, and triangular birds. Again she felt it hard to catch a breath as the past enveloped her. This thing of beauty had been made by the hands of her own mother. Suddenly she thought of her sister and brothers. She opened her mouth to ask about them just as Charbonneau poked his shaggy head inside the tepee and yelled, "Little Bird, you must come. *Les capitaines* say you be in their council."

"What did he say?" asked the old squaw with the mirror close to her face.

Sacajawea made the sign for a meeting. "There is a

powwow between the white men and the chiefs. They asked me to come."

"Awww," the old squaw said. "You are asked to the council where there are only men?"

A tittering rose among the women. Shoshonis would never permit a woman in their councils. Willow Bud's eyes were wide with curiosity.

"Are you something special to these white men that they cannot powwow without a woman sitting among them?" asked Willow Bud. Again the squaws tittered.

Sacajawea folded the precious robe over her arm and tried to explain. "It is not because I am a squaw and they are braves. It is because I can speak the Shoshoni tongue and the white men cannot. I can speak for you to them."

The women slowly nodded. "*Ai, ai,* we understand that." And with a clucking noise made with their teeth and tongue they showed that they approved of this and she should go at once.

Willow Bud followed at a little distance, then, getting up courage, asked, "May I care for him?" She held her arms out for Pomp.

Sacajawea handed the sleeping baby to her girlhood friend, kissing him first.

"What is that?" asked Willow Bud, making a smacking noise with her lips.

"It is a sign for love." Sacajawea crossed her arms over her breast in the manner of a woman greeting her man when he returns from a hunt or war. "See?" And then Sacajawea kissed the startled Willow Bud on her cheek.

Captain Clark was formally seated on a white robe in the Council Lodge improvised with willow boughs, his face still smudged with vermilion paint, an ermine collar clasped closely about his neck. Captain Lewis sat beside the chief, who was tall and sat with his back straight and proud, his black eyes looking intently into the faces of the strange white men, reading what he could of their intentions here among his people.

Besides putting an ermine collar around Captain Clark's neck, the chief had tied six small white seashells in his hair. These ornaments from the Pacific

Coast were highly valued among the Shoshonis. The
men had removed their moccasins.

Sacajawea was to translate from Shoshoni to Minnetaree; Charbonneau was to translate from Minnetaree into French if he could not find the English
equivalent; then Labiche, nearly as dark as any Shoshoni, would translate into English. It was a very slow
way to manage translation, but it was the only way
there was so that everyone could understand what was
being said.

Sacajawea left her moccasins by the entrance and
sat quietly between Charbonneau and Labiche.

The chief wore a headband made from eagle feathers
and dyed vermilion and yellow; the small white breath
feathers came over his cheeks. His shirt was doeskin,
as were his leggings, and embroidered with red-and-
black porcupine quills. His face was painted with radiating yellow lines, proclaiming the beginning of a
new day. A large yellow dot was drawn in the middle
of his forehead and encircled in red, indicating friendship and peace. In his hand he held his pipe. He moved
into the circle and lighted the pipe by placing a coal
from the fire in the green stone bowl. The pipe was
longer than the chief was tall, its stem decorated with
tufts of horsehair. He held it toward the sun, which
stood over a range of hills in the west, and then he gave
it to the four directions, finally turning and placing it
in the hands of Captain Clark. Clark closed his eyes
and blew the smoke from his lips. He held out the pipe
to Captain Lewis.

As Lewis drew on it, he was aware of a murmur
among the men seated around him. It was as if a rustle
had swept through the watching Shoshonis like a slight
breeze through a grove on a hot, still afternoon. The
murmur died, and the oppressive silence came again.
Friendship, he thought; this means friendship. This is
a miraculous thing. We come in here and smoke with
them, in their country, and now we're going to talk
some more, and if they wanted, they could wipe us off
the earth this day. We are a great people, a fearless
people; we go in where angels fear to tread. They cannot
want to kill us; or if they do want to, they're not going
to do it without their rituals. They're going to smoke

and talk Lord knows how long, and then maybe they will let us have it. No, the chief is a wise man. We're worth more to them alive than dead.

The pipe was gone, and the chief was talking. His voice came from deep within him, from down under the tooth necklace and the yellow slashes on his ribs. He patted and smoothed the white doeskin of his open shirt and made a sign to the earth and to the distance and to the natives around him; and he began to talk, directing his remarks to Sacajawea, waiting as she began to translate his expressions of honor and approval of the white men in the Shoshoni camp.

The depth of the chief's voice, the way he held the pipe, the way his black eyes probed into her soul, brought more memories to Sacajawea. The reality before her was mixed with the memories, as in dreams. Suddenly, instead of the gaunt, hollow-eyed chief, she heard her father speaking. She heard him speaking to the People. Her eyes narrowed to see better. A small hoop wound with rawhide suspended one red feather over his left ear. A wave of pulsating excitement flashed over her body.

"Cameâhwait! Never Walks! My own brother!" she cried, jumping up to embrace him. She threw the robe their mother had sewn over this tall, silent chief. She wept profusely. "We are of the same family, my brother!"

The chief was visibly moved. "Boinaiv, my baby sister! No—I thought it could not be you. We mourned you as dead. But you are here. The Great Spirit has looked upon us today with gladness."

Sacajawea tried to control her weeping. Between sobs she asked, "Our sister and brother?"

The chief, greatly agitated, shifted and blew his nose between his fingers. Finally, more composed, he said, "Gone into the land of the spirits with those who were our father and mother."

"*Yiiiee*, gone!" Again she burst into sobs.

"My sister, hush. There are strangers present. It is impolite to display emotion with such abandon. Control yourself. There are two that live."

"Two? But you said—"

"*Ai*, our brother, Spotted Bear, and our sister's papoose, who is called Shoogan."

Chief Cameâhwait gently placed a hand on his sister's arm. "Boinaiv, we shall talk of these things after the council."

Sacajawea tried to control her emotion, but the situation was overpowering. She had no strength to stop. She felt helpless, powerless, exposed, and naked in her deep emotion before all the People, yet she did not see anyone but her own flesh brother. She was seized by dizziness and a shivering weakness. A thunderous wind seemed to surge within her; the earth itself rocked and swayed under its power. She clung to Charbonneau for support until the dizziness passed. She heard Chief Red Hair saying, "It's all right, Janey. You need not feel guilty about your tears. Your homecoming has moved many to the edge of tears. I saw Captain Lewis rub his eyes, and Labiche has blown his nose more often than any of us."

Charbonneau surprised everyone by standing up and extending his right hand toward the chief. "How do, my brother-in-law," he said, with a swagger of his shoulders. When he sat again, he adjusted the kerchief about his neck and eyed the ermine collar worn by Captain Clark. He thought he would get his ermine collar out and wear it around camp. The chief would then know that he was somebody, all right.

Captain Lewis rose. "Tell Chief Cameâhwait that we come in peace, and that we go across the mountains to the salt sea to open the way for white traders. We must go swiftly ahead of the snow, and we have brought tobacco and bags of corn as presents. Others will follow, to trade kettles, awls, hatchets, axes, guns and powder, for the Shoshonis' beaver, otter, and ermine."

Chief Cameâhwait looked pleased. Guns and powder, this was what his people needed to keep them better supplied with game. He rose, dignified and in full control of himself. "I understand, and I am pleased. But why would our enemies, the Sioux and Blackfeet, not capture the white traders and their goods before reaching here? I think they would."

Captain Lewis rose and told the chief about the Great White Father in Washington who wanted all the Indian nations to live in peace. "You are now children of the

Great White Father, and it is he who sent us here. And it will be he who sends traders to you."[1]

Chief Cameâhwait was astonished. "Can this Great White Father send my sister to lead so many men to our nation? Can he keep peace among nations who have warred for years?"

Captain Clark rose. "He sent us to tell the Indian nations to lay down their weapons and be peaceful and trade with each other so that each may live better. We brought Janey—Sacajawea—with us so that she could speak to you, so that you might understand what we had to say. She is a wise young woman."

Sacajawea tried desperately to control her tears.

"Stop sniffling, you squaw," ordered Charbonneau. "You delay the powwow."

Sacajawea bit her bottom lip and clenched her hands into fists. She was bewildered. The sudden joyous shock of it all still shook her, and the responsibility of the translating now included having to pass on a compliment about herself.

"My brother, these white chiefs—Chief Red Hair and Chief Captain Lewis—are strong leaders. They keep their word. They—" Once more, sobs shook her.

Charbonneau was impatient and fuming. "I ordered you to stop that bawling."

Captain Clark touched Charbonneau on the shoulder and shook his head, saying, "Don't. She can't help it. Can't you see she is greatly moved to find some of her family still living? Family ties are strong with these Shoshonis." He motioned to Captain Lewis.

"We think it proper that this council continue tomorrow after one of our interpreters has had time to talk with her brother and meet more with her own people. We'll begin tomorrow when our men arrive with the canoes and supplies."

The Council Lodge was immediately cleared; however, Captain Clark had to drag Charbonneau out by his shirt. The métis was protesting, "He is my brother-in-law. My family. I want to stay and talk with him."

Alone with her brother, Sacajawea suddenly found herself tongue-tied. She watched him remove his headband of feathers. He motioned for her to sit on the white

robe, watching her. She seemed more beautiful than
the memory of his mother, yet she was so similar. All
her movements were rhythmical. Her eyes were red and
swollen, but by tomorrow they would shine again. He
noticed the fine stitching on her tunic, her wide belt of
blue beads. He saw that her hair was neat and she was
clean, and that her beauty came from health; she was
not half-starved as were many of the women in the
tribe. She was also a stranger to him, a woman with a
white man, a swaggering, wind-blowing kind of man.
She could speak several tongues, and she was treated
as an equal by the two white chiefs.

Sacajawea felt a great pride rise within her. This
brother had followed in the footsteps of their father. He
had earned the office of chief, the respect of the Agaidükas. He was someone to be pleased with.

"Spotted Bear is at our camp in the mountains," he
said. "We will go there soon, and you will see him. You
will notice he still has long white marks on his face
from the fight with the great yellow-and-black-spotted
bear."

"And the papoose?"

"Oh, Shoogan. He is yet a child and cared for by
Spotted Bear and his woman."

"What is she called—the woman of our brother,
Spotted Bear?"

"She is called Cries Alone."

"And your woman—what is she called?"

"Dancer."

"Our sister?"

"She left to be with the spirits two winters back. She
had mountain fever, cough, and pain in her chest during
the Season of Snow Melting. Her man, the son of Red
Buck, was struck with an arrow from our enemy, the
Blackfeet, during a battle for horses. From that time,
all the color began to fade out of her cheeks. She would
scarcely eat or speak."

"Shoogan—how many summers?" she asked, her
hands dabbing at her eyes.

He held up three fingers. "He is going to be as fast
a runner as his grandfather if he ever learns to pick
up his feet more carefully." He grinned.

"I must see him. I will care for him as my own. Pomp would like a brother."

"Pomp?"

"*Ai*, Willow Bud holds him. He is seven moons and kicks as if he would be walking if we let him stay on the ground instead of carrying him in a blanket." She demonstrated by throwing the small handmade robe over her back and pulling two corners around her neck. "You must see him."

"You care for Shoogan. With you he will have a full belly."

Then he turned to show the side of his head where the long hair was partially cut in mourning. "The Blackfeet took many of our horses and killed eight of our best warriors and made off with three women and one small boy. The loss was large."

She wondered how the Great White Father so far away could possibly hold any peace between lifelong enemies.

Cameâhwait wondered at her silence. "Were you treated well?"

"The white chiefs treat me well. They are straight-tongued. Chief Red Hair is gentle and kind. The other is quiet and thinks to himself, but he is also fair in all dealings."

"*Ai*, I saw all that at the council." He looked directly at his sister.

Sacajawea felt the blood rising to her cheeks. "My man means well," she said, then looked at her feet and went on. "You will help these white men over the mountains. Help them, and they will help you and the People. They have promised to send traders with food and guns."

"The People then can take their rightful place among the other nations and defend their lodges and women and horses. We will have strong warriors."

"The day will come," she said. She looked up to see Chief Red Hair coming into the willow lodge. "My brother," she said in the soft tongue of the Shoshonis, "I would give my life for this man. He has saved mine as the river came rising up a cliff to wash us away. And he chose me to come here where I found my people. His power is strong. He is like a rock. He made my belt of blue beads." She showed it off proudly.

"There is a special feeling between you?" Chief Cameâhwait looked down at his sister.

"He hunts the buffalo and keeps us well fed," she said. "He would share his hunt with you and all the Agaidükas."

"*Hou!* My people's hunger will be satisfied, and we can sit comfortably as we talk with the white chiefs," said Cameâhwait.

Captain Clark put his hand on Sacajawea's shoulder, with the other making signs. "Ask your brother to join us at the riverbank. The canoes are just beaching, and we will make presents."

Sacajawea interpreted, "We will go with Chief Red Hair to the river and see more white men and their goods, and the big dog—as big as a colt—and the black man, who will be your friend."

Chief Cameâhwait blinked unbelievingly at his sister.

Big Moose

Lewis relates the following complication which arose from Sacajawea's unexpected home coming:

> *The father frequently disposes of his infant daughters in marriage to men who are grown who have sons for whom they think proper to provide wives. The compensation given in such cases usually consists of horses or mules which the father receives at the time of the contract and converts to his own use....Sah-car-gar-we-ah had been disposed of before she was taken by the Minnetares. The husband was yet living with this band. He was more than double her age and had two other wives. He claimed her as his wife, but said that as she had had a child by another man, who was Charbono, that he did not want her.*

Reprinted by permission of the publishers, The Arthur H. Clark Company, from *Sacajawea, Guide and Interpreter of the Lewis and Clark Expedition*, by Grace Raymond Hebard, 1957, p. 64.

There was confusion at the riverbank. Sacajawea watched her older brother lead the Shoshonis in a ring around the white men, hallooing, whooping, singing, embracing, with more Shoshoni red-paint smearing. She saw the chief spot Ben York and motion for York to peel off his buckskin shirt. York stood patiently as Chief Cameâhwait tried to rub the black off his arms and chest, and pulled his kinky hair. The chief was gesturing to his men that this black man was the greatest medicine by far.

The canoes were unloaded and turned bottom side up on the level embankment near a stream flowing into the river. Soon the Shoshonis were examining kettles, axes, boxes, and soft robes. The sight of the flintlocks made their eyes gleam like fire points. They had never seen so many at one time.

"We will take shooting-sticks for the horses you want," gestured Chief Cameâhwait flatly, pointing a long bony finger at Lewis's flintlock.

The situation was touchy because the expedition had few guns to spare. Clark patiently used hand signs to explain that trade with other Americans would take place only when this party had gone to the Pacific Ocean and come back. "The more help you give us now," he motioned, "the sooner the traders can come and the sooner your people can have rifles and ammunition. We cannot give you rifles now."

With great dignity, Chief Cameâhwait motioned that he understood. Lewis presented him with a small Jefferson peace medal to wear around his neck, a blue uniform coat, a shirt, scarlet leggings, and tobacco. The chief went back to York, who was rolling his eyes as he sang a Negro spiritual, waving his hands and swaying his great body.

"See, you got to feel it," said York, thumping the chief on the chest, "you just can't sing it when you not warmed up to it."

The chief shook his head, not understanding a word, but trying to outshout and outmoan York, who was now bent double with laughter as two subchiefs, medals hanging around their necks and colored strips of ribbon grasped in their fists, came to join the chief in imitating York.

"You all sound like conjure men or preachers—too much monotone. Push it out from the bottom of your belly to the roof of your mouth. Just think of a fantastic tale and let it talk for you."

The chief laid down his gifts and clapped in delight as the subchiefs rolled their eyes toward the sky and shouted in their monotone, singsong voices.

When Captain Lewis fired the air gun, he sent the Shoshonis huddling in fear; then, sensing no imminent danger, they yelled in unison at the wonder of such great magic.

The Shoshoni dogs nipped and yipped at Scannon, who stood very still and held his head high. To get him out of this predicament, Captain Lewis put him through his routine of tricks. That sent the natives into vocal fits of admiration.

Captain Clark sauntered over to where York was entertaining the chief and his two subchiefs.[1] He watched for a few moments, then with hand signs he asked the chief about a river passage through the mountains. Chief Cameâhwait repeated the hand signs, then squatted on the ground and drew a river in the dust, showing with pebbles that it had many falls, and one place where the falls were higher than those of the Great Falls of the Big Muddy. With the dust he built mountains that were so close along the riverbank that no canoe could pass through. The ridges continued on each side, perpendicular to the river. Worse yet, there was no way to get out to hunt. And if there was some unknown way, it would be of no use—there were no deer, elk, or any game in that country. It was a dead land.

Sacajawea saw the disappointment on Captain Clark's face as her brother described the passage through the mountains. She moved closer and helped with her hand signs and few words of English to interpret the problems to be faced going farther west. There would be seven suns over mountains of solid rock, with no vegetation, followed by ten suns of sand and gravel, with no game and no water unless there was snow. The snow could be deep or blizzarding, making travel nearly impossible and frostbite almost inevitable. But beyond all that was a fertile country with small game and fish in the river, and still a great many suns farther was the stinking lake—the ocean.

That day it was arranged for Clark, Sacajawea, Charbonneau, and some of the men to go ahead to the main Shoshoni camp in the mountains to bargain for horses. Lewis decided to keep a few of the men behind with him to cache extra supplies and sink the remaining canoes out of sight in the river. Lewis and his men would then pick up Clark and his party at the main camp, and with horses to carry the packs, they would follow the mountain passage drawn by Chief Cameâhwait. Even knowing the dangers they faced, all the men were delighted—they were sick of canoe travel.

To Sacajawea it was nearly unbelievable—she was here, looking at the broad, level valley, Shoshoni Cove. This was the gateway to the highlands, where there was but a narrow opening, through which the river narrowed and chiseled its way forward. Along the cove's high edge were spruce, pine, aspen, and alpine willow. As if trying to show the life history of the region, the mountains at the western rim of the cove showed their ancient strata; the old fossilized strata rested upon younger strata rich in fossils of clam and oyster shells and the backbones of fish and fern. The old Shoshonis called these highlands "mountains without roots."

Sacajawea remembered what this pass meant to the People. To the west of it they were safe, though they lived like bears on roots and berries; to the east was the land of plenty, but they had to be in constant hiding because of the Blackfeet. The soft-spoken, prophetic words of her grandmother came to her: "Boinaiv, you are destined to be a leader of the People, to bring them full bellies and contented faces." She began wondering if perhaps she could persuade Charbonneau to stay now with her people. He could be here to meet the men who would come after this expedition to build trading posts. She could show the women how the Mandan and Minnetaree women embroidered their tunics with dyed quills.

They rode four days alongside the river, today called the Salmon, where the bed was rocky, the water rapid, and the mountains amazingly steep. They passed places where there were no more spruce forests or aspen, no crowded stands of lodgepole pine or montane meadows, only rocky alpine heights, with bull thistles.

One of the Shoshoni men found a tomahawk that Clark had lost in the grass after chopping heads from a good mess of rainbow trout. A tomahawk like that was worth a great deal to the Shoshoni, because he had no steel knives or hatchets. He split wood with a wedge of elkhorn and a mallet of stone. He made a deal with Clark to trade his horse for the tomahawk when they reached the main camp. Through all the hidden meadows and valleys this Shoshoni spread the word that a horse could buy a good tomahawk. The braves began to ride horses, unshod but surefooted, over the rocks, down steep slopes, and through narrow passes to the main camp for trading.

Clark's party passed several small encampments of Shoshonis who were hunting or digging roots in the mountain valleys. Naked children played with the horses in the small camps. The squaws fed the horses the inner bark of cedar trees. Always the horses were decorated with eagle plumes in their manes and tails. This was the insignia of the Agaidükas living in the Rocky Mountains. Chief Cameâhwait explained, "The People would die without their horses. They are true friends. My horse knows my voice, and he listens when I speak. He warns of the enemy and informs of nearby game."

As Clark's party neared the main Agaidüka encampment, Sacajawea's heart beat fast with excitement. She rode beside Chief Red Hair and her brother, and made herself sit very still, even though Pomp cooed and jabbered and caused Willow Bud to smile the whole day. She looked up at the glistening mountains that guarded the valleys and lowlands and willow-brush lodges on the bank of the clear river for the People. Her eyes moved from the birch and aspen and red paint-brush flowers of the foothills to the belt of spruce above, then to the top where the wind-tortured lumber pines and white-bark pines grew in grotesque shapes. She studied the summit, trying to visualize where pockets of kittentails or dwarf clover grew, their life span only

a few short weeks. A mountain jay scolded a lone pipit.
She breathed the invigorating air and knew that the
foothills, and the mountains behind, were something
certain and enduring, something in which she could
believe when there was uncertainty in life.

Willow Bud pointed out late-blooming bear grass,
windflowers, blue columbine, purple clematis, pearlike
everlasting bedstraw, and then the yellow goldenrod.
They chattered about the times they had made chains
of flowers in their girlhood. And then, before she knew
it, they were at the camp and the People were coming
along the wide trail from above to meet them.

Sacajawea's exaltation died. The People were ema-
ciated from hunger and grown old with work. She had
forgotten how starved they had been. But their faces
were happy and smiling, even gay. *Ai*, these were her
people. She felt close to tears. The women still let their
hair fall loosely over their faces and down their shoulders, she saw; not many women braided it as her mother
had done. The men divided their hair by means of
dressed leather in two equal queues, which hung over
their ears and down their chests; many had cut the hair
to the neckline because of the loss of relatives in recent
skirmishes.

Willow Bud swung down from her horse and hurried
to a group of women, and then the women pushed toward Sacajawea, jabbering and cooing at Pomp, feeling
the soft doeskin tunic on Sacajawea, and fingering the
wide belt of blue beads she wore. They picked up her
two fat braids and wound them around Sacajawea's
head, laughing. Over and over they said that this was
something unbelievable. A middle-aged woman came
up carrying her grandchild on her hip. She brought him
close to Pomp. The babies reached out toward one another.

"See," said the grandmother, "he knows this newcomer is an Agaidüka." Then the woman called, "Hush,
sshh! Women of the Agaidüka, look at the one called
Boinaiv who has come back to us. Look closely. You
can see she is like another who lived among us years
back. She stands with her back straight like the other;
she wears her hair like the other; she looks around at
us with questions in her eyes like the other."

Some of the women blinked tears, so great was the resemblance of this young woman to her mother, whom they had dearly loved as the wife of one of their great chiefs. The younger women, who could not remember but had heard the stories of greatness, stared and smiled. Sacajawea smiled as they called her Boinaiv, clenching her teeth together so that her tears would not spill out. She opened a pouch tied at her waist and gave the nearest ones a few kernels of dried corn, the first they had tasted. She poured a few kernels in her hand and gave the woman with the grandchild the empty beaded pouch. She put her arm around others and whispered in their ears, "I am one of the People." She charmed them. They were delighted with her baby. She had a hundred nursemaids for Pomp.

Then the women began to notice the man of Boinaiv. He held his head high, smoothing out his mustache and hitching up his bright, multicolored sash. Some of the younger women giggled behind their hands at the hair on Charbonneau's face. "He is like a big brown bear," said one. "No, like a porcupine," said another, a bit bolder than the rest.

"He is my man, called Charbonneau," said Sacajawea. "He cooks for the pale eyes."

"*Hai, yi! Yip!* Cooks! A man cooks? That is the duty of the woman. What do you do? Do you hunt for the meat?" They turned now to sarcasm, looking at her strangely.

Willow Bud spoke quickly. "It is a custom of the pale eyes. It is the way things are done. It is a fine custom. It lets the women have time to play with the children and tell them stories."

The women nodded, hushed, thinking carefully on that. Slowly they began to thread their way among the willowbrush lodges to the center of the camp where the skin Council Lodge stood. Chief Red Hair had already entered. Sacajawea asked Willow Bud to care for Pomp, and, to the surprise of many of the women, she left her moccasins at the door and boldly walked inside to sit in the place for interpreters. She was about to sit on the hard clay floor when she saw a small child before her, and beside him a warrior whose cheek was whitened by four long, deep scars. Instantly she recognized the warrior.

"Spotted Bear, my brother!"

"Boinaiv!" In one sweeping motion he pulled the robe from his shoulders and covered her shoulders also. "Boinaiv, we had all mourned for you as dead. We did not dare speak your name!"

"Many times I have seen you in dreams," she said, tears running unchecked down her cheeks. "Many times I thought of the time you fought the yellow-and-black-spotted bear alone. I recall how our father found you behind a windfall, red with your own blood, and the bear red with your blood and his. We feasted that night, singing with the Medicine Man to make you well again."

She grasped his hand, letting the robe fall to the ground, and noticed the long black hair of an enemy scalp fastened at the string of his breechclout. "You are still fearless," she said with pride.

The child, ignored so far, rested his hand lightly on the robe, waiting for the adults to end their conversation. Sacajawea glanced down. "Shoogan," she said with a certain intuition, and pulled the naked little boy to her. He came shyly but without resistance. She lifted him in her arms and held him out to look at him. The child scowled back at her, his mouth puckered as if pulled together by a drawstring, and curled his legs around her waist. The child had a mop of snarled hair, and his feet and legs were laced with scratches. His knees were gray from crawling in the cook-fire ashes, and his small hands greasy from dipping into the meat pot. He was no dirtier than any other Shoshoni child that had grown too big for dry-moss swaddling but was not yet big enough for clothes.

"And so, he is the son of our sister?" Sacajawea beamed. "And it is you, Spotted Bear, that I see in this papoose."

She gave the child a little pat on his naked bottom and set him on his feet on the ground. The child backed away and planted himself solidly, his lower lip pushed out stubbornly and his eyes clouding up darkly.

Quickly she scooped him up in her arms again. "When I return, I will raise him with my papoose. He will have two mothers, your woman and me." She looked at the round, hollow-eyed, undernourished child. "You will have a little brother and you will call me *umbea*, mother."

The toddler, no longer afraid or shy, put his head against the beaded yoke of her tunic.

"My woman, Cries Alone, has no babies yet, and he is the light in our lodge" said Spotted Bear softly. "He lives with us."

Sacajawea shifted her feet, and her eyes moved away from the hurt and sadness she saw on her brother's face. She thought, He believes I would take the child away. "When your woman lets him come to visit me, I will tell him stories about the pale eyes."

Spotted Bear's eyes lighted. "She is my first woman. She is good. There is no hole in her moccasins from running around. She stands by me. She loves the boy as if he were her own. She would bring him to visit in your tepee. So—you can see we have thankful hearts he did not die when it was discovered he was deformed. He was considered a curse, but my woman would not listen when others requested that the little one be interred with his dead mother on the scaffold. His cries would have followed us through the night across the hills, long after he was out of sight. His spirit would have followed us forever. My woman knew."

Now Sacajawea could see why the child was named Shoogan. His left foot was turned in slightly and was smaller than the right, a clubfoot.

The child stared with his two black robin eyes as Sacajawea examined his foot. His pink-brown mouth pursed, and he spoke. "I go. Father goes. You go. I go. I like you." He beamed, and then he went to Spotted Bear, who had picked up his robe and was preparing to leave, for the men of the council had taken their places.

Sacajawea took her place beside Charbonneau.

Chief Cameâhwait brought out his stone pipe and lighted it with a coal from the small smokeless fire. He drew a few puffs, then held it up, stem outward toward the west, intoning in a controlled, ceremonial voice a prayer, moving the pipe to the other three directions, then toward heaven and earth. He passed the pipe to the left, each man making a few motions and smoking. Captain Clark was constrained by a strong, incongruous feeling that he was in church. He breathed deeply, and then spoke to the Agaidükas.

"As you know, our Great White Father, who lives in a large village toward the rising sun, has sent us to you. We have come to blaze a trail for traders who will bring guns and blankets and axes in trade for your beaver and ermine pelts."

After a while, Chief Cameâhwait spoke.

"It is believed that the white man's magic smoking-stick will make the difference between full bellies and starvation. The Agaidüka has always hunted his meat with bow and arrow, testing his skill and courage in the chase. His medicine is good, and for this he has a skill beyond the white man's.

"But the white man has strong medicine, and now he is offering to teach us his skill with the smoking-stick. So—let us hunt the buffalo, killing them where we find them, the women dressing the meat where it falls, bringing it into camp, as is their right. This is the Agaidüka way. In a little while we can dance with round bellies and sleep in peace. I say we learn the white man's skill and hunt meat with guns."

There were murmurs of approval from the Agaidü-kas.

Sacajawea interpreted the chief's words to Charbonneau, who in turn gave the words in French for Labiche to translate into English.

While the translation was proceeding, Sacajawea proudly watched Cameâhwait, who was handsome this day with a tippet over his leather shirt. This neckpiece was about four inches wide, cut from the back of an otter skin, with nose and eyes on one side and tail on the other. Attached to this collar were hundreds of little rolls of ermine skin, which fell down over his shoulders nearly to his waist, so as to form a sort of short cloak. The center of the collar held oyster shells. It was elegant.

Then, like thunder in a cloudless sky, a deep voice boomed in the gutturals of the Shoshoni language, interrupting the proceedings. "Where is this woman, Boinaiv? Where is this woman?"

Everything stopped, the air still as before lightning. All eyes moved toward the open flap, where an unkempt, thick-necked warrior stood.

Sacajawea stared at the man. What could he want? She felt acutely uncomfortable. Had she violated some custom or law that she had forgotten or did not know?

"I want this squaw," the man said. "Three horses and a Spanish saddle were sent to her lodge many seasons ago as a gift to her father. She is my woman. Mine!"

Heads turned to look at Sacajawea.

Sacajawea put her hand to her mouth. So—this was Big Moose, the son of Red Buck. But he was old and had bad manners! Her mind was confused. It raced here and there trying to untangle what was happening. She did not understand how she had let herself into such a situation. She forgot to interpret his words.

The chief held his hand up imperatively. "Hold on, we are in council."

The man shook his head and spoke again. "I paid for her before she was out of the cradleboard."

"*Ai*, Big Moose, we all know that is true," said Cameâhwait. "Your father, Red Buck, made the arrangement with my father."

Sacajawea was unable to move, stunned, but she knew this to be the truth. Her sister had been betrothed to the brother of Big Moose at the same time. Then she felt a chill, for Big Moose was staring at her.

"She must come with me," Big Moose said.

"She sits in the council of chiefs." Cameâhwait spoke sternly.

"This is no place for my woman. I paid good horses," Big Moose repeated.

"Your father paid the horses," said Chief Cameâhwait. "You could not afford them at the time. We will powwow with you after the council. Go, sit in the front circle with the other warriors," he ordered.

Slowly the big Agaidüka pushed his way forward, every eye now fastened on him. There was a humming of voices, a sign of apprehension. The Agaidükas sensed trouble.

"Have you admitted this woman to the men's council to make me ashamed? Do you know how much I am ashamed for her?" Big Moose pulled angrily at the tuft of drab hair above his ear. "These white men have brought this woman here to torment me because she looks like the lost Boinaiv. I wish they would tell me why they do this."

"You know this is Boinaiv," said Cameâhwait.

"Then I claim her! She is to share my lodge with my other squaws, Leaf and Smoky Robes. Come now, Boinaiv. We go. Do not make me more ashamed by remaining in council with men. This is not the way things are done. Do not dishonor my lodge!"

Charbonneau shifted his feet under him. He could not understand the angry Agaidüka, but he sensed the tension had something to do with his woman. He began to feel anger rise in him. Who did this clod think he was, anyway, yelling things at his woman and interrupting the council?

"What did he say, eh?" he demanded. "Why aren't you telling us? He seems worked up about something."

Sacajawea began to speak. The man had come to reclaim her. This was the way things were. She had dishonored him. She belonged to another.

"*Mon dieu!* Pah!" Charbonneau exploded. There was no sense to it. She was his woman. He had won her fairly in the game of hands. He glared at the man. "I spit on you, *bâtard*! You *grandpère*! You old fart! You dirty old buck!" He did not stop to reason that he and Big Moose were about the same age, more than three times that of Sacajawea. "Tell him," he told his woman, "tell him that I am your man and that you are the mother of my son." He pointed through the flap toward the circle of women where Willow Bud sat with Pomp's head buried against her shoulder.

Sacajawea spoke, her voice thin and high-pitched at first.

Big Moose looked bewildered as he saw Willow Bud cradling a fat, clean papoose. He looked at Charbonneau, who was shaking his fist and smoothing out his mustache at the same time. His shoulders sagged and his head fell, his voice barely audible. "I am a man who does not need a squaw with a paleface papoose. I have squaws and plenty papooses. I do not wish for a son with skin the color of milk." He looked at Pomp. "Ugh," he said in disgust. "He is probably so weak he will never have thoughts of his own." Big Moose stepped toward Charbonneau, his foul breath causing the Frenchman to lean backward. Big Moose's lips blew out with the bubbling noise of marsh gas bursting through soft mud.

"May your food turn to ashes in your mouth, you fuzzy-headed raccoon," Charbonneau muttered under his breath.

Captain Clark nudged Labiche, who could not keep a straight face or a twinkle from his dark eyes as he told the story as Charbonneau had gotten it from Sacajawea.

"Lord Almighty! What can happen next?" asked Captain Clark. Then he turned to Charbonneau, who was wiping his brow with the end of his yellow cravat. "We ought to keep peace and make up for this old warrior's loss. Charbonneau, you open the pack over there behind the lodgepole and give him your old leggings and waistcoat and the yellow silk scarf around your neck. Maybe some tobacco."

Charbonneau's eyes were bugging out. It seemed as if suddenly he were a good three inches taller. His voice was doing the same trick it always played on him when he was excited; it had climbed up and up, and he was standing on his toes now with his heels raised off the ground as if he were trying to reach up to where his voice was. The more he tried, the higher his voice became. His breath was getting short, too, and he had started to sweat.

"My waistcoat and yellow scarf? I am not to be blamed for his loud, stinking bellowings, or for some moldy promise made years ago. Tell him to take his shock of coarse black hair and get out of here. Look at him sitting there like a puffed-up toad, thinking he can take my woman. He's not going to have my coat or my leggings, either, Capitaine, sir. He gets nothing."

"My words were an order," snapped Captain Clark.

"*Zut!*" Charbonneau said, and reluctantly brought out the clothing and tobacco and passed them to Big Moose, who smiled broadly, promptly rubbed his grimy face against Charbonneau's, and turned toward the lodge opening, hugging the gifts to his wide chest. He considered it a fair settlement for a debt he had given up long ago as uncollectible.

The humming in the council started again. Charbonneau, angered, thought they were making fun of
him, and he stared at the circle of Shoshoni faces, ready
to burst into a tirade about their uncouth manners. But
soon enough he sensed that the people were not making
sport of him at all. They approved of him; he was a big
man to give away such fine gifts. He began to smile
then, soon dropping his anger.

Sacajawea turned to Captain Clark. "I am grateful
to Chief Red Hair," she said softly.

Captain Clark, involved beyond all previous experience in protecting this young woman, felt the joy that
this role of protector gave him. He sat with his head
held high.

Chief Cameâhwait held the long-stemmed jade pipe
high as a signal for silence and order. "Let us continue,"
he said. Then his voice rang throughout the open lodge.

"Mighty chiefs and brothers, this year will be remembered in the legends of the Agaidükas as the Time
Many Palefaces and One Black Face of Great Medicine
Came among Us. In my family it will be remembered
as the Season Our Sister Came from the Land of Our
Enemies. We have friends among these palefaces. We
do not fear them. You see for yourselves what good care
they have taken of our sister, and how generous with
gifts they are to our brother. Now, Chief Red Hair will
speak of what he wants from us. Listen."

Captain Clark stood, his bare feet upon the white
robe, spread for chiefs. The fire seemed to light up his
face, and the Agaidükas noticed the similarity between
the sacred red flames of the council fire and his thick
thatch of red hair, drawn and bound in a queue behind
his ears. He was great medicine indeed. He held out
his arms as if to gather all of them unto him, and his
friendly smile won their complete confidence.

"Great Shoshonis, we need your help. We need your
horses to carry our supplies over the mountains to a
river where we can build canoes that will take us to
the Great Waters of the West. I ask now for two things:
a guide to show us the trails over the mountains, and
horses to carry the supplies. We will pay you well. Will
you do this?"

Sacajawea interpreted slowly so that the People would

understand well. Then, on impulse, she added to the translation:

"People of my own blanket, my heart is filled with so much happiness I find it hard to keep the tears off my face." Her voice was childish; she paused, then started again more slowly. "But my heart is filled with sadness to see you hungry. I had forgotten how it was. While I have been away from you, I have seen unbelievable things. I have seen lodges that keep out the winter wind and summer heat. I have learned how to put seeds into the earth to grow into foods that cause the mouth to water." She smacked her lips and rubbed her belly. "There are ways to store these foods for winter. I have seen traders come for the foods with knives, awls, kettles, axes, and blankets. Hunt and save your pelts for the traders who will come here. You can trade horses for unbelievable good things. This will fatten the Shoshonis so that you will not perish as the game in the mountains has perished. Help the white men. I have spoken."

Shaking from nervousness and the excitement of her impulsive speech, Sacajawea sat down and lowered her head in the manner of a proper Agaidüka woman.

The chief was moved by her speech of love for the People. However, it was not in his Agaidüka nature to let his emotion be shown outwardly. He rose impassively and addressed the members of the council. "Do you wish to help these friends who have traveled a long trail to be with you now?"

"*Ai*," was the unanimous reply.

"So—it shall be. You have spoken." Chief Cameâhwait turned to an elderly man. "Our bravest warrior, you have the most knowledge of the trails west over the mountains. Will you act as guide to these white chiefs?"

The old warrior, whose face was as dark as weatherworn leather and wrinkled as a dried persimmon, nodded approval. "*Ai*, my four sons shall come, also."

"Good," said the chief. "Now I wish to honor this Chief Red Hair who has shown kindness to my blood sister and shared his food with my people. To this white chief I give my tippet of furs, and to the black white man I give a *poggâmoggon*."

Ceremoniously, he placed the snow-white tippet across the shoulders of Captain Clark, and in York's hand the chief placed an instrument consisting of a handle about the size of a whip handle, about two feet long, made of wood and covered with dressed leather. At one end was a thong, two inches in length, which was tied around a stone weighing about two pounds and held in a cover of leather. At the other end was a loop of the same material, which was passed around the wrist so as to secure the hold when striking a severe blow to a small animal or some other game food.

"I also give to this Chief Red Hair my name, Cameâhwait." By signs he showed it meant "One Who Never Walks." "I will keep my war name of Tooette-cone, Black Gun. My people know this war name and know that it was given to me by an enemy warrior during a fight. I had fallen from my horse and saw a long black smoking-stick as I got to my feet. I pulled it from the hands of a wounded Blackfoot, and he yelled my new name as I hit another enemy across the back with the stick. The stick jumped from my hands, shot lightning, and ripped open the man I had hit. Again the enemy yelled 'Black Gun,' and they ran down a hill for a cover of trees."

Modesty about personal achievements had no place among the Shoshonis. When a man did something big, he told it and retold it.

"Henceforth, I shall be known as Tooettecone," said the chief. "This will be as a reminder of the black shoot-ing-sticks the traders will bring to us when they bring the trading post close to our camp. And hereafter, among the Agaidükas, this Chief Red Hair will be known by the name of Cameâhwait."

To give a friend one's own name was an act of high courtesy and a pledge of eternal friendship among the Agaidüka Shoshonis.

"Chief Black Gun," said Captain Clark, moved by the gifts and the bestowal of the name, "I am honored greatly. I would like to think of you as a brother, as does Janey here—the one you call Boinaiv."

The chief's dark, impassive face broke into a wide grin. He was very pleased.

York opened up the pack sack on orders from Captain

Clark, and he and Sergeant Gass passed out mirrors, beads, paint, and fish hooks to the pleased Agaidükas.

"That about skins it out," said York, shaking the empty sack.

The next day was windless, with an unnatural warmth, as if summer had finally reached beyond its peak. In the morning, John Collins and George Gibson brought in several buffalo. Near noon, Hugh McNeal and John Ordway came into camp with three deer. Sacajawea went with some of the women to dig turnips in the valley beside the River for the People. Early in the afternoon, Captain Clark sent word to Chief Black Gun that the white men would like the Agaidükas to have a feast with them.

As the crier went around the lodges telling the people of the meal with the white men, wild whoops were heard and the Agaidükas descended on the camp. Without waiting for the meat to roast on the cooking sticks York and Charbonneau had placed around the fires, people began to eat and tear at the meat as if they had not seen any in weeks. They fought over their shares, pulling and jerking and greedily devouring the warm, dripping, raw flesh; they pulled great handfuls of Mandan corn from the kettles with their bare hands, not seeming to mind the heat.

"Do your people always act this way?" Captain Clark asked the chief. He was appalled by the scene.

"Game is scarce for us. Usually each hunter keeps what he kills for his own family. This is the first time many have had fresh game in weeks," said Chief Black Gun sadly. He was standing next to Sacajawea, who looked on in silence.

Captain Clark turned his back on the blood-smeared scene and ordered Ordway and Collins to divide the three deer with the Agaidükas. In addition, he distributed what was left of the Mandan dried corn and beans.

"It won't be many years before these people can live below the mountains and feed on corn, beans, and squashes," said Captain Clark. "If they put their minds to it, they could become good farmers."

Sacajawea turned away. "Good farmers," she mimicked. "They have no taste for it yet."

"They've eaten enough Mandan corn and beans to get the taste," he flashed. "Lord knows, they could poke seeds into this ground in the spring."

Sacajawea shook her head sadly. Then suddenly she looked at Chief Red Hair, her mouth rounded. "Please," she said, "I would like to boil a little squash for my brothers to taste. Lord knows, they would like that. And I can show them how."

Forgetting herself, she bolted for the cooking fire. Out of the tail of her eye, she saw Chief Red Hair settling down on a boulder and chuckling.

Chief Black Gun and his woman, Dancer, Spotted Bear and his woman, Cries Alone, Shoogan, Willow Bud and her man, Yellow Neck, ate the orange squash greedily. Sacajawea watched their mouths rounding as she pushed squash toward Shoogan.

"Leave me half my thumb," she hooted.

As she fed the child the fragments left in the kettle, she hummed an ancient tune that lost itself now and then in her pleased chucklings.

"Miss Janey!"

Her song stopped short. York's voice was not loud, but Sacajawea caught its excited pitch. "Whooo! You look here. I'se fetched something sweet for after supper." York had a sly smile on his face, and a crowd of children behind him. The children were sucking their fingers. He handed her a handful of sugar cubes and put more on the ground beside Chief Black Gun. "It appears like it's the first time they'se had such fine tastes."

"These sweet stones are finer than anything I have ever dreamed of eating," Yellow Neck told Sacajawea, smacking his lips loudly.

"Will the white traders bring these?" asked Spotted Bear.

"*Ai*, they will bring all good things to the People," she answered, and then began to show them how to put squash seeds into little holes in the ground and cover them, then look for the rain clouds and wait for the green shoots and then the fruit.

"Yes, sir," York told Clark later. "They'se wild, but they'se like children when it comes to liking sweets. Lord, they'se still be licking their fingers. If the traders bring lots of sugar, there will be no reason to be scared of Injuns."

A feeling welled up in Clark. York knew, right enough. He knew how to make friends. He knew people. Of its own accord, his hand reached out and took hold of York. "Thanks—I'll make a note of it in my journal this minute."

"Write how Miss Janey looked when she saw her kinfolk. You could've lit a lamp wick off that smile. I'se never seen the sun rise up in nobody like it done in her then—just as sudden as the rain pour down like it never going to stop."

CHAPTER

21

Divided

Now that he had begun to succeed in getting horses,
Lewis evidently thinks that Sacajawea deserves a reward for her help. He gives Charbonneau some merchandise with which to buy a horse for her. What effect
this has on her Indian women friends one can only guess.
Certain they must be startled, since in their tribe it is
the man of the family who rides if there is only one horse.
If he owns a second animal, his wife and children may
share rides, unless the horse is too heavily loaded with
the family possessions. Possibly the women are jealous
of Sacajawea when they see her mounted while they have
not only to walk but help carry the white men's baggage
as well. Perhaps this is the beginning of her second separation from her people.

NETA LOHNES FRAZIER, Sacajawea, the Girl Nobody
Knows. New York: David McKay Co., 1967, p. 71.

Captain Lewis and a couple of the men busied themselves packing and caching supplies for their return trip. They sank the remaining dugouts in the river. It was time to start on the portage over the mountains.

But Chief Black Gun was not interested in having the white men hurry on. He was enjoying the food the white men provided, and the entertainment they gave each evening around the campfire. The chief sent Big Moose, Spotted Bear, and several other hunters to look for buffalo in order to prepare the winter's supply of meat. It was now the edge of the cold weather, and he had known throughout the last days of summer, when the autumn taste was in the air, that he would make the annual hunting trip sooner than usual, sending out most of the good horses with his hunters. Each year these Shoshonis joined their neighbors, the Flatheads, to go down into the plains with the hope of getting a winter meat supply before the Blackfeet could drive them off. The hunters took their skin sleeping rolls and leather sheaths filled with arrows and rode out leading the best Agaidüka horses.

When Lewis expressed impatience with the lesser grade of horses left at camp, the chief said, "Wait a few days until my hunters come back with the good horses packed high with meat."

"Three days—I'll wait no longer," Captain Lewis told him. "Then I'll buy horses from some other tribes—maybe the Flatheads, your neighbors." In anticipation, Captain Clark and some of the men went on ahead to set up a forward camp.

Before leaving, Clark asked Chief Black Gun for several Shoshoni men to accompany him up a fork of the river he had named after Captain Lewis.[1] No one but the old persimmon-faced warrior and his four sons volunteered. Even these five men looked as if they would turn back at any moment. Sensing their reluctance, York grabbed the hands of the four sons and jigged in a circle with them. Then he pulled the old warrior into the circle and began chanting. The warrior smiled, thinking that York had praised him and his sons with some great medicine. "I give you a name like one of us," York said solemnly. "Here after we'se going to call you Toby." He pointed a long black finger at the old man. "Toby—Old Toby." Then he used hand signs to show it was a name.

The old warrior pushed out his mouth, and the corners quivered when he tried to speak. He appeared nearly to cry, he was so pleased. It must have been a considerable time since anyone had given him any sort of gift.

Captain Clark, Drouillard, and several others, under the guidance of Old Toby and his four sons, set out to explore the river and set up a camp. Once they stopped to watch some Agaidüka fishermen who used bone gigs fastened to short lengths of thin rawhide tied to poles. The gig struck the trout so hard that the sharp end passed through and caught the other side of the fish. They went on, following the river north, then turned west with it, after the entrance of a north fork. Then they saw the first canyons, whose steep sides and swift, rock-filled rapids caused Captain Clark to pronounce this a completely nonnavigable river. Toby pointed out that the Agaidükas called it the River of No Return.

By the next afternoon Captain Lewis was impatient when Big Moose and Spotted Bear had not returned to camp. The chief busied himself sending more men and some women with butcher knives made of chipped flint and more horses to the hunt. "Hunting is good when they stay!" the chief laughed.

Captain Lewis knew there was game in the area. His own hunters had come back with buffalo and antelope each morning, dividing their kill with the needy Shoshoni families, but now Lewis felt as though there were a cold wind blowing on him. The good horses were being sent out of camp! No, by God! The expedition was not going to be stuck here all winter, then have to turn back east in the spring. Suddenly he realized what Chief Black Gun was up to. He should have realized it by the way they had been greeted by these savages. The Indians were not only hungry for food, they were starved for comradeship. The expedition was made up of men who were compassionate and friendly. Chief Black Gun was trying to delay the expedition so that the Agai-dükas would have food and company through the winter. That was why Charbonneau was encouraged to swagger around wearing his soiled ermine collar and to brag about his hunting ability, thought Lewis. By convincing Charbonneau he was a big man in camp, the Shoshonis thought to persuade him to encourage all the white men to stay for the winter. Well—they had the wrong man.

And Janey? Did she want to stay with her relatives? It would be a natural thing. But the expedition would be the loser. She and Pomp had kept the men's spirits up when the going got tough, and she would be a continuing indication to future tribes that the expedition was peaceful. I will have to play my hand close to my chest, thought Lewis. All at once he laughed. "She's the one. Thank the Lord for Janey!"

Captain Lewis devised a plan that afternoon with Sacajawea to get the goods carried over the foothills to the steep incline of the mountains where Captain Clark would be waiting. It was impossible to carry all the expedition's supplies on the few horses the men had bought, so Sacajawea would ask the Agaidüka women who had strong backs to carry the heavy packs. The women would not say no; they had eaten much of the expedition's dried corn and meat, and would be glad for a way of saying thanks.

Sacajawea moved from one tepee to the next. Finally she was standing in front of Willow Bud's tepee. She felt a deep pain go through her when she noticed Willow Bud standing near the outdoor cook fire exactly as she had seen her own mother stand a thousand times, her arms folded across her bosom, quiet, as steady as the mountain behind the camp itself. Sacajawea felt like a child again, come home, eager to be enfolded in strong maternal arms, eager to be protected against all harm and hurt. Once again tears flowed down her face as she put her arms around her friend.

"I'm glad you are home," said Willow Bud.

At that moment Sacajawea wished she could turn back the years, see her father strong and laughing once more, hoisting her to his shoulder, carrying her around the camp while he pretended to be a horse and she clutched at his hair and laughed and kicked his ribs. She wished she did not belong to Charbonneau, had never traveled with the white men, had never seen the Minnetarees and Mandans.

"It's life. It has to be," said Willow Bud, wiping away Sacajawea's tears, her voice low and sad, but calm. Sacajawea remembered her own mother saying, "If it has to be done, then it has to be done." It was as if the Agaidüka women had a pact with fate, as if they said, "What must be, will be, but nothing will ever defeat us."

Then Willow Bud said, "Each day you look more like yourself. I think it is because you gave away all your clothes and now wear those of the poor Agaidüka Shoshoni. You are one of us."

"That is what I want to talk about," said Sacajawea impulsively. "I want to know if I can stay in your lodge if my man goes on with the white men over the mountains."

"But he will stay here with some of the white men for the winter. The chief—your brother—thinks they will bring us food and keep the Blackfeet out of our camps."

"So—that is it!" Sacajawea saw things more clearly. She understood why Charbonneau insisted on wearing the ermine collar and why Black Gun was so friendly to him. Charbonneau did not want to go. He was a big man here. "But my man has promised the white men he will go as far as they go. He cannot stay." Then, looking at Willow Bud, she said, "I can stay. The white men needed me to lead them to this camp so they could buy horses to get over the mountains. Now my work with them is finished." She made the cut-off sign for emphasis.

Willow Bud moved backward a step or two. "I have not thought about this. I know my man would not be happy to have another woman to feed, especially one that has a white man's child with her. The child will have to eat. In this lodge there is hardly enough to feed the two of us in winter." Willow Bud hung her head and kicked at the earth beneath her feet. "Why not go to Spotted Bear's lodge and talk with his woman. If you stay there, we will visit back and forth."

"*Ai*," Sacajawea said. "I will."

"Let me know what she says." Willow Bud looked up. Sacajawea had already turned and was walking slowly toward her brother's tepee.

Cries Alone was inside with Shoogan. Sacajawea pulled a red blanket from her shoulders and took Pomp out of its folds so that he could sit near Shoogan. "See how they like each other," she began. "Cousins, they are nearly like brothers."

In the end, Cries Alone sent Sacajawea to Chief Black Gun's lodge, explaining that Spotted Bear also had all the mouths he could possibly feed, but Black Gun was not only her brother but the chief, and he would surely find room for her and her half-white child.

Sacajawea shook her shoulders as if shaking off her thoughts, and picked up Pomp. She tried to see that it was for the best. Still, all the old ways had returned to tempt her. She thought she had only to say she wanted to stay and she would be welcome—freely, gladly, tenderly welcome. She thought of the paths her feet knew— across the rocks, to the meadow, to the creek, up the ridge to the clearing, to the berry bushes, to the tepees, to the cook fires, to the sleeping couch.

But as she thought about the peacefulness and security she had known as a child, she knew deep beyond the thinking that she could not stay, and she knew that the peaceful feeling would not last—it actually had not lasted through her childhood, she thought, remembering the raid of the Minnetarees. So, even as she thought of the familiar pathways, she remembered the good food among the white men and the good hides for clothing. She had gone on a journey, and she could not turn back; she had a man and a child.

As Sacajawea stopped in front of Black Gun's lodge, Dancer came out to greet her. "Um," said Dancer, "there is no need to ask. I know your brother would not let you stay in this lodge. But then, he would be glad to see you here if you stayed with your own man in a tepee of your own and your man went out for winter meat. All the white men should stay."

Sacajawea nodded. She had half expected that answer. She was welcome if she stayed in the camp of the white men with her half-white child. "Well, then, if you

want, you could help pack some of the baggage over the
foothills. The white men are going west. Has an Agaidüka been as far as the big sea?"

"No, because it is a bad journey, with hardships and
only the mountain sheep." Dancer reached out a strip
of dried meat toward Pomp.

"I am going to see that big sea and taste its salty
water," said Sacajawea stubbornly.

Dancer's eyes grew large, and she made the sign for
a split tongue. She said she could not believe a woman
would go on such a trip.

Sacajawea could not be angry with these women;
they had done what was expected of them. But she felt
an inner disquiet; she was deeply shaken. To have been
turned down by her best friend and relatives went
against every courtesy she felt the People should have
shown. She did not stop to ask anyone else to carry
goods over the foothills but went back to her camp and
Charbonneau.

The next morning Captain Lewis carried out the remainder of his plan. He gave Charbonneau a tomahawk
and an old pair of woolen leggings and told him to buy
a horse for Sacajawea.

"By gar, if we aren't staying the winter here with
my brother-in-law and his people, maybe I ought to
have a horse, too."

"Oh, Lord, I should have thought of this," said Lewis.
He gave Charbonneau another tomahawk and a couple
of steel knives. Charbonneau was able to buy two horses
and a mule from some men he had entertained with
hunting stories.

Sacajawea's having a horse of her own caused some
commotion among the women. They had never seen a
woman riding a horse around the camp. Their tongues
wagged. This was Boinaiv, who seemed to have a way
of doing what no woman did. Sacajawea looked around
at their faces and wondered why they had not thought
of using a horse to carry the water jugs from the creek
and back to the tepees. It was a long walk. She asked
for jugs and shortly had them all filled and tied to the
sides of her horse. Others came with their jugs. The
women stood in line during the afternoon laughing and

gossiping, half-afraid their men would come back from the hunt, see them doing this new thing, and accuse them of being lazy.

"Boinaiv does not see a woman's place as we do," said one woman, clicking her teeth. "I should say not," said another within Sacajawea's hearing. "She behaves like a man. Look, she can carry a pack for the white men on her horse, and we promised her to carry packs on our backs." Someone tittered. "*Ai,* I saw that man of hers cooking, so I should not be surprised if he were the one to go to the birth lodge. She is the brave; he is the squaw." More tittering and some loud tee-hees could easily be heard.

Nothing they could have done, however, could have hardened Sacajawea's stubbornness more. At first, the laughter pierced her and hurt; slowly it became simply a sound, a concert of sound. She stood alone. It was pride that came to her rescue, pride that refused to be humbled. She felt publicly humiliated and stoned with words. Standing, listening, it came to her that these women were like half-grown children. She felt shame for them, and pity. Then to herself she thought, You cannot recover childhood, nor can you ever find your home in your past. Slowly she led her horse to the other side of the camp where York was entertaining some children by dancing barefoot in the dust, wiping a bit of red paint from his body and daubing it here and there on theirs.

The children gathered about her, admiring the horse. York was kind and commiserated with her. "We'se both without folks. But we'se lucky to have acquaintances in two nations, ours and the white man's." Then he said, bristling with indignation, "I'd like to take a hickory stick to those spiteful women." Sobering, he predicted, "Troubles never come singly. There's some in those mountains. I'se getting hunched. These damned Shoshonis know there are hazards up there. I'se been praying: Lord, hold the buzzards back so we'se get out of here safe and sound and be on our way home to the States come another year."

Sacajawea followed his words as best she could. "Buzzards?"

"T'se don't lie to you, Janey. I'se scared. Those mountains are pure rock and straight up."

She straightened Pomp more comfortably on her back and made hand signs, saying, "I'm a rolling stone, pulled by whatever new thing lies over the mountains."

"Janey, you'se stubborn. If I said not to jump over that yonder fire pit, you'd jump clean over it before anyone told you it was impossible."

Now she laughed. And the children laughed as York jigged around the horse.

Three days after Captain Lewis had lost patience with Chief Black Gun, the remainder of the expedition started out to catch up with Captain Clark and his party. Many Agaidüka women carried heavy packs on their backs, and the few horses the men had purchased were loaded heavily. Willow Bud carried Pomp. Sacajawea led her horse which was also packed high with supplies. Many of the Agaidüka men rode their horses beside the white men. They would stay until Chief Red Hair was found. The Agaidüka men considered themselves degraded if compelled to walk any distance. Were a Shoshoni warrior so poor as to possess only two horses, he would ride the best horse and leave the other for his baggage and his women and children. If there was much baggage, the women followed on foot carrying the remainder. The children walked or rode on the drag.

The trail was short because Captain Lewis was called back several miles to attend Pete Wiser, who had become quite ill. At about the same time, the Agaidüka woman who had been leading two packhorses stopped beside a small creek, a mile behind the main party. She did not return, although she sent the horses along with another squaw.

Sacajawea asked her brother, "What has happened to the woman?"

Chief Black Gun looked unconcerned, but replied, "My sister, called Boinaiv, where are your eyes? Her time was at hand. She will meet us soon."

The men had dismounted and led their horses to graze near a spring where the grass was green. They would wait for Captain Lewis. Sacajawea and Willow Bud sat on the parched buffalo grass beside the trail.

Sacajawea nursed Pomp before he whimpered with the first midmorning hunger pangs. The child's eyes closed as he suckled lazily, his small brown hand walking on his mother's chin. Willow Bud sang softly, something she made up about the trees looking over the small animals and good friends.

They waited several hours for the return of Captain Lewis. Then the chief ordered that camp be set up for the night.

The Agaidüka woman came into camp carrying her newborn papoose in a tattered robe slung across her back. "I am here," she said, a grin crinkling the skin around her eyes.

Sacajawea laid Pomp on the grass and hurried to see the new infant. She begged the mother to lie down and rest while she had this opportunity, and brought her a bowl of broth that she sweetened with sugar. The new mother seemed grateful for the nourishment and the fussing around her, but she repeated that she was fine and ready to start again. She looked at her tiny daughter, then hitched her dress up a little to check the goose-down packing she had used on herself. She pointed to the parfleche beside her. "I have collected the breath feathers all summer for this time," she explained.

In the grayish cast of the short twilight, Captain Lewis returned with Pete Wiser, who was recovering slowly from an attack of stomach cramps by medicating himself with small doses of peppermint and laudanum. He found there was no moving on; the Agaidükas had set up camp for the night. "Lord in a bush," Lewis swore under his breath, "we could have made ten miles more before sundown. The damn Shoshonis don't want us to leave."

"Your brother does not wish to trade with the white men for horses," said Willow Bud. She sucked her cheeks in and then worked them up and down, scrubbing her teeth with them.

"What?"

"The raids of enemies have taken half our horses. They are our only protection. There are not enough now for all the People to ride. The Flatheads have come to the Three Forks. The hunters must go more than once

to the buffalo country before the Season of Deep Snow.
They must meet the Flatheads. Every horse our chief
trades to the white chiefs may mean the life or captivity
of a woman or child."

Sacajawea winced. A sick feeling took her. "But the
men in council said *ai* to the trading."

"The People do not always think deep," Willow Bud
answered. "They are ruled by the time and how they
feel today. Their thoughts do not take them to tomorrow
and how they will feel then. A tribe is not held together
by feelings alone."

Something had surely gone wrong. Sacajawea could
not figure it out. She'd thought her people could help
these white men. Yet on the other hand she could not
forget that she had not so long ago been a captive. It
was something she would never wish on anyone. The
sick feeling tightened like cramps in her belly.

Willow Bud then asked her a painful question. "How
long before these traders come?" She waited patiently
for the reply. Then she became uneasy at Sacajawea's
silence. "You think many snows?" she asked suspiciously.

Sacajawea nodded. The cramps rose up into her
throat.

"So—as I thought. The way is long."

Thinking of the Agaidüka courage word, Sacajawea
used it. "*Puha*," she said, but the word came thin and
puny from her lips.

"*Ai*, your brother sees the white men have changed
you. You no longer think courage in the Agaidüka way.
You no longer remember the women's courtesies. You
speak out. You give orders to your man. Your thoughts
are traded and confused with those of the whites."

"Is that bad?"

"No." Willow Bud sniffled, then sighed. "Two minds
trading thoughts cause each mind to grow stronger. In
the end each mind loses the identity it had in the beginning. Look at your son. He is fat and beautiful. His
beauty comes from the white men and the Agaidüka.
He is both; yet he is neither."

Sacajawea felt her blood warming. "Now you listen,"
she said, her voice pinched. "Pomp is beautiful because
he is the best of two nations. Here is an example. When

the black man first came to the Five Villages, those people were impressed by his strong body and agile mind. The men bought his favors with furs and robes and tanned hides so that their wives could hold his seed and grow his children. They believed that the children would be strong and quick-witted warriors, strengthening their villages."

Willow Bud clapped her hands to her mouth. The Shoshonis did not volunteer the service of their wives as did the Minnetarees or Mandans. Willow Bud now had much to think about and said no more.

Sacajawea spent the night with alternations of emotion in her heart, and she recalled the voice of her father saying, "All that lives is round. The stem of a plant, a tree, the body of a man, the sun, the moon. The sky and the whirlwind are round. The day and the night circle the sky. The seasons add themselves onto the circle of life, and death closes it. The closed circle is a symbol of life, of time, of the earth."

The morning sun came up over the foothills into a sky that was red as the coals of the council fire. It touched the snow-peaked mountains above the camp and moved swiftly down the sides. The horses had begun morning grazing. It was a new day.

Sacajawea tied several small packs to her horse and rode it to the Agaidüka camp. Black Gun was talking to Yellow Neck and two subchiefs. She overheard him say, "Break camp today. Meet me tomorrow at the yellow cliff in the pass. Then we will go to the buffalo country in the plains with the Flatheads. They are near the Three Forks. We do not need white men to kill our food."

"You told them you would help," said Yellow Neck. "They brought your sister to you. They are good with gifts."

Black Gun's face became dark. "The People come first. We must meet with the Flatheads for the buffalo hunt."

Sacajawea watched the subchiefs go with the message. Her heart beat fast. So—Black Gun, her brother, was breaking the word he had given in council. He would desert the white men and let them get over the mountains as best they could, alone.

She felt conspicuous walking through the camp looking for Captain Lewis. He was packing supplies on a fidgety horse who stomped off the flies. It was to be a warm day. She knew she must not make her judgment too quickly; she must turn this knowledge over slowly.

Captain Lewis started the procession rolling, with the chief and two of his braves next. Scannon followed, trotting ahead of the Shoshoni dogs. Then came the heavily burdened packhorses; then the women and children straggling along beside. Warriors mounted on roans and pintos brought up the rear. Sacajawea mounted her horse, looking over the women and children for Willow Bud and Pomp. Her head swam; her heart still pounded. Should I tell what is within me? she thought.

"The People come first," Black Gun had said. And that thinking was what kept the People together; it was what made him their chief. It was life or death for them to get food. The buffalo would supply food to last several months. She could understand that, but it was not like her brother to behave with a split tongue. This was a bad thing. She pulled her horse to a stop and motioned for the squaw with the newborn baby to ride for a while.

Sacajawea took the red wool blanket that she used to carry Pomp on her back and pushed it into the mother's arms. "For the Month of Howling Winds," Sacajawea said and smiled.

"*Hou!*" Signs of approval went through the women. The new mother gratefully mounted the horse, her infant bouncing in her leather shawl on her mother's back. Captain Clark would be pleased, thought Sacajawea, to have his blanket used by a full-blooded Shoshoni papoose.

These people borrowed kettles, knives, and axes from the white men, and they returned them when finished with their chores. They were generous with what they had, supplying the men with berries and wild vegetables and giving gifts. They met poverty and distress with their heads held high and determination in their hearts, and rejected any more responsibility whenever possible, she thought as her mouth twisted wryly. Yes, a chief should think of his people first. Her brother was right.

But what if the white men did not have enough horses and were forced to go back down the Big Muddy to their Great White Father and say the Shoshonis were people with forked tongues? Then the white men would not build a trading post at the Three Forks. The People would remain hungry and live in fear until they were completely driven under. Oh, no! The People must not be destroyed! So—it is better to have trouble today and be alive for tomorrow.

Sacajawea shifted the lead string of her horse to Willow Bud and pushed ahead.

It was midday, and the men were halting for the noon meal. Sacajawea ran past Charbonneau and her brother toward Captain Lewis. Hesitantly, she told him what she had heard of her brother's plans.

Captain Lewis raised his eyebrows and looked at her with his cold blue eyes. "Why didn't you tell me earlier? Right away this morning?" His voice was harsh. "Always tell me immediately when you hear or see something that will affect this expedition. Lord, woman, don't you know what this will do to us?"

"*Ai.*" She nodded, her tears close.

Controlling himself, he took out his pipe, tamped it, and lighted it with a stick in the Shoshonis' small fire. Then he walked to Chief Black Gun, sat on the ground, and took off his moccasins.

Sacajawea had an inspiration. She sat next to Captain Lewis and took off her moccasins. She scowled so at Charbonneau, who had trailed along, that he sat and removed his moccasins. Then the gathering Shoshonis followed silently, watching Captain Lewis. Chief Black Gun kept his eyes on the ground. Charbonneau gave his woman some hard nudges when Captain Lewis was not looking, but she would not speak to him.

Finally Captain Lewis stood. "My brothers, you have taken off your moccasins as a pledge of your word. Is that right?"

Sacajawea fidgeted, doing her best to translate.

"*Ai, ai!*" they said.

"In our council you promised not only me but also Captain Clark to help us with horses over the mountains. Now I find that you will break camp and meet your hunters in the mountains, then go east to buffalo country. This makes it impossible for us to trade for more horses."

Sacajawea translated, conscious of her brother's dark face upon her, his eyes accusing her of deserting the People for the white men.

There was silence. A dreamlike quality prevailed, for Captain Lewis knew this impromptu council could change suddenly to a situation of horror if not handled just right. He wiped his neck and forehead with an already sweat-stained handkerchief. He turned to look at Chief Black Gun. "Is this so?"

"*Ai!*" Black Gun said in a tone that somehow implied a doubt.

"Where are your two subchiefs?"

"It was my order," answered Black Gun. "I sent them on as messengers."

"We have proved we speak with a straight tongue. We are your friends. Once more I say that you made a promise to help us over the mountains."

Chief Black Gun looked directly at Captain Lewis. "The Flatheads have arrived at the buffalo hunting grounds. We must have food for the winter."

"And once more I say that a great lodge can be built near the Three Forks by the Americans. You can trade there for food and guns. Will you speak with a straight tongue?"

"I will not speak with a forked tongue." Chief Black Gun's voice was low and deliberate. He motioned for silence and looked off into space for many long minutes.

"Shoshoni brothers," Charbonneau said then, unable to stand the silence, "I think—"

"I think you had better shut up," Captain Lewis said, and Charbonneau closed his mouth.

Finally Chief Black Gun spoke. "The People will wait a few more days before all go on the hunt. We have time for hunting when you have gone."

Captain Lewis rose and in a ceremonial manner presented his remaining unsoiled white handkerchief to Chief Black Gun, who gave it to Yellow Neck with instructions to ride ahead and overtake the subchiefs, and countermand Black Gun's first order.

Then Captain Lewis hastily gave out billets entitling the Shoshonis who were helping with the transport to receive merchandise when their job was completed. Only one deer was killed that day. The captain gave it to the Shoshonis to divide, and he went without supper.

On August 29th, the men of the Lewis and Clark Expedition were reunited and ready for departure. Captain Clark's party had hunted successfully and had several deer, elk, and antelope and many trout with them. The food was divided with the Shoshonis, and the billets were exchanged for flour and sugar, which the Shoshoni women cooked with dried berries. It was a dish Captain Lewis had taught them to make.

The expedition made some good last-minute trades and brought the number of horses up to twenty-nine. Lewis branded them with a hot iron that read: U.S. CAPT. M. LEWIS.[2] Clark got the last two horses from Yellow Neck by trading with him a pistol, a flintlock, balls, and powder. There were murmurs of approval from the nearby Shoshonis. The weapons made Yellow Neck a big man in their sight.

Chief Black Gun presented Charbonneau with a large willow-woven pot made watertight with hardened pitch. The pot held a supply of horn spoons made from the bighorn sheep.

"We make a present to our brother. We make this present to you who can prepare a feast with the help of no squaw."

Charbonneau looked about him. No one appeared amused. Yet he sensed amusement in the air. Was this some little joke the chief was making and the others enjoying? All the Shoshoni faces were devoid of emotion. He took this to be an exhibition of esteem on their part for his fine cooking.

"*Merci beaucoup! Merci beaucoup!*" he said with his hands moving rapidly, much flattered.

Sacajawea could imagine how the People would double over in laughter when Charbonneau was out of sight. She looked at her people, then at the white men, and then at her own man. She felt pulled in half. She had given Willow Bud a tiny pair of Pomp's outgrown moccasins, saying she was certain there would be another papoose for her arms to enfold. She had slipped a braided horsehair chain around little Shoogan's neck, saying, "Do not forget me. I will come back." The child ran to show his gift to Cries Alone.

Sacajawea stood by her brother, who was seated on a white horse, and touched his hand good-bye.

"Our ways are no longer yours," he said.

"I have seen this," she replied sadly.

"You must stay with your man. That is the Shoshoni way. He will not come here again." He said the words slowly, looking past his nose.

She knew she had promised to come back. Now, deep inside, she wondered if it were a falsehood. She started toward her horse, then stood between the two bands. She felt she belonged to neither. Black Gun's eyes drilled into hers, and she could not look at him, feeling something akin to a foreboding. She forced a smile and raised her hand in farewell to the People.

Captain Lewis watched Sacajawea move ahead on her horse, and he knew Clark would approve of the purchase, and even his motive behind it.

Book Three
THE CONTINENT CONQUERED

In Governor I. Steven's report on the Pacific Railroad surveys of 1853 to 1855 the following statement was written:

"At the crossing of the Snake River, at the mouth of the Peluse (Palouse), we met with an interesting relic. The chief of the band ... exhibited, with great pride, the medal presented to his father, Ke-Powh-kan, by Captains Lewis and Clark. It is of silver, double, and hollow, having on the obverse a medallion bust, with the legend, 'TH JEFFERSON, PRESIDENT OF THE U.S., A.D. *1801,*' and on the reverse the clasped hands, pipe, and battle axe crossed, with the legend, 'PEACE AND FRIENDSHIP.'"

OLIN D. WHEELER, *The Trail of Lewis and Clark*, vol. II. New York: G. P. Putnam's Sons, 1904, p. 124.

This may be the same medal discovered more than a century later, at the same location in Franklin County, Washington, in 1964, where the Palouse River empties into the Snake River.

Washington State ethnologists found it in a canoe burial while excavating an ancient village site. It is much like the Chief Yellept Medal found in 1890 in size and composition and structure. It differs, however, in that it has a perforation immediately above Jefferson's head. Erosive effects have destroyed the finer details of this piece. Lewis and Clark made no mention of presenting medals to Indians at the mouth of the Palouse, though they did give one to Chief Cutsahnem at the confluence of the Snake and the Columbia Rivers.

On March 1, 1899, an engineer named Lester Hansaker, was doing some excavations for the construction of a roadbed for the Northern Pacific Railroad when he came across an Indian grave at the mouth of the Potlatch River (called Colter's Creek by Lewis and Clark) in Nez Percé County, Idaho. In the grave he found a Jefferson Medal, which is now located in the American Museum of Natural History, New York. It was wrapped in many thicknesses of buffalo hide. This may be the same medal with the suspension ring which the captains gave to Twisted Hair, the Nez Percé chief and tewat.

The Oregon Historical Society has a Jefferson Medal that is silver, of the shell type, with a diameter of about 2¼ inches. It was found in the early 1890's in a grave on an island near the mouth of the Walla Walla River and lacks the suspension loop and has suffered considerable damage due to unknown causes. This medal may be the one which Captain Clark presented Chief Yellept on the Expedition's return journey. The explorers met Yellept's Walla Walla tribe below the mouth of the Walla Walla River on the west bank of the Columbia, in what is now Benton County, Washington.

Recently some Indian treasures have been found at the ancient Chinook village of Wishram, in the state of

Washington. Among the treasures was a silver dollar with the date 1801 on it. Also two Washington Season Medals of silver, 1¾ inches in diameter and perforated. Originally they may have had suspension loops, though they are missing today. On the reverse the inscription "SECOND PRESIDENCY OF GEO. WASHINGTON MDCCXCVI" has been completely eroded away, and the marginal wreath of oak and laurel leaves shows distinct wear. On the obverse all detail is gone except that the outline of the man sowing wheat and, below, portions of the letters, "USA." These two medals are on loan to the Maryhill Museum, Washington, from Mary Underwood Lane, a granddaughter of Chief Chenoweth, a famous Cascade Chinook, who may have lived in a village just west of the present North Bonneville, Washington. As to the history of these medals, no one actually knows, but they might be the very ones given to the chiefs Chillahlawil and Comcommoly on November 20, 1805 by Lewis and Clark.

PAUL RUSSELL CUTRIGHT, "Lewis and Clark Peace Medals," *The Bulletin*. St. Louis: The Missouri Historical Society, vol. 24, no. 2, 1968, pp. 160–67.

Over the Mountains

Since snowshoes were used for walking, the lightest possible construction was wanted. Easily made "bear-paw" snowshoes were a bit less than a foot wide and about a foot and a half long. They were roughly egg shaped to spread the weight of the wearer, and the more pointed end was the front. Bear-paw frames were often crooked. They had two thwarts, and all the spaces were filled in with coarse twined weaving, very open, so as to pick up the least amount of snow.

EDWIN TUNIS, *Indians*. New York: The World Publishing Co., 1959, pp. 50–1.

A week later, Captain Lewis had already moved his people to Clark's forward camp, and the expedition was once again together. By this time, the outfit was left with Old Toby and only one of his four sons, Cutworm, as guides. The other Shoshonis accompanying the white men had turned back home. This was a relief to Captain Clark, because during the days just before turning back, the Shoshoni women had become so jealous of Sacajawea's having her own horse and such a favored position with the expedition, that he was afraid there would be some outward confrontation to settle. If that happened, he knew he'd put the blame squarely on Captain Lewis's shoulders, where it belonged. Some scheme! he thought. Giving Janey her own horse was like planting an overhot powder keg in the midst of a Shoshoni powwow. It served its purpose to keep her with the expedition, but did not keep feelings from reaching a boiling point.

Sacajawea was furious with the women's attitude and tried desperately to make them understand her position. They all pretended not to comprehend and made malicious remarks behind her back and spoke cattishly to her face. For example, even Willow Bud said on the day of departure, "Don't cry. When we see you next year, maybe you will be chief of these palefaces."

The remark stung and brought more tears to Sacajawea's eyes, but for once she held her tongue.

The expedition moved forward through the precipitous canyon of the North Fork of the Salmon River and headed northeast toward the Bitterroot Valley, where Old Toby assured the captains he could easily pick up the trail by which the Nez Percés crossed the mountains to the buffalo plains. The Shoshonis had sold them a total of twenty-nine horses and two strong-backed mules for packing.

The wind was the master, but the men blessed it since, while it blew, the haze of flies was held impotent in the shelter of the rock lichens or hidden in favored canyon niches where there were a few scrawny spruces, none of which stood more than a yard high.

Just before dusk, the hunters joined the main party, empty-handed. For several days Sacajawea had looked for game signs, but saw not a bird nor an animal track. This land seemed deserted. Then one morning a faint animal smell came in with the wind, but she could not place it. It was neither deer nor rabbit; not ground squirrel, fox, or bird. Then the odor vanished and Pomp's hungry cry rose above the moan of the wind.

As this day faded, Three Eagles, chief of the Selish tribe of the Flathead Nation, was scouting for horse thieves, but to his astonishment he saw in the canyon valley a line of men that belonged to no tribe or nation he knew of. Not one brave in this line wore paint on his face or a robe on his back. He thought perhaps horse thieves had robbed them also, because to his knowledge all men wore robes in this cold, windy weather. He noticed that there were two men riding together at the head of the string. A few men walked, leading pack-horses, and they made their way openly, not secluding themselves behind rocks or the poor, ugly little trees like a war party. They had only one squaw among them, and she carried a papoose on her back. War parties never permitted women and children in their midst. Three Eagles wondered where the other women of these men were. Had the horse thieves taken them also? Then he saw one huge man, painted all black for war.

The string of men seemed to be heading straight for his village. Hurriedly, he ran off to the village, where he ordered all horses driven in beside the tepees and everything prepared for defense. Then he stood on a rise, hidden behind a boulder, and watched the strangers come on. Some were bone white. Were they all sick? They did not ride or walk like men who were ill. Curious about these visitors, he went back to his village and greeted the men with quick, deft movements of his hands, and he asked his squaws to find buffalo robes among the people of his village to replace those that must have been stolen from these poor men.

Then Old Toby stepped forward and interpreted with hand signs for the captains. He told the chief that the white men had blankets in their packs, but used them only at night to sleep in.

"This bone-white tribe has strange customs," said Chief Three Eagles.. He was a big, swarthy-faced man with long, flowing hair, and not overly clean. He invited the expedition to stay the night. There were about thirty-three tepees. Captain Lewis estimated eighty men, three hundred women and children, and at least five hundred horses.

Lewis thanked Three Eagles and promised that his party would stay the night in their own camp a few hundred yards upstream. Sacajawea recognized their odor as that which had come fleetingly on the wind, and she knew these people were of the Flathead Nation. The expedition was treated to a meal of boiled venison after they gave out a few gifts of colored beads and ribbons. The Selish Flatheads laughed and chatted with a low, guttural clucking, resembling that of so many turkeys.[1] They did not seem to have definite words, only a soft crooning to their chatter.

Old Toby asked the whereabouts of the trail to the Nez Percé's camp. Three Eagles pointed out a trail to the northwest that was no more than a faint game trail winding through stones and deformed juniper. "It leads to the Nez Percés, who live on the other side of the mountains. The trail is empty." The chief rubbed his belly and bent double to show hunger pangs for want of food, indicating the trail held little game.

"Praise the Lord!" shouted the elated Captain Lewis, ignoring the fact that game would be scarce. "I knew it! There had to be a way across these mountains."

The next morning, the captains bought thirteen more horses and three colts, and exchanged seven that were worn out. They then traded for half a dozen bags of jerky from the Selish before moving north down the Bitterroot Valley. Hunters were sent out during the day and found no large game, but fortunately came in with several cranes and some pheasants for the evening meal.[2] That day the horses took much punishment from the cold, bitter winds, little grass for food, and the steep rocky terrain. "A high-grain diet would help the beasts ward off the cold," sighed Captain Lewis.

Riding became dangerous. The men slipped and struggled forward over slabs of rock that dipped steeply over the sides of the trail. The trail skirted the moun-

tain slope, then dipped and swung to the west. The
expedition found itself in a grove of tall pitch pine. Some
trees must have been up to one hundred and sixty feet
in height, and many had fallen. The trail twisted and
turned to avoid them, so much so that the head and tail
of the outfit was frequently in a position to reach over
and shake hands from opposite sides of some huge log.
Even winding around, and jumping everything they
could possibly get over, the men still had to cut the trail
open in several spots.

The evening was gray, cold, and still, with a threat
of snow in it. Nothing was stirring, and there was no
sound—not even from the stream, which here fell swiftly
and quite silently through level flats of an old lake
basin. It was as if the stillness of death lay on the
camping place. A mist crept along the walls of the tiny
valley like a gray, formless, frozen ghost, and the mountains were hidden from the party by a low canopy of
leaden clouds. Not even the Flatheads had used this
place in many years. There was a place where the men
off-saddled, a knoll, where a fire had been made—but
the sign was old. Grass and dry seed heads of dead
flowers were poking through the ashes; moss covered
the blackness of the charred logs. A set of tepee poles
was piled against a rock, but it was long since the poles
had been used and they were all rotten. Not far from
the poles were three circles of boulders, half-hidden in
the moss and lichens. Sacajawea walked into the center
of one of these tent rings and found under the dry grass
the blackened embers of a center fire. Near the dead
fire she found a ladle of elk's horn and a bone sewing
awl. She wondered what made the women of this lodge
hurry away so fast, leaving behind a hard-to-fashion
ladle and awl.

Before sunup, she was wakened by the whimpering
of Pomp, who was hungry. She snuggled him to her
breast. When Pomp was again asleep, she rose and
walked away from the camp to relieve herself. Along
the edge of the old lake basin she found rows of small
stones set up by children playing and perhaps twenty
tepee rings scattered here and there. Around the rings
she found a bone fish hook and other tools of the people
who had once lived here. A wooden ornament for some

woman's hair was discarded in the moss. Beside it lay
a section of bow with a good spring still in its fibers.
Nearby was an empty stone cache. Normally it would
be used to hold the excess meat during the winter. It
looked unused, not stained with blood or animal tissue
or hairs. Why had these people left so suddenly? What
terror could have made a woman abandon the beautifully woven vegetable tray—a thing of enduring value—
to split and whiten under the summer suns and winter
snows? And how could men flee when their bows and
fish hooks remained in the deserted camp?

Before she left the camp of tepee rings, the ancient
inhabitants seemed to speak to Sacajawea and tell her
of fleeing from an insidious enemy so quickly that there
was no time to pack all hunting gear and household
goods. On second thought she believed they did not
rush, they just didn't pack well because they didn't care.
The enemy had left them weak and debilitated. As the
sun came through the peaks of the mountains, there
was no other sound than the harsh piping of the newly
rising wind. No birds, no chipmunk chatter, no scurrying of field mice was in the air. The enemy was starvation.

As she walked around the back side of the rings, she
found a large block of blue argillite up-ended to form
the marking of a burial mound whose roof had been
constructed of the owner's cradleboard. The openings
had been neatly filled with rocks and thatched with
willow, and the whole was so well made that the crypt
had remained almost intact. Beside the grave were
child-sized deep spears, bow drills, and arrows, indicating that the dead child had been a boy. These would be
needful things for the boy to show that he had left the
world well prepared to face the next. It was a peaceful
grave. But when Sacajawea turned back, she found half
a dozen more children's graves, and beyond them were
ten or eleven adult graves. She found herself hurrying
away and felt an almost hysterical desire to see living
men again. She almost ran the last few yards to camp,
where she was greeted by York and in turn greeted the
man with an effusiveness that startled him. York then
told her that the hunters had been sent out once again,
but there were no signs of game around the camp. This

was small comfort, for the party had counted on stocking up with meat before they continued climbing into the higher ranges of the mountains and into the unknown lands to the northwest. The expedition's food supplies bought from the Flatheads were almost exhausted. The short rations were beginning to undermine the strength and to some extent the morale of the party.

Captain Lewis brought out the portable soup, which was an experimental ration he had made up in Philadelphia. It was made from dried vegetables that had been fortified with iron, in the form of ferrous sulfate. No one liked this soup, which had a stronger, more bitter flavor than the wild grouse, but it was better than chewing on moccasin leather. Thinking of the people of the rings, Sacajawea ate all of her soup, saying nothing about the way it set her teeth on edge.[3]

As they left the area of the old lake basin that morning, the sun was suddenly covered with sullen storm clouds and the long moan of the wind rose above the noise of the horses' hooves clattering over the blue-and-green talus. Along the stark rocky meadows that soon lay beneath the expedition, Sacajawea saw the old camps of those unknown people. Beyond, the little rock mounds rose above the stone surface like gray boils on the bones of the land.

"It would be no marvel if that black sky sent us rain and the rain turned into sleet by midday," hollered Charbonneau, blowing on his hands to keep them warm. "Or even snow."

During the morning the hills came closer to the streams until they passed through deep gorges, where the roar of the torrent floated up to them from below. They were forced to wallow across in deep water, and the horses somehow clambered their way up the scarp of shale. Paths wound in every direction. But they were not game trails, only washes from wind and melting snow. The hunters found no game. In the evening they again had portable soup. It was getting harder to find wood for the night cooking fire. And this night the wet clothing had to be dried.

The precipitation had not come by the end of the next day. But the temperature dropped by nightfall,

and the men knew they would sleep fully clothed in
their blankets because the exertion of staking out the
horses, hunting the few spare sticks of firewood, and
setting up camp caused them to sweat easily. They felt
weak with hunger. The small fire would not dry out
sweat-dampened clothing and also make the watered-
down portable soup. It they took off their damp clothes
they would freeze up, and next morning they would
never get them back on.

During the night Sacajawea caught Pomp's nose
gently between her thumb and forefinger, her palm
over his mouth, to stop his crying. Her milk was not
rich enough. When he began to twist for breath, she let
go a little—but only a little—and at the first sign of
another cry, she shut off his air again. She did not want
him to wake the others. She crooned ever so softly as
she did this, a growing song of the Agaidükas, to make
the boy straight-limbed, strong of body and heart. She
held him tightly, keeping him warm; feeling that his
fingernails were long enough to scratch, she bit off each
nail to the tip of his fingers.

The next morning, Old Toby and Captain Lewis
walked to the top of a nearby ridge to survey the route
with the good spyglass. There was nothing to be seen
but rock and steep terrain. The ground was bare, except
in the gullies, where a light powder snow had drifted
some days back.

The constant climb was treacherous, and the horses
had a rough time of it. For three more days, the expedition faced cold and wind that did not let up once.

Sacajawea confided to Charbonneau, "I must have
circles under my eyes and a bend to my shoulders, like
poor Willow Bud in the Season of Snow. It is cramps
from being constantly hungry."

Charbonneau's belly contracted, and he yelled,
"Damn you! That kind of talk will bring cramps to
everyone. Shut your mouth!" He pulled off a leather
whang from his sleeve. "Chew on this."

She turned from him and sniffed, pulling the sharp
smell of a wind-tormented mountain cedar deep into
her lungs. At least the smell made her feel good. In a
way it did; but in another way it didn't. It made her
think of food. Her mouth watered as she thought of the

sweet ground corn of the Mandans—she could lap up
the meal and drink a little water from a gourd, hold
the meal and water in her mouth and knead it with
her tongue while she rode. The thought didn't do her
belly any good. She gave it up and pushed her horse on
ahead of Charbonneau to ride at the side of Old Toby.

Ahead, Captain Lewis had halted at a spring before
angling up the next ridge. The horses pulled at some
sparse yellow grass. Then the rocks on the trail shuddered as a packhorse snorted and rolled down the embankment. The trail didn't shake, but it seemed to as
another packhorse followed the first, going sideways
down the bank. They were hurt, but not badly. With a
rope, several men had them back on the trail. Their
packs were still in good shape. But before making night
camp, the pack on the horse carrying the prized desk
of Captain Clark loosened and caused the horse to mis-
step. He rolled forty yards down from the trail and
lodged against a stunted juniper. The horse was not
hurt, but the desk was smashed. Captain Clark insisted
that the pieces from the desk be packed up so that he
could repair it at the first opportunity.

The worst part of seeing the horses back on the trail
was the feeling that if they had been hurt badly, they
could have been used for food. Sacajawea had not got
it through her head until now that the white men would
not shoot a packhorse, unless he was in total misery.

Before moving on, Captain Lewis looked down into
the blue, shadowy valley they'd angled away from. It
faded out of sight into the dim haze of twilight, and
there seemed to Lewis a feeling of mystery about it that
he could not catch and set down in words in his journal.
The sight moved him. He thought there was a softness
to it, almost as if he could feel the breath of the Pacific
coming from over the mountains. It drew him like a
dream, like a place he'd seen before.

They all rode on in silence, hoping to make a few
more miles before night came down upon them. Coming
over the side of a slope, they rode down into some fallen
timber that was hard to cross.

Day by day, Old Toby picked their way of ascent. He
was an excellent guide, for he knew how to read the

ridges and gullies and he was gracious about pointing out things of natural interest—the winter colors of the saskatoon, a cluster of thin-stalked, yellowed mountain laurel, the gray of the deer moss. He knew much and enjoyed talking Shoshoni with Sacajawea, who also had Indian eyes. For it was she who first spotted the creamy white object that seemed to be no different from the surrounding rocks.

"Chief Red Hair," she called.

"Yes?"

"There is a sheep not far, up in the rocks. Old Toby says he will be needed to keep away frostbite."

"There!" Captain Clark said. "I see him."

"I see him, too," answered Lewis. "He's nearly a mile away. I don't know about frostbite, but I'm sure he can take away our bellyaches. Drouillard, come here. What do you think?"

"I could go up," he said, already measuring the distances and looking to the priming of his rifle. The powder grains lay there, crisp and dry. He closed the pan and gave the butt a mild jolt on a root to snug the charge down in the barrel.

"See that overhanging rock? If that moves, half the mountain will start rolling. Watch yourself," warned Captain Clark.

"Lord, it looks like a good meal walking away," Captain Lewis sighed as the sheep disappeared. Drouillard was soon on the slope, to the left and heading higher in pursuit of the sheep. All eyes were turned on him. He was climbing a series of zigzag ledges that were occasionally narrow enough to throw him into view. It looked impossible. It was a sheer precipice. Suddenly from above came a *thunk-a-thunk-a* sound as rock pounded down the mountainside. The men gasped as the sheep passed right over their heads and struck a slope of scree behind them. Climbing downward from the argillite outcrops was the small, agile figure of Old Toby.

Seeing the way things were going with Drouillard and the loose rock, Old Toby had carefully climbed above the men to a shelf of rock, and being able to see the sheep when they could not, Old Toby had moved close enough to make a magnificent shot with his bow and arrow.

It was the years this old ram had spent climbing around these hills that made him the toughest meat any of them had ever tasted, but the soup made from the mutton was delicious.

During the day, while the mutton lasted, Old Toby stretched the sheep's hide between the rocks at each stop, and at odd times he cut and sewed four moccasins for Scannon, for the dog's feet were bruised by sharp stones.

And long after the mutton was gone, and the outfit no longer slept with full bellies, each evening Old Toby told how he, with a bow and arrow, had made the magnificent shot that had kept the white men from starving. "Smoking sticks, *paugh*! No good for sheep." But the feat was not repeated.

On Friday, September 13, 1805, the expedition came upon several hot springs, which Old Toby called Indian baths. A frenzy of scrubbing and scouring and washing possessed them.

Sacajawea bathed and scrubbed her clothes clean with sand, and bathed Pomp and scrubbed his clothes, hanging them on the stunted subalpine firs growing near the blazing fire York had built up. She rinsed her hair until it made a squinching sound between her fingertips. Then she bathed Pomp again and poured handfuls of water down his round back. "You must swim," she told him.

Others waited patiently, pleased with the sight of Janey giving Pomp a swimming lesson, and though it was an indulgence, for already snow was smothering the peaks, they camped early that day and Captain Lewis led a hunting party to scour the rocky ledges for game. Old Toby found a small shrub with curled, oval, fragrant leaves. He skinned the leaves from the stems and urged York to boil them with water. It made a tolerable tea. Everyone sipped, but remained hungry. No game was found, and tempers grew short.

Shannon lost his patience with Sacajawea when she could not pronounce the English word *tamarack*. "Land

alive, Janey! You're as bad as a schoolchild. Stop fid-
geting. Sit down." She sat down meekly and quickly.

"I see a tree. It is a tamarack," he said.

Sacajawea knew he could not see it. There were no
trees that tall among the rocks here.

"Janey!" Shannon's voice darted at her, as brisk as
his knife. She jumped as though he'd pricked her.

"I see a tree. It is a tam-aw-rack," she recited, and
then stopped Captain Clark from picking up Pomp, who
was crawling near the fire.

"No, no. Do not stop him," she said. "He must learn
to make his own decisions, take the responsibility for
his actions. It is like I hear you tell the men."

"At this incredibly early age?" gasped Captain Clark,
rubbing his chin. Sacajawea could hear the whiskers
scraping like two dry pines in a high wind.

"When he begins to crawl, no one cries *no* and drags
him from the enticing red of the coals. I am watching
that he does not burn. He must learn himself the bite
of fire and to let it alone. See how he jerks his hand
back?"

The baby whimpered, and with a tear-wet face
brought his burned fingers to Captain Clark, who was
nearest him, for soothing. Clark immersed the baby
fingers into his now-cold tea.

"See," Sacajawea continued. "His eyes do not turn
in anger toward his mother or any other person who
might have pulled him back, defeating his natural desire to test, to explore. His anger is now against the
red coals. So—he might creep back another time, but
cautiously. So—soon he will discover where warmth
becomes burning." She let her hands fall into her lap,
and Clark handed the child to her. Automatically Sacajawea pulled aside the slit tunic, cupped out her left
breast, and gave it to the papoose. The child's lips quickly
found her dark-brown nipple. When Pomp fell asleep,
Sacajawea took soft cattail-down mixed with dried moss
from a leather box and pressed generous handfuls between Pomp's chubby legs and wrapped him in his blanket. The feathery down made the baby sneeze, but he
did not wake.

"Go on, Janey." Shannon stopped whittling and

looked around. "La, what's come over you? I vow you ain't got your mind on learning."

She thought his neck seemed too thin to support his head. His ears protruded. He hadn't shaved for the last few days, and there was a trace of blond hair on his pale upper lip and thin cheeks. She wondered if he were sickening with this teaching.

"You can go," Shannon told her. "I'm in no mind for lessons, either. My mind's plaguing me this last hour with thoughts of food we don't have. Well—" Shannon picked up the knife and swung it toward the ground, making it stick. "Oh, get along now, Janey."

Other tempers were short. Pat Gass swore, "God grant there's no worse place on earth than this cursed damned mountain country." And he said more to make the air blue as his horse stumbled during the night picketing and lost its load, sending the packs flying in every direction.

That night, cold and hungry, they killed the youngest colt for supper.

For several days beyond Colt-killed Creek,[4] the Nez Percé trail continued to head west, following ridges, not valleys. The view they saw when they finally reached the stony plateau was the view of a new world.

In the foreground the land dropped steeply through a thrust into a gorge that seemed to converge to a central trough. But it was not the foreground that held Sacajawea's eyes—it was the immense, airy sweep of the snowfields and ice pinnacles beyond, and the tall peaks soaring into the blue.

Soon most of the men had rubbed ashes under their eyes and put bear's oil on their arms and necks to avoid sunburn. The mountain sunlight was dangerous.

"I doubt I'd burn much," said Shannon. "I'm already brown as I can get, but just to be safe—" He took a handful of ashes from the dead fire and rubbed them on his face and forehead. He stared at the scene without a word now, without even an exclamation. At last he drew a long breath and edged over near Sacajawea. "God!" he said. "Them's the biggest mountains in North America, and only you and me has seen them, and a few of the men, and maybe some Indians, like Old Toby and Cutworm. It's going to be a blasted country to travel. Lookee there at that black gash in that dip. I reckon that's where the Columbia River flows, and it'll be hell's own job to get down to it."

The cold blue sky beyond the mountains dulled to a colder gray, and all light went out of the landscape. More cold weather was trying to get through; it was not making much headway, but the pressure was there; a switch in the wind and the snow would be driving down the Bitterroot Valley by nightfall. They made camp against that possibility and put up elk-skin lean-tos. The snow came as ice splinters. Soon there was nothing but white around them, except the tops of the little gnarled firs.

The next morning, Old Toby pushed large squares of wool pads cut from the old mountain sheep's hide into the hands of each member of the expedition. He explained carefully how to rub cheeks and noses with the oily wool pad to prevent frostbite. He made certain the wool moccasins on Scannon were secure.

That day the thin, cold air seemed to cut through their clothing, but the sun was out for six hours. Sacajawea, after sniffing the air, pronounced on the weather. The first snow had fallen, so there would be three days of cold and more snow, then for maybe ten days there would be a mild, bright spell, then the big snows and fierce cold would come. The mild spell would enable the party to finish the ascent before the deep cold set in.

"Where'd you learn that?" asked Drouillard.

"I have listened to Old Toby tell it to Cutworm," she said.

Old Toby and Cutworm rested after the day on the trail, but this evening they were sorting out many small pliable willow sticks in the snow.

"And where did they find those?" asked Drouillard, pointing to the willows.

"They have carried them in that large pack for this time on the mountain," said Sacajawea. "They knew we would have deep snow above the timberline."

Old Toby began twisting the pliable sticks into "bear paws," or snowshoes. Cutworm helped by holding the sticks over the fire to make them bend more easily.

These snowshoes were lightweight, constructed in a round shape to spread the weight of the wearer. Two separate rods were joined by the toepiece and raised in front at a sharp angle. The centers were of finer willow crisscrossed in a large mesh and whipped around the outside edges. On such shoes, Old Toby explained, an active man could easily travel forty miles a day on the level. All the men who wished to walk and lead their horses had snowshoes. Old Toby spent considerable time showing the trick of walking without tangling up both feet.

The day-old snow lay deep, and under the strictures of the frost, it was dry and crunchy, so that Old Toby went first, followed by Cutworm, to break the trail. In the dry snow, Old Toby's efforts did not make a firm track, so that the stages had to be short, and by the midday meal the men were at the end of their tether. Some horse broth revived them, but their fatigue was such that Captain Lewis ordered camp made an hour before nightfall.

The next morning, they felt the same penetrating cold. The wind was gusting, sharp flurries picking up the powdered snow and swirling ice particles around them, forcing the men and horses to turn their faces away from the painful blasts. The men soon learned to keep their faces covered with a kerchief or the end of a blanket, and to rub their faces frequently with the pad of sheep's wool Old Toby had given them to tie on the back of their mitts. Between each gust was an eerie calm, when it became possible to hear the crunching of the horses' hooves on the snow and the soft scuffling of Scannon's feet, and when the men's cheeks felt suddenly hot in the momentarily still air.

Charbonneau tried to brush the ice from his beard. He'd had that beard so long now. How many years since he'd first grown it? Maybe twenty—he'd started it back in his early trapping years. He'd kept it, worn it like a badge of maturity when he was drinking at the Hudson's Bay Post when Toronto was no more than a couple of log cabins and half a dozen skin tepees. The beard and the peeling face—he'd even been foolish enough to feel proud the first time he'd got a touch of frostbite. He rubbed his face with the oily wool. He could just make out Old Toby leading the party in the dim distance ahead, with the horses moving along in a string behind. Then the whiteness all around him thickened—rose up in a cloud—seemed to be piling in. Whirls of snow flew high over the lead horses—sometimes the horses themselves disappeared. He sighed and moved up closer to the rest of the men. He felt his legs beginning to stiffen. He had the strange feeling he was being drawn into a nightmare. "This is going to be one goddamn stinking storm," he shouted into Drouillard's ear.

Once again they made camp early, using the old tepee skin Charbonneau had brought from Fort Mandan, and lashing the lean-tos together. By now some of the men had frostbitten fingers, which functioned clumsily. Even taking the job of making camp in relays, their hands went numb in a few minutes; and even with the aid of the wool pads, some of their faces had frozen in the combination of deep cold and strong, gusting winds. Along most of the trail, they had been riding right into the wind, and it is impossible when snowshoeing to keep one's face averted from the wind all the time. Shannon's nose and cheekbones were showing frostbite, and Pat Gass's nose was badly frozen. Captain Clark had a patch of frostbite on one cheek, and his other cheek had a tiny patch of white in the center.

Just by being in out of the wind under the enclosed lean-to, they were a little warmer. No one bothered to take off his boots at night, and they all slept with their hands tucked down in the groin—the warmest part of the body. That night on the high scarps the men neither ate nor talked about food. No one bothered to hunt under the snow for the scarce sticks. No one went out to chop the stunted firs. The expedition was thoroughly exhausted, and the men could do nothing but roll up in their blankets.

Scannon was not happy that night, either. He was cold and shivering and weakened because he had not been fed. Captain Lewis had been forced to hit him to keep him moving. At a time like this, he could not afford to be easy on his dog; if he didn't keep going, he would drop and freeze to death.

Scannon had walked along slowly, and every now and then had stopped and stared after the party. He had been left farther and farther behind. Sacajawea really liked that dog and had called to him, and he had come walking on, wobbling and staggering. She'd waited and patted him and talked to him, and once she had asked Lewis to put him up on a horse right beside where she was walking so she could keep her arm around him. But he was not accustomed to riding and had been frightened, so that he struggled under the blanket Lewis had tied around him to keep him on the horse. Sacajawea had patted him with her hand. She was certain that a rest would perk him up, but he kept struggling feebly and once he had fallen off. Lewis swore that he was too tired and cold and miserable himself to be kind-hearted, but he had gone back and picked him up and hit him to make him walk. After a while, instead of plodding along as usual with his hands tucked up under his arms for warmth, Lewis had put Scannon back on the horse and, along with Sacajawea, kept an arm across the side of the dog. Lewis had felt his hand freezing. His face was giving him some trouble with frostbite by this time, too.

When they stopped to camp, Sacajawea noticed that Scannon just dropped when lifted from the horse. She knew that a dog would normally dig down into the snow and curl up to protect itself from the cold. Using one of her blankets, she built a windbreak around Scannon to keep the wind off.

The party pushed on through the next day. They didn't make many miles, and the horses were visibly weakening. The captains were worried. Sacajawea kept rubbing Pomp's face with the soft patch of wool and crooning to him. She ate handfuls of snow, trying to keep her thin milk from drying up altogether. Dinner was some old bear's grease Lewis had found in a pack. Scannon refused to eat even the bear's grease. This refusal seemed to signify what really alarming shape the outfit was in. They had another cold camp that night.

The next day was a nightmare. If anything, the weather had deteriorated. They snowshoed through quite steep country now, cliffs that rose up and rolled down. There was nothing to do but keep going, indicated Old Toby, beckoning with his arms. At the noon rest

the men noticed that one of the packhorses had gnawed
at his groin and rear legs where he was getting frostbitten. His flesh just seemed to split and become a raw
wound, and he had tried to bite at the pain or lick at
the frozen places because they hurt. Captain Lewis had
a couple of the men distribute the packs from this horse
on several that were not heavily loaded, and then he
shot him. The carcass froze after it was skinned out.
Without wood for fire, the men ate the meat in raw
hunks, letting it thaw in their mouths. Sacajawea urged
Scannon to stay beside her. She fed him pieces of meat,
little by little.

Captains Lewis and Clark, Toby, and Drouillard sat
up most of the night discussing their situation. It had
taken the others a long time to fall asleep in the cold.
It was still blowing, and they would have more ground
drift to contend with in the morning. So the four of
them sat there in that cold and knew they might not
last another day if something weren't done. As they sat
there, Clark's eyes fell on a twenty-pound canister of
tallow candles. Suddenly an idea came to him.

He dumped out the candles and stood the tin canister
on its end. With his ax he cut two holes in the side and
a larger one at the top. He then rummaged through
some of the gear until he found a couple of smaller tins.

By using the small tins, the men fashioned a crude
stove with a stovepipe. Then they put the old tepee skin
and all the lean-tos closer together, pushed snow around
the outside for warmth, made a hole between two lean-
tos for the stovepipe to fit through, and closed over the
gap with a piece of elk skin, so that the snow wall would
not melt when they got a fire burning. Clark brought
in the battered remains of his prized desk, which was
quickly chopped up and set ablaze. Everyone stood there
with their mitts off, coughing and choking on the soot
and smoke, but enjoying the first warmth they had felt
in days.

Sacajawea's hands felt so numb that she could have
put them right on top of that hot stove, and even though
her hands would have been sizzling, she would not have
felt the pain. To begin with, the warmth felt good, but
soon she was in agony, as were most of the others. Her
hands and nose, cheeks and chin had all been frozen,

and now they suddenly began to thaw out. Huge frost blisters burst out on her face. Clark had a blister down one side of his nose and others across both cheekbones. Lewis had one across his chin. Charbonneau had one all across his nose and under his chin whiskers. Many of the men had swollen fingers that had turned dark red in color as the skin became stretched and shiny.

Old Toby had told them that the sudden warmth would cause trouble with the frostbite, but he could think of no option. The best way to fight frostbite, he advised, was to put the affected part in water. Clark had laughed, telling him, "There are too many affected parts."

Then Old Toby laughed, pointing out that the biggest problem was the white men's whiskers. "Only greenhorns wear beards outdoors, or men in desperate trouble. Beards are a nuisance in cold weather. I notice the breath freezes in a man's beard, and he soon faces trouble." He was looking at Charbonneau.

"Well, with no hot water, we have been unable to shave for some time," Charbonneau answered.

"Looks like you have not seen hot water in several years," kidded Drouillard.

The moisture frozen deeply in the beards of the men had indeed contributed to frostbitten chins and cheeks, and now the warmth of the fire made those bearded faces sting as though they were on fire. As soon as they had thawed out and dared move without suffering excruciating pain, the men looked through the gear until someone found a big kettle in which to melt snow to make soup from the horse meat.

The soup kettle bubbled and poured forth steam, and the air inside the lean-to became soggy with moisture. Everyone's clothing became wet as the embedded ice crystals melted.

No one complained that the soup lacked vegetables or that the larger hunks of meat were not entirely cooked. Some men carefully sipped the broth, finding that chewing moved muscles that hurt their frostbitten faces. Others pulled chunks of meat from the liquid with their fingers because it was too painful to put the hot broth near their lips. Sacajawea took pieces of meat out of her tin cup with her fingers, ate them, then coaxed

Pomp to sip the broth, which held more nourishment for her baby than her own milk.

Feeling full and warm, the next thing she did was to give some of the cooked meat to Scannon, doling out a little bit at a time so he could handle it. Lewis decided the expedition should stay in this camp for a day to rest the horses, to enable the men to put medication on the legs and feet of the horses and feed them some inner bark from the few stunted fir trees in the area, and to let the men get some needed rest themselves.

A day later, the horses were much improved. Then the mild time, forecast by Old Toby through Sacajawea, began. There was a shuddering undercurrent of cold, but the sun shone, and though it gave light rather than warmth, it took much of the bleakness out of the landscape. On the scarps the little firs were bent and ragged with the winds, and the many bald patches were bleached by storms.

The party plodded on; the horses marched forward, and Sacajawea walked, even in snowshoes, with her queer toed-in stride. They saw hanging glaciers, cirques, and arêtes with poised avalanches. The expedition followed a network of ridges and seemed rarely to lose elevation; they passed gullies and glens, but nevertheless they had been descending steadily. The expedition had crossed Lolo Pass and were coming down the Clearwater watershed.

One morning Sacajawea found she could hardly move. Her face was still raw from the frostbite, and her legs and back ached. She was sweating under her blankets. She looked up and saw York standing near with Pomp on his shoulder.

"You'se played out," he said. "We let you sleep in. But not this Pomp. He's been walking on my chest as I try to rest on my back. We all laugh at the sturdy push of his legs. Frost never touched him."

Sacajawea smiled, but found it took some effort. She was filled with a sick lassitude, an increasing loss of will to do anything, and, worst of all, persistent diarrhea.

"Today we rest. Tomorrow we go slow," promised York.

Tomorrow, she thought, will I be wretchedly ill, or

indifferent to any feeling at all? What has suddenly happened to me? She fell asleep as if drugged.

"That woman of yours is worn out, same as the rest of us," Captain Clark said to Charbonneau.

"She's got the mountain sickness," puffed Charbonneau, who had an armload of firewood. "No goddamn stamina. She could die, like a stinking squaw."

Captain Clark's reply was an angry shout. "By God, she'll get well, you bloody-minded Canuck. You know if she were a man she'd be a chief. She's made of strong stuff."

Charbonneau squirmed himself around inside his shirt and gave a forced, awkward laugh. "Squaws are like spoiled pelt—no good except that a man has them to keep him warm. That woman right now couldn't bring much more'n a rabbit fur would."

"Listen, you can't tell fur by the price it fetches. I've heard traders working on a drunken Osage, telling him his pelts were no good, giving him a gourd of watered rum for prime beaver that would buy a whole year's outfit. Man, can't you see Janey is prime squaw? She could bring about an understanding of the Indian as a human being to the whites, given half a chance. I've been thinking about this."

"Capitaine, she's more like trade goods that the Northwesters peddle. She don't always wear so well."

"For God's sake, Charbonneau!" Captain Clark sounded as though his patience had about run out. "She's an intelligent human being."

"*Zut*, a sick *femme* is nothing but a burden," Charbonneau mumbled as he walked away.

The next morning Sacajawea felt better, but there were others with the unpleasant illness. Stopping at frequent intervals off the trail was hard enough with snowshoes clumsily in the way, but the deep apathy made it even worse.

Then, partway down a ridge, they could see below them a level plain spread out like a tabletop. The plain was dotted with pines. Captain Clark said, "To my dying day I'll never forget this. What beauty below." He strapped Pomp between some bedrolls on one of the packhorses and let him ride there all day instead of on Sacajawea's back. Despite their persistent diarrhea, the morale of the men bounced upward. Surely there would be game among the pines below.

By late afternoon they were caught in a blinding blizzard of wet snow, which drove down out of the north and blew straight in their faces.

For ten miserable miles they walked straight into the eye of the storm. Wet snow plastered their caps, trousers, leather chaps, and Mackinaws; it whitened the horses and piled up in between the packs. They walked with their heads down and without speaking except to shout at some wandering packhorse. They suffered—and when the storm stopped abruptly, they were all deeply grateful.

Late that afternoon, Captain Lewis scanned over the rocks and fallen trees with the spyglass. Finally Captain Clark said, "Here, let me look." Then the glass was passed from hand to hand, but there was no mention of anything unusual until York spoke.

"I see them tough sheep," he commented, handing the glass to Shannon. Shannon saw the band of sheep, their yellowish coats almost invisible against the snow, coming down the cliffs. There were between fifteen and twenty of them, including several pairs of ewes and lambs. Passing the glass from hand to hand, the men and Sacajawea watched as the lambs were taught to handle themselves on the face of a mountain. The ewe would come down some steep and dangerous place to the ledge below. Then she would turn around and look up, obviously telling the lamb that it was safe to follow. Nothing doing; the lamb would stand there hesitating, looking down and not liking what he saw, timidly putting first one foot and then the other forward. The ewe would go again to nuzzle the lamb and tell him to have confidence—then down again to show the way. Usually he followed; but on one or two occasions a mother had to perform the climb as much as three times, and once a ewe gently pushed her unwilling offspring until he had to go. Once they moved, the lambs were surefooted. They had to be, for a slip in this place meant death.

In the morning Captain Clark took nearly half the party ahead to hunt. They quickly dropped to the tree line, where the air was warm and sheltered from the wind. Captain Clark left a note on the inner face of a hunk of pine bark, which was pushed into an over-hanging forked tree branch, for Captain Lewis. It told that the hunting was good and the country was level—easy going. They had shot two thin elk.

When the two outfits finally met again, Captain Clark's party was in high spirits, even though a couple of the men were still suffering from the lingering diarrhea. They had reached what they thought to be a navigable branch of the Columbia, and it was only a day's march ahead. They had met a stray horse, killed and butchered it. They had breakfasted on the horse meat and saved the rest for Captain Lewis's group. The horse meant that Indians were in the vicinity, and, in fact, two days later they had walked into a small village of Nez Percés. They were good people who had given them a pack of dried salmon and some flour made from cam-ass root.

The party under Captain Lewis had not been so fortunate. They had eked out their small stock of horse meat, then killed a coyote and a crow. More of the men had come down with dysentery. Sacajawea had made a concoction from chokecherry bark, which she fed freely to the men. They took it, thinking that a Shoshini ought to know what was best to counteract the effects of the damned mountain sickness. To add to their discomfort, they had been plagued by the constant assault of in-satiable flies that rose from the soft snow at their feet until they hung like a malevolent mist and took on the appearance of a low-lying cloud. The black flies and mosquitoes came in such numbers that there was sim-ply no evading them.

Charbonneau·complained, "If I have to expose myself once more to those flies, it will be impossible for me to sit down. I pray to the Madonna that these runs dry up."

To stop for rest or a ration of food was torture. At times a kind of insanity would seize not only Sacajawea but some of the others as well, and they would plop wildly on their snowshoes in any direction until they were exhausted. But the pursuing insect hordes stayed with them, and they got nothing from those frantic efforts except a wave of sweat that seemed to attract even more mosquitoes.

Sacajawea felt them from behind her ears, from beneath her chin. A steady dribble of blood matted into her clothing and trapped the insatiable flies until it seemed she wore a black collar made up of their struggling bodies. The flies worked down under her tunic until stopped by her belt. Then they fed about her waist until her tunic stuck to her with drying blood.

The land they were passing over offered no easy routes to compensate for the agonies the flies inflicted upon them. Captain Lewis and his party had hit rolling country, and across the path ran a succession of mounding hills whose sides and crests were strewn with angular rocks jutting out of the softening snow. On these rocks their snowshoes were cut and split and their feet were bruised until it was agony to walk at all. The horses all had bruised feet. Each valley had its own stream flowing down its center. Though these streams were less than five feet in width, they seemed to be never less than five feet in depth. Around these streams the snow fleas came out in swarms, smelling like rotten turnips, and blackened yards of snowbanks with their jumping, twitching bodies.

The men's faces were doubly aggravated from the frostbite blisters, which had not healed. Most were bearded, with ragged whiskers growing out through their frostbite and blisters and insect welts. It was too painful to even think of removing their whiskers at this time.

For their reunion they shared the dried salmon for supper, and York made flat, parchmentlike bread from the camass flour and water. Luckily they had found a ridge where a little breeze played and held back the flies.

Charbonneau came running up from the brush to receive his share of salmon. He pulled off his old felt hat and waved it above his head. There was a pasted-down line around it from the sweat under his hat. He curled his upper lip, showing his yellow, gappy teeth, and making his mustache jerk. His nose was red and peeling. "I don't know about the rest of you," he cried, in a forced voice that was too high, "I don't know about you, but I've had enough walking, especially among these damn pesty flies. Do we have rights as men of an official expedition, or don't we? We're tired of wearing out moccasins in broken-down snowshoes."

"Well, sure we are," answered Pat Gass. "What's that got to do with how you feel?"

"Considerable. We gotta get down to them trees there and make canoes. If we wait, them fish-eating Indians could scalp us. This is ambush country. I can feel it."

"They ain't showed us no inclination to part our hair," said Shannon.

"What do you mean you can feel it, Charb?" asked Cruzatte.

"I'll tell you! *Sacre*! The Indians down there know this country. We don't. They have been surveying us for days now. I can feel their eyes on the back of my neck. For that matter," he yelled, raising his voice higher, "what if that river ain't a branch of the Columbia? We sweat ourselves sick and freeze ourselves to death and get eaten alive by flying beasts, and then what if we find that Old Toby led us right into these bloodthirsty Indians!"

"You're getting edgy for nothing," said Drouillard. "The frostbite, trots, and flies have got to your brain."

"When I'm wrong I'll say it." The words came all at once now. Charbonneau spurted words the way a keg does whiskey when the bung is started. "By *Jésus*, men, I ask you, are we going to slink behind trees and walk in hiding toward some great stinking pool of water? If we stand here yapping, we'll have all those thieving Indians at our backs. I can almost feel the arrows whizzing past my ears now. I say stretch our legs toward the canoe country or turn back—to hell with seeing that big stinking ocean. What you bastards say?"

He had jolted the men. Captain Lewis began to listen to Charbonneau.

"He's bit off more than he can swallow," said Captain Clark quietly. "The trail through the mountains took a lot out of him."

"Took a lot out of all of us," whispered Lewis. "He just scares easily."

"Scared men do things a drunk man wouldn't do," answered Clark.

Charbonneau was sweating, and he stared around at the men, rolling his bloodshot eyes, scratching one shoulder, then the opposite thigh. And he was not yet finished. He wiped his face on his sleeve and blew his nose between his fingers, and when he spoke again, his voice went up so high it cracked. "I say we get out of this country. We do it fast. We go back to the Shoshonis. We just get our asses out of this bloody fool country."

He twirled his cap between his hands. His breathing became audible. He rocked back and forth on his toes, his voice high-pitched, as though someone were pinching his windpipe.

"I'm going to get my horse and gear and *femme* and head east. If nobody else wants out of this hellhole, I will go it alone." He stood still, breathing hard, looking from one man to the other.

Now Captain Clark wanted to say something. He raised one hand, his face tight, expressionless. At his salute the men quieted. "No, Charbonneau, you're not. You try going back over those mountains and I'll have you tied tighter than a queue done up in wet green hide. No one leaves the party now. Is that clear?" Captain Clark stood looking straight ahead, still as a rock, hardly breathing.

The men stood in unison and shouted that they were with the captains all the way. Old Toby and Cutworm yelled "*Ai!*" with the men, not actually understanding what it was about. Those two knew that Charbonneau had the mountain madness, but in two or three days he'd be back to his old self. Old Toby shook his head because to him it was incredible that so much ferocity had not killed Charbonneau long ago, weak and whimpery as he appeared at other times. Instead, his blustery talk and fuzzy thinking made him stronger.

Charbonneau had turned, and he now groped through the men; he did not even put his black felt hat back on. He wheezed, and his lower lip stuck out, reaching for his mustache. He looked as though he were close to tears. His throat bulged with the sounds inside it. "There's times the Capitaine Clark acts like living among the Indians has turned him red inside. He can freeze his face up as blank as any redskin I've ever met. *C'est fantastique!*" He walked off into the brush to cool off.

There was about half a minute when there was no

expression on Clark's face. And not one of the men had the guts to say a thing right away. There were no sounds at all except their breathing and the little *scuff-scuff* of a man's hand rubbing back and forth across his bearded chin.

"Well," Clark said quietly, "that's all. Let's get to work setting up the night camp."

That evening, Old Toby and Cutworm gathered the snowshoes, explaining that there was no more need for them. They would be out of snow country in another day or two. Several of the old snowshoes made a good fire to melt a pot of snow for drinking water and for boiling some of that dried salmon. The rest were saved as convenient firewood for later on.

Two days later, Charbonneau seemed quite normal. Riding through tall grass with him, Sergeant Ordway looked at the plains spreading out below them. "Rich and delightful for cultivation. I'm a farmer at heart. I'd like to have me a big farmhouse in the middle of that green land."

"You're asking for plenty of backbreaking work," said Charbonneau. "But it's the richest land I've ever seen since we left the Missouri bottoms."

On the south bank of the Kooskooskee, as the Nez Percés called the Clearwater River, where the north and south branches met, Captain Clark found an ideal campsite. Several more of the men fell ill. Captain Lewis himself could hardly stay in the saddle. Three men were unable to walk to the camp and lay beside the trail, waiting to be brought in by packhorses. Others, able to stagger along, had to lie down before they could manage the last couple of miles into camp.

Hunters brought in four thin deer and two large, fresh salmon. Sacajawea found the camass root and began digging. York was soon down on his hands and knees, helping. Captain Clark came over the hillock abruptly and had to swerve to miss going over York's body. The horse threw him so that he hit the ground hard on his left hip. It was most painful for him to walk for several days.

"I'd feel fit if my hip didn't aggravate me so," said Clark. But by the following day he didn't feel at all fit; he had a fierce case of diarrhea and deep lassitude.

It was then that Old Toby turned physician. That evening he took the tallow candles that had been removed from the tin canister, put them in one of the iron kettles, and melted them. When they were a lukewarm liquid and not quite congealed, he told Clark to drink what he'd poured in a cup. Then he went around to every member of the expedition and told them to drink; it would cure their trots.[5]

Strangely, the men did not think it tasted so bad. Clark ordered the men to go to bed early, and he did the same. By morning, Clark and the others were completely cured. They could not believe that ordinary candle tallow could do this. Some admitted that the night before they were actually greedy for the stuff when Old Toby brought it to them, but ordinarily tepid lard would nauseate them.

The next night, Clark felt well enough to attack the illness forthrightly with Dr. Rush's infallible Philadelphia pills, a powerful charge consisting of ten grains of calomel plus ten grains of jalop. He supplemented this with Glauber's salts and tarter emetic and offered the concoction to anyone who might want it. He had no takers for his medicines. However, many men went with Sacajawea back to Old Toby for more melted candle tallow. Old Toby told Sacajawea that the fat would find its way into her milk. No one except Old Toby had understood they had been suffering from a deficiency of fat; the active men could not function in that cold country on lean meat and at a level near starvation.

23

Dog Meat

Clark's Journal:

> October 10th Wednesday (Thursday)

all the Party have greatly the advantage of me, in as much as they all relish the flesh of the dogs, Several of which we purchased of the nativs for to add to our store of fish and roots etc.

BERNARD DEVOTO, ed., *The Journals of Lewis and Clark*. New York: Houghton Mifflin Co., 1953, p. 246.

In a large meadow, called the Weippe, which was watered by streams from the snowcapped mountains, Nez Percé women dug the camass root with bone hooks. The root was round, like an onion. Little heaps of them lay here and there on the ground where the expedition hunted a suitable place for a campsite one late afternoon. Whenever one of the explorers wandered over the meadow or went close to the hills, the Nez Percé women would scream and run to hide in the brush. Little girls hid behind baby brothers and sisters and then peeked out to get a sight of these strange palefaces who had come to camp on their land.[1]

Early the next morning, the chief of the village, who was also a medicine man and called Twisted Hair, came to visit. Captain Clark smoked a pipe with him and told him of the Great White Father in Washington who had sent the white men to visit the people of the Far West. He said, "After a few days we will move on to visit other river camps."

Twisted Hair then spoke with hand signs, and a halting translation through Old Toby and Sacajawea again took place. "We have no Great White Father in the East, but we will be friends." His face was square with sharp features as if pinched out of clay. Shining brass rings decorated his ears, and brass wire was twisted around the end of a braid of hair that hung down the side of his face. Twisted Hair pointed to the many horses around the Nez Percé camp, saying, "Our horses are far sleeker and stronger than the ones you ride. I recognize yours come from our friends the Snakes on the other side of the mountains."[2]

Late in the afternoon, Chief Twisted Hair drew on a white elk skin a chart of the rivers to the west for Captain Clark. Clark stroked his beard. According to this chart the Clearwater joined another river a few miles from the camp the expedition now occupied. Further study showed that two days by canoe toward the south the river joined with another, larger than the first.

"The Nez Percés fish on this second river. It is called the Snake," indicated Twisted Hair.

Clark saw that five days' journey by canoe on the Snake was a very large river into which the Snake emptied itself, and from the mouth of that river to a great waterfall was a journey of five more days.

Twisted Hair blinked and moved his hands. "On all the joining rivers, as well as the main river, are many Nez Percé villages."

Then Clark gave Twisted Hair an American flag and a handkerchief in payment for the map and information. Clark made a sign for the chief to wait. He rummaged around in several wooden crates and came up with a steel knife, another handkerchief, and some twists of tobacco. "I want to trade for some dried salmon and skins suitable for clothing."

Twisted Hair rolled sidewise on the ground, showing that he would bring the trade items immediately. He returned with a dozen baskets of salmon, some elk skins, and ibex, or goat, skins. Again he rolled on the ground in a paroxysm of almost inaudible laughter.

"No, no," corrected Clark. "I am not going to cook and sew. Sacajawea and Old Toby will sew. York will do the cooking."

Twisted Hair rested his chin in his hand. "That would have been something to see. A white man doing a squaw's work." His belly shook with laughter.

During this time Captain Lewis was in the center of the village buying up the fattest dogs he could find. He traded an ax to one man for several dogs. The man was so pleased that he buried the ax at once for safekeeping. Another man exchanged a dog for a flint and steel, and he was so delighted with his trade that he completely wore out the flint that same evening with repeated demonstrations.

Lewis brought the dogs back to camp on leather leashes and ordered them killed, skinned, and roasted. He was certain the meat would not only taste better than the constant diet of rotten fish they were having, but be necessary to ensure the men's health.

Captain Clark felt a bit squeamish about eating the dog meat. He talked to Shannon. "I got Lewis's think-

ing; I understand him. But I can't help thinking about
a retriever bitch I once had. The best hunting dog I ever
knew, and together we had some great times in the
hills. She could track a beast all day, and minded a
blizzard no more than a spring shower. Well, she got
something mortally wrong with her innards and was
dying. One morning I missed her from her bed beside
the stove, and my brother, George, told me he'd seen
her dragging herself up through the woods in the snow.
I followed her trail and found her dead in a little laurel
grove, the place she'd been happiest when she was well.
She wanted to die on her feet. I reckon that's the best
way for men and hounds."

"Sure," said Shannon, "maybe Captain Lewis feels
he's right—but how many of these here codgers would
give up their lives for a dog?"

That evening, the mealtime was very quiet. One by
one the men gingerly nibbled, then succumbed to the
dog meat. Charbonneau thought it was the finest meat
he had tasted. This truly disgusted Sacajawea. She
begged Captain Lewis not to butcher any more dogs.
Her people would eat horses in desperation, but never
dogs, no matter how hungry they became. She also remembered her friend Dog from the big Hidatsa village,
and her throat constricted. She could eat no more. "You
would eat your dog, Scannon?" she asked Captain Lewis.

"Of course not!" he exclaimed. He was not looking
at her; he just kept his head down and was quiet. Finally he looked up, explaining, "This is not breaking
any law nor a sin with these Nez Percés. My sensation
of right and wrong is my conscience. The men in this
outfit need red meat. If we don't find it hunting, but
find it in the village in the form of a dog, then we'll eat
the dog. I am bound to build the health of the men in
my charge, so I am forced to give them something that
is not considered fit for eating by some, but a delicacy
by others." Lewis nodded his head toward Charbonneau. "You know, some people eat those bitterroots,
boiled until they are mush and still too bitter for my
taste—besides that, they give a man so much gas he
can scarcely breathe. And there are some who eat crickets and ants. This does not make them sick; it keeps
them from starving and actually keeps them fit. This

fat dog meat will keep our men well. You can understand that, can't you, Janey?"

"I see how you feel about the men, but I do not have to eat dog meat, and neither does Pomp." Her mouth was drawn down so that she could keep it firm.

Captain Lewis now looked directly at her. "It doesn't make any difference. You don't have to eat that meat if it bothers you, so long as you stay well. But if you get sick on rotten salmon or too many damn roots, I'll hold your nose and make you drink dog-tail soup!"

She looked at him in alarm, her eyes wide. Captain Lewis thought her eyes looked like a doe's. In fact, she sort of makes me think of one when she walks, he thought to himself. Quick and light, and she always seems to be watching out, curious, as if she saw something waving in the grass ahead and she would go to find out what it was. Lord, like a little animal.

By October 5, everyone was feeling well and preparing to move on toward the Pacific. The expedition now had a total of thirty-eight horses. Captain Lewis gave the pack mule Charbonneau bought from the Shoshonis to Old Toby and his son. Lewis and a couple of the men heated up the iron and branded the horses that had been purchased since leaving the Shoshonis. Then they cut off the foretop hair of all the remaining horses, thus marking them twice for easy identification. Three Nez Percés, two brothers and the son of Chief Twisted Hair, had agreed to take care of these horses until the expedition returned the next year. Clark and some of the men built caches near where five ponderosa pines had been cut to make new dugout canoes. They buried the saddles, some canisters of powder and balls, and the branding iron in the caches during the night and carefully laid the turf back in place, hoping no one would detect these freshly cut holes in the ground. The five huge pines were trimmed, then hollowed out, first by burning and then by scraping, to make seaworthy canoes.

Word traveled fast by the *wearkkoompt*, the Nez Percés' grapevine, that five dugouts were coming downriver filled with white men who traveled with a squaw and a papoose. At the last minute, Chief Twisted Hair

and his subchief, Tetoharsky, wearing long leggings of
goat hide, decided to accompany the party to the Columbia River. Both men had beaver pelts tied around
them, going over a shoulder, with the hair next to the
skin. Their arms were bare; chest and back showed
nakedly between the loops of pelts. Each wore a gut
belt, and each looked about with an agreeable unconcern about time. They squatted in the dugout with Old
Toby and Cutworm, a picture of contentment, oblivious
to the shifting of the cargo to make room for them, and
not seeming to care one way or another what the next
step would be.

The men of the expedition noted happily that this
part of their travels would be entirely downstream. This
meant no paddling, no poling, no labor at the tow rope,
and hopefully no portages. But their dreams of floating
down a broad and pleasant stream were soon rudely
destroyed. On the second day out, Sergeant Gass's canoe
hit a rock and swung in the current; hitting another
rock, it split, filled, and sank. As usual, the men who
could not swim were in the canoe that had the accident.
The water was no more than waist-deep, but the danger
in rapids is not depth. The capsizing canoeist is more
likely to die by being swept underwater and being held
against a rock by the force of the current, if he is not
brained against a rock. There was nothing to be done
but land, dry out the baggage, and repair the damaged
canoe with plenty of pine pitch, elk hide, and strips of
pine.

By noon the canoes were moving fast through some
turbulent water in a deep canyon. Suddenly Nat Pryor's
canoe grounded and its cargo was thoroughly drenched.
The men were stranded midstream where the water
was only thigh-deep, but on either side the swirling,
gray-green water was over a man's head. Charbonneau
had a hard time keeping his feet on the bottom of the
river. The water was moving fast enough to push him
over. "*Jésus!*" he yelled, holding on to his felt hat. "Save
me! *Allez!* Get a rope!"

"Don't get excited, Frenchy," said Pryor, doing some
swearing himself.

"Hurry!" cried Charbonneau. "My feet are slipping. I'll be a goner! Holy Mother!"

"You ain't no goner," growled Pryor. "It's against nature. Hang on."

"L'aide!"

"Keep your shirt on!" called York. "I'se throwing out the rope." He first grinned at Charbonneau, who was kind of simpering in his beard, then stabilized his own feet and threw a rope to the closest man stranded mid-river. He worked quietly, easing each man out, and he smiled, pleased with himself, in the way of a man doing something for friends.

"Thank you, sir," said Pryor, shaking York's hand and slapping him across the back.

"Merci," Labiche said, smiling.

"Zut! That water, she is like ice. My feet are blue," said Charbonneau, pumping York's arm emphatically up and down.

"Bonjour," answered York, grinning broadly.

Again that day there was baggage to dry out and the damaged canoe to repair with braces of pine wood.

That evening, Cruzatte had his fiddle out, ready for songs and dancing with the Nez Percés who lived nearby and had come to see these strange pale ones. He offered the violin to Sacajawea, saying, "I made a promise to you a long time ago. Before this trip is over, you'll be able to play a tune on this old fiddle. Hold the bow straight and curl your fingers this way." She tried; and the more she tried, the more the Nez Percés mimicked the screech owl. The air was filled with screeching and laughter until Cruzatte, sides aching from his own laughing, took the fiddle back. "Janey, all you need is more practice."

"Ai, this box lacks something from me," she agreed.

Looking around the next morning, Sacajawea could see nothing but stones, sand, and a wide sagebrush plain. She could smell nothing but the stink of drying salmon. It seemed as though the entire Nez Percé nation lived on the riverbanks, and all they did involved salmon in some way. They ate salmon, slept on salmon, burned dried salmon, and traded with salmon.

In the late afternoon each day, Old Toby and his son wandered among the small thickets of sage that stood out like black islands in a tan sea of sand. They found no game and came back to a supper of cold, dried fish or, if the expedition were fortunate enough to find fuel for a fire, fish soup and boiled roots.

"This is not food," Old Toby exclaimed one day when York handed him a plate of steamed salmon. "We sleep on the bare ground, where it is wet and cold, so we need more fat or all of us will have the belly cramps and die doubled over in pain."

Twisted Hair and Tetoharsky shook their heads and picked at their salmon, eating every morsel they could put in their mouths.

Old Toby motioned toward the river. "A roast duck. Watch for the ducks on the river; then, when it is roasted, eat every last drop of grease." He picked at the fat lying along the back of his salmon. "This is not the best grease," he complained.

Captain Lewis, feeling a touch of the cramps and diarrhea again, tried a few agonizing swallows of more fish, then decided he wasn't hungry. He moved away from the eaters and dozed with Scannon pressed against his legs in the sand. Before breaking camp in the morning, he said to Drouillard, "We need more meat. See if you can't find some river tribe that will trade us a few fat dogs in the next couple of days."

For the next two days the canoes tossed in the wind from storms that hovered on the hills or swept over the chasm of the river. Thunder roared in the distance, and lightning struck on the hilltops, twice starting landslides.

Once they approached an island and were almost upon it when Sacajawea saw the dark mass heave. What had seemed a sandy shoreline was the yellow foam around an enormous raft of drifting sagebrush, jammed together by a combination of wind and fast water. Branches and roots were scattered through the mass and waved like ponderous monsters as they rose and fell in turn with the rapids.

Old Toby and Cutworm stopped paddling to watch the drifting sagebrush, and they talked in low tones with Twisted Hair and Tetoharsky.

Charbonneau's mouth was open. He said, "What are they saying?"

Sacajawea turned her head to answer, "Something about evil spirits living in the river that do not want men in their river."

"By gar, they are superstitious," mumbled Charbonneau. "I'd almost rather be sitting in Pryor's canoe than hear them make up such stories and complain about the fast water we have to go through. Those savages have lived in this country all their lives. Why should the river frighten them? But I've never seen such swirling white water since the Missouri's Great Falls."

Toward the end of the fourth day, the hills receded, the banks leveled into sandy beaches, and the slopes became covered with blue-green clay. The wind died altogether, and the waves quieted. As the unexpected silence deepened, the crashing of water on the shore became the only sound, and a sense of apprehension grew in Sacajawea's mind. She watched Old Toby and Cutworm. They seemed to take surviving too easily. There were no more complaints or retelling of Shoshoni superstitions. They seemed as calm as Twisted Hair and Tetoharsky. All four now seemed relaxed and indolent, expressing nothing but lazy curiosity. Something was up, but what?

"What is it?" she asked. Her voice seemed startlingly loud without the wind to snatch it away.

A violent, unexpected gust of wind hit the canoes like a padded blow, and Sacajawea gasped at its heat.

"What?" hollered Charbonneau on the crest of another gust, which bent the grasses on shore, flattened the water, and swung the dugouts sideways.

"Sit back!" Captain Clark gasped. "You're upsetting—us!"

Charbonneau gripped the thwart. At each stroke the dugout lunged forward, settled, seemed to coast an instant of its own accord, and then, just on the verge of balancing to the motion, it snapped his head again. There was only a second between strokes. Charbonneau's paddle trailed in the wake of the others. Sweat smarted in his eyes as he balanced on sore knees and bruised toes, groaning aloud. Culminating all his misery was the large felt hat that he had to keep from slipping about on his greasy hair.

"We are going to get the storm now," Sacajawea yelled

above the wind, pointing to the solid black mass of
clouds racing over the sun, breathing dull flashes of
lightning.

Drouillard, their bow man, hesitated, looking toward
the nearest land.

Now Sacajawea was apprehensive, and she agreed
with Drouillard that this was no place to be fool-
ing around in a canoe; they should head for shore.
The canoes swept around a point into a long bay that
widened at its end where the Snake met the Clearwater. Rain streamed in dark, alternating streaks
with the direction of the wind gusts. Sacajawea could
see it was not just a matter of heading for shore,
because when the canoe was headed to run downriver,
it was not controlled and tended to surf, ending up
beam-on to the river, and then it could turn over. She
could see Drouillard trying to ease off the wind and
work his way at an angle to the shore, sidling in
toward land.

Old Toby gave a shriek, and Charbonneau blurted,
"Rocks!"

Petrified, Sacajawea watched rocks rush at them,
then fall out of the way by inches. When they reached
the mouth of the Snake, big, heavy rollers came.

Captain Clark must be frightened, too, thought Sacajawea. But he didn't show his worry, and to steady
the crew and perhaps himself, he said, "It's all right.
Head for deeper water—there will be long, easy swells."
He handed Sacajawea a section of the battered tepee
skin Charbonneau had brought from the Mandan camp.
The river was running whitecaps now, and every time
it broke over the canoe, a mass of frothing white water
deluged them. It was like having a great bucket of cold
water constantly dashed in their faces.

She finally stuck her head under the tepee skin,
mumbling that her face was clean enough and she didn't
need it washed anymore, and she didn't really enjoy
looking at those waves. She kept down under the skin
and bailed with a canister until she was exhausted.
Suddenly Charbonneau announced that he needed to
take a leak. Twisted Hair and Tetoharsky proposed to
join him. They laughed. Captain Clark yelled, "Hold
it!" Old Toby and his son gave them sidelong glances

of disgust. Finally they just remained kneeling in the canoe and added to the river in the bottom. Old Toby shoved the bailing canister into Sacajawea's hands, grabbed Charbonneau's felt hat, and bailed with it as fast as he could, grunting pointedly in the direction of Charbonneau and the two Nez Percés.

There was a rocky reef halfway between the canoe and the shore. The canoe shot right over that rocky reef, and Sacajawea, head out of the tepee skin, could see it inches beneath the canoe. She drew in her breath. She could hear Old Toby grunt and Captain Clark's breath whistling on her neck.

The canoe raced toward the shore, where Sacajawea could see waving and leaping forms where a crowd of river natives had gathered. Hands seized the gunwales and stopped it with a sudden shock. The other four canoes were stopped in similar fashion along the shoreline.

Lewis called loudly to Clark, who was trying to shake off a native who had lifted him bodily up out of the canoe. "They're going to carry us all out!"

Sacajawea gasped as she felt arms circle her shoulders and legs and swing her out over the water, then set her down safely on the shore. The canoes were beached by another wave of naked chests and shoulders that swept on toward the shore.

Above the shoreline, women, wearing long leather skirts trimmed with shells and pieces of bone, were looking for dry sticks or dry pieces of salmon to start their fires. Some were grinning and shaking their fists in the direction of the departing storm clouds, and others were hunting belongings from the debris strewn through the sand and setting up the windblown scaffolds that were used to dry the split salmon. The village was thirty or forty yards from the shoreline. The three dozen tepees were made without skins, but of large grass mats, woven together in blocks, then put together like a patchwork quilt. The lodges were rectangular, supported by poles on the inner side. The tops were also covered with mats, leaving a hole in the center to admit light and let the smoke pass out.

"I have never been so relieved in all my life," said

Captain Lewis. "I think we were all close to drowning in that storm."

The men were running up and down the beach to warm up. They were a bedraggled, wet sight as they hugged each other, glad to be out of the canoes. Old Toby *kiyi*-ed with his son and vowed that he would never leave land again, and never go anywhere in a canoe again. The men stomped up and down until they were warm, then unloaded the gear and spread out the blankets. They were tired, and it seemed like the perfect campsite, right beside the confluence of the Snake and Clearwater, a pebbly beach protected from the wind by a stony bluff.

Sacajawea relaxed and noticed that she had been holding one arm behind her back across the legs of Pomp, who was asleep. The men hardly had time to lay out the baggage to dry and reclean and oil the guns before this village of Nez Percés were upon them again. A Nez Percé lifted each member of the expedition up and through the wet sand to the center of their village. There a fire was roaring and the familiar smell of roasting salmon was in the air, overpowering any other smell.

The chief talked to Captain Clark through Drouillard and Chief Twisted Hair. Clark suggested York bring up a box of trinkets for the chief and the important men of the tribe. York turned to leave and was bodily carried by two Nez Percés to the stores lined up on shore in front of the canoes. "Hey, men, I'se too tired to mess around," complained York. "I'm too pooped to argue, but I'd rather walk on my own feet." The men smiled and hitched York up for a better grip on his wide shoulders and legs.

Drouillard pushed his fatigue to one side and used his knowledge of Chinook jargon[3] on these Nez Percés, with good results. He explained to the Nez Percés that the expedition would build their own camp rather than stay in the lodges as they suggested. In the morning when the expedition was rested, they would come to the village and powwow with the chief and his subchiefs. The chief was called Live Well. Drouillard could not interpret the meaning of the subchiefs' names. "Too complicated," he said, shrugging his shoulders.

Chief Live Well lifted his eyebrows, and his lean

forefinger pointed toward the soggy gear on the beach. He took a flag handed him by Captain Clark and wrapped it around his shoulders. Clark gave him a small season medal and a string of red beads. The chief held out his hands for more. Captain Lewis shook his head, but Clark rummaged around and brought up a pewter mirror from the pack York had brought back.

Drouillard could hardly control his laughter as he interpreted Chief Live Well's next words. "He believes that the storm brought us to their shore as a kind of unexpected gift. He thinks the river gave us to his village. That's why they carry us all around. We belong to them, so they will take care of us."

"We are something to be prized and treated with care," agreed Captain Clark.

"But not carried around. Not worshiped like something rare and exalted," added Captain Lewis.

"They want us to eat with them, and I think we'd better," said Drouillard.

York groaned, "More parboiled fish. Wagh!" He kicked up two mats made of reeds, half-buried in the sand. A young, clean-looking squaw ran in and grabbed them up, running back to repair her lodge with them.

York watched her go, his nostrils wide to recover that fleeting fragrance of sage and wet rushes. "I'se like talking with her. Can't you teach me this jargon? What kind of talk is it, anyway?"

Captain Clark made hand signs signifying that the expedition would be glad to have their evening meal with the villagers.

Drouillard turned to York. "I learned that talk years ago and was assured that all Northwest Indians understood it as easy as most understand the universal hand signs. That old codger who spent a winter teaching me was right as rain. You've noticed that a thirty-mile trip runs us through six or seven changes of natives, all Nez Percés according to Twisted Hair, but they have different ways of speaking, sort of like the British, the Northwesters, and you. I've been trying out this Chinook jargon on Twisted Hair and Tetoharsky, and I decided to try it tonight on these Nez Percés. They understand a lot, and I get about half what they say."

The sun was below the horizon, and the river was

now flat and calm. Sacajawea sat next to Charbonneau and nursed Pomp. She was so tired she could eat only a few mouthfuls of the boiled fish that was served on large platters of rushes. Charbonneau complained that the fish was gritty with sand. "I think my piece was dropped before it was put on the platter," he said, pulling the bones out of his mouth and dropping them at his feet.

"I can't eat another mouthful of fish," Captain Lewis said. "Every village we pass has only this maggot-infested food. I can't swallow another bite. I'll go to our camp and relieve Goodrich on guard duty. Maybe he'll enjoy some of this."

"You don't look well," said Captain Clark.

"I'm not. My insides are on fire. I think I ate some salmon that was really rotten."

"There's some physic in the medical stores that might help."

"I'm running every few minutes now. It's mighty weakening. Humiliating, too, with those fellows carrying me every time I have to go. Can't we stop this nonsense?"

"Let them carry you back to camp. I'll have Drouillard trade for some dogs, and I'll try convincing them we can walk, but if I'm not successful, watch for them carrying York and Drouillard back to camp to fix you a bite of stew."

Two grinning Nez Percés carried Captain Lewis back to his camp. Lewis immediately rolled up in his damp blankets and tried to sleep. It seemed only seconds before Drouillard tapped his shoulder.

"We have some stew for you."

"I feel terrible," Lewis said. He sounded querulous to himself. "I think I'm hungry. Did you bring the stew with you?"

Drouillard handed him the tin cup, and he curled his lips on the smooth tin and sipped loudly, pressing to tilt it more, inhaling the vapor as he drank. When the cup was empty, he looked up questioningly.

"There's more. And more meat."

He drank a second cupful, then chewed the meat from small bones that Drouillard gave him one by one.

When he lay back with his eyes closed, he felt much better.

"Thank you, Drouillard," he murmured.

"York is cooking seven dogs in all. No one liked that gritty salmon, and everyone is tired and out of sorts. Captain Clark thought it would help the men sleep better this night. As far as I know, only the Shoshoni guides, Janey, and Clark himself have turned down the roast dog meat."

Captain Lewis was surprised and opened his eyes. "So—those four would starve themselves amid plenty?"

"They'll eat the camass root Janey dug a couple days ago and some kind of greens Old Toby found to counteract the gas those roots give a person. Old Toby would like to go out looking for a deer or elk in the morning. But I don't want to stay long enough for hunting. I don't like being carried around by these Nez Percés."

Captain Lewis, even through his low-grade nausea, was laughing at the situation. "Everyone is a little snappish from being cramped together in the canoes today and from constantly eating and breathing salmon. But have you noticed Twisted Hair and Tetoharsky? They put fish away like they haven't eaten in a week. That also turns my stomach."

"Mine, too. I don't think they take time to chew. And Captain Clark hasn't talked himself into eating dog yet. You should have seen Charbonneau eat dog meat under the nose of Janey. You know how she hates him showing off. When he passed a tender morsel to Pomp, she eyed him fiercely and said, 'You, you dog-eater!' Then she pushed Pomp into York's lap so the child would be out of Charbonneau's reach." Drouillard chuckled and went to his blankets.

The only light in camp was from the roasting fire. The whole expedition was worn out. They rolled up in their blankets with their feet toward the fire. There was no singing or dancing this night. Reuben Fields, known for his teasing, was lying next to Charbonneau. "You're a regular dog-eater, ain't you? I bet if I shook out your blankets I'd find a big piece of dried dog meat."

"*Oui*, I do like it," admitted Charbonneau, turning over, "but don't talk so loud. There are them that don't favor it."

Fields looked sideways. "Like your little woman?" he whispered. "And Captain Clark?"

"Shut your damn mouth," Charbonneau told him quietly. Charbonneau's wide, thick-lipped mouth was tight at the corners. He spoke in a husky voice. "Don't tease me about my likes and dislikes and the behavior of my *femme. Tu comprends?*" He reached a hand out and punched Fields in the belly.

Fields looked bewildered. "Sure, I'll forget it. I was only teasing a bit for fun. What else is there to do for a laugh? Aw, come on, Frenchy, I didn't mean nothing."

"I got a different notion," Charbonneau said.

"But why?" asked Fields, sitting up and beginning to chatter. "What have I done? I haven't done anything. I was just funning, friendly-like. No offense." Then he got hold of himself and said more slowly, "Aren't you going to forget it?"

"*Non,* I don't forget."

"Not just some fun?" Fields asked foolishly. He put a hand behind himself for a brace and ran his tongue back and forth along his lips a couple of times, as if his throat and mouth were all dried out. He looked around, and it was not encouraging to him. There was a solid ring of faces, and they were not serious, but smiling, waiting expectantly for someone to punch someone else in the nose.

Fields said, "You don't want a fight, now, do you?"

Nobody replied. Then Captain Clark came out of the tall grasses, being carried by two Nez Percés. "I understand what Lewis feels—this is so ridiculous," he said, waving the two men off toward their own village. "I don't like being lifted here and there and watched over as I take a leak. Whatever brought us to this village was a mistake."

"No mistake," whined Charbonneau. "This here man makes smart remarks to me. No man is going to call me yellow, if that's what it means by calling me a dog-eater. And no man is going to imply that my *femme* and you are in cahoots."

Captain Clark sighed, not knowing what the men were arguing about, but knowing that Reuben Fields was just a harmless tease. "Of course not," he said smoothly. "You know we have a number of men here only too willing to eat dog instead of that gritty, greasy salmon—Captain Lewis for one. And as for Janey and me, we only agree that dog meat does not suit our taste. You know Fields—he teases constantly; it even becomes tiresome. So—no more fuss. Go to sleep. You'll feel all right in the morning."

Charbonneau pulled his dirty blue capote over himself. "Well, I am not one to make a mountain from a molehill, but I still say I don't like to be made fun of."

A few of the men looked hard at Charbonneau, but most pretended that they had not heard him and rolled over to sleep. Captain Clark said quietly, "Tomorrow after supper I'll keep time by beating on a pot with a dog bone while you dance with York for some other group of natives down this river. They'll think you're a big man."

Sacajawea could not sleep. She was curled up off to one side with Pomp, and she watched the bluff above the camp, but it was all blackness now. All the time Charbonneau was fussing with Fields she wondered how she could get to Captain Lewis without being noticed. Now she wrapped the blankets around Pomp and inched her way to Lewis, who was slumped against a low rock, snoring.

"I have to talk," she said, pulling on his sleeve.

"It's the middle of the night!" he said in surprise.

"I had to wake you. Something is going on with Old Toby and Cutworm. I thought you would like to know right away. You told me, 'Anything you hear or see that affects the expedition.'"

"Janey, what's going on?"

"This afternoon, when it was yet daylight, when we were at the village, they built a signal fire on the stony brow of the bluff."

"Why the signal?" Lewis asked uneasily, wondering fleetingly if there were hostile bands watching. What would it be like to be struck with terror instead of delight over the fact that unknown human beings were moving about in this country? He put the thought away and waited for an answer, balancing on an elbow.

"Old Toby signals the tribe we left a day ago. He advises them that he is returning."

This made Lewis sit up. "They are not staying with us to the Pacific Ocean?" He shifted irritably. "Why?"

"Mostly," Sacajawea said, looking directly at Lewis, "because they see no reason for making the rest of the trip. They do not like river travel, or the food. They see you have no need for more interpreters, with Drouillard talking to the river people now and the two Nez Percé guides."

"Oh, they're just a little jealous. I think they'll get over that. I have to be sympathetic," said Lewis.

"But you do not agree?" Sacajawea asked quietly. "The Shoshonis never do anything that seems useless or without any pleasure attached to it."

"Can't you persuade them to stay? They have been of great service to us. I will repay them well."

"I don't think I can do anything, but I'll try because you are a friend and I am on this journey with you."

"Janey, this journey is precariously balanced between acute misery and bearable hardship. I should not ask you for help, but I am pleased that you feel you owe it to me. I am grateful for the information, and we'll settle this in the morning."

Sacajawea sat hunched over for a few moments thinking she ought to leave. Then she said, "When I think of the times to come, the frightening river travel, the constant stink of fish, and the freezing nights, I could go crazy. But I don't think of just that, and the time goes smoothly enough. There is pleasure for me being here with you white men. One day follows the last without much trouble. I see land that Shoshonis have never seen and meet tribes not known to them. It is a satisfaction more than a pleasure. When I wander away and come back into camp, it is inviting, and I find companionship here, strange and indescribable, but satisfying—something I could never have dreamed when I was a child or when I was with the Mandans."

Lewis propped himself on an elbow as Scannon came crawling toward him, fawning with ears laid back and mouth wrinkled over white fangs.

"Even this dog gives me pleasure."

"Of course," Lewis said. "He is a loyal friend to all of us." Lewis lay back.

"It is time for sleeping," said Sacajawea, and she crawled back to her blankets.

Lewis could not go back to sleep. This was rare for him because normally he could defer a pressing problem until the next day, knowing that a night's sleep would help him solve it to the best of his ability the next morning.

But tonight there was the perplexing question of the two Shoshoni guides. How to repay these men?

He became introspective. Curious how they had come and helped the expedition through the pass, knowing how to fashion the snowshoes at the right time, to use the sheep's wool and add fat to the diet, even how to cut and sew clothing. Then the two Nez Percés came as the Shoshonis were leaving. It was fate. Stranger still was the presence of Janey. He could not have imagined her while they made preparations and wintered at Wood River almost two years before. Life hides many things until the time is right, he thought.

Before Captain Lewis was awake to settle the situation next morning, Old Toby and Cutworm had had enough of useless canoe-riding. Without a word to anyone, they packed their few belongings and left on foot.

Sacajawea thought she had seen them for a brief instant at a distance, running up the river's edge, shortly before the morning meal.

"They didn't say a word of farewell," said Captain Lewis.

"*C'est extraordinaire,*" Charbonneau said.

"Maybe it was the dogs I bought for breakfast," suggested Drouillard. "They eyed them while I skinned them out and sputtered some Shoshoni vituperations before sunup."

Twisted Hair made hand signs and with his jargon to Drouillard said he knew they had made up their minds to leave when they had seen the drifting sagebrush the day before. Then, after riding through the rain and rough water, flopping around like soggy brown bears, they knew the river spirits were angry. So—they weren't going to leave land again, not even to fish from a canoe.

"They didn't even wait for their pay," said Captain

Clark. Then he asked Twisted Hair if a Nez Percé could ride a fast horse out to bring them back so that they could receive their pay, at least. The chief nodded his head from side to side.

"No, no, if the white men gave the Shoshoni guides goods for payment, the Nez Percés would only rob them on their way home. If they think they need payment, they will take something from the cache you white men left by the five big pine stumps, or they might take a couple of your horses along with their mule back over the mountains with them."

There was regret in everyone's voice, and disappointment. Old Toby and Cutworm had been useful guides and good friends.

The expedition began packing their gear in order to leave before the village became wide-awake. But Goodrich, on guard, alerted the captains that there seemed to be a babel of voices coming toward camp. Clark looked up, and his first startled impression was that the whole tribe had moved into their camp, but when he counted there were only twenty-four. These men were dressed in skins and had decorations of shells tied in their hair and at their ankles and wrists. Each had a thin bone pierced through his nose. Chief Live Well made signs that they wanted the expedition to come to their camp for some kind of ceremony.

"Tell them we'll come if they don't carry us," said Lewis, who was still feeling a bit weak.

Drouillard and Twisted Hair spoke with the men. Drouillard told Captain Clark they wanted everyone in the camp to go with them. Clark thought if they spent the morning keeping these Nez Percés happy, Lewis would be that much stronger when they were ready to go downriver in the canoes.

Sacajawea permitted herself to be shuffled along as the Nez Percé surrounded them and led them to the center of their village, where most of the villagers were already assembled and dressed in good skins, with their faces decorated with white, blue, and greenish paints.

As the pipe was being passed around, she tried to assimilate the feeling of sadness she experienced with the absence of Old Toby. It had been a kind of link with her relatives; now it was broken. She felt as though her heart lay on the ground.

Captain Clark gave the chief a handkerchief and a small hatchet. The four drummers sat at the four compass points and beat a one-two tattoo. A Medicine Man dressed in goat skins stepped into the circle and placed a tray made of woven grasses on the ground by the small fire. Beyond the ceremonial circle was a corner where many women were cooking over several larger fires. They were roasting meat over a scaffolding.

Suddenly Drouillard turned to the captains, his face white.

"I can't believe this!" he cried. "They can't be serious!"

"Tell us," urged Captain Clark, quickly indicating that Twisted Hair and Tetoharsky could help Drouillard in the translations.

"They want us to become members of their village."

"No problem with that," said Clark. "If that makes them happy, let's get on with it."

"Look at the pile of pointy bones on the grass mat. They will put every last one of them through our noses so we will be true Pierced Noses."

"Not through my baby's nose," said Sacajawea, pulling out of her sadness right away and tugging on Charbonneau's sleeve. "And not through mine. I want to breathe."

"They have counted us and have the exact number— one for each," said Drouillard.

"Pierce our noses!" exclaimed Shannon. "No, by God, not mine!"

"I'll not stand still for that treatment!" shouted Gass.

Charbonneau shook his head as if he had just tumbled to the situation. "And not me—*allons!*"

"Wait!" shouted Captain Clark. "There must be a way out of this. Think, all of you. I'll talk with the chief as long as I dare."

Captain Lewis scratched his head and wondered if more trade beads would satisfy them. He had Drouillard ask. The chief's face lit up; he would take the beads, then go on with the ceremony. The drummers beat faster.

"Fire the shooting-stick in the air," suggested Sacajawea.

"Start a fire with the phosphorus matches," suggested Cruzatte.

"I don't want to start a war," said Clark between his teeth.

Chief Live Well began lining up the people of the expedition. First York, because he was the only black white man with the group. Then Sacajawea, because she was the only squaw, and then her child. The chiefs of the group next, Lewis and Clark, and then the rest of the men. This was to be a big celebration. It would take a long time to pierce so many noses. But when such a fine adornment was to be added to the gift the wind had brought them, time was nothing. *"Huru!"* Chief Live Well shouted, bending over the thirty-two bone pieces, honed needle-thin on either end.

York was lifted by two men with large bones in their noses and greenish stripes along their arms. The Medicine Man was carefully selecting the correct bone. Suddenly York jumped about in a jog. This delighted the villagers, and they rocked back and forth in a shuffle, grinning.

York was talking to Drouillard in a singsong voice. "I have an idea, and it might save us from this nose-piercing. I might have done it anyway, so it's nothing to be excited about. Remember that pretty Nez Percé gal we saw yesterday who took the mats for her lodge? You tell that chief to get me something like that and I'll give these people something they can keep to remember us by. By and by that gal will have a little baby." He kept on dancing, moving his hips in front of the women and rolling his eyes at the men.

Drouillard's mouth dropped. Captain Clark took over as he read Twisted Hair's hand signs. "Sounds daft. But we don't have many other ideas."

Chief Twisted Hair and Tetoharsky laughed, making suggestive finger signs and urging the chief to accept York's proposal. Soon all the villagers understood what York had suggested. It appealed to them. This was much better than giving the white men something—they would have something to keep and show off. They knew the principles of eugenics; they practiced it with fine horse breeding. York was tall, broad shouldered, thick chested, and his arm and leg muscles were hard as cedar wood. His offspring, either male or female, would improve the tribe. Any eligible woman would be honored and proud to have a child by this magnificent, healthy specimen.

The chief finally leaped beside the dancing York. He shouted a kind of rhythmic chant and moved with wild gyrations, and slapped his thighs and rubbed York's arms to show his tribesmen that the black did not come off.

The women formed a circle behind the men and danced heel, toe, heel, toe. A few threw their heads back and moaned, low and guttural.

York continued his dance, moving his hips in a manner Lewis thought risqué. He smiled and showed his even, white teeth. He flashed his eyes daringly. He looked at the undulating circle of women and wondered which ones belonged to the chief. A couple of men sat in the sand close to Sacajawea and other members of the expedition and pounded on skin drums held between their legs. Their moving hands and fingers were a blur to York, who was now fearful he would choose a woman not belonging to the head chief, and that this whole scheme would blow up into a fighting riot. York's mouth felt dry. He glanced at the chief who grinned and bounced his hands off his thighs. York shrugged his shoulders and pointed to the women's circle, meaning, "Which woman would you have me take?"

The chief was not stupid. He pointed to his middle woman, who up until now had given him no children. All the women were pleased and there could be no jealousy or bickering over the chief's choice. York jogged toward the woman, put his big hands on her bared shoulders, and led her to the center of the circle. He pulled her close to him and the Nez Percé moaned in unison. He pushed her away at arm's length and did a little jig. The Nez Percé groaned together again. After a short time the drums increased the tempo. York felt the perspiration run in streams down his back; his breath came in short gasps. Suddenly he picked up the woman and cradled her in his arms like a small child. He walked around the inside of the ring of brown, laughing faces, then he broke through and walked around the outside of the ring. All the time he grinned. The woman's arm

was tight around his neck and he felt her fingers in his
hair. She gave a sharp tug to the right. Baby, he thought,
now that I'm worked up for it, you've just shown me
the way to your lodge.

The circle of women broke with squeals of delight as
York carried the woman through the skin covering of
the reed and brush shelter. Captain Clark sighed with
relief, glad to have his nose left unpierced. Drouillard,
his hands sweaty, said he was grateful to York for vol-
unteering for this act of bravery. Gibson gave out a low,
wolf's call. The other men began to relax and rub their
unmarked noses in thankful relief. Several older women
stood in front of the lodge where York and the woman
had disappeared, shouting words of encouragement and
making jokes of the coarsest kind: "Is the penis black?"
"Is it too large for the hole?" "Move slowly!" The villagers roared with laughter.

Drouillard tried to translate, but his neck turned
crimson and he tended to stutter. The more clinical the
advice and joking became, the more hilarious it seemed
to the Nez Percé. They rolled in the sand with gales of
laughter. Embarrassed, Drouillard gave up, saying,
"You know, the drift is all sex."

The Medicine Man in goat skins made hand signs to
tell the two captains he wanted them to eat with him.
Lewis had noticed some women bring bark platters of
food and reed mats from the lodges, placing them in
the center of the dance area. They were standing back,
waiting for the men to eat first. When the men sat in
the sand beside the mats, more platters of freshly roasted
salmon and boiled dog meat garnished with wild onion
were brought out.

The men began to transfer their animal excitement
to the eating of meat. Only Charbonneau mumbled that
he wished he were in York's shoes.

"Why?" asked Pat Gass. "His shoes are there in the
sand. I bet they're too big."

Charbonneau pushed his bottom lip out. "I mean ..."

"Sure, we know what you meant," said Gass, laughing. "But, man, you got yourself a woman. That's more
than York or any of us on this here trip."

Charbonneau picked a string of meat from between
two molars and leaned over to say confidentially, "Might

as well have no *femme.* Shoshoni squaws stay away from connection until the papoose he is one year or stops nursing. Which comes first?" He paused and noticed that not only Gass was listening, but also Gibson and Drouillard, so he continued, "Holy Mother, Nez Percé *femme* are appetizing when one has big hunger." He licked the grease on his mouth.

"Hey, control yourself," said Gass, slapping Charbonneau on the back. "Do you want little Canucks scattered all along these river villages? What would your woman think? You got Pomp, and he's the handsomest papoose I ever saw."

"Zut!" answered Charbonneau, reaching for a left-over piece of salmon and stuffing it in his mouth, then wiping his hands in his hair, Indian-fashion. "Look at me! I am a man. *J'ai besoin de plaisir."*

By the next morning, Captain Lewis was feeling nearly back to normal, and the expedition left the river village early in their five canoes. The morning was still dark, and the stars were bright. The village came to say their farewells. Some of the villagers held torches made of dried salmon. This made the shadows monstrous. Dogs whimpered and yelped occasionally, and Scannon growled. The men with the torches looked for York, then bent to look at his reflection in the inky mirror of water, their bodies luminous with fish oil. They murmured their approval when they saw his reflection as clearly as their own. He was surely one of them. They patted and rubbed his arms and back. He was something great.

Other men dashed into the water and lifted the loaded canoes, heading them downriver with a mighty push. The people on the bank shouted as the canoes shot past the village. To Sacajawea the dugout again leaped ahead with some mysterious life just as she was adjusting her sitting position with Pomp on her back. She was flung backward into Charbonneau's lap. Charbonneau's short arms, like the whipping branches of a tree, pushed her forward into York's back, who turned around and gave a triumphant, challenging laugh. Sacajawea caught the gunwales as, once again, the canoe seemed to tear itself from the water with the force of the paddles.

Another cry from the men in the canoes behind, and York turned and shouted back. York's neck swelled, and the veins stood out in his temple as he opened his mouth and roared excitedly.

On the beach the crowd waved, and up on the bluff four torches smoked in silent circles. The sky was brightening. The Snake River, a sheet of silver behind, swept at right angles, curved, and was lost to view in the gloom. Then they entered a series of canyons and gorges. The towering mountains closed in, and at their stony feet the water was black. The water had seemed calm in the little bay. As they went downriver, the waves became heavy under a wind that was blowing along with them.[4]

Charbonneau could not wait to talk to York. "How was she?" he asked. "Was she good? Did she bounce up and down or did she just lie there?"

"She was good," York replied. "Her man was at the foot of the robe with us, and her mother and sister were in the lodge. They all laid down and pretended to be asleep, but all ears were wide open. I'se can't say it really helped my performance. On the other hand, it didn't stop me."

"Oooh," Charbonneau said, rolling his eyes, "*plaisant.*"

24

The Columbia

Captain Clark attributed the friendliness of the river tribes to the presence of Sacajawea. He wrote in his journal: "We find she reconciles all the Indians as to our friendly intentions. a woman with a party of men is a token of peace."

Each day the group of Nez Percés that followed along the riverbanks changed. These groups helped pilot the canoes through rapids and rocks. The canoe in which Sacajawea rode, with Drouillard as bow man, struck a large rock and overturned. Some of the trade goods were lost. The water was waist-deep, and they walked the canoe to the shore and picked up the baggage to dry out. After that, the canisters with gunpowder, food, and gear were tied in the canoes, along with the rifles and blanket rolls.

All the Nez Percés remained friendly, always ready to make gifts of their dried salmon and talk with the captains through Drouillard. The men found no game on the shore. The terrain was mostly sand, with a few sagebrush growing here and there, which was not good firewood. The expedition often traded with the Nez Percés for a few dry sticks or bought dried salmon for their cook fires. Soon they came to country that was even more open, with no hills or obstruction to an equally featureless horizon that was hazy now with fog. Chief Twisted Hair pointed out that soon the land would become dense with trees and river travel would become more difficult because of large rocks and fast water.

Four days after Drouillard's canoe capsized, another canoe was driven crosswise by the current and hit a rock. Waves dashed over the canoe and it was filled. The crew held the sinking canoe until another was unloaded on shore and sent to pick up the men and drag the heavy, waterfilled canoe ashore. Despite the careful lashing down of the gear, some shot pouches and tomahawks were lost. One of the Nez Percés from the nearby tribe swam out and rescued two floating paddles.

Nat Pryor and Si Goodrich found some split timber, parts of some old Nez Percé Council House, buried under large rocks. There was no more wood in sight. Captain Clark argued with himself for a time before using the timber for firewood, because he had always made it a point not to take anything belonging to any tribe, not even their wood. This time, however, he violated that rule in order to warm the men and dry their goods, as well as to cook the evening meal. Fortunately, this once, there were no Nez Percé camped nearby. While checking the canisters of powder and food, the men found everything dry and well preserved except for one large container that held some camass-root bread. Nat Pryor tasted the bread, made a face, and spit it out. The taste was moldy, sharp, and sour. The Indian bread, soggy and yellowed, lay in a solution full of tiny bubbles. "If you eat this and burp, the aftertaste will be like fish coming back over the riffles."

John Collins came by, picked up the discarded canister, smelled cautiously, and put his finger in the juice and tasted. He paused a moment or two before he set it back on the ground. York was slicing dried salmon and Collins wandered over to talk to him about the fermenting bread. York told him the mess was to be thrown out; the can could be used for something else. Finally Collins talked York into tasting the soggy bread. He ate a little piece and wrinkled his face. "It will never amount to much," he said, "but if you want to give it a try, go to it. Add sugar and water. I won't interfere with any more noise than an oyster."

Collins added a full two cups of sugar and carried the canister to a sandbar by the river. He removed the tight-fitting lid and added water by dipping it up into the lid. He took the mixture back to the cooking fire, stirred it with a thin piece of driftwood, and placed it on the ground where it would stay warm, but not boil.

No one asked about the bread until the following day. The men were packing the gear to move on when someone noticed the lid had popped off and that a nauseous odor filled the air. Collins replaced the lid and gingerly pulled the stinking mess away from the morning fire. He wrapped it in a woolen blanket, being careful to keep it upright, and placed it in the bottom of the canoe he would be in that day. Several men asked what was in the blanket, but Collins only smiled. That evening it was unwrapped and again placed near the cooking fire. The lid was not tight. Sacajawea held her nose and said to York, "Something died there."

York seemed to know what was in the canister, but his lips were sealed. Charbonneau volunteered for guard duty, though. He seemed to understand there was something important in the vile-smelling container.

In the morning the captains were busy trading for some twenty pounds of dried, fat, horse meat with important men of a nearby Nez Percé camp, and Drouillard and Twisted Hair had gone along for the translating and bargaining, so that Sacajawea could not ask them about the importance of the mysterious can. She looked for Shannon and found him with York. She showed them the canister, which was now close to the river cooling in wet sand. The lid was half-off and foam dribbled down the side. York found a tin cup and scooped out some of the foamy juice. He sniffed and then laughed. He called Collins, who took a taste from the cup. His mouth puckered and his eyes closed. "Damn good!" he said.

Sacajawea said she did not know how it could be so good when it smelled so bad and made his mouth bunch together.

Collins handed the cup to Shannon, who tasted a sip of the liquid, made a face, and coughed. Then he smiled, saying, "I might learn to like it."

Sacajawea pulled at Shannon's sleeve. "Let me try."

The men standing around the bubbling vessel grinned as Shannon passed the tin cup to her. She held her breath, then she sputtered and wiped her eyes. "It makes the warmth inside same as rum, but the smell is not good. It is some kind of poison." She left the men standing around, laughing. Collins put the lid back on and placed it back near the live coals of the morning fire.

The captains learned from local Nez Percés that by canoe travel the Snake River would join a larger river in one day's time. Both captains talked with Twisted Hair, studied his map, and decided everything was in order.[1] Captain Clark treated several of the Nez Percés with silver nitrate solution for red, inflamed eyes. He discussed the Indians' health with Lewis. "Most of them have sore eyes. Must be from looking at the water with the sun reflecting off it as they fish. Or the reflection off snow and ice in winter. I'd guess they fish through ice or in fast water even in winter."

"Or the constant blowing of fine sand," said Lewis.

"And have you noticed the bad state all these river

Indians' teeth are in?" asked Clark. "Rotting down to the gum line or no teeth at all."

"That must have something to do with this constant diet of sandy fish," said Lewis.

That night Collins volunteered for guard duty and sat around with a flintlock on his lap eyeing the canister, which now seemed to have a life of its own. The lid often worked loose, and then there were small whisperings of escaping gas; at times the lid could not be kept tight at all. In the morning he again stored the softly gurgling container in the bow of his canoe.

At midmorning, Sacajawea pointed to the sky and the little bay ahead of her canoe. "This is what Old Toby said to watch for," she called to Captain Clark. "Ducks we can eat!" The sky was dark with blue-wing teals, and many were feeding on the shallow shoreline of the bay. Clark motioned for the other canoes to hold back as he loaded his rifle and shot. Before the five canoes had gone downriver four miles, they had enough ducks for their evening meal. The thought of a meal without fish picked up everyone's spirits.

By afternoon, the canoes were among rocks, rapids, shoals that ran from bank to bank, and a narrow crooked channel. Just as spirits were slipping with the work and worry of keeping the canoes upright, the channel opened and they could see the confluence of the Snake with a large river.

"It must be the Columbia!" shouted Clark. "Nothing else would be that wide. Beautiful!"[2]

Drouillard looked for a place to beach and found sand all along the shoreline. As soon as the canoes were pulled up and the men were unloading the gear to set up camp, the neighborhood Nez Percés were greeting them. This group came with beating tom-toms, singing and dancing, then forming a ring around the party and swaying to and fro.

"At least they don't carry us around," said York. "I'll choke the next one that tries that!"

Captain Clark had several blankets spread on the sand and asked the chief and his important men to sit and smoke with him. This gave York and Charbonneau time to clean the ducks and start a fire with dried sagebrush they pulled from the sand. While the ducks

roasted, they sat with the others and watched Captain
Lewis give the chief a Jefferson peace medal, a shirt,
and a handkerchief. The second chief was given a small
Washington medal and a handkerchief. Then Lewis announced through Drouillard that if the Nez Percés would
trade for some decent firewood the white men would
dance for them after they had eaten. This was the first
night on the Columbia—a night for a big celebration.
There was no doubt now that they would soon see the
Pacific Ocean, the Stinking Waters as the Indians called
it.

Sacajawea bathed Pomp and pulled a new shirt over
his head before she came to join the men at the evening
meal, the first in a long spell with no fish on their plates.
Some were already finished when she sat down with
her plate of savory roast duck. Charbonneau sat himself
beside her and fed Pomp some of the soft, well-done
meat and gave him a bone to try his newly cut front
teeth on. As she ate, Sacajawea noticed that her man
did not have his capote on and he was bright red in the
face, as though he had been heaving an ax against a
large tree. Sweat appeared across his forehead.

"Are you sick with a fever?" she asked.

"*Non.* I am celebrating." He stood up and began dancing clumsily while repetitiously singing an old Mandan
three-note song. When he came close Sacajawea smelled
the sour, moldy bread on his breath. Some of the men
were laughing at his attempt to dance.

Sacajawea saw the canister on the sand. It was lid-
less and the liquid inside was down from the top. The
men were freely dipping their tin cups for swallows of
the sick-smelling, pale-yellow liquid. They were careful
to avoid dipping up the brownish froth or any lumps of
sour bread.

Charbonneau was kicking up sand with his dancing,
laughing and weaving this way and that, careful not
to tip his cup too far on its side. He took Captain Clark's
cup, managed to fill it about a quarter full, and did the
same with his own cup. Then he announced boldly to
Clark, "You get the dog bone and beat on this here big
canister tonight. Soon now, she will be empty, then I
am going to dance for those Nez Percés right along with
York." He threw back his head and drank greedily.

York moseyed over and decanted a little of the pale liquid into his cup. "Ah! That there is mighty fine beer!" He grinned at Collins. "Aren't you glad I saved the spoiled bread for you?"

Collins grinned back, then joined Hugh Hall, who was singing. At first the songs were soft and slow, then Hall's voice rose and gained power. Sacajawea stared at him, scarcely believing what she saw and heard. He had always been quiet and shy. It must be that the drink has a magical power, she thought.

Charbonneau stopped his awkward dancing and sand spreading long enough to pass his cup to Sacajawea. "Drink, *femme*. She is good for you."

The smell was like rotting food scraps that only camp dogs would touch. Sacajawea held her breath to try again. The mouthful of liquid burned her throat and she felt it glow in her belly like heat from a live red coal. She saw Captain Lewis sample some as he talked with Shannon, who also had a cup of the foul liquid. Slowly she drained the cup and passed it back to Charbonneau.[3]

Wiser called out sleepily, "Man, it's hot out here tonight!" He took off his shirt and dropped it on the sand at his feet.

Charbonneau and Collins had begun dancing, their arms around each other. They were singing, but each a different song, and Charbonneau was singing in French. The two songs did not blend together; they sounded terrible. Charbonneau started laughing. His booming voice shook Collins, so he stopped singing, but kept right on dancing.

A strange, magical power had grabbed everyone. Sacajawea felt the ground move under her feet. Shannon took her hand and began to move around her in what he supposed was a heel-toe dance, laughing foolishly and encouraging her to follow him. She saw from the corner of her eye that York was tipping the canister over his empty cup, decanting the last drops of juice— most of it dripping into the sand at his feet.

The Nez Percés had formed a circle around the camp to watch these strange white men entertain them. They seemed to be staring in amazement. Collins walked around shaking hands with the Nez Percés. Cruzatte

walked around playing his fiddle with his eyes closed.
Gibson hummed along beside him with a funny grin on
his face. LePage spun around, with his arms out like a
bird. Ordway started dancing. He had not entered into
dancing much before, but now he started off whirling,
bending his head, and stamping his feet in wild imitation of a buffalo about to mate.

Charbonneau grabbed the smelly container, turned
it upside down, and watched the scummy bits of sour
bread and dark froth run out on the sand. He had a
bone in his right hand which he whacked on the bottom
of the large metal can. York heard the drum-beating
Nez Percés trying to keep time with Charbonneau, the
men laughing, and he began dancing around the fire.
The light made his black face shine and reflected off
his white teeth. Sacajawea looked up, noticing that he
wore the clothing made by Old Toby, which compli-
mented him in every respect. His basic garments, shirt
and leggings, were of the finest, softest goat skin bought
from the Nez Percés back on the Clearwater and worked
to a pleasing sepia tone. Over these he wore a perfectly
fitting knee-length frock of the same material, the hem
and seams accurately cut into frills an inch or so in
length. At his wide elk-hide belt he carried an excellent
nine-inch-long razor-edged knife in a strong leather
sheath, and his favorite weapon, the war club made of
a heavy smooth stone the size and shape of a large goose
egg sewn into wet rawhide that had dried and tightened
around it to a hard finish, with a strip of this same
rawhide covering a strong hickory handle. This was the
poggâmoggon given to him by Sacajawea's brother. On
his feet he wore very soft buckskin moccasins covered
over by a rougher over-moccasin of heavy elk hide, which
reached to his knees.

John Potts linked his arm with Cruzatte's and
brought him to the center of the ring. "A square dance!"
Potts announced, calling out, "Allemande left, dos-a-
dos, cast off," as most of the men joined in to dance.
Shannon brought Sacajawea in, and it seemed to her
that she was tall as a lodgepole with long, straight legs.
The papoose on her back weighed as much as a handful
of breath feathers.

"The men needed a bit of fun," sighed Clark.

"I certainly am glad that fermented mash is gone," said Lewis. "Lord, there would be hell to pay if this fun got out of hand."[4]

Slowly, a few at a time, the Nez Percés crept into the center to dance with shuffling feet around the square dancers. Some of the Nez Percé women became bolder and began feeling Colter's shoulder-length blond hair, shaking their heads in amazement over the light color. When they saw the red hair of Captain Clark, the women put their hands over their mouths in disbelief that hair could be that color at all. York laughed loudly, yelling, "Now you know how it is to be so different that people touch and pull at you. Ha, ha, ha! As long as I dance they'll leave me alone."

He was right. The minute he stopped to catch a breath, the Nez Percé women were at him, the greatest wonder of all, their wet fingertips finding his arms, pulling his frock up, working their hands under his shirt so they could see his chest and back as they tried to rub the color off. When a couple of the older boys boldly pushed a few women aside so they, too, could try the old wet-finger test, York exploded.

"I'll take your ears off with this long tooth"—he waved his knife in the air—"and I'll feed 'em to the dogs. I'll make a fierce face at your chief and he'll fall over with a bellyache!" His voice boomed as he waved the war club about his head with the other hand. "I'se sick, sick, sick of wet fingers and mauling my black body. If anyone touches me, I'se the one to say who!"

The women and boys screamed and moved back. Nez Percé children ran to the back circle to hide.

"Stay away from me or I'se pin you to the earth and leave you there to dry out with all your flea-bitten salmon!" He tested the knife edge with the edge of his thumb.

There was a sudden silence as a Nez Percé warrior jumped into the circle close to York waving a flint knife and with hand signs making it clear he would use it before York could use either of his weapons.

Sacajawea steadied herself as she saw some of the other Nez Percé men pull out their flint knives. This could get out of hand, she knew.

The Nez Percé in the ring with York slapped his

chest. He was solid, with muscles that stood out gnarled
as weathered bark. His arms were as thick as most
men's legs. Sacajawea had been right; here was trouble.
York looked around at the now silent faces and staring
eyes and knew that he could not refuse the challenge.
He did not want bloodshed, but could it be avoided?

Sacajawea kept her eyes on the ground so that it
would not sway or heave upward, and she began to sing,
her voice at first soft, then ringing out strongly. She
moved slowly, with short, toe-heel steps along the circle
of men. She told York to put the knife away. He slipped
it in the sheath and stood quietly as she added more
words to her song, telling the men to dance slowly in
place as she sang. The Nez Percés copied and they, too,
danced toe-heel in place. This was something new to
them, a woman leading a dance and singing aloud in
public.

Captain Clark moved in close to York. "That song
is something you taught her. It worked once, and it is
working again."

"Yes, sir, something I'se taught her." York smiled
and relaxed a little, putting the war club under his elk-
hide belt. "Women—ain't they something else, though?
She saved me from myself."

"You sit down and let the others dance. You've had
enough celebration tonight."

"But, sir, I was looking at a pretty little gal who
looked like she was all moon-faced for me."

"How can you be woman-hungry after the other
morning?" Clark said, mostly teasing, relieved now that
York was not the center of attention and the knives
were all out of sight.

"I'se just looking. Ain't that Janey a pretty sight?
She's just a-swaying those Nez Percés to be peaceable
and singing out orders to us. She can use our words
about as well as her old man can now. She's kind of
like one of the family." Then, glancing over his shoulder, York saw a young squaw moving up closer to him.
"Just look at that little gal there"—he pointed her out
to Clark—"she's asking for it."

"Your kinky hair will be scattered clear across the
North American continent, from the Mississippi to the
Pacific Ocean," chided Clark.

Charbonneau never remembered how the dance ended because he and Collins were sitting out in the sand, back to back, snoring deep in their throats. McNeal, who was on guard, checked on them once in a while during the night to make sure they were still there.

Sacajawea remembered the dance afterward. Her head was perfectly clear before it ended. She could hardly wait for morning so that she could ask Captain Clark about the sour bread in the canister and how the men had turned it into a powerful medicine that could cure shyness.

When all but the guard were asleep in the camp, Sacajawea left Pomp wrapped in her blankets and walked through the grass to the water's edge. The wind pulled at her loose hair, and she slipped from her tunic, carefully folding the blue-beaded belt. The wind was chilly. A quarter moon rode low over the river, the expedition's camp, and the Nez Percé village. She threw her arms up toward it. She moved knee-deep into the clear, cold water and bent to fling it over her body.

She prayed to the Great Spirit in the Shoshoni tongue, making all her thoughts known. But when she thought of her man she could not form a prayer—she did not know what she desired for herself with Charbonneau. *Ai*, she knew, but she could not bring it out in the open, even for the Great Spirit. She secretly wished Charbonneau were like Captain Clark, wise and kind.

She stepped from the river shivering but refreshed. She stood naked long enough to let the cold night wind dry her before she slipped into her tunic and tied the beloved beaded belt carefully, then shook down her hair. Still she lingered, standing quietly in the pale light from the moon. She turned at the sound of a cough, thinking it to be McNeal, and said, "I was bathing."

"I know," answered Captain Clark, still visualizing her creamy-brown shoulders and small, high, pink-tipped breasts, the curve of hips and thighs that melted into the perfect legs and tiny brown feet highlighted with moonlight.

He could not explain his feeling of the moment. He was used to the nakedness of Indian girls and women and generally felt no desire. Yet tonight his face fevered and his hands were hot in the cold wind. He thought that it was well she was unaware of his feeling.

She bowed her head, understanding instantly why Clark was staring at her.

They went silently back to camp, nodding at McNeal, who thought the captain had gone to get Janey out of that cold river before she came down with pneumonia. Before leaving for his blankets, Clark said, "I was restless after all that excitement tonight. We all owe you much for keeping things peaceful. I am always grateful we have you with us. And now I can better understand the temptations of York." To himself he thought, I did not mean to say that last to her. What is the matter with me? I seem to be addle-brained from Collins's beer. "Goodnight, Janey."

"Goodnight. I am glad to be near you." She hurried off through the grass to her blankets, passing Charbonneau leaning against Collins, snoring loudly, sucking in and out the ends of his mustache. I know one thing, she thought. Chief Red Hair thinks of me as I think of him when we are busy and not near one another. And he thinks of his men in the same way. He is the protector of us all. She fell asleep thinking of the next canoe ride on the cold blue water.

The next morning, Charbonneau and Collins walked around holding their heads and groaning. Captain Lewis accused them of exaggerating. The other men told each other about how much of Collins's beer they had drunk. Sacajawea knew that if they had consumed as much as they told about, there would have had to have been three canisters instead of one. Captain Clark thought this was as good a time as any to lay over for a day. He explained to the men that he wanted to explore the Columbia about ten miles upstream to see if there was any game in the vicinity.[5]

Captain Lewis stayed in camp and reorganized the gear. He made sure that the packs with the trade goods were easy to get at. He counted out the number of medals they were carrying and decided that they could give them out a bit more freely than before.

When he returned, Captain Clark told how astounded he was at the number of salmon in the island-dotted river. And noting that a large percentage were dead or dying, he asked the men to eat only the ones that were well dried or freshly killed. He said he would continue to buy dogs from the Nez Percés. Silently, Sacajawea wished he would buy horse meat. Each tribe they passed seemed to have an abundance of horses.

For the next two days, the canoes had no navigational problems and the river Indians remained friendly. On the third day, the expedition was again met by the Nez Percés in the vicinity as they made night camp. About two hundred men formed a half circle around the entire expedition and sang to the beating of four drums for some time. The principal chief was given a Jefferson peace medal, and the second chief a medal of smaller size. Lewis thought it necessary to lay in some meat, so he purchased forty dogs in trade for bells, thimbles, a few red beads, and a roll of brass wire.

In the morning, a young-looking chief called Yellept, from a Walla Walla village downriver, came for a visit along with some of his important men. These people lived in peace with the Nez Percés, and like them shared characteristics of both mountain and prairie Indians. Part of the year they fished the rivers, dug for the camass root, *kouse*, and other edible tubers. In the early spring they mounted their horses and rode to the mountains to hunt deer and elk. Sometimes they made the long trek over the Bitterroots into Blackfeet country for buffalo, the hides of which were used for moccasins and robes.

Yellept wanted the white men to stay a few days so that his villagers might come to meet them. Lewis gave him a Jefferson medal and several twists of tobacco. Chief Twisted Hair and Tetoharsky understood his language, although it seemed to Drouillard to contain more clacking sounds than the Nez Percé tongue. The captains promised Chief Yellept they would stay a few days at his village on their return trip. Before leaving, the chief drew a map in the sand indicating that the Columbia contained a great falls several days from this place. Noting this, Chief Twisted Hair jumped around saying, "So—it is as I have told you. Now you know for certain you will come to a place in the water where you cannot use the canoes. I told you so!"

Chief Yellept named a few of the tribes the expedition would encounter as they went on. The Nez Percés would be left behind. First they would meet the Yakimas, then the Chopunnish, and when they were close to the Stinking Waters they would find the Chinooks, "a shabby group." Around the mouth of the Columbia the white men would find the Clatsops and Tillamooks. Captain Lewis asked through Drouillard if there were deer or elk in the country of the Yakimas. Chief Yellept shook his head. "Only salmon and water birds this time of year. The land is a sandy plain, with few trees and little firewood."

By evening the expedition had met the Yakimas. Sacajawea watched women take dead fish from along the banks, split them open, and put them on their drying scaffolds. There was no tree in sight from which the scaffold could have been made. Curiosity got the best of her. She stood close to a group of women for minutes, then with hand signs asked how the wood was brought to this place. "Oh," said a short, pregnant squaw with many small white shells around her neck, "our boys mount their ponies, slip into the water, position themselves at the four corners of rafts made of willow pokes and buffalo skins. They ride downriver where the trees grow. That is easy. Coming back, everything must be lashed to the rafts. The horses shuttle back and forth from one bank to another coming upstream. That is very hard. Sometimes a horse or a boy is lost."

"Where do you find the shells?" Sacajawea asked, indicating she thought they made nice decoration.

"Sometimes we trade buffalo hides to those who live near the Stinking Waters. Shells are nothing to them. But look." The squaw pulled up her tunic and revealed a pair of black woolen trousers she was wearing.

Sacajawea was astounded. "It is the clothing of white men. How could you have that?"

The squaw smiled, pulled down her tunic, and patted her abdomen. "White men come to the Stinking Waters. They trade for skins and furs. Their canoes are so much larger than the ones your white men brought here, so that I do not believe you are of much importance." The squaw turned and started splitting salmon down the back, ignoring Sacajawea.

Sacajawea did not notice. She was hurrying to find Captain Clark. He was talking with some of the Yakima men. She rushed into the circle and spoke as best she could, then used hand signs. Twisted Hair gave her a reproving look. She sat beside Drouillard and tried to speak more slowly.

"Janey, it must be important, but can't you see how you distract these Yakimas? They do not approve of a woman coming into their meeting. Can't this wait?" said Captain Clark.

"*Ai*, but I know there are white men at the Stinking Water."

"You know this for sure?" asked Drouillard, dumbfounded.

She began to tell her story, but before she was finished, the Yakima men had left in disgust. Captain Clark did not know whether to scold or praise her. "Next time you have anything so important to tell me, go to Captain Lewis or to Charbonneau and tell them; they will come and tell me and not make my guests leave so abruptly. Damn, I would have liked to have asked those men about the ships and the people on them at the Pacific. Oh, hell, I suppose we'll find out soon enough. Don't forget, unless I ask you to interpret, don't barge in on a meeting or powwow. Still, the men didn't say anything half as exciting as you learned from that woman."

By the next afternoon, everyone had noticed that the bunch grass grew much thicker and there was no more sagebrush to be seen. The expedition made their night camp near a small river that flowed into the Columbia. There was an encampment of about thirty grass lodges arranged in the form of an irregular V, with the apex downriver, to the north. There seemed to be nearly a thousand ponies here, munching the grass contentedly. When Captain Clark saw a white crane gliding over several grass huts, he took careful aim and fired, thinking of the roast bird for his evening meal. For a moment the people of the village, who had witnessed the bird drop from the air, were transfixed with wonder. Suddenly their minds grasped the horror of it, and they fled for their huts, hiding.

Captain Clark took Drouillard and Chief Twisted

Hair with him to the village beside the small river and
called to the people. No one came out of the huts. They
opened several doors and called. Drouillard tried explaining how the bird had fallen. Slowly some of the
people came out with bowed heads, wringing their hands,
waiting for the blow of death to hit them. In one hut
Clark raised the chin of a little boy and smiled at him.
He offered the child a tin spoon. Then he offered gifts
of tobacco and white beads to the older members of the
family. No one reached out for the gifts. In another hut
he lifted the chin of a little girl and smiled at her, giving
her yellow beads. Finally, in the center of the V made
by the huts, he stood with those bowing their heads and
calmly took out his pipestone calumet from the leather
sheath fastened to his belt.

"All tribes know the meaning of the peace pipe," he
said loudly so that Drouillard and Twisted Hair could
hear as he sat crossed-legged in the center of this village. Slowly the people raised their heads, and others
peeped from their doors, not yet daring to go out. Clark
took off his tricornered hat and laid it beside the pipe
on the ground in front of him. Still nothing happened.
He picked up his hat and began slowly and carefully
to improve the crease in it with his big, rawboned fingers. Several children came out and stood close to their
doorways. Clark took that for his cue and strolled over
to one particularly large hut where several men huddled together. He lit his pipe from a stick in their fire,
then knocked out the fire and refilled his pipe, relighting it with his magnifying glass from the sun's rays
that came through the smoke hole. The men shrieked.
Clark tried to pacify them. Not one would touch the
pipe lit by the sun.

Captain Clark sat on a rock outside the large hut
and smoked by himself. Using hand signs, Drouillard
tried gently to persuade a couple of children to go to
Captain Clark. A man came out and watched Drouillard; finally he said, using signs, "The one with flame
for hair is not a man. We saw him cause a bird to fall
with great thunder from a stick. Now I saw him bring
fire from the sky to light his pipe. No man can do that."

Twisted Hair sat with Clark, telling him these people were called the Chopunnish and they had never seen

white men before. "What about the Walla Wallas who have traded with them?" asked Clark uneasily.

Twisted Hair shook his head, saying, "These people do not travel on the river much. There is enough fish here to keep them in food, and they can buy skins from their neighbors or use horse hide for their moccasins." Twisted Hair then tried to reassure the Chopunnish man with soft cluckings they both seemed to understand. "It will be dark soon," said Twisted Hair, "and you will see he lights his pipe from the coals of the fire, same as any man."

Still that was not enough to show that Captain Clark was harmless, so they would touch his pipe. Finally Clark asked Drouillard to bring Sacajawea and Pomp to him. "Tell her she is needed to get this meeting started," he chuckled. "I hope she is not stubborn after I told her yesterday she broke my meeting apart. Tell her it's important and I want her here."

Sacajawea's presence was their reassurance. At the sight of her placing her papoose close to the feet of Captain Clark, the brave called to others, as he pointed toward Sacajawea and her child. They peered at Pomp, who smiled back with baby chatter and patted the old, worn hat Clark had left on the ground. Then Pomp picked the hat up and popped it onto his own head. His eyes were covered, and he bent his head back in a comical way so that he could see. The Chopunnish laughed at the baby. Finally someone said, "No squaw goes with a war party—still less a baby."

Soon they were smoking with Captain Clark, Chief Twisted Hair, and Drouillard, but with their own pipes. Never would they touch the magic pipe of Captain Clark. Sacajawea let Pomp wander among the Chopunnish, hanging on to each one for support as he half crawled and half walked from one to another, smiling and jabbering.

In the morning before leaving camp, Captain Clark climbed to the top of a bluff about two hundred feet above the small river and spied a mountain peak, a perfect cone. Some days later the whole expedition saw snowcapped Mount Hood far to the south. Beyond the Umatilla River and the Chopunnish village, the expedition saw the signs they were eagerly looking for—

there were Indians wearing scarlet-and-blue blankets,
and one wore a sailor's pea jacket. Now they knew they
were coming closer to the coast, where ships had stopped
to trade with the natives.

During the next few days they saw a rusty flintlock,
a sword, brass kettles, brass armbands, large beads,
overalls, shirts, pistols, jammed beyond working order,
and tin powder flasks. Some of these river people wore
white and pink seashells in their noses, and some startled the men with their use of four-letter English words.
However, the captains, with the help of Twisted Hair,
Tetoharsky, and Drouillard, could get almost no information about white men, white traders, or large seagoing vessels. These river people were getting the white
men's goods secondhand by trading with other natives
farther down the Columbia.

Sea otter began to appear in the river, which was
now much of the time too dangerous for the canoes, and
long, tedious portages had to be made. Charbonneau
continually crabbed about carrying all his gear, including the bedding. "I'm not a packhorse," he snorted.
"There's no great rush," he told Sacajawea sharply. She
hurried ahead of him with bedding and clothing under
her arms and her baby slung across her back.

"We have all day," he said, but not so loud. "*Jésus*,
I work my tail off getting the gear around one bad spot
in the river, only to find another one waiting down
below. That's sense now, ain't it?" He waved his old
black felt hat around in the air. "I suppose if there was
forty-eight hours in a day you'd just keep packing for
les capitaines." He trotted after her, cackling.

She did not look around, but she could still hear him.
"*Allez! Jésus*, why hurry?"

She felt hot and angry, but she knew she would do
nothing, not even say much. She plodded along in her
toed-in way, and at a clump of sword fern stopped to
suck in a couple of mouthfuls of air and get hold of
herself. One thing she could see: if her man could make
her so angry when there was nothing she could do about
it, then a lot of the men must get stirred up with him,
too.

"Do we have to be punished like this only because
we cannot swim?" asked Charbonneau at another point

where the river had so many whirlpools and rapids that Captain Clark sent all the men who could not swim ashore, loaded with the firearms and precious papers, to haul them overland. Actually, Charbonneau was against almost any kind of work that made him perspire and breathe heavily.

"This is the most fatiguing business I've been engaged in this week," admitted Pat Gass. "But I guess this shows those old buck Indians on the shores watching that we are men. Real men."

These were the Chinook Indians they were passing by, and each village seemed dirtier than the last. They were crawling with lice and did not seem to notice.

A handful of Chinook braves offered assistance with their horses on an especially long portage around the Celilo Falls. Then they took their own pay by pilfering the stores for hatchets and a canister of black powder. Below the falls were stacks of salmon, dried, pounded, packed in grass baskets, heaped into bales, stored in mat huts, and cached in deep holes in the sand.

"I'd take a basket of pounded salmon just to get even," said Shannon, "but I hate to add more of that to my belly. I don't think it'll ever wash out of my hair or ears, and I'll always smell this way."

At the end of the evening meal, Chief Twisted Hair and his subchief, Tetoharsky, sat with Captain Clark, who had been talking with Sacajawea and bouncing Pomp on his lap.

"We want two horses," said Twisted Hair. "We do not trust the Chinooks, and we want to get out of here. You saw how they took your goods without asking. We are much afraid of the men who live beyond this part of the river. They fight over nothing and make war with everyone who passes." They made hand signs to indicate they had been growing uneasy for some time about the Chinooks.

Captain Clark sent York to trade for two horses for the Nez Percé guides. "We'll smoke the pipe before you leave," suggested Clark.

Twisted Hair looked pleased and said he would conduct the ceremony according to his custom. "This is the time for you to smoke, and anyone can talk on whatever serious subject he wants to. The woman can also talk.

Don't talk too long." He looked pointedly at Sacajawea. "Just say what you want to say if you have a notion. Just say a few words." Now he looked at Captain Lewis. "You can talk again. Don't talk too fast." He looked at Drouillard, who interpreted his speech. "If it is the Great Spirit's will, you will all live long. If you talk out your words too fast, you won't live long; that is what we all believe. When you go visiting us on your way back over the mountains, if we don't give you a gift, that's all right. If we give you too much too often, you might not live long. If you get horses on the warpath, don't go again too soon. You might get killed. Conserve what you have. Do everything in a measured way. The Great Spirit wanted us to live on this earth, and here we are. These are the things that the Great Spirit gave us— the camass, the sand and salmon, and deer, and other things—and we must take care of them. We cannot throw away or waste anything. We cannot know what is going to happen in the future."

Tetoharsky began, "This is your time to talk. We are not in a hurry. If you have a story to tell, tell it. I would like to leave before the sun is in the sky one more time. I want to see my woman and her children."

Drouillard spoke. "I would like to see the Pacific Ocean. How do the rest feel about that?"

There was much nodding of heads, and then Captain Lewis spoke. "I am going to get a hundred pounds of ammunition out tonight and make sure everyone knows where it is."

Si Goodrich said, "Good idea, in case these Chinooks are not too friendly like the old chief here says."

Captain Clark thought this an opportunity to make peace between the downriver villages and those on the upper river, and he begged Chief Twisted Hair to stay.

Several of the men made some remark on these matters, then Shannon proposed that they all shake hands with the two Nez Percés to show their appreciation and friendship.

Sacajawea stood up, but Charbonneau pulled on her skirt, saying, "Sit down, *femme*. None of the other fellows stood up to make their speech. Why should you?"

She scowled at him, then looked at the Nez Percés and said in English, slowly, "We have spoken. We are friends. Goodnight and thank you." That broke up the ceremony. York was back with the horses.

Before sunup, the expedition was ready to move farther downriver and saying farewell to the Nez Percés. "We go back to look after the white men's horses staying at our village," called Chief Twisted Hair, waving both arms and bouncing on his horse.

After Chief Twisted Hair's warning about the warlike nature of the Chinooks in front of them, the captains were wary, but the ammunition Captain Lewis issued was never used. The Chinooks were infested with lice, squinty-eyed, excellent at swiping small items, but quite friendly. Many of the Chinooks flattened their babies' heads with a board attached to the cradleboard, and their language was a series of tongue clacks, which was hard for Drouillard to distinguish.

The Pacific

On November eighth the ocean was sighted. "Great joy in camp," wrote the usually unemotional Clark. "We are in view of the Ocian, this great Pacific Ocian which we have been so long anxious to see, and the roreing or noise made by the waves brakeing on the rockey shores [as I suppose] may be heard disti[n]ctly." The estimated distance the explorers had traveled from St. Louis to the ocean was four thousand one hundred miles.

From *Sacajawea*, by Harold P. Howard. Copyright 1971 by the University of Oklahoma Press, p. 83.

At the Short Narrows of the Columbia River, the water rushed through steep rock walls not more than forty-five yards apart. Travel here was dangerous, but a portage around the rapids was next to impossible because the banks were too difficult to climb. Captain Clark took the riverman, Cruzatte, with him for a walk along the narrow shore to examine the wild water.

"This is a bad stretch," said Clark.

"We've had worse," said Cruzatte. "It's not going to be bad as long as we can let the canoes down with ropes. It's when we have to take them out of the water that it's misery."

The canoe in which Cruzatte paddled stern reached some willows, then was caught in a stronger current. The men in it bent to their paddles. Still it swung sharply away from the bank.

"They have gone too far!" shouted Clark.

"Watch out!" someone else yelled.

"Work her in! Work!"

"Make into the shore! Hey—they'll need a rope!" called Captain Lewis.

The backs of Cruzatte, Gass, Labiche, and Colter were bowed under the strain. The canoe shot from beneath them. It stood up on its stern, then spun like a twig, danced, and lunged through foaming water with the four men clinging to it. It swept in toward the bank, danced, slipped up on a rock, and caught. Cruzatte, Gass, Labiche, and Colter were on the rock. Then, chest-deep in dangerous water, Cruzatte pulled the canoe in close to shore. "Hang on!" Lewis shouted to the other three, then swung a braided elk-skin rope over their heads.

The rope sailed across the water, and Gass was the first to catch it. The four men, chest-deep in the water, braced themselves as the rope jerked taut. Then the dugout was slapped violently across the water and against the shore. Hands waited there to grab them and drag them to safety. Taking up the rope from Captain Lewis, Cruzatte carefully brought the other four canoes through safely, one at a time.

Charbonneau commented on the fast-swirling water, "Looks like a horrid, agitated gut, swelling, boiling, and whirling in every direction." That evening he brought out his French harp, to the delight of the expedition and the local Chinooks. Cruzatte played his violin in accompaniment until Charbonneau's wind gave out.

The day after the Short Narrows was also bad because the Columbia passed through hard, rough, black rock, from fifty to one hundred yards wide, swelling and boiling all the time. The men called this the Great Shoot.[1] Here the river dropped sixty feet in two miles. Cruzatte admitted the canoes could not make it through and doubted if a man would get through alive. The men began the portage over the rock-strewn shore, along the edges of the cliffs, sweating, panting, chanting, wet with spray, half the time waist-deep in dangerous water, numbed to the hips. They made camp at a flat place that had been used recently as a camp by a tribe of Chinooks. When the men cleared away the dried grass and fish skins, they discovered they were covered with fleas and had to strip and duck in the cold water in order to get the insects off their legs and bodies.[2]

Across the river was a small encampment of Chinooks. Their lodges were different from any yet seen. They were made of wood with roofs, a door, and gables, like frontier cabins. In the front of each lodge were stacks of salmon.

"Ten thousand pounds," wrote Captain Clark in his journal that evening, "all dried, baled with twisted grass rope, and probably bound for traffic further down the river. What a smell."

Moseying near Charbonneau, Reuben Fields said with a teasing glint in his eyes, "Hey, when the wind comes over the water just right, I swear I can smell your boots on the opposite bank."

"My boots," replied Charbonneau, squinting his eyes to peer through the slits, "will smell the way you do every day when they have gone through this damn river country. *Poulet merde!*" He held his nose and walked away, not wishing to enlarge on the subject.

The terrain began to change, and more trees grew along the riverbanks. Mountains, large and glistening white with snow-covered peaks, were seen ahead. The expedition passed ancient burial places where the dead were stacked one upon the other and the whitened skulls were placed in a circle on a high platform in the trees. On either side of the river channel they saw rocky palisades, green-mossed and dripping. Waterfalls came down the slopes and fell in a rainbow mist to the river.

One morning Pat Gass felt his head after passing under a burial platform beside a falls and said, "I sincerely hope it is the mountain mist that bedews my top hair, and not some disintegrating remnants of someone's great-grandmother."

A river flowing into the Columbia was named after Baptiste LePage, and another after Pierre Cruzatte. On the rocks around these rivers lay many sleeping hair seals. Sacajawea pointed them out to Pomp, saying, "See, the river people are out there taking a rest."

One evening a local Chinook stole Charbonneau's old blue capote and hid it under the roots of a tree to pick up later. Sacajawea found it and took it to Charbonneau. He scolded her for letting his coat get full of muck and wet leaves and crawling with fleas. "Go wash it!" he yelled.

The Chinook tribes they now saw tattooed their faces by putting charcoal under the skin in intricate designs in the belief that it improved their looks.

York was panting for breath when he found Charbonneau. "I'se been looking quite a spell for you," York said. "There's this fellow who looks like his face was made permanent blue with huckleberry stain, with your coat rolled under his arm and moving, like he's expecting to be shot, for the other side of camp."

"My capote?"

"Did you trade him that coat for something? Man, you'se going to need it. The nights are already cold."

"My *femme* found it. Damn thieving Chinooks! Hey, don't tell her I know a Chinook swiped it."

"Why not?"

Charbonneau acted like he did not hear the last question and did not seem in a mood for conversation, so York sauntered on to talk to some of the other men about the peculiarities of the Chinooks.

"Did you notice how all those squaws look alike? I can't tell one squaw in a family way from another in a similar condition. Do you suppose they all belong to the same ladies' aid society? Watch! See how they go around sucking in and measuring each other with their eyes? I'll bet my beaded moccasins and woolen stockings they're getting ready to unload all at once. Each squaw will have a papoose to carry around to be admired at the same time—almost like what happens back home when the church ladies carry their prize johnnycake in a fancy covered dish to the parsonage for a circle meeting, all holding up their creation for the admiration of all and feeling good for the effort put into making something beautiful."

The men laughed. Thus reinforced, York went on, "And can you guess the diet of these folks? They eat olives. It's a kind of pickled acorn, flavorsome enough if you don't know what they was pickled in, and they eat dogs—that's why they raise so many inside their villages—and then they have a chaser, which is a kind of watery stew made of fish eyes. Listen to this: I seen one big buck eat fire. Honest! He licked it right off a chunk of pine pitch and snorted a big stream of it eight foot out into the air. I think he eats it on his boiled fish like it was pepper sass."

The men guffawed and pounded York on the back.

"Them natives is an outfit, all right," agreed Gibson.

For the next couple of days the expedition was in the valley of the lower Columbia, the home of the warm Chinook wind. The country was one of long slopes, running against the sky. The hills and swales were still green, and the air was warm and moist with rain. Swarms of swans, geese, ducks, cranes, storks, gulls, cormorants, and plover flew overhead. They were a delicious change in diet from the salmon. For a time the canoes drifted smoothly, then suddenly they descended into deep river canyons, and then in a little while they were back on smooth water between rapids again. There were the unique wooden huts of the Chinooks on both sides of the river. The huts always had racks of drying salmon around them, and everywhere the banks of the river were strewn with fish skins, making a sickening stench.[3]

When the expedition passed by the Hood River inlet,

the Chinooks ran from their outside chores into their lodges. All were terrified as though they had never before seen white men. They could not be persuaded to come out, and they never ventured near the expedition's camp. This tribe was dressed in skins from the shaggy mountain goat. Beside each hut was a wooden box with salmon, halibut heads, and roe, putrefying. Holding her nose, Sacajawea showed Clark the carved goat-horn spoons and wooden dishes, elaborately carved, that lay inside the boxes. She pointed out that this might be a tribal delicacy, comparing it to the Hidatsas' liking of rotten buffalo flesh. She laughed when Clark made a face and held his stomach. They called to the people as they passed lodges and racks of salmon and other fish, split, dried, and some boxed with oil. Finally Clark left a few gifts near a large cache of dried fish. The odor of decaying fish and rancid oil lay heavily over this village.

Below the Hood River there were abandoned wooden huts, which the captains examined. They were built of split red cedar with a top smoke hole, or roof well, that could be opened for light or shut by an arrangement of sliding boards. The entire hut depended on notching and mortising; no pegs were used. The dead were placed in open wooden boxes, which Bratton found in an area to one side of the abandoned village. Inside, the bones were weathered white. Some of the boxes contained baskets made of spruce and cedar roots woven together. There were bowls beautifully carved with a kind of sea monster. The features were a mixture of bear and shark, with curved lines on the cheeks representing gills, a shark's tail, and bear's paws. The men found carvings in stone and baked clay in the grave goods. Sacajawea half believed that the spirits of those people might not wish to be disturbed, so she fought her curiosity to look inside and looked instead inside the forsaken huts. She found a tiny amulet of a human figure, carved from a beryl; the knees were slightly bent and drawn up against the chest, the kneecaps were flattened, and the feet were merged with the base. The head was large in proportion to the body, almost equaling the shoulders in width. The figure lay discarded in a corner, and she found it because its reddish coloring attracted her attention. She squealed with delight and ran out to find some discarded rope or sinew that could be used to tie around the little doll. She found some braided, hairlike twining in another hut and placed the doll around Pomp's neck. His baby fingers examined it, then he popped it into his mouth, sucking on the feet. Sacajawea belatedly remembered the captains' policy of not taking anything from any village unless it was especially given as a gift. She knew Captain Lewis would judge her more harshly than Captain Clark.

"Why didn't you tell me you wanted a toy for the child?" chided Clark.

"I didn't know until I saw this. It is a gift to him from me."

"I should have had one of the men make Pomp a doll. Gass could make a toy to amuse the boy. I was not thinking or would have had something made weeks ago."

"Now he has it," she said, her face brightening. "I do not have to put it back?"

"It did belong here, and if the former resident came looking for it, what would he think if he found it around your son's neck?"

"The right size for that child," she said, holding her breath a moment.

"You believe the child who owned it before grew up and discarded it?"

"*Ai.*"

Clark was amused and put his arm around her shoulders. "Let your son enjoy it, then."

Sacajawea was more breathless than after an uphill run. She was weak in the knees. Then it came to her that being with the white men was happiness. Some days were hard, *ai*, but there was always happiness. And here with Chief Red Hair outlining her eyebrow with one finger gave her more happiness than her heart could contain. It ached. And she thought that this was a pain that only more pain could cure; like some sickness, she'd feel worse before she felt better.

That day the canoes passed by villages of Chinooks who had flatter heads because of the practice of strapping a padded board across the head of every infant.

"It is *l'malade!*" Sacajawea cried, imitating Charbonneau's French.

"I don't like it, either," agreed Clark.

"Worse even than putting a bone through the nose," said York.

In the evening they camped upriver from a village that was packing fish into large canoes. The expedition had not seen such long, light craft on the river before. These were tapered at the ends, wide in the middle, and the stern and prow lifted into beaks like a Roman galley. The projecting bows served to repel wave action in rough water and prevented swamping. The canoes were painted red, brown, black, or white, and had carved figures at the bows.[4]

"Good Lord," said Lewis, "those craft will carry sixty men and maybe three tons of fish."

The canoe was paddled with leaf-shaped paddles with a crutch-top handle. The steersman in the bow had a longer paddle.

"They use sails," remarked Shannon, pointing to a canoe with very thin planks reinforced with strips of wood and sewn at top and bottom. Then he pointed again. "Two canoes lashed together. See, there!" Two canoes were tied and a plank deck was being laid over them.

Not far from the canoes was a platform over a stream. The women there were gaffing and netting the tightly packed fish as they moved upstream.

"These people look too busy to be interested in visiting with us," said Drouillard.

Around the expedition's camp the cedar timber grew scant because the ground was too sour and weak for it. Only a few dwarf trees grew between black-mud marshes full of cattails and dwarf elder bushes heavy with bunches of mouth-puckering blackberries.

Before sundown the wind came up and brought in a rank sea smell, along with great marsh hawks and a flock of sandpipers and dippers looking for a tasty mouthful in the stream's backwater.

"Oh, is that the smell of the Stinking Waters?" asked Sacajawea.

"Janey, the Western Sea can't be far," said Lewis, twitching his nose, "but the ocean smell is so mixed with rotting fish, it is no wonder it is called Stinking Waters. Lord, will I ever smell anything but decaying fish?"

"I am wondering if we'll ever get to the ocean. Constantly now, I ask myself, what will the terrain be like? What sort of natives live on its shores? Will we meet with a sailing vessel? Lewis, I can hardly wait for the days to pass now until we get a view of that ocean," said Clark, nudging a little tree toad off a deadfall into the lush ferns.

York brought in a few wild blackberries. Sacajawea went out to gather wapato root from the marshy soil.[5]

Sacajawea chased a long-toed salamander, colored like the dark mud and with a wide yellow band from the back of its head to the tip of its tail. All of a sudden she stopped. She was face to face with a black bear digging lily bulbs or grubs from the mud. The bear backed a few feet away from her, but continued to dig. Saliva ran from its mouth. Sacajawea turned slowly, and still looking over her shoulder to make certain the bear did not leave, she hurried back to camp to find Captain Clark. "I know a hunter can have a good shot. Wouldn't fresh bear steaks be good?" She licked her lips and rubbed both hands over her braids, as if wiping off the bear's grease already.

"I'll get McNeal and Hall to go after it," said Clark, his mouth watering.

One crack from a rifle was heard, and before the men had time to argue who had shot it, the two were back in camp with the bear over their shoulders. It was the best meal the expedition had had in days. The men stuffed themselves as though they would not get any meals the next day. About all they could do that evening was sit around the fire and sing and tell stories.

Slowly the Chinooks from across the river came over, inspected the five canoes of the expedition, then sat quietly listening to the white men sing. The captains smoked with the chief and learned that these people smoked dried clover. In fact, the clover patches seemed to be privately owned, and small areas were marked off by grass ropes. The chief explained through Drouillard and with hand signs their fishing habits.

"When spawning time comes, the salmon ready to

spawn make their way back to the freshwater streams from which they came, leaping falls and overcoming all obstacles. We have five to seven salmon runs a year." He held his fingers up. "The fish going upstream are ready for the taking."

Then he surprised Drouillard by telling his belief in the supernatural power of the salmon. In fact, he taxed Drouillard's interpretive powers and he was not certain he got the story straight. "The fish allows itself to be taken in our nets, or by our gigs. Its spirit, released by death, returns again and again, provided the proper care is taken that no offense is given. The salmon live in great houses under the sea. There they assume the same form as you and I and have feasts and potlatches among themselves." Here, Drouillard shook his head and told the captains he was not sure his interpretation was what the chief meant, but it was some Chinook mythology that they had believed for a long time. "So," Drouillard went on, "only when they assume salmon form do they sacrifice themselves. And so—it is our custom to return their bones to the sea, just as those dead salmon are seen returning downstream; then they can assume their human form under the sea and can come again to us."

The chief waved his arms all around. "To throw salmon bones carelessly away would prevent the return of the spirit to the sea and give great offense. The salmon might withhold themselves, and the humans on land would suffer. My village asks you to please return all the bones to the river." The chief crossed his arms in front of his chest and sat silently a few moments.

Captain Clark noted that this particular group of Chinooks had a cleaner-looking village than most because they did not leave the fish skins, heads, and bones lying around.

Lewis wondered how this village dealt with the villages farther upstream, who were so much more careless with the salmon leftovers and did not appear to honor this myth.

"I think they ignore them," said Drouillard. "Once they had a smart headman who knew a way to keep the stink down and have a cleaner place for his people

to live. This village remembers those ideas; the others
have forgotten over the years."

"I would have thought other smart men would have
seen the same thing and done something about keeping
villages cleaner," said Clark.

"The rain cleans things up," said the chief after
Drouillard had tried to make the captains' questions
clear to him.

The following evening the wind came down off the
snow peaks with a stiffening coldness, and the expedition camped in the protection of a cliff. The wind
snapped at their fire and brought rain. Rain fell
throughout the next day from low, leaden clouds, which
concealed the snow mountain. They ate the bear meat
until it was gone, then had wapato stew.

The rain continued. Beneath the grasses the earth
was now a level, dark brown floor. The weather was
foggy, cold, and raw. The wind grew more violent, and
the waves in the wide river became higher. The water
became brackish. It was so salty that a few of the men
became ill from using it to prepare the dried and pounded
salmon, which, after the bear was finished, had again
become the mainstay of their diet. No other game was
seen anywhere. They searched the water for beaver,
but it was too salty.

The tips of the snow peaks dropped lower in the
northeast and at last vanished beneath the floor of the
earth. The wind stirred the cold sand of the wide valleys
and lashed the men's faces with it. Sacajawea pulled a
robe high around Pomp's face for protection against the
biting sand. The valleys were bordered by ridges whose
rim lines were scribbled across the sky.

The blankets and robes were continually wet and
mildewed, and there was no way to replace them or
slow down the growth of mold. After two weeks of this
wet weather, even their clothing was rotting away to
rags.

If there had been large game, there would have been
no time to tan the hides. The shores on each side of the
river were steep and rocky, with pinnacles rising up
and up. Once the canoes passed over a forest of gigantic
submerged tree trunks. One small stream after another

came tumbling down, free of rock, in cascades of white,
frothing water. The north shore was an unbroken bat-
tlement of beautiful multicolored rock. None of the men
had dreamed of such a magnificent land. But neither
had they dreamed of this raw wind, and rain, and penetrating dampness.

"Vicious, beautiful country," Clark remarked.
"Rather think I'm dreaming, or can it be as bad and as
beautiful as it seems?"

"Oh, *Jésus*, worse," said Charbonneau, sniffing and
coughing and shivering, "much worse. We have to keep
working to keep from shivering to death."

The expedition spent the night of November 8 in
Gray's Bay on the north side of the Columbia River.
They all felt miserable. Sacajawea sat huddled in a
blanket, with Pomp wrapped in a small robe, trying to
keep him from fretting. He was too old now to be happy
confined to a robe all day. He squirmed and whined and
nearly wore his mother out rocking him and singing to
him. He wanted to walk or crawl and explore his surroundings as any ten-month-old would.

Wind, rain, cold, and waves were never-ending. The
brackish water was bitter, undrinkable. The hills came
so close to the shoreline that there was no level ground
to sleep on. The baggage had to be piled on a logjam to
keep it above the incoming tide. As the tide rolled in,
one of the canoes was inundated by a huge breaker. It
sank before it could be unloaded. The tide brought in
immense trees, two hundred feet long, four to seven
feet across, dashing them against the beach. Two other
canoes sank during the night from the breakers rolling
over them. It was all the men could do to keep the canoes
from complete destruction. No one was dry. The men
shivered as they worked or ate or rested.

Sometimes it was a case of each man for himself.
Some found shelter in rock crevices, others on the hillside among the many varieties of toadstools and mushrooms, none of them looking like an edible variety. Fog
shrouded the water, and debris was driven against the
shoreline, where precipitous banks alternated with spits,
points, and what Clark called "nitches." Cold rain fell
constantly. Drouillard and the captains camped on some
logs that had jammed upon the rocks with the tide. They

erected poles and spread cattail mats on top, umbrella-fashion, to keep the rain off. There were no robes, no blankets, no clothing that was not moldy, worn, and soaked.

Shannon worked lashing the baggage down and hardly ate anything. He was sick of fish and talked about hunting large game. There was no game in the area that any of the men could find. By evening Shannon sat on the logjam and shivered. Cruzatte tried to get him up to help lash in the canoes, but he did not seem to hear. Charbonneau offered him his Mackinaw. Shannon just sat in a stupor.

"Hey!" yelled Charbonneau, "something's wrong with this kid. He shivers, and he does not look right!"

Clark was beside Shannon in a minute, asking him to the shelter. Shannon jerked to his feet and tried to walk, but his feet would not move. His arms jerked in the direction of the shelter. He did not talk.

"He probably has a cold or sore throat," said Captain Lewis, feeling Shannon's head and hands. "Lord, feel the boy," he said to Clark, "he's not hot, he's cold!"

They carried Shannon to the shelter and took his wet clothing off. They dried him as best they could, put a pair of woolen socks on his feet, and wrapped him in Charbonneau's large wool Mackinaw. They then rolled him against the back of Lewis's big dog to keep the warmth in his body.

Lewis rubbed Shannon's hands and arms to bring the warmth back into them. Shannon moaned, but he was still shivering. He did not seem able to respond to any questions asked him. By morning he was sleeping and the shivering had stopped. The captains decided to stay another night so that they could be certain Shannon was all right.

When the fog lifted just before noon, there was much hollering in the camp. "That is the Pacific Ocean!" shouted Clark, peering way out beyond a piece of land that jutted into the wide river. "I am certain it is the Stinking Waters. I can feel the big breakers shake the earth under my feet here."

"I think I can see those breakers rolling in!" shouted Lewis. "We have finally arrived at our destination!"

The men were all smiling despite the rain. Sacaja-

wea sneezed and tried her best to keep Pomp amused
and warm if not dry.

"Keep wool next to your skin," Cruzatte advised.
"Then you won't get the shakes the way Shannon did."

"Keep working. Don't get chilled," someone else advised.

"Don't get chilled," Charbonneau mumbled. "Everyone in camp is chilled, even the dog. We need wool
trousers under these leather ones. That would keep us
warm, even if they were wet."

"Let's think about getting to the Pacific," suggested
Pat Gass.

The men did think about their destination. They
talked about how far they had come to see a fog-covered
sea. Shannon woke for a while and let York feed him
a few pieces of fresh salmon. Instead of being cold, he
was now feverish, and wanted to kick off the blankets
piled on him.

Because the men thought they had seen the ocean
that day, there was some singing in the camp that night.
The singing came from various shelters as the men
bedded down. To Sacajawea it sounded like echoes
bounding back and forth in the mountains.[6]

In the morning Shannon was awake, feeling a little
better, but still weak and feverish.

"We'll stay in this miserable place one more day,"
announced Captain Lewis. "We'll build a fire and dry
out as much as possible."

"What will we build a fire with?" asked Charbonneau.

"Everything is soaked," said Gibson.

"There must be degrees of wetness," said Clark. "We'll
find driftwood under this logjam that is not as wet as
that on top."

When the fog lifted after midmorning the men could
see a Chinook camp across the bay. The cedar plank
lodges were quite large, square, and set on top of a swell
of ground. There were a few dozen men with rabbit and
fox furs draped over their shoulders, napping on reed
mats just above the high tide line. They were short and
paunchy with broad, flattened heads and muscular arms
and legs. They did not rouse from their sleep to ac-

knowledge the waving and shouting from the strangers on the opposite bank.

Later in the afternoon the fog was again a thick shroud and the explorers could not see the large ocean breakers they believed were vibrating the ground under their feet.

Next morning, when the fog had dissipated some, Drouillard signaled the Chinooks. One man idly made hand signs saying, "We cannot bring trade goods over to your side until the tide goes out. You newcomers should make fun of this rain and fog."

Flocks of gulls swooped in on the flopping salmon washed up on a mud spit in front of the Chinook village. With the least amount of fuss someone would stroll into the cluster of screeching gulls, shoo them out of the way with a wave of hands, and drag the salmon back up to a drying rack. Drouillard guessed the salmon averaged thirty or forty pounds apiece.

"Looks like they can bring in three hundred pounds of food an hour during low tide," said Drouillard. "No wonder these people aren't too excited about food gathering."

Sacajawea sat cross-legged on the sand with Pomp in her lap, watched the Chinooks drag up a dozen large salmon, and then she stood and stated that she would be back. She carried Pomp down through the brush looking for a place to rest and watch the tide go out without miring halfway to her knees in the mud. She found some old rough boards, probably from a collapsed Chinook plank·house, and she made a crude lean-to over a large, flat rock. She squatted there with Pomp, half dozing in the shelter.

By late afternoon the tide was out, and she waded across to the village. This was no mountain stream they were camped by, but a big tide-reach nearly half a mile wide. She made hand signs and traded her ratty woolen blanket for two nice-looking, cream-colored goat hides. The hair on the hide was exceptionally thick, and she was pleased with her trade. She pulled out four pairs of outgrown beaded baby moccasins from the robe around Pomp. These people had never seen colored trade beads and were much impressed with the bright colors on the little moccasins. These she traded for two dozen weasel tails. The weasel tails were the largest and finest she had ever seen, of the purest white, adorned with black-tipped tails, faintly stained with pale gold. She hid these away at the bottom of Pomp's robe. As she was leaving, several Chinook women ran after her, pointing to her belt of blue beads. Sacajawea shook her head no, not for trading, no. The women moved closer to feel and exclaim at the beauty. One woman held out a conical hat made from cedar bark, large enough to keep rain off a man's shoulders. The woman looked disappointed as Sacajawea walked back across the bay's shore, not interested in trading her belt for the hat.

Clark had put up the remains of Charbonneau's old tent across the back of the shelter for more protection against the wind and rain for Shannon, who was now sitting up and talking some. Sacajawea laid one of the goat hides over Shannon's knees. "Wear this in the rain. It will keep you warm and the rain will fall off it."

"Hey, Janey, where did you find it?" he said. "It's better than any of my old, worn blankets. Thanks!"

Charbonneau ambled by to see how Shannon was doing, and when he left, he mumbled something about his *femme* not bringing him a new robe, and he didn't even have his Mackinaw to wear, only the heavy, old, musty capote. That night he pulled his tattered buffalo hide over himself and did not even bother to look for more shelter. He snored in the rain.

Sacajawea slept in the shelter with Pomp rolled up in the new goat hide. Clark lay at the edge of the shelter so that he could keep an eye on Shannon.

Sacajawea wanted to sleep, but could not. Her mind kept hearing the wind. They were so close to the sea now that its booming jarred the timbers under her head. The waves sounded like a herd of horses coming on a dead gallop, and whenever she started to doze, it roused her with a scared feeling that she was about to be run over by them. It was much more restful not to sleep at all, so she lay awake and considered her situation.

She was feeling more and more as though she belonged with these white men. They accepted her as one of them. She was learning to speak their tongue. York and even Shannon had dug roots with her. York sometimes carried Pomp. She had acted as an interpreter and was at times treated more like one of the men than like a squaw. She then wondered if these men really had much sense. They gathered wood and set up the camp. This was actually a squaw's work. Then there was another way of looking at things. She had learned to play Cruzatte's fiddle some, had fired a rifle, and had sung in public. These were things done only by men. But here, with these people, it made no difference. Life was good here, despite the rain and cold and Charbonneau, who did not bother her overmuch.

She opened her eyes wide and looked at the few inches between herself and Chief Red Hair. Suddenly she longed to fill those few inches and place her body close to his. She wanted to lie secure where he might put his arm over her.

In the darkness the wind blew the elk skin from one of the pegs. Clark refastened it and then, not realizing Sacajawea was awake, wiped her damp face with his handkerchief. He wondered at her endurance and uncomplaining nature. He thought she was learning more of the outgoing ways of the whites, leaving some of the submissive, slavish ways of the squaw behind. He overcame a sudden desire to hold her in his arms and shelter her from the rain. Then he thought, A man's not clearheaded at night. Night's like a room; it makes the little things in your head too important.

The first grayish hint of dawn crept over the camp and faded Sacajawea's thoughts, so that she was no longer sure of them. She wondered if there were a kind of insanity coming from being under a roof of any kind, even a tattered elk skin and cattail mats. I'm too cooped up and cannot look at these thoughts against the real size of things. She lay quiet, feigning sleep until Pomp awoke, cold, wet, and hungry. She dried him as best she could, put the goat hide around his head and back, and moved outside to a dead log to nurse her baby in the fog.

The next day Shannon was well enough for the expedition to leave in the slow, misty rain. The river splashed under them. There was nothing to eat but soggy fish. They made camp early in the afternoon and immediately a few neighboring Chinooks were among them haggling over a few fish they had to trade. These

Chinooks were a sight with vests and breechclouts of woven cedar bark. Before they left they had stolen two blankets, a cooking kettle, some fishing gigs, and several of the men's moccasins drying near the fire. Clark told them to lay the stolen goods down or he would shoot. He leveled his rifle at them, and they put the goods on the sand and ran.

On November 12, thunder, lightning, and hail were added to the misery of bailing water out of the canoes and wringing out wet clothing and bedding. Then the misery became worse when the rising waves began to threaten their camp and they had to move half a mile inland, leaving their baggage on the rocks to care for itself that night. The canoes were filled with stones and sunk to protect them from the battering waves. The next morning, the local Chinooks had taken some of the baggage and two of the canoes. Drouillard and Lewis had to go into the Chinook camp and demand that these things be returned. Seeing rifles leveled at a couple of the men in their village, the Chinooks sullenly returned the stolen canoes and baggage, including a peace pipe. They all seemed to be well informed on the power of the rifle.

"I don't see any evidence of rifles in their village," said Lewis, "but they all seem to know what it will do. This is evidence that someone was here with guns before us. And these people seem to think that if we do not present them with gifts right away, they are free to take whatever they wish. Where do you suppose they learned that?"

"These Chinooks are different from those back up the river," agreed Drouillard. "Either they've forgotten manners, never had any, or were taught some bad habits by someone."

In the morning one of the local Chinooks came dressed in a sailor's jacket and trousers and made signs that he had some friends that could speak the white man's tongue and act as interpreters. This was a new surprise. Clark immediately gave the man a small penknife and asked him to bring the men to the camp. The expedition sat in a circle on the sand waiting for the men who could speak English, wondering if they were white men, or Chinooks who had learned the language. The three men who came back were Chinooks, dressed in cedar-bark vests and sailor's trousers. They knew a total of four English words among them; "Damn, Haley" and "Come here," and used this linguistic gift to cover the theft of a hatchet. A search of their greasy, grimy persons did not restore the hatchet. The captains sent them back to their village and decided to continue to rely on Drouillard as interpreter among these people.

"When we get to the coast do you suppose there will be white men in a camp or on a ship anchored in a bay nearby?" asked Shannon.

"I would bet on it," said Lewis. "I would guess that there might be some traders from England there with all the things we've seen on this river. And maybe there will be ships from China or even Russia."

"Let's move on and see what is actually on the coast," suggested Clark.

The river was nearly five miles wide at this point and very choppy midway across. The riverman, Cruzatte, said it would be best to travel along the shoreline. Even there the waves were so high that the canoes could hardly ride them. Sacajawea was the first to become seasick. Some of the men gently teased her. "The canoes do so much heaving that it causes those inside to do the same!" "Green is not your best color, Janey!"

Then nausea gripped Charbonneau's stomach. LePage turned greenish and felt ill before some of the other men began to retch from the violent motion of their small canoes. Then the tide, which swelled the river, added to their troubles, and Captain Lewis ordered the canoes to turn in toward the shore. The expedition spent the next day at Point Distress,[7] where a large shelter of brush was built on a hillside and a fire burned constantly in the front. They tried to dry out clothing and blankets and robes, even though the rainy mist and fog did not clear up. Sacajawea busied herself mending the men's moccasins and trousers and shirts with what little good leather was left.

On the night of the fifteenth, the expedition camped in Haley's Bay[8] in huts made from the boards of a deserted Chinook village. The fleas had not deserted, but the huts were dry and that was heaven. The sight outside the next morning was unbelievable. The sun shone, clear and beautiful, and the men with sick colds and chest coughs saw the Pacific roaring up to the sand beach before them. Their joy was near hysteria. They tumbled out of the huts and ran along the sand barefoot. Some ran in the water and splashed those running beside them.[9]

"Never did I think I could be so miserable, nor so wet for so long," said Captain Lewis. "That was some trip down the Columbia." His dog, Scannon, lay contentedly in the warm sun.

"Maybe we'll sight a ship that will give us all quick passage home," laughed Captain Clark. "But not today. Look how clear that ocean looks—not a ship, canoe, or even a log on her. There's water clear to the horizon."

"Oh, am I glad to be here!" shouted Drouillard. "How about giving me and a couple of the men permission to look around for some kind of game? Maybe we'll find a camp of Englishmen! Wouldn't it be something if we had the company of white men instead of Chinooks this day? And it would be something if we had meat instead of fish to offer them."

"Yes, of course, go," said Clark, "and please find some meat."

Suddenly George Gibson was standing out on the beach in his bare feet. It was a rare treat to hear him play his fiddle. He placed it under his chin and played several tunes. Pomp danced around and clapped his hands, finding it hard to stay on his feet in the deep sand. He laughed every time he fell.

Someone yelled, "Hey, Cruzatte, where's your fiddle?"

Cruzatte pulled it out of one of the packs and rubbed his hand across his whiskered face. He plucked the strings and said, "Oh, well, what the hell, any music is better than none." He played an accompaniment with Gibson, and then noticed Charbonneau off to one side playing his French harp. Pomp was dancing around the three men and laughing out loud, not only when he fell but when his father, Charbonneau, took a deep breath.

By now the entire expedition danced and cavorted and sang as though they were all children again, with complete abandon. York took Sacajawea's hand and skipped in a circle with her while he sang loudly, "Praise to the Lord! We'se here!" over and over.

"Hey, get the water out of that music box!" Shannon, feeling quite well, teased Cruzatte.

"It ain't water," Cruzatte called, pointing his violin bow at Shannon and wagging it to and fro, "it's sand you kick up with your feet as you jump around like a hyena. You act like you're getting rid of fleas!"

Drouillard and a couple of the men came back with two deer slung between them. The outfit welcomed them with a loud cheer. York built a fire with driftwood right away, holding back the really wet pieces until the fire had a good start. The meat was skinned out and put on spits for roasting. "We saw no sign of Englishmen today—we'll look again tomorrow," promised Drouillard.

CHAPTER

26

The Blue Coat

*All the coast Indians coveted, and demanded blue, or
"chief," beads, but unfortunately the expedition had exhausted its supply of blue beads. One visiting Indian
had a gorgeous sea-otter robe that the captains were
determined to secure. Sacajawea gave up her belt of blue
beads so that a trade could be made for the robe. In
compensation she was given a coat of blue cloth.*

From *Sacajawea*, by Harold P. Howard. Copyright 1971
by the University of Oklahoma Press, p. 84.

The Chinook chief, Comcommoly, reminded Sacajawea instantly of Chief Kakoakis, for he had only one eye. The empty socket was filled with yellow matter, half-dried, half-oozing. His right eye was small and beady. He was short and stocky and wore a high-crowned, woven cedar and grass hat on his flattened forehead. Around his shoulders was an otter robe that covered most of his squat body but did not hide his bare, crooked, fat legs. His teeth were brown, jagged, worn down to the gums. He smelled like putrefying fish.

Captain Lewis, unable to sit calmly seeing Chief Comcommoly's beady right eye darting here and there, and the festering left socket, offered to wash the soreness away with alcohol and medicate it with the expedition's famous eye ointment, dilute silver nitrate solution. The chief was grateful, and after that, he showed great consideration for the men of the expedition and admitted he had been quite suspicious of them at first.

Chief Comcommoly and Chief Chillahlawil from nearby villages had come accompanied by a few people from each village to trade around the white men's fire. The visiting women squatted beside the campfire while the men began to bargain with Captain Lewis over woven rush mats, fish, cranberries, and fish gigs.

Sacajawea tried to keep her distance from these inquisitive Chinook women, who were so flea-infested that a bath was needed after each close contact. The women were eager to paw over Pomp, to examine his clean buckskin shirt and his tiny, quilled moccasins.

Captain Lewis had smoked the pipe with the two Chinook chiefs and given each a Washington seasons medal. He gave a flag to Chief Chillahlawil, who had a big head and huge shoulders, and nostrils that continually quivered, opening and closing, as though he were trying to pick up a fleeting scent. Comcommoly held out his hand for a flag. Captain Lewis shook his head no, and pointed out by hand signs that he had his sore eye medicated, so they were even.

After the two chiefs had admired their medals and

smoked again, Captain Lewis began his usual harangue about the Great White Father in Washington who had sent the white men as friends to keep peace with all the Indian nations and to encourage the nations to make peace with each other so that there would be an end to all fighting and sadness in the Chinook families.

There was some shuffling around as one of the men in an otter robe got up, blew his nose clear with a loud blast, and spoke to a woman who was picking at the quills on Pomp's moccasins. The woman left. The man was tall, had great muscular bulk, and big hands. His face was rough, like the back of a toad. It was more round than oval, with rolling, flashing eyes. There was an air about him suggesting that on the least provocation he was ready to go down the violent path with someone. Soon the woman returned carrying a medicine bag, which she gave to the man as he danced energetically in the sand. He danced in front of Captain Lewis and sat down, opening his dirty, red-striped medicine bag, pouring out fourteen dried fingers in the sand. These, he explained by hand signs, were from his enemies. He had a way of talking all over, with his face and hands, and even the muscles of his body. "If the white chief is pleased that I so bravely took the lives of so many enemies, I will paint these fingers red and never kill again."

Captain Lewis tried to stand up to the man's eyes, but found he was not quite up to it. It was the first time he had seen anything except the scalp taken from an enemy. "That is exactly what I want. No more killing and only peace from now on." Then Captain Lewis really looked at the man's otter robe. It was the most beautiful robe he had seen. It was made from a pair of closely matched sea otters and seemed to have a denser, finer underfur of dark gray-brown, overlaid with a heavy coat of long, straight, glistening dark brown guard hairs, than any he'd noticed. He began to move his hands, telling the man how much he admired his robe. The man stood up, and his feet danced close together. His eyes began to glow. Cautiously Captain Lewis began to bargain for the robe.

The man shook his round, flattened head no. He did

not want to trade his robe. Then he shook his medicine bag. He would sell the fourteen fingers from his enemies for an ax. Captain Lewis shook his head no. The man then explained that his woman had spent many hours making the robe beautiful for him and it was hard to get the sea otter.

Captain Clark came into camp with his party of men. They had explored some of the coastal region around their camp. Clark started to tell Lewis about the huge pine he had carved his name in, then stopped and stared at the otter robe on the man. He saw its beauty instantly. Clark knew otter was hard to trap or shoot, since they invariably sank and were lost. Pat Gass was with Captain Clark. "That there is the finest set of furs I ever saw," he said, reaching out to feel them. For a few moments they watched Lewis bargain desperately for the Chinook's robe.

To all of Captain Lewis's offers the Chinook glanced scornfully at the trade goods offered and shook his head no.

"Two thick blankets. Very warm," offered Captain Lewis.

"No."

"Five blankets, pretty colors."

"No."

"Beads?"

"*Tiacemoshack?* Blue chief beads?" His hands made the signs as he spoke the Chinook jargon. His feet were still.

The captains had discovered before that one of the few errors they had made in planning the supplies was the large store of red, white, and yellow beads. They never dreamed the natives across the continent preferred blue beads. To all nations they were the only valuable kind, fit for a chief, and so called "chief beads."

Captain Clark could stand being an onlooker no longer. He moved in closer and offered his pocket watch, a handkerchief, a string of large red beads, and a silver dollar. He pointed out that the dollar could be worn around the man's neck like the peace medals of the chiefs if a hole were punched in the top.

"No," the Chinook sniffed.

Captain Clark was thinking how Judy Hancock would

look in the luxurious otter robe. Into it, he thought, she will disappear almost completely, wrapped up like a queen in a mantle of softness. He took out a pocket knife and added to the pile he already had on the ground for the trade.

"No."

Sacajawea had been out of the way of the Chinook women, but watching the bargaining for the otter robe. "Blue chief beads." The words pounded in her head like the surf pounding against the rocks when the tide rolled in. She could feel the light blue flowers worked in the pattern of darker, sky blue beads and the row of green leaves on her belt. She loved the belt of beads made by Chief Red Hair. It was the only material thing she prized except for her sky blue stone on the thin leather thong. She knew it was precious for its own sake, but only to her. If it was the only thing that would buy the otter robe for Captain Clark, should she give it up? To be able to do something for Chief Red Hair was what she wished. This would be doing something. She would give the belt, and in return he would have something he prized highly. That would surely be putting the precious belt to its best use, she thought. After all, the beads did come from the captains' stores in the first place. She unfastened the belt and, without looking directly at him, handed the beaded belt to Captain Clark.

"Buy the robe," she said almost inaudibly.

"I have nothing the Chinook wants," Captain Lewis said to Clark, spreading his hands apart. "Good Lord, Clark, buy the robe if you can. You'll never get another chance like this!"

Captain Clark stood motionless with the belt in his hands, Sacajawea's body warmth quickly leaving it. Her face was always alert and her mind swift. Her expression changed readily with her changes of thought these days, so that a man who was used to her could tell what was in her mind even when she wanted to conceal it. He studied her. She tried to remain impassive, calm.

"Go ahead; it will make me pleased," she whispered.

Captain Clark's eyes focused on the belt. He fingered the leather thongs that had tied around her waist; they curled because of the tying. He thought of the moment he had given her this gift, a token of his appreciation to her for saving his life. He haggled within himself over his own exact shades of feeling. He looked up at the black wall of spruce behind the camp and the long heads of white timothy jarring and shedding seed with the boom of the sea. The wind was sticky with salt. He did not think about Judy Hancock now. She had faded from his thoughts.

"A sensible man would trade it for the robe he wants," urged Captain Lewis.

"I'm taking it, Lewis," said Captain Clark, with a sudden feeling of sadness overcoming him. "And thanks a lot for knowing what this fellow wants," he said, turning to face Sacajawea, who neither smiled nor frowned.

The Chinook's wolfish eyes danced. His pocked face glowed like pitted pipestone in the sunlight. He stared intently at the belt. Finally he held the beaded belt with his dirty fingers, squatting near Captain Lewis. His smell was very strong, and his rotten-fish breath hit Clark squarely in the face. The Chinook became so excited that he broke into song. *"Tyeekamosuk, aye, aye!"*

"Sell, now?" Captain Clark asked him.

The Chinook sniffed a quick, nervous breath, then expelled it with a blast. He burned a fixed, unwavering eye upon Clark. "Sell, sell, sell!" Greedily he grabbed the belt and held it with his mouth as he pulled the otter-skin robe off. Saliva dripped over the beads and off the thong ends.

Sacajawea ran her hands down her tunic. She drew it in. Something was missing, lost. She recalled how she had always liked putting on the belt and adjusting it over the folds of her tunic. Never again would envious women feel it and smile and cluck and ask her to take it off so they could feel and feast their eyes on its beautiful pattern and workmanship. Never again would Pomp pull at it with teasing baby fingers. She would have never grown tired of it. Never. Now she would never forget what it had looked like.

Then her logical mind turned. Why did Chief Red Hair want the robe so much? Was it for himself? Was it for the Great White Father in Washington? With a stab of jealousy she wondered if it might be for the pale-eyed girl in his village, the one he called Judy. A sob shook her shoulders, and she could no longer control her stoic expression. Tears ran unchecked down her cheeks. The rain began slowly matching her tears; then it came faster and faster.

Captain Clark found her standing by a giant white pine, clinging to it for support.

"Janey, you'll catch cold out here," he said. "We've all been looking for you. Pomp is beginning to think that York is his mother. Come—" He stopped, surprised at her sobbing. "What is it?"

Sacajawea pushed herself back hard against the tree. She straightened so she faced the rain, ashamed of her emotion.

Captain Clark understood as soon as he looked at her loose, unshapely tunic, once held so snugly around her graceful form by the beaded belt. She is a girl, little more than fifteen or sixteen, with a yearning for feminine finery that all lovely women have. Regret struck Captain Clark. He had not dreamed that he would feel, standing with a Shoshoni girl at the edge of a camp where they were surrounded with a choking scramble of vegetation, as if he were in the middle of a city that boiled and roared with a different kind of life from this. This life fought and destroyed itself in a million different forms and paid no more attention to her than people in the heart of a busy city do to a shade tree or a vacant lot.

"I'll remember what you did this day," he said, too shaken now to think of a better way to put it.

Sacajawea tried to free herself from his arms.

"Janey, are you sorry that you gave me your belt?" She looked into the gray mist.

"I can see you are. I should not have taken it from you. I am a fool sometimes. What can I do to make it up? Can I give you something to take its place? What would you like from the supplies? Anything you choose."

"Nothing," she said in English in a small voice.

He pulled her head against his shoulder to console her. She shut her eyes against the rain, and he told her that she must not mind, that he would fix it so everything would be all right. He moved his head so that his

lips were close to brushing hers, and he noticed that
her skin was damp and a sprinkling of green-white
moss from the tree bark stuck to it. The thick brush
walled them off from everything except themselves—
the earth under their feet, the gray sky overhead. He
knew that a moment's decision could mean something
dangerous and dishonest, and that it would have to be
paid for. It would be worse to stay and in an unguarded
moment let her release all holds on herself, and let go
his check on himself. Short-breathed, unable to speak,
he released her, not daring to risk looking back.

When she was breathing quietly again, she started
back to camp. She slipped in beside Charbonneau, who
was talking in a loud voice to a Chinook chief, Delashelwilt. Neither man paid any attention to her until
Charbonneau stopped his bragging and hand signaling
with the chief.

"What is eating you? *Jésus, a cheval sur une gre-
nouille!* I do not like bragging *bourgeois* Chinooks."

She did not answer.

"I thought you liked excitement," he said. "Listen to
this. The chief says his own *grandpère* lived in the dirty
hut he now lives in. He thinks that is class. Now you
help me be the big man around this camp and we show
him who's got class."

"The men know you are not such a big man," she
said softly.

Charbonneau hissed at her angrily, and turned toward the chief.

"Chief, your woman is one smart squaw. Your
daughters are smart also."

Sacajawea lifted her eyes, wondering when Charbonneau had seen the chief's woman.

"*Jésus*, if she brings pretty young squaws to our
camp, she is smart. She will get white men's goods."
His hands moved swiftly.

What is he talking about, thought Sacajawea, as she
watched Chief Delashelwilt jump up and hurry off with
a limpy gait to his own village.

"*Bonheur, ami!*" Charbonneau yelled. "I like them
plenty young—no old trade goods for Charbonneau."
And he broke into loud laughter.

"My man, what are you planning?" she asked.

"Squaw, it is best you keep out of this. It is something only for the men. Chief Del's woman will help me be the big man in this camp. So—now you do not be so inquisitive."

He left her sitting alone under the canopy of tattered old elk skins with her confusion of emotion and thoughts.

Sacajawea did not like these Chinooks and wondered why they were so dirty and infested with fleas, lice, and filth. Worse than the Hidatsas, she thought. Anyone could see that once they had been a powerful people who had managed to maintain a distinct language, religion, culture, and set of taboos and traditions against the encroachment of surrounding tribes. But that had all gone to pieces. Was it the few years of casual trading with palefaces that had proved so destructive, or was it outright hostility from other tribes? That would take some thinking, she knew.

These Chinooks were friendly, easy to get acquainted with when treated courteously. But what was Charbonneau so interested in peace, friendship, and understanding for? What had he been talking about? Why should the women of the chief interest him? She had seen these Chinook women stir their pots with their hair hanging loose in every direction and even falling into the stew. They cleaned the children's bottoms with their fingers, then, without a wiping or a wash, dug out hunks of fish from the pot and popped them into their mouths.

They had many white man's goods: brass pots, bright red, blue, and green blankets, ribbons for their hair, brass bracelets. One squaw even had a pair of high-top black shoes, and she looked quite ridiculous with her pigeon-toed gait in those unwieldly hard-soled shoes. Her legs were tattooed with different figures, and on her left arm were some letters of the white man's writing: "J. Bowman."

The following day, Sacajawea washed some of Pomp's garments in a clear, fresh stream. She heard angry women's voices. Then she heard the voice of her man shouting something to Captain Clark. Curiosity made her hurry back to camp to see what was happening.

Standing very close to Charbonneau was an old woman whose nose was long and pointed. Her hair matted and stuck out in every direction, and her dress was red trader's cloth wrapped loosely around her sagging form. She shook her fists in the face of Captain Clark. Sacajawea counted six young women with only woven rush skirts on, tossing coquettish challenges at the men who stood about.

Clark raised both his hands.

"Now just one moment! Charbonneau, both Captain Lewis and myself have told you before there will be none of this going on in our camp. You have seen the state of filthy unwash these people are in. You have this mother and her daughters packing out of here immediately. And see they stay in their own village. Our men have enough temptations without this!"

"But, Capitaine," pleaded Charbonneau. "These redskinned maids have pleasing features. They will comfort the men. Madame Del, here, will find you one that will make your blood fairly boil. Maybe she will make them wash up a little. Eh, what do you say?"

"I say you'll be horsewhipped by myself and then by Captain Lewis if these women are not removed from our camp within ten minutes. Only a very desperate man would look twice at these stinking squaws."

One of the young girls, who had many strands of colored beads and string drawn tightly around her legs, began to reach out toward Captain Clark. He pushed her aside in disgust and slapped at his itching wrist.[1]

"The morals of these women may be nature's way of evening things up," said Clark to Charbonneau. "Any man who falls, I'm willing to bet, will pack away a tangible memento of the occasion, which might and might not get cured."

"You could go to their village as rabbits under the grass," suggested Charbonneau to several men around him.

Bob Frazier flapped his arms. "I'm turning into a bird. I'll get there fast."

"We can put on buffalo skins," said Hugh Hall, laughing, "and sneak over."

Captain Clark shook a finger at them. "You heard me."

"I wonder sometimes how you ever got out of your hole, Charb," said Ordway.

"He has big feet to dig with," Gass said.

Sacajawea felt humiliated by the action and words of her man. She thought, Why does he think only of this one thing? He is lazy and unclean, and he thinks everyone is like him. If he worked harder, he would not have the time or the energy to behave this way. Why can't he be more like Chief Red Hair?

She tried to hide herself in extra work for her baby all day. She pretended to play cheerfully with him, letting him crawl and pull himself up to walk with the help of Captain Lewis's supply chest. When he became tired and his fat legs wobbled, she laughed and picked him up.

"Janey, I wondered where you were," said Captain Clark, coming beside her, squatting on his heels so that he could watch the baby walk by holding on to anything he could reach.[2]

"I think he'll be walking home," Captain Clark said, winking.

"With such short legs?" said Sacajawea.

Captain Clark began spreading some trinkets for Indian trading on the ground. There was a hide scraper, a couple of long-handled knives, an awl, a pewter cup and spoon, several colored handkerchiefs, Indian bracelets and necklaces, and tins of red beads. This would have been a tempting assortment to any squaw. He tossed aside his faded old blue coat in which he had wrapped these things.

"Now, you choose whatever you wish, Janey," he said. A smile of amusement played across his freckled face as he watched her hold the baby close to her breast so that he would not get into the gay array. Then she picked up some of the articles, feeling and testing them. It was a momentous decision. She wished to take something that would please Chief Red Hair, but on the other hand, she found nothing she really wanted. Nothing could replace the blue belt. Then suddenly she knew. To his surprise she pointed to his old blue coat. He'd worn it out on the long journey to the Pacific Coast.

"That coat," she said.

"That old coat?"

"*Ai.*"

"But it is worn out. I threw it away. Find something new."

"The coat was worn by you. It is like a part of Chief Red Hair," she said shyly. "That is what I want."

Captain Clark looked at Sacajawea and felt humble in the presence of this girl who could not have shed her conscience so offhandedly. When anything bothered her, she showed it. A flood of compassion engulfed him.

"If that is what you want—" His hands trembled as he picked up his blue coat. God, he thought, what have I done now? First I unwittingly took her beaded belt and traded it for a gift for young Judy Hancock, and now I have taken her heart and tossed it out along with my old coat.

With a woman's innate intuition, Sacajawea sensed his thoughts. She put her fingers over his mouth, so that his words turned into a kind of confused whaw-whaw-whawing. "You are a boy," she said. "Nobody but a boy would be so hesitant about giving something so old and worn to a squaw."

She pressed the coat to her breast and quietly walked, with her back straight and her toes pointed forward, not inward, out of the circle of the camp.

She walked slowly and deliberately, her head high, until she came to the sandy beach. She put Pomp down by the side of a sheltered embankment and gave him a pretty shell to play with. Waves were pounding and beating the shore with as cruel a force as that of her own emotions, and between this turbulent sea and her heart she felt a deep common bond. Her eyes searched the gray sea far out over the vast expanse of water where there was only infinite grayness and the soft falling mist. This was her future—infinite grayness with no definite pattern. She put one arm into the coat, then the other. She pressed the worn sleeve against her cheek, wetting it with her tears. There was a strange comfort in the familiar scent of the garment. She whispered into the wide folds of the coat, much too large for her small body, the familiar words he had taught her.

"Do unto others as you would have them do unto you."

Almost involuntarily, her arms fell crossed against her breast in order that the sleeves might stay up past her hands—the Shoshoni sign for love.

27

Weasel Tails

Clark's Journal:

> *Christmas Wednesday 25th December 1805*
>
> *at day light this morning we we[re] awoke by the discharge of the fire arm[s] of all our party and a Selute, Shouts and a Song which the whole party joined in under our windows, after which they retired to their rooms were cheerful all the morning. after brackfast we divided our Tobacco which amounted to twelve carrots one half of which we gave to the men of the party who used tobacco, and to those[1] who doe not use it we make a present of a handkerchief, The Indians leave us in the evening all the party Snugly fixed in their huts. I recved a pres[e]nt from Capt. L. of a fleece hosrie [hosiery] Shirt Draws and Socks, a pr. Mockersons of Whitehouse a Small Indian basket of Gutherich, two Dozen white weazils tails of the Indian woman, and some black root of the Indians before their departure.*

BERNARD DEVOTO, ed., *The Journals of Lewis and Clark.*
New York: Houghton Mifflin Co., 1953, p. 294.

"Umbea, umbea, um-be-a!" called the toddling papoose. His feet were bare, and his knees bruised and scratched. He wore only a small leather shirt with a single row of red and white beads across the front yoke.

"Here I am," called Sacajawea, brushing the sand from her brown-leather skirt and the large old blue coat. Her hair was neatly braided and wound about her head. She wore no ornament except the small, sky blue stone on the thin thong of her throat. To wear many ornaments was the prerogative of the male, she believed. Her baby laughed as she grasped him about the middle and swung him into her arms. Her son clung to her and snuggled himself into the folds of the coat. He put his arms deep into the wide pockets.

She began to feel better, watching the carefree baby. He poked one wiggly brown foot into a pocket. His round face was solemn. She knew he was playing a game and enjoying himself immensely, yet he was not loud or riproarish. He played entirely for the fun of it, because he had nothing but the present moment to worry him. She spoke aloud to herself: "Like my son—I'll take each sunrise as it comes." In her resolve she must have squeezed her baby, for he gave a little yelp.

She sat with Pomp in her lap on the damp sand and looked over the expedition's camp. It was a good place, even with the sand in the clothing, bedding, and food. Pomp's eyes were heavy with sleep. He stubbornly refused to lie on the big blue coat, denying that he was sleepy. Sacajawea coaxed him to curl up in her lap; one arm was still in a pocket.

The day was still, and she felt drowsy. She thought of the latest talk among the men. They wanted salt for their food. Chief Red Hair had spoken of it more than once. And they wanted a better campsite for the winter months. She knew the expedition was going to stay in this area through the winter because no one would survive the trip back upstream and over the mountains at this time of year. Anyway, the men were exhausted. Sacajawea could see the fatigue in their eyes. Their clothing was in shreds and they all needed red meat in their diet.

Shannon came out on the sand and sat beside her. He was quiet for a time; then he said, "I hope a trading ship or two come before spring. Maybe we wouldn't have to go up the Columbia and over those blasted mountains if it did. We could all get on that ship and sail home."

Sacajawea looked at Shannon in disbelief.

"Well, I heard the captains talking about it. You know Captain Lewis has a letter of credit from the American government, so there would be no trouble in dealing with traders who might come to our camp from some seagoing vessel. I think the captains hope the traders can supply them with trade goods, trinkets, for the different tribes on our return trip. You know there's a shortage of colored beads, looking glasses, and combs. The captains just gave away too much. And to make it worse, these Chinooks ask for too many fish hooks and awls for their wormy salmon."

"Shannon," she said seriously, "we will collect all the seashells to use for trading. The river tribes love them." She picked up two small pink shells and handed them to Shannon.

"That's an idea!" He made a heap of them beyond the tide line. "Hey, I almost forgot, there's some Chinooks in camp. Let's see what they are talking about."

Everyone seemed to be talking at once, using hand signs, to find where the best hunting was. "Deer," one Chinookian answered, "is most plentiful farther up the river." "Elk," another Chinookian said, "are found on the south shore of the bay. Everyone knows elk are larger, give better meat, and are easier to kill."

After the evening meal there was a council. The men discussed the best site for the winter camp. Each member of the expedition was given a chance to talk if he wished. Ben York suggested laying in a large supply of elk hides so that he and Janey could sew moccasins, so there would be enough for the return trip. Shannon spoke up and said he would be willing to help Sacajawea make trousers if they could be stored in a dry place so that they would not have green mold when they were ready to be worn. "Damn damp climate," the nineteen-year-old snorted.

"Would you rather camp in them mountains?" hooted Pete Wiser.

"If they are drier," said Shannon.

"We get to them mountains and there's bound to be ten, fifteen feet of snow. I had enough of froze feet, myself," said York.

"A camp on the south shore would be best for making contact with a trading ship that might come by," offered Sacajawea, surprising everyone. "And I'm in favor of a camp where plenty of *quamash* roots can be dug for bread and beer."

"Hooray!" shouted Pat Gass. He was on his feet hopping around in a show-offish manner, and the men laughed, waking Pomp.

Pomp climbed off his mother's lap and trotted after his father, then with a giggle seated himself in Captain Clark's lap.

Gass knocked a toe against a rock, hopped around, holding his toe with both hands and cutting loose with curse words. "Something in that damn rock got it in for me!" He eased his foot down. "Damned ambusher, that rock!"

Captain Lewis raised his arms, announcing that there would be a vote on the place for the winter campsite. "For a yes, raise your right hand. Who would like to stay here?"

A little moment of silence came. No one moved. Then Sacajawea, who had stood up, put in a question. "Here? No one wants to stay here. We all know the south shore is best. Anyone who does not raise his hand for the south shore can stay here and eat fish."

Clark laughed into his hand and was so amused by Janey speaking out in quite good English in the expedition's council that he set her words down in the official journal that evening.

Captain Lewis was not so amused. "Wasn't it a bit irregular to have a squaw and her man, who's a citizen of Canada, and your manservant, York, and Shannon, a boy barely nineteen, vote as though they were U.S. citizens with the rest of us on this military expedition?" He paused and took a deep breath. "This was an important decision."

"Now, Lewis," pacified Clark, as the sweetest of smiles

wreathed his.lips, "isn't this whole expedition unorthodox in so many ways?"

"Oh, Lord! You're so right! But I must say I call it bad manners—downright bad manners—for that squaw to speak up so—" He broke off abruptly and cast a glance at Clark.

Clark ran a finger along the neck of his leather shirt, as if to ease his throat. "A woman! A mere girl at that— she took the words from your mouth. Go ahead, admit it. You were going to say the exact words in your next breath. You wanted the men to vote for the south shore and plenty of elk meat!"

"Yes, I did! But Lord help me, the next time she speaks up and asks for something—"

"Takes the words from your mouth, you mean," teased Clark. "You'll probably grant her wish. You know she doesn't ask much. I daresay your grandchild won't read the history of the United States without reading of you and me and of her, with fearless men crossing the prairies and mountains, enduring hardship and privation. We are a close-knit group with a terrible and rigid goodness that comes with work and self-denial." Clark feigned enormous dignity.

Lewis looked a little sheepish and said, "For Lord's sake, forget I said a thing."

There was more rain and high waves as the expedition crept back along the shore the way they had come, looking for a place where the estuary was narrow enough to cross to the south shore. It was hard to find firewood that was dry enough to burn. The blankets were wet again and mildewed. The big leather tent was in shreds and no protection at all. Some of the men used their frayed blankets to make crude lean-tos, but they were so full of holes that nothing was kept dry.

During the last of November, there were a few days that were warm, when the leaves browned, and the grass ripened in the sun, and the reflection of light from the water lasted until long after nightfall. But afterward the sky blackened and rain fell, and from that time until spring the rain never totally stopped and sunlight never shone over the land or sea. Except on the line of surf, the sea itself was like ink. The tre-

mendous winds that blew out of it carried fierce twisters
of rain that turned everything inside out as they passed.
The shifting winds blew smoke from the campfire into
the men's eyes, which soon became painful from that
irritation. Then they began to wonder how they were
going to get along when they found deer but no elk;
even geese were wary of hunters.

Ben York noticed that the weather was hard for the
papoose. He was by turns unruly and listless. He told
Pomp tales that were Negro folklore, handed down by
word of mouth through the years. Like the songs Sacajawea remembered her grandmother singing, these
were primitive accounts of the sorrows and tribulations
of a wronged people and their inevitable reward in the
afterlife.

"And the angel say to him, he say, 'Mose, come up
on this here throne and eat 'cause you are hungry, and
drink 'cause you are thirsty, and rest you weary and
aching feet.'"

Sometimes Pomp rode on Clark's back and heard
stories that invariably began with the magic words,
"Once upon a time just like this—" There would follow
a nursery tale or one of Aesop's fables. Pomp remembered the English words and repeated them— "fox, rabbit, wolf, horse, man, woman." That the listener was
hardly a year old and incapable of comprehending what
he heard made no difference to Clark. He was determined that the boy learn English and was pleased when
he responded so quickly.

A few days later, the expedition, tired and wet from
riding in the canoes, came to a knob of land projecting
about a mile and a half toward a shallow bay, and about
four miles around. The neck of land, which connected
it to the main shore, was more than fifty yards wide.
Lewis called the projection Point William[2] for William
Clark, and there the men landed the canoes and set up
another temporary camp. The stones on shore were brilliant reds and greens and white. Sacajawea scooped up
handfuls for Pomp to play with.

One of the canoes had a wide split and needed repairing. Before that job was finished, the wind shifted
to the northwest and blew with such fury that trees
were uprooted near the camp. "We must move out of

here right away," said Sacajawea. That night there was rain and hail; sleep was fitful and miserable.

The next day, the rain let up, for several hours. Sacajawea spread out blankets and clothing to dry, then sat on the beach to watch the birds. Eagles, hawks, ravens, and crows picked up small salmon floundering on the shore where they were washed in. She liked the beach. It was clean, away from the snakes, lizards, and spiders, but not the sand fleas that seemed to follow her everywhere. Then there was rain that night and the next day. Her nerves wore thin as she bucked mud, sand, and wet brush for the sake of a bit of dry land.

Captain Clark sighed, "How long? Can it rain forever?"

Even the Chinooks turned short-tempered and asked for two axes, three knives, and a good blanket for one fifty-pound fish, though they had been around this area for generations of continuous residence to get accustomed to the climate.

The men lost weight and color, and squabbled incessantly. Captain Clark's stomach became upset, probably from so much pounded fish and salty water.

Sacajawea, always watchful, pulled out a soggy piece of bread from under her blanket folds. It was made of wheat flour, not the wapato roots everyone had come to loathe. She had been saving the good bread for Pomp. She now offered it to the ailing Chief Red Hair. The ancient and dubious biscuit was a little sour, but Clark ate it with relish, saying, "That is the only bit of food I've had in weeks that was not fishy or salty and that sits firm inside my stomach." He tweaked Pomp's little brown nose. "I ate your muffin."

Pomp replied with a wide, baby grin, "Num, num, num."

The next afternoon, soon after the canoes were beached, Sacajawea lay Pomp on the blue coat for a nap while she hunted colored seashells. Clark sat with her and put some he found in an empty canister. The two became so engrossed with the beauty of the shapes and designs and colors, and the small, smooth stones of agate they saved, that they did not at first see the dark clouds forming to warn them of the coming storm. Sacajawea jumped up and pointed skyward and began to run toward camp with Pomp. Clark followed. York came toward them and took Pomp in his arms and hurried him safely back to camp. Sacajawea and Clark followed. Then both stopped to look back. There was the black center of the storm coming in from the water and churning the flat water into a wall of foam ten or twelve feet high. Clark started on to keep the wave from overtaking them, but Sacajawea was fascinated and climbed to a high, flat stone.

"Let's let it catch us!" she called, daring him. "It won't hurt us here—will it? Come see what it does."

Suddenly the wind hit so hard that Clark staggered and had to sit down. Sacajawea ran to him, and water plastered them in a solid sheet. Through it she saw in a kind of blur that Clark was laughing. When she opened her mouth to talk, the water beat on it and stopped it so she could not say a word. The rain slackened and passed on, and the two ran down the beach, now trying to overtake it and face it down again, but it outran them. They were drenched but laughing. He drew a great breath and let it out again as Sacajawea ran into his arms. He pushed the hair from her eyes and smiled at her. The touch of his firm, callused hand was like running fire.

"You smell good, like the crushed ginger weed." He sniffed and sighed, still holding her. He found himself suddenly throbbing with love. He thrust his right hand behind her head and bent to kiss her full on the mouth. She took hold of him and held her arms tightly around the small of his back, not wanting to let him go. His lips were warm, and she marveled at the strength of them and how their strength was transferred to her own lips.

"You have used sorcery on me, Janey. I could not help myself," said Clark, pulling away and smiling into her eyes. "We must hurry back now, before it is too late." He looked sideways at her and felt a rush of gentleness toward her because she, too, was trying to hold back the power that had risen with the beating of their hearts.

"*Ai*, York will come looking, thinking the ocean has swallowed us." She felt her lips and wondered how they could feel like burning coals and her knees weak as water.

She's got me roped as tight as a horse plowing a field in spring, and I don't know that I have any more to gain than the horse, he thought as he followed the figure in the brown tunic with his eyes until she disappeared in the trees this side of the camp.

He crossed the rocks beyond the beach and walked in the same direction. He stopped and arranged some of the baggage and inspected the repaired canoe. Then he talked to Bill Werner, who was on south guard duty. He felt he had his emotions in control. He vowed not to let himself be carried away by his heart, not to let his guard down again. He was a captain of the United States Army and responsible for this outfit. His first duty was to his men and to his co-captain. Janey, God bless her, had a man.

After the storm, dozens of huge birds swooped down for the easy food. The men called the big birds vultures, but they were larger than any vulture anyone had ever seen before. Baptiste LePage shot one down, and it measured nine and a half feet from wing tip to wing tip, three feet, ten and a half inches from the point of its bill to the tip of its tail. The tail itself was fourteen and a half inches long, and the head and beak six and a half inches.[3] York added the vulture to the three hawks and three ducks the hunters brought in later that afternoon for the evening meal. The hunters had seen elk sign, and the news brightened everyone's spirits.

Captain Lewis managed to get a small canoe across to Point William, only to find that there were swamps on the south shore that would make overland travel impossible. He turned back to Meriwether Bay[4] and found a site along a little river called Netual[5] by the Chinooks. This place was ten miles from the Pacific Ocean, but within hearing of the dark, angry breakers. Selecting a high point on the west bank of the Netual, so that the permanent camp would be out of swampy land and the incoming high tide, Captain Lewis went back for the men to start work on shelter and fortifications.

* * *

Captain Clark and Drouillard walked northwest, exploring the coast. They were often in mud and water to their hips, walking through bogs where the weight of a man would shake a half acre of ground. Drouillard was eager to explore and leave the cedar cutting for the winter cabins to the others. Clark was dubious about finding anything in the way of game, so he kept his notebook out so that he could sketch an unusual tree or plant. Clark was feeling a little uncertain about himself at this time, but he was eager to see this new country and talk to natives he had not seen before. Besides, the farther away he was from Janey, the better. If Janey wanted him for some silly advice or to answer some fool question, she could think of someone else. As for this exploring, if he didn't find anything he would quit, even though he had told Drouillard they might be gone a couple of days.

It was afternoon when they came upon a small group of Chinooks. One of the men came forward and shook hands with both Clark and Drouillard, cleared his throat, and said, "Sturgeon very good." After the initial surprise wore off, the men felt disappointment because apparently that was the only English the man knew. Drouillard sat with the man and used hand signs and jargon as they passed a pipe back and forth. The man said that once in a while the Chinooks attacked the white men that came off the ships, but they had not planned to attack the men of the expedition because there was not so much to gain. The expedition did not have many trading goods the Chinooks wanted. Drouillard found that the Chinooks were mainly interested in alcohol.

Around dusk they found a quiet, grassy spot protected from the wind where Clark could write in his notebook and sort out the day's leaf and twig specimens. Silently several Clatsops, from a village on the south side of a line of boulders, crept close to the two men to observe them. Clark saw them and drew rough sketches of these silent observers. They were dark, their complexions running to deep brown rather than reddish. All seemed fat, and their faces had a combination of stupidity and covetousness. The females were tattooed on their lower lip with charcoal embedded under the skin, which left them with a line of dusky blue, as though they had spent the day in an elderberry patch.

The next morning Clark and Drouillard visited the Clatsop village. The people knew they were Clatsops, but somewhere in all the years of their existence they had forgotten or found it unnecessary to know the name of their particular tribe. They used strings of mussel shells ground into cylindrical beads for money, but were willing to go along with the barter system if they could purchase metal fish hooks. Their houses were built from the abundant supply of cedar planks and were window-less and rotten smelling. This was partly due to un-washed bodies and no ventilation, but mainly because of the small, dried smelt that were fastened by the tail in shell and pottery bowls and placed all along the walls. When burned they gave off a white light.

"They are as good as our candles, if you like the smell of putrefying fish," commented Drouillard.

They ate this little candlefish with the villagers. Clark called them "anchovie," and put several on the end of a wooden stick to roast. They were so fat they needed no additional sauce.

These Clatsops lived mostly on fish. They did trap some game and killed it with a bow and arrow at a range of from two to five feet. Clark and Drouillard watched them trap wild ducks by setting decoys on a brush-covered hole in the marshes, hiding under it until a flock landed, then grabbing their legs and pulling them underwater to drown.

They learned the Clatsop trick of treating the little creeks with a few bushels of hemlock bark. Then the stupefied speckled trout would float up by the bucket-ful.

Vegetable products were scarce; besides wild crab-apple, the Clatsop women picked a coppery-tinged wild sorrel, which, after cooking, Clark thought had the fla-vor of rhubarb.

The second evening at the Clatsop village Clark brought out his sketch materials. His first subject was a child sleeping in a cradleboard with a flattening board covering the top half of its head. While sketching, Clark thought of the ease with which these people lived, with food and shelter and clothing at their fingertips. Yet, he could think of nobody who would trade places with them. They had not perfected any great skill in arts or crafts or thinking; their easy living was not conducive to creativity. On the other hand they were not warlike and did not even try to explore new places along the coastline.

By the third day both Clark and Drouillard had seen enough of these self-contained, contented people, so the two men headed for the expedition's camp. They discussed the unknown past and future of the indolent Clatsop band. Had the Clatsops' ancestors landed on the shore in some small craft, or had they trekked overland in small hunting parties in the prehistoric past? Had these people once been warriors and recently tired of that uncertain life? At present they seemed to be going nowhere. If they all died out suddenly no other tribe would grieve. This one group had followed a trail to nonentity. On the other hand, the men argued, these people had no stress and were happy with the way things were.

Clark and Drouillard noticed the strong mixture of odors from the wild flowers and vegetation that hung in the thick forest's unmoving air as they made their way back to camp. The balsam poplar buds were covered a glistening, freeze-resistant, winter coat of resin, making them look as large as peace medals. This ball of sticky resin was delightfully fragrant. The mosquitoes were a great annoyance and didn't seem repelled by an application of rancid bear's oil.

Back at camp the two men could not contain their curiosity and asked Sacajawea what she knew about the woody substance a few of the idle Clatsops chewed that turned their saliva blood red. She thought a moment, then said it was probably from the inner bark of the red alder and that the people probably chewed it to ward off diarrhea. Intrigued by this information Clark and Drouillard made a study of the alder that grew as large as three feet thick in every damp place. They found that the fresh wood was satiny white, but turned cherry red when it had been aged. Drouillard guessed that the bright color was tannic acid in the alder's sap, which also explained the medicinal power of its inner bark.

During the weeks the men worked to get the winter cabins finished, they were troubled with dysentery, colds, aching muscles, colic, and boils because they worked out in the constant rain.

Clark and Drouillard tried the red alder medicine to relieve the distress of their dysentery. They soon found it worse than the disease. The moist, inner bark was so astringent that their mouths puckered for hours and the red juice made them look like they were bleeding to death. The soft wood tasted harshly bitter and biting and left their teeth ugly brown, which both men feared would become a permanent discoloration like the Clatsops'.

"This here timber makes the finest puncheons I ever saw," said Pat Gass, with a carpenter's appreciation of good white pine and cedar. "They can be split ten feet long and two feet broad, not more than an inch and a half thick."

The logs were rolled up Boonesboro-fashion into winter shelters, made from some abandoned Clatsop boards that the Indians gave permission for the white men to use, fleas and all. By mid-December the men were chinking and mud-daubing the cabins. Using elk hides for weatherboards, they tightened up the cabins and began cutting doors.

The hunters had found plenty of elk by then, and the roasted meat helped cure the dysentery and colic. Mallard ducks settled wherever there was swampy ground, and the men managed to bushwhack a few with guns. Then they began to find plenty of deer, but complained because they were so small.[6]

Sacajawea stayed to herself, mending the tattered clothing and sewing new shirts, trousers, and moccasins as the hides became available. The issue of where she was going and whether she was headed directly there did not arise, for she knew she would spend time somehow—sleeping, eating, loafing—so she might as well spend it here; she would not die any sooner because she was here among white men. What is ahead in life is usually unknown.

She did not want to be troubled by the problems of her man, Charbonneau. She did not love him, but her life because of him was good, so she felt a loyalty toward him. She wanted to be as free of him as possible so that he could not cast a net over her made of the strings of his dependence on her. Yet it was this avoidance of Charbonneau's net that had run her directly into the strings of affection woven by Chief Red Hair.

It was to some extent to take her mind from him that she turned back to her memories. Those of her early childhood were pleasant. The memories of her later childhood were sharp and painful. Since her life with the white men, she had felt a belonging and a realization of their hold on her. They had their claws in her, like the sharp nails of a hawk fastened into a ground squirrel. It was not their conscious effort, but their endemic kindness. This kindness would remain with her, later not a memory of the past but of the present. It clinched her existence and her nature and twisted her, and she resented it in a kind of tender and anguished way. Why do I want to be like these white men and still be one of the People, especially when my childhood is a chaos of events?

By Christmas Day the fort was nearly done and the expedition men warm and dry, their colds nearly gone. They were living in the most luxurious quarters ever erected in Oregon country by 1805. They had spring water close by and wood enough down the draw. The cabins were sixteen by thirty feet. The south cabin contained a huge tree trunk that could not be removed. It was Shannon who had the great idea of smoothing off its top and making a table, and since it was rooted to the ground, the cabin had to be built around it.[7] The doors of all eight cabins faced inward on a parade ground, forty-eight by twenty feet. The outer walls were joined by a stockade, eight feet high, with a gate and sentry box at the south end. The north buildings, for the non-commissioned men, were divided into three rooms. Each room was sixteen feet square with a fireplace in the middle. The south building had two officers' rooms, each with a fireplace, and a separate storehouse, which was good—both for them and for the field mice and the wild rats that sneaked in at night. The sentry box was manned night and day. The gate was locked every night.

One sergeant and three privates constituted the guard,
which changed each day at sunrise. All the natives were
asked to leave at sundown, with the exception of one
party of Chinooks caught barefoot in a freezing snowstorm late one afternoon.[8]

Captain Lewis had forbidden the "thieving Chinooks" to enter the fort without a special permit. Even
on Christmas Day the guard was alert and stopped a
small man with a hawklike face. He was bare to the
waist and his breechclout seemed too big for his body,
but he looked as though he had the strength and vitality
to match even bigger clothing. He, like any Chinook,
smelled of fish and carried lice. He said, "No Chinook!"

"Who, then?" asked the guard.

"Clatsop," the man said, entering with wapato roots
and cranberries.

"Beautiful," said Captain Lewis, looking over the
berries, "and they come on Christmas Day." He gave
the man a couple of files for the trade. The man squatted
on his heels and poked the berries, not yet ready to
leave.

While he was poking, Lewis called Drouillard to use
his jargon with the man. The man puttered around the
roots and rearranged them and chatted with Drouillard
in a friendly manner, but rarely said more than "Yes"
or "I think so."

Finally he laced his fingers across his middle. "You
know," he said, "I talked those ignorant Klatskannins
out of an attack on your camp. I told them your men
were better hunters. They told me you would let the
fish in the river die of old age while you tramp in the
swamps after ducks and use the shooting-stick for the
deer. But I think you know what you are doing. I have
never seen such a lodge for keeping the wind out as
this." Then he settled back on his heels, looking small
in his weather-bleached clout, but by his manner, clearly
at ease with the strangers.

"What name do you go by?" asked Drouillard, all the
time wondering if the Klatskannins were a large tribe
and if there were any others in the vicinity who had
similar ideas.

"The other tribes call me Yanakasac Coboway. My
own tribe knows me as Chief Comowool."

Lewis brought out some red beads and gave them to the chief. But he pushed them back at Lewis and pointed to the files, indicating that he could use more.

"Why? What for?" asked Lewis.

"We carve the designs on canoes with chisels made from iron files."

Finally Drouillard stood up and stretched, saying, "The berries and roots are fine. Glad you came. Come to see us again. Tell the neighboring tribes we are peaceful; we have gifts for them."

Chief Comowool chuckled, and from a small leather pouch pulled out some yellowed paper and began to roll a cigarette as white men do.

"Where did you learn that?" asked Lewis.

"Haley. He gives us all many gifts. He will be here in three moons to trade. He, too, is peaceful."

"Where does he come from? Tell us in which direction his ship comes." Lewis was excited.

Chief Comowool pointed to the south but was not able to give any other information about this trader, who seemed to be a favorite with the Indians.

By the time Chief Comowool left, several of the men had gathered in front of the officers' cabin to sing carols. York boiled the wapato roots for the men's noon meal, and Lewis surprised the men while they were still at the tables in the mess hall by dividing the remaining stock of tobacco, twelve pigtails into two parts and distributing one among them to the men who smoked. The rest was set aside for trading on the return trip. Sacajawea and the men who did not smoke were given a silk handkerchief.

Cruzatte took out his violin, and there was some dancing. He let Sacajawea play the violin while York tried to teach Pomp the polka. Pomp giggled so hard that he lay on the floor and kicked his fat legs in the dappled light from the fireplace. His tiny fists waved in the air, and he gurgled in his throat with delight over so much attention. He was a glorious specimen of man-child. His light brown skin was hardly a blemish in the eyes of his mother.

"He is a show-off," said Sacajawea, handing the violin back to Cruzatte, who was pleased because she had not forgotten the tune he'd taught her.

York took her around the waist for a polka around the room. She learned fast, and LePage came forward to dance with her. "I am proud of my little namesake," he said. "I am glad that your baby has my name, Jean Baptiste, because I can see you are going to bring him up in the right way. He's not even a year old and he can walk!"

Shannon, not to be outdone, cut in to show Sacajawea the schottische. She got her feet mixed up, but kept a straight face and time to the music through it all. The men began to clap, and soon almost everyone was clapping or dancing.

"I want to begin the talking lessons again," she said.

"You want to continue with the English?" asked Shannon. "I thought you were tired of it."

"I thought you were sore at me because I learned too slow."

"I'm glad you won't give up."

"I want Pomp to learn when he talks."

"That's easier than you think. That's all he'll hear if he stays around us.

"Can you teach me some of this jargon or some more Minnetaree and Shoshoni, if I don't get it all mixed up?"

"Why would you want to know all that?"

"I might want to come back into Indian country," he said. "Maybe I'll set up a trading post. Fort Shannon. Boy, what a name, bejesus!"

"What a name, bejesus!" agreed Sacajawea. "The trading will be at the Three Forks for the People?"

"I'll be a bull-tough mountain man out there," Shannon answered.

Sacajawea picked up Pomp so he would not get in the way of the dancers, and he struck at her face. Every blow of the little hands touched the heart of Sacajawea. This son of hers would beat many a man twice his size. She would see that he learned the manners of the white men, and their language would be his language.

Outside the snug cabins there was wind and rain, making the ice slick. The slushy snow had frozen. The hunters had come in empty-handed. John Potts said, "Funny thing out here in the snow—I could see it take shape and bound away right before my eyes. It was white moving on white, white with dark eyes and a gray tuft of tail, white that was jackrabbits, but they ran before my gun was aimed."

The food for this Christmas dinner was the boiled cranberries brought by Chief Comowool and sweetened with the last of the sugar cubes and some poor elk, so putrefied that they all ate it only from necessity. York had roasted it until it was dry, then added a few wapato roots for moisture.

Some of the men exchanged small gifts. Clark received a shirt, drawers, and socks from Lewis, moccasins from Whitehouse, and a woven basket of rushes from Goodrich.

Gass gave Pomp a set of pine blocks, made from the wood he used for the floorboards. Then the men's eyes twinkled as if with some delightful secret as Clark cleared his throat and motioned for York to bring in something. It was a pine cradle for Pomp that the carpenter, Gass, had made from Clark's instructions. At the headboard was a crude carving of a wild rose, made by Gibson, and at the foot was a bird, carved out by LePage. The men crowded around to see the look on her face.

Sacajawea could not hide her emotion; her whole heart was loosened and dissolved. "Oooo," she said with her hand over her mouth. It was fearfully difficult to keep her eyes dry and her voice under control. "Beautiful! I say thank you. Pomp will say thank you by sleeping in this cradle."

The baby climbed in unaided and rocked himself back and forth until his eyes closed and he was quiet.

"Merry Christmas, Janey," said Clark.

She looked up, startled, but Clark smiled and made it easy for her to feel relaxed. *"Hee-hee tum-tum,"* she answered.

"A laughing heart to you and everyone," Clark called out, translating her Chinook jargon.

Lewis had been watching her accept the cradle, and he thought to himself, Lord, that Janey has more emotion than I believed. He had brought a basket of blackberries in from the storage room. They were about the size of a cherry and dried. "Look what Clark has brought for me, everyone." He shoved the basket on the plank table. "The Clatsops call them *shelwell*. I hope your bellies are grateful and they sit well."

The men laughed and went over to try them. "*Oui*, let's eat again," said Charbonneau.

When the berries were almost all gone, the men relaxed and sang and told about other Christmases spent with their families. Sacajawea gave York a pair of beaded moccasins and shyly held out a leather bundle to Clark. "I bargained myself for this. It is a gift for a great chief. Merry Christmas," she said in her fair English. Then she went on as though she were a spring that could not be stopped unwinding. "This is the birthday of the son of the white man's Great Spirit. This day, long ago, a star stood guard over the lodge where the papoose slept in his cradle. It is a day to be happy and to make others happy."

She caught everyone unawares with her knowledge of Christmas. Shannon had spent several hours with her that afternoon explaining the meaning of the white man's big medicine day. Charbonneau, wearing a wide necklace of white shells around his neck, and much oil in his hair, was surprised at his squaw's knowledge. He had not remembered gift-giving himself, but she had entered into the spirit of Christmas as if she had celebrated it all her life.

Clark let out a long whistle, and everyone stopped talking to look his way. "Wheeeiii! Great balls of fire! Where did you find these, Janey?"

The leather bundle held the two dozen white weasel tails. Tails such as these were one of the most prized forms of decoration among the North American Indian tribes.

"You must not give them away—not to a white squaw," she said slowly. "Because squaws are not allowed to possess or wear tails the length of these. These are for a great chief's ceremonial robe." She fingered the snow white tails with the black at their very tips and a faint streak of palest gold staining the black.

Clark's eyes were moist in the firelight. "Janey, it is one of the nicest things anyone has ever done for me. I'll never forget as long as I live." His hand momentarily brushed hers.

Charbonneau was still eating bits of dried berries

and once in a while pulling off bits of meat from the tin platter in the center of the table. He ate the meat like an Indian, putting a piece in his mouth and cutting it off under his nose with a flip of a hunting knife. "*Mon dieu*," he said, holding the knife poised close to his face, "I do not like bragging, but I have a collar of such tails, a gift to me." He cut off a mouthful of hard, dried meat and forced it down his throat half-chewed.

"It was a very short-tailed collar, more for a child," said Sacajawea, almost whispering.

"Hey, Charb," called Ordway, "you blow a lot of wind and it's meant mostly for the other end!"

Gass pointed his finger at Charbonneau. "Your ma never had to throw cold water on you to keep you from holding your breath."

Charbonneau looked around at the men, then at Sacajawea. There was nothing of self-satisfaction in her expression, nor of egotistic basking in victory. Her face seemed drawn with weariness, the brown lids half-closed, and for an instant she seemed oblivious to those around her as she contemplated the lines in the framing timber of one wall.

"Oh, shit, squaws exaggerate." Charbonneau flushed and stomped out, slamming the door. The afternoon rain had melted most of the snow and ice. He walked from the fort to the beach, where he could almost see the bay run out into the sea. He stood for several moments. As far as his eye could see, the beach sloped gently into the somber forest. The gray sea and the gray covering of high clouds domed together to the horizon. The tide was being sucked rapidly from below where he stood, silent and motionless. A mysterious force drew the water outward. Each wave ran the length of the shore, falling a foot or more below the previous one. In half an hour, a mile of dark, uneasy bottom was laid bare. Then the same mysterious force started climbing toward the forest.

The sand quivered faintly under his feet. Tiny bubbles rose and remained; small holes opened and gasped. Curious shellfish materialized and scurried meaninglessly across the sand. Gulls came and hunted them down. Well, he thought, the devil take me if I was not exactly right. There was nothing but the distant wind in the treetops on one side of him and the distant waves on the other. Between the two he moved alone. If he stayed, only the sea would roll itself to his feet and slip away again, over and over in a terrifying vision. He laughed with jarring loudness.

Within the next couple of days a warm, moist, southwest wind blew off the sea. "Talk about a midwinter thaw," said Lewis. "This is it."

"The meat is spoiling, and we must have salt for curing," said Clark. "I've said this before. Now I'm forced to organize a salt crew."

The following day five men were dispatched with five of the largest kettles to build a cairn for the manufacture of salt from seawater. The saltmakers' camp was erected near Tillamook Head, about fifteen miles southwest of the main fort. The men built a neat, close camp, convenient to wood, salt water, and fresh water from the Clatsop River. They kept the kettles boiling day and night, scraping them out only when they had boiled dry and the salt was thick and crusty.

Ben York was ill with a cold that had settled in his lungs from the strain of lifting the heavy logs to put in the pickets around the fort in the cold rain.

In the evenings Sacajawea brought him herb tea and hot, flat bread from camass roots.

"You are the best gal in this whole outfit." He pounded his knee and laughed, then had a fit of coughing. She pulled his arms above his head. Then she pounded him on the back so he would breathe deeper. "Me old aching back," he complained.

"You will feel better, by and by," she said.

Later Lewis came into his quarters, highly agitated. "Where are the meat bones for my dog? You don't suppose some flea-bitten buck has walked off with them?"

Clark laughed out loud and wiped the ink off his quill. "Janey knows how to make the most of things. You won't believe it, but I found her breaking up the bones. She boiled them and it was amazing the quantity of fat and good food she extracted. She flavored the broth with dried sage and fed it to York. He likes it and he's some better tonight. When she's through with those bones there really is not much left for a big dog like Scannon."

Lewis rushed out to the mess hall to retrieve any other bones before Sacajawea could get her hands on them.

A young man, who caused some excitement, came to the fort with several Clatsops just before sundown on New Year's Eve. He was much lighter-colored than the Clatsops. Both Clark and Drouillard thought he looked like a Mandan. He was freckled, with long, dusky red hair, and was about twenty-five years old. Lewis and Gass left their checker game to see if they could communicate with him. The man appeared to understand English, but he did not speak a word of it, using Chinook jargon instead. He held out his arm so that they could see tattoed on the outside: "Jack Ramsay." He indicated that was the name of his father, but he never knew his father himself. He believed himself to be a full-blooded Clatsop. Lewis bought some roots, dried fish, mats of woven rushes, a small deerskin, and some Clatsop tobacco, made of dried clover leaves and heads, in small rush bags, from this son of Jack Ramsay and his Clatsop companions.[9]

In the morning Sacajawea was awakened by the discharge of a volley of small arms. These were fired at dawn to usher in the New Year. The men spent the afternoon anticipating where each would be the first day of January 1807. Their evening meal was little better than the Christmas dinner—boiled elk, wapato, and cups of water. Toward midnight they went to their beds of pine boughs and were lulled to sleep by the falling winter rain. Some awoke with fits of coughing because the fireplaces smoked terribly, and some woke from the cold coming in the doors left open to get rid of the smoke.

For the most part, the winter was mild. When the snow melted, the grass was green underneath. Spring flowers opened in late January. (The moist Japan wind gives the Oregon coast the temperature of England.)

CHAPTER

28

The Whale

Clark's Journal:

Wednesday 8th January 1806

we arrived on a butifull Sand Shore, found only the Skelleton of this Monster on the Sand; the Whale was already pillaged of very Valuable part by the Kilamox Inds. in the Vecinity of whose village's it lay on the Strand where the waves and tide had driven up and left it. the Skeleton measured one hundred and five feet.... The Kilamox although they possessed large quantities of this blubber and oil were so prenurious that they disposed of it with great reluctiance and in small quantities only; insomuch that my utmost exertion aided by the party with the Small Stock of merchindize I had taken with me were not able to precure more blubber than about three hundred lb, and a fiew gallons of oil; Small as this stock is I prize it highly; and thank providence for directing the whale to us; and think him much more kind to us than he was to jonah, having Sent this Monster to be Swallowed by us in Sted of Swallowing of us as jonah's did.

BERNARD DEVOTO, ed., *The Journals of Lewis and Clark*. New York: Houghton Mifflin Co., 1953, p. 306.

Most of that winter the firm stump in the center of the captains' cabin was spread with maps and papers. Books were written and records were made of plants and trees, birds, fishes, and animals. The men named rivers and measured mountains. They prepared a geography of this new land to carry back to the States. Lewis was busy with Indian vocabularies, learning the Chinook jargon and setting it all down carefully in a journal. Clark busied himself with maps and the drawing of plants, animals, and the natives.[1]

The saltmakers' product was not so coarse as the rock salt the expedition had obtained in Saint Louis, or that which they had made in Kentucky. Soon all of the fresh game was salted and mealtime became more interesting. Charbonneau was back making *boudins*, his sausage, in which the large intestine of an animal was stuffed with heart, liver, lungs, kidneys, and fillet steak, minced with suet, onions, sage, and then boiled.

York was not ill for long and teased Sacajawea most every chance he had all winter long. "I'll have sweet potatoes for supper today," he'd say, holding up a fistful of rush roots.

This was the happiest winter Sacajawea had ever known, with her baby toddling around her, pulling her robe around his chubby face, or tumbling over his pine cradle. She could not really understand how the presence of her child and herself gave a touch of domesticity to that Oregon winter. Once in a while the Clatsop women, dressed in woven cedar skirts, came to see her. They sat with their backs against the wall without saying a word, watching her every motion. They always left colored shells and shiny seeds so that she could use them on moccasins and shirts. Sometimes she helped Charbonneau with his spits turning slowly over the cooking fire outside, or with the roasting of elk tongues, or his boiled sausage. She became good at making trapper's butter, boiling up the marrow of a shank bone with a pinch of salt. She learned to make candles from elk tallow, which were used in the short days of winter,

when darkness came on in midafternoon. No one suggested they try the black, dried candle-smelt.

Early in January the Clatsops gave the saltmakers
some blubber from a whale stranded on the sandy shore.
It was palatable and tender, tasting much like the fat
from beaver or pork. Bill Bratton left the salt camp,
taking some of the blubber to the men at the main camp.
Clark was so enthusiastic about it that he planned to
go back the next day with Bratton, two canoes, and ten
of the men to look for the whale.

When Sacajawea heard about the enormous fish, her
eyes burned to see it. She spoke first to Charbonneau
about it. "I can go. York will watch Pomp for me."

He told her definitely, "*Non!* You can't go off leaving
your papoose like that. Besides, I am going and you will
have to watch the roasting meats." That evening he
spoke to Captain Clark about his *femme.* "That ornery
femme wants to see the whale, but I told her she couldn't
take *l'enfant,* so she must stay in camp with him."

Clark was busy with his preparations and only half
listened to Charbonneau, finally agreeing with him just
to get him out of the way. "She can look after the cooking pots here. That is woman's work, anyway."

Charbonneau grunted his satisfaction and hurried
back to Sacajawea. "*Les capitaines* say you cannot go.
You have to stay with the cooking."

Sacajawea struck her hands together. "You'll have
sand in your meat!"

Charbonneau just smiled smugly. "I am sleepy," he
said, going to his quarters to lie down.

Sacajawea sat down, disappointed, hugging her knees
and bending her head back, watching the gray clouds
as they swirled in and out of view and wondering how
she could see that huge fish. She had learned to figure
logically that one or two favors can bring a correspond-
ing favor. And so, with a plan in mind, she left a handful
of seashells and colored stones for Pomp to amuse himself with and went to see Chief Red Hair. She knocked
on the half-opened door.

"Yes, what is it, Janey?" said Clark, pushing the door
open wider so he could see her.

"Remember when we came to the river that broke
into two arms and you did not know which one to follow?

I showed you the one. I helped you say words to the Shoshonis. I made a good bargain and found chief's weasel tails for your Christmas."

Clark nodded, but his eyebrows pushed together in a frown. He sensed she was trying to tell him something else.

"I traveled a long way to see the Stinking Waters. I climbed mountains and kept my papoose out of the way of the working men. I did not let him cry at night, even when he was hungry. Now—I want to go to see this unbelievable fish."

Clark watched her face with the large, pleading black eyes and knew she was going to see that whale. She had not come this distance to be stopped by a little cold wind and someone suggesting she stay behind and cook, when something so fascinating lay so near. He was not surprised at her determination to see beyond the next hilltop, and the next. This was the very thing he longed to nourish in that quick mind of hers. Her logic amused him.

"But now I have to go back on my word with Charbonneau. I told him you would look after the cooking pots."

"No, not back on your word—I will look after the cooking pots, on the trail to and from the giant fish."

"And if Charbonneau wants to come along, he will have to carry that little dancing boy, Pomp."

Lewis came in just as Sacajawea impulsively ran over and pumped Clark's hand up and down in gratitude. Together they watched her run to her quarters, and both hoped that Charbonneau would take the news like a gentleman.

"I think you let that squaw wrap you around her little finger," said Lewis. "I'm inclined to agree with old Charbonneau. Staying in camp, tending the cooking is woman's work. What good will it do her to see a stranded whale? Lord and glory"—he cleared his throat several times—"you're a little soft in the head when that squaw is around."

The next morning, twelve men, Sacajawea, and Pomp breakfasted by candlelight. "Best eat a bite and get moving," York whispered to Sacajawea. It was gray dawn and cool with the night's frost on the grasses when

Sacajawea stepped out ahead of all the men, following the trail Clark and the saltworkers had blazed weeks ago. Charbonneau looked at her back, shifted the baby from one arm to the other, but said nothing; he only breathed loudly through his open mouth. Clark found two of their canoes where he'd put them, safely hidden in the brush near the Netual River. As they climbed into the canoes, Sacajawea took Pomp from the relieved Charbonneau.

"It is better I put him in a blanket on my back. I am used to him there, and to me he is no trouble," she said.

"This boy no trouble?" muttered Charbonneau. "He moves all the time. My arms are black and blue from the pounding of his legs. He is like a fish—I almost lost him because he wiggled so much. Whew! I'm glad your back is strong." Charbonneau lay back against the side of the canoe with his head propped on his arms. Someone handed him a canoe paddle. He shook his head and put his hand on his stomach gravely. "I am hungry."

"Everyone pushes a paddle," said Clark, "and eats later."

Charbonneau groaned. "Christ's blood, my hands will be one big blister. I was meant for better things."

"We all have to paddle. Even Janey will have her turn," said Clark quietly. He wanted to shout, How dare you be so lazy and act so moronic? You've been a free trapper and worked twice as hard as this on your own many times. Why do you act this way in front of people? You make a fuss over all the small things. You upset me and upset Janey. I want to tell you that I despise you.

Charbonneau began to sing in his French-Canadian patois, keeping time with the men's paddles. Some of the men hummed along.

At once Clark's anger began to fade. How can any man be angry for long with a fellow who is so changeable in his moods? "We'll eat when we leave the canoes and begin hiking."

The sun rose clear, burning through the morning haze that hung over the two canoes as they floated smoothly over the Netual into Meriwether Bay, heading southward along various creeks and streams until they had to abandon the canoes, eat, and move overland. They stopped once near a herd of fat elk in the midst of a violent thunderstorm; barely a drop of rain fell, and soon the sun was shining through the clouds again. Bratton shot one of the elk, and they all helped cut the carcass and pack the fresh meat in the hide so it could be easily swung between four men. They made night camp underneath enormous cedars and looked across the water to see the tall, clean-trunked white pines, each as round and straight as a cannon, and each with a little tuft of foliage at the very tiptop. They were surrounded by tall, coneless Sitka spruce, mountain hemlock, honeysuckle, and low-bush huckleberry. The party moved on across the small inlet, fording the warm shallow water.

By noon of the second day, they had reached the salt camp. They examined the kettles of Jo Fields, George Gibson, Bill Bratton, and a couple of others that were under a rock arch. Pat Gass and Bill Werner had their brass kettles on two huge stones with a hot fire between, boiling seawater into a gallon of salt per day. This salt camp was close to four cedar houses belonging to some Clatsop families. These people fed the visitors dried fish and thick thistle root dipped in whale oil. While the men were still eating, Clark went to one of the houses and talked with a squat young man who was wearing a rolled Navy neckerchief as a belt for his breechclout. Clark hired the young man, called Twiltch, for the price of a steel file, to guide the party to the whale. Sacajawea talked in hand signs with some of the women, who were curious and had formed a ring around her. They asked why she and her child traveled with many men. Sacajawea explained that she was the woman of the party. The Clatsop women put their hands to their mouths and cackled loudly.

"Imagine," said one round-faced squaw, "having so many men. Hee-hee-hee! There must be no time for sleep at night. Hee-hee-hee!" Sacajawea turned red beneath her brown skin, but she did not attempt to explain that she was the actual woman of only one of the men. These women enjoyed this joke so much that they could not help but carry on with it.

"Twiltch will lead you to the great fish, but do not make soft eyes with him. He has two women who do not wish to have him shared by another—especially one with so many men to entertain." They fell into a fit of laughing again.

Finally, recovering herself, an ugly squaw with ears pierced so that links of rusty chain hung from them asked, "You have some big medicine you use on men? I would buy some of it for this." She held out a beaver hat and a flag of China. "If I had the big medicine, I could get a man. Couldn't you share a small part with me?"

Sacajawea smiled and held out her hands to show she had no big medicine. The women grabbed at her hands and tunic.

"Come on, we're busting away!" shouted Pryor as the men began to follow Twitch.

Thinking fast, Sacajawea bent close to the homely woman, held her breath, and pressed her lips against the cheek of the astounded Clatsop squaw, who immediately let her go. The other squaws let go, and Sacajawea hurried to catch up with the men headed south, forgetting to collect her payment of hat and flag.

"Oooo, big medicine!" murmured the squaws, all smacking their lips.

Twitch led the party to Tillamook Head, about thirty miles south of Cape Disappointment. Bill Bratton had been given permission to leave his saltmaking awhile longer and travel with them to see the whale. They paused on a hillside, named it Clark's Point of View, and looked out over the boisterous Pacific.

This was the first warm day of that year. A warm Chinook wind eased in from the direction of China, and the high tide built glossy ridges of green water into draft-horse waves that smoked spray into the sun and collapsed booming among the dozing sea gulls on the hard sand. The beach at high tide was not a good place to walk because every inch of sand above the high-water mark was piled with mountains of driftwood—stumps as big as tepees, dead trees, sprawling roots and branches overhead and underfoot, beams and old timbers, broken lumber from wrecked ships, even trimmed logs from Tillamook tribes' dugouts that had gone loose from their towlines.

Sacajawea smelled the sea, the wet kelp, and the salt

air, and looked a long way out over the water. She saw,
riding big combers behind the surge, a great flight of
white gulls diving for fish. The comber broke and the
birds flew back with it, then drew back into the surf
and came in again, looking for more fish. She could see
one side of the Columbia where it widened into bays
that were dotted on the shore with the lodges of various
Chinook tribes—Clatsop, Tillamook, Cathlamet, and
Cayuse. On the other side of the river were white-barked
quaking aspen, bracken fern, and young Douglas firs.

Down the steep rocks that overhung the sea, the
party followed Twiltch to the Tillamook village, where
the great whale lay stranded on their shore. But Clark's
outfit was too late. The Tillamooks had stripped off
everything that could either be eaten or boiled down
for oil. Only the skeleton remained. Some of the Tillamooks were still there storing whale oil in bladders
and the whale's own entrails. Clark managed to buy
three hundred pounds of blubber and a few gallons of
oil by offering them brass buttons, tiny bits of wire, and
a steel file.

Sacajawea walked, unhurried, around the huge skeleton, her tongue making clicking sounds within her
mouth. Clark said it was a small whale, but it was the
largest animal she had ever seen.

"The water must be very deep to have such huge
creatures live in it," she said to Charbonneau as she
let Pomp walk inside the whale and peer between the
rib bones.

"*Femme*," said Charbonneau with an authoritarian
tone, "there are many monsters in the sea. Big ones
like this eat the next big ones, like the seals. The seals
eat the salmon, and the salmon eat the smelt. The smelt
eat minnows. That's what happens all the time in the
sea. The big eat *les petites*."

"Why?" she asked, wondering why creatures could
not live without fear for their lives.

"*Pourquoi*? They are hungry. To swim all the time
makes them hungry."

"Ah, *ai*." She studied the whale carefully so that she
might be able to describe it to the People when she
returned. I will return to the People with so much to

tell, she thought. It will be something to see their faces
when I tell of this fish as large as a tepee.

Charbonneau pulled Pomp out of the path of some
barefoot children where he had wandered. The children
were walking logs in the brush to avoid the snakes that
lay curled on the damp ground. A child sidled up to a
sluggish snake and boosted a path through the weeds
for himself with one toe.

"This is a place you like?" asked Twiltch, watching
Charbonneau carefully. "You come over for a visit?
Maybe we get up a stick game. Everybody likes the
stick game."

Charbonneau hitched Pomp a little higher on his hip,
smiled so that his yellowish teeth showed in the sunlight, and said with hand signs that he would do that
when he had the time, certainly.

"You bring round coins," said Twiltch.

"You mean money?" indicated Charbonneau, astounded.

"Money," answered Twiltch, not making any hand
signs, but taking a buckskin sack off his belt and clanking it for the answer.

Charbonneau bent forward to see the contents. "*Capitaine*!" he yelled. "This here Chinook, he is a rich man."

Clark looked over the sack of coins. "Looks like a lot
of British Northwesters medals to me, and a couple
Russian, and see here, a Spanish piece. Interesting, eh?
This might be Chinese." He held one up for a better
look.

"He won them in the stick game," said Charbonneau
excitedly.

"Must be a lot of white trading going on up and down
this coast. Yes, sir, maybe more than we have thought."

"You have coins for the stick game?" Twiltch moved
his hands fast.

"*Non*, not me," said Charbonneau with his hands.

"You can't play?" said Twiltch, making a noise in
his throat as if he had choked on something bitter.

There were five cedar cabins in this Tillamook village, which was beside a freshwater creek. Sacajawea
called it Whale Creek and chased after Pomp, who made
it a game to run between the lodges just out of his
mother's reach. The lodges were sunk four feet into the

ground and covered with ridgepoles making sloping roofs. The sides were boarded with rough slabs of cedar, laboriously split with elkhorn wedges and stone hammers. A door in the upper gable admitted the Tillamooks to their half-underground home by means of a ladder outside and another inside. Around the inner walls, pallets of rush mats were raised on scaffolds, two or three feet high. Under the pallets were skin boxes of dried berries, roots, nuts, and fish. In the center was the fireplace, six to eight feet long, sunk in the floor, and surrounded by a low cedar wall and mats for the family to sit on. The walls, lined with mats and cedar bark, formed a warm shelter.

Sacajawea saw large wooden bowls, spoons of horn, skewers and spits for roasting meat, and beautifully woven, watertight baskets. She noted that each squaw carried a knife fastened to her right thumb by a loop of rawhide and hidden under her robe when visitors came. These knives, bought from seafaring traders, were invaluable for digging roots, cutting wood, meat, and fish, splitting rushes for mats, baskets, and the tall crowned hats, and cutting animal skins.

Sacajawea's mouth dropped open as she heard some Tillamooks talking with Twitch. Interspersed among their native words were English: "damned rascal, musket, knife, son-of-bitch, powder, heave the lead, bloody redskins." She asked questions, but they seemed to know no other words, or other foreign language. None had any idea where the traders had come from or where they went on their floating lodges; they just pointed southwest and shook their heads,[2] then asked Sacajawea why she asked so many questions. "Are you chief of these men?" asked a Tillamook, who thought Sacajawea was bad-mannered for speaking out and asking too much. The Tillamooks turned their backs toward her, but Sacajawea broke in unexpectedly, using hand signs and the jargon she had picked up.

"I just want to ask one more thing. Do you set aside anything for trading? For instance, do you save spuck[3] pelts to trade for these?" She pointed to three rusty British muskets leaning against a lodge and a brass kettle in the yard.

Now the Tillamooks were all nonplussed, not know-

ing whether to ignore her and talk with only Captain
Clark, or to answer her last question.

"This tribe and my tribe both collect weasels and
spuck for trading with the inhabitants of the floating
lodges." Twiltch's voice was brittle and unfriendly as
he spoke for the Tillamooks. The Tillamooks then
grunted an imperious affirmative and stepped away
from her and closer around Captain Clark and his men.

This tribe is touchy, Sacajawea said to herself. I will
be more careful. She looked up in time to see Pomp
slide down a mud-slick bank and dive, head first, into
the creek. She ran to pull him out, all the time thinking,
I have committed another discourtesy. I have not kept
my thoughts on my baby, who is slippery as a fish,
sliding from my eyes the moment I take an interest in
something else.

"You stupid *femme!*" yelled Charbonneau. "You are
not here as an interpreter. You came along as the cook."

"I think you are to be the cook also, as on the trail
to this place. We both turn the meat."

"I am not doing squaw's work," he said sullenly, looking away into space. "And make your child stop hollering. I hate that noise. God curse him. He's wet. Do
something with that mess!"

She removed the baby's clothing, wrapped him in
her blanket, and slung him over her shoulder, saying
to herself, Thank the Great Spirit for keeping the truth
of this baby's wetness from his father. She built up the
cooking fire. Pomp slept the rest of the afternoon while
his mother cooked and the men stayed on at the Tillamook village and held a council. Sacajawea put chunks
of elk meat on sticks over the fire and turned them at
intervals to roast evenly. Curious how that huge fish
came out of the sea just at this time. Is it an omen?
Strange how he landed when I was here with the white
men so I could look at him. No one has ever seen a
whale on this beach before. It is sad! The fish has no
future, and we can know nothing of his past, only of
this, now. One thing is certain, he is a part of the land
now, forever.

Her ears heard almost imperceptible approaching
footsteps. The footsteps stopped behind the rise going
to the white man's camp. Then she heard Pat Gass's

voice. "There is good indication the Russians and Spanish have not been here too often."

And Chief Red Hair's voice. "Janey was the one to find out the Tillamooks and Clatsops store up weasels and spuck for trade with incoming ships. I think we can get this trade in the hands of the United States. I believe that is exactly what Tom Jefferson had in mind when he sent us out here. Damn those Tillamooks for their customs! I would have liked Janey to sit in on that meeting with them. Her questions are pertinent."

The men, Sacajawea, and Pomp went back to the salt camp on January 9, spent the night there, and the next day returned to Fort Clatsop.

Two days later, the Clatsop chief, Comowool, from the village on the south bank of the Columbia, and Chief Comcommoly, from the north side, came to visit the white chiefs. Clark was ready with more questions about ships and traders. The native chiefs huddled beside the fire in the parade ground of Fort Clatsop. Comcommoly was muffled high about the face in a three-point blanket from the Hudson's Bay Company, so that only his hooked nose and his beady right eye showed above it. Comowool's shoulders were bare. His legs were covered by a pair of moth-eaten navy blue woolen trousers.

Clark pointed to the royal blue blanket. "Who brought this?"

Comcommoly raised his hand and made signs, saying the name "Haley" and indicating, "Three masts, brings presents. We like him."

"Tell me when he will be back," said Clark.

"Three moons."

Clark nodded, then prodded the men more. "Name others who come in ships to trade. Tell me something about them."

Comcommoly's face wrinkled with a smile as Drouillard sat beside Captain Clark and spoke fluent jargon with him. "Maybe we'll learn something today," Drouillard said as an aside to Clark, and he gave both of the men a pair of gray wool socks with the toes and heels completely worn out.

Comcommoly said, "Tallamon, not a trader; Callalamet, wooden leg; Fallawan, floating lodge has guns which killed some of my people. He does not trade now. Davidson, no trader, hunts elk; Skelley, only one eye." The chief pointed to his own empty socket and was silent as the pipe was passed for smoking.

Finally Chief Comowool shrugged his bare, scarred shoulders and shifted his weight on the woven backrest he had brought with him.

"Moore, comes in four-masted ship, maybe he will be back in two moons to trade; Captain Youens, he will come in one moon for trading."[4] The chief went on with a weasely voice, "Swipton, Mackey, Jackson, Balch— all traders with three-masted ships."

When the two chiefs left, Clark walked along the bay with his spyglass pointed out to the gray-green sea. He saw no ships, but he ran across a slough lined with hundreds of beautifully carved canoes. These were coffins, with burial gifts still around the passengers; the skeleton feet all faced the sunset. Clark passed two old Chinooks fishing with nets, and he pointed up toward the bayou. The old men shrugged; they did not know whose bones they all were. They indicated, "Those old, old people. Long ago the skin broke open, and they lay in their lodges, on the sand, in the brush."

The other old man bowed his head, his hands moving quickly, "There was great mourning along the river at one time."

Clark guessed that hundreds of Chinooks were cut down long ago by smallpox.

It was much milder than it had been at Fort Mandan the winter before, but the continual rain, fog, and murky skies were depressing. Boredom was a problem, created by the sedentary routine in the wake of months of strenuous activity and danger on the westbound journey. The captains did all they could to keep everyone busy, but this was not always possible, and onerous chores were resented. Sacajawea, York, and a couple of the men sewed moccasins from the elk hides they dressed until they had an average of about ten pairs per person. Sacajawea saw moccasins in her sleep. Any excuse was used for a change of pace from the daily routine.

On February 11, York announced after the morning

meal, "This is to be a celebration for the first birthday of Master Jean Baptiste Charbonneau, known to us as Pomp."

The men sang and danced with Pomp during the day. Some told him stories, or held him on the back of the dog, Scannon, so that he could have a "pony" ride. The dinner was elk's tongues and candle-smelt. At the finish, York brought out a large round sheet of flat bread made from wapato root and topped by one elk-tallow candle. Charbonneau complained that the bread tasted sour.

"You feisty old bastard, put salt on it," said John Potts.

Shannon put one of the Chinooks' conical grass hats on the baby's head. It almost covered his eyes, and he moved his head up and down, trying to see.

Lewis held up both hands for quiet. "I bought many of these hats and will give them to all of you to keep the sun and rain off your heads on the way back to the States."

There was a loud clapping, and someone cried, "Hup, hup, hooray for our captain!"

Bratton came in from the saltmakers' camp with a barrel of salt and a string of tiny yellow matched shells for Pomp to wear around his neck. Bratton was fed, and when he finished, he sat Pomp on the mess table to put the shells around his neck so that all could admire them. No one noticed that Pomp pushed the soft, half-burned tallow candle to the floor. Bratton took a step backward to look at Pomp, and his moccasins slipped in the greasy tallow.

"Hey!" he called, trying to hold himself up. He lost his balance and went down flat on his back. "Curses on the poxridden joker," he said, trying to get up.

Some of the men close by were laughing at the way Bratton's feet flew in the air as he fell. "You looked like a puppet on a string!" laughed Shannon.

"Shut up! My damn back is broken! I can't move!" Bratton's face was red and his upper lip wet with perspiration from the pain in his lower back.

Lewis carefully moved his own hands over Bratton's back and said, "I don't think any ribs are broken, and the vertebrae seem all right. Maybe it is a pinched

nerve. I think York could try to pull out your spine and
line it up. If it is a pinched nerve, that might just relieve
it."

"No way!" Bratton snapped. "Don't touch me! The
pain—oh God, it is great!" His head rolled to one side,
and all the men were quiet as they saw that Bratton
had passed out.

The light from the fireplace flickered, making the
sweat-streaked face of Bratton seem grotesque.

"*Femme*, spank that child!" Charbonneau ordered.
"He threw the soapy candle on the floor. He is responsible for this terrible accident. Warm his bottom with
this." He held a kindling stick in his hand.

"No, that is not making Bratton's back whole again,"
said Sacajawea, shaken. "That is cruel. I will not allow
you to touch my baby." She could never raise her voice
to reprimand a child, and never used corporal punishment. What was treated as a catastrophic event by
Charbonneau, a white parent, was regarded with casual calmness by Sacajawea, a Shoshoni.

"In that case you are responsible for that bloody candle on the floor. Where were your eyes?"

Sacajawea thought, You're a cruel, cold-gutted,
heartless bastard. She was hard put to hide her distaste.
"I cannot bear to be near you!" She picked up the frightened Pomp and took him to her quarters, putting him
to bed in his cradle. She searched in her sewing scraps
and found a long, soft, leather strip.

She was certain she had not caused Bratton's trouble, but she would do all she could to help him. She
would not blurt out at her man because if she did she
would surely lift his head right off his shoulders. In the
mess hall she heard Chief Red Hair say, "He is like a
tiger with boils on his ass, but I'll give him some laudanum and he'll behave himself." To her relief she heard
Lewis say, "Yes, he'll be all right."

Sacajawea gave Captain Clark the leather strip and
suggested hot and cold packs be used alternately during
the night after wrapping his back with the leather to
give it some support.

In the morning and for the next couple of days, Bratton felt no better. Once she watched while Clark gave
him more laudanum and sponged his face. She saw the

taut mask of Bratton's face, the way he accepted the painkiller without pleasure and the cold towel with cold thanks.

Charbonneau kept looking at her as though it were her fault that the accident had taken place. Clark told him once, "Lay off her. It was something no one saw. The baby is too young to know what he did. The best we can do is take care of Bratton and see that he can walk again."

She watched Charbonneau walk off talking to himself; she was furious that he wouldn't help minister to Bratton. She managed to get some strips of cedar bark and long grass for weaving from the Clatsop women. She and York wove a sling to carry Bratton in. You're foolish and without manners, she told herself, for expecting this man to smile and act grateful for all this fussing. He feels that the accident should not have taken place. He wants to be back with the other saltmakers instead of here where a baby runs the day's activities.

"We are all sorry and would like to take away the time of the accident. But it has happened. Pomp meant no harm. He likes the yellow shells," she sighed, her voice soft and honeyed so that even Charbonneau in one of his most foul moods would have been soothed. "It was my fault. I should keep my eyes on that child. He is into everything this winter."

Bratton smiled but said nothing. During the next few days his face turned pale and he lost weight.

Day by day, the winds came up and warmed the land so that the marshes became softer and oozed. Clouds sat low and dark on the skyline. The grass began to grow taller, and out of somewhere came magpies. The days were dull at Fort Clatsop.

The Clatsop girls were providing amusement for the men. Lewis warned them time and again of venereal diseases.

"Those are the very germs that are responsible for the miseries of McNeal and Goodrich. Furthermore, we have little trade goods left. We won't have anything for the home trip if you men trade it off for those Jezebels' favors!"

Unanimously the men promised to have nothing to

do with the girls they knew were afflicted, which were only two or three. All these young girls practiced only what they knew as notions of hospitality in their tribe, and a sort of fertility rite, in which their tribe might gain new and stronger bloodlines.

Sacajawea felt no compunction to keep the men's activities a secret and pointed out to Clark that some of the Clatsops mixed pounded beaver castoreum with bear's oil and rubbed it on their body to heal the scabs and ulcers of syphilis and the oozing of gonorrhea.

"Does it do any good?" asked Clark.

"The beaver glands do have an odor that travels ahead of the wearer some distance," explained Sacajawea, "but it does not rid anyone of the sickness. He must endure it and die early."

"Well, it would be a good idea to put medical dispensaries in American forts," said Clark firmly. "Eyewash, salts, laudanum, and the new mercury salves could be stocked. I imagine it will take some months of fast talk and statistics to convince others of this need."

"First, you could tell Captain Lewis."

"That's exactly what I will do."

Life seemed to creep back into the men as the sap crept up into the tree trunks that spring. Since most of the men either smoked or chewed and they missed the tobacco habit, it was not long before the smokers discovered the inner bark of red willow mixed with bearberry and the chewers found the crabtree bark.

One March evening just after dusk, Chief Delashelwilt waddled nervously to the fort wearing a Hudson's Bay multicolored blanket coat stained with fish oil and soot, to talk with Charbonneau. He also wore a little medicine bag suspended from a braided bit of moosehair that ran around his neck. In the bag, Delashelwilt was convinced, his immortal soul was lodged, and if he stroked the bag frequently, his influence over men would be invincible.

The men talked for some time until Delashelwit was told by the sentry the fort was closing for the night. Delashelwilt and Charbonneau shook hands. Charbonneau looked about as Delashelwilt left. The gate was barred, and Charbonneau quickened his step. He began to hurry to his quarters.

Sacajawea saw him come in and close the door. He dropped several gold coins on the top of his bunk. He began to dance in an awkward way in front of the coins.

"Is everything all right?"

"*Oui*, everything is perfect."

The next night Chief Delashelwilt came to visit Charbonneau again, but this time he was accompanied by half a dozen squaws.

When they left, Sacajawea asked, "What did that knife-scarred chief want with you?"

"We are friends."

"What friends? I know friends—and I know enemies!" Sacajawea whirled back to Charbonneau. "They are paying you to make some kind of deal. I can feel it. Why don't you let them crawl out of their holes and stand in front of the captains to make their deal?"

Charbonneau stared back malevolently.

"They are not friends. They will cause you trouble."

"Why don't you hide your head in a hole like a prairie dog when the hawk sails over him? Then you would not see what is my business, not yours!" He put several more coins in a leather bag with the others.

In her mind Sacajawea could see Delashelwilt's woman—the big breasts, the big bottom, the little feet and fat wrists, and the hunger for goods. She did not like the faces of his squaw friends, nor their leering, jeering glances. And, most of all, she detested in them their lack of dignity, for they all wore more beads and shells and foofaraw than the chief himself did, and most of it came from the diminished stores of the expedition.

They are all childish and foolish, but what can one expect from a flea-bitten Chinook, she asked herself. The expedition is low on trade goods. What right does my man have to give it away? He does not collect shells to restock them. I cannot rant over these normal things and act like a madwoman. I need some plan. I have seen extraordinary things and have been to strange places. I must be able to think of something. I can only think of Chief Delashelwilt as a liar and cheat, and my man acts out his wishes with no thought of his own. Charbonneau, you are so stupid, Sacajawea wanted to shout. I want to tell you I hate you. You cause more troubles.

Chief Red Hair would have a solution. He would give her strength and release her from this torment.

"Come in," Clark answered to the timid knocking. "Janey, I'm always glad to see you. Here, let me take my dancing boy, Pomp. He is getting brighter every day." Clark hummed as he stood Pomp on the floor and skipped around. Pomp loved it. His feet kept time to the song as his eyes stayed fastened on Clark's face. Sacajawea suddenly felt the familiar wild beating of her heart. She trembled.

"You came for something?"

"*Ai*," she said, wondering why she did not try some words to say while she was by herself. She felt miserable. "The Chinook squaws are unhappy, and we will make them happy."

"Chinook squaws?"

"*Ai*, the woman and friends of Chief Delashelwilt." She glanced at the doorway, distracted as York came in.

"That moronic, flea-bitten buck. I told him not to come around here with those girls!" Clark was angry. York backed out the door and closed it softly. "That dumb Chinook! How did he get in?"

"He came as a friend."

"You can find friends in the manure pile sometimes," said Clark.

"He is not my friend," she added quickly. "He brings coins to buy friendship and wants trade goods from the stores in return. The trade goods should not be handed to him. It can be used later for things the men need. Now the squaws would be happy if they had tiny pieces of colored ribbon to sew on their tunics. They will go home and cause no trouble. The chief will have to go home with them, and he can be given some of that new kind of tobacco the men are smoking. There will be no fight. Charbonneau will have his coins until he plays the stick game with Twiltch."

"So—it was Charbonneau who was behind this. Who says there will be no fighting?" roared Clark, glaring past her toward the door. "Who knows what tomorrow will bring?"

"Tomorrow is in the hands of the Great Spirit."

Clark looked in bewilderment at Sacajawea. "Who cares about tomorrow!" He left his quarters with the door swinging wide open. Charbonneau's the key. How are you going to handle him? he wondered. He slowed his pace. Janey told me how to avoid a battle. It is strange, but it is true. The plan will work. He strode to the front gate of the fort and was not surprised to see Charbonneau sitting on the outside watching Chief Delashelwilt come through the trees with his covey of females. His body stiffened and became straight. His face was gray with anger, but he did not falter.

"Sit still, you ape," Clark said to Charbonneau when he strode past him to meet Delashelwilt. "Stop, you dogs!" The Chinooks could not understand his words, but his manner was unmistakable. "Delashelwilt, your scalp is loose on your head and I would like to take it!" Clark's eyes shot toward Charbonneau, who was backing inside the fort. Clark's muscular arm shot out and grasped Charbonneau's hand. "Get red, white, and blue ribbon and a sharp knife from the stores. Right now!"

"Oui!"

Clark hoped Charbonneau could find an extra knife. The goods that the expedition was depending on for the purchase of food and horses during the four-thousand-mile homeward trip could all be tied in two handkerchiefs.

Clark cut the ribbon into tiny pieces, almost like confetti, mixed the colors, and handed a few to each girl. The girls at once compared the number of various colors. One girl moistened a few on her tongue and stuck them to her face, to the delight of the others.

"Take the pouch of makeshift tobacco off your belt," ordered Clark. "Give it all to the chief." Clark then made the final cut-off sign with his hands and pointed toward the trees beyond the fort. "Go home before you spread your infection to any more of my men." Then to Charbonneau he added, "I'm surprised a sensible man like yourself would be seen with scum like that. Especially those women who all have the clap."

Behind him there was a growl of rage from Delashelwilt when he found he could take the tobacco, but not the knife. The chief pulled his little medicine bag from the braided moosehair and stomped it into the ground. He pointed a finger at Charbonneau and said in plain English, "Paleface, jackass poop!"

Book Four
HOMEWARD

Washington, U.S. of America. July 6, 1803

Dear Sir

In the journey which you are about to undertake for the discovery of the course and source of the Missouri and of the most convenient water communication from thence to the Pacific ocean, your party being small, it is to be expected that you will encounter considerable dangers from the Indian inhabitants. Should you escape those dangers and reach the Pacific ocean, you may find it imprudent to hazard a return the same way, and be forced to seek a passage round by sea, in such vessels as you may find on the Western coast but you will be without money, without clothes and other necessaries, as a sufficient supply cannot be carried with you from hence. Your resource in that case can only be in the credit of the US for which purpose I hereby authorize you to draw on the Secretaries of State, of the Treasury, of War and of the Navy of the US, according as you may find your draughts will be most negociable, for the purpose of obtaining money or necessaries for yourself and your men: and I solemnly pledge the faith of the United States that these draughts shall be paid punctually at the date they are made payable. I also ask of the consuls, agents, merchants and citizens of any nation with which we have intercourse or amity to furnish you with those supplies which your necessities may call for, assuring them of honorable and prompt retribution. And our own Consuls in foreign parts where you may happen to be, are hereby instructed and required to be aiding and assisting to you in whatsoever may be necessary for procuring your return back to the United States. And to give more entire satisfaction and confidence to those who may be disposed to aid you, I Thomas Jefferson, President of the United

587

States of America, have written this letter of general credit for you with my own hand, and signed it with my name.

Th. Jefferson

To
    Capt. Meriwether Lewis

E. G. Voorhis Memorial Collection, Missouri Historical Society, St. Louis.
Also in:
REUBEN GOLD THWAITES, ed., *The Original Journals of the Lewis and Clark Expedition, 1804–1806*, Vol. 7. New York: Dodd, Mead and Co., 1904–5. Reprinted by Arno Press, N.Y., 1969, pp. 254–55.

Ahn-cutty

Back around Warrior's Point Clark came, whence the
Multnomahs were wont to issue to battle in their huge
war canoes. An old Indian trail led up into the interior,
where for ages the lordly Multnomahs had held their
councils. Many houses had fallen entirely to ruin.

Clark inquired the cause of decay. An aged Indian
pointed to a woman deeply pitted with the smallpox.
"All died of that. Ahn-cutty! Long time ago!"

EVA EMERY DYE, *The Conquest*. Portland: Binfords and
Mort, 1936, p. 269.

Each morning the weather seemed warmer. Sacajawea often sat where she could see the shoreline and the seals playing in the sea and sunning themselves on rocks. She was convinced that the white men had made no effort to kill the plentiful seals for food because they were a strange race of people who lived in water. Her own people had believed in water spirits for ages. Even Shannon had told her of their "wonderous homes" underwater, one time in a teasing mood. She could hardly picture herself as a grandmother, but thought, If I am ever with grandchildren, they will be amused with stories about these water people who sit on the rocks and stare at us who live on land.

The men began to talk of going home. Bratton, still carried in the grass sling, was certain the warmth of the spring sun could bring healing to his back.

In preparation for the return journey, Captain Lewis "borrowed" a canoe from the Clatsops in return for some elk meat they had "borrowed" during the winter. Comowool, the Clatsop chief, evidently did not think it necessary to go through his trading routine with Lewis. He watched as Lewis looked over his canoes with the ornate prows. Later in the afternoon he stayed with Lewis, who was fishing with a couple of men, taking the line of first one and then another, while they took a look for better places to fish.

Lewis was thinking, Why doesn't he just tell us where the fish are and then go sit in the shade and let us fish? Actually he liked Comowool, had found him cleaner and easier to be around than some of the other chiefs at the various Chinook tribes. But his very liking was for some reason a source of irritation, as much toward himself as Chief Comowool.

The men were working their way back toward camp by the middle of the afternoon when the row of ten or twelve Clatsop canoes came into view along the bank just ahead. Lewis pulled in his line, walked past Comowool, and said to the others in English as casually as if he were commenting on the weather, "We'll take the middle-sized one, second from the left, in payment for the half an elk he and his men took a month back."

George Shannon paused to wipe his forehead, gazed out across the swampy land in the opposite direction from the canoes, and said, "I'd take that long-prowed black on the other side."

"I haven't had a chance to study them," Pete Wiser said. "Is that big red one any good?"

"Too big," Lewis told him. "We have to take it past some fast water on the way out of here. We need something small and maneuverable."

"I'll help you get it and have it well packed for the home stretch," Joe Whitehouse said.

They took delight in this game of mild revenge against the Clatsop chief who fished beside them. Lewis thought that the others probably found it sweeter than he did. How many times they had faced the language barrier when they were around the Chinooks and felt their shortcoming of not trying to learn the language, even the jargon! They discussed the merits of the canoes—which ones might be best for shallow water, which ones appeared to be watertight, which ones were most beautifully carved. Sometimes they looked at the string of canoes in order not to appear to avoid them. They enjoyed the sense of their own cleverness, the audacity, the hint of danger in it.

The next morning, Lewis went back to the same place and bought a canoe from Comowool with his gold-laced uniform coat, the long-prowed black canoe. Comowool briefly checked the outside of the canoe for cracks, then began to pull it away from the main string.

Lewis caught movement in the low brush above the bank and looked hard. Three men were coming on foot. He said to Comowool, "Looks like some others are coming here."

Comowool looked, frowning, then laughed and used jargon to talk with Lewis. "Yes, they are hunters from my village."

All three men came close and grinned in a friendly manner. One man's hair seemed to have oil on it to make the black hairs stick together and form stiff points at each shoulder blade. He said, "Good day to be breaking camp and heading up the river."

"Pretty good," Comowool said.

"What I wanted to see you about— How much is half a good elk worth? Maybe a small canoe?"

"Yes, about that."

"I guess the white chief can borrow that one." He pointed to the middle-sized canoe, second from the left.

"He knows you borrowed that elk meat."

"Well, he didn't make a fuss over it, so he must have known we had some hungry people in our camp."

It seemed as if they were trying to outdo one another at grinning.

Comowool asked, "Why do you stand there? Pull that canoe over against the first one I sold you."

Lewis began to grin. "All right. I'm much obliged. I'll borrow this canoe. You fellows are all right."

Comowool chuckled. "Move out!" he said to his three hunters. In a moment the three of them had departed through the trees.

Lewis was aware there had been a sense of comradeship and humor among the four Clatsops but that it was turned against him. He suspected that Comowool understood more English than he let on. Comowool started to follow his three men, then returned to Lewis, who was puffing as he pulled the borrowed canoe away from the others. The chief clicked his tongue, pointed to Lewis's head, and put his hands together in the shape of a wedge. With more hand signs and jargon he said, "Friend, you are not as backward as some I bargain against. So, then—I am surprised that you people do not put your heads against the board as the Chinooks do. It would improve your looks."

Lewis was startled and confused. Was this more native humor or was it actual criticism? He took a deep breath, rested a moment before replying, and gathered his thoughts. Of course, he had seen Chinook mothers with their babies strapped to a cradleboard covered with soft moss. Across each baby's forehead was a smooth slab of bark held on tightly by a leather band passing through both sides of the cradleboard. A grass pillow was under the back of the baby's neck for support. Sacajawea told him the practice was vile and pointed to an infant whose mother was collecting seaweed. The baby's eyes seemed to be about to pop out of his head from the extreme pressure of the flattening bark. Sacajawea told him that a baby was strapped in such a manner for the better part of his first year, thus causing the front of his skull to be flat and higher at the crown. She said, "The papoose cried when the mother cleaned him and quieted when the head lashing was again in place. Pagh! It is a practice for savages!"

Lewis cleared his throat, pointed to his own head, and said, "We might try it, if it improved our minds."

The chief's head bobbed up and down and his eyes twinkled in enjoyment of this competition of words. "How will you know until you try?"

When Lewis told Clark of the incident he said, "These natives are not slow-witted. They can even outsmart us white men at times!" They both laughed out loud.

On the day of departure, Captain Lewis gave Chief Comowool a certificate indicating the kindness and attention they had received. Then the captains made him a gift of the cabins and furniture in the fort as more substantial proof of their gratitude for his cooperation.[1]

Comcommoly, the one-eyed Chinook chief, was given a certificate along with Chillahlawil and several other important men of the tribe. The fat Chief Delashelwilt was given an "Indian Commission" to keep him peaceful. These papers were seven and one-half by twelve and one-half inches and filled out with the name of the man being honored.[2]

Just before leaving, Lewis posted a paper inside the officers' quarters, which read:

The object of this last, is, that through the medium of some civilized person, who may see the same, it may be made known to the world, that the party concisteing of the persons whose names are hereunto annexed, and who were sent out by the government of the United States to explore the interior of the continent of North America, did penetrate the same by way of Missouri and Columbia rivers, to the discharge of the latter into the Pacific Ocean, where they arrived on the 14th day of November, 1805, and departed on the 23rd of March, 1806, on their return to

*the United States, by the same route by which they
had come out.*[3]

Both captains had given up the idea of the expedition's returning by ship, even though they had carte
blanche letters of credit, the main reason being that
they sighted no ship during their stay on the west coast.[4]

Departure day was gray, dreary, and wet. Sacajawea
felt a lump in her throat when the canoes were loaded
and they took final leave of the fort at one o'clock. Her
head reeled as her canoe left shore and the water waved
beneath her. When she looked back, the fort had sunk
from sight beneath the low swell of the bay. She waved
to the Chinooks packed on the shoreline. She wanted
to weep.

For two days the dugouts tossed in wind from storms
that hovered over the land. Thunder roared around
them. Lightning struck on the hillsides and twice started
fires that quickly went out with the downpour of rain.
Then the wind died altogether and the waves quieted.
The unexpected silence deepened; the crashing of water
on the shore became the only sound, and a sense of
apprehension grew in Bratton's mind as he lay in the
bottom of a dugout, his back in great pain.

"What is it?" he asked. His voice seemed startlingly
loud without the wind to snatch it away.

"Another storm somewheres," Pryor said, and his
words, too, seemed loud. He spoke to Collins behind
him and then said, "See, there? Over the far point.
Drouillard and his men have found us a campsite. They
are beaching their canoe; let's follow."

Charbonneau was in Drouillard's canoe, dipping in
time with the movements of fish-oiled backs before him.
Sweat smarted in his eyes as he balanced on raw knees
and bruised toes, remembering how he had asked for
the poling job, saying if he had to have his share of
upstream work, he'd do his now while the water ran
wide and smooth. He readied himself to jump overboard
and help pull the canoe onto the shore. His palms were
gummy with sores from the paddling. While the other
canoes were pulled in, he let Sacajawea wrap his hands
with soft, pliant leather. "They will heal faster wrapped,"

he winced. "But until they are better, I cannot hold a paddle or pole."

Charbonneau woke the next morning and found he could not move without sharp pains; even his fingers were curled stiffly and felt like swollen growths.

Mosquitoes had plagued the expedition since the weather warmed, and a new rash of bites began to itch excruciatingly. Charbonneau scratched a chain of welts, staring about and waving peevishly at the clot of gnats whining around his head. Sacajawea sat beside him and wordlessly offered him a bladder of fish oil.

"I rub that on my hands and they will slip on the pole. I rub it on my back and I smell as vile as the rotten fish. You rub it on my aching shoulders." He picked his teeth with a twig.

"It is time to push on," she said, rubbing some of the soreness from his shoulders. "The canoes are ready to go. Some have already started along the bank on foot to hunt elk. Come, Chief Red Hair says you will paddle again."

"With these hands? I can't."

"*Ai*, you can with the leather protecting them. I promise you will feel nothing today."

He followed her numbly into one of the waiting canoes. She sat near the back with Pomp held between her knees.

On March 30, the campsite was on flat, green prairie where the hunting was good.[5] Trumpeter swans beeped over green patches of sedges, and flocks of brant made rolling, guttural honks that blended into a babble of noise that carried far into the distance.

Wood smoke from the evening fires of a Shahala village rose into a high dusky sky trail that lay above the western larch with its soft, short bundles of green needles. When the expedition settled around their own fire, the Shahalas came to inspect them. They were dusky brown and their bodies squat from sitting most of the days in the bottom of a canoe. The man who seemed to be their chief had his hair cut shorter than the others, ragged above his ears.

"*Katah mesika chaco?*" Lewis asked him in Chinook.

"*Halo, muckamuck*," said the man, shaking his head and rubbing his protruding belly. "Fish are gone, and there is nothing to eat, *muckamuck*. The salmon will not come until the next full moon."

"Do you hunt the deer and elk?" asked Lewis, again in Chinook.

This thickset chief chuckled with amusement. His people had no weapons for large game. They netted fish and made snares for only small animals.

For ten days the party camped near the Shahala village.[6] They needed meat for the mountain crossing. A dozen men went out to hunt the abundant game while the rest were kept busy cutting and hanging the meat on maple-stick racks over smoldering fires to dry.

With the leather bandaging off, Charbonneau rubbed the raw palms of both hands with fish oil. The flaps of dead skin were dry and horny. He stood beside Sacajawea, who was cutting meat into thin strips. "Shouldn't these flaps be cut off?"

She inspected his hands and seemed to hesitate a moment, then went to her leather pack and thrust around inside, coming out with a mat woven from cattails, which she placed on the ground for Charbonneau to sit on. She began paring off the flaps and some of the horny skin around the wounds on both palms with her butcher knife.

Charbonneau slipped off his moccasins. Sacajawea said, "The time to cut your toenails is during wet weather. Not a day like today." She began working on his toenails with the hunting knife. Sacajawea alternately wiped the knife on her skirt and dug at his toenails. Then she started on his fingernails. Charbonneau sat there mumbling now and again when she seemed to cut too close to the skin. "Damn *femme*, take it easy. I need toes and fingers."

Suddenly a noise rose above the camp and came toward them. Dogs jumped into view, barking deliriously. Children ran after them, laughing and squealing. The rest of the Shahala population came straight through the trees, singing and tramping over the blankets and gear stacked around the base of a large fir.

Charbonneau gazed, terror-struck, at the freshly yellow-painted faces. He stood up, and his knees trembled with an impulse to run; he felt Clark and York pressing against him.

"Sweet Jesus," York breathed. "If I didn't know they'se peaceful—"

Charbonneau crossed himself.

Clark shouted so close that Sacajawea's ears rang. "Whoa! Stop right there! Hold back!"

The Shahalas stopped. There was absolute silence. Then the chief with the short hair stepped forward and Sacajawea gasped. The man was weeping. The tears rolled down his expressionless features, along the furrows of skin that was freshly painted in white-and-yellow bands.

The women divided and moved behind Sacajawea. They all had yellow paint in their ears.

Clark put his hands on the bony shoulders of the chief, looked him in his gaunt face, then spoke to him about this sudden visit of all the tribe. Clark nodded, understanding, and rubbed his stomach, announcing loudly, "We will let this whole crowd eat with us. They have had nothing much for nearly two weeks and won't have anything much until the salmon move upstream for spawning in a month or so." He motioned for Sacajawea to cut off no more strips for drying, but to help York and Charbonneau set up spits to roast the remainder of the elk for the starving village.

There was a deafening clamor as the villagers scrambled up close to the roasting fire and pressed forward to sit in a tight circle, men first. Halfway through the meal, two other men wandered into the camp wearing nothing but cedar-bark breechclouts. No Shahala looked up to notice them, but continued to eat greedily. They rubbed their bellies and stood outside the circle, waiting patiently for someone to invite them to eat.

First Clark asked where they came from. *"Kah me-sika illahee?"*

"By the falls of the great river flowing into the Columbia from the south," answered one of the newcomers.

With a stick, the other drew the river in the sand. "Multnomah."

Lewis nudged Clark. "We saw no river in the south. What are they talking about, do you suppose?"

"Feed them; then I'll go with them," Clark suggested.

In the middle of the afternoon, Clark followed the

two men on a level stretch of land through which a
river wound out of sight between high, grassy banks.
They used a dugout canoe to come to the mouth of the
river, which had been so masked with islands that the
expedition had failed to see it. Clark walked inland with
the two men to a slough where many native women
were carrying long, slim canoes on their backs. The
women plunged, waist-deep, into the cold water, frightening up ducks and geese. They loosened wapato with
their toes. The bulbs rose to the surface and were tossed
into the small canoes.

Clark stopped at the village, called Clackamas, where
the two men lived. "Will you trade a basket of the wapato bulbs for these awls and fish gigs?" he asked, taking the awls and gigs from his pocket and placing them
on the ground before the two men.

The men shook their heads no. Then they explained
that the wapato was the only thing they had to keep
themselves from starving until the salmon came up
their river. Nothing was valuable enough to trade for
their wapato roots.

If Janey were with me, she'd dig in with her brown
toes same as these women, thought Clark. She'd keep
our camp supplied with these roots. Then he had another thought. He looked around and saw that the
women had stacked much of the wapato to one side, as
though they were stockpiling it. To Clark that meant
they would not starve if they sold him a couple of baskets of the roots. He took out a piece of artillery fuse
from the leather pouch hanging on his belt.[7] He dropped
it into the fire outside the nearest bark lodge. Then he
took out his pocket compass and a small magnet and
sat himself down on a rush mat. The fuse blazed up
into a bright red flame as he made his compass needle
follow the movements of his magnet very quickly. The
people were astonished with the magic he held in his
hands. Some who watched were actually terrified and
ran to their lodges crying, *"Meschie! Meschie!* Big medicine!"

Some of the women began piling several baskets of
wapato at Clark's feet. They begged him to put away
the pieces in his hand and put out the terrible red fire.
Clark assured them he would do this right away, and

almost immediately the portmatch was exhausted. He put the compass and magnet in his pocket. Then he paused to shake his head in thanks for the roots and to light his pipe from a burning stick. Before smoking the dried willow bark, Clark moved the pipe as if sending bits of the smoke to the sky and the earth and the four winds. He drew four acrid puffs and passed the pipe to the men. They smoked and talked in low tones. Clark shoved the awls and fishing gigs toward the women; then he turned and walked away, carrying a basket of roots. The two men who had brought him to their village picked up a basket apiece and carried them out to the canoe beyond the slough. The people of the village had turned and were chanting something in unison as they left the bank.

"What are your people saying?" Clark asked.

"Oh, they repeat a legend, as old as many grandfathers, that says a great chief will come to lead them to a land of feasting and plenty. They wonder if you are that chief. They looked closely and saw plainly that your face is brown like theirs. The legend says the man is white on his face, like the fine beach sand."

Amused with the superstitious legend, Clark impulsively rolled up his sleeve, and the two men stared at the whiteness of his skin. When they beached the canoes, the men indicated they would also carry the basket Clark had and the pack on his back. They insisted, waiting patiently for him to pull it off. Clark bent to drink from a small spring. The men waited with an agreeable unconcern about time. They did not drink.

"You don't believe that legend about a white chief, do you?" Clark asked finally.

"What is there to believe? The legend is old. The white chief must have died long ago on his way to our village. He looked, but he could not find us."

Two days later, Clark took seven of his men and two of their canoes to explore the Multnomah River once more.[8] At one view they could see five snow peaks. Clark took soundings in the uniform flow of the river. "There seems to be water enough for a good-sized ship," he said. "And I feel certain it could supply fresh water far down the southern Pacific Coast." He measured at least two-thirds of the width and could find no bottom with his five-fathom line.[9]

Clark and his men examined the low-growing plants, the mullein, hawkweed, tansy, yarrow, thistle, butter-and-eggs; the soil, black humus; the bushes, vine-maple that grew low at the edge of the wood with a pinwheel leaf; the timber, one-hundred-foot-high incense cedars, a yew with long, spreading branches, glossy dark top, and deep yellow-green on the underside, white oak, dog-wood, red alder, Oregon myrtle. They measured a white fir that had fallen and found it to be three hundred and eighteen feet tall.

Two days later in camp, Clark sat on his haunches watching Pomp sniff wild rose blossoms and told Sac-ajawea of several empty villages he and the other men had found while they examined the inlet on the south side of the Columbia. "The lodges were not entirely empty. Inside was furniture, sleeping pallets. Actually, everything was left as if the people were coming back in a few moments. Yet everything was quiet. There were no dogs, no old people left behind. There were grinding mortars and pestles, canoes by the doors and along the beach, mats, bladders of fish oil, baskets, bowls, trenchers—all undisturbed. The fires were dead ashes. Where are those people?"

"Where?" she asked.

"They all went to the Clackamas village to wait for the coming of salmon." Clark winked.

She made a face. "More fish? Are you going to follow them?"

"Who said I wanted to net stinking salmon? I'd rather the men hunted elk and you stripped out the meat and dried it for us."

Again she felt the familiar pang that took her breath away, and she longed to put new moccasins on his feet and bring him food. However, she was sure that he would never bring his thoughts out into the open be-cause she was Charbonneau's squaw. She also knew that she was expected to suppress her feeling and never let it come to the surface again.

That Frenchman will never appreciate her, thought Clark as he turned to smile at her. "Janey, tell me—"

"Ai?" she asked faintly, keeping her face away from

him, and the spirit of her voice was as quiet as a deep
river that lets no storm raise foam upon it.

He shifted his feet on the rocky ground and said,
"Today my men and I rounded the Old Warrior's Point
and went up a well-worn trail to an old village. The
Multnomahs lived there. Their lodges have fallen to
the ground, and there is no sign of the Multnomahs
anywhere. Where did they go?"

She looked at him with laughter in her soft brown
eyes. "They went to the Clackamas village to wait for
the coming of salmon?"

"No." He shook his head but noticed how beautiful
she had become. He thought, That full, rich Shoshoni
womanhood is striking. "It was something else. Some
unknown thing. There is no longer a tribe called Multnomah, only the river."

She did not answer immediately. She spread her
hands out. "*Muckamuck*, nothing, but rotting lodges?"

"*Muckamuck*," Clark answered.

Now her face was a mask. "I will find out."

She moved among the bark huts of the Shahalas,
watching the women and children in the mud from the
afternoon drizzle. Where she could, she walked on grass.
The leaves of the alders dripped water. The smoke of
the village hung like a fog around the tops of the huts
and among the upper branches of the trees. The camp
smelled soggy.

Two women were pulling their drying rack and
grinding equipment under the shelter of a broad awning of patched leather in front of their hut. The women
squatted in the doorway and surveyed the area under
their shelter. Both wore long fringed skirts suspended
from the waist down past the knees. These garments
were made of the inner rind of cedar bark, twisted into
threads which hung loose, and flapped and twisted with
each body motion, and giving the women a kind of duck's
waddle.

A new flurry of rain began, and Sacajawea took it
as an excuse to walk over and take refuge under the
awning. She asked, "Is it all right for me to stand here?"

The women grunted.

"I'd like to ask something."

"I don't have any roots to trade," said one woman with wisps of tousled hair poking out of her grass hat.

"No, I do not want to trade for food."

The women looked at her with black, suspicious eyes. "What did you want to talk about?" asked the other woman, who had badly decayed front teeth.

"Well, it seems that I have a lot of questions about women's medicine. You see, the white men know nothing about how a woman feels or what is best to keep her well."

The women shook their heads slowly. The one with bad teeth said, "Men! We know how that is. What society do you belong to?"

"Society? I am Shoshoni, that's all."

The woman laughed and said, "Oh, if young people would only listen to their elders these days. If they would listen to those with more experience, they could learn something."

The woman with the hat went into the hut and came out shortly with a red-hot coal held between two sticks. She dropped the coal in a small fire pit dug in the center of the sheltered area. The butt of a dead limb extended into the hole; the coal sent a little puff of smoke out, and two thin yellow flames licked over the wood. Sacajawea held her hands outstretched over the faint warmth. Since she was wet, the fire felt good.

"I guess there's plenty that women like you would know that someone like me doesn't. About the old tribes. What they did. Where they went. What their women did about cramps."

The woman with the hat went back into the hut and came out with three mats of woven grass, which she placed on the ground around the fire pit; she sat upon one, cross-legged. The other woman sat, and Sacajawea could see that they were willing to talk. She asked, "What can you tell me?"

"Well," said the woman with bad teeth, "first you get in a woman's society. If you don't already belong to one, you have to start at the bottom. The Red Salmon society teaches you how to dance in the right way and what foods to avoid so you won't suffer cramps. And my advice for that is plenty of hard work; stand up, sit down, stand up, sit down, bend, straighten, bend, straighten, and you feel no cramps."

"So—don't forget," said the woman with the hat, "the members of the Red Salmon learn how to lure the fish up small streams close to the village. Many women belong to these societies. Societies are not just for men. When you belong, you have to be able to plunge your arms in boiling water and complain that it is cold. Could you do that?"

"Why is that?"

The woman with the hat looked at Sacajawea as if she thought she was deliberately slow-witted. "Because it shows you are a person who can take hardship and still not call it hard." The woman snorted. "You don't know much. I can easily see that living with only men has not done you much good."

Sacajawea wondered if she could point her questions in the right direction without arousing suspicion or antagonism. She was the newcomer, the person who was different, and she was smart enough to know newcomers were never well accepted at first. "Have the women of your tribe always worn these easy-to-make, one-piece skirts?"

The woman with the conical, woven-grass hat bent forward. "You can see we sew well. Your eyes are sharp anyway."

Sacajawea thought that the skirt only deserved praise for its simplicity. "I can see that on a quiet day those threads hang in place until you move or walk, but in a breeze you cannot be covered by much, and in a hard wind—*kiyi*—if it is the month of snow, the place where your legs come together will suffer frostbite. Could you weave the threads in a solid piece?" As soon as she had finished she was sorry. Her words were wrong. She looked from one woman to the next. Her neck and face felt warm. "I am only asking you to help me understand your customs," she said weakly.

"We can tell you need plenty of help. For your information, in the month of the shoulder moon we have blankets to wear that are woven from dogs' wool. It takes five or six good dogs. A matting of bark threads is for canoe sails."

"Shoulder moon?"

"Shoulder-to-shoulder around the warm fire."

"Uumm," said Sacajawea, wondering how to go on using her limited Chinook jargon. "What do you eat—besides salmon?" She used hand signs as she spoke.

"Are you hungry?" asked the woman with the rotting teeth. "Would you like to gamble for something to eat? Dried salmon, boiled crab or clam? Some fresh fish oil? A box of smoked pigeon breast?" The woman got up and with her ducklike gait went inside the closest hut. It was built of split cedar planks set on end. The roof was gabled and supported by posts and covered by overlapping boards. She came out holding a red, square-cornered, cedar box. She pointed to the box, then pointed to the moccasins Sacajawea wore.

Sacajawea took the box. She had never seen anything like it. The thin cedar boards, when thoroughly wet from steaming, had been bent around partial cuts, and the box was tight enough to hold even liquids. The corners were sewn with fibers, and the lid was decorated with inlaid shells. "*Skookumchuck!* Something good!" Sacajawea decided to say only complimentary things.

Both women nodded. The one with the bad teeth said, "Inside is much fish oil. Oil can be used to flavor fruit, or to rub on your face, all over, and in your hair. Keeps you young. Now you give me moccasins. You gamble nothing else."

"You want to trade—make a bargain?" asked Sacajawea.

"Gamble, bargain, trade—*ai.*"

Sacajawea shifted her weight on the mat and saw that the woman with the bad teeth shone with oil from her greasy hair to her shiny feet, which were bare. The woman with the umbrellalike hat wore moccasins with thick, ugly leather soles and tightly woven grass tops.

"Good medicine too," said the woman, reaching for Sacajawea's moccasins, which were soft, buff elkskin.

"Medicine?" asked Sacajawea. "The same oil used by the ancients? The Multnomahs?" She looked under the lid and found a yellowed bag of transparent gut, tied with stiff sinew to keep the oil from exposure to air, so it would not become rancid right away. She pulled her moccasined feet up under her tunic, pretending she wanted more time to talk before deciding on the gamble. "What happened to them?"

The woman with the hat opened and shut one fist in the air several times, rapidly. "You ask more questions than can be answered. The words in your mind mill around like salmon before jumping up white water to spawn. Is that what you learn from all those pale eyes you are with?"

Sacajawea bit her lip and looked from one woman to the next. "I just want to learn about your ways."

The woman with the hat picked up a stick and threw it at a scruffy dog who was sniffing around the drying rack. "Well—it is no secret that the Multnomahs gambled with men whose faces resembled the brown bear. Those people learned to depend on the gambling between themselves and these strangers. They were nothing until the big canoes came in sight and those men came ashore. They stopped attending the yearly salmon festivals or the horse fairs for their gambling. Then the strangers laughed at their important rituals and made them learn their tongue. They became nothing. But they thought the strangers made them more important than all of us—"

The woman with the bad teeth interrupted, "At least you and those men you are with try to speak our tongue. That is in your favor." She spat in the fire and smiled at Sacajawea when it sizzled. "My people speak the language of the strangers, but it means nothing."[10]

The other woman continued. "Those white men came to their village on floating lodges and stayed. They made their homes there and tried to get the Multnomahs to behave like they did. This was all long ago. The white men tried to break all the societies and set up something new. The Multnomahs hid, then practiced their personal medicine and held their society rites, anyway. They showed those foreigners every hospitality. But in time they learned those men were nothing. They were *tilikum*, common people." She spat in the fire.

The woman with the bad teeth said, "They were not real chiefs, like the ones you travel with." She squinted into the fire that had blazed up. "Yet you can never be too sure. Best to take every precaution and be on the lookout for anything not just right. The Multnomahs made that mistake. If they were here, they could tell you plenty of advice along that line; they learned it all the hard way. If the slightest hint of any sickness, especially *ahn-cutty*, comes your way, duck into the nearest sweat lodge, then dive into the cold water. That washes out your system. The Multnomahs just lay around their lodges until it took them away."

"Where? Where did they all go?"

Both women grunted at the same time.

"You are dumber than I thought," said the woman with the bad teeth. "They died of *ahn-cutty*." She pecked her face and arms with one finger. "The white men brought it to them. That was the fine gift they brought and gave to the Multnomahs in return for friendship." She spat into the fire.

"They were all sick?"

"Everyone—young, old, men, women, fat and thin. Everyone, except the white men who were *tilikum*, and left when they realized there were no people to take their orders or follow their commands. I will say one thing, though, the white men put all the bodies in canoes, stacked one on top of another, and let them float in the bog away from the village. I believe that was the only desire of the Multnomahs those men carried out. I'm too young to remember. But their history is passed on along the river. They were a kind, good-hearted people, long ago."

Suddenly it occurred to Sacajawea that she had been gone a long time and she probably had all the useful information she needed. She rose and said, "I enjoyed talking. I have to go now."

"If you ever want to join the first woman's society, I will sell you a membership in the Red Salmon. You could stay right here with us. There is usually plenty of work to keep you busy," said the woman with the hat.

Sacajawea slipped out of her moccasins and handed them to her and pulled the sewing awl from her blanket and handed it to the woman with the bad teeth. "Thank you," she said and walked out into the rain. She hoped she had learned enough to satisfy the curiosity of Chief Red Hair.

That evening, Clark stared at the sodden sky. He

had hunted most of the day and was so tired he did not want to move. He ruminated vaguely on the difference between his weariness and Sacajawea's liveliness. I drop in my tracks, he thought, and she sighs and continues to hunt for edible roots. Then in vexed admiration he saw her coming toward him, her feet hardly distinguishable because of the mud on them and on her legs. She sat with her legs folded in front. She did not say anything for some moments, then, *"Ahn-cutty.* The whole Multnomah village died, long ago."

Clark sat up.

"Smallpox. I talked with two old women while you hunted today. One showed me deep pits on her own face and said, *'Ahn-cutty.'"*

While she told her story, Clark noticed that she had a feather ornament knotted in her hair. He felt a warm glow he had not experienced until she came into his life. He dragged a piece of driftwood to some dry sand by the cook fire and settled against it.

Sacajawea moved with him. She hugged her muddy knees and waited with growing confidence for some expression of his satisfaction, feeling that the moment would last forever in her memory. She picked her teeth with a splinter and spat in the fire; yet she did not offend him. She met Clark's gaze and stared back with the remote peacefulness of an animal.

The next day she and some others traded their seats in the canoes to those with weary feet. She carried Pomp on her back in a thin blanket. They walked on a trail beaten leafless, which wound about, considering only the shortest way between boulders and broken cliffs. They kept to the bank of the river, which seemed to cascade from pool to pool or splashed over rock-strewn rapids. The woods receded around a succession of small fields. As the hours wore on, Sacajawea noticed that Clark always waved to the natives they passed. He talked with his men, and laughter surrounded him. It was a desire for friendly contact with him. She watched him gesticulating, wiping sweat from his face with the sleeve of his leather shirt, hitching his belt, emptying his moccasins, stretching out on his back with arms spread in the grass. He enjoyed everything.

Charbonneau's feet were hot in a short time, his shirt stuck to his skin, and his hair was tousled.

After three miles of dense green timber, of pines and spruces, the trees began to stand apart in groves or small irregular groups. They found sugar pines and tasted the sugary pitch that exudes from the heartwood when wounds are made by ax or fire. The pitch comes out in kernels, crowded together like white pearl beads. Charbonneau ate considerable and was the first to learn of its laxative properties. By late afternoon they were back down to the grassy banks of the river. Charbonneau's legs were weary and achy, and his shoulders drooped with fatigue.

The canoes were already pulled up on shore. The mosquitoes were an intolerable agony. Lewis groaned aloud when he could no longer refrain from baring his naked hindquarters close to the ground, where the mosquitoes were a black layer of piercing needles.

Charbonneau was tired enough to fall and simply lie on the ground. The mosquitoes invaded his reasoning so that the most thoughtless, necessary action was torture. He slid down the embankment as if he had orders to do so, and placed one foot into a canoe. He knew that it was only on the water that he could find rest from the insects, somehow, while working.

"Is this my canoe?" he called to Cruzatte, who was already kneeling in the middle.

"Sure. We'll go only a short distance before finding a campsite for this night."

Charbonneau was cautious about shifting his weight, and he had barely knelt in the canoe when it lurched unsteadily, moving off the shore. The next canoe, led by Lewis, was already being paddled upstream.

A sigh escaped Charbonneau; he did not know whether it was for his misery or contentment.

With the first strokes of the paddle, the agony of the land suddenly became a wilderness through which he sped in the canoe at will. It was even strange that nothing hindered his escape. He simply knelt in the bottom and departed.

With dizzy elation he began to sing a voyageur's chant as he paddled against the current. Muddy water swirled through bushes on the low banks. The ground

was black, the pines and hemlocks stood out among
naked trunks, but the top of the forest was a filmy cloud
of opening buds. Patches of snow glinted in the light.

The hardships of winter showed in Charbonneau. He
was lean and his muscles tougher. He gazed at the
budding hazelnut trees, and at the violets and fern-tufts
on the rocks lower down. He paddled in time, remembering the blisters, aching tendons and cramping joints.

At first paddling upstream relieved his tired feet.
Then he glanced up and saw the rain clouds gathering.
The wind was channeling along the river blowing the
rain that came fast into a spray. The canoes moved to
the shelter of dell copses and large trees where everyone
caught their breath. Charbonneau's shoulders and neck
were loose with the work. The river, already bank full
from snow melt, slowly spread out over its banks, covering sand flats and meadows. The alders and willows
were bent against the current. Within minutes the storm
was in full bloom. The men stayed close to the bank,
shoved their paddles inside the canoe, and stood to pole
against the sand, which often gave way in a mad swirl
of eddying water. Charbonneau said he could see only
new misery every hour, and was there not anyone who
remembered that they were only going a short way?

Several times he opened his mouth to shout at Cruzatte, but the bent figure, poling evenly, gave such an
appearance of obliviousness to the surroundings that
he choked the words down in a rage. They went on over
the smooth water where the rain danced.

Toward evening, they pulled up under a looming
cliff. There was just room to pull up the dugouts on a
strip of beach, and Charbonneau stood in the water
while the others unloaded; then he crawled under one
of the overturned dugouts. Lewis distributed dried meat.
Charbonneau chewed unhappily.

They sat quietly, waiting for those coming on foot to
catch up. Ordway spread some fir branches on the ground
and after a time started a smoky fire. Charbonneau sat
shivering now in his drenched clothes.

"Hey, Frenchy," called Collins. "It ain't so cold if you
come do a little work." He was chopping down a small
tree for dry firewood.

"Hey, down there!" called Clark. "We are all here

but Charbonneau. I have two men out looking for him along the driftwood a mile or so back."

"Bring your men here where it is dry!" called Lewis. "Your man Charbonneau is with us. Rode in the dugout all afternoon. Thought you sent him."

A breeze stirred, mixing with the mutter of the river. "Damn," sighed Clark, at the same time firing his rifle as a signal to his men. He scrambled down under the cliff, growling at Charbonneau, who feigned sleep.

They made camp and hunted for two days. Sacajawea watched her man relaxed and indolent. She said nothing to him. Lewis came in with an otter and two porcupines the last night under the cliff. The men gathered by the fire, where York boiled fish. York stirred the pot with a stick, and built a spit for the small game.

In the morning, they were moving up the wide river in the first grayness of dawn. A cool breeze came up, but there was no rain. By evening, the balmy weather had changed. A cold wind circled the shores and their cook fire roared fitfully, shooting sparks. The men built shelters with huge pine branches. Just before nightfall, a black cloud appeared to the south and spread across the sky. It was a flock of migrating birds, and everyone stared in disbelief as it broke into pieces overhead and the parts fell toward the earth, just out of sight up the river. In the gray dawn next morning, they poled slowly along the shore and came on the ducks in a reedy bay.

By April 7, there was enough dried meat and salmon to carry the expedition safely back to the Nez Percé country. The men began to look around for a village where they could find at least a dozen packhorses to use during portage and to carry Bratton, who still could not walk, around the Narrows and Celilo Falls. They had very little to trade for horses, and the natives wanted eye dags, which were a kind of war hatchet. The expedition had no eye dags, and all the blacksmithing equipment was on the other side of the Divide in a cache.

The cold rain clouds seemed to dissolve.

One night the men watched Skillute fishing canoes move slowly across the water by the light of pine torches. Clark and Charbonneau had not talked together since the afternoon Charbonneau had climbed into the canoe to rest his feet. Now they watched the spectacle of the black smoking lights side by side, brooding silently. Charbonneau was tired from the long days of poling and stretched on an elbow near the fire where he could not see Clark, sitting near his head. "I will make roast of the porcupine tomorrow," he remarked, suddenly bored with the strain between them.

"I got two beaver today you can use," Clark replied at once.

"Wagh, they would be better used to buy horses," suggested Charbonneau. "The Skillutes have some—I have seen."

Clark flung a piece of wood into the fire, wishing he could be sure Charbonneau spoke the truth. But to his surprise, he realized that his emotions were a mere echo out of the past months, more than an expression of his present feelings. He did not know how he considered Charbonneau at this moment—the fact that he himself had not seen the Skillutes' horses was puzzling. Truthfully, this complaining, bragging squawman had a keen knowledge of the land and the inhabitants and the signs they left. He was actually better able to care for himself than he appeared. Clark turned to face the river. The fishermen were coming in, their shadows vague and monstrous as the torches waved. They pulled up the canoes and their low talking was clear in the quiet camp. Only their dogs whimpered and yelped. The Skillutes who carried torches stayed for a moment by the shore, bending to look at their reflections in the inky mirror. Then they quenched the flames and drifted silently downriver to their own village. Clark answered their greetings without moving. The stars glimmered faintly on the black water.

Charbonneau rolled up in his blanket and abruptly fell asleep.

When Clark awoke in the misty dawn, Charbonneau was helping York build a fire from the coals under the ashes. Clark watched them a moment, silently.

"Good day," Charbonneau said unexpectedly, glancing up with a smile. "Meager comforts to this life."

Clark stretched, then stood up shuddering. He walked along the shore a short distance, relieved himself, and came back, scratching his head and yawning violently, to stand close to the flames with outstretched hands. He felt rested and looked about at the others packing their blankets, getting ready to move out.

"Not so fast!" he called to them. "Take time for some jerky this morning! I'm going to take a look around the Skillute camp and possibly dicker over a couple of horses there."

"No horses at that village," said Shields, brushing insects and cobwebs from his hair. "I just wandered through the woods in that direction and didn't see anything but those flimsy bark canoes."

"Well, maybe they don't want us to know about their horses," said Clark quietly. "I heard they have some. I want packsaddles made when I return."

Charbonneau looked up from the fire, his face warm and red under the dark whiskers, but he said nothing.

Lewis began to call out names for hunting that morning.

Clark dickered for the rest of the day with the chief of the Skillutes for a couple of horses. The squaws fed Clark boiled onions, and still they could not come to terms on the horses. The men wanted more fish hooks. When they were put with the bundle of other things, the men nodded and said with signs that the horses were all in a valley where the women were gathering roots. They would send out and bring in horses the next day. Then the men began to ask for articles Clark did not have. They looked through the bundle of articles he had brought and complained it was not half enough for two of their fine horses. Clark could think of nothing to do but return to his camp. Then he noticed something he had not seen before. He bent to examine the deep, running sores on the left leg of the chief where a bear had pawed him several weeks before. Clark indicated he was something of a medicine man and would like to dress the wounds. The chief's face brightened, and he stretched out his leg. When Clark was finished, one of the chief's squaws complained of a sore back. Clark rubbed a little camphor on her temples and back and placed a warmed piece of flannel over her shoulders.

"I have not felt so well in many seasons," she said, smiling broadly. "I will give you two horses."

That afternoon, Charbonneau went to the village

with Frazier and returned with a good mare for which he had given his belt, some elk's teeth and a packet of paints.

But the following morning, the chief and several bucks came back holding out a bundle with all the articles used to purchase the horses. They wanted to return the purchase price and get their horses back. This was an acceptable practice among the natives. Charbonneau stepped forward, removed his woolen shirt, and gave it to the chief for the horse he was riding. The Skillutes asked for more woolen shirts and brought in more horses to trade.

That night, Charbonneau neglected to hobble his horses and lost one because it wandered off.[11]

On April 22, Charbonneau's other horse became frightened with an elk-hide saddle and wool robe on his back and ran full-speed down a hill, leaving Charbonneau wheezing behind on the trail. Near an Indian village the horse threw off the saddle and blanket. An alert Indian hid the blanket in his hut.

Lewis sent Charbonneau to overtake the horse and baggage. He gathered up the baggage and found the saddle in the village, but not the blanket.

Sacajawea had seen the Indian skulk off with it, and she told Lewis she would find it. "The blanket keeps my child warm at night."

Lewis turned to Clark. "Those pirates better deliver that blanket or I'll burn their damned, flea-infested huts. I've had enough thieving. I'll not forgive them the time their cousins, several villages back, tried to keep old Scannon for their camp dog."

While they were swearing at the Indians, Sacajawea was getting the blanket. She told a squaw in the hut where she saw the man take it that her baby was blue with cold. She let the squaw hold Pomp while she searched for the blanket. She found it under a pile of rush mats, and the squaw seemed pleased and smiled. She let Sacajawea hold her papoose, who had a runny nose and sores on his face and shoulders. Sacajawea was happy to take back Pomp and the blanket.

"My papoose is the most handsome," she told Clark.

On the twenty-fourth, Lewis decided that the canoes were of no more use as the river was getting narrower

and the large boulders and swift water much too frequent. Lewis asked some river Indians if they would
exchange horses for the canoes. The Indians shook their
heads no. Instead, they held out strands of colored beads,
the same the expedition had traded for salmon the year
before, and indicated they would trade beads for the
canoes.

"We want horses," said Drouillard in Chinook.

"I do not think they will trade their horses at all,"
said Sacajawea quietly behind Drouillard. "Maybe so,
then, you take their beads and give them the canoes.
You can use the beads later in trading. Take the beads."

Drouillard turned and scowled at Sacajawea. Her
fine tanned tunic was worn and grease-stained. She
held her back straight and looked directly at him. In a
moment he decided she was right. He reached for the
beads. Sacajawea barely seemed to move, yet she was
standing in front of him putting out her hand, indicating that two strands of beads were not enough for the
two well-made canoes. An old squaw with an opaque
film over one eye added several more strands to the pile
in Drouillard's hand. Sacajawea made a low grunt inside her throat and stepped closer to the canoes. A large
buck pulled a strand of blue beads from his neck, and
several other men followed his gesture. Sacajawea nodded, but her face remained impassive. There was a pile
of beads at Drouillard's feet now. She walked around
it once, examining it slowly. The expedition men stood
in quiet wonder. A squaw added some bright pink seashells on a long thong. Sacajawea looked up and smiled
at the Indians. She placed her palms together and held
her hands under her chin.

She looks like a child praying, thought Clark, looking around at the incongruous situation.

The Indians smiled in return and seemed highly
pleased with the canoes. They were pushed into the
water and floated downriver faster and faster.

Drouillard was overwhelmed by the actions of Sacajawea. That evening around the fire he told Clark,
"She does not speak to me often, but when she does,
she is eloquent."

They stored the beads in a leather pouch and tied it
to the pack on a pinto pony.

CHAPTER

30

The Sick Papoose

Clark's Journal:

Thursday 22nd May 1806

Shabonos son a small child is dangerously ill. his jaw and throat is much swelled. we apply a poltice of onions, after giveing him some creem of tartar etc. this day proved to be fine and fair which afforded us an oppertunety of drying our baggage which had got a little wet.

Tuesday 27th May 1806

Shabono's child is much better today; tho' the swelling on the side of his neck I believe will termonate in an ugly imposthume, [1] a little below the ear.

R. G. THWAITES, ed., *The Original Journals of the Lewis and Clark Expedition 1804–1806*, Vol. 5. New York: Dodd, Mead and Co., 1904–5. Reprinted by Arno Press, N.Y., 1969, pp. 57–8, 72.

The gear and baggage were now carried by horses. Bratton, still not able to walk well, and several others with bad stone bruises on their feet, rode the few horses the expedition had. The rest walked. The stones along the river's edge were hard, and the sand between was soft. This caused aching feet and legs. Sacajawea took Pomp to the water for a bath one evening and found York bathing his aching feet.

"My feet is plumb worn down to my legs," he said. "Janey, we'se on our ways home. We'se homeward bound."

"*Ai.*" More and more she heard the word "home" in the men's conversation. "Home." They said the word tenderly, as though they had good memories to go back to. Sacajawea dried Pomp with soft doeskin and hugged him close in her arms. This was "home" to her—the best home she had known since she was a tiny girl. She slipped from her moccasins and eased her own bruised feet into the cool water.

"This little fella will sure have a lot to tell his little friends."

"Will he remember?"

"Naw, not rightly. But you and I will. Some men would give a whole lot to have been on this here trip. I wouldn't mind staying with some of the natives we seen. For instance, those Nez Percés or even your Shoshonis and them Mandans."

Sacajawea smiled. "You would miss home."

"Home—that's where the heart is. Say, this stream is mortal cold, ain't it?"

She saw that he had on only a torn leather shirt and short leggings.

"I have a robe if you want it."

"Thank you just the same, Janey," he said. He chuckled a little sadly. "It takes all my hands to cook supper, and I never did learn the knack of keeping a robe held on."

"You will learn if you become chief of some tribe," she teased.

616

"I never thought of that." He chuckled to himself. "You'se got a way of teasing that makes it easy to take."

She left her moccasins and ran to the camp bouncing Pomp on her hip. She rummaged through her bundle of clothing, then sat Pomp on a leather robe and ran back to where York was pulling his feet from the water and letting them dry off on a rock.

"Here." She held a blue two-point blanket out to him. "I would rather have a lighter robe. This is too warm for me."

"I'm all used to the cold now, and you'll catch your death not wearing something on your shoulders." He was shivering and wanted the blanket. His blanket had long ago been traded for the favors of some pretty squaw to keep him warm one night.

Sacajawea wrapped the blanket around his shoulders. He protested, but she talked cheerfully and he let her put it on him.

"Sure's a fine blanket," he said happily. "I'll learn to hold it on and cook at the same time. I'm getting warmed up a mite. You really think I could be a chief?"

"*Ai.*"

"I've argued that with myself, but it don't help the feeling I owe Master Clark my services. If he set me free, then I'll be an Indian chief. I'll be like something you never knew." He said it as if he were joking. "I'll be a black man that's looked up to and leads his people to prosperity."

"The Great Spirit will look at you pleased," she said, wondering if he were still joking or a little serious.

"God is in us, Janey," he said seriously. "He works through us."

She'd miss Ben York when this trail came to an end. Sadly, she slipped on her moccasins.

On April 27, the expedition met Yellept, chief of the Walla Wallas, waiting in the green hills, wrapped in the United States flag Lewis had given him.

"Come to my village for food and horses," he said, happy to see these white men once again.

The expedition was happy to see Yellept and his people at the mouth of the Walla Walla River. The squaws began to unpack the horses and sort out cooking pots. Sacajawea tried to catch up to them, but the streaming of squaws, dogs, and children forced her back. She stumbled up beside Clark, whose pack had been snatched off his back.

"These people don't know what stealing is," Clark said encouragingly, waving his hairy arm. "Not like Chinooks. We'll get everything back."

"I wasn't worried," Sacajawea shouted back.

Chief Yellept brought the first armful of wood for the cook fires as the women cut up mullets for the kettles. Several bucks brought in four dogs for the feast.

Clark and Sacajawea gorged themselves on the mullets, then laughed at each other, remembering their vow not to eat any more stinking fish. But under no circumstances would either eat the dog meat.

Sacajawea wondered why these Walla Wallas were willing to exhaust their own food supply, even their wood and clothing, in a day or two of feasting, never replenishing the stock until they were shivering and hungry again. Was it a sense of sport, a contest against fate and each other? Or was it simply laziness? She did not extend her thinking beyond the mountains to her people or any of the other tribes she'd been with. She'd just now noticed this fact of Indian living.

In that village there was a captive Shoshoni woman. The captive and Sacajawea were invited to a council. The captains explained who they were and the object of their journey. The prisoner translated the words given her in Shoshoni by Sacajawea into the Walla Walla tongue. The woman was short and fat and wore nothing more than a long leather dress with no sleeves and the sides open. The dress was held together with a woven grass belt. She was highly honored by being invited to a council, and she felt that Sacajawea had reached a height of esteem never before dreamed of by women. She believed that the great medicine of these white men had been transferred to Sacajawea, making her something great, not only to the white men but to all Indian nations as well.

Sacajawea showed Clark an infected slash made by the captive woman's digging knife as she dug roots. "I'll clean it and dress it with linen strips soaked in borax water," promised Clark.

The woman excitedly told Chief Yellept about the healing powers of the white chief.

"Opposite our village is a short route to the Kooskooskee."[2] The chief waved his arms in gratitude for the white chiefs. "A road of grass and water and plenty of game."

Clark estimated that this cutoff would actually save eighty miles if they left the rest of the canoes behind, detoured the Celilo Falls, and traveled on the high land above the canyon.

"But don't leave yet," begged Chief Yellept. "Stay a little longer." He had sent out invitations to the Yakimas, the Cayuses, and the Salish. The healing power of the white chiefs was talked about all along the rivers. The lame, sick, and blind began to press around the expedition's camp. The number of unfortunates was prodigious, reminders of Indian battles, hunts, neglect, damp weather, and exposure to the constant blowing of fine sand.

Clark was the physician, and Sacajawea the nurse. They distributed solutions of lead and zinc salts, eyewash, splinted broken bones, gave out emetic pills, and used sulfur ointment for skin ulcers. They employed camphor liniment and quick massaging to relieve rheumatism.

In gratitude Chief Yellept offered a beautiful white horse in trade for a single blackened cooking kettle one of the women had not returned to the camp.

"This here is the only large kettle with no hole in its bottom," said York. "If this goes, we can cook like the Indians in grass baskets."

Clark looked at York and gave him the beat-up kettle. "If you like it that much, keep it," he said.

Then Clark gave the bewildered Yellept his sword, together with one hundred bullets and some powder for an old musket Yellept had and some pieces of red ribbon for his squaws.

That evening the Walla Wallas formed a half circle around the white men and watched them dance. Cruzatte brought out his violin, and York sang some songs in Chinook that tickled the Walla Wallas so much that they rolled on the ground holding their sides as they laughed.

Yellept hung his new sword at his side and danced around the ring.[3]

The next day, following their chief's example, two minor chiefs gave a horse apiece in return for medals, pistols, and ammunition.

Lewis wrote in his journal: "I think we can justly affirm to the honor of these people that they are the most hospitable, honest, and sincere people that we have met with in our voyage."

For three beautiful days the expedition traveled through new grass beside small streams. It was so warm that most of the men were stripped to the waist, tying coats and shirts in a bundle on the horses. Yet the nights were still and cold, with stars that shimmered brilliantly.

On May 7, Red Robe, the brother of the Nez Percé chief, Twisted Hair, visited the expedition and took them to a large lodge housing six families. Lewis invited all six families to accompany him back to his camp for a dinner of horse beef. One of the men of the lodge brought along two canisters of powder, which he claimed his dog had led him to. "It was buried in a bottomland near the river only a few miles away."

"They are canisters we buried ourselves as we came downstream last fall!" exclaimed Lewis. He gave the man a steel firemaker for being honest. The man was pleased with himself and followed Captain Lewis around for half a day grinning and indicating by hand signs that his tongue was not forked.

In the evening a Shoshoni man who had been captured as a small boy by the Chopunnish, a tribe of Nez Percés, came to the expedition's camp because he had heard there was a young woman of his nation. The man was called Shadow. He talked most of the evening with Sacajawea, asking about her nation in the mountains. He told her he was of the Kogohue tribe of Shoshonis and he thought his people now lived south in the plains, feasting on the buffalo every day.[4] He said, "My people never come north anymore, but now they stay where the summers are hot and dry because there is more food and even more horses to be raided from villages still farther south."[5]

Led by Red Robe and Shadow, the expedition moved on toward the larger Nez Percé villages. The mountain peaks were still covered with snow, and even some sides were covered below the tree line. No one could get through the passes until more snow melted. "After the next full moon," said Red Robe.

During the next several nights, the coarsened drifts turned to stony hardness and trees began to fall, torn in half by their loads of ice and snow. Twisted Hair's village had black snow around the lodges, where layers of soot concentrated.

Everyone in the expedition was surprised to find Chief Twisted Hair cool and distant, breaking into violent tirades with another chief, Neeshneeparkeook, Cut Nose.

Drouillard was unable to translate the fast-flying Nez Percé words of either chief. There seemed no way of finding where the horses were that the expedition had left in Twisted Hair's care.

Drouillard tried frantic hand signs. Charbonneau tried hand signs. Both Lewis and Clark tried hand signs and Chinook jargon. Everything seemed useless as the chiefs spat out Nez Percé faster and louder than anyone could understand.

Sacajawea appealed to old Shadow, who knew the Nez Percé language, and through her could interpret the angry words of the chiefs. But to her disappointment Shadow was a stickler for etiquette. He explained, "It is improper for me to interpret a private quarrel between two important chiefs. Even for the friendly white chiefs I cannot repeat those words, nor try to interrupt and pacify them."

The expedition's men hoped that the quarreling did not mean trouble for them, and finally went to make their camp. After supper, Lewis sent Drouillard back to Chief Twisted Hair's village in hopes that the quarreling was over and the chief would come to smoke with him. While Drouillard was gone, York strutted around the relaxed party mimicking the angry chiefs. Pomp jumped up and down laughing. Clark picked the child up and sat him on his shoulders, then danced around with York, shouting shrill, incomprehensible, guttural sounds, stomping the blackened snow.

Shannon rolled in the hard snow, holding his sides laughing. Sacajawea laughed until tears rolled down her cheeks. At this moment, Twisted Hair arrived in their camp. Lewis had to quiet the men because he was fearful the situation could become less than a laughing matter. But Twisted Hair acted as if nothing had happened. He smoked a pipe with Lewis and told through hand signs that his two subchiefs, Cut Nose and Tunnachemooltoolt, Broken Arm, had grown jealous. To make them feel important he had let the two of them care for the white men's horses. They had had free use of the horses, who were nearby, munching tender blades of spring grass. But if the white men wanted the horses right away, it would take some time to round them up. Twisted Hair said, "And your packsaddles are no longer in the cache because it was poorly made." He pushed his hands downward to show how some of the earth had fallen in. "I buried them in a new cache, which I made myself."

Suddenly Cut Nose and Broken Arm appeared before the captains. They shoved and pushed Twisted Hair to one side.

Cut Nose said, "He is bad and wears two faces."

"He did not really let us take care of your horses. He let his young warriors ride them fast and hard," said Broken Arm. "But now the two good friends of the white chiefs have intervened and saved your horses from careless use, which would spoil them. You, white chiefs, are fortunate to have such good friends as us, who can tell you about the bad old man, Chief Twisted Hair."

Chief Twisted Hair said nothing. He kept his face averted and remained sitting with his back against a stone. Soon all the horses were returned to the captains. Then Twisted Hair invited them to his lodge. There he told them that two horses were missing, but they were the two Old Toby and his son, Cut Worm, had taken back to the Shoshoni nation with them. Then he invited the captains, Drouillard, Charbonneau, and Sacajawea to eat with them. Sacajawea sat back against the wall with the other squaws, who passed Pomp from one to the other. Each examined his beaded shirt and moccasins and stared in wonderment at his winter's growth.

Clark burned his finger trying to snatch half-boiled pieces of meat from the kettle, and he used the tops of his moccasins for napkins. "Makes them waterproof." He winked at Charbonneau, who was wiping his hands on the legs of his trousers. Twisted Hair wiped his hands on any one of the two dogs in the lodge when either came close enough in their frantic scramble for meat bones.

Twisted Hair took the men to the new cache where their saddles were stored along with the ammunition. Lewis stopped by a spring to wash his hands.

"I do sincerely believe that Twisted Hair is about as hot-tempered as they come," said Drouillard, wiping his hands through his long hair. "But I think he is honest."

The Nez Percés brought in over sixty horses to the men of the expedition. One horse was wild, and they tired of struggling with him. On the good advice of Charbonneau, the horse was made into steaks and roasts. When some of the other stallions proved hard to control, the Nez Percés showed a couple of the men how to geld them.[6]

During the next few days, the sun ate steadily into the sodden snowdrifts. The Nez Percés discarded most of their clothes, even going barefoot in camp where the snow was packed hard as earth. The forest swayed its ice-free branches, and the nights suddenly became warmer. The stars were often covered by a film, and there seemed to be a vast and restless whispering everywhere.

"Rain," Sacajawea said. "I can smell it."

The rain started that night. At noon the next day, the men were huddled in Nez Percé lodges built on a framework of long poles laid in a circle to meet at the top, where strips of birchbark were spread, leaving a hole over the center. The skin of elk or deer hung as a door. Branches of spruce and pine were spread on the ground against the heaped-up snow, which had nearly melted, and which made the lower wall of the lodge. The men slept like the Nez Percés, feet toward the fire in the center, curled in tortuous positions to keep their legs out of the coals. The smoke, like a greasy blanket, did not escape through the hole overhead, but packed itself into every cranny on the ground. Even the dogs burrowed their tortured snouts into the arms and legs of the coughing sleepers, searching for a breath of filtered air.

The village was in a small clearing separating the forest from the riverbank. The wet ground was trampled everywhere, littered with ashes, burned wood, and bones—everything useless was simply thrown out the door. A film of soot stretched like mosquito netting under the trees.

When the rain stopped, the expedition moved their camp to Commearp Creek,[7] to the village of Broken Arm. This chief received them formally under the flag they had given him the previous fall. Broken Arm gave the expedition two horses, two bushels of *quamash*, dried salmon, and four large flat cakes made from *kouse* flour. Broken Arm refused payment and instructed his women to set up a special lodge for the white chiefs and their important men.

The unexpected pleasure of privacy in a lodge gave the captains a chance to enlarge the hole in the top. They preferred the added cold with the reduction in smoke.

"Yes, the smoke keeps some warmth," said Clark, "but I think it would be more comfortable to freeze than to choke to death."

"I have noticed that the dampness on the coast seemed to hurt more than the drier cold in these regions," observed Lewis.

The frogs shrilled in every sodden hollow, and small birds and squirrels racketed on leaf-budding branches. Indians from neighboring villages came to the white men's camp. When four principal Nez Percé chiefs came with three subchiefs, the captains took the opportunity to have a council, because here seven chiefs were present according to Nez Percé tradition for a successful council. Lewis explained the nature and power of the United States. One chief made a rough map with charcoal on an elk hide, showing the pass across the Divide through the mountains. The council took half a day because of all the interpreters. Sacajawea translated in Shoshoni to Shadow, who was still with the expedition, and he translated to the Nez Percés.

The Nez Percés were great politicians. They had kettles of food made. The chiefs yelled out "*Ai!*" to the white men's ideas of keeping peace with other nations, then further signified their approval by helping themselves to the food. Those who wished to vote "No!" could do so by staying away from the food. The "*Ai*'s" defeated the "No's" unanimously.

Further friendship was deepened by the expedition's medical supplies. Realizing that they no longer had sufficient trading goods to buy provisions, medical fees became their only means of bargaining. Clark and Sacajawea treated as many as fifty people a day. In some cases Clark refused treatment unless the Indians let him have dogs or horses in payment so that the expedition would have food. The Nez Percés had plenty of dogs, which they never ate themselves, and they understood the payment for medical treatment because they paid fees to their own Medicine Man. One squaw was so grateful to Clark for opening a large abscess on her back and allowing her a good night's rest that she gave him a beautiful gray horse with white spots all over.

The Nez Percés were a pleasant-mannered people for the most part, who moved around, digging camass and fishing in the spring, hunting and berrying in the mountains through the summer, fishing in the fall, and gambling and horse-trading during the winter.

Sacajawea found that they called themselves Lema, People, just as the Shoshonis referred to themselves as the People. They traveled enough to know there were other subdivisions of their nation, and they were identified according to location: Meli Lema or Pakiut Lema, standing for Grass Country People or Canyon People. Wandering had kept them from getting dull and stupid, as some of the west coast tribes were.

One morning Sacajawea took her child to the village smokehouse, which had been built on the ground above a pool where the stone fish traps were. Beside the smokehouses were dugouts covered with old hides to keep from splitting in the warm spring sun.

Some naked children shouted that there were more salmon in the river than stars in the sky. Pomp slipped in the sand and fell on his hands and knees. Sacajawea pulled him up before he could object and continued walking toward the smokehouse, curious.

"Are you going to open the smoke hole and get a fire going?" a boy ran to ask her.

Sacajawea shook her head and indicated that she did not know this method of smoking fish. The boy found a pole ladder and climbed to the bark roof. He lifted the sticks and hides covering the smoke hole and threw them to the ground.

A squaw the boy called "mother" opened the low door and stepped back, for the bitter odor of smoked wood stung her nostrils. She was fat and round-faced, but had a good-natured smile. She wore many shells and thongs wrapped around her ankles and arms. She built a fresh fire, all the while smiling at Sacajawea as the heat was carrying the air up through the smoke hole and drawing fresh air into the wooden smokehouse.

Sacajawea let Pomp play in the sand with the older boy. She helped the mother bring in more driftwood, which had been hurled along the beach by the winter's williwaws. Once she ran into the water after Pomp, who had decided to poke his bare toes into wetter sand.

The Nez Percé women had built salmon traps by making large enclosures surrounded by stone walls, which were covered with water. As the water flowed down the river, draining through the stones, the salmon were caught in shallow water and could be picked up with their bare hands. Sacajawea saw the flat shells of mussels on the rocks and waded out to pry some loose with her stubby old knife. Once she stopped to watch minnows dart above helgrammites that barely moved with the flow of water, as delicate as flowers in the wind.

Suddenly the boy, clad only in a breechclout, darted toward her. "There's a many-legged fish under the ledge! It will grab your leg!"

She raced to shore. "Would it bite?" Sacajawea asked, running beside the boy.

"It would grab your leg and pull you down, down," he panted.

His mother was feeding the fire again, and Sacaja- wea could hear her loud chuckle and the click of her tongue.

There were no octopus in the Kooskooskee River, but there must have been stories about them in the river closer to the Pacific, and the stories had reached these Nez Percés.

Other brown, naked children had gathered at the shore and were laughing at the good joke. Sacajawea crossed her legs and sat on the sand laughing with them as she realized it was only a funny joke to play on a stranger.

"I got enough large mussels, anyway," she said, pointing to the pile. "You can have a feast." She began shelling, silently putting the meat on a flat piece of driftwood. Happily she thought of nothing, vaguely aware of the sun on her back, the nearness of her child, now asleep in the warm sand, and her Nez Percé friends. The feeling of contentment enclosed her.

In the afternoon, Sacajawea went to Clark and asked if York could help treat the natives with the magic eye-water because she was busy at the smokehouse. "Just this one day. I will bring you some large mussels I have smoked."

Clark could never refuse her. "Keep Pomp with you!" he called. "York is not likely to be a good nursemaid and medical assistant at the same time."

For his supper Clark ate the tender white mussel meat, smoked and salted to perfection. "Ummm, better than salmon," he said.

"There is enough for all to try." She urged Clark to distribute the bundle of dried, smoked fish. "I did leave some to the Nez Percé squaw who built up the smoke-house fire, and she fed many children."

The men smacked their lips; Pomp crawled to Clark's lap and fell asleep.

"Squaw, put that *enfant* to bed!" yelled Charbonneau.

"Shhh," warned Clark, "no need to wake the child. Let his mother enjoy the festivities in her honor. She went to some trouble to clean and smoke these mussels as a surprise. It is good to honor her once in a while."

"No need to honor a squaw. I have said that before. Wagh!" Charbonneau sulked. "She is supposed to know how to catch fish and cook. But look, I am the one that has done most of the cooking around here. Then she goes off to enjoy babbling with other women and cooks over some greasy, louse-infected wood the Nez Percés have."

Clark looked amused. "Tomorrow you catch, clean, and smoke some salmon, and fix greens for us. Janey will help me with the medicines. Then during supper we'll have York sing to you."

Charbonneau stalked off to wash the tin plates. Having his bluff called, he wished to say nothing further.

Clark sat back with his pipe and said mostly to himself, "What can we do for Bill Bratton? He's as stove up as that old chief, Tomatappo, those Cayuse brought in some days ago."

"We'll try a sweat lodge," replied Sacajawea impulsively.

After a few moments of silence, as Clark enjoyed his pipe, he swatted his knee. "Well, I'll be danged! I should have thought of that a long time ago. For two months Bratton's been carried by canoe, and horseback, and treated with liniment and powders. Nothing has really worked. The sweat bath can't be worse. We'll have a sweat tonight!"

It was dusk when Clark told a couple of the men to build a little tent of skins, barely large enough to accommodate two people. They scraped the hole from the loam and filled it with ashes.

"We'll roll hot stones from the fire outside onto these ashes," Clark explained. "Sweating is a treatment as old as the oldest Indians. The Mandans prescribed it for any ailment."

Clark sent for Charbonneau. "Go to the Cayuse camp. Have their men bring their old crippled chief here. We're going to do a sweat. I want him to keep Bratton company because he's never had one before. Do 'em both good, maybe."

Charbonneau hurried off, happy again to be an important messenger for the expedition.

When Tomatappo was brought in, Clark went to Bratton.

"Come on, old man," he said, "a sweat will do you good."

"I know," Bratton said in a weary voice. After a moment he allowed himself to be carried by York to the small skin tent. He undressed and crawled inside. The warmth had an unexpected effect. He gasped with pleasure and sat on a thick heap of boughs spread with a hide, in pitch-darkness, and tried to stretch out his legs. They touched someone's feet.

"This is fine," Bratton exclaimed. "I am going to be thoroughly warmed."

The old, naked chief chuckled, and Bratton could hear him settling comfortably.

The flap of the tent was pushed aside, and in the dim light from the outside fire, Bratton saw shadowy hands rolling a stone with sticks. The stone was jostled along the earth to the pit. The sticks smoked from the contact and were thrown out. Someone poured water on the hot stone and pushed a small jar of water to sprinkle on the stone toward Bratton. This created as much steam as the two in the tent could bear. York pushed in two steaming cupfuls of strong horsemint tea for the men to drink.

"*Tomonowos*," said Bratton after he had taken a huge swallow. "Powerful," he had said in Nez Percé.

The old chief said, "*Oho*," and drank noisily.

Bratton felt the water stream on his chest and arms. The atmosphere became stifling, and he opened his mouth to breathe. But delightful shivers ran through his body, to his very marrow, and there was a tingling in his joints, so that he felt he would sleep the night through in the first real rest since leaving Fort Clatsop.

"You must stay only a short while the first time," said Clark, pulling Bratton out. York helped to support him as they took him to the river to be plunged twice in the cold water. Then he was sweated again for another three-quarters of an hour.

The chief snuffled out a dreamy chant.

Then the flap was opened and Bratton crawled out. Clark wrapped him in blankets and allowed him to cool gradually. He chewed the meat Clark handed him and reached for more. He was still sweating profusely, and he wiped his face with the corner of the blanket.

"When is that old man coming out?" Bratton asked.

"His people will bring him when they feel he has had enough. The Indians never do anything that seems good by small degrees," Clark said, lighting a twig.

"But he will melt to skin and bones."

"They would not let him stay if they felt he was not getting some pleasure from it." Clark put the twig to his pipe and sucked on the stem.

Tears were starting to drop from Bratton's eyes from the campfire's smoke, and he lay down.

The chief was brought out and wrapped in a fur robe and placed on his back beside Bratton. He indicated he was hungry. Clark nodded to one of the Cayuse men that old Tomatappo should have something to eat from the white men's cooking kettle. York passed the man a plate of boiled meat. The old man asked twice for the plate to be refilled.

"He cannot remember when he has felt so good," said Shadow, the old captive Shoshoni. "Look, he can move his hands and arms and feed himself."

Tomatappo's arms and legs had been paralyzed for three years. In two days, he began to wiggle the toes of one foot and move the leg, while the other had tingling sensations in it.

Bill Bratton was able to walk about the next day.

The weather now alternated between bad spells of cold and then sunny days when the natives swarmed into the expedition's camp with their aches and pains to be treated. On a good day Sacajawea was heating flannel strips to lay over an old woman's aching joints, when she realized that her child had been whiny and would not play contentedly by himself. The papoose was not fifteen months old and had survived more than most any other child had been subjected to. Almost from birth he had been traveling, sometimes on horseback, sometimes in a canoe, and sometimes slung over his mother's back in a cradleboard or in the fold of a thin blanket. He had escaped drowning twice and had shared the cold, rain, and semistarvation that had laid low one after another of the grown men.

Sacajawea knew he was cutting teeth, and it was hard to keep the steady flow of water from his mouth wiped off. How messy growing teeth are, she thought. He's cranky today with it.

Ben York noticed something different in the child's

actions. "Why you'se stick close to your mammy, child?" he asked.

Pomp hid his face behind his mother's leg.

"Something's wrong with this here Pomp. He's not a bashful type."

Sacajawea put her hand on the child's head. It was warmer than usual. She kept her hand there for a few more seconds to make sure. Then she pulled the child on her lap and saw that his eyes were bright with fever. She and York looked inside his mouth. His throat was red.

"This here baby's got a sore throat from wading in that icy river water." York picked the child up and placed the little head on his big shoulder. "Come on, soldier, we're going to get you a cup of tea." He patted Pomp's head, and the child began to whimper and then cry out as if in pain. Sacajawea held her arms out for him. She felt her child's neck, then upward toward the ears. Behind Pomp's left ear was a swollen area that caused him to cry out when touched.

In the afternoon, he became restless and his fever increased. Sacajawea kept him wrapped in his robe of rabbit furs. He tried to push the robe away.

York brought clover tea, but he refused to swallow. "He has a nasty earache there," York said, shaking his head slowly.

Clark came to look at Sacajawea's child. He brought hot wool packs for his neck and ear. He eased the pain with drops of warm oil mixed with laudanum in the child's left ear.

"The Lord, he knows this little soldier is sick," York comforted Sacajawea. "He's watching and going to keep him safe."

"I want him to be a man like Chief Red Hair," she murmured.

During the night, she thought of a medicine man who could work a chant for a sore throat. But she did not even know how he would work up such a thing. She thought about what she might do and remembered her grandmother. Quietly Sacajawea found a place between two tall birches, a place where she stood among the wild green ferns under the night sky. She stood quietly, drained, letting herself go, letting her thoughts flow where they would. The Great Spirit is aware of my child's sickness, she thought. Her mind turned to the healthy child he had been. For many moments her brain would not clear. Then, as if under a hypnotic spell, she heard the child's laughter over and over. She thought, Time flows over some as the Kooskooskee flows over leaves and flowers that are whirled away and gone. Time flows over others as over a firm stone that does not float away. My son is like a stone. He is not a delicate flower.

She stepped slowly away from the clump of ferns and birches. She was satisfied that her continued love and care would bring her child through the bad sickness to good health. She slept peacefully for several hours.

In the gray, misty dawn, Clark made an onion poultice for the reddened swelling under the child's ear and gave him a cream of tartar slurry to swallow. Pomp had to be coaxed. He could not swallow comfortably.

The next morning, Clark made a fresh poultice and let the child sleep. Sacajawea stayed close, letting Clark take care of the ailing natives alone or with the sporadic help of York.

"Don't think me selfish not helping you with the sick natives," she said once, "but I cannot leave Pomp today."

"Janey, you must stay with him," said Clark. "You must tell me if there is any change, either way, better or worse. This child is more important to us than all those Nez Percés with aching backs."

The child slept, and she sat beside him in a makeshift lean-to of hides and pine branches. She noticed the Nez Percés as they waited their turn to be doctored by Clark.

The men were stout, portly, good-looking, rather like her man, Charbonneau, without his facial hair. They were better dressed than the Chinooks, Clatsops, or Walla Wallas. Their tunics were clean and white, as were their leggings of deerhide. They wore bandeaus of foxskins like turbans on their brows. The women were small, with good features, and they dressed neatly in tight-fitting woven-grass caps and long buckskin skirts, whitened with clay.

Then she watched several small boys carrying a wicker coop with some young eaglets from one lodge to another. They raised the birds for their tailfeathers. She daydreamed of Pomp dressed in white leather with a vermilion breastplate.

The child whimpered, and she darted quickly to his couch. She rocked him in her arms and sang to him. His feverish eyes opened, sought restlessly for some object, and rested on four black puppies nipping at the heels of two small girls. The girls began to run after Lewis's big black Newfoundland, Scannon. They were trying to show him the puppies. It dawned on Sacajawea that the puppies were, in fact, Scannon's offspring. The huge dog stopped and sniffed at the pups. Then he pushed one off its feet, then another and another. He barked for them to get up, and he romped through the camp with the puppies following. And so—he is proud of his children, thought Sacajawea.

Pomp's eyes shifted and rested on Clark, who had come into the lean-to. "My throat hurts," he whispered.

"I know," Clark replied quietly. He looked at the child's swollen neck. Pomp cried out when his fingers passed over the left side. "Get Charbonneau to hunt more onions."

Sacajawea laid the child in Clark's arms and ran to find her man.

"That boy, he is only cutting teeth," said Charbonneau at first. But seeing how concerned she was, he followed her to the lean-to and looked on as Clark fed Pomp another dose of warm water with cream of tartar. Much of the slurry trickled from the corners of his mouth.

"The neck, she is puffed. My son is ill. Do something now, for he must get well!"

"Well, now, you get some onions," said Clark, giving the child to his mother. He reluctantly left to help York give out more eyewater and laudanum to the ailing natives.

Charbonneau then turned to face Sacajawea. "Do not give the boy any of those dirty Indian cures, like putting some magic bone on his neck or plastering it with horse dung. I'll get a beaver castoreum to rub on the redness and cover it with the beaver's tail. That is the best cure for this poison."

She shook her head at the old French-Canadian coureur de bois treatment and shook her finger at the onion poultice. "Chief Red Hair's medicine is best."

Charbonneau sulked off with a sharp digging stick so that he could easily ply the onions from the dark loam.

The following day, Pomp was no better, but he was no worse. He was too warm and fussed a great deal. Twice Clark applied a fresh onion poultice, and twice he threw out a wad of beaver fur that Charbonneau had slipped in the swath of bandaging that held the poultice.

Sacajawea ate little during mealtimes, but hurried back to see if her child would begin nursing. She held him as though trying to pour a bit of her strength into his weakening, feverish body. Clark managed to get a few drops of water into him several times a day. The child needed fluids badly. Discarding the onion poultices, Clark tried a salve of pine resin, beeswax, pitch, and bear's oil.

Within a week, the abscess began to ooze. Clark decided not to lance it because he was certain the tissue would scar less if he did not cut it open to drain. He was certain that the child would have a large enough permanent scar from this infected mastoid. As the abscess continued to drain, Clark continued to apply the hot pine resin.

When the abscess stopped oozing, Charbonneau was certain his son would be well. He begged Sacajawea to leave him on the pine couch and help with food preparation for the outfit. Sacajawea would not go. She rocked the child back and forth as he slept. Sometimes he shivered in his sleep. Other times he perspired profusely. She could see his body was no longer plump, and his rosy brown coloring was only a grayish tan.

The day that Pomp eagerly searched for her breast and nursed hungrily, Sacajawea, too, was certain her child would be well. His fever now subsided quickly. Even though he was weak, he smiled and chattered baby talk. Sacajawea took him out in the warm afternoon sunshine to see the doves cooing and the camass flowers covering the prairies like a deep blue lake. She picked yellow glacier lilies growing at the edge of the pine forest, the pink moccasin flower, and the paired yellow flowers of the honeysuckle. She showed Pomp the delicate petals and stamens. Then she looked eagerly for the tall, dense racemes of beargrass with its slippery, grasslike leaves, a sure sign that the snow had receded from the foothills. Returning to camp, she nuzzled the warm body of her child and thought, I could hold him in my arms forever.

For years he would be her most precious and prized possession. In a country where material goods were few, men found some token or talisman to prize above all other things. It was their innate instinct to have something, no matter how small or insignificant. Often a warrior prized one certain arrow and would give his woman or daughter up before he would loose that prized possession. A man could always take another woman and have another child, but never another arrow with the magical powers of the prized one.

The child meant many things to Sacajawea. He was of her flesh, and he was white, like her beloved Chief Red Hair. He was a symbol of joy and laughter. He had gone with her on this long trail into many strange nations, and his eyes had covered much land, sky, and water. He had endured hardship, and shared in the plenty the men had enjoyed. He could speak words of several languages. And she knew, as a mother knows, he would be great among her people and among the white men.

CHAPTER

31

Retreat

Clark's Journal:

Tuesday June 17th 1806

*our baggage being laid on Scaffolds and well covered,
we began our retragrade march at one P.M. haveing re-
maind. about three hours on this Snowey mountain. we
returned by the rout we had advanced to hungary Creek,
which we assended about two miles and encamped. we
had here more grass for our horses then the proceeding
evening, yet it was but scant. the party were a good deel
dejected, tho' not as much so as I had apprehended they
would have been. this is the first time since we have been
on this tour that we have ever been compelled to retreat
or make a retragrade march.*

BERNARD DEVOTO, ed., *The Journals of Lewis and Clark*.
New York: Houghton Mifflin Co., 1953, p. 405.

The expedition moved several miles down Commearp Creek on May 18, then turned north along the Kooskooskee, which was very high and overflowing its banks at many places because of the melting mountain snows. The next day, the expedition forded the river at a wide, shallow spot and swam the horses over, with the baggage tied securely to their backs. York found a circular area about thirty feet in diameter sunk nearly four feet in the ground and surrounded by a three-and-a-half-foot-high wall of earth.

"That is something very old," agreed Sacajawea. "It was used for defense against enemy attack. Many men could hide inside behind that earth wall."

Captain Clark suggested the men erect shelters of sticks and grass facing outward, and within the sunken area erect a shelter from skins and place the baggage there.

The Nez Percés told the group that they could not cross the mountains for three or four weeks at the earliest. "The snow is too deep to walk in, and there is no forage for your horses." Each day the men looked at the snow-covered Bitterroots and confirmed the Nez Percés' statements among themselves.

The free time available while waiting for the snow to melt gave the men considerable relaxation. Footraces were run with the Nez Percés, and many dances were held. Baptiste LePage and Charbonneau went to the Nez Percé village to test their skill at trading elk's teeth and squirrel tails for more camass roots. "Janey will pound those roots dry, and York will make that good, crisp flat bread," said LePage.

During this time Shannon, Collins, and Potts traded for a Nez Percé canoe, which they used to cross the Kooskooskee to trade in another river village for *kouse* roots to use as vegetables. One day late in May when they landed on a narrow strip of beach, the canoe swung broadside against some trees and filled with water. Potts had to be pulled out because he could not swim. While pulling him out, Shannon and Collins had to leave a couple of blankets, a capote, and all their trading beads in the bottom of the canoe so that they could fight the rapids. Shannon told Captain Lewis, "We lost all our goods, sir, but we saved good old Potts."

When Charbonneau heard the story, he snorted, "Damn careless! Those blankets and things should have been tied in that canoe. They would be wet, but not lost for good." Then, two days later, LePage and Charbonneau themselves lost a dressed elk skin, packets of vermilion paint, and their packs. They were going to trade for more camass roots, but they had not tied the packs on securely, and as they forded the river, the packs loosened and were lost in midstream.

That afternoon, both Lewis and Clark cut buttons off their threadbare blue Army coats and gave them to Hugh McNeal and Ben York, along with eye-water and pine salve to use in trading across the river. By evening, the two men had returned with three bushels of camass and some flat bread made of *kouse*-root flour.

That same afternoon, Drouillard came back from a trading mission to report that some Nez Percés had taken a couple of tomahawks that belonged to the expedition. "And one of those we all prized highly, because it belonged to Sergeant Floyd.[1] Those God-cursed, thieving savages."

Captain Clark could see Drouillard was in a temper and tried to calm him down. "Go back to those coots who stole the tomahawks and see if you can trade something to get them back."

"That whole outfit stinks like polecats in rut! They make my guts boil," said Drouillard.

"Here are some pink scallop shells Janey found on the beach above Fort Clatsop. They should catch their eye. Try to get the tomahawks back for these." Clark handed the shells to Drouillard, who seemed to be calming down.

"For Christ's sake, those men had better trade back those tomahawks. They are offal, but what can one expect from people who are childish and without manners. I'll get them back. You can count on it!"

"That's what I want to hear," said Clark. "I'll personally return Floyd's tomahawk to his family when we get back to the States."

I ought to put their heads on spikes, thought Drouillard. He did not say his thoughts aloud, though, because his fit of temper had somewhat subsided. It left altogether when the Nez Percés gave the tomahawks back for the scallop shells.

Each day, the captains watched the rising river and melting snows from the mountains. Bratton was so well now that he rode in the bareback horse races. Pomp ran about with Nez Percé children watching the games and pitching quoits.

One day a young woman, her hair tied back with a thong, brought her dark-skinned, kinky-haired newborn to show off proudly to Sacajawea. The new mother wore only a skirt and a leather vest carelessly untied over her breasts. "See, how big he is already! And he came two moons early," she said proudly. "He is strong like the father."

"Something good. *Skookumchuck*," said Sacajawea, cradling the papoose and humming to him while he slept. She knew York had fathered this papoose on the westward trail. "He is called York?" asked Sacajawea.

The young Nez Percé mother sat on the ground, her body half-covered, but she was totally unconscious of affectations. "*Ai*, York," she smiled, her eyes crinkling. "Small Man York. He will be something great in this tribe. See, he does not cry even now. There is no other papoose like him in any village."

Sacajawea did not say what came to her mind. She thought there were probably several others that York had left in the various villages the expedition had visited. And maybe, she mused, half-white papooses had been left by some of the others.

The evening she first heard the piercing, eerie singing, she began to think that some of the Nez Percé women were a little flighty. The night was still and the sound was easily carried over a wide area.[2] She noticed that it made Ben York shift uneasily, put another log on the fire, and look around anxiously at the others, as if he wanted to move out somewhere. He finally did sidle back to the edge of camp and then lope off into the woods.

Sacajawea could not imagine what had got into him. He had been holding Pomp and making the child laugh

and giggle. He stopped and just seemed to sniff the air
and listen. Most of the others didn't seem to hear it, or
ignored it as some wood noise.

No one paid him any attention as he went away to
the edge of camp and then disappeared. Why am I wondering? thought Sacajawea. York can take care of himself.

She washed Pomp's hands and face and took him to
the back of the camp, where he knew what was expected
of him before going to bed. Quickly he pulled off his
leggings, relieved himself, pulled off his shirt, and ran
back to his mother. Sacajawea cleaned him with a handful of leaves. She patted him goodnight on his pile of
pine boughs and pulled a robe up to his chin. The fur
tickled and he pushed it away, turned on his side, and
was asleep in a moment.

The whistle came again, this time close to the edge
of the camp. Curiosity, always high in any woman, especially an Indian, got the best of Sacajawea. She stepped
away from her sleeping child and tried to follow the
strange, shrill whistle. It seemed to come from the edge
of the clearing, then from behind a tree. Just when she
thought she was close, it moved. It was neither a bird
nor an animal. Suddenly she saw a pretty young Nez
Percé woman standing in an opening, with tall pines
on either side. She was dressed in a deerskin shirt and
leggings, which were fringed. A leather band around
her forehead kept her long black hair off her face. She
moved with a subtle rocking motion, blowing through
her hands, which she held in front of her mouth. Sacajawea waved to the young woman. The woman did
not seem to notice her. She turned her back and whistled again. From behind a tree came York, his white
teeth flashing in the moonlight. He ran for the young
woman.

Sacajawea hurried back to the campfire, chuckling
to herself, thinking how York followed the whistling
like a buck deer followed the sashaying of a desirable
doe. That excited Nez Percé woman was leading him
all over the Nez Percé country, through the brush and
between the pines and through the tall prairie grass.
She would be caught sooner or later, and maybe before

next spring the fun-minded woman would be the mother of another curly-headed Nez Percé papoose.

On June 10, Lewis announced, "Strike camp. We are moving a little farther into the foothills so that the hunters can find more game."

None of the Nez Percés followed the camp. Shadow left the expedition that evening on the pretense that he wanted to go down to the river to fish. He never returned. Sacajawea knew that he had become more Chopunnish than Shoshoni now and did not actually wish to go over the mountains to see any of his Shoshoni cousins. She tried to explain this to Clark. "It is not surprising that he does not want to go with us over the mountains. He is now like the people of the Nez Percé nation, who did not wish to travel outside their own territory often. He misses his adopted tribe and wants to be with them."

"We'll miss him. He was good with translations around here and understood the art of negotiation when we traded with the Nez Percés. I'd hoped he'd escort us across the mountains and parley with the Nez Percés for several more guides. So—if our guide leaves us, we'll go over the mountains by our own wits," said Clark.

Five days later, Lewis made another announcement. "Collect the horses, pack the baggage, and strike the camp. We are moving up over the mountains onto the Lolo Trail early tomorrow morning. I have already sent Windsor and Colter out with their rifles to look for deer, wolf, fox, or rabbits for our meals."

Two hours after dawn the next morning, the two hunters were ten to twelve miles ahead of the main party. They stopped to examine the gray sky. "Looks like snow," said Windsor.

"Those can't possibly be snow clouds," answered Colter, squinting in the sky at the grayish overcast.

"You can't deny those are snowflakes," said Windsor when the huge flakes began drifting down.

Slowly the men tramped upward in the mountain tanglewood. Then they noticed that the firs were bent from wet snow and they were walking on a path only by guess. "I can tell by those dead branches hurtling down and the occasional dead tree falling that the wind

is stronger than usual," said Windsor, turning to face
Colter. He turned more quickly than he had planned,
and his rifle struck a boulder. It broke near the muzzle
and was impossible to fix.

"I hate like hell to make this suggestion," said Windsor, "but it looks like we'd better turn around and see
if we can't locate the main party before we get lost in
this storm and they find us frozen solid as that damn
rock that broke my rifle."

"You're right. The sooner we find them, the better,"
agreed Colter.

Sacajawea carried Pomp in a blanket on her back.
The air was cold and crisp. She blew on her hands, often
tucked them up under her blanket, but it was difficult
to ride the horse and lead the packhorse with no hands.
The weather seemed to take hold of everyone, so that
after a while each man's mind was aware not of arms
and legs, but of sky and land; the snow clouds an intimate part of the body, the horizon one's eye. By afternoon the snow was two feet deep. Hours passed and the
horses began to stumble. The heavy, blowing snow, piling, drifting, piling again, took away the old shape and
face of the land.

Finally, Clark had to admit that none of the landmarks he had expected had come in sight. They were
lost. The men were tired, but Clark's words snapped
their minds back to the need to plan for the night—
how to keep off the cold, how to be alive and able to go
on when morning came. They began to complain about
cold feet, and with so much snow there was no grass
for the horses and no game for the stew pots. They had
found no sign of the two hunters who had been sent
ahead. In that swirling snow they could not see the
tracks of mice and squirrels. The wind blew with a
hundred voices, and the shadows of the trees mingled
indistinguishably with the black trunks.

Clark found dried wood after patiently scraping away
snow, and tried sparking his flint, but the wind and
endless swirls of snow ended any hope of a fire. They
camped in a small ravine. The next day their march
was shorter. Each day, the hunters from the main party

hunted less; each day, the cold deepened and their fear increased.

The main party was camped in another small ravine when the blizzard broke. They stared at each other with glittering eyes across a hoarded fire, against the back of a pine-bough lean-to, wondering if they would starve to death before getting through the mountains. It was then that Captain Lewis's mind shook off its paralyzing agony in an overwhelming urge to think.

"A man must keep moving to keep his blood running," he said.

All the men had been cold before, and each knew that if it got through the skin and the frost bit into the bloodstream to harden it, he might be crippled for life, or there would be fever and then death.

"We must go on, not rest," said Lewis. "If your hands, arms, feet, or legs begin to feel warm, that is dangerous; then the frostbite is setting in."

There was no inclination now to talk about how thick and cruel was the snow, how dumb to be caught in the middle of it. All their wit and strength had to be given to figuring how they might keep their feet and find the trail back.

Lewis was looking at Sacajawea. Her hair, dull and lifeless, fell in strands on her shoulders. Her face seemed shrunken so that he imagined he saw her skull more than her features, the wide jaw and far-apart eye sockets. She held the eighteen-month-old child's face automatically against her breast, and the child made unconscious sucking movements with his mouth.

Which of the men should he send back? Lewis dropped his head on his knees in a wave of dizzy weakness and clung despairingly to one clear thought. "Clark," decided Lewis.

"What?" Clark sighed.

"Take the squaw and the child back to the Nez Percé village. We will follow." He saw that Clark agreed. There was a better chance if they went back now.

"Horses can't go without food longer than five days," said Clark. "We'll take them back, too. But leave the baggage here that we have no immediate use for. It can

be a sign to Colter and Windsor that we have gone back.
We'll pick it up the next time on our way up."

"This is madness," said Gass. "Tomorrow we might
be more bewildered than today."

Clark said, "'A pioneer is never lost, but occasionally
bewildered.' That's a phrase from my old friend Daniel
Boone. Funny I'd be reminded of that now. Janey, I'll
carry Little Pomp for a while. Come on, tie him to my
back."

Clark led the retreat, with Sacajawea and the others
following slowly behind. No one talked much; they
seemed to live only in brief thoughts that seemed hours,
even days apart. The descent was never steep. A thaw
came with rain and melted much of the snow. An occasional slope of mushy snow had footholds that were
bad. They lost four horses and the mule when the rain
turned to snow again.

"Here's a beaver dam!" Clark yelled back. "Maybe
we can get a beaver or two to roast."

The men milled around the beaver dam. York built
a small fire. Sacajawea heated water in a kettle on a
tripod of sticks. York found some dried fish and *kouse*
roots to put in the boiling water for a fish stew.

Colter and Windsor meandered into camp while the
men were standing around with their tin cups, sipping
the hot meal. "Hey, if you guys had stayed in one spot
we would have caught up with you two days ago," said
Colter. "Thank God we are here. That snow and wind
was bad. I'd forgotten how cold it could be."

While the men were crowded around Colter and
Windsor, John Potts was still at the beaver dam stubbornly trying to chop a hole in the ice so that he could
bring out a couple of the animals. Suddenly he was on
his hands and knees yelling for someone to help him.
"Help! I cut my leg! Help! The ax slipped on the ice!"

"I'm coming!" yelled Lewis. He saw that Potts had
cut a vein in his leg and the blood was gushing from
the wound. It was touch and go for a while as Lewis
tried to stop the bleeding.

Potts was given a cup of the fish stew and then put
on his horse to continue the downhill ride until evening.

Sacajawea, free of Pomp, helped York clean up the

tin cups and put the fire out before joining the others on the downhill trail.

Windsor and Colter were each riding horses now near the end of the line. Sacajawea and York brought up the rear.

"Hang on!" York yelled out as Colter's horse reared and bucked. But it did not help. Colter fell on the rocks in the middle of Hungry Creek. He clung to his rifle and his blanket. Sacajawea and York stopped their horses in the middle of the creek and watched Colter whirl downstream, get a shaky footing, then climb out of the ice and water. York gave him a dry blanket to replace his wet, frozen clothing. As York was picking up the stiff, wet clothing, a porcupine fell out of a tree. He surprised the three of them. Sacajawea quickly climbed from her horse and threw a large stone on the head of the animal, crushing it. Still shivering, Colter skinned out the frozen flesh and chewed some off the bone. "He's frozen solid. You didn't have to hit his head."

"Hey, I roast that for you," said York.

"No need," laughed Colter. "I'll have it eaten by the time you get the fire going. Here, have some." He passed around pieces of frozen porcupine to York and Sacajawea. They ate, enjoying it. Then they rode up to the rest of the expedition. There was no view, for the clouds hung low on the wooded ridges, and streamers of mist choked the aisles of the trees.

Exertion seemed to take the sting out of the cold, and now the men's senses were alive. There were no smells, only the bleak odor of sodden snow, but the woods had come out of its winter silence. The hillside was noisy with running water and the drip of thawing firs.

That evening, Cruzatte brought in a mountain delicacy, several dozen large morels. These were mushrooms that the Nez Percés rarely ate. York roasted them. Cruzatte, Drouillard, and Clark ate heartily. Sacajawea, York, and Colter were not hungry, for they had finished off the raw porcupine. Charbonneau and Lewis thought when the mushrooms were cooked in this fashion, without salt or grease, they were truly an insipid, tasteless food. Charbonneau gnawed maple twigs with some of the other men and fed his mushrooms to Pomp.

Now the thought of fat salmon, fresh from a well-fed winter in the sea, became irresistible. The men, with few fish hooks left, fell back on the infantryman's last resort. They bayoneted salmon.

Sacajawea was kept busy making a smooth cut the length of the belly and scraping the guts and blood out of each fish. The head and tail cut off, she made a cut from end to end, close to the backbone. The fish lay open, held together only by the skin of the back. She made the next cut by slipping the knife under the exposed bone and removing it from the other side of the fish. She removed the backbone without waste. When the hunters brought in deer and a black bear, their diet improved. Their heads cleared, and their cramps became almost unnoticeable.

During one night the wind changed, and the cold became so severe that it stirred the men out of sleep and set them building up the fire. Sacajawea awoke to air that bit like a fever, and a world that seemed to be made of metal and glass. The cold was more intense than anything she had ever imagined. Under its stress, trees cracked with a sound like shots from machine guns. The huge morning fire made only a narrow circle of heat. If for a second she turned her face from it, the air stung her eyelids as if with an infinity of harsh particles. To draw a breath rasped the throat. She kept Pomp inside her tunic next to her own warm body.

The sky was milk-pale, the sun a mere ghostly disk. The world seemed hard, glassy, metallic, with no shadow, no depth or softness.

The cold cowed the dog, Scannon, and he lay close to the fire with his eyes partially shut.

"Iron freezes instantly to the skin," said Drouillard. "Must be sixty below. If there was any sort of wind, I reckon we could not break camp. We'd have to bury ourselves all day in a hole. But we ought to make good time. Might even make Cut Nose's camp by noon tomorrow."

The hunters found one of the horses had foundered in a drift the night before and was frozen. They drank the blood from the animal's throat and rested an hour. They carved as much meat as they could carry from the carcass and took it into camp. The next day they went back for the horse. The others gathered firewood, roasted the meat, slept, and ate.

"I could spend some time in one of those smoke-filled lodges and not complain about choking to death," said Pryor.

"How long you think this cold'll last?" asked Shannon.

"*Zut!* A couple days is enough!" answered Charbonneau, holding a mittened hand over his dripping nose. "Maybe three days, not more. Big freezes often come between the thaw and the real spring. In the north the Chippewas call it the Bear's Dream. This cold pinches the old bear in her den and gives her bad dreams."

The men were surprised that the violent weather, instead of numbing them, had put life into their veins. They walked stiffly, but felt as if they could go on for hours.

One day Charbonneau's eyes burned with a different ache from that from the cook-fire smoke, and piercing flashes of pain shot through his head. The snow blindness kept him inside a lean-to for several days. He waited, with bandaged face turned in Sacajawea's direction, for the times she left to turn the smoking horse meat or to gather wood, and then he sat in terror as the wilderness came toward him with gigantic steps. Once he was sure the wind had torn the lean-to away from his head; he tore off the bandage and rushed out to stumble into Sacajawea's arms. He lost all sense of shame, following her, whimpering with the cold, while the others worked to keep him warm and fed.

During this waiting, Pryor and Windsor froze their feet and hands out hunting. Clark immersed their feet and hands in warm water. The men yelled out in pain. Sacajawea sat near watching. Suddenly she could take no more. She said sternly, "No warm water; do not bring those men near the fire; wait and let the strength in the rest of their body help heal and restore slowly."

As the men's feet thawed and blisters came on the skin, she opened the larger blisters with a sharp bone, heated momentarily over the fire, and in the night she crawled from her robe to lift their arms vertical, tying them upright with thongs to pine branches. Later—she seemed to know when it was needed, and was not the

shy girl she had been last fall in these torturous mountains—she rubbed their legs and soothed their muscles
and coaxed the lagging blood circulation.

Neither Clark nor Lewis interfered with her treatment. From what they knew of such bad frostbite, the
men might have lost an arm or leg.

One morning Drouillard volunteered, "Shannon and
I will go down to look for game and see if we can locate
the Nez Percés."

Clark agreed and found some forgotten beads in his
pocket. He sent Joe Whitehouse along to buy salmon
with the beads, in case they found some Nez Percés.

When the three men returned in two days, they had
with them the brother of Chief Cut Nose and two other
Nez Percé men, who had volunteered to serve as guides
over the Divide for a fee of two rifles. Apparently no
one wondered how three Nez Percé men were going to
share or divide two rifles.

That evening the three Nez Percés, stripped down
to their breechclouts, set fire to the lower branches of
the pine trees around the camp. It took the chill off the
mountain air, and transformed the trees into towering
columns of flame.

Sacajawea woke her child to see the sight. The men
were reminded of the Fourth of July celebration. The
Nez Percés explained that this was done to bring fair
weather for the journey ahead.

Gradually Windsor's thawed hands came back into
use and the pain in Pryor's arms grew less and the
muscles of his arms became obedient to their owner.
On Windsor's left wrist was a bracelet mark of healing
blisters over the raw skin.

"That there is an emblem," he said to Sacajawea.
"There the mitten did not reach the end of the jacket
sleeve, and the cold wind bit deep." He stretched up
both arms. "God, I'm thankful for good arms, fully restored. Janey, you knew when to pick each mischievous
blister, when to lift the arms, when to rub them and
tease and cajole them. I give you my name for all that."

Sacajawea laughed. "You will call me Dick Windsor,
then?"

Windsor laughed. "Truthfully, I like Janey much

better. And can you imagine the names the men would think up for me if they found you had mine?"

They both laughed.

"Say, tell me, what good is a moth-eaten piece of beaver fur on frostbite?"

"None." She sobered.

"Well, that is what I told Charbonneau, but he insisted it is a cure for anything from hangnail to ringworm. I told him to wrap it around his mouth, because I noticed he did not use it so much when his eyes were sore."

"He tries, but how can he know the medicines of my old grandmother?"

"I'm surprised he knows as much as he does. Listen, Janey, he's really a knowledgeable woodsman. Only one thing—he panics fast. Now, take me; I never panic, but I don't know enough to come in out of the cold."

She smiled as he walked off toward the group of men skinning out a fresh buck deer.

The snow began to sink beneath the weight of sunwarmed air. The snow melted to ice; the ice became rotten, and water seeped through from beneath.

One of the Nez Percé men complained of not feeling well. He wanted to go back down to his village for a few days to recover. This caused some concern because sometimes such complaints with a native meant he was going to abandon any enterprise he was not well pleased with. Three days later, the ice was gone, and to everyone's delight the man had really been ill. He came back. He helped collect the horses and pushed the outfit on while he was still recovering.

As the crows began to caw and small birds whistled in the bushes, Sacajawea found time to dig the knobby quamash roots. Pomp gathered the bright, blue flowers in his chubby fists and brought them to his mother.[3]

"This makes a man gentle," she tried to explain to him, "to notice delicate, short-lived beauty."

Clark could not restrain himself, but he watched her boldly. He saw that her eyes laughed much of the time. Her features were not merely exceptionally attractive, but were arranged so that her expressions showed in a subtle way the restless harking of her soul. He could not read her deeper thoughts and wondered what it would be like to take her thin-boned head in his hands, like a skull, and look inside to satisfy his longing to know. He imagined for a moment he could see the very blood under her bronze skin change with her emotions. There she was, a Shoshoni squaw, whom he admired. She was another man's woman, yet he had come to depend on her for knowledge of herbs and edible roots, medicinals, and sewing his clothing. She amused him. Once, when the others were fishing and hunting, he had let her arrange his hair the way she liked, with braids over each ear and a necklace of small shells about his tanned neck.

"And so, still, you are nothing but an impostor with those red braids and sky blue eyes," she said to him, suddenly smiling. "I cannot make you over." She then shaved his cheeks, feeling that disturbing fluttering inside her breast. She wondered if white women felt the wings fluttering inside when they were near the man they cared for, or was it only a weakness felt by herself for the man she so admired and respected? She did not know.

He looked at her low, smooth forehead, the good, straight nose, full mouth, round face with the triangular cheeks, and small ears that flared out from her head. Suddenly he thought of some small, brown-skinned, quick-pulsed, furry being—some early human creature whose bones were buried under layers of sand, clay and dust.

32

Pompeys Pillar

On the afternoon of July 25, 1806, a stop was made on the south side of the Yellowstone River near a remarkable sandstone formation. It was located about 250 paces back from the river and measured some 400 paces in circumference. Clark estimated its height at 200 feet. He named it "Pompy's Tower" after Sacajawea's infant son, whom he had nicknamed "Pomp" or "Little Pomp," but today it is known as Pompeys Pillar. Clark and some others climbed the only accessible side, the northeast. Near a spot on the path leading to the top where Indians had etched animal and other figures in the rock, Clark inscribed his name and the date. On the grass-covered soil of the summit, the natives had piled two heaps of stones. The surrounding countryside was visible for a distance of 40 miles.

ROBERT G. FERRIS, ed., prepared by ROY E. APPLEMAN, *Lewis and Clark*. Washington, D.C.: U.S. Department of Interior, National Park Service, 1975, p. 228.

On June 26, the expedition was back where it had stored the baggage for the retreat down the mountainside. The men had placed the packs on scaffolds in the trees. Nothing had been damaged. The snow here was seven feet deep and hard. The Nez Percé guides warned the men that they would have to hurry to reach the place where there would be grass for the horses. "Horses are again hungry," they said.

The outfit welcomed a visitor in their camp that evening, a Chopunnish warrior who wished to accompany the white men to the Great Falls of the Missouri. Now the expedition faced the snowy mountain barrier with four guides, who they hoped could traverse this trackless region with instinctive sureness.

Later, Sacajawea asked this Chopunnish warrior if he knew of the man called Shadow, who had been captured by the Chopunnish when he was small, but by birth was a Shoshoni.

"No," the Chopunnish said. "That man must come from a different tribe in this great Nez Percé Nation."

The next day, the expedition stood on a high peak where some natives had built a large stone mound and put a tall tamarack pole in the center. All four guides insisted on stopping to smoke their pipe. This was a sacred spot to them.

Looking about, the captains realized both grandeur and danger in this savage country. "I doubt that we could find our way alone," said Clark. "We are entirely surrounded by mountains and at this moment it seems impossible to escape them."

"I am eternally grateful that those blizzards are over. Good Lord, I doubt we could have lasted another day or two in that," said Lewis.

The fresh meat was soon exhausted, and Charbonneau was told to use a pint of bear's oil with the boiled roots Sacajawea brought in. This was an agreeable dish.

Clark checked Pott's healing leg at least once a day to make sure it was not breaking down. The swelling was now down, but the leg was black and blue and so stiff it was hard to walk on. Clark put pounded roots and leaves of the wild ginger on the wound and wrapped it with a strip of wool.

"That ginger is great for pain," said Potts. "Or the wrapping is so tight, I feel very little in my leg."

Clark also kept an eye on Sacajawea's child, Pomp, seeing that his head and ears were covered in the cold, driving winds. Several times he carried the boy ahead of him on his horse with blankets wrapped tightly about him. The boy remained so warm that he was sleepy much of the time as the horse jogged over the snows of the mountain pass. Pomp's abscess was nearly healed, but there was a deep-pitting scar that would remain forever behind his left ear.

Two days later, the four guides were promising grass ahead. And, true to their word, early in the day they found rich patches of new grass scattered among the rocks. The horses needed it badly. In the afternoon, the snow's softness made the going difficult. The air became almost mild. They camped under a rock shelter where they could all lie well away from the fire and sleep in comparative dryness.

Early in the morning, Lewis walked on the soft grass and paused to listen to the melting snow rushing into tiny streams. He was cheered to hear spring coming for certain to change places with winter. He bent to look into the water covering some dark silt and saw his own reflection.

He was startled to see in the water-mirror an unfamiliar, lean, lined face, surrounded with a scraggly beard. The nostrils were ringed in red, the brown lips cracked. The tanned cheeks were taut against the high bone, then sagged against the jaw. The blue eyes were embedded deep within their sockets and the eyebrows looked pale and brittle, like old winter grass. Tangled, overgrown whiskers hid insect bites. A bony hand scratched at the loose skin around one jaw. Sandy hair, now dark with an accumulation of oil and soot, was held away from the face by a grimy, black fur cap. The leather shirt was smeared with grease and mud and hung loose on jutting shoulder blades.

He was surprised to see this frightful scarecrow, who looked crafty and nervous as a trapped animal as it licked its dry, crusty lips. Lewis sat back on his

haunches, an easy, familiar posture by now. He pulled
off his cap and his hair fell in strings against his neck.
He scratched his head with short, broken fingernails,
then deliberately pulled off his shirt. He stood and kicked
off his moccasins and baggy leather trousers, then
scrubbed the gaunt body with translucent gray, melting
snow. His nose wrinkled with the foul body smell when
he pulled on the filthy shirt and trousers and pushed
his bare feet into the soiled moccasins. He ran a cold,
wet hand through his hair and beard and sighed loudly
at the tangles. Back in camp, he felt as if everyone was
aware of his vanity. He felt guilty and ashamed for
wanting to be clean when the others neglected a bath
in ice water and waited for a warmer time.

Then he saw himself, a man who had been President
Jefferson's private secretary. A gentleman who had lived
in the executive mansion in Washington, D.C., he was
picking bits of horsemeat from a blackened kettle and
enjoying it. In a smoke-filled skin and pine-branch lean-
to, he lit his pipe and passed it to half-naked natives
before he took it from the savages' mouth into his own.

Lewis sat, expressionless, and looked at the man with
whom he shared the honors of this expedition. Clark
seemed an equally grave and dignified scarecrow. Lewis
had the sudden mad desire to shout with laughter and
roll on the ground in hilarity.

The next day, they saw only patches of drifted snow
as they came down the northeast side of the Rockies.[1]
Roots were the only food left.

As Sacajawea slogged over the soggy loam, each step
seemed to drag along some of the hillside. Her thighs
were numbed, and she had a sickening ache in her back.
She managed to struggle down to the tree line, and
then collapsed on a damp, mossy bank. Charbonneau
picked her up and set her on some rotted bark. She got
up and started down the hill, but again fell. A whistle
from Shannon brought Clark back, and a glance showed
where the trouble lay.

"You got to ride, Janey. There's plenty of horses. If
you don't ride, you'll be sick. There's no camp for a sick
squaw until we get into the big timber."

Charbonneau spoke up. "Squaw walks. Her legs are

strong. Horses carry the baggage, and the hunters need to ride. So—there's no room for a squaw on horseback."

"Shut up!" Clark said in French. "She obeys my orders. She rides."

She obeyed and finished the rest of the descent in a miserable half doze, her arms slung through baggage thongs to keep from falling off. Clark kept Pomp in front of him on his horse.

They found a deer carcass lying on the trail where the hunters had left it. Sacajawea began to sing a sad song in her soft Shoshoni tongue. Bratton and White-house packed the venison on a horse, and she did not hear them shout their thanksgiving for the fresh meat. Her mind was buried inward, upon dying, winter-starved people. She imagined the men were in great sorrow. Clark watched her constantly.

To her he was an enveloping shield, and she felt protected merely by the sounds he made near her, so that nothing could intrude across the invisible circle. And she felt completely alone. She did not care what the others did and never looked at them. If occasionally she was separated from Clark, a restlessness began in her mind and grew steadily, like the wind in the trees moving down to move the snow into great drifts. Sweat formed on her face and hands, and she would start out after Clark. With only a glimpse of him in grease-stained leggings and shirt laden with soot, these sounds would retreat.

She refused to eat, and slept little.

"Janey needs the sweat bath," said Bratton. "She suffers the mountain sickness."

The next afternoon, the expedition found a luxury— a hot spring that the natives had dammed with stones and mud to make a bathing place. The men had baths, and the four guides remained in the hot spring as long as they could, then ran to plunge into the creek, which had ice at its edges.

At the campfire Clark urged Sacajawea to go bathe her child at the spring. "Do not go near while she is there," he warned the men. "Perhaps she will go in with the child, and it will warm her bones as much as a good sweat. Maybe Bratton is right. This will do her good."

The child giggled and gurgled as she held him in

water that made his brown skin pink and glowing. The
pitted scar behind his ear was a vivid red. She ran her
fingers lightly over it. It is a mark, like a reminder, so
I will remember how precious a life can be, she thought.
It is not an ugly mark. It is beautiful and sets my son
apart and shows for all to see how he overcame the
badness in his body. "*Skookumchuck*, something grand,"
she said to him in Chinook, laughing with Pomp. She
sat him on a blanket and slid from her greasy tunic
and swam in the delightfully warm water, first looking
around so that she could see Clark's back where he sat
by the fire. She took great handfuls of sand and rubbed
her hair to remove the old, rancid oil. When she was
finished, she sat on a stone and combed her long hair
over and over with a two-pronged stick, forgetting to
keep her eyes on Clark, but watching her child and
hearing the low babble of the men's voices from over
the rise. She braided her hair, dipped her tunic into the
water, and cleaned it with sand and hard rubbing. She
squeezed it dry and smoothed it over her thin body,
knowing her own heat would dry it before night. Slowly
she slipped in beside Clark and Charbonneau at the
fire, her eyes bright, her face glowing. She held her
child and listened to the men and saw her child asleep
in her lap. He is my *skookumchuck*, she thought again.

By low grunts and hand signs, the native guides were
telling about barefoot tracks they had seen in the loam
that morning. "It was a Flathead fleeing from a Blackfoot," they said.

The four Nez Percé guides regarded the trail of the
white men into the country of their hereditary enemies,
the Blackfeet, as a venture to certain death. Now they
were close enough to Blackfoot country. They rapped
on their heads, significantly drew their knives across
their throats, and pointed far ahead into the star-filled
sky. They wanted to go back to their own country. The
four Nez Percés quietly left the campfire that night and
started back up the mountain. Lewis ran after them,
begging them to direct the expedition as far as the East
Branch of Clark's River, so they would be headed in
the direction of the Missouri. Lewis gave the brother
of Chief Cut Nose, Yomekollick, a small seasons medal.
Yomekollick gave his name, Folded White Bear Skin,

to Lewis in exchange, and agreed to stay a few more days.

The day after, Sacajawea stood petrified with fright as Lewis rolled with his horse forty feet over the edge of a cliff. Ordway scrambled after him and found Lewis unhurt but shouting, "The horse, the horse! We must get him up! Put him on his feet!"

To Sacajawea's surprise, the horse was also unhurt and stood up. With an effort she shook off her fright, shoved Pomp into Shannon's hands, and scrambled down, heedless of briars and stones, to guide the horse back to the trail. Ordway pushed Lewis back up to the trail. The men on the top of the embankment shouted encouragement and stretched out hands to bring the three up over the edge, and at the same time, the horse scrambled to the trail with Sacajawea following, nearly breathless.

"That was a close enough call for me," sighed Lewis, wiping his hands on his leggings.

By nightfall they were back in their old camp, "Traveler's Rest,"[2] where they had stayed early in September of the year before. By the firelight Sacajawea pulled thorns from her scratched legs and rubbed bear's oil in the cuts. She sang in English the songs the men sang and chatted easily with them about the next day's trial. She had overcome the mountain sickness. She looked at Lewis. "I am glad we did not have to eat your horse."

During the winter at Fort Clatsop, the captains had decided that when the expedition returned to Traveler's Rest they would divide. Lewis, with Yomekollick as his guide, decided now to go on to the Great Falls by the route the Nez Percés had told about, which was shorter than the one they had taken nearly a year before. His party would go up the Hellgate and Blackfoot rivers, cross the Divide, and go down to the Great Falls by way of either the Dearborn or Sun River. From there, Lewis wanted to go to the Marias River and see if it had a northern branch. Pat Gass, Drouillard, the two Fields brothers, Frazier, Werner, Thompson, Goodrich, and McNeal were going with him. The last three men would go as far as the Great Falls portage. They would make camp there, raise last year's cache, put the equipment

in order, and wait for Clark and his party to join them
along the river.

Clark said, "I want only the good swimmers with me
if we are to float."

Sacajawea's heart sank because Charbonneau could
not swim, and so she was certain she would be assigned
with him to Lewis's group.

But Clark continued, "I'll take Janey. She is invaluable at retrieving goods from a canoe that ships water.
However, we might have to tie her man to the supplies
so that he'll get pulled out in case of an accident."

Charbonneau laughed heartily, but his face was black
from an inner hatred of being teased.

Lewis and his party turned north. Clark, with the
remainder of the outfit and fifty horses, went south
along the Bitterroot Valley.[3]

The expedition found the valley pink as a rose with
the delicate bloom of the bitterroot. The soft violet and
pink shooting stars pointed their yellow tips toward the
fair sky. Wild strawberries still bloomed, along with
raspberries and thimbleberries. The outfit hiked, leading the horses, through old, bearded forests, past moist
alpine gardens, alive with sparkling water and the vivid
green of moss, sheltered in the heart of the mountains
from wind and burning sun. They passed marmots and
rock rabbits, and the smell of white serviceberry blossoms was pungent and sweet on the air.

Deer ran before Clark's party, leaping across the
clear streams. The men saw herds of bighorns on the
mountains at the edge of snowbanks. When they rode
horseback in the bright sunlight, the ground threw back
heat. The grass became dry, the trees parched, and small
stream beds dry. Once they rode the horses slowly along
a stony watercourse. Clark stopped and pointed upward
where none of the others had been looking. They had
ridden through a gap in the stone into a kind of rocky,
waterless cirque. Looking up, Sacajawea was first to
see what Clark pointed at. It was hard to see exactly
what it was.

She dismounted, left her horse in the dry creek, and
scrambled up a short slope of broken stone to the foot
of the cliff. There, worked in some red pigment, low
down on the cliff face, was a small representation of a

tepee. Smoke rose from the smoke hole, and in the left foreground stood a dog. The whole thing looked like the work of some native child, and the men who had come to look stared wonderingly.

"What does that mean?" asked Shannon as he backed down the slope a few paces to get a better sight of the bluff.

And then, maybe twenty feet up, he saw a painting of native hunters. It was old and faded; the full glare of the sun made the figures nearly invisible. The figures of men were scattered about, some hunting buffalo, some smoking peacefully, some walking under a huge red sun.

"Just look at that!" exclaimed Clark. "To reach the high point on the face of that rock, those artists must have built themselves a scaffold of poles lashed together with thick thongs."

"How old?" asked Sacajawea, looking upward.

"Fifty years. I don't really know, maybe much older," said Clark, who seemed struck with delight over the fact that unknown human beings had moved about in this trailless country long before he came.

"This ancient place may be the meeting ground of a buffalo hunt, and the people made pictures while waiting to pass the time," said Sacajawea.

"Aw, these drawings are supposed to bring in the buffalo," suggested Shannon.

"And it's a might weighty thing to send to President Jefferson," teased York.

The party went on across an intervening coulee. Then they had to lead the horses and try to keep ahead of them. The horses came up the steep slope with a rush. Charbonneau's horse began running loose. He had somehow got ahead of the group in the coulee. Charbonneau ran behind his horse, leading the packhorse. All he could do was watch that monstrous rump up above him, clawing and scuffling away at the mountain and hurling down rocks, which those below had to dodge. Charbonneau urged his horse on with horrid threats and a quirt whenever he could reach him because if the horse hesitated and fell, he would sweep the whole lot with him. And there was no question of turning back. That horse could not have turned around on so steep a slope, with so poor a footing, let alone go back down it. Up went the party, hoping. It was all they could do—and fortunately at the top there was a gravelly, rocky slope. They could see where to descend into Ross's Hole. There were some signs of recent occupation—a fire still burning and fresh sign of two horses—but no sign of the native Flatheads or anyone else.

Charbonneau looked uneasily at Clark and wondered fleetingly what it would be like to know that hostile bands were watching them, to feel that stalking enemies were on the lookout in that desolation—after all, hadn't they come across the ashes of other men's fires? Charbonneau put the thought away deliberately and laughed nervously.

They followed an indistinct trail across the Continental Divide down into the large valley of the Jefferson River.[4]

In that valley Charbonneau spotted a buffalo. He kicked his horse into action and primed his rifle as he rode, but he did not keep his balance as he watched the buffalo and worked with his rifle. He was thrown to the ground and remained stiff and sore for a week. George Gibson fell off his horse and landed on a sharp snag, which ran nearly two inches into his thigh. This lamed him so badly that he had to be carried in a litter made of poles lashed and woven across by rawhide thongs.

Sacajawea rubbed rancid bear's oil on the face and arms of Pomp to keep off mosquitoes. She passed it to Gibson and Charbonneau. The mosquitoes were small and penetrated the netting covering Pomp at night. Some of the men slept facedown against the ground to keep the insects off. Pomp's face became red and swollen like some huge puffball even with bear's oil and protective netting.

"Deer in these parts are poor on account of these torturous insects," Clark grumbled. "The ravenous pests have sucked away most of the animals' blood."

There were large and aggressive rattlesnakes that the horses had to sidestep. There was a close call when Sacajawea comforted her child and did not watch the trail carefully. Her horse stepped into a nest of small rattlers, but the horse pulled out so fast there was no time for any to strike.

The following day, they came to Shoshoni Cove, where they had buried canoes the year before. Now in the Shoshoni country, everyone kept a lookout for the Agai-dükas. Sacajawea found the meadow grass waist-tall when she stopped to gather camass roots. Always she hoped to see somewhere women of the People out gathering roots. She saw no one and no marks of a recent camp. The trees were full-leaved, and the whole wide cove was spread green. The rimrocks seemed silver around it, and the sky like a sheet of blue silk.

Charbonneau looked at this valley in high summer and said, "I would call it Bayou Salade."

At midday Sacajawea pointed to old beaver dams making a small stream wide. "Here my people have trapped." Even the trees seemed familiar. Hours passed, and the dusk before dark came on. There was still no sign of the People.

Worn and tired, leg muscles stiff, the men made night camp.

"I have given my word that I would return to see the People," Sacajawea said, more to herself than to anyone else in particular.

"This outfit will not wander all over these foothills looking for some people who are on the move—who have probably moved more than once since we last saw them," scolded Charbonneau. "*Femme*, what you think? We could never be certain of finding them. And there is Capitaine Lewis's party—waiting for us. The men—they want to be home before the Missouri freezes. *Femme*, you come with me. We will make our camp with the Minnetarees. They will be your people. Huh?" Charbonneau scratched through the hair on his chest and cleared his throat. He noticed Sacajawea's bowed head, but did not see the tears that touched the blanket across her knees.

"Time will work for me," she mumbled. "I will see the People again." Sacajawea knew that Charbonneau would rather be where he could pretend he was a big man. She knew also that he would never understand her feeling toward the People, or any one person. This was his way. She knew, too, that her own brother, Chief Black Gun, had told her she must stay with her man because that was the Shoshoni way, but he had also

said that Charbonneau would never come back to the
Shoshoni. *Ai*, she thought, Black Gun knew then. The
foreboding she had felt when leaving her brother was
due partly to the intuitive knowledge she herself had
had that she would never see Black Gun again.

She sat still for a time, wondering. Finally she heard
Charbonneau laugh huskily and saw him go to sit with
the men around the fire.

Captain Clark found the canoes safe and the cache
of supplies intact and dry. Inside the cache the men
found tobacco. They acted as though that were the most
important find of the day. The chewers had long ago
tired of crabtree bark, and the smokers coughed on their
mixture of red willow bark and bearberry leaves. Now
that the cache was opened, smoke puffs and brown spit
flowed freely, and the men began to feel that the hard
part of the trip was behind them and now it was something to tell big stories about. They counted the mile-
stones. They had passed Willard Creek,[5] gone on to the
Jefferson River, and camped in Shoshoni Cove.

The next morning, Clark left Nat Pryor in charge of
six men to bring on the horses overland. The rest of the
outfit climbed into the canoes. In three days the canoes
covered the distance that had taken more than a week
on the way upstream the year before.

Pomp dangled his hands in the river and chattered
with Ben York. The mountain streams that fell into
the river were full of sticks and fallen saplings where
beaver built homes and the water was calmed to a placid
pool. The beaver, with otter and muskrats, basked along
the banks. Sometimes a beaver slapped a tail around
a canoe, angry at the invasion of his security. The beaver were often eaten now and pelts saved to take back
to the States.

On July 13, Clark met Pryor and his six men with
the outfit's horses at the site of their old July 27, 1805,
encampment. That evening, Clark sent John Ordway
and ten of the men downriver in the six canoes with a
letter for Captain Lewis. Ordway's party was to camp
at the Great Falls and wait for Lewis. Clark took the
rest of the party overland with the forty-nine horses
and one colt. The rocks and prickly pear were hard and
sharp on the hooves of the unshod horses.

Sacajawea walked with Clark and York. "The People put moccasins on their horses before the hooves are worn down to the quick and are as painful as this."

"Moccasins?" asked Clark, at first unbelieving, thinking Sacajawea was making a joke, then wondering why he had not thought of so simple and logical a thing himself long ago.

"*Ai*, made from green buffalo hide because it is strong."

After the last meal of the day, Sacajawea showed Clark and York how to make moccasins as best she could remember, for the horses that were most lame. York saw how the moccasins helped, and he made more as the party continued over the stony plains.

And York carved a willow whistle for Pomp as they rode past the small timber in the rain.[6]

Sacajawea kept looking backward, hoping to see a thin wisp of smoke—something to tell her that the People were near. She stopped frequently and breathed deeply, then took small, shallow breaths, smelling the air. She could detect no camp or horse herd or group of people nearby. To leave this land of the People was one of the hardest and loneliest steps of Sacajawea's life.

"Don't lollygag around here," warned Charbonneau sharply. "Come on, *femme*. The outfit, she will leave you behind. *Faire allons!*"

Clark, coming up from the rear, sensed her desire to linger at this last edge of Shoshoni land. He wanted to ease her hurting heart.

"Janey, there is a time to plant and a time to pull up that which was planted."

She looked at him, her eyes wide. He really knew how she felt. He knew it was hard to pull away from all her childhood memories. He knew she was aching inside and that by tomorrow this land would be something in her past. Slowly she drew herself to her full height.

"You brought me to the land of my people; now you take me away. Is that your right?" The words flashed from her, each word deliberate and each meant to reproach and sting. Her head was held high, her hands making a talk of their own.

In an instant it dawned on Clark that she cared

deeply about him and wished for him to feel her hurt
as she rode through her people's land without so much
as saying a farewell to them.

She knew also that the things she had submerged
and made to stay sleeping in her had come awake. Then
she thought how impossible even to speak of this deeper
feeling between them. This feeling had roots between
them, but the roots could never be nourished and kept
alive when the well of feeling had to be kept buried. It
had to be a river that never dried up.

Her vehemence went down like a storm wind and
faded.

Clark said nothing as he watched her ride ahead. He
thought that what he had heard and seen were fragments and ripples of her personal identity as an individual. It was as though a wish had been granted and
he had seen inside her skull. He saw she was becoming
herself and finding her purpose, no longer cowed by the
shackles of Shoshoni or any other native tradition or
behavior. She was behaving as a white girl, or any girl,
might, given the opportunity to find herself.

On July 18, Charbonneau saw a thin line of smoke
rise to the southeast in the plains. Then he became
excited when he thought he saw an Indian on the highlands on the opposite side of the river. He rode back to
Captain Clark, "*Mon dieu*, you talk with my son and
make jokes, but *Jésus*, don't you see that smoke and
that man? There, see? He is a Prenegard, a Crow with
slanting brown eyes, opened wide, and a single black
crow feather in his hair."

"How could you have seen a man's eyes from this
distance? I did see a line of smoke," Clark said, wiping
the palms of his hands on his buckskins, "but I don't
see it now."

"You saw the smoke, and that means Indians somewhere," Charbonneau said, standing up to him.

Some of the other men became jumpy when Charbonneau told about the thieving Crows who were
watching the camp constantly. The men became especially uneasy when horses actually began to disappear,
one or two at a time, always at night. Only the best

horses were missing. When half the horses vanished one night, doubt was no longer possible.

"*Sacre*! Now you believe me," said Charbonneau. "I saw a Crow Indian, a damned, thieving Crow."

The remaining horses were so nervous that they stampeded one morning when Pryor approached them. He took a search party out and failed to find a single horse, but he brought back a length of Indian rope and a moccasin, still wet around the sole, which seemed to indicate it had been worn a few hours earlier near the water. Shannon found the tracks of the stolen herd, being driven at full speed down the valley. So—perhaps the Crows were around, though no one ever saw them— except old Charbonneau.

Clark ordered Pryor to take Windsor and Shannon and go directly to the Mandan villages. From there they were to go north to the Assiniboin, find Hugh Heney, the Canadian trader they had met in 1804, and give Heney a letter asking him to persuade Sioux chiefs to visit the President of the United States in Washington, D.C. Clark made it clear that he would pick up the three men and the chiefs with his canoes on the way down the Missouri.

These three men were trailed by the Indians, which kept them in a constant state of excitement. One night a wolf came into their camp and bit Pryor's hand while he slept and was about to attack Windsor when Shannon shot it. "We have two hopes," said Shannon. "One is that we find Clark again, and the other is that the Indians will not find it necessary to take our scalps." They shouldered their packs and headed for the river.

Unaware of the three men's trouble, Clark ran his canoes swiftly down the Yellowstone River, enjoying the scenery. The days were hot, but the nights were cool. Now and again, buffalo dotted the landscape, under the shade of trees, or standing in water, like cattle, or browsing on the soft green hills. Deer and elk were shot from the canoes. Sometimes they heard the booming subterranean geysers hidden in the hollows of the mountains.

On July 25, Clark ordered the dugouts to land. He wanted to examine an unusual rock. Its tall sides were

covered with animal figures; the top was flat except
that it had two rock cairns built at the summit that
seemed to mesh together because there were Vs in the
rim aligned like Vs in a rifle sight. Clark examined the
top of this unusual rock, which rose almost sheer above
the broad, flat plain of the Yellowstone Valley. There
were no loose stones on the top. Clark surmised that
some people had to carry the stones for the cairns up
the steep, accessible northeast side, a hundred and fifty
to two hundred feet from the valley. Inside the cairns
were bird bones, together with several small clay bowls
painted black and several others painted white.

"Too bad we did not find this earlier," sighed Clark.
"It might be some kind of structure to measure the
solstice. We could have tested it with spring stars. I
wonder who made use of it."

Clark was busy examining the carvings, then pointed
out some interesting markings to Sacajawea. She ran
her hands over the rock and found more carvings of
deer grazing. As she bent close to the rock, Pomp, in a
blanket on her back, reached out and touched one primitive animal representation.

"Bear," he said plainly.

Clark reached for the child's hand. "I name this pillar
Pompy's Tower," he said ceremoniously.

York laughed and said, "Some folks'll think this rock
was named for a little pickaninny instead of Janey's
firstborn."

Looking down to the base of the pillar, Clark saw a
creek flowing close by and announced, "I dedicate the
creek below to my little dancing boy, Pomp, and name
it by his given name, Jean Baptiste's Creek."[7] Before
climbing all the way down the rock, Clark paused to chip
his name and the date in the side. "Pryor and his men will
know we've been here if they pass this way," he said.

"I could chip a buffalo in the rock," quipped Charbonneau, "but I could not spell my name. Maybe someone would do that for me?"

"Aw, come on down carefully. It would be better if
you roasted us some fresh buffalo hump. I saw lots of
those big beasts below us just waiting for some hunter
to shoot," said Clark, grabbing for the small brush to
steady his downward path.

33

Big White

The Mandan subchief, Sheheke, or Big White, was named because of his blueish eyes and white hair. He went down the Missouri in 1806 with Captains Lewis and Clark. From St. Louis he traveled to Washington D.C. to meet his Great White Father. His safe return to the Mandans caused many problems for the United States Government.

Lewis and Clark presented Big White with a Jefferson Peace Medal that is three and three-sixteenth inches in diameter. The suspension lug soldered to the collar is small and the medal weighs one and a half ounces. It is a near miracle that the medal still exists and has not been bent or scarred more than it actually is. Big White treasured the medal and passed it on to his son, White Painted Horse, who passed it on to his son, Tobacco. Big White's grandson, Tobacco, passed it on to his son, Gun That Guards The Horse. So it was given to Big White's other descendants: Good Boy, Four Bears, Four Turtles, Red Buffalo Cow, and Black Eagle. Finally it came to the great, great, great, great grandson of Big White, Burr Crows Breast of Elbowwoods, North Dakota. Burr Crows Breast sold the medal to the western history lover and *general practitioner, Dr. K. O. Leonard of Garrison, North Dakota.*

PAUL RUSSELL CUTRIGHT, "Lewis and Clark Peace Medals," *The Bulletin*. St. Louis: The Missouri Historical Society, vol. 24, no. 2, 1968, pp. 165–66.

Once Clark had the men pull all the canoes into shore because the river was blackened with buffalo fording from one side to the other.

"We have come nine hundred miles down to the Yellowstone by my estimate," said Clark.

When they were under way once again, Sacajawea kept smelling the air and looking toward both riverbanks.

"What do you look for?" asked Charbonneau suspiciously. "Are there Indians near?"

"Not natives, but *ai*, people. It is difficult to understand."

"You are the one that is difficult to understand," sighed Charbonneau.

"Oh, no," said Sacajawea, "I only say what I feel."

"Your thoughts go one way, and your tongue only just points after them. There is a lot to imagine to follow some of your words." He watched her working in the bow of the heavy canoe; the child was tied to a crossbar behind her. She paddled as steadily as any man.

Clark and some of the others heard her words, but could not imagine who could be near. Pryor and his group were far overland, they were sure, and it was not yet time to meet with Captain Lewis and his party.

"There is a group of people near," she repeated.

Clark did not believe in prescience and told her so. She only smiled back, her face, in the strong reflection from the water, cheerful but stubborn.

When they reached the junction of the Yellowstone and Missouri rivers, Clark began to wonder if Sacajawea might be right and maybe Lewis's outfit was close, so he wrote deep in the wet sand of the riverbank: W. C. A FEW MILES DOWN ON RIGHT-HAND SIDE. For two nights Clark's group camped on the right-hand side of the river. The mosquitoes drove everyone crazy. On the third day they were pushing the canoes back out into the river when Sacajawea pulled at Clark's sleeve, grinned, and pointed upstream. Coming down the Missouri in their bull boats were Nat Pryor, Dick Windsor, and George Shannon.

At noon four days later, there was a loud cry and waving of caps from the men as they sighted the canoes of Lewis's party. Sacajawea smiled broadly at Clark. He shook his head with wonderment. Her talent was something that civilized white men seemed to have little intelligence about. Then Clark turned to watch the canoes land, and he began to have a sinking feeling in the pit of his stomach. Something was wrong. He could not see Captain Lewis anywhere.

"Where is he?" shouted Clark, running forward to examine the oncoming canoes.

Pat Gass looked up, jerking his thumb toward the bottom of his canoe. "Here! It's shot he was!"

"Good God! He's—all right? Is he hurt badly?" Clark ran to the beaching canoe with the others all following. Oh, God, don't let anything happen to that good man, he thought. How could he have been shot? Had they run into some unfriendly natives? His fears were quieted when he found that Lewis had only a buttock wound. Then he could not hold back his relief and laughed heartily when he was told that the nearsighted Cruzatte had mistaken his captain for an elk.

Lewis lay pale but smiling in the bottom of the canoe. "Cruzatte is probably the only soldier in any army known to have shot his commanding officer in the seat without punishment."

"The man should have looked where he was pointing that muzzle," said Clark. Gently he and York lifted Lewis up out of the canoe and carried him to the camp on the river's edge.

"Oh, it was a mistake, just an accident. It is nothing," Lewis said softly.

Cruzatte looked shamefaced at Captain Clark. "Sir, I never should have gone hunting! I will stick to fiddle playing from now on."

"I keep telling you it will heal in twenty days, a month at the most. Don't berate yourself for an unavoidable accident," said Lewis slowly.

Clark, taking no chances, examined the wound. It was still so painful that Lewis fainted as Clark cleansed it. He dressed it with fresh patent lint from the medical stores.

Sacajawea went to York and said, "Strong clover tea

might revive Captain Lewis. Then he needs to eat meat for more strength."

"You'se make the tea and I'se get him some cold elk roast we have left over," said York, rushing around the cook fire.

By the following evening the wound was so sore and Lewis's legs so stiff that he would not leave the canoe. He slept there uncomfortably. Somehow he found the strength to write one last lengthy and technical botanical note about the Missouri cherry tree. From that evening on, he let Clark keep the only written journal for the last few weeks of the expedition.

The next afternoon, the entire group started out in five canoes and the white pirogue Lewis had brought with his party, as well as two lashed-together canoes that Clark had built. The two bull boats were left behind. In two days the canoes came alongside the large village of their old friends, the Mandans. A firing of guns brought swarms of natives to the beach.

Sacajawea felt as though she were awakening from a dream. It was hard to realize it was all over. She found herself in the midst of familiar landmarks as she stepped from the canoe. She was back far too soon. A part of her life was gone. From now on, she would not rise in the morning with an untrodden trail ahead holding new sights to see. This was a familiar village with familiar habits. She began to feel like a caged bird.

Shouts, laughter, an involuntary cry, and then a sudden din rose from the natives who surrounded the returned men, who remained in a cluster, smiling, clinging together still. For a moment Sacajawea had an impulse to flee the cage of people surrounding her, and she sensed the same urge in her companions. Then the vision of hardship and hunger flashed through her mind, and she looked at the Mandans as people who could offer an enchanting world of warmth and lazy well-being. She seized the hands of the nearest squaws and suddenly laughed. She noticed the look of veiled timidity in their eyes and saw their expression change to startled wonder when she laughed. For the moment she did not try to understand or ponder or explain or hear explanations. She wanted only to enjoy her sensations.

"Squash! Corn!" she shouted and continued laughing. "Lodges, people!" She waved her arms and embraced the women. But beyond the emotions of welcoming, a false heartiness was reflected in the eyes of these women. Their expressions seemed tinged with fear and apprehension.

"Look!" Sacajawea shouted, now longing to see something more in their dark eyes. She pushed the hair back from the left side of her child's head. "He almost went under! His whole body burned for many days. Chief Red Hair had healing salves. Others were sick. We ate our horses."

"When?" some disbelieving squaw asked.

"During the winter." She released Pomp. "We were afraid to sleep because of the cold."

"*Ai*, it was cold here last winter."

She shook her head emphatically. "Not like that. Some of the men froze their hands and feet. Some wanted to lie down and sleep on the trail." She paused, looking from one to the other. "It is wonderful to see you."

A babble broke out, and the din of the villagers drowned her words. "What? What?" She seized the wife of a subchief whom she knew, pulling her closer. "Did you expect us? Have you wondered about us? I cannot hear you speak. What is wrong? Why do you look as though you do not believe what you see?" Suddenly Sacajawea felt so uneasy she turned and twisted to see over their heads.

"Red Hair! Red Hair! Chief Red Hair!" she called. She pushed the squaws aside and elbowed her way to Captain Clark. In the crowd she saw some of the other men's familiar faces. The noise was deafening. She grasped Clark's arm and tiptoed to scream in his ear, but she hardly knew what she wanted to say. She wanted only to be near him, and near the others—Captain Lewis, York, Shannon, Cruzatte, Gass—all the familiar faces—for the Mandans had become strangers and she felt alone. Captain Lewis stood uneasily, supporting himself by makeshift crutches propped under his arms. The dog, Scannon, stood protectively near. York reached out and pulled her back into the group of men just as Charbonneau broke away and made for the crowd of squaws. He saw Otter Woman with the boy, Little Tess.

"By *Jésus*," Charbonneau shouted, "you look good!

And is that my boy Tess? He is big." He pointed excitedly to the youngster who stood barefoot alongside Otter Woman.

When Otter Woman was close to Sacajawea, they stared at each other, and finally Sacajawea asked, "And where is Corn Woman? Didn't she come with you?"

But Otter Woman was staring through Sacajawea. She hardly saw her; she had eyes only for her returned man, Charbonneau. He was a hero who had come home to her. Charbonneau put Tess on his shoulders and went through the crowd. He had been ordered by Captain Lewis to invite all the chiefs to a powwow with the white men.

Clark turned to Drouillard. "Go to the lower village of the Mandans and ask René Jussome to come and do some interpreting for us. Let's hope he is around."

Then Clark brushed a lock of black hair from Sacajawea's forehead and clasped her shoulders with his hands, holding her firmly against him for several minutes before breaking away to walk through the crowd in the direction of Black Cat's village, Rooptahee, in order to invite him personally to smoke the pipe and talk once again with the captains.

"We are going to ask some of these village chiefs to accompany us to Washington," said Captain Lewis, now sitting in the canoe where York had lifted him.

York was going through some of the baggage, trying to get together the makings of a suitable pallet for Lewis to use while the men were camped on this beach. "That Kakoakis won't," said York, chuckling. "He's fearful that the Sioux wait behind every tree for him with a tight bow."

Late in the afternoon, during the powwow, the captains found that the Minnetarees had broken their pledge and had continued raids against other tribes, especially the Sioux. Each tribe was ready to jump at the others' scalps. President Jefferson's peace plan is not working well, thought Captain Clark.

Gass threw deadwood on the council fire, and the flames sprang up, lighting the faces in the ring around the fire.

Sacajawea felt someone nudge her back and whisper

in her ear, "Go to your mother in the lodge. She has
lost all hope." Turning she saw it was Fast Arrow. He
was pointing in the direction of his lodge. "She does not
believe you will ever return."

"Grasshopper does not know I am here?" she gasped.

"She has been told but does not hear. Let her see
you."

Sacajawea stood and embraced Fast Arrow. He
pushed her aside roughly. "I have watched the river all
winter."

She left the council and followed the path.

Sacajawea pushed the plank door open, walked
through the low entrance, and the familiar smells of a
Minnetaree lodge overwhelmed her—leather, cooking
meat and fat, drying squash, and cornhusks.

"Mother?" she whispered. Cornhusks on a pallet rustled, and suddenly quiet weeping answered her. She
bent down into Grasshopper's outstretched arms and
no longer felt like a stranger among familiar faces. For
several minutes old Grasshopper could not stop weeping. Finally she dried her eyes, sniffed once or twice,
and said, "Oh, my child, I did not believe I would ever
see your face again." Slowly Grasshopper began to talk
of the things that never passed away from the heavens
and earth, and after a while she was silent. There was
a sadness such as Sacajawea had never known mixed
with her love for this mother.

For the first time in nearly two years, Sacajawea
and Pomp did not spend the night in the camp of the
expedition. She was in the lodge that Otter Woman had
kept neat during the time they were gone. In the morning, Grasshopper felt well enough to venture from her
lodge to come for a visit with Sacajawea. The old woman
sat herself against a wooden lodge support and held the
squirming Pomp in her lap, cooing and fussing over
him. She smacked her lips over a bowl of stew and asked
for another. Settling back against the wooden post, she
slept for a while. Sacajawea and Otter Woman cleaned
the lodge and smoothed out the sleeping couches. When
she awoke, Grasshopper, with regret in her voice, told
of the day the white men's fort burned. This was not

many days after the expedition went up the Missouri to the west.

Sacajawea stopped her work to listen.

"Chief Kakoakis took some of his men and some supplies to the abandoned fort the same day the white men left. The British, under the leadership of Charles MacKenzie, had coveted the fort for a trading station and for living quarters for their men. There was some loud argument between MacKenzie and Kakoakis. MacKenzie took his men away, saying, 'No one will use this fort.'"

Grasshopper put her hand on her chest and rocked back and forth a few moments as though trying to catch her breath. "There was no more talk about the affair for many days. Then, on a hot, dry day, someone noticed ashes falling from the sky. Before that we had several days that were blazing hot and dry with high winds. But on the day the ashes fell, I can remember Fast Arrow coming into our lodge upset and covering his feeling with a shortness of speech."

Grasshopper clicked her tongue rapidly. "Fast Arrow said the white men's lodges were in the middle of a red blaze. It was those high winds that kept the flames on the move. The wind leaped over the walls and spilled the flame out onto the prairie. The wind swirled this way and that as the Great Spirit moved it. The people from all the villages came to watch, and the flames moved beyond the fire line made two winters ago by the white men. The fire-killed trees standing gaunt and gray, tinder-dry, became ashes on the blackened ground. The humus around the tree roots smoldered, and when the roots weakened and released boulders sitting on them, the boulders leaped downward, gaining speed, jumping, smashing their way through brush, dislodging others that were larger than themselves." Grasshopper twirled her hands around each other to show how the boulders rolled downhill, gaining speed. "Red-hot rocks leaped across the creek, hummed in the air, and buried themselves in the drifts of fireweed. There was much smoke by now, so that the whole sky was hidden and there was no sun. An unnatural darkness settled on the Five Villages at midday. The Great Spirit was angry—even Kakoakis could see that. Grasshopper shifted her weight.

Charbonneau had come in while she was talking, but had not paid much attention to the women at first. Now he slid a little farther down on his spine. "I'll be damned," he said softly. "Who started it?"

"No one knows. But the women in this village say the man called Mackenzie went north behind the hills." Grasshopper's chin pointed. "He is no good?"

"Maybe," said Charbonneau. "What does it matter now? We'll have to keep an eye peeled, is all. It was not very clever of MacKenzie, maybe. The time will come when either Kakoakis or the Americans will catch him out."

Grasshopper was talking again. "The villages braced themselves, much as a man does who expects to receive a blow. That is it, they thought. The darkness seemed to thicken, and who could tell that above the smoke the rain clouds were gathering? Then the first great drops came down through the smoke, and all the Minnetarees and the Northwesters looked up and wondered if this were real or part of some terrible dream. The skies opened, and soon the rain was drumming down in blinding torrents. Everyone ran for shelter, and gradually the smoke was washed down out of the air and the prairie appeared once again. The fire choked and steamed and spluttered, and slowly died. That was the end of it." Grasshopper clucked and thought that she should add something. "I am sorry the white men's lodges were eaten by fire. It leaves a scar on our land and on our hearts."

The expedition had set up their temporary camp opposite the village of Rooptahee, where old Black Cat was chief.

After a few days of rest, Clark asked Jussome to try to talk one of the important men of the villages into going to Washington. Jussome left grumbling that maybe Charbonneau ought to do some of this hard work also. But soon he was back in a cheerful mood with good news. One subchief had consented to go. It was She-heke—Big White, as the Northwesters called him because of his blue eyes and nearly white hair. Big White

had agreed to go if he could take along his woman,
Yellow Corn, and his youngest son, White Painted Horse,
and if Jussome and his woman, Broken Tooth, and their
two children, Toussaint and Jeanette, went.

Captain Lewis limped around his camp pondering
on those terms. No other chief would go downriver with
the expedition. Finally Lewis said, "This is probably
the only way the expedition is going to get a member
of the five Upper Missouri tribes to meet Jefferson."

When Sacajawea heard that Jussome and Broken
Tooth were going to Washington, she knew Charbonneau would not be needed as interpreter on the downriver trip. She knew, too, that Jussome had seen the
grand welcoming given Charbonneau, who was now a
big man with the Mandans, and that Jussome was jealous. So—what else? He had arranged with Big White
so that he could also be thought of as a big man.

A few days later, Sacajawea learned of one of the
men from the expedition taking advantage of opportunity. John Colter asked Clark if he could leave the
expedition to go with two trappers, Joe Dickson, from
Illinois country, and Forest Hancock, from Daniel
Boone's settlement on the Lower Missouri, back to the
Yellowstone.[1] Dickson and Hancock were glad to have
Colter accompany them and share their trappings. He
would be a useful guide, having just come from that
country, which was all new to them.

Colter had gotten used to being called Seehkheeda,
White Eyebrows, by the Indians of the Five Villages,
and he knew he would be politely considered eccentric
by the whites in any city. He had become "bushed,"
meaning that he was used to the unending struggle
against the elements and the hard physical work it took
to live in the beauty of the unspoiled wilderness. He
could not live away from the majesty and dignity of
plains and mountains, the greatness of it, nor its challenge.

Captain Clark explained to the other men that they
would grant this special privilege to Colter only if all
the others agreed to finish the journey into Saint Louis—
except Charbonneau, who had made arrangements to
stay in his old lodge in the Minnetaree village where
the captains had found him.

The men agreed. They were all eager to go home.

When Colter got around to leaving, there was none of the ritual of formal farewells. The men all came to say good-bye. Sacajawea was there with Pomp and Charbonneau. A handshake, a "So long," an occasional "*au revoir*," or even a casual nod or wave of the hand sufficed. These men and the woman and child were his close friends, and by now they had become as taciturn and undemonstrative as any native, so Colter understood their sincerity thoroughly, regardless of fanfare or display. He needed no other proof that they were his friends than the fact that they had made an effort to see him off.

"I have not forgotten the most important lesson of the expedition." Colter nudged Charbonneau. "An outfit never takes a woman with them except on peaceful business. I think we need to find a woman to accompany us. Do you think she'd go?" He bent his head toward Sacajawea.

The men guffawed. Sacajawea suppressed her grin. Charbonneau shifted restlessly, and his bright, pinpoint eyes searched every face to make sure no one was making sport of him.

All day Otter Woman asked endless questions. She asked about the Shoshonis and the Blackfeet. She asked about the mountains, trees, and water. She barely listened as Sacajawea told of the men so hungry they ate horsemeat and even dogs. Otter Woman was thinking what to ask next when Sacajawea told about the water people, the seals, sliding up and off the rocks. Then she told of the skeleton of the great whale. Otter Woman did not know what things to believe, and so she asked more questions. To her these events were unimaginable.

Pomp seemed happy to have an older brother and followed Tess around like a shadow.

Charbonneau was happy to be back in his old lodge where Otter Woman would take off his boots and bathe his feet. "By gar, one of these days I am going to Big White's village and give him some advice for living with the white men, and then I will see if Corn is willing to leave her *maman* and *papa* to come back here with me."

The next day was hot; by afternoon it was depressing. Charbonneau opened the lodge door and called inside, "*Les capitaines* will leave, and you will not have said your last *merci, femme*. Come on out here."

Sacajawea scooped up Pomp and followed Charbonneau, who was winding his way through the curving streets to the water's edge. Charbonneau wore a dark scowl on his fat, bearded face. He was obviously disappointed over Clark's decision to take Jussome as interpreter on the Saint Louis—bound trip, so that Big White would go along.[2] He did not think how he had told Clark he planned to stay in the Minnetaree village and trap and act as interpreter for the incoming traders, a life he was already accustomed to.

On the street of the village they were joined by some Minnetarees, some Mandan warriors, women, and children—who all looked at Charbonneau and chanted in unison, "Whoohoo, whoohoo!" Charbonneau stopped, and his worried face lost its scowl, his features forming a great half-moon reaching from the bottom of his ears to his chin, all wrinkled with laughter. He waved and tossed his head in the sunlight. "They are glad I am back! They call me Chief of the White Men's Canoes. I told them how I poled to keep the canoes on a straight path and how I prevented them from shipping water by keeping out of rapids. See, I am a big man among these Five Villages!" Others ran past calling, "Whoohoo!" They waved to Charbonneau, who continued along ahead of his woman as the crowd at their heels cried happily, "Whoohoo!"

They passed the village of Mahawha and walked across the freshly broken camp of the expedition. Sacajawea was not sure she could keep her tears back. They went to the canoes, which were almost loaded. Sacajawea could see Captain Lewis half reclining in one canoe with an account book in one hand. Pomp pulled away and ran toward Captain Clark, who was supervising the last-minute loading. He caught the child and tossed him in the air, catching him with a kiss as he fell back into his arms. "Go, go, good-bye," the child squealed in English. Clark put him down and began explaining sadly that Pomp would not be able to go on this trip.

CHAPTER

34

Good-Byes

Clark's Journal:

Saturday 17th of August 1806

Settled with Touisant Chabono for his services as an enterpreter the price of a horse and Lodge purchased of him for public Service in all amounting to 500$ 33⅓ cents....I offered to take his little son a butifull promising child who is 19 months old to which they both himself and wife wer willing provided the child had been weened. they observed that in one year the boy would be sufficiently old to leave his mother and he would then take him to me if I would be so friendly as to raise the child for him in such a manner as I thought proper, to which I agreed etc.

BERNARD DEVOTO, ed., *The Journals of Lewis and Clark*. New York: Houghton Mifflin Co., 1953, pp. 457–58.

"**H**ey, Charbonneau!" Captain Lewis waved. "You are just the man we want to see. We want to settle with you."

Charbonneau sauntered to the canoe.

"You have quite a sum coming. Not only for services rendered at twenty-five dollars a month, but we owe you for the leather tent and a horse that the elusive Crows ran off with. Man, we sure made good use of that tent—wore it out. Clark and I figure you earned five hundred dollars and thirty-three cents. Is that satisfactory?"

"Mon dieu!" exclaimed Charbonneau.

Lewis made out a government money order. As he reached for it, Charbonneau's eyes gleamed. He had never had that much money at one time before.

"You have to take it to a United States trading post or to a bank in a town to get the actual cash, you know. That will buy a lot," Lewis explained. He grasped Charbonneau's arm and looked into his face. His eyes narrowed against the glare. "We have completed our journey. There is nothing but thankfulness in my heart."

Charbonneau turned away when he saw Jussome push Broken Tooth and their boy and girl into the next canoe. But Lewis's slim hand tightened its grip. "Surely you feel happiness and some sense of accomplishment."

"Capitaine, do not think that I feel any resentment that I cannot complete the trip to Saint Louis."

Lewis dropped his hand. "We owe you nothing!" he cried angrily. "You stated you'd be more at home among the Minnetarees. We gave you friendship, and now you have been fairly paid for your services. There is no reason to become sulky. Can't we part happily?"

"Maybe we can talk him into coming to Saint Louis and buying a parcel of land with that money order," said Captain Clark cheerfully, coming to supervise the fastening together of two of the canoes with poles tied across them so that Big White and his family and the Jussomes would have a place to ride together.

"That's nice," said Charbonneau, staring blankly at

681

Lewis for an instant. "I'm not certain what to do with it yet."

"Here is your Army discharge," said Lewis, handing Charbonneau another paper. "That might come in handy if you ever want to buy land in the States. You can show them that you worked for the government in the capacity of an interpreter for the U.S. Army. That ought to make a good character reference."

"I was thinking about the blacksmithing tools," Clark said. "Charbonneau can have those. We have no further need of them." Lewis nodded his agreement.

"Wish we could show our appreciation to your *femme*, Janey. If anyone deserves compensation—for interpreting, and caring for all those sick natives, and keeping up the general good spirits of the men—she does. But we can't list a woman on our Army payroll—no way."

"Oh, that is all right," said Charbonneau sullenly, watching his woman talking with the other men. "She is a squaw; she don't need nothing."

"Well, there is something else I've been thinking. Why don't you change your mind and come with us? We'll make room. We could, couldn't we, Lewis?"

But before Lewis could answer, Clark was speaking again with Charbonneau. "Come on and try to live among the whites. I'll take you down to the Illinois. You can buy a piece of good land and farm—horses and cattle. Or you could hire out on the river boats; or you and I could be partners in some sort of small-scale fur trade."

Charbonneau's eyes were on Jussome, who was pushing Big White here and there. Charbonneau's shoulders sagged. "As a voyageur I have no real prestige with the whites."

Sacajawea had come next to Charbonneau and now tugged at his arm. "This is opportunity," she said.

"You'd be better off than among these Indians," said Clark. "Even Janey knows some of the white ways now, and she can speak fair English and French. It will be hard for her to be content anymore among the Minnetarees and Mandans."

"*Ai*," said Sacajawea, pulling at Charbonneau's arm until he stepped away.

"*Non, non,*" he said, scratching his shaggy head. "I have no acquaintance or prospect to make a living below. I know no business except trading with Indians. We starve in Saint Louis." He continued to watch Jussome. "I—I stay and live in the way I have done—with the Minnetarees!" Charbonneau cried in sudden consternation. "I have said this before."

Clark had been watching Sacajawea, who was slightly taller and much slimmer than Charbonneau. Her face was better proportioned, with its shapely nose, black eyes, bronze skin, and dark hair. Clark knew that Charbonneau regarded her only as a possession, a symbol of wealth. He knew that she had learned to be intensely perceptive; she was intelligent. He was aware that he could find prettier women—to the white man's standards—in a ten-minute stroll down the streets of Saint Louis, but there would be none who would adore him so. And she was the squaw of one of his employees. She had become quite indifferent to Charbonneau, but she was devoted to her child.

Clark had also grown fond of the child. "Think! I offer you a better life, not only for you but for your child. Yes, let me give him an education. Let me raise him, send him to school, like a white child."

Sacajawea pulled her child close, not in fear but in bewilderment. She knew now for certain that Chief Red Hair felt a deep tenderness for her child, for why else would he offer such a great thing? But she knew, too, it would break her heart to send her son away alone if Charbonneau would not go himself and permit her to go also.

Lewis shifted uncomfortably in the canoe, his wound still bothering him. What is the matter with Clark? he thought. He should know that Janey won't give up that child. Does he hope by that kind of ruse to get her to come to Saint Louis? I knew he was fond of her, but not this much. Lewis could not see her face, but it had become transfused with yearning. She longed for her son to have the advantages Clark had had himself as a child, as the bears long for spring to ripen the berries, or as buffalo trapped in the mountains hunger for the plains.

Charbonneau answered, "When the boy is weaned, you ask me again."

There was silence. Clark raised his head and stared at the men, some of whom had left smoldering ashes and were walking slowly toward the canoes.

"I will tell you something because I know in your heart you respect me," said Clark, wiping his forehead with his leather sleeve. "You have asked for help, looked for servility, and demanded special privileges. The men have secretly laughed many times at your wild scrambling, but never when you were eager to join and do your share. They were sorry for your tortured hands and miserable condition, but they were proud when you showed the least doggedness and courage. There were times they deliberately tested your daring, and there were times you showed you could stand up like a man."

Clark had unbuttoned his shirt and was fanning himself with a branch of cottonwood leaves. Charbonneau stared at him in openmouthed surprise. Clark chuckled. "Now I have flattered you enough. What I want to say is this. The men feel"—he laughed—"that they alone are responsible for turning a weak, helpless Frenchman into a man with whom any one of them would be pleased to hunt or trap. They trust you according to the rules that make a white man a desirable companion in the wilderness. You are not an Indian. What do you say now?"

"You do not lie?" Charbonneau flushed.

"So—it pleases you. And will you now realize how badly you have treated Janey, who deserves as much or more than you for the success of this trip?"

Charbonneau plucked at the whangs on his sleeves and pictured himself the owner of many fine horses and fat cattle, with a farm of tall corn and fat bolls of cotton. In his imagination he saw his sons, Tess and Pomp, going to school in Saint Louis. He saw Sacajawea's grinning face, Otter Woman's flat smile as they sang beside the cooking fire. And then they all turned to Clark and held out a brimful bowl of stew and an ear of roasted corn before turning toward Charbonneau.

Remorse filled Charbonneau. He had repulsed friendship, and now he wondered why Clark had not, in turn, deserted him. How had Lewis been able to bear

his insults? Where had they found the kindness to stay
at his side? Now he felt shame and turned his head
away from Clark's gaze.

"Well," said Clark, "bring the child to me in a year
or so. I will take him and bring him up as my own son.
This I can do as a favor for Janey."

"All winter I have thought of my son learning to
read and write," she whispered. Tears welled in her
eyes, and a sob broke in her throat. She could not speak
more. Scannon made a low moaning sound in his throat
and jumped to her side, nuzzling her hand; then he went
quietly back in the canoe with Lewis.

Scannon had developed for Sacajawea something as
akin to a feeling of human affection as he was capable.
For her part, Sacajawea respected and admired the ada-
mantine spirit of the dog's unsubmissive soul.

She turned her head to the other men. Most of them
wore only the leather trousers she and York had sewn.
Except for their beards, they were hardly distinguishable from the breechclouted Indians. In the crowd she
saw York elbow his way to the canoes. Now the noise
from the natives seemed deafening. York grasped her
shoulder and bent down by her ear, but she hardly knew
what he said. In his eyes there was the familiar, the
well known, the intimate. He had been crying, and Sacajawea's gaze struck fresh tears to his cheeks.

"It is all over, Janey," he said, and though Sacajawea
could not hear the words, she read them on the trembling brown mouth.

Hard, squeezing fingers sank into her shoulder, and
she was twisted about violently against Clark's chest.
She threw her arms around him and kissed him on his
hairy face. "I will bring my son to you. It is a promise."
She was barely able to hold back her tears. She turned
away from both men abruptly so that they would not
see her crying.

"She is proud," York said to Clark with an amused
inflection.

Clark, composed and standing in his canoe, felt that
somehow he had deserted Sacajawea. He stared at her
with unhappy, searching eyes.

Then Pat Gass called to Charbonneau, "Hey,
Frenchy, fur companies aren't run by men chewing bear

meat around a native campfire." Gass's broad face was deeply weathered, his lips wide and set in a manner that drew a crease line from each side of his straight, short nose to the corners of his mouth. His raven black hair was thick and long against his neck. His eyes, cool blue, always suspicious and seeking, warmed as he smiled and called, "The rules of the game are set up in Saint Louis these days. I'll be there, and you should be, too."

Charbonneau seized the hands of the nearest bucks and laughed suddenly, shaking off his remorse, and appearing now to have only hurt feelings. "Do you think I don't know what I should do? I am a man of experiences." He tapped his forehead. "And ability. I speak three, four languages, and I have a number of words I use with impressiveness."

Gass called from the floating canoe, "*Au revoir!*" The canoes moved downriver fast. Far out, two men on the forward canoe fired a rifle. For some time Sacajawea remained there gazing at the empty river. Her son clung to her side. A series of clouds came up to cover the blazing sun.

The natives were speaking their feelings in a jumble of voices. "Our hearts are heavy." "In the wind at night we will hear the white men's voices, and in the day the sun will paint their shadows." "Do not forget us, for we will be lonely."

She listened until she felt that she must turn away to hide her emotions once again. Now the villagers talked of the stars, the earth, the water, the sights and sounds of the world that were everlasting. She had been away for two years, but as she looked inside herself she found that the time was not a succession of years or seasons, but a single unit of rich experience and lessons learned. She had gone on the expedition's trail with a certain amount of indifference, as a follower, a slave to her Frenchman, Charbonneau. The chastening process had begun abruptly and had been complete. The learning had come more slowly, but it was thorough. She was genuinely sorry to be left behind.

Even under the cloud cover the day was hot and humid, and she flexed her knees and tried to hold back her tears.

* * *

Dropping below their old 1804 winter quarters at Fort Mandan, the two captains saw but a row of blackened pickets left. The cabins lay in ashes. Clark halted the canoes to go ashore. His private thoughts ran uninhibited in his head as he wandered among the ashes and the gray, wrinkled mushrooms that now covered the blackened grounds. His journal was objective and impersonal about the burned-out fort.

He shook his head at the blackened cabins and stamped the ashes off his feet. He moved from the heat-cracked boulders and blackened trees down toward the waiting canoes. He'd seen enough. His thoughts were dark as he stepped into an open glade that formed a gentle hollow in the center of a shallow basin to which the rains of centuries had brought a depth of rich soil. It was completely covered with asters, tall and pale and scarcely moving in this somewhat sheltered spot—no other flower grew there. The asters shone in the pale yellow light of a cloud-hidden sun like their namesakes, the stars.

Clark was strangely moved. He bent down over the flowers for a moment, and when he raised his head, his eyes were shining. "I don't think I've ever seen anything more beautiful," he said aloud, from the heart. "The fire did not come here—it could not burn everything." And he bent once more over the asters, which shivered a little as a warm breeze passed through the basin, and then were still again.

Now Clark was thinking of home, the safe, peaceful plantation, and he saw the vivacious blue eyes of Judy Hancock as he gave her the gifts he had brought. She was called the most beautiful girl in Virginia, with her light auburn curls. So, he thought, I have two girls—Janey, a brown-eyed fawn, and Judy, a blue-eyed red fox. Clark jumped aboard his canoe and dipped the paddle into the water.

Lewis had settled himself in the white pirogue, moving his leg back and forth to relieve some stiffness. It would be nice to live like a gentleman again, with hot baths and no beard.

The expedition was leaving behind the grizzly bears, wolves, rattlesnakes, hostile Sioux and Blackfeet as they

swept downriver, covering eighty miles a day. They no
longer thought of a diet of roots, dog meat, and pounded
salmon, the prairie heat and mountain cold, the prickly
pears, wild roses, and blue camass, and the endless
native powwows. They thought of home, with the smell
of corn pone and molasses and the sight of women in
calico dresses. The Corps of Discovery was soon to be
heard from.[1]

Sacajawea, her son enfolded in her arms, was unconscious of the crowd waving and shouting toward the
canoes as they became small dots upon the muddy water.
She was unaware of the rocks and sticks under her feet.
She stumbled forward toward the empty, rolling hills
under the hot mid-August sun. She did not hear the
whimpers of Pomp as she brushed past rosebushes and
stinging nettles.

She stopped at the top of a long slope that rose easily
from the river, a benchland where the village was situated. She turned to the west and saw that the plain
reached out to high yellow hills that formed a ragged
line against the sky. That way there were no trees, and
the surrounding valley swept away on either side, empty
and barren and immense. Land benches tilted upon one
another like great red and amber slabs driven through
the irregular contours of the tossing hills. She saw horse
herds grazing on the plain. At the foot of the slope,
round bull boats swarmed like fat-bellied polliwogs.
Some of the villagers had followed the expedition downriver for a while and were now coming back, bobbing
and twisting as they moved toward the shore. The river
was half a mile wide, but the cries from the opposite
shore, the barking of the dogs, and the beating of drums
came clearly across the water.

Sacajawea's thoughts ran past the yellow hills, past
the shining mountains, onward through the haze to the
great Stinking Waters of the west. They came slowly
back over the Lolo Pass to the Great Falls, and to the
land of the People. There a child waited for her to come
back. Shoogan, her sister's child, waited as the People
waited for white traders to come with guns and ammunition. She thought of the enemy, the Blackfeet. If

they had guns, there would be no peace; it would be a season of wars and sadness in the two nations.

Slowly she turned to face the blazing sun. Down the yellow Missouri to a land she did not know went her white friends and the great black one, naked to the waist, his head wrapped in a red kerchief that fluttered against his wide, shining neck. She imagined the muscles of his back and thick shoulders as he paddled, sweat glistening in the sun on the knobs of his spine.

She was not the same as she had been before in these river villages. She knew things not known by her foster mother, Grasshopper, or Otter Woman, Fast Arrow, or even the one-eyed Chief Kakoakis. She would not be content to stay in this place long. She had goals and a horizon to follow. She had hope. She would teach her son these things. He would learn to read and write.

She wept in the dry brown grass where no disapproving Minnetaree could see her, away from the taunting eyes of her man. Pomp sat beside her, picking up stones and placing them in a small heap between his knees. A rush of self-pity filled her lonely heart. Her man did not care what happened to her. He would find another young *femme* when it pleased him. Otter Woman was glad to see her only because the lodge work could now be shared and she could have more time to visit, sit in the sun, and gossip. Today, the thick-walled lodges of the Minnetarees seemed oppressive with filth and darkness, because she had lived for two years almost completely outdoors, except in the coldest part of winter, in the clear air and next to Mother Earth. The wooden cabins of the white men were light, not filled with filth, even though at times smoke-filled. She thought, Squaws belong where they are, the way the buffalo belong where there is grass and distance. But not me. I do not wish to be thought of in the same breath with prairie dogs. They belong where they are. They were put there. I have moved. I have changed. The village is here and the same. I do not belong in it.

"*Umbea.*" Pomp tugged at her leather tunic and patted her arm. His face was bright and full of laughing. A deer mouse scampered off, and the child tried to follow.

Sacajawea caught his hand and walked in the direction of Grasshopper's lodge.

"I am happy you came first to see me after your friends left," said the old woman. "You are a true daughter." She clicked her tongue and smiled. "You are sad. I can see it. Sit and listen to your old mother for a while. The world will go on if you are not here. Boats will go up and down the river."

Looking up, Sacajawea said, "I worry about my people and the strength of their enemies, the Blackfeet."

"We are your people." Grasshopper took a willow fan to Sweet Clover, who sat near the fire stirring the stew made with fresh corn. Sweet Clover did not look up, but began fanning her face vigorously, and her stirring became faster, so that Grasshopper began to shake with laughter. When the old woman looked at Sacajawea, she made herself calm and said, "The Blackfeet will kill and be killed. The sun will shine, and night and day will come. You are on Mother Earth to live and die. You can do and think what is best, but there is no use fighting things. You help others when you can, work, and live as best you can—that is all." Her face puffed in and out in thought. "You can fight for what is right. It does not matter so much how you fight. It is what you fight for. A grandmother once said, 'You have to stick to the row you are hoeing.' In this life it is a person's first right to live, even if he has to shed blood for that. And what you think is right has to come while you are alive. It is no good to you when you are dead. Am I telling you too much?" The old woman looked fondly at Sacajawea. "I am wearing on you?"

"No," Sacajawea said quickly. "I need your thoughts."

Grasshopper said softly, "It is good to hear you say so, my daughter."

"You have a right to hear this," Sacajawea said. "Chief Red Hair asked to take my son to his village, to teach him understanding of the markings on paper."

"Your little Pomp?"

"*Ai!* My son would have much in his head."

"You are young and silly. I doubt if you'll take my word for it, but I will tell you. You think the white blood of a father dominates the mother's blood. That is not even sensible."

"Sensible!" Sacajawea's mouth was wry upon the word. "How can you judge that?"

"Well so, then maybe not. I've done many things that were silly. If anyone had told me, three or four months ago, that you'd find your way back here, I maybe would have said he was in the world of spirits. And the day I took you into my arms and said you were my daughter—well, so there are times one has to be a fool. I did not have room to choose."

"That's it. That's my feeling. My son could learn the white man's ways." Sacajawea looked around the lodge slowly. Sweet Clover had fallen asleep beside the cooking fire.

"You were forced on me. Was this offer for teaching your son to be a white man forced on you?"

"I could do like my man and ignore it, as if it were never spoken."

"Why don't you? Maybe that is the sensible thing to do. It doesn't sound like sense to me to make a person into something he never was."

"Who can say what a person can be made into? I have been changed."

"You want your little son to be like the whites?" Grasshopper looked incredulous. "You like men who boast, who cannot shoot a straight arrow, who hit women, who want their meat fully cooked?"

"So," said Sacajawea calmly, "I never dreamed you thought all white men were like the one we call Charbonneau. Pah! He is but a dry bean dropped from a rotten pod. He's a bad smell. There are others who have no fear of cutting out new trails, who can cut their feet to pemmican on the rock and half drown in the river, let the flies eat them, freeze, and eat their horses to keep from starving; and before they sleep they can make marks with a thin stick in what they call journals." She was pacing up and down the lodge, her arms shaking. Her head tossed from side to side. "This other kind of men know of lands beyond the seas. But they have not been there. They learn of them from journals. This reading can do much. It is something I want for my son."

Grasshopper could see Sacajawea's intention was as firmly fixed as her determination that Pomp should take on the characteristics of the white man. "And so—

you would not be afraid to send your son to the white
man's village?"

"Afraid?" Sacajawea thought that Grasshopper did
not even try to understand. She drew in her breath and
held it, watching Pomp as he pushed a tiny red coal
back into the fire with a discarded bone. "I do not believe I fear any place where Chief Red Hair would be."

Grasshopper told herself that she could name on her
fingers ten times over squaws who lacked the courage
to do what Sacajawea had in mind for her son; and yet
just now she looked more like a wistful child than a
squaw—even a squaw of only fifteen or sixteen summers.

"And you speak this out loud? What if I should say
the same words sometime to your man?"

To your man. Startled, Sacajawea realized that it
was the first time since coming back from the west that
she had thought of herself as belonging to Charbonneau. The thought angered her; belonging to him meant
nothing but drudgery. She shifted her weight to the
other foot. She would do all she could to see that her
son was not bound by the same kind of life. "I do not
fear your tongue."

Grasshopper began to laugh. She sat with her hands
flat against her broad thighs and roared with laughter
that stung because there was so much to laugh at, that
stung the more because there was so little humor in it.
"And so—it is this Chief Red Hair who has tied your
heart in knots, so much so that you would even let him
take your firstborn son from you! Ho—ho—ho—OOO!"

Sacajawea began to laugh also. There was no good
reason to laugh. It was foolish; she sounded foolish to
herself. For two years she had given her heart to one
of the captains of the expedition, but her body had belonged to her man and her body had felt nothing; it had
been dead. Her heart beat with its own life. She could
see Clark, gentle and tough at the same time, and his
red hair; it needed only sunlight to set the red sheen
shining in it.

"So—it is my daughter who seeks out the highest
chief among the white men and permits him to take
her heart. My daughter, who has a man—no, a dried
bean—is to be commended because she does not tell

either man her feelings. Sometimes it is good to stay inside yourself and not let on. My own mouth is sealed. Now it is time for something to eat. Your son must have a full belly to match the full head he is going to have. And your belly must not go empty, my daughter."

But emptiness came of another hunger. Forbidden hunger, and a forbidden man.

Otter Woman and Tess were outside Charbonneau's lodge when Sacajawea returned.

"Where did you go?" asked Otter Woman. "Our man is looking for you. He wants you to clean these fish for cooking." She pointed a dirty finger at the half-dozen fish with blue flies buzzing over them. The fish were not fresh.

"How long have they lain here?"

Otter Woman looked up, surprised that anyone would be that inquisitive. "Two, maybe three suns. Our man left them here under the wood so that the coyotes could not get at them."

"They have spoiled in this heat and will give us bellyaches." Sacajawea threw them out toward the refuse heap in the back of the lodge. Then she made a broom from willow branches and began a vigorous sweeping of the lodge. Otter Woman sat on her sleeping couch wondering what had taken possession of Sacajawea since she had been gone. No squaw ever worked so hard, so fast and furiously. By evening the lodge was in order, clean above Minnetaree standards, and the couches were neat and sweet-smelling with sage laid in between the musty hides and blankets. There was fresh corn soup and antelope chunks sent from Grasshopper's lodge in the kettle when Charbonneau returned. He glanced briefly around and shrugged.

"The place shines like a new-minted louis d'or. *Nom du bon Dieu*, my women also are as golden clean. It is past believing. Let me have some of that meat."

"That meat," said Sacajawea, glancing at Otter Woman, who had done nothing but eat all afternoon, "has been saved by me from the wolves who infest this lodge and eat like a famine is to come."

"That could not be me," said Otter Woman inno-

cently. "But it could be your sons who have been in and
out after food all day."

"*Zut!* If my sons are *Canadiens* like me, they are
mangeurs de lard," laughed Charbonneau. "With some
disrespect, too."

"I would not mind being a pork-eater when there is
meat like this." Sacajawea filled a dried gourd with
boiled meat and corn.

"*Oui*, it is good." Charbonneau chewed a mouthful
slowly. His jaw muscles stretched his beard, and his
bobbing head flung it from side to side. "You have become a nice housekeeper and fine cook since I have been
gone. You are glad I am back? *Oui*. Keep your eyes
there on my bowl. She needs refill."

Otter Woman smiled, accepting the compliment and
refilling his bowl. She ran her fingers through his greasy
hair.

Sacajawea's hands balled into fists.

"*Ma petite furie*," he said. "Little storm, do not scratch
a man's eye out. Cut those long nails." He pulled away
Otter Woman's hands and laid his head in her lap. "I
have needed a squaw like this—one with big tits a man
can hang on to."

Otter Woman giggled and began rubbing his shoulders, bending low over him.

Sacajawea's fists dropped helplessly, and her voice
dropped with them. "Come, little sons of the man called
Charbonneau, it is your time to eat this tender meat."
It struck her suddenly that there were streaks of white
in Charbonneau's hair that were beginning to overrun
the black.

"Kakoakis, that old one-eyed chief, wants to hear
more stories. He likes the one about me killing the
grizzly. She had the biggest mouth I ever saw. *Oui*, the
biggest. And I shoot right into that bear's mouth. *Pouf!*
She is dead. The chief listened to me tell how I kept
the canoe from upsetting in fast water. Your man is
important. *Le grand esprit* guides me. You a lucky squaw
to be in the lodge of such a big man in this village." He
pulled Otter Woman close and whispered something;
then he sat up and looked at Sacajawea, who dipped
small gourds of water for the boys.

"Where did you go this afternoon after the boats left?

Kakoakis would not believe the story of the whale, and I looked for you to tell him it was so and to clean some fish he gave to me three, four days ago."[2]

Sacajawea did not answer, but began to stir the meat after pouring more water in the kettle.

"I am giving orders. Next time I want you, you be in this lodge. You hear, Little Bird?"

"*Ai*," she said, not wishing to begin an argument.

"Give me some tea." Charbonneau talked to the fire. "If you do not do as I say, I will take a tough leather thong and smack your legs with it. My squaws behave. You will not act like you did when Capitaine Clark was around. And you keep your mouth shut about that trip. It had nothing to do with you. It was a trip for soldiers and strong men, not sick squaws. So do not brag about your part or I will tell how you lay in the bottom of a *bateau* for many days moaning and letting spittle slide past your lips."

Sacajawea blinked. Then she noticed on each side of his leather shirt hung pieces of bright green ribbon. "Kakoakis will be jealous of your shirt's ribbons."

"Le Borgne says I sing my life away and strut like a *jeune coq* to be gazed at and admired. That means *rien du tout*—nothing at all—to me. You are right, he is jealous. From now on, Little Bird, you say nothing, only answer my questions." Charbonneau's eyes were like dark molasses. He took up a tin cup for tea. Being French, he had a feeling for drama and its uses, and for the details that made if effective. Expression, costume, gesture—all these were important. A gesture was often more than the mere turn of a palm or the shrug of a shoulder—he included his whole body and its attitudes.

Sacajawea could see that Charbonneau loved living among people before whom he could brag and strut. He had no real desire to return to the land of his father. He preferred this life, where he could be lazy and blame his slovenly ways on his squaws.

"If you do not behave, I will do exactly what Kakoakis does."

"What does he do?" asked Sacajawea, wishing right away she had not asked.

"He is master of his household. One of his women

disobeyed. She spoke out of turn. She went to stay with her parents, where she thought she had protection. But Le Borgne followed her. He entered the lodge, sat upon the ceremonial robe, which was presented him as a distinguished caller, smoked a peaceful pipe with the squaw's father, rose, and excused himself. As he passed this squaw, he raised her by the hair and murdered her before the eyes of her mother and father. So!" Charbonneau drew his finger dramatically across his throat. "Let that be a lesson to any squaw who opposes me!" Scowling fiercely, he retreated to his sleeping couch, where a hushed and trembling silence greeted him.

Finally Sacajawea ventured to ask another question, "Did anyone defend the poor girl?"

"*Mon dieu!* You fool! *Plus on est de fou, plus on rit.* The sillier it is, the more one laughs." Charbonneau guffawed and crossed himself. "Fear of Le Borgne is so great that no one rises to defend his squaws. That girl's death will remain unavenged."

"*Qui ne sait pas être fou, n'est pas sage.*" Sacajawea's voice rebuked him. "It takes a wise man to make a fool."

"I am not wise—me? You think that, *hein*?"

Otter Woman sucked in her breath, and her hands trembled as she poured more tea into Charbonneau's cup.

Sacajawea bit her tongue and was grateful when he drank the tea and stomped out of the lodge, motioning for Otter Woman to follow him to Chief Kakoakis's lodge. There the men listened eagerly to the things Charbonneau told, but they did not believe all he said because they remembered his old habit of exaggerating; often that evening, they let him know they thought he used his imagination generously by laughing uproariously, as if all he said were a great joke.

"It was not all *la fête*," he said darkly.

When night came, Otter Woman came to get food for her man and his friends. Sacajawea had both children sleeping on their pallets. Wrapped in blankets, the small boys looked like carelessly dropped sacks of Indian corn.

"Our man loves storytelling," sighed Otter Woman. "He told that I was the daughter of a great war chief, named Burnt Knee, and that he had to pay many pure white horses to get me from my father. There was no

Chief Burnt Knee that I know of, and he never had many white horses. His tongue is so crooked he could not say he bought me from a Blackfoot brave for a knife that had no blade, only a shiny handle, and that the Blackfoot was glad to get rid of me because I ate too much. Now, you tell me the story of that whale once more," begged Otter Woman.

"This is not something I made up." Sacajawea sighed deeply. "Even you know there are people and animals and trees on the other side of the mountains." When she finished, Otter Woman could almost see the huge whale bones on the sand.

No, Otter Woman thought, Sacajawea's eyes do not need a wash, she saw those things. No one could make up such a story. She backed out of the lodge carrying the kettle of stew carefully. Her hands became stiff gripping the cornhusk wrapping wound around the metal handle to keep off the heat.

Charbonneau spent more than half the night eating and telling stories, which grew more absurd as the morning drew closer.

Sacajawea lay on her couch wondering why Charbonneau did not go to the Rooptahee village to bring Corn Woman home. Why didn't Corn Woman herself come back? Didn't she know her man was here?

And when Charbonneau announced the next day that he was going to go up to the Mandans to bring Corn Woman back, it did not greatly surprise Sacajawea.

Otter Woman gasped, composed her face, and hurriedly fixed a small parfleche of jerky for his trip. Her mouth was clamped shut. She did not utter a word of farewell to Charbonneau, but brushed his hand lightly with hers.

For the next several days, while Charbonneau was gone, the lodge became filled with buzzing women who wanted to hear the story of the whale and saltmaking. Otter Woman began to tell things as though they had happened to her. Sacajawea kept her mouth shut. This sent the women into gales of laughter. At first she resented their laughing until Otter Woman pointed out, "See, it is a real achievement to cause all this merriment. There was so much to see and do on your trail. There is no harm in me telling the stories. It gives you a rest. Our man did not forbid me from talking. To give enjoyment is a good thing."

Late each afternoon, Sacajawea escaped the giggling women by taking a bundle of wash and going to the long sandbar at the river. The bar curved in from midstream and formed a small cove under some cottonwood trees. Here she washed Pomp's leggings or her tunic, then stretched her weary limbs in the cool air. Once she pulled on the old blue jacket Clark had given her, which she had hidden in the center of her wash bundle.

Thought after thought crowded her mind. She tried to relax and clear the thoughts. In the small leather pouch around her neck she kept the stone that was like a piece of blue sky. The stone reminded her of childhood and how far she had come since that time. She felt the smooth sides and put the coolness of the stone against her cheek. She tied the thin string around her neck, trying to see the chip of blue upon her breast in the graying light. She closed her eyes. She saw the stone bright in her mind. After a while, she replaced it in the pouch.

She took out the now-tarnished peace medal Sun Woman had given her for good fortune on the long journey to and from the ocean in the west. Someday, she thought, I will let my son wear this around his neck— when he is someone important among the white men. Next, she held the rusty red piece of glass with the white bird raised on one side. This, she thought, I'll always keep to remind me that my name is Sacajawea, Bird Woman.

Inside the pouch were several blue jay feathers, a red feather, blue ribbon, and also a small bone comb and a pewter mirror. She combed her hair, thinking of the time Clark gave the comb and mirror to her. She imagined him saying, "We will meet again, Janey," his freckled face smiling. She pulled the jacket around her bare shoulders and smelled the coat's familiar odor, breathing deeply into the folds. This was her medicine. This was the thing that preserved her courage and reminded her of places beyond the river villages. It was more tangible than memories.

Like the young brave when he grows into manhood, she, too, needed a medicine. It was something to give

her strength to meet the hardships of life. The young
brave found his medicine by praying alone long hours
with arms extended toward the sun, not eating until in
a dream his totem was revealed. She thought of the trip
to the Stinking Waters as her medicine dream—for
now it seemed only a dream.

She saw Charbonneau coming between the lodges
alone. Why hadn't he brought Corn Woman? She hastened her steps and was about to call out when she saw
that his head was bent and his shoulders hunched in a
look of complete dejection. He walked with a bent-kneed
slouch, deliberate and swift, his lips pressed tightly
together. His face was like oiled deerskin. His mustache, whose uneven curls hung down on either side of
his mouth, increased his melancholy look. The cries of
the locusts came in broken chirps.

"Where is she?"

Charbonneau folded his bent legs under him and sat
beside the hard-packed trail. "She went to the Land of
Shadows during the deep snow." Even and patient and
never stopping came the song of the locust. All else was
silence. Behind the clear, close sounds were others, more
distant, and still others, more faint.

Sacajawea sat, placed her clothing bundle between
them.

"She had a coughing sickness, and bad smell. She's
white as bone and food come up from her belly. She's
light as feathers and not wake up again. *C'est vrai!*"
He crossed himself. "The family say she is my fault. I
think they lie. Listen, how can it be my doing when I
am not here?" Even sitting down, with his legs under
him, he managed a most creditable swagger as he
brushed off his hands. He wiped them clean of the incident, even though it still lingered to trouble his mind.

Sacajawea stared at the dusty trail. Her memory of
Corn Woman was as bleached as dry bone. She could
not imagine what she had looked like. She thought the
locust sound was like the blowing of wind, spreading
everywhere across the prairie, always there ready to
be heard by those who wished to listen. It was a help,
a familiar thing. But she could not put it into words
for the man who sat with his head in his hands.

"La malchance me poursuit! I am cursed with bad

luck! They say I left her too long with no hope of me
returning. Those dirty Mandans! They knew I would
be back! They are the ones. They let her die, telling her
all the time I was gone and would never return. 'Do
not think of the man who has fled with palefaces,' they
said. She sat, never speaking, only coughing. One time
her family, they scolded her for not eating. But she only
sat watching the river, and when they said the boats
of palefaces never would glide there again, she screamed
and cried on her pallet. Her family say I am an ungrateful heart. *Dieu, que je suis fou vous le demander!*
I am ashamed of myself."

"It is no fault of yours. They miss their daughter and
look for someone to take the blame for their loss. You
are faultless."

Charbonneau stared at the woman who spoke with
understanding. He marveled at her this moment. She
had a man's logic in that slim body that was like a
child's. She was soft and slight; to have such a hard
stubbornness about her seemed out of place.

"Her memory cannot be taken from you. It lives forever within your heart." She looked down at him.

She spoke like a grown woman, he thought. "A memory, she is cold like my Corn Woman. I want something
warm and soft. *Pouf!* You are here. You are warm. *Ma
pauvre* squaw!"

Sacajawea smelled the dampness among the tules at
the edge of the river, and felt the unyielding roughness
of a stone under her hands.

Charbonneau boldly pushed aside her clothing bundle, then pushed upward on her tunic. His hands were
knotted, tanned by the weather. They ran down the
sides of her body, feeling with a surprise and familiarity
that it was firm and warm.

"Otter Woman lays soft and warm in her couch waiting for you," Sacajawea whispered, repulsed by his boldness, sympathetically aroused by his grief.

"*Mais non!* It is not Otter I feel my hands tingle for.
It is for you I have the hotness in my belly. I want you
here, in the twilight, struggling on Mother Earth beneath me." His hands were shaking as he crossed himself.

He pushed her down before she could escape. His

breath was hot on her face; she let out a strangled groan. She felt the silent texture of the stone with her hands, and the powdery dust of the earth—like a thing heard, like the locusts.

"This is your duty to me," grunted Charbonneau. His leather trousers lay around his ankles.

35

Saint Louis

Clark was able to provide education for two, perhaps three, of Charbonneau's half-breed children, and he also cared for René Jussome's daughter. By eighteen-ten old Charbonneau, almost certainly accompanied by Sacajawea, had come to St. Louis, bought land, and tried to settle down.

Excerpt from p. 438 in *Lewis and Clark: Partners in Discovery* by John Bakeless. Copyright 1947 by John Bakeless. By permission of William Morrow and Company.

When the air began to feel crisp, and the daddy longlegs were grouped in clusters outside the lodges, a sure sign of fall, Sacajawea found time to visit her dearly loved Grasshopper.

Rosebud stirred the fire outside the lodge door. Sweet Clover sat on a skin pallet in the autumn sun. She smiled vacuously. Grasshopper helped her eldest granddaughter, Chickadee, sew a leather pouch.

"You have come in time to see me huge as a mountain with this kicking papoose inside!" Rosebud shouted with glee. "I hope that this is a boy who smiles as much as your Pomp."

Pomp had seated himself beside Chickadee, and he laughed as she awkwardly pushed the bone needle in and out of the leather.

Sacajawea could feel the welcome; it lay warm all around her.

After a meal of boiled squash, root of the yellow water lily, and white turtle meat, Grasshopper persuaded Pomp to stay with Chickadee, and Sweet Clover to wash out the gourd bowls so that Rosebud might rest with her sewing. Then she invited Sacajawea to go to the village of the Dead.

Not a word was spoken as they walked outside the village stockade and across the prairie, where the sunflower heads had lost their long gold petals and only the seeds were left. Goldenrod blossoms waved across the land like wands. The two women, one waddling at a slow pace, the other gliding along with the unhurried steps of youth, approached a ring of chalk white skulls. Then Grasshopper spoke.

"On a warm day after several of rain, I came here, some time ago, alone. The scaffold where the body of my man rested had broken and fallen to the ground. I used my scraping knife and dug a hole for everything left, except this skull. It was beautifully bleached and purified. See!"

Grasshopper led Sacajawea to a skull that sat upon a bunch of wild sage in a circle of other skulls, numbering about a hundred. The skulls were eight to ten inches from each other, with the faces all looking to the center—where they were religiously protected and preserved in their precise position from year to year.

There were many of these circles made of bleached skulls on this part of the prairie, but Grasshopper knew precisely which one was her man's. She had brought a half-filled bowl of turtle stew, which she placed beside the skull. She told Sacajawea she would return for the empty bowl in the morning. Scarcely a day had passed on which she had not done this since she had placed the skull in its circle of companions. The two women sat cross-legged beside the white skulls. Grasshopper began to talk to the skull in front of her in a pleasant and endearing way. She told how her child, Sacajawea, had come home and how beautiful she was. She told how winsome and bright her part-white grandson was. She kept up a conversation with the skull for quite a while; then she took out a pair of moccasins from a parfleche swung across her back and began beading them with quills. Now she told the skull of the expected grandchild and how pretty and strong all of Rosebud's children were.[1]

Sacajawea sat quietly enjoying the sunshine, unable to recall anything like this ceremony among her own people. The Shoshonis left their dead on scaffolds or in trees and did not speak of them again—and probably never saw them again.

Grasshopper put her sewing away, brushing her skirt for the journey home.

A week later, Sucks His Thumb came to Charbonneau's lodge with a message for Sacajawea. Rosebud had a new papoose, a girl named Sparrow. Sucks His Thumb sat near the cooking fire and ate what Sacajawea handed him on a bark plate, boiled corn. Otter Woman suggested that they start right away to make a cradleboard for the new papoose. She sent the children to the river to find good, pliable willow stems for weaving a head protector on the board.

Sucks His Thumb asked questions about the father of his two companions Tess and Pomp. "Why does he not pull out the many face hairs? What does he do with the beaver pelts he packs in such large bales? Are there

more white men where he came from? Why do more
and more white men from the northeast come into the
Five Villages?

"For beaver, of course," answered Tess.

"Why, then, doesn't your father go to the white village and trade his pelts there? Maybe the white men
would give him wonderful things for those good pelts."

"Wonderful, like a hole in the middle of the back,"
answered Tess. "Little brother," Tess said, strutting to
and fro like his father, "the white men do not want our
people in their villages, but they want to come to ours."

"We welcome them," said Sucks His Thumb.

"*Ai*, we have manners," said Pomp.

Charbonneau traded one of his compact bales of beaver pelts to a British free trapper from Lake of the
Woods region for a new-fashioned, percussion system
flintlock with a horn of fulminate powder and leather
bag of lead balls. The trader said the gun and fulminate
compound had recently come to the Hudson's Bay in a
shipment of regular flintlocks. Charbonneau was skeptical, but he thought the balance of the rifle suited his
short-fingered hand exactly, so he was happy with the
trade and did not question the origin of the gun too
closely. He rubbed the stock with bear's grease and held
it up to admire the shine of the wood's grain. Every day
he took it out and aimed it at anything that moved—
squirrels, ravens, gophers, a striped skunk, and once a
skittish mule deer that hightailed it off before he could
find it in the gun sight. Charbonneau blamed the fact
that he could not hit anything on the faulty position of
the sight. He picked up a piece of sandstone to rub,
work over, and enlarge the V of the sight with several
dozen well-placed strokes. When that did not work he
blamed the novel percussion powder that the Britisher
had bragged about to him.[2] "The slightest nudge makes
this fulminating salt explode—bam! Be bloody cautious, my friend."

This new powder was placed in a tube connected to
the bore of the flintlock and then struck with the hammer, the flash being strong enough to ignite the charge.
Charbonneau was told that he did not need priming
powder, there was no pan for free sparks. However, he

nearly always put pinches of powder on the flint for
good measure. He told himself that it was the same
precaution the Indian took when he used fire sticks.
They would put a little black powder down before ro-
tating the hard stick in a block of softer material and
the powder would make a big spark for certain ignition.[3]

Charbonneau's women expected him to bring home
plenty of game after strutting around the lodge talking
about his beautiful new thunder-maker. It seemed to
be a prized possession. He kept it handy at all times,
and at night it was under his couch for easy reach.

Blowing out the ends of his mustache one day, he
said to the women, "My new gun, she is hoo-doo. You
know what I mean. I hunt but bring home nothing.
Little Bird, you are going to have to buy more meat
from your adopted brother—what's his name?"

"You mean Fast Arrow?" Sacajawea asked. "What
do I trade? Maybe some dry tea or your smoking tobacco?"

Charbonneau pretended not to hear the question. He
wondered why he did not take his family and leave this
blamed village. He could find a place where he was not
considered weak and ineffective, where the people would
look up to him for his physical and mental abilities. He
went to bed and lay on his side, where silently he
watched Otter Woman scour out a kettle with sand and
balsam twigs, rinse, then fill it full of water. As soon
as the water steamed Sacajawea added dried squash
and left it to boil.

Before daylight Sacajawea was wakened by the sound
of beating hooves, then thrashing and the cracking of
trees. But she knew there were few trees in the village,
only the upright poles of the security fence which enclosed the village. She threw off the covering robe, pulled
on her tunic and rushed outside.

An entire band of wapiti was on the move. They were
charging through a big break in the fence, thundering
into the ditch behind the fence and up through the
center of the village, kicking up dust and panic. At first
the leaders of the herd were stymied by the wide, three-
to-four-foot-deep ditch, which held a few feet of water
whenever there was a hard rain. Several wanted to
follow the ditch around and one or two wanted to climb

the steep bank and charge through the village. When the followers bunched up behind these leaders, they took off pell-mell in both directions.

By this time other Minnetarees were awake and coming out of lodges with bows and arrows, long, pointed, chert-tipped spears, steel knives, and their preferred flintlock rifles. Sacajawea ran back into the lodge calling for Charbonneau to get outside. "Here is your chance. The wapiti—the big deer, the elk—have come!" She shook him until his eyes were open. "Break the hoodoo. Wapiti are close. You go right up and boom it falls to the ground. They are so close you could hit one on the head with a large grinding stone!"

Charbonneau was slow getting out of bed, pulling on wool pants and a red shirt to cover his bearded chest, tying a scarf around his throat and a red bandana to hold his neck length hair in place.

"No time for boots!" shouted Sacajawea. "Grab the gun!"

"It is hardly light out there," complained Charbonneau. "Every man, woman, and child in this here village is out. I can hear them. What is this excitement?"

"Ai!" shouted Sacajawea. "There is enough wapiti to last two winters. They are here! For you to take!"

By this time Otter Woman and the boys were up and dressed and outside, curious to see what was going on. Sacajawea pulled the gun from under Charbonneau's bed and followed them. "Come on!" she called.

"She is black as *le diable* out there," mumbled Charbonneau.

Once outside his eyes adjusted to the first gray light of early dawn. Twenty yards away on the grassy, flat area two bucks were battling. Harems of three or four cows for each buck were standing off in a disinterested fashion munching grass. Unusual and exciting as that was, the sight of several dozen wapiti coursing around the inside ditch was spectacular—something the Minnetarees had never seen before. Charbonneau moved up to stand with a group of men with guns who were laughing and shouting and aiming at the animals. Several wapiti were already dead on the bottom of the ditch or lying on the edge. Charbonneau was close enough so that he could see the arrows in the dead animals' necks

or briskets. He could see the prominent facial glands
below the eyes. The rest of the animals were nearly
hysterical—stampeding, hardly looking for a way out
of the ditch or out of the village.

The villagers were in danger of attack by the elk, of
being impaled by antlers or slashed with hooves if they
moved out into the wide ditch where the animals were
moving back and forth, round and round.

Charbonneau heard the crack of a gun and looked
to see where it came from just as the whir of a spear
sang over his head and the *chuk* of it hitting the shoulder of a cow thudded into his ear. Charbonneau ran
back to the side of his lodge for safety. It was obvious
that if he stood out in the open he could be in the middle
of crossfire. He was truly frightened, and crouched close
to the lodge wall with his arms around his knees to
keep from shaking.

Sacajawea and Otter Woman with the two boys stood
with a group of women watching the fighting bucks,
who had now locked antlers. The women knew that
given time, someone would throw a butcher knife or
two at the bucks or stone them to death and thus save
the animals from dying of starvation.

Sacajawea remembered that she carried the long
flintlock, powder horn, and bag of lead shot. She backed
up to find a spot where she could take aim on a wapiti
running in the ditch and not worry about being in the
path of an arrow or lead shot. The gun was heavy and
longer than she was tall. She rested the stock across
an old heap of garbage and pulled back the cover of the
tube next to the bore.

"Filled," she whispered to herself. She dumped in a
little powder and rammed in a ball. Then she noticed
a long forgotten, dilapidated bull boat, and moved the
barrel to rest on that. She felt the trigger; she heard
the flint crack on the steel. Any other noise was covered
by the shouts of the villagers. The kick of the gun
knocked Sacajawea from a squatting position to flat on
her back, and to her disappointment the ball hit one of
the upright posts and lodged there. "Damn, son of a
bitch," she said, remembering what she'd heard white
men say in similar situations. She reloaded, letting the
gun rest on the rotting bull boat. She put her head down

to the gun and sighted for some brownish hide, then for the white on the chest. This time the ball hit right on target and was swallowed into the chest cavity, and the wapiti fell over on its side with legs twitching.

Sacajawea sat up and rubbed her aching shoulder. There was smoke hanging low over the entire village and the strong smell of gunpowder. She felt an elation and smiled. Charbonneau had been right at first—this was a fine gun. Ram home a bullet, pull the rod free, and spark from the flint does the rest. There was no worry about getting the priming pan wet with sweat when holding it too close to the lock. She could still hear Chief Red Hair telling Shannon never to hold a flintlock close to the lock when carrying, because "your sweat will run down and damp the pan."

She looked around for Otter Woman and the boys. They were huddled down at the side of the lodge with Charbonneau. Otter Woman was wailing, tears running down her face. Sacajawea put the flintlock over her shoulder and said, "What is the matter? I have shot a wapiti for our lodge."

"Look for yourself," said Charbonneau, his eyes wide. He pointed his stubby forefinger to the place where the bucks had been locked together in battle. They lay spraddled on the ground, still locked by their antlers, but with a score of arrows and knives growing out of their chests and sides. Several cows were down, the rest had disappeared, and in their place were four Minnetaree women with bloody backs and shoulders, their arms and legs flung out from their bodies.

"What happened?" asked Sacajawea.

"Ai," whispered Otter Woman, beginning to wail louder. The boys clung to each other.

"Everyone threw their weapons at once, like crazies. They wanted to kill the wapiti, and they killed themselves. Stupid! Stupid!" said Charbonneau, shaking his head as if coming out of a bad dream. Suddenly his head snapped up and he looked at Sacajawea. *"Nom du bon dieu,* what are you doing with my brand-new gun?"

"I shot a wapiti," she repeated.

"How do you know how to shoot? Are you trying to show me up?"

"Chief Red Hair let me shoot at targets pinned to a tree—only once or twice. I was never good."

"This was beginner's luck then," said Charbonneau, and his face brightened. "So—the gun, she works. The hoo-doo is broken. Give it to me and I'll show you some real shooting." He grabbed the gun and walked to the ditch, hoping that the frantic animals were still racing around it. He checked the gun, rammed in a ball, and felt the trigger. Holding it to his shoulder and remembering its kick, he wondered how Sacajawea took that jolt. Her shoulder is black and blue, he thought. He lowered the weapon when he saw that several women were already bent over dead animals, butchering them. Men were loading up packhorses. The remaining elk had stampeded through another break in the rotting pole fence, and Charbonneau walked over to join several men who were examining the exit. The men moaned that they could have gotten at least another six or seven animals if they had only been quicker.

"I got me a wapiti," Charbonneau told them, and then walked on.

He passed a group of keening women. A young boy lay on the bloody ground. He had been caught in crossfire and hit in the back by an arrow but he was alive. The Shaman was called to suck out the arrow head.[4]

In an unusual burst of philosophizing, Charbonneau cursed at the waste of humankind in such a frenzy to save each other from hunger. Out loud he said, "I've seen death while people go for food, and death while people go without food. Where is the Great Spirit in this?"

Several men came up to Charbonneau, and they talked about the power of the Shaman, a power that could bring wapiti right into their village when the front gate was locked. One man said, "The Shaman and Chief Kakoakis conjured something big last night. I heard plenty singing and dancing in the chief's lodge."

The Minnetarees had killed two dozen wapiti, with an average weight of at least seven hundred pounds apiece. That would supply each lodge about a hundred twenty-five pounds of meat.[5] This called for a feast and celebration that would last a couple of days.

Charbonneau went back to make sure his women

had started butchering "his" wapiti. If they got it all
cut up and pulled into the lodge, out of sight, he reasoned, maybe he would not have to divide it with another family. After all, he thought, there is no meat in
my lodge at this moment and I have two squaws with
big mouths and two growing boys to feed.

Otter Woman cried off and on most of the day as she
and Sacajawea made strips for jerky inside their lodge.
At the edge of the village where the bodies had been
lifted to burial platforms, the families of the dead
mourned with a high, ululated keening. Charbonneau
spent the rest of the afternoon cleaning his gun, rubbing
it with oil, watching the women work with the meat.
He guffawed when the two boys complained that they
couldn't find the wapiti's gall bladder. "You saps," he
said, "you have now learned what every man and woman
already knows—that the wapiti does not have a gall
bladder."

Charbonneau felt let down. The excitement had worn
off and he had not used his gun. He glanced at Sacajawea and wondered if she was really good with his
newfangled flintlock. He was a little afraid of her. If
her temper came to a boil she might grab the gun again.
What could he do about it? Maybe he would be better
off getting out of this damned place—go out trapping
for a while.

Later in the afternoon Chief Kakoakis came to the
lodge door. He and Charbonneau talked about how one
of the larger wapiti was shot.

"I sure got me a big one for this lodge," bragged
Charbonneau. "There are plenty of hungry mouths here.
My gun shoots straight—never misses."

"You divided with a needy family?" asked the chief.
"All people share. Your women will show you where
extra meat is needed. I heard how the ball from your
flintlock lodged directly in the wapiti's heart. A perfect
shot...and by a woman."

Charbonneau felt the blood rush to his neck and face.
He looked at Sacajawea, who was speaking to the boys
and seemed to be paying no attention to him. "Well, I
was standing back from my woman, protecting her in
case the wapiti came out of the ditch; I had this newfangled flintlock, see. I took careful aim and bam! That's

all I had to do. Aim and shoot. Her shot went into the fence. Mine went to the heart. It is a natural ability."

Kakoakis laughed and put his arm around Charbonneau's shoulder. "You bring some of the white man's rum to my lodge and we'll celebrate your ability."

"I'm out of rum," said Charbonneau, with some regret in his voice.

"Get some," said Kakoakis, leaving.

Sacajawea looked at Charbonneau. The look made him shiver and feel guilty. He was afraid she might take some of his meat to that old woman, Grasshopper. Or worse, the old woman and her half-witted girl, along with the one who had all the papooses, might come for a visit in his lodge. If they did that, he did not want to be around. "I ought to go up to one of the Canadian posts," he said. "I could get some things for the chief and do some trapping on the way."

No one said anything to his suggestion. He rubbed bear's grease into the stock of his new gun and thought of picking up a piece of firewood and beating both women. Then they would talk to him, and pay him the attention he deserved as the man in the lodge. I could cut their noses off and send them out, he thought. Then I could find a couple nice young girls that appreciate me. But he knew no young thing would come willingly to his lodge if he did that bloody deed. And he would not do that because he preferred his squaws good-looking.

Charbonneau found a better way to hide his disgrace than disfiguring his women or getting drunk with Chief Kakoakis. The Britisher who had sold him the flintlock returned late in the afternoon, and the two men left that night. They trapped the rivers of the Côte Noire. He was gone nearly a month.

Most of the women were in the fields harvesting the fall crops. A Canadian trader on his way to Fort Assiniboin, then east, stopped by a belt-high stone fence and called out, *"Bonjour, mes amies!"*

Sacajawea looked up and squinted her eyes into the sun. She could see him talking to one of the women, his hands jerking. The woman wiped a hand across her perspiring face and motioned toward Sacajawea. "He calls in the same tongue as your man. I think he looks for the one called Toussaint Charbonneau, sometimes called Chief of the Little Village."

"*Ami!*" she called, and walked to the narrow passageway in the rock fence. Out of the field, she noticed the man was short and his black hair trailed down his neck through a bone ring. There was no bridle on his horse, only a single rein tied to its lower jaw.

"*Alerte!*" The face of the French-Canadian turned redder than the inner bark of the red pine. He licked his lips and spoke in French. "I want to speak to the man Charbonneau. You know where I can find him?"

"*Oui,*" said Sacajawea, nodding her head. She also spoke in French so that this stranger would know that she spoke with a straight tongue. "He has just returned, this same day, from the Côte Noire."

The man stared unbelieving at the sweating squaw who laid her hoe against the rocks and motioned him to follow. He began unscrewing the cap of his powder flask, and pulled from the flask a cylinder of tightly rolled paper. Just inside the lodge were fur bales that Charbonneau hoped to exchange later for supplies. The man looked at them, then looked into the center of the lodge where Charbonneau was pouring water into a sack of flour to make *galette*.

Sacajawea tied the man's horse to Charbonneau's, which was hobbled at the side of the lodge. She saw a twitching around Charbonneau's mouth, the beginning of a grin that anticipated a meeting with an old friend. But he did not know this man.

The stranger took Charbonneau by the arm. "Charbonneau—Toussaint?"

"*Oui.*" He let the water go unkneaded in the small flour sack. "What you want with me?"

"I am André La Croix. I have a letter." He unrolled the bit of paper.

"Wait! Can you read it?" Charbonneau reached for the paper. "Name of a name, who would write all this to me?"

"We find out who he is." André La Croix read the letter. His English came with difficulty, his lips exploring every sound.

Sacajawea looked over La Croix's shoulder and drew

in her breath. She stared frozenly. To her the neat script meant only one person, Chief Red Hair.

> *August 20, 1806, in board*
> *Pirogue near Ricara Village*

Charbono:

Sir: Your present situation with the Indians gives me some concern—I wish now I had advised you to come on with me to the Illinois where it most probably would be in my power to put you on some way to do something for yourself. I had not time to talk with you as much as I intended to have done. You have been a long time with me and have conducted yourself in such a manner as to gain my friendship; your woman, who accompanied you that long dangerous and fatiguing route to the Pacific Ocian and back, deserved a greater reward for her attention and services on that route than we had in our power to give her at the Mandans. As to your little son (my boy Pomp) you well know my fondness for him and my anxiety to take and raise him as my own child. I once more tell you if you will bring your son Baptiest to me I will educate him and treat him as my own child— I do not forgit the promis which I made to you and shall now repeat them that you may be certain—Charbono, if you wish to live with the white people, and will come to me, I will give you a piece of land and furnish you with horses cows and hogs—If you wish to visit your friends in Montreall, I will let you have a horse, and your family shall be taken care of until your return—if you wish to return as an interpreter for the Menetarras when the troops come up from the establishment, you will be with me ready and I will procure you the place—or if you wish to trade with the Indians and will leave your little Son Pomp with me, I will assist you with merchandise for that purpose, and become myself concerned with you in trade on a small scale, that is to say not exceeding a perogue load at one time. If you are disposed to accept either of my offers to you, and will bring your Son your famn Janey had best come along with you to take care of the boy until I get him—let me advise you to keep your bill of exchange and what furs and pelteries you have in possession, and get as much more as you can, and get as many robes, and big horn and cabbra skins as you can collect in the course of this winter. And take them down to St. Louis as early as possible. Enquire of the governor of that place for a letter which I shall leave with the governor. I shall inform you what you had best do with your furs pelteries and robes, etc. when you get to St. Louis write a letter to me by the post and let me know your situation—If you do not intend to go down either this fall or in the spring, write a letter to me by the first opportunity and inform me what you intend to do that I may know if I may expect you or not. If you ever intend to come down this fall or the next spring will be the best time— this fall would be best if you could get down before winter. I shall be found either in St. Louis or in Clarksville at the falls of the Ohio.

Wishing you and your family great success, and with anxious expectation of seeing my little dancing boy Baptiest, I shall remain your friend.

William Clark

Keep this letter and let not more than one or two persons see it, and when you write to me seal your letter. I think you best not determine which of my offers to accept until you see me. Come prepared to accept of either which you may choose after you get down.

Mr. Teousant Charbono, Menetarras Villages.[6]

"Read it once more," urged Sacajawea.

Charbonneau made a noise in his throat that signified nothing. "What does it mean?"

La Croix sucked in his breath and expressed exasperation. He had an owllike face and round, lightless black eyes; he was darker than Charbonneau. His fat shoulders and short back were blackened by the sun and wind. He wore a white mussel-shell necklace with a pendant of bear claws.

"Did you see Chief Red Hair?" Sacajawea ran her hands lightly over the paper.

"When I left him, he and his men, they were going to Saint Louis." He read the script again.

Charbonneau shook his head in two short, impatient jerks, as if the suggestions had enraged and awed him. He was in a quandary. Which offer was best for him? How should he get down to Saint Louis? When should he go? Should he go at all? He argued and considered, and then decided not to go. He did not have enough pelts yet.

"Pouf!" said La Croix, fastening his belt up another notch, "you're too damned toplofty for your good, my man. A chance like that? You decide not to do anything. A bigger fool I've never seen." He pulled on glossy skin gloves and went out to mount his horse.

Sacajawea turned so the firelight touched her eyes. They were half-closed, narrow; their polished gleam was no wider than two splinters of sharp flint. They were hostile, and her voice was hostile. "You have shown yourself to be a jackass and a fool."

She darted after La Croix. "We have pemmican and *galette*. Eat; then you'll be ready to start out."

"Merci; au revoir. A free trader like myself ought to be moving before sunset, Madame Charbonneau. I was paid fairly to get the letter into Charbonneau's hand. Now that the job is finished I'm heading toward the Lake of Rains—there's a long enough trail ahead. If I sit around, I hear things that are not there—the wind in the grass, the sound of running hooves on the earth, the murmur of water about a canoe bow, the beat of a skin drum, the chanting of watermen. So I go back to trapping and living among Assiniboins and Ojibwas. *Savez-vous*? I like white man's luxuries, though— mashed potatoes with salt."

"Vous attendez." Sacajawea ducked inside the lodge and was back in a minute with a handful of sugar cubes. Some were stained purple because they had been kept in a bag with dried currants and plums.

"Merci!" called La Croix as he rode off, first looking up and around to orient himself by the sun as Sacajawea stammered her gratitude to him for bringing the letter. Then he rode on in a beeline for the north, going through the back gate of the village and keeping on across the prairie to the edge of the forest.

Sacajawea shivered with sudden anticipation. She thought of holding the letter, looking at the markings that Chief Red Hair had made. She thought, He does think of us as I think each day of him. We will meet again.

Charbonneau went to Fort Pine to trade his furs. The days turned to winter, and the country was changed. Sacajawea's memories crowded together and moved in a tightly woven parade, overlapping and merging until they blurred before her eyes as if in a whirl of snow-flakes. When she could stand it no longer, she reached into the sack that held Charbonneau's valuables, such as his government money order, his French harp, three or four tallow candles, and Clark's letter. She looked at the markings on the paper in the light of the lodge fire and found some that were similar. But she could not read them.

She now lived in the present, using events gone by only as a measure of comparison, as a guiding experience for the future, which never emerged. There was an inherent vitality in Sacajawea's coppery figure, an ability to adapt, a placidity and devotion to her child, that gave no sign of weakening. Otter Woman observed this vital force in Sacajawea through the searing monotony of the days when the snow spread a white cover over the quiet hills and the river froze.

When Charbonneau returned from the north, he was in a black mood because he felt he had not received enough for his fine pelts. He began to grumble over the food his women brought him. He did not like the steady diet of corn and squash and elk jerky. Both women explained that he had not brought in enough other meat to use in the stew or to make pemmican.

Grimacing, Sacajawea told Otter Woman of the steady diet of fish that winter in Fort Clatsop.

"Fish would taste good now!" exclaimed Otter Woman, pulling her soiled woolen blanket more tightly around her shoulders.

"We will get some, then," said Sacajawea, and she told the boys to pull on their warm leggings. They walked upstream to fish through the ice, away from the places where the young boys of the village fished, so that none would tease or taunt them with shouts of how their man could not provide enough food. They caught small bass. Sacajawea told how the white men did not eat the insides, not even the heads of fish. Otter Woman shook her head, thinking of all that good food going to waste.

In the evening, Charbonneau was cheered for a few moments as he ate several fish rolled in flour and fried crisply. The two women chatted in Shoshoni, softly, so as not to bother him as he ate. The winter was getting him down, with nothing in his trap line, no traders in the village, and the family of Corn Woman demanding more meat and hides in payment for the life of their daughter. The less Charbonneau did, the less he wanted to do this cold winter. He spent the afternoons playing the stick game with Chief Kakoakis. He never asked anymore where the evening's fresh fish came from. He reasoned that they could be from the old woman, Grasshopper, who came to visit his women often.

Charbonneau did not know exactly what day it was, but one morning when the sun shone on the sparkling white snow he declared it was Christmas, crossed himself, and played his French harp.

Sacajawea recalled the merriment and gift-giving of the white soldiers. She gave Pomp and Tess the last little sugar lumps, and Otter Woman was given some short pieces of blue satin ribbon.

"*Nous avons envie de danser*," suggested Sacajawea.

"*Mon dieu*, dance then," said Charbonneau. He watched her strong legs and vigorous body as she danced around the lodge with the little boys following. She was no longer *petite et delicate* as she had seemed the night she sat on the blanket for the hand game. He had known this change for many months and had asked himself questions for which he had no ready answers. She was the leader. It was obvious as she moved to the center of the lodge with quick, certain steps, and there was an excitement stirring within her, as if she were again making her own plans to see the country in its immense richness. Charbonneau told himself he disliked energetic, headstrong women. Still, there was a nymphlike quality about Sacajawea. He was most attracted to the elfin, submissive qualities of very young girls.

In the spring of 1807, there were moccasin telegrams sending word that "American trade boats are coming up the Big Muddy." One group was going to the mouth of the Bighorn. One group would build a trading post at the Five Villages, and another would bring Big White and his family home.

"That subchief on his way home?" Charbonneau shook his head. "A man can't do a thing nowadays without it getting upstream faster than a bird flies away from winter. There will be too many people around here presently."

"Jussome will be coming, too," Otter Woman reminded him.

"Pah! This is something to think about. My eyes won't hurt none to have another look at his ugly face. I have missed that old Picardois. I think he is one fine bird. This time next year I will have him pluck, *non?*"

Charbonneau's round belly and winter fat shook as he chuckled. It was plain he thought well of his joke. "Jussome will strut around the street of this village, and I will pull those tail-feathers out of him. *Hein!* I think his feathers turn to dry leaves when he gets home, *pardieu.*"

"Who will build the trading post on the Bighorn's mouth?" asked Sacajawea, her lips quivering.

"*Les rats de la rivière ne reconnaissent pas leur ancêtre maternelle une fois partie,*" Charbonneau swore softly. "It will be the first fort built above the Five Villages. I would like to be there."

"Could you go?" asked Sacajawea, her eyes wide. "It is not far from the camp of my brother, Chief Black Gun. The People will dance when they see traders coming."

"*Ah, ça!* It is not that easy. *Nom d'un nom,* you make it so simple. Can't you see the job for me is here? I can be an interpreter here for the men who come up the river. Many will be coming, and I will have much to do."

There was a timid knock on the rough plank lodge door. Otter Woman turned to Charbonneau, who sat

with his eyes shut, leaving morose creases in his face.
"I was not expecting anyone."

"It is visitors, though; the knocking continues."

Charbonneau opened his small eyes and opened his
hands and fairly flung them at Otter Woman.

She went to the heavy door, made from soft cottonwood cut to size with an ax and chiseled to fit the opening. It was hung with wide leather strips tied around
the doorframe and the first plank in the door. The whole
thing was stained a deep ocher with clay mixed in bear's
grease. The door swung open slowly and strained the
leather bindings, making a groaning sound.

A young woman, wrapped in a bright orange piece
of blanket, with a girl near the same age as Little Tess,
smiled at Otter Woman. Otter Woman made a croaking
sound. The young woman spoke. "Don't you remember?
This is Earth Woman, and I am called Sun Woman."

"Sun Woman!" Sacajawea cried out, running to embrace the squaw, whose cheeks flamed because she had
not been recognized. Her tunic was quilled across the
shoulders. Her moccasins and leggings were clean,
showing she'd ridden a horse.

Sacajawea sent Tess out to tether the guest's horse.

"We have come to hear your stories," said Sun
Woman, dropping the blanket shawl on a wall peg. She
wore thin ankle bracelets over her leggings. Her child,
already walking with the usual in-toeing, was dressed
in the same manner. "My man, Four Bears, went on a
hunt and rode this far with us." Her black eyes warmly
lighted the shadows in the lodge.

"Come," said Sacajawea, taking the child, who carried a cornhusk doll wrapped in rabbit skin, by the
hand. "You may sit in the place of distinction."

"I will tell some good tales," offered Charbonneau,
stepping forward. "You come to hear what I say?"

"No," said Sun Woman timidly. "I only came to visit
with the women of your lodge."

"So be it. But it is my turn to talk today." Charbonneau's smile taunted Sun Woman. She held her small
body erect. Charbonneau thought she looked like a bird
trying to be dignified, small and unsure of herself. "My
women, they go to plant early squash." He waved his
hands toward Sacajawea and Otter Woman.

Sacajawea looked from one woman to the other. Sun Woman shrank against the wall.

"What for? It is hardly time yet. What for?" But Sacajawea knew. She interposed her body between Charbonneau and Sun Woman.

Sun Woman was embarrassed. Her child, Sak-weahki, Earth Woman, moved slowly toward Pomp. There was a stillness in the lodge like the sudden quiet of slack water at the foot of a high falls. There was danger in slack water. It had a way of gathering itself imperceptibly, of rolling smoothly, without warning, into the irresistible, tumultuous chute of another sault.

Charbonneau passed behind Sacajawea, whose face was white. Her enormous eyes stared. Charbonneau smiled, put his hand on the edge of Sun Woman's short tunic, his finger pushing up along her warm thigh.

Otter Woman put her hands over her face, chagrined.

"Little Sunshine—" Charbonneau felt his voice shake.

Sun Woman made a gurgling noise in her throat. It was Sacajawea who moved beside them and spoke. "Our man was leaving to visit Chief Kakoakis. He is leaving now." Her tone was low, reassuring. Her fingers touched the back of Charbonneau's collar, pushed down along the cold skin at the back of his neck, closed tightly on the woolen cloth.

At the same time, Earth Woman tapped Pomp on his shoulder and in a girl's high voice said, "My father sent you a white pony. It is because you can travel far and come home safely."

"Pony!" cried Pomp.

"The white pony?" Little Tess suddenly appeared from the middle of his sleeping couch. "I saw him. Come, I'll show you."

The boys' legs moved as fast as they could go for the door. Charbonneau's hand dropped, and he stared after the boys. He put the women aside. "Pah! A pony, you say? I will see for myself. *Dépêchez-vous, mangeurs de lard!*" he called to the boys and trotted after them. His quick step carried him through the entrance and out the door.

Otter Woman let her breath go out, *pouf*. Sacajawea felt her dignity go. "I hate you!" she called, then crum-

pled. Then she summoned her composure and sat on
Otter Woman's couch beside Sun Woman. Otter Woman
began making herb tea.

"Is it true?" asked Sacajawea. A curious embarrassment seized her, but she tried to appear calm.

"*Ai*," said Sun Woman, her voice shaking yet. "Four
Bears has a special liking for you and your son. He has
been happy since he heard of your safe return. I think
he makes a special effort to watch over your household.
He feels that you need more care since you live with a
white man. I understand that concern now."

This last caused Otter Woman to put her hands to
her mouth and laugh nervously. Soon the three women
were looking at one another and laughing behind their
hands, knowing that there had been three of them and
only one Charbonneau. He had been powerless, in fact.

Once Pomp came in for dried plums to share with
the children. Otter Woman gave him a handful of dried
corn for the new horse.

"The pony is not here," said Pomp. "He was ridden
through the village for showing off by my father."

Then the three children were inside, listening to the
story of the Nez Percé fish trap and the burial canoes
of another nation. Sacajawea showed Sun Woman the
red, puckered scar behind Pomp's left ear, which was
all that was left of his dreadful sickness when he was
on the expedition. She told of the kindness of Chief Red
Hair and how he used medicine to make Pomp well
again. Pomp moved away and showed Earth Woman
how Ben York had danced, making her laugh.

"Music," said Pomp. "We should make music like the
fiddle."

Sacajawea looked out the door and saw that for certain their man was gone. Cautiously she sorted through
Charbonneau's belongings in the sack until she found
the French harp. She also opened the leather pouch that
held the peace medal.

"See, I still keep this shiny round totem safe. A gift
like this is always valued. When Pomp is older I will
give it to him to keep in his own safe place."

The medal was not so shiny as they remembered.

"It darkens with age," said Sun Woman. "We'll look

at it again after another snow; then see if the face there is as black as the man you call York."

"*Ai*," said Otter Woman, and she retold of the repeated wet-finger tests on York's black skin by the strange tribes along the rivers, just as though she had been there and seen it all herself.

Before she was finished, Pomp repeated, "Music. We want to dance."

Sacajawea put the medal away and put the French harp to her lips, blowing softly at first, barely breathing in and out on the top. When she felt more accustomed to the music, she played louder—no specific tune, but with a definite rhythm to her composition. The children laughed and danced, hopping on one foot, then the other. Otter Woman and Sun Woman clapped their hands and chanted with the notes. Finally the children complained of being thirsty.

Otter Woman poured the herb tea in tin cups.

"It is the best time I had for many moons," said Sun Woman, her face flushed. "Please come to Rooptahee for a visit. Send me word when your man is gone, and I will come again."

"We'll all ride the white horse," laughed Earth Woman.[7]

When the visitors had gone, Sacajawea replaced Charbonneau's French harp and told Otter Woman to keep her mouth sealed about the instrument. Then she cautioned the boys not to say anything about the good time they had just had.

"Your papa would not understand that we only enjoyed ourselves and it had nothing to do with him," she said.

Charbonneau came home at twilight. The weather was mild with the promise of spring in the air. He ordered the women to put the children on their couches. "They have had a busy day and are nothing but cranky!" he yelled. "Nothing is worse than a whining half-breed kid."

After he had eaten a little elk jerky, he had Otter Woman remove his moccasins.

"Why are your feet so tired? Didn't you have a fine white pony to ride?"

"What pony? There is none. I gave it to the family

of Corn Woman so they would not bother me, but now they want three good buffalo robes besides. Greedy. *Mon dieu*, greedy Indians."

"You—you gave away a gift that belonged to your son?" asked Sacajawea, shocked and angry with this big, foolish man.

"I had to or they might have taken my scalp. *Jésus*, they are a mean, *sauvage* bunch. It was a pretty horse," he sighed. "All white, except his mane, which was more cream or yellow. Nice."

Sacajawea went mad. She became a wildcat. She beat her hands against him like an infuriated sparrow hurling itself upon a moose. "Why did you come back? I hate you. I do, I do!"

Her dignity was gone. He lifted her, scratching, kicking, clawing, and set her down on her couch. The lodge door slammed. Charbonneau went to Chief Kakoakis.

There were more moccasin telegrams about boats carrying white men up the Missouri. One was captained by Manuel Lisa, a wary Spaniard who had come past the Sioux, as far as the Arikaras. Kakoakis swore he'd stop this white man from trading beyond the Five Villages. Mainly he did not want the Shoshonis armed and fed. They were a good source of horses and slaves. Kakoakis could not stop Lisa, and soon there were more boats. One party was led by Auguste Chouteau from Saint Louis, who was bringing Sheheke home. The Arikaras fired on the boats, killing three white men and injuring three others, two of whom were Jussome and George Shannon. Big White was forced to return to Saint Louis.

Chief Kakoakis came to see Charbonneau the evening the news of Sheheke's retreat came. He was exultant. "See, now, I was right. The United States is only a small nation. I was smart to stand by the British. Sheheke was foolish to visit the Great White Father. He will never get home—not alive, anyway." He grinned his lopsided smile and blinked his one good eye.

Charbonneau had worn himself thin boasting of the great exploits of the Americans and, patting the letter from Clark, bragging about the job offers. His position among the Minnetarees was by now none too comfortable while Chief Kakoakis was supporting the British.

About this same time, there were squabbles among the British and Americans for fur-trading rights in the west.

During the spring, Sacajawea and Otter Woman softened the old buffalo hides Charbonneau had left behind. He had taken a pack of pelts to Fort Pine. The women made clothing for their own use and some to sell to traders who might come upstream. Sacajawea had learned to drive a good bargain, and she understood most of the French or English traders, which was a great advantage. Otter Woman grew to respect Sacajawea's ability more and more. Charbonneau began to resent it.

When Charbonneau returned, he seemed in a great hurry. He had plans. He had a purpose! He was going to "Red Hair's town." There was a great fur market there. He had heard about it from men who came in from Michipicoten. "There are many who are transporting their furs across Lake Superior to get them into Prairie du Chien or down to Saint Louis," they had said. Charbonneau was impatient and ill-tempered. He ordered both women to get ready. He was confident his plan would work. He was going to take both boys to be educated by Capitaine Clark. He felt it was a foxy move. He knew that Clark would not have the heart to send Little Tess back to the Indians, or keep him out of school, so both his boys would have an education and do something great for the Charbonneau name. Even his relatives in Montreal and Toronto would hear of the Charbonneau boys being educated in Saint Louis. *C'est le monde renversé*, he thought, they won't believe such a thing can happen. He raised his eyebrows and sucked in his round cheeks just thinking of their astonishment when they heard this news.

Sacajawea was dazed by this surprise move of her man. It had been a dream, but now it was a reality. She and Otter Woman were packed within a day's time. Then Sacajawea began to fret and worry. Would there be room for all of them in a boat returning to Saint Louis? There has to be, she thought. Charbonneau had made it clear they were all to go. *Voilà!* So there it was.

But she remembered he sometimes did not check into details too carefully.

The next morning, she asked, "May I use your horse to visit Grasshopper? She is getting old, and I would like to see her once before I go away from this village. I would like for her to see our growing son."

"*Oui*," said Charbonneau before thinking. "You go and show off our son. He is quite a boy. Let him dance for old Grasshopper, eh? Tell her he will one day not be a *sauvage*, but a gentleman that reads and writes like the whites."

"*Oui, merci!*" she said, grateful that he did not remember he had planned entering his riding horse in the Minnetarees' spring races in the next couple of days.

At Grasshopper's lodge there was much commotion as the children crowded around Rosebud. "See," said old Grasshopper, her face grained like the scum on cold corn porridge, "it is a fresh-born beaver. Fast Arrow found it hunting two suns back. Its mother was so thin and scraggly that he let her go to fatten up. See how the children love this new pet."

Sacajawea saw a tiny animal, no bigger than a large fist. She felt its quick breathing and its tiny pink tongue on the palm of her hand. She held it for a few moments, then handed it to the small girl, Chickadee. Then Sacajawea surprised them with her announcement of going down the Big Muddy to Saint Louis.

"Alone? Are you going alone? Does your man know about it?" asked Rosebud, astonished. "We won't breathe a word."

"He knows. We are all going. My man has word of trappers coming in from the Red River of the North and passing here in two or three days. We are traveling by canoe with them."

Grasshopper pushed two grandchildren from her lap and shook her head. "An Arikara chief, called Anke-doucharo, went downriver to visit the Great White Father, and now that is ended; he is dead. The Arikaras do not like white men. There is a rustling in the dry grass that seven hundred Sioux are ready to fight anybody that is white and traveling up the Big Muddy. These same Sioux would like to come fight the

Mandans, or Minnetarees, anyone—they are blood-hungry."

"You worry," sighed Sacajawea. "You are more like a grandmother each day."

"I am a grandmother, and I am wise. Men do not stop fighting just because someone who is kind comes to make a peaceful gesture to them. They forget and fall back into their fierce ways soon enough. It is the way men are. The Great Spirit knows this. And so—does the Great Spirit of the palefaces know this truth?" She reached out her gnarled old hand to examine the neatly braided hair of Sacajawea. Her hand moved to Sacajawea's nose, fine and straight, and to her pure, unblemished copper skin. "I have friends and relatives killed by Sioux, with whom our village has battled forever. It will not stop unless the white men kill them all to the last man. But you, my daughter, are not meant to wither and grow old in this prairie nation. The Great Spirit plants wiseness behind your eyes. Care for your handsome son. He, too, will be wise in the ways of two people, the white men and the Indian nations."

Sacajawea bent to one of Rosebud's little girls. "I like girl-children," she said, nuzzling the child in the neck so that the girl laughed. "They let me hold them longer than boys."

"Dance with me," cried the little girl. They danced in the manner of a jog. Soon all the children were dancing with Sacajawea. Rosebud sat on the floor inside their circle so that she could watch. She was nursing the beaver cub. Finally she could stand sitting no longer and reached for a cupped bark dish by the cooking fire and pressed milk from her other breast into the dish for the beaver. Then she joined the dancers while the cub lapped up the milk and Pomp pulled at its broad tail. The beaver made a crying sound, almost like that of a baby. Pomp dropped its tail and scooted back to the dancing children with a grin on his face.

When the trappers came into the village before daybreak, Otter Woman and Sacajawea were waiting at the water's edge. They carried Charbonneau's baggage and some dried corn and jerky, their own change of dress and extra moccasins, and the boys' clothing. Charbonneau ran in little trotting steps to the *patron*, who was crouched over a campfire; only his blue felt hat with its fur tail showed plainly.

"Can we come aboard now?" Charbonneau asked, looking at the three dugouts.

With one hand the *patron* pushed his black mustache up from his mouth as if to clear the way for his words. His voice was sharp; the flesh of his face was dark and cracked like leather that has seen too much rain and sun. The pouches under his eyes sagged and showed pools of red, like those of a bloodhound. He breathed audibly through his mouth, blowing at his drooping mustache. He had on boots, leather trousers, and a shirt.

"You'll have to split up. You in this pirogue and one squaw and papoose in this, and the other squaw with papoose in the other *bateau*." He wiped his hands on his fringed shirt. "You did not tell me you had two squaws with you. *Sacre crapaud!*"

Sacajawea did not stand around to hear the men argue about why Charbonneau had not said anything about bringing both women and children. She quickly stepped into the canoe designated for one squaw and child and settled herself among her baggage with Pomp on her lap.

The Missouri's current did most of the oarsmen's work. There was little struggling against it with poles and oars and ropes. They had plenty of game and fresh wild fruit. They swept past the Arikara village. Each night the camp was silent, except now and then for the matter of one man talking to another and the clink of spoons against metal plates. The fire glowed and died and glowed again as the breeze played with it. Against the river the canoes were black logs.

Sacajawea and Otter Woman sat together sopping up bean juice with dry corn bread and feeding it to their children. Sacajawea swallowed the last of her bitter coffee. The food was good, and she was glad to be back tasting the fare of white men. Her thoughts strayed to the unknown Saint Louis.

Charbonneau got up and looked at the men about the fire. His eyes fixed on the *patron*. As if to crack the silence he said, "I be dogged, Miquelon, if we keep on with these white beans, I do believe we'll blow your *bateau* to Red Hair's town." The men looked at him unsmiling, their eyes catching glints from the fire.

"It is an idea," said the *patron*, "if only the rest could make the wind like you." He lighted his pipe with a brand.

Charbonneau went to his buffalo robe and half covered himself with a blanket. Soon his snoring was audible. Sacajawea and Otter Woman laid the children on buffalo robes and rolled themselves up in blankets beside them.

On the third day out, they met a band of Teton Sioux. Sacajawea huddled in the bottom of the canoe, holding tight to Pomp, who was asleep.

Miquelon said, "Quiet, *écoutez* now, all. *Non* song, *non* curse. To the *passe avant*. *À bas les perches.*"

Charbonneau lowered his ash pole and felt it catch on the riverbed. He brought the ball of it into the hollow of his shoulder and set his legs to driving, feeling the canoe give under his feet. The canoe slid through the water. *"Lève les perches!"* The boatmen whispered and straightened and caught their canoes before the current pushed them into a sawyer, and then it was push again, step by step, to get their *bateaux* into the main stream again, while the ball ground into Charbonneau's shoulder and his lungs wheezed.

Sacajawea could see Charbonneau trying to pole and slipping his pole against the rocks, inefficient and puffing. The dark bank moved by, its trees and undergrowth a picture of filtered sunlight and light shadows on the faded leaf carpet. The leaves were soft and moist; beneath them was rich black humus. Lying against the humus were moss-etched logs, returning their elements to the soil to feed future generations of trees. The ledges and sand came out in full sight, and the blue spiderwort was everywhere. The Sioux stood painted on the shore, some with bows at their shoulders, others with rifles at the ready. The water murmured against the canoes. They slid swiftly downriver from the waiting Sioux.

"Steady," said the *patron*, Miquelon. Only the smothered grunts of the crew sounded and the whisper of the waves along the canoes.

"Nigh perfect," said one of the hunters as the Indians

were left far behind. "There's a good bunch of willow. Here, you."

The alcohol gurgled in its short flag kegs as Miquelon lifted it from a cargo box. He brought the kegs over the side. The men who stood in the water waded ashore.

"*Assez*," said Laurier, a hunter. "Enough."

"How much of the whiskey you allowed?" Charbonneau asked the hunter.

"Gill a day for each boatman, when the going gets rough, but it lasts about four months only. The bigger outfits do a sight better. Take the Northwesters or Hudson's Bay. I've knowed land brigades to get a gill a day for a whole year for each man, making out they was boatmen, and of course not a boatman in the lot, as everybody knowed."

They dropped their blankets near the willows and brought out the kettles. "Might as well make a little soup and sleep," said Laurier. "It's a long way yet to Saint Louis."

For three days the wind was right; the canoes moved along, and the rowers sang songs and only played at rowing. That suited Charbonneau better, as he had begun to rue the day he told these men he could row, cordelle, and paddle any craft that man could fashion. Early every morning, while darkness still lay on the river and woods, two of the men, hunters, slipped out of their blankets and went ahead to hunt, meeting them later on the bank or hanging game on a limb where it could not be missed and then going ahead to hunt some more.

Sacajawea saw that from their association together the boatmen had developed a kind of slang peculiar to themselves. They had a quickness and a vulgar smartness that amused her.

"By littles the damn pole is pushing clean through my shoulder," complained Charbonneau, swinging Little Tess to his shoulder and grabbing Pomp by the hand. "They dance and it will make these men laugh."

He walked to where three Frenchmen, sitting cross-legged, were singing. Sacajawea guessed it was a love song. They made mouths over it, and their eyes rolled. Two boatmen wrestled on the ground, tumbling over and over and laughing as they tumbled.

"Donkeys," Otter Woman said. "Just donkeys. Out of the harness they roll and heehaw."

One of the boatmen jumped up and yelled, "I'm a son of a wildfire—half horse, half alligator, and a touch of the earthquake—I've got the prettiest sister, fastest horse, and ugliest dog in the States, and can kill more liquor, fool more varmints, outrun, outjump, throw down, drag out, and whip any man in all Kaintuck."

Everyone roared a mighty laugh. Charbonneau took this as his cue and started playing the French harp. The boys held hands and toddled around him, sometimes with a toe-heel step, and sometimes just running. The men grinned and clapped.

"This child is dry as a powder horn," said Charbonneau. "Might it be time for the keg to be opened to wet down our whistles a little?"

Miquelon opened the keg and was followed by the greater part of the men.

The cook beat a pan with a long-handled spoon. The songs broke off, the wrestling ceased, the drinking was finished in fast gulps, and everyone pushed forward. There were beans again, and parched corn, and wild turkey. Charbonneau heaped his plate and sat down against a tree, smiling to himself as the squaws squatted at the water's edge washing the face and hands of the boys. *Jésus*, who cared about a dirty face?

Two days later, they passed the mouth of the Vermilion River. They ran down as far as Floyd's Bluff.[8] Two weeks out from the Mandan villages, the three canoes met a trading pirogue belonging to Auguste Chouteau, the Saint Louis merchant and trader. To the delight of the crew, the Chouteau craft started for the bank. Miquelon caught its mooring rope. "Come ashore, the food is warm. Coffee we have. *Beaucoup*."

The paddlers rested their oars. "Sounds grand," said one. "My ass's breaking."

Stiffly the men rose and stepped out. Most of the men had on red-flannel shirts covered with blue capotes, moccasins, and each had a knife hanging from a broad leather belt. They had sugar in the Chouteau outfit. More coffee was brewed, and a quarter cup of sugar was in the bottom of every tin cup before the coffee was poured on top. The general joy of the after-

noon was marred only by Charbonneau and Otter
Woman. Weary with so much travel, they argued about
who was going to hold Tess. The little boy relieved his
own discomfort by squalling. Miquelon gave the child
some sugar water, and he was immediately quiet, sipping the sweet, cool liquid. Sacajawea put her finger in
the bottom of her tin cup and stirred a little; then she
let Pomp lick her finger. She did this until the cup was
clean.

Miquelon tossed the painter back to the Chouteau
crew and with his foot started the canoe into the current. The paddles glistened, and the patch of black receded until Sacajawea could not tell what was canoe
and what was wave in the twilight.

The next day, they met another party of French traders, and they feasted on venison and wild onions together. They sang French songs far into the night. The
next day, the voyageurs sang to the stroke, songs that
Sacajawea had come to know by heart, though she did
not know all their meaning.

The French rivermen make me think of devoted dogs,
thought Sacajawea. They are not the stuff of which
warriors are made, they are not fighters, yet they are
industrious and loyal soldiers. They seem tireless, and
they move into unknown country with an ever-ready
quip and a chant on their lips, even as they look fearfully at the hills ahead and cross themselves as the
shades of night conceal the world. She was certain that
their religion had made them see life through a veil of
mystery and distortion, and had instilled an unquench-
able fear in them.

Sometimes Pomp squirmed and tried to drag his fat
hand in the brown water. Sacajawea joggled him until
he laughed and stretched his legs out, keeping time
with his feet.

Otter Woman sat slumped over in one of the canoes,
and little Tess dragged one hand in the water. Charbonneau looked sharply at them, praying Little Tess
would not fall into the brown water. The sky was blue
and patched with slow white clouds. The sun looked
down, bright and hot.

Sacajawea, tired of sitting in the bottom of the canoe,
asked one of the voyageurs if she could take the long

blade. The man laughed, then said, *"Je chanterai."* Carefully she took his place; he held Pomp in the bottom of the canoe and began to sing.

She pulled to the rhythm of the tune, laying the long blade far back and pulling it through, trying for the easy skill of the voyageur she was spelling.

The party passed old Mr. Dorion, the Sioux interpreter, in a pirogue with some French traders who were going up to the Yankton Sioux for beaver pelts.

Laurier and another hunter were sent out, and the canoes continued all night because the evening was wet. Thunder rolled up the river and rumbled down on them; the wind was not strong. Miquelon called, *"Hallez fort! Hallez fort!"* and the paddlers steadied down on the oars as they felt the wind coming now at their backs. By morning they were passing the little French village of La Charrette, the home of Daniel Boone. Sacajawea had long ago given the voyageur back his blade. The canoes angled for shore, and the men began to sing again, softly, relieved that they could finally rest and be through with work for a few hours.

Laurier and the other hunter came in, and the party had steaks from deer flanks. In three or four hours they were back in the water. Sacajawea saw her first cows grazing on the bank.

"Cross between buffalo and horse and the Rocky Mountain goat," Laurier explained to her.

"Extraordinaire!" exclaimed Sacajawea, clapping a hand to her mouth.

They passed a high rock slope where a cool copse of aspen stood trembling in the breeze. One of the men told Otter Woman, by hand signs, that the aspen's wood had been used in the cross and ever since the Crucifixion the leaves of this gentle tree had trembled.

"Ai," answered Otter Woman, never comprehending the Crucifixion story. "I know the wood is good for fuel. It has little odor and does not taint the meat." She moved her hands slowly so the man could read them.

The next day was even more exciting. They passed a dozen canoes of Kickapoos going out on a hunting expedition, and more grazing black-and-white cows on the banks. In the afternoon they saw the village of Saint Charles. Sacajawea waved to Otter Woman in the next canoe, pointing to the white ladies walking in long, puffed-out skirts along the bank.

With cheers and the firing of guns they landed at the village.

The men traded some pelts for beef and pork, and flour, sugar, and tea. They had a great dinner on the beach of pork steaks fried in flour, and tea with much sugar.

Miquelon finally waved his arms. "Get aboard! Everybody! We're moving. Get on!"

A waterman took up the big pot full of tea from the fire and leaped into his canoe with it. The others threw blankets and guns into their canoes. There was some cheering, and a voyageur began to sing. Laurier let out a long, wild yell, and someone fired a gun. The noise of the shot thundered into the village; it was caught by the bluff behind the shadowy town and thrown back at them.

"On to Saint Louis," called Miquelon.

Just above the junction of the Missouri and Mississippi rivers loomed the mud chimneys of the log Fort Bellefontaine, where Colonel Thomas Hunt was in command and Dr. Saugrain was chief surgeon. Sacajawea listened as the men talked. She knew of the use of Dr. Saugrain's pills. She stared intently at Colonel Hunt walking along the bank as he was pointed out to Charbonneau. Hunt had a large face, burned brick red, graying hair, pale blue eyes, and a quick grin for his little daughter, Abby, who walked beside him.

Pomp and Little Tess climbed out of the beached canoe. The little white girl, Abby, ran toward them. Her eyes sparkled. "You are like the children who came with the other two Indian ladies a long time ago. One of the men looked like him." Abby danced up and down and stared at Charbonneau.

"That was two years back, my dear," said Colonel Hunt. "That was a more important party than this, I daresay. Lewis and Clark were on board those canoes."

Abby giggled and put her hand to her mouth. "There was the manservant—he was a big black Indian. I remember."

Sacajawea's heart leaped. It was probably Jussome

who reminded the child of Charbonneau, and the other men Sacajawea knew for certain.

Two days later, in August 1808, they sighted the old stone forts of the Spanish in Saint Louis. The frontier village was noble, rising on a high terrace from the rock-bound river. They landed the three canoes in the center of the village beach. Down the banks came people to greet them. These people never suspected, as Colonel Hunt had not suspected, that three members of this small party were from the famous Lewis and Clark Expedition.

"Laurier!" called a small, black-eyed Frenchwoman in blue.

"Susette," called the hunter, and with a leap he was out of the canoe and upon the shore.

"*Mon dieu!*" cried Charbonneau. "Many people. It is like Montreal. And where do we find Capitaine Clark?"

CHAPTER

36

Judy Clark

"I have become quite a galant and somewhat taken with the fair creatures," Clark wrote his brother Edmund from Washington, but his real interest was in Judy Hancock, whom he soon persuaded to marry him.

When Clark confided his engagement to Mr. Jefferson, that constant friend presented him with jewelry for Judy—a necklace, two bracelets, earrings, a pin and a ring, of pearls and topaz.

Judy set the date of their marriage as January 1808.

Excerpt from p. 383 in *Lewis and Clark: Partners in Discovery* by John Bakeless. Copyright 1947 by John Bakeless. By permission of William Morrow and Company.

Late in the afternoon, Charbonneau left his two women and two sons on the rocks beside a pier. He went to find William Clark.

The sun streamed like a red glaze over the limestone bluffs that stood behind the town, filtered through the trees and smoke of grass fires, and glinted on the surface of the Mississippi. The street above the river was filled with confused and unfixed shadows, the clash of voices, and the strains of fiddle music. In this hour before sunset the street was raucous with voyageurs, tanned and sallow, quick of gait, graceful and gay; black-eyed Frenchwomen, and little French children in red petticoats; here and there a *coureur de bois*, a Kentucky hunter, lank and lean; Creole *engagé*; and the Negro, breed, and Indian *filles de joie* who filled the shops and bars.

That summer there had been heat and no rain. Now there were grass fires burning in the Grande Prairie beyond the bluff; small orange tongues licked at the yellowed grass, and smoke rose above the land diffusing the strength of the sun and forecasting an ominous end to summer.

Sacajawea looked about, feeling small and frightened. She searched through the crowds that milled about the pier. Could that be Broken Tooth, Jussome's woman, there, sweltering in a dirty cerise blanket, speaking sharply to the children beside her? And was that She-heke dressed in the blue coat with gold braid and the eagle feather worn proudly in his hair? She was not sure who these people were, and her head swam with so many unfamiliar things in view.

"Well, bless my soul," said a voice at her elbow, "it is the little dancing boy. I thought my eyes played tricks." It was big, grinning Ben York.

"York! York!" Sacajawea was overcome with joy to find a familiar face. She pushed Pomp toward him, but the child was shy.

"How do? You all remember me? You were only a papoose when we left you standing on that Mandan beach. I'se your old nursemaid. I taught you to dance.

See?" York took a couple of quick jog steps despite the rocky ground.

Pomp slowly imitated him, then smiled up at York, who picked him up in his big black arms. Tears streamed down his face. Pomp put his cheek against York's. "I looked for you," the child said softly.

"I would have come back looking for you, but I'se a slow walker," said York. Then, pointing, he said, "Who's that?"

"Tess, my brother. His *umbea*, Otter Woman—see? There."

"How do?" said York, remembering now that Charbonneau did have more than one woman. "Your man, that rascally Charb, come with you ladies?"

"*Ai*," said Sacajawea, shading her eyes with a hand because she thought she recognized someone else. "Pryor! It is you!"

"Certainly, it's me," said Nat Pryor, laughing. "I see York found you first."

Pryor was the official escort for Sheheke and his family and now took the job of being escort for the Charbonneau family. Charbonneau came trotting into sight, and Pryor took them by horse and buggy to the barracks of Saint Louis. They were housed with Sheheke's family under the protection of the militia.

Sheheke did not have on a blue coat, but a black cutaway.

"This lodge is so large I could be lost in it," said Otter Woman.

Sheheke laughed, amused that once he had felt the same way. "You will not get lost if you sit in one corner and do not move."

"Master Clark will be along soon," said York, finding a lump of sugar somewhere in the depths of his pocket for Pomp, and one for little Tess. Then, suddenly, he had an ear-to-ear grin on his perspiring, shining face. "I think Master Clark like me to fetch you all to his house. Come, you hear? You young'uns, too."

Charbonneau followed him down the long steps, and Sacajawea, with her hand tight on Pomp's, came close behind. Otter Woman held Little Tess by one arm, stating flatly she preferred to stay behind listening to the tales Sheheke's squaw, Yellow Corn, was telling about the white man's food. She was really afraid to go out into this unfamiliar, noisy village.

Sacajawea's shoulders jerked slightly under her loose deerskin tunic. "We will go without you."

Otter Woman had turned her back.

Outwardly, Sacajawea was composed, almost stoic, but inwardly her heart throbbed violently. York turned and picked up Pomp so he could ride on his wide shoulders. Sacajawea looked first at York, then at Pryor. She could scarcely keep up with them on the hilly street to Main and Pine. Charbonneau paused frequently to peer into doorways, speak with Canadians, and observe the gamblers knotted about buffalo robes on the dirt floors of bars. York led them to a small wooden building adjoining a shining white one-story house. They were inside the stuffy Council Hall—General Clark's Indian museum.

Clark came in. He was clean, shaven, beautiful—more beautiful than Sacajawea had remembered. In the warmth of the summer afternoon, he had opened the chest flap of his blue cotton shirt. The wrappings of his moccasins held brown homespun breeches snugly about his ankles. Under his reddish brows his eyes remained a cool blue. His hair, a red-orange shade the sun might have created in its burnings, was thick and long against his neck and tied with a leather thong.

"Janey!" Clark gasped. "This is the best surprise I've ever had. Why didn't you tell me you were on your way downriver?" he said, turning to Charbonneau. Then: "Pryor, did you know they were coming?"

"No, sir. It was a complete surprise to see Charb, here, in the middle of the cigar store, Le Bureau de Tabac. Then I found Janey, here, and Pomp talking with York."

"No time; we get ready; we leave." Charbonneau shrugged his shoulders under his sweat-stained buckskin shirt. The shirt was fringed at the shoulders and embroidered with strands that once had been brightly painted, but now were stained and blackened.

"Well, I'm glad you are here. Welcome to Saint Louis!" Clark shook Charbonneau's hand as if he could not let go.

Sacajawea controlled herself, although she wanted

to run beside Clark, throw her robe about his shoulders, and weep for joy. But seeing him here, in his own lodge, made him seem different, larger. He was shining, clean. She glanced at her tunic and robe. She was embarrassed and wished she had changed to clean ones, and fresh moccasins.

"My little dancing boy, Pomp, come here." Clark stooped to pick up the child. "Come, let me see how you've grown."

The child drew shyly away.

Clark was visibly disappointed. Sacajawea bent to whisper to her child; he looked into her face for an instant, then, reassured, stepped out into the center of the room.

"Watch, Chief Red Hair," the child said in a soft voice. Then he began to dance with his tiny knees bent, moccasins barely touching the floor, in perfect rhythm to his mother's clapping hands.

"Wonderful!" said Clark, now satisfied and pleased. The child went to him and was pulled onto Clark's lap.

Sacajawea had never seen chairs with arms and a back like the ones York brought in. "Sit here, Janey," said York. "It's better than the floor."

She sat, but she felt stiff and uncomfortable. Soon she was on the floor, Indian-fashion, listening as the men spoke of getting in touch with the fur companies so that Charbonneau would get an interpreting job.

"You did get my letter, then?"

Charbonneau grinned, nodded, and reached into the bag hanging from his belt. He drew out the paper that had sung to Sacajawea. "I keep it safe, with me."

"Let me have it, will you?" asked Clark. "I'd like to keep it in my files." Clark took the letter, smoothed it flat, and slipped it into the back of his desk drawer at the far side of the room. Had he known it would turn up a century later to be studied and his intense interest in the Charbonneaus debated, perhaps he would not have preserved it so carefully.

Coming back to his chair, Clark said, "You should not have stayed behind so long, Charb. You and Janey should have gone with us to see President Jefferson last year when I took Sheheke."

Clark explained to Charbonneau that each of the

enlisted men of the expedition was entitled to three hundred and twenty acres of land, and that included Charbonneau. "And there has been talk of giving each man double pay. Lewis was given sixteen hundred acres of land; and I, one thousand. Can't you just see Lewis when he heard about it? He wrote to the powers in Washington, and you're right, I was given sixteen hundred acres also. That's really more than I can use. Charb, if you want to buy some from me with your extra pay, you are welcome to do it."

Charbonneau muttered something and blew on his mustache.

Nat Pryor scratched his head and spoke. "I know that Ordway bought the claims of LePage, Werner, and Goodrich, paying two hundred dollars for the first two and two-fifty for Si's. So he got himself nine hundred and sixty acres."

"Yes," said Clark. "Young Shannon also bought extra, snapping up Tom Howard's claim. Say, did you know Lewis was made governor of Louisiana, and he resigned his commission in the Regular Army a year ago last spring?" He did not wait for anyone to answer. "I was made brigadier general of the Louisiana Militia. That could mean some work if war breaks out. We all know the British will attack." He slapped his knee. "I don't think Lewis cares for those Britishers much, either. A more interesting job was also given me. I am agent for the Indians—Pryor works for me."

Clark immediately saw the question in Sacajawea's eyes. "I am a go-between for the Indians and whites. I help them with their problems. And they both have problems."

On impulse, Sacajawea spoke up, clasping the sky blue stone that hung around her neck for courage. "Will you help the People? The Agaidükas need guns to hunt food and to keep away the Blackfeet. They have promised to trade well for guns and ammunition."

"*Femme*, shut that mouth. The men are talking now. What's the matter with you?" said Charbonneau, getting his blood up.

"I had to ask," she said softly.

"Now, now," said Clark. "I want to talk to all of you. Charb, leave her be. And if I ever hear of you mistreating Janey, I'll see that she leaves you, and I'll have her well provided for."

Charbonneau flushed. "She'll be spoiled worse than a dead horse on the prairie."

"I've not forgotten the promise we made to your brother, the chief. Manuel Lisa—he lives here, on Second Street—tried to reach your people, but he was sent back by angry Yanktons. Then Colter went. He was met by the Blackfeet. And Jefferson sent some men last year, under a Lieutenant Pinch, to build a trading post at the junction of the Lewis[1] and Salmon rivers. Some of those men talked to me before leaving, and they were going to try to protect the tribes who are without arms against those who have been given British flintlocks."

Sacajawea sighed, relieved. Chief Red Hair never broke a promise. Her people would be reached and strengthened.

"Charb, there are men in this town organizing the Missouri Fur Company. They will build a number of trading posts, just as we planned a couple of years back."

Charbonneau nodded to Clark, understanding.

"The largest post is to be at the Three Forks of the Missouri."

Sacajawea drew in her breath.

Charbonneau scowled at her.

A soft, musical voice called from an inner doorway, "Will, may I come in?"

"Yes, do."

Sacajawea looked up from her seat on the floor. Her eyes met the face of a smiling young woman with brown, curly hair framing her pink-and-white face. Her mouth was large, with thin lips over white even teeth, and her dark eyes were set wide apart. Sacajawea's brown eyes bored deep into the white woman's, which danced and fluttered at the Indian girl's sudden, keen interest.

The young woman's eyes rested on Sacajawea's face, seeing her skin, ruddy from sun and wind, her straight nose with wide nostrils, her white, unbroken teeth showing but little when she smiled. Sacajawea's face was a trifle gaunt, her cheekbones high, and there was a deep purplish hint to her raven black hair.

Clark stood with his arms outstretched to meet the young woman. "Please, come in, Judy. Janey is here, and her son, and Monsieur Toussaint Charbonneau. I want you to meet them, especially Janey. You've heard me say she was worth more to us on that trip than some of the men who were along."

Pryor stood and bowed toward Judy Clark.

Charbonneau let out a burst of air. *"Nom du bon dieu!* My squaw already got the big head and thinks she was guide for all those men. Soon she will have nothing to do with us at all. She be too good. All the fat will be in her goddamn head." Charbonneau's face reddened as he looked at Clark's wife. "Excuse."

Judy Clark smiled and extended her hand to Charbonneau and then to Sacajawea, who had risen and still stared at the beautiful dress—light, fluffy, yellow, flowing to the floor.

"Janey, this is my wife, Miss Judy. She is my woman," said Clark proudly.

Suddenly Sacajawea was making the past come alive again. She saw ropes and towlines and thongs of tough leather weave through swirling brown waters; then she felt the almost invisible shimmers of fine mist that joined her and Chief Red Hair and this young woman. Sacajawea extended her brown hand as Charbonneau had done. Hers was roughened by work, and she tried to smile, but civilization had not yet taught her to look pleased when in truth she was far from it.

And so—my belt of blue beads traded for an otter robe to give to this woman. And so—this is the squaw Chief Red Hair named the clear, sparkling river after. The honeysuckles smelled sweet, and violets nodded on its banks, she thought.

Again Clark read Sacajawea's thoughts. "Remember the river I named Judith?"

"If that name stands, Will," Miss Judy said with a teasing in her voice, "it will show you that you didn't know me any too well."

"So," admitted Clark, taking her hand, "so I named it the Judith River, instead of Julia. It was your nickname, Judy, that confused me."

"There's no harm in it—you were thinking of me," she said, laughing.

"We've got to find a lodge for Janey and her son and man."

"Will, I know just the place," Miss Judy said quickly. "The cabin you let traders and hunters use. It's vacant. They'll have a roof over their head—I can help Janey fix it up."

"W-w-what!" stuttered Clark, unable to hide his surprise. "That is just the place. I wouldn't have thought of it. And will you show Janey how to make curtains and things?"

"Yes, yes. I want to," Miss Judy said, kissing Clark over his left ear, after pulling him down to her height.

"*Diable!*" blurted Charbonneau.

"Then I'll make arrangements for your boy to go to school, as soon—"

"But, Will," interrupted Miss Judy, "this child is no more than three; four at the most. He's just a baby."

"Three and a half. But time takes care of everything. You know what I have told you. No matter what I did for Janey, I couldn't do too much. I actually owe my position to Janey."

Charbonneau squirmed. "No squaw's worth that much," he said more to himself or the floor.

Miss Judy said, "Of course, Will, you told me. I have not forgotten."

Sacajawea felt a mixture of embarrassment, shame, and fear.

Miss Judy saw the uncertainty in Sacajawea's face and said, "I offer my hand in friendship. I shall do all I can to make you acquainted with Saint Louis and get you settled in your cabin." Then she did a quickstep and two swift turns, bowed low before each of the adults, and patted the top of Pomp's head.

"You have gone daft," said Clark, chuckling to himself. "There may be a spell on you."

"Let's all go and look at the cabin," said Miss Judy, twirling once and standing at her husband's left shoulder.

"*Eh, bien!*" Charbonneau stood up, charmed by the antics of Clark's beautiful wife. "*Magnifique!*" He made a round circle with thumb and forefinger and blew threw it. "My Otter Woman and Tess, my other son, they are here also."

"Where are they?" asked Clark. "You didn't leave them outside?"

"*Non*, they are with Sheheke, where our baggage is."

"You old rogue," said Clark, not at all fooled, but much amused by the trick the métis had played on him. "We'll get them and put them up in the cabin, too. You fox, I will educate your boy Tess. Now what do you think of that?"

"*Merci, mais oui.* That is nice," said Charbonneau, feeling very cagey.

Miss Judy led the way, skipping, her body drawn fully erect and her lips parted.

The log cabin had two new windows, and the thick waxed tarp that had covered them still lay at the side. The windows were the six-pane kind, with the unpainted wood still bright against the weathered gray of adjacent split logs. Inside the door the whole place looked neat. Shelves of new wood on the wall near the stone fireplace held dishes, and on a wider, low shelf stood buckets for water. There was a battered kitchen table and a single straight-backed chair made of birch. There was nothing else to sit on except boxes, or the hand-hewn bed, which was fastened head and side to the walls, the only post standing at the outer corner. A curtain of thin old blankets strung on wire partitioned the cabin and left about eighty percent of the space for the kitchen–living room. A wooden crate had been nailed to the wall over the table, and it contained grayish white flannel sheets and a heavy, folded four-point Hudson's Bay blanket, dark blue with a black stripe at either end. Beside this box hung a huge calendar, in both French and English, showing the Saint Lawrence Valley divided into two provinces, Lower Canada (Quebec) and Upper Canada (Ontario). Over the head of the bed hung a watercolor sketch of the bleeding heart of Jesus. This lodge will take some getting use to, thought Sacajawea.

"There is plenty of wood out back," said Clark.

Charbonneau touched the glass in a window and then went out to examine the wood ricks. "I'll send over some buffalo meat. Be a good idea to have your women dry some so they'll have supplies when you go trapping," Clark said to Charbonneau. "I'd like to see you settle down and get a little patch of land. You could raise most of your own food and maybe some sheep or cows. Be good for you. You're not getting younger, you know."

"I first would like to be an interpreter for some trader around here. I need to get used to this country." Charbonneau had his head down as though he were thinking. "This is much farther south than I'm used to. I might take some land, but I don't think I'd like raising potatoes, string beans, or *les oignons*."

"Then you could try cotton," suggested Clark, "or tobacco."

Inside, the women were chattering about where to make sleeping pallets for the children. "The bed is fine for a man, but I would fall to the floor and so would Otter Woman," giggled Sacajawea, who had never seen a sleeping couch so high off the floor before.

"The boys should sleep there," suggested Miss Judy. "They ought to learn to sleep in a bed if they are going to school."

"*Ahh-i*." Sacajawea pulled up a big sigh from way down inside herself. "Who will catch them when they fall in the middle of the night?"

"They'll have to learn to stay under a blanket. There are other things they will need to know, and you have to help," said Miss Judy, her eyes challenging Sacajawea.

"That's right," said Clark, moseying back inside. "The boys are here for an education. You don't want them to be as ignorant as old Jussome, who needs someone to sign his own name, do you?"

"*Mais non, merci*." Charbonneau, who could neither read nor write, shook his head. "Never will they be like that old weasel."

Miss Judy plumped a battered coffeepot on the table. "I can boil some coffee. See, there is a box of sugar and a can of coffee on the shelf. Let's hope it's not stale and rancid."

Even though she was tired from the trip and the excitement of meeting old friends, Sacajawea began laying a fire, using a substantial cone of sticks, the larger ones on the outside. Clark bent to light the fire with a phosphorus match. The small sticks blazed, burning quickly. Sacajawea pushed on larger sticks. Miss Judy set the big pot of water on the iron arm above the fire, then threw in coffee and sugar and let them boil.

"Say, speaking of writing, Charb, did you know that Pat Gass's journal of the expedition was published early last year? An Irish schoolmaster, David McKeehan, corrected Pat's spelling and grammar. I talked with him, and to hear him tell it, Pat needs schooling himself. His spelling must have been dreadful. Now Lewis and I have to get ours in shape. Jefferson asked about the journals last year."

"Why don't you send York after the other lady and her little boy and the Charbonneaus' baggage?" asked Miss Judy.

"You have a fine *femme*," said Charbonneau, who felt himself an expert in those things. He poured a third cup of coffee. It was strong and sweet.

"Yes," agreed Clark. "That is a fine suggestion, Judy. And Charb, you still have a good eye, eh? Judy is an angel, she dances and talks too much, but she has not one mean, spiteful hair on her head." Clark planted a soft kiss on his wife's hair. Then he took her hand and led her out the door saying they would be back soon.

The two squaws worked for days drying the meat that was sent to them. They cut it in thin strips and hung it in the sun on a scaffolding made of cottonwood saplings. Miss Judy marveled at the stamina Sacajawea showed when she began a task. Otter Woman soon grew tired of drying meat and sat on the door stoop.

Often Miss Judy sat in the shade, telling nursery tales to the boys. Soon they were all singing together:

> "I climbed up the apple tree
> And all the apples fell on me.
> Make a pudding, make a pie.
> Did you ever tell a lie?
> Yes, you did, you know you did,
> You stole your mother's teapot lid."

"What's a teapot lid?" asked Little Tess.
"The top of a teapot, silly," answered Miss Judy.
"Do we have one?"
"I don't know. Do you like tea?"

"I like mine with sugar, same as Papa. We don't have any now."

"Next time I'll bring some and we'll have a tea party," said Miss Judy, swinging each boy around once or twice, then sitting down again, laughing.

Otter Woman stretched herself and moseyed over to sit beside the children and Miss Judy. She had on a gingham dress she'd made from some red-and-blue cloth Miss Judy had brought for window curtains.

"Why work so hard on that meat?" said Otter Woman, pointing a ragged fingernail toward Sacajawea. "There will only be more. Chief Red Hair will take care of us. We do not have to work our fingers to the bone. We don't even have to gather the wood. We don't have to work anymore. We can play with the papooses, like you do. We can wear our new blankets and walk along the river to see the boats and the pale-eyed ladies."

Miss Judy laughed at Otter Woman; then, her eyes still twinkling, she said emphatically, "You'll never appreciate anything if you do not work for it." She moved her hands so that Otter Woman could understand, but she was slow with hand signs. "I will teach you how to sew if you promise to make curtains with the next gingham, and no more dresses stitched up the sides with leather string."

"*Ai*"—Otter Woman kept her voice low and flat—"after window dresses, I make dress like white squaws. And so our man thinks he has a white woman, tee-hee-hee."

Sacajawea's head went from side to side, and her voice had a dry harshness. "Otter Woman, you could help finish cutting this meat today. Do you want our man to throw firewood at us because there is no jerky?" Sacajawea's hands were blistered from the cutting knife, but finally she had all the meat cut and hung in the sun to dry.

Otter Woman's shoulders hunched together, and she coughed. "Much smoke in the air. I hope it rains."

"Oh, me, too," said Miss Judy. "Something has to put out these brushfires. I don't want them moving close to town. This smoke is bad enough."

"When the wind is right, my eyes sting and I can't stop the coughing," said Otter Woman.

The next morning, Sacajawea surprised Otter Woman by saying, "Let's take the boys walking along the riverbank." Despite the heat, Sacajawea took her blanket so that she could carry Pomp on her back easily if he became tired.

Otter Woman talked a stream of inane chatter because she was so excited about going out to look at the new sights. She coughed as she combed her hair until it shone; then she put on her red-and-blue gingham. Little Tess skipped from the cabin and threw sticks down the trail.

Saint Louis was about fifty years old. It had begun as a French trading post, and only in the last four years, since the United States had acquired it from France with the Louisiana Purchase, had it really grown. At one time it had been a Spanish possession, and so now people from both Spain and France lived on the banks of the Mississippi River. There were also a few people from England, some Canadians, Indians from many tribes, métis, halfbreeds, Creoles, Americans, and blacks living in or near the village.[2]

The two squaws watched, and as they learned about these people, their wonderment grew. "It is like a Mandan summer fair," said Otter Woman. "So many people in this village."

There were about a thousand people living in Saint Louis at this time.

A few scattered log huts, warehouses, and docks were strung out along the river's edge. They walked slowly through the French quarter, with its narrow, crooked streets, and high-balconied houses with ladders reaching up from the ground to the top rooms. Everything seemed tilted at crazy angles, as if the dirt had settled one way, then another, leaving the buildings leaning sideways, or more often just forward, like the heads of gossiping old ladies.

Then they walked slowly uphill from the river to some new board houses and warehouses, all raw and ugly in the late-afternoon sun. They were surrounded by the noises of hammering and banging, dogs barking, and near-naked, dirty-faced children yelling.

"It is not like the sleepy Minnetaree village," said Sacajawea.

After a few more turns, they went straight up a long street and came to a very broad store building with two galleries and warehouses to either side and behind; the whole was advertised by a split-log sign that had a white birch rim all around.

"I wish that I could speak those words that the white man writes," said Sacajawea, pointing to the sign.

"The board is large and the markings deep. That is some important person in that lodge," said Otter Woman.

Men pushed through the doors carrying supplies, other men ran from warehouse to warehouse, wagons were loading at side doors, and a dozen horses were tied to hitching posts out front. A black boy, about the age of Little Tess, dressed in a beautiful scarlet jacket and black-silk top hat, was watering the horses from a wooden trough, then tying them up again. Some men threw the boy coins and poked him playfully as he bent to pick them up.

When the men were inside, Sacajawea went up to the boy and asked in her best English, "Whose beautiful lodge is this? What is the chief that lives here called?"

The boy's face broke into a grin. "They is no chief. But it sure enough is a beautiful lodge. This am the trading post of Mr. Chouteau. You gals want to borrow a mule?"

"No." Sacajawea smiled. "We are walking. Thank you."

"Don't fret, you ain't the only ones walking," said the boy. Then he went back to watering the horses.

"Even so," sighed Otter Woman, lifting her blanket from her face on the way home, "I miss our village. Things were more convenient there, and the river not so far away."

Sacajawea had put Pomp into the blanket and hoisted him on her back. Little Tess ran along ahead of the squaws. "Did you notice these men always busy, never sitting in the sun or loafing around?"

"I saw only the fine stitching on the women's dresses," said Otter Woman, coughing in the smoky late-summer air. "It is as neatly done as our quillwork."

One day Sacajawea shyly asked Miss Judy to show her how to embroider.

"You don't want to do that on window curtains!" Miss Judy was amused. "They look fine with their red roses."

"I want to make a shirt for Pomp. I want to make a shirt like the white boys wear," Sacajawea explained. "A shirt with prairie flowers down the front."

"A white shirt with full sleeves? The kind the French children wear?"

"*Ai*, that is it," said Sacajawea. "He can have it for school."

Miss Judy helped Sacajawea, who painstakingly made a white shirt for Pomp with pink roses on the front. Otter Woman, not to be outdone, made a pair of white trousers for Little Tess, with a cotton drawstring at the waist.

"Ah, wouldn't Grasshopper exclaim over these garments. She'd feel the fine texture and the smoothness of the flowers," said Sacajawea proudly, her eyes shining.

Ben York brought venison and left the two deer hams on the kitchen table. He stopped to admire the sewing. "You gals can do anything you puts your minds to. I'd sure enough like one if you have nothing else left to do someday, Janey. One of them shirts, fancy trim and all, uumm. When I go to Kentucky, people's eyes will sure enough pop out looking at that on me."

At first Sacajawea thought he was teasing, but watching him look at Pomp, she knew he meant it. She wondered if she would be able to get enough white muslin to make a shirt for York.

"Why do you make things for others?" asked Otter Woman, putting a hand to her mouth to stifle a cough.

"Oh, Otter Woman"—Sacajawea's breath grunted out—"it's doing something for a friend."

"Pah! Make something for yourself. Don't you want to look fancy like the white squaws?"

"I don't think about them too much," said Sacajawea. "Only about Miss Judy and her kindness to us."

"Well"—Otter Woman's mind was working slowly— "I am making a dress to wear when I sit in the shade against a fence and watch the white squaws pass along Rue Royale. Wouldn't you like to wear a white squaw's dress and come with me?" Otter Woman's eyes beamed admiration as she held up the red-and-yellow cotton

print she had been stitching. It had very little shape—
a hole for the head and two for the arms. She would
not follow the pattern Miss Judy had laid out. "Too hard
to follow," she complained.

"There is much learning before I wear a dress in the
manner of the white squaw. It is hard yet to eat with
a knife and fork. I want to teach our sons not to eat
with the fingers. At school they will eat the way the
white boys do."

Otter Woman snorted. "That is a long way off."

"They will sleep on beds with many pieces of cloth.
And they will wear a shirt when they sleep."

"A shirt?" Otter Woman said it with some heat.
"Whoever heard of such a thing! Will they be on guard
for the enemy to strike at any moment and so must
sleep with moccasins also?"

"No, but it is the way of whites to have a shirt for
sleeping."

"What a waste. Shirts should be worn during the
daylight. Besides, at night a shirt would keep one too
warm," Otter Woman said stubbornly. "I will tell Little
Tess to wear his shirts for day, and nothing for night.
Maybe he can teach white boys a sensible thing or two."

"Little Tess teach the white boys—you think—
ah—" Sacajawea cut it short—what was the use, she
thought.

That night, Otter Woman tossed on her pallet of pine
branches thinking of other things she had noticed. White
women could not make peace inside their lodges. Day
after day they fought dust and dirt. They made war on
everything—clothes, pots, floors; fighting with lye soap,
scouring ashes, straw brooms, and feather dusters. Otter Woman felt sorry for these white squaws who did
not realize that dust and dirt were just a part of life to
be endured like a bad cold, hunger, or mosquitoes.

As the months in Saint Louis slipped away, Sacajawea came to realize there was another change within
herself. The beating of her heart had calmed when she
was near Clark. Her tongue was no longer tied. The
gnawing pain of living close to him had eased. She was
fond of his woman, Miss Judy, and felt no resentment,
no bitterness, but now a soft affection and adoration for

the man, such as had possessed her during the first
winter with the white men at Fort Mandan. Clark was
a great man; he was someone to be respected and to
serve. She was growing wiser, more mature. She realized they could not share a bond of love between them
as man and woman could, and as he surely did with
Miss Judy, but she knew she would always have a special place in his heart. It is now a good road that we
walk together, she thought. There are times I think I
am wise and can see the foolishness of others. I put
myself above the passions of youth. But I do not believe
wisdom is what throws off passions; it is age.

In June 1809, the Missouri Fur Trading Company's
barges and keelboats left Saint Louis outfitted to establish posts all along the Missouri. Clark made a special trip to the cabin in the woods to visit Sacajawea.
"The largest post will be at the Three Forks. Close to
your people, Janey. This will give them regular food
and some protection from the Blackfeet," he said.

"I have been thinking," she said, "that it is really
you who represent the image of the Great White Father
to my people. You are a hero."

In Saint Louis, hero worship was at its height. Here
the ideals were Meriwether Lewis and William Clark,
who had been west, traced the Missouri to its source in
the mountains, and carried the United States flag to
the Pacific and back.

Hero worship is characteristic of youthful, progressive peoples. George Shannon was a hero. He had been
shot in the knee by an Arikara's flintlock while he was
with the crew taking Sheheke back to his Mandan village. Dr. Saugrain saw blood poisoning in Shannon's
leg and together with Dr. Farrar performed the first
thigh amputation in this region—without anesthetic.[3]
Shannon lay at the point of death for eighteen months,
but he rallied and regained his strength so that he could
go to Lexington. There he studied law, finally becoming
an eminent jurist and judge, and was known as Pegleg
Shannon.

Ben York was a hero. Trappers, flatboatmen, frontiersmen, and Frenchmen spun long yarns at the Green
Tree Inn, but York outdid them all with thrilling in-

cidents that never failed to inspire an audience. He had
been to the Pacific Ocean and seen the great whale,
sturgeon, and porpoise; that put all inland fish stories
in the shade. Once, Auguste Chouteau's manservant
said, "Me and the colonel met in Ben York for the first
time someone greater than myself."

Sacajawea and Otter Woman often explored Saint
Louis shops while Charbonneau was away trapping.
There were things they had never seen before and whose
use they could not imagine—things like flatirons, butter churns, cigar rollers. They were constantly amazed.
They watched men trade pelts and hides for food in
tins. Others traded paper money for clothing. This paper was the white man's magic. Both women decided
to make moccasins and trade them for money or food
in tins.

Several weeks after that decision, Sacajawea was up
in the gray-lavender light of false dawn. She had moccasins in a parfleche. She didn't hurry, but she didn't
loiter either until she came in sight of the trading post
on the corner of First and Washington. She went inside
the stone wall that surrounded the store. The Chouteau
family lived on the second floor. Reaching nearly to the
second story were tall fruit trees—some with apples,
others with pears.

A good many bearded, tobacco-chewing men had con-
gregated in the big room downstairs. They talked,
laughed, and spit upon the floor; sometimes they hit
one another on the back. Sacajawea saw piles of skins—
shiny blue, black, and brown—tied up carelessly with
string, lying on both counters and floor. There was a
little balcony office in the rear where Pierre Chouteau
sat and wrote in his books. Sacajawea had a glimpse of
him when an old trader, wearing a patchy coonskin cap
with one ear flap hanging down, left the office door
open.

With the money she received for the moccasins, Sacajawea bought three yards of snow white linen to make
York a shirt. She held out her hand. "Is that enough
money?"

The red-faced clerk moistened his pencil in his mouth
and did some figuring on a piece of paper, then gave

her back some change. She found some packets of bright pink floss to make roses on the shirt and again held out her hand. "Is that enough?" She bought white thread, then needles, paying for one thing at a time to be sure she had enough to buy the next item.

The clerk became uneasy as she looked and fingered the new things. Once he spoke to her sharply. She answered him in French, which surprised him. She told him she knew that some people took things that did not belong to them, but she, never. She told him she had as her friend Chief Red Hair and that she lived in his town because he had invited her there. The clerk did not seem impressed—in fact, he did not really believe her—yet he did think it strange that this squaw could speak both French and English. She continued to explain to the clerk that she would teach her people that it was wrong to take things, but now her people thought all white men were like themselves—whatever belonged to one man belonged to all.

The clerk looked quizzically at her, then asked, "You belong to anyone? You got a husband? Someone who eats your stew?"

"*Ai*," she smiled. "He is Charbonneau. He is also a friend of Chief Red Hair."

The clerk turned and, looking up, called to Chouteau. "Boss! This here squaw speaks French and English and claims she knows General Clark. She says her husband is a man called Charbonneau. Know him?"

Chouteau looked over the balcony. He was taller than most Frenchmen, slender, with dark, flashing eyes, very carefully dressed, and with an easy manner, as if he had long ago decided not to be bothered by little things.

"*Oui*, I know him. He lived with Indians many years way up north. He's the squawman that likes brandy and *les jeunes filles*. He was an interpreter for Lewis and Clark on their trip to the west. The men on that trip tell stories about him—not too flattering. That could be one of his squaws. Which one I wouldn't know, but if she says she knows General Clark, I daresay she does. How do you do, Madame Charbonneau."

Sacajawea saw him bow toward her. "*Merci*. I am fine. How do you do, Monsieur Chouteau," she said.

The clerk said nothing. There was, he thought, nothing worth saying. After that, the clerk was kind to her and tried to help her understand about money and the many things in the trading post that she did not know.

One day he was astonished to find that she claimed to have gone along on the Lewis and Clark Expedition. Glancing at her, he was unreasonably annoyed by the truth in her eyes. There was decency about her; she was not one to conceal facts or prevaricate. This squaw had nothing to hide and did not pretend with stories. After that, he could not do enough for her when she came to the trading post.

Sacajawea always told Otter Woman all she had seen in the post and begged her to come, but Otter Woman was shy because she could not speak or understand enough French or English. "I will teach you," suggested Sacajawea.

"No, I cannot learn. It is too much for my head. I will listen to you and pretend it was me there in the town. You continue selling the moccasins I make and bring me the cloth so that I can make myself soft, brightly colored dresses." She actually preferred taking care of the boys or sitting out of the way in the shade of a building and watching the passersby, drawing her shawl over her face if anyone seemed to look at her. She listened to the white ladies talking together and wished she could be so gay. She admired their dress and curly hair. But at the same time she missed the more familiar things in a Minnetaree village. "A cooking fire in a mud lodge is easier to keep hot than this one in a cage of stones." She complained about the fireplace in the cabin. She complained about the wooden floor. "It has to be swept more often than a hard-packed dirt floor."

"I will tell you something strange I have learned," Sacajawea told her one evening as the days grew shorter. "White men, like Chief Red Hair, have only one woman, no more." She clapped her hands to indicate the finality of "one."

"Are they so poor? Can they not afford more?" asked Otter Woman.

"No, not poor; they could buy many. They do not want more. That is the way of the white men. But when they live with us, they take our ways, as our man has done."

"It is the best way. I would not like to do all the work in a lodge," said Otter Woman, clearing her throat. "I am glad to have you to help here."

"And more," said Sacajawea with her hand over her mouth as if she were about to divulge a secret. "The white man does not buy his woman. Women are not paid for with horses and other valuable goods. They are not won in games. A white squaw does not belong to a man unless she wishes it to be."

It was unbelievable to Otter Woman. "It would cause great trouble, I think."

"But then," said Sacajawea, "is our way always best?" She was thinking how her father had sold her to Big Moose when she was only a papoose—too small to understand. "White men have black people to help with work. Like our friend Ben York. There are black squaws, too. The white men called them servants."

"Our way is best. Squaws are the servants. I do not mind being a squaw." After a moment, Otter Woman's eyes went to the floor, and she shuffled her moccasins back and forth. "That is not true. I would like to be called *lady*."

Sacajawea looked at Otter Woman, surprised.

"*Ai*. I like their dresses and the shell combs in their hair. They are prettier than we are in our drab skin tunics. But they could not gather wood, smoke jerky, or skin a deer in a dress."

"And so—you would rather wear a dress and not be able to do your work?"

"I prefer the cool cloth of the white squaw's dress. And the warmth of her long, fringed shawl."

Sacajawea laughed at her. Otter Woman began to laugh at the absurdity of her desire until a coughing spasm began that left her weak.

37

Lewis's Death

During the summer and early autumn of 1809, Meriwether Lewis found his problems as Governor of Louisiana Territory growing and his personal popularity decreasing. He was at odds with Frederick Bates, Secretary of Louisiana, who privately did everything he could to undermine Lewis's position. Lewis feared his health was failing, and dosed himself continually with pills and medicines, in addition to drinking heavily.

On July 15 the Secretary of War wrote refusing to honor a draft of $500, which Lewis had drawn to provide Pierre Chouteau with tobacco and powder for Indian presents, to be used by the expedition that was taking Sheheke, the Mandan subchief, home. Lewis had to go to Washington to straighten out this mess.

In September, before he left Lewis appointed William Clark and two other friends as his attorney with full power to dispose of his property. On the eleventh of September he made a will. Then he wrote to his friend, Amos Stoddard, to forward his mail to Washington, D.C., until the last of December, after which, he expected to be back in St. Louis.

On October 11, 1809, at Grinders Stand in the last cabin on the border of the Chickasaw country, Governor Lewis died at the age of thirty-five. No one is sure if it were suicide or murder. Thomas Jefferson believed he was murdered. The evidence for murder is not strong, and the stories that came from Fort Pickering, the army *post at Chickasaw Bluffs (Memphis) where Lewis had once commanded, strongly suggest suicide. None of the evidence is really conclusive.*

ERNEST KIRSCHTEN, *Catfish and Crystal*. Garden City, N.Y.: Doubleday and Co., 1965, pp. 771–72.

Charbonneau came back in early fall in a dither because he had not trapped enough furs to see him through the winter, with two squaws and two children. When an offer to trap for a fur company on the branches of the Arkansas River came, he accepted. He would be in Comanche country. He had heard that the Comanche language was similar to Shoshoni. "Comanches, they are relatives of the Shoshonis, first cousins, like." He had lied a little to get the job. "I have two Shoshoni women," he'd said. "And if a man cannot learn to talk to his squaws, he must surely starve and have no moccasins made for him. I learn to talk Shoshoni plenty fast. So—I speak Comanche also, if they are the same."

"You are our interpreter, then," said the *patron*. "We leave day after tomorrow. Get yourself extra clothing and traps, and be here at dawn."

Charbonneau took the paper notes from the man and rode his horse to Chouteau's trading post. While Charbonneau was gone, Clark came to his cabin to tell the family good-bye for a time and to leave a hindquarter of young deer.

Clark sat on a packing crate warming himself before the fire. "I am going to talk with some important men. Charbonneau's heard of them—Governor Harrison, General Johnathan, and my own brother, George Rogers Clark, also called general. I am going to talk about keeping on good terms with the Indian nations. It is my job to keep peace between tribes and nations. And my job to prevent or punish murder, drive squatters off the Indian lands, keep the Indians off land they have sold to whites, recover stolen horses and kidnapped children, punish robbery, and keep whiskey from the thirsty Indians. I am going to get these men to help me. And York is coming with me to Kentucky. He's found a girl, says he's in love with Kentucky—but I believe it is Cindy Lou."

"York?" Otter Woman giggled. She liked the big black man. "So—he is moving toward the sunrise as he said he would."

"We'll go east, all right," said Clark. "To Louisville, then on to the cotton plantation where Cindy Lou lives."

"Is she all black?" asked Otter Woman, her eyes wide with curiosity.

"Oh, I'm sure of it. According to York, she's a tiny black girl who laughs and sings all day. I have it in the back of my mind to set York free, to let him be his own master. I would like to set him up in business with a wagon and team of four to six horses, hauling freight between Richmond and Nashville. He can have a job and a wife and be a free man."

"Will he like that?" asked Sacajawea, puzzled. "Will he like it after looking after you for so long? Do you think he can change his thoughts and habits?"

"Certainly he can. That is the burning desire of all manservants these days—to be freedmen and run their own lives. York deserves this. He's worked hard for me."

"I have something for him," said Sacajawea, looking for a piece of leather to wrap around the shirt she'd made for York.

"Let me see that," said Clark, holding up the shirt. "Oh, York will be mighty pleased. I can see him showing off with a jig or two when he puts this on. Can't you?"

"*Ai,*" said Sacajawea, glad she had finished the shirt in time.

But given his freedom, Ben York was not happy, and he had little success as an independent businessman. He did not take good care of the six horses Clark gave to him. He let two of them die and drove a bad bargain selling the remaining four. He sold them because the freight run was too long. York was away from Cindy Lou from early spring until midsummer, then from fall until winter.

"Damn this here freedom," he told Cindy Lou. "I have never had a peaceful day since I got it." He felt certain his business had been poor because the whites preferred dealing with other whites; they seemed to feel a black, even a freed one, was not to be trusted with valuable freight.

Eventually York left Cindy Lou to come back to General Clark. He told her that he would send for her as soon as he was settled in Saint Louis once again. But she did not hear a word from him. Once an itinerant black preacher told of a freedman who had died of cholera in Tennessee and was buried there as an unknown. "That man was free, but he was sick and poor and had no folks to care for him. Sometimes so much freedom does not suit a man," said the preacher. Cindy Lou questioned him, and it seemed to her that the description fit her husband. She sent word back to General Clark by way of the preacher that York was dead.

"I just can't believe it," said Clark. "It does not seem like York to go off to die alone. Mark my words. That unknown buried in Tennessee is not my Ben York."[1]

In the fall of 1809, there were many days of freezing rain around Saint Louis that glazed the foot trails with a sheath of ice that was like hobnail glass. Then a warm wind from the south came in, and the ground became soft as mush, overlaid with widening pools in low spots. The sunsets were orange under the low, scudding clouds.

One evening, Otter Woman was mending moccasins and coughing in the funny choked way she had developed that fall. She coughed deeply, but she tried to cut the cough off before it came from her throat so that it would not be so noticeable. "I think it is the smoke from the old prairie fires," she'd say when she was outdoors; or, "Too much smoke blows back from this smoke hole," she'd say if she were in the cabin sitting next to the fireplace.

"Maybe it is caused by the warm winds," said Sacajawea, who went out back to find dried grasses and seed pods to put in the granite bowl on the windowsill, as she had seen Miss Judy do. The boys, who had suffered from cabin fever during the freezing rains, were outside pretending they saw black bear or wolves coming through the maple thicket. Suddenly Tess stopped.

"Someone's coming!" he shouted. "I heard feet splashing through water, and a wet moccasin spat on the oozy trail."

Sacajawea looked past the cabin. A black-caped figure was running up the path. The moist air was warm, too warm this evening for a thick cape. Who was it? She stepped quickly around the side of the cabin to the front. Miss Judy was knocking frantically on the door.

Otter Woman let her in as Sacajawea and the boys quickly followed. Miss Judy's eyes were red, and she looked frightful. She stood in the middle of the floor and looked from one woman to the other, shaking her head.

"What is it?" Sacajawea asked.

"Oh, Janey," Miss Judy whispered. "I had to come as soon as I heard. I had to tell you."

"What?" repeated Sacajawea.

"It's Meri. Lewis. He's dead."

Sacajawea's hand went to her mouth. It was not true. Not the sandy-haired co-leader of the expedition, dead. Not after all he'd been through and survived as healthy as anyone. A cry escaped her lips, a soft moaning, a high-pitched keening, not loud but intense; then she stopped, sensing that Otter Woman was perplexed.

"Get coffee warmed for our guest," said Sacajawea softly to Otter Woman. "Take her robe. It is warm. Open the door."

Otter Woman muttered something about being treated like a servant. She looked at Miss Judy, who wept quietly, then she closed her mouth and ran to do as she was told.

Miss Judy sat on the edge of the bed, composed herself, and slowly told as much of Governor Lewis's Tennessee tragedy as she knew. "Pierre Chouteau came to tell me so that I would know when Will comes back. Even Rose York, Ben's mother, felt the sorrow and kept saying she wished Ben were here to sing prayers."

Still stunned, Sacajawea could find no words to explain to Otter Woman how she felt. Her sorrow made her lash out with commands to hurry Otter Woman in making their guest feel welcome. "Get the chair for Miss Judy."

"*Ai*," said Otter Woman, scraping the chair across the floor to where Miss Judy could easily move from the bed to the chair with only one step.

"Meri sent us his favorite pair of ivory-handled dueling pistols as a wedding present," Judy said, as if to herself. "Will was so pleased that he promised to name our first boy after him. And you know we did. Will begged him to come live with us when we first came to Saint Louis. But in that charming way of his he said,

'Thank you, but no, I'm going to move in with Auguste Chouteau. It is better for two wayward bachelors to live together.'" Miss Judy pressed her face with a small white handkerchief.

Sacajawea sat on the floor close to Miss Judy's chair. She could not hide her sorrow; tears ran down her cheeks.

Otter Woman sat the boys against the wall and gave them each a granite cup filled with a mixture that was half sugar and half bitter coffee.

"The guest is fed first," Sacajawea said, sniffing and glaring at Otter Woman, who hurried to fill a cup with coffee for Miss Judy.

Otter Woman was careful not to spill anything on Miss Judy's black wool skirt and ruffled, white-lace blouse. She kept her eyes downcast, then asked Sacajawea why they wept over a white man who had died far from Saint Louis and never came to see them as Chief Red Hair had done. She put her hand to her mouth to stifle a cough, then said, "I do not understand this deep feeling for this man."

Miss Judy straightened, wiped her nose, and reached deep into her black-velvet handbag. "Here, I nearly forgot this. I brought you a throat balm. Dr. Saugrain made it up. It's pine pitch and honey." She handed Otter Woman the bottle and a pewter spoon. "Meriwether Lewis was a friend—more like a relative. A brother."

"*Ai*, a brother." Sacajawea nodded, her eyes still wet.

Otter Woman licked her lips and tried a spoonful of the cough syrup. She bent to let Tess have a taste from her spoon. Then Pomp hitched forward and took a taste.

Sacajawea made clucking noises, and the boys moved against the wall, their backs straight. Their brown eyes watched Miss Judy.

"I call our baby Meri, but Will calls him Lew, or sometimes Looie."

Otter Woman spoke up. "I know about that. I wanted to call mine Kakanostoke, but my man say *non*, he is Little Tess."

"What is that name?" snapped Sacajawea.

"It is Blackfoot for Owl; it means Ears Far Apart."

"I like it," said Miss Judy, settling further back in the chair as she sipped the coffee.

The little cabin darkened in the deepening twilight. Sacajawea got up, her face now calm, closed the door, lighted two candles she took from the wooden shelf, and put them on the kitchen table. She put bowls on the table and poured stew from the pot beside the fire. She took a bowl and a large spoon to Miss Judy. Otter Woman sat beside the boys and ate her stew, letting them dip their spoons into her bowl. Sacajawea did not eat, but when she thought the boys had had enough, she pushed them outside, saying, "Stay on the step." Soon they came in quietly, and she pushed them up on the hand-hewn bed; she took off their moccasins, shirts, and trousers, and placed them neatly on the shelf. "Too warm for a blanket," she said.

Otter Woman sat on her couch of furs in the opposite corner and complained it was too dark to sew. Soon she was snoring.

Miss Judy pulled one of the gray-white blanket sheets from the shelf and spread it over Otter Woman, who coughed in her sleep. Then she blew out the candles and sat on the floor beside Sacajawea. Both stared into the flames of the fireplace; neither spoke of the grief that drew them together. When the fire was only coals, Miss Judy curled up on the floor, using her arms to rest her head, and said, "He was always kind and fair. He took in that old Creole, Piernia, and made him decent again. He liked to hold our baby son. He told how he was afraid at first to hold your little son. Said he'd never seen such a small human before. Oh, Janey, tell me what he was like to you."

"He made dumplings for the men, and they teased him, but they ate and asked for more. He saw a bent fern and knew what size animal had been by. He found flowers and seeds no one else saw. He loved that big dog, Scannon. He traveled past plains barren of trees, beyond the mountains that shone night and day. He followed the river that flowed westward into the Stinking Waters, and he went right on until now he journeys to the Land of Everfeasting. We cannot speak his name," Sacajawea whispered.

Shortly after daybreak, Sacajawea awoke, refreshed by a deep sleep. Her eyes, still puffy from weeping, moved to the corner where Otter Woman still lay, then

to the boys, who were grinning at her from their bed.
She moved to the empty pallet where Charbonneau
slept when he was home. It was mussed, as if someone
had slept on it. The door opened and Miss Judy pushed
her way in, carrying a load of wood for the fireplace.
She dropped the logs, took off the black headkerchief,
and her dark curls flowed down her back in long ropes
of braid. Her large brown eyes were serene, but the lids
were still red and swollen. She said not a word, but
found a straw broom and swept the room, smoothed out
Charbonneau's pallet, showing she'd slept there, then
straightened Sacajawea's pallet, put moccasins and
shirts on the boys, and began preparing porridge. She
showed a complete familiarity as to where things were
and what to do. As she mixed the meal to go in the pot,
Sacajawea spoke softly, "Why do you do the morning
cleaning and cooking as though you, too, lived here?
Why?"

"We need more water from the spring," Miss Judy
said to the boys, then faced Sacajawea. "Janey, I could
not stay in my big house alone—without Will, I mean.
I kept thinking how he will feel when he hears about
Lewis's death. And I kept thinking about what that old
dog Scannon will do now without him. Rose talked to
me, but it was little help. Finally she suggested I come
to you. She said you'd understand more than anyone
that the Lord had called our good friend to his side
because his work on this earth was done."

Miss Judy scrubbed the kitchen table and laid out
the bowls and spoons Sacajawea had just washed.

Sacajawea went to the shelf and brought down a
small leather pouch. She pulled up the old packing crate
and seated herself at the table to open the pouch in her
hand.

"See this blue ribbon? Your man gave it to me. And
this comb and looking glass. See this red feather? Hold
it. It reminds me of my father and my brother. Our
friend gave it to me when we came back over the mountains in the snow. And so—here is the chip of blue sky
on the leather lacing. I like to wear it. It was once my
mother's, then my grandmother's. I do not know where
it will go after I leave this earth. And see, here is my
chief money." She took out the peace medal Sun Woman

had given her. "Here is a red piece of glass I made myself. See the bird on it? These are things, but they bring memories. Things can be taken away, but never memories. You and I cannot ever forget our friend, the sandy-haired white chief."

Miss Judy put the red feather back into Sacajawea's hand. "And so, you keep it to remind you of our friend." Sacajawea dropped the cardinal's feather back into Miss Judy's lap.

"Janey," Miss Judy began, deeply touched, "we are about the same age, yet I feel you are so much wiser." Her voice became a whisper. "I do not understand, but I accept. I have seen goodness and love." She bowed her head. "Oh, Lord, this has not been our will, but yours. Now, while my heart is tender, speak to me, Lord."

Sacajawea was moved by this conversation between Miss Judy and her Lord. She felt a strength come to her as she sat quietly listening.

"Blessed are they that mourn, for they shall be comforted," Miss Judy whispered.

Otter Woman stirred and said that she would get up after she had taken another sip or two of her cough syrup.

Quietly Sacajawea washed the boys' faces in a wooden basin and sent them outside to dry off. She gave Little Tess a bucket to fill with spring water.

"Why wash faces? Who is to see?" asked Otter Woman, grabbing a bowl and spoon from the shelf, then moving toward the hot porridge.

"Dishes are on the table," said Sacajawea. "I will serve you there."

Otter Woman looked surprised. "At the table? Just for eating? I don't want to eat at a table. I'd feel like it was in that school Miss Judy tells about with those desks."

"Otter Woman! You should not speak that way with guests," said Sacajawea.

"I like to sit at a table," said Miss Judy, dragging up the birch chair.

Most reluctantly, Otter Woman also dragged up a crate. Sacajawea looked relieved, but Otter Woman asked, "Miss Judy, do you always eat at a table?"

"Whenever there is company," Miss Judy said.

"Sometimes Will has his journals and scrapbooks on it, so there is hardly room for anybody but him to eat there."

"But," objected Otter Woman, "here there is no company. We all slept here together last night; there is no company."

"There is a friend who is our guest," Sacajawea insisted.

"That is true," Otter Woman agreed, "and because she is my friend she should not have to eat at a table. We'll eat like last night. Fill my bowl. I am hungry."

"But Otter Woman, you are thoughtless. Miss Judy wants to eat at a table, and the boys like to also. The coffee is ready. You pour it."

Otter Woman stared at Miss Judy as though she found it hard to believe. "I'll get the coffee. You get the bread," she said belligerently to Sacajawea.

Sacajawea piled cold fried bread on the table and began ladling out the porridge into the bowls from the pot hanging near the fire. Pot was the right word, for it was the tall type of granite-ware chamber pot with a wooden handle on a wire bail. A smaller pot was on the hearth holding the stock for stew.

Miss Judy tilted her head, listening. "There's the sound of a horse coming. Someone is singing. A man, I think."

"I hear it, too," said Sacajawea.

The door swung open, and there stood General William Clark. He had been in Kentucky with Cindy Lou when the news of Lewis's death arrived.

Otter Woman came to a standing position, holding back a coughing spasm. Sacajawea stood. One of high rank had entered.

"Rose told me I'd find you here, the three of you gaining strength from one another. Sit down. I'll have some of that hot porridge, too. Smells good."

"You have come to mourn the loss of our friend?" asked Sacajawea in a whisper.

"Yes," said Clark, "and no. I have also come to fetch Judy, to bring you news of Charbonneau, to praise the Lord for such a fine day, and to tell you I believe York has gone out west somewhere."

Sacajawea snatched up the peeling knife and began

to push it down on the first knuckle of her right little finger.

"Janey, what are you doing? Stop that!" shouted Clark.

Miss Judy looked from one to the other, her face pale.

"You wish to do the cutting of your own finger for mourning our friend first?" Sacajawea asked, bewildered that Clark did not understand her action.

He understood. "Don't mourn for Lewis in that way. The white man's God does not require him to mutilate himself to show his sense of loss." He wrapped his handkerchief around the cut and bleeding finger. "Lewis would not ask you to do that for him. You know what he wants us to do?"

Sacajawea shook her head. "You must not speak his name."

"That is something else we do differently," Clark said, sitting on a crate beside Sacajawea.

She felt somehow ashamed that she had displeased him with traditions deep-seated within her—something that her nation and even Minnetarees did. She had wished to show she honored Lewis as much as one of her relatives. She held up her left hand so that Clark could see where she had cut the first joint from her little finger years before.

Clark touched her quivering shoulders and spoke softly.

"Lew's brother, Reuben, is up the Missouri somewhere, so it is up to me to get his affairs in order. Lewis's papers and baggage have been sent here to me. He left everything to his stepsister, Lucy Marks. See, the white man can tell from a piece of paper who should have his possessions after he leaves this earth. I am going to get all the diaries Lewis kept, and those I kept on the trip west, and make a book. It is up to me now."

Sacajawea understood. The talking book was something both white chiefs had worked on. Lewis had asked her about flowers and roots that were edible. He had asked her about leaves and bark that were medicinal, and she had shown him what she remembered from her childhood or had learned from her Minnetaree captors.

Clark looked into her tear-swollen eyes. "I will ask

you questions about our trip so that I will have everything correct in the book people read. You'll help me?"

"I cannot read," she said.

"Pomp will learn. He will read to you from our book."

"*Ai*, that will please me." Sacajawea looked at Clark and tried to smile.

"Early this morning I came home," continued Clark in a voice faintly touched with humor, as though a man cannot help his voice. "I was muddy, weary from riding, but there was no wife to greet me at my home, only Rose, the other servants, and my young son, Lew, howling for someone to feed him."

Miss Judy looked up, almost tearful again, but Clark took her hand across the plank table and continued, "I think I will ask Nick Biddle to edit the journals for me and to visit us at your old home in Virginia."[2]

Judy's face brightened. "Oh, are we really going to have a holiday in Virginia?"

"I am ready," said Clark. "Do you think you can get your howling young son ready?"

Sacajawea sat quietly, thinking. She did not know this Nick Biddle, but she knew George Shannon and she knew he was studying to be a rule keeper[3] to help the white men and Indians keep rules and live peacefully. She had little fear anymore of speaking up when she had an idea that seemed good in her own mind.

"How far is it from that Virginia to Kentucky?" she asked.

"Well, Kentucky is on the way to Virginia," answered Clark, now dangling Pomp on his knees and winking at Little Tess, who was on his other side.

"I think Shannon will do best with the talking book. He was there."

"That's a thought! George would like to do it, too. He's a fine scholar. For that matter, he's a good teacher— taught both these women English," he said, winking at his wife. "On the expedition he sometimes asked me what words were most important for Janey to know."

"You told him the words I learned?" Sacajawea was surprised.

"No, not really. I told him to teach you as much as he knew."

They laughed, seeing the absurdity, and Clark remembered how Shannon had struggled to get Otter Woman to pronounce any English word correctly. She always had trouble with the *b, f, j,* and *l* sounds because those did not exist in the Minnetaree tongue. At times she sounded as though she had a cleft palate, and her Minnetaree speech patterns made her English sound so matter-of-fact that dramatic effects were heightened. Her tense and word order struck him as hilarious, and now Clark tried to remember choice examples, but these and other qualities of her early English eluded him.

"If only you'd been here last night," said Miss Judy. "What would you have done with one simple gloomy thought?"

"We will be neither simple nor gloomy. We have work to do, and we will keep the memory of our friend alive forever," answered Clark. "That is an order. Come home now, Judy. Let these women set their house in order. There is a change in the air. Winter will be here. And that old rascal Charbonneau is coming home. That is what I came to tell you." He stood up and took a step toward Sacajawea. "Before he left for the Arkansas, we had a long talk. There will be school next fall for these two boys. Why don't you ask him to take you and Otter on a trip before it gets too cold?" Clark put his arms around the shoulders of both Indian women, who were now standing beside the door. Miss Judy filled the mugs with hot coffee and sent the boys outside on the front step. When the coffee was gone, they were all outside saying good-bye. There was laughter, there was hope, and there was work to be done.

Otter Woman went back inside and began washing the cups and bowls, complaining of the mess left for her to clean. She ordered Sacajawea to put fat meat in the simmering stew because if Charbonneau were on his way, he'd certainly be hungry when he got home.

38

Otter Woman's Sickness

April 2, 1811

We have on board a Frenchman named Charbonet, with his wife, an Indian woman of the Snake nation, both of who accompanied Lewis and Clark to the Pacific, and were of great service. The woman, a good creature, of mild and gentle disposition, was greatly attached to the whites, whose manner and dress she tries to imitate, but she has become sickly and longed to revisit her native country; her husband also, who had spent many years amongst the Indians, has become weary of civilized life.

LEROY R. HAFEN, ed., "The W. M. Boggs Manuscript about Bent's Fort." *Colorado Magazine*, vol. 7, 1930, pp. 66–7.
   Also in:
REUBEN GOLD THWAITES, ed., *Early Western Travelers*

1804–1807, "Journal of a Voyage up the River Missouri," by Henry M. Brackenridge, vol. VI. Baltimore: Coale and Maxwell, 1816. Reprinted by The Arthur H. Clark Co., Cleveland, 1904: pp. 32–3.

Two days after Clark came to the cabin for his wife, Charbonneau arrived, asking for more beaver traps. He'd lost two on his trip to the Arkansas. General Clark offered him four and urged him to take his family on a short trapping trip before the winter wind and rains came. "It will prevent cabin fever," Clark said.

"I know there is buffalo on the Platte, and these squaws can skin them out as fast as I shoot them. It is far—cannot stay long with *deux femmes* and *enfants* on a trip. Plenty beaver there, also. Yi-eo-ow-ee! I go!"

Charbonneau led the way, his squaws riding a single horse, his boys riding another that was piled high with baggage. Twenty-four days out of Saint Louis, they passed the mouth of the Platte River. Here, a few miles downstream at the mouth, and a few miles upstream at Council Bluffs, a dozen or more fur companies had posts built for the Pawnee, Omaha, Oto, Ponca, and Iowa trade. The Charbonneau family pitched their skin tepee near one post and watched Charbonneau go to buy more supplies and exchange stories with the French-Canadians at the post.

"By gar," he said, "it is good to hear someone play the French harp again."

"There's some music in everyone," said an old trapper who sat with his back against the vertical logs at the front of the trading post.

"Who's that!" yelled a voice from inside.

"It's Charbonneau, on his way to get a few beaver plews before winter gets going."

"Well, son of a gun, Big Tessie. I remember when you took that purty little Arapaho into your tent, and consarn my picture if her pappy wasn't mad because you didn't give him a horse in trade. I'll swear you stood up to him and in hand sign, with the delicatest kind of a tremble coming in your hands, answered him back that some of these here days he'd have a papoose instead. Haw-haw-haw, was that there old coot mad. When he give his rusty rifle the waking touch, you squatted as if her bark was going to bite you!"

"*Oui*, and I bet I left the papoose," said Charbonneau, laughing exultantly.

"You were gone the next morning afore the sun came up. You're powerful with the women, sure 'nuf."

"How long you been in charge of this here post, Jake?"

"Since I last hear you come down from Red River of the North. You been among those métis and roughnecks of the Hudson's Bay lately? Or the muskeeters too much for you?"

"*Non*, I been thinking of trying a farm in Saint Louis. That is not considered a business for a mountain man, but by gar—I might be able to raise some nice sheep or goats." Then he looked at the old trapper. "Hey, you want to sell that harp poking out of your pocket there?"

"This here French harp?" asked the old trapper. "That's certain, if you got a pint of good whiskey."

"It's with my gear. Brandy. I will get it for you. Then I play you a tune on that French harp. I always have one, but lost mine somewheres."

"I'm coming to get my pint, you varmint," said the trapper.

"I got *deux femmes* and *enfants* with me. You like to come out and meet them? They went to the west with me and back again. Capitaines Lewis and Clark made that trip with us. My squaws act like the white women now. They never are satisfied with nothing. They like the calico dress. *Jésus*, it is an expense. And *Jésus*, muskeetairs are big on the Columbia—big as the buzzards that follow us all the way from the Upper Missouri."

"Well, I ain't going turn down a chance to see some good-looking squaws and little breed kids running around naked."

"You corn-dodger mill, my kids are not naked. My kids are going to school next year or so."

"Trapping must be good business for you, I swear. You with the XY or Nor'west?"

"Independent," answered Charbonneau. "Capitaine—he's now Générale—Clark, he sends them to the school. He thinks my family is worth all that for what we did as interpreters to the Pacific."

The old trapper shook his head. Sacajawea and Otter Woman nodded to him. He told the boys how to play crack-the-whip and played with them until he was winded.

Charbonneau gave him a pint of well-watered brandy and sat down to play the French harp. Sacajawea was pleased to hear such happy sounds around the camp.

"Imagine taking these here two squaws and chilluns to the far west," sighed the old trapper. He sat on the doorsill of the post, a shriveled little old man with hair and face gray as ashes. He had dark Indian eyes, high cheekbones, and a long, sickle-shaped nose.

Charbonneau played a couple of old French tunes and sang some dirty words. Then he and the old trapper sang one together, laughing heartily. Stridently they took up each last line and, repeating it three or four times, kicked holes in the ground to the rhythm of it. Otter Woman began to dance as she gathered up firewood for the evening. Little Tess and Pomp sang with their father, who recited to them a new verse about how he took his Arapaho girl to the schoolhouse for to learn her reading and writing and ordinary living, and as it was quite original and unprintable for those times, the old trapper and post clerk laughed and swore joyfully.

"You, big braves, sing loud on the other side of the post. It will make you feel good, and it will make me feel good not to know what the words are you sing," scolded Sacajawea.

"See, I said they are becoming like white women!" Charbonneau eyed her, but obeyed.

The trapper pointed a long, bony finger, curved almost to a hook with rheumatism, at Charbonneau. "You remind me of a Canuck I once knowed. He wore a Nor'west capote, same as you, and a one-shot gun rifle. He made that shoot plumb center when he got buffler. He got his fixings from old Chouteau, but what he wanted out there in them mountains, I never just rightly knowed. He made some pictures of the Injuns and their horses. That were a hair of the black bear in him. Leclerc knowed him in the Blackfoot. The boys still tell how he took the bark off the Cheyennes when he cleared out of the village with old Elkhorn's squaw. His gun was handsome—that's a fact."

"Might be that he was me." Charbonneau's chest swelled. "I been those places and hightailed it out of

Elkhorn's village with his little *femme* one night," he bragged.

The old trapper looked through squinted eyes at Charbonneau and grinned. "Why, you couldn't draw the hinder part of this chile's foot. You ain't got nothing to crow about here. You aiming to pick up supplies from Jake?"

"*Oui.*"

"Better git moving. Them there Omahas are coming in for tobaccy and firewater. Jake will close this here post if they git too pestering. Black Harris came through a week ago and couldn't git nothing for two days. This chile's not leaving until Ashley's party come through. But you with women and chilluns, looks like you ought to move on."

"Obliged to you for the warning. I'll stop back before the snow to press the plews," said Charbonneau, tapping the spit from his French harp on the back of his left hand.

"I could just go with you."

"*Non*, thanks, I'm pushing on in the morning." Charbonneau wanted to go alone and work in secrecy—plews were too valuable to take on a doubtful partner.

Charbonneau finished his purchases, and they pushed out the next morning. They passed circles of buffalo skulls that Indians had made to draw herds of buffalo to the area. They camped beside the Platte again, and Charbonneau set his traps in the small streams heading into the large river. The boys learned to build rafts that floated in the streams. They fished and waded in cold water, wearing only breechclouts. They learned to imitate the call of the wolf, coyote, whippoorwill, and mourning dove. Sacajawea told them meanings for each howl and bird call.

They worked the meadow streams where the water ran slowly enough to be dammed by beaver. Charbonneau set his traps late in the afternoon, between sunset and dark. They worked upstream, because signs of other trappers or Indians might come downstream, and because Charbonneau believed the country grew safer as they moved higher. His was a trapper's mind. Even though slow and bungling in many ways, when he hunted beaver he read the country, recorded his route, watched for hostiles, and planned for all eventualities. He was not always wise in his plans, but he was a mountain man, with ruggedness and a knowledge of living with the country.

Little Tess and Pomp explored the beavers' dams and tried to imitate them upstream, only to find that the dams they built were washed aside by the stream overnight. The beaver built his house of small branches, with a five-inch plastering of mud for roof and outer walls, on the edges of the pool his dam made. It was almost six feet high and twice as broad. In the middle of the earth floor was a pool, sometimes two or more. They were the exits of the tunnels that had been dug down through the earth to the stream bed above the dam. Weighted down with mud and water-logged snags was the winter hoard of saplings and branches whose bark was the beavers' food.

One day Sacajawea showed both boys how the Agai-dükas hunted beaver by blocking tunnels. She chopped through the roof of the house and dug out three good beaver. The boys were delighted with her prowess.

Otter Woman, not to be outdone, pulled out a two-arm span of heavy linen thread, a needle, and a snippet of yellow buckskin from a small bag hung on her belt. She knotted one end of the line, threaded the needle, then pierced the tiny piece of buckskin and drew it down against the knot. That was all she needed to catch trout, she explained, turning her head and trying to suppress a cough. "It might be better with a grasshopper added." So, with the needle still threaded, she walked away from the creek, watching in the grass. It was late for grasshoppers, but she caught two. One went into the bag, while the other was threaded and drawn down against the buckskin.

Back at the creek, she took a turn or two of the line around her index finger and let the bait drift down a sunny, shallow riffle. Within seconds, a nine-inch trout had fought his way up over the gravel, the water bulging and breaking from his glistening green back. When he'd had time to swallow the grasshopper, she swung him fast and low in a wide horizontal arc to the bank. The next one was caught as swiftly and as easily. She handed the line to Little Tess.

Sacajawea moved with Pomp upstream to a pool behind several old logs and brush, and she lay on her belly in the grass within reach of the brush that grew from the water. A trout shot away as she dangled both hands, her fingertips moving gently, almost touching, deep in the shaded pool. Her hands grew numb, and she scrambled up, showing her son how to dangle his fingers in the water to attract trout. A good-sized one came up, and Pomp was so excited that his fingers scarcely moved as the fish rubbed his back against them. Pomp warmed his hands a little and tried again, but after a while had to warm them again. Otter Woman shouted that she and Little Tess had ten trout on the bank. That made all the Charbonneau family needed for the evening meal.

The next day, Charbonneau took them to the spot where he had set a trap at the natural runway of the beaver, just inside the water where a path came down from the bank. The other traps he baited and set in places for attracting the beaver and for drowning him when he was caught. The bait was the musky secretion taken from the beaver's prepuce. Charbonneau used it straight. "Some doctor this with bear's grease or powdered stink bugs," he explained. He called the bait "medicine" or "castoreum," and carried it in a plugged horn bottle at his belt. Otter Woman did not seem to mind its perfume, but Sacajawea was not attracted to it and tried to stand upwind from Charbonneau whenever he baited the traps.

Charbonneau selected the proper places for his traps meticulously, setting them in water of the proper depth and driving a stout, dry trap pole through the ring at the end of the five-foot steel chain into the bed of the stream. He patiently told the boys this latter was to keep the beaver from dragging the heavy five-pound trap out of the ground and into the air. For if he did that, he would escape by gnawing off the paw by which he was caught. When every other preparation had been made, Charbonneau smeared a little medicine on a twig or willow, which he arched just above the surface, directly over a trap's trigger. The scent attracted the beaver—reminding Otter Woman of a pet dog's behavior when there was a bitch in heat around the Minnetaree village—and when he approached the bait stick, he was caught by the foot.

Charbonneau had waded into the stream at a sufficient distance from his selected place, carrying his set trap, and he waded several yards downstream before getting out. He splashed water over his own trail and made sure the man-scent was eliminated.

Next morning before sunrise, Charbonneau went out to raise the traps. One beaver had struggled and unmoored a trap, but it was too late. The float stick showed where the carcass was. Little Tess waded out to bring it in. Charbonneau's line was four traps. The women skinned the beaver on the spot. He had been killed by drowning. A full-grown beaver weighed thirty to sixty pounds and the pelt a pound and a half or two pounds when finally prepared.

The women packed the pelts and medicine glands back to camp. Camp was never located in the same place for two nights straight. The boys carried the tails, for they were a delicacy when charred in the fire to remove the horny skin, and then boiled.

The rest of the day was spent playing games with the boys, blowing on the French harp, or dozing. Sacajawea and Otter Woman were busy, with no time for dozing. They scraped the flesh side of the pelts free of tissue and sinew and stretched the hides on frames of willow, rather like large embroidery hoops, and then the pelts were given the cool fall sun for a day or two. When they were dry, they were folded with the fur inside and marked with Charbonneau's symbol, *C*.

Little Tess was as full of blunders as his father. Pomp accompanied him on his afternoon rambles and saved him from passing into the next world several times. Pomp would show him the lower ford, which he could never seem to find for himself, generally mistaking quicksand for it. He recommended that his brother not shoot his arrow at a deer in the moment when Charbonneau was passing behind the animal on the farther side of the brush. Pomp did not lose his patience, but seemed to take it as his lot to have an older brother who had to have his horse brought back to him, which ran away because Little Tess had forgotten to throw the reins over his head and let them trail.

"He'll always stand if you do that," Pomp reminded him. "See how that horse stays quiet over there?"

Little Tess would not answer. He watched his small brother's tiger-limberness, and his force that lurked beneath the surface, and his dislike for him grew. Little Tess found the company of his half brother more and more disagreeable.

One afternoon, the boys went duck-hunting. They found several in a beaver dam, and Little Tess had sent his arrows through two as they sat close together, but they floated against the dam, out into the stream, some three and a half feet deep, where the current was about to carry them downstream.

Little Tess's anxiety over the ducks caused him to pitch into the water; he crawled out slippery but triumphant. Pomp's serious eyes rested upon his brother, a spectacle of mud-caked leather shirt and leggings, and he said nothing, except "Won't be hardly enough for this night's meal." Pomp tied the birds to the saddle.

"I'll get more," said Little Tess, his face strangely pinched. His eyes were inky slits.

"I reckon you won't be so lucky and stay undrowned next time," said Pomp, handing him his bow, which he was about to leave deserted on the ground behind him. They rode to camp together in their usual silence. The inky slits fastened on Pomp.

Charbonneau looked at his mud-covered son. "Looks like the cap on your head was the one mark showed you were not a snapping-turtle." Little Tess's eyes, still narrow slashes, turned with his body, and he did not come into camp for supper.

"It is not right to tease the boy so much," said Otter Woman.

"Anyone could fall into the creek. It is just good that Pomp was there to help him out," said Sacajawea.

Charbonneau was not exempt from the mountain man's occupational disease, rheumatism. His joints creaked, and before dawn he was up limbering his legs and arms at the fire. Every year when winter was near, he believed the water got colder.

The days shortened, and the blue of the canyon shadows deepened. They discovered a dust of snow in the meadow one morning. Another morning, ice had formed along the edges of a stream when they checked the trap lines.

"Time to think of wintering beside the roaring fire," said Charbonneau, sending the women back to camp with the pelts and letting the boys stay to collect the traps in preparation for heading back to Saint Louis.

Coming over a rise where the knoll was covered with fallen sycamore logs and low-bush sage, they saw a cow elk standing alongside a log with her back to them.

"If we brought her into camp, our man would have no trouble finding something for supper," said Otter Woman.

The cow was as big as a young steer and quite awkward-looking. Her hams were patched with a thin yellow color. Sacajawea thought, if she runs, I will laugh because those patches will jerk back and forth so stiff and idiotic-looking. Maybe she was put here for some joke, because there is nothing so funny about an elk's ability to cover ground. The cow took one squint over her shoulder at the two women and, without any backing for a start or other preparation of any kind, jumped over the log sideways, came down facing them, and hightailed it off into the brush with her hindquarters working like pale yellow streamers in a fast wind. Sacajawea and Otter Woman laughed until Otter Woman began coughing and had to sit down before she could stop.

"A person has to be badly crippled to starve in this place," said Sacajawea, still laughing.

"Or own a couple of foolish women," grumbled Charbonneau, who had come along beside them with his rifle loaded.

The women packed the beaver skins and the tepee and strapped them on the back of the packhorse. It was their job to keep the pelts dry in case of rain, to dry them if they got wet, and to safeguard them on the trail. They would stop at the post again and press the packs into compact bales of about a hundred pounds apiece with a machine. Some small posts rigged up contraptions of logs and stones to compress the packs.

While Charbonneau went back to help the boys find the traps, Sacajawea picked up the French harp and played; Otter Woman laughed and danced until again she began coughing.

Sacajawea played and danced. Otter Woman doubled over, trying to catch her breath, not knowing whether to laugh or cough. Just at that moment Charbonneau came into camp, sooner than the women had expected him. He threw down the two clanking traps he carried.

"Squaw, give me that!" He wiped the mouth organ off on his trousers and swung Sacajawea around by one of her braids. "No *femme* of mine is touching my harp. Stay out of my gear!" He pushed her against a tree and swung his big moccasined foot at her. He missed and swore in French.

"But—I have done nothing, really. Nothing to hurt you." Sacajawea could see that his blood was up.

"Lie down," he ordered. "Or I will shoot you." He pulled his rifle from where it stood against the tree and drew it to his shoulder. Sacajawea obeyed and crawled to the ground. Charbonneau dropped the rifle and grabbed some rawhide thongs used for tying the packs. He tied her hands. He then tied a long thong to the saddle on his horse. He pulled up the reins so that the horse might walk or run, whichever he fancied. All the while, Otter Woman stared as Charbonneau swore he would shoot if Sacajawea moved. He groped for his rifle, shouldered it, and watched the horse begin to graze. Sacajawea was dragged behind in the fashion of a travois. Charbonneau seemed to enjoy that as fun. Sacajawea stood it as long as she could; but soon it became unbearable, and she screamed for Otter Woman to untie her. Otter Woman stood as if frozen, looking from Sacajawea to Charbonneau, unable to say anything.

Sacajawea was immediately ashamed of her cry. She knew that it would only goad her man to leave her tied longer behind the horse.

Otter Woman was stiff with fright. If she helped Sacajawea, Charbonneau might make her lie down and be tied to the horse, too, or he might whip her with leather thongs for interfering. He was the master. He did what he wanted, and the women obeyed. She had learned to submit, to be a slave. It was better to watch in fear and horror than to be tortured. It was better to muffle a cry, than to be beaten by the hands of this man.

Ancient memories seeped into Sacajawea's brain and shielded her flesh from pain. In her mind she saw a young brave with a quiet face. His hands were tied to a high stake where he was swung around and around, his feet not able to touch the ground. He spoke of good hunting while heavy weights were tied to his feet, his face always calm.

Sacajawea did not permit herself to ask when her man would free her. No tears came to her eyes, no other sound from her lips. Then she heard another command.

"*Umbea*, Mother, get up."

She pulled up her hands slowly and felt they were free. She pulled herself up; she did not cry or limp as she walked. Needles were in her flesh, which screamed to her silently. Her brain was numbed, but it woke and she could hear the words of Chief Red Hair speaking to Charbonneau, "If you mistreat Janey, I'll see she leaves you." She smiled inside herself; she had a friend.

"Come here, Mother." Pomp and Otter Woman rubbed her with bear's oil. Her raw flesh burned. She tasted blood in her mouth, where she had bitten the tongue that made an outcry—a hateful tongue that would try to dishonor her.

"Mother, it is good Little Tess and I came into camp right away."

Now she stood still, savoring a feeling of bravery, feeling the pain absorbed into a deep, dark sense of well-being. The small boys had not seen her flinch nor heard her cry out. Pomp had cut her hand bonds. Little Tess shrugged and sauntered off.

Pomp's short legs leaped after him in one noiseless bound, like a mountain cat's. He spoke quickly in Shoshoni. His hard *k* sounds drummed like hail on a tin roof. "I say my mother must never be treated like that again. You are a coward if you walk away from her."

"*Ai*," replied Little Tess thoughtfully, speaking in English now. Then with one strong brown hand he reached out swiftly and gave Pomp's yellow shell necklace a fast, strong jerk and a twist. The gesture was at once an insult and a threat. "I say—" Suddenly Little

Tess stopped. He opened his mouth, and there issued from it a sound so unearthly as to freeze the blood of anyone within hearing. It was a sound between the crazy laugh of a loon and the howl of a wolf. It was the death howl of the Shoshonis, taught him by Sacajawea, who had said that when a brave howled in that manner it meant destruction to anyone in his path.

Pomp's face turned a dough gray, and he stepped away from his brother, who ran like a streak of brown buckskin behind the nearest clump of trees and vanished.

"Parbleu! That'll learn you not to be blowing in my harp when I'm not around." Charbonneau spat at the ground, his face dark.

They had an evening meal of boiled beaver tail and tea. Darkness circled the trees and grew up over them. The distant hills slipped away. The fire of green cottonwood burned slow. Charbonneau tossed under his blanket. Little Tess reappeared with light steps and lay at the edge of the campfire, his eyes dull, dead black. Soon he was sleeping.

It was early January when the Charbonneau family returned to Saint Louis. The first big snow of winter held them in the snug cabin for several days before Charbonneau could get out to sell his pelts to Chouteau. Otter Woman's cough had become worse.

Sacajawea hunted barks and dug roots, which she boiled together in a small iron pot for Otter Woman. The potion was black and extremely bitter. Otter Woman complained as Sacajawea squatted on her haunches to see that she drank it. The herb mixture sent a warm glow of relaxation and sleepiness through Otter Woman, so she slept the night away despite chilling winds, sleet, or snow. The boys went on short hunting excursions with their father. Sacajawea stayed behind to care for Otter Woman, who breathed hard at the slightest exertion.

In the spring, Sacajawea coaxed Charbonneau to see General Clark about some land. She hoped Charbonneau would try his hand at farming. She thought that way he would be back at the cabin more often and would see that Otter Woman needed the help of a white medicine man—maybe even the famed Dr. Saugrain.

"If we were back in the village of Metaharta, the Medicine Man would know what to do. I would not have this cough," said Otter Woman. "I wish Charbonneau would take us back up the Big Muddy."

"You are not fit for travel," chided Sacajawea.

During the summer, Otter Woman gained little strength. Her back and legs were weak, and when she struggled to her feet, she walked with much difficulty.

When fall came, Charbonneau said, "*Femme*, if it is land you want, I'll get what is coming to me from Générale Clark. Then we'll see if we can make it at farming. Maybe the boys will be in school, and I ought to stick around here some."

This should have made Sacajawea happy, yet she was still worried about Otter Woman's health. Miss Judy had sent Dr. Saugrain twice, but he only shook his gray head, mumbling something about Indian squaws not being cut out to live as whites and breathe the germs for which they had no ready-made immunity. Sacajawea could not understand him. He was brusque and did not wish to visit or drink the tea she offered. He did leave a medicine that quieted Otter Woman nearly as well as the black bitter-herb potion. Sacajawea thought it was made from laudanum because it was so similar to the sleeping medicine Clark had used on the trail west. When Sacajawea asked about it, Dr. Saugrain squinted his beady eyes and puffed out his cheeks, mumbling again about dumb, half-educated squaws.

On October 30, 1810, Toussaint Charbonneau purchased a tract of land on the Missouri in Saint Ferdinand Township from Clark. Charbonneau tried to build himself a cabin on this land with the help of his two women. But summer had passed, and the chilled air made work go slowly. Wild geese winged south in crying wedges. The nights when the ducks clattered in the river, and the dawns when the whooping cranes rose in clouds from their feeding in the lowlands, had passed. Fires swept across the prairies, transforming the dun color of autumn into a black waste.

Now the prairie was covered with a thin layer of

white snow. The Charbonneau family found itself in a leather tepee the whole winter. The boys were unruly and fought together. Otter Woman complained of smoke and drafts. She wanted to move back to the trappers' cabin at the edge of Clark's property in Saint Louis. She seemed discontented and at the same time uncomfortable, like a sick person who cannot find an easy way to rest. She played the plum-pit game with the boys to keep them from squabbling. Sacajawea noticed that she tired quickly and seemed to forget what she was saying. She seemed to be moving into the spirit world.

One day Otter Woman said abruptly to Little Tess, "You'll like the people in Metaharta. Aren't you going to learn to hunt for the village?"

"*Ai*," said Little Tess, thinking that he must be crazy to answer such a ridiculous question. He wasn't going to hunt for any Indian village. He was going to learn the trapping trade.

"How much can you bring in before the snow closes in on the entire village?"

"*Umbea*, Mother," Little Tess said, exasperated, "you can see I'm not a hunter yet. We do not live in any Indian village. You said yourself, earlier this morning, that I was going to school in the white man's village. What is the matter with you?"

"I remember your father years ago. He didn't always want to hunt for our lodge either." Otter Woman stared straight ahead and breathed through her mouth.

"Those were the old days," he said looking at Pomp, who made the hand sign to indicate that Otter Woman was tired and needed to rest.

"You will have to look for your helper among the animals. Some animal that you can call on when you need help in a good hunt." Otter Woman clumsily shook the plum pits in her hands. She then held them and seemed to forget she was playing a game with the boys.

"Where do I look for a helper?"

"It's up to you. You have to seek it. It's there and you have to know which animal it is that wants to help you. That is only natural. It's up to you."

"I'm not sure I'd know what to do to find the right animal. Maybe I should ask someone else if it is important."

Otter Woman gasped for air as she spoke. "That's the trouble. You don't know what is important. There is no one here. You have to grow up in the village. There's understanding!"

"But, *Umbea*, is this important?"

"Important? Of course. You are mixed up now, but when the time comes—you'll see. You have to have an animal helper in order to live. That's your power—it's you!"

"I want to be like Papa. He doesn't have a helper. He doesn't talk about it."

"He's more white—so he does not believe." Otter Woman coughed. Her hands balled into fists, and her body shook. She could not seem to catch her breath. There was a rattle in her throat as though she could not cough. Then her face turned red and she fainted. Her breathing eased and her face became calm. It was no longer red.

"*Umbea*, come back from the spirit world," Pomp cried over her.

"She's coming back," said Little Tess, relieved.

Sacajawea was on her knees bathing Otter Woman's face with water. Pomp was beside her, holding one of Otter Woman's hands.

"She didn't even remember we are going to school. I think she lives in the past. She's getting old." Little Tess went outside.

"Is she getting old?" asked Pomp.

"She is sick," Sacajawea answered.

For the next couple of days, Sacajawea kept Otter Woman in bed so that the coughing would not become worse. Charbonneau sulked around the house because it was too cold to fish, and too cold to hunt, and the meat supply was low. Finally he snowshoed into Saint Louis to sell a meager supply of furs to a British trader, Charboillez. Then he agreed to act as the trader's interpreter among the Pawnees at a small wage for the remainder of the winter.

By early spring, he was back at the tepee. Otter Woman was no better; in fact, her coughing spells seemed as severe as before and closer together. She was unable to do many heavy household chores without having a coughing fit.

By midspring Charbonneau was tired of hearing his boys arguing, and Otter Woman coughing, and looking out of his tepee flap at some land that belonged to him, but which seemed far too vast to plow and seed. He decided to move out and sell the land. He took his family back to the trappers' cabin near Clark's place and sold his tract of land back to General Clark for one hundred dollars.[1]

"Now my man can take me back to the Metaharta village," sighed Otter Woman, holding her hands to her chest as she coughed. The stews no longer fattened her, so that she was pale and thin. "Sacajawea, look after the boys while I am visiting the Metahartas. I'll have lots to tell when I come back."

Charbonneau looked wearily from one woman to the other, then stomped from the cabin, mounted his horse, and headed for the city.

"Maybe he goes for Dr. Saugrain once more," suggested Sacajawea.

She was out digging sassafras roots to store with the dried fruit in order to keep bugs out when Charbonneau came riding back. He pulled a fifty-pound pack of hard biscuits from his saddle pack and handed her the reins, then lurched toward the cabin. "Hey!" he called, "there's a party going up the Missouri tomorrow morning with Monsieur Lisa. I've entered his service as interpreter."

Sacajawea hurried with the watering of the horse, tethered him, and ran back to the cabin. "I can take care of Otter Woman while you are gone. I will have Miss Judy bring Dr. Saugrain."

"*Non.* First you pack Otter Woman's things. She is going with me. Next you make certain that General Clark gets the two boys in school. You know I am sick of hearing about the Metaharta village and how good it is. I am going to take that squaw back there, and we are going to see if it is all that good. And she can see the Medicine Man there. Maybe that is what a squaw needs."

Sacajawea's mouth fell open. Surely he knew that Otter Woman was too ill to travel. If there was bad weather, Otter Woman might not make it upriver to the Minnetarees. "She is very ill," she whispered.

"All year I have heard nothing but crying for the old village. Shut up and get her things ready!" He reached into a sack for his bottle of brandy. "Don't say nothing to me. Pack!" He put the bottle to his lips and gulped two or three times. Then he threw the empty bottle, hitting Sacajawea on the shoulder. It spun her around so that she lost her balance and fell to the floor. She lay there a few moments, stunned. "Get up!" He had a rawhide whip in his hand.

She rose to her knees and grabbed her shoulder; the pain was great. Finally she was on her feet helping Otter Woman gather her things.

"Oh, I can show off my beautiful white-lady dresses," Otter Woman said with a smile, feeling a small surge of strength from the anticipation. "Broken Tooth is back at the village with her man, Jussome. I heard they got back before Big White and his family. I'll make that woman jealous with the nice things I have. Hers are probably worn out by now. It will be so good to see the old village." She bent double with coughing.

"Rest all you can on the boat," said Sacajawea.

On her pallet that night, Sacajawea could not sleep. Her own thoughts flew back to the Mandan corn festivals, to Sun Woman and Chief Four Bears, to Grasshopper, to Antelope and Catches Two and the ugly, one-eyed Chief Kakoakis, and to the Five Villages where Otter Woman was going.

The Charbonneaus were riding their horses across the fields at dawn. Already there were farm women digging with sharp paring knives, gathering feathery greens—dandelions, lamb's quarter, violet leaves, tender blackberry sprouts, wild turnip, and lettuce. The clouds were tossed about the sky, and they had to lean hard into the wind. The day was warm, and the song of the peepers came sweetly over the hills from the ponds. The starlike flowers of the spring beauty, the hepaticas, blue violets, and fuzzy mullein leaves were in their path. The redbuds splashed their color on the hillsides. In the deep mulch laid down by eons of past vegetation Johnny-jump-ups blossomed so thick that they made a petaled carpet. Buttercups glistened like jewels in the warm morning sun, while over all were the wings of butterflies.

"I will never forget this land," whispered Otter Woman, riding behind Sacajawea. Sacajawea could not answer, for the lump in her throat was large. She would miss Otter Woman.

Even Otter Woman had some doubts about leaving now. Her cough made her chest ache, and she was afraid to think of her illness. Deep inside, the fear penetrated her every bone that she would never return to see her son, Little Tess. This was the last time for seeing these beloved people. She was overcome by the sadness of departing. At the riverbank she turned her pale face toward Sacajawea and whispered hoarsely, "Take care of Little Tess."

"*Ai*," promised Sacajawea, tears behind her eyes.

Little Tess reminded his father to return soon so they might hunt bear up north. He did not look at his mother, Otter Woman. He disliked sniveling women.

Pomp clung to Otter Woman's hand a moment, then let her go. He waved and shouted his good-byes.

Charbonneau stood in the prow of the keelboat and waved both hands dramatically. He looked sideways. Beside him, Otter Woman stood, her face calm, stoic, with no trace of emotion. Her eyes were wide, as if in fear, but tearless.

She's rather pretty, keeps her mouth shut, serves only me, Charbonneau thought. She is really my favorite; she has surprisingly long, arched brows. Then Charbonneau's waving ceased because he had recognized his old friend Jussome on the deck. "*Zut!* You dog-faced rascal!" he shouted. Jussome slapped Charbonneau's back in greeting.

This was April 2, 1811. Charbonneau was in the service of Manuel Lisa, going up the Missouri. Otter Woman stood on the deck in her red calico dress waving a yellow handkerchief as she had seen white ladies do.

When the keelboat was out of sight, Sacajawea led the horses back to the trappers' cabin. She was content that summer just knowing she was near friends and taking care of the two boys who called her mother.

* * *

Judy Clark often came to visit, telling about important people in the city. Most often, Sacajawea asked about school. She could not picture the nature of such a thing for learning.

"The man who founded Saint Louis, Pierre Laclede, went to school at the University of Toulouse. He brought most of his books to his home here," said Miss Judy.

Sacajawea understood the talking books, but the university was an enigma. She smiled and shook her head. She listened and tried to understand.

"Father François Neil and half a dozen cathedral priests have opened an academy for boys. They call it the Catholic Academy.[2] This is the school where Will has decided to send Little Tess. I heard him say that Father Neil emphasizes that students of all faiths are welcome and that 'no undue influence will be exercised in matters of religion.'"

"*Ai*, there is much to learn. Isn't Pomp going at the same time? I thought—"

"Oh, Janey, of course your Pomp is going. But Will has decided to send him to a different school. He thinks it would be good for the boys to be apart, so that they don't always have to compete with each other. Pomp is going to the school run by the Baptist minister, Mr. Welch.[3] Don't look so forlorn. Both boys will be back with you on holidays. You could even go to visit them once in a while. I'm sure Father Neil or Mr. Welch would understand."

"Our life has changed," said Sacajawea.

New Madrid Earthquake

The weather had been unseasonably warm. For several weeks a comet had been visible. Superstitious Missourians predicted the end of the world. Indians left the territory. This was the fall of 1811.

When the calamitous phenomenon appeared, it was in the form of an earthquake—one of the greatest earthquakes ever known on the North American continent. This tremendous disturbance continued through December to March, 1812. Two thousand shocks were reported. Cracks opened through forests and fields; landslides swept down hillsides. Rivers changed courses, wiping out sand bars and islands that had been landmarks. During a hard tremor the Mississippi receded from its banks, arching to a great mountain in the center. Suddenly, with a frightful roar, the water pounded back toward the banks, but surging and reversing, so that the water swept upstream rather than downstream. Thousands of trees were mowed down and cemeteries were turned upright so that rows of coffins were exposed in the village of New Madrid.

Teacups rattled in Philadelphia, clocks stopped in Boston and church bells rang in Virginia, as the tremors were felt over one million square miles. Moderate to heavy damage was reported in St. Louis, Cincinnati, and

Louisville, and minor damage occurred as far away as Columbia, South Carolina, and Savannah, Georgia. Later geologists found that some 30,000 square miles had been lowered from six to twenty-five feet, while other areas had been raised a similar amount.

MYRON L. FULLER, *The New Madrid Earthquake*. Washington, D.C.: U.S. Geological Survey, Bulletin 494, 1912.

Sacajawea was up before dawn, mostly because it was too cold to sleep. The fire had gone out, and the horses were stamping around, noisy and restless. There had been a bear in the woods during the night, and the horses had not settled down. She studied the tracks around the tethered horses, knowing full well that bears attack a horse only if they are feeling ornery enough. She patted the four horses Charbonneau had left behind, saying to them, "Shhh, brighten up, a bear's natural outlook is a grouchy humor." The horses were ready to move. She moved the first three farther out into a clearing where they would have grass to munch, and then she put a woolen blanket on the fourth, and a buffalo robe over that, and tied it all down with leather straps.

She took her calico dress off the hook where she had hung it the night before after ironing it smooth with the flatiron Miss Judy had given her. She changed her leather tunic for it. She took up the fawnskin pack, which held moccasins and beaded shirts, and thought about Chouteau's store, where she would exchange the pack for dried beans, bacon, tea, and hard candy. She could not make up her mind which thing was the greater wonder—the bacon or the hard candy.

It was something to find meat so fat and salty and ready to boil. The hard candy was something to taste and savor a long time.

Everything that happened to a person, it seemed, was hooked up to something else that had already happened to that person, or was going to happen. Nearly six summers ago, her brother, Chief Black Gun, had sat on a stone in the Agaidüka camp and told how he thought sugar lumps were the finest things he had ever tasted. Now she was going to trade for some for herself. She could trade for her own!

She rode past a farmer running his horse around a freshly plowed field. Presently she was riding past a noisy bar where the street was full of traders, rivermen, and a handful of Indians. Then she rode through the French quarter. She passed rainbows of people—Parisians, Spaniards, Africans, Austrians, Germans, Scots, British, U.S. military men, a Shawnee chief, dark-suited preachers, white women dressed in pink and blue. This was the United States drained prismatically through Saint Louis. Sacajawea looked among the men, bearded and tobacco-chewing, ganged around the broad store building, until she noticed one who was familiar coming around the corner of the warehouse.

"Seehkheeda! White Eyebrows!" Here eyes were wide with surprise.

"Janey, is it really you!"

"*Oui.*" She flushed under her copper skin. "You look like a Mandan warrior."

John Colter flushed under his bronzed skin. "I was thinking you looked like a white woman in that fancy dress. Know where I can find General Clark?"

"Follow," she said and led him into the dark inside of the building, past the piles of skins, to a clerk she caught by the sleeve. She asked if he would take the moccasins and shirts for the supplies she needed. The clerk, with an easy manner, showing he had known her for some time, told her to find what she needed. He unrolled the fawnskin pack and laid a beaded shirt on the smooth oak counter. Then he arranged the half-dozen pairs of moccasins beside it, and laid out the other two shirts, bright with small colored beads around the edge. Sacajawea cupped her hands twice at the barrel of dried navy beans. The clerk put two double handfuls of beans in the small muslin sugar bag she handed him. She showed him where to slice off the slab of salt pork, then picked up two tins of hardtack and pointed to the hard candy in a jar on the counter. She made her fist into a ball. The clerk understood. He scooped out an amount similar in size to her fist and weighed it in the sugar bag with the beans. Wetting the tip of his pencil, he figured the price by subtracting the weight of the beans alone. She pointed to a five-pound can of tea and one of coffee.

"*Merci,*" she said with a polite shake of her head.

"Good day to you, ma'am," said the clerk, who was dark, like a Frenchman, and carefully dressed.

"Here, let me carry those," offered Colter when she'd wrapped her trade in the fawnskin.

"*Non*, it is squaw's work," she insisted and fell into an easy stride with him. She tied the pack to her saddle strap and mounted. Colter caught up on his horse.

"A race with the Blackfeet? Is what we heard true?"

"Sure is. Potts and I were trapping on the Jefferson near your Beaver Head."

She nodded.

"They riddled Potts, stripped me, and then gave me a chance to run for my life. I made it to the Madison, found a beaver's house, and crawled inside. Those Blackfeet hunted up and down all around me. When night came, I headed for the pass to the Yellowstone."

Sacajawea put her hand to her mouth. John Potts dead! At the hand of the old enemy, the Blackfeet! She did not speak until they reined up in front of Clark's Spanish house on Main and Pine Streets.[1]

"There are stories about you meeting devils, and boiling water shooting from the earth, and trees made of stone."

"Looks like the grapevine talk beat me here." Colter shook his blond hair from his eyes and laughed. "I had to stop telling those things; men thought I wasn't quite right in the head."

It was Sacajawea's turn to laugh. "The people in the Minnetaree villages did not believe me when I told about the fish as large as two lodges. They said I had a forked tongue."

"Well, Bill Clark will listen and believe," said Colter.

"Come," said Sacajawea, dismounting. "Chief Red Hair knows we tell what our eyes see."

"Janey!" cried General Clark as the two started up the stone steps. "And Colter! Balls of fire! Where have you been? Come in, come in." He led them into the Indian room, where the walls were lined with robes, hides, and maps, with stories marked on many of them.

"Well, sir, last month I was at the Three Forks."

Clark gasped. "And you are here in Saint Louis already?"

"Yes, sir. Came down that river in thirty days."

"That breaks all records."

"Yep, guess it does, at that. Colonel Menard and Andy Henry have started a fort on that strip of wooded grassland between the Jefferson and Madison. Droui-

llard and I trapped around there and camped with them.
Had to be on constant lookout for skulking Blackfeet.
Say, I was certainly shocked to hear about Captain
Lewis's suicide. Doesn't yet seem true."

Clark's face puckered; his eyes opened. "You feel that
way too?"

"Yes, sir. What a shame. Say, I heard Shannon is
called Peg Leg and gets about as well on his wooden
leg as any of the rest of those university fellows."

"Can't keep a good man down long," agreed Clark,
showing them to a place at his plank conference table.

"Where's that son of a gun, Ben York?" Colter looked
around the room.

After a short silence, Clark began speaking in a low
voice, looking toward Colter with a long-focused gaze,
as though he were transparent or not there at all. "He
is a good man," Clark said with seeming irrelevance.
"Ben York. That son of a gun. I do miss him. I took him
to Louisville, where he worked as a freedman. Then he
wed a little gal on the next farm. But he didn't stay
long. Left Cindy Lou and came back here to me. He got
to hanging around the Greentree Tavern and the Union
and Missouri hotels telling wild tales and drinking the
grog the men gave him. It was not his fault entirely.
The *engagés* and rivermen liked to hear him tell how
the Indians marched admiringly around him and pushed
their fairest daughters on him. He impressed them with
his powers of strength, and then he got to acting like
he was the only black being on earth, and some kind
of high chief. I had to warn him several times. But he
didn't think I was in earnest. Something had to be done.
So I got Cindy Lou freed and sent him back to Louisville
so that he could settle down, raise a family and have
some decent work, hauling freight with a wagon and
team of six horses. He seemed pleased when he left,
maybe because Janey made him a fancy shirt with big
roses on front and back. Oh, Lord, he seems to have
disappeared—we have no actual word from him. He's
just gone." His mouth puckered, and he shook his head.
He searched the faces of his listeners with a vaguely
grieved, apprehensive look. There being no denials or
questions, he changed the subject. "Janey, tell Colter
what our little dancing boy is doing."

"Oh, he's living at the school!" she said, squinting at him with suppressed amusement in her eyes. "He has the talking books and looks at them more often than at me when he visits."

"Tell what he's learning," Clark insisted, fumbling for some tobacco in a long buckskin sack.

Sacajawea waited until his pipe was lit and he'd drawn a few puffs. "He can read and write. Reverend Welch tells him about lands across the Great Water. Once he said he wished to go to see that land himself. And Tess is at Father Neil's," she said proudly.

"Tess?" Colter asked.

"Oh, I'm sorry, don't you remember the other small boy Charb had at the Mandan village? The son of one of his other women—Otter, her name was." Clark passed his pipe to Colter, who puffed with hollowing cheeks.

"I remember her," Colter began, speaking out of a slowly thinning fog. "She was the one Shannon took a fancy to; he tried to teach her some English words."

"She's the one. Caught on slowly, but she tried, which is more than can be said of that rascal Tess. Father Neil says he is either sleeping in the schoolroom or acting like a clown."

"Pah!" said Sacajawea. "He needs a leather strap. Otter Woman was too soft with him."

"Now don't you go telling her what I said." Clark's fists hit the table.

"*Ai.*" Sacajawea sniffed, then smiled. "She has not yet returned with our man, remember?"

"You know me; I forget who is where most of the time," said Clark. "I had a talk a fortnight ago with Welch about clothing and books for Pomp—they call him Baptiste. That lad is bright. Catches on fast, and no problem with his behavior. The other kids like him."

Sacajawea chuckled and was still. Colter passed the pipe back to Clark.

"Where is Charb?"

"Charbonneau hired out with Manuel Lisa as interpreter so that he could take Otter Woman back to the Minnetaree village. She's not well. Charbonneau insisted that the Medicine Man was what she needed."

"Some man, huh?" said Colter winking. "All heart and soul. Say—where's Ordway?"

Clark smoked awhile. "He's in New Hampshire. Bought some land there. And Windsor, too. Whitehouse sold his land to Drouillard and reenlisted in the Army."

"Drouillard went under in a skirmish with the stinking Blackfeet." Colter cleared his throat. "Thought maybe you hadn't heard. Where's Pryor?"

Clark raised his head and seemed to come back slowly from a distant place. "I'd heard. Pryor got his discharge, and now he's gone out to the lead mines to trade with the natives. Friendly with the Illini and Osage, he is. I hope he has no trouble with the Shawnee out there. And speaking of trouble, there's a strong feeling in Congress for war against Great Britain because of her seizure of American ships and seamen."

"I've heard." The bright look went out of Colter's eyes.

"Go on," Clark jogged him. "What have you heard?"

"Not much." Colter sat looking at his hands, as if he were puzzled by them and trying to fit them together. "So help me," he said solemnly, "some say it is best to strike at England through Canada, using the friendship of the Indians to help our Army."

"Why?" Sacajawea spoke sharply. "The British are befriending the natives as fast as they can and turning them against us."

"Against *us*," repeated Clark with a smile. "Now you speak like an American. And Americans know that the British can't fight. My God, they whoop like a pack of Blackfeet, but they'd drop dead if they ever got close enough to hear a Blackfoot whoop. They'll come tricked out in hunting shirts, when they've been turning up their snouts for years at settlers that had nothing else but hunting shirts to wear. They'll play Blackfeet, letting on to burn a man's insides, while he's still alive, but when their neighbors are being burned alive not twenty miles from them, they won't lift a finger. They'll be yelling 'Down with Yankees!' when the only thing they ever put down is their breeches! That is not fighting."

"It does not prove they wouldn't fight if they really had a call to," said Colter.

"You'd be surprised how deaf they could be if anyone called them. They can't fight in this country. Don't know how, never did, and most likely won't learn. But it could be a mess if they started."

Judy Clark came into the room then. Her face shone like the sun. "Oh, Will, I didn't realize you had company—and it's Janey. Why didn't you tell me?" She skipped past the men and sat beside Sacajawea, tossing her brown curls and smiling at Colter.

"This is John Colter, one of my men from the expedition," said Clark, standing.

"I'm pleased to meet you." She smiled and indicated that the men should sit down again. Her eyes twinkled. "Janey and I can go into the parlor, and you men can talk." She motioned for Sacajawea to follow her.

"Come, I'll play the piano for you. We just had it sent here from New York."

Sacajawea had to keep her hand over her mouth when she saw what a piano was. To her the keys looked like a long set of teeth. The music was unimaginable; she'd never heard so many different sounds.

By midafternoon, she knew she'd better start for home, and promised to teach Miss Judy how to make jerky if she'd let her touch the piano keys.

"Will says so often he has a yen for dried meat." Judy ran around the piano as Rose York came into the room with a plate of cookies.

Sacajawea took a handful and pushed them inside her dress so that she could save them for the boys when they came home from school on holiday.

In the fall, Clark sent Sacajawea part of a buffalo so that she could have meat when the boys came home from school. And Clark was shrewd enough to know that she often had Indian guests come to her cabin so that she could show other women how to sew or embroider or cook like the white women. Sacajawea was a leading lady in the Indian community of the riverfront city.

One afternoon, Miss Judy came with Clark and their boy, Meriwether Lewis Clark, to visit Sacajawea. Judy sighed as she saw the one-room log cabin, with an indolently smoking chimney, squatting in sullen destitution. Before the door a ramshackle wagon stood waiting for nothing. Down yonder in the brushy draw,

an almost roofless shed stared listlessly upon the bright
blue sky.

"See, Will has brought more meat. I'm going to stay
and learn how to make the dry strips," said Miss Judy.

Clark rode off on business of his own—something
about "Red Sticks" uprising along the frontier, a Creek
war faction.

"Did you see the comet last night? The star with the
tail?" asked Miss Judy cheerily as she spread an old
quilt on the ground for the baby to lie on. "We watched
for an hour or more."

"The fire tail?" asked Sacajawea. "*Ai*, some of the
Indians are leaving for camps away from Red Hair's
town. They were fearful last night and said that Mother
Earth is at her end."

"Posh!" laughed Judy. "That is superstitious nonsense. You'll see, by next year the old earth will still
be here with us on it."

Sacajawea chuckled and showed Miss Judy how to
hold the butcher knife and cut buffalo meat into inch-
thick slices and strips and score it crosswise. They spread
the strips on the cottonwood poles in front of the cabin,
high to keep it from dogs, wolves, and vermin. There
was a smoky fire under the frame to make the meat
sweeter and tastier.

"You are like a sister. It is no one's fault how she is
born, and your heart is as much Shoshoni as mine."
Sacajawea's eyes shone with a merry light.

Three days later, Miss Judy came back to see if the
meat was done. Sacajawea smiled and pulled off a small,
stiff piece, which she put in baby Looie's fist. He seemed
to enjoy tugging and chewing on it. His chin dripped.

"Warm sun is good for your papoose," said Sacajawea, gently holding the baby close to her breast and
patting his little back. Then she put him down on the
quilt. She patiently showed Miss Judy how to strip the
sinew and gristle from the dried meat. "Jerky," she said.
Then Sacajawea's arm took in all the racks of finger-
width strips of meat. "Pemmican—that is in a class by
itself."

Miss Judy learned how to pound the dried strips in
a wooden mortar until they were pulverized and then
packed loosely in clean parfleche bags. Sacajawea poured

melted buffalo fat over the open parfleches. Then the women sewed up the mouths of the bags. "This pemmican will keep for many seasons," explained Sacajawea.

"Will has told me what a splendid high-energy food it is. He said it's a complete diet in itself. It can be eaten uncooked or fried, roasted, boiled, alone, or in combination with anything on hand."

"*Ai*," agreed Sacajawea. "It is best when mixed with dried, ground-up fruits."

"Can't you just see Will when I tell him I made jerky and this whole bag of pemmican? He won't believe me, I know."

Sacajawea wiped the perspiration from her forehead with an old scrap of deerskin. She would do almost anything to please Chief Red Hair, and she was delighted with this young woman who was his wife.

Miss Judy, singing "Skip to My Lou," sat beside her son and watched Sacajawea take the long strips of buffalo fat, which had lain along the back of the animal, from the drying rack. The fat had been slowly fire-dried. Sacajawea cut it into sticks and put it in leather pouches. The kidney fat was dry, and she sliced it to be stored for later use with corn or beans in the cooking kettle.

"It's hot for November," said Miss Judy, fanning her face with her hand.

"*Ai*," agreed Sacajawea. "We must store up the warmth for a long, cold winter."

"Don't you miss Charbonneau and Otter Woman?"

"I miss Otter Woman and often wonder if she is in the Minnetaree village. I have never seen the coughing sickness cured." For a time Sacajawea seemed unconscious of Miss Judy as she worked with the strips of meat, turning them over to get the smoke on both sides.

"Janey," said Miss Judy, drawing closer to Sacajawea, "if it is the decline, the sun and air will do her good. Maybe she stayed in the cabin too much all day and did not get enough fresh air. She needed rest. Charbonneau won't insist she get up early and get his meal, will he? He will let her sleep, won't he?"

"You know he is as stubborn as an old donkey," Sacajawea said at last in an explosive whisper. Her mouth was pulled together, as if she were trying to keep from saying too much. "If she does not do what he expects, he will say he cannot afford to keep her any longer and trade her for a red blanket to the first person who comes along."

"That's outrageous!" burst out Miss Judy, shocked.

"I did not mean to talk so much." Sacajawea stopped and tried again. "The thing is, with herbs and broth, the Medicine Man will help her. You've no need to worry. Would not do Otter Woman any good, anyway."

Miss Judy did not speak. She just stood up and stared for half a minute, then picked up her baby and the extra parfleche and doeskin-wrapped package of jerky.

"Here." Sacajawea took the baby while Miss Judy tied the package to the back of the saddle, then pushed the bag of pemmican in between and lashed it on tightly. A meditative mood was strong upon her.

As soon as Miss Judy left, Sacajawea felt a wave of loneliness, a feeling of foreboding. She thought of Otter Woman's good fortune at being able to go back to the Minnetaree village. Or was it good? She'd be going back to the old ways. Here near the river town, things changed and the ways were new and exciting.

Red Hair's town was growing. Each year a few more stone houses were built and more good furniture and good cloth came up the river. Often a trapper or trader brought his Indian partner downstream with him for a winter in town. Then he introduced him hospitably to the civilization they had talked about in camp. Saint Louis was full of transients—Canadians from Montreal, like Charbonneau, who had arrived to become *engagés* for Chouteau or Lisa, and mountain men in to buy new guns and to spend their pelt money, as Charbonneau did. And always there were Indians, unabashed in their curiosity about the white man. They came to town with birchbark sacks of maple sugar, skins of wild honey, horsehair lariats, moccasins, herbs, buffalo tongues, and bear grease to trade for blankets, horse gear, coffee, tea, tobacco, knives, tin cups, and the like. The trappers, who customarily acted as their interpreters, did not try very hard, if at all, to keep them from buying rotgut whiskey, too.

Sacajawea thought of the braves who loitered around

Chouteau's big stone warehouse, where the "fur rows" smelled to high heaven. When the braves were bored, a band of them would mount their ponies and race madly down the main street, shooting blunt arrows at every dog and cat in sight. She said aloud, "My boys will not be like that. They will learn self-control."

Most of the Indians never did understand why the white men so sternly forbade these races. There was much they did not understand about the white men. For example, why did Mr. Boujou, the watchmaker, always wave his arms and scream *"Sacre!"* when the braves sauntered into his shop to examine his collection of glass eyes? Sacajawea chuckled a little to herself at that thought. In his best blanket and wearing his tomahawk like a dress sword, an Indian went where he felt like going. He knocked at no doors. But black cooks screamed and sometimes hurled hot water. And their white mistresses screamed and sometimes fainted. There was no such silliness if a brave stayed with the men down near the levee. That was where there was rotgut, big talk, and sometimes a melee.

Sacajawea heard more talk of the comet in the sky. Some said that it meant the coming again of the white man's God. Others, more pessimistic, said the earth was going to explode and fall apart all over the sky.

Tecumseh, the famous Shawnee chief, had moved into the southern part of Missouri to quiet the tribes and negotiate peaceful land settlements with the white settlers. It was generally recognized that open war with the Indians would necessarily be part of the June 1812 declaration of war against the British. Sacajawea wondered how much Tecumseh understood of the problems of both Indians and whites.

In mid-December, the month before the snow covered the ground, Sacajawea was shaken from her sleeping couch. She heard a roaring and groaning in the earth. The cabin creaked and seemed to be moving. She staggered to the door and crashed drunkenly against the cabin wall. Winds rushed from many directions and mingled and cried in the upper air. Lightning leaped out of the dark, and fireballs danced in the distance. Then all seemed quiet. Sacajawea leaned farther out

the door and waited for the rain, but no rain fell. There
was only the leaping lightning and the crying winds.
A wolf howled, deep-toned, near, and there was no answer. She listened to the winds and heard voices shouting. "Come, come to us," they called. She pulled her
blanket closer and shivered. Again she heard the voices
calling her. The voices of children calling to their mother
in the black of night. Frightened children calling. The
lightning leaped, and she saw the wolf, low-bellied to
the ground, running past the cabin into the dark. The
floor began to roll, and the meager furniture seemed to
walk. Her head reeled, and her breath came in short
gasps as her throat tightened with fear. In the brightness of the next lightning flash she saw great numbers
of wolves pressed close together following the low-bellied one. Across the grassland the earth seemed to roll
in waves like the Stinking Waters of the west. Now the
shivers ran down her back.

There had been stories all fall at Chouteau's trading
post from the rivermen who had been awakened by
tremendous noises and violent agitations of their boats.
They told of trees falling on the shore and the sea gulls
screaming. Many a *patron* tried to sooth his men with
"Restez-vous tranquil, c'est un tremblement de terre."
But men could not understand as the perpendicular
banks above and below them began to fall into the river.

Trappers who came up from Tecumseh's territory
near New Madrid in the Missouri delta told about great
chasms four feet in width forming with the shocks. Some
noticed that every earth shock was preceded by a roaring kind of groan, and that the shocks uniformly came
from the same point and went off in an opposite direction. The river was reported to be covered with foam
and driftwood, and had risen.

Sacajawea gathered her butcher knife, firesticks, and
a pouch of the fresh-made pemmican and followed the
same trail as the wolves had taken, the trail to town.
She walked. She was afraid to ride a horse on ground
that rumbled. The way was hard in the dark. There
was nothing now in her mind but fear. Only when the
lightning leaped could she see the ground stretched
before her, opening with sounds like tremendous claps
of thunder followed by a diminishing cracking, like the

grumbling of a great sheet of ice. The lightning showed
the trail, and it led her up along the creek toward town.
She came against rocks that had tumbled into the creek
bed. Frightening rumblings were discharged like the
explosion of artillery. The ground heaved and rolled in
a succession of earth tremors, six or eight minutes apart.
She huddled against the stones, then climbed over them
where the ground seemed smoother under their dried
grasses and she could move easily. She could not make
out the trail, but thought by some instinct she would
reach the home of Chief Red Hair.

The winds died some, and the lightning ceased. She
passed circular holes, resembling the vents of small
volcanoes, from which only minutes before gases, steam,
and water had shot high in the air. Some glistening
black protrusions of rock and substrata were exposed
along the trail, but she could not remember them from
before and wondered more and more if she were going
in the right direction. The darkness was thick, the air
acrid and sulfurous; far ahead she thought she saw a
glimmering in the weeds. The glimmering faded, then
came again. She stumbled, watching it become larger.
Then she saw faces shining in the light of a campfire.
All were stupefied by the great Mother Earth rumblings and openings that spewed the sulfurous fumes,
blasts of carbonized dust, or great geysers of water and
steam. These fugitives had sought refuge on a hilltop
while they tried to see the continuing devastation below. They were now composing themselves for death by
frantic hymn-singing and prayers. The noise of these
white farmers and their families was as frightening as
the roar from inside the earth.[2]

Instinctively Sacajawea moved in a wide circle around
the campfire. Her right foot reached out in one instant
to meet only air, and she pitched forward, downward.
Her body twisted, and her hands caught at the sod edge.
Her fingers gripped and held. She dangled into deeper
darkness, and her mind whirled in circles and her legs
thrashed as she sought to swing them up and crawl
back over the edge. Slowly her fingers slipped, and she
fell downward, her left ankle striking a dead-white pro-
trusion of rock. She lost consciousness as her body lay

folded upon itself on the mud at the bottom of a yawning crack in the earth.

She lay surrounded by the earth; only the dark sky, now veiled by a yellow haze as dawn approached, looked down at her. She seemed close to the inner heart of the rumblings, and yet she could hear the outer winds whispering among the grasses. The ancient magic of her beginnings was there.

The winds whispered through grasses and were the voices of spirits that lived in Mother Earth. Her mind knew such spirits existed. She had learned of them when she was a child. The sighing winds, streaks of lightning, images of a low-bellied wolf in fright, heaving earth, frightened palefaces chanting around a flickering fire, and small animals running scared were all signs to her as she merged into the natural forces that surrounded her. These were the things that brought her to the bottom of the crack in Mother Earth.

She was somewhere between her lodge and the lodge of Chief Red Hair. She was a bit of human life in a mud-walled well, alone.

The wind sighed, and the rain fell. The drops gathered a chill from the high openness of the sky. The cool wetness brought consciousness back to the dreaming Sacajawea. She stirred; waves of pain swept through her body, and she was unconscious again. The rain stopped. Mother Earth rumbled deep inside herself and far away.

A sickly yellow dawn spread over the land and filtered through the oaks and hickories. Awareness came to Sacajawea. She lay in a heap. Her tunic was mudcaked, and clotted blood clung to her left leg. It was twisted grotesquely beneath her, but not broken. Pain swelled and receded and swelled again in her throat with each in-drawn breath. She stared upward at the yellow-gray clouds overhead for a long time.

The sun was almost straight above her when she moved. Agony streaked inside her as she moved her left leg, pushed down a little, and pulled it around in front. She could not remember what had happened. She could not recall the terrified look on the white faces in the firelight. She did not know that she was the woman called Sacajawea. She did not recall that she was running away from some unknown terror. She imagined the cry of an infant who longed for the comfort of its mother's arms, then recognized her own whimperings. She was a primitive, elemental creature looking about herself now for the primary substances of survival. Her eyes found the pouch of pemmican where it had fallen in mud when she pitched over the edge of the earth crack. She inched her way toward it, wondering what was inside the leather pouch. Her back ached, but did not seem more than bruised. Her mouth felt dry.

She sat up and looked around again. The crack was long and turned sharply to the left about a hundred yards in front of her. A butcher knife lay half-buried in the mud at her feet. She tucked it inside the leather belt at the waist of her tunic. She pulled herself upright, pulling at the dirt along the side of the crack. Her left ankle throbbed, and she could not put her full weight on it. She gripped the pouch and pulled at the dirt, trying to raise herself out of the crack. The dirt and mud crumbled under her hands. But she knew she had to find a way out. She limped to the turn and found the sides were all equally steep. She put her hand into the leather pouch and found the fine-pounded meat laced with blackberries. She put a pinch in her mouth. It was dry and hard to swallow. Her head ached. She crammed two more pinches into her mouth and let the juices form slowly, slowly from the dryness. The dried meat was pounded finely and needed little chewing. A convulsive constriction of her throat forced it down. She reached for more, and in the reaching stepped down on her left foot. A blackness surrounded her, and unconsciousness took her again.

Daylight disappeared and darkness grew. A half moon rose over the land, and its silver light moved slowly across the grass to the crack in Mother Earth. The pale light touched the limp figure. She stirred and opened her eyes. Her unconsciousness had passed into sleeping, and the sleeping finally into awakening. Her eyes looked at the drifting moon. She knew who she was. She was Sacajawea, mother of Baptiste, friend of Chief Red Hair. She did not know where she was. But the moon in the dark sky was the same moon that she had watched from her cabin door so many nights. It had not changed. The sky had changed. No longer was the comet visible, and the sickly clouds were gone.

Her muscles were very stiff and sore. To move was to call back the pain. Her left ankle was discolored and swollen. But she was Sacajawea. She could grit her teeth and fight the hurt. She ate a little more of the pemmican. She limped along the floor of the crack to a large stone that she had not seen before and pulled herself up to it. She looked around. She could see grass hanging down from the mouth of the crack. She reached through the moonlight to touch it. It fell, and some stayed in her hand. It was wet. She remembered the rain. The moonlight moved across the bottom of the crack, close to the wall of mud above the large stone. It beckoned her upward. Almost involuntarily she reached for the knife in her belt and began to cut footholds in the side of the wall. The pain in her muscles had subsided into an aching that could be endured. The pain in her left ankle was a mounting torture. She fought it and dug. She fought it and was defeated. She rolled from the stone to the damp earth and shuddered. Then she was still.

The sun warmed her. She scraped the mud from her leather tunic, kneeling on the ground, with her weight on her right knee. Her left leg touched the ground little, doing only the job of helping her keep balance. She finished cleaning her tunic, then sat with her back against the stone. She shivered. It was cold. She limped back to where her blanket had fallen, then sat again with her back to the stone. She tucked the blanket around her legs. She listened and heard nothing. No one came. The pain in her ankle had numbed. There was no one to come. No one knew she had gone into the night. No one knew that she had been afraid and had started toward Chief Red Hair's lodge. No one knew that she was concerned over the well-being of her boys, Baptiste and Tess. Not even she admitted that, but she knew that was why she had fled into the night. She knew it as well as she knew she was the one called Sacajawea. But she would not say it aloud as she would not say her own name aloud. No hunting party would come here. No trapping party would come out here far from the stream.

She held the knife firmly and all afternoon dug niches in the mud wall. The wind did not touch her; she dropped the blanket, and the working kept her warm. She felt small tremors in the earth, but there was no rumbling and she kept digging. Finally, before the night fell, she dug deep into the pouch for pemmican and ate the last mouthful of pounded meat. She dug her feet deep into the niches, and her hands gripped the edge of the niche above as she pulled herself upward. She remembered the firesticks, but did not go back down to look for them.

Out on the grass she rested, then looked for the path that led to the town. The winds sighed softly in the upper air. She drew the blanket tightly around her body. Her breath came in short gasps. There was a tingling in her hands and arms. Her ankle had swollen more. She lay beside the long wide crack and thought that the Great Spirit searched for her. He came in the form of rabbits and ground squirrels. He leaped and laughed and mocked her, and his laughter was terrible. "Look at this squaw," he said. "She climbs up out of Mother Earth and is afraid of the dark night." A rabbit sniffed at her and turned its tail toward her saying, "She follows the crying of papooses, but is afraid to go to them. Afraid she will find herself in another crack."

Her breath came more easily, and her ankle throbbed into her inner-most being, awakening in that being an anger that filled her. A shout rose in her mind and traveled to her lips. "A mother will face anything to comfort her child! Move forward!"

She sat up and, cutting off a wide strip from the bottom of her tunic, bound her ankle tightly, pulling the soft leather until it was smooth and shiny. For a few moments she crawled along the ground, feeling for cracks. She saw the hills swell up boldly in front of her. They were gentle hills, and the swales between them broad. She knew if she could not find the trail she could stick to the high ground. One oak ridge would lead her to another; if she took the bottoms, they would lead to other bottoms. They were not like the mountains. The mountains were far away, in a dream. She'd have good going; no mountains to get in the way. She'd had enough ups and downs. It seemed as though there was no such thing as level going; it was all up and down and in and

out. There was no sense to the troubles she faced trying
to reach town. "Good Lord," she said aloud, using one
of Lewis's favorite terms, "I could use a little level going."

She limped along the slope of a hogback and heard
the rushing of the small creek. The ground was smooth.
It felt good to her feet. It felt familiar, somehow. The
woods smelled familiar. It was like coming home. In a
way it was. It was like getting back to something that
she'd been away from. She thrust her hand into the
water and brought it out, cupped, and drank deeply.
Again and again she drank. She felt a rise of nausea
but fought it down. Soon she was on her feet, slowly
feeling her way along the trail. The moon rose and
lighted her way. She skirted two more cracks in Mother
Earth. As the backbone of the ridge behind shut out
the terrifying days, the notion took her that it was not
only the feel of the ground, nor the woods' smell, nor
the rolling hills that gave her that queer feeling. It was
the same feeling as in the aftermath of the flood when
she and Chief Red Hair had stood alone, except for her
papoose. She was alive. She was at the edge of the town.
She knew that the glow from the place closest in her
line of vision came from the live candles in Chief Red
Hair's lodge.

Things had not changed much. Six years ago she'd
been obliged to Chief Red Hair, and she still was. He
was sending her boys to school. And they'd taken to
spelling books and cropped hair like a bear took to sugar.
She wondered if she'd ever be of much use to the boys
again. She had set so much store by reading and writing
like the whites. But now the boys had changed. They
were not so pleased to have her hands on them anymore.
Her lips quivered. She set her jaws together, hard, and
pulled her cheeks in tightly against her teeth. The muscles at the corners of her mouth made knots and pulled
her lips out straight.

But then, she was not bad off. Charbonneau was not
home to badger her. Chief Red Hair kept her supplied
with meat and skins. Nothing was so bad. She had
moved ahead on her trail of life, that was all.

She eased her feet along the ground. The moon rose
and lighted her way. She went around to the back of
General Clark's home. The door opened. Old Rose's eyes

were wide. "Oh, child, what's the matter with your leg? Come in here to the kitchen."

Sacajawea limped in. Rose, her hands running over the swollen ankle, her fat cheeks fluffing in and out, reassured herself that the bone was not broken. She wrapped the ankle in cool, damp cloths.

A kind of pleasant stupor was stealing over Sacajawea as she sat by the kitchen hearth. She was placed on a pallet beside the hearth. She slept and dreamed that Miss Judy held one new papoose after another in her arms. No celebration was held for one papoose, however, as it was a girl, a thing to be cherished, but not as important as a boy.

For the next several days, Sacajawea's thoughts moved about, but she did not. She seemed drawn to the pallet and lay on it, motionless as a stone. She took no note of the lapse of time. She knew when anyone besides Rose entered the kitchen. She could understand most of what was said, but she could not answer. To open her mouth and move her limbs was nearly impossible. Miss Judy and Chief Red Hair appeared in the kitchen once or twice a day. They whispered above her.

"It is well that Rose heard her at the back door that night."

"Yes, she might have been dead next morning. I wonder what she went through to get here?"

"The rumblings and quaking ground were enough to frighten her out of her wits, alone, way out there in that desolate cabin. Primitives are slaves to their environment."

On the third day, she was better, on the fourth she could speak, move, rise, and turn on the pallet. Rose brought her gruel and dry toast, which she ate with relish and felt stronger for it. On a chair beside the pallet were all her things, clean and dry. The traces of mud were removed from her tunic, the creases left by the rain smoothed out, and the bottom sewn with fringe. It was quite fine. Her moccasins were cleaned and softened. After a weary process she dressed herself. The tunic hung loose, but she pulled it tight at the waist with a leather sash and smoothed out her braids. Then her nose noticed the fragrance of new bread. Rose was baking.

"Ah, this here morning when another earth tremor shook us all from our beds, you don't notice a thing, child. Now you is dressed." She smiled. "Come sit in the rocking chair." Rose bustled about, looking at Sacajawea from the corner of her eye every once in a while. She took the loaves from the stone oven. There were more tremors during the day; dishes rattled, and pots slid from their hooks.

"I can help cut up the potatoes," offered Sacajawea, as Rose brought out a pan of them.

"You ought to rest, child."

"But I must do something," pleaded Sacajawea. "Let me have them."

Rose consented and brought a clean scrap of muslin to spread over her tunic. "Lest you soil it."

When the potatoes were pared, Sacajawea asked where Chief Red Hair was that day.

"Gone to fetch the children. They ought to be back soon."

"Children?" asked Sacajawea.

"Yes, ma'am. The boys from those schools in town."

Then they came in by the kitchen door. Clark had Baptiste by the hand, and with the other he shoved Tess into the room.

"Janey, I've brought you a surprise. I hope you're strong enough to stand the chatter from these two. Schools are closed early so that Mr. Welch can have the chimney repaired on his main building. Father Neil said he no longer had control over the boys and sent them to parents or guardians until after the holidays."

"The noise of a chimney falling woke everyone. We thought the sleeping room had split apart," laughed Baptiste.

"A brown bear wandered into the yard around Father Neil's quarters," said Tess, edging closer to Sacajawea. "He was looking for a place to hide from the ground grumblings. But I was not scared."

Sacajawea nodded her head, her eyes wide to show she knew how the bear himself felt—afraid.

Baptiste said, "Mr. Honoré, who keeps our records and gets our wash done, told us to get up and look at the school. Bricks were all over the yard from the chimney. Then he took us to his parlor and showed on a slate how there was a shifting within the earth. When this shifting settles down, everything will be quiet again."

"I was not scared when the candles went out and my cot bumped the wall," bragged Tess, his thumbs stuck under his belt. "I closed my eyes, and it felt like I was in a canoe going through white water."

"Come here, Tess, let's see who is the taller," said Clark. The boys stood with their heels to the kitchen wall and let Clark make a mark with charcoal above their heads. "Well, Pomp," Clark coughed, "I do believe Tess is eating more meat. He's the taller."

"But I learn more at my school," insisted Baptiste.

"What do you know?" asked Tess. *"Rien du tout."* He spoke French, the language he learned in school.

"Yes, tell your mother what you've learned," said Clark, sitting down beside the hearth with a cup of tea in his hand.

"I know what is the shape of the earth."

"What?" asked Sacajawea. "All sensible persons know it is about the shape of Rose's pancake, round and flat and smooth except for the mountains on top. The sky— why it is all over just like if that kettle were turned over the pancake."

"Do we live on the inside or the outside?" asked Rose.

"We live on top of the pancake, which is under the kettle sky. That kettle sky covers us all over just like Miss Judy's parasol," said Sacajawea.

"Under there we would all smother," said Baptiste, wrinkling his nose.

"Well, take my strainer instead of the kettle then," said Rose.

"No, the earth is round, and we live on the outside," said Baptiste.

"Good boy," whispered Clark, grinning.

"All round? Where did you get that foolish thought?" said Rose.

"I learned it in my geography. Now, this big gourd hanging by the door—"

"Don't you take that gourd!" cried Rose. "I keeps my best sage and herbs in that there gourd. Why don't you experiment with that nice round pumpkin over there on the table. But don't go bustin' it."

"I won't. I'll just stick this pin in here on the top, and we'll pretend that's you."

"That's pretty thin for me. It'd better be your mammy."

"Then I'll stick another pin near the bottom, and that is a black man in Africa—like old York, a long time ago. Now I'll light this candle."

"Who's that, the light of the Lord?" asked Rose.

"That is the sun. Now, the earth moves slowly up to the sun, and it gets lighter and lighter until it's daylight."

"Don't you drop that even if it is getting lighter," said Rose, her brown eyes wide.

"Then it moves around until the earth gets right under the sun. That's noon—dinnertime at school."

"Careful, now, or there won't be a dinnertime."

"Then it goes around, and it keeps getting darker on your side until it gets here and it's night for you."

"I'm standing all alone in the dark?" asked Sacajawea, marveling at her son and his knowledge—or foolishness.

"But look at the man, old York, in Africa—he is in the daylight. Then the earth moves around again, and you are again in the daylight. Now, all this time the sun has stood still, and the earth has been moving."

"I think you should put the pumpkin down and stop this moving foolishness. You ask me to believe that nonsense?"

"It is true. Mr. Welch said so."

"You expect me to believe that I live on a slippery yellow ball that goes sailing round and round with my head now up and now down? You can't fool this old squaw that is your mother. You better go to York on the other side of that pumpkin. See if he will listen. I'm no ignorant, uncivilized savage that knows nothing."

Miss Judy had come in, and she began to dance around the kitchen, giggling to herself. Clark guffawed twice, then stopped when Baptiste looked crosswise at him.

"*Umbea*, don't you understand it?" Baptiste asked Sacajawea. "You have lots of imagination."

"*Ai*, I do. But I have sense enough to know that if I

was like that pin, hanging on the side of that pumpkin,
I'd just fall off and break every single rib in my body,
and when the world turned over, I'd just pitch headfirst
to the who-knows-where, and then crack my head clear
open, and when I get around again to this side, I'd fall
over backward and break my neck."

"But, *Umbea*, the pin does not fall out."

Tess began to laugh and stomp his feet on the floor.

"You are a foolish child, my son. Foolish! That pin
is sharpened down to a point and stuck in the earth,
but am I sharpened down to a point? Look at me and
say so. Now, if that was the case I'd stand right here
and you'd starve to death. If what you said was so, I'd
be afraid to go to bed at night—afraid I'd roll off to
nowhere. And besides me, what would happen to the
soup kettle, the water pails, and the woodpiles? What—
wake up in the morning and find everything spilled
and gone way down to nowhere? Uuuhh, not me!"

"But, *Umbea*, Mr. Welch says it is just as if there
were a great strong man in the center of the earth that
holds the ropes that you are hitched to, and the same
with the water buckets, and—"

"Now stop that right away! That nonsense is like
telling lies. You can hear Chief Red Hair laughing at
you, and Tess is stomping his feet, and Miss Judy is
making fun by dancing around you. Suppose there was
ropes hitched onto things, wouldn't the water get out
anyway—you just can't hitch water to anything, son.
You just can't. And I know there are no ropes tied to
me."

Rose rolled her dark eyes and nodded her head,
agreeing with Sacajawea.

"I didn't say there were ropes hitched to you." Baptiste flung his arms out toward his mother. Then he
said slowly, "I said it was only as if there were, and
you are not really trying to learn, and I do not think I
like you anymore, because you don't believe what I'm
trying to teach you. You'd rather be an ignorant
squaw."

Sacajawea stared at Baptiste. She felt as though a
dirty trick had been played on her and she knew it but
she wasn't sure yet what the trick was.

"There, now, my son, don't mind my ignorance. You

won't, will you? I'm as dull as that old meat ax over there. Certainly the earth is round. It is rounder than the roundest apple that was ever grown on Monsieur Chouteau's apple trees. And it always was, and always will be. I'm the fool if I can't see it. My eyesight hasn't been good lately. Maybe I'm getting old. Can't even stay on my feet. See?" She pushed out her tightly bandaged ankle. "One day you won't have your old *umbea* hanging on to this earth sharp as a pin no more."

"You aren't old and sharp. You're young and round just like the earth, and I'll stick to you even if you don't believe in geography."

"Woof!" shouted Rose. "Look at that pancake just from the oven. Burned to a crisp! That what come of ignorant people like me listening to talk about people way on the other part of the earth that are all black like my old man, Old York, God rest his soul."

Miss Judy's face loosened. "Rose, make us another pancake, and we'll all have tea with it."

"Someone better get Tess some tea or he'll choke," laughed Clark, pointing to Tess, who had stuffed his mouth full of freshly baked bread.

"I certainly will, and I've a mind to swat his snitching hands," sighed Rose. "Lordy, what they going teach in the school next?"

Book Five
LIFE AND DEATH

Henry Brackenridge, an author, statesman, and lawyer from Pittsburgh, wrote in his daily journal that Charbonneau and his wife, "who had accompanied Lewis and Clark to the Pacific,"[1] were along on the same keelboat as he, going up to Fort Manuel in the spring of 1811.

There is no doubt that Charbonneau talked with Brackenridge as he did with Jussome, who was also on Lisa's keelboat. If he told Brackenridge his wife accompanied Lewis and Clark, the assumption is that the woman was Sacajawea. Yet Charbonneau was known to be a braggart and not above a lie or two. If the woman was not Sacajawea, but Otter Woman, she may not have understood all the English words. If she did, she would not have contradicted her man in front of anyone. Jussome would not have bothered to straighten out Brackenridge if the woman was not Sacajawea, but in all probability would have added to Charbonneau's story for his own amusement. However, there are many who believe that this woman was actually Sacajawea going to Fort Manuel with Charbonneau in 1811.

The Missouri Historical Society, Saint Louis, has an unsigned journal, found in 1912, telling about the life at Manuel Lisa's fort on the Missouri River in northern South Dakota during the years 1812 and 1813. The writing in the journal has been established to be the work of a clerk, John C. Luttig, of the Missouri Fur Company.[2]

There were about sixty-five persons living in the fort. Each day Indians brought news of tribal wars and threats of attack on the fort. In this journal, Luttig wrote that Toussaint Charbonneau made wild overstatements of dangers from Indians in order to excite fear among the engagés. Luttig could not understand why Lisa kept Charbonneau on his payroll as an interpreter.

On December 20, 1812, Luttig wrote:

> *This evening the wife of Charbonneau, a Snake squaw died of a putrid fever; she was good and the best woman in the fort, aged about 25 years; she left a fine infant girl.*

In March 1813, the fort was attacked, and the Indians killed many of Lisa's men. Charbonneau quickly escaped and left for Mandan country, leaving his small daughter in the care of an Indian woman belonging to another engagé at Fort Manuel. Some historians think the Indian woman may have been the squaw of Charbonneau's old friend, René Jussome. Many historians believe that this entry in Luttig's diary is about the death of Sacajawea.

Luttig thought that Charbonneau had been among the men killed in the Indian attack, so that when the remaining men and their families were sent downriver to Saint Louis, in June 1813, the baby, Lizette Charbonneau, was sent along. In August 1813, Luttig made an application at the Saint Louis Orphans' Court for appointment of himself as guardian for the children of Toussaint Charbonneau, deceased:

> *Toussaint Charbonneau, a boy, 10 years old*
> *Lizette Charbonneau, a girl, 1 year old*

The girl would be near her brother, Tess, whom Luttig recalled Charbonneau saying was attending a school for young boys in Saint Louis. No one knows why Luttig did not add the name of Jean Baptiste, the eight-year-old son of Charbonneau. Perhaps Luttig did not know that Charbonneau had another son, or Luttig knew that Charbonneau had left Sacajawea in Saint Louis, and she was the mother of Jean Baptiste. In this case Jean Baptiste would not be orphaned.

General Clark was not in Saint Louis in August 1813. When he returned, he heard of the Indian attack on Fort Manuel and some days later crossed Luttig's name off the guardianship papers and wrote his own after Toussaint and Lizette Charbonneau. In this way he kept his promise to care for and educate Charbonneau's children. But he did not make application at the Saint Louis Orphans' Court for appointment as guardian of Jean Baptiste. Thus, some believe that he knew Sacajawea to be alive and living in Saint Louis at this time.

The baby, Lizette, was not heard of again—until perhaps April 23, 1843, in Westport, Missouri. Then a child, Victoire Verifluille, daughter of Joseph Verifluille and Elizabeth Charbonneau, was baptized. Elizabeth Charbonneau may have been the baby girl, Lizette.[3] However, some historians believe that the baby died shortly after coming to Saint Louis, as no further word is heard about her through General Clark.

In the South Dakota Historical Society publication Wi-Yohi for February 1957 there is a reference to a cash accounts book that William Clark kept from May 25, 1825, to June 14, 1826.[4] There are records on one hundred and thirty-two pages, plus both inner endpapers. Of prime importance is the record Clark inscribed on the front cover, telling what happened to the members of the expedition. Clark wrote:

Men on Lewis and Clarks Trip

Capt. Lewis   Dead
    Odoway   Dead
    N. Pryor   at Fort Smith
   R^d Windser   on Sangamah Ills.
    G. Shannon   Lexington Ky.
    R. Fields   near Louisville
    Wm Bratten   near Greenville Ohio
    F. Labieche   St. Louis
    R. Frazier   on Gasconade
Ch. Floyd Dead   Al^r Willard   Mo.
P. Gass Dead   Geo. Drulard   Killed
J. Collins do.   Tous^t Chartono   Mandans
J. Colter do.
P. Cruzate Killed   Se car ja we au   Dead
J. Fields do.   Tousant Charbon   in
S. Goodrich deadead   Werten-
G. Gibson Deadead   burgh, Gy.
T. P. Howard
H. Hall
H. McNeal dead
J. Shields do.
J. Potts Killed

J. B. Le Page dead
J. Tomson Killed
Wm Warmer Vir.
P. Wiser Killed
     Whitehouse
     Warpenton
     Newman

Clark was wrong about listing Pat Gass as dead. He was in Virginia from 1825 to 1828. His listing of "Tous^t Chartono" as being with the Mandans is correct, for old Toussaint Charbonneau was not killed during the attack on Fort Manuel as Luttig believed, but went to the Mandan villages. Also, it was not Toussaint Charbonneau who went to Germany. It was Jean Baptise who visited Württemberg. Therefore, Clark's last entry is wrong.

Although Clark's notations here are not conclusive, they cannot be dismissed lightly. It does not seem justifiable to say, "If Clark is wrong about Gass, and the misnaming of Jean Baptise, then perhaps he is also wrong about Sacajawea." The cases are different. Gass had gone back to Virginia and severed his contacts with the west, but Sacajawea, Charbonneau, and their children were Clark's concern for many years after the expedition. He cared about them and felt a responsibility for them. It is difficult to believe that he would have been wrong about Sacajawea's death.

However, he was in error in his last entry, for it was Jean Baptiste who visited Germany. It is a mystery why he did not write out the name Pompy or Jean Baptiste here.

Dale Morgan, of the Bancroft Library, one of the most competent authorities on Western American history, suggests that Charbonneau only had two children, Jean Baptiste and Lizette, and that Jean Baptiste was sometimes referred to as Toussaint, his father's name. Does this account for the use of both names in General Clark's expenditures as superintendent of Indian affairs for school expenses?[5] Dale Morgan said to me in a discussion of the cash accounts book:

On the basis of this evidence, I submit that the

earlier date of 1812, is the correct date for the death of Sacajawea.

Dr. Merle W. Wells, well-known historian and archivist for the Idaho Historical Society, wrote to me in October 1967:

> A list of the members of the expedition prepared by William Clark around 1825 indicates that the original Sacajawea had died before that time. Clark, of course, could have made a mistake, but that is terribly unlikely.
> Therefore, instead of Charbonneau's sickly squaw, Otter Woman, going to revisit her native country, it may have been Sacajawea who went on the keelboat with Manuel Lisa's party up the Missouri. This is the present belief of many historians.[6]

The diary of William Clark Kennerly, nephew of General Clark, dated 1843, is in the Missouri Historical Society, Saint Louis. In his diary, Kennerly states that Jefferson Clark, the general's youngest son, and Baptiste Charbonneau, son of Sacajawea, went to school at Reverend J. E. Welch's. Kennerly wrote that he remembered both of Baptiste's parents very well and often saw them walking together along the streets of Saint Louis.[7]

Kennerly told Eva Emery Dye, author of The Conquest, a work of historical fiction based on the Lewis and Clark Expedition,[8] that he knew the mother of Baptiste Charbonneau, the woman known as Sacajawea, and she lived in Saint Lewis while Baptiste went to school during the years 1815 to about 1820.[9] While making arrangements for the centennial of the Louisiana Purchase Exposition in 1902 in Saint Louis, Eva Dye wrote this information in a letter to Grace Raymond Hebard at the University of Wyoming, December 18, 1906.[10]

In 1932, Dr. Hebard, professor of political economy at the University of Wyoming, published her book, based on thirty-four years of research about Sacajawea. She claims to have found that Sacajawea left Charbonneau after a family quarrel-and wandered south to live for nearly twenty years among the Comanches in the Oklahoma Territory. Dr. Hebard was the first to rediscover that Duke Paul of Württemberg took Jean Baptiste Charbonneau to Germany in 1823 and returned with him in 1829.[11] However, some of the facts in Hebard's book cannot be verified today. For instance, she has a reference in the book from the Salt Lake City Desert News of October 1, 1856, about a Snake Indian named Baziel and an Elder Isaac Bullock.[12] Nothing can be found in that newspaper about either man.

In December 1924, Dr. Charles A. Eastman, a Sioux Indian and a college graduate, was appointed by the U.S. Department of Indian Affairs to visit the Shoshoni, Hidatsa, and Comanche reservations where Indians might still remember Sacajawea, or know her by tribal tradition, and locate her actual burial place. Dr. Eastman made his report to Washington on March 2, 1925.[13]

Dr. Eastman's informants stated that Sacajawea left Charbonneau after a quarrel about 1822 and went south to a Comanche tribe, where she lived for a number of years. She left the Comanches to search for her firstborn, Jean Baptiste. She found her own people under the leadership of Chief Washakie, at Fort Bridger, Wyoming. Sacajawea lived the remainder of her life on the Wind River Reservation, Fort Washakie, Wyoming, until her death on April 9, 1884. She lived near a son, who called himself Baptiste, and near her sister's son, Shoogan, or Baziel, the latter name given to him by the Mormons. The U.S. Commissioner of Indian Affairs at that time accepted this report and agreed with Dr. Eastman's findings.

If Sacajawea did quarrel and leave home, and Charbonneau and the boys could not find her, they would probably assume she was dead. Baptiste and Toussaint were in school in Saint Louis. They might have seen Clark and told him Sacajawea was gone. Old Charbonneau might have said he thought she was probably dead. With these facts Clark would certainly write "dead" after Sacajawea's name in his 1825–1828 cash accounts book.

It is now known that both Dr. Hebard and Dr. Eastman were incorrect in their belief that Jean Baptiste was
buried at Fort Washakie, Wyoming. Jean Baptiste Charbonneau is buried on the Inskip Ranch on Cow Creek
in Jordan Valley, near the small town of Danner, Oregon, close to the Idaho line.[14]

Who, then, was the man who called himself Baptiste
Charbonneau at Fort Washakie? Could he have been an
intruder, as Dale Morgan believes, or could he have been
the other boy, Toussaint, who was Otter Woman's son?
Neta Frazier believes the latter might just be the case.[15]

History has a way of being lost or misrepresented.
Personal testimony has a way of being slanted or fal-
sified to please the questioner. People die, so statements
cannot be checked. On the other hand, a statement in
print tends to become fact when in truth it may not be
fact at all, but only a myth written down.

It seems that no one will ever know positively Sacajawea's fate. No one knows with certainty the date of
Sacajawea's death.[16] But if she lived longer than December 20, 1812, and the old Comanche and Shoshoni winter tales reflect her later life and travels, she did influence
many of our famous military men, mountain men, traders, trappers, chiefs, and their women. So, for the moment, assume that it was Otter Woman who died at
Manuel Lisa's fort and that the evidence found for Sacajawea's living a long life is inspiration enough to continue her story as if she truly lived until April 9, 1884,
and was buried on the Wind River Reservation, Fort
Washakie, Wyoming. The remainder of this novel is based
upon these interesting Comanche and Shoshoni stories.

CHAPTER

40

Lizette

My little breath, under the willows by the water-side we
*   used to sit,*
And there the yellow cottonwood bird came and sang.
That I remember and therefore I weep.
Under the growing corn we used to sit.
And there the little leaf bird came and sang.
That I remember and therefore I weep.
There on the meadow of yellow flowers we used to walk.
Alas! how long ago that we two walked in that pleasant
*   way.*
Then everything was happy, but alas! how long ago.
There on the meadow of crimson flowers we used to walk.
Oh, my little breath, now I go there alone in sorrow.

MARK VAN DOREN and GARIBALDI M. LAPOLLA, ed., *The World's Best Poems,* "The American Indian—A Lover's Lament," by H. J. Spinden. New York: The World Publishing Co., 1946, pp. 616–17.

On December 24, Sacajawea and the two boys dressed warmly. They strapped saddle blankets to two of the horses that stood close together in the drafty stable behind the cabin. They were going trading at Chouteau's.

Inside the store, Sacajawea traded several pairs of thick-soled moccasins for a small sugar sack of hard candy—a Christmas treat for the boys—a canister of tea, and a sack of dried beans. The boys listened to the rivermen standing around the potbellied stove telling stories of how the land around New Madrid rolled and burst open, shooting water, sand, and black, oily slime into the air during one of the larger earth tremors.

"This here child seen birds frozen with fear so's they couldn't fly," said one old-timer.

On the trail home, the surface was swept with a screaming wind. The trail was broad as it ran through the heart of the city. The air was full of sifted white snow, and the wagon furrows were rapidly filling. The horses panted and struggled as they plodded forward. Through the muffled scream of the storm Sacajawea turned and shouted back at the boys, "Stop there, at the lodge of Chief Red Hair!"

The boys grinned and nodded. Her order needed no explanation. She always had good reasons for her actions. They remembered she had kept aside a small pair of leggings and a small shirt at the store, telling the clerk she did not wish to trade anything for them. They were to be gifts for the two youngest children of Miss Judy and Chief Red Hair. Inside Clark's kitchen she emptied her own sons' half of the hard candy into the sack of dried beans. She tied the cloth sugar sack down tight against the remaining candy. "This is for the older children, Looie and Mary," she said, half to herself.

Tess and Baptiste tethered the horses and stomped snow off their moccasins as they followed Sacajawea through the back door into the kitchen. Sacajawea had dropped the half-filled sugar sack of hard candy on the kitchen table, telling Rose to try a piece before dividing it between the two older children. Beside the sack she laid the neatly folded packages, explaining that they were for the two younger children.

"There are only two children in this here family," said Rose, peering closer into Sacajawea's face. "Has the quake left you addlebrained?"

Sacajawea smiled and took a moment before answering. "Oho, there will be three boys and one girl adding to the laughter and to the crying in this house before long," she said in a prophetic whisper. Then, in a louder voice, she asked, "I wonder where Miss Judy is? She is as affected by chills as the little girl will be. You will have to remember those two are frail. Care for them even more than the others." Now her voice cracked and ended in what sounded like a sob.

"She and Master Clark, they'se taken their horses out somewheres," said Rose. "With this wind a-blowing they'se be back shortly. You stay. Get your thoughts straight. That snow and cold wind is getting you as muddled as some far-seeing sorceress who dreams up happenings so close to the truth that it makes a body's hair stand straight on end."

Sacajawea stepped toward the back door, nodding her head to indicate that the boys, Tess and Baptiste, should prepare to leave. *"Merci.* We go to our lodge before the snow is deep and before I have to sleep in your kitchen once again."

Rose laughed but shook her head and smoothed down her kinky hair as from the window she watched the small boys mount their horse and follow Sacajawea along an invisible white trail. "Watch out for them earth cracks—hear?"

Rose's voice was snatched away by the wind. A pall of white enveloped the figures. Upon them beat a wind of stinging sleet. The snow was getting deeper. Once or twice Sacajawea's horse stumbled, but he did not fall. The words Tess shouted up to Sacajawea were almost lost in the roar of the shrieking wind.

"...helluvatime...riding."

"Not far...up ahead is our lodge," she shouted back, trying to keep the boys as close behind her as possible. Her attention then concentrated on sticking to the back of the horse. Numb though her fingers were, she had to keep them fastened tightly in the frozen mane of the animal. At the cabin she pulled the boys off their horse and sent them inside to start up the fire.

"Got to stable the horses," she yelled, and hurried with the chore.

After a time she was standing before the warmth of the fireplace, and circulation was flooding back into her veins. She endured a half hour of excruciating pain. She had to clench her teeth to keep back the groans that came from her throat as she walked the floor and nursed her hands and fingers.

When the storm moderated enough to let her go out with safety, Sacajawea went to the stable to check on the horses. When she came back she was triumphant. Upon the table she dropped two packages held in the crook of her arm.

"The makings of our Christmas dinner," she announced with a grin. "Chief Red Hair has been here. We just missed each other. He left a supply of meat and hides in the stable and these two tins of plum pudding, a favorite of the white man." She had not noticed the gifts the first time, when she'd put the horses in and been no numbed with cold. "He came to see us while we were at his lodge trying to see him," she repeated.

"Merry Christmas!" shouted Baptiste.

"Aw, let's eat," said Tess. "I'm nearly starved." He snatched a hunk of frozen meat from under Sacajawea's butcher knife.

"Put that down," she said. "You will have your food cooked the way the whites prefer. My boys will grow up civilized and not eat raw meat with blood dripping from their mouths. You are not savage Blackfeet."

That winter and all next spring, Sacajawea had strange dreams in which a spume of whirling, blinding snow clung to everything it touched. The snow was wet and soft. Once she thought she saw Charbonneau with snowshoes heavy with white slush. But each time she saw densely laden spruce boughs brush Otter Woman's face and shower her with little avalanches. Otter Woman's face was white and her voice low, saying, "Oh, my sister, keep my papoose as your own." Then there was no sign of life in the vast whiteness, only a mass of ice and snow. The dreams were always similar. There were more earth tremors that winter.[1]

General Clark brought more meat and hides. The first week in January, Sacajawea sent the boys back to school with him. Then she busied herself making moccasins and leggings and shirts to sell at Chouteau's store for her other needs and the luxury of hard candy.

Soon after his appointment as territorial governor of Missouri, Clark came for a visit.

"You have come to tell me about Charbonneau," said Sacajawea, making a pot of tea and slicing some cold roast venison.

"Well, I have. How could you know?"

"I'm not sure, but I had the feeling."

"And there is this little girl." Clark unwrapped the bundle he held on his lap. Inside was a dark-haired papoose, about a year old.

"Ooo," said Sacajawea, making sucking noises with her mouth. "Where did you find this little owl—on the trail to this lodge?"

Clark handed the papoose to Sacajawea, who rocked her gently. "She is Charbonneau's daughter. Her mother, Otter Woman, died last December. The baby was about four months old then." Clark watched Sacajawea, whose expression changed subtly.[2]

Slowly she stopped the rocking motion. Her dark eyes swam with tears, but she did not let them roll down her cheeks. She was more beautiful than the young woman Clark remembered from the expedition.

Clark's mouth sagged partly open. He blinked against his own tears; then he stood up, scraping the packing crate on the floor. "A man belonging to your people would leap from a cliff before he would cry," he said gruffly.

"But you are not Shoshoni. You are a white chief," Sacajawea said, surprised at the excess of her own feeling.

"The clerk at Lisa's Fort Manuel came to Saint Louis in August with this baby girl and left her at the Orphans' Court. She's been nursed by a squaw living near the barracks. When I found out about her, I put my name on her guardianship papers. I want you to take her. She'll be good company while the boys are at school. Raise her as your own. Otter Woman would have asked that. Teach her to sew and to sing."

"Mon dieu! It cannot be. Yet I know it is. Otter Woman is not coming back." She began shivering. "Where is Charbonneau?" she asked as if afraid to say his name aloud.

The baby cried. Sacajawea rocked her to and fro.

Clark paused and kicked at the crate. "Luttig, the clerk, says he went out with a party of Northwesters and never came back. He suspects he was killed by the Sioux during one of their attacks. It's been pretty bad up in the Missouri." Clark's head was lowered.

"It is hard to believe." She shook her head. "Everybody is dead. All those we knew; never to see them again."

"I am so glad you did not go up the Missouri," said Clark, "that I don't even care if you let your tears roll down your face. We will both miss that old rascal Charbonneau."

"I will keep her." She hugged the baby eagerly, while anxiety and grief fought in her heart. She knew that any moment now she might let the tears slide down her cheeks. She felt, deep inside, that where the frail Otter Woman had succumbed, so also had her tough, hardy man. Their life's trail had ended.

When Clark tried to speak, his voice broke. "Janey—little Janey. You're safe. Thank God, I still have you."

The tears brimmed over. Then, somehow, she was weeping in his arms. A stress of emotion had swept her into his arms. Now she drew away from him shyly, peeling the blanket from the baby. The maturity of her own experiences asserted itself.

"Does this papoose have a name?" She was deeply moved by the presence of Clark and his admission of fondness for her; she was also embarrassed by the display of so much sentiment.

"The baby is called Lizette." Clark could not take his eyes from her as she held the sleeping papoose lovingly in her arms. It seemed that a bird sang in his heart the gladness he had tried to express. He saw her primitive beauty vivid as a flame. He was now her sole protector. He thought her rocking movements a miracle of supple lightness. Her body had the swelling roundness of vital youth, and her eyes were alive with the eagerness that time dulls in most faces. They spoke little now, but drank tea from hot granite-ware mugs. Clark allowed his feelings no more expression. Love for her ran through his veins like old wine. He knew she lived in a world primeval. Would she waken to real love one day, or more disillusion? Now there was only wonder at the world in her soft eyes, he thought.

"Little Lizette," she said. She stopped rocking only after she had drunk her tea.

Clark held out his hand to say good-bye.

She gave him a quick, shy little nod, turned without shaking hands, and moved outside, carrying the baby under one arm. She took up the reins of his horse and handed them over to him.

All through the remainder of that day, happiness and grief flooded her heart. She was not ashamed. She would tell Tess about his mother, and she would continue to care for her boys. She would tell the boys the good things about their father. A man goes his own way. In a country of strong men, he could stand shoulder-high to most and command the admiration of friend and foe alike, even when under their breath they called him an old rascal.

Sacajawea sang like a lark in springtime while caring for the yearling girl. Baptiste and Tess taught her to take her first steps, and each vied with the other in showing off to make her laugh.

Sacajawea carried the baby in a small red-wool blanket she slung over her back when she rode into town to trade at Chouteau's.

Once Monsieur Chouteau came out of the little balcony office at the rear and peered at the child at her back.

"What is this?" he said. "Is it the latest half-breed child that Bill Clark has appointed himself guardian for?"

"*Ai*," said Sacajawea, shifting so that she could look at Chouteau. "I am the mother of this Kloochman."

"And you speak in the west coast jargon, too? Remarkable. Bright eyes. They watch me wherever I move. Bill Clark takes a liking to Indian kids. He's educating your son and another half-breed, I hear."

"*Ai*," said Sacajawea proudly. "I am mother of both boys."

"You don't say? Mother of all the kids Clark fancies, eh? Say"—he rolled a cigarette with one hand—"I recall another squaw that used to come around here with you. She sat outside against the post and pretended to be asleep, but she watched people." Chouteau laughed and his deep-set eyes crinkled at the corners. He gave Sacajawea a small paper bag of hard peppermints.

She shook her head no. She had nothing more with which to pay for the candy.

"No, no, keep it. It is a present for Kloochman, the Little Woman," said Chouteau.

"Thank you," said Sacajawea. Her heart became large toward him, and she felt it important that she pay for the gift of candy somehow. She bent her head, pulled off her beaded leather headband, and held it out to him.

"Why, thank you." His eyes flashed. "But this beadwork does not look Shoshoni to me."

She was startled by his remark. "You know that I come from the Land of the Shining Mountains?"

"Oh, yes, Bill Clark told me how you found your family there and helped him get a good supply of horses to ride overland. It's remarkable. Even Clark said to me, 'She's quite a woman.'"

"*Merci*," said Sacajawea, a little flustered by the thought that Chief Red Hair would discuss her with this carefully dressed, easy-mannered Frenchman.

"Please tell me where you learned to make designs like this?" He held up her headband.

"My people do not have beads to sew with, only quills and teeth and shells. I get beads here. I make the designs. No tribe's designs—mine. It is a mixture of what I learned from the People, the Minnetarees, and Miss Judy." She collected her package of bacon and sugar and coffee and shuffled toward the door. She could hear Chouteau chuckling to himself. Then she heard the clerk speak in a soft voice to Chouteau.

"Imagine what General Clark would say if he knew that his wife's influence on the bead design of that squaw was rated with the influence of several Indian tribes. It is rich, isn't it?"

* * *

Then during the Month of Picking Blackberries, Lizette slept fitfully and began to cough. Sacajawea rocked gently with the baby night after night, trying to soothe her restlessness. The baby now cried too easily and clung to Sacajawea for security.

"She is so frail," said Miss Judy one morning; she had brought several of little Looie's outgrown dresses for Lizette. "Oh, this poor brown baby. She will not see another summer sun if she does not stop that coughing."

"Will you take her to Dr. Saugrain? Please?" asked Sacajawea.

"I will see if he will come here. I will ride to him this afternoon," promised Miss Judy.

The doctor was not home. He was off on a trip visiting with his friend John Audubon in Kentucky. He never came to see Lizette when she needed him.

Sacajawea did all she knew to do. She boiled sassafras tea and spooned it through the baby's fevered lips. She bathed the thin little face with tepid water. "Little Woman, Little Woman, your eyes make you look like an owl, they grow so large and your face stays so small," she crooned.

In December there was a week of days when every morning Sacajawea had to carry baskets of dried grasses from a pile behind the cabin to the horses. The snow was too deep for them to forage on their own. They stood patiently waiting in their crude stable of oak boards.

The winter air was dry and crisp, and Lizette seemed better able to breathe. Sacajawea made cornmeal mush and watered it down for the child. In the evenings she held a stone on her knees and with a smaller one cracked hickory nuts for Lizette. The child followed Sacajawea everywhere like a shadow. Sacajawea fixed one of the old packing crates so that Lizette could stand upon it and watch the dishes being washed. Sometimes Lizette helped dry them on the muslin toweling Miss Judy had brought. "Good Little Woman," crooned Sacajawea happily.

One morning she bundled Lizette into warm clothing and tied her on the back of the gentlest horse so that she could watch Sacajawea chip stove wood and stack it in the rick by the door. By noon Lizette was tired

and coughing. She refused to eat more watery mush.
While she slept, Sacajawea dug a bushel of potatoes she
had buried below the frost line in October, and brought
them into the house. A light snow was falling, and she
tucked the red-wool blanket more tightly around the
wan little body. "Little Woman needs Father Sun," Sacajawea said aloud. She took three arrows, the bow, and
a knife and went about a mile along the creek, following
deer tracks. She sighted the animal, shot it in the neck,
and saw it fall, jump up, and run. About ten minutes
later, she got her second shot at the weakening animal
and killed it. It was big, and she skinned it late that
afternoon.

The next day, she gently placed a wet poultice of
boiled onions and raw venison liver on Lizette's chest
and bound it with a warmed flannel cloth. The child
coughed hard, then slept fitfully, sweating under the
red-wool blanket. The sweating pleased Sacajawea. It
meant the fever was broken and the child was getting
better. She went back to the deer carcass and carried
several of the better cuts home, tied to the back of a
horse.

The following morning Lizette slept late, and Sacajawea went for more venison before other animals
found an easy meal. When she returned, she called to
Lizette, "Little Woman, Little Woman, see what I have
brought you—the tender tongue." The child did not
stir. Sacajawea went to the corner opposite her bed,
where Clark had built another bed, barely two feet wide,
but nearer the fireplace. The child's feet, a grayish brown
color, hung over the edge. Sacajawea lifted them gently
back under the blanket. She cried out in surprise. The
child's feet were cold, dead cold. There was no life in
the little body. "Poor Little Woman. Poor Little Woman,"
she crooned.

Sacajawea did the best thing she knew to do. She
bathed the cold body in warm water and dressed it in
Looie's white dress. She slipped small beaded moccasins
on the little feet. She painted the part in Lizette's neatly
combed hair red. She painted the sunken cheeks with
vermilion. Sacajawea looked through her folded robes
and blankets until she found a small quilled fawnskin
robe. She felt the designs around the edge, which were

intricate, intimate circles, suns, and triangular birds. She had used this robe her mother had made only on special occasions to wrap Pomp. As she wrapped Lizette's body, she thought of the day she was given this robe by the kind Shoshoni woman. She turned over the packing crate Lizette had stood upon and eased the bundle into the crate.

Sacajawea dug in the ground at the back of the cabin under a tall, scraggly red cedar. It took her two days. The ground was hard on the surface and wet clay below. Snow blew into the hole. When the hole was the right size, she wrapped a blanket around herself, got a horse ready, and went to tell Chief Red Hair. She was going to bury Otter Woman's girl-child in the way of the white mothers Otter Woman had so admired.

Sacajawea found that Dr. Saugrain was having supper with the Clarks. He decided to follow his host and hostess to the pitiful squaw's cabin. He was a little man, wrinkled, dried up, and soured, and even on his horse he looked old and frail. But when he spoke there was something overpowering in his manner, something knowledgeable in his eyes. Sacajawea felt intimidated by his belated examination of the dead child. He shook his head. "Filthy stuff," he muttered, dabbing at the bright red cheeks with his immaculate handkerchief. "Nothing could have been done for this infant. She must have contracted consumption from her mother—or some close relative—before she was even sent downriver. Her short life was in a decline before it began." He rewrapped the body, sniffing distastefully at the soft skin robe, and he pushed the bundle back into the box. He turned to Sacajawea, who, standing apart from Chief Red Hair and Miss Judy, felt like an outsider in her own lodge. "Best clean out this place thoroughly. Burn the baby's clothes and bedding. Sprinkle wet tea leaves on the floor before sweeping. Then burn them at once."

Governor Clark buried the baby under the red cedar, swearing once as the short needles prickled his face. He bowed his head and said the Lord's Prayer. Miss Judy put a flat gray shale stone at the head of the mounded grave. Her tears spilled on the shale, making dark circles.

Dr. Saugrain would not drink the hot tea Sacajawea

prepared, but he sat haughtily on his horse until Governor Clark and Miss Judy came out of the cabin. "My only hope is that you did not breathe that overly contaminated air too long or too deeply," he said, riding off down the trail without looking back to see Sacajawea standing alone in the doorframe, tears streaming down her face.

School

Jan. 22, 1820. No. of vou.—118. Payments, to whom made—J. E. Welch. Nature of disbursements—for two quarters' tuition of J. B. Charboneau, a half Indian boy, and firewood and ink. Amount—$16.37½.

March 31. L. T. Honoré. For boarding, lodging, and washing of J. B. Charboneau, a half Indian, from 1st January to 31st March, 1820. Amount—$45.00

April 1. J. and G. H. Kennerly. For one Roman History for Charboneau, a half Indian, $1.50; one pair of shoes for ditto, $2.25; two pair of socks for ditto, $1.50 (one Scott's lessons for ditto, $1.50; one dictionary for ditto, $1.50; one hat for ditto, $4.00; four yards of cloth for ditto, $10.00;)—one ciphering book, $1.00; one slate and pencils, 62 cents for Charboneau.

April 11. J. E. Welch. For one quarter's tuition of J. B. Charboneau, a half Indian boy, including fuel and ink. Amount, $8.37½.

May 17. F. Neil. For one quarter's tuition of Toussant Charbonneau, a half Indian boy. Amount—$12.00.

June 30. L. T. Honoré. For board and lodging and washing of J. B. Charboneau, a half Indian boy, from 1st April to 30th June. Amount—$45.00.

October 1. L. T. Honoré. Nature of the disbursements—For boarding, lodging and washing of J. B. Charboneau, from 1st July to 30th September, 1820, at $15.00 per month. Amount—$45.00.

December 31. (Voucher) 233 (Paid to) L. T. Honoré,

for boarding, washing, and lodging from 1st October, to 31st December. For J. B. Charboneau, a half Indian, $25.00.

GENERAL WILLIÁM CLARK, *Abstract of Expenditures as Superintendent of Indian Affairs, 1822.* Washington, D. C.: American State Papers, Class II, vol. II, no. 5, 1834, p. 289.

During the Christmas holidays, the boys, home for a week from their school, grieved with Sacajawea over the loss of their small sister. Baptiste, particularly, stood silently in the back of the cabin staring at the small brown mound of earth covered only with a skiff of snow.

Both boys spoke in French, the language then taught in the schools of Saint Louis.

"*Pauvre petite fille*," sighed Baptiste.

"You get my goat," scolded Tess. "You're weak, mourning with the squaw who is our mother. You'll bog down on the trail. A man has to have guts," he grumbled. "A papoose is not worth all that sadness. *Jésus!*" He spat on the floor.

During January the boys watched the flatboats dodge floating cakes of ice on the Mississippi. They went duck-hunting where the palatial Planters' House was to be built later. Nothing could have prevented them from hunting, fishing, trapping, and generally learning about the land when they had days off from school. Tess became possessed when he saw other boys with a single-shot rifle. By the time he was ten years old he had sold enough snowshoe rabbit hides at Chouteau's to own a rifle himself. He and his friends would pick off cottontail and snowshoe rabbits, an occasional duck, and sometimes a grouse, which they sold at Chouteau's, or to the Union Hotel for those who liked to eat wild game in the city.

Other times the boys brought home their small game to broil on sticks over the fire Sacajawea built at the side of her cabin. When the larger game failed, they netted bullfrogs, or caught them on a fish hook baited with a scrap of red flannel. They hacked off the bullfrogs' legs and roasted them. The boys took an old frying pan from Sacajawea's cupboard, and on Friday afternoons they would go to their hideout, where they had supplies cached. They would fry up a panful of chubs or a big, intricately boned catfish. They spent one whole Saturday wading in the shallow yellow water, hunting clams in the sandy bottom. They boiled a saltless, emetic chowder and bravely ate it. Baptiste found a distorted

little knob of a pearl in a clam that he smashed open
on a rock, and had a dream of instant fortune.

Once in a while, a minor bonanza did come their
way. During the war of 1812 the peaceful citizens of
Saint Louis were stirred to nervous tension. A battalion
of soldiers was organized and quartered at Fort Bellefontaine, where the old stone towers and fortresses were
refitted. Most of the voyageurs and *engagés* stayed in
Saint Louis, afraid to go out into the wilderness with
the Indians skulking for whites. "Always the savages
lie thick as copper snakes in the woods around us," they
said. "The whites are outnumbered two to one, maybe
more." They all believed this statement.

With the trappers staying in town, the boys found
that the price of furs rose until a good slough muskrat
brought three dollars from *engagés* at Chouteau's. The
river rats were smaller and less valuable, but more
within their reach, and the traps that in summer were
used for gophers, they used for muskrats quite as well.
From the time Baptiste was nine until he was nearly
twelve, he and his brother trapped the river with a good
deal of persistence. And when they bundled up their
take one spring they had fifteen muskrats, nine ermine,
and a beaver that they had skinned closed; they had
not opened it up by cutting through the belly, which
would have rendered it worth next to nothing.

The boys made small change by picking wild cherries, blackberries, gooseberries, wild raspberries, currants, or persimmons for home-canning housewives.
Picking gooseberries at ten cents a quart, even when
the berries hang on the underside of the prickly stems
in heavy rows, is not a way to get rich. The meagerness
of their total earning power was an analogue of the way
their mother worked and the rewards she got. There
were afternoons when the boys would crawl under the
plank sidewalk in front of the hotel and search among
the dirt and papers and old tobacco cuds for coins that
had fallen through the cracks.

The discipline at school was not very rigid for either
boy. At Father Neil's the boys were allowed to smoke
at any and all times, and the smoke from the black
cigars the students bought just outside the grounds was
often so thick that one could hardly see across the room.

On weekends the boys liked to see who had learned to inhale deepest. Tobacco for Tess was a step in the progress of education, as was the hard liquor served with meals to the students at William and Mary College in the days when General Clark attended that institution.

The good Catholic brothers at Father Neil's school taught a kindly companionship combined with a certain manliness that would stand the boys in good stead when battling with the rough frontier life they faced. The congenial brothers made frequent trips with their students to all places of note in the vicinity. Tess was much interested in visiting a wonderful cave with subterranean vaults and chasms where they heard the roaring of water. No one ever found the source of the water. But they found the cave infested with thousands of bats. Tess often went with other boys to catch the bats, carrying them in a bag and turning them loose in the school dormitory. This always gave any new boy a little excitement and caused him to forget his homesickness for a time.

Baptiste explained to his mother during one Easter holiday, "I cannot always tell if I am Indian or white. I was taught to endure pain. I can put a hot stone on my flesh and not cry out. I can sit in the icy river and not jump out right away. But it is hard for me to study. This makes me Indian. The white boys are not made to endure pain, and they seem to study easier. But I can make my bed, wash my clothes, and keep my room neat. This makes me white. I can catch more frogs, snare more rabbits than the white boys, but I can sleep as easily in a soft bed as between two buffalo robes. I can eat with a fork and a spoon and keep my fingers dry, or I can use my fingers and wipe them dry in my hair."

"To be strong against hardships is good, my son. You will know the ways of the whites and be liked by them. You will know the ways of the Indians and be liked by them. In this way you can help the understanding between two nations, whites and Indians."

Baptiste thought about the time when he was a small boy in the woods. He looked back and saw his life stretching like a cord behind him. And the brightest piece was when he ran free in the woods. It had a glory

that school did not. He dug into his leather bag and
found his knife, its blade well protected by the tallow
he had rubbed on it. He tested the blade with his thumb.

"You can use my oilstone," said Sacajawea.

He sat before the fireplace whetting his knife on his
mother's stone. "Then sometimes I believe the Indian
in me is dying," he said. "I think I have poor eyesight
and a limited sense of smell, just like the whites."

Quietly Sacajawea talked to her son. "I taught you
to speak with a straight tongue. I showed you right and
wrong. I bound you to my heart with strong new vines.
Now these vines have rotted and they tear apart to let
you stay at the white man's school so that you can
become a man. This is a new way of living where there
are whites coming to live on the land that once belonged
to Indians.

"Your father taught you game signs and animal habits and where to find them. He taught you to hunt and
shoot a straight arrow. You give me no shame as a
hunter or trapper. I have told myself on winter days
that when I am old, when my bones creak, my son will
keep me in bear's oil and venison. When the ashes of
life cool, you will kindle the fire to warm my old age."

Baptiste heard his mother and was deeply moved.

"My mother," he said in French, "I would rather
follow my father into the woods and be a trapper or an
interpreter. I can learn the languages of the different
tribes easily. Their language is much easier than those
the white teachers put in books for me to write and
speak. The French of my father is easier than the French
of a textbook."

Sacajawea looked at him with sternness and pity for
many minutes. "Pomp," she said, purposely using his
baby name, "you were born under unusual circumstances. The very first clothes upon your back were the
soft blanket clothes of the white man. You were not
dried with soft doeskin, but with white cloth. You were
not wrapped in rabbit fur, but in a woolen robe. You
did not have the power of animals rubbed into you, so
you will never develop the instincts necessary for survival. That is why the Indian in you has died. Can you
smell a deer upwind? Or count the tailfeathers of an
eagle in flight?

"No."

"Your ancestors could. The People still can. After you are in school more time, you will enjoy it. It will be easier. There is much white blood in your heart. It has been planned that way. Your father was half-white. He understood the whites and the Indians, but he did not really care about either, only himself. You will never be a small man like that. The Great Spirit has put you in the stream of life with Chief Red Hair, so you must do what comes into your life and do it well. Do it in the manner of a chief. A chief must be strong, kind, honest, and wise like Chief Red Hair. Be polite without groveling. If you are ever afraid of anything, do not deny it, but behave as if you feared nothing."

The boy's mouth was stopped. He could say nothing, only look at his mother, whom he had always loved. He knew as well as if she had come out and spoken the truth that his mother had loved Governor Clark when they had been together on the western trail so many years before. She respected him, but she had never respected, or really loved, his father. His mother wanted him to attend school because it was Governor Clark's desire.

Sacajawea's life moved along in this settled and quiet routine. She often discussed the Indians' problems with Governor Clark, who was worried about his charges. The Indians were adopting the white man's evils, not his good qualities. The Indians' spirit was being subdued; their lands were being taken away; their language, which ran untroubled as a spring brook, was decaying into hoglike grunts; their stalwart men were being corrupted by the firewater of the greedy trader; their women were being diseased by filthy white men.

"Janey," Clark said to her, "the Indians need a friend they will listen to and trust. Somehow your people have escaped all this corruption and disease because we have not been able to get a fort established for any length of time near them. Maybe your Great Spirit has seen a way to keep them from losing their souls by keeping them in their homes in the Shining Mountains, even though they suffer a bit from hunger. Isn't that better than losing dignity?"

The new thought startled her. It was certainly a
strange way to consider the People's misery. Then she
realized that she, too, had found it a struggle to adjust
her ways to those of the whites. She still would rather
do her cooking outside over an open fire than in the
fireplace. She could see that her boys were going through
a time of adjustment, but for them the path was smoother
through reading the talking books and living with white
boys at school. She wondered if the People would ever
need to adjust to these new ways, or if they would live
forever in the way their fathers had.

"There is a boat in the water that has no sails and
no oars, but it moves," bragged Tess. "I have seen it."
"No," said Sacajawea, "you are telling me this for a
joke. It cannot be!"
"It's true!" shouted the boys together.
"You will see," said Tess. "It is a steamboat. You
have seen the steam rise when the water boils for soup?
Mon dieu, that is the power."
Sacajawea shook her head; she did not understand.
"It is strong when it is shut up; it makes a lid dance,"
Baptiste tried to explain. "Sometimes the lid pops off,
and the water foams out of the kettle. That is power,
like a man working. Man has harnessed the steam like
a horse and makes it work for him. It pulls the boat on
the river."
"That takes much thinking," said Sacajawea skeptically.
Early the next morning, they followed the crowd to
the levee. Others also wanted to see this new wonder,
the steamboat. It was true—there were no sails, no
oarsmen bending their backs, no cordellers. It was a
magic boat that sailed alone by an unseen hand. People
danced and sang. They all could see it with their own
eyes, yet it was unbelievable. Sacajawea shared with
the white men something that was new to all. It seemed
to her that she was pulled closer to them from this
instant on. She looked at the ship. "White man's magic,"
she said softly, feeling that it affected her as much as
any of those standing around her. She joined in the
shouting: "Hurrah for the steamship!"
Ten days later, Tess witnessed a duel between

Thomas Benton and Charles Lucas. Lucas, who lived on Main Street, exchanged angry words with Benton in court. Benton was a large man of powerful build. He had the dignity of a great statesman and orator. Lucas did not like him because of that quality. Their dislike for one another smoldered and waited for any small thing to cause it to flare. It flared at the polls on election day, August 4, 1817, because Lucas contemptuously asked if Benton had paid his tax in time to entitle him to vote. This small comment was justification enough to these men for a duel.

They met on the morning of August 12, 1817, on Bloody Island. Tess was there with some schoolmates to witness the fun. Each man fired one shot; Lucas was wounded in the neck, while Benton received a slight contusion below the knee. Benton would not let the matter rest. He said he expected Lucas to meet him again as soon as his neck wound healed.

Tess followed Benton to his boat and taunted, "*Zut*, you fight like a squaw. I bet you couldn't hit poor old Lucas again if you stood only ten feet apart! Does that scratch on your leg pain much?"

Benton pulled up one of the boat's oars and threw it at Tess, which only made Tess laugh more.

Tess and his friends huddled together several times after classes in the next few weeks. Then, their scheme well in hand, they sent a messenger to Lucas's home on the morning of September 27, asking for a second duel.

Most of Father Neil's students waited several hours for the big scene, which they viewed with all the frivolity of children at a circus. Never once did it cross these young boys' minds that this duel would be considered one of the most regrettable ever fought in Saint Louis. The two men met once again on Bloody Island and took their positions, ten feet apart.

The men fired at the same time, and Benton's ball penetrated Lucas's heart. Lucas lived a half hour longer—not long enough to get him off the island, across the Mississippi, to Saint Louis.[1]

Tess took great delight in telling Baptiste the gory details of Lucas's fatal wound the following weekend.

"Scare Bleu! Blood all over. I did not know a body held so much."

As he spoke, he saw Baptiste's and Sacajawea's shining brown eyes intent upon him. His heart seemed to swell, and he felt important. So he added more to the story, with expressions of horror on his face, aiding his words with the movements of his hands. He said that it had rained on the island and Lucas's powder became wet, but that Benton had protected his powder by keeping it in his armpit until it was time to be tamped down the barrel. That was why he had won. That was why he had been able to shoot right into the heart of Lucas.

The mood of the story was shattered as the door of the cabin was thrown open. In stalked a short, heavyset man whose face was framed in a matted, graying beard. His hair was uncombed, and his face was lined and drawn. The old man was followed by a young, plain-looking Indian girl. Her skin was smooth, her forehead broad, her nose fine, her mouth straight, and when she walked she did not bounce overly much. Her flesh was as rigid and solid as stone. She was perhaps fifteen summers old.

Startled, Sacajawea jumped to her feet and started toward them. But she drew back, quivering. "Charbonneau! My man!" she blurted out, frightened by the appearance of a man believed dead.

"Horreurs," laughed Charbonneau, "you look like you have seen a ghost. You ain't happy to see me?" He had a devilish grin as he approached her. "Come, give me nice big kiss for welcome home."

Sacajawea could not speak. She just stood staring at the apparition. Her shoulders dropped and her mouth pursed as though she were trying to hold herself together.

Charbonneau looked from one boy to the other as their faces flushed under his scrutiny. *"Sacrée Marie,"* he muttered. Time had slipped by him, he could see that easily enough now. He faced the older boy.

"I am your papa, Little Tess." He stretched his greasy hand out to shake. "I come back."

Tess shook hands with his father. He had no hard feelings toward him and remembered the fun of the old days, trapping for beaver.

Baptiste, too, timidly extended his hand.

Finding himself welcome, Charbonneau nodded to the woman in the doorway. "This is my new squaw. She's called Eagle. She's Minnetaree, niece of Kakoakis. Remember him? Ha, same damned, filthy buzzard."

Sacajawea's heart had fallen to the floor. She saw the peace of her little family dashed apart. Her whole being cried out against these two intruders. With nausea in the pit of her stomach, she watched Charbonneau, uninvited, take off his leather coat and toss it into a corner. Very much at home, he sat down expectantly at the supper table, while the woman, Eagle, stood stolidly in the doorway.

"How is—what's his name now—Générale Clark?"

"He is away."

"When will he be back?"

Sacajawea's mood was not improved by this conversation. She felt perspiration standing out in beads on her forehead and upper lip, which felt as cold as ice. What to do? This man was the father of her boys. Sacajawea bit her lip, sucked in her breath once, stepped over to the young woman, and said gently, "What's wrong with young people these days that they don't show more respect to their elders? Come inside and close the door. It is cold out there. Inside we have hot tea."

Charbonneau looked sharply at Sacajawea. She had developed into the full bloom of womanhood while he'd been away. He admired and at the same time resented this. He knew she was different. She knew when to speak and how to put words together.

That summer, Governor Clark and Miss Judy moved to a new home that they had built especially for their growing family of three boys and one little girl. It was a two-story brick house set on the southeast corner of Vine, running half a block south on Main toward the river. Miss Judy could hardly wait to show the wing attached to the south end to Sacajawea. It was called the Council Chamber and was a great room, a hundred feet long and thirty-five feet wide. At night it was lighted by massive chandeliers hanging from the high ceiling.

General Clark displayed all his Indian trophies there. Sacajawea saw feather headdresses, brightly colored ornaments, canoes, shields, bows, arrows, projectile points, clothes, cooking utensils, pipes, knives, dishes, agricultural and musical instruments, war bonnets, snowshoes, moccasins, cradles, robes and hides, and even a rare Roman coin found by a Fox chief on the bank of the River Des Peres.[2]

During the summer, Miss Judy's health failed, and even though it was a crucial time when the Missouri Territory was fighting for admission to the union as a state, Clark took his wife to the sulfur springs in Virginia. She did not rally, but became worse and died. Clark was heartbroken. It seemed as though the sun had fallen from the sky. His enemies took advantage of his time away from Saint Louis and his deep grief.

"He favors the Indians at the expense of the whites," some said. "He is too good to the thieving Indians," others whispered behind his back. "We want a new man for governor!" And the sounds spread like a brushfire in dry leaves.

When he returned, Clark found that Missouri had become a state and Alexander McNair was governor. And to add more sorrow to his grief-stricken heart, his little daughter, Mary, had taken ill and died at the home of her mother's cousin.

Charbonneau said, "It has nothing to do with us. Stop your wailing, woman, and make me a pair of breeches. If I find you wandering off to somewhere, like to the Clark mansion, I will beat you with my bare hands."

Sacajawea looked at Charbonneau and grieved in silence for her dear friend.

Late in the summer, Charbonneau announced he was going to Sante Fe with De Mun and Chouteau. Before he could even suggest that the boys go along, Sacajawea pointed out that they would be going to school in several weeks. Charbonneau said nothing, but studied Sacajawea, then laughed, showing his stubby yellow teeth.

She flung her arms fiercely around both boys. She heard the woman called Eagle gasp. She felt Charbonneau pull her back and heard him draw a deep breath.

"Little Bird, take your hands off the boys! They are

growed now. Let them decide if they want to go to school. Don't decide for them."

Sacajawea winced. To her the boys were not yet grown, yet by Indian standards they would both have been on their own even a year ago. She looked at Charbonneau's face with its graying beard. She looked at his hair—long, wavy, gray, shaggy at the neck, curling at the ears—and imagined it suspended high on a stick in a dance around some Blackfoot fire.

"I'm going back to Dr. Welch's," said Baptiste softly. "I—I really want to. I'd like to go trapping during the next summer vacation, though."

"He wants to be an educated white man!" cried Tess. "He's sickening."

Sacajawea did not move or look up, but her fingers stirred restlessly over her mouth.

"Can't sit around waiting for summer. Gotta earn a livelihood. Gotta get the good pelts now—this fall." Charbonneau's lips were pressed firmly together.

"I can get some gear and grub together and be ready to pull out whenever you say," Tess said, looking expectantly at this father.

Charbonneau stared. "Little Tess, you growed a lot."

"Everybody calls me Tess now."

Sacajawea stared at Tess with her soft eyes wide and questioning. Her lips moved, but no sound came out. In her mind Charbonneau had closed a door and put his hand upon another. He was taking away one of her sons.

Baptiste saw her eyes and the remote sorrow that had suddenly come into them so swiftly, and his warm heart reacted at once. He said, "Mother—something hurts you. What is it?"

She did not answer him, did not even seem to know him. Baptiste had never seen her like this before, and yet the urgency of her hands moving over her mouth struck a chord of understanding within him. Whatever it was that bothered her, he knew she needed help.

Silently, he went to face his older half brother, and with his eyes he beckoned his father.

"I want you to tell Tess to finish this last year with Father Neil. Governor Clark has made provisions for us both to be in school again this fall. Clark says good

words about your cooking on that trail west. He tells
many people of your worth. He is paying you back for
those good services by giving us a chance to learn of
the white man's world at a time when many half-breeds
have to stay in the saddle just to keep alive." There
was no anger or outrage in his face as he continued.
"By next summer we can both go out trapping with you.
Zut! That is something to look forward to."

"Hell," said Charbonneau, "you're telling the truth.
I am also interpreter for the expedition. I saved some
of the Army men from drowning and from falling off
the mountainside. That's straight. The world's ahead
by me." He got out his tobacco and took a serious bite.

Eagle brushed her hair back from her eyes.

"I can load a smooth-bore flintlock fast as the next
Army man. Ever hear about the grizzly I shot so my
friend, Drouillard, wasn't mauled? It was near the River
That Scolds All the Others, and the day was calm, after
a night of hard wind and rain. I had just—"

"A man," interrupted Baptiste good-naturedly, a
flicker of a smile touching his face, "naturally does a
heap more shooting with his mouth than with his gun.
And for two reasons. One, he's a surer, quicker shot
with his mouth; and two, it costs less ammunition. A
man can load and fire his mouth off twenty times with
a big swallow of whiskey."

Charbonneau grinned knowingly at his younger son
and began to rummage around in a large bag for a bottle
of brandy. He tipped it up, jammed the cork back tightly,
and wiped his mouth on the back of his hand.

"To be sure," he said, still grinning. "I wouldn't want
you to call my bluff—but I never invited no ragtail
half-soft son to come to Santa Fe. That is a man's trail.
Tess, you just stay put another winter and get toughed
up. You're growed all right, but still soft." He kept
looking Tess up and down.

Tess said, "You're just a part-white man that is also
part dog. I may just bury you in that there bag."

"I'd turn you in for murder." Charbonneau's smile
was slow to come, but it was broad when it got there.

It was as though a great light grew in Sacajawea.
She had not dreamed that her own son, Baptiste, could
use words in such a way. His words were like the thin

edge of a knife, persuading and whittling away at the thoughts of a man so that he was turned on another path. She was no longer afraid to look at him, to see his youth, and to smell the freshness of him. She laughed aloud and squinted her eyes as if something stung them.

Looking at his mother, Baptiste saw that her eyes were swimming with tears, and they made him wonder. He guessed that maybe women always cried at a moment when they knew they had what they wanted, and his own sensitivity told him that Sacajawea seldom had what she wished, but accepted what came as her lot.

Taking a step toward his half brother, Tess said, "A white man's liver with his own gall squeezed on it might be too bitter to eat. I am going to try yours with goat gall if I ever decide to kill you."

"You shut your gab," said Charbonneau.

Eagle said, "You are the talkingest tribe I ever seen. Did you know that?"

"Let every man skin his own eel," answered Charbonneau, tipping up the brandy bottle again. Then his voice went high. "Why do I have to keep reminding the whole mess of you that I'm heading southwest? Somebody get the leather around my horse and bring up the packhorse. I want to get going." He looked at Tess. "I never reckoned you could be so wool-brained."

Clark kept himself as busy as possible and soon found good reasons to do so. The Indians were buying more and more trader's liquor.

He proposed a lesson for the Indians. His idea was a long row of kettles placed on the grass in his front yard, all filled with whiskey. When many Indians were assembled, he struck at the kettles, spilling the whiskey to show that strong drink was an enemy to the Indians. But as Sacajawea had warned him, this method was much too sophisticated. The Indians' main feeling was deep regret for the lost whiskey.

Clark confided in Sacajawea, "Even the Indians are laughing behind my back now. They expect some kind of miracle from me. And now my children need me at home to be a father and a mother."

"What do your children expect?" she asked. She was all poise. The gentleness of her face betrayed no indication that Charbonneau slapped her around whenever he took the notion.

"They expect—and need—a firm hand. Rose is getting too old to take care of them."

"So then—what about a younger woman? A mother for them?"

"It would take a lot of qualifications to be my wife, Janey. That woman would have to be intelligent, soft-spoken, and for my boys, imaginative. She would have to be someone they already know and respect." Then he surprised her by holding out a small portrait, which had been in his breast pocket. "This is Harriet Kennerly Radford. She herself has two small children, Mary and John, and a twelve-year-old son, Bill. She has no man to help raise them. I'm thinking of being that man."

She had known in her heart that Chief Red Hair would take another woman to help care for his lodge and children. Her suspicion fulfilled, she tried to hold herself so that his words would not cut. But the hurt was deep and it was all she could do to keep her hands from clutching at her heart to ease the pain. She knew this Harriet woman was the cousin of Miss Judy. Harriet! For a moment she thought of fleeing so that she would no longer hear him, when he suddenly took both her hands in his and said with surprising tenderness and deep sincerity, "Janey, no one can push you out of my heart."

Her heart was so full that for a moment it threatened to choke her. After a while she managed to say, "I would like to see this woman called Harriet. I will tell her of your bravery, that you do not exaggerate, and that you make a good showing anywhere."

When Clark was silent, she said, "Maybe she will be the best-looking woman in Saint Louis."

Then he laughed. "She is a good-looking woman." Then he quickly added, "But, Janey, you don't hurt anyone's eyes either."

On November 28, 1821, William Clark married Harriet Radford. She was a great beauty and much admired by the small social set in Saint Louis. The following summer they had a son, who was named Jefferson Kennerly and called Pomp by Clark.

When this Pomp was a year old, Clark threw him in

the water of the quarry he owned. Clark stood by to rescue him if necessary, but the child managed to swim out, furiously kicking his legs and thrashing his arms.

This incident delighted Sacajawea. She felt great joy in the knowledge that Clark called his own new son Pomp. It was the same nickname she gave to her firstborn. A surge of pleasure made her face glow. She knew that her life was more varied than most Shoshoni women and it was due to friendship given her by all the men of that west expedition. Her sons were educated in the white way. She could come and go as she pleased, talk to whomever she wanted. She was no longer bound to her environment. She could make her own decisions.

Duke Paul

June 21, 1823

The homes of the fur traders, two large houses, were scarcely more than a half mile further up on the right bank of the Missouri. I went to that place in order to visit the owners, the Messrs. Curtis and Woods. Neither of them was at home but the wife of the latter was there. She was a creole, a daughter of old Mr. Chauvin, with whom I had spent the night near St. Charles. The whole population of this little settlement consists only of a few persons, creoles, and halfbreeds whose occupation is the trade with the Kansas Indians, some hunting and agriculture. Here, I also found a youth of about sixteen years of age, whose mother, a member of the tribe of Shosho-nes or Snake Indians, had accompanied the Messrs. Lewis and Clark, as an interpreter, to the Pacific Ocean, in 1804−6. This Indian woman married the French interpreter, Toussaint Charbonneau. Charbonneau later served me in the capacity of interpreter, and Baptiste, his son, whom I mentioned above, joined me on my return, followed me to Europe and has since then been with me. I remained for dinner with Mrs. Woods and after the meal went to the Kansas again.

PAUL FRIEDRICH WILHELM, HERZOG VON WÜRTTEMBERG, *Erste Reise nach dem nördlichen Amerika in den Jahren 1822 bis 1824*, vol II, 1835. WILLIAM G. BEK, transl.

and ed., *South Dakota Historical Collections*, "First Journey to North America in the Years 1822 to 1824," vol. XIX. Pierre, S.D.: State Historical Society, 1938, pp. 303–4.

The following year when the land was losing its dead-brown color and tender, bright green leaves were coming back on the willow, with its blooms hanging like fuzzy caterpillars, and the redbud, dogwood, and haw stood in patches of pink and white, Sacajawea worked beside Eagle preparing packs. They were going on a trapping trip up the Missouri to the mouth of the Kaw River.[1] Clark had told Charbonneau that a Mr. Woods was waiting in a small settlement for an interpreter and trader among the Kansas Indians. Clark suggested that Charbonneau take the job and take his family with him so that the boys could do some trapping.

"My God, that is what I say," said Charbonneau. "Big boys like this should be out working, not inside turning white with their nose between book pages."

Eagle wore her best tunic and leggings and a matted blanket held loosely about her shoulders. Her hair part was painted vermilion, and her hair hung loosely down her back. Tess, nearly twenty now, poked her in the side and hissed in her ear, "I would pay a good four-point blanket and a beaded belt to have a woman like you."

"Your father paid ten ponies," Eagle lied, grinning.

Shocked, Tess rounded his eyes at the young woman and lapsed into an affronted silence.

Sacajawea, in a plain tunic with fringe hanging to her knees, picked up the packs and took them outdoors. She went to the shed and brought the four ponies, one by one, to the front door so they could be saddled or loaded. She knew the men would each ride one and she and Eagle would share the fourth. They would each carry part of the gear needed for the summer trip.

Sacajawea's work did not claim her full attention. Her mind was restless. When the last horse was tethered, she stepped to the back of the cabin and pressed herself close to the back wall, looking at the mound of soil with the gray slab of shale at its head. Spring beauties were growing near the small grave, and the brown needles of the cedar were sprinkled over the top. Her hands touched the rough logs of the cabin. It made her think she could hug the child close, as if she could get back the child who had been irretrievably lost. She wept, thinking of all the vigorous life in that little body that was so quickly used up. She knew it was not right for her to feel this way—strange, how quickly the end had come! The end—when she should have been in the cabin with the child. She was weak. These were hopeless tears. She dried her eyes, knowing there were dangers for all life. This was not life, but eternity itself.

"Nobody gets cabin fever this summer, *hein*?" Charbonneau asked as he checked the leather straps around the bundles. His eyes squinted at Sacajawea, but she did not answer. He had never once asked her what had happened to Otter Woman's child. She had tried to tell him, but he would never listen. She wondered if he knew who lay under that small mound of earth. She wondered if Tess or Baptiste had ever told him. She thought not. He probably would not have heard them. He would probably change the subject to something more to his liking, or to something he could brag about.

She sat back on the horse, looking down at Eagle, who carried a bundle on her back and was walking first. She gave one last look at the cabin, whose door was now closed. It was not locked against thieves, for there would be none. A hungry trapper might wander by, but he would take no more than he needed and leave the rest as he had found it, even chopping more wood to replace what he had used. This was the code of the times.

The Charbonneau family made their night camps where they found water. The horses grazed as they slept. The boys took turns at the night watch.

They pushed through hilly country and came down to the broad, sandy river. Clouds covered the sky. Eagle and Sacajawea erected the leather tepee near the small fur-trading settlement. Charbonneau went to find Mr. Woods. This was the only trading post in the Kansas country. Before this time the Kansas Indians had been served by itinerant traders who brought their loaded pirogues up the Missouri from New Orleans, or who came overland, as had the Charbonneaus, with loaded horses from Saint Louis. The settlement was only about three or four years old.

Woods and Curtis, who operated the post, were traders licensed to do business with the Kansas Indians. Their wives were Creole women, and the rest of the population consisted of half-breed hunters and trappers who worked for the post.

Slowly Sacajawea became aware of sounds all around her. She looked and saw nothing but the few cabins of illegal squatters. She looked in a freshly leafed oak and saw a squirrel barking, then a skein of crows, noisy as they strung off from the top of a post oak, then a jay scolding from the top of a cedar. She blew out a gusty breath. For the first time she could see for herself the white settlers squatting illegally on Indian land. The Kansas tribes were being squeezed and pinched. Clark had told her this was one of his major problems. The Indians were bewildered and perplexed and angry, and Sacajawea felt they had every right to be. She was on the side of the Indians, and she herself had felt confused about their problems much of the time when Clark had discussed them with her. The U.S. government was determined to move the Eastern Indians west of the Mississippi. They had transferred tribes from their ancestral homes to this new country. Sacajawea often thought the Great White Father in Washington must be about as confused as anyone as he struggled to try to make everyone happy—the white men of the East, the Indians of the East, now the Plains Indians whose homes were being disturbed, and the settlers who were always moving westward.

Out of that huge land Jefferson had bought from Napoleon, there was so much territory that the eastern land could be freed from Indians so that the eastern land could be used only by white men. The government had promised the Eastern Indians it would move them, paying for their land, west of the Mississippi. There was land that was not occupied by white men and probably never would be wanted by them. The land was wasteland—only flat prairies, not good for farming, only good for the herds of buffalo roaming over it, eating the short, tough gamma grass. Sacajawea knew that Chief Red Hair was honorable and Nat Pryor a good man—he was acting as a go-between for the Osages and the whites. Their hearts were increasingly heavy at the way things were going. It was not their fault promises were broken. She had taken Chief Red Hair by the hand and did not mean to let loose of it, yet seeing what was happening to the Indians was enough to make her despise all whites. The wind blew cold. Rain began to fall.

Sacajawea and Eagle ran about, gathering fallen branches for firewood. Before night they had built a snug camp, and the cool spring rain seemed good.

The next day, light showers fell. The women sat in the tepee sewing and stirring the fresh venison stew. They watched squirrels chase one another and hide in the tall grass.

Tess and Baptiste, tired of sitting around the damp camp, moseyed over to the settlement and found that one of the large log houses there belonged to Woods and his brood of dark-skinned children. The other house belonged to Curtis, who had fenced in his field of corn, beans, and potatoes.

"Look there," Tess said, pointing. "Every spring that man plows and plants. All summer he pulls weeds and his back is tired. In the fall he gathers, and in winter he fences, cuts wood, mends, and patches, and not often can he take his gun to go in the woods. I'm going to depend on my gun for food, and go where I please, do what I please, and be as free as the wind."

Baptiste looked at his half brother and grinned. "So— you pretty much do that now. I heard you were gravel in Father Neil's throat most of the time, doing what you pleased."

"You have got to make your own way."

"A man has his own notions of what is best for him."

Charbonneau met the boys. He'd found Woods, who thought that trapping would be complicated by the high water, but he thought this produced the best furs. Charbonneau puffed out both cheeks. "We're going to set them traps tomorrow, early."

Both boys learned that it was hardly too much to say that a trapper's life depended on his skill. He not only worked in the wilderness, he also lived there, and did so from sun to sun by the exercise of total skill. Instead of becoming tired of a trapper's life, these boys, fresh from school, thrived on it. They used their heads, and intelligence, which had so recently been used in proving complicated geometric theorems, and their language mastery in English, French, German, and Spanish. They were awed by their father's skill in the wild, and argued with each other as to whether Charbonneau had any specific craft, technology, theorem, or rationale, or whether it was only a rule of thumb that dictated his code of operating procedure. They agreed it was a total pattern of behavior.

They learned the whys, whats, and hows from Charbonneau, who was more of a braggart than a teacher. Why do you follow the ridges into or out of unfamiliar country? he would ask. What do you do for a companion who has collapsed from want of water while crossing a prairie? How do you get meat when you find yourself without gun powder in a country barren of game? What tribe of Indians made this trail, how many were in the band, what errand were they on, were they going or coming back from it, how far from home were they, were their horses laden, how many horses did they have, how many squaws accompanied them, and what mood were they in? Also, how old is the trail, where are those Indians now, and what does the product of these answers require of you?

Buffalo are moving downwind, an elk is in an unlikely place or posture, too many magpies are hollering, a wolf's howl is off-key—what does all this mean? A branch floats down stream—is this natural, or is it the work of animals, or of Indians, or of trappers? Another branch or a bush or even a pebble is out of place—why? On the limits of the plain, blurred by a heat mirage, or against the gloom of distant cottonwoods, or across an angle of sky between branches or where hill and mountain meet, there is a tenth of a second of what may have been movement—did men or animals make it, and if animals, why? It was unlikely that Charbonneau himself could detect 60 percent of these things accurately, but he knew what should be known. He knew that as a trapper's mind dealt with these puzzle pieces, it simultaneously performed still more complex judgments on the countryside, the route across it, and the weather. The boys learned to modify their reading in relation to season, to Indians, to what had happened. They could modify it in relation to stream flow, storms past, storms indicated, and modify it again according to the meat supply, to the state of the grass, to the equipment on hand. Trappers must master their conditions. Tess and Baptiste not only mastered their conditions, they enjoyed them to the utmost.

Later these boys saw soldiers, gold-seekers, and emigrants come into their country and suffer where they had lived comfortably, and die where they had been in no danger.

The days became warm, and the heat inside the tepee oppressive. The mosquitoes came in droves, and the women kept their skin covered with rancid bear's oil. This only added to their discomfort in the heat as they perspired under the oil. They sat under the post oaks waiting for a cool breath of air. Their hair was tied against their necks with thongs as slick from grease as their moccasins. Whenever they passed the trading post, they left behind a strong smell of wood smoke and rancid grease.

"Them there squaws of old Charb's keep to themselves and don't buy none of that whiskey the others do," remarked one of the itinerant traders to Curtis, who rubbed his chin, his blue eyes reflective.

"Yeah, but have you seen the one son? He's in here with two, three pelts and asking for his pay in whiskey nearly every fortnight."

"Sure, but the younger breed is the opposite. He don't drink, and he stays out with the traps."

"They're both more like Indians than whites, even though they got some schooling," said Curtis. "I heard that Governor Clark himself educated them two. He hopes they get into politics or Indian affairs one day."

"This here chile bets they both end up living with Indians. You can't never hammer out a gold piece from wet clay."

The men looked up toward the north sky and saw clouds gathering. "If you don't like the heat, it'll soon be cooler," said Curtis, moving off the steps to the inside of the post.

The trader shaded his eyes and looked at the churning, boiling clouds. The weather shifts fast on the prairie, he thought. A few minutes ago, I saw nothing to indicate a storm, only a low red haze against the northern horizon.

A spatter of heavy, noisy drops hit the dust, and Eagle hurried for shelter. Sacajawea pulled the kettle off the tripod and brought it into the tepee, placing it upon the floor. The handle was hot.

"Roasted fingers?" Eagle inquired mildly.

That night, a thunderstorm deluged the settlement and threatened to wash away everything, but it did not cool the air. It became sultry and hot. The short street in front of the post and the two cabins was knee-deep in mud. A couple of small boys rode their horses wildly down it, splattering the mud in every direction.

"My boys would like that horseplay," said Sacajawea, ruminating.

"The sun is setting clear. Maybe the rain is over. Our man ought to be back. The streams are probably running bank-full and overflowing. He'll have words to say if he loses some of his traps," said Eagle.

The next morning, the rain came down hard again. The wind turned to the northwest, and the sultry heat was somewhat broken. The Missouri had flooded the lowlands, so that but little could be done by way of trapping or hunting.

"Well, it is time they came in," said Eagle, watching Baptiste and Tess riding through the mud past the settlement. She craned her neck suddenly, looking down toward the gap in the trees where the mouth of the Kaw began to widen. "Strangers coming in, too."

"Our man with some trappers, I expect," said Sacajawea, braiding a bridle for one of the horses.

"No. Strangers. Several of them. Walking."

Sacajawea put down the horsehair rope and rose quickly to join Eagle outside the tepee. "Coming from the river?"

"Ai."

They watched as the small group of men made their way, slipping and sloshing, heads down, across to the post. Sacajawea counted them. "Two—three—four." As they watched, the men reached the end of the street, and Eagle chuckled as they sank over their boot tops in the deep mud and floundered, heaving to lift themselves step by step through the muck.

"Hey, we should have laid some planks down for these gentlemen," said Baptiste.

"Not me," called Tess. "It is plumb funny to see them, mired, not able to hardly move. If someone shot a rifle above their heads, they'd make that mud splatter."

The four strangers had beached their pirogue at the mouth of the muddy Kaw. Now they looked about curiously, noticing the naked children on the ponies, the unkempt squaws carrying wood in their arms, the bleak-looking log houses. The lead man waved a hand that took in the street, the children, the squaws—the whole settlement—and said something to his companions in a voice too low to hear.

"He's telling 'em to leave this squaw village at once," Tess said.

"Shhh," Baptiste warned, and began unloading his gear and traps and pelts from his horse so that he could meander closer to the four newcomers.

The strangers made their way through the mud to the wooden porch of Woods's house. There they scraped off as much of the slick clay as they could before the tall one knocked.

Rita Woods stood at the door. She was a woman in her early thirties, beginning to carry a little extra weight, to broaden in the hips and thicken at the waist. She was dark-skinned, almost swarthy, and her hair, which had been as black as a moonless night when she was younger, had gray wings along the temples now. She was a handsome woman, but not really pretty. The stranger spoke in halting English.

"Shhh," Baptiste warned again as Tess pressed in close behind him, moving closer to the side of Woods's house so they could see and hear better.

"Is this the home of Mr. Woods?"

"*Sí.* He is not here, but running his own trap lines to the south."

"I spent a night with a Señor Chauvin in Saint Charles. I promised him I'd stop to see his son-in-law."

The woman smiled, showing flashing white teeth. "That Señor Chauvin is my *padre.* I am the wife of Mr.

Woods," she explained. The men had difficulty understanding her Creole Spanish. Finally, she called a small, nearly naked child to her, and gave him some instructions in Spanish. She smiled at the four men and sat quietly to wait. The men—one named Caillou, another Louis, and an elderly Canadian called Roudeau—sat timidly on chairs while the fourth man sat back and relaxed, perfectly at ease, waiting for what would come next.[3]

The child ran straight to Baptiste and Tess and explained that his mother wanted them to come at once. "You know Spanish," said the child. "You learned it at a school?"

"Yes," said Baptiste, sensing something urgent about the child. "Then, come, you help Mama talk to the men."

"Maybe we can earn us a gold piece," said Tess. "What's your name?"

"I am called Juan," said the child, running back toward the house.

Tess and Baptiste stood on the porch a moment so the mud and water would run off their boots. Baptiste knocked. The child, Juan, answered and brought them into the sitting room.

"I beg your pardon, Juan would not even let me take my muddy boots off first," Baptiste apologized. "He said it was urgent that I come in." He spoke to the woman in Spanish.

She smiled and indicated the four men with her outstretched hand. Baptiste understood at once. "She wants us to interpret for her," he said in English.

Tess stood behind his brother, looking from one man to another.

"*Ja*, go slow so that I understand all she says," said the tall relaxed man, who had a German accent.

"Do you speak German, sir?" asked Baptiste.

The man was surprised and said quickly, "*Ja, ich bin Deutsch.*" He took Baptiste's hand and shook it, then spoke in a deep, rich voice, using his native tongue. "We have been as near drowned as men can be and still breathe. The water has been overhead and underfoot. Oh, Caillou, Louis, and Roudeau here are gentlemen of my party. I am Paul Wilhelm. At home I am Duke of Württemberg."

"I am Baptiste Charbonneau. And this is my brother, Toussaint."

"It is my pleasure to find you in this wild country," said Duke Paul. "I have sailed from Hamburg to New Orleans and was granted permission by Mr. Adams, your Secretary of State, to enter and travel at will through the United States. See, here is the note he has signed."

Baptiste took it and, after reading it, translated for Rita Woods. "John Quincy Adams writes that the federal authorities of the west are to provide this man and his party with every means in their power to further and safeguard his movements and to furnish him military escort when it should be necessary. He's someone fairly important."

Rita Woods nodded her head. "*Sí*, he stayed with my father downriver."

Baptiste gave out a long, low whistle. "Did you meet with Governor Clark in Saint Louis?" He winked at Tess, never figuring that Duke Paul had even heard of Governor Clark.

"*Ja*, he gave me a passport from the Secretary of War to travel up the Missouri. I wish to explore for my own instruction. To learn the natural science of the country and to hunt."[4]

Baptiste and Tess were stunned. Clark had talked with this duke. The country was getting smaller.

The duke was a young man in his mid-twenties, of medium height, rather slender, passionately fond of his pipe, unostentatious, and he spoke very broken English. He wore a white slouch hat, a black-velvet coat, and probably the greasiest pair of leggings Baptiste had ever seen. He had long black sideburns, curving forward to his pursing mouth, and hot brown eyes showing intense, fanatic concentration. Baptiste counted fifteen buttons on each side of the greasy leggings. He wondered where the party was going.

"I have a keelboat on the Missouri. It is waiting there for me to explore this Kaw River. Then I'll travel up the Missouri to visit various Indians along the way."

Rita Woods suggested that the men all stay for supper and dry out their boots by the fire. She pulled up a bench, and the men took off their soggy boots, outer coats, and hats, and held their chilled hands toward the fireplace.

Caillou was a man of medium height, thin, slope-shouldered, narrow-faced. Louis was a small-featured man, with a large nose and cleft chin. The elderly Roudeau was stocky, with swarthy skin and a shock of dark hair that was graying at the hairline.

That afternoon, Baptiste learned that Duke Paul had received military training in Germany, but not caring for military life, he had chosen to study botany and zoology. The King of England was his uncle, and he had suggested that the duke search for material in the New World. Duke Paul was fascinated by the life of an explorer. He confided that he had talked at great length with Clark about the famous western expedition.

"Herr Clark told me that he had educated the baby that was carried halfway across the continent during that trip. He said the boy was out on a trapping expedition with his father. How I would like to meet that young man."

Tess coughed and nearly choked.

Baptiste drew in his breath quickly. Then he made his face bland and innocent-looking. He studied a thorn scratch on his thumb, rubbed it thoughtfully, and took his time about speaking. "I am the papoose of the expedition," he said finally. "My mother is in our camp. She can tell you much about that long trail." His eyelids were heavy over his narrowed eyes, only an edge of white showing beneath them. "My father is still with his trap line. He was interpreter and cook with the expedition." Baptiste continued to examine the scratched thumb.

Tess squirmed in his seat, wondering what he could say about himself that would attract the attention of these important men.

"Do I understand you, sir?" asked Duke Paul. "You are the baby of the expedition?"

Baptiste looked into his face. "Yes, sir, I am that baby."

Duke Paul inclined his head and studied Baptiste. Then he slapped his right leg, shouting, "*Merkwürdig!*"

"My mother is a full-blooded Shoshoni. I expect you know."

"*Ja.* Well, I should have a talk with her before I go to the river again. Incredible. I still cannot believe my good fortune."

Rita Woods was impressed with her dinner guests, but Sacajawea was not impressed with the strangers. There were many travelers going through Saint Louis, she said, and they were all much alike. But when Baptiste explained to her and Eagle that the duke had also crossed the Great Eastern Waters to get here, they were amazed.

Sacajawea had always thought that the Great Waters would stop the white men, as they had stopped the expedition. Hadn't they camped the winter beside the Great Western Waters, then turned around and come back? But this man had come from the east! Now nothing could stop the white men. Her interest in this stranger grew. She began to ask him questions. "Did you walk overland from the Great Eastern Waters?"

"*Nein*, we traveled around the continent to the Mississippi Delta. We traveled up the river from New Orleans. *Ja*, we had to change to a smaller boat."

Tess eyed the strangers suspiciously and felt a pang of jealousy as Sacajawea offered them food and hot tea with plenty of sugar to drink. Baptiste asked many questions about the homeland called Germany.

Eagle crept back inside the skin tepee. She could not understand the words of these strangers, and she could stare at them better through the front flap without seeming so discourteous. Her wonder at Sacajawea grew as she watched her talk with hand signs and English words slowly with the four men. The men seemed to enjoy their visit with her. Sacajawea wore her soft buckskin gown loosely belted at the waist, beaded moccasins, and a narrow band of beadwork across her forehead. Her long black hair was parted in the middle, oiled back in smooth wings, and hung nearly to her waist in two long braids. Her smile was like a flash of lightning across a cloudy sky.

Eagle's face was somber and passive as she watched Sacajawea shuffle around the cooking kettle. The men were offered portions of tender meat from the kettle.

The duke shook his head and held his belly. "*Nein*,

danke." He had eaten much not long ago at the table of Rita Woods.

Never before had Eagle heard a guest refuse food. This rude refusal did not seem to disturb Sacajawea. She ignored it and went on making hand signs and talking with the men. Eagle watched, her face lowered, wondering what it was in the eating courtesy she had missed. Then she saw with her own eyes Sacajawea take up the horn spoon and dip into the kettle for a large piece of meat. She held the meat so that it cooled, then slowly picked off strings of it and ate as she talked with the men. Baptiste did the same, which was acceptable. But a woman talking and eating with guests—with strangers!—with men! Eagle shook her head, thinking, I have come to live with a family that is half-savage, with no manners—brazen. What if our man should hear of this?

Tess pushed aside the tepee flap and stepped inside. A thin blanket was wrapped around his middle. Eagle drew back. Tess's gaze was silent and fixed. Eagle spoke. It was true that his mother did not observe the proper courtesies expected of women.

"So—you would have me speak to my mother about being corrupted with evil white ways?"

Eagle stretched her stiff, bent legs, and straightened her back. "I would have you speak to your own father."

Tess had a fine beaver pelt in his hand, which he wanted to show off to the visitors. He stood in the doorway scratching his dirty red-wool shirt. "What the hell!" he said. "You trying to start something?" Then he was outside explaining how easy it was to trap such fine specimens to the man called Caillou.

The duke was still talking with Sacajawea. "I would like to make a request," he said. "I ask your permission to take your son as an interpreter for me."

She looked swiftly into his face.

"We are going up the Missouri. He will be well fed and paid for his efforts. He is the first young man I've found who can translate so that I fully know what he is talking about. His mind is most agile."

Baptiste blushed as he translated for his mother. Sacajawea drew a deep breath and puffed it out slowly, with silent thanks. She smiled and nodded her consent.

"*Ai*. He will go. His papa will like it. He thinks the boy should have a job."

The duke gave her a straight look. "We start in the morning to catch the rest of our party. Have him meet with us down at our pirogue." He shook the boy's hand, nodded his thanks, and filed down the trail, through the mud, to his pirogue and camp on the Kaw. Not one of the other men said a word until they were halfway to the pirogue; then Caillou, Louis, and Roudeau began to talk at once. "A boy for an interpreter," they laughed.

Charbonneau came in telling how the Kaw had overflowed the bottoms until it was several miles wide, three or four miles above the mouth. It was a sea of water; the banks were gone; only the slow eddies down the middle showed where the main channel was. Traveling was difficult, even by horse, and he was glad to be home. His horse was loaded with beaver pelts. Charbonneau ate his supper in silence; then he began to storm. "The boy is too young! That is a job for me! Is it true that a German duke was here who speaks French?" He faced Baptiste.

"Yes, quite well," answered Baptiste, stiff-lipped. "Some English, mostly German, and he does not know Spanish. I had to translate to Mrs. Woods for him."

Charbonneau eyed Tess. "You said you translated for the Woods woman."

"We both did," said Baptiste quickly, gently.

Charbonneau's dark, wrinkled face remained a rusty iron mask. "I will speak to this man."

"Speak to your older squaw first," suggested Tess. "She is the one who made the arrangements and ate, like one of the men, with the strangers."

"My woman?"

Tess closed his eyes and stalked peevishly back and forth. "That there duke," he said, "is an idiot."

"The man," Charbonneau said bluntly, "he is a damned fool." Then he added, "He is a fool who can't see beyond his own nose that there are older, more experienced men around who make excellent interpreters."

"Tell him I should be the one to go." Tess opened his

eyes petulantly. "I can speak French and a little German."

"But you don't know Spanish," said Baptiste.

"Pah! You make me want to puke!" said Tess.

Charbonneau hesitated. He had the feeling that this matter was the beginning of something larger. Abruptly he caught Sacajawea's wrist and twisted her around to face him. His whiskers had grown, making his face look shaggy and dark. The rusty mask was broken. His mouth was half-open, and his breath came in small gasps. "I should beat you." He picked up a long leather thong and wound it around his wrist to lash against her. She sank to the ground and covered her head with her arms. She kept silent and bit her upper lip so as not to cry out.

Eagle watched from one side. She was truly half-sorry to see her friend treated so roughly—and half-sorry that Charbonneau did not lash out harder. After all, Sacajawea had entertained four men and had eaten with them. That was wrong. Yet Eagle also knew that Sacajawea seemed to do things easily, with no conscious thought of Indian etiquette. She used either the white man's or the Indian's manners whenever it suited her purpose.

Charbonneau lashed out with a loud snap of the whip. It caught at the back of Sacajawea's tunic.

Eagle also knew that she wished she had the easy-going ability to talk with strangers that Sacajawea had. She watched their man puffing, his whiskers moving in and out as his cheeks moved with his breathing. His forehead was red and perspiring. She dared not interfere or she would also be whipped.

Both boys shouted for Charbonneau to stop. Baptiste tried to grab at Charbonneau's hands, but he was pushed away.

Sacajawea seemed to crouch lower, but still no sound escaped her lips. She endured five strong, deliberate lashes. Her dark eyes gleamed.

In a burst of courage Baptiste dragged his mother out of the whip's reach. Charbonneau let the leather thong fall to the ground. He spat and walked over the black string of leather, leaving Sacajawea to her shame.

Sacajawea stood up. Deliberately, before all of them,

she spat toward Charbonneau, then walked slowly, contemptuously away.

Away from the camp, she threw herself on the wet ground and opened her proud and stubborn Shoshoni shell and wept. She lay facedown, her arms outstretched above her head, her fists clenched.

"A man has to keep his woman in line," sniffed Tess. "I would never have a woman who speaks up the way our mother does. She matches wits with anyone, man or woman. That is not proper for a squaw. She acts as though she has been to the white man's school herself."

"She thinks and can express her thoughts," said Baptiste.

"Would you like your mother to speak up to your schoolmaster? To Mr. Welch?"

"Well—"

"See—that would be an embarrassment. If she went to my school and spoke up to Father Neil, he would soon have her muzzled. No one speaks up to him. Our father is master of this camp, and he knows how to run it. His blood boils fast, and this is good. I will be like him."

"What a temper you'll have!" sighed Baptiste.

Near dawn, Sacajawea rewrapped her braids with thick grass stems, brushed off her skirt, and strode back into camp.

Eagle bathed the long red welts on Sacajawea's back and arms, making guttural sounds in her throat the whole time. Charbonneau left the tepee but soon came inside and took a bowl of water from the water bucket and rummaged around in his roll of clothing for a straight razor.

They did not see Charbonneau all day. He had gone to the camp of Duke Paul with Baptiste. When he did come into camp, he looked triumphant.

"That duke fellow, he hired me; Baptiste, he stay here," he announced. "He agreed to wait one more day before pulling out. He was impressed with my knowledge of the Big Muddy. Maybe we go up as far as the Mandans."

"You have a job as trader for Woods," Tess reminded him. "I thought you'd talk him into taking me. I'm older than Baptiste."

"You keep your mouth shut or I give you the whip. I am the man. I do as I please. I am boss."

Tess backed away, and Charbonneau spoke more briskly. "Do this, do that! Get the job for me! *Zut!* You get your own work. You go to hell! I decide what I do!"

Sacajawea felt heartsick. She had hoped that Baptiste would have a chance to be on his own for a few weeks—maybe learn how to do interpreting well so that he could get away from Charbonneau. Yet, there was something else. She could not look at Charbonneau without pulling her blanket up over her mouth to hide her laughter. His face looked as if it had been put together from two faces that did not match. The upper half was deeply tanned and weathered. But his cheeks and chin were as white as those of Chief Red Hair's new woman, Miss Harriet, who never went outdoors without a veil to shield her complexion. She tried not to stare, but she could not help giving a quizzical glance now and then at Charbonneau's face where he had shaved off his whiskers so that he would make an impression on the strangers. His dark eyes bored into hers.

"You want more of that whip, Little Bird?" he asked.

"If you do it again, I will leave and you will not see me again," she said, her eyes hard and black.

By the next morning, Duke Paul was anxious to move up the Missouri, and he came to help Charbonneau carry his gear out. He watched Baptiste brush the horses to get the mud out of their hair. The boy smiled. The duke began to talk with Sacajawea and motioned for Baptiste to help translate for them. Again he remarked on Baptiste's likable personality and responsiveness. Sacajawea felt pleased and puffed up a little. She made him a cup of tea with extra sugar.

Charbonneau cupped his hands and shouted to the other three waiting men.

"Patience," said Duke Paul. "I want to ask your good woman's permission to take that young boy, Baptiste, to my homeland. I will stop in Saint Louis for him in the fall."

Baptiste looked at his mother. "He said he would be in Saint Louis when the aspen grow orange and the oaks are fire against the sky. He will take me to his home across the waters."

Sacajawea was dumbfounded. This man from the far-away land wished to take her son with him. When would he let him come back?

"He says I should stay a year, maybe two, maybe three." Baptiste held up his fingers. "I am to learn his tongue even better than now, and speak to his people about the land here." His heart was pounding.

"*Ai*," answered Sacajawea quietly. "Now ask your father."

"Oh, all right, if you want to go for a while," said Charbonneau with no thought, eager only to get on with this trip.

"It is then a promise," said Sacajawea, smiling. "He will go with you. You will take care of him, then return him to me."

"You can be sure of that," said the duke, his face reflecting his astonishment that the Indian mother would be so willing to have her son travel to a land she'd never heard spoken about before.

He did not know her thoughts. She was thinking about all the things her son would have in his head when he came back. Maybe as much as Chief Red Hair. This was the thing to do. Let him go. Her love for her firstborn shone from her eyes. Could she be without him? Not know what he was doing? She looked at the duke and saw his brown eyes soften and felt his great strength, and she knew he was the one to finish making a man out of her son. He would not break the gentleness in the boy as Charbonneau would. Her heart would drop without him, but it would break if Charbonneau took over the training of him.

For a long time there was silence. No one noticed Tess edge up until he spoke. "He gets pay for traveling to your homeland?" he asked laconically.

Duke Paul whirled around. "I never cheated anyone."

Baptiste reached out to shake the duke's hand on their agreement. "When the aspen change, we will leave."

"I will be at Chouteau's store inquiring about you, you can bet on it."

The sun rose high and warm. The men walked on the high spots, trying to avoid the mud holes.

"We cast off now!" shouted Charbonneau.

"Fine," said the duke, bowing low toward Sacajawea and Eagle, who had followed the men for a last farewell.

"I know this river well," said Charbonneau, nodding his head up and down. "We'll use the poles as long as we're in the overflow here. When we get farther upstream, there is a point that rises high and pushes out into the river. The river has not overflowed there because the banks are high. We'll tack across to the other side."

Roudeau nodded, understanding. "We'll take the ropes, then."

"I'll handle this," Charbonneau continued. "We'll take to the bushes."

"Bushwhack?" Roudeau said slowly.

"Certainly—grab the bushes, hang on, and pull the pirogue along by hand. This is the best way."

"Won't that be slow?" asked the duke.

"Nothing's slower. Maybe when we get to the bluff we can use the sail. You have one?"

Roudeau nodded. Then the men took up their poles and at the duke's signal felt the bottom and pushed away from the shore. Slowly the pirogue moved forward as the men fell into a sort of rhythm of walking and hauling. When they had made a hundred yards of progress, Eagle waved and turned to return to the tepee. Sacajawea waved and shook her head wondering how long it would take Duke Paul to discover that her man did not know how to counsel others, especially about river travel. Charbonneau was a hog. She thought, Perhaps he will speak to the duke about going across the water to his homeland in place of his son, taking this other thing away from Baptiste also. She felt certain that after the river trip the duke would come to Saint Louis and ask only for Baptiste. He would be glad enough to let Charbonneau stay behind.[5]

CHAPTER

43

Kitten

Somewhere in what is now western Oklahoma and Kansas, the polygamous old interpreter took to himself another wife. This was a Ute woman, beautiful and youthful enough to become a discordant element in the household, and before long she and Sacajawea were engaged in a bitter domestic feud.

Reprinted by permission of the publishers, The Arthur H. Clark Company, from *Sacajawea, Guide and Interpreter of the Lewis and Clark Expedition*, by Grace Raymond Hebard, 1957, p. 153.

"Tess, you continue on the job as trader for Woods," suggested Sacajawea. "Baptiste will help run the trap line."

But Sacajawea's thoughts were heavy when she looked at the boys—the one becoming the exact shadow of his father; the other, her own son, more like someone remembered in the past, more like her own father. I saw this boy's eyes open, his small limbs harden to play. He has been mine all these years. He is still mine! He is going away, but he will return. He will no longer be a boy. He will not see me, perhaps. I am a mother. What mother can understand why her son should be taken? I said *ai*, he could be taken. I understand. Oh, Pompy, my loved one, come to *Umbea*, before you leave her; come before you lose her.

But Sacajawea, looking at her son and the son's half brother, feeling her heart cry out with anguish, said, "It is going to blow."

Already the sun was hazed over and a dark gray cloud was forming in the west. She watched the dark cloud, weighing the speed of its wind against the chances of getting the pirogue across the river before the squall hit. They could make it, she decided, and began to pack a parfleche with jerky for the boys.

The boys knew what was expected of them. They cleaned the traps and loaded their horses, ready to pull out before that stiff breeze could blow up any more rain clouds.

For the remainder of the sultry, oppressive summer, Sacajawea and Eagle dug roots for eating, tanned deer hides, and dried sour purple grapes. The grapes would be used later in pemmican, despite their seedy quality.

Sacajawea and Eagle watched trappers and buffalo hunters come and go. The weather alternated between bad spells of heat and severe thunderstorms, which were a relief from the hot days and the scourge of stinging insects.

Tess, who looked like his father, with his mouth drawn down at the sides, his brown eyes squinting, shoulders rounded and somewhat humped, gave an impression of not fully understanding what was taking place around him. He continued to trap for Woods, but did not care for the mosquitoes and blue-green blow-flies. Just before it was time to return to Saint Louis, he hired out as an interpreter at the Washita post, saying he'd be back in the cabin before Charbonneau.

Baptiste hung around the settlement, working with Woods and Curtis, trading with the Kansas Indians. On one occasion he went as far as the villages of the Iowas, Otoes, and Osages to trade for their fox pelts and tanned buffalo hides.

One evening Eagle sat at the fire long after the sun had set in a brilliance of red and gold. She called to Sacajawea, who had gone to sleep inside the tepee, "Come see, the moonlight is going out! It is finished! I see no clouds! What can this mean? Eeeiii!"

Sacajawea stood by her side and watched an eclipse of the moon. Then a small cloud sailed past the moon, and it seemed to be hanging close to the earth, a dark red. The left surface seemed lighter than the right, and a deep cleft or valley seemed to be visible on the moon's surface.

"I believe the time for snow and ice is coming," said Sacajawea. "This unusual sight is an omen."

Eagle pulled her blanket closer. "I was afraid of that. What can it mean?"

"We must go back to our cabin."

"We must go as soon as Baptiste arrives from his trap line?"

"*Ai*," sighed Sacajawea. "Tess will find us already back in the warm cabin when he returns. We will keep it warm for our man."

The fire burned out. Eagle and Sacajawea watched the moon return to normal, and they went to their sleeping robes.

On the day the first snowflakes fell, Charbonneau came galloping into the yard. Baptiste came from behind the horse shed where he had been cutting wood. He had heard Charbonneau coming, singing one of his favorite French songs about a lover and his young bride. Charbonneau was drunk. "Hey!" he called, not seeing

Baptiste standing against the side of the cabin, barging
through the door and throwing his pack down. "You
two squaws come on out and see what your man has
bought with the pay Monsieur Herr Duke Paul Wilhelm
of Württemberg, nephew of the King of England, cousin
of King Friedrich I of Württemberg, gave to me." Charbonneau pointed proudly toward a black stallion pawing the earth impatiently and then to the young, shy
girl standing beside the horse. She was emblazoned
with all the trappings and painting of her Ute tribe.
Her ears were pierced four times on the rim, and several
long blue-and-white glass beads were pushed into the
holes. She wore a string of these glass sticks around
her neck; otherwise she was naked.

"She is my new bride," announced Charbonneau,
leering in her direction. "And that is not all." He swaggered around outside the front of the cabin. "I found a
barrel of brandy in the sunken wreckage of an old double pirogue two days from here. Wahoo! What drinks
have come from that barrel!" Unsteady, Charbonneau
untied the straps holding the barrel to the stallion.
"Chief Wakanzere and his Kansas band traded her to
me for about half of this fine brandy. She was taken in
a raid not over three weeks ago. He said she was too
young to be his woman and too old to stay with his
children. Some brave, whose face was painted with red
stripes and whose head was shaved as smooth as my
nose, said the chief was pleased that I'd take her off his
hands. He really wanted rifles for his braves, better
than those the British make. So—I promised him I'd
bring in a load of good American rifles soon as I got
back to Saint Louis. He's still waiting there for me, by
gar!"

Eagle gave the Ute girl, who now did not look too
shy, a wicked glance.

A covey of partridge, alarmed by the stamping of the
stallion's feet, took to the air, and as they passed over
a prairie-dog village, there was a shrill, quarreling bark
among the creatures, angry over the disturbance, de-
fensive at once. Sacajawea thought, Brave, empty sounds
they made, retreating instantly when real danger
threatened. Some people, she thought, were like that.
All talking and no doing.

The newcomer stared at Sacajawea and Eagle. Her face was daubed with vermilion.

"She is younger than your youngest son. She is a papoose who does not yet wear clothes!" shouted Eagle, her hand over her mouth the instant the words were out.

Charbonneau stumbled inside and hunkered over the front of the fireplace, steaming.

Sacajawea looked at him. He had seen more than sixty winters; his hair was long and salted with white among the dark, mangy curls. She waited for him to tell what he would about the trip up the Missouri.

"Remember Charlie McKenzie? They call him King Charlie now. He's with the Arikaras for trading."

Baptiste came into the cabin and squatted on his haunches near the fire, watching his father, then the newcomer, the Ute girl.

"One whole day, canoes of Ashley's men came downstream." Charbonneau looked into the fire. "Most of the men were wounded. They had a fight with the Arikaras after they'd fished up a brandy keg and were for the most part drunk as hoot owls."

He would not tell much about his trip. He had left the duke at the Grand Detour post, where he was visiting with the agent. Charbonneau had come to Council Bluffs in a dugout he'd found among some cattails. He was certain that the duke was on his way down the Missouri by now.

Baptiste nodded. "The aspen are orange and the oaks red and yellow against the sky. He will be here soon."

"The duke lost two of his hunters from overexertion and heat. *Sacre*, it was hot." Charbonneau rolled his eyes remembering how the two men showed symptoms of a nervous and gastric fever. Then the duke had asked him to act as hunter in their place. He had refused, reminding Duke Paul he had been hired as interpreter. The duke had insisted Charbonneau use his rifle and hunt game. He had given Charbonneau his interpreter's pay and said from that day on he was engaged as a hunter. Charbonneau explained how he had been able to leave at night and get out of the camp. It wasn't defeat; Charbonneau saw it as keeping his pride and protecting his feet from the prickly pear, rocks, and mud they would have trod upon if he'd become a hunter.

In two days Tess rode in from the Washita post, tired but glad to see that his father was there.

"Even less room now for that painted papoose," grumbled Eagle.

"She is a little thing—you will make room," said Charbonneau.

Eagle looked at him. "With two grown boys, this is no place for her unless you wish to raise her as a daughter."

"She is right," said Sacajawea. "Your sons learn the white man's way. One woman. How can they learn from a father who has two women and brings home another?"

"Sons no trouble," said the Ute girl coquettishly. Men and boys were her stock in trade. Her father had often gambled off a night or two of her alluring company to traders. Now she felt her luck changing. She would not have to serve this old, wrinkled mountain man, but she could use her charms on the sons. She looked at the stocky Tess, who saw her from his squinted eyes as though seeing her through bright sunlight.

"My old man knows good merchandise!" exploded Tess. "Just look at those straight, strong legs."

Baptiste stood with his mouth wide open, staring at the Ute girl. "Doesn't she have a name?" he asked finally. "For a couple of days we just stare not knowing what to call her."

"We could call her Kitten, huh?" said Tess. "I bet she is playful."

Sacajawea seemed resigned to the whole affair, feeling that the girl was actually too young to influence the boys. She looked at Kitten as if she were an errant child. In fact she treated her as a child. She combed her hair in the mornings and scrubbed her face in the evenings. She sent her on errands and showed her how to mend moccasins.

Charbonneau, strangely, was not jealous of Kitten's flirting with his sons. He seemed quite amused by the entire situation. Perhaps it was amusing to him because he knew very well that Eagle, now about eighteen summers, previously the youngest of his women, was now seething inside. She was jealous of this adolescent child.

The snow lasted a week; then the weather warmed, and one day it was sunny. "Duke Paul will be here any day to get supplies before he goes south to New Orleans," said Charbonneau. "I would rather be on a trading trip with the Sioux than meet him right away."

"You are leaving?" asked Sacajawea.

"*Oui*, by tomorrow night. I will take my son on a short hunting trip."

"You will not take Baptiste. You have given a promise that he will wait here for Duke Paul. The leaves are turning red. He will be here soon now."

"*Femme*, how could I forget that?" sighed Charbonneau. "Each evening that duke reminded me of it and what he could do for my son. He said the same words Générale Clark uses. 'Your son is one smart fellow, but you, his father—no brains that show.'"

Sacajawea put her hand over her mouth and smiled. She thought how peaceful it would be while Charbonneau and Tess were on the hunting trip. She hoped maybe she and Baptiste could visit Chief Red Hair once while he was gone. Then she remembered that Baptiste, too, would be leaving before the next snow. She was ready for Baptiste to go, but the thought of the day of his return made her want to sing. That would be the time she would set her face toward the sun.

The wind blew cold that evening, and Charbonneau sat on the floor with his sons playing the game of plum pits. Sacajawea sat sewing. Eagle was looking through her belongings for a missing necklace and beaded belt. Kitten sat close beside Tess. She was covered by a loose gingham Mother Hubbard that Eagle had given her. Kitten had left one shoulder free and had belted the dress around the middle with a blue-and-scarlet sash. Her waist-long hair rippled free over the glass sticks in her ears. She wore a silver squash-blossom necklace and a string of dark brown seeds.

"*Zut*, I would like to take that trip to the duke's fatherland," grumbled Charbonneau. "I could be a big man when I came back with all the knowledge from there."

Abruptly Sacajawea stopped her sewing. A song stuck

between her teeth. Her face went dark and dead. She sat staring. Eagle looked up at her. Sacajawea was jerked out of her daze by Eagle's words.

"Our man is foolish—nobody at home—you know." She pointed to her head. "No one would take an old man to a strange land across so much water. The water sickness would affect him."

Sacajawea pushed hard to get the needle through two layers of hide, and pricked her finger. She frowned and sucked at the tiny drop of blood, then set her face and fixed her wary black eyes on Charbonneau.

"I need some warming before I high-tail it to a hunter's camp." Charbonneau pulled Kitten closer to him.

"The papoose is too young for any warmth," warned Sacajawea, remembering her fate among the Minnetarees with sudden remorse. She clicked her tongue and thought now about getting Baptiste away from this situation.

After several games, Charbonneau wiped his face with a red bandanna. "Play something with a good stake—something worthwhile."

Tess nodded, his eyes glistening and his breath coming fast with the excitement of the game and the glances and sly handclasps of Kitten stirring him.

"Me!" suggested Kitten boldly, smiling at all three men.

Baptiste drew in his breath and let out a low, shrill whistle.

Sacajawea exploded. "No!" she said. "You will never do this."

Charbonneau laughed and tugged at his beard. "She is mine for tonight. If you win, Bap, she is yours tomorrow."

Tess nodded. "And mine the next?" He burned with desire.

Charbonneau went on dipping his hand into a bowl of bear's oil and tree sugar mixed with hominy and venison. "You learn to cook like this, and you be number one around here," he said, winking at Kitten and licking his fingers. At this single moment Charbonneau felt contentment about the coming deep fall days, and he thought nothing could approach the joy of having two nearly grown sons and three fine-looking women

to keep him feeling young. Afterward this evening
seemed more like a dream. It was nearly a dream now,
with shadows in it. Kitten snuggled near Baptiste, side-
stepping Charbonneau to get near him.

Sacajawea appraised the situation quickly. She noticed the bare feet of the girl, ankles tied with colored
leather cords, the long gingham dress making her young
body seem shapeless, yet the one bare shoulder revealing its soft skin, the small parfleche Kitten wore
at her waist, now bulging, where it had been flat several
days before.

Kitten, suddenly conscious of Sacajawea's eyes,
turned her face toward her. "*Pase*," she said in Spanish.
"Come in. You wish to play the game?"

Sacajawea remained quietly sitting, her hands in her
lap.

"This house is yours also," Kitten said. "You keep it
clean. You can play." The tone expressed contempt.

"No! You stand!"

The flat, terse answer halted Kitten's look. She slowly
drew her eyes from Tess and turned to face Sacajawea
with her whole body. What she saw was a mature squaw
who threatened her friendship with the two boys. Kitten's face held an expression of indolent cunning. She
had known squaws long enough to know the arrogant
assumption of some that all men bowed to the wishes
of the eldest squaw in the lodge.

"So then, you do not have to. I would be the last to
force you to play the game," she said affably. "You can
come and watch. Maybe you will learn how it is played,
then." She paused, and in a conciliatory voice that did
not mask her disregard of Sacajawea's demand, she
added politely, "Sit with us and have some boiled coffee."

Kitten was resolute enough to know that to this polite offer should be added the casual gesture of turning
around and going about the game. But she could not.
The deathly quiet of Sacajawea held her, and the look
in her eyes. They had hardened like obsidian. Kitten
saw behind the look too late.

As she slowly got to her feet, Sacajawea was already
standing, weight balanced evenly on both feet. Sacajawea reached for the small parfleche.

"Let us see what sort of beading is done by your people."

Kitten held the bag close to her waist and lowered her sulking eyes.

Tess looked up, his eyes bright. "Come on, Kitten," he pleaded. "I would like to see what you make. Do you have Ute trinkets in there? Beads you have strung?"

She took a step backward.

Tess lurched toward her and grabbed the bag, breaking the strings that held it to her waist.

"Do not lay your warty hands on that, you filthy son of a bitch!" she cried in her pigeon English learned from white traders. She scratched at Tess.

"See, she is plenty strong." Tess grinned. "And wild like a kit of the mountain lion."

Kitten staggered back to swing her fist, her feet spread apart. The movements of Sacajawea caught her eye and froze her an instant too long. Before she could drive in a blow, Tess had an arm around her. They went down in a heap.

Sacajawea had emptied the bag's contents upon the floor before the amazed eyes of the family. All sorts of trinkets and jewelry spilled out. There were pearl earrings belonging to Sacajawea, a gift from Miss Judy. Eagle reached for her missing necklace of pink seashells and her multicolored beaded belt. There was Sacajawea's small snap purse of American coins she had saved from sales at Chouteau's, and the peace medal, which took up all the back space in the purse.

Kitten, flailing with her fists and pushing with long, strong legs, pulled away from Tess. With slashing dark eyes she grabbed the bag and began scooping the trinkets into it. Sacajawea shoved her aside and began searching for her own things. She found the blue stone, the piece of sky, still attached to its thong. Beside it was her pewter mirror and bone comb, and the round, rusty red glass with the white bird raised on one side.

Eagle moved closer to gather her things, laughing shrilly, almost hysterically. "I knew time would be an enemy and soon we'd know what kind of girl you are!"

Kitten seemed like a captured animal. She had a thin face, a bit pockmarked. Her shoulders were straight. Her rounded buttocks quivered. Then she did not move except for her eyes, which now constantly turned this way and that to watch the boys, Charbonneau, and the kneeling women beside her.

Tess panted and wiped his sweating forehead with his hands.

Clutching her stolen belongings, Sacajawea half rose from the floor; with a quick push of her knee she threw Kitten flat on her back, and with her free hand scratched at her face and bare shoulder. Kitten clung like a panther. She clawed toward Sacajawea's throat.

Over and over they rolled, scattering the stolen goods on the clean-swept floor. They rolled against the far wall. Kitten reached for the inside of her blue-and-scarlet sash. Sacajawea came back with a swing of her arm that knocked the butcher knife from the Ute girl's hand. A kick from her foot sent the knife clattering out of reach.

Kitten let out a low whine. The accuracy of Sacajawea's timing, the safe parry of the butcher knife, kicking it out of reach, tempered her anger with a spot of fear. There was a cold deliberation about Sacajawea's attack that froze her again an instant too long. Before Kitten could reach for her opponent's long braid, Sacajawea had pushed her fist into the hollow at the base of Kitten's throat. Just as her other hand came up to scratch at the Ute's thin face, there was a sudden and terrific explosive crack above them. Both women lay as if stunned for an instant. Then Kitten, with a heave, broke loose and staggered to her feet.

Sacajawea rose to her knees. She saw Kitten standing before her with glazed, frightened eyes, staring at a long rip down the side of her cotton dress. This revealed her tawny pubescent body.

Charbonneau could no longer stand the situation and had pulled the horsewhip from its wall nail. He had snapped it with such force that it had caught the thin dress of Kitten and ripped it.

With a frantic howl Kitten cried out to him, "Go to it! Go to it! Crack it good over the crone's back!"

Thus encouraged by the hatred and fear that was on the girl's face, Charbonneau lifted the whip and struck once.

It fell like a great tree. The impact on Sacajawea

was like the heavy trunk of a cedar and a moment later the lacerating sting of its branches and needles.

Oh, Lord, Sacajawea thought, I am finished. I will not stay in this place with a man who humiliates me and a child-squaw who has sticky fingers. Her face was set into an impassive mask.

The next blow struck her like a bolt of lightning. She heard the deep rumble of thunder, the sharp crack, and the hiss of flame all at once. The impact dazed her an instant. To clear her swimming gaze, she looked up. Baptiste was clutching the butcher knife. He did not move. He drew a target on his father, near the breast-bone, in his mind. Still, his hand did not move; his mouth went dry; his knees trembled.

Eagle, crouched beside the table, shouted. "Do something! He will kill her!"

"*Ai, ai, ai,*" said Kitten, her tone expressing admiration for the old man.

The third blow pushed Sacajawea forward on her face. Her body felt no pain; there was only an irresistible, bodiless force that hit her from all sides, a roaring in her ears. She rose to her knees.

Her thoughts were above her body. She remembered how Charbonneau had looked when he shaved off his whiskers—as though he had two faces. *Ai*, he did have two faces—one, conceited and fun-loving; the other, uncontrolled and unthinking. She thought of Duke Paul, who was taking her son Baptiste out of this lodge, with gratefulness. She thought of Chief Red Hair and knew he would encourage Baptiste to go to that unknown land across the Great Eastern Waters. Her face relaxed, and she smiled with shining eyes, as if nothing were happening. *Ai*, to her this whipping was an unreal dream that would soar away, forgotten. She thought of her own words: "If you whip me again, I will leave and you will not see me again." *Ai*, she would leave. There were other lodges, other people for friends.

Baptiste gripped the knife with trembling fingers. Impossible! He gritted his teeth; this time he would stop the horrible whipping. His glance fell to his mother, crouched close to the floor but with her head held up. He saw this peculiar thing about her face. There was no anger on it for Charbonneau or the young Ute girl;

no shame for herself; neither pity nor sympathy. It was relaxed and smiling. His gaze plumbed the dark pools of her eyes. Baptiste could not believe them. They were deep with the greatest love he had ever seen, and turbulent, as if stirred by leaping trout in the joy of spring. They were triumphant with a strange exultation.

Another blow came, and her head felt large with pressure. She came up gasping as the lash uncoiled around her. A warm trickle ran down her side under the shreaded tunic.

Two more blows came with long pauses; they lacked vigor. Did Charbonneau hold back, or was it the strange, kind smile and look of exultant triumph in his woman's eyes that made him stop?

Sacajawea rose slowly, panting. With calm dignity she walked forward to her son.

Baptiste met her. He felt shame that he had no power to use the knife on the one who had left long, bleeding welts on his mother's back. Angrily he threw the knife so it struck the floor and stood, handle up. She faced her son as if nothing had happened, her face relaxed and smiling, her eyes shining.

"The duke will come for you before the next snowfall. Go." She said it in a low, curiously vibrant voice.

Baptiste felt as though he were standing alone, high on the edge of a fathomless chasm, the world lying far below. His mother's face smiled with understanding. A new strength filled him.

Charbonneau rolled and lit a cigarette and walked toward the fireplace, hands thrust deep into his pants pockets.

Like someone driven by an unconquerable obsession from which she was not yet freed, Sacajawea mechanically gathered up her blanket and placed it beside the door. The others watched as she and Baptiste walked slowly, in quiet dignity, as if nothing had happened, through the opened door.

Sacajawea felt the darkness cover her, and the pain across her back became sickening. She gulped the fresh air to subdue her rising nausea. Then she slumped to the ground. Presently she heard Baptiste talking with someone. She tried to stand on her feet. Eagle came to her with wads of old faded-blue strouding.

"I have waited until our man snores with sleep," shushed Eagle with a finger over her mouth. "I come to wash your back."

At the tiny stream behind the shed, Eagle washed Sacajawea's back, sopping off the blood with the wads of trade cloth. She put a fresh tunic carefully over Sacajawea's head.

Baptiste squatted in the darkness, thinking. He thought in the morning he would see General Clark. Clark would know of a place for his mother so she would not be in danger of another whipping from Charbonneau. He wanted now more than anything to get his mother away from this place.

Sacajawea shivered with a chill.

"Our man is a beast," said Eagle with disgust. "We ought to take a rope and tie him to a tree."

"The mare," Sacajawea said. "Get it for me."

"Let me bathe your face first," begged Eagle.

"There is no time," said Sacajawea. "I am leaving."

Eagle went into the shed for the mare. Sacajawea stood, unsteadily at first. She went back into the cabin and quietly searched for a few belongings.

Kitten stirred, sat up in her robes and said, "There, now, cut out her heart!" She pushed her butcher knife toward Charbonneau, who was by now half-awake, and drew her finger dramatically across her throat, making a foolish clucking noise.

Charbonneau frowned at her a moment, then looked away. Kitten came back and began to slash the air around him as if to cut his body into chunks. He jerked back, dodging her thrusts as well as he could, then he stayed still and merely frowned at her threatening movements, watching Sacajawea putting things into a large leather bag.

"She is my woman many years," he said sleepily, staring at Sacajawea, half-frightened now at the continued violence the Ute girl displayed.

The smile of triumph faded from Kitten's face. "Then let us skin her like a beast."

"You are from the *diable*," said Charbonneau, sucking in his cheeks.

"We have human meat for the next meal," said Kitten smiling, looking at Sacajawea. "You'll stay?" She was moving out of her blankets.

Sacajawea said nothing, but packed her things and took a leather box of jerky from the shelf.

"We'll take her hair. Quickly!" Kitten, on her feet now, pushed Charbonneau's hand, which held the butcher knife.

He shrank back, wondering what the girl would do, and hoping it would not be a cruel thing. The night's episode was finished; it was now time for sleep.

"Get the hell back in your robes!" muttered Tess. "I want to sleep." He took Kitten by the arms and held her against him. He laughed with great delight as she tried to bite his hands and arms. "Oh, Jesus!" he stormed.

A thin, bitter smile slashed the Ute's mouth. Instantly it changed to a sullen frown as she saw Sacajawea pick up the snap purse with the medal and coins and pearl earrings, the pewter mirror and bone comb, then the sky blue stone on the thin thong and the red marblelike glass, and drop them inside her bag. The glow of the fire brought out the deep rose red in Sacajawea's dark, round, unlined cheeks. She had not lost her dignity. She did not scream or jump, but moved quickly and quietly. She slipped on the old blue coat with the worn sleeves, letting the wide folds and familiar scent of the garment engulf her. Her eyes turned to Charbonneau.

He had never seen her quite like this. She seemed to tower high above him. She said no word. Her face showed a look of rapturous triumph. He felt his strength gone, and he feared this strange beauty that seemed to radiate from her black eyes, which were sharper than knives.

"Dear God, the blessed Jesus, Mary, and Joseph, now where the hell are you going?" he howled with exasperation. "What is this, anyway?" He pushed his fear away and concentrated on her face. "Little Bird Woman! Oh, Madonna, protect me from the females in my household!" He was now enraged, but he knew that he was as helpless as an infant tied in a cradleboard.

Sacajawea saw his shoulders beginning to sag. She felt pity, but pushed it away. She had pitied him before. She carried the bag to the door, found some steel firesticks, and picked up the folded blanket. She pushed the door open and walked through without looking back. Outside she said calmly to Eagle, "Send Baptiste to the homeland of the duke."

"*Ai*," said Eagle, trembling. "It is done. I promise. That Ute girl makes me so angry. If she were on fire, I would not spit on her."

Sacajawea heeled the mare and was gone.

Thundering out of the cabin, Charbonneau lifted his fist, his face now livid. "Damn! Where the *diable* is she going?" he asked in desperation.

"Who knows?" It was Kitten's answer to life and death alike.

Charbonneau swung his head from side to side, glowering helplessly from beneath his shaggy eyebrows.

Tess was outside searching through the night air for a sound that might lead them to her. "Can't track anything this night. In the morning we can track that horse easy."

One thing stood out to Charbonneau like a sore thumb as he looked toward one face, then another, then toward the empty blackness beyond. His life suddenly had come tumbling down like a house of cards. It was the strange female power he felt Sacajawea possessed. It sought to dwarf his manhood, and against it he had no means to rebel. He felt as though he had been trampled by buffalo. His mouth had the taste of a magpie's nest. He grunted and spat on the dust. So—maybe this was good riddance for the rest of the night. Tomorrow, early, they would track the damned horse. By evening things would be the same and he and Tess would go out on a fall hunt, just to gather a few fine beaver pelts and maybe a deer or young elk. In any event he planned to be gone when Duke Paul came to Saint Louis. Charbonneau felt he could not endure a tongue-lashing from the duke right now.

Eagle was certain this was the dark night that had been predicted weeks ago when she watched the moonlight go out with an eclipse. If she had only known then what the omen meant, she could have warned Sacajawea. Tears were in her eyes. She heard a low sigh in the darkness.

"Umbea." It came from Baptiste as he let his breath out as if he'd been kicked.[1]

Sacajawea was gone!

Jerk Meat

After Sacajawea left Charbonneau, she apparently wandered about for some time, finally making her home with a band of Comanches, called the Quohadas, or the Antelope Band.

HUGH D. CORWIN, editor of Prairie Lore, *the journal of the Southwestern Oklahoma Historical Society*, personal letter, 1967.

Sacajawea sat wrapped in her blanket behind a small hillock. The night wind did not touch her aching back. The mare was tethered close by. The pitch blackness of the night, the fireflies, the silence, the tragic, soundless rushing of the great earth through time—it caught at her breath, her heart.

She held no resentment, no bitterness. Life was more than what she saw, heard, and sensed. It extended beyond the visible, the audible, the sensory limits. She was certain the moon in eclipse had foretold this parting from her family. It was a path in her life and could not be avoided. It was her weakness that had held her from sensing, weeks ago, this predetermined change in her life.

Then daylight came. The sun's rays filtered through high clouds. The mare, staked Shoshoni-fashion, browsed on the dried grasses.

She lay very still, listening, so still that not even the yellowed grass under her rustled. There was no other sound than that of the mare getting her first meal of the day. There was no neighing, no creaking of leather. The only other audible sound was the loud beating of her own heart.

She wondered if Eagle would take a beating for having helped her get the mare. Her scowl changed to a smile as she thought that this mare was one of the best horses belonging to Charbonneau. Charbonneau would not dare punish Eagle severely, for she might leave and go to her own people.

Sacajawea said aloud to the mare, "Charbonneau, you would then have no one to mend your leggings or sew moccasins or boil your tea. The Ute child will not stay long if she has to do squaw's work. She will run to some other white trapper who has foofaraw that takes her fancy."

Her monologue was accompanied by small, scandalized clucks and tooth clickings, glottal explosives, and offended, swallowed gutturals. The mare said nothing.

"You always did like young squaws. I have heard men tease about your 'daughters.' Below your face hairs

you turn red and angry as though it were some unnatural thing to hide. I feared that violent temper more
than thunderstorms."

Tongue clicking and head shaking, she smiled at the
cloudless sky and rolling hills. She decided to move
south with the warmth for the winter. She wadded a
strip of jerky against the inside of her cheek.

Facing the sun she said, "Thank you, Great Spirit,
for giving me the courage to leave my man at the time
he was no longer safe to live with. Thank you for directing the path of my boys. Thank you for guiding me
down the trail south where the sun warms the earth."

Sacajawea was thirsty. Her mouth was dry. Her legs
were stiff. Her back ached. Her eyes searched the ravine. She saw only the scrub timber, brown-leaved oaks.
She pulled at the buckskin tether of the mare and rode
easily through the center of a dry creek bed.

She did not build a fire that night for fear it might
be a signal to Charbonneau. She rested awhile, then
when she discovered the full moon, she decided to travel.
The land began to fall slowly underfoot. Twice the mare
slipped into natural dips in the land, jarring her enough
to rattle her teeth. The mare stumbled into wet, sloggy
mud. There were tall bulrushes. She pushed through
to the other side of the rushes. A fringe of trees loomed
over her, a darker patch of black in the night. She
stopped to listen, head bent, loose and flowing hair
hanging to one side. Somewhere ahead, water was running over gravelly shallows. She moved through the
trees. The horse walked on grass, then gravel.

At the edge of the stream Sacajawea dismounted,
pulling the horse along until she touched the edge of
the running water. She drank from cupped hands. The
mare drank. She bathed her face and arms, then her
neck under her flowing hair, and let water run over
her tensed, aching back. She dug out a comb from the
leather bag. It was made from dried buffalo tongue, a
prickly slab. She wondered why she had brought this
along when she also had the bone comb from Chief Red
Hair. She shrugged her shoulders, cringing from the
pain in her back. She combed her hair from her forehead
back and then down to the hair ends hanging about her

hips. She braided it and used small strands from the bulrushes to tie the ends.

She walked, leading the mare. She went over hills, sometimes through thick underbrush. Several times the horse could not walk through the deep, wet muck of a slough. It took time to circle the sloughs. She had time.

For many days Sacajawea slept part of the morning, then traveled by horseback until nightfall, when she tethered the mare and wrapped herself in the blanket to sleep. Each morning the pain in her back was less noticeable.

One morning the supply of dried meat ended, and from then on she subsisted on the meager fare of the land. Game was scarce, and it was a rare day when she could bring down a rabbit or a quail with a stick or stone to cook over a small fire of dry wood, started by her steel firesticks.

She counted ten suns before reaching a west-flowing river. The river was shallow when she first found it. By the intaglio of many hooves, which her mind recreated as the dancing movement of horses waiting to cross, she saw that people, possible friendly, had forded the river. She followed. She crossed, made night camp, and listened to the purling against boulders and sycamore trunks. The morning was cloudy.

Along with high humidity and a feeling of uncomfortable mugginess, the low-lying clouds brought swarms of no-see-'ems—small, biting gnats that made her arms and legs itch. The back of her neck was crawling with them and it felt like each had a tiny, jabbing lance. The mare shook her head, switched her tail, and whinnied. She might have bolted if the rawhide tether had not been held tightly. Sacajawea wondered if this were a warning to turn back.

Sacajawea led the mare through a natural redoubt of wind-torn scrub pines and boulders. Suddenly a fierce rain squall came up out of nowhere. The horse whinnied, and Sacajawea had to hold the lead rope firm.

The wind died quickly and the rain grew gentle. Soon the sun shone faintly through the clouds. A blue jay sitting on a windfall scolded.

She climbed a rise to thick yellowed grass and saw not a moving thing except the river, which had risen

and was flooding muddily through the little canyon.
She checked the tether of the mare and spread the blanket out on the thick grass to dry in the last rays of
sunlight. She emptied the pack sack, piled her loose
belongings on a huge flat-surfaced boulder, then sorted
them and placed them where they caught the breeze
and would dry. She took off her wet tunic and spread
it on the boulder. She put on the old blue coat, smelling
the dampness of it the second it came out of the pack
sack. She lay down. She was asleep in an instant.

When she woke she was as tired and achy as when
she lay down the night before. The gray woolen blanket
was nearly dry, holding only the dampness that was in
the humid air. She folded it and began to repack her
things when she heard a loud scraping. She glanced
around, wondering if she were alone with the mare.
Nothing seemed out of place. The crows were still
perched in the trees overhead. She put the old blue coat
into the leather bag, which was stiff from yesterday's
rain. She rubbed her tunic between her hands to soften
it before pulling it over her head. The sound of scraping
came again and this time it made her jump. The mare
calmly munched the red clover and prairie acacia. Sacajawea looked on either side, then her eyes moved
upward. Two post oaks were rubbing branches in the
wind, making a scratchy, creaking noise. She laughed
out loud. She was not only tired, she was hungry and
thirsty. She looked at the muddy river and wondered
if she could find clear spring water. Tossing the blanket
on the mare's back and tying the leather bag on top,
she swung one leg over and pulled herself up on the
horse. The waist-high grass seemed greener after the
rain. But signs of game, large or small, were washed
from the red soil.

At midday when the sun was hot Sacajawea saw a
lake whose wavy shoreline seemed less than a mile
away. However, it continued to move just out of reach.
The hills that rose out of the flat plain looked like islands in the lake. Once she stopped and made the horse
go backward several yards. The shoreline moved forward toward the horse.

By sunset she was walking, leading the mare through
grass and dried mud. The air was drier and cooler and

she trudged on, enjoying it. Her gait was pigeon-toed, the usual squaw-walk, the toes kept inward to keep one's balance while carrying heavy loads.

Shortly past sundown she sat on a rock and bent with the mare to drink great handfuls of water from a spring that oozed from the black leaf mold at her feet. She was warm, almost feverish. The autumn air seemed hot and dry. She put water on her face and wrists. She felt refreshed and took off her moccasins and bathed her feet in the small well of cool water, muddying it. She noticed signs of deer in her path. Hunger gnawed her insides. The hills rose like great loaves of brown bread taken fresh from Rose York's oven. Sacajawea dug roots and chewed their juices dry.

In the morning, she stood to look from a great height on a green river that found its way in the open along a great distance. This sight gave her much relief. She thought if she moved downward toward the river she might find a village. In the evening, she worked on a crude bow and a couple of arrows, using the hard maple and strips of leather from the bottom of a tunic and her butcher knife.

Each day seemed like the one before, but the land changed slowly, subtly. The hills were not rolling, but rose right out of the flatland. The land across the winding river seemed boundless. A loneliness engulfed her. She shot a squirrel one evening. She ate berries and roots and padded her frayed moccasins with the squirrel hide. The land seemed limitless. The horizons did not express the limits of a valley; they told her there was more beyond, that this bare, treeless land stretched away and away. She felt small and dry. She chipped the local stone crudely to make more points for the arrows.

The plains seemed to have less game, water, and vegetation. Heat waves lay over the bare grass. The mare carried her along. She did not direct her, but let the Great Spirit guide her path from one bit of brittle grass the mare munched to the next. Her hunger was not sharp, not demanding as it had been during days gone by when she had been with Lewis and Clark but it was there, a part of her.

A horned toad scrabbled away toward the west. She

pursued him, thinking he might make a sort of meal
and give her strength to find a spring before sundown.
She took quick, jerking looks around to all sides, furtively, like a savage in the wilds. She was looking for
something to drink, something to eat. She was a hunter.
And then, far down a slope against a wall of yellow
rock, she saw buffalo with little birds sitting on their
backs riding across the prairie. Surely there was a hunting party out for such a fine herd.

She looked at her small bow and short arrows. She
longed for a taste of good, roasted buffalo hump. She
began to eye the mare as she tethered her for the evening. Then, hurriedly, she caught half a dozen locusts
and pulled their legs off so they could not jump away.
She let them dry on a flat stone, then chewed them,
swallowing cautiously. She did not think of what they
had been; she thought only of food to sustain herself. I
believe I could eat dog meat today, she thought. Chief
Red Hair would find it unbelievable that I could be so
hard put for something to eat.

It was a day to remember, with the sound of wolves
howling far along the prairie, trailing the great herd
of buffalo, and no hunters following or even aware of
all the good meat and robes walking away. In the twilight she tried out her bow and arrows on the bull bats.
She hit one and spent the whole evening skinning and
roasting it, but the meat on its skeleton was so scarce
she was left even more hungry.

The wild, hard land of the southwest rolled on forever. Day after day, Sacajawea clung to the back of the
mare feeling light-headed. At night she slept under
mesquite brush, inert, palsied with weakness.

One evening she stopped in an arroyo where wild
cedars grew dark green. The sun sank in a sickly yellow
cloud bank casting a blood red streak through it. On one
of her quick, furtive looks she saw a pronghorn buck.
It was directly behind her on a rise, not more than a
hundred yards away. The thought came to her mind
that this was some kind of a foretoken. She could not
think what it meant. Cold sweat was on her hands. She
moved slowly away from the cedar in order to see the
pronghorn better. He had not moved a muscle, but stood
with his head high and his nose in the air, a sentinel.

His black horns rose straight above his eyes. His face was very white, and the three white bars on his throat stood out shiny in the fading light of day. A bubble of white spittle dripped down from the left side of his mouth as he finished chewing the last bit of cud, then fell to the rocks at his feet. His little tufted tail twitched slightly. Sacajawea could hear his breathing distinctly. She could smell his warm, heavy, animal scent. The long white hair on his buttocks rose and expanded into bunches, yet he did not move. Then, slowly, his head turned, and she looked straight into his yellow-brown eyes. She blinked her eyes. He was gone. His movement was so fast she could hardly remember his leaving at all.

Shaking with excitement, she ran across the cap rock to where he had been. She fell to her knees, her hands searching frantically. *Ai—iii!* There it was! A small, dark, wet spot, a drop of spittle where he had stood. She was certain of it. It was still wet to her touch. She sat, and her mind began churning. Had he been waiting for her? Was this a vision? Was it an omen? And so— what was the meaning of the pronghorn that seemed to look her over the way a father might look over a daughter in a new tunic? Slowly she made her way back to the mare who was patiently waiting. The horse was drinking. Sacajawea had not noticed the spring at the foot of the cap rock. She lay beside it, searching her mind. Why had she not seen the spring? The water poured into her parched body like a river of ice. It stabbed at her insides. Her stomach cramped in pain. Her head swam. She lay very still until the dizzy spell subsided, looking upward at the sky in twilight. She saw silhouetted against the blackening sky four twisted cedars on the cap rock near where the pronghorn had stood. She closed her eyes against their burning. Four—the medicine number of the People!

Her stomach hurt terribly, but that was nothing. Her wonderment was too big for pain. She would rest until she was stronger and could think on it more clearly. There was no need to hurry. She had a lifetime of years ahead. Maybe the Great Spirit would speak to her in dreams and tell her what she was to do. She lay quite

still, waiting for the cramping to stop and thinking
about the pronghorn.

In her night dream she saw four yellow, glacial lilies
trembling in the wind against snow patches at her feet.
The magnificent pronghorn came to sniff at the lilies,
then walked across them, not once looking at her.

"No, no," she called, "do not trample such beauty."

The pronghorn turned and seemed to smile at her.
His mouth opened, and he spoke in a deep, resonant
voice, "More will come in their time and be as beautiful;
do not be troubled, my daughter."

The morning dawn was gray. The wind stirred
through the rocks. The air was filled with tiny cold
teeth. Sacajawea's mind cleared. Desperately she longed
for another human, someone to tell about the dream,
someone to talk with. She began to wonder about the
unseen people who had crossed the river with many
horses days before.

She was tired of living on snakes, horny toads, and
dry grass roots. Her tunic was filthy with dust and dirt;
her moccasins were but patches from various hides of
small animals. Her hair hung in greasy strands. Her
hands were dark brown from the sun and callused from
leading the mare through rocks and small canyons, along
dry creek beds. Now she rode and held loosely to the
reins as the mare put one foot ahead of the other on
and on in the cold day's grayness. She was certain that
the pronghorn was a talisman, a protector for her. Had
he not called her daughter and told her not to be troubled?

She came to leafless willows at the edge of a shallow
river. She sat in a slight dip in the land as protection
from the cold wind. Her legs wobbled. She felt weak.
She lay back between several stones. The earth was
cold. She closed her eyes a moment, then opened them
abruptly to check again what she thought her mind had
told her was in the willow. A small, straight branch
did not seem to belong. She stood up and worked it loose.
It was a broken arrow shaft, about a foot long. It was
bound with thin rawhide, and on the end that had been
embedded in the tree was black obsidian. The head was
cut in a manner that caused Sacajawea to turn it over
and examine it more carefully.

"My people!" she exclaimed out loud. "Great Spirit, you must not play tricks with me."

She knew well enough that this was too far south to be Shoshoni country. The dizziness came back, so she sat for a moment. Without much thought she began pulling her fingers through the tufts of ripened grass, collecting the tiny dropseeds in her skirt. She pinched some between thumb and forefinger and put them in her mouth. The little seeds were hard, but when chewed made a nutty-tasting, gummy paste that was quite good. She spent most of the day by the shallow river collecting seeds and putting them in the leather bag. She walked past several charred mounds that looked as though fires had been built there recently; beside the mounds were small piles of chipped black obsidian. She saw these things, but her mind did not connect them with any human occupation, for she was preoccupied with keeping the dizziness to a minimum.

She looked to see where the mare was and was startled to see dark gray-black clouds piling up in the distance. She could see small puffs of dust being blown up by the wind under the clouds. It grew darker and the wind began to blow, flattening the prairie grass. She noticed a sick, yellow-green color at the leading edge of the clouds as they swooped lower toward the earth. Dust devils whirled along the ground, closer now, carrying sticks of dry mesquite and stalks of dead plants along with sand and dirt.

With fascination she watched a spiraling cloud grow and slant down, bending and twisting from the heavy, dark cloud. Like the drooping tail of a coyote it dragged across the ground, roaring and sucking up mesquite and whole cottonwoods and willows. This slender tail of a cloud pulled up for a moment, then dropped again, picking up more dirt, gravel, trees, and grasses. It veered away from Sacajawea, moving quickly upriver. Within minutes she felt the fierce gusts of wind that trailed behind the long finger of the cloud, and heard them rush through the tops of the trees. Yellow streaks of lightning flew across the sky and she pulled the horse close among the willows for protection. She picked up the arrow again and took a closer look at it. The shaft was grooved from the end of the feathers to the head

of the arrow point. There were two straight black grooves
on one side. She turned it over and saw two red spiral
grooves. Many times she had seen her own father cut
just such grooves using a bone containing a circular
hole with a little projection inside.[1] *Ai*, she thought to
herself, can this possibly be a Shoshoni arrow? She
crouched close against the willows. Suddenly it began
to hail, and the horse twitched and flicked its tail as
though it were being attacked by bloodsucking, green-
headed flies. Sacajawea spoke softly to the horse so that
it would not bolt away through the waist-high sage.

Sacajawea's head ached, and she pulled her old blue
coat over herself as protection from the pelting of the
corn-size hail. She thought about the grooved arrow and
she shivered. The hail did not last long, but the cold,
blustery wind felt like it would blow forever.

She scraped at the melting hail with her toe. Just
then a ruffed grouse flew up and away down the riverbank, but she did not try to chase it with a stone or
with her bow and arrow; by now her hunger pangs were
beyond feeling. She did not even think of hunting buffalo chips for a fire to keep off the cold. Her thoughts
seemed more a dream than reality.

Sacajawea imagined she would get up soon and would
then see Eagle fixing the morning meal. Baptiste would
be there, his sturdy back straight as a lodgepole. He
would smile as he told what had been done the day
before in school. Her dreams faded; she slept. It was
dark when she awoke. There were no stars in the sky.
She pondered the funnellike cloud that had sucked up
the land and growing things. Was it some device of the
sky-people, sent for her to see? Did it have an important
meaning? Was it related to the pronghorn experience?
Was it a foreshadowing? She buttoned the old blue coat,
thankful for it, and pulled her wet blanket closer about
her shoulders.

The wind had now died down, and Sacajawea took a
deep breath. Her mind cleared a bit, and she could detect a familiar odor in the air, but she could not name
it. She pinched her nostrils tight and blew hard. Again
she sniffed, taking only small amounts of air at a time.
Then she knew. A wild dog or coyote was near. She
heard the mare whinny. She wondered if the coyote was

nipping the mare's legs. Then she remembered coyotes usually went after much smaller prey, unless it was carrion or something foul smelling. That was it! Foul smelling! She scrambled to her feet and grabbed the lower branches of a cottonwood. In doing this she had a whiff of her unwashed body. That caused her to hurry and she pulled herself painfully up into the tree.

From her perch she saw a restless, doglike animal pacing back and forth near the tree. The mare snorted once and moved away into the tall, brittle grass. Sacajawea could hear the swishing of the stems. The farther away the sound retreated, the more alone she felt. Her stomach knotted and her eyes watered. One foot was jammed uncomfortably in the fork of the tree, but she knew she had to stay put until the coyote left. Toward morning she saw another coyote join the first. They circled in opposite directions around the tree. Once she pulled off a branch and threw it at them but they only growled and ran faster. Her arms and legs grew heavy with fatigue. Her eyelids closed, but she dared not let herself fall asleep or relax her hold on the tree.

In the first light of dawn she saw slender shafts of white smoke rise in the south and merge with the pale sky. The smoke seemed to come from a broad gully three, four miles away. The coyotes had snuck away and she worked her foot loose. She wanted to see the arrow shaft again and she looked around for it. She wondered if the coyotes and the arrow were dreams or reality. Her eyes burned—they were puffy from crying and lack of sleep. Her head felt dull and oversized. She saw her mare munching a patch of Indian grass. Close by, staked to a low, scrub juniper, was a strange pinto pony. She rubbed her eyes, making them sting, and squeezed them down into narrow slits in order to see better. *Ai*, there were two horses and both were on rawhide tethers.

She moved her head and was surprised that she did not feel dizzy. She saw an orange flame between herself and the two horses. Hunkered over the fire, replenishing it with small mesquite sticks, was a strange man. She stared.

He appeared taller than the average Shoshoni, but she could not be sure until he stood up. His bare chest was wide and thick and copper-colored. His shiny, braided black hair was long, falling below his shoulders. On one side of his head he wore a round silver plate, about the size of Sacajawea's hand. She wondered if it were some good-luck token or his all-time helper. He wore close-fitting leggings attached to a leather string around the waist. The material was fringed, loose, and flapping beyond the seam. His moccasins had high buckskin tops, similar to the Shoshonis, with the seam down the heel. The fringe from the lace to the toe was short, but that along the back seam was six to eight inches long and it had bits of silver tied in the ends. A band of rawhide was wrapped around his left wrist so that he would not feel the sting of his bowstring.

He glanced up, his eyes meeting hers. They were slanted slightly upward and his wide, full mouth matched their curve. His nose was hooked like the hawk and his chin was round and firm.

Sacajawea licked her rough, chapped lips. "Who are you?"

"Comanche."

To Sacajawea the word Comanche meant, *I am a human being*.[2] She smiled at this answer and tried again. "Why are you here?"

"We are going to my lodge. You are a gift for my sister."

She had to listen intently to his twang, and the way in which he flapped the *r* by placing his tongue against the roof of his mouth and letting it drop fast. When she understood she pulled herself up, her heart pumping. "I am no gift! No slave! I am Shoshoni! Maybe lost, that is all!" She was indignant.

"Shoshoni!" he sputtered, making the in-and-out, weaving movement with his hands. "So—that is why your tongue is different, but the same, if I listen carefully."[3] He looked at her closely.

She was embarrassed, knowing that she was dirty, unkempt, and had not bathed in weeks. She was still in the cottonwood.

"Come down." He reached into a leather pouch and held out his hand. "*Wadzewipe*, Lost Woman, try this with *penat*."[4] He held a narrow piece of ordinary pemmican toward her. In his other hand he had a small skin container and he motioned for her to dip the pemmican in the container. She hesitated, took a deep breath, then jumped out of the tree into the sand. She crawled on hands and knees toward the food. A clear, viscous, golden brown liquid clung to the stick of pemmican. She put her tongue to it and the taste was sweet and delicious. She licked off the honey and dipped again and again, her hunger awakened. She was starving.

The Comanche laughed and slapped the side of his leg. "You have more hunger than manners, my cousin. We have more honey. It is gathered in the summer near the black sage, where there is much thorny chaparral. The gatherers are either stung by the honey bees or thorns."

She looked sideways at him. His upturned eyes were brown and clear. Many adult men had eyes that were muddied, the whites yellow and streaked with red. Slowly she got to her feet so that her stomach would not cramp. She shuffled down to the shallow river to drink. She cupped her hands and sucked in the muddy water, then stayed in the squatting position for several minutes to rest. She was glad this day's dizziness was not overpowering. She put her hand to her head, scratched vigorously, and again wished for a bath. She was surprised to see that the Comanche had followed her to the river. He washed his hands and drank.

"I saw you yesterday. I imagined your village sent you away for some punishment. I watched you examine my spent arrow. It was meant for the speckled grouse, but the fool bird got away two, three times. Later, I found a skinny, young pronghorn, and shot it for food for my old grandfather. During the twisting wind, I yelled for you to seek shelter. You did not listen to my warning. You will like my sister—my mother—"

"Stop!" she snapped. "I am not going. I will never be a slave! Never!"

"Well, so—now, I hear what you say. Anyway, you come with me, cousin. So, fix yourself."

"Fix? What? This is me! How can I be fixed?"

"How? Comb your hair. Wash your face. I think there is beauty somewhere, but it is deeply hidden. Fix yourself!"

She was so startled that she actually started for the

river, then stopped and looked him in the face. He had delicate little laugh lines at the corners of his mouth and his nose twitched. He stepped forward, as if to push her toward the water.

"You smell of sweat and trail dirt. Anyone standing downwind can tell you have traveled far." He looked from her louse-infested head to her scruffy, makeshift moccasins.

Reddening, Sacajawea turned and hurried out of his gaze to a place behind some thick willows along the riverbank. "I might go to that camp, but not with you! I will not belong to anyone!" she called back.

He raised his voice so she could hear. "Shoshoni women are same as Comanche. Talk, talk, when there is little time and much work. I have butchering, if you know how."

She felt weak and so kept her mouth closed. She shivered with the cold air when her soiled, ragged tunic was off. She rubbed small gravel mixed with water over her body, not only to clean it, but to warm it as well. Soon her skin burned as if the water were boiling. Using fine sand and water she scrubbed her hair. The wind dried her brown back with the long, white scars and she felt more alive than she had for many days. Finally she washed her tattered tunic, put on the old blue coat, and wrapped the gray woolen blanket about herself. Near the fire she put the tunic on a large mesquite branch to dry. Only then did she notice that he had hung pieces of a small bull antelope in the same mesquite tree.

"Can you cut and pack that in the antelope's skin so that it can be carried on your lowly mare?"

"Lowly?" she asked. "Because you prefer stallions does not mean you can make base comments about my mare. She is patient, loyal, and probably can walk longer without complaint than your patchy-looking pony."

He said nothing.

She closed her eyes and hoped she was not going to feel dizzy-sick. She found her butcher knife with her firesticks in the leather bag tied to her mare's back. She managed to cut the meat in smaller hunks so it would pack well. She cut off a small piece of fat and rubbed it on her lips and over the scratches on her legs and arms. Then she chewed it, hoping it was not too rich for her griping belly. Neatly she tied the finished pack with strips of antelope hide, but she knew there was not strength enough in her arms to lift it to the back of either horse. She sat on the gravely riverbank to rest, her back against the meat pack.

The Comanche brought her more pemmican and the honey bag. She found it hard to keep her eyes open. Finally he took away the food and pulled the meat pack up to the mare's back. Sacajawea lay on the ground a moment, until a voice above her said, "The sky is heavy with snow clouds. Come before the snow. The Quohadas are waiting."[5]

Her tunic was dry. Behind the big mesquite she took the blanket and coat off and slipped on the clean tunic. The fresh smell pleased her. She saw the parfleche in which he kept pemmican next to the pinto and pointed to it.

"I would have the strength to go, if I ate a little more."

"Ha! Just like a woman to only think of her belly when it is time to move on. A little at a time is best, Lost Woman. I, Jerk Meat, will give you more when it is time."

"How do you know what is best for me?" Sacajawea was somewhat irritated and reached out for the parfleche.

"So!" he laughed and slapped the side of his leg. "Your manners are worse than a spoiled child's. Or is this the usual way for my cousins who live as hunted animals in the Rock Mountains?"

She jerked her hand away, and her face turned crimson. She knew he was right. She had been too long by herself, not remembering manners. She combed her hair smooth with her fingers, wishing for her buffalo-tongue brush from the leather bag she'd left tied to the mare. She parted it down the middle as best she could and braided each side, wrapping small cottonwood sticks around the ends.

Now Jerk Meat looked at her and smiled his approval. Then he picked up the tattered blanket and threw it into the highest limb of a cottonwood, far beyond her reach. He looked at it and held his nose.

Then with no warning, not listening to her protests, he pushed her down by a flat stone. She did not have strength to resist. He laid her braids upon the stone and cleared his throat.

"I will keep them clean," she pleaded once more.

"It is a buck's privilege to wear long hair. I would be much degraded to bring in a squaw with hair longer than mine." He hacked each braid off below her ears with his knife. He picked up the braids and stuffed them inside his leather jerkin. "You won't need another bath until summer."

Holding the cut ends of hair, she sniffed and said angrily, "No buck will push me around. I'll take as many baths as I wish between now and spring."

"Horsetail," he said, provoked with this talkative squaw he had picked up and spent so much time bringing back to life.

The clouds grew grayer, and snow began to fall in large flakes. Sacajawea walked behind Jerk Meat. She led the mare with the meat and antelope hide tied to its back. Now she did not shiver quite so much and wanted to talk. She was like a well overflowing. It had been so long since she had spoken to another human that she could not be stopped.

She told the Comanche of the beautiful sunsets on the prairies, of the meadowlark's song from a nodding sunflower. She told him of the first rattlesnake she had eaten and of the lightning and heavy rain and the terrible heat, then cold. He nodded. He did not ask questions about more of her past. He let it sleep. He called her Wadzewipe, Lost Woman.

The ground was covered with white snow, but she did not feel cold. She was exhilarated by companionship. Jerk Meat told her that when the grass was green and the winds hot, great animal herds came to these Staked Plains. Brown bands of buffalo moved into the wind, herds of wild mustang with manes that flowed against the rose of a late summer sky, and the graceful antelope bounded, playful in a soft sea of grass. "We are called the Antelope tribe. The Quohadas! We hunt, raid ranches in Texas, and cross the Rio Grande to trade with Mexicans. Ten pounds of coffee can be traded for a good horse, or a keg of whiskey for a few mules. The

Quohadas are rich—their horse herds number in the thousands."

As Jerk Meat talked, Sacajawea watched the trail made by the small leather tassels attached to the heels of his moccasins in the skiff of snow. Then she studied his hair, which contained buffalo fur. The proper placement of the fur made his own hair appear longer, as though it reached below his shoulders. It was daubed with pine pitch and vermilion paint. Then she noticed the tip of each ear of her mare had been slit—the same as the ears on his pinto.

She asked him sharply about it.

"Have you seen the white man?" he asked her.

"*Ai*," she said.

"They do such things to make it known which horse belongs to which man. This is my mark."

"But that is my mare."

"You brought it to me for bringing back your health. So—we are even." He laughed.

"Can women ride horses in your village?"

"*Ai*, some do."

"Then I will work and earn my mare back," she said soberly.

He looked back at her quizzically, asking how it was she knew much about the white man when she came from the Land of the Shining Mountains.

"Traders who are white will come to my people," she said, avoiding his question.

He was truly surprised. "White traders in the mountains?"

"*Ai*, and so my people will not be without guns and ammunition for long. They will hunt more game and have full bellies."

"Ugh, guns make people hate one another," he said, thinking she made up that about white traders to impress him, and he spit at a pine. "Now, do you need the iron kettle of the white woman to cook in, or can you make a basket from willow?" he teased.

"I can make a good cooking basket," she answered, and to prove it, she tethered the mare and stepped into a willow grove and with her butcher knife cut some small branches. She worked quickly, making a deep basket. Jerk Meat hunted for the backside of a hillock sheltered from the wind. When he found a place, he curled himself up inside some dry leaves and went to sleep. Sacajawea built the fire with his rubbing sticks and heated two stones red-hot. She put snow and strips of antelope flank into the basket, then the red-hot stones. When the snow melted and the water boiled, she added more snow quickly so that the water covered the meat. After a while she tasted the meat. Delicious. She tasted some more. Wonderful. The snow almost put out her cooking fire. She gathered more sticks and heated the stones again and cut more flank meat. Then Jerk Meat was standing beside the fire, his toe pointing to his rubbing sticks.

She was embarrassed that she had not asked permission to use his sticks and that he would find she had eaten the meat before he had had any. She hurriedly put the fresh strips into the basket and put in handfuls of snow. With two green sticks as tongs, she dropped the hot stones in one by one.

"A fine cooking basket," he said, one side of his mouth turned up. "And so—I also see you have yourself gained much strength from that old father antelope."

She was too ashamed to reply. She owed much to this man, and she was rude and unthinking. Tears of humiliation came to her eyes; she blinked them back and sat very quietly.

He ate with his back to her. Then he turned and said, "If we move quickly, we will be in the village by evening. Come. A warm tepee is better than sleeping in a bed of snow."

She longed to ride the mare as he rode his pinto. Her legs began to ache, and her feet were numb. Her body became weary. She sneezed and coughed. Her throat ached. She knew she dare not say a word. Soon she could make out a small stream with big trees along it. Among the trees nestled the village, made up of some fifty or sixty lodges. Most of the hides that covered the tepees were decorated, but Sacajawea could not see this in the evening light. She saw only the warm, friendly yellow showing through the conical tepees. The snow stung like porcupine needles on her bare arms and legs now. Her hair was wet, and the top caked with snow.

The lodge of Jerk Meat was near the center of camp.

It was made up of a larger tepee, where Jerk Meat's mother and father lived; a small tepee, where Sacajawea was given sleeping room with two others, a young woman and an old man; and the smaller tepee, where Jerk Meat slept.

The young woman was Spring, sister of Jerk Meat. Spring had recently lost her man on a raid across the Rio Grande. Sacajawea also learned that the old man was the grandfather, Big Badger. Jerk Meat's mother was called Hides Well, and his father, Pronghorn, was a chief.

That first evening, she held back her sneezes. She lay down and her mind was clear, as a warm, clean buffalo robe was pulled over her by Spring. Sleep came almost instantly. She did not hear the drumming and singing as the village celebrated the coming of more hunters with good catches. It was a celebration for the food that would keep them through the cold winter. The early snow foretold a long, cold winter.

In the morning, Hides Well came to the tepee and motioned for Big Badger and Spring to leave. She motioned for five or six squaws to come inside. They crowded around the buffalo-hide couch staring at the sick Sacajawea.

"Wadzewipe," they repeated among themselves. "Lost Woman." "*Avajemear*," said one short, fat squaw with a single thin silver loop dangling through one pierced ear. "She went a long way."

All afternoon, women trooped in to gaze at the woman who had come from a long way, alone. They poked their fingers and elbows in each other's ribs as they jabbered about the newcomer as if she had no ears to hear. Big Badger, outside against a cottonwood tree, watched from slitted eyes and grunted each time he shifted his weight for a more comfortable position. Finally, he pulled himself up to his full height and then bent double to enter the tepee, scattering the women to the outside with a wave of his big boney brown hands.

"Enough. The woman must rest to gain strength."

For a week, Sacajawea lay most of the time on her robe inside this tepee. She fought off high fever and a sore throat. Once, in delirium, she spoke of the black man who danced with her baby, and then of the white man who beat her upon the back.

The old grandfather, Big Badger asked, "Who is this young woman? Where did she come from?"

Jerk Meat replied simply, "She is Wadzewipe, Lost Woman."

Big Badger had a drooping face with a few scattered white hairs that he did not bother to pluck since he did not care about his appearance. His hair was white and thin, drawn into slender braids.

"There, and so—we must end her sickness," Big Badger said one morning. "Call Kicking Horse."

Kicking Horse had red and yellow feathers tied to his wrists and ankles. Large silver loops hung from his ears. He carried a buffalo's scrotum made into a rattle in his left hand; in his right he carried a quirt. He hit the ground around the sleeping couch furiously with the quirt, driving the hot devils out of the tepee. He turned to Spring and spoke so softly that Big Badger could not understand him. Soon Spring was back with a paunch full of water. He ordered Spring to remove the robe and tunic from the sick woman. Laying the quirt to one side, the Medicine Man sang in a monotone, his eyes rolling toward the top of the tepee. He turned without losing a beat in his song, and asked that the paunch be emptied over the woman. Sacajawea drew in a fast breath as the cold water hit her hot belly. At first it felt cooling and refreshing, then she shivered uncontrollably. Spring and Kicking Horse moved her to a dry couch and quickly covered her with a heavy skin. She was near the smoke hole in the center of the tepee. Her shivering stopped. She felt weak and did not like the shaking of the rattle that Kicking Horse insisted must be done through the night.

Usually Big Badger seemed sad and hardly alive, of little account. But a smile drew all the sag out of his face as he watched Jerk Meat reverently roll himself on the ground in the four cardinal directions, invoking powers that governed the great mountains of the north. Jerk Meat made signs of power and safety in the air with a twig from a lightning-struck tree and placed the dried wing of a dead turkey over Sacajawea's heart to give her life. He did this while Kicking Horse rattled and danced the fire dances he performed for curative purposes. At dawn, Kicking Horse went to his own lodge.

By morning, Spring was crouching near Sacajawea with a horn filled with a thick, hot soup.

Sacajawea took only a few mouthfuls before lying back and sleeping again.

"She wandered many months," said Jerk Meat to Big Badger outside the tepee. "She must have been lost when her people moved to a winter camp. She must have stopped to look at the flowers or talk with birds. She is that kind of woman. I saw her talk with a buck antelope just before I shot him."

"Aha," said Big Badger, hopping about on his spindly legs, which seemed hardly able to carry his stooped body. "She babbles about a baby, a white man that is a scoundrel, and a white man that is black. I never heard of black white men. She is perhaps a Medicine Woman, with special knowledge?"

"She is Wadzewipe," answered Jerk Meat.

"Aha," answered Big Badger. "You are right. She is a woman, not a girl. Perhaps she has seen thirty summers. She already has much knowledge of life. You can see that plainly. Someone has made lash marks upon her back. She was sent to us, maybe. The Great Spirit has reasons unknown to us for what he does." Big Badger went inside the tepee to look at Sacajawea and shake his head at her thin cheeks, but when he looked the cheeks were not burning with fever, and he smiled and called the others.

Spring brought water in a skin paunch, and they watched Sacajawea gulp it down. Big Badger showed Spring how to chew yucca roots, warm the residue by the fire, and apply it to the lacerations on Sacajawea's feet, which were too slow in healing.

In a few days, Sacajawea's strength began to return. A warm stirring of thankfulness ran through her. These were humans showing kindness to a stranger. She marveled at the warm feeling such action could bring.

For the first time, Sacajawea moved her eyes around the tepee. She saw that the floor was swept and the poles at the sides held cooking utensils and clothing, neatly hooked. She counted the skins around the tepee—ten—this was a small tepee. The skins were dou-

bled at the botton so that at night when light from the
fire showed through, the figures inside would not cast
shadows for the outside world to see what was going
on inside. The tepee was well made. She could see that
the tanned buffalo hides were well sewn and stretched
tight, flesh side out, over twenty, maybe twenty-two,
straight, slender poles of cedar that had been peeled,
seasoned, and shaved smooth to the same diameter.
Each lodgepole was about twenty feet long, with pointed
ends so that they would stay fixed in the ground. The
Comanches used the four-pole foundation, as did the
Shoshonis, which gave a grouping of two poles on each
side, unlike the three-pole foundation—forming a kind
of spiral, that was used by Cheyennes, Kiowas, and
Arapahos.

Sacajawea remembered the times she had helped her
mother, grandmother, and sister tie the four lodgepoles
together. The remembrance brought a constriction to
her throat. The women had pulled, pushed and steadied
the pine poles to get them upright, then tied them securely near the top. Sacajawea sighed. She swallowed
and set her mouth in a firm line after wiping the water
from her eyes. She and her sister, Rain Girl, would pull
the bottom ends of the poles out into an egg-shaped
circle, then the rest of the poles were laid against the
top crotch and pulled out to form the complete ellipse.
The long leather rope that was left dangling from the
top was then pulled tight and used to tie these other
poles in place. Rain Girl stood on their mother's shoulders to do this. Old Grandmother would always say,
"Tighter, tighter, pull tighter. What weaklings girls are
nowadays. This lodge will fall with the first hint of a
breeze." It never did as far as Sacajawea could remember. From on top of her mother's shoulders Rain Girl
used a rock to pound the poles solidly into the soft earth,
keeping them three feet apart from one another.

Sacajawea remembered how it felt to grab the end
of that rope and pull it outside the framework. She
walked with the sun, went clockwise four times—the
medicine number—pulled the rope upward as tight as
her arms would permit. She could still hear the snapping of the rope as it whipped up into place. She left
the rope hanging near the center of the floor inside, so

that Old Grandmother could fasten it to the anchor stake as tight as she wished. The anchor stake was about a yard long, two inches thick, and driven into the ground toward the back wall a few feet beyond the center fire.

This had been a happy time, Sacajawea thought. My mother sang and munched on dried fruit. Sometimes for more security Old Grandmother would set short stakes at an angle across the lodgepole, pounding them in the ground with a stone so that the lodge would be safer in harsh gusty winds.

The buffalo hide covering was pushed upward from the inside by a long pole. Rain Girl stood on her mother's shoulders to fasten the covering at the top. Then it was stretched around the outside of the poles and fastened at the front with finger-sized wooden pegs on either side of the door flap. Those lodge cover hides were usually replaced every two years, because of wear and weathering.

The widest part of the floor was from the entrance directly to the back wall. The place of honor was next to this rounded, back wall, where the man of the lodge slept. Beds of the other occupants were on both sides of the egg-shaped floor space. The beds were elevated above the ground about six inches with poles and rawhide slats. Buffalo robes were spread on top for bedding. Pillows were made of rabbit skins and stuffed with sweet-smelling grass. Sometimes a buffalo hide was hung between beds for privacy.[6]

Sadly, Sacajawea wondered if she would ever see those Shoshoni tepees again. From her resting place she looked through the open front flap of the tepee. The snow had melted. Jerk Meat was at work wrapping arrows in front of a fire.

Big Badger was slouched down beside the cottonwood tree facing the tepee, his eyes closed against the bright winter sunshine. Big Badger was thinking, Our horses have never been more numerous, and our donkeys are fat. We have nearly one hundred warriors, and our tepees are mended. We are like a mighty bow drawn taut, ready to shoot arrows in any direction with force. The Great Spirit has brought us to this superb condition.

Approving what he saw of the equipment of his village,
the old man next studied his tribe. It was well organized, faithful to the one unifying Great Spirit, disciplined, vigorous. It was as cohesive a unit as could then
have been found in the desert regions—less educated,
perhaps, since no member was able to pound silver or
polish turquoise—but unified as no other tribe of the
Comanches could be, for it had been Big Badger's stern
command in the warriors' secret society, of which he
was headman, that no strangers be allowed to enter the
Quohada tribe without a period of indoctrination so
rigorous as to repel most applicants.

Sometimes a Mexican lived in the Quohada village.
Often the Mexican was captured as a small boy and
held as a slave by a blood covenant with one of the
warriors. Blood was taken from a vein in the captive's
arm to signify he was a slave and had a right to life,
food, and protection. No one dared molest him as he
was chattel property. Of course, the owner could sell
him at any time, and then the blood ceremony was
repeated.

When the Mexican captives were grown, they could
become members of the tribe. Some of the Mexican Quohadas made excellent warriors. After a successful raid
they were usually given a Comanche name and even
allowed to take a Comanche wife.

With women, the problems were different. In their
constant raids with other tribes, the Quohadas often
took prisoners, and generally the women, if enticing
creatures, were kept and never traded back to their
rightful owners. In those early years, not even Big Badger's son, Pronghorn, stayed away from the women prisoners. Big Badger was smart enough to realize his
impotence in this matter. Rape of women captives was
not looked down upon, as it was with the true Quohada
women. Jerk Meat had taken a Kiowa woman as his
wife nearly ten years ago in order to protect her from
Kicking Horse, the Medicine Man, and some of the other
more brutal Quohadas. The woman was loyal and a
strong worker. Big Badger respected her as a true Quohada. She died from injuries received when the horse
she was riding put its foot in a gopher hole and fell on
top of her. Her child was born dead and she died two

days later. Big Badger's grief was great and it was many weeks before he could smile again. Jerk Meat also grieved long and deeply. He could not eat for days and he found it hard to carry on a conversation. He suffered constant pain in his belly, and found no joy in a successful raid or hunt. At the end of that year Big Badger advised that he find another woman.

One morning before Sacajawea was barely awake, Hides Well came into the tepee and began cutting off the remainder of Sacajawea's hair. All but her most tattered tunic had been taken away, and now she was warned not to use much water, nor to rub grease on her head or skin. By now she was well enough to perform the menial tasks required of the women of the Quohadas—cutting and fetching wood, pounding corn, dragging away dung, carrying water, and helping the other women scrape flesh from pegged-out hides.

Although some of her strength had returned, she felt depressed. This was a new life. But she was a slave, something she abhorred. She had grown accustomed to living in the manner of the white people, and it had been much easier than this hard existence in this harsh land. She was determined to make the best of her situation and complain to no one. The Quohadas had willingly taken her in, and they were kind to her—she would comply with their rules of living. She rested frequently between tasks and each time discovered that she was an object of great curiosity in the village. She saw eyes watching her from the tepee doors or from underneath tepee flaps. Wherever she went, she felt curious stares. Children were fascinated by her. They constantly followed her, saying, "Tell us stories. Are traders white-skinned? We have seen the Mexicans, and they are brown."

Jerk Meat went hunting and in two days came back with an elk, which he took to Kicking Horse for healing the fever of Wadzewipe.

Soon Sacajawea lost herself in the satisfaction of the work, and the depression lifted. Sometimes she hummed one of the Quohada songs with the women while she worked or was in the process of making a good thing, and she felt satisfaction at this accomplishment.

But after these times of forgetfulness, she would suddenly see clearly and feel guilty. How could she, a mother, have forgotten? She would feel as if she had been unfaithful to her son who loved her. She believed that one day she would find her son, Baptiste, when he had returned from the land across the Great Eastern Waters. She felt that the boy Tess would follow in the tracks of his father and become a trapper and trader, working more easily with the white men because he had gone to the school.

Early one morning she was up helping roast the antelope and elk that would be part of a feast day with games and contests celebrating the winter sun before it was lost from sight behind snow clouds.

Spring, who was pleasing to look at, with a broad face and kind black eyes, stirred the outside fire under a roast. There were no regular eating hours in Comanche families. Food of one kind or another was always kept in readiness for whenever any member of the family became hungry. As Spring turned the meat, Sacajawea noted the thickening around her middle. Hides Well came up with bark plates and said, "And so—she is going to have the child by early spring. Big Badger will be delighted to have a boy to train and teach the ways of a warrior."

It was the custom in most tribes, when there was no father left in the family, for an aged relative to take over the training of the child. If it were a boy, Big Badger would teach him to be an expert with a child's bow and teach him to harden himself by the time he was twelve summers, so he could run seventy-five miles a day through the cactus and mesquite-laden country, up and down mountains and canyons, with a tirelessness that would be the despair of the white men who tired to follow him.[7]

Sacajawea caught her breath as she thought, And so—the child might be a girl. Oh, joy, I will help in the small one's training. I will show her how to sew beautiful designs on fine white doeskins with dyed quills and antelope teeth and small, polished bones. I will teach her the Shoshoni way of weaving baskets of strong, tough grass.

"I am thankful my brother found you and had sense enough to bring you home," Spring said to Sacajawea.

"I am thankful to have friends," said Sacajawea. "Have you been eating finely ground uncooked bone? You must so your papoose will have strong bones and your own teeth will be preserved."

Spring looked up, startled. "Wadzewipe, you talk like my older sister."

"And so—I feel I am." Sacajawea smiled. "You must be strong to raise a child with no father. I will help you teach her."

"I was thinking—thinking about finding myself a man." Spring giggled behind her left hand.

"*Ai*, and deprive Big Badger the great pleasure of training your small boy? It would make the old man live again. It would put a sparkle in his eyes and quicken his step. He would look at the new day with eagerness. Now he is only sad and wonders how long he must wait before he enters the Happy Hunting Ground. Would you take away my pleasure of training your small girl? I think of it each day and make plans."

Spring giggled again. "One of you will be disappointed. I can't help but think Big Badger has already found someone that lights his day. He has a sparkle in his eye when he looks your way. He wonders about where you have come from. What are the black white men?"

Sacajawea looked sharply at Spring.

"It's true you said something about one when you were burning with the fever—a white man and a baby. Where did your trail begin?"

Sacajawea lowered her face. "So—I have told you I come from the Shoshonis, from the land of deep snow and spring flowers. My people are proud; they have feast days and merriment and are not always hungry."

Spring stared at Sacajawea for a long moment. "Why did you leave them?"

"I was taken by an enemy when I was a small child to be a slave. I am looking for a day to come when I can be of more help to my people. Then I will go back," said Sacajawea softly, her head lowered so that Spring could not see her eyes.

"There is more to your story—but I will wait until

you are ready for the telling." Suddenly Spring giggled
so her shoulders shook. "I do not think my brother wishes
for you to go. I have seen him also look at you in a way
that men look at women when they are thinking—"

"Oh, it cannot be. No man thinks of me," gasped
Sacajawea. "I am not young. I have seen plenty of winters. But it is nice of you to say this. And it is good to
know that he is not sorry he brought me to his camp."

Big Badger came from his tepee dressed for the day
of festivities, a leather band around his forehead and
new drags on his moccasins. He came to the fire and
tasted the roast by poking a stick into the side and
pulling off a small piece. He licked his lips and smiled.
"You women cook good."

"We will cook all day if you feast on our meat. Why
don't you try some of the contests?" asked Spring.

"The young are all alike, sharp of tongue and no
respect," said Big Badger, wiping his fingers down his
buckskins. "None of my women spoke to me that way
or I would show them the sting of my hand across their
face. They would not like that sting. They always talk
nice to me."

Sacajawea moved quickly away from the old man.
Her thoughts were of Charbonneau. Quickly she composed herself, looking more closely at Big Badger.

"Oh, Grandfather," said Spring, "you never could
discipline your women. Mother tells how kindly all your
women were and how good you were to them, and you
had many. You would never disgrace them with a slap
of your hand." She sighed and put her cheek against
her grandfather's. The old man laughed silently, his
belly shaking.

Sacajawea sighed.

The contests were held in a small canyon. The ground
was packed firm from many tramping feet. When Sacajawea and Spring came to watch, there were eight
boys standing in a straight line. Chief Pronghorn was
talking to them in his slow, resonant voice. In his hand
he held a small gourd of water.

"Each of you take a mouthful," he said, "but do not
swallow it. Hold it in your mouths. You are going to
run four miles with no swallowing." The eight boys,
dwarfed by his size, nodded eagerly. They took the water

in their mouths, and then, at a signal from Pronghorn, they started out trotting. Pronghorn ran behind the boys to see that they did not rest on the way. Big Badger called out derisively, "Pronghorn, try to keep up with those young ones—you are like an old turtle. Ha-ha-hee-hee."

When the boys returned, they again lined up, and then, as Pronghorn walked from one to the other, they spat the water on the ground. All the boys but one had held the water without swallowing.

"And so—what happened to you?" Pronghorn demanded sternly of the unfortunate one.

"I stumbled and swallowed the water," he said miserably.

"Go. Your tepee."

The boy turned away without a word. His father, sitting among the other men, rose and followed him silently. He was much ashamed.

Sacajawea half ran to catch up with them. "Do not feel too badly," she said. "There will be other times. Your boy can be a leader of the Quohadas. There will be many changes before he is a grown man. Tell him to keep his eyes open and watch the changes and understand them. He will find his own opportunity to show his worth."

The man stood stock-still. Never had a woman talked to him in such a bold manner. Sacajawea realized she had acted on impulse and out of empathy for the father and son. She did not hang her head; she looked the man in the face and smiled. She felt a strange elation at breaking a strict code. Or, she thought, was the elation for causing the father of a fine boy to think not just of the present but of the future? She turned and made her way back to Spring; yet her head did not bow.

Spring had not missed her. Two twelve-year-olds were wrestling. They wrapped their wiry arms around each other and struggled for a hold. The men and other boys squatted, watching silently. Soon bets were made as the boys twisted and tightened their holds. A boy called Wolf grabbed his opponent's wrist and, twisting his arm around his back, began to exert an upward pressure. The smaller boy, Turkey, fought to get away, but Wolf continued to force the arm upward and Turkey began

to bite his lips. Wolf raised the arm another degree,
and the smaller boy's face contorted in pain as he strove
to keep himself from crying "Enough." The men watched
stolidly. Wolf kept up the leverage until Turkey thought
his arm would break. Then quickly he managed to twist
around and catch Wolf under his leg with his free arm
and throw him down. Before Wolf could recover, Turkey
was on top of him, his knees digging into his groin, his
arms pinning Wolf's shoulders to the ground. Then the
smaller boy moved swiftly and got a headlock on Wolf
and wrapped his legs around his waist and began to
squeeze. Wolf's face filled with blood, and his eyes began to bulge.

The men and boys watching made no move.

Wolf suddenly relaxed, but he still did not cry quits.
Turkey squeezed still harder; then Wolf fainted, and
his head rolled loosely on his shoulders. Turkey rose,
and Pronghorn threw water on Wolf's face.

"It was brave," Sacajawea said so that all could hear.
"The boy you call Wolf did not give up."

"*Ai*," Kicking Horse said. "He is my son. I will pay
all bets."

"But he did not give up," said Sacajawea.

"And so—it is true he did not utter a word," agreed
Big Badger, standing up and facing the men. "And so,
then—let all bets be canceled for this contest. We will
go to another."

Next the boys were given slings and led to a flat
place where there were many small round stones on
the ground. They lined up with four on one side and
four on the other. They separated to a distance of about
twenty-five feet and then, at a signal from Pronghorn,
picked up stones, fitted them into the leather slings,
and hurled the stones at each other. They had to hurl
the stones and try to dodge the stones thrown at them.
The stones were not light, but they were expertly thrown.
Some hit arms and legs. One boy was hit on the chest.
Another struck a boy near his eye. Blood streamed down
his face, but he did not stop. With one eye blinded, he
continued to hurl and dodge stones. Wolf, a little groggy
from his wrestling, was not as fast as he might have
been, and a stone struck him on the wrist, causing it
to snap back. He tried to continue to pick up stones and

throw them, but the pain was too great and he dropped out of the contest without a word and walked away.

Sacajawea noticed that he went to a small creek. When she was sure no one would follow him, she moseyed toward the creek. She spoke firmly to Wolf, who was staring at his hand; it dangled oddly at the end of his arm. She held the arm and hand gently in the cold water, then quickly pushed the broken bone together and tied it, with the tongues of her moccasins serving as a sheath, and the lacings the bindings. She pushed the arm and sheath in the creek, explaining to Wolf, who lay beside the creek, his face pale, that when the sheath dried, it would become a tight band holding the bone in place until it was well grown together.

"Come back to me when the winter wind howls around the tepees," she told him. "Then your arm will be like it was when the sun shone on it this morning."

Wolf shook his head. Never had he known of a woman who took over the healing. He would tell his father, Kicking Horse, about this Medicine Woman.

After the sling contest, the boys took small bows and arrows and shot at each other. Then there was a foot-race to a point four hundred yards away and back. Wolf came to watch, sitting not far from Sacajawea. The boy with the bloodied eye moved close to Wolf. Soon Wolf motioned for her to follow them back to the creek.

At Wolf's request, Sacajawea cleansed the boy's face. The eye was not damaged, but the soft skin underneath was cut so that a flap hung loose. The bleeding had subsided, but the boy was quite weak from the loss of so much blood. With his eye closed he said, "This will make a large scar when it heals."

"*Ai*," murmured Wolf. "That is life."

"No," said Sacajawea. "I will show you how to sew it with a fine bone needle."

"Sew it?" asked Wolf, even more curious about this woman who had not been in their village long, who spoke so boldly and acted with confidence. He followed her to her tepee, where she found a small bone needle among Spring's sewing. Quickly returning to the creek, she told Wolf to push a wad of soft grass under the injured boy's head.

"It will hurt a few moments, but your face will not

be scarred when it heals. After one full moon, pull out the stitches."

"And you do this for the son of Twisted Horn?" asked Wolf incredulously.

"*Ai*. Who is this Twisted Horn?" Sacajawea asked, taking several long hairs from the boy's head.

"He can no longer hunt or go raiding because his legs grow weak and he cannot stand. His woman must beg food for her lodge."

The boy groaned and rolled his head to and fro on the ground. "I will be able to hunt soon," he said weakly.

"Hold him so that he will not cry out or thrash me with his arms," she ordered Wolf. She sewed the boy's face together with his own hair as sutures. When she was finished, she laid the fine bone needle in the hand of the son of Twisted Horn. "Put this in your medicine bag. Always use the hair from the head of the wounded one."

She got to her feet and was moving toward the crowd to see other contests when she was aware of a woman standing near. It was Gray Bone, the mother of Wolf. The boy indicated to his mother that Sacajawea was a friend. "She is Wadzewipe," he said.

"A brave boy," murmured Sacajawea. "He will one day be a medicine man or a brave warrior."

"You heal his arm? You did not let his father do that?"

"And so—I did not know his father to ask. His father did not step forward to look after your boy."

"His father is Kicking Horse! You are a she-dog!" Gray Bone moved on hurriedly, her face red with anger.

Wolf was already on his way to other contests, holding his broken wrist close to his chest. The son of Twisted Horn had walked slowly to his own lodge.

Gray Bone turned back and faced Sacajawea, her lips tight against her teeth. "You want my son to be a baby?"

Sacajawea did not know what to say. "Well, so—of course not. Your boy will be strong and endure all things. He cannot grow strong if he is broken before he grows into manhood—if he has only one hand to use."

"Aha," spat Gray Bone. "You draw attention to yourself and disgrace our sons by treating them like babies. Their wounds will heal without your interfering."

"There is a thing called rotten flesh that makes wounds grow large and red and slowly kills a strong body. Surely you have seen it. This can be kept small by a wash in clear water."

"Aha, what do you know? You are a stranger, not one of us. You are a woman who does not keep her tongue tight, but lets it hang loose for all to hear." Gray Bone spoke in a tight, high-pitched voice.

"The Great Spirit does not wish fine Comanche boys to die. He does not wish for you to weep for your son because he has a crooked wrist."

"Do not talk!" shouted Gray Bone. "It is enough to have Quohada boys treated like babies, their wounds healed by a squaw, a stranger, and not by the Medicine Man. Remember it was Kicking Horse who brought your health to you. Are you so ungrateful that you cannot call him for healing wounds?"

"He did not make a move to help the boys," repeated Sacajawea, trying to plead innocent in the face of these loud accusations. "He sat with the men, watching the contests and betting."

"You did look at him?"

"Well, so—*ai*, I did look to see if he was going to help."

"You—you flirt, Nyahsuqite!"

"My eyes are clear," Sacajawea said, her anger up now. "A cloud has descended and now covers the vision of some people."

"How would you know what I see? You do not have a man. You do not have a child. You could not feel as I do about my son. I do not wish him to grow into manhood being treated like a baby or a girl."

"I treated him neither way. He was not disgraced. The others know of his bravery." Sacajawea tried to control her rage with this crazy woman who could not seem to understand that she had only wanted to help. "There was no intent to insult," Sacajawea said, hating herself for speaking so before this woman.

Gray Bone continued, "You leave my man and boy alone. Or I will see that Hides Well knows about your flirting. Perhaps Chief Pronghorn will have your nose cut off. Then you would be good for nothing except to satisfy the passions of men who have no women. Your face would not be so beautiful, ha-ha. They would take you in the bush only on moonless nights so they could not see what they had. You—you Nyahsuqite!"

Sacajawea turned and walked away, keeping silent.

For most of the early winter, Sacajawea kept busy helping Spring and Hides Well make clothing with the buffalo hair on the inside, even on the moccasins. Strips of buffalo and elk meat were dried. When they were stiff, hard, and almost black, they were carried to a ledge at the back of the village and pounded in shallow holes in rocks until they were a powderlike meal. Then the meal, whitish with a few dark fibers, was put in large rawhide boxes, covered with a layer of pounded meat, a sprinkling of shelled pecans, a layer of dried plums or sand cherries, and another layer of pounded meat. When the boxes were full, the women poured boiling tallow, rendered out clear, over it all and let it soak in.

"There is no need to be a stranger here," Hides Well said. "You can be one of our people."

"*Ai*," Sacajawea said, looking from Hides Well to Spring. "Your family has been kind to me."

"It is said that there is a new name by which some call you," mentioned Hides Well, swinging her close-cropped hair back and forth.

"*Ai*." Sacajawea hung her head. "I do not behave in the manner expected of a woman. I have been too long without a village of my own people."

"Pah, it is a name bestowed by jealousy." Hides Well's words were not emphasized, but Sacajawea flushed.

"I have gone by several names, as the custom of our people is to have a name that fits the appearance or some deed we committed."

"So—Gray Bone is a wise and brave woman; the name she awarded is the name you prefer?"

Sacajawea looked around in discomfort. She felt she was losing face, and she did not know how to stop it.

"Do you wish to talk of my name?"

"*Ai*," said Spring, coming for more hot tallow. "You have not forgotten the ways of your people. You have been among others and seen more. You do things in a different manner—with a different attitude. And so— it is the attitude."

Hides Well growled at Spring, and then suddenly there was a crack of her hand against the young woman's thigh. Sacajawea jumped. Though watching, it had taken her by surprise, but Spring did not wail. Instead she giggled, a sort of chuckling, water-over-stones sound that made Sacajawea smile.

Hides Well seemed to fill out until she was larger than herself. She threw back her shoulders, and her face grew stern. "My daughter, Spring, will keep silent. I speak to just one here." Then, turning to Sacajawea: "You lived among the whites?"

"*Ai*," Sacajawea answered. "I suppose it must be told. I had a man who was part white, part Sioux. I lived near the white village, Saint Louis. I saw two boys grown. One was all mine. The boys went to the white man's school and understand markings on paper. They work for white men." Briefly she told about her trip to the Great Western Waters. Hides Well looked at her with disbelieving eyes. Sacajawea could not go on. She bit her tongue.

"You say this of yourself?" Hides Well's face, dark already, went darker still.

"I do not hide anything from you. You have asked me a straight thing, and I have answered straight, as a man speaks to another man, to explain himself."

Hides Well was long in replying. As if the sight of Sacajawea bleakened and soured her, the cords of her neck tautened and her mouth became flat. Her black eyes seemed to look at Sacajawea from across a great distance.

This distance is the difference between myself and these people, Sacajawea thought, and it has to be crossed now if I am to remain here. She twisted her hands together. She had to get to Hides Well from where she was.

"You are a brave woman to tell me of this," Hides Well said at last. "You speak with a straight tongue, maybe."

"Good Lord! There is no fork in my tongue," said Sacajawea. "If permitted, I will live with your people a few winters. Then I will leave to find my own son and

live with him. I cannot go to him now. He is gone to a
land across the Great Eastern Waters, but only for two
or three winters."

Hides Well looked from the west to the east, then
shook her head.

"I have spoken to you not knowing whether I will be
permitted to look for my son. The end of my time may
be today—or tomorrow. Only the good Lord knows,
damn it to hell!"

Hides Well belched profoundly and satisfyingly, and
Sacajawea's anger fled. Sacajawea flexed her knees and
grinned at the woman. Hides Well grinned broadly,
delighting in the white man's profanity Sacajawea had
used. She nodded wisely, covered her laughter with her
hand, and made the sound of amusement and astonishment, "Hooo-hooo."

"Hooo-hooo, yourself," Big Badger said, coming into
the center of the women's work area. "I heard what you
said. I listened carefully. Why should my people do anything to help a woman who has lived among the whites?"
His voice was icy.

Sacajawea's heart fell to the ground.

"For many a harvest I was friend of some whites. I
protected them against bad Comanches. I received only
treachery for my actions. For the lives of whites I saved
I was paid in death of Quohada warriors. Other white
traders came to us with promises and left us death."
He spoke of the times the white men had gathered the
Comanches together promising to make peace and then
instead had poisoned their drinking water.

When he finished, Sacajawea replied, "You do not
yet tell the whole story. You are correct, but your hatred
blinds you to something. I can tell you as many more
as you have already told me of Indians who have stolen,
broken promises, traded spoiled meat for good axes, and
caused death and sorrow among the whites."

"You tell me white men are good?" Big Badger adjusted his robe. "They kill us, so we kill them."

"*Ai*, there are bad whites. There are also bad Comanches."

"You ask me to now be your friend when you have
been a friend of our enemies?"

"Still, there are white men who have caused your

people no harm, and yet they are hunted like animals
and killed. Do your people try to find which white men
are good and which are bad?"

"No."

"I ask you to be greater than that."

Big Badger gazed at her in bewilderment. "You are
a strange woman, and you ask strange things. You ask
favors. Only men ask favors."

"I am speaking as a man speaks to another man. A
man can give favors only according to his own size."

Big Badger stood up and walked away. Sacajawea
looked at Hides Well, who had been greatly amused by
the outspoken Sacajawea. There was now a comfortable
understanding between the two women. There were no
hard feelings. Hides Well nodded her head toward Big
Badger. Sacajawea followed him until he stood at the
edge of a huge stone.

"It is quiet here," she said.

"*Ai.*"

"It is good here."

"*Ai.*" Then Big Badger began to speak, at first more
to himself. "This is the country of the Quohada Comanches. This is the country where they belong. The
hills and valleys and day and night belong to us. It was
so from the memory of the oldest man, and that memory
came from the oldest man ahead of him. There was
nobody but Comanches here and the land was filled
with food and the Comanches could make a living for
themselves. The Mexicans came, and we defeated them.
The white men come again with more treachery and
arrogance. The white man thinks he is better than any
other man. He makes his own laws and says those laws
must be obeyed. Why?"

The old man took his pipe from the folds of his robe
and smoked. Sacajawea let a little time go by before
speaking. Then slowly, careful of her words, measuring
them, thinking of their effect, appearing casual and
unworried, she said, "Comanches have laws, and when
a white man lives among them he must obey them."
She added, "I have broken your law. I do not control
my tongue. I broke another when I set the bone in the
wrist of the son of Kicking Horse and sewed the skin
of Twisted Horn's son so he would not be disfigured.

And I am breaking another by sitting here talking with an important man in your tribe?"

Big Badger stretched his arm and touched Sacajawea's shoulder. The muscles of his upper arm were banded with silver; there was an expression of serenity on his face.

"Wadzewipe," he said, "I respect you." His words came slowly, and were as careful as Sacajawea's had been. "We are friends."

Although the touch on her shoulder was light, she felt its calming effect. She felt a great peace come over her. She knew inexplicably that the outstretched hand was a bridge to cross the abyss. She felt secure and very alive. The old man spoke once more.

"You will find a way to show the Quohadas you are to be respected, and you will answer to the name Wadzewipe."

Sacajawea looked unwaveringly at him. "I do not know how I will do this."

"We will talk often. You are welcome among the Quohadas always."

Sacajawea looked away from Big Badger, into the blue, hazy distance. "Through his life a person is content if he finds a friend. Through that one friend a person has more contentment than he can have with hundreds of others."

"You will begin your new life here as one of us." Big Badger rose and adjusted his robe.

"I find it good here." Sacajawea scrubbed her face with her hands to make the memory of her past go away. She dropped her hands and met the old man's eyes.

"Your boys will find a new life for themselves. They are grown. To find your son one day may be something the Great Spirit only knows about. You will rest with the Quohadas."

They walked silently to the village, Sacajawea following Big Badger, to the tepee that stood near the center. In the sun before it sat Hides Well. She was pretending to sleep. Sacajawea knew that she was waiting for them and that she watched through small slits in her eyes.

Big Badger drew his robe over his chest, grunted to

indicate the conversation was finished, and bent to enter his tepee.

Hides Well stirred and looked up the street at some
yipping dogs. "He is considerable man," she said.

Before going to sleep that night, Sacajawea thought
of all the people she had known. Their names sounded
foreign in her mind, as though they were now people
of a strange land.

As the winter wore on, there was less and less work
to do and Sacajawea learned to recall the forgotten words
of her native language, and to give them the Comanche
accent. Big Badger spoke Spanish at times, which he
had learned from the Mexican traders. She quickly
picked up his limited Spanish vocabulary.

Pronghorn was chief leader of hunts. In that capacity
he called on Kicking Horse, the chief Medicine Man, to
perform the hunt ritual. Kicking Horse asked Bites
Hard and Dancing Foot each to carry a secret charm
chosen from his medicine bag. Kicking Horse put on
his sacred mask made of the whole skin of a buffalo
head with the horns still attached. He moved the mask
skyward, then toward the four corners of the earth in
a prayer to the guardian spirit. He prayed that the
spirit would direct the buffalo to the Quohada hunting
grounds. He turned four times, moving his outstretched
hands in a curved line so that they formed an imaginary
ring. Everyone believed he was powerful enough to draw
a large, invisible ring around any herd of animals.

In the morning Pronghorn led the hunters to the
hunting grounds. They found a good-size herd of buffalo
and they rode in from all directions. The men on horseback rushed the animals closer and closer together. The
buffalo dashed recklessly around like a gigantic pinwheel. The hunters moved inward, shrinking the outside circumference as they whistled wildly. The sound
was like a tremendous wind rushing through tops of
gigantic oaks. The tramping of the frantic animals'
hooves was like a constant, earthshaking thundering.

Kicking Horse was left on a little knoll far outside
the ring. He watched closely and suddenly pointed his
medicine bag at a gasping bull. The animal fell from

exhaustion and was trampled to death. That was the
cue for Bites Hard and Dancing Foot to fling the charms
away and to shoot their arrows. After their chosen animals were dead, the other hunters took their turn.[8]

Kicking Horse enjoyed showing off his power. However, there was one person he had no power over—his
first woman, Gray Bone. She was given to fits of incoherent rantings. Her hair was coarse and uneven at
the ends and her eyes were beady and hard. She was
fat and usually slow on her feet.

Flower, Kicking Horse's second woman, was made
to work hard by Gray Bone, who was also unpleasantly
jealous. Sacajawea had had a taste of that jealousy, and
wondered what could be done to counteract it and replace it with friendship.

The weather during the last part of winter alternated between bad spells of cold and sunny days when
the film of ice at the creek's edge would melt by the
middle of the day. On some good days Sacajawea went
with Spring and Hides Well to bring wood or dig roots
for eating. Sometimes Jerk Meat came into the tepee
and sat in a corner watching the women work.

Jerk Meat was tall and lanky, unusual for Comanches, who were generally built short and stout. He always wore the silver plate in his long hair. He smiled
and seemed friendly with everyone in the lodge. He was
always helpful and kindly and did not talk too much.
Once he put his hand on Sacajawea's arm to help her
balance an overlarge load of firewood. Sacajawea
thought the touch was as nothing to him, but from it
she felt fire course through her body. This she interpreted as gratitude that he had brought her to his village.

Living close with them, Sacajawea began to notice
that Jerk Meat's face was smooth and deep red in color.
In a far-off way he sometimes reminded her of Chief
Red Hair, but his face was broader and he had great
jaws and wide cheekbones. His manner was gentle, and
he continued to treat her like a child. His hair was
always clean. Often his sister, Spring, combed it for
him. It was greased and slicked down on top; then the
two braids, which started at his shoulders, were wrapped

in bearskin with long whisks of buffalo fur tucked inside.

Jerk Meat was one of the honored warriors in a tribe
where warfare was highly regarded. He was taught to
ride horseback well as a young boy, to stand water and
food deprivation. He knew that success in defeating an
enemy was rewarded with tribal respect and admiration, and he believed that death in battle was a thing
of glory, guarding a person from the terrible miseries
of old age.[9]

One day two young visitors came to the large tepee.
One wore dirty old pieces of thick buckskin tied around
his left wrist. It was Wolf. Sacajawea was pleased to
see him. He had come to have the tough buckskin cast
removed. She led him close to the fire so that she could
better see where to cut the old lacings. She nodded and
pulled out her butcher knife. She had to make sure she
did not cut too close and pierce her own fingers. Wolf
sat on the floor when the buckskin was peeled. He held
his arm in his lap.

"The tingling will soon be gone," Sacajawea assured
him. "See how pale it is. It needs exercise—slowly at
first. In a few days it will be all right."

She looked into the second youth's face. The deep
gash under his eye that she had sewn with his black
hair had healed into a thin pink ridge. Her fingers ran
over the ridge lightly.

The son of Twisted Horn smiled and pointed to a
man who was at the door of the tepee. It was Kicking
Horse, dressed in his finest clothes, as though it were
a feast day.

"My father comes to see you perform your healing,"
explained Wolf. "He believes your medicine is nearly
as great as his."

Kicking Horse came inside and examined Wolf's
wrist.

"It is healed. See, it hurts and needs to learn to work,
but I can twist it around and pick up little things. My
mother said it would be forever stiff. It is not."

The son of Twisted Horn darted out of the tepee, then
came back with a basket woven of heavy grass brought
back from some Mexican raid.

"I thank you," said the boy.

Wolf said, "My father brings you a gift."

Kicking Horse laid several large silver loops at her feet. Sacajawea stepped back and nodded her appreciation.

"My mother, Gray Bone, is not well," said Wolf. "She has a fever and coughs. My father prays over her when she sleeps."

"Have you tried the sweat bath?" Sacajawea asked Kicking Horse.

Kicking Horse looked startled. "That is only for the men."

Sacajawea looked about her. The lodge of Pronghorn sat perfectly still. "I am sorry," she said quietly. She wondered why it was she always forgot that women took a secondary place.

Jerk Meat stepped out from the shadows and grinned, not knowing how winsome the uncertain, one-sided smile was. "You said yourself Wadzewipe had some power for healing. And so—then you, the Medicine Man, could arrange a kind of sweat bath for your own woman as Wadzewipe suggests."

Kicking Horse scowled, then nodded.

Jerk Meat saw Sacajawea's mouth soften and twitch a little as if she might be trying to keep from smiling.

"There is no harm in trying, even though it is not usually done," said Kicking Horse. Then he looked Sacajawea fully in the face. "Are you a Shaman?"

A chill settled over her. "No, I can do nothing that is magical. I know little compared to the knowledge of the white men who are called doctors."

Kicking Horse began to speak, but at the same time Spring had gone to the tepee entrance and suddenly let out a cry of surprise. "Horses! Who would tie all those horses to the entrance of this tepee?"

Kicking Horse made a small sound in his throat.

The boys, Wolf and the son of Twisted Horn, laughed. "Ask her," they said together. "Kicking Horse, tell her why you are here."

Kicking Horse made the small sound again and cleared his throat. "I have come to ask Lost Woman to live in my tepee and share her medicinal powers with me. I come to take her. I leave my finest horses to replace your loss."

Sacajawea moved back stiffly. Dryly she repeated, "I have no power."

Kicking Horse glanced around the lodge, embarrassed. He pulled at the one silver loop that ornamented his left ear. He rubbed a thumb on it and mumbled, "The Lost Woman will come? There is no reason to hesitate. My offer is generous."

"She does not have any powers to share," said Chief Pronghorn sternly, looking down at Kicking Horse, who had hunched his shoulders.

"I suppose I should say she is soft," said Big Badger, moving the boys aside so that he could speak directly to Kicking Horse. "She cannot carry much wood. And her water kettle is only half-full."

"She is my sister," said Spring, giggling behind her hand. "And she helps around the lodge less than any one of us women."

"And she does that hastily," added Jerk Meat, his words coming queerly thick, as if pushed out of his throat over some obstacle. "She is constantly in hot grease with someone for giving of her clumsy help and bad advice."

"I call her bossy," said Big Badger tautly.

"Does she boss you?" asked Kicking Horse, backing toward the tepee opening.

"She'd better not!" said Big Badger.

"Well, then, maybe I can handle her," Kicking Horse said, coming back into the tepee. "I can take care of my women, Flower and Gray Bone, well enough." He moved swiftly toward Sacajawea. "Will you come as my third woman?"

She smoothed her short hair, not yet grown out more than two or three inches from the cropping she'd received more than four months before. She pulled at the neck of her tunic, shook out her skirt, and went—had Kicking Horse known it—through all the motions a woman makes when she is confused and nervous and wants to gain time—a necessity for setting herself to rights before she sets a man in his place. All Kicking Horse saw was a composed young woman whose voice was cool, whose eyes were not, and whose mouth was puckered.

"My fingernails are long; they scratch. I have not

washed. My stench is stronger than the polecat's. Your
horses, out there"—pointing to the six that were tethered to a stake in front of the tepee—"have never been
brushed, so their hair is dull. The Comanches must
learn to brush the hair on their horses before they will
have anything compared to those of the white man."

Kicking Horse tried to think of something to say, to
find an excuse for his presence, for his intrusion. There
seemed to be nothing that would not make matters
worse, so he said nothing. He simply stood awkwardly
before her, twisting the silver loop around and around.
Carefully he kept his face composed, knowing that to
stammer, to utter some inanity, would only incur her
swift wrath and bring it down on his head. It was easy
to tell she was seething, that all she needed was his
first word to start boiling over. He knew he could not
endure another woman with a sharp tongue in his tepee. Gray Bone was more than enough for him. He had
no idea that this Lost Woman was so free with her
tongue. He did not like Pronghorn, but today he felt
sorry for him with this woman in his family. Meekly
he turned, picked up the several large silver loops, and
shuffled through the opening, blinking in the light of
day, motioning for the silent boys to bring the horses
along home with them. "In Pronghorn's moccasins I
would lodgepole that woman. It would be a good thing."
The boys laughed, but made no reply. It was not good
to venture opinions in family matters.

"Is it true you think our horses dull?" asked Jerk
Meat wryly.

Sacajawea stared at Jerk Meat, who met her look.
Color flamed in her face, turned her warm-red. "But
then, your horses, they are even more beautiful than
those owned by my people, the Shoshonis."

"You are now truly one of us, Granddaughter!"
shouted Big Badger, dancing with tiny to-and-fro movements. Then he stood before his grandson Jerk Meat.
"Would you like this woman as your own and have
many sons by her?"

Jerk Meat looked at Big Badger awkwardly, as if off
balance. Then his eyes shone and his mouth worked to
keep from smiling. "She is one of us. You just called

her granddaughter. Does a man take his own sister?"
He struck out for the open air, trotting up the main
street of the village, leaving Sacajawea standing with
her mouth open, bereft of the last word.[10]

CHAPTER

45

Comanche Marriage

For the ordinary Mexican mule and donkey caravans, existence was purely nomadic—the finding of an Indian encampment, the making of presents, then the spreading of trade goods on the ground: bolts of calico and a few Navajo blankets; some knives and beads and mirrors, the hard, sweet bread the Mexicans baked in their outdoor ovens; beans and pumpkins, which the Indians relished as a change in their all meat diet. Generally there was Taos whiskey, too, and it is not likely that the Comanches eschewed its use. Once the goods were displayed, prices were set by the use of counting sticks—this many pumpkins for a pair of moccasins; this many buffalo robes for a Navajo blanket. Haggling was interminable. Every article was traded for individually, never in lots. But finally the bartering was done and then probably there was a feast in the lodge of the chief, story telling, gambling at the game of hands, horse races, and quick, urgent amours.

DAVID LAVENDER, *Bent's Fort*. New York: Doubleday and Co., 1954, pp. 130–31.

The spring weather was fine; gum trees showed red branches, and sweet acorns, known by the Spanish name of *bellotas*, grew in small fat clusters. Sacajawea worked with Spring to remove the bitter tannin from the *bellotas* saved from last fall by boiling the kernels several hours before grinding. Then the women soaked the *bellota* meal in hot water with occasional changes until the bitter flavor was lost. When the meal was dried and parched in an earthen oven, it tasted much like cornmeal.

During the time when the warm spring winds blew through the short, greening buffalo grass, Spring's baby was born. It was a fast, uneventful birth. For days afterward, Spring cuddled and cooed over the round brown papoose.

"He is like a ripe, fat plum," said Big Badger. "I will teach him to tie a taut bowstring."

"Lost Woman will teach him the healing art," said Jerk Meat practically, "and then he will be a man of great worth to the Quohadas."

When the camp traveled, it carried everything it owned by horse. The very old and very young were carried by travois. They broke their winter camp and traveled only twelve days to a new temporary camp on the Red River. Then in the middle of spring the lodges were struck and the entire Quohada camp moved again to a place called Hungry Horse.

Before reaching Hungry Horse they traveled north through hot, dry countryside. They ate little, forded rivers, and when the woman found an area of fertile land containing beds of yap—the tuberous roots of Indian potato—they stopped. The women boiled the roots and sweetened them with crushed mesquite beans. The Quohadas consumed all the yap they could find, not attempting to preserve any. Their attitude when food was plentiful was that it might spoil unless eaten.

The Quohadas moved along with cool showers to a valley. The river became a broad, muddy torrent. Some of the boys tested the current on horseback. Some found it necessary to slip from their horse's back and swim

holding on to their horse's tail. This crossing was too
hard for the old and very young. They made a temporary camp to wait for the river to slow and to construct
rafts from the cottonwoods. Sacajawea was among the
women helping to bring in the huge cottonwood poles.
Suddenly her mind began to work and she took to the
river's edge to chop off thick willow branches. She made
a crude frame and stretched a piece of old rawhide over
it, in the manner of making a bull boat. The other
women scarcely paid any attention to her as she set her
boat in the water and loaded it with goods from Pronghorn's lodge. She pulled off her tunic and got into the
water beside the spinning boat. Paddling and kicking,
she pushed across the wide water and dumped the supplies on high, dry ground; then she was in the water
pulling the boat back across for more goods. The supplies and equipment of Pronghorn's lodge were across
the river in one day, and many of the rafts were not
yet constructed by other women.

"Ah, look, such a thing is truly knowledge from a
great totem," one woman pointed and whispered. Gray
Bone spotted Sacajawea by the water's edge showing
Jerk Meat and several other braves how to construct a
bull boat. The men made two that were larger than the
one she had used. They were very pleased with them.

"She is a constant lover, always looking for a man,"
snapped Gray Bone to some women. "Her true name is
Nyahsuqite, the Flirt."

Big Badger came toward the women, and Gray Bone
closed her mouth and worked hard tying her raft together, her face scarlet.

. "The Lost Woman is one of our people," he said softly,
stopping to inspect the raft. "She is more valuable to
us than three sharp-tongued squaws," he snapped and
walked away.

The next morning, Sacajawea walked close to Gray
Bone, saying evenly, "We have only to get the small
one, Wild Plum, across in the round boat. I can see you
have several days' work left on your raft. I will give
my round boat to you when I am finished so you can
start moving your household goods right away."

"Well, so—ah," sputtered Gray Bone, "it is small,
but I suppose I can make several trips and get my things

over." She left her partially finished raft and sat on the bank to watch Sacajawea swim out into the water, twirling the bull boat that carried the sleeping infant safely across the river.

At the end of three days, all the Quohadas had crossed. The tribe went on across the prairie to a sheltered canyon where a small creek ran. One evening Sacajawea asked Big Badger, "Do your people ever go to the Kaw River where it meets the Big Muddy?"

He turned toward her and said slowly, "That is hard to say. There are many rivers, and some have more than one name."

Big Badger was not much help. She had been thinking more and more of Baptiste. Perhaps, she thought, if he were back from across the Great Eastern Waters he would go where those rivers met because the trapping was good.

Sacajawea stood alone early one morning, on the little hill above the camp. She could look in all directions and see the skyline. She could see the young boys already at their play. In reality they were practicing a skill that would only be perfected when they reached manhood—trick riding. The small boys picked up sticks, moccasins, anything from the ground, while their ponies galloped as fast as they could. The oldest boys were grabbing at blanket rolls, cooking pots filled with stones. On a long sandbar three young men rode their ponies at full speed and swooped down, almost underneath the running animals, to grab a companion from the ground and swing him across a pony. Already the young men knew the importance of rescuing a companion who fell in battle, or on a hunt.[1]

She turned to see a group of little girls playing beside the creek. Most of them wore breechclouts similar to those worn by the adolescent boys. The small boys wore nothing. The girls carried sand in baskets, pretending it was mesquite flour. They tied a harness with short sticks to the backs of pet dogs to make a kind of old-fashioned travois, using it to carry their play robes and toy household material.

Sacajawea moved so that she could sit comfortably in the warm morning sun on a flat-topped boulder. She knew that Charbonneau had never been able to ride a horse the way even these boys did. Certainly, she had heard him boast about sticking to his horse, never letting light show between himself and the horse's back, but he couldn't know what sticking tight meant until he'd seen these boys.

She watched several of the older boys tie a looped rope around a gelding's neck. A young man slipped the loop over his head and under his arm. He jabbed his bare heels into the horse's sides and with both hands nocked an arrow in his taut bowstring and let it fly, lodging it in the trunk of an old, dead cottonwood tree. Nothing showed but the leg of the rider hooked over the scrawny back of the horse. No wonder these people were sometimes called Lords of the Plains, she thought. Oh, if only Baptiste could see this! Where was he now? Would she ever have news of him?

She figured that by now Baptiste must be someone of importance among the whites, because he had been to the land far beyond the big waters with the one called Duke Paul. He must be back by now. What wonderful tales he would have to tell! She wondered how she might send word to him that she was fine. She looked beyond the creek, across the Quohada village. She saw what looked like a wagon train kicking up clouds of red dust across the plains. That's it! She sat up straight and shielded her eyes from the sun with one hand to see better. She'd ask the white people in that wagon train. A tingle of excitement ran up her spine. Then she sighed and let her shoulders droop. Would the whites understand what she wanted to know? What would they do if they saw her in Comanche clothes? Maybe they would shoot! She felt stymied for a moment. Then she figured they wouldn't shoot if she came to them speaking in their tongue. It had been nearly two years since she had said anything, except in Comanche, but she was confident she could speak the white man's tongue as well as before.

She stood up again and cupped her hands, staring hard at the continuous puffs of red dust. "What is new from St. Louis? How is Mister Jean Baptiste Charbonneau? Have you heard? *Kiyi!* Listen to me! He is my

son! We are friends of Captain Red Hair! And—Duke
Paul! What is the latest news?"

She wanted to run ahead to see if it was truly a white
man's wagon train. But logic told her it was more than
five, six miles away, and by the time she could find
their trail they would be far gone.

She drew in her breath and felt her stomach tighten.
She opened her mouth to exhale slowly. What had suddenly come over her? If she had attracted the attention
of the whites, would they come straight for the Quohadas? Would they shoot into the tepees? Would they
care about a man she called "son"? She couldn't be sure.
The dust plumes were farther away now. Would she
risk these people's lives for news of her firstborn? If she
started, she could reach them. The train would stop for
the night. She spoke out loud. "I'm a lousy squaw. Those
whites do not know me. They will laugh, make fun, and
send me away. If I can believe what the Quohadas say,
they will shoot me in the back." Tears welled up in her
eyes and spilled down her face. She could not hold them
back. Finally she brought herself under control. She
looked around and saw that the play areas of both boys
and girls were empty. The sun was already past its
midpoint. When she got back to the lodge everyone
looked at her, then resumed work, as if she had not
been gone all morning.

Only Jerk Meat said, "Lost Woman! Why did you go
out by yourself?"

"I watched the children at play and marveled at the
boys' horsemanship," she said.

"You called out in a strange tongue?"

"*Ai*—once I learned some white man's words. It was
nothing."

"They made you sad?"

"Well, they make me mad," Pronghorn said. "More
white men are coming into our country this year and
taking out more buffalo meat."

"Our scouts saw a long string of them today," said
Big Badger. "And they had guns that glinted in the
sunlight."

Pronghorn's mind ran ahead to the next season. "In
summer, maybe we'll find two or three trains coming
through. They already are thinking too well of them-

selves. We'll teach them who is the stronger. We will dance under their scalps."

"No, we ought to get some presents from the whites."

"You think they'll give us presents because they fear us?"

"And so—well, I know that the Quohadas take what they want. You got some fine things from the Mexicans. I think we'll never be friends with the whites. If you act friendly, they ask you to move your camp to a certain place, and they want to hunt on your land."

Sacajawea began telling stories on the long, lazy summer evenings. She told of the Beaver Head and the clear running water in the streams of the north and how the mountains shone with glistening brightness when the sun was upon them. On these occasions Jerk Meat moved close to the smoldering fire and closer still to Sacajawea and seemed entranced by her stories.

"Well, she makes them up," he said one evening to Hides Well before he moved out to his own sleeping tepee. "No woman could have come from that country to this, alone."

"My son," said Hides Well, "she has given us no reason to doubt."

Spring laughed and made a face as her brother moved to his tepee.

Time seemed to move fast, and before long the prairie was again covered with snow, an unbroken sheet of white. The herd of horses was allowed to roam in order to browse and find grass. The men came in with rabbits, and one time with a lean elk that was hard to divide among fifty-two lodges. Some were so hungry they ate things they would not think of as food at any other time, such as boiled rawhide, toads dug out of holes in the mud banks, turtles from the frozen backwater of the river.

When they were in the Season When Babies Cry from Hunger Pains the Quohadas were nearly desperate for any kind of food. One man waded through the snow to the largest trash heap and snared a dozen rats. The rats were made into a thin soup and anyone in the tribe was welcome to eat it as long as it lasted.

Kicking Horse, the Quohadas' Medicine Man, pulled

an old buffalo hide from under his bed and painted a picture of a buffalo on the flesh side. He twirled that hide around four times, then threw it out the door of his medicine tepee. He went to see the direction the painted buffalo's head pointed. The hide had landed in a heap and the painted head looked up at the sun.[2]

A rumor spread that Kicking Horse was having a spell of difficulty with his magic that he used to find grazing buffalo. The difficulty was caused by someone walking behind him while he was eating. Everyone knew that caused a medicine man to lose his power.

When the snow was nearly gone, the son of Twisted Horn found the buffalo grazing on short, green grass in a valley lined with pecan trees. He came racing on horseback into camp, screaming and hollering that he had seen buffalo. The Quohadas eagerly went out on their first spring hunt.

Sacajawea and Spring stood in front of the trees, whose leafless branches were covered with yellowish clumps of evergreen mistletoe. They walked to a place where they could hide.

"I can taste a good hump roast already," said Spring.

"Just the sound of it makes my mouth water. I'll wager Jerk Meat gets the first kill," said Sacajawea. Her self-assurance was outward. Inside she felt fearful and confused. She was secure in Jerk Meat's presence; without him she felt alone and moody. It was something she could not explain. She did not intend for any one person in the Quohada band to become too important to her.

The hunters had discarded all clothing except their breechclouts for the dangerous but exciting work of the hunt. They rode their ponies against the wind in a semicircle and stayed out of sight of the buffalo. The men on ponies slowly spread out until the herd was surrounded everywhere but on the windward side. Pronghorn sounded the signal. Immediately, the whole circle was closed. The men ran their ponies around and around the buffalo, yelling and driving them into a tight bunch. The bulls, protecting the cows and calves massed in the center, milled around the outside, making targets of themselves for the hunters.

The women knew that the meat could spoil quickly

if the animals were run too long and were overheated
when they were killed. They each hoped the men could
move in fast and get plenty of meat for the curing racks.
The heavy work of skinning and butchering was done
by the men.[3]

The killing done, the hunters pushed the bulls over
so the bellies were on the ground and the legs stuck
out in four directions. They left the cows where they
had fallen so that the women could get to the full ud-
ders. With each animal they made a low cut on the neck
and pulled the hide back. The front quarters were cut
at the joint and pulled out. The hide was separated
along the spine. Each man was adept at keeping the
sinews uncut during this operation. Jerk Meat strung
all the sinews he stripped out on the short prairie grass.
He knew the women would want most for sewing, but
he wanted some for wrapping around spear points that
he fitted against a straight shaft. Sinew smeared with
blood for glue held the stone points tighter than anything he knew.

Most of the hunters were now pulling the hide farther back, cutting the hind quarters at the joint and
pulling them out. The flank and breast were rolled into
one large hunk. Ribs were separated from the breast
bone and the entrails removed. The young children who
had been allowed to come with the women gobbled the
raw entrails, pulling the greasy guts through their
clenched teeth in order to strip out the contents.

For a moment Sacajawea saw her own Agaidüka
Shoshoni of years ago, for they behaved similarily after
a successful hunt. She brought herself back to the present, and watched Jerk Meat cut between the ribs of a
large bull, pull up and out—groaning with the hard
work—then break some nice rib steaks from the spine.

Most of the women were now down the hill and
crowding around their menfolk. Some, like Spring, went
down on their haunches to carve out the hot livers and
immediately savor the rich liver seasoned with exploded gall bladder salts. Hides Well had her blood pot
next to a cow with its udder slashed, catching the milk
mixed with blood—a nutritious drink to be fed to children and nursing mothers.

Sacajawea found a calf suffocated under the weight

of the large cow Hides Well was working on, and she
and Spring pulled it out. They stabbed their butcher
knives in the calf's belly and pulled back to make a
slit. Inside was curdled milk. Pronghorn and Jerk Meat
left their butchering a few moments and dipped their
hands into the slit. With great relish they scooped this
delicacy into their mouths. With their appetite somewhat dulled they went back to their butchering.

The women took whole stomachs of buffalo up the
hillside to the cooking fires. The entire sac was slowly
cooked over hot coals. By now women, children, and
men alike were blood-smeared from faces to feet.

Finally the men were nearly finished. They took the
horns and hoofs because those would be useful later on,
but the heart was left intact with the skeleton so that
the buffalo spirit might live on and continue to replenish the plains. All the meat was packed in the hides,
loaded on horses, and brought up the hill to the women
for further processing.

Triumphantly, Hides Well chatted with some of the
women. She waved her arms to show all the empty
skeletons cradling hearts, with rump and head left for
vultures, coyotes, and wolves. The Quohadas now had
plenty of food for many days. And with the help of the
sun the blood on the meat would glaze and the flies
would leave it alone.[4]

Back at camp, they scraped the skins and let them
soak while preparing the meat. After three days they
would peg the skins to the ground and stretch them in
the sun. The brains of the buffalo were saved. These
were worked in very hot water until they were malle-
able, and the sun-dried skins would be put into a solution of the brains and worked until soft. Then they
would again be stretched out on stakes on the ground
to dry and be pulled and stretched. Sacajawea kept her
eyes lowered while she worked, but always she watched
the form of Jerk Meat; the blood in her veins warmed.
However, she did not think that he noticed her any
more than any other member of his family, maybe less.
She remembered how, when she had lain near starvation, Jerk Meat had nursed her and built a soft couch
near his campfire and broken her fever. And he was a

good hunter, always sharing his catch with friends and needy members of the tribe.

For days Sacajawea kept to herself, turning everything over in her mind. Perhaps Jerk Meat had a way of contacting the whites. Maybe the Mexicans in the south that he talked of would know about the things that went on in the village of Saint Louis. She felt her loneliness was for her son, Baptiste. During this time she thought of her firstborn and believed her attraction to Jerk Meat was a reflection of this terrible yearning.

One morning long after the buffalo hunt, Sacajawea walked along the river alone and came upon a thicket of orangewood—*bois d'arc*, it was called by Chief Red Hair. This wood made the finest of bows. Her heart began to jump as though it had a life all its own. She wanted to run to tell Jerk Meat about this find of such good bow wood. She wanted to tell him how the Shoshonis and white men each made their bows so that he could make use of the best ideas she could bring him. Then she stopped, trying to will her beating heart to be still. It had suddenly dawned on her that she was not scheming of a way to get Jerk Meat to help her find her son, but she was scheming. She was ready to pick up any idea that would give her an excuse to be near Jerk Meat. She opened her mouth and poured out a single whoop that rang in the still air. Then she ran back to the village. I am a woman of more than thirty summers, feeling like a girl of fifteen, she chided herself. But she did not make any attempt to wipe the smile from her face, the sparkle from her eyes, when she approached Big Badger.

"I am looking for Jerk Meat."

"And so—how is it that a young woman seeks out a man?" Big Badger grunted, his dark eyes snapping.

"The *bois d'arc*, by the river—I wanted to tell him about it."

"The what?"

"The orangewood for bows," she said simply.

"And so—then why did you speak of it in a strange tongue?"

"I forgot myself and spoke the tongue of the white man."

"Your tongue will cause you plenty trouble, young woman. And now, tell me what is it between you and my grandson?"

"Well, so—what could it be? He is my brother," she said, turning scarlet.

"Good! I can tell you it is better if the young man seeks out the young woman. He is already at the orangewood thicket."

She hurried back to the clearing, where a sandbar sloped down to the clear stream. For a fleeting moment she thought, *Jerk Meat was at the orangewood thicket when I was there. He must have heard me holler and dash back to the village. I am acting like a silly girl half my age.* She slowed her step and inhaled the sweet smell of the season, warm and pleasant. She scrambled through vines until she was near the grove of orangewood. Jerk Meat was cutting finger-sized shoots and bending them to test their strength. His eyes lighted when he saw her, and the corners of his mouth lifted.

"And now, you are coming to tell me how to make a bow?"

She said, "I immediately thought of you when I saw the orangewood earlier. I ran back to tell you so that you might have the first choice of these good straight branches."

"Isn't there anything else you want to tell me?" A quick flash of delight was in his black eyes, but his face remained impassive and he purposely narrowed his eyes.

She saw the look in his eyes and said, "*Ai*, there is something I have just discovered." Now her eardrums pounded with blood because of her boldness.

"That is strange. I thought you had known all things forever," he teased.

She thought it had been wrong for her to come back here. She was fearful now that he did not feel the same as she. Was she only acting like a child struck with puppy love? She bent and splashed water on her face for cooling. She stepped back in order to leave quickly and put an end to this foolishness. Her foot caught on a root. She stumbled and fell into the water. He did not move to help her but slapped his hand on the sides of his leggings and laughed a deep, hearty guffaw. When he could control his merriment and she was pouring water from her moccasins, not feeling embarrassment, but actually feeling more at home than when she was in the tepee with Spring, he said, "Would five horses be enough, or do you think you are worth six?"

She gasped with astonishment and covered her face with her hand to hide it. "My brother?"

"Words," he said and put his hand over his heart, making the sign of love. "I, too, have made a discovery, but I made it many moons back."

She wanted to tell him that she was honored and that she felt great pleasure, but she felt tongue-tied. She lowered her eyes and watched him move his bow stocks out of the way with his moccasin toe.

"So—maybe you ought to take the wet tunic off and wring the water out."

She looked up and saw that he had stepped back as if waiting for her to move next. A warm tingling grew at the point where the tops of her legs came together. She untied the yoke of her tunic, slid her arms out and let it drop at her feet. She felt the air on her skin. She shivered and the tingling ran through her entire body. She stepped out of the tunic and was pressed against him, his hands moving over her arms, over the white scars on her back, down across her rounded, firm bottom. With one hand he pulled her closer, with the other he worked loose his breechclout.

"It is the perfect time," he said. He put his foot against the backs of her feet, bent his knee, and gently brought her down to the grassy ground.

She forgot the wet tunic. She brushed her lips against his closed eyes, over his nose, and down to his lips. She lingered there, kissing him. He forgot the orangewood bow stocks.

"*Ai*," he whispered, "my Shoshoni sister has magic in her lips. What you do is good."

"It is loving," she whispered.

For a while they were aware only of their own heightened feelings. This arousal was something wonderful to be savored and fully enjoyed.

Freely and honestly they had admitted their love, and with the simplicity of a man who always goes straightforwardly toward an objective, Jerk Meat felt that the next hurdle should be taken. They loved each other, and they had said so. There had been no arrangement between families; this love was something they had felt for themselves.

"I shall round up some of my best horses this minute and put them outside Pronghorn's lodge. I think you should be my woman very soon."

"Oh, not yet, not so soon."

"And why?"

"Can we leave things the way they are awhile longer? When everyone knows, it will not then belong only to us. Let us keep it to ourselves."

"I do not want to keep it," said Jerk Meat flatly. "I want to tell everyone. Why are you afraid to face up to it?"

"Oh." She leaned against him and knotted and re-knotted the fringe on his shirt. "Face up to it?" After several seconds she began again. "Oh, I face the fact I left a man I did not love. I thought I would leave here after a while and look for my son. I would live with him. Now I do not want to go." Her face was troubled, and her eyes lowered. "I did not think I would ever take a man again. This feeling is something I have not planned, but it is strong with me."

"Can your son take care of himself?"

"Ai!"

"So—then you must get used to that and think that maybe he is what you trade for me."

"But then—" She thought for a moment. "There are things you do not know."

"There is much time for me to know them."

"I should tell you about the time I was ready to leave camp and follow the wagon train." Sacajawea felt she must tell him. She did not look at his face. She kept her eyes on the ground, speaking slowly, but telling it all to the end. She admitted she was not an ordinary squaw. Her life's trail had already passed by more experiences than many pass in one long lifetime. When she finished, she looked at him. Instead of being shocked as she expected, he was ablaze with indignation and tears were close to spilling from his eyes. He did not hide anything from her.

"I watched that day. I knew you were thinking of

leaving. I wanted to bring you back. Then I wanted you to go to the whites and never return. I scolded you for going out alone, but I wanted to shake the devil from you. I wanted to tie you so that you would never be able to leave. And then, the time Kicking Horse brought horses for you, I wanted to jam his big silver earring around his scrawny neck and pin his green foreskin between two stones. His offer of six horses was so generous that I cannot see why Pronghorn turned it down."

"So—maybe he is sorry," she said, making her eyes squint at him and her mouth turn up in a smile.

Stoutly Jerk Meat replied, "Well, then, I shall offer my father two or three times as many horses, and he will have to make you my woman."

The mild weather stayed, and there were those who chose to take advantage of it. Jerk Meat hurriedly talked four other braves into going south to Mexico with him on a horse raid. Big Badger shook his head in wonderment over the folly of this grandson who would traipse off in search of a raid when he could have the excitement of a marriage ceremony. Big Badger's eyes were not blind to the feelings between Sacajawea and Jerk Meat.

One afternoon the camp crier rode through the village. "Trading tonight! Trading and feasting! Bring your robes and trade goods!"

Hides Well and Spring made a pile of all the things they wanted to take for trading that night. There were a couple of leather boxes, several good buffalo robes, moccasins, and some clay cooking vessels. Sacajawea helped the women carry the trade goods outside the village where there was a grassy flat spot next to a small, nearly dry creek bed.

Sacajawea stood openmouthed with surprise. She had thought the Mandans and western river Indians were the only ones that held trading fairs. Here were several huge fires with delicious-smelling meat held above the flames by long poles.

Spring moved close to Sacajawea and said in a low voice, "Do not get hungry for that meat. It is probably swine."

"So?" asked Sacajawea.

"Well, no good Comanche eats meat that is associated with mud and filth."

Sacajawea was about to tell Spring that white men ate pork with no bad effects, then closed her mouth. She saw the dark-complexioned men wearing trail-stained wool trousers, holding up colorful gourds, strings of beads, woven reed mats. One man held up a squawking chicken. He had more in a wooden crate at his feet. These men wore wide-brimmed hats and had silver spurs attached to their leather boots. They were trading their wares for all the *anta blanca*—well-tanned buffalo hides—the Comanches could furnish.

The Mexicans also had large, dried tobacco leaves displayed for trading. The Comanches that bought the tobacco later cut the leaves into strips and pounded them to shreds after adding some dried, crushed sumac leaves. The Comanches rolled their cigarettes in cottonwood leaves or blackjack oak leaves. Both men and women smoked, though some preferred to smoke pipes.[5]

The Mexican traders brought metal barrel hoops, metal box bindings, and iron frying pans that could be used for fashioning arrowheads and spear points. They sold files to work the arrowheads and spear points so they would be symmetrical and sharp.[6]

The Quohadas made it clear by pointing and motioning that they wished to trade for everything they saw. Moccasins for a dried gourd, a wing-bone whistle for a yellow crook-neck squash, a rabbit skin for a small woven mat. Some were interested in the chickens.

Kicking Horse squatted on a flat stone and laid out a thick mat into which he inserted wooden pegs. He covered these with the halves of dried gourds, six of them, which he moved here and there on the mat. Two braves squatted in front of him. Sometimes one pointed to a half gourd, which he lifted, then they would shout gleefully. When several of the Mexicans gathered around to watch, the Quohadas, by hand signs, persuaded them to point to the half gourds. The pegs did not seem to stay in their old patterns after they were covered. At first the Mexicans pretended to be unaware of the point of the game, but the Quohadas took it seriously, even though they doubled over with laughing. The stakes were the chickens.

An impulsive hope ran through Sacajawea. Maybe these men would know of the one called Baptiste Charbonneau. She could send a message through them. She looked warily about, her eyes seeking something in the faces of the leather-clad visitors. She could not find it. Instead of friendliness she saw something hard, knavish, and shrewdly acquisitive. She sensed that these were not honest merchants who were trading powder and cartridges for beautiful furs and well-tanned hides. The traders carried weapons, but the Quohadas outnumbered them ten to one, so she walked from the side of Spring and went directly to the largest Mexican she saw, somehow believing size meant rank and knowledge.

"Señor, I am *umbea, madre*, mother," she stammered in a pidgin mixture of English, Comanche, and a little Spanish she'd picked up from the Quohadas. "My son is smart man, like you. He is important in the white man's village—the one called Saint Louis. Have you been there?"

"Out of the way, squaw, I want no traffic in women. Sell your wares to your own chief. *Adiós!*" He pushed her roughly to one side, and the men around him glared rapaciously.

"Baptiste Charbonneau? You hear of him? He can read the markings on paper. He is important in trapping. You know?"

"I know much, but I don't want a dirty, stinking Comanche squaw telling me anything, no matter how good-looking she is. *Vamos!*" His black mustache curled over thick lips.

She lowered her eyes and walked away. She was humiliated. Her cause was hopeless, and there was no way to make these traders understand. How could they ever believe she was the mother of a boy who could read and make the marks on paper?

"Did you see the wonderful travois!" exclaimed Spring breathlessly. She pulled Sacajawea forward to look over the wooden carts. Never before had she seen such large wheels. The Comanches never used wheels.[7] "There has never been anything like this!" She pulled again at Sacajawea. "Come, Lost Woman, you can trade later."

Hubbub and confusion reigned. Sacajawea tried to

get Spring back to the trading tables where braves
stalked gravely from tent to tent, boldly fingering the
articles on display and demanding to be waited on first.
Women, loaded down with robes, pressed behind their
men, jabbering excitedly and admiring the goods with
the zest for shopping typical of women of all races.

Spring ran her fingers over the wooden carts. She
pointed to the many sleek horses and the few mules
that were night-grazing on the prairie grass. Sacajawea
pulled her over to see the hawk bells on the mules'
harnesses. She laughed as she rang each one. Every
trader packed a generous supply of the tiny bells, which
had been used in the East in the sport of falconry.

"I'll trade for some. A present for you," said Sacajawea.

"Oh, Lost Woman, I do like them." Spring shifted a
strap on her shoulder that held Wild Plum's cradleboard. "A string of elk teeth ought to bring a handful."

Sacajawea did not answer. She had suddenly heard
a forgotten but beloved sound. She listened as she looked
at the Quohadas haggling over clusters of beads, vermilion, looking glasses, shells, awls, iron buckles, steel
rings and bracelets, copper wire, buttons, ribbons, and
other trinkets spread on a dirty Navajo blanket. The
Quohadas could not resist the foofaraw. Some had left
the noisy game of the half gourds to paw through the
looking glasses. The strange musical sound cannot possibly be out here, thought Sacajawea. It is the sound of
a French harp, but surely this is impossible. Her eyes
sought the player of the harmonica. Her footsteps were
directed to the sound.

Indolently playing the harmonica was a Mexican boy
who looked to be about the same age as Sacajawea remembered her own son, dark-haired Baptiste. But the
Mexican's nose was broad and his face was pitted with
tiny scars. The whites of his eyes were yellow in the
firelight.

He leaned against a stack of newly acquired tanned
hides, eyes not focused on anything in particular. His
cheeks moved in and out with his breath as he played.

Sacajawea gazed in wonder. By firelight the dented,
scratched, tarnished brass glowed, radiating a sensation of warmth. She stood close enough to see the in-

strument move back and forth in the Mexican's mouth as his hands went one way, then the other. The haunting sounds floated out into the evening air. Once he stopped and pounded the harmonica on his leg to clear out the saliva. She crowded in closer. She felt her temples throb. Impulsively she bent over and said in pidgin English, "Señor, I like to blow once."

The boy looked up. His brown eyes were wide open.

Sacajawea made hand signs as she spoke. "I used to make music for my son. A boy about your age." For the first time she noticed a strand of copper wire threading through the brass plate on one side of the mouth organ and encircling the shoulders of the player. She saw that the loop was large enough for him to slip over his head. The boy said nothing, but raised his hand and motioned frantically toward an older man.

The Mexican was greasy-looking and busy eating a piece of roasted meat. He talked with his mouth chock full. "José, I said if any of the bucks gave you trouble. Don't call me for some skinny, doe-eyed bitch. She ain't going to skin you alive."

Sacajawea watched, not understanding his Spanish. She decided the two resembled each other. He is giving the boy some fatherly advice, she thought.

The man blew smoke from his brown-paper cigarette into Sacajawea's face so that she coughed.

The boy said, "She wants to blow in my harmonica."

"So let her. What harm is there?" said the man.

"Maybe she puts lizards and snakes in her mouth."

"Her spitting in that music-maker might just keep these thieving redskins in good humor while we get away with all their leather goods."

The boy looked sullen.

Sacajawea ran her finger over the harmonica. She smiled at José and his father. She pointed the instrument toward the north, east, south, and west, then with a wide flourish of her arm, toward heaven and down to the earth. She felt it necessary to show appreciation to the Great Spirit for this lucky opportunity. She was also thankful Jerk Meat was not around, because she was working on a plan. If she could attract some attention, maybe one of the Mexicans would listen to her, then she could ask him a question, and he would listen and give an answer.

"She makes the sign of the cross," said José with surprise. "You said they are heathens."

"Well," the elder Mexican stuffed more meat in his mustached mouth to give himself time to think. "Hell, it is some *sí*, some *no* with these people. Some are, some not." He motioned with his hands.

Sacajawea was still rubbing her hands on the smooth, hard, warm brass. She noted the worn, dirty reeds and their wet, fetid odor. She slipped the braided wire loop over her head and placed the harmonica up to her mouth.

She puffed and made a long, sustaining, plaintive note in the night. Then she inhaled for a longer, deeper note. The low, gurgling sounds startled her and she pulled the wire back over her head and tapped the harmonica on her skirt in order to drain it.

She sat down on the sandy red earth not far from José, tucked her moccasined feet under her skirt, and slowly started to play "Skip to My Lou." The rhythm was not right. She stopped, hummed a little to herself, licked her lips, and started again. Her throat was tight, her breathing was hard to control, her hands shook, but after a few minutes she relaxed. Her tongue moved over the holes more easily. She inhaled and exhaled and darted her tongue here and there to cover the wind channels. Old tunes came back to her. Suddenly she was playing the mountain men's and traders' songs taught her by York and Cruzatte.

Someone started to keep time on a skin-covered, hollowed-out section of a log. Others were dancing the heel-toe step. José stared in disbelief, as if he had never heard the harmonica played. Sacajawea's breath hummed its way into whistlelike music, and with a fluttering of her hands cupped around the harmonica, out came the song of a jay, a catbird, a meadowlark, a mockingbird.

Big Badger came to the edge of the crowd and stared as if he half expected the harmonica to explode in Sacajawea's hands and the big Comanche cannibal owl, Piamuhmpits, to fly out. Soon he was caught up in the rhythm. He swayed on the balls of his feet, the quill-work on his leggings glittered in the flickering firelight.

Sacajawea recognized Spring, Hides Well, Kicking Horse, Flower, Bear Woman, and Hawk Feather.

Sacajawea finished with a flourish, paused, and stood up clasping the harmonica in her hands. She turned to José's father and spoke in her simple Spanish, always using hand signs. "I look for Baptiste Charbonneau. He is with white men. I am mother—" She hesitated, looking at the man's blank face, then in a burst of desperation said, "The Chief Red Hair, he knows. You know him?"

"I do not know Red Hair." The man's mustache quivered.

José dropped a handful of hawk's bells in her lap. Each bell was no larger than the cap on a post oak's acorn. As Sacajawea nodded her appreciation and lifted one for admiration, she felt a tug on the copper wire around her neck. She figured José was demanding his harmonica be given back. All at once the wire was pulled tighter. It cut into her throat, shutting off the air to her windpipe. She tried to call out, "*Aiaught.*" Sacajawea clawed, fighting with outstretched arms. She could not breathe and her face darkened to almost purple. She wondered if she were going to suffocate. In one last effort she concentrated all her energy on the act of pulling herself backward and down to get away from the cutting wire. She felt someone grab her arms. She twisted her body and brought her head down. The wire slipped up over the back of her head. She gulped in deep breaths of air and recognized Gray Bone's cackle and She Cat's snicker.

Gray Bone pushed She Cat out of the way, picked the harmonica off the ground, pitched it down against a flat stone and pounced on it with all her weight. It crunched and crumpled beneath her moccasins.

"White man's squaw!" spat Gray Bone. "You are not Comanche!"

Sacajawea pulled away from She Cat's grasp and jumped toward the broad Gray Bone like a coyote leaping after a gopher. The Mexicans shrank back. This was a fight between squaws. They gathered up their belongings, loading the carts and mules fast.

Hatred blazed in Gray Bone's face. She grabbed a stone and pounded Sacajawea. Sacajawea tried to call out to José or his father, but no matter where she looked there was no one to help. Her throat hurt from the strangling as much as her body did from the beating she took.

But this beating and near fatal choking was not the only price she paid for her few moments of music. Next morning as she came up the path from the bathing place she met Gray Bone with her two companions, She Cat and *Kianceta*, Weasel Woman. She Cat, a large, old woman, wore jangling circles of silver wire in a half dozen holes along the rim of one ear. Weasel Woman's hair was cut short. Sacajawea thought perhaps she was in mourning for a lost relative, and felt pity for the woman. Even outdoors their bodies smelled of smoke, dogs, and rancid grease. Most Comanche women morning-bathed frequently, but it was obvious these two either slept too late or did not bother with the washing ritual.

The three women walked close to Sacajawea and pushed her toward a grove of scrub oaks. She struggled to free herself, but they threw her in the sand, holding her arms and legs. Wild fear gushed through her. They began staking her arms out, then her legs. She strained against the bonds, but they held. She called out to them asking what they were doing and why. They were silent.

Gray Bone drew her bone-handled knife out of a small parfleche she had tied on her belt and stared down at Sacajawea, her eyes glittering mercilessly. She wiped her knife once across her tunic and motioned to her two assistants. Obediently they crowded, one pushing her hand firmly over Sacajawea's eyes to block her view of the proceedings, the other lying heavily across her stomach to pin her securely to the ground. A wad of soft leather was pushed tightly into her mouth.

Sacajawea's body felt hot as fire despite the coolness in the ground under her, despite the morning breeze. She wondered what they were going to do. She thought she felt a rawhide band being slipped around her head. "No, no!" she tried to cry out. She imagined that next they would throw water on her head and then the bandage would feel tight. She knew that dying of a rawhide band around her head would be slow. She would feel only a small headache at first, growing, growing, until— She screamed silently until she ran out of breath. Wouldn't anyone look for her? No one knew she'd gone for her bath; the others in Pronghorn's lodge were yet asleep.

The morning sun was just topping the nearby ridge, throwing off hues of pale orange, pink, and the glistening yellow. It gave more light. Gray Bone, knife in hand, stepped to Sacajawea's head and squatted. In an agony of despair Sacajawea mumbled through the wad of leather, "Great Spirit, take the cloud from their eyes. They do not see what they are doing."

Coolly Gray Bone went to work. She adjusted the headband so that Sacajawea's hair would not get in the way. Now Sacajawea knew what she was doing. For she felt an excruciating pain in the area of her nose. This was the Comanche way of branding a woman a prostitute for life. It was over in half a minute. Gray Bone knew what she was doing. She did not fully sever the nose, thereby giving her the mark of a loose woman. Gray Bone wanted only to disfigure Sacajawea so that no one could be sure if she were an upstanding woman or one of questionable quality. Her disfigured face would leave her life a question to others; it would leave her a nothing; no one would pay her any attention.

Sacajawea lay writhing in pain as the two fat, stinking assistants cut the bonds on her arms and legs. Blood soaked the sand as the women marched backward off toward the village, their right hands outstreched toward Sacajawea, thumb between index and second finger, in the gesture of scorn.

"And your ears should be cut off, you—flirt," sneered Gray Bone. "Now the one called Jerk Meat, the son of our chief, will bring fine Mexican horses in trade for my own sweet daughter, Round Belly. She mooned over him all winter and he did not see her. Now he will see he can do no better than take the first daughter of the Medicine Man as his woman."

When they were out of sight, Sacajawea thought, let this not be the morning of my going to another world. She managed to feel her nose, all the while breathing through her mouth and tasting the bubbles of blood that dripped along the back of her throat. The nose was

cut back to the bone. She fainted. Coming to, she realized she must do something or she would bleed to
death. She pulled herself to the water and washed her
face carefully. There was much pain and she was afraid
of fainting again. Slowly she pulled the leather headband down over the nose to hold it in place. The effort
was great. Sacajawea's mind whirled with the words:
Round Belly—Jerk Meat.

Her world blackened. When she came to, she heard
the gentle *pit-pat* of the late spring sap from the oaks
dripping on their newly formed leaves. Some of the sap
hit the sand, making it sticky. It dripped on Sacajawea.
Her arms were sticky. There was some fluff of the cattail nearby and when she moved her arm it stuck. It
stuck to her fingers when she tried to pull it off. The
trees were rich in spring sap. Cattail fluff! She opened
her swollen eyelids wider, then gingerly felt her throbbing face. The face was swathed in the soft fluff and
tied firmly with wide rawhide bands. A piece of wood
or bone was shaped over the top of her nose. She could
not breathe from the nose, but she no longer tasted
blood. She was weak and exhausted and could not remember bandaging her face so expertly. She tried to
pull her thoughts together. I must leave the Quohadas.
I'll go north and ask about Baptiste, maybe I'll go as
far as the People in the mountains. I am disgraced. Jerk
Meat must never see me. He would scorn me, and I
could not bear it.

She slept for a time, gaining strength. She imagined
something soft as cattail fluff touching her hand and a
voice as far away as a dream, "We raided the Mexican
traders. They have fewer horses and one less well-fed
trader. Ha-ha-hee-hee."

She thought only of Jerk Meat and his steady, trust-
ful eyes, his gentleness and understanding. The soft
fluff touched her hand again and again. She awoke, and
the sky was as black as smoke-hole soot. The only sounds
in the dark were the whiffling sniffs of a horse as it
cropped new grass, the drip-dripping of the oaks, and
the sliding water sound of the creek.

Sacajawea awoke next on her own pallet. Her stomach hurt, as if pinched, and her face felt like a huge
puffball. She was thirsty constantly; the water she drank

from the skin bottle Spring brought did not quench her
thirst. Her throat felt swollen, and her mouth was dry
and hot as if she had a fever. Then she remembered
her nose and her vow to run away.

"Why did you bring me home?" Sacajawea asked,
conscious of her rudeness, but driven by her own necessity to know. Her teeth chattered so that she could
hardly speak between them. She clenched her jaw hard
on them.

Calmly, taking no offense, Spring answered, "Gray
Bone's boy, Wolf, told our brother to find you by the
stream, hidden in the oaks. He said you had fallen and
cut the side of your nose. It is good our brother looked
for you. Kicking Horse said you would not have lived
through the night if you had been unattended."

"Kicking Horse?"

"Well, *ai*, he helped Jerk Meat push the cut together.
He did it in the same manner that you held together
the cut on the son of Twisted Horn's face. They were
quite pleased with their sewing!"

Spring had fastened the tiny hawk's bells to the fringe
of her skirt, and when she moved they made a gay,
tinkling sound.

Wild Plum gurgled from inside his cradleboard hung
on a pole peg in the tepee.

"Sewing on my nose?"

"Your ears have heard," Spring said quietly.

Her face ached, and her heart stayed on the ground.
She could only think, what if Gray Bone tried more
retaliation? She resolved to keep the secret of what had
happened. "Jerk Meat?" she asked.

"He has many horses and a few mules. He hunts and
rides to show off his new herd."

The day came when the pain in her stomach eased,
and the fever cooled, and the chill was gone. She felt
only a dreadful, draining weakness. The binding was
removed from her nose, and she helped Spring with the
easy chores. She gave thanks to the Great Spirit for
keeping her life and for the sharp edge of Gray Bone's
knife, because there was only a thin line across the
front of her nostrils and a thin pink ridge on either side
to prove her nose had been severed at all.

Jerk Meat did not come to see her, and she felt flame

on her cheeks when she dared imagine he went to see Round Belly.

One afternoon Big Badger lumbered into the tepee and sat down with a wheeze. When he was young he could lasso an enemy and drag him to death. It was many years since he had thrown a lariat or gone out on the warpath, but he was still looked up to.

"Everywhere I go there is some talk," he grumbled. The fatty sacks under his eyes quivered. "What is there now between you and your brother? If there is anything, let us get on with it. I see Gray Bone grooming her daughter as a wife for my grandson. Wagh! The only reason I can see Jerk Meat going to that lodge is for talk with Kicking Horse about healing medicines."

"I would like to have you show me how to make a bow so that it shoots straight."

"That is a brave's education. What do you want with that kind of knowledge?"

"There may come a time when I will need to know more than I do, Grandfather."

"I can no longer fight, but I do not expect you to do it, even though you know more than most women of your age. And you do not have to hunt meat for me. I expect you to find a man among the Quohadas who will care for me in my old age." He straightened out his thin, rheumatic legs with a groan. "I have not had good luck with many great-grandchildren. There is Wild Plum. I'd like more for this lodge. Well, then, it might serve Jerk Meat right if that fat daughter of Gray Bone's caught him off guard and he ended with her for his woman. She is built for childbearing." Big Badger eyed Sacajawea carefully.

She did not blink an eye, but listened intently to the old man's complaints.

"My granddaughter, Spring, has no time to take care of an old man like me. Her man died in a raid on the Utes. He was rich and had many horses, but those horses have dwindled in the lot of Pronghorn. I think he butchers them for winter meat. So—by a miracle I have a new granddaughter. But she has another man's brand on her—and so she believes she is not enticing to men. Well, in my opinion—"

"Grandfather, you know perfectly well that I will

take care of you all the time I am here." Sacajawea stroked the white strings of hair on the old man's head.

"And will you now consort with your brother?"

"Grandfather!"

"All right," he said petulantly, waving his hand. "I did not mean to put it exactly that way. But I know how you both have looked at one another. Gray Bone acts disgraced before the whole band by me and my family because Jerk Meat does not offer a fine horse or two for Round Belly. She knows he has a distinctive, white horse that would more than serve as a bride-price with any family in this band."

Hides Well came into the tepee. "There are things beyond ordinary understanding. We should be grateful to have Lost Woman in our lodge. She must follow her own path."

"The woman, Gray Bone, sickens me," mumbled Big Badger.

The next day Sacajawea brought a big load of firewood back to the lodge on her back. It was tied together by wide leather bands. The load was heavy and she was perspiring, in no mood to stop and gossip with the women who stood in front of their tepees waving to her. Inside the lodge Sacajawea bent way down to slide the load off her back. She rested a moment then asked, "Where is Jerk Meat? I saw his white horse tied outside."

Spring said, "He told us he was going south, maybe as far as the Red River. I believe he is looking for mustangs."

"Why didn't he ride the white gelding?"[8] Sacajawea was puzzled.

"I suppose he wanted you to care for it," said Big Badger after he cleared his throat noisily.

"It ought to be with the rest of the herd. There is not enough grass around the lodge anymore." She went out to lead the white horse out to the pasture on the other side of the village, where everyone let their herd graze freely.

"She didn't notice the horse was loaded with gifts," burst out Hides Well, clapping her hand over her mouth.

Sacajawea was back, dragging packs and leather boxes from the back of the horse into the tepee. She said, "I suppose he left these things for us in exchange for taking care of his favorite horse. If we did not know better, we might think all this a gift to the family of a bride. Just look at these Mexican blankets. Beautiful! I like the red. And baskets of silver beads! They could be from some great warrior." She hung a long strand of silver around Spring's neck and gave the baskets to Hides Well. A box of rough onyx stones she gave to Big Badger for making bird points.

She gave a whole pack of eagle feathers, including the blanket it was wrapped in, to Pronghorn. He said, "Thank you," cleared his throat, looked at Big Badger, and wiped a hand across his face as though trying to hide some huge secret.

Big Badger suddenly had a coughing fit. Afterward his eyes snapped. He was obviously enjoying the whole situation.

Sacajawea looked from one to the other. "Have you been thinking what I am thinking—that some man found Jerk Meat's horse staked out front and thought it a handy place to leave his gifts? Honestly, I think somebody wants Spring to be his woman. Oh—I am stupid! Forgive me—they were not things for me to give away." She was confused and embarrassed.

Spring spoke up, "Listen, if all this were for me, I'd divide it exactly the same way. You keep the red blanket, my sister, and the string of little silver beads. I'll keep the many-colored blanket and the little gray and black one for Wild Plum."

"But who? If you accept the gifts, you—you must know who left them," stammered Sacajawea.[9]

"My brother left them and you already accepted," hooted Spring. "So, take his revered white horse to join the herd of your father, Pronghorn. And remember—it was you who called yourself stupid, not one of us." Spring was bent double with giggles.

The whole lodge, except Sacajawea, were holding their sides, convulsed with laughter.

Sacajawea felt like a buck deer with its antlers caught in the brush. "Jerk Meat is away. How will he know I put his horse with our father's herd?"

Big Badger put his knotted, arthritic hand over the catch in his side, then straightened and wiped his eyes. "I have not had so much fun since I stole that Apache's horse while he relieved himself behind a tall cactus. He probably believes to this day that some night spirit made that horse invisible. Tee-hee! My grandson asked me to be his go-between on the day he gathered orangewood sticks for arrows and forgot to bring the sticks back when he returned. Woogh! Would you like to tell us about that day, Granddaughter?"

Sacajawea's face was flushed. She shook her head. She knew there were few secrets kept in any village, but she wondered how much Big Badger knew for sure.

"You are my family, now," said Sacajawea shyly. "I like all of you and it is known the one that is not here is special to me. So, then, when did Jerk Meat say he would be back?"

"He gave Spring and me time to make a marriage tepee," said Hides Well, thumping the pile of hides with her butcher knife.

"I would like to make a fresh tunic, if there are skins enough," said Sacajawea on impulse.

"*Ai*, take your skins from the pack that was on the white horse," said Big Badger. "Looks like my grandson thought you'd say those exact words. And so, if I'm not being overly bossy as a go-between, get that white horse into Pronghorn's herd. It's no secret that it is something he has wanted to own ever since Jerk Meat brought it in from that raid beyond the Brazos River."

"*Ai*, Grandfather," said Sacajawea. "The white horse will be cared for."

"Looks like you will be cared for also," said Pronghorn, pointing to Hides Well and Spring, who were already laying out the hides to be used as the marriage tepee cover.

Jerk Meat was with two companions who knew of a place on the plains where many young ponies were driven out of a large herd each year by the old stallions. Each man took a string of eight to twelve gentle mares with them as bait. These young wild ponies sniffed the mares, milled around in their vicinity, and in a few days some were ambushed at the closest water hole. They fed out on the prairie, but when the mares were hot and thirsty the ponies followed them to water, even a dozen miles away. The men easily took the mustangs when their rock-hard bellies were full of water.

Jerk Meat and his friends spent the next couple of days breaking the wild horses. They lassoed a pony, threw it to the ground, and blew into its nostrils. This ritual made the mustang the blower's property. The hairs around the mustang's eyes were pulled by two hand-held sharp stones. Then each pony had a loop of rawhide rope brought up under its jaw and tied around its neck. The end of the rope was tied to the neck rope of one of the mares so that it would not escape when it recovered from overguzzling water and charged with lowered head, or bucked. During this time the owner talked with a calm voice, loaded it with a heavy pack and in about two days set it free. It usually followed the mare around. Then the mustangs were driven into the water hole before the men mounted any one of them. Riding in deep water eased most of the bucking and was easier on the men if they fell off.[10]

Jerk Meat returned to camp at the end of a week with one new mustang for each of his twelve mares. His two companions were equally lucky, and each spoke of the future father-in-law who one day might receive a couple of the best ponies from their herd. One asked, "Jerk Meat, what will you do with your mustangs? Save them for meat during cold weather. Your new sister, she must eat much. We've seen she is no infant, but full-grown."

"I thought of something like that," said Jerk Meat, who knew well enough what he was about to do, but didn't want to let the squirrel out of the bag, in a manner of speaking, until the water was boiling or the deed was done.

Jerk Meat's friends drove their horses out to their family herds, but Jerk Meat gave a wave with one hand and drove twenty-four horses right down the center of the village, past the tepee of Kicking Horse and on to his own father's large lodge. Quickly he tied each mustang to a mare and let the rope to the mare's hackamore trail on the hard-packed red earth.

Big Badger was out first to check on the commotion. He waved to Jerk Meat and indicated everything was going the way they had planned. Big Badger was careful how he walked among the milling horses. "I'm going to announce the marriage myself," he said with pride. Lost Woman took your prized white horse to Pronghorn's herd and was as nervous as a bat in a high wind waiting for your return. You made a good choice. Everyone likes her. She is a cheerful worker. But, maybe you have overdone the gift giving. No one has ever given two sets of presents, and I've never seen a whole herd of horses driven through the village and set before a lodge in my whole life. You might be starting something. Lost Woman might get a swelled head when she sees all this." He waved both hands around, pointing at the horses.

"Grandfather! You know we planned this. You are my go-between."

"Grandson, you smell like horse. As your go-between, I suggest you soak in the creek while waiting to see what Lost Woman does."

"Ai—get me clean leggings, quick!"

Big Badger ducked inside the lodge after a careful walk through the restless herd. He tried to avoid stepping into the fresh dung.

Then, tossing a change of clothing to Jerk Meat, he called, "Run! Everyone inside is coming outside. Their curiosity is worse than the antelopes'."

Jerk Meat swung his leg over his pinto and dashed for the bathing creek. He rode so hard that he did not hear laughing, nor the slap of the stiff hides of tepee flaps banging shut. Everyone had heard him bring the herd of horses into the village and they watched him, but they would not be caught staring.

Spring and Hides Well followed Big Badger outside. They could not believe what they saw.

"Our lodge area will smell worse than a swine wallow, with all that fresh dung," laughed Hides Well. "My son has lost his mind."

Sacajawea came out with Pronghorn. They wandered among the horses examining them.

"Now who is asking for a woman?" asked Sacajawea.

"You know this is not for me," said Spring. "I confided to you six days ago that there is no one in camp that interests me."

"Well," sniffed Hides Well, "it certainly is not for me. I have a man. But he was never this generous."

Finally catching on, Sacajawea shouted, "You mean Jerk Meat is back? Where is he? I must see him. Oh, so—an ordinary thank-you will hardly be enough. What can I do?" Suddenly tears were running down her face and she couldn't talk. She looked from one to the other and whispered, "I am a woman who has once had a man. I am not worthy." The tears came in torrents.

Spring was at her side. "We have put some planning into this marriage celebration. We think you are plenty worth it."

"I can never live up to your high expectations. I must leave before it is too late for any courteous action." She cried harder and made sniffling sounds. She realized she didn't really want to leave.

Big Badger put his rough hand on her shoulder. "Granddaughter, you and Spring talk this over while you take this herd of miserable mustangs out to pasture. Just look at their ragged coats. Not one is sleek and shiny. In a year, after good care, they will be wiser and more beautiful. Think on that. If you put the wild ones in Jerk Meat's herd, no one will criticize, but the first present will all have to go back to him also. It will be all right. You will still be a member of this lodge. You have won our favor and kindest feelings."

Sacajawea put her arms around Big Badger and buried her head in his shoulder.

Pronghorn looked away from so much emotion.

Big Badger saw him, grunted, and turned Sacajawea over to Spring. "Women!" he sputtered. "No man was made to understand one. Keep her in line with frequent beatings and she follows you like a pup. Give her everything and she threatens to leave. It turns my stomach!" He went back into the tepee and pulled Wild Plum from the cradleboard, nuzzling him and clucking at him, making the little boy laugh.

Hides Well followed him into the tepee. There she got out her paints and goose grease. She laid Sacajawea's new tunic on her sleeping couch and marveled at the quill design on the yoke. It was different from anything she had seen. In fact it was not even a Shoshoni design. It was something Sacajawea created from her imagination. Usually this was not done in the Comanche nation.

Spring grabbed a loose rope and untied the mustangs. Sacajawea followed her, then all of a sudden jumped on the bare back of a little, shaggy-coated, wild pony and rode through the village toward the pasture with the herd racing ahead of her. Spring had seen her action and was right behind on a pony, yelling, hair flying along with manes and tails. Sacajawea turned and grinned. Spring waved to everyone along the way, thinking, Big Badger will not have to announce this marriage. Everyone already knows!

The two girls walked back and saw that Big Badger had on his best shirt and leggings. Hides Well painted the inside of his ears red, then he ducked out the lodge door and walked through the village.

"My grandson, Jerk Meat, will take the woman we call Wadzewipe. Let no other wooer interfere with this partnership. I am their official go-between." His voice had an exuberant ring.

Inside, Sacajawea pulled off her tunic and wiped the dampness off her face and arms with a soft hide. She rubbed her back and front, then legs and feet. Hides Well painted the part in her hair with vermilion and put a little of the greasy, red paint inside her ears for a beauty accent.

Suddenly there was a noisy rushing about close to the lodge. Pronghorn, feeling in the way, was glad to go see what was going on. Sacajawea laughed nervously, saying, "It is probably people welcoming Jerk Meat as he comes from taking a look at where I put his herd of mares and mustangs."

But the voices sounded angry, and the noise increased. Hides Well sighed, put the paints aside, wiped her hands and went out. Sacajawea followed.

Gray Bone was in front of the tepee shouting at Pronghorn. "You let your son take your own daughter as his woman! Evil! Evil! What kind of chief are you? That woman should be killed for tempting your son." Two other women pressed toward him. Sacajawea recognized them immediately.

She Cat yelled, "Ai, only in your family could such a vile thing take place!"

Sacajawea shivered as the fear inched along her spine.

Pronghorn held his clenched fist toward the heavens. "I am your chosen chief!" His voice was loud. "My word goes. And so—while I or any one of my family live in this band, Lost Woman will be treated as if she had always been one of us. Big Badger is go-between and he announced that they will live together. I give my consent to this union. That is enough talk now. Get out of the way. Forked tongues do not scratch my skin." He stepped aside, head up, looking over the hushed crowd gathered in front of his lodge.

Twisted Horn's woman spoke up. "There has never been such rich gift giving for a woman in the history of the Quohadas. So, there is bound to be jealousy. I say, let the young people alone. This is their affair."

"*Ai!*" shouted a man. "A marriage is nothing to divide a band's feelings."

"Right!" shouted another woman, who was jumping up so that she could see better. "We should think of our own happy marriage day."

From then on the shouts took on a more erotic turn. The Quohadas laughed and made earthy jokes about marriage customs and sex. One man said, "Is it true women have a hole with blue lips and no teeth?"

Gray Bone, Weasel, and She Cat glanced neither right nor left, neither up nor down, but stared only straight ahead. Their legs moved jerkily as they sulked back to Gray Bone's tepee, put down for the day at least.

Sacajawea breathed a sigh of relief and went back to fold her old blue coat and collect her other possessions. She helped Spring tie Jerk Meat's bow and arrows, steel-bladed knife, winter moccasins, extra leggings, shirt, and rusty pistol into his buffalo robes.

This day would now date passage of time for the Quohadas. They would retell what Lost Woman wore and how her hair shone. They would say, "She was a woman that was found half-dead out on the plains, brought to us to mend, and became one of us. She was a hard worker and full of laughter. I knew her personally."

Sacajawea's thoughts ran deep. She and Jerk Meat met and from that moment they were never strangers. They were sensitive to the feelings of one another. She felt he was the only person she could fully trust with her innermost spirit and her outer body.

Hides Well and Spring left to make the last minute arrangements in the marriage tepee. Sacajawea was left alone with Big Badger and Wild Plum. Pronghorn had gone to look over his increased herd of horses until he could calm his fury with Gray Bone and her friends.

"I feel a need to eat," said Big Badger. "Do you suppose you could fix a little fire in front of the lodge so that I can sit out there and keep my bowl of stew warm? I'd enjoy seeing people stand around and gossip."

"*Ai*. It will be good to use the time to do something you desire, Grandfather," said Sacajawea, moving beside him, patting his thick-knuckled hand. She leaned closer and kissed him on the forehead. "You are the best go-between in the band."

"Tee-hee! That is something magic you do with your lips. Will you teach this to the little grandmother on the other side of the village for me? Tee-hee!"

Sacajawea looped a worn blanket under Wild Plum so that he hung against her hip, and she went to the fire hole and dug a coal from the ashes and pushed it with a piece of bark to the front of the lodge. She broke a few twigs over it and fanned a flame alive. She put stew in a small clay pot and nestled it down against the little bed of smoldering sticks, then called for Big Badger to come out. He brought his willow backrest and settled himself against it, smiling.

The neighbors pointed down the path in front of some tepees. It was Jerk Meat coming back from his bath, carrying his dirty clothes in a roll under one arm, and in the other hand the heart of a fresh-killed horse from his herd.[11]

Spring and Hides Well met him behind the village, finished butchering the horse, delivered the meat to those who were most needy and gave the untanned hide to the same little grandmother Big Badger had mentioned living on the other side of the village.

Jerk Meat hung the bloody heart on a wooden closing peg of the tepee flap.

"What is that?" asked Sacajawea, clicking her tongue. "I like your clean leggings and white moccasins."

"I like the design on your dress. I see you can sew,"

Jerk Meat said. "This heart is for one ceremony my Shoshoni cousins may have forgotten. You roast it, divide it, and we eat it. It keeps our two hearts on the same trail for life." Jerk Meat sat on his haunches near Big Badger, who grinned toothlessly.

"Then you go to the marriage lodge," whispered Big Badger, slapping Jerk Meat on the back.

Sacajawea thought she understood, and liked the meaning of the heart ritual. She found a thick green stick in the lodge's wood pile. She pushed the heart on the stick and held it over the little coals. When it was browned and tender she let it cool in the evening air, then nervously divided it into two parts. All the while the villagers were looking, talking, laughing, gossiping, but not coming too near the tepee. They knew they should go home, but they were reluctant to leave. Jerk Meat ate two or three bites from his half. His face shone and his eyes were bright as he watched Sacajawea. She picked at her half, not daring to look Jerk Meat in the eye because of the excitement that was building inside of her.

The dark was almost in. Jerk Meat whispered, "Let us leave." He wiped the meat drippings from his hands on his freshly braided hair.

The small fire threw shadows on the outside lodge wall. A soft whisper went out from mouth to mouth, "They are leaving. They are going." The men stepped back into the darkness, and the women gathered in groups, their hands over their mouths as they whispered with their eyes cast down.

Sacajawea and Jerk Meat stood up. Then she kneeled, picked up both their packs with a leather carrying strap, and hoisted them on her back. They walked together to the newly built tepee at the edge of the village.

Neither was aware of the twinkling stars, the curious camp dog that pushed a cold nose against the back of Sacajawea's legs, the chirping crickets, nor the howling coyote.

Inside the marriage tepee they stood side by side. Sacajawea was overcome with shyness after unpacking the sleeping robes, and took a few twigs from the wood pile to place on the red coals of the center fire. Jerk Meat touched her hand and motioned to the pile of

robes. He too felt bashful and had to say to himself,
this is my woman. Sacajawea crept to the far side of
the buffalo robes and removed her moccasins and tunic
and drew a robe about her shoulders. She lay quivering,
every nerve of her flesh alert. She watched the slow,
silent movement of her man pulling off his shirt and
coming beside her. Gently he pulled her close to him.
The thrill was strong. Both felt the explosion at the
same time.

46

Joy and Sorrow

Sacajawea had five children while with the Comanches, but only two lived beyond infancy, the oldest, a son, Ticannaf, To Give Joy, and the youngest, a daughter, Yagawosier, Crying Basket.

CHARLES A. EASTMAN, *Report to Commissioner of Indian Affairs*. Washington, D.C.: Department of the Interior, March 2, 1925, pp. 1–69.

The tepee at the edge of camp was hidden by burr oak and wild grapevines. It was small, built for two, with highly colored paintings on the sides. The paintings were of the sun, depicting happiness, the moon, depicting restful nights, rain, meaning a good harvest of roots and berries, and at the sides of the door flap were fastened six silver bells. The hawk's bells were cut from the fringe of Spring's skirt. When the air stirred, the bells moved lightly with it.

The inside of the tepee was filled with branches of oak and sweet-smelling sassafras.

When Sacajawea woke in the morning, she glanced at Jerk Meat. He was still asleep under his robe. She smiled and brushed her hand along his long side hair. She sat up and threw off her robe and rushed from the tepee. The sun was high. She started a fire outside and listened to the distant barking of dogs, the creeping of the breeze through the oaks, and the soft speech of the villagers, barely audible. She ran on down through the trees to the creek's edge. She knelt. Nose touching the water, she sipped a drink before bathing. She heard Jerk Meat call as she hummed softly to herself, letting her hair dry in the sun and by the heat of her small fire.

"Where have you been?" he asked.

"Bathing."

"Why did you not waken me?"

Her dark eyes crinkled. "You were sleeping with a smile on your face; I could not waken you." She took his head in her hands and pulled it down to her own.

"It was bad to wake and not find you at my side." He stroked her streaming hair. "Why did you not wait for me?"

"Come, let us go swimming together, then."

"Together?" he asked, startled.

"*Ai.*"

"A man and woman do not swim together."

"Why not?"

"No one does," he said. "No one ever does."

"And so—would you like to—with me?" she cupped his chin and kissed him. He moved his lips against hers.

"Do I do it right?" he asked. "I like to touch your lips."

"*Ai*," she said. She kissed him again. "You do it right."

He cupped her chin gently and kissed her. His hand moved across her firm, round breasts and fingered the sky blue stone in the hollow of her throat.

She could see the wisps of smoke rising from the tepees of the village.

"We have everything here," she said happily, pointing to the inside of their tepee. Inside were parfleches of mesquite bean cakes, roasted yucca fruit, ripe acorns. Even the necessities for preparing the food had been left by Hides Well. Spoons of buffalo bone, water gourds, fire drills, and woven grass containers.

"Are you happy?" he asked.

"Happy?" she repeated. "Even more happy than I have ever been. More happy than when I was with my son, and the other one, called Tess. More happy than when I was with the white soldiers."

"White soldiers!" He jumped backward, and his dark eyes blazed.

"*Ai*," she said. "I will tell you how it was that I was chosen to show them the homeland of the People."

"Chosen?" he asked, more perplexed.

"It is something I could not tell everyone. They would have thought my tongue the most forked in the whole Quohadas band."

"Tell me," he commanded.

When she finished, however, it was not soldiers he was indignant about. "What a stupid, cruel man—that one, Toussaint Charbonneau!"

Sacajawea slumped against Jerk Meat with an inner amusement mixed with a draining sense of relief. She thought, Who can ever tell how a man is going to react. In her moccasins most women, especially a woman of the Quohadas, would have held to a rigid adherence to the ideas of the tribe. She would have shaken her head and said it was a squaw's duty to follow along with her man and take whatever he gave. Instead, Jerk Meat had immediately and emotionally identified himself with the captains. His whole reaction was masculine, personal, and uncritical. Charbonneau was the only one at fault.

"A squaw should not talk of these things—maybe. The Quohadas would say it is not modest. But I must tell you so that you can know me and know that I am not like all other squaws. But it must be between only you, my man, and me. No one else must know all these things. They would not believe. They would not understand how such things could be true."

"*Ai!* Tell me what I already know. How are you not like other women?"

"Last night I was happiest of all. When we came here, the feeling was so good it seemed as though it could not go on. It seemed that surely I must die, and when I was with you as one man-woman that I could never live again and be happy alone without you. I have never felt that way. I found something new. And then, this morning I did not want that feeling at all. I woke and looked at you and touched you and felt your face and hair and listened to you breathe and there was nothing I wanted different. This is how it should be! I thought. And I have never before known of it. I am a grown woman, but I do not know very much. Then when I left you, I knew I could have remained at your side. Then the coming-back thought gave me the feeling of my heart coming through my skin.

"And at the creek there is a deep place and the water against my body makes it feel good because my body was clean with you, not used in whatever manner traders and mountain men deal in sordid acts with squaws. I kept thinking what you did to me, and I loved my own body because it had given you happiness." She pulled away from him, blushing. "I think now it is not modest for me to reveal inner thoughts to you. You asked me if I was happy," she said defensively.

"There is no modesty between us," he said. "I had another woman once. I know something of what a woman thinks."

"A woman should not talk too much, though. Pronghorn and Hides Well would be shocked."

"No," he said, "between us everything can be said. We are two people, yet one unit. Everything can be said. The good and the bad, the most beautiful and the ugly. There must be nothing secret, no words that we cannot listen to from each other, nothing we cannot do with each other. We are bound together, yet separate."

"You are more wonderful than I thought. You think deeply. You are gentle. You understand. You are a man. I give my love to you." She put her hand on her heart and made the sign of love and held her hand out to him.

"Now listen to me." He held her off, surveying her brown body, frowning at the white lines of the old scars on her back. "Each time something is held back, it builds part of a wall. Each little thing, no matter how small, builds on that wall. And then one day you will find you are on one side and I am on the other and it has become so high there is no climbing over. For a time we have each lived within ourselves, alone, and now we must start something new and share everything together. Everything. We must not grow alone in any way."

"*Ai*," she said, "like two wandering streams that come together. Can you feel the same happiness I do?"

"*Ai*, I can feel it. It is as though I have never felt happiness before. Let us not lose our good feelings. Each person thinks he or she alone has these feelings, as though the feeling were created each time. And each person is right. No one feels the same things. They go by the same names, but they are different, just as faces are different."

She squatted by the glowing fire pit and dipped a flat bean cake in the meat stew she'd started earlier. "I must be a good woman and feed you."

"I have forgotten about food."

"You must eat," she said seriously. "Many seasons ago my own mother used to say that a man judges his woman by the way she prepares his food. I do not want you to think I have no skill." She hastened to the inside of the tepee for a cooking basket. She quickly brushed a tear aside and desperately wished she did not feel so much like weeping at this very moment of joyousness. "Go for a swim in the creek."

"If you will come with me," he said shyly.

"No. If we went together, we would not come back for a long time."

"*Ai*, you little fox."

"The water is maybe too cold for you?" She lifted a

leather lid, reached in, and threw out a piece of brittle
bread at him. "That is the direction of the water," she
said, and pointed with another piece of bread.

He made a little joke. "Do not eat all the stew before
I return."

She arranged the bread with pieces of dried meat on
it. She combed out her soft warm hair and pinned it
behind her ears with a piñon stick for the sweet smell
it gave. She remembered the white tunic Hides Well
had left in the tepee. She felt more like a woman than
she had ever felt before.

The food was ready when he returned. He started to
eat. "Why do you not eat?" he asked.

She shook her head and bit her lip. "I somehow cannot."

"I cannot, either, then," he said.

"Oh, please, you must."

"Why do you cry, Little Fox?"

"Oh," she said, "I am not certain. Maybe because I
am so happy. It is the weeping of joy."

He moved toward her, seeing how beautiful she looked
in the white doeskin tunic, which was very plain, with
fringes at the bottom and the armholes. The neck had
a little blue quillwork, and a narrow, blue-dyed doeskin
belt encircled her waist.

"Do not come to me now," she said softly. "Let me
look at you."

He ate a few more bites, then put the bark plate
down and went to her.

"You should have finished your meal. But I am glad
you came over to me." She shivered against him and
buried her face in his neck. "I will try to outgrow this
quickly." Her voice quavered. "I know how a small baby
feels when it first begins to walk. I know how a rabbit
feels when it opens its small eyes for the first time. The
beginning is beautiful, but it is so new and so big a
feeling, it is frightening." She lay beside him on the
grass. "You will never grow tired of me?"

"Never. But will you grow tired of me and then go
back to that wandering in search of your grown son?"

"Never will I leave you, my beloved," she said, meaning every word. "There is nothing outside to which I
belong. Nothing anymore. I belong only to you."

"You will tell me that often," he whispered. "We must never forget that, no matter what happens."

He carried her up a little hill into an oak grove. He carried her as if she were no more than a sack of breath feathers. The hill sloped into a small gully, which was packed with years of fallen leaves. "This is a couch made for us," he said. "Remove the white tunic and sit in the sunlight. You are as beautiful as any young girl on her first day with a man."

She still felt shy with him. She obeyed and liked the feel of the sun on her back. She watched him take off his vest and leggings and sit beside her. He sat for some minutes, waiting for her shyness to recede, then he began to stroke her body with the tips of his fingers. She kissed him on the forehead, eyes, and mouth. He kissed back hungrily.

"You are like no man I have known."

"You do not like me?" he questioned gruffly, tugging at her short hair.

"I do like you! *Ai*, I love you. You give me a feeling I never knew anyone had."

He lay with his head on her outstretched arm. "I have a new joy and a wonder because of you. I wonder at the sights, sounds, and feelings because they appear larger and more clear than before. It is like seeing things through a flattened drop of clean water. Always stay close to me. I want to touch you."

He loved her and she felt an explosion in her belly. They clung to one another in ecstasy. The fierce, urgent emotion had been so great that it caused her to cry. The tears wet his shoulder and he stroked her forehead. They slept undisturbed.

The days passed one after another as beads strung one behind the other on a string. He swept out the tepee and arranged the cooking things. She folded sleeping robes and cleaned their clothing. He hung a buffalo paunch on four upright sticks and she filled it with water. Rocks were heated and forked sticks were used to place them in the water. He added strips of dried meat to that boiling water and she added wild carrots and onions dug from the edge of the creek. He showed her how to make a dressing from wild honey, buffalo tallow, and water to use over the cooked meat.

Jerk Meat practiced regularly with his bow and arrows and sometimes let her try. They ate and swam and walked through the trees. They lay in the sun and listened to the songs of the birds. At night they sat by their small fire and smelled the burning wood, and after the fire died they lay on their backs and looked at the sky and asked each other many questions.

She told him of her childhood and of her capture by the Minnetarees. She told him of the sea people who live in the Great Western Waters, the seals that bark and play so close to land that they amuse the people on the banks with their antics. She told him of the flood in the Rocky Mountains and how Chief Red Hair had saved her baby and herself and how Charbonneau had cried out like a pregnant squaw. She watched his eyes widen when she told him about the carcass of the huge whale on the sands of the Great Western Waters.

He told her of the time he was nearly captured by the Tonkas, the flesh-eating Comanches of the south. He had saved himself by quickly digging a hole in the sand and burying himself until the band had passed. He was alone that day seeking his medicine.

"Did you find your medicine? Did you dream a great dream?" she asked eagerly.

"I did not dream. The nights were not cold enough, and I did not starve long enough. But I found my medicine in the skull of the buffalo. I was trapped two nights in a place where many buffalo had died. The timber wolves were all around hunting for small animals. They would have had me, but I stayed in the middle of that dying ground with the skulls all about and the wolves did not come near. From that time on, the buffalo skull has been my special protector."

"And when did you take a woman?" she asked.

"After I joined the young men's Foolish Society. The Foolish Society is open to those who feel bold enough to disregard caution and ride up to an enemy and strike him using as his only weapons a quirt and a buffalo scrotum rattle. If he manages to escape death, he is then acclaimed a warrior for his valor. In spite of many casualties, there are always those who are reckless enough to take this chance.[1]

"My first woman thought I was brave and daring

because I hit a Ute during a big horse raid. She was the foolish one, because truthfully I was frightened to death. She was the daughter of a Kiowa subchief, and a quiet, well-behaved woman. She caused me no sadness until she was crushed by her horse and our girl-child was born with no breath. She was called *Tu-Pombi*, Black Hair. I missed her."

Sacajawea undid his braids and combed his hair gently. "You speak of your woman who has gone away and say her name. This is against our beliefs."

"We already have done things not done by Comanches, but I do not regret them. They are good between us. Perhaps some of the white men you have named and spoken of are not living. You do not know. Perhaps the big black man we have laughed about is not living. Oh, I wish I had seen him just once. A man like that— black all over—*oooay*. Unbelievable!"

She braided his hair and tied the ends with thin leather strips and put the small piece of buffalo jawbone, worn shiny, back into the left braid just behind his ear. "You are handsome, my man."

"You talk with sand in your mouth, my woman," he said pleased, grabbing her by her short hair. "Come, we will swim together."

Later she would remember how she stood in the deep part of the creek, the cold water reaching her waist. "I had one child—but maybe I cannot give you children." The thought was new to her. She had not wanted another child with her white man.

"Then you will be my woman and my girl-child also," was his answer.

She put her arms around him from behind and held him as though she would never let go.

"I will wash your back," he said, and more softly, "you tell how the scars were put on you." He worked the loam from the creek's bank around her body as she told of her past. Next she scrubbed him, working the sandy soil into his hair, under his arms and across his chest and back. They rinsed clean by swimming into the deep hole under the overhang of willows. Then they lay on the sunny bank to dry. She noticed that the cottonwood leaves were beginning to turn yellow and there was the slightest chill to the evening air.

Jerk Meat boiled the water for the dried meat while Sacajawea found cress at the edge of the creek for salad. As he ate, Jerk Meat held his left jaw.

"Do you have a toothache?" she asked.

"It is not bad," he said. "We will look for the mushroom to kill the pain when you finish."

They walked along a game trail. Sacajawea found a tree fungus that she knew would ease pain when heated and held on the wound, but Jerk Meat was looking for a little brown mushroom that grew close to the ground near rotting wood. It was nearly dark when he found it. He dried it on a rock near the fire and stuffed it in the molar's cavity. Sacajawea held the warm tree fungus on his jaw, then when she thought he ought to be feeling better she kissed him on the mouth.

"Woman," he said, "a man can do nothing with you around. I believe the wise man who said that a man who has been with a woman lately is prone to wounds because arrows and bullets are drawn toward such a man. He must have known a woman like you."

"Phfft," she said, "there is no enemy band near here. See how quiet the village is."

"There are always enemies in the land," he said positively.

"You have strong medicine, and nothing will harm you. It won't, will it?" she asked.

"No, but we must always be ready." He took out his knife and cut down a slender branch of ash. He came back beside her and sat on a flat stone. He began to adze the branch down. "Here, you try some." He handed her the branch and pointed to her knife at her waist.

"For a bow?" she asked, holding the clean white wood, and he nodded *ai*. He moved away and indicated that he was going to look for a buck deer they'd seen at the water hole early that morning. They needed the fresh meat. She watched until she could not see him, then cut the wood a certain length, measuring from her right hip across to her extended left fingertips, the way Big Badger had done. With the knife she beveled the bow with grooves cut down the back.

Over the evening fire Jerk Meat boiled the deer hooves and tendons until they were a sticky glue. He spread the glue over the back of the bow in several thin

layers and pasted on two sinews with the wide ends
together in the middle. "Watch and do not forget," he
ordered. He spread on more glue and powdered it with
white clay. He told her to repeat that treatment several
times. Then she wrapped a piece of buckskin the width
of a hand around the middle of the bow. Several days
later she made the bowstring from the deer's rear-leg
tendon. Done, she set the bow aside to dry well.

He searched the bottom of the creek bed until he
found a black stone that satisfied him. He gave it to
Sacajawea to hold while he made a flintmaker, a tool
with a long wooden handle tipped with a piece of deer
antler. A burr oak handle fitted exactly under his right
arm, from the tip of his middle finger to the point of
his elbow. He set the butt of the handle against his
chest to form a steady fulcrum, then, setting the antler
point against the edge of the black stone held in his
left hand, pressed firmly. Presently the stone fractured
and a small flake flew to the ground. Flake after flake
jumped off around the entire rim of the stone. He worked
both sides.

While he was busy, Sacajawea chose a half-dozen
chokecherry shoots, second growth, and cut them to her
liking.

It became dark; they moved closer to the fire. Jerk
Meat worked until he had six gleaming arrow points,
perfectly tipped. Sacajawea had found feathers of the
wild turkey and placed them tightly in the butt end of
the chokecherry shoots. Seeing that the arrow points
were properly grooved so that blood could flow from the
wound they would make, Jerk Meat fastened them with
glue and thin strings of buckskin onto the chokecherry
shoots. He set the arrows several feet from the fire so
they would dry gradually. To Sacajawea there was a
magical sense of rightness in all they did together.

He murmured his satisaction and moved to his sleeping robe and closed his eyes and folded his hands over
his lean belly, composing himself for sleep. Sacajawea
lay quietly beside him. She liked this calmness by the
outside fire, and she felt humbled in his presence. He
was a man of discipline, yet one of gentle humor and
logical good sense. Her love for him was deep.

One night, late-fall heat lightning flashed across the

sky. The wind rose and caused acorns to pepper down
like hailstones. Jerk Meat turned and placed his hand
across Sacajawea's shoulders. "Are you awake, my
woman?"

"*Ai.*"

"We must go back to the village in the morning. We
have stayed long. Maybe too long."

She questioned him.

The thunder rumbled far away.

"See, the thunder tells us it is time to go back to the
village and live with the Quohadas. We must begin to
store up our own food for the winter."

"I like being lazy with you," she said like a petulant
child.

"You must fold the tepee skins, woman, and pack
the cooking things. We belong now in the village."

In the morning she obeyed, knowing there would be
other good things, but it would never be quite the same
again, anywhere.

Most of Sacajawea's time now was spent keeping her
tepee neat, making clothing, talking with other women,
and preparing the foods her man liked best. When he
brought home a deer she learned how to mix the raw
brains and leg marrow in a way he liked. The curdled
milk from the stomach of a fawn, still young enough to
be nursing, he considered a delicacy. Liver cooked with
marrow and the raw tallow from around the kidneys
she fixed especially for him. She smashed persimmons
to a pulp after removing the seeds and dried this paste
by spreading it on rocks in the sun. It was stored in
large rolls. Hackberries were pulped in the same way,
then mixed with bear's fat and made into balls to be
roasted on a stick over a fire. If she worked alone, invariably the thought of Jean Baptiste came to her mind.
She wondered what he was doing, if she would see him
again, and if he thought of her. She did not tell these
thoughts to Jerk Meat.

Once Jerk Meat and some of the braves—on a spring
trip to trade robes to Mexicans for shawls and silver
and a rusty harmonica—witnessed the strange procession of white men stripped to their waist marching
through the street of the small village called Santa Cruz

de la Cañada. Jerk Meat gave the harmonica to Sacajawea and asked her to play for him. When she finished,
they discussed the strange parade far into the night.
He'd seen men pulling large *carretas* with immovable
wheels, the harnesses, made of horsehair, galling and
painful. The men all wore caps and black masks and
whipped themselves until the blood ran down their backs
and covered the yucca-fiber whips. One man walked
alongside the whippers playing a *pito*, a homemade flute,
and close by him another twirled a *matraca*, or noise-
maker. They sang short songs continuously. He told
her of the strange, cruel thing done to one of the white
men who was pinned to two crossed poles and carried
up a small hill. The man's hands and shoulders were
bleeding, and a headband made from the thornbush was
pushed low on his forehead. The man was slapped and
spat upon, until finally his head sagged on his shoulders
and the life passed from him. Then there was a great
moaning and wailing as the *matraca* made thunderous
noises.

"Why?" he asked, puzzled.

"It is hard to say why men are cruel to one another,"
she answered, and thought of the Mandan Okeepa, the
Torture Dance. Some men lived and some died during
that ceremony. "The Mandans were as cruel when
leather thongs were threaded into the muscle sinew of
a man's chest and back. The man was made to walk
around crossed poles in the center of the Medicine
Lodge." She told Jerk Meat how Fast Arrow was chosen
by Four Bears to take part in the Okeepa Ceremony.
"It was a long time before he recovered from that ordeal.
It is strange that both the white men and the Mandans
used the headband of thorns and the crossed poles."

"Huh," sighed Jerk Meat, "that is the strange thing.
In many ways men are similar, no matter where they
live or what tribe they belong to."

"I believe, now, that it is far better to be gentle with
each other," said Sacajawea. "I am certain the Great
Spirit does not wish us to harm ourselves for foolish
reasons. It is like killing more antelope than we can
eat and then throwing away what spoils."

"You talk like a squaw," chided Jerk Meat. "I think
it is not good to have an able-bodied man laid low be-

cause of self-inflicted wounds. What if the enemy chose that time to make a big raid on his horses? That man is not good to anyone. What if this torture ceremony left him crippled, without the use of an arm or leg?"

"The Mandans believe it is the way to show bravery. I have often wondered why other nations did not use such ceremonies."

"Woman, they do other things. If they had thought of this torture ceremony, they would try it. Men are that way."

By spring, Sacajawea knew she was pregnant. The thoughts that had disturbed her through the winter did not rise to the surface for a long time. A child to raise, to hold close to her breast, to sing for, to teach, enjoy, laugh with, and watch grow—this engulfed all her thoughts—and in good conscience she put off thoughts of her hunt for her grown son.

One morning when Jerk Meat was out hunting, she walked toward the river with a digging stick and her grass basket. She looked for wild roots. She stopped suddenly and bent down. She had found a cache, empty now, but exactly like the ones made years ago by the white soldiers under the direction of Chief Red Hair. She looked more carefully, her thoughts carrying her back to the time she had carried Pomp on her back. She easily lowered herself inside. At the cool bottom she scraped the soft dirt floor and found a metal awl, rusty but usable. She scraped again and found another. The thoughts and memories of her firstborn engulfed her. She found small seashells and blue and red beads and silver ear plugs. Climbing out with no difficulty, because of moss growing along the sides which made the footing easy, she put her find in her upturned skirt. She carried her treasures secretly back to the camp.

The next morning, she said to Spring, "Come with your digging stick and basket. I will show you something new." Spring took Wild Plum to Big Badger, who was teaching him to spin wooden tops.

The women found two more caches and scratched in them for half the afternoon. At times Sacajawea hardly listened to Spring, but lived in the past. "I wanted to come back alone," admitted Sacajawea.

"Oh, you must not be out alone now," said Spring. "Your time is near. Someone should be with you." She bent for red beads and found a granite drinking cup. They left the pits and dug roots. All at once, Spring called, "Look, there is snow!"

"Foolish one, this is summer," laughed Sacajawea.

"Lost Woman, I swear it," said Spring, "come with me and see." She ran through the buffalo grass pointing all the while to the field of brilliant, sparkling white. Sacajawea sucked in her breath and wiped the sweat from her forehead. "How can this be?"

They knelt on the light crust, and it cracked through. It was not cold, but hot as the sun beat upon it. Sacajawea said, "My sister, this is salt. Salt of the highest quality, not brown like the blown salt we have dug from sand. Beautiful, beautiful salt."

The women filled their baskets with the clean salt. Their meat would taste good this winter. Other women were sent to gather salt. This find of a prized preservative was one more reason for the Quohadas to look upon Sacajawea as something uncommon, different. When the hunters brought in buffalo, she showed a few women how to salt-cure meat, using the same method the soldiers had used at Fort Clatsop. The anticipation of the salty, smoke-cured meat made her mouth water and occupied her thoughts so thoroughly that she scarcely felt the first twinges of her labor pains.

She did not have a difficult time delivering her son. Hides Well and several others who were proficient in midwifery came to assist. She clung to the birth posts as they bathed her loins with water containing herbs. They were about to give her yucca leaves mashed with salt to help the birth, but she pushed down deep within herself and gave a guttural moan as the child was delivered. Her face was glassy and wet, but she had not cried in pain. She lay down exhausted and fell into a soothing sleep, not knowing if the child were boy or girl, knowing only that Hides Well would take care of her small one. Later she became aware that someone was near. "Can I tell Jerk Meat he has a son?" It was Spring kneeling beside her, holding the healthy baby. Pronghorn had taken Jerk Meat for a long walk into the sandstone bluffs, since fathers never stayed around while their women were giving birth.

"Quick, send Big Badger to tell Jerk Meat the papoose is here," said Sacajawea. "*Ai*, tell Big Badger just to say, 'The papoose is healthy and cries as loud as a cougar. The mother is well.' Jerk Meat will guess whether it is a boy or girl all the way back."

The monotonous songs of the women immediately changed to rejoicing and some exuberant laughs. Not to tell the new father the sex of the papoose was the sort of joke that the women thoroughly enjoyed.

The umbilical cord was cut and Hides Well wrapped it in a square of soft doe's skin and then hung it in the elderberry bush behind the lying-in lodge.[2]

The papoose was bathed and oiled and wrapped in soft skins. Sacajawea was fed thin broth; she was not allowed to eat meat because it made blood and could cause a hemorrhage.

Jerk Meat was at the birth shelter in minutes. It was as if he had put scrapings from deer hooves on his moccasins to give him swiftness.

Sacajawea opened her eyes as she heard someone saying loudly, "Today we have a new Quohada."

She saw a glimpse of Jerk Meat and was sure that he jumped into the air so far the weasel tails dragging at the back of his moccasins just barely touched the ground. A woman brought the small bundle in soft doeskin quickly past him, then placed it across Sacajawea's breast. "Old Grandmother, is he a boy or girl?" stammered Jerk Meat.

"This is a healthy child," answered the woman with eyes twinkling. "See the good color, like a sun-dried strawberry."

Propriety forced Jerk Meat to leave the birth shelter until his woman could come home under her own power. Still he did not know his child was the son he had dreamed about.

The Medicine Man, Kicking Horse, came to make certain the papoose was not deformed or diseased in any way that he could tell. If he found that the papoose was unfit, he would leave it out on the plains to die.[3] He nodded when he found that Sacajawea's papoose was well and healthy. He kept his eyes averted from Sacajawea. Before he left he painted a large black spot with charcoal on the outside of the lying-in tepee door to show that the new Quohada was a future warrior and his presence would strengthen the band.

For the first few days the papoose lay in soft hides and a rabbit-fur robe beside Sacajawea, where Hides Well could give him constant attention. When Sacajawea could get up, she bathed herself in the fast water of the creek. She felt weak, but noticed her belly was folded up, becoming flat again, and happiness filled her mind. The next day she took her time cleaning the papoose, greasing and powdering him with dry-rot dust from a cottonwood tree, packing him with soft, dry moss, wrapping him in one of the thin hides and placing him in the basket she had made of rawhide stitched to a flat, angular board.[4] She was ready to go to her own tepee.

The wife of Twisted Horn was first to come to see the new papoose. She brought a gift of black crow feathers to tie on the basket to keep away evil spirits. It was customary for the new papoose's father to give the first visitor a gift of some value in return. Jerk Meat gave the Twisted Horn family a black-and-white Mexican blanket. A week later Sacajawea was ready to go on an antelope hunt with Jerk Meat and help him butcher his kill and pack it on the extra horse. Before they left, Big Badger tied a stuffed bat to a corner of the basket so that the papoose would have even more protection from any unseen evil forces.

There was no set time for giving a papoose a formal name. Generally a person of distinction was invited to name the papoose.

"You will not ask Kicking Horse to name our papoose. I do not believe anything he would come up with can give him a longer or more useful life," said Sacajawea as they rode along.

"*Ai*, he could give him a name that would cause some injury or sickness. So, then, wait until we think of something special."

"I'll call him Summer Snow. He almost came to us at the salt find. I think the salt drew him out."

"*Ai*." He grinned broadly. "You call him that for now. I'll name him later. Listen to Big Badger."

"He has never been on a hunt since I've been with the Quohadas."

"That is true. Listen."

Big Badger's deep voice seemed to come from the bottom of his moccasins, pulsing strongly on the long-held notes, then trailing to the ground at the end.

Sacajawea rode up to him.

"What are you singing, Big Badger?"

"There are no words to this song. It is singing for my happiness and your happiness. The song belonged to my uncle. I paid him three pack dogs for it. That was before we had many horses." He sang more, then said, "This is the first time in many summers I've felt like singing. I dreamed last night of my youth and of how it felt to do those high-spirited things. Then I saw Wild Plum and Summer Snow and I knew I would teach them to be men with high spirits and always be laughing with happy hearts."

They set up the temporary camp late in the afternoon below some wild currants and pecan trees near a spring. The women went to find the trees to cut and trim into lodgepoles.

In the morning, the men ate early and set out looking for the herd of antelope the scouts found. The women put water on the new-cut poles and turned them in the sunshine so they would become seasoned without splitting.

Gray Bone walked past. Her hair was shaggy, and her stare arrogant. She patted Sacajawea's baby on his cheek. Sacajawea felt her spine tingle as she readjusted the cradleboard on her back.

"He seems small and puny to me," Gray Bone said. "Maybe his mother has thin milk." She pointed a finger at Sacajawea. "Look at your insignificant breasts. You are hardly a squaw."

At that moment the sound of the wing-bone whistle was heard, and the women in camp knew the men had found the herd. The taunting stopped and Gray Bone moved on.

"Think nothing of what she said," advised a young woman. "That old Gray Bone is jealous of anyone who is more intelligent and more beautiful than she. Which is almost everyone in the band. She is the most quarrelsome squaw in the camp. Not many follow her. Most pay her no attention."

Big Badger held Wild Plum as he climbed to the top of a small bluff where they watched the hunters. A scout dressed as an antelope crawled out of the brush on all fours.

Care was taken to come in toward the wind. The hunters moved slowly into position to kill as many antelope as possible before the rest of the herd realized that they were in danger. A curious old buck moved toward the scout, several younger animals followed. Suddenly they all stopped to stare and sniff. The scout pretended to chew grass. He knew curiosity was a strong trait in antelope.

The old buck moved and the younger ones followed still closer to the disguised scout who moved into tall grass near a slough. The scout pretended to drink. The old buck moved up and drank. Soon the other antelope had crowded in, their hooves making a sucking in the mud.

Wild Plum nudged Jerk Meat and each nocked an arrow and drew his bowstring taut. The other hunters also chose targets as the herd moved unsuspectingly into the waiting semicircle of motionless men on horseback hidden in the high marsh grass.

The scout, on hands and knees, moved away from the gathering herd, through the muck and grass, to the opposite side of the slough. The hunters let their arrows fly. The old buck sprang up and raced back across the meadow. The rest of the herd followed, moving into the hunters' flying arrows.

Wild Plum *kiyi*-ed with glee when he saw Jerk Meat's arrow plow into a young buck's lungs. Big Badger smiled with anticipation of the taste of a roasted antelope ham.

The Comanche hunters were well spread out with their kill. Each man butchered swiftly, often glancing at his horse's ears to see if they waved alternately. If so, it was a sign that coyotes or wolves were near. The men brought the meat into the temporary camp, and it was time for the women to work, slicing the meat into thin strips to hang on racks for sun-drying. The hides were laid out on the ground and fastened down, flesh side up, to be scraped for tanning later.

When her work was done, Sacajawea walked to a cluster of pecan trees and pulled her baby from her back. She undid his bindings, cuddling him and talking to him. "You will be a successful hunter, like your father," she said to him. Summer Snow woke and felt hunger pangs. With his open mouth, he nudged around for food. Sacajawea sat with her back against a small pecan tree, closed her eyes as she nursed her baby. This is my happiness, she thought.

Back in the village there was an Antelope Dance with the smell of the juicy meat roasting above several small fires. The dance broke up in midafternoon, and Sacajawea took Jerk Meat's packhorses to the grassy pasture and freed them. She walked back along the stream, then saw women ahead, waiting for her. There were three of them. Gray Bone was in the lead.

Sacajawea felt her hands shaking and her insides knotting. She knew their motive. They would try to taunt her into an impulsive act so that they could beat her. She looked about for the sight of a friend. They had chosen the time well; there was no one about, except some children playing in the sand by the stream. She was instantly thankful her baby was inside the tepee. She feared what lay ahead.

Then she remembered some advice Big Badger had once given her! "Do not turn around from trouble." She walked boldly down the path toward them. When she tried to pass, Gray Bone stepped in front.

"You are not Comanche," Gray Bone said. "You are a stranger who has come among us to live in a land that is not yours. You have visited our hunting ground and were lucky. That old blind antelope must have run into your man's arrow. The Great Spirit intended for the Comanches to eat these antelope, not intruders. Leave the Quohadas at once and take your louse-infested son. Leave our village or I will take your life."

She Cat stepped forward, her face hard. "You think because a Comanche family adopts you and then lets you marry their son you have the right to look and act like a Comanche?"

Weasel Woman pointed derisively at Sacajawea's simple tunic and at the single flower design in the yoke. "You do not wear the dress or embroidery of a Comanche. You are a foreigner. What's the matter? Aren't our sewing customs good enough for you?"

Gray Bone's suspicious eyes squinted, and her fingers curled into tight balls. "You are not like us in other ways. We do not like those who are different."

Sacajawea thought. She needed some time to plan a way to leave these women. She needed time to think over a plan as a thing experienced. She moved backward, wanting to gain a moment or two. She knew a plan made and visualized was reality, not to be destroyed, but easily put into action. She looked about to measure distances quickly.

Gray Bone whipped out a butcher knife. "I see your ears are whole, yet you are living in evil with a brother. Now, leave this land forever as furtively as you came in. And so—before you go, I am notching your ears so that the next time we meet I will know who you are."

Sacajawea stood very still, focusing her wits. Gray Bone's knife did not frighten her. She knew a couple of ways to take it from her. It was best to let this wicked, mean woman talk. When she had talked out most of her hate, perhaps she would cool off.

"Look how straight and proud she stands," Gray Bone sneered. "What has she to be proud of? She is married to her own kin, yet she does not have a drop of Comanche blood in her."

Sacajawea could feel her face flush. Why was this woman continually taunting her? Why was she considered an outsider? Wasn't she a Shoshoni, cousin to the Comanche? Hadn't she kept Wolf's wrist from healing in a deformed manner? Wasn't Wolf Gray Bone's son? Was it that she yet wanted Jerk Meat for her marriageable daughter? Or was it that things strange and unknown were always hated with a malice that melted toward fear?

Triumph gleamed in Gray Bone's watery eyes. She thought she had found the way to goad this one called Lost Woman.

"Listen, Woman Who Sleeps with Her Brother, I forbid you to consider yourself married, or to live with this band, or raise your child as a Comanche. If you do any of these things, I will spill out all your black blood and let it drain on the ground."

Sacajawea's pulse began to race. A loud kind of music began to pound in her head, and her heart beat out a heavy rhythm. She crouched down. This dirty old woman deserves more than just being deprived of her butcher knife, she thought. She deserves to have her heart cut out. A song throbbed in her head—if she had been able to speak of it, she would have called it the Song of Action. Her teeth bared, and fury flared in her eyes. Sacajawea moved fast as lightning.

Whap!

Gray Bone reeled from the stinging slap. Recoiling, she charged and struck out at Sacajawea with her butcher knife. With swiftness, Sacajawea withdrew her body, turning it to the left as the knife went past her breasts. She caught Gray Bone's wrist with both hands, pulled her in the direction she was going, unbalanced her, and in a flash twisted the butcher knife out of her hand. It fell, and was kicked aside as the women dodged one another.

Gray Bone's eyes were entranced, and she felt the wary, the unknown waiting for her. It was shadowy and dreadful; it threatened her and challenged her. Her eyes were wide; she charged, then struck out at Sacajawea, who raised her hand to stop her. Then, instinctively, Sacajawea's right hand went for her own bone knife, polished thin on one side, held by her waistband. Gray Bone's mouth opened in terror. Sacajawea thrust the thin-honed blade of bone upward. She could feel the knife bite in, feel the weight upon it. Gray Bone crumpled, struggled to rise, her face distorted in stunned disbelief, her hands wrapped about the deep gash in her neck. She felt the unknown all about, hidden in the wash of the stream, in the willows, and behind the boulders, hovering in the air.

Sacajawea bent to pick up Gray Bone's butcher knife, and her eyes flicked to a rustle beside her. It was the other two, moving forward almost soundlessly. She froze a moment, and then her lips drew back from her teeth like cat's lips. She whirled on the two women, a knife in each hand. Motionless, they stared for a terrified moment at Gray Bone's butcher knife, then at Sacajawea's tipped bone knife, then last at Gray Bone kneeling in the buffalo grass. Surprise spread over their faces. Turning, they ran into the brush.

Sacajawea was surprised at how easy it had been. Big Badger's advice had been sound. Sacajawea's timidity had probably saved Gray Bone's life. In her rage she had missed the artery, inflicting only a cut through the skin layers. The blood came through the cut bright red on Gray Bone's fingers and formed tiny scarlet puddles in the dirt at her feet.

Sacajawea was relieved and then exhilarated, as if a very sore boil had been opened and the poison drained out.

Then a feeling of guilt came over her. Gray Bone had received what she deserved. Still, a small voice deep inside Sacajawea kept saying, "It is wrong to kill another human." She had tried to kill a human being, failing only because she had not the boldness to push harder on her bone knife. She did not ever want to be cruel or violent as she knew that some were—Comanches, Shoshonis, and whites. Every step of the way back to her tepee she thought about what she had become in such a short time.

Outside the tepee she stopped and looked down at her hands. The rage had left her, and a sick disgust took its place. She leaned over and vomited. She went inside, buried her head in her hands, and cried with great, heaving sobs. Only the crying of her small son could rouse her from the feeling of depression and guilt. She freshened him with clean cattail down, then held him close and nursed him. What was this thing that had made her half-insane? she thought. In her woman's soul she knew that there was a savage in everyone. And yet it was the control of this savage that made the difference between humans and beasts. Reason, good sense, love—these made humans.

The tepee flap lifted. Jerk Meat, ducking because of his height, rushed inside. His dark face was stamped with concern. An angry hum of voices came from outside.

"Gray Bone's relatives and friends have come for you," he said. "They are angry because they say you cut her up and left her alone to die. It is a bad thing when members of one band fight. There is always trouble over it." He was daubing on his black war paint. The noise outside grew louder, and dogs began to bark.

"So—she cut my nose once!" Sacajawea yelled to her man. "It must be a bad thing when a Comanche woman cuts another without good reason."

"*Ai,*" he said quietly, "I saw you with a dangling red nose. Quite a sight. But it healed with hardly a show of a healing line. Good medicine runs in our lodge."

Sacajawea heard voices very near. Someone said, "Let's go inside and bring her out."

Jerk Meat picked up his long lance. Facing the door, he began singing his war song.

Shaken, Sacajawea stood by him, bow and arrows ready. She steadied herself. Sacajawea loved this man. She could not now imagine life without him. There was no question; she would follow him. She wished with all her heart that this were not happening. It seemed so senseless to die for knifing a witch like Gray Bone.

Then another voice was heard outside the tepee flap. A deep, strong voice. It was the voice of Kicking Horse. "I have stanched the flow of blood from my old woman's neck. The wound is not deep. It will heal. Now, whoever fights will have to fight me also."

There is nothing to do but to save ourselves, thought Sacajawea, throwing away the past.

Everything became quiet. Kicking Horse, standing stiffly outside Jerk Meat's lodge, knew the capabilities of his woman and what her insane jealousy could do. He called her cohorts and said gruffly that any more ambushing would have to be punished, even if it meant his own woman being thrown out of her tepee.

"It was my woman who started this trouble." As he spoke, She Cat nodded her head up and down. "Gray Bone was first to draw her butcher knife. Children playing nearby came to tell me. Members of the Quohadas band, what is a woman to do—a woman alone—when three large bodies cut her off from the path and threaten her? What is she to do when one draws her butcher knife and tells her she is going to notch her ears? Should she run? Should she climb a tree and hide?

"Our women are taught from the time they are small to use their butcher knife in case of any danger." Kicking Horse kept on talking, slowly, calmly, and clearly,

and so great a talker and Shaman was he that Gray
Bone's friends, She Cat and Weasel Woman, gradually
forgot their quarrel and went home. The other people
slowly tired of his haranguing and went back to their
tepees. The excitement of a real fight was talked out.

Kicking Horse scratched at the tepee flap. Jerk Meat
quickly admitted him. His black eyes were somber. On
his back were arrows in a leather quiver, and he carried
his bow.

"Our friend—" began Jerk Meat.

"Hush," said Kicking Horse. "It may not be good to
call me that. I wish to say that this is what makes a
man—or woman. To be able to fight and not to be afraid."
He came to Sacajawea, put his hands on her trembling
shoulders, and patted her affectionately. His face seemed
wet with tears. "I envy your man. I will be his friend
forever." He bent beside her sleeping couch and picked
up his woman's butcher knife, but first he eyed the bone
knife lying beside it. Then, as suddenly as he had entered, he left.

"Now you will tell me what happened out there today
to make them so angry," growled Jerk Meat, leaning
his lance against a tepee pole and indicating that Sacajawea should wash off his paint. "The last time I saw
you, you were full of roasted antelope and had started
to take the horses to feed."

She told him.

Jerk Meat sat on the dirt floor with a grunt. "Little
Fox, you've done all right. You have fought twice with
Gray Bone, and won once. Who can tell, perhaps at the
next feast I'll have you relate stories of your bravery."
A smile turned his mouth up. He moved so he could
put his arms around his woman. Something swelled in
her breast, something proud and grateful and heart-
warming. A great humility swept over her, and an overpowering weariness.

Before summer was over the women cut thick buffalo
hides into squares that the men could use to protect
their heads and backs from the relentless sun that beat
down on the hot, treeless plains as they hunted. For
the first time in their lives the men complained that
the buffalo herds seemed scarce and thin.

Sacajawea made a new shield for Jerk Meat during
the summer with the shoulder hide of a tough old buffalo bull. The hide was heated over steaming hot water,
rubbed on a large, rough rock to get most of the flesh
off, then scraped to finish the fleshing. Her heating and
steaming thickened the hide by contraction. Then she
used a smooth stone to pound and rub the hide to take
out all wrinkles and make it pliable. A circular piece
was cut and stretched flesh side out over a circular
wooden hoop two feet in diameter. Another piece was
cut and stretched on the opposite side. These were sewed
together by pulling rawhide string through holes
punched around the edges of the hide. The space between the layers was about an inch thick and she packed
it tight with goose feathers.[5]

The surface of the shield was stretched into a saucer
shape that would readily deflect an arrow and in most
cases deflect a rifle bullet unless it struck straight-on.

At the end of summer the band was ready to move
northwest even though they had not had a good buffalo
hunt. They were moving across the tableland called the
Staked Plains. The rivers, lying far apart and cutting
across the Staked Plains southeastward, were serpentine, low banked, silty, and bitter tasting—not fit for
drinking.

To Sacajawea it seemed as though they were on the
roof of the world. It was a strange, wild, hard land that
rolled on forever beneath an endless sky. When the
rains came, water would rush out the sides of a draw
and Mother Earth would drink it dry, and sometimes
lakes would be made in shallow basins, then birds would
fill the sky and frogs would croak in the mud. Jerk
Meat told about the land in early spring when it rippled
with the delicate wild flowers in waves of gold. In summer it was scorched and blasted by sun, and the mesquite and scrub oaks were little more than bushes. The
grass became brown, brittle, and sparse. The blue
northers howled through the gray winter days.

The Quohadas were secure in this land where the
Mexicans never came. They made winter camp by a
cold little pond. Pronghorn had chosen this place well.
The water had gathered in a small depression that was
lower than the level of the surrounding plains. The

camp was in a kind of bowl. They could not be seen unless a man rode up to the very rim of the bowl and looked down. The camp was safe.

Above the camp were colored logs of petrified wood, and not far away were giant bones from great lizards that once had lived on the plains. These caused Sacajawea to recall the great whale skeleton she had seen on the western coast. And she thought about her first-born son. And again the longing for him rose to the surface.

Along a meandering creek valley they found canyons for protection, grass for their horses, but no expected buffalo and antelope for winter meat. Hungry Kiowas came to visit and share their meager food supply. The Kiowas brought a little parched corn that they traded for some horses with Mexican *comancheros*. In this depression they were protected from the full force of the wintry blasts from the north. The hungry friends visited several days until both corn and meat were all gone.

The women burned off the sharp spines from leaves of the prickly pear cactus and fed them to the horses, keeping the sweet-tasting fruit for their family. The ice over the pond was broken and melted in tightly woven grass baskets. The women put mesquite brush tight against the sides of their tepees to keep out the cold wind that whistled across the plains.

The men killed several older horses for food. Jerk Meat and several others went out after small game. They found none and came in before nightfall with eyes swollen almost shut, bloodshot, burning, and smarting, tired and stiff with the cold.

That winter seemed to be a procession of trials— days with bitter winds that lashed and stung the face with dry sand snow, icy nights, white freezing fog in the mornings, so that the horses had to be held together in the spooky white by ear, afternoons when white-coated Mother Earth flashed up such a glare that a horse rider closed his eyes to slits, or went nearly blind, in spite of painting his cheekbones with charcoal. Skin and lips cracked as crisp as the skin of fried fish, and grew black with sun. Eyes smarted as tears seeped through swollen lids. Babies cried because of hunger pains. Sacajawea became thin, but she continued to drink plenty of snow water and nurse her child. The boy was not content with watered-down milk, and he cried out in the night. During these times Sacajawea played softly on the rusty harmonica Jerk Meat had given her and she sang:

> "Rouli roulant, ma boule roulant,
> Rouli roulant ma boule."

For a while they would forget their hunger and the cold, frozen bed robes.

They heard the wolves' hunting noises far off, back up the plain on some creek bottom. They seemed to cry from great distances as life immune to cold and hunger and pain, hunting only for the wolfish joy of running.

Jerk Meat told Sacajawea the weather could not last, as they began to feel there was nothing between them and the north wind and the wolves but the skin tepee, so thin that every wind moved it, its sides so peppered with spark holes that lying on their robes at night they caught squinting glimpses of the stars.

The weather warmed early, and the summer was hot and dry. The Quohada band did not move from the little basin, but stayed near the fresh water of the pond and the shade of the few cottonwoods and willows. Once or twice they made temporary hunting camps as they went out to find the great herds of buffalo. The herds were small that year, and often the hunters came back with reports of white men making great killings and leaving most of the meat for the buzzards and wolves, taking only the hides.

Sacajawea gave birth to a second child late in the summer, another boy. Jerk Meat renamed Summer Snow, Ticannaf, because of the happiness he brought to their tepee. The baby was called No Name until the time when an appropriate name could be found.

That winter, the horses that lay down in the ice and froze to death were thawed and eaten.

A blue norther came and leaned its wind on the tepees in strange erratic patches, as if animals were jumping on the skins. The Quohadas went outside to try to keep their tepees from blowing away. The men hauled large boulders to anchor the tepees, and the women tied long, stout leather ropes to the lodgepoles and hooked them to the wooden pegs nearly buried in the frozen ground. The old men pointed to the sundogs and said they meant something. The early winter weather could not last, but they feared what might replace it.

One night the darkness was full of snow pebbles, hard and stinging, that beat their faces, shutting their eyes and melting in their hair, but freezing again. The camp slept most of that time, two or three days. Then, when the wind eased, they dug their way out, and the tepees were surrounded by dunes of snow. There was no sign of the horses.

Buffalo Bones, Coming Home, and Jerk Meat hunted until they found the horses downwind. They came back before dark and reported dead coyotes that the wolves had left when the storm drifted in. The next day, they brought in half a dozen half-eaten coyotes frozen stiff on the backs of the lost horses.

That evening around the cooking kettle, Jerk Meat spoke of rich pemmican with dried fruit and nuts mixed in as he sucked on a coyote bone with little meat on it. Sacajawea spoke of roast duck and boiled pumpkin. Before dawn, that night, the wind reached down out of the north and rushed in a new blizzard. They fought and groped through the wind and snow to fasten down their tepees even tighter with more boulders and rawhide ropes. They heard the beating of hooves as antelope came down to their depression for shelter. The Quohadas cursed them as they stumbled over guy ropes and tore one of the tepees down, snorting and bolting into one another. The men tried to take a few for food, but found their hands so stiff with cold they could not hold their bows straight and taut.

In the morning, the sky remained gray. Whenever anyone had to go outside he looked at the horses, which were picketed so they could move around or bunch up to keep warm. The women went out and fed them fleshy, pulpy cactus leaves or cottonwood sticks.

Fuel ran low, and they could find none in the snow, so after meals they let the fires die and crawled under their robes to sleep or tell stories. Talk flared up and went out again. Once or twice Sacajawea went out and carefully scraped the worst of the snow off the top of their tepee while Jerk Meat watched inside with concern because a careless poke of the stick would easily cut through the skintight hide, leaving them exposed to the storm.

Jerk Meat talked with Ticannaf in the cold afternoons. "I played *nanipka* when I was your size. I went over a hill and waited until the other boys hid themselves under buffalo robes; then I came back and tried to guess who was hidden under each robe." He told of his first antelope surround and the coyote stories he'd heard himself as a boy from Big Badger. Sacajawea kept the baby, No Name, under the robes with her and put Ticannaf under the robes with Jerk Meat. The wind slammed against the skin tepee in furious gusts.

Sometime before one gray afternoon howled itself out, Sacajawea bundled her baby and went outside. The rest of the camp lay in their robes. She went to the lodge of Pronghorn and Hides Well. A jet of white breath followed her. The tepee of Pronghorn shook and gave way, then shuddered stiff and tight again. Sacajawea was inside, and Hides Well was tying the flap tightly shut. "This one's the worst yet," said Pronghorn.

"I came for antelope chips," she said. "We are out of fuel, and no one can find any under that snow."

Hides Well held up two steaming chips from near her fire. "Take these. We have only a few also."

"Thank you," said Sacajawea as a numbness like freezing death stole through her.

"Is the child all right?"

"*Ai*, he dozes and listens to his father tell stories."

"Is the baby all right?" Pronghorn laid his pipe aside and stared at the bundled baby.

"*Ai*, only hungry and getting thin."

"Aren't we all?" asked Hides Well.

Back inside her own tepee, Sacajawea slipped inside her robe without starting the fire up again, only laying the two soggy chips near the cold fire. She fell asleep nursing No Name.

She awoke, hearing the awakening sound of Jerk Meat and his soft calling, "I must be fed, woman, get up."

She sat up. "The wind's died."

"*Ai*, it will be me next if I don't get something in my belly."

"Shall I kill one of the horses?"

"No, not yet. I'll talk to Pronghorn. Maybe he'll call a council."

Sacajawea hustled to the flap and looked out. The sky was palest blue, absolutely clear, and deep drifts lay all around the tepees. Other women were trotting their horses up and down a long, narrow space, getting them warm. The breasts, rumps, and legs of the horses were ice-coated. There was not one among them whose ribs did not show plainly under the rough winter hair.

Jerk Meat swore, "More snow blindness!" He stepped past Sacajawea and blew his nose with his fingers— first one nostril, then the other—and again studied the land. There was no color in the landscape, only the packed white sheet running off into the east, where the sun was just rising.

Pronghorn was out calling a council. It was decided to move to a more sheltered spot. "We'll try to move the horses," he said. "They maybe can make it, but unless we get a *chinook*, it is starving time for them."

The women pulled down the tepees and packed their belongings, and the band rode out straight into the sun. They kept the horses going hard.

"Hurry!" warned Kicking Horse. "I do not trust the weather any more than I do my older woman."

Near noon, far to the south of the basin they had lived in, they came to a wide stream, angling down from a canyon wall. The vegetation was sparse, but it held some elk. They quickly moved in and got all they wanted for food and new hides. As the day wore on, it changed from a pale blue to lavender, then to a faint pink, and then the sun was gone as if it had slid off the ice-slick horizon. Pronghorn pushed them on. Their breath froze all over them.

Sacajawea, her face stiff, her shoulders aching clear down across her collarbones into her chest from the papoose on her back, glanced briefly at the frosty stars in her night sky. She found the Dipper and the North Star, her total astronomy learned from Chief Red Hair in another place, during another time. Then she wondered if Pronghorn knew where a sheltered place was. The band could not possibly take much more of this. They had been on the horses since sunrise and had eaten nothing but a little raw elk meat. What if the horses should give out?

Pronghorn stopped a little farther on. No one had said, "Can we stop now?" Pronghorn seemed to like what he saw. The low, flat place behind a cutbank in the turn of the stream was a good camp. The dry grass was partially exposed at the edge of some drifts. There was much running water. He stuck a willow stick into the ground. Instantly the tired squaws tumbled out the lodgepoles and unfolded the leather tepee coverings. The men all sat huddled together talking, stupid with cold and fatigue. Children screamed and cried as their mothers tried to hush them.

Finally camp was set up. Everyone seemed too exhausted to eat the elk meat that roasted on the large center fire made from some downed cottonwood logs. The men let the heat beat on their faces and gleam in their bloodshot eyes. Some went to their tepees; others stayed and slept around the huge fire. A few came out from their tepees and stood in a row and made water, lifting their faces into the night air that was mistier and warmer than any night since the first snowfall.

"I don't know," Kicking Horse said, sniffing for wind. "I do not quite like the looks of the sky."

"But it is warm," the other men said, almost with reverence in their voices, thankful for a night without wind and snow.

The mild air might mean more snow, but it also might mean a thaw coming in, and that was the best luck they could hope for. They kicked the snow around, smelling the night air soft in their faces; it smelled like a thaw, though the snow underfoot was still as dry and granular as salt.

"This must be the break," added Jerk Meat, leading Ticannaf inside the tepee for a good night's rest.

Sacajawea hardly heard him. Her eyes were knotted, the lids heavy with sleep. But not even her dead-tiredness could lift from her the habits of the last couple of weeks. In her dreams she struggled against winds, she felt the bite of cold, she heard the clamor of people and

animals and knew that she had a duty to perform—
she had somehow to locate the baby for his feeding. She
called, but she was far down under something, struggling in the dark to come up and break her voice free.
Her own nightmarish sound told her she was dreaming
and moaning in her sleep, and still she could not break
free into wakefulness and shove the dream aside. Things
were falling on her from above; she sheltered her head
with her arms, rolled, and with a wrench broke loose
from tormented sleep and sat up.

Jerk Meat was kicking out of his robes. There was
a wild sound of howling wind. Sacajawea leaned over
the fire, stupidly groping for cottonwood bark, as a
screeching blast hit the tepee so hard that Jerk Meat,
standing by the flap, grabbed the pole and held it until
the shuddering strain gave way and the screech died
to a howl.

"What is it?" Sacajawea asked idiotically. "Is it a
chinook?"

"*Chinook!*" Jerk Meat said furiously.

He janked his stiff leggings on and groped, teeth
chattering, for his fur-lined moccasins. He dressed as
fast as his dazed mind and numbed fingers would let
him. Sacajawea broke more bark in her hands and
shoved it into the fire. At that moment the wind swooped
on them and the tepee came down.

Half-dressed, Jerk Meat struggled under the skins.
Sacajawea was still crouched over the fire, trying desperately to put it out. She saw Jerk Meat bracing a
front lodgepole, and she jumped to the rear one; it was
like holding a fishing rod with a thousand-pound fish
fighting the hook; the whole saillike mass of skins
slapped and caved and wanted to fly. One or two rawhide ropes on the windward side had broken loose and
the wall plastered itself against Sacajawea's legs, the
wind and snow pouring like ice water across her bare
feet. "Somebody out there—tie us down," Jerk Meat's
grating voice yelled. Buffalo Bones crawled toward the
front flap on hands and knees. Braced against a pole,
Big Badger was laughing. The top of the tepee was
badly scorched and there was a large hole burned around
the edges, but the fury of the wind had put the fire out.

The skins could be repaired. Pronghorn came out to help.

Ropes outside jerked; the wall came away from Sacajawea's legs; the tepee rose nearly to its proper position; the strain on the poles eased. Eventually it reached a wobbly equilibrium so that she could let go and send Ticannaf outside with his father and she could locate the baby, No Name, in the mess of her own sleeping couch. The outsiders came in gasping, beating their numbed hands. In the gray light of storm and morning, they all looked like old men; the blizzard had sown white age in their hair.

"Ohhh!" Sacajawea cried. "Our baby does not breathe! His head is crushed flat. No, no! This cannot be true!"

"The front lodgepole," whispered Big Badger, wiping away an icicle from under his nose. "It fell. *Ai*, it fell where he lay asleep."

"He is solid, frozen," said Jerk Meat aghast. "How long has he been this way?"

Sacajawea could not answer; her grief was too much. Her heart lay broken on the ground.

Big Badger held the small, undernourished body. "He was not sent to the Great Spirit by the lodgepole, but much earlier in the night by the cold finger of frost. The winter was too much for such a small boy. The Great Spirit made certain the boy made a safe trip to the Land of Warmth and Everfeasting by cutting off his earth life twice," he said as great tears rolled down to his chin.

Pronghorn walked from the tepee trying to control his emotion. He sent Hides Well and Spring to console Sacajawea.

For the remainder of the night, the men pulled and strained and fastened the rawhide ropes on the tepee. Spring brought in a half-cured elk hide to cover the burned top skin and sewed it neatly while the men held the poles down. Once the whole middle of the windward side bellied inward; the wind got under the side, and for an instant they were in a balloon. Ticannaf thought for certain they would go up in the air. He shut his eyes and hung on, and when he looked again, the men had grappled the uplifting skirt of skins and pinned it down.

The women started the death howl, shrieking. Sacajawea lay prone on her robe. She could not think. She did not want to move or speak. She felt as though an avalanche of ice and snow had hit her in the back and a herd of mustangs had stampeded over her midsection. She felt torn apart so that her heart lay on the ground. Her stomach felt full of knots. Her grief was deep.

Jerk Meat was stunned. He knew that he had lost something he could never have again. A son, yes, but more than a son. He had lost a piece of his life with Lost Woman; the web that reached from the present to the past was broken. There would be no other boys like little No Name. The new ones would be different. The baby had died without becoming old and useless. So— that might be good, thought Jerk Meat.

As in a nightmare where everything is full of shock and terror and nothing is ever explained, Sacajawea looked around at the numb huddle of friends and saw only a glare of living eyes, and she believed she saw a question on Jerk Meat's face. The question was directed to her: "Didn't you know the boy was freezing?"

Hides Well slashed herself on her arms. Spring began to cut off the first joint on her small left finger. Jerk Meat pulled out his knife and began tearing at the flesh of his little finger.

Sacajawea raised her head. Suddenly she was up, grabbing at their knives. "No, no!" she cried. "It is not necessary to do that!"

They looked at her, puzzled. Bewildered, Jerk Meat sat beside his woman. "Then I will throw away my beautiful orangewood arrows."

"*Ai*, if you feel that is proper," she said softly. "Please, do not let anyone else mutilate his body for the death of someone he loves." Her words were not her own, but those of Chief Red Hair years ago when she had tried to cut a finger joint in mourning for their friend Captain Lewis. Now she herself sat around in the cold, unwilling to build a fire and feel the comfort of its warmth. That morning brought news of others, small children and old ones, who had died during the cold snap.

Sacajawea went from tepee to tepee, preventing the slashing of arms or cutting of fingers, and preventing those who had cut themselves from jerking the scabs from those self-inflicted wounds, causing them to bleed again. She tried to explain that it was somehow wrong to search for relief from sorrow in pain. The women sobbed and broke down. She said, "Crying is no good. We must work to keep the living alive."

The usual burial place was a deep crevice in the rocks or a cave, but the weather was too cold to search for a suitable spot. The face of each corpse was sprinkled with powdered local rock containing enough mercuric sulfide to be scarlet and the eyes were sealed shut with moist, red clay. If possible, before the body was cold the knees were bent to the chest and the head pushed to the knees, then it was wrapped in a robe and held together with lashings of rawhide rope. The women cut many poles that day from the thin cottonwoods and built a pen around the bodies. Some wanted to build individual pens, but because of the scarcity of poles they had to place their beloved ones all together. The poles were pounded into the frozen ground. Into this enclosure they placed the personal effects with the deceased—saddle and bridle, tomahawk, scalping knife, bow and arrows and lance, or in the case of a squaw, her favorite tunic, cooking kettle, tools for dressing skins.

Pronghorn had forbidden them to kill any horses for burial because the Quohadas still living needed horses for food and travel. There was some discussion about this because the band believed in a kind of resurrection in which the dead would rise and march eastward to take possession of their land. The personal items were left with the dead because the Comanches supposed their souls would have need of them in the other world.

The penlike enclosure was roofed with bark and willow branches and covered with mud. The work was exhausting. The women sat on the ground awhile and did not look at the burial hut, ugly brown against the sky and unmelted snow patches. Sacajawea sat with the women, her robe over her head, wiping her leaking nose against the edge of the fur and feeling slick ice there as the temperature began to drop. Suddenly she threw off her robe and moved toward the burial place that held the small bundle of No Name.

"He did not even have a name. He could be driven off into the barren wasteland crying for years among

thorns and rocks, thirsty, hungry, and in pain because
he was not named when he lived. Oh, my baby!"

"Our old grandmother was fond of small ones," sobbed
a young woman crouching before Sacajawea. "She will
hear your baby's cries and carry him into a warm valley. She will give him cool water, pounded corn, and
elk meat. She will set him upon a horse that is fleeter
than the wind just to hear his laughter."

It was wonderful the way the Quohada tribe kept
track of itself and all its various family units. If every
single man, woman, and child acted and conducted himself or herself in a known pattern and broke no walls
and differed with no one and experimented in no new
way—then that unit was left safe and strong, alone.
But let one man or woman or child step out of the
regular thought or the known pattern, and the people
knew, their suspicion ran, and their thoughts traveled
over the camp.

Sacajawea was now watched more than ever. She did
not conduct herself in familar patterns. The people began to watch her as they realized now it was she who
had held them back from the tradition of cutting their
own bodies while they were in the deep hole of grief.
They had not yet made up their minds whether to be
grateful or angry toward her. She had broken another
wall in their life.

Darkness came. The night was dominated by the
wind. Sacajawea searched the center campfire for her
man. She called his name. She did not realize others
watched her. When she found Jerk Meat, he took her
to their patched tepee. They huddled together under
their robes, comforting their remaining child, Ticannaf.
He said it was the first time he had been warm since
they moved camp. It was not until the next morning
that Sacajawea noticed what the whole camp already
knew: Jerk Meat had cut off his long, flowing hair.

That morning the cold had settled in, freezing the
muddy ground. Pronghorn called another council, and
they decided to move camp farther up the canyon toward the south. He sent a party out first with some
skins for a lodge and to start a fire going for the others
who would come to the new camp cold and tired, dragging their thin horses.

Some of the women of the second party had to take
turns walking because the first party had taken horses
for their supplies and many had been slaughtered and
eaten by the Quohadas during the past weeks. Step by
step they moved through the canyon, panting, winded,
crying encouragement, forcing themselves to keep up.

Sacajawea sagged and started to sit down, and Hides
Well climbed from her horse and barely managed to
hold her up. Sacajawea could not see more than a bleared
half-light. She could see no objects. Her tears were ice,
her lashes stitched together. Savagely she wiped her
face across the snow-slick fur of Hides Well's blanketed
shoulder. With what little vision she could gain, she
looked straight into the wind and snow, hunting for the
huge white conical wall that would be the lodge. Spring
and Wild Plum rode a horse, and Jerk Meat rode with
Ticannaf sitting in front of him. Sacajawea tried to control her tears, knowing they might mean blindness and
death in the wind that drove itself down her throat. To
talk was like trying to look and shout up a waterfall.
The wilderness howled at her, and she stopped, sightless, breathless, deafened, and with no strength to move
and barely enough to stand, not enough—desperately
not enough, she slid down and away. This was the end.
It was not hard. It was easy.

Then pain stabbed through her eyeballs as if she had
rubbed across them with sand; something broke the
threads of ice that stitched them shut. She looked into
the gray, howling wind and saw a loom of shadow in
the dark murk; she thought in wonder, Have we been
here going around and around the lodge? The darkness
moved and the wind's voice fell from whine and howl
to a doglike barking, and Hides Well was there shouting
in her face.

She heard the unmistakable crackle of a fire going
inside the lodge. She felt an arm around her, the urging
of someone else's undiminished strength helping her
along through a deep drift that gave way abruptly to
clear ground. Her head heard one last scream of wind,
and the noises from outside fell, the light brightened
through her sticky eyelids, and her nostrils filled with
the smells of roast elk, tallow, and the delicious odor
of spicy cedar bark. Someone steered her around and

pushed on her shoulders. She heard Jerk Meat whisper, "Little Fox, you cannot be finished so easily. You belong to me." She felt safety like this was pure bliss as she eased herself down on the old buffalo hide that was spread for her. Later she sat with aching feet in a basket of water, and when the pain in her hands swelled until it seemed the fingers would split, she felt this safety was only misery. She could not numb the ache into bearability. Her eyes were inflamed and sore; in each cheek a spot throbbed with such violence that she thought the pulse must be visible in the skin like a twitching nerve. Her ears were swollen, and her nose was so stuffed and swollen that she gurgled for air. She knew how she looked when she saw Kicking Horse, who had let his women ride their two good horses as he walked.

Kicking Horse said to her, "Feeling anything?"

"*Ooo, ai*," answered Sacajawea.

"Better let those feet stay in the water awhile," Kicking Horse said when she pulled up her feet. "The slower they come back, the better."

"I think my face is frozen, too," she said.

"Well, we'll be sitting around for a couple of weeks now," said Pronghorn, looking at his own painfully swollen hands.

Weatherbeaten and battered, the Quohadas crowded into the one big lodge. They huddled back against walls and away from the center fire, and each retired within his skinful of pain and weariness. Sacajawea, with pain enough to fill her to the chin, locked her jaw for fear of whimpering. She made a note that none of the Quohadas whimpered, not even Gray Bone, not even the children—least of all her own son, Ticannaf, who sat sound asleep on Jerk Meat's lap. The worst she heard was a querulous growl when anyone moved too fast. Big Badger, the old one, unfrozen except for a touch on the fingers and ears, moved between them in moccasined feet and flipped the cooking pot with the edges of his palm, saving his tender fingertips, and looked in. The mystic smells of brotherhood were strong in that lodge.

CHAPTER

47

Gray Bone

*The once roaming bands of Texas, Oklahoma and New
Mexico are Comanches, a branch of the great and widely
distributed Shoshone family. Their language and traditions show that they are a comparatively recent off-
shoot from the Shoshone of Wyoming; both tribes
speaking practically the same dialect. Once the tribes
lived adjacent to each other in southern Wyoming, then
the Shoshone were beaten back into the mountains by
the Sioux and Blackfeet, while the Comanche were driven
steadily southward by the same kind of pressure. How
soon the Shoshoneans turned into Comanche Plains Indians remains uncertain. They passively took on Plains
features, absorbing essentially material rather than social and religious traits. The earliest unquestionable reference to these people goes back to 1701 and places them
near the headwaters of the Arkansas (Colorado); in 1705
they were found in New Mexico. Since Comanche and
Shoshone differ only dialectically, their separation cannot date back many centuries.*

ROBERT H. LOWIE, *Indians of the Plains*. New York:
McGraw-Hill Book Co., 1954. Reprinted by The American Museum of Natural History, N.Y., 1954, pp.
216–17.

When the cold snap broke, the Quohadas moved on and made camp in the bottom of the southern end of the great canyon, which was sliced through by millions of years of cutting water, sculpted into twisted shapes by storms and sand-edged winds. It was not steep-walled; the sides sloped into massive steps banded with many colors of rock, not too steep to be climbed. The stream that had cut the canyon was there, on the floor, washing over the red clay. There were groves of scrub cedar and a few age-old sycamores primitively growing only the inner layer of its bark every year.[1] The Quohadas knew the sycamores were ancients, surviving fungus diseases, storms, and floods to lend their branches for strong arrows and digging sticks. The Quohadas showed each tree respect by choosing each branch carefully before hacking it off with knives or axes.

The men found small game rabbits and fox to shoot with the polished sycamore arrows. There were wild carrots and parsnips near the stream that could be dug easily with the hardwood digging sticks.

The men planned a buffalo hunt as soon as the weather warmed enough. The hair on the beasts was loose this time of year, but it did not matter as the hide was to be used for tepee covers, anyway.

Sacajawea did not plan to go with the hunters because she was a third of the way through her time. She was pleased to have another child, but not as ecstatically happy as she had been a year ago. She was almost afraid to feel great happiness, as though it would be an omen of bad times ahead. She stayed in the main camp and watched after Ticannaf, Wild Plum, and Big Badger.

The sun was back in unbelievable warmth, and the stream flooded its banks. The canyon was faintly tinged with fresh green shoots. Big Badger took the small boys swimming in a quiet spot under some willows in the stream. For being only five summers old, Wild Plum swam well, his arms and legs churning through the water much the way a dog swims. Sacajawea had a

1017

great pot of boiled rabbit ribs ready for them when they returned.

One day the sweetish, slightly sickening smell of bloated buffalo carcasses filled the canyon. The familiar smell brought Sacajawea's girlhood with the Minnetarees sharply back to her mind. She wished to see for herself and suggested a walk to look for carrots to go with the boiled rabbit. Big Badger nodded and motioned for the two little boys to follow along. They pushed through soft clay where the willows were gnawed down to stubs, broken, mouthed, and gummed off by starving animals. The floodwaters covered the low spots. Sacajawea held her nose, then let go and smelled the rich, rotten, stinking carcasses as the redolent smell rolled upwind the way water runs upstream in an eddy.

She wondered why she had combed her hair so carefully and put on her best tunic, tied the sky blue stone around her neck, and put the small pouch with her few valuables on the string at her waist, just to walk in this horrible stench. It is like going to meet old memories, she told herself.

Wild Plum tugged at her skirt saying, "Wheee-ou! What is that smell?"

"You will see soon enough," promised Sacajawea, noticing Big Badger hold his nose.

The floodwaters forced them out of the bottoms and up onto a wide ledge. Below, Sacajawea saw the stream, astonishingly wide, pushing across willow bars and pressing deep into the cutbank bends. She heard the hushed roar like wind as the water rushed below. There were the buffalo balloonily afloat in the brush where they had died. They saw a cow float around the deep water of a turn with her legs in the air, and farther on a heifer, stranded momentarily among flooded rosebushes, rotate free and become stranded again. Then, abruptly, ahead of them dead eyeballs stared from between spraddled legs, horns and tail and legs tangled in a mass of bone and hide not yet, in that cool bottom, puffing with the gases of decay. They must have piled against one another while drifting before one of the winter's blizzards.

She clung to Ticannaf's hand and with the free hand

each pinched his nose shut. A little later the stench was so overpowering that they all breathed it in deeply as if to sample the worst, and looked to the left where a huge bull buffalo, his belly blown up and ready to pop, hung by his neck and horns from a tight clump of alder and cottonwood where the snow had left him. They saw the breeze make cat's paws in the heavy winter hair.

"*Ai*, that is enough, when you find them in trees," exclaimed Big Badger. "We will go back with no carrots for our meal. This is a bad year. You can see the bad. You can smell the bad."

Sacajawea looked at Big Badger, weathered and scarred as the country had left him. His eyes were black and steady, though, marksman's eyes. His long fingers plucked a strand of new rice grass. He bit it between his teeth. His head went slowly up and down.

"Lost Woman, you have been here before?"

"No, Big Badger, not here, but far up north, where the same thing happens to the buffalo—and the people"—her breath caught—"eat the soft, putrid flesh."

"*Pobrecita*," he said, "we would all be so ill with belly cramps we would die."

"I could not eat." Her eyes came down and found Ticannaf watching her steadily. "There are more beautiful things. We must find them for the boys."

They hurried back toward the village, holding their noses. Wild Plum hung back and pointed. By his toe was a half-crushed crocus, palely lavender, a thing tender and unbelievable in the mud and stones.

"Beauty," said Big Badger, "is here, where you find it."

Sacajawea bent to pick it up. Smelling the mild freshness she handed it to Wild Plum, who said, "It will not take the place of wild carrots."

"So—who can eat after this stink," grumbled Big Badger, putting the five-year-old on his shoulders and trotting homeward. Sacajawea and Ticannaf trotted behind.

Big Badger suddenly made the "stop" sign with one hand, slashing it in the air behind him. There was movement in the Quohada village. The camp should be quiet at this time of day. Only the grandmother of Wounded Buck was left behind, and she was asleep in her tepee. He held his hand behind him, slowly moving it back and forth, meaning, "Be still." A dark figure moved without sound, as in a dream. It carried a rifle. It mounted a saddled horse. Another figure did the same. Sacajawea could see they had on blue jackets or coats. Her breath caught. They were white men. She felt a curious splitting sensation, as though she had suddenly divided into two people. She wanted to run to those men and ask them questions, to look into their eyes to see what they knew of her grown son, or of Chief Red Hair. Then her other half wanted to run, hide, get away from them; they were the enemy and she their prey. She was afraid of them.

The four of them waited, crouched down behind red sandstone and some sparse cedar. The village looked like a camp of the dead. There was no sound in it now and no motion. Suddenly the echo of gunfire came along the canyon walls. Acrid blue-gray powder smoke mixed with the rotten-carcass odor. Then some other men on horses came down into the canyon. They sat calmly and formed two lines, then waited. Then there was a piercing noise, familiar to Sacajawea. "The sounding horn," she whispered. The charge had been sounded.

Twenty-two men let out a holler and rode madly into the canyon. There was no resistance. When they charged, they charged. The mud was churned up. They pumped bullets into the tepees. A man fell from his horse, then another, hit by their own lead ricocheting off the rock walls.

Big Badger was furious. He swore constantly in the Mexican-Comanche tongue.

The camp had been swept through by a scythe. The crumpled tepees were empty and covered with mud. Smashed drying racks lay broken in the sunshine. Cooking pots were overturned and left behind. Buffalo robes and discarded clothing were strewn all over the ground. Lodgepoles were scattered.

The white men seemed weary and disgusted that they had found no Comanches. They kicked at the pots and spat, then mounted their horses. Enough was enough. They put the two dead men across their saddles and led the horses up the canyon walls.

"Lie still," warned Big Badger when Wild Plum

squirmed in the damp grass. "These men are out for revenge. It may be that they were attacked by Apaches and many were killed. The white man considers all Indians the same."

"But, Big Badger," said Sacajawea, "we did nothing to them."

"*Ai,* nothing. But we are Indians. Indians killed their comrades."

"That is not fair," said Wild Plum. "Quohadas are peaceful, not ferocious like the Tonkas."

"*Ai,* we know that even among the Comanches there are good and bad, but they do not. They have no understanding. It is bad," sighed Big Badger.

The white men were not quite finished. Two men rounded up the Quohadas' ponies and mules, and two others stayed behind to set fire to the tepees, then fled up the rocky wall. The lodgepoles burned, and then a stink of scorched hides filled the air. In less than thirty minutes the great village of the Quohadas was an inferno. The crackling tepees burned like torches, and then the ancient sycamores began to burn.

Deep inside her belly Sacajawea felt the knotted sickness of hatred for these white men.

The afternoon breeze fanned the flames, and tepees collapsed in showers of orange sparks. The old wood of the lodgepoles cracked with loud reports as the licking flames found their hearts.

Greasy smoke hung like strange clouds. It was hot in the canyon.

"A large village can make a lot of smoke when it burns," said Wild Plum, lying with Ticannaf in tearless wonderment.

All night they watched the fires burn and smelled the stink that boiled up out of the earth. It was the first time Sacajawea had been fully aware of the enmity of the white man. She had no idea why they had come or where they had come from. She began to wonder if they were all like the Mexicans—friends one time and enemies another. She was hurt and confused. Now the only certainty in her life was the love she felt for her man, Jerk Meat.

"It is gone," said Big Badger. There were tears in

his eyes. Wild Plum lay close to him and asked, "Is my mother all right?"

"That is the one thing we can thank the Great Spirit for. The early hunt took everyone out of the village."

"And we can thank Lost Woman for wanting carrots for her stew," added Wild Plum.

"*Ai*," agreed Big Badger. "We wait here one more night to make sure the palefaces do not come back. Then we go down and look."

"I'm hungry," whispered Ticannaf.

"This is all the jerky I have. Chew it slowly," said Sacajawea, pulling a piece of hard, stringy meat from a small leather pouch attached to her waistband.

They dared not build a fire, and they could feel the damp, cold earth through their clothing. When it became dark, they huddled together for warmth. Sacajawea slept fitfully with her legs curled around the small body of Ticannaf. The night dragged. Daylight brought no comfort. The place did not seem like home. When the sun rose, it helped. Big Badger went over the cap rock to scout around for the white soldiers. He was gone a long time.

Sacajawea and the boys played games with small stones as they lay in last year's damp weeds. "Can we have a fire?" Ticannaf asked.

"No, it is better not to make any more smoke," she replied.

Big Badger came puffing up the side of the yellow rock. He spoke fiercely. "Do not think about what you see. Go down and wrap the body of Wounded Buck's grandmother. She was shot five times. Those white men are brave to shoot an old, helpless grandmother and then burn down a deserted village. Yaaagh!"

As Sacajawea went down the slope toward where the village had been, she was shocked by its appearance. A few of the lodgepoles had not burned. The whole area was trampled by horses' hooves. Wild Plum hung back among the scrub cedars. "What is it?" she asked.

"My mother's sewing basket is over there. See, all the things are spilled in the red mud."

"You pick them up and wipe them off, then bring the basket and whatever else you find to the far end of the village. Big Badger is there cleaning off some lances and war clubs."

Sacajawea gathered up the body of the old woman and gently laid it on a scorched buffalo robe. She rolled the body in the robe and tied it securely. She built a small fence for the burial hut from odds and ends of sticks. She put an iron kettle inside with the body and several of the better robes, along with a bone spoon and a skinning knife with no handle. She did the best she could to make a roof over the burial hut from sticks and mud and stones.

Then she began to pull out bedding and extra clothes that were not burned beyond use and put them in a pile. Big Badger was looking through the mess for tools and cooking gear. They put what was usable at the far end of the camp and covered it with extra robes. There were not many lodgepoles left. Pronghorn would have to move the camp to a place with lots of trees.

Wild Plum found the old blue coat that Sacajawea cherished, but there was nothing else to be found except some small blue beads and a couple of hawk's bells around the burned hole that had been her tepee.

By late afternoon, clouds had come rushing over the sky. Big Badger made a small fire with twigs and dry grass. They ate some pemmican they had found in a leather sack half-buried in mud beside the stream. They slept. When they woke, the fire was out and a fine mist was falling.

The hunting party came back through a driving rain. The night was black and wild around them, and that was good. There was no chance of being seen.

Their scouts had seen the *taibo*, white men, and they had been able to travel around them without being seen. They were tired. They had ridden hard and long and with heavy loads. Their hunt had been successful. But they were shocked at the desolation and destruction in their camp. They were disheartened at the news that all the extra horses and mules were gone. The women began to make temporary shelters from the scorched hides and robes that Sacajawea had piled up. No one complained that someone else was using her robe. They were too shocked and worn out. They worked together to make a dry place for the children to sleep, then built themselves temporary lean-tos. The smell of smoke and wet, burned leather was strong in their noses that night.

Spring and Hides Well asked Sacajawea to sleep in their shelter. It was small but warm, with the men on one side and the women on the other, making no space at all in the middle. They all slept fitfully, listening to the water run down the lean-to and drip off the ghost-white sycamores.

They woke late. The rain had stopped, and the hides were damp and steaming. They loaded the scorched remnants of the village onto the shivering horses and moved out, seeking a fresh spring camp.

The evening winds blew across the purpled plains. The pecans that lined the muddy stream whispered in their dark branches. Doves called softly to each other. Sacajawea cooed softly to her small son, Ticannaf. She had found peace again. She and Jerk Meat were together, and the village was whole again in a sheltered place where the food supply was good. No one spoke of the Time of Blackened Tepees.

Sometimes scouts came in with reports of white hunters in the base area of the mountains and along the wide river. Pronghorn did not understand how the presence of the white men could be so widespread.

Jerk Meat delighted in Sacajawea's changing moods. Sometimes she was like a small child, and then she would be altogether a woman, as complete and as complex as a woman could be, passionate and eager, strong as he was, sometimes so violent that he fell back drained and aching with the hollow pain of his love for her. Sometimes she was almost like another man; they walked and hunted together, and it was not correct to say he loved to be with her in the forest. She was the forest. She was everything he saw and listened to and smelled. She was the same as the birds and the wild animals they found. She was the waters of the stream and she was Mother Earth.

He learned laboriously to speak her broken English and French, the love phrases first, and then in the depth and extent of her passion with him she forgot the alien expressions and reverted to her own Shoshoni tongue. He was studious and eager in his quest to find that which she loved best when they were together, and it was not long before she forgot that she had ever known a man before him.

When he went on raids he came back and told her everything he had done during the time he was away. As she listened gravely, he found himself remembering unimportant little things he thought would amuse her and in some way bridge these short periods of separation. He pictured his world as being filled with people and events of only minor importance; he wanted her to know, as he knew, that his lodge and his life was with her.

And she was as full of gossip when he came to her as he was. He listened to all the things she told him with great soberness.

One night they entered their tepee, and, seeing Ticannaf asleep, she slipped out of her clothes and felt the quickness in Jerk Meat. She could never get over her feeling that there was something of the untamed animal in him. He pawed at the earth in pretense of tackling a black bear alone with only his hunting knife. His hand moved toward the unseen beast. Quickly he plunged the knife at the throat. He made the death roar of a bear deep in his throat. He pantomimed butchering the bear and offering a choice bit of meat to the east, west, north, and south. He pretended to shove the meat into his mouth. He wiped his hands on his bare thighs and chest.

"Woman, wash me!" he commanded.

She brought the buffalo paunch full of warm water and poured it over him. "I will get more." But he grabbed her up in his arms and danced around with her on the muddied ground of the tepee.

"My Little Fox, my woman. Together we live."

Neither cared about the muddy floor as they danced until they fell. They rolled until they were wedged against a tepee pole and a leather storage box.

Later, lying next to her, half-asleep, he asked if they could revisit the place where they had spent their first days and nights.

"You know it should never be," she said.

"Why not? For us?"

"*Ai*, for us, but if we do all these things that we

believe are all right for us, and others do the things they think are all right for them—no one will obey the tribal laws and there will be no respect for anything."

"You are getting older and wiser, Little Fox."

"So—we can think of that time," she added, "but we must not try to relive it or go there."

He stroked her body. "I thought about you all the time I was in San Fernandez trading with the Mexicans."

"Are there pretty women there?"

"No, I can see no pretty women but here, Pajarita."

"You call me Little Bird?"

"*Ai*, you are beautiful and your voice is music. Remember the times you played the metal mouth box, the harmonica? What sounds! Would you like me to trade for another in Mexico so that you can sing our papoose to sleep?"

"But Little Bird? Why?"

"Oh, Pajarita! I am so much in love with you."

Softly she said, "That was my girlhood name."

"Oh," he said, smiling. "It is a most suitable name. I should have thought of it before. I shall always call you Little Bird. You are my Bird Woman." Then his eyes shone and he teased, "Still, you are foxy at times." There was laughter in his voice. "Why did they not notice that also when you were a girl?" He kissed the soft part of her neck.

"It is good here," she whispered into his ear, holding his hand very tightly over her heart. "There is nothing between us, nothing. Remember how you said we would be just one, you and I? That is how we are. You and I know it is the custom not to make love from the moment we are sure of making a new life until the child is weaned. Yet we have never heeded this custom."

"*Ai*, customs—we have broken many, you and I."

"What about others? I have thought about that."

"Perhaps—no one talks."

He lifted her chin and kissed her.

By late summer Sacajawea had a papoose strapped to her back. The child was named Surprise, because she was the first female grandchild for Pronghorn and Hides Well.

One afternoon as Sacajawea added wild parsnips to her cooking pot, she looked up and saw how things seemed stained a sickly yellow by a weird cloud light. "I hope there is no more rain in those dirty gray clouds," she said.

"We ought to get some nice hide for moccasins tomorrow if this heavy buffalo sign means anything," said Jerk Meat, unconcerned about the coloring over everything.

Wounded Buck wandered by, then stopped to talk and smoke with Jerk Meat. He swatted his arm. "That buffalo gnat—" He looked around for a stone, found one, knocked out the dottle from his pipe, blew through the stem to get the spittle clear, and started again. "The buffalo gnat is a no-see-him—no bigger than a speck of dust in the tail of a man's eye. He will bite you on the hands and face and make you think someone is poking at you with a burning stick. Or maybe with porcupine needles. He will crawl under your shirt and leggings and in your moccasins and pinch you until he is full and fat with your blood. He will leave a bump as big as the mound on the front of a prairie dog's hole"—he held up his thumb to show the actual size—"and as sore as a moccasin blister."

"I've been eaten by some in my life—it was nothing," said Jerk Meat.

"No, by themselves they are nothing, but in clouds or swarms thick enough to choke a mule, they are something."

"Like what?" asked Jerk Meat, scratching himself.

"Like"—Wounded Buck stretched the statement long—"like causing the horses to stampede, run wild in all four directions." He pointed four ways.

The cloud of gnats drifted in shortly after the Quohadas had eaten their evening meal. For several hours the people in robes, the horses at the pickets, and the loose herd, tail-slapped, bit, brayed, scratched, cursed, or groaned—each in his own way fighting off the waves of invisible insects.

After a little letup came a second, thicker horde out of the night sky. The suffering of the Quohadas and their animals became more intense. Ever the camp dogs yipped.

Jerk Meat's face was a beefsteak of welts, his hands
swollen and puffed until they could scarcely open and
close, yet when he went out to the horses with some of
the other men, he found he had just begun to suffer.
There was a fearful whining hum of the tiny winged
invaders, and the mules were braying and kicking, the
horses whinnying, and the children crying. Ticannaf
tried to stay under his robe, but it did no good. The
baby, Surprise, kept up an incessant screaming, her
tiny eyelids swollen shut. Sacajawea found it was all
she could do to keep from screaming herself. She wished
for rain, snow—anything to stop these invisible sting-
ers. She tried keeping Surprise under a robe, but it was
too warm and the baby cried. She scratched and thought
she must be going insane as the hum became louder.

A third swarm hit the camp. The horses broke before
it to go plunging and whinnying off into the night with
the braying mules, the hammering drumfire of their
panicky hooves rising briefly above the ear-ringing hum
of the insects and the screaming, helpless curses of their
human pursuers.

Then there was nothing but the continued whine of
the whirling black host muffling the bitter profanity of
the weary, nerve-worn Quohadas.

The morning following the gnat stampede was spent
in riding into prairie draws and gullies, rounding up
what was to be found of the horses. Several of them
were so swollen and totally blinded that the men shot
them. They had lost half the herd.

The people were hideous with puffed, inflamed faces,
splitting lips, bleeding ears and noses. Some of them,
too, were actually blind, their eyes swollen to sightless
slits.

Surprise's eyes and mouth were so badly swollen that
she could not nurse. On the seventh day, her fever
burned so hot that her small body could not be cooled.
Her stomach cramped, and her screams turned to moans.
Sacajawea made a salve with squashed yucca leaves
and rubbed it on the infant's face, arms, and shoulders.
This was as good a remedy as any. It was simple and
did not cost anything. Hides Well came in and questioned the salve. She thought perhaps it lacked authority, and she wanted to call the Medicine Man,

Kicking Horse. Sacajawea said she could not imagine
what else Kicking Horse could do, and anyway, he was
busy applying salves to others with swollen faces.

The news of the baby's illness traveled quickly among
the tepees, for sickness was second only to hunger as
the enemy of the Quohadas. And some said softly, "It
is a shame to lose so many babies. It brings any mother
to her knees." Some of the women nodded and went to
Jerk Meat's tepee. They crowded in and make little
comments on the sadness of sickness affecting such a
small one, and they said, "She is in the hands of the
Great Spirit." An old woman with swollen hands squatted down beside Sacajawea to try to give her aid if she
could, and comfort if she could not.

Kicking Horse hurried in, scattering the women like
prairie hens. He took the child and examined her and
felt her head. "I will try," he said, "I will try my best,
but I have little hope." He placed the down from a dried
milkweed pod on the baby's feet to give her power for
running later in life. He shook his rattle and squatted
by the unconscious child. Twice he spread his spittle
on her closed eyelids and prayed deeply. She died before
the sun reached its midpoint in the sky.

Again Sacajawea was engulfed by grief. She was
afraid to be alone. She begged Jerk Meat to take her
hunting, on raids, anywhere. She cried, "Do not leave
me alone with my thoughts." She pleaded with Jerk
Meat to let her go to Mexico. "I will skin your animals
and pack your meat. I will be no burden. Spring has
already told me Ticannaf can stay with her." She knew
that with the concentration required by physical effort,
time passed rapidly. It was the passage of time that
would heal her broken heat.

"My Little Bird, you are a fox today," said Jerk Meat,
picking at anything to bring strength back to his fragile
woman. She had always been obedient and respectful
and cheerful and patient, but now she was none of these.
She could stand fatigue and hunger better than most
men, but now she would not eat and she was constantly
tired. She could arch her back in childbirth with hardly
a cry, but this grief made her weep until her eyes stayed
red and swollen.

"I was wondering," said Jerk Meat hopefully, "how

I would get all the meat packed and put on the one extra horse I am taking. Now I have the answer. I will take two extra horses and you."

"*Ai-eee!*" she cried. "I am happy. Thank you."

The next morning they started, passing old buffalo wallows, shallow ponds with a few puddles of muddy water. The water was fouled with green scum and dead flies. It smelled bad. Some of the Quohadas dismounted, broke off handfuls of grass, spread it on top of the water, sucked the muddy fluid through the grass. Sacajawea was not that thirsty. A few stemless yuccas dotted the sand, and some stunted piñons began to appear among the jointweed. A river flashed its crystal waters as it tumbled out of the tableland. Now Sacajawea became unbearably thirsty.

Pronghorn guided the party down a series of natural steps in the stone, hitting the bank of the river without trouble. For a long moment nothing could be heard but the sucking sound of water going down hot throats. To Sacajawea's surprise, the river was shallow and the water tasted warm. They forded to the opposite bank, and along a similar series of rock terraces, which looked as if they had been carved centuries before, they climbed out onto grassy tableland. The air was cool and refreshing. There were Mexican traders under the mesquite trees. Their oxcarts stood on the gray-green galleta grass that stretched into the distance.

Three days they camped here and feasted with the Mexicans, playing games of chance, pocar robado, pocar garanom, and showing off their horsemanship, the Comanches riding so that only the toe of one moccasin could be seen over the top of the horse. They would swing under the horse and come up on the opposite side. All the while they shouted, "*Hiii-eee!*" There was much tequila drinking.

On the third day, Kicking Horse saw a small pistol lying near some silver trinkets and brightly colored rebozos. He picked it up and turned it over. He liked it. "How much? What do you want for this?" he asked the first Mexican trader he saw.

"*Quién sabe?*" answered the trader, swaying and staggering after one of the señoritas who were with his party.

Kicking Horse found another trader. "*Con su permiso,*" he began.

"*Lobo,* give that to me!" The trader grabbed for the pistol. Kicking Horse hung on, and as he did so, the pistol was fired, hitting the man in the foot. Instantly the camp was pandemonium—Quohadas fleeing, Mexicans running to their carts for protection, firing helterskelter at anything that moved. In the confusion a young Mexican girl, near twelve or thirteen, and her baby brother, about two summers old, ran to the opposite side of the camp and found themselves surrounded by Quohadas. Kicking Horse tried to fire the pistol at pursuing Mexicans, but there was no other bullet. He waved the gun about. Other Quohadas were nocking their arrows into bowstrings, then fleeing for their horses. Sacajawea was mounted and into a grove of gnarled piñons before she stopped to look around for the others. She spied Jerk Meat, then Wounded Buck, Pronghorn, and Red Eagle. Then she saw Kicking Horse coming toward them at a fast gallop with the Mexican girl and her baby brother tied in front of him.

"Let's get out of here!" ordered Pronghorn. They rode fast and hard for the rest of the afternoon. By evening they were camped under a heavy, orange-colored sky. Then they learned that Wolf, son of Kicking Horse and Gray Bone, had been left behind, dead, on Mexican ground.

The Mexican girl sobbed quietly, her brother asleep in her arms. Sacajawea offered her water from a skin paunch. The girl spat at her.

"*Agua fría?*" Sacajawea asked.

"No, never!" shouted the girl in Spanish.

Sacajawea knew of the custom of the Comanches, to take women and children from other villages to use as slaves. The small children were adopted and raised as Comanche children. They were loved and treated well. She also knew that the Quohadas seldom took slaves. Her heart went out to this dark-haired half-child, halfwoman Mexican. The girl's hands were bound tightly. Sacajawea spread the soothing juice from a crushed yucca on her arms and wrists, but she could not undo the binding. The girl submitted with teeth clamped shut and eyes tightly closed. Sacajawea bathed her face with cool water and gave the baby a drink and a strip of dried jerky to chew on.

"Try to rest. You will not be treated badly. I will promise you that," she reassured the girl in broken Mexican and with hand signs.

From then on, they traveled slowly, stopping when any shade appeared on the trail during the heat of the day, camping here and there a day or more to hunt antelope and buffalo or pick wild fruit.

A week after the skirmish with the Mexicans, they were nearing their permanent camp when they all heard a strange noise carried by the warm wind. Some rode a bit faster. The noise sounded to Sacajawea like the cackling of wild geese. She scanned the heavens but saw nothing. As they drew nearer, some said the noise sounded human.

With a loud whoop, Kicking Horse dug his heels into the flanks of his tired horse. The horse dodged over-hanging branches of mesquite as it plunged forward, urged on by strikes from Kicking Horse's quirt.

Then they all heard the voices, wild and savage. In the clearing was Gray Bone in the lead, mounted on a large roan with a stripe of white paint on each of its flanks and a black stripe running down each hind leg. A few other women were mounted on ponies; others ran awkwardly on foot, holding on to the legs of the mounted ones. They were all moaning the death chant. The scouts had arrived in camp in advance of the main party and spread the news of Wolf's death. Then someone in the hunting party shouted, "Tell her about the two children you have brought to take his place, Kicking Horse! Tell her not to grieve! She has two for one!"

The wailing of the women stopped. Sacajawea looked around her as the women headed for Kicking Horse. He watched them for a few measured minutes, then pointed to his short-cropped hair—the mark of mourn-ing—then to the two Mexican children. Without warn-ing, he shoved the girl and baby off his horse to the ground. The girl, shaken, looked at the approaching women running straight for her. She bent over her brother as the women felt her arms and legs and pinched her here and there. All agreed that she was plenty strong and would be a good worker in the lodge of Gray

Bone. Gray Bone stepped forward and struck the girl across the head and shoulders with painful blows. As she beat her with her fists, her cries rose to maniacal fury.

Sacajawea thought of the time she was a girl and a captive of the barbarous Minnetarees. She kicked at the flanks of her horse and rode through the crowd. "Stop!" she shouted. None could hear. "Stop, she is only a child. She is badly frightened."

The crowd fell away and turned to greet their men, brothers, and fathers. Gray Bone turned her back and ignored Sacajawea and the Mexican children. Sacajawea saw Spring, who grinned back broadly, but looked as though she had run for miles in the heat to meet the hunting party.

Sacajawea dismounted. "Ticannaf?" she asked first.

"He can ride better than Wild Plum. He has learned to make a slingshot and has a skinned knee." Spring gave Sacajawea a quick glance, then looked at the Mexican girl holding the baby. "We have missed all of you and had no idea you would bring strangers to us."

Kicking Horse, leading his horse, walked to the girl, pulled her to her feet, and indicated she was to lead the horse. Amidst the mob, he carried the baby boy triumphantly on his shoulder to his lodge.

"The girl is afraid," said Spring.

"*Ai*. The Quohada life is strange to her."

"I hope Gray Bone is not strange in her ways with her," sighed Spring.

At her tepee Sacajawea had a sudden desire to pull her son up into her arms, but she knew she must not show that much emotion. She rumpled his long black hair and saw him run off to greet his father.

Every young Comanche boy learned to be self-reliant. By the time he was five years old he could manage a pony and a year later he could use a bow and arrows. He learned the signs and tracks of birds and animals. He learned the customs of the band and was seldom reprimanded. He learned to catch the night-flying bull bats with arrows whose foreshafts were split horizontally and hummingbirds with arrows whose foreshafts were split vertically. He was adept at shooting the large, prairie grasshoppers with the hummingbird arrows. The young Comanche enjoyed eating the grass-hoppers' large, muscular legs.

The winter camp was five days south of the camp that had been burned by the bluecoats. The Quohadas were heavily loaded as they moved through the rough country hoping to find Mexican traders so they could buy more guns. Some of the men wanted to make a trip into Mexico before the cold came; some even suggested going to Fort Sill for revenge against the bluecoats. Others, including Chief Pronghorn, thought the blue-coats would leave them alone because they had fought a dead camp and did not want to be so tricked again. A few said they would like to find a wagon train and raid it for supplies.

After they settled in the winter camp, a council was called and the men decided to go to Mexico, attacking any wagon trains they found along the way. No women were allowed to go on this journey. Six-year-old Ticannaf begged to go and prove his bravery. Sacajawea held him close and pointed out gently that Big Badger was staying behind, and his cousin, Wild Plum, who was older by several winters, was not going.

Jerk Meat looked at his son. "It is time you had man-training. Do not let your mother teach you squaw-cook-ing or berry-picking while I am gone. Go to Big Badger. Tell him you wish to learn the art of arrow-making." Jerk Meat made his eyes small slits and looked at Saca-jawea, who was still hugging the boy. Ticannaf sud-denly cried out in some distress. Sacajawea freed him and watched as the child put his forefinger in his mouth and explored. After a moment Ticannaf grinned and showed his mother and father a small white tooth. He rolled the tooth in the palm of his hand. He was a sturdy child with olive-brown skin and a mop of raven hair, which had never been cut. "Why did it come out?"

"It all began when Old Man Comanche walked be-side a big river looking for trouble." Sacajawea began laughing down at her son.

"Do not fill our son with made-up foolishness, Little Bird," growled Jerk Meat, taking his shield from Saca-jawea. He had four or five horse tails and a couple of mule tails attached to the rim to indicate he was an accomplished raider. These tails were attached with leather thongs to the underside of the shield. An outside cover of thin hide protected the shield, and around the rim of the cover were six feathers held in place with sinew.[2]

As they watched the men leave, Sacajawea continued with her story. "Old Man came to some ducks swimming in the reeds. They asked what he had in the skin pouch over his shoulder. Old Man told them it was songs. They asked him to stop and sing so they could dance. 'I'll sing you a legend of the People,' he said, 'if you keep your eyes shut.' He was thinking how good they would taste on a roasting stick. Old Man sang, and the ducks came out on the sand and danced. Then he took a stick and hit them on the head, one by one. But the last duck was suspicious and opened his eyes in time to save himself by flying away. Old Man built a fire and found a roasting stick, but he found one duck was missing and went off to look for it. While he was gone, Coyote came along and ate all those delicious roast ducks. Then he filled the empty carcasses with stones and put them back on the stick before he slunk off. Old Man came back empty-handed and hungry. He bit into the first duck, and all his front teeth broke off. He was madder than a mud dauber whose home is trampled on by a thick-skinned moose. He spit blood and swore and could not find anyone to get even with, so he picked on the small, teasing boys—like you, my son. He said that from that time on, all the young children would lose their teeth."

Ticannaf laughed, pushing his tongue in the gaping hole in front of his mouth.

Sacajawea pulled a chunk of venison from the cooking pot over the outside fire and carefully handed it to Ticannaf on a cedar stick. "There are no stones in this," she said, and went inside the tepee to pick up clothes for mending for the coming winter.

Buffalo were still present in the canyon, and some of the old men left behind went on hunts. Big Badger brought down one. The buffalo hair was good and thick at the start of winter, and the women decided to make a new bed robe for Big Badger. Spring and Sacajawea cut the meat in thin strips to dry on the rack. Hides

Well saved the heart and liver to dip into the gallbladder as delicious snacks for the next couple of days. Try as they would to shoo them away, flies, sweat bees, and yellow jackets gathered on the raw meat. Ticannaf washed his snacks off before eating. Wild Plum teased him, but he explained it was a protection that his mother had learned somewhere long ago among some strange people she had been with.

One afternoon as spring approached, Ticannaf tired of boiling hooves for arrow glue. Sacajawea took him with her as she rode up the rim of the canyon and onto the broad plain. They felt good. The early spring sunshine was warm on their faces. Ticannaf was beginning to ride very well.

He stopped and pointed down into the flat river valley where a stink was coming up on gusts with the wind. There were acres of whitening bones and the meat that had not been pulled off the slaughtered buffalo carcasses by scavengers was black with blow flies and putrefying in the hot sun. They were accustomed to the stench of bad meat, but this smell combined with the sight of the awful, plundered waste sickened mother and son.

Sacajawea was angry. As far as she could see, there were enough buffalo on the ground to feed the entire Comanche tribe, all the different bands, for nearly half a dozen winters.

"What did this?" asked Ticannaf.

"It must be the white men," she answered slowly.

"Why?"

"They wanted only the hides to make them rich so they can live better than their neighbors. It is a greed that some men have."

"What is this greed?"

"Oh, my son, it is a desire beyond reason for things— food, clothing, tobacco, guns, buffalo hides—or to manage other people. Greed makes men disrespectful of their friends, dishonest, and unkind. It is all bad."

"No entiendo."

"Men sometimes want things so much they will destory to get what they want. These terrible white men have destroyed good meat to get the thick hides of the buffalo. They can trade these hides for many supplies and lots of tea, tobacco, coffee, even for the women they wish."

"Were they *soldados*?"

"Quién sabe?"

Sacajawea gazed at the scene for a long time, thinking that the great beasts had been dead more than a week, and no one in the Quohadas' camp even knew the hunters had been so near. Her heart was on the ground. She knew that not all white men were friends. She turned crosswind back to camp in the secluded canyon.

She wanted to call a council immediately, but most of the important men were not there and it was not the place of a woman to call a council.

Sacajawea was angry.

She waited four days. In the meantime she talked with several of the old men as they left the Smoke Lodge, where they usually gathered each evening to smoke and talk. No boys or women were allowed in there with them. They went because they were mostly interested in the past. As they smoked they could enjoy the latest gossip or talk about deeds they performed long ago. Sometimes they had fun asking each other such embarrassing questions as, "Did you ever run away from the enemy?" They had no need to struggle for prestige and were wise, giving sound advice to prevent quarrels and the making of enemies.

They told her what they had heard or seen. White shooters could kill as many as thirty to forty buffalo a day. Each shooter had a dozen hide skinners and they came with white-topped wagons. The skinner stripped off the buffalo hides, leaving the carcasses along with the big woolly head. They sold the hides to other men in the forts. It was hard to understand why the white men needed all those hides.

She stood in front of the Council Lodge and called everyone to listen to her news. Those that saw a crowd in the center of the village came to see what was going on. She began by telling about the thousands of skinned buffalo lying in the river valley and ended with, "The white men are trampling upon our hearts. What are we going to do?"

"Hey-yah!" There was general agreement. A solitary drum began to beat slowly.

Sacajawea moved away from the circle, letting some old men step forward to give their ideas. She went close to Spring, who had Ticannaf and Wild Plum beside her. Wild Plum was making faces at the young girls who were skipping among the crowd. The sun was sinking toward the treetops.

"I think we had better all go to our lodges and get our evening meal," said Hides Well, moving among the women but staring intently at Sacajawea. "The men are not here, and we cannot do anything yet about the white raiders of our buffalo."

A few of the women got up to go. A few more followed. The singing continued, and Sacajawea heard *"Hey-yah"* over and over as some of the older women stamped their feet when they sang.

Big Badger passed from the old men's circle on his way to his lodge. "Bad, bad"—he shook his head—"this will be a bad night."

Sacajawea did not understand his remark. She was still angry from seeing all those wasted, rotting buffalo. It was hard to fathom the irresponsibility of the act. The night air had a chill on it. The smoke of fires hung everywhere.

While Sacajawea and Ticannaf were putting their bone spoons away, they heard someone singing. It grew louder, like a death chant. Sacajawea felt her pulse pounding in her throat. Something unusual was happening in the center of the village.

They walked until the lodges thinned out and they came to the center of the village, where the ground slanted downward into a natural arena. Here half a hundred women squatted along the gentle slope on all four sides, with twice as many children and half again as many old men. At the sight of Sacajawea, a heavy silence settled over the crowd. Nobody moved; they were watching. Everyone knew that a turning point was at hand. Gray Bone's lodge witnessed the first struggle. Not long before, Gray Bone had come out carrying the Mexican baby and dragging his resisting sister.

"It takes more than barking dogs to drive the fox from cover," someone had called.

And Gray Bone had answered back, "And so that non-Comanche, Lost Woman, talks fire to you, but her deeds are ashes! I make the flame!" She directed the placing of two posts of newly hewn cottonwood into the ground. Leather thongs were hung from each post. Several gaunt-faced women, shockingly pale, and a lone woman drummer sat in an open space beside the posts. A fire of cedar was kindled nearby. Its light glanced off the feverish eyes and bared teeth of the women, who began to sing and whose fervor increased as the Mexican girl and her brother were dragged to the fire.

Contempt was on Gray Bone's dark face. She moved to the center. The air was rent with her arguments for punishment. "We must not shrink from any measures!" she shouted. "These are offspring of the vile dogs who kill the buffalo, taking away our meat and hides! I have proof. This girl also takes. She takes extra broth for the wretched, squalling boy here. She steals a robe to cover herself at night. *Hey-yah!* I knew these two were sent to this village to gorge our food, pilfer our robes, so that we starve and freeze. Then their relatives will come and take over our village and our land. They are the enemy living in our camp!"

The children were bound hand and foot. The Mexican girl kicked and struggled; the baby cried.

Sacajawea sucked in her breath. She knew that Kicking Horse had kept them in his own lodge, treating them as well as his own children. The girl helped Gray Bone and the younger woman, Flower, with the lodge chores, and she seemed well liked. The baby was being raised as a son by Kicking Horse. He was to take the place of Wolf. Sacajawea pressed forward, using her elbows, until she reached the front row. In her everyday voice she ordered Gray Bone and the others to set the Mexican children free. "That," she said, "is not the sort of children they are. They are innocent. They can be Comanches, and we will be proud to have them in this tribe. So—that should be your choice. Take them home. They are frightened."

A few women raised objections. They wrangled for some time. Sacajawea repeated that Gray Bone had no other choice. The children were captives of her man,

Kicking Horse, and it was Gray Bone's duty to care for them.

"I'll take care of them!" Gray Bone shouted back.

Disconsolate, Big Badger moved behind Sacajawea, smiling helplessly. "You must come back, Lost Woman," he said.

Sacajawea stopped, and the crowd behind her was suddenly silent. Her face was as gray as the skins in her tunic. She stared at Big Badger as though she did not know him.

"You must come back, Lost Woman," Big Badger reiterated, nearly weeping with distress. "You cannot stop it now. You will only be hurt."

But Sacajawea took one step farther and began to shriek, "Children, can you hear me?"

The Mexican girl flung her head up and screamed.

"Can you hear me?" shrieked Sacajawea, waving her arms like banners. "We are not savages who mistreat children. I gave you my promise. No one will mistreat you. We all know Gray Bone has seen justice done and now goodwill is to come." Her Spanish was bad, but she used her hands out where she thought the girl could see.

A few in the crowd laughed; the rest were silent. A coarse voice cried, "Wait until Pronghorn comes—he'll put a stop to it all." Other voices joined in; the whole arena roared. Big Badger, near tears, pulled Sacajawea back. Still she shrugged off his hands.

"Free the children. They are not slaves!" she shrieked.

His eyes agape, Big Badger receded a step. His neighbors right and left quickly put out their arms to bar Sacajawea's way. It grew very quiet, and Sacajawea suddenly realized she stood alone in the empty space between these Quohadas and the others, Gray Bone's friends. Her knees gave; she reeled. Hides Well leaped forward because she thought she had been pierced by a skinning knife from the others, and supported her with her arms. The rest surged forward, too, and the empty space was obliterated by the crowd that pressed around the Mexican children.

There were several old dried scalps swinging from peeled white-willow wands implanted in the dirt. These seemed a clue to the occasion.

Gray Bone was in the center. In a shrill voice she recited glories that the Quohada men had performed in battle and then bragged about the number of slaves they had brought back from raids. Sacajawea could not recall anyone ever mentioning any other captives used as slaves since she had been with the Quohada band.

"And from now on, this tribe will punish anyone who kills our relatives or rips hides from our cousins, the buffalo! That is good, good, good," Gray Bone sang in a high, reedy falsetto. "We must give our enemies a lesson if they do not behave."

Some of the spectators' mouths tightened at the effrontery of the boasting, but a few of the women applauded with approval after each recitation, stamping their feet, clapping their hands, and vigorously shaking their gourd rattles.

"We must punish them."

Again there was agreement with hand-clapping, gourd-rattling, and shouts of *"Hey-yah!"*

A dancer in a long-fringed tunic with vermilion-and-black stripes painted on her face and arms, her beaded ear pendants and copper wire wristband glinting in the firelight, burst into a frenzied gait. It was She Cat. With a long, slow sweep of her hands through her hair, down her sides, and over her hips, she indicated that her enemy was the Mexican girl. She Cat crouched and looked wildly about, as though her victim had escaped. She bounded after her and, with a grunt of rage, went through the action of grabbing her by the hair and swinging a club downward.

Sacajawea's legs began to shake uncontrollably. The pantomimist pulled a knife from her bosom, stooped, and pretended to tear off the scalp. Then Gray Bone decided there had been enough pretending and snatched up one of the scalp poles. The black hair on the small willow hoop stirred in the air. Flourishing it triumphantly, she whirled around, arms spread, facing the four directions, one after the other, and tapped the Mexican girl on the head with the wand. A roar of approbation echoed off the canyon walls.

A wave of anguish overcame Sacajawea.

The Mexican girl and her brother were lashed to the two posts, back to back, the right hand high on one post and the left high on the other. Their bound legs were loosed so that their ankles could be secured to the bottoms of the posts. The two-year-old cried in pain, turning his head from left to right and keeping his eyes shut. Tears streamed down the girl's face, and her tied-up arms twitched again and again as she wanted to wipe the tears off.

Sacajawea looked from right to left at the women clustered about. She was remembering that when an enemy kills a Comanche, the Comanche's tribe kills or tortures its enemy captives in return. And at this remembrance a seed of fear germinated in the pit of her stomach.

Everything grew ominously quiet. The drum was hushed. All around, the audience stood gravely still, as if waiting for a new and more significant scene to start.

Big Badger moved with deliberation to the center, his arms flapping to the crowd. "Something is growing here that is bad," he said, trying to shout above the women, who now began to chatter. "Stop and all go home. Take the children home. Our chief is not here to advise us. Nothing must be done this night that we cannot undo or that would cause the men who are gone to look upon us with shame."

Gray Bone was not listening, She Cat was not listening, and the drummer, who was Weasel Woman, had begun again even before Big Badger finished. His head hung on his chest, and he was swallowed up by the crowd. Feet stamped in a rhythmic beat on the dirt to the beat of the drum. There they were, led by She Cat, the dancer, a long line of painted squaws with their hair plastered upward with cactus spines and river clay. Each carried a skinning knife in one hand and a gourd rattle in the other.

Sacajawea stared at them, entranced by the deliberateness and confidence these women showed. They seemed in no hurry, advancing slowly, with a half shuffle. They glided forward; then back, left and right. The onlookers remained still.

Sacajawea gaped at Gray Bone. Her stomach twitched, her buttocks jiggled, and the strands of hair poking up from the cactus spines waved in the wind. Bowlegged and pigeon-toed, she looked old and wiz-

ened, her slit-eyes boring hypnotically into the eyes of
the crowd. The rattling gourds grew louder, and Sacajawea braced herself. If Big Badger could not stop them,
how could she? Ticannaf was clinging lightly to her
skirt, yet his eyes were fixed on the spectacle in front
of him.

The Mexican girl screamed shrilly. With a swift, dex-
trous stroke of Gray Bone's knife, a tiny patch of thick
black hair was scalped off. Next, the women dancers
drew their knife points across the midsection of the girl
and small boy, ripping their clothing and cutting deep
red gashes.

Rage and revulsion shook Sacajawea. The chanting
women formed a serpentine line. Sacajawea called out,
"Stop! Stop! Do not harm them! They have done nothing
to you!" The line slithered around the children, slashing
at them. Sacajawea lifted her gaze to the stars. She
sucked in a long gulp of the night air and began to pray
to the Great Spirit. "Stop them, stop them, stop them!"

She heard the barbaric uproar, the advancing and
retreating. Her legs were locked in terror and in an
effort to keep them from shaking. In another moment
a dull rushing of air sounded in her ears, the sky turned
black, and the singing retreated to someplace far away.
She felt ill. Hides Well again pulled her up. Her legs
were so deadened that she found it difficult to walk.

"Do not do anything more!" Sacajawea croaked. "Go
home! These are only children. They are frightened and
hurt. Take them home!"

Gray Bone made more slashes across the shoulders
of the girl. Her knife stabbed at the baby. His howling
stopped. Blood flowed down from his chest to the dirt.

Sacajawea began to push forward.

"No, not now," Hides Well said. "You cannot stop
this. Even together we cannot stop this."

Sacajawea had seen the dull fish-eyes of Gray Bone
and the great sadness that lay like a lake behind her
pupils. She also saw that the Mexican girl no longer
breathed. The girl's face was mutilated with knife
slashes. Her entrails lay bloody upon the ground.

Gray Bone yelled, "They killed my son, but they will
kill no more! Dirty Mexicans!"

Sacajawea realized Ticannaf was standing at her side.

She put her hand on his shoulder and wished he had not witnessed this evil thing. She thought there must have been something of the same kind of brutality, the same indifference to suffering and rights of others in those twenty-two white men who raced through the empty Quohada village, setting fire and burning tepees in a furious desperation to destroy the thing that would not fight back.

She could not sleep. She heard the restless turning and moving about that Ticannaf made in his bed. Her logic finally made her admit calmly and quietly in the middle of the night that it was she, Sacajawea, who had stirred up that great, black, ugly thing in Gray Bone and the other Quohada women this night. She had not meant that to happen, but not meaning such a thing did no good. It was that impulsive thing in her—the thing that caused her to speak before the women and children and old men as if she were a chief in council— that had been bad. She was the bad influence. She bit her tongue. Jerk Meat would have a perfect right to beat me, she thought. I am truly a bad squaw. Her tears of self-pity spilled into the darkness.

The next morning, Sacajawea rose in the gray dawn and with quick steps hurried to the center arena. There the two cold bodies hung lifeless, mangled, and crusted dull red. Sacajawea unbound them, stuffed the cold entrails into the gaping cavity of the girl's belly, and dragged them to her own tepee, one at a time.

"Mother!" cried Ticannaf. "What do you do?"

"I am washing my conscience," she told her son. She washed the bodies with warm water and wrapped them in clean white doeskins. She then wrapped them in heavy buffalo hide and bound them up together. The load was much too heavy for her now. She went to the lodge of Hides Well.

"Mother, I must have help. I must have help in making the burial hut for the bodies of the Mexican children so they will be safe from wolves and coyotes."

"You, Lost Woman, have prepared their bodies for burial?"

"*Ai*, my mother. It is I who killed them."

"I have thought of that. I have also thought it was bound to happen because I think something evil possessed Gray Bone. Maybe you started her last night, but if you had not been so angry with the white hunters, and had kept your tongue silent, something else would have unleashed the dark spirit in Gray Bone. It is tangled with the heavy grief she carries for the death of her son."

CHAPTER

48

Shooting Stars

On November 12, 1833 a dazzling shower of meteors blazed across the night sky. All America saw them. In Independence frightened Missourians were convinced that heaven was protesting against recent mobbings and whippings of the Mormons. In Santa Fe horrified Mexicans were sure that the state had brought a flaming curse on itself by denying certain privileges to the Church. While the skies dripped fire, while William Bent and the other traders watched from Bent's Fort's unfinished walls, the visiting Cheyennes decked themselves in full battle regalia of feather and paint, lance and shield. They could not fight this fearful tumbling down of the stars, but at least they would die like men. Women cried and children shrieked. The dogs howled back at the chorusing wolves. Chanting their death dirges above the din, the warriors rode in single file around the tepees, under the shadow of the mud bastions.

The next morning the sun shone again. The young men laughed at their alarm and stories of the night the stars fell passed into folk tale.

DAVID LAVENDER, *Bent's Fort*. New York: Doubleday and Co., 1954, pp. 143–44.

The warriors returned from Mexico in a state of gaiety. No Quohada had lost his life, and they had traded hides for awls, axes, knives, kettles, a few old guns, and silver bracelets and earrings for the women. There was to be a celebration.

Sacajawea hurried out to meet Jerk Meat. She found him in front of the tepee of Kicking Horse. The men were talking, their faces dark and grave. They saw her and came forward.

"Is it true that you provoked Gray Bone into this murderous thing?"

"I do not think she—" began Jerk Meat.

"Let her tell her story," said Kicking Horse.

Sacajawea told first how she had come in angry, and without thinking had told all the people about the wasted buffalo.

"You acted like some chief woman?" asked Jerk Meat.[1]

Her head hung low. She was much ashamed. Kicking Horse had his pipe out and was making little sucking noises, as though impatient to get on with the rest of it.

"We saw white men load hides on carts drawn by mules and go toward the white villages. Many hides and no meat," added Jerk Meat.

"Let her speak," said Kicking Horse, pointing to Sacajawea with his pipe.

She told the whole thing as best she could remember, even telling how she had dragged the bodies to her tepee and prepared them for a proper Comanche burial. She told how Hides Well had helped. She pointed in the direction of the newly made burial hut.

"Woman," said Jerk Meat, without seeming to move a muscle, "do not speak with a forked tongue. Hides Well had no part in this hideous thing."

"*Ai*, the load was heavy for me. I asked her to help. We talked. We talked about the spirit that sometimes possesses Gray Bone."

Kicking Horse was very quiet. He stopped sucking his pipe. "It is difficult to face truth about someone you

1047

once thought you loved," he said, then walked away
with his head hanging low.

Later in the day, shrill cries and the sound of blows
came from the direction of Gray Bone's lodge. She bolted
out screaming with pain. Behind her moving nimbly,
ran Kicking Horse. He held a cedar club in his right
hand. Overtaking Gray Bone, he struck her from behind and knocked her flat on the rough ground.

"Do not go sniffling and hiding your face like a child
when I am talking to you. When I tell you to pack, do
it. Take your things and get out. From this day on, I
will say I do not know you. I have never seen you.
Vamos!"

Gray Bone sobbed harder, trying to rise, red welts
showing on her arms and neck.

"Stop that howling and move. You are no longer fit
to be a Quohada Comanche. I will endure no more from
you." Kicking Horse swung the club again with all his
strength. Gray Bone tried to stifle a pain-crazed cry.
Scrambling up, she got to her feet and stumbled back
into the tepee, moaning. Kicking Horse dropped the
club and seated himself under a tree. He began to smoke
with sucking noises. In the tepee behind him, Kicking
Horse knew, Gray Bone was composing a prayer, her
face set rigid and her muscles hard, to force the Great
Spirit to give Kicking Horse compassion. She would
tear the compassion out of the Great Spirit's hands, for
she needed it desperately this time, and because the
need was great and the desire was great, her little secret prayer was louder than she would have wished.

Kicking Horse's eyes were dark, but in decency he
pulled himself up straight and stood in front of the tepee
until Gray Bone had packed her things and moved away,
alone, from the village.

The news traveled fast. Kicking Horse was without
one of his women. All manner of people grew interested
in Kicking Horse—people with no thought about his
powers as Medicine Man. The news stirred up something curious in these people. Every father with a full-
grown daughter not yet married wanted her to parade
inconspicuously in front of Kicking Horse's tepee. Every
mother with an eligible daughter urged her to groom
and clean herself and keep a pleasing smile on her face.

Later, Jerk Meat came to Sacajawea with a dark look. "You must prepare to move."

She drew in her breath, and her mouth made a small O. Jerk Meat explained that Pronghorn was furious about the wasted buffalo meat. He was still ranting, and because he thought the camp was in danger of being discovered with white men coming so close, he had called the council and decided that the entire camp must pack up and move out.

"My man," said Sacajawea, wanting to know why Jerk Meat had this black mood over his soul that he did not rub out, "do you feel you must banish me from your lodge as Kicking Horse has done with his woman?"

Jerk Meat shuddered; he ground his teeth together.

She touched him. At her touch he shivered. She thought she could understand his mood a little. She knew she had been outspoken, but it was not the first time a squaw had warned of impending danger. She had not been too far out of line to tell about the destruction of the buffalo and the nearness of the white men. And how could she have known Gray Bone would act like that? But that was it. If anyone should have known that Gray Bone would use such an occasion to draw the attention to herself, it was she, Sacajawea. "Speak to your woman. I would know what your trouble is. We are as one."

He shuddered some more. He spoke. His voice cracked. "Oh, my woman, Gray Bone, who once lived in the same lodge with our friend Kicking Horse, has said she will banish you from the Quohada band whenever her opportunity arrives. She declares you are the chief troublemaker for the band."

"Do you believe that?"

"No, but I believe that things happen because people cause them to."

"That woman can do nothing to me. Do not believe what she says to you."

"I had a dream. In the dream you were forced to leave the Quohadas. Again you wandered in the plains with no one to care for you."

"That was a dream, my man. I will stay with you. I will not go away."

A massive breath made his chest shudder. He swallowed again and again. "Oh, Lost Woman, my Pajarita, I could not live without you. It would be like losing my right arm and leg to have you gone. It is a feeling so deep that I think it very rare and valuable. I think not many men feel so about their women. I could not do as Kicking Horse. I do not want another woman. You never complain about working alone. Many men's women would."

Sacajawea fell silent. What could she say to comfort her man? "I am yours and you are mine. I love you as I have never loved any person. I shall never love a man after you. You are all."

Suddenly a voice from behind the tepee shouted to them. "Look! Come see!"

It was Ticannaf, and there were six small brown trout in his willow net.

Jerk Meat said, "My son, did Big Badger teach you this art of catching fish?"

"No, it was my mother," said Ticannaf, smiling. "She puts the water worms, peeled from their stony homes, inside the net and tells me to lay it in the foamy water." The boy's hair had the shine of a burnished crow.

"Mother of Ticannaf, come here," ordered Jerk Meat. "In my leather pouch I have something for you that I found in Mexico. It is a light-maker."

She turned the wax candle around in her hand and admired it. A smile made her lips upturned, and her eyes sparkled. "It is beautiful. I like its color of red. And I will tell you something. I will tell you how this stick was made." She began telling the astonished man and boy how she had watched Judy Clark make candles from lye of ashes and tallow. In the evening she showed them how the light could be moved from dark corner to dark corner to make it light. Jerk Meat and Ticannaf were fascinated by the tiny yellow flame and did not want her to blow it out until daylight. Then it was melted down to a nub of soft wax. Jerk Meat thought his woman knew more than five other Comanche women put together.

In the morning, the women struck the tepees, and the band moved out to search for a fresh campsite. They met three members of the *Nokoni*, Wanderers, band who had been to San Carlos. They were loaded with colored shawls and trinkets. They rode beside Prong-horn and Jerk Meat and discussed the nature of the whites and their coming into the Comanche lands. They were also disturbed about the skinned buffalo being left for the buzzards.

"Of course," said a young man with great silver disks in his hair plaits, "the Great Spirit knows the whites' disposition. He gave them books and taught them to read so they know what is right and wrong. We Co-manches know that without a book."

Sacajawea was about ready to say something, but Jerk Meat caught her look in time and made a face that meant, "Hold that tongue, woman."

"There is talk of a big raid on one of the white forts past the Moving Mountains. You Quohadas could come and help," said another Nokoni.

Jerk Meat rather liked the idea of traveling a great distance and raiding the white men's fort. That would be something to discuss on long winter nights.

That evening, the three Nokonis were made welcome by Chief Pronghorn. Kicking Horse danced around the fire for them in his finest headdress. He had taken a new woman to share the lodge chores with his young woman, Flower. The new woman was *Pahahty*, To-gether, a widow with two small sons. Kicking Horse was like a grandfather with the boys; he wanted to show them to all the Quohadas in one evening. He could not stay away from their side; he wanted them to know about his medicine, and his raiding abilities, and his horsemanship. The little boys were only hungry and sleepy; they wanted to curl up in their mother's lap. Together was a pleasant-looking young woman whom Sacajawea had seen around the camp. She wished them both much happiness.

Together served hot broth to the three Nokoni strangers at the request of Kicking Horse so that the good cooking ability of his new woman would be known by all the camp.

Round Belly came simpering outside the tepee and eyed the warrior with the large silver plates in his hair. She moved a little closer to him, until finally she was very near. He looked at her and forgot to drink his broth. She asked him a question. He nodded his approval. Round Belly ducked into the tepee and came out with a dried buffalo tongue and began to undo his long braids, taking out the silver plates. She brushed his hair all the while the men spoke of planning a raid against the white men.

"We do not want the white men to plan a raid against us," said Pronghorn. "There are white men and more white men. There are only this many Quohadas," he said, extending his arm around his camp.

The men talked more. "Will you come if we plan a raid?" one warrior asked once more.

"No, we will not go on large raids against the whites, only small ones to keep them back. Small ones are irritating and keep them from moving into our lands completely. We like the old way of keeping to ourselves unless provoked."

"Then you will not stand up as our brothers?"

"We will help your old women and old men and children when you are all killed by whites," answered Pronghorn.

One of the warriors pulled on the fellow having his is hair combed.

"The only way you can get her to stop is to take her as your woman," said Kicking Horse, joking.

"I will take her, then," said the Nokoni warrior, laying all the hammered silver disks at the feet of Kicking Horse; then he brought the horse he was leading over and tied him at the side of Kicking Horse's lodge.

Round Belly smiled shyly and went inside the tepee. In minutes she came out dressed in her finest tunic, with whangs at the bottom, and her hair slicked with deer tallow until it shone. Flower said, "Your father will miss you." Together said, "Obey your man, my daughter. Send us word when you can." Round Belly smiled as she mounted the Nokoni's horse behind her wooer.

Kicking Horse himself was dumbfounded. He was attracted to the silver disks, but he never in the world believed that his daughter would find someone who would take her, and he never believed he would have such fascinating medicine objects as the silver disks. His smile of approval came finally and was broad, showing his straight, horselike teeth.

The Quohadas cheered and clapped as the three No-koni men and Round Belly rode off. "She was lucky to find a rich and brave man," they said. "She was lucky."

In the year following that summer, Spring was given trinkets by Wounded Buck, who had lost his woman during a siege of the winter sickness. Wounded Buck had taken Wild Plum out on short excursions looking for deer and antelope. Once when he brought Wild Plum back to Spring, he told how the boy had shot the deer. Spring was proud. "Now, my son, you can supply our tepee with meat."

"It is my place to do that," said Wounded Buck. "I am going to care for you and the boy as my own." After that, their ensuing marriage was the talk of the camp.

Wounded Buck had proved himself a strong warrior, but not until he had brought in a Kiowa scalp. Before that, the most he had done was to steal a rifle and a couple of horses. He had lost the rifle before he got back to camp, and the horses were not staked one night and wandered off.

The women talked about the match. Some said they were surprised that Spring had not taken a man sooner because she could have had her pick of the bachelors. Someone even suggested they were surprised Kicking Horse had not chosen her, because he was always at the lodge of her brother, Jerk Meat, eyeing and jab-bering with the one called Lost Woman. A few laughed at this sly joke.

Wounded Buck brought three fine horses to the lodge of Pronghorn. He and Hides Well came out dressed in their best; then Big Badger came out and acted sur-prised. Spring led the horses to her father's herd, and Wounded Buck led her shyly to the tepee that Sacaja-wea and Hides Well had fixed for them. Pronghorn sent Big Badger around to announce the event and declare Wounded Buck a member of his family, which everyone already knew.

Before the exciting day was over, Sacajawea felt the first stab of pain go from her abdomen around to her back. She hated to miss the fun, but quickly she dragged an old robe behind a thicket of low-growing piñons. She did not want to have the others miss the festivities by

stopping to build a birth lodge for her. It seemed to take
a long time to get to the flat place behind the chaparral.
The baby was born quickly. It was a girl. Sacajawea
was glad, even though there would be no celebration
for a girl. She wrapped the papoose in a thin, soft skin
after tying the cord with rawhide whangs from her skirt.
Then she dozed off and on for the rest of the afternoon.
The sun was beginning to turn the thin streak of clouds
bright pink when she awakened and lazily watched a
brown butterfly hover over the sleeping papoose. Sacajawea got weakly to her feet and drank several handfuls of cool water from the stream. She cleaned herself
slowly, then cleaned the baby, who cried as the cold
water hit her little back and front. That evening, the
women ooed and ahed over the new Quohada. "Tiny,"
someone said, "but well formed. See her hands flutter
like the butterflies."

They moved south for the winter, which passed easily. The stream around which the camp was centered
froze, and the boys and girls slid and played games on
it. The stream did not go dry; sometimes the antelope
came to drink from the holes the men had chopped in
the ice, and the men would lie in hiding to kill them.
The Quohadas had fresh meat regularly. They had not
seen any sign of the *taibo*, white hunters, or their wagon
trains for some time now, and they were feeling more
secure and free in their own lands, more like the old
times.

The members of the band now seemed to accept Sacajawea. They spoke to her freely, and when she had a
heavy load to lift, any of the women might come over
to help. She felt more relaxed and willing to help when
a mother came to her with an ailing child. The Medicine
Man, Kicking Horse, did not seem to mind that she had
special knowledge, such as how to cut a cross on a rattlesnake bite, then suck the poison out.

One time, a warrior came to her with a huge piece
of lead lodged in his side. The side had become red and
inflamed. She had him go to the spring and stand in
the pool waist-deep, bathing the wound. The warrior
could not stand straight. After a while, she commanded
him to stand up and push out on his stomach muscles.

The warrior did with great effort, and the black blood oozed from his side. The second time he did it, the lead popped out in his hand. Sacajawea had him stand with the wound in the water for several minutes. Then she warned him not to put his hands near the wound, nor to put the fur of a beaver over it, nor wet buffalo dung. "You must keep only clean grass and a strip of soft skin over the hole." Her reputation as a wise woman grew in the band.

As the seasons followed one another, she taught many little girls to sew and make beautiful patterns of flowers and trees and animals on the yokes of their tunics. This knowledge she had gathered partly from the memory of her own grandmother's teachings, partly from the Mandans and Minnetarees, and partly from Judy Clark. The Comanche women had never seen anyone so creative. They encouraged their girls to learn her patterns of embroidery with colored quills.

One evening, Jerk Meat stared into the dying lodge fire thinking that it was now time for Ticannaf to go to his place of dreaming. To him, the boy did not seem old enough, although he had been alive fourteen summers. "I know a place Ticannaf must go," said Jerk Meat.

"That is only part of what you know," teased Sacajawea. "Our boy must go alone. You cannot help him. That is the way."

"*Ai*, but I must show him the place." He leaned forward. "All this—the stars, the tepee fires, the ways of our people—all this is good. But I know other things. There are now dead buffalo on the plains; there are soldiers and hunters on our hunting grounds."

"My man, there are no soldiers around here."

"They will come."

"And so—the Quohadas will move."

Jerk Meat smiled. "The Quohadas will fight."

"I have heard those words many times," she said. "You will fight, and I will fight with you when the time comes. But before that our son must go to his place of dreaming. And we will think of a better way than fighting."

Jerk Meat looked across the fire. Ticannaf and Butterfly were already asleep on their robes.

At daybreak, Ticannaf called to his father, who was getting out of his sleeping robes. "Let's go! Come on! We can race the wind!"

"Take me! Take me!" Butterfly held up her arms to her big brother. "I will not cry. I will not make any trouble."

"This is no trip for girls," Ticannaf growled. "It is only for braves."

"You are not yet a brave," said Butterfly, pulling at the tassels that hung from the back of Ticannaf's moccasins.

"I will be in four suns. Count. I will be back in four suns."

Father and son were gone.

Sacajawea tried to tell her small dark-eyed daughter how it was for a young man to go off alone and seek his personal medicine. "It is a time when Ticannaf has only the wind for company. He will not eat or drink. He will let his spirit flow with the animals and plants. When his spirit is free he will talk in a stronger voice than the others and he will remember it all his life. That one will be his protector, his personal medicine. From then on, in any time of need for himself or his people, Ticannaf will be able to talk with his protector and he will receive advice. This is a time for strengthening from the inside for Ticannaf. When we see him again, he will be a man. This is the Comanche way."[2]

Jerk Meat and Ticannaf rode until dusk. They made camp in a small grove of wind-stunted oaks where there was grass and a spring for the horses. The place was familiar to Jerk Meat. They built a fire. The evening was not cold. They ate the pemmican in silence. Jerk Meat waited for the sun to go down completely. Then he called his son to his side.

"You are here," he said.

"I am ready," Ticannaf nodded.

"From this very spot many years ago, I set out for the Hill. It is now less than a day's ride. Can you find it?"

"Ai."

"You follow the stream toward the river until you come to the two hills that rise above the plains like the breasts of a woman. The hill that looks down upon the other is the Hill. The signs are good, I think."

"I will find my protector."

"Here, take these things with you." Jerk Meat gave his son a bone pipe, tobacco, and an old fire drill in a buffalo-horn case. The boy had a good buffalo robe of his own. "Cleanse yourself in the spring tonight; go on in the morning." Jerk Meat thought of the Hill sitting in a twisted, rough world of blown sand and jutting rocks, where brown-yellow canyons slashed the earth and the buttes reared into the high, searching winds.

"I will return with the *puha*, medicine power. I swear it."

Jerk Meat's sharp-lined face was dark and grim in the early blackness. "You are my only son, *tua*. Come back. Do not take risks. There are unknowns in this country. You will be weak from the fasting and nights with no sleep—"

"A man must go himself when he seeks the vision," Ticannaf said. "Nothing can harm me when I have my medicine."

"So it is said." Jerk Meat wanted to tell him that he had seen many men die who had good medicine. That Big Badger was not always correct in his teachings, that good medicine was not everything, that he, Jerk Meat, was beginning to wonder if it was really anything. But he could not say these profane things to his son. Not at this time. "You must take great care."

Ticannaf was excited. He was in no mood to listen to words of caution. "I will remember what you have said. I must go now to the spring and make myself clean."

Jerk Meat watched his fourteen-year-old son, graceful as a young buck, as he ran toward the water. Slowly Jerk Meat went to his horse and headed toward the Quohada camp to sleep by the side of his beloved, Lost Woman.

Halfway home, he saw the small white tents of the soldiers. He saw the horses staked behind the tents. There seemed to be only one cart carrying supplies, and the horses still wore their packs. The small fires were barely visible through the mesquite. At first he did not understand this camp, then slowly it came to him— this was a war party camping. He crept closer to count the horses and tents. There were enough to fill both hands three times. He crept back to his horse, mounted quietly, and turned to circle the camp, avoiding the vedettes, the mounted guards, around the outskirts.

Then he rode his horse to a lather, not bothering to picket him as he ran to the lodge of Pronghorn. He reported the party of white soldiers camped near. Between them they decided the soldiers would sleep through the night and move out during the daylight. "Let our warriors sleep," said Pronghorn, "they will be more prepared to fight tomorrow."

"I cannot sleep until I know what these *taibo* intend to do," said Jerk Meat.

"They are not looking for us. We have done them no harm," said Pronghorn.

"But Comanches have raided against the wagon trains and the small groups of whites in the forts," said Jerk Meat.

"We wait. By tomorrow night they will have moved out and be gone. I will send scouts out to watch them."

The alarm sounded before dawn. A party of mounted soldiers was seen approaching in the direction of the village.

Some of the women were building the morning fires when the warning came. They gathered their belongings into baskets, boxes, and neat piles. The men were ordered to burn the tepees. Sacajawea collected her belongings and supplies, put on the old, worn, and faded blue coat, tied her leather bag of small treasures to her waistband, and placed a small bundle under Butterfly's arm.

Pronghorn deployed the men quickly and ordered the women out of the area of burning tepees, over the stream and into a small canyon. Sacajawea slipped a clumsy bundle of extra clothing for her family on her back.

Pronghorn had sent half of his warriors around the enemy's right, a trick taught him by the Mexicans, to move the point of combat away from the camp and give the women an opportunity to get away.

The white soldiers had already received their in-

structions. Instead of moving in to fight off the coun-
terattack from the right, or moving back to hinder
encirclement, they split their forces, half of them going
on the flank attack and the other half moving forward.

The women struggled across the stream and down
the sides of the canyon. Hides Well seemed to be in
command. She motioned to this one and that. "Hurry,
hurry, over this way, duck down. Drop the baggage,"
Hides Well panted. "It is of no importance."

"Where is Spring?" asked Sacajawea, slipping the
bundle from her back, glad to be rid of the clumsy burden.

"She is coming. Save your breath and do not hurt
yourself on these rocks."

Sacajawea looked around. Spring was coming down
between two large rocks. Butterfly stood and waved to
her. Then the child lost her footing and fell. Her foot
wedged between a knotted cedar and a large boulder.
She screamed. Sacajawea scrambled to her. She knelt
and tried to loosen the child's foot.

"My leg," sobbed Butterfly.

There was a shrill cry from above. The soldiers had
pushed their way across the camp, across the stream,
to the edge of the canyon. The air was filled with smoke
from the burning lodges.

Sacajawea lifted the cedar to free the tiny brown foot.
She gave her child a pat to reassure her the foot was
not hurt badly. "Hurry on," she said. Butterfly straightened and moved toward the bottom of the canyon. Then
a bullet struck Butterfly in the middle of her back, and
she fell forward, sliding a little on her face.

Sacajawea screamed when she saw Butterfly try to
stand. The child's mouth overflowed with blood, and
she fell again. Her face lay on a jagged rock. Her breath
came in shallow wheezes.

Above, the soldiers had left the edge of the ravine
and were milling around the smoking camp. They could
not see anything in the blinding smoke. They were at
a disadvantage. The Quohadas knew every inch of their
ground and fought as individuals. The soldiers finally
retreated.

Pronghorn ordered his men to the ravine to join the
women. He sent others to get their horses. He hurried

down the steep incline, his eyes watering from smoke. He stumbled over Sacajawea, who held Butterfly in her arms. He bent down and saw the bright red stain on the child's back. He gently lifted her and put her over his shoulder, then continued down the ravine, motioning for Sacajawea to come down beside him.

The women had gathered in a shelter at the far end of the canyon. Sacajawea gently prodded Pronghorn's elbow and motioned for him to lay the child on the cool sand. She bathed the little brown face with water from someone's waterskin. Butterfly opened her dark eyes.

"Do not be angry with me, Mother," she said.

"Oh, no!"

Blood spilled down each side of her mouth. She looked at Sacajawea and smiled. Sacajawea held her in her arms and gently rocked back and forth. Tears streamed down Sacajawea's face. The child was not breathing.

Sacajawea covered her face with black mud. She wrapped her girl-child in a hide and placed her at the end of the ravine where she had died. Sacajawea piled stones around the body, then covered it with stones so that wolves and other prey could not get in. This was in the manner of the Shoshoni when there were no trees to put the body into. She sat at the side of the grave and tried to feel the presence of her little girl. She sat there through the rest of the afternoon and through the evening and into the night, picking up little stones and dropping them, staring at the grave.

Near the middle of the night the sky seemed aflame with stars that were falling. Sacajawea watched, bewildered, feeling that the sky would forever after be black with no stars at all. At length she hid her head and listened to the death wails and shrieking of the others who were camped above the ravine. She wondered if Jerk Meat was in camp and decided he must be rounding up the horses with some of the other men. Could he see the sky? she wondered. She was afraid to move. When she looked up again the sky was streaked with the blazing meteors. The meteor shower continued for some time. She thought she heard the wolves howling above the camp's mourning cries, and she imagined that other women had covered their faces with mud or ashes and torn at their hair until it fell loose.

A long shudder racked Sacajawea. She pulled her knees up under her chin and folded her arms across them and laid her head on her arms again. Her shoulders shook. No sound came from her, but she was racked with a terrible shaking. Finally she looked at the sky and saw a brightening toward the east. The shooting stars had quieted, and there were only a few long streaks lighting up the dark sky. She thought, Could it be that they are lighting a path so that my child can easily find her way to the Other Side? *Ai*, that could be it. "Hold your chin up, my child, the path is well lit," she whispered.

In the afternoon, Sacajawea went up into the camp. She found Jerk Meat sleeping by the picketed horses. She sat beside him and told him quickly how his daughter had been killed. "Do not hold yourself in," she said. "Even a man may cry."

Jerk Meat cut off the hair on the left side of his head and said nothing. He walked around the burned-out village and then walked to the top of the ravine and stared at the pile of stones. He sat beside the grave, mourning and refusing to eat.

Sacajawea tried to change the expression of his turned-down lips by talking of the night's shooting stars. She asked if there would be stars left for the coming night, but it was useless to talk. He continued to mourn in silence, but on the third day he began to smoke and pray.

Sacajawea gave away all of her cooking utensils and her sewing box and materials. All of the dead child's clothing and toys, trinkets and ornaments were pushed into the ravine by Sacajawea. There were times when a powerful nausea came over her and she had to sit and breath deeply to overcome the feeling.

In the night when it rained she put an old buffalo robe over Jerk Meat's shoulders and sat with him. He ignored her. On the morning of the fourth day he walked back to the burned ashes of the tepee, then to the temporary camp the others had set up. He looked around and slowly went back to the ravine for Sacajawea.

"Come, our son will be back. He must not find his mother and father gone." He could not control his voice. He reached for her and clung, sobbing. He let the tears fall freely down his cheeks. After several moments he pulled away and put his hand on his woman's thin brown one. "We must not talk of the child again. We will never forget the Night That the Stars Fell. In the camp everyone was afraid. Kicking Horse said it was a warning that many Quohadas would fall out of sight. Pronghorn said you were caring for the child. I thought you comforted her."

"You must not speak of her." Sacajawea paused and brushed her hand across Jerk Meat's lips. "A part of me is gone. My heart is on the ground, and I cannot pick it up."

"*Ai*, mine is there beside yours."

They helped each other up the embankment. Other families mourned their dead. The Quohadas had lost four young men. Hides Well came to them, her eyes reddened. "Have you heard? Father is dead. Some of the men found him crouched against a tree with a hole in his chest. His bow was in his lap, and an arrow was clutched so tightly in his hand that they could not remove it."

Sacajawea stared at her, then shook her head as if to clear it. "I'll help with the burial preparations."

Hides Well put out her hand and shook her head. "No. Pronghorn means to make a long distance today. We have been in this place too long. We are moving out right away. Are you ready?"

Jerk Meat left to get the horses.

"But who will wrap Big Badger?"

"There is no time. We are leaving. He is not important any longer." Hides Well tried to cover her grief.

Sacajawea walked slowly along the *bajada* to the horses. She found Jerk Meat standing around, doing nothing, as if he did not know what to do next. "We will wait at this place for our son. And we will give the grandfather a proper burial," she said.

"Hides Well will like that," he said.

The Quohadas finished loading their few belongings and left just before the clouds parted and the sun went behind the hill. Hides Well waved from the top of the hill. Spring called, "I'm sure you can follow our trail to the new camp."

Then Sacajawea and Jerk Meat used their last good

hide to wrap Big Badger. "Take care of our girl-child," Sacajawea whispered in Big Badger's dead ear. They tied him tightly and spent much time on the burial hut.

"I hope he finds a good fat antelope in the Happy Hunting Ground," said Jerk Meat.

"I have been wondering if white men will be with us in that place where there is always dancing and feasting," she said.

Jerk Meat looked at his woman quizzically, but said nothing. He was remembering his childhood and the good times he had had with his grandfather as they rode on the plains in the hot sun or in the cold rain. He remembered the straight arrows they made together and the first time he shot a bear. Big Badger had jumped up and down for happiness. The lodge of Pronghorn would never be the same anymore. It would be like a tepee with a large hole ripped in its side.

Sacajawea dreamed of the pleasure she felt when Big Badger took over the manhood training of Ticannaf. She dreamed of the enjoyment he had showing Butterfly the trick of pulling plum pits from his ears. She cried for the sadness Ticannaf would feel when he returned to find no small sister in his tepee and no greatgrandfather to tell his medicine dream to.

In the morning, Sacajawea asked, "Could we travel forward a short distance to meet our son as he returns?"

"That would be good. But we must not get close to the Hill for fear of destroying the new manhood of him."

"I do not intend to go get him. Just meet him on his way back."

"All right, get those packs on the horses," said Jerk Meat.

Toward evening they spotted him, a solitary figure on the hot, empty plains. He was jogging along in the general direction of the old camp, and he was taking his time. His roan horse blended in with the mesquite and the brush and the dark yellow earth. He seemed not to have a care in the world.

Sacajawea grinned. Jerk Meat rode a little faster.

"I had a vision! I am a man!" They heard his joyous voice call, and they waved their arms to him.

Then suddenly, when he was close enough, he sucked in his breath a little. "What is wrong? Where is Big

Badger? And the others? My crybaby sister? I want to
tell Big Badger about my vision. Maybe he can see
meaning in it."

Sacajawea could not hold back the flood of tears. For
a moment she could not speak. The young man looked
from one parent to the other. Jerk Meat told him of the
battle with the soldiers who turned tail and ran from
the Quohadas. Soon Sacajawea was filling in details.
Ticannaf wept and vowed he would shoot two white
men each for the death of his sister and great-grandfather.

"Do not make rash claims at the moment of sorrow,"
warned Jerk Meat.

The Comanches lived with danger every day, so that
death was a reality anticipated. They lived life with
joy, but death was greeted by the tribe with great passion and ritual. Sorrow among the living was deeply
felt.

The family of Jerk Meat lived near the lodge of
Pronghorn and Hides Well in the new winter place.
Spring and Wounded Buck lived near. Wild Plum was
eyeing the girls. It would be no time before he had a
woman of his own.

Ticannaf was given a special invitation to attend the
first council held in the village that fall. He was to sit
in the first circle of men and tell his medicine vision.
The Shaman, Kicking Horse, was to interpret the dream
if there were questions as to its full meaning.

Ticannaf was nervous about what he was going to
say in front of all the important men. He practiced day
after day in the tepee so that he would not forget and
leave out some small but important detail.

Sacajawea listened, but kept her mouth closed.
Women were not supposed to hear about the holy vision.
It was for men's ears only. Ticannaf did not consider
his mother's ears; in fact, he was so engrossed in his
own thoughts of manhood and his vision that he hardly
noticed her at all.

His speech was long. He started from the time he
could see the Hill. He could not mistake it. There it
was up ahead, tall and silent. His father had dreamed
on the same Hill, perhaps his grandfather, Pronghorn,

and his older grandfather, the one now gone. Perhaps the Thunderbird himself lived on the Hill. The Thunderbird was immense and colored dark blue with jagged yellow markings, like the lightning that rent the sky. He had seen one of the sacred places where the Thunderbird had touched Mother Earth. There was a mark, a broken tree, ripped down the center, the white wood exposed and splintered. The branches of the tree hung outstretched on either side to form the shape of a huge bird. The dried grass at the base of the tree was charred black. He had seen this himself.

He was not afraid and never once considered turning back. There was only this one way to go if he wanted to become a man, a man with horses of his own, and a woman of his own, and the respect of the Quohada band.

He staked his horse near a muddy spring at the foot of the Hill where there was plenty of grass. He took the packs from his horse and took only his robe, tobacco and pipe, and the fire drill in its case of buffalo horn. He began climbing the Hill. It was not hard. He was used to climbing. The sun did not see him, and the wind touched him every now and again through the brush. The wind had tiny cold teeth, but he hardly felt them.

At the top of the Hill it was perfectly flat, with room to put up ten tepees across the top from ridge to ridge. There was nothing but four cedars, wind-stunted, growing near the south side. Four. That was the medicine number.

He could still see Earth, the Mother, below him, and to the east he thought he could see the even rows of small white tents of the white soldiers. He could not be sure—the light sometimes played tricks at such heights. The night wrapped around him, and the stars sparkled overhead. He told how he felt that this spot was outside of the horizon, beyond Mother Earth, even. This place had been waiting here forever between the sky and Mother Earth. It had been here when the whole Comanche nation had come out of the north, when the first buffalo had been born. It would always be here.

Mother Earth, guardian of the young below, took on a silver sheen as Mother Moon, guardian of warriors on a raid, rose above the rim of the world. The tiny fires of the imagined white men's camp seemed to be only reflections of the tiny stars in the dark sky.

He spread his buffalo robe near the four dwarfed cedars and lay down facing the east. He tried to sleep. He could feel the forces around him, hear them whispering in the trees. He waited to hear the Voice that would speak to him. Suddenly it was daylight.

His eyes felt the glare of Father Sun. He got up from his robe and faced Father Sun, staring straight at it with narrowed eyes. He reached his palms upward, reaching out for the sky. He could feel the power of Father Sun. It warmed him and filled his body with strength. This was a good feeling.

He filled his bone pipe with dry tobacco, tamped a dry piece of Spanish moss into the hole of the wooden drill block, and took out his fire drill. He twirled it between the palms of his hands. It was slow, but finally a little smoke curled up from the edges of the hole. The tinder had caught. Instantly he took out the hardwood drill, scooped the burning moss with a bare hand, and put it in the pipe's bowl. He puffed carefully until the pipe caught. He offered the burning pipe to Father Sun and then to Mother Earth and then to the four directions. He smoked and prayed until there was no more tobacco to burn in the bowl. The harsh smoke had made his mouth dry, but he was not thirsty.

He sat, waited, as Father Sun climbed high into the sky. There was little shade from the stunted cedars. The sun grew warm; the rocks and dust were hot. He did not feel the heat. The wind dried his skin. He sat motionless, eating no food, drinking no water. He felt pangs of hunger. He was used to hunger, and it did not bother him. He could not see the spring at the foot of the Hill, nor could he see his horse when he was at the very edge of the cap rock. He could not see the little rows of white tents. He was sure now that he had imagined the white men camped out there. The day passed. He sat very still. Then he thought he heard something.

It was a Voice, a whisper. It was familiar. He shook his head to clear it. It was only the wind in the scraggly little cedars. He could not be fooled.

He felt the cool light of stars upon him and saw the calm Moon Mother. He thought he saw the tiny thorn pricks of yellow fires in rows glowing up at him. He blinked his eyes to make them water and squinched his lids down to see better. It was only the starlight reflecting from some placid stream far below. His imagination could not trick him.

He did not sleep, but suddenly he was aware of a light that had not been there before. It filled the air and danced over the gray stones of the Hill. He had never seen a light like this before. He pushed aside the robe and got to his feet. He could see every detail of the cap rock vivid with this silver glow. The sky was covered with blazing streaks, like arrows of white light, showering down on the land as far as he could see. The dripping fire seemed to radiate from one point in the sky. He raised his hands, offering himself to the brilliant silver light, to the four directions, and to Mother Earth. He felt faint. His head felt light. The four Holy Cedars seemed to jump out at him, and their shadows were long fingers pointing toward him.[3]

Then it was there on the desert floor below him— the yellow-orange reflection of the flaming arrows in the sky in a neat row. Now he knew there was no water in that place. This was his vision! He was having a Holy Dream. Ticannaf could hear himself breathing. He listened for a sound from the flashing sky. There was no sound from those vivid silver streaks, not even the wind, only his own breath moving in and out. Then he heard it—the Voice, a whisper, and it was familiar. The Voice was his own great-grandfather, Big Badger, speaking from the fiery sky.

"This is your medicine, the night sky filled with stars. The stars push one another off their path of life. See them fall from their trail. They fall as enemies in battle. They fall as white soldiers fall before Quohada warriors. Below is the steadfast reflection. It has nowhere to fall. This is security against enemies. You will dream up this vision of the firm yellow lights when you need protection. It will make you strong. Keep a piece of the yellow light with you forever, for courage and patience. I will leave it for you. Remember how I appeared to you."

Ticannaf blinked, and the shimmering sky was quiet. The morning star blinked at him from her proper place.

No stars were falling. Ticannaf shook with excitement.
He ran across the cap rock and looked far below. He
looked beyond, down into the plains. He could see nothing but grayness. He fell to his knees, looking, looking.
Ai-iii! There it was, a tiny, crystalline rock. A piece of
yellow light. It was a clear rhombohedral prism of cal-
cite. Ticannaf felt one of the corners depress his fin-
gertip. It was real. He held it tightly in his shaking
brown hand. His heart was hammering against his ribs.
A piece of yellow light. The soft dawn came up over the
rim of Mother Earth. He laid the crystalline prism before him in a soft shaft of light. It seemed to give off a
fluorescent glow. He examined the pale yellow crystal
in his hand over and over, then held it up so the shaft
of dawn pierced it. A tiny rainbow stood against the
crystal. Many times that day he made the rainbow appear.

The sun moved in and out of clouds. Once a thunderstorm rumbled overhead, but no rain fell. The air
was hot and stifling; his mouth felt dry as dust. But he
was not thirsty enough to wish for water. He could not
sit still. He climbed down the hill; his legs were weak.
He patted his horse and then went to the spring. He
stared at it, then put his whole head in the muddy pool
of water. But he did not drink a drop. When he straightened up, he felt faint. He put his head in again and let
the water run through his hair and over his eyes and
mouth. He did not open his mouth.

When he went up the Hill again, it was a steeper
slope than it had been the first time. It was much harder
to climb. He wondered if he should stay through the
whole four Holy Days, then told himself there could be
another vision, so he had better stay the prescribed
time. He was light-headed and dizzy. He seemed to have
no control over his legs. He had to drag them over the
cap rock, and his hands were cut on the rocks, but he
did not mind.

In the evening the rain fell, and he wondered why
he had gone down to the spring to wet his head. His
head buzzed; he shook it to clear it. The day had passed.
The night passed.

The third day was gray. He kept the pale crystal in
the palm of his hand. He could not see the rainbow

beside it. Occasionally the rain drizzled. Toward evening, the clouds disappeared and the stars shone. He watched all night. None fell from their place. Everything was calm. A breeze dried the rocks and made Ticannaf shiver. Mother Moon shone on him, but her light could not make the rainbow come from the crystal in his hand. It is locked inside, somewhere, he thought. I will try to get it out again during the day. He pulled his robe tighter around his chest. The night passed into the fourth day. This day he was not a boy. He had passed the Four Medicine Days. Ticannaf was a man.

He scrambled down the hill, skinning his knees and hands on the sharp rocks, but they did not hurt him. His horse nickered at the new man he saw. Ticannaf ate a strip of jerky from the parfleche near his horse. Then he fell on his belly at the spring and ducked his head; then he opened his mouth and drank. The muddy water filled him, stabbing at his insides. He did not mind. His stomach cramped. He lay down, hardly feeling the pain. He slept before going back to the village. He did not have to hurry. He had a whole lifetime before him.

CHAPTER
49

The Raid

Sacajawea lived approximately 26 or 27 years among the Comanches when her husband, Jerk Meat, was killed in a battle. It is a fact this was the first husband of her own choice and apparently she was devoted to him, therefore at his death she was heartbroken and very much depressed. At that time she was not in harmony with the relatives of her husband, therefore she declared she would not live among them any longer. When she said this the people did not take her seriously.

Reprinted by permission of the publishers, The Arthur H. Clark Company, from *Sacajawea, Guide and Interpreter of the Lewis and Clark Expedition*, by Grace Raymond Hebard, 1957, pp. 154–55.

During one of the hot, dry days of summer when there was no wind at all, only swarms of cicadas stridulating in the mesquite, Sacajawea gave birth to another female papoose. She was pleased with this papoose, who was small and perfect as her others had been. She hovered over the papoose, protecting it, keeping this link to her own mortality from the ravages of desert life, of Quohada living. She made a stout basket from willows in which to lay her new daughter. It was not in the manner of the Comanches. It was not in the manner of the Shoshonis, but more like the cradle that her first born, Pomp, had lain in while he slept at the edge of the Mandan village. She liked the basket. It was convenient to hang a strip of rawhide to a lodgepole, or from the limb of a tree while she worked outside. The baby was strapped in with wide leather straps so that Sacajawea could fasten the basket to her back, or take the papoose out easily to clean her, then hammock her in a soft blanket in a loop that placed the papoose close to Sacajawea's breast. The other women did not make fun of her, but rather were curious and asked how to make such a baby basket for a daughter who was expecting or for a favorite grandchild.

Hides Well was amused. "Why must you always do things differently? Are the Comanche ways of making a cradleboard so awkward that you have to improve on them?"

"No, my mother, it is only that it pleases me to make my child warm and secure for the winter months."

This new papoose affected Pronghorn. It helped him forget the death of Butterfly and the old, intelligent Big Badger. He would come into the lodge when Sacajawea was there with the child, and no longer did he seem to have the feeling of something missing slap him in the face. He found that his words were coming back to him and he was again remembering what was on his mind to tell the women, or in the council he could stand up and talk without a lump coming to his throat or an angry blaze in his chest when mention of white soldiers was made.

Also, it seemed that Jerk Meat was suddenly more cheerful and did not try to fill the conversation with inane speech such as "The berries seem bitter this year" or "The snow is white."

The early winter weather was pleasant, and the sun shone warm and thin. The men were able to bring in many fat antelope for winter clothing and food. All the women were busy tanning hides, drying strips of meat and the soft, dark plums. They chopped pecans to add to their pemmican.

Sacajawea made tallow candles, with the dried fibrous mesquite stems as wicks, for Wild Plum and his young squaw, *Hebo*, Walking Against the Wind.

Jerk Meat teased Ticannaf one evening after a good meal. "Do you have many horses, my son?"

"No, my father. One for riding and one for carrying supplies. Why, do you wish to use one?"

"I do not wish to use one, but old Dancing Foot might like one or two."

"Why would Dancing Foot need my horses?"

"If he is to be your father-in-law. I have seen you eyeing his youngest daughter, Happy Heart. So—your mother has also."

Ticannaf reddened. He moved a step toward his mother, then added, pointing to his baby sister who cried in a fit of hunger, "Mother, aren't you going to do something about the *Yagawosier*? That Crying Basket is loud enough to attract the mother instinct of female wolves." Then he lifted the tepee flap and stepped into the night breeze. It was true that he had been seen walking with Happy Heart, daughter of Dancing Foot, many times lately.

"Crying Basket," Sacajawea crooned as she put fresh cattail fluff in the leather pocket between the baby's legs before nursing her. "Our papoose has a name. *Yagawosier*, Crying Basket."

Jerk Meat watched the smoke drift up and out through the smoke hole just below the top of the tepee. He moved to the back of the tepee and sat cross-legged on the buffalo robe that covered his slightly raised couch, watching Sacajawea nurse Crying Basket and prepare the baby for the night. His woman always dressed with care, and this pleased him. The sky blue stone looked good against her brown throat. The beads on her long deerskin tunic glittered in the soft light of the tiny fire. Her dark eyes were outlined in yellow paint.

"Come and sit," said Jerk Meat.

She knelt on the floor beside him. She did not speak. Her close-cropped hair framed a face that was good to see in the gentle light; the strong line of her jaw was softened.

"I am glad that you have come to me." Jerk Meat stood up, but made no move toward her. It was as though their bodies had never joined and he was greeting a friend. He felt uncertain, like a boy.

Sacajawea said nothing, but she looked at him openly. Her eyes shone. She seemed ageless, yet quite young somehow. He could remember her when she had first come to the Quohada camp. She had sometimes played bull-roaring with the young girls, swinging the flat cedar board through the air, holding it by the thong tied to the handle, listening with delight to the whirring noise it made. Her eyes were as bright then as now.

"Tonight I feel the time passing," Jerk Meat said abruptly. "Our son is a man ready to take a woman. Together we have seen many good things and many bad. We have been happier than most and sadder also. I sit with wonderment at my wiseness so many moons back when I chose you among all the beautiful Quohada girls."

"Tell me," Sacajawea said. "I will listen why you chose me instead of a beautiful Quohada woman."

Jerk Meat knew an instant of shame, shame that he chose his words wrong, that he did not tell his woman he thought her the most beautiful woman he had ever seen and this feeling had never diminished through all the years he had lived with her.

"I will always love you. You make life strong and worthwhile; you give me health; you give me happiness. A man could want no more. Many have less and are content."

"I feel that for you also," Sacajawea said, stirring the tiny fire until it seemed to fill the tepee with light. "We have held our hearts in our hands and laughed. We have found our hearts on the ground. In time we have picked them up and lived again. We grow closer together with time. You are the handsomest horse rider among all the Comanches."

"Woman, I believe you talk with sand in your mouth," Jerk Meat laughed, pulling her on the couch beside him. She nipped once at his ears. He did not wait, could not. He took her body, took it with a violence that was more than hunger; it was more need to love and be loved. When it was over, they were both weak and trembling. It passed, and their bodies stilled. Jerk Meat felt a warm, comfortable drowsiness, akin to lovely tenderness.

"Sleep now," she said, her breath soft in his ear. "I will stay with you." She pulled the buffalo robe over herself and lay close against his curled back.

Jerk Meat slept. Sacajawea slept. Crying Basket slept. Ticannaf crept inside the tepee, lay on his couch, and slept. Their dreams were good.

Mother and father were awake before dawn. They whispered and lay close together in the chilled air. They came together again, slowly. There was still plenty of time before the others awakened. It was like a greeting, a comfortable greeting filled with all the warmth and good wishes exchanged by longtime friends with great respect and admiration for one another.

Sacajawea roused herself and built up the fire. They talked. He dressed. "The times are getting worse," she said slowly. It was not good for a woman to complain. "This is a good winter with plenty of meat for us, but there will be sad times ahead. There will be sickness. Even the Comanches cannot withstand the sickness the white men bring in. Other nations will suffer."

He shook his head. "It is shameful. It is wrong for some tribes to be herded like the *taibo* cattle to live in a place chosen by white men. This is Comanche land. The buffalo are still here, and the Quohadas will stay here. We are free."

"For how long?" She looked at him, her yellow-rimmed eyes filled with words that could not be spoken. "The old days are gone. They were gone when I came here to you. The white men can move over all the land, and will."

"*Ai*, but what of that? There has always been someone taking land from someone else. We took this land from the Apaches. We can fight the white soldiers."

"Perhaps. It is not for a woman to say, but you know that I must say I do not believe so. I believe that we must all learn to live in peace and there will be less Quohada blood spilled on the plains."

"You have always talked much for a woman," laughed Jerk Meat deep within his throat. "I like the way you do it."

"And I have been thinking."

"My *pia* talks and also thinks," grunted Ticannaf sleepily from his couch.

"I have been thinking that the nations of Indians need someone like a go-between to talk to the whites for them, someone who understands both people."

"My *pia* talks like some chief," Ticannaf teased his mother.

"Someday this may come," said Jerk Meat seriously.

"It will come," said Sacajawea. Suddenly she thought of her old friend, Chief Red Hair. He could understand both people, talk with either, live with either, and be friends with both. Then, as suddenly, it dawned on her that she was the mother of a *cholo*, half-white, half-Indian. She was a go-between herself already. She would save this to tell Jerk Meat when they were alone again. It would help him to understand that the whites and Indians could live together.

In the spring the band moved again into the buffalo range on the rolling plains. Ticannaf had a woman, Happy Heart, the daugher of old Dancing Foot, to whom he'd given his two horses. Sacajawea made a beautiful marriage tepee, painted in reds, blues, and yellows. Happy Heart fastened her tepee next to the tepee of Jerk Meat and Sacajawea. She was part of their lodge. In time Dancing Foot, a widower, came to live with them.

Jerk Meat told Happy Heart that she must have plenty of strong braves because he had only Ticannaf, who was not even brave enough to spank his woman the night she fed him cold soup. Happy Heart smiled, remembering the evening she had visited with Sacajawea and her cooking fire had gone out. For Sacajawea, the everyday work went much faster with someone to talk to and laugh with like Happy Heart.

The next spring, plans were made for a small raid into the Mescalero country to replenish the dwindling Quohada horse herd. No women were going. But many young braves were going who had not been on more than one or two raids. Bites Hard, the elder son of Kicking Horse and Gray Bone, was going. Ticannaf and Wild Plum were going. Ticannaf was busy for a day painting himself and checking his shield and bow; then he and the others danced the War Dance with the older warriors, trying to keep from showing too much either of pride or nervousness. That night, all members of the raiding party moved out in the dark.

The camp settled into the waiting period. The old men left behind watched the small horse herd, leisurely hunted antelope, worked on weapons, and slept. The women did not worry much. They knew that the raiding party had been strong in numbers and had gone for sport as much as for serious raiding. Jerk Meat, Ticannaf, Pronghorn, Dancing Foot, and Wounded Buck had gone. Sacajawea worked as she saw fit, going often to visit and gossip with Hides Well and Spring.

Sometimes Sacajawea sent Happy Heart to take the horse kept hobbled near camp to graze in the grass meadow. Sacajawea sometimes went out to the meadow to dig roots, Crying Basket strapped to her back. The sweet peas were beginning to put out their pale-lavender flowers, and she dug their roots for food. Occasionally she went for an hour's walk from camp to a hill where yucca grew thick and where the soil was easy to dig. The roots of the yucca were good to use in bathing and washing things, also to put in a tanning mixture.

Out by herself, she would take Crying Basket from the basket and hold her under the arms, teaching her to walk. When the baby was tired, she would let her sit and crawl in the grass, poking at the bright wild flowers. Sacajawea thought of her life with the Quohadas and felt it was only good and satisfying when Jerk Meat was home.

It was nearing the time for Happy Heart's child to be born. Sacajawea spent more and more time with her. The girl did not want to be left alone if her time came early because some old woman had predicted that if

that happened the baby would not take a breath. Sacajawea was making a robe for the new baby from the
tattered remnants of her beloved old blue coat. She had
opened up the sleeves, which had frayed cuffs and holes
in the elbows. She tried to sew them to the top and
bottom of the coat, but the material was old and rotten.
Finally, she gave up and sewed the coat to the underside
of a soft white doeskin. Now the small robe reminded
her of the quilts Judy Clark had shown her so many
years back.

Happy Heart was pleased with the new blanket for
her coming papoose. "It is the warmest robe a Quohada
papoose has ever had," she said, feeling the soft thickness of it.

"*Ai*," agreed Sacajawea. "That blue coat has kept me
warm for more seasons than I can count on my two
hands. The man who gave it to me must be a grandfather several times over now."

"A man? Not your man, Jerk Meat?" asked Happy
Heart in surprise. "I thought probably Jerk Meat took
it in a raid on a white man's fort and brought it to you
as a gift."

Sacajawea clapped her hand over her mouth, instantly realizing what she had said to the girl. "Well,
and so—it was from a *taibo*. This white man lived in
a fort. He saw my need for warmth and gave me the
coat. Even though you think the whites are our enemies, there are some who are friends and who do not
have forked tongues."

"Oh, Mother," said Happy Heart, wide-eyed. "It was
Jerk Meat who brought you to our camp. And then you
were cold and hungry. He brought the warmth back
into your body. Perhaps your mind wandered when you
were so hungry and you supposed it was a white man
who gave you the coat. Maybe it was Jerk Meat after
all. You have forgotten."

Sacajawea answered, "*Ai*, my daughter. Starving
causes the mind to wander outside the body and see
things no one else sees. You are right." She thought,
The man who gave me that coat had the reddest hair
and the bluest eyes I have ever seen. His deeds will be
told among the whites for many seasons. He will never
be forgotten.

Several days later, some of the old men decided one morning that they should go to check on the raiding party in case they needed help. Two days after some of the old men had left, three scouts came back. They galloped to the center of the village. One of the men said, "They are coming soon now."

Everyone asked at once about their own men. The scouts would say no more. Some women began to push their way back to the edge of the village. Some of them stopped first to paint their faces and put on their best clothes to meet their men, or fathers, or brothers.

Sacajawea hurried to her lodge and painted the pretty yellow circles around her eyes and tied the sky blue stone on the thin thong around her neck. She put a leather band around her flying hair and tied a string of blue-and-white trade beads around her waist. She went out with Crying Basket hung in a blanket on her back, following the crowd in anticipation.

One look at the dejected men, whose eyes were glued on their shuffling moccasins, caused Sacajawea's heart to fall. She looked for Jerk Meat. Spring and Hebo ran out to look for Wild Plum. Some of the women were already keening with high-pitched shrieks. Sacajawea's eyes fell on a couple of mules and a few spent horses, all with no manes or tails. Wild Plum had long red gashes along his arms, soot on his face, and a shorn head. He hardly looked at his woman, Hebo, but went directly to the front of the Council Lodge.

Sacajawea's mouth was so dry she could not speak. She hardly recognized Ticannaf, who was skin and bone. A hard knot grew in her belly as she looked over the worn-out riders and did not find Bites Hard, Kicking Horse, Dancing Foot, Pronghorn—nor her beloved Jerk Meat. She wanted to sit in the dirt and pour dust over her head. It was unthinkable, but obvious, that no others were coming back.

Ticannaf kept his head low. It was hard to hear his words. "All I bring is a tick-infested mule and this Mexican captive.[1] Her name is Choway."[2]

The girl had not been noticed. She hung back, her black eyes darting from one to the other. She was about twelve or thirteen summers.

The women began crying and moaning. Some fell

upon each other's necks sobbing. Sacajawea was stunned. It just was not true. This could not happen. Jerk Meat was coming over the hill in a few minutes now. He would be here.

Hides Well was sobbing, "Pronghorn! Pronghorn! Where have they left you?"

The men who had returned got up and went to their lodges. The village was in mourning. During that first black night Happy Heart delivered a stillborn boy. The Mexican girl stayed outside Ticannaf's lodge, bewildered and frightened.

The story of the unsuccessful raid finally took shape through visiting and sorrowful talking. The men had gone deep into desert country, then on past El Paso, finding it well guarded. They spent one night on the desert and began their return the next day. In the region between the lower Pecos and the Rio Grande, they camped at a spring coming out of a cave. This was a deep rock well with a large basin of water, and on each side a cave ran under the rock from the water's edge. During the night they were surrounded by a large force of Mexican soldiers, who killed several of the horses and forced the Quohadas to take refuge in a cave. These Mexicans had several Mescalero Apaches with them. Even though the Apaches were enemies of the Comanches, they called out in the Comanche language several times for the Quohadas to hold out.

Inside the cave, the men were without both food and water. The Mexicans watched them so closely that they could venture out to the edge of the water only under cover of darkness to get a drink or cut a few strips of flesh from the dead horses. They ate the putrefying meat raw. Kicking Horse was shot in the leg while getting a drink of water. The smell of the dead horses was almost unbearable, but the hunger and thirst were even worse. The men were brave, but they suffered. Some of them, led by Pronghorn, explored the cave to see if there was any way out. They found that it ran along at a long distance and at the end there was a hole opening to the daylight. Pronghorn climbed up and thrust his head out, but he was seen by the soldiers and shot. The men buried him behind a huge rock in the cave. The soldiers closed the hole with large boulders.

The Mexicans were afraid to attack the Quohadas and were determined to keep them penned up until they all died of starvation.

Soon the decaying horse carcasses made the water unfit to drink. After about one moon of suffering, they realized that a longer stay meant dying in the cave, so they decided to make one last desperate attempt to escape in the night.

Before starting the escape, Jerk Meat and several others chanted the Death Song, in which they hurled defiance at death.

The walls were steep and difficult, but there was a cedar growing from a crevice, its top reaching nearly to the top of the cliff. The men thought that it might just be possible to use the cedar to climb out. They managed to get to the top without attracting the attention of the Mexican guards. Only one, Kicking Horse, who had been shot in the leg, was unable to climb the steep incline. He begged his friends to leave him. They did not. Jerk Meat fell twice with Kicking Horse on his back. Wounded Buck said it was the life of Kicking Horse against theirs, and if they stayed with him or lost more time trying to get him out, they would all perish together in the cave. The men urged Kicking Horse to have a strong heart and die like a warrior. He calmly accepted the inevitable, saying, "When you get home, rest. Then come back and avenge me." Then he sat down beside the wall to await daylight, then death, when the Mexicans would see him. He was a brave man.

Jerk Meat pushed and pulled the men to hurry them to the top. Wounded Buck was first, and he saw the fires of the Mexicans burning in many directions about the mouth of the cave. The Mexicans had good ears and heard something. They fired in the direction of the cave many times and wounded Jerk Meat, who was shot through the left side. Dancing Foot was shot, and Long Hand was hit in the back. Several others were killed, and more were wounded. The rest found horses to carry the wounded. They hurried away from that place until they reached the Sun Mountain Spring. The wounded men were placed near the spring and given water. Ticannaf stayed all night beside his father. Jerk Meat died in the early dawn. Long Hand and Bites Hard died soon after. The men covered the bodies with stones to keep wolves away and moved the wounded under the shade of an old mesquite. As they prepared their horses to ride, one of the men heard Dancing Foot's death rattle and found him with his face in the spring, dead. They pulled him back and placed his body near the others and piled on more stones. Toward midday, the men spotted a band of poor Mexicans traveling slowly in the opposite direction. When night fell, Wounded Buck and Ticannaf went back and raided the Mexican camp, killing no one, but getting two old mules and the girl, Choway, who had run after the Quohadas waving an ax and shouting Spanish obscenities.

The men set fire to the prairie grass to hide their trail. They killed several skunks and dragged them behind their horses to stop the Mexicans from sending dogs to follow them.

Sacajawea wanted to go back and gather Jerk Meat's bones to be brought home for burial. The men said it was too far and too hazardous. They would not let her go. Much of the time she sat alone at the edge of camp in an area of rocks and stunted cedar. Her grief was deep inside. She could not weep.

The sense of awe and of uncertainty hung over the Quohadas' actions. They went about their activities quietly. Hides Well took the medicine bundle of the dead chief and placed it in the creek. She took down the big tepee of Pronghorn, which had always dominated the center of their camp, and burned it along with his other belongings.

The wives of Kicking Horse, Together and Flower, distributed his belongings to members of the band that did not seem to have too much. They burned all his medicine things. Those that would not burn they placed in the creek under a large rock.

Ticannaf visited his mother often, giving her Choway, the Mexican girl, as a gift to ease her sorrow, but the sorrow was something he could not reach. She existed, but did not live. She moved about and prepared hides Ticannaf brought to her; she kept the kettle full of stew meat; she kept Crying Basket clean and well fed; but she did not speak to the child, or pat her, or hold her in the evenings. She ignored Choway. She did not throw away the possessions of Jerk Meat, but left them where he had left them. Other women eyed her uncertainly, and some began to talk and discuss her past idiosyncrasies. Hides Well was appalled at Sacajawea's behavior, and Spring looked at her, saying, "You never could behave in the proper Comanche manner."

Some of the men talked about the need for a council. They talked and waited in uneasy silence. No one took the lead to do anything.

Sacajawea sat by the drinking spring one morning. It was gray and gloomy. Clouds hung heavy across the sky, and a little rain drizzled down. Her thoughts wandered back to the time long before she came to live with the Quohadas. She was near the Pacific Ocean with Chief Red Hair, and it was raining, raining, for days it rained. The men were not sad. They played games, joked, managed to keep things fairly dry. They even made little wooden toys for Pomp. Pomp was a beautiful child. He was happy. Was he a fine-looking man? she wondered. Was he now working with the whites? And Tess, where was he? He had the same terrible temper his father had. Had that temper pushed him into trouble? She swung her head from side to side.

Happy Heart came with a kettle for water. "Oh, my mother, please go to your tepee. It is not good to sit on the wet ground in the rain. The other women talk. They say you do not know if it rains or if the sun is glaring down hot and dry."

Sacajawea laid her thin hand across the young woman's and looked into her face. She was pretty. She was a good worker. She loved her man, Ticannaf.

"Who do you suppose they will choose as the new chief?" asked Sacajawea.

"They might choose Red Bull or Tabananikah, Hears the Sun Rise, or the man of Spring, Wounded Buck. Or they might choose Ticannaf, but he is young, without much experience. It takes a lot of qualifications, my mother. The man must have made a name for himself in war and mean something to the other bands."

"When another chief is chosen, I am leaving this band."

"Mother! Why? You can't do that!"

"Yes, it is the thing for me to do. You have a good

man, and he will love and look after you. You do not
need me here. No one really needs me here. The others
talk behind my back. Even Hides Well and Spring look
at me as an outsider. It is not their fault; it is the days
we go through."

"What about Crying Basket and the Mexican girl,
Choway?"

"I will take Crying Basket. You may keep Choway.
She is a good worker. Find her a good man."

"Where will you go?"

"I will go north, maybe to your cousins, the Shoshonis. I may try to be a go-between with the whites
for our band here. Maybe not. I have not yet decided."

"See, you are not serious, *pia*. You would not go to
see our enemies, the whites. You would not even be a
go-between; that is something a man would do, a man
who was as well-thought-of as a chief or shaman. For
a little while I thought you might be serious. But you
are only joking."

When the first flecks of snow fell, slanted in flight
by the wind, the band headed south to get away from
the place where memories of the dead warriors were
strong. Sacajawea carried Crying Basket on her back,
and Choway led the two packhorses. They had walked
only a few miles when Sacajawea saw something in the
brush, a movement. She turned and stepped outside the
procession to investigate. Behind a mesquite thicket
was an old woman with a mangy dog and a small travois.

"It is cold," said the old woman. "I am going south."
She looked thin and cold; her tunic was torn and dirty.

"Do you have food?" asked Sacajawea.

"A little," said the woman, not wanting to admit she
had none.

"Let me see," said Sacajawea.

The woman opened a small parfleche. Inside were
three or four kernels of parched corn, that was all.

"That was from a Mexican supply cart," she explained. "They were camped by a water hole, and in
the night I was hungry, so I filled my sack, but the food
is hard and dry."

"Come, travel with us a few days," suggested Sacajawea. "You will be fed, and I have extra clothing to keep you warmer."

The woman looked at Sacajawea, and it seemed tears came to her eyes. It could have been the way the light shone.

The two traveled a little way side by side.

"Kicking Horse? How is he?" the old woman asked.

Surprised, Sacajawea looked at the stranger for several moments before answering. "You cannot speak his name." Then she looked still closer and this time recognized the old woman as Gray Bone. She did not know what more to say to her. She looked around at the others, but none had recognized Gray Bone. They were buried in their own thoughts or trying to keep warm in the wind and biting snow. "There was a raid in Mexico. Many of the men did not return," she said finally. The moment she said it, Sacajawea was sorry. Gray Bone did not need to know that the Quohadas were so vulnerable and unprotected. Gray Bone was pathetic, but she was trouble.

Gray Bone grinned broadly, so that her broken, rotting teeth showed as a jagged yellow slash across her face. She trotted up ahead and pushed herself into the procession along with her scraggly yellow dog pulling the small travois.

At the midday rest, Gray Bone had found her friends and was chatting freely with some of the older women. She had come back to the band. She had been invited back by Sacajawea. There was no one in command to keep her away. The council had not yet been able to agree on a new chief. Spring shook a finger in Sacajawea's direction but did not come to talk with her.

Sacajawea kept her promise and took a fresh tunic and some clean but worn leggings and moccasins to Gray Bone, who grabbed for the clothing.

"I see that you are not so generous with your old friend. These leggings have holes in them. You were about to throw them away." Gray Bone gave the leggings a toss over her shoulder. She Cat let out a stifled tee-hee. Gray Bone stared at Sacajawea. "You cannot throw me away like cast-off leggings. I am still a Quohada Comanche. And I have some knowledge that would interest you, Lost Woman. I have been as far north as the white men's fort. For the use of one of your horses, I will tell what I know."

Sacajawea shook her head, but said no word. She could not tell if Gray Bone were truthful or not. She went back to her packhorses and pulled out dried meat for Choway and Crying Basket.

Hides Well shuffled by and shouted a warning, "Gray Bone is there!"

"I have seen her," said Sacajawea.

"Who invited her to travel with our band?"

"I did, my mother," said Sacajawea.

Instant anger showed in Hides Well's words. "Woman, there is talk that you act strangely. Now I can believe it. This is a black day."

"She was cold and hungry."

"She is trouble. Her mind is evil."

"Perhaps she will live quietly with her friends."

"Hah!" said Hides Well. "She watches us from the corner of her eye right now. You have become soft and stupid. Maybe you should have been kicked out of the band also."

Sacajawea wiped a piece of stringy meat from the chin of Crying Basket, but made no reply.

They traveled through rough terrain and much snow, finally coming to a small valley with red-clay slopes. In the valley were other Comanche villages: *Penatuhkas*, Honey Eaters; *Kotsotekas*, Buffalo Eaters; and *Tanimas*, Liver Eaters. The Quohadas chose a winter campsite upstream from the other villages. The Tanimas told of a white man named Bill Williams, who had spent two winters with them. They said he knew all the white men in that part of the country and those up north.

Sacajawea hoped Bill Williams would come back this winter. His woman and child were with the band, so he might be back.

The change of camp and talks with other bands were good. The Quohadas gained a clearer perspective and began to believe that their lives would go on as they always had. After their great grief they needed this change, and now they were able to laugh, to send children to play games, and to visit back and forth with the other bands.

Some scouts brought back messages of white soldiers in all directions—north, west, south, and east. They talked of a man named José Castro in the southwest, who wished to attack white traders, especially one named Frémont.

Sacajawea was bewildered by the fact that white men were fighting or attacking other white men.

The Buffalo Eaters told of the Kiowas, who had bought blankets in the spring from white traders. They were good woolen trading blankets, but children wrapped in them to keep the spring winds out at night fell ill with high fevers and red blotches on their bodies. If they were rushed to the cooling stream to halt the high fever, they were dead by morning. If they were not and the fever burned within their bodies, some died, some became blind, and others survived but were dull-witted. Very few of that Kiowa band survived the disease that was in the blankets of the white men. The Buffalo Eaters warned all the bands not to buy the white men's trading blankets. They told the bands not to trust any white man.

One day four Penatuhka men rode into the Quohada camp. Wounded Buck invited Wild Plum and Ticannaf to sit with them in front of his lodge. The Penatuhka were polite and ate and smoked before talking.

"We traded beaver pelts to some white men on Prairie Dog Town River," said the man wearing a red flannel shirt. "There white men said one day all of us will live together in one big camp. What do you make of this?"

"I've heard that whites tell plenty lies," said Wild Plum, picking at his teeth with a straw.

"Well, and so, one of the whites said they had men ready to show us how to put eyes in the ground to grow something called potatoes."

"How can anyone have confidence in white man's words?" said Ticannaf.

Sacajawea was inside the tepee listening. She pushed aside the door flap and blurted, "White men, did you say? Was any of them called Chief Red Hair?"

The four Honey Eaters looked at her dumbfounded, then whispered together in low tones. The man with a silver belt buckle in his hair said, "Do you Quohadas

always let your women interrupt men talk? We Penatuhkas consider such a woman highly unmannerly."

"This is Lost Woman," said Ticannaf, trying to cover
his embarrassment. She used to live with some whites
and is anxious to hear news of them."

"*Ai*, one old man had red hair and a red and white
beard. He knew how to speak with several tribes. He
said he lived at the edge of the Father of Rivers, the
Mississippi."

Sacajawea felt like a bubble about to burst. "What
was this red-haired man's name?"

"This man you could not know. He was a truly great
chief among his people. He traveled far across the land
to the Shining Mountains and the Great Stinking Waters
of the West. I do not remember his name."

"It is him!" shouted Sacajawea. "So—he is still here!"
She let out a great sigh and her eyes lit up as she
continued questioning. "Did he talk about houses that
float on the river, and the iron moccasins for horses,
and the thin, snow white robes used on sleeping couches?
Did he? Were his eyes sky blue?"

The four men again stared at the woman asking all
the questions, and whispered among themselves. The
Quohadas were staring at Sacajawea. Then their whispering began. "How does she know of these new things?
She never told us about them before. Do you suppose
she could be a spy? Her ways are strange."

"Say, Quohadas, do women usually speak up in your
councils?" asked a Honey Eater with a blue blanket.

Now all eyes were on Sacajawea. She trembled and
mumbled, red flames of excitement in each cheek, her
piercing black eyes seemingly on the ground, but she
saw the Honey Eaters. "I am sorry. I listen to white
traders and hear things. It seems many of these things
the white men offer are not bad. There is some good."
Her legs shook. She sat on the ground.

"Ha!" exclaimed Broken Horn. "The voice of Lost
Woman is like that of the Honey Eaters. She hears
things that are new and she thinks they are good."

After thanking Wounded Buck for his hospitality,
the four visitors did not stay much longer.

Once or twice, some of the bolder women asked Sacajawea how it was she knew so much about the way

the whites lived. She was evasive in her answers, usually saying she listened to traders talk. The women suspected more, but did not say so in front of Sacajawea. The gossip came back through Hides Well.

"The women are uncertain about you and ask if you ever lived in a white village," said Hides Well.

"Tell them I lived many places," she answered. "Tell them here I have been the happiest."

"Sometimes I find myself looking at you in an uneasy light. I'm not saying I actually distrust you. But you did ask the crazy one, Gray Bone, back into the band. You gave her food and clothing. And from what I know, you have every right to stay completely away from her. Then there is this. You save meat fat. You make something like the yucca washing juice, only much better. It is true you do not hide your knowledge because I know several women who now save ashes in a parfleche and pour water over them, then collect that dripping water to mix with their leftover meat fat. Their tunics and leggings have never been cleaner. Now, I am wondering where all your knowledge came from."

Sacajawea's heart sank. "My mother, there is a bond of friendship between us. Let us not break that. I will show you how to make the washing liquid this afternoon."

"Is it true that you are some kind of woman Shaman?"

"No, my mother," said Sacajawea, aghast, "that is not true."

"And so—now how do I know?" Hides Well walked away to her own tepee, not waiting to be shown the wonders of crude soapmaking.

Late that summer, Ticannaf and Happy Heart had another son, this one very much alive. They named him *Waigon*, Thunderbird, because his cry was as loud as any thunder that woke them in the night.

Gray Bone came to the tepee of Sacajawea several times. She did not stay long, but the women of the village were aware of those visits. One day late in the afternoon, she came in bringing a dead turkey with her.

"I wish to give you this," she said and moved around as though restless.

"Thank you," said Sacajawea, reaching for the bird swinging by its neck in Gray Bone's hand.

"You do not know what it is like to catch a bird with one's hands.".

"Is that how you got the gash on your arm?" asked Sacajawea, bending nearer to see the wound better.

"Not exactly," said Gray Bone. "It happened on a hunt. I ran into a coyote. She turned on me. Afterward, she drank much water and did not turn on me again. The wound is not new, but takes its own time healing."

"Let me look." Sacajawea took the woman close to the tepee fire.

"Many have said that the sister-in-law of the new chief has special medicine powers. I recall something like that—but at times my mind wanders. Can you heal it?"

"New chief?" asked Sacajawea.

"*Ai*, your sister's man, Wounded Buck, has been named the civil chief of our band. So—it is true they do not tell you everything now. You are becoming the outcast!"

Gray Bone then did a peculiar thing. She put her hands to her mouth and rolled her eyes heavenward. She shrieked and screamed and tore at her hair. Sacajawea tried to calm her with herb tea, but Gray Bone pulled an old, broken rifle from under her robe and tried to swing it at Sacajawea. She missed, and it hit the other side of the tepee wall. Gray Bone seemed unable to swallow. She had great difficulty breathing. Finally Sacajawea calmed her, but the spittle continued to roll down the sides of her mouth as though she could not swallow.

"You have eaten something bad?" asked Sacajawea.

Gray Bone shriveled, her eyes opened wide, and the muscles of her mouth and larynx moved with spasms. She moved around and around the tepee. She could not speak.

"Rest here," offered Sacajawea. "I will take care of you until this sickness passes." When Choway came in, she handed her the dead turkey. "Get rid of this. Destroy it. It is not fit food. Those who eat turkey become

cowards and run from their enemies in the same fashion
turkeys run away. Keep Crying Basket with Happy
Heart for the rest of the day."

Then Sacajawea sat back on her heels looking at
Gray Bone. She had never seen anyone act this way.
What have I done? she thought. Now I am obligated to
care for this woman, and I do not really like her. I hate
her. I am frightened of her. Once she cut my nose. Would
she again? Perhaps in the middle of the night?

By the next morning, the whole village knew that
Wounded Buck was chief. He was young and could fight.
He understood the old way and could see the coming of
a new way.

For the next two days, time dragged for Sacajawea.
Gray Bone seemed to get better; then she would become
feverish, restless, and want to walk outside. Sacajawea
and Choway tried to keep her tied down to a sleeping
mat with thick rope. Choway bathed her face, but her
maniacal behavior discouraged much washing or cooling with water.

On the third day, a whippoorwill swooped low over
the camp, trailing behind him his mournful yet urgent
cry. The Quohadas heard this and during the morning
looked at one another asking themselves, "Who?" They
believed the cry of a lone whippoorwill flying low over
a camp meant violent death to some particular member
of the band.

Sacajawea pulled her tired limbs from between her
robes and crouched over the fire, which had gone out.
Crying Basket began to whimper with hunger pangs.
Sacajawea looked toward the child. Then she saw the
empty sleeping couch, clothing torn off hooks, a parfleche of pemmican partly emptied on the floor, the
tepee flap partially open. Gray Bone was gone! She
woke Choway. "I've got to find that old sack of bones,"
said Sacajawea. "Who knows what she can do? She's
rotten as an egg lying too long in the sun." She left the
fire unlit and asked Choway to straighten the lodge,
light the fire, and look after the child.

"What is her disease, *pia*?" asked Choway. "She looks
very sick. I do not like the smell of her."

"I think it is from the coyote that cannot swallow

water. It is bad. I should have fed her mayapple roots
when I first knew."

"There are no such roots here, *pia*," said Choway,
shaking her head.

"Well, so—there are other death powders." Sacajawea packed jerky in a parfleche hurriedly.

"*Pia*, my mother, please, no—" called Choway, but
Sacajawea had turned toward the entrance of a gully,
riding her horse swiftly along the slow-winding curves
of the dry course.

Gray Bone was not there. Sacajawea soon realized
the search might take all day. She listened and heard
only the twitter of a small bird, the thumping of a rabbit, and the gnawing of a porcupine at a cottonwood
stump. It is quiet, she said to herself, surely. Then she
corrected herself: Nothing is sure.

Some of the gullies had rocky steps beyond which a
horse could not go, and in those, brought up short by
the rock barriers, she turned back. In others the sandy
bottom ran clean and free all the way to a far rim, and
in those she saw nothing, not even a snake or lizard.
The catbirds and jays went about their normal business,
making it certain that there was nothing new around.
The sun pushed beyond a grove of stunted oaks filtering
a sickly green light to the ground.

About noon, she saw plants growing in lush profu-
sion below two strong jets of clear water. The stream
fell straight down the rock wall for a small distance,
then was broken by the banding of rock into a sequence
of short falls, as water might run down garden steps
during a heavy rain. This was an oasis of greenery that
contrasted agreeably with the otherwise arid aspect of
the land shimmering under dry waves, heralding a heat
that would crack the ground, already sucked dry by a
thirsty sun. A cascade of scarlet monkey flowers tumbled down the slope, the whorled stems of horsetails
grew thickly among the rocks, and everywhere the shiny
leaves of poison ivy glistened in the sun. How ivy had
found this place puzzled Sacajawea. She had not seen
any in all her years with the Quohadas. Mother Earth
provides a small secret place and somehow sees to it
that the plants find the place. I must find the secret

place of Gray Bone, thought Sacajawea. She may be near the spring, resting.

She led the horse to the cold and delicious water. She ate a small piece of jerky. The horse grazed on the grassy bottom for a while, then came back to her. She led it to the bottom again. The animal tossed its head and pulled back. Then Sacajawea knew that what she had sniffed a few moments back on the gentle breeze was not her imagination. Twenty yards away, beside another pool formed from the waterfalls, lay a dead coyote, her head near the water, as though trying to take one last drink. Sacajawea left the horse and examined the animal. There had been a considerable scuffle. She could see moccasin tracks. The coyote's skull had been crushed. Near it lay an old, rusted muzzle-loader. The rifle had once been the pride of Kicking Horse. The stock was broken in half at the breech. The butt was smeared with the blood and brains of the coyote.

The coyote was not large. It was female. Her muzzle and lower jaw had a mottled look from dried froth that extended clear back to her eyes, which were open and peculiarly yellow. The moccasin tracks led away across the other side of the water.

Sacajawea jogged her horse slowly, keeping the pigeon-toed tracks before her. Far ahead, she could see that this clear land was becoming broken again. During the warm afternoon, she went up a slight incline to a plateau, beyond which a rise of catclaw-dotted hills foretold more abrupt walls of limestone. The wind was hot even in the coming evening. The sky was clear. There was small chance of rain washing out Gray Bone's tracks. The great dome over Sacajawea filled with twilight as the sun went under.

Sacajawea hunched herself down on the horse for an evening's ride. She looked behind every small bush. Once she held her horse still, straining all her senses, and she became aware of the little sounds, the hollow call of an owl, now there was no wind, but she heard the rattle of a dusty mesquite, and knew some creature was stirring about a night's business. She heard the singing whir of some insect at work or travel.

The night became black. She hobbled her horse and

slept in a shelter formed by an overhanging stone ledge. She woke at daybreak, ate some jerky, and resumed her ride. She came to a place where there was a milky, warm stream. The stream was only one or two feet wide, but from the size of the canyon it had cut, it was obvious that it could be quite formidable in a flash flood. The sandy banks cut from the rocks were thickly grown with mesquite and catclaw. The gravelly benches were a desert garden. Sacajawea stopped to look for telltale moccasin tracks in the sand by clumps of orange mallow and yellow flowers. She tied her horse to a mesquite and bent to search the sand where it was crisscrossed with lizard, mouse, and insect tracks. There were no moccasin tracks. An occasional butterfly drifted in and out through the patches of yellow and shade. The voice of the creek was soft. The motion drifted into the heart of the little canyon where the sun filtered through the leaves in a sickish warm green. The swell of the white sand dunes, the soft bubblings of the milky water, the yellow of the rock across the stream, and the arc of blue sky seemed a clean, bold contrast to the nauseating incubus of green that flowed through the small chasm, like a scrim in the hot breeze. Farther down the canyon the stream was gone, dried to dust in the ovenlike heat.

Something caught Sacajawea's eye. She climbed from her horse. Nestled among the pebbles and sand was a small potsherd, about two inches square. Its gray-white surface was decorated with black Vs. The inner V was further embellished with little black dots. She picked the fragment of clay pottery up, then looked around her feet and saw the ground strewn with dozens of other ancient shards. Some, like the one in her hand, had white-and-black lines; others had designs on a white background, or black on red. Still others, probably from vessels of a more utilitarian nature, were unpainted but adorned with a corrugated design, as if the wet coils of clay had been pinched by the maker and marked with his fingernails. She crouched back. The Ancient Ones had lived here. Still squatting on her heels, she continued examining the fragments. Suddenly there came to her a premonition of danger. It seemed a shadow had fallen upon her. But there was no shadow. Her heart had given a jump up into her throat and was choking her. Then her blood slowly chilled, and she felt the sweat in her tunic cold against her flesh.

She did not stand up or move; her eyes darted around the ground. She was considering the nature of the premonition she had received, trying to locate the source of the mysterious force that had warned her. She felt the imperative presence of some unseen thing. There was an aura too refined for the senses to know. She felt this aura, but could not tell how she felt it. It seemed that between her and life had passed something smothering and sickening—ghosts, as it were, that waited to swallow up life.

Every force of her being impelled her to turn and confront the unseen demon, but her soul dominated and she remained squatting, in her hands a black shard. She did not dare look around, but she knew by now that there was something behind her and above her. She looked at the shard, examined it critically, rubbing the sand from it and noticing tiny dull red dots that formed a circle at the edge. All the time she knew something above her was looking and watching her.

She pretended interest in the clay fragment in her hand, listening, but she heard nothing. She realized her predicament; she was caught in the camp of the Ancient Ones.

She shifted her weight ever so slightly, but stayed squatting on her heels. She was cool and collected. Her mind considered every factor. She would have to rise sooner or later, move from this spot, and face the incubus that stared at her back. As the moments passed, she knew she was nearer the time she must stand. She wanted to run, to rush to her horse and on to safety. But her intellect favored a slow, careful meeting with this thing that she could not yet see. And while she debated, a loud crashing noise burst on her ear, like a stone falling down a wall. At the same instant she felt a stunning blow on the left side of her back. She sprang up, noticing a wide niche in the yellow wall far up a steep, rocky slope, but her feet crumpled and her body fell like a leaf dried by the rays of the all-conquering sun. The air was expelled from her lungs with a sigh, and her body lay upon the hot earth, defeated, but it only appeared so. The human body, a vast and inventive organization of living cells, survives even when it seems lost.

Above, on the yellow ledge, another great stone in her hand, Gray Bone looked for a long time at the motionless body beneath her. After a while she replaced the stone and went away from the ledge toward the wall. She was breathing hard when she reached the niche. Set back under an overhang were five or six little rooms, each about six feet long, four feet high, and three feet deep. Each had its own door to the ledge where she stood. The sticks that served as lintels of the doorways were perfectly preserved in the dry air.

Gray Bone panted for breath and fought the ominous feeling that she was on the private property of others and they were squeezing the very life-force from her lungs to remove her from that property. She bent to examine a tiny corncob, much smaller than the corn she had seen. Her head ached, and her throat contracted with spasms as she tried to gulp the hot, life-giving air. Her skin prickled as the breeze went through her tangled hair.

She looked down the slope to the bottom of the canyon where she'd last seen Sacajawea. Her eyes squinted in the fading sunlight, but she could not locate the body of Sacajawea she thought she had left for dead a few moments before. She wiped her hand across her eyes, but she could not see clearly. Her hand slid down across the side of her face where a rush of flame went through her flesh. She moved to the edge of the cliff and began descending, resting on each stone cut. She wanted to see the dead body of Sacajawea just once more.

Slowly, in a peculiarly disjointed fashion, she walked to the dry creek bed. Gray Bone did not go in a straight line. She trembled as though shaking off the ghosts of the Ancient Ones who lived in the walls of the cliff's overhang. The apparition in front of her stood out like an overlord, a protector, in the twilight.

It lifted a hand and made a motion to come on. The sand dune was circled with piñon and deadfall. Gray Bone made her way cautiously. Her tunic was torn and hanging in ribbons. Her arms and legs were deeply scratched and bruised. Her face was hard, with dry skin over the skeleton to defy desiccation of the small inward moistness. One side was red and swollen where the flesh had been torn from the cheek to the chin. The gashes were scabbed over, but the wounds were inflamed. Through the shredded right leather sleeve, Gray Bone's arm was exposed. It was badly scratched, and it, too, looked swollen and red.

"I have not much patience with curiosity-seekers," rasped Gray Bone. Her voice was thick, as though retarded by some fleshy barrier. "There is no way to get me back to that camp, which stinks from human and dog excrement and rotting horseflesh. It is an eyesore upon Mother Earth with its ragged skin lodges and poor inhabitants."

She had fallen into the loner's habit of soliloquy. She tried to smile. It broke open the scab on her cheek, and the wound started to ooze. She wiped her mouth on the back of her hand, and then wiped her hand in the sand at her side.

"The thought of water is good. I wish I could drink. Smells nice in the desert." Jerkily she inhaled the hot, sweet breath of the canyon through nostrils that dilated and quivered.

"Ever know a camp that stunk more?" She moved down the dry creek a few steps. Not once did she take her eyes from the form at the creek's bank. "Out here there are no old crones named She Cat and Weasel Woman pawing over you, pretending you used to be something. When you know you are not anything, only a creature confined to a narrow band of time."

She leaned forward in a confidential manner. "At least Coyote is like me, conscious of certain things, whether she is conscious of time or not. She was my sister, and she turned crazy on me!" Her voice rose to a tight pitch. Her eyes half closed in the faded memory of that painful fight. She folded her feet under her and sat on the ground still talking, frequently pausing to gulp deep drafts of air. She babbled about how Kicking Horse had protected her. She rambled on about how she had fought with Kicking Horse many times, but in the end she had won because death had claimed him and his arguments. She wiped her mouth again.

Gray Bone constantly looked at Sacajawea, who was not dead, but sitting quietly on the sand and listening.

A flicker of awareness showed in Gray Bone's sunken eyes, to be replaced by an expression of scorn.

"And your man is gone. And your white man has gone under." Her laugh was like the screech of a crow announcing it had found carrion on the canyon floor. "He was named Charbonneau. I heard your talk with the Mexicans. So—I have asked around since leaving the Quohada stench. That Charbonneau was in the village named Saint Louis two summers past. He was with one called Joshua Pilcher, who gave him wampum, money, so he could buy a hunting knife. He then returned to his young Ute woman. This old weasel, Charbonneau, bragged about a Snake woman he had. This women, he said, went with him and white soldiers to the Stinking Western Waters with a son on her back."

Sacajawea could say nothing. Her head pounded; her back ached and throbbed. She started forward a little, then stopped and watched Gray Bone, whose hands covered her throat as though it was a great effort to speak.

"That old weasel liked women young. That is why he let the Snake go. He wanted a fresh child to keep him warm. I could understand a man like that," she croaked. "I like young girls with slim, firm bodies. They make my blood run and my head swim. My man beat me for looking at my own child when she was ripening." She wiped her mouth again and gasped for air.

Sacajawea realized that Gray Bone never swallowed—that she could not.

Gray Bone pointed a clawlike finger at Sacajawea. "You were that Snake woman! I know it!" Then she swayed and it seemed she could not speak more, but after several moments she seemed to have a second wind.

"This Charbonneau died near a white man's fort up north. It was a frightened young Sioux woman who buried him under layers of damp earth, where he will no longer see blue sky. You wonder where I learned this? It was from the mouth of a white man, Charles Larpenteur. He said that old man never carried a gun, only a hunting knife, and wore a red trading shirt, and offered his young women to any man in camp. It was some custom with him."

Gray Bone's hand twitched. She leered into the darkening air with contempt.

Sacajawea bent forward, rubbed her back, and felt a large stone bruise. She knew the disease of the coyote had nearly taken possession of Gray Bone's body, but her mind was working. She had heard many times that lucky ones bitten by crazed animals took only a few days to die—but the unfortunate ones took weeks. Gray Bone was fortunate.

"There was a chola—part Shoshoni, part white—who came to a fort, far north—Bill Bent's—with furs on a donkey charrette. He could scratch on paper. Once I hid in the fort at the side of a building, a lodge of logs, and watched." Gray Bone's head nodded, and her hands went to her throat. Sacajawea feared the words would become incoherent. She wanted to ask questions, but was afraid Gray Bone would say no more. "I put things together. The one with the furs was called Charbonneau. Sometimes Bap. So—he is the son you asked the Mexican trader about?"

Sacajawea could not answer. She could not speak. And now Gray Bone seemed unable to stop. She exulted when Sacajawea sat motionless. She looked about herself until she had established the continuity of her existence and identified Sacajawea's form sitting passively across the dune from her.

"Now I was not so bashful. I found an opportunity when this Bap was walking alone and went up to him. I asked in good Comanche if he had a *pia*, Wadzewipe, or Lost Woman. He looked and asked for a repeat of my words; then he said no, his *pia* ran away and was never found. She is dead—maybe eaten by a coyote." Gray Bone laughed raucously. "I said his mother lived with the Quohada Comanches. He said no, she liked to live like the white people." Gray Bone tried to lick her parched lips. Her voice was hoarse. She choked, then quieted, and her voice was no more than a loud whisper. "I told him I know his *pia*. He laughed and gave me chewing tobacco. Nice man."

Sacajawea shivered as a breeze stirred the dead gray dawn air. Gray Bone's mood varied. "The wind," she groaned. "It will skin me alive." She ran her left hand lightly across her bosom and down her thigh. The touch seemed painful. As the breeze grew, she groaned, "Can't you stop it? See what it is doing to me?" She wiped her mouth and seemed to forget Sacajawea was there. She began to explore her body with her fingertips, muttering something about heavy clothing.

"Where is this place—Bent's? The chola—where is he?"

"What?" Gray Bone rasped, straightening up abruptly, an expression of wonderment and awe overspreading her face as she peered at Sacajawea. Her mouth twitched. "The white men are north."

"How far?"

"Six, eight suns by horse, maybe farther; it is hard to say." Her face moved as if in a spasm, and she hesitated a few moments. She again pushed a hand against her throat, then wiped her mouth.

"Can I get you water?" offered Sacajawea.

"I cannot drink it. Do not bring it near." Her voice was hardly audible.

"I will go for help."

"No, I cannot use help. Do not leave." She pierced the stillness with a shrill laugh. She moved closer to Sacajawea, then with one swift motion struck out with arms and legs.

Sacajawea's legs felt a jerking grip that overthrew her. Swiftly as the grip had flashed about her legs, just as swiftly Gray Bone brought a stone down, grazing Sacajawea's left hip. And like the crack of a beaver's tail on water, Sacajawea hit Gray Bone with the flat of her hand on the good side of her face, and with a quick thrust of her other hand, struck Gray Bone's hand. The stone was thrown out and thudded into the sand. The next instant Gray Bone felt Sacajawea's hand grip her wrist. The struggle was for the butcher knife Gray Bone had grabbed from Sacajawea's waistband, each woman striving to hold it. Gray Bone could see only dimly; then she was blinded by a handful of sand deliberately flung into her eyes. In that moment she slashed the knife across Sacajawea's shoulder and her grip slackened. In the next moment Gray Bone felt a smashing darkness descend upon her skull, and in her brain the darkness filled with nothing.

Sacajawea had grabbed the stone. She hit again and

again, until she was sure Gray Bone was not breathing, except for the dying of the pulsing heart. Sacajawea tossed the stone over the white dune; she was breathing heavily. She sat beside the body of Gray Bone. Sacajawea sobbed and panted for breath. "That old woman wanted me on the trail to the Unknown with her!" Sacajawea was half crying from anger and exhaustion. "Why would I want to go with her?" She peered at Gray Bone's bloody face, with the eyes staring at the sky, the head twisted to one side and sprinkled with fine particles of sand. It was difficult to distinguish the features.

Sacajawea scrubbed her hands and arms with abrasive sand, instinctively knowing she had touched the unclean body of someone diseased. With her hands she covered Gray Bone's body with clean white sand from the dune. She carried half a dozen large boulders to place on top. "That is the best I can do," she said aloud, cleaning her butcher knife with sand.

She thought she heard the wild, half-human scream of a *chimbica*. She moved toward her horse in the mesquite thicket. She had never heard a cougar cat scream in the afternoon before.

She mounted and left the body of Gray Bone as she would leave a scrub oak leaf fallen in the winter's wind. Leaving the past, she rode down the dry canyon, across the bits of potsherd poking out of the sand. The cry of the cougar cat became a whisper as she passed under the niche in the wall where once life had lived in balance with nature, simply and happily, until something had abused and abased those Ancients and they no longer walked on the sand or watched the flight of birds, but passed on to the trail of the Unknown.

Book Six
ON THE
FINAL TRAIL

While he was in charge of Bent's Fort on the Arkansas, August 30, 1842, Jean Baptiste Charbonneau was described by a traveller there as one "who proved to be a gentleman of superior information. He had acquired a classic education and could converse quite fluently in German, Spanish, French, and English, as well as several Indian languages. His mind, also, was well stored with choice reading, and enriched by extensive travel and observation. Having visited most of the important places, both in England, France, and Germany, he knew how to turn his experience to good advantage.

"There was a quaint humor and shrewdness in his conversation, so garbed with intelligence and perspicuity, that he at once insinuated himself into the good graces of listeners, and commanded their admiration and respect."

RUFUS B. SAGE, *Scenes in the Rocky Mountains by a New Englander.* Vol V. Philadelphia: 1846.
LEROY R. HAFEN and ANN W. HAFEN, eds., *Scenes in the Rocky Mountains, 1820–1875,* "Rufus B. Sage, His Letters and Papers," Vol. II. Glendale: The Arthur H. Clark Co., 1956, pp. 52–4.

CHAPTER

50

Bent's Fort to Lupton's Fort

*There is a Mexican girl who was captured by her son,
Ticannaf. This girl lived with her until the old lady
disappeared and her son's family would not live with
her, so they gave her to a man for his wife, although she
was only 14 or 15 years old. This girl knew a great deal
about her but even she never knew her past history.*

CHARLES A. EASTMAN, *Report to Commissioner of Indian
Affairs.* Washington, D.C.: Department of the Interior,
March 2, 1925, pp. 45–6. "Statement given to Dr.
Charles A. Eastman, Feb. 15, 1925, in Lawton, Okla.,
by Wesuepoie, mother-in-law of Tahcutine, youngest
daughter of Ticannaf, concerning the traditions of
Porivo, or supposed to be Sacajawea, or 'Bird Woman.'"

In the next dawning, Sacajawea saw the thin streams of smoke rising into the quiet air. She was on high ground, riding toward the Quohadas' camp.

In the village a feast was going on in honor of the new chief, Wounded Buck.

Sacajawea looked at these people who called themselves Quohadas. Their faces were happy once again and full of confidence. They had ridden through the time of having no chief and were now whole and alive.

Hides Well pushed through some women and came to meet Sacajawea. Hides Well's lips were drawn tight. "Get off that horse and show some respect for the new chief. What about old Gray Bone? Did you find her? Where is she?"

"Shh—do not say the name. She cannot return to this camp."

"She has gone away?" Hides Well's mouth began to turn up into a smile.

"*Ai*, she has gone with *los muertos*."

"Dead? You saw her die?"

"*Ai*, I helped her, my mother. She was crazed by the mad coyote's bite. We fought."

"You are bringing her remains in for proper burial?"

"No, *pia*, she is under sand and stone in the little canyon. The body was not fit to carry."

Hides Well looked out of the corner of her eye at Sacajawea. "Lost Woman, she was a Quohada and deserved that much. The people will turn from you, remembering who invited her to be a member of this band again."

"Even while living she was putrefying."

Hides Well did not argue with Sacajawea; yet she did not agree, either. She walked off to her lodge.

Choway, who was now close to fifteen summers, and Crying Basket, who was nearly four summers old, ran out from the crowd to welcome Sacajawea home.

"I do not know whether to laugh or cry," said Sacajawea softly as she nuzzled her child and wet her neck with tears.

At times such an aching loneliness came through

Sacajawea that she could not stay in the tepee with Choway. She moved out under the open skies and sought some nameless comfort in the sage and mesquite. At night the aching became a weight against her very breathing. The people pointed to her and whispered behind their hands. Hides Well no longer visited with her, and Spring became so busy with her own family that she seldom went out of her way to see Sacajawea.

Sacajawea began to wonder more and more about her firstborn. Her wonderment grew and fed on itself with the memory of old Gray Bone's last words. Was it true she had seen Baptiste? Had he reached Saint Louis? Was he working for Chief Red Hair? Was it possible she could travel north and find him? She felt isolated and alone on the barren plains, with no one to turn to. Sometimes she pulled Crying Basket into bed with her so that she could hear the child's breathing and faint cries, which seemed a comfort.

At sunrise one morning, her mind was made up. She brought her horse to the tepee door and tied a large package of dried meat to its side. She filled a water bag and fastened it to the animal's other side. She kicked at the old lodgepoles behind the tepee, which had been discarded at the beginning of spring. She tied them travois-fashion to the horse. She went inside and brought out a bundle of old tepee skins and tied them on the travois. Then she brought out her clothing and the clothing of Crying Basket.

By this time, Choway was up. "What are you doing?"

"I am leaving."

"But where?"

"I am not sure," she said. "I cannot stay here and be at peace with myself any longer. Everyone looks cross-wise at me, even my own family, since I did not bring the crazy woman's rotting bones back to the camp for a Comanche burial. They looked the same way when I let her into the camp. I want to go away."

"I do not understand," said Choway.

"I will try to pick up the threads from my other life. It will not catch up with me, so I will try to find it."

"I still cannot understand."

"Tell my son, Ticannaf, I have gone a long way, *ava-jemear*, and do not seek me."

"But you know he will."

"*Ai*, but he will not find me. I will be many miles from here."

"You can't go. You will be back before nightfall—within two suns. The Wichitas will tell us where you travel. You are my mother now."

"You may have this tepee as your own," said Sacajawea. "Ticannaf will bring meat and hides to you. You have been a good helper for me. I have not been a good mother for you. But just the same, you have become a good Quohada, and that is something to be proud of."

She was ready. She took up Crying Basket and tied her to the travois. Sacajawea took another horse from the herd and put a robe on its back. "Ticannaf may have the rest of his father's horses. Tell him and he will know for sure I have gone."

Choway nodded, knowing she would miss this squaw who had been kind to her. But Choway had sensed there was conflict between the Quohada band and this woman they called Wadzewipe.

Sacajawea mounted, pulled on the rawhide of the packhorse, then, relenting, she touched Choway and said in Spanish, "I love you and these people. Only there is something beyond this that I must go to. I do not know where it is myself."

Once, Sacajawea looked back, and it seemed tears were streaming down Choway's face. Sacajawea could not be sure. Her own tears were a continuous stream down her face. She had spent more than twenty-five summers with the Quohada band, and now she was going into some unknown kind of life.

She headed straight north across the country. She traveled fast at first through the arid, unproductive country, where a broad, shallow river, some six hundred yards wide and only a few inches deep, seemed to struggle for its life among yellowish white quicksands. The first few days Sacajawea sang, and the words floated back to Crying Basket. She tried to think of English words she'd learned, then of French words. Many were lost to her. She could remember better a little Spanish. She sat astride her horse as if it were part of her. She watched the sun set, then stopped and made camp for the night.

They wound around hills and dry creeks. Crying Basket sat up front on the horse with her mother for company. Occasionally they could see the timbered course of streams out to the right or left.

Sacajawea wondered what the white man's fort was like. She was certain it would be made in the same way as Fort Clatsop or Fort Mandan, with logs. She thought of bluebonnets that bloomed in damp areas, the purple violets, and white buttercups. She could see her first-born picking spring flowers. She tried harder to visualize more detail. Actually it was hard for her to remember exactly what Baptiste had looked like—round face, black eyes and hair, like any papoose.

They came to a little valley where there was nothing but dry, strawlike grass for the horses. The dried meat was gone and they found little water. They were exposed to the burning sun and the only water they found in two days was in a stagnant pool in which several stray buffalo wallowed. With her horses she drove off the buffalo, then the horses put their noses down and sucked up the alkaline water. She deliberately pulled them away before they had their fill, knowing that too much would kill them, and no water at all would also kill them. She washed Crying Basket's face and then her own with the warm bitter-tasting liquid. She permitted the child to suck her fingers, only to avoid distressing cramps. They rode around overhanging limestone cliffs and through rough sandstone gullies. The soft skin on Crying Basket's arms and legs became dry and parched. Her face was scaly and her lips cracked. Sacajawea tried to keep the child covered, but it was hot and the child pulled the clothing off. Sacajawea longed for animal fat to soothe the child's dry skin and relieve her own itching.

One night they stopped in the bottom of a little dip where water ran down a rocky channel into a tiny bed of grass. The water was sweet, but could not be dipped up without mixing it with mud. Sacajawea showed her child how to lie on her belly and draw the water up through her lips. They chewed on the grass stems, pretending they were the wild potato. She let the horses drink several times and before morning the little patch of grass had been cleaned off the red earth. She filled

the water paunch with the muddy spring water and
they moved on in the morning.

They rode over sharp stones and through thorny brush
to the base of a high bluff. They followed the bottom of
the red sandstone bluff until they met a gap in the wall.
The gap was a pass that sloped upward and she turned
the horses in, clambering through the scree until they
reached a ledge nearly a third of the way to the top.
There was no way to continue the upward climb so they
stopped there before the sun was halfway across the
sky. There was grass and some other plants growing in
the sheltered places close to the high-cut bank.

It was hot and muggy. Clouds hung low in the east.
Crying Basket ran naked on the red earth. Finding a
little shade among the chaparral, she sat there and dug
in the dirt with a small stick. Sacajawea found a few
wild onions and several small sego lilies in the bunch
grass. She cleaned them on the bottom of her tunic and
pushed them close to the hot coals of her small cooking
fire. She turned the bulbs frequently and let the coals
cool. She watched her child and noticed the small body
was thinner than when they had left the Quohada camp.
Crying Basket did not say she was hungry until the
afternoon wore on and the clouds grew. Sacajawea peeled
the outer skins from the onion and lily bulbs, which
were still warm and very soft.

Sacajawea felt wet all over, yet there was no rain.
The air was heavy and hard to breathe and made her
feel anxious. She balanced the child on one arm and
moved closer to the bank where the horses were tied to
a stunted, post oak covered with a catbrier vine. She
pulled the robe from her riding horse and spread it on
the ground for the child to sleep on. She sat on one
corner, brushed the dark hair from the little girl's face,
and kissed her cheek. She had not used this white man's
gesture much on this papoose.

The thunder roared like a long tattoo on a tight skin
drum. Sacajawea watched the chain of lightning in the
clouds. She sang an old Shoshoni lullaby that had come
to her:

> "This day is good,
> The baby sleeps,

Content with food.
Under dark clouds,
The voice of thunder
Sounds soft to her ear."

It seemed that Mother Earth was talking as the rumbles of thunder penetrated even into the ground. Sacajawea got the bundle of old tepee skins and spread them over her back and around her child. It felt good; the gusts were cold.

Lightning flashed more frequently as the clouds rolled in like dirty water boiling in a kettle. Crying Basket moved, pulling her knees against her chest for warmth. Sacajawea remembered an old saying of her mother's. "Roast the porcupine and when you have eaten it, mash the bones, then the frozen rain will come." The wind blew dirt into her face, so that she pulled one of the skins higher for protection. The grass was pushed nearly flat. The horses stayed close to the wall with their heads down. The dust swirled one way, then another just before the hail peppered them. Sacajawea held the skins over her child and herself as best she could in the thrashing wind.

Crying Basket woke up and climbed to her mother's lap, clinging from fear, her eyes wide. She did not cry, but her tiny heartbeat quickened. The hail fell in streaks and bounced on rocks; the horses shone in the frequent flashes of lightning, their hooves smeared with gummy clay. Then the wind slacked off and the rain came, but did not last long.

The roiling clouds moved away, and their grumbling was not so loud. The bright stars seemed to hang low in the sky. Sacajawea was soaked. She found a partially dry skin and wrapped the child in it. She lay down, trying to forget the wetness and was soon asleep.

Sacajawea was awakened suddenly by some subconscious sense. She was stiff and sat up slowly. Her eyes became accustomed to the starlight as she looked around. Her eyes fell on a small hole nearby where the ground had been kept dry by the robe. The robe corner was now folded back so the movement at the hole was visible. Two dark, hairy legs were feeling the outer edge. Then the hairy body of a wolf spider emerged, looking for food. Silently it moved on long, fuzzy legs to examine Crying Basket's exposed foot. Sacajawea involuntarily stiffened. She breathed deeply and forced herself to remain motionless. She knew any sudden movement might make the creature lunge and drive its fangs deep into the tiny, bare foot, releasing its poison.

She sat quietly, praying to the Great Spirit that the child would not move. The hairy, dark spider backed away by inches, fell off the robe into the dirt, and scrambled away silently and out of sight. Sacajawea let out her breath, closed her eyes, and thanked the Great Spirit for the creature that intended no harm. For all living beings life was a constant hunt for food and avoidance of enemies. She could have squashed the spider, taking its life, but what would have been the purpose of that?

In the morning, Sacajawea repacked the damp skins, led the horses farther along the ledge, and checked the end horse hitched to the travois. She scooped up Crying Basket, tied her in a blanket, and swung her over her back. The ledge narrowed, then circled around a sharp sandstone point. On one side was a high bank of rock, with some precarious overhangings that looked as if they could fall at any moment. On the other side was a sheer drop-off down to the plains. Far below, the river looked like a pale green satin ribbon thrown carelessly on a red-brown floor. The lead horse would go no farther and there was no room to turn around.

Sacajawea could not look down without feeling a helplessness that fostered the urge simply to let everything go and topple over the edge. Forcing the thought away, she took a deep breath and looked only at the ground where the horses' hooves touched. She inched forward hugging the wall, to investigate further.

To her surprise and joy, on the other side of the point the ledge widened and a broad incline led all the way to the top. Carefully she coaxed the horses forward inch by inch. She held her breath when the travois teetered once, then let her breath go when it settled upright.

She finally got to the summit and could see what appeared to be another wide, expansive plain, carved with dips, crevasses, and small canyons. Below, the river still meandered.

As the morning sun moved higher and bathed the

high plain with light, Sacajawea, with Crying Basket still on her back, moved down a game trail to seek a way to the river. They found a crevasse in the sandstone and came out on a wide ledge. A fog bank had now moved in above the river and was only a few hundred yards away. It was like a wide wall in front of them. Sacajawea stood at the edge of the stone shelf, feeling stimulated from the exertion and clear-headed in the warm rays of sunshine. She turned and caught her breath. There was the most astonishing sight.

Mirrored on the fog's wall-like surface was the side view of an enlarged shadow of a woman carrying a child on her back! Sacajawea moved, and the shadow moved. She made a quarter-turn to face the fog bank and held out her arms. She made a shadow image of a large bird, larger than any thunderbird she had ever seen drawn inside rock caves or on high rock cliffs. She moved her arms and the bird's wings seemed to flap as if readying itself to soar into the sky.

Then she noticed a glow, similar to a rainbow, encircling the upper half of the shadow picture. She stood motionless, her arms widespread, transfixed with awe. She was certain this phenomenon had some significant meaning for her. Sacajawea moved so that the silhouetted woman and child were haloed by the light. The colored, concentric rings all about her larger-than-life shadow could only mean one thing, she thought. The disk of colors was a protector: it was a totem to care for her and the child in this harsh land. What else could this extraordinary sight possibly be?

Sacajawea was so overwhelmed that she could not make a sound for several long moments. Her mind searched for some supernatural explanation. Slowly and deliberately she lowered her arms and turned for another side view. Awestruck, she felt the presence of the Great Spirit all around as she reverently gazed at the image of mother and child with a spectrum of violet-through-red around their heads.[1]

The sun rose higher and the shadow slowly disappeared. The wall of fog evaporated and Sacajawea clearly saw the river and another game trail.

For many days after that her mind dwelt on the shadow picture. She was unable to connect it with any

natural cause and effect, such as relative position of
the sunlight, thick fog, and where she stood on the rock
ledge or reflection, refraction, and dispersion. Thus, she
turned to superstition, to some powerful, magical force
that was a sign to her. She decided it was a sign that
she was to have a large, full life, that she was headed
in the right direction and that she would be protected
by this rainbow light. This explanation satisfied her.

Each night Sacajawea was more exhausted. She
climbed from the horse, pulled the packs off, and lay
on the earth with her child sheltered in her arms. Each
night she looked for the North Star in order to start
out in the right direction in the morning. Crying Basket
licked cracked lips and asked for water more often. Sacajawea longed for meat to put flesh on the bones of
Crying Basket and herself. Their diet had become one
of bare subsistence.

There was a breath of winter in the sharp, dry air
as they rose into the shaggy foothills bordering the
plains. Now they found berry bushes with ripe fruit.
They crossed old beaver dams, but saw not a beaver.
The beaver had once been rich in the small streams,
but by this time were gone. Unknown to Sacajawea,
the spot was too accessible to trappers. She guided the
horses through black junipers and scrub piñon, then
back to the grizzliness of blade-leafed soapweed, grease-
wood, and cactus. The going grew rough. Eventually
they forded another river. It was hard now to separate
one river from another, or how or where the crossing
had been made.

One day she saw dust feathering out against the sky.
She knew it meant men on horseback.

Forgetting the riders that night, Sacajawea built a
fire to keep the chill away. Crying Basket's legs were
covered with scabs, and her feet were scratched and
cut. Sacajawea cut an old tepee skin to bind them. The
child's nose seemed pinched and pointed, and her
scrawny fingers all thin bone. The horses were thin and
gaunt. She looked at her own feet, which were bruised,
swollen, and torn, with blackened nails. Her hands were
rough and cracked. As she cut bindings for her feet, she

thought neither she nor her child could travel many more days; even the horses were ready to drop.

Sacajawea lay in a stupor with Crying Basket in her arms. She had heard the horses coming, but had no strength to hide. And then she heard the horses stop, and opened her eyes, and saw Mexican soldiers with broad hats staring down at her. There were many of them.

"*Con su permiso*," the nearest soldier said. "*Pobrecita*." He pointed to the starving child, then to the two thin horses. Most of the soldiers were mounted on fat black Mexican horses.

"*Agua?*"

Frightened, she slowly sat up with as much dignity as she could muster. She answered, "No water. It is gone."

A man offered her a drink from a *copita*, a small silver cup. She gave it to the child first. In a few moments the soldiers, or dragoons, had all dismounted and were setting up a rest camp.

"We travel again, before sunup," explained the first soldier in slow Spanish and with hand signs. Someone brought a plate of pinto bean paste and *panocha*, a gluey brown pudding made from dried wheat sprouts. Crying Basket dipped fingers into the food, then licked them noisily.

"Are you lost?" another soldier asked in Spanish, also using hand signs.

"I am going north to the white man's fort," Sacajawea answered, less frightened and more curious about these soldiers who had found her path. "I look for my son."

"Your *muchacho* is lost?"

"No, he is cholo—too grown to be lost." She measured a full-grown man with her fingertips held high.

"Ah, he is half-white. You have a white husband?"

"No." She shook her head, wanting to ask the man questions herself, but a deep weariness overcame everything and her hands dropped back in her lap.

A man with a red serape came to her. "I'll take the papoose."

Her mind woke, and she felt ill from eating much too fast.

"No, no! Do not take the child! No!"

"I am sorry," the man's face was reddening. "I did not mean to frighten you, señora. I only wanted to help so that you could rest before we travel. You may ride with us to the fort. We will call when we start. I will leave the child. But if she is hungry, we have more food."

He was gone before she could reply. Crying Basket was asleep, curled beside her. Sacajawea tried to think her situation out, but fell asleep long before the sun set.

Long before the sun rose, the man in the red serape was back. "I mean for you to ride this horse, señora," he called softly. She stirred and rubbed her eyes. Patiently he held the reins of a sleek black mare. "You will ride with us. Your horses will follow in our pack train."

"Where?"

"We go looking for *americano* fur traders in Mexican Territory. The men who steal mules from Mexican towns. We ride to Bent's Fort."

"Bent's?" she asked, fully awake.

"Who else, the white *conquistadores!*" shouted one of the mounted soldiers.

She saw her horses being led to the back line, the travois in place. She nudged Crying Basket.

"I will ride beside you and hold the child for a while," the man said. "You do not look too strong."

Sacajawea mounted the black mare and tried to keep up with the man who carried Crying Basket.

That evening one of the soldiers gave Sacajawea a pair of huaraches in place of the leather bandages on her feet. Another Mexican soldier gave her some soothing oil to rub on the child's dry skin and parched lips. For the first time she saw the pack train and the mules and muleteers. Their conical hats were covered with oilcloth peaked above their long dark hair. Their heads were thrust through holes in coarse, bright-hued blankets, and their leather pantaloons were split down the sides, revealing a loose pair of cotton drawers beneath. Enormous spur rowels jangled on their heels; their saddles bore sweeping leather skirts and wooden stirrups. To her they were ridiculous-looking. As soon as the mule team was hitched the next morning, one muleteer mounted the right-hand wheel mule, and another climbed aboard the left-hand mule of the span behind the leaders. The rest of the hands armed themselves with whips and took positions on either side of the team. At a shout from the chief muleteer, all fell to, whooping, spurring, whipping. The mules brayed and plunged. This was brutal but effective; they set themselves into the collars in fine, smooth style. Sacajawea's thin horses were tied behind.

The next evening, she was given a *capita*, a small cloak, to ward off the night chill. And a soldier dug deep into his pack to find a bright yellow shawl for the child.

In a few days Crying Basket's eyes were bright in the night firelight. She danced while the men sang. She is like Pomp was, Sacajawea thought to herself.

Slowly the dragoons moved over the northern Mexican Territory until midmorning one day when the horses were stopped. Someone pointed, and all eyes were on the north bank of a river. "*Americano!*" someone shouted.

Sacajawea squinted her eyes and saw an American flag, red-and-white stripes, similar to the ones used by Captain Lewis and Chief Red Hair. It was flying in the front of an adobe structure. She had never seen anything like this. Beyond the white-walled fort were low sand hills; at one side were small chalk bluffs and ledges of rock. Bordering the river were bottomlands that high water might flood, but in good seasons there would be enough grass for many horses. The man in the serape pointed far southwest to two humps. "Spanish Peaks," he said. He pointed far northwest to a dim dome. "Pike's Mountain," he said. Directly in front were sunflowers and the lark sparrows dipped. "Bent's Fort," said the soldier.

The rectangular fort faced eastward toward the approaching train of Mexican dragoons. Sacajawea noticed that on top was a high watchtower with holes to look through. She did not know that in the tower was a large telescope through which one could see for miles around. Musketry and small field cannons were mounted on top of the walls. They approached the main door made of wood and almost completely covered with heads of nails to prevent Indians from cutting through it or shooting their arrows into it.

Sacajawea could see that this was not ordinary. The fort stood out like beautiful white walls of a canyon. The door opened, and the dragoons went in, followed by the muleteers.

A small man, walking briskly, came from the back part of the buildings inside. He had a tanned, clean-shaven face. "Bill Bent," said someone. He shook hands with the dragoon captain and talked several minutes, then smiled and motioned for the men to lead their horses and mules to the corral. Sacajawea saw her two horses being led to water and a meager pile of hay. Crying Basket clung to her mother's tunic once they were dismounted, her eyes wide.

Bill Bent was aware that this year, 1841, Governor Manuel Armijo had denounced his fort, together with all similar American posts near the Mexican border, as "shelters of thieves and contraband, instigators of Indian forays against Mexican citizens, and a constant menace to the welfare and independence of New Mexico." Bill Bent was friendly. He wanted to trade with Mexicans, for the fort needed flour and salt.

The dragoon captain had come to trade flour, beans, salt, and pepper for American guns and ammunition and to look at the mules in the corral. Some just might have been stolen in Mexican Territory and brought here. It was his business to find out.

A young Cheyenne woman, neatly dressed in a long-skirted gingham dress, came out to the *placita* and, seeing Sacajawea standing apart from the men, opened the swinging iron gate. She motioned for Sacajawea to come through.

"That's Owl Woman, Bill Bent's wife," said the man in the serape as she walked past the gate.[2]

"*Ai*," said the woman softly to Sacajawea. "You have come a long way. I would like to hold your child. She seems so small." They sat together on a wooden bench on the narrow porch. Sacajawea tried to talk in Comanche, then Shoshoni, and then with hand signs and a smattering of Spanish and English she was able to make herself understood. Owl Woman used her hands constantly as she rocked to and fro with Crying Basket on her lap.

"My man will see that the white medicine man takes a look at your baby. He will have a salve for her legs and feet."

"The Mexican soldiers were kind and gave us some oil," Sacajawea said.

"Do you go back to Taos with them?"

"Oh, no," said Sacajawea.

"Is one of them your man? The one in the red serape?"

"No." Sacajawea grinned. "I came alone. Our paths came together. I am looking for one called Jean Baptiste Charbonneau." Sacajawea's heart beat faster at the mention of her quest. She watched Owl Woman.

"No, he is not here."

Sacajawea's heart fell. So—it was a wild-goose chase after all. Her son had never been here.

"He was here a few moons back, at the ending of winter."

"You saw him?" Sacajawea's heart jumped into her throat.

"*Ai*, Bap Charbonneau gets supplies and packs his buffalo robes here. He goes by boat down the Platte River to Saint Louis."

Sacajawea's hands flew to her face, covering her mouth. Tears stung at the back of her eyes. Baptiste had been here. At this place! She was not able to be stoic and hold the flood of tears back. They poured down her face.

"That Bap—he did something terrible to you?"

Sacajawea could only raise her hands in the Comanche manner and look toward the heavens and give prayful thanks to the Great Spirit for keeping her tired and worn moccasins on the right path. Finally she whispered, "He is my firstborn. My own."

"You? You are Bap's mother?" asked Owl Woman in amazement. "Once he told me his mother carried him to the Great Western Waters on her back. I think he joked with me."

"*Ai*, he told the truth. We were with white soldiers and one black one called York."

"York?" Owl Woman looked puzzled.

"*Ai*, and Chief Red Hair. We have lived in Saint

Louis, and my boys went to the school. They can use the talking leaves and make marks on paper."

"Read books? Your boys?"

"*Ai*. Baptiste and Tess."

"Tess?"

"Did one called Toussaint come with Baptiste?"

"No," said Owl Woman, shaking her head in confusion. "I know all who come here. And I know Baptiste. Handsome. Cheyenne girls make eyes with him. But he does not take a woman. He is strong. Good on a horse. Old Comanche woman, is this your son? True?"

Out in the corral there was an argument going on. Bill Bent was trying to calm several dragoons. "None of the men who work for me make runs in your territory," said Bent. "They are aware that you will confiscate their money and furs and jail them."

"Señor Bent," said one dragoon, "we had mules stolen near Santa Fe. We overheard the men say they were coming this far north. We have tried to follow them."

"You know who they were?"

"No, we do not know the names of these mule thieves."

"No doubt they are renegades and a long way from here by now."

The men seemed satisfied for the time being and moseyed back into the *placita*.[3.]

"See," said Owl Woman. "Small White Man there? He is my man and will feed those soldiers and their muleteers and they will buy supplies and go on by tomorrow. There will be no trouble here."

"Baptiste? Will he come back?"

"Perhaps. We will ask Small White Man when he is finished with the men. Come now."

Sacajawea followed Owl Woman, who still held Crying Basket, into a lower apartment off the *placita*. Without saying a word, Owl Woman took an old washtub from a large nail in the whitewashed wall. She handed the child to Sacajawea. "I could not fill this with water with my arms full," she chuckled. She filled the tub from a pump and put her hand in the water. "It is not too cold. Come." She pulled the child's soiled tunic over her head and placed her in the tub of water. Gently, Owl Woman splashed the water on Crying Basket and cleansed the sores on her feet. She scrubbed the child's head with broken bits of desert soapweed, making a thin, sudsy lather. The child kept her eyes on her own mother and did not say a word or cry out. Owl Woman gave Sacajawea a piece of white strouding, coarse trade cloth, to dry her child, then disappeared. In a moment she was back with a thin, gaunt man who carried a small black valise.

"This mother and child need medicine," said Owl Woman in broken English. "They have come a long way looking for the man we call Baptiste."

"Handsome Bap! Ho-ho! Is this his squaw?"

"His mother."

"Oh, well"—the doctor cleared his throat—"I just never figured Bap had a mother at all. How do you do, ma'am."

He pulled the child on his lap and sat on a wooden bench. Cupping his two hands one on top of the other, he listened to the child's breathing from her chest to her back. Sacajawea watched to see what great medicine this old man had for her child. She wondered about the way he tapped his fingers on her back and belly. Was that good?

"Ahh, fine. Some salve and clean cloths on the feet and she'll be running around in a few days. Ichthyous salve. Keep the baby clean, absolutely clean."

"*Si,*" said Owl Woman, wondering how she could keep the child clean with that black, tarlike grease on her feet. "And the señora?"

"Umm, she must have a bath and dress her wounds with the black, greasy salve. Each must bathe twice a day. They need food. Can you get milk for the baby?"

"*Si.* Pretty Feather has no child to nurse since hers died of fever."

Pretty Feather, a fat, comfortable Cheyenne squaw, was called to nurse Crying Basket. The child was four and had not nursed during the long journey with her mother, but she quickly snuggled down in the lap of Pretty Feather and suckled hungrily, then was fast asleep. A broad grin was on Pretty Feather's face.

Sacajawea quietly got up, going outside.

Pretty Feather followed. "Why do you look for the gate? Are you leaving?" she asked.

"I am dirty," answered Sacajawea with fast hand signs.

"Pah, Comanche always more dirty than Cheyenne. You take bath in same tub as baby." Pretty Feather grinned, and gently prodded Sacajawea back into the lower apartment. Then she sat and crooned to the sleeping child still in her arms. Owl Woman brought out a red dress made from strouding. Sacajawea put it on after the bath, which she thought hilarious, because never since the Fort Clatsop days had she seen a warm pool of water carried in and out of a lodge. That was certainly something only a white man could have thought of doing! She felt sleepy and her head nodded as she ate the hard bread and buffalo meat Owl Woman brought in. Owl Woman laid a buffalo robe at the side of the room. Sacajawea slept there with Crying Basket curled next to her the rest of the day and part of the next.

The following afternoon, Bill Bent, who was actually called Small White Man by his Cheyenne woman, found Sacajawea in the *placita*. He sat on the log bench, cleared his throat, and said, "Two years ago your son brought the first *bateau* load of furs down the tricky Platte. Late this spring he went down the Platte again with an even larger load of furs for Saint Louis."

"I will wait for him to return," said Sacajawea.

"Well, I have been thinking you'd say that. So while you wait, you can work with Pretty Feather, cooking for the men here. She will show you what you need to know. Cleanliness is first. The Cheyenne women are clean. You Comanches can learn something from them."

Sacajawea did not like his implication; she had heard the same words before, and had liked them no better earlier. "Comanche women are clean when in camp, but traveling even the white man does not stay clean. In the mud, rain, and wind, he can stink." She was standing with her back held rigid, her hand over her nose, before Bill Bent.

Bent was surprised at the squaw's quick defense. He looked more closely at Sacajawea. "You speak quickly. You are not the regular subjugated squaw."

She looked at him, a man of light complexion and stocky build. "I am Shoshoni," she said. "My father was a Shoshoni chief many moons back. My brother is chief of the Agaidükas, Salmon Eaters. They are north in the Shining Mountains."

"But you came from Comanche Territory?" he questioned.

Sacajawea looked into the man's pink face and saw his eyes intent upon her. She heard Owl Woman playing with Crying Basket and laughing. She knew she must tell this man her story so that he could be certain she was the mother of Jean Baptiste Charbonneau. Her English came slowly, and was mixed with Spanish-Comanche and a smattering of French phrases with hand signs. By late afternoon Bill Bent had heard the incredible story of this wandering Shoshoni woman. He was so impressed that he not only found a place for Sacajawea to work in his kitchen, cooking for the thirty or more regular workers at the fort, but he let her stay with Owl Woman in her lodge at the Cheyenne camp. During the day Owl Woman cared for Crying Basket.

Sacajawea noted immediately that Bill Bent commanded great respect among the trappers and Cheyennes, in the same kind of manner that her friend Chief Red Hair had once done. He opposed the sale of the crazy-water to the Cheyenne.

Winter came, and with it came much snow. Then one day the snow began to thin and the air felt warmer. Early one evening Sacajawea passed outside the fort and walked down through the Cheyenne camp to the river. The sky was milky with light. The air was brisk with frost, and the edges of the river, when she reached it, were ribbed with thin, webby ice. She cracked the ice and sucked on a thin piece. The back of winter was broken now. The ice was thinner and thinner each day. The iron-hardness of the ground was slowly thawing. The willows along the river were reddening down their trailing streamers, and soon the small yellow threads of leaves would appear. She sniffed the smells that came to her nostrils—the acrid smell of wild sage, the tonic smell of sweet gum, the muddy, spongy smell of thawing ground, and from the lodges, the smell of pine smoke. They were good smells. It was April, the moon when geese lay eggs, and spring was on its way.

She returned to the lodge of Owl Woman and took

her place before the fire. She took the horn ladle handed her by Owl Woman and ate from the wooden bowl of boiled pounded corn. There was no meat in the Cheyenne lodges as there was in the white man's fort. There would be no meat until the spring hunt. Sacajawea still could smell the dripping meat juices in the fort's kitchen. But she had not eaten there. The pounded corn had cooked to a mush, and it was good. She ate hungrily; then she moved to her sleeping robe with Crying Basket beside her.

"Small White Man has sent for me tonight," said Owl Woman bending over Sacajawea. "He has a guest who comes in from the north, Fort Lupton. Sit up, you will be interested. The man's name is Rufus B. Sage. This man knows the man Baptiste Charbonneau."

Sacajawea was suddenly sitting up. "Perhaps I could go in your place and talk with this man," suggested Sacajawea, poking Owl Woman in the side and laughing.

Pretending shock, Owl Woman rounded her eyes at Sacajawea and lapsed into an affronted silence; then she suddenly slapped her side and laughed, saying, "My man would not allow it. He want one woman. Me."

During the conversation that night, Bent mentioned Sacajawea to Sage, and asked him for any news of Baptiste.

"Well, you know Bap was with Louis Vasquez and Bill Sublette in thirty-nine, and that son of a coyote has been to Europe. He can spin a yarn half the night and play euchre the other half. Now tell me about this old woman."

Rufus Sage was fascinated with the story of the old squaw with the young child who claimed to be Bap's own mother. "Look," he said now, "what if I take the squaw back to Fort Lupton with me? Bap's coming back to Fort St. Vrain before summer to take those furs from Céran down to Saint Louis. She'd have a better chance of seeing her son if she were closer to St. Vrain's."

"I don't know," Bent said. "My Cheyenne woman here has grown fond of Crying Basket, and that Shoshoni squaw is a good worker in my kitchen. She's cleaner'n any Comanche I've ever seen and minds her own business."

"I was thinking how other things go, too." Sage lowered his voice and bit his pipe. His nostrils stood wide as he inhaled. His black hair was pulled to the back and tied with a small piece of buckskin. "I was thinking of Fontaine up there at Lupton's. You know that man has a half-breed kid to care for and no one to leave her with. His woman's people wouldn't take the baby after they found out she had the pox and did not die with her mother."

Bent rubbed his hands together, beginning to see what Sage had in his mind; he sat waiting patiently for Sage to say it outright.

"They will have nothing to do with Fontaine or the child, even though both are as healthy now as you or me. This here squaw, the one who is supposed to be Bap's mother, could take care of the kid and cook for Fontaine. Maybe he'd feel like raising vegetables or herding sheep again."

So that was it, thought Bent. Sage was well respected for his concern about the welfare of his fellow white men in this territory, and his mind traveled straight to solutions. "I'd rather miss her," said Bent, relighting his pipe and motioning for Owl Woman to replace the dried meat platter with a fresh one. "But, all right— we'll ask her."

While Owl Woman went to fetch Sacajawea, Rufus Sage traded with Bent for several canisters of sugar and other supplies. He was happy to be going back to his base fort with a surprise for Fontaine.

Jacques Fontaine had been a free trapper. He had come from French-Canadian stock and worked his way down to Lancaster Lupton's from Canada's Fort McLeod. He had found himself a pretty Ute woman and stayed at Lupton's. He became a fur trader for Lupton and a hard worker. One year he raised a few sheep; another he grew a fine garden that fed the fort. When his woman died of the pox he was lost and did not seem to care if he stayed in the fort or if he sat outside against the wall with the Indians in the sun.

* * *

Early the next morning, Sacajawea gathered her belongings, packed her horses, and prepared to go with Rufus Sage to Fort Lupton.

"I will ride north with my man in the late spring to visit you," Owl Woman promised. "Maybe your great son will be there so that I can again pass my eyes over him." Owl Woman's face was impassive, and her eyes narrowed as she watched Sacajawea. She would miss her.

A flash of quick delight in her black eyes indicated Sacajawea's pleasure in the words. Then both women covered their mouths with the back of their hands to hide their amusement as Sage mounted his horse from what was to them the wrong side. Then Sacajawea arranged herself and Crying Basket, and the small party left Bent's Fort.

When Sage reached the timber that began a few miles north of Bent's Fort, he pulled his horse up in a stand of jack pines and rested a little while. The air began to thin and cool. Sacajawea was grateful for the moccasins and Navaho blankets Owl Woman had given her in trade for the huaraches, *capita*, and yellow woolen shawl. She wrapped one blanket around herself and the other around Crying Basket. Sage pulled a buffalo robe around himself. When they were nearly four thousand feet above sea level, Sacajawea caught a glimpse of a mountain peak. Then others came into view. The peaks were covered with gleaming snow. She told Sage and Crying Basket that they were like the beautiful Shining Mountains in the far west. Sage smiled at her delight in the scenery.

During the sixth night out, they were awakened by a miserable, cold spring rain flowing in from the north, and by the afternoon of the next day, the temperature had dropped low. They huddled in blankets and robes and rode down off the last of the foothills that rolled away from the snow-covered mountains, the pack mules of Sage strung out in a little line and Sacajawea's packhorse behind.

Before them unfolded a majestic panorama. In the foreground facing west was Fort Lupton, situated on the east side of a small river. Three miles northeast was Fort Jackson, and beyond that was Fort Vasquez.

Beyond Vasquez to the north, hardly visible, was Fort St. Vrain. Except that St. Vrain was larger, the rival trading posts were similar, with adobe bastions at two corners, and smaller wooden blockhouses protruding over the entrances where American flags fluttered from tall masts. The whitewashed walls rose imposingly against the background of hills covered with coarse grass and scattered with pines and cedars. Crowding the plain between the forts were several hundred Indian tepees. The course of the small river was dotted with willow, box elder, ash, and cottonwood. Behind Fort Lupton, Sacajawea could see about an acre patch of cultivated ground. It seemed incongruous, yet she was not surprised by it; white men can do these things, she thought. She wondered if this were the farm of Monsieur Fontaine.

"The first monument on the prairie is Lupton's," said Sage, pointing. "Old Fontaine will probably take you visiting all them forts if he ever comes out of his shell. He used to take his Ute Woman visiting and show her off at all of them. Céran St. Vrain was especially fond of his little girl, and old Lupton was like a granddaddy to her."

Sacajawea learned that in the years since the four forts had been built there'd been no trouble between them. But if anyone wanted to start a trade war, things could get awkward.

They rode down a small round plateau circling toward Fort Lupton and the Indian tepees. Sage stopped and looked again, first at Fort Lupton on one side then at Fort Jackson on the other. Sacajawea looked at the white-skin tepees, the streamers of smoke against the sky, the dogs and children running helter-skelter among the tepees.

Finally Sage said, "I'm half-starved." He kicked his horse into a run and fired his rifle.

They rode in through the arched passageway beneath the blockhouse. The squaws and near-naked children by the wall clustered around them in the small courtyard. Coming from the blacksmith on the opposite side of the courtyard was a man with white whiskers and heavy white hair.

"Hey, Lanc, this old Comanche woman is here to take

charge of Fontaine's baby. Can you guess who she claims to be?"

"Is this what you got at Bent's, you fool?"

"Aw, I got the sugar and salt pork, but who do you suppose this squaw is?"

"Pocahontas?"

The old man's eyes twinkled bright blue as Sage dismounted and helped Sacajawea and her child down. Someone came up and took the packs off the horses and led them to a small corral and water.

"Rub the horses good, Charley!" yelled Sage, then he said, "This here is Bap Charbonneau's mammy. She was the woman with those captains—Lewis and Clark. Can you ever imagine?"

"Hell's fire! Never would have dreamt a thing like this. Is it true or are you pulling my leg?"

"True, true," replied Sage. "She knows too much about that there expedition for it to be anyone else. Been living with bloodthirsty Comanches in Mexican Territory for a time, looking for her son. Left her old man in Saint Louis. Incredible, eh?"

"Madame Charbonneau," Lupton addressed Sacajawea with a bow. "Madame Charbonneau, are you certain Baptiste is your son?"

"*Ai*," she said, wondering why the white men needed the story over and over again.

Lupton shook his white head. "I'll get Mrs. Ducate, the washwoman, to show you around."

"Take her to Fontaine," interrupted Sage.

"She'll take you to Monsieur Fontaine," said Lupton; then he turned again to Sage. "Rufus, I have some traps for beaver I want you to set out. Come get them before we all have supper."

The men walked away, leaving Sacajawea, Crying Basket, and their packs. Soon a large, pleasant, red-faced woman came toward them.

Mrs. Ducate did not hide her surprise when she found that Sacajawea was not a white woman in the red dress. "We'll have a bath first off," she said, taking Sacajawea into the tiny washroom where she worked. She took a bucket out to the pump and filled it with water. She placed the bucket on the hot wood stove. The room was very hot. Crying Basket was asleep on her mother's shoulder. Sacajawea sat on the floor in a corner opposite the stove and watched.

Mrs. Ducate poured the hot water into a big wooden tub. She went out, pumped water into the bucket, and added it to the tub to cool the hot water. Sacajawea again marveled at the white woman's pool for bathing. This tub was larger than the tub of Owl Woman. The water was soothing. Crying Basket sleepily clung to her mother as Sacajawea pulled her dress off.

"Soap," said Mrs. Ducate, handing Sacajawea an uneven yellow bar. Crying Basket tried to take a bite from the soap. Both women giggled.

"It is much like the soap of Miss Judy," said Sacajawea with surprise.

Mrs. Ducate was even more surprised at the squaw's English. She ran her hand over the brown smoothness of the little child's back. Then she noticed the faint white scars across Sacajawea's back.

"You've been treated mighty poorly in your time, poor thing," she sighed aloud.

Sacajawea looked up. "Time is better for me now."

"For me, too," laughed Mrs. Ducate. "My Charley is the clerk at the fort, and between the two of us we make out quite well. Took a long time to get this far."

Sacajawea examined Crying Basket's feet and legs. She was pleased the sores and scabs had disappeared. She scrubbed Crying Basket vigorously with the soap. The child whimpered when soap got into her eyes. Sacajawea splashed the water on her face, and soon the child was singing and splashing back. Mrs. Ducate brought out a faded blue-gingham dress for Crying Basket and fresh undergarments for Sacajawea.

These underthings were new to her. Sacajawea was used to living free from such bindings, but she stood patiently as Mrs. Ducate fastened them to her. That evening she took them off, never to wear them again, except for the petticoats. These she did not mind wearing, as she imagined herself to look as pretty as Judy Clark had looked with her petticoats swishing about her bare legs.

Then Mrs. Ducate brought in a little dark-eyed half-breed girl, about a year older than Crying Basket. "This is Suzanne Fontaine."

Sacajawea looked at the child, who wore her hair in short dark braids. "She is beautiful."

Mrs. Ducate smiled and braided Crying Basket's hair and tied strips of red cloth around the ends. Sacajawea then thought her own daughter beautiful. She bent to hug both children.

Mrs. Ducate announced, "Suzanne, this is Madame Charbonneau, who will cook for you and tidy up around your place." Then, abruptly, she turned to Sacajawea and asked, "Why is old Lancaster Lupton so interested in you?"

"Maybe because the one called Sage is interested in finding my son."

"And why don't you speak like other squaws?" Mrs. Ducate shook her head. "You are a somebody, I can see that. But who?"

A grin crept over Sacajawea's face. "I am the mother of Baptiste, and a long time ago I lived near the village of Saint Louis. I saw how the white women spoke and lived. I have been at the place called Bent's and have learned more. I can talk your tongue now, huh?"

"Oh, oh." Mrs. Ducate stared at Sacajawea in a placid, measured way, trying to piece things together. She dropped herself into an unpainted chair and stretched out her legs.

It was not long until Sacajawea was settled in as housekeeper for Monsieur Fontaine, who was neither young nor old, but had white hair, a gray pointed beard, and smoked his pipe continually. Sacajawea kept his rooms cleaner than Mrs. Ducate thought possible. Suzanne loved having Crying Basket as a playmate and companion. Often she asked to sleep in the single robe in the corner of the living room where Sacajawea and Crying Basket slept each night. Monsieur Fontaine did not allow it. He thought his daughter should sleep in a proper featherbed. And he made sure that the sleeping robes were neatly folded and stacked early each morning so that no hint of a bed showed in his front room.

Sometimes Sacajawea took both little girls visiting outside the fort. They visited the camps of friendly Utah and the Tukadükas, or Sheep Eater Shoshonis, living near the walls of the fort. The girls ran with the camp dogs and played ring and pin, hoop and pole with the Utah children.

When travelers came to the fort, Sacajawea sat in the yard to hear of where they had been and who they had visited. She was aware of trappers going out of the fort and who was carrying furs to Mexico or east to Saint Louis.

One morning after breakfast, Monsieur Fontaine got his pipe and motioned for Sacajawea to stop sweeping the floor a moment.

"I have to ask you, Madame Charbonneau. Was old Toussaint your husband?"

Sacajawea was startled, and a chill crept over her. She looked carefully at Monsieur Fontaine, whose face told her nothing. "*Ai*, many years back."

"I met him at Fort Union on the Upper Missouri back in thirty-five or so, and he was then claiming to live with the Mandans. Since then, those people were wiped out from smallpox. He had trouble speaking the Mandan language without mixing French phrases with it. With no more Mandans, I wondered what happened to old Charbonneau. I would not have thought him to be the kind of man you would live with. He often talked about his boys and their education in Saint Louis, but he was a damned scoundrel himself."

Sacajawea had to keep a hand over her mouth to keep from showing her amazement. "Our paths have not crossed for many seasons," she said. "But the Mandans—gone? It is not possible."

Monsieur Fontaine rose and began to pace. "So you had sons who were schooled in Saint Louis?"

"*Ai*," she answered, wondering what he was to say next.

"Old Lancaster Lupton has a West Point education. What do you think about education for girls? I am serious."

"You mean read the talking leaves?"

"I most certainly mean that, madame. How else are these young women going to get on? Your son went to school with backing from General Clark, and so did that other, called Tess. The time is coming when everyone will be expected to read and write. The white man is going to force the red man to be civilized. I know it is coming."

"But you mean these little girls, here, learn from books?"

"I've been thinking about this for some time. Have you met Céran St. Vrain? Maybe we could take them to Fort St. Vrain and have Céran work with them on the teaching himself. He has books. You could teach the sewing. I've watched you. Your work is equal to any white woman's."

Sacajawea shook her head.

Monsieur Fontaine resumed his pacing.

Then, with no more discussion of such an important subject, he left the room; a snatch of a whistled tune came from the yard, and the iron gate of the fort opened and slammed.

Sacajawea ran out after him. She stopped and saw him in the unkempt garden digging and still whistling, throwing out weeds here and there from a row of pole beans.

CHAPTER

51

St. Vrain's Fort

An Indian woman of the Snake nation, desirous, like
Naomi of old, to return to her people, requested and
obtained permission to travel with my party to the neighborhood of Bear river, where she expected to meet with
some of their villages. She carried with her two children,
who added much to the liveliness of the camp.

The Shoshone woman took leave of us near Ham's
Fork of the Black Fork on the Green River, expecting to
find some of her relations at Bridger's Fort, which is
only a mile or two distant, on a fork of this stream.[1]

JOHN CHARLES FRÉMONT, *Report of the Expedition on the
Rocky Mountains in the Year 1842, and to Oregon and
North California in the Years 1843–44*, 28th Cong., 2nd
Sess., Sen. Doc. no. 174. Washington, D.C.: Gales and
Seaton, Printers, 1845.
also in:
Donald Jackson and Mary Lee Penal, eds., *The Expe-
ditions of John Charles Fremont, Travels from 1838 to
1844*, vol. I, Urbana: University of Illinois Press, 1970,
pp. 430, 457–58, 468–69.

Mrs. Ducate stopped Sacajawea at the water pump one morning. "Say—you've got him out of his shell. He was whistlin' and hummin' this morning when he went out to that garden. Next he'll be wanting to take you and the little girls to the other forts. He'll want to show them off. Let's fix them up. I have some pink gingham and we can make them dresses and hair ribbons."

Sacajawea was delighted with the idea, and indeed, Mrs. Ducate was right. By the end of the week Monsieur Fontaine's face was a shade tanner from working in his garden, and there was a twinkle in his eyes. "I want to go visit St. Vrain. Bring the children. We might hear something about that roving, handsome Baptiste. He ought to be in Saint Louis by now. Maybe St. Vrain has heard," he said to Sacajawea.

Sacajawea could not wait to tell Mrs. Ducate. "See there, I told you," was her reply. The two women chattered and scrubbed the little girls. "They look beautiful in that pink with their dark eyes and black, shining braids," said Mrs. Ducate, walking around each little girl.

"*Ai*," said Sacajawea, just as pleased with the effect. "Will Monsieur Fontaine like their looks?"

Monsieur Fontaine brought the horses from the corral. He was most pleased with what he saw.

Sacajawea wore a yellow flowered dress. It had been Mrs. Ducate's once and was big for Sacajawea, but she had taken in the waist with a belt of woven grass. Underneath she wore two petticoats.

Suzanne rode in front of her father and Crying Basket rode in front of Sacajawea as they set out.

During the ride Monsieur Fontaine turned his head slowly every so often and stared at Sacajawea. Slapping a gnat that had lit on his nose, he remarked once that this country sure did get as hot as the inside of a buffalo. Sacajawea reluctantly understood that he was one of those people who could ride through a land full of glory and never see it. To Jacques Fontaine, beauty meant a clean shave, and shining boots, and his own reflection in the stillness of a deep pool. He had hauled furs in

1132

and out of the country, herded sheep, farmed, but never noticed a mountain or a sunset in his life.

So Sacajawea did not talk about the spectacle around them. But that evening she gazed at the declining sun that sent long blades of light among the rocks, striking fantastic colors from their walls, and the shadows that lay purple on the ground. They arrived at Fort St. Vrain as the sun slipped behind one of the far towers, and the light around them was a thicker purple, though there were still crowns of gold on the top of the fort.

The Indian women inside the fort gathered around the little girls in pink and ooed and ahed, and touched their soft dresses.

Charley Bent came out.

"He is called White Hat by the Indians and is Bill Bent's brother," explained Monsieur Fontaine.

Charley Bent was happy to see the old *engagé* Fontaine out for a visit again. "You'll be trapping by fall," was his prediction. Then he winked toward Sacajawea. "Another woman now, huh?" asked Charley Bent.

"No. She's my housekeeper."

"Of course." Bent winked. "Come through the blockhouse to the main quarters." Descending the blockhouse stairs behind Sacajawea and Monsieur Fontaine, holding a spyglass in his hand, was a stocky, round-faced man. He was distinguished by a hedge of black whiskers and deep brown eyes, and his gray cassinette pants and red-flannel shirt set him apart from the buckskin-clad trappers and the Mexican dragoons with their colorful serapes. This man was Céran St. Vrain, first in authority here.

"We would like to wash up a little before the evening meal," said Monsieur Fontaine. "We want to stay overnight. I don't want to take these babies back to Lupton's in the dark."

"*Oui*, you may sleep inside the fort, Monsieur Fontaine. I did not know you were remarried," said St. Vrain.

Monsieur Fontaine colored. "I am not, but I have a fine housekeeper for my little girl. This is Madame Charbonneau and her daughter, Yagawosier."

"Charbonneau?"

"French, huh? Baptiste Charbonneau works for you

and Bill Bent? *Oui?* He worked for Louis Vasquez? *Oui?*
This woman is looking for him. He is her son."

"Vasquez?"

"Charbonneau, Baptiste."

St. Vrain slapped the side of his leg with fine calfskin
gloves. "That man is one of the finest men in the mountains, on foot or in a *bateau.* He always wears his hair
long—down to his shoulders, sort of Indian-style. I
loaded him down with furs early this spring, and he is
on his way down the Platte to Saint Louis. Probably
there now. If not, he's camped somewhere reading to
Jim Bridger. Ha-ha. Those two even argue about what
Bap reads. Bridger can't read a word, but he's got a
thinking head. That Bap has had a good deal of education. And you say Bap is *her* son?" St. Vrain looked
at Sacajawea.

"*Ai,*" said Sacajawea. "You know my boy well?"

"Do I? That fellow has been working for me since he
came back from Germany. He can get a mule or a man
to do anything he says."

"Did the Duke Paul come here again from his village
across the Great Eastern Waters?"

St. Vrain stared at Sacajawea and brushed his hand
across his mouth. "First time I ever heard a squaw say
so much in good English and make sense. By God, you
just could be Madame Charbonneau."

"I am!" flared Sacajawea, moving herself so that her
skirt rustled on the floor.

"Now I can't wait until he comes back up here from
Saint Louis," said St. Vrain. "But he may just go to Bill
Bent's or across the mountains to that ramshackle Fort
Bridger first. He and Bridger talked about doing some
trapping."

The bell for supper rang, and Sacajawea and the girls
followed the men into the large dining hall. Wooden
benches lined each side of the plank tables. Many of
the workers at the fort were men with Indian women
and children. These women looked curiously at Sacajawea in her gingham dress and the little girls in pink.

Across their table sat St. Vrain next to his young
wife, who was languidly beautiful, dark, and serene.
Sacajawea thought she looked more Mexican than In-

dian; then, when she looked again, she could not be sure.

The food was good. There were chunks of fresh mutton stewed with peppers and dried onions, slabs of goat's-milk cheese, and fat red Mexican beans. In place of bread there was *atole*, a cornmeal from which was cooked hot mush, and *pinole*, a mixture of parched corn flavored with sugar and cinnamon. St. Vrain told Sacajawea that mixed with hot water, *atole* and *pinole* made good porridges for children.

Next to Sacajawea sat a mountain man. He was thickset, towheaded, blue-eyed, bandy-legged, and quiet-spoken most of the time. This man was telling about a skirmish with the Blackfeet. He pointed to the shoulder in which he had been shot. "Not even beaver fur would stanch the wound," he said. "But the subzero temperature of them mountains saved my hide. My blood froze, and the wound closed."

Sacajawea made some derisive noise and spoke the name of the Blackfeet in Shoshoni. The sun-haired mountain man looked at her and spoke in the Shoshoni tongue. She was delighted and asked him how far away the mountains were from here.

"Long ways," he said. "Long. But they are worth gaping at." The mountain man looked at Crying Basket and then at Suzanne. "Them yours?" he asked.

"This one," she pointed.

"I have a little girl not much older. She is in school in Saint Louis. It's been a year since I've seen her. Her mother, Waanibe, an Arapaho, is not living."

"Shh," Sacajawea warned him. "Do not speak the name of those who have gone away."

"Hey, it's been awhile since I've seen one of these," he said, reaching behind Sacajawea so that he could tug at the necklace her child wore. It was a narrow wooden paddle, whittled from a willow and pierced for the woven and beaded buckskin necklace. "That's a goose stick. Every time the wild geese migrate, a notch is cut on the stick. Right? This here papoose is five winters old."

"*Ai*," answered Sacajawea, pleased that the man knew what the necklace meant.

"Are you Yankton, then?"

"No, Shoshoni." And she made the special movement like weaving in and out in a grass basket. "But I have learned from others about counting winters." She then looked fully at his face. "I have a son. Maybe your age."

"So—you cannot be that old," teased the man.

"*Ai*," she said. "My son works in the white man's forts and goes to Saint Louis."

"So—has he a name?"

"Baptiste. Jean Baptiste Charbonneau."

"Well hang the boots and saddles! I'm Christopher Carson. And I would not have believed what you have said unless I'd heard it."

She smiled and waited for him to say more.

"Your son, he left Bent's Fort last year and came here to St. Vrain's. He took furs into Saint Louis."

She nodded; she already knew most of this.

"He was to check on my little girl. He knows his way around that town. Went to school there himself. Buys books in Saint Louis to read during the long winters in the mountains. That sound like your boy?"

"*Ai*," said Sacajawea; then softly: "I was in Saint Louis while he went to school. He and Toussaint."

"Not old Toussaint. You're pulling my leg. He never saw the inside of a school!"

"No, Little Tess."

"Yes, seems I remember that one, too—dark and rather thickset and short—about same build as me. He likes firewater and fights. Last I heard he lived down with the Utes or Crows, maybe. He has a woman there. He's not the man Baptiste is, if you don't mind me telling you."

"*Ai*."

St. Vrain came to the side of the table and bent to Kit Carson.

"So—you've met this woman who claims to be the mother of Bap Charbonneau. She'd like to see him when he comes in for more furs."

"I think her best bet is at old Gabe's Fort, on the Black Fork. It's not so much, just some logs and a sort of stockade. I heard that Louis Vasquez, down the table there yonder, helped Gabe with the building. Fantastic the way it holds together. Say, this squaw—she speaks a fair sort of English and knows more than most about them Charbonneaus. How do you account for that?"

"I believe her." St. Vrain then stepped over toward Monsieur Fontaine. "Why don't you stay tomorrow? It is the Fourth of July, and we'll shoot off the cannon and pass out some bacanora or cognac. I'll start some book learning with those girls. And I'll give you some books so that Lupton can help for a while this winter. In the afternoon the little girls can see horse racing and the games. They'll enjoy the festivities. So will your Madame Charbonneau. Some Cheyennes are coming in for trade, and with them Gray Thunder, the daddy of Owl Woman. You know who she is? Bill Bent's Cheyenne woman."

"Will Owl Woman come?" asked Sacajawea softly.

"It's possible. Knowing that his brother Charley is here, Bill Bent might just come in with his woman."

"Hey, Jacques," called Charley Bent from another table to Monsieur Fontaine, "tomorrow you show us how you can ride your horse and what a good shot you are! We'll get a few bets going."

The next day before noon, John Charles Frémont and his party, including Tom Fitzpatrick, arrived at St. Vrain's Fort. There was much shouting and celebrating. They were invited to eat in the mess hall with St. Vrain and the others. During the conversation St. Vrain asked Frémont if he had heard any news from Saint Louis of Baptiste Charbonneau.

"Of course. Just last summer I met that old grizzly-fighter. He was taking peltries to Saint Louis. Said he was working for you and Bent."

"True," said St. Vrain.

"Well, he ran into a snag—that is, the spring rise had been too low to carry the boats, so they gave up and sent for horses. Didn't you get word and send him some?"

"No, but maybe Bill Bent did."

"Well, he had the nicest little camp not far from Fort Morgan on an island. Called it Saint Helena. Sounds like him, doesn't it? There was this big grove of large cottonwoods and the tents were pitched under them." Frémont waved his long arms about and moved his mouth around as he talked. "He made us mint julep from horsemint. Very good, as a matter of fact. We had boiled buffalo tongue, and coffee, with the luxury of sugar."

"See there"—St. Vrain pointed down the table to the vicinity of Sacajawea, who could eat none of her noon meal as she overheard their conversation—"that is his mother."

"Now, Céran. You must be coming apart. That is a squaw in a gingham dress, but the mother of Bap? Wagh! He's an educated man. He studied some years in Europe."

"She knows a lot about his early life in Saint Louis," said St. Vrain.

"Probably heard something from white traders. Those Indians will tell you anything that pleases. You know that."

After eating, Frémont and half his party moved south to gather news from traders and trappers at Lupton's about passage over the western mountain range. Then they planned to move down to Bent's for mules. Tom Fitzpatrick stayed behind with the other half of the party to gather further information about travel through the mountain passes.

The sun was high when Gray Thunder's band came in sight. Already the Utahs and Shoshonis were having a riding competition. Sacajawea and the little girls watched dancers. Two tepees had been pitched together, the poles crossed, and the lodge skins rolled up to form a large pavilion. A half-dozen men beat time on a hollow-log drum, while another half-dozen squatted in a row and played on tight leather hand drums. All seemed orderly confusion. Elderly men moved about quietly. Women with infants openly at their breasts, and others with small children, were arranging pallets on the ground in the little shade they could find from piñons and chamisa.

Louis Vasquez moseyed around the fort before taking his supplies, including two bags of salt, back to his own trading post a couple of miles north. St. Vrain insisted Vasquez first meet the Shoshoni squaw who claimed to be Bap Charbonneau's mother.

Sacajawea smiled politely and asked slowly, in Spanish, when Vasquez thought Bap would be back around these forts.

"I'll be a ring-tailed racoon," said Vasquez to St. Vrain. "The woman does speak fair Spanish and knows more about that dude Charbonneau than you or I together." Then he turned to Sacajawea and said, "I think that son of yours is on his way to Gabe's Fort. Then he'll be in and out of this area sooner or later." Vasquez was still shaking his head in wonder over the Shoshoni woman who talked Spanish with French phrases scattered here and there, as he left St. Vrain's Fort that afternoon.

A noisy game of hands was in progress. It was a game Monsieur Fontaine had played many times—the Indians' version of the old shell game. He loved it. Sacajawea watched the drummers beat time on hand drums and heard everybody sing a noisy accompaniment to the rhythmic movement of the one-who-hides-something, who manipulated the small, polished bone. She found the game did not intimidate her. The unpleasantness of my girlhood is a thing of the past. Those bad things have healed over, she thought.

Kit Carson seemed bored with the games and went out along the other side of the fort to the horse races.

Old Bill Williams nudged Monsieur Fontaine. "Let's get in that there game," he said in a thin, cracked voice. Bill was about six feet, one inch, gaunt, redheaded, with a hard, weather-beaten face, marked deeply with smallpox. He was all muscle and sinew. He had heard of the festivities going on at St. Vrain's Fort and being in the vicinity had come in to see the goings-on. Generally he avoided crowds. He preferred his own company. He had lived with one Indian tribe or another for years. He was called Lone Elk by his friends.

There was a log-sawing contest, and Sacajawea moseyed there with the girls to watch.

Gray Thunder left his men, who were unpacking, preparing to do some trading, and he came straight for the games. Monsieur Fontaine spoke his regards to Gray Thunder and offered to let him play hands in his place. Bill Williams seemed to look neither to the right nor the left. He did not look at Gray Thunder as he spoke,

but seemed to be thinking of something else as his voice
whined out, "Once you sit here, there can be no exas-
peratin' hagglin' over where the bone is. I hain't gonner
stay if this game gets slow and bound up."

The wrinkled, tough-minded Gray Thunder sat down
to play the game with vigor. Monsieur Fontaine, now
standing, watched as the Cheyenne Medicine Man lay
his tobacco pouch on the blanket. Others followed Gray
Thunder and put down their bets. Gray Thunder tossed
in two silver dollars on top of the pouch he'd just put
down. Bill Williams bent forward, which gave him the
appearance of being humpbacked, and moved his head
from side to side. The Cheyenne singing commenced.
Gray Thunder moved his hands in time to the singing,
allowing occasional glimpses of the bone as he passed
it from one hand to the other. Bill pointed to his right
hand, but it was empty.

"*Ee-yah!*" exclaimed those who had bet on Gray
Thunder. But the round was not over, the Cheyennes
having merely gained the advantage. Gray Thunder
smiled as he handed the bone to Bill Williams. If the
old Indian guessed right, he would win. Bill Williams
gently placed his worn Bible on the blanket. "Lucifer,
get behind me," he said.

Gray Thunder guessed right and won. "That there
Bible will do you no good, but it will do you no harm,
either," commented Bill. "I'll get my Good Book back,
you varmint."

Both Gray Thunder and Bill guessed right on the
next round, so no bets were exchanged—though some
additional wagers were made by the onlookers. It was
fairly even for a while; then Bill Williams began winning more consistently. After a long losing streak, Gray
Thunder looked at Bill admiringly. "Lone Elk, he is
much alive," he said.

Monsieur Fontaine, sitting cross-legged next to old
Bill, glanced briefly at Gray Thunder. Gray Thunder
smiled quickly, his little twinkling eyes everywhere,
then he resumed his masked emotions. Monsieur Fontaine thought about these two travelers, Bill and Gray
Thunder, of merging trails, who did well to keep an eye
on one another's attitude. Fontaine felt alive himself
this day, and he was enjoying himself more than he

had in many months. He felt now he had something to live for, a motivation. He was going to have both little girls educated so they could read and write and make something of themselves.

As the stakes in the game increased, Fontaine's confidence increased, and he spoke aside to Sacajawea, who had come to sit beside him so the girls could watch the game. Bill Williams once in a while paused in his game to make laughing grimaces at the two little girls, who in turn hugged their knees in laughter.

"Madame Charbonneau, get St. Vrain. Tell him to bring something for higher stakes. This will be my day! Gray Thunder is finding he cannot stretch Bill Williams on the fence to dry!"

St. Vrain came back with Sacajawea. Both were laden with trinkets and a roll of white strouding. The Cheyennes began leaving the circle of the game to reappear carrying loads of furs. They could not resist the white man's trinkets and cloth. The game resumed and new bettors arrived and others entered or withdrew as their luck prompted them. Besides quantities of foofaraw, Monsieur Fontaine was soon betting good three-point blankets to entice the Indians to risk their whole winter caches of beaver and fox.

Gray Thunder played it cautiously, sometimes sitting out a game or two and letting one of his warriors play. The games were now fairly even and the Indians were well satisfied until Old Bill had another run of luck and took three games in a row. "I gotter keep that white cloth for the two pretty little papooses here. They plumb took my fancy," he said, closing down on one eye as if to wink at Suzanne and Crying Basket. Because of the number of Indians betting against him and also the size of the stakes, Old Bill's winnings were beginning to make an impressive pile. St. Vrain lifted the pile of furs and skins off the blanket. "Nice easy way to trap," he commented.

"Aw," said Bill, "you all know I have no glory except in the woods, and my ambition is to kill more deer and catch more beaver than any other man. But these here I'm giving to this here Fontaine so's he can give his papoose some book learnin'. I say it won't do 'em much good, but it won't hurt 'em, neither."

Just then, Gray Thunder looked over at the huge pile of furs and skins. He stood up using hand signs as he talked. "Your winnings against what I have left."

"Hi! Ti! Good! Agreed!" shouted the Cheyennes behind him.

"One pile of furs," Old Bill said. He broke a stick in two and set half of it, to represent the pile, at the edge of the blanket.

Gray Thunder matched the half stick and nodded to the Cheyennes to sing.

Old Bill nodded toward Gray Thunder's left hand and missed, but when he, too, succeeded in concealing the bone, Gray Thunder lost the advantage. St. Vrain sat at the edge of the blanket letting himself be drawn into the merrymaking. Old Bill passed the bone to St. Vrain, and a new game was started. Old Bill withdrew his precious worn Bible from the blanket.

Gray Thunder placed a whole marker at the edge of the blanket. "A horse." St. Vrain matched the bet. The round was deadlocked. The sticks increased until both St. Vrain and Gray Thunder had bet a fourth of their animals. Old Bill clapped his hands and yelped in a voice that left the hearers in doubt whether he was laughing or crying. Then St. Vrain guessed wrong and Gray Thunder guessed right and won the game. A riotous shout went up from the Cheyennes. They knew they could sell horses at their own price to the loser. The dancing gyrations became wild, and Monsieur Fontaine feared it could lead to mayhem. He looked at the Cheyennes' dark faces and knew it would not take much to start trouble. Other traders had had their hair lifted for less. He shrugged and tossed the short length of polished bone to Gray Thunder.

"Start it off, *ami,"* said St. Vrain, who was determined not to be beaten. St. Vrain lost the round and was minus at least half his horses. Monsieur Fontaine shook his head. "That *enfant*'s a fool to even have started in a chance game," he said to Old Bill.

Bill sniffed the air, and even though he appeared to look straight ahead, his eyes were everywhere. Gray Thunder resumed the game. St. Vrain won a round, and another. Then Gray Thunder won. The stalemate began again. The Cheyennes became as possessed,

swaying back and forth, in and out, stamping their feet
and raising their arms with the beat of the drummers.
Some called to the players to move on more quickly.
Bill Williams edged around beside Sacajawea and
tweaked the nose of each little girl; then he whispered
something to Sacajawea and moved his hands rapidly
so that she'd be certain to understand. Her eyes rounded,
and she caught her breath a moment. Then he seemed
to reassure her with a touch of his hand, as he held the
old Bible toward the heavens.

"*Ai*," she nodded and left to move inside the fort,
leaving the girls watching the game.

Bill Williams sniffed the air and remarked boldly,
"Do'ee hyar now, boys, thar's sign about?" His high-
pitched voice quavered. "This hoss feels like caching."

"Don't go off and hide now!" called Monsieur Fontaine. "The fun is just beginning." But off he went to
find his horse and then make himself scarce in the
woods again. Though most mountain men sensibly believed there was safety in numbers, Bill was known to
leave a large group when he sniffed the possibility of
Indian attack.

"He's crazy as a hoot owl," said St. Vrain. "But nobody can say he's not shrewd, generally acute, and original—and far from illiterate."

Monsieur Fontaine, who was daydreaming again, felt
a light touch on his shoulder. He turned, half expecting
to see Bill Williams again, but it was Sacajawea, who
hurriedly indicated that she wished to enter the game—
on the side of Gray Thunder and his Cheyennes.

"*Sauvage*," he chuckled and nodded toward St. Vrain.
He studied Sacajawea, wondering what had prompted
her, a squaw, to get into a man's game. There seemed
no reason for her wanting to enter the play, but it certainly would do no harm. He and St. Vrain had lost
much already. To lose a little face by having a squaw
play opposite them and win a few rounds would please
the Cheyennes and might be a way to finish the game
more quickly. He shrugged. Sacajawea wedged in between St. Vrain and Gray Thunder.

She put several pairs of white moccasins on the blanket and touched the ones she wore so that the others
could see their beauty and value. Gray Thunder gave

a deep grunt of displeasure. This was no place for a
foolish woman. Ignoring him, Sacajawea looked along
the line of bettors opposite her. Her blanket slipped off
her shoulders. Her eyes sparkled and there were red
spots in the center of both cheeks.

"Against one fine horse of St. Vrain," she said in her
best Comanche English and fast hand signs.

"*Ai*," Gray Thunder agreed, his face still dark.

"I will be the one who is hiding something," she said
and picked up the bone from Gray Thunder's hands.

St. Vrain looked at the woman and then looked at
the hoard of skins Gray Thunder had won back. "Go to
it, *sauvage*," he sighed, signaling for the Cheyennes to
begin their song once again.

Gray Thunder shrugged, and Sacajawea manipulated the bone. The onlookers stood a moment, hyp-
notized, as St. Vrain successfully guessed the hand in
which Sacajawea held it. Then she guessed his hand
correctly.

Then he pointed to her left hand. It was empty. A
rumble of disappointment arose from the Cheyennes.
There would be no sale of horses. St. Vrain had won
back all his animals.

Gray Thunder looked across at St. Vrain and began
making arrangements for delivery of the horses, and
Sacajawea sent for the one horse she had lost to St.
Vrain. In the moments of going to pick out and deliver
the horses, gunfire was heard beyond the fort in the
direction of the Cheyennes' horse herd. The alarm was
relayed through the various Indian camps, and Sacajawea heard, "Horse thieves! Many horses stolen!" There
was instant tumult. Monsieur Fontaine was forgotten
as Gray Thunder and a group of his young men broke
from St. Vrain and scattered for their camp. Sacajawea
watched the Cheyennes leave, then she reached deep
into her blanket. Only Monsieur Fontaine, who had
been bundling up some of the peltries St. Vrain had
won back, saw what she did. She had cheated Gray
Thunder that last guess. The bone had not been in either hand.

Monsieur Fontaine's eyes narrowed. A man did not
always hanker to be beholden to any fool squaw, but
sure as he was no drinking man—his tastes ran more

to horse liniment for horses—St. Vrain owed something to this *sauvage*. On second thought, maybe it was Bill Williams he owed it to—what had that old coot said to her just before he left, anyway?

Monsieur Fontaine watched while Sacajawea went leisurely in the direction of the fort, followed by the pair of little girls. Then he hoisted a bundle of furs to his shoulder and went toward the fort himself, thinking he'd better get his horses and hightail it inside the fort before they were raided out here.

Coming in from the horse races, Kit Carson turned toward the fort. With Cheyenne horses driven off by enemy raiders, there would be a chase and likely a fight. He would not miss that. Carson felt it lucky for his friend St. Vrain. If the white men could help the Cheyennes recover their horses, without a doubt Gray Thunder would not be reluctant to pay off his losses. And the Cheyennes would do more trading at St. Vrain's Fort than at the others nearby. In the joy of victory, Cheyennes would do anything for brave warriors, red or white. Carson went off to saddle up and follow Gray Thunder's men in search of the raiders.

Monsieur Fontaine, out of breath and panting from carrying the bundles of furs into the fort, began to hunt out his fast horse in the corral. Sacajawea could be counted on to look after Suzanne while he was gone, he was confident. Other men from the fort came for their horses to join the Cheyennes in their chase.

In the Cheyenne camp, the warriors hurriedly painted themselves and their horses; they were beginning to sing their war songs for courage. Then a wolf cried out. It was a long, quavering trill of sorrow, indescribably mournful.

The spell was not so easily broken. Monsieur Fontaine kicked his horse into motion and fell in beside St. Vrain. He seemed eager to be on his way as the great wolf's sobbing cry still echoed down the hills, and even riding his horse he remained in a tense attitude of listening long after the final eerie note trembled in the distance and was lost in the *kiyi*-ing of the warriors.

St. Vrain's eyes narrowed as he looked at Monsieur Fontaine. "The wolf calls to you, monsieur? What does he say?" asked St. Vrain.

Monsieur Fontaine looked sharply at him. He was startled. "Do you ridicule me?"

"Of course not, *ami*. I only observe your reaction to the howl of a prairie wolf."

"Some say the French are superstitious." He returned to what seemed an endless gaze into the low hills. But he came back. "This day has been something so different from my usual days and I have felt so blessed to be alive and the wolf's cry did seem to come directly to my ears. Gray Thunder would say, 'It is a good day for dying.'" Monsieur Fontaine paused. "Céran, am I not truly blessed to have such a fine woman to care for my little Suzanne?"

St. Vrain smiled, then laughed, and rode past Louis Vasquez and Charley Bent to the front riders beside Gray Thunder.

Sacajawea stood just inside the gates to the adobe fort wondering how such a fine day could change so rapidly. She let her musings carry her to other summer celebrations with the white men. She could almost hear Cruzatte's fiddle as Chief Red Hair danced and the tall pine crackled into a fiery blaze.

Tom Fitzpatrick remained inside the fort with his men to celebrate the fading Fourth of July with tin mugs half-filled with bacanora, a clear white liquor distilled from cactus juice. There were some Utes at the gate asking to buy the crazy-water. Fitzpatrick sent an order that the few barrels of bacanora his party had left could be sold to the Utes if it were watered half and half.

Sacajawea took the little girls back to the cell-like single room she had been given by St. Vrain the previous night. She left the door partially open so that there was some light so she could wash the children with water from the pump and put clean doeskin tunics on them. She washed their calico dresses at the pump and spread them over the single bench in the room for drying. She felt she needed a bath, but did not dare go outside the fort now. She let the pump water run over her face and arms and neck. In the room she removed her calico dress and petticoats and slipped on a simple tunic. She rinsed out her dress and laid it beside the girls'.

The bell announcing supper rang. She was not sure she should go into the dining hall without Monsieur Fontaine. The girls were hungry. She slipped to the courtyard and stood by the mess hall. A Cheyenne woman looked at her and made a clicking noise with her tongue. "You are not in the white woman's dress, so you cannot go into the place of eating." Sacajawea's heart sank, but the woman came back almost immediately with a plate of pinto beans and corn bread and a mug of steaming black coffee with a layer of sugar syrup at the bottom.

"You hear *el lobo*? Señora, when the wolf cries before dark, it is a bad sign. It means someone is marked for death." The woman walked away rustling her huaraches.

Sacajawea let the children eat the warm corn bread as she blew on the coffee to cool it for drinking. Suddenly she felt exhausted. This was a new life. Each day was so different, with so much to think about and put in the right place in her mind. To try thinking of tomorrow would surely fatigue her. She fell asleep with the coffee half-drunk beside her on the dirt floor. The little girls were already curled up together on a bright Navaho rug.

At sunrise, Sacajawea was up and standing by the mess-hall door. Someone told her to vamoose. She stepped a little way from the door, and someone else put a tin plate of steaming biscuits and a cup of black coffee in her hand. At that moment she saw St. Vrain come past on *her* pony, headed for the corral inside the fort. My horse, she thought—oh, no, it is his since yesterday. He was leading another horse with the rider thrown facedown across the saddle. There was a small hole in the rider's back from which blood had oozed, but it was black and dried now.

"It's a shame"—St. Vrain beckoned to her—"old Fontaine was shot in the back."

Sacajawea's hand shook, and she spilled a little coffee.

"We were behind some boulders with Gray Thunder's men. Nine Crows made a dash for a stream. Mon-

sieur Fontaine waited until they were within fifty yards;
then he fired on them. He hit two before they turned
back. He missed a third, and the Crows charged him.
He was a good rider, but could not get around the rocks
fast enough. The bullet struck just as he dodged for the
far side of his horse, hanging by one foot. I got that
Crow with my old Silver Heels, and we managed to
recover the horses for the Cheyennes. A savage sport."
He spat at the ground.

Others gathered around them. "Gray Thunder and
his men are just coming into their camp," someone said.

Sacajawea stepped close to the body. Monsieur Fontaine had been a quiet, peaceful man who had gained
back his life only to lose it quickly. She looked away.
St. Vrain had brought out a double blanket, and Carson
was there helping spread it on the ground. The body
was laid on it. She bent to set the plate and coffee on
the earth, then she moved in and pushed the white hair
from the cold face and brushed the sleeves and straightened the jacket.

A fine man was gone. She felt sorrow and loss of
something irreplaceable.

"By your garden, in the manner of the whites," whispered Sacajawea to St. Vrain. By this time both little
girls were standing beside Sacajawea. Suzanne stared
at the form in the blanket, not understanding that it
was the last remains of her father.

Someone opened the gates. Carson and St. Vrain
grasped the ends of the blanket and carried the body
to the back of the fort. The garden was lush and green.
There were blue lupines near the front. One of the men
from the blacksmith shop came with shovels. Finally
they stumbled to the loose earth, and some six men
lowered the body into the hole.

They dumped the earth into the grave. The clods
bounced on the blanket. After some minutes Fitzpatrick
took a shovel and the hole was filled and mounded over.

The men carried rocks to cover the mound. Sacajawea sat beside the row of lupines; her face was pale and
trembling. The two little girls sat in front of her, somber.

The rocks left something lacking. Carson cut down
a tall aspen and trimmed it down so that two side

branches were left on the main stock to look like a cross. He inserted it in the loosened earth at one end of the grave and propped it with stones.

Spirits were low inside the fort, but a supper of potatoes, frijoles with chilis, corn bread, and buffalo roast seemed to lift them.

The following day, Sacajawea made ready to go back to Fort Lupton. St. Vrain quietly made her a present of half a dozen good packhorses, some tins of coffee, and bacon and flour. Some of the squaws living inside the fort brought moccasins for the little girls, beaded in bright designs. The squaw who had given Sacajawea food from the mess hall gave her a leather packet of jerky.

Tom Fitzpatrick shook her hand, Carson patted the children, and St. Vrain said something about if he were a few years younger he'd keep her. "I'd keep them, too," he added, chucking the girls under the chin.

The news of the raid and chase for the horses had already reached Fort Lupton. Monsieur Fontaine's death was not news when Sacajawea entered the fort. She stayed on helping in the kitchen under the watchful eye of Mrs. Ducate and Lancaster Lupton.

Sacajawea was mending a calico dress belonging to Crying Basket when Lupton sent for her.

"Madame Charbonneau, a Ute runner has come to my post only a few minutes ago. He brings news of the explorer John Charles Frémont, who is at St. Vrain's Fort now. It seems the Mexicans are getting tough and have stopped all commercializing with Americans. At any rate, Frémont left Bent's Fort with mules and supplies and did not attempt to go farther south for more trading. He is back earlier than expected because of the new Mexican laws, and he has sent word that he is going to Gabe's, Jim Bridger's Fort, and you might like to travel with his party. There are Shoshonis camped outside Bridger's Fort, and they might be of your tribe. And the latest word from Bill Bent is that your son is coming to see Bridger before winter sets in. So—if you still wish to trail after that elusive son, here is another chance."

Mrs. Ducate said over and over how hard it would be to find a replacement for Sacajawea in the kitchen.

Lancaster Lupton wished her luck and checked her six horses and the packs strapped to three of them. She seemed to realize that another part of her life was closing as she left Lupton's. It was a heart-tugging moment at the fort's gate. Amid laughter and good wishes, Sacajawea was pale and serious for a moment. She looked into Mrs. Ducate's eyes and said softly, "*Adiós.*"

She rode with Crying Basket in front and Suzanne in back of her. No one questioned her right to mother Suzanne, the half-breed child left behind by Monsieur Fontaine's death. Suzanne herself called Sacajawea *umbea*, Shoshoni for "mother." Mrs. Ducate wiped her eyes on her apron as she bade them good-bye. Afterward she said to Lupton, "That there squaw is a saint. A genuine saint."

The Ute runner rode close to Sacajewea, explaining in hand signs that a party of dirty Crows had attacked the Arapaho camp not far from St. Vrain's the day before. Sacajawea clasped her mouth with one hand and scanned the hills. The Ute laughed and *kiyi*-ed for a moment, then assured her there was no need to worry as the Arapahos were too strong. The Crows had made a fast retreat this time.

Tom Fitzpatrick, whom the Indians called Broken Hand because one of his hands had been crippled by the explosion of a gun, was still at St. Vrain's selling watered bacanora to the camps outside the fort. With furs and peltries he received as payment, he planned to repay St. Vrain for board and room for himself and his men these past weeks at the fort.

From St. Vrain's Fort, on July 23, 1843, Frémont left with Carson as his guide, Charles Preuss, map-maker, Louis Zindel, Prussian expert in explosives, and Sacajawea and her two little girls. Fitzpatrick's portion of the party consisted of Alex Gody, hunter and scout, much of the heavy baggage, and most of Frémont's men. They had decided to split because they could find no one who knew the character of the mountain passes due west. They were heading straight for the ford of the Green River beyond the mountains. Fitzpatrick took the emigrant road by way of the mouth of the Laramie

River to Fort Hall, the Hudson's Bay Company post on the Snake River.

Frémont's group set out to cut through the mountains of the South Pass by way of the Powder River Valley. Soon they found themselves in one of the wildest and most beautiful parts of the Rocky Mountains. Sacajawea's heart was singing. She could almost feel herself as a child in the land of her people, the Agaidüka Shoshoni, even though these mountains were more tree-covered than those she remembered from her childhood home. She began to feel more certain she would find Baptiste, and then daydreamed a little about reuniting with her own people. There were towering walls all around where they traveled; the sides were dark with pine forests. There were long waterfalls coming down the sides of the mountains to the river below. The river bottom was covered with flowers—shooting stars, buttercups, yellow bells, and trillium.

Sacajawea busied herself digging *yampa* roots in the low-timbered river bottom. She took them to the expedition's cook and showed him how to make them into a fine mashed vegetable for the men's supper.

"Wagh," said Carson. "I'm half-froze for meat and we get mashed dill roots, which we have to pretend are turnips."

"But there is turkey tonight," promised Frémont, who had sent four men on a hunting party.

From here, their way, even in the smoother parts, was made rough by dense sagebrush, four to six feet tall. Then the party counted itself fortunate in spotting a small herd of buffalo. For two days they camped about two hundred miles out of Fort St. Vrain to dry the buffalo meat for future use. Sacajawea made herself useful whenever possible and with her skinning knife cut strips of fresh meat thin so that it would dry quickly over the smoky fires.

The summer air was hot, and the charrettes[2] moved with some trouble along the ground. The little girls were permitted to ride in one of the charrettes. Kit Carson had perched them high on top a pile of rolled pelts and skins.

Several days out from the meat-drying camp, the horses struggled over deadfall and huge rocks. Frémont

looked around, then rode ahead to a high point and saw
a range of mountains in the north that he felt sure were
peaks of the Sweetwater Valley Range.

"Yes," said Frémont, grinning, "those peaks would
break our backs. No sense rambling about it, we'll abandon any further efforts to struggle through this im-
practicable country and head back to St. Vrain's."

"I'm sorry as all glory!" said Carson. "I'm more than
a little sad to turn around. Let's keep going for one
more day or two northward."

The party proceeded north-northwest along the east
side of the Medicine Bow Range until it reached its
northern extremity, then they moved west,[3] crossed the
North Platte, and moved slowly up the Sweetwater Valley and over South Pass ahead of Fitzpatrick's division.

Sacajawea put her hands on the little girls at night,
but said little. There was not anything to say. The children's eyes were big as plums as they saw how the land
changed from plains to mountains and hidden valleys.
They passed porcupines sitting in fir trees eating and
sleeping there so they could chip away the outer bark
with beaverlike teeth, then cut off and eat the tasty
inner bark, leaving the bare wood showing. Some of the
dead trees and deadfall showed evidence of the eating
habits of those porcupines. The slow-moving porcupine
can do more damage to a grove of fine timber than
almost anything but a forest fire, thought Sacajawea.

Frémont did not find a more southerly route to Oregon and northern California than this one. Sacajawea
found she was not truly accepted as a member of the
party as she had been with the Lewis and Clark Expedition so many years before, but no matter, she was
going closer to the land of her people and her firstborn.
Carson was friendly and spoke often with her. She
watched him pull off the dry leaves from the jimson-
weeds, powder them between his fingers, and sift the
powder into thin papers that he rolled and moistened
with his tongue to hold together so that he could smoke.
"Relieves my congestion in this high country," he whispered to her in a confidential manner.

Sacajawea shrugged, knowing that the weed gave a
lift to his spirits as he smoked.

When Frémont's party reached the Oregon Trail on

the banks of the Sweetwater River, they found a broad, smooth highway where the constant passage of emigrant wagons had beaten the sagebrush out of existence. It was a surprise and a happy change from the sharp rocks and tough shrubs through which their horses had been pushing. From this point onward, their path was easy and, despite dust and heat, progress was rapid.

Each evening now, Sacajawea took the little girls to a stream for bathing. She washed out their tunics and hung them over a rock or on a tree limb to dry. She let them dance by the campfire, even encouraged them whenever the men began to sing. They learned the words to the mountaineers' songs, not always understanding their meaning, which was bawdy, or sad, but always about a woman left behind.

"Wish I had some of that lettuce in the garden at St. Vrain's," said Carson wistfully to no one in particular one evening. "You know, if you take a handful of lettuce, crumble it up in a ball, and put a little sugar on it, you'll find it tastes pretty much like an apple."

"This child's hankerin' for some apples right now," said one of the mule cart drivers.

Sacajawea left the firelit circle and came back with her skirt full of small wild plums, which she had cached at the edge of the camp.

"These will fill my hankerin'," said the cart driver, diving in with both hands.

"I didn't see any plum trees," said Frémont. "That Snake squaw has a nose for eating off the land. Those were fine blackberries you brought in that cold night on the mountains, ma'am." When he spoke to Sacajawea he looked where she'd been standing. She had disappeared, but not for long. She came into the firelight again with a grin as broad as the Mexican cart drivers' sombreros.

"By jing!" Carson turned to Sacajawea with a grin as wide as her own. *"Ay, muchísimas gracias."* He bowed with mock gravity. "This watercress will be as good as lettuce from Céran's garden. This is a wondrous thing. All I did was wish and here it is true. Sugar, *amigo*?" Carson had turned to Frémont.

Twice within the next week the expedition passed

the new-made graves of emigrants, and once they fell
in with a stray ox wandering aimlessly.

Carson came riding back after scouting a mile or so
ahead of the party late on the hot afternoon of August
18, 1843. "You're here, Madame Charbonneau!" he
called. "See up there? That is Ham's Fork, on the Green
River. Jim Bridger's Fort is a mile or two southward
down the wide path. There."

She could see. Her heart began to thump as she pulled
her packhorses from the train. What lay ahead she was
not sure, but she felt she was closer now than she had
been for many years to her firstborn.

"If you are still at Bridger's Fort when I come by
here again, I'll stop and say 'Greetings,'" said Carson.

Sacajawea wished to thank Frémont in some special
way for taking her this far, but she was at a loss to say
anything when he handed her a small leather tent.
"Take it. I no longer have any use for it, and it will be
a place for you and the little girls to sleep if you have
to live outside the fort."

Sacajawea did not protest; instead, she put her hand
out to shake Frémont's in the manner she knew white
men did to seal a bargain or show good friendship.

Then she waved her farewell to the others, and the
little girls called "*Adiós*," shaking their brown hands
as the expedition of Charles Frémont went on to catch
up with Fitzpatrick and the rest of its party.

At this place the river valley was wide and covered
with good grass. Cottonwood timber was plentiful. The
streams looked cool and clear.

Fireweed and wild hollyhock grew on either side of
the trail. Blue harebells were scattered alongside. The
trail was marked with wagon wheels and vaguely resembled the streets of Saint Louis.

Sacajawea was pleased to see the good timber and
plentiful grass near this fort, which was made of a log
wall eight feet high running around the buildings of
logs and white clay between. The roofs were made of
branches and poles, covered with grass, leaves, and dirt.

Outside the wall were several Indian lodges and small
wooden houses. Sacajawea was sure white men lived in
the log houses. It did seem a shabby concern compared
with Bent's Fort and St. Vrain's and Lupton's. She

climbed from her horse and hoisted both children down.
Then they walked slowly into the Indian village, leading the string of six horses. Suddenly Sacajawea noticed
that the markings on some tepees were Shoshoni. There
were a few camp dogs and some near-naked children
staring as she passed. A young woman carrying water
in a huge grass bucket stopped and asked in Agaidüka
Shoshoni, "Mother, have you lost your way?"

"Is this the home of one called Jim Bridger?" asked
Sacajawea in stumbling Shoshoni.

The squaw signified that she had heard so from many
lips, but he was out now, trapping beaver on the Sweetwater with many braves.

"Will he be back before winter?" Sacajawea then made
the sign of the Shoshonis to indicate she was a member
of this tribe. The squaw put her hand to her mouth in
surprise. She turned away.

"*Café, señora?* Coffee?" Sacajawea called.

"Huh—no *café* here," said the squaw, turning back.
"We have not had coffee for a long time."

"*Sí, señora.*" Sacajawea ran to her packs and brought
back a little sack.

"*Café bueno,*" said Sacajawea, giving the sack to the
squaw and dropping back into her Spanish-Comanche
tongue. "I will live here among my people and wait for
the man called Jim Bridger."

Sacajawea chose a small, grassy spot to put up the
leather tent Frémont had given her. She staked the
horses. When there was an evening campfire, she took
the girls and sat on the outer circle listening to the
Shoshonis talk about the land from which they had
come, the Shining Mountains. Some of the women who
came to the campfire were wives of the trappers who
lived in the little wooden cabins outside the walls of
the fort. They talked about their chief called *Washakie*,
Gourd Rattle. Sacajawea longed to ask about Tooette-
cone—her brother, Chief Black Gun—but she did not
open her mouth. Soon she learned that Washakie was
the civil chief and he had several smaller tribes under
him. The tribe of Nowroyawn was due at this camp
anytime now.

The next morning, at the water hole in the nearby

creek, Sacajawea spotted the squaw she had given her
small bag of coffee to.

"Nowroyawn?" asked Sacajawea. "He is a chief? Of
what band?"

"*Ai*, he is chief. He was recently chosen to take the
place of the great Chief Black Gun." She spoke softly,
speaking the name of their dead chief quickly. She continued, all the time studying Sacajawea, "Three summers ago, Black Gun was killed in battle against the
Apaches. Nowroyawn was chosen partly because of his
slowness to bring the tribe into war and partly because
he is nephew of Black Gun and the one called Spotted
Bear."

Once again Sacajawea was struck with information
she was not prepared to receive. She sat down and stared
openmouthed at the squaw. When her mind cleared she
asked softly, "So—then, where is Shoogan?"

The squaw drew in her breath. "You come as a
stranger, yet you know the name of the chief's cousin!
Who are you?"

Feeling dizzy, Sacajawea whispered, "Black Gun and
Spotted Bear were my brothers. Shoogan is my sister's
baby. She died and he was left with Spotted Bear."

"What?" asked the young squaw, leaning forward
and showing her wide-spaced teeth.

"I have come home to the People," Sacajawea said.

"For what?"

"To be with my relatives. I was taken captive when
I was a child."

"What does that have to do with coming back? Things
have changed."

So she told the young squaw at the water hole she
was looking for her firstborn, who had accompanied her
on a visit once before to the People. "Does anyone in
the tribe recall that visit when many white men came
up the river?"

"*Ai*," said the squaw. "My own mother told the story
often. Are you the one called Grass Child who returned
with a child on her back?"

"The same one," said Sacajawea in a whisper.

The squaw looked and finally nodded approval. This
could be. For had not Grass Child come once before as
a young woman, and now she was here again as an old

woman. She did not have an infant son, but two little girls this time.

The next day, the young squaw, who was called Toward Morning, unseen, followed Sacajawea and the little girls to Black's Fork, where they spent the morning fishing. When Toward Morning could no longer stand to sit still and watch, she came out of her hiding behind the brush.

"How do you catch the fish?" Toward Morning asked.

"We use the metal hook," answered Suzanne with hand signs, pulling her line from the water. "See, I put a strong grass string on the cottonwood pole, then the hook is fastened to the string. It is a new way. Much like the way of the white men. It is easier than the old way of making a willow or grapevine net, my mother says."

"*Ai*, I can see that," answered Toward Morning. "Your mother knows much. She should be called *Porivo*, Chief Woman."

Sacajawea came up to the squaw, wondering if she were criticizing or approving.

"Can you sew in the white woman's way?" asked Toward Morning.

"*Ai*, there are metal needles and string finer than thinnest rawhide."

"If I can trade for metal needles inside the fort, will you show me tomorrow?" asked Toward Morning shyly.

"*Ai*, of course. I will show you how to make designs on tunics that will make your friends' eyes widen," said Sacajawea, pleased that she would have a friend to sew and chat with.

"Porivo," said Toward Morning as she left.

From then on, Sacajawea was called *Porivo*, Chief Woman, by the Shoshonis.

She noticed in this tribe some relaxing of the strict old ways. First was the mentioning out loud of her dead brother's name, even in a soft tone, but it had been mentioned. She noticed, too, that some of the women spoke of themselves by their own names. To have a name was something sacred and meant some trait or deed of the bearer. The name was never to be spoken out loud by the bearer for fear of losing some of its sacred power from overuse. Some of the women told

Sacajawea their names as in the white man's intro-
duction of new friends.

Sacajawea showed Toward Morning how to fry fish
on a flat stone near the cooking fire to make it crisp.

"You do not put fish in a pot of hot water?" asked
Toward Morning.

"No, then they are mushy. Much better this way.
Try one." Sacajawea put the crisp brown fish on a board.

Toward Morning was amazed. "Good. Good."

"Better with salt." Sacajawea sprinkled on a little
unrefined salt she had in a leather pouch.

"Ummm. This something."

Toward Morning asked Sacajawea to sit with her
during the evenings' campfires.

"*Ai*, we have come home," repeated Sacajawea.

"Home!" said Crying Basket, sucking the first two
fingers on her right hand—an indication of the sharing
of the family food, or being at home.

52

Bridger's Fort

It was on a lovely evening in April, 1843, that the opportunity came for my first trip across the Great Plains. William Sublette was elected as chief guide, as he had been all over the western country several times. Sir William Drummond Stewart, from Scotland, was going along to hunt Buffalo. One of the cart drivers, Baptiste Charbonneau, was the son of the old trapper Charbonneau, and Sacajawea, the brave Indian woman who had guided Lewis and Clark on their perilous journey through the wilderness. He had been born about the time they built Fort Mandan, far out in the Dakota hills and had been carried as a papoose on his mother's back all through the Indian country. By a singular coincidence he was now again to make the journey and guide the son of William Clark through the same region.

From *Persimmon Hill*, by William Clark Kennerly. Copyright 1948 by the University of Oklahoma Press, pp. 143–44.

The sunlight filtered through the crevices in the adobe walls to dabble the hard-packed ground. Inside Fort Bridger there was a blacksmith shop and a trading store and more log cabins. Many Shoshonis crowded into the store to trade and gossip. Some had furs and leather leggings for trading. The flies buzzed around their heads and walked about on their seemingly intractable faces.[1]

When it was her turn, Toward Morning traded new-made moccasins for three large metal needles. Sacajawea placed willow baskets on the counter and pointed to the little squares of hard peppermint candies, which she thought were sugar cubes.

"Hey, Louis, haven't seen anything like this before!" called the storekeeper, a plump, baldheaded man whose fringe of hair made a wispy halo around his elfin face. "Are these here Shoshoni basketry?" he asked in French. The other man, Louis, sorting out pelts behind the broad plank counter, was nearly hidden from view. He grunted and made some motions with his hands, but did not hurry to look at Sacajawea's baskets.

"*Oui*," she answered in French. "I learned a long time ago when I lived with my people. Then I showed the Comanches, and they showed me something different. Now I show you Shoshoni know-how woven with Comanche know-how."

Both men looked at her incredulously.

She continued in French, "You like these?"

"Louis," said the plump man, "did you ever hear a squaw talk French patois?"

Louis squinted his eyes and tapped his long fingers on the counter. He was almost as dark as the Shoshonis.

Sacajawea recognized him. "You are the man called Vasquez!"

He recognized her. "And you are the Comanche woman. The one who claims to be Madame Charbonneau! Well, I'll be! *Sacré amigo!*" (Louis Vasquez's parents were French and Spanish, and often he mixed the languages in a single sentence.) "Hey, Jake, this here fool squaw was at St. Vrain's when the Crows came

1160

raiding horses off the Cheyennes. She claims to be *la mère* of Bap Charbonneau, that Frenchman."

"*Oui*, Baptiste. *Je le connais*."

Sacajawea leaned over the counter to look more closely at Jake, and offer by way of friendship her out-stretched hand. Patient-faced, he took it and stepped back so that he could trade with those Shoshonis who had formed a line beside Sacajawea. Vasquez hand-pumped heartily.

Jake turned from his new customer and said, pow-der-soft as the fall of a moccasin in deep trail dust, "You know, Bap was through here six, eight weeks ago. He traveled from St. Louis with some prosperous Scots-man, Sir Stewart. What a party!"

"I didn't know Bap had come back west," said Vas-quez, his eyes sparkling like chipped obsidian as Jake's soft voice rose to what seemed a shout to Sacajawea.

"They even had Bill Clark's young son, Jeff. Fanciest hunting party I've ever saw."

Toward Morning was jerking at Sacajawea's arm. "Come, let us begin sewing. We have needles."

Sacajawea pulled her arm away and pressed Jake further. "Where were they going?"

Jake was a half-breed Cheyenne, hard-reared among his mother's people. He had spent his early manhood learning and walking the trails of the trappers and traders. There had always been trouble in the camps of the white men for Jake Connor, and he belonged neither there nor in the old Cheyenne camps. He was neither white nor red, until he met Louis Vasquez, who seemed to feel some empathy for the strange, friendless man who carried the fires of only one ambition in his breast—to belong to the white race of his father.

"Going? Why, they was on an enormous game hunt along the Oregon Trail."

"How many men?" asked Sacajawea, flushing, start-ing to stammer, the yearning for sugar cubes now for-gotten. "What does he look like? And Chief Red Hair's son—what does he look like?" She stopped in mid-sputter and asked, "Who else was there?"

"Well, I don't know exactly," said Jake quietly, hand-ing out a tin of coffee for three pairs of moccasins. "There was Bill Sublette—he was the leader for that Scotch dude—and Geisso Chouteau, Cyprian Menard, Bill Kennerly—all from St. Louis—and young Jeff Clark, the spittin' image of his old man."

Sacajawea's hopes soared before the narrowed eyes of the half-breed. "It is close to thirty winters since I have put my eyes on my firstborn." She held her hands up and opened the fists three times to show thirty. "I am looking for him."

"That Bap is handsome as any breed I've seen," said Jake, his face coloring. "I mean he is not too short and squat, but rather tall, and he holds his head high. He's mostly a white man and knows how to use tools and wear a button shirt, went to school and learned names of strange lands and wars. But one thing he never learned—to wear boots. He prefers moccasins."

Sacajawea never took her eyes from Jake as she spoke. "He loved the woods, and the river, running along quiet, but he also craved new things. He went to the land called Germany with a man called Paul—Duke Paul."

"C'est fantastique, amigo! She is right. That is Bap!" cried Vasquez, his black eyes snapping as he came up from behind the broad counter.

Jake nodded to the next Shoshoni in line, but kept his eyes on Sacajawea as he talked. "Old squaw, you've come to the right place. Jim Bridger can tell you most. He's been with Bap on hunting parties. He's had Bap read to him. Bap is the readingest fool anybody's seen. Brings books from Saint Louis so that he can read and argue with Jim."

Toward Morning stood sulking beside Sacajawea. She couldn't get into perspective the curious fact that this woman could speak another tongue and get so excited about something these men were saying.

Sacajawea turned to her and said in Shoshoni, "Take the girls to the lodge. I will be there soon. It is important to talk with these men. I have to talk now."

Toward Morning shrugged her shoulders and walked to where the little girls were petting a large yellow dog. She beckoned to them, then left through the open front gate, still puzzled by the behavior of her new friend.

Jake leaned toward Sacajawea just a little, saying, "Now, just tell me a thing. What you want to get by tracking someone you haven't talked with in thirty years, besides maybe a kick in the backside and a heart-ache?"

Sacajawea looked thoughtful and bland. "So what?" She made quick hand signs. "He is my papoose. I can rest easier if I see for myself that he is a man." She shook herself and disturbed a dozen flies that had set-tled on the blanket covering her.

Louis Vasquez came to the other side of the counter and frowned. "Jake is right. Let me ask you, old woman. You ever think about what's in front of tomorrow?"

This French-Spanish trapper and trading-post op-erator was glum and serious. He pointed his finger ac-cusingly. "You're not so young anymore, and you might find it hard to reckon with the way your son lives and thinks. Haven't you ever thought that he might not want to meet up with his mama particularly?"

Sacajawea looked skeptical as her mind worked. "Do you ever think about having somebody look after you when you can do nothing?" She looked at Vasquez ap-praisingly. "My people," she went on, "take care of fath-erless children and the old. They are proud to help. When I am old, it will be in my own way and I won't beg from my son." For a moment Sacajawea's eyes clouded with anger; then they were devoid of expres-sion.

"I understand what she's saying," said Jake. "If she no longer belongs with her son, she wants to know, and she'll make out best she can. Happen she gets hurt, she'll crawl off to lick her own cuts."

Vasquez grunted. "Well," he said obliquely, consid-ering Sacajawea, "it's none of my business."

Sacajawea smiled as if to acknowledge an apology. "*Ai*," she said. "It would give me a fine feeling to know someone worries about me."

Jake smiled and nodded, motioning her to follow him into the blacksmith shop. They left Vasquez trading with the remaining Shoshonis. Sacajawea put her hand over her mouth, not able to speak as she looked at a suit of armor hooked up on pegs by the inside door. Jake lifted the metal visor to show there was no one inside. Never had she imagined such clothing. She won-dered how a man could walk or ride a horse in such a suit. Finally she asked, "What manner of tribe wears this?"

Jake spat between his feet. "I only know that the man who financed Bill Sublette's party, that Scotsman, Sir William Drummond Stewart, brought it from England and gave it to Jim Bridger for letting all his party rest at this here fort. Thought you'd enjoy seeing the suit Bap rigged Jim Bridger in. When he had him locked inside, Bridger tried to mount a horse. He fell. Bap rolled in the dirt with laughter. And that same day I heard Stewart tell about them Sioux at Fort Laramie—thirty, forty lodges of 'em. Some of the chiefs—Red Bull, Bull Tail, Little Thunder, and Solitary Dog—came to visit the party when it stopped. Those chiefs recognized young Jeff Clark right off because he looked so much like his old man, Bill Clark—red hair and everything. They all knew old Bill Clark."

Sacajawea drew in her breath.

"And I remember Bap adding something to that there conversation. He said he'd been on a long trip with his old man, and Bill Clark was leader of that trip. Then he said the funny thing. He said he and Jeff were given the same baby name—Pompy."

"Pomp!" she gasped. Her hand slapped against her mouth in astonishment.

"Yea, that's it!" shouted Jake. "That's what Jeff said it was. Them chiefs were so impressed they invited Jeff Clark and Bap Charbonneau to a real feast of boiled dog."

"*Non*, not dog," said Sacajawea, her eyes large.

"Oh, it was. The Sioux think it the greatest kind of meat."

Sacajawea shook her head.

"The etiquette of them Sioux would not allow a single scrap to be left in the wooden bowl each guest had. After that there feast, the pipe was smoked and the oldest chief, Red Bull, made a speech, through an interpreter, who was your boy Bap. The speech was mostly about that Chief Red Hair, who was Bill Clark."

Sacajawea could not speak.

Jake spat between his feet again and went on. "That man Stewart would have made your eyes bug. He dressed like a fop, in a white shooting jacket, colorful shepherd's plaids, and a broad-brimmed white hat. The trappers at the fort laughed at such an outlandish outfit. But even more surprising, he had wagons piled with tins of meats, jars of pickles, and wines, and tea and coffee in packages straight from England, plenty of sugar, and barrels of flour. When the trappers were not guffawing, they gaped in wonder. How could such a dude get along in the woods? Their ridicule turned to respect and liking. That man was a rider and as good a shot as the most expert trappers—near as good as Bap hisself." Jake winked at Sacajawea. She was still thinking about meat in tins and could not make a mental picture of such a thing. "And when it came to skirmishing with the Crows or Blackfeet, he was just as brave and cool as the most experienced mountain men. Best of all, he was hospitable and shared his supplies with all. And they came to accept him on equal terms. Now, I think in the same way you'll get along with Bap. You have the patience to trap him down, and he'll be on equal terms with his ma once he gets to know her again."

Sacajawea's eyes were on a distant place. "You are right," she said. "Things change. But the mountains are still here, and the green spring hole where trout hang and look as big as a man's arm." She looked up at Jake, and her eyes softened. "There are things he won't forget, and we can start there."

Jake chewed on the end of his cold pipe and mulled this over.

A door slammed, and Jake jerked guiltily.

"Why, where's Louis?" demanded Juanita Vasquez. She was short and plump. Her apron was freshly starched. "What are you doing? How dare you hide back here with this—this squaw."

Sacajawea felt confused.

"Miz Vasquez," said Jake. "I was just showing Miss Charbonneau the iron suit. She's the ma of Bap Charbonneau. You know, the cart driver with that fancy Stewart party?"

"Jake, you fetch Louis right now and tell him to come for supper. Then you close the blacksmith shop. You know it's off limits to Indians."

Jake was discomforted. "I meant no harm, ma'am. She's a friend of Louis's, too."

Sacajawea seemed unsure of what to do next. She moved out of the doorway and toward the gate in the wall of the fort.

"Good night," she said in clear Spanish. She moved slowly away from the fort.

"Well, she speaks Spanish. She can't be all Indian. What did you say her name was?" asked Juanita Vasquez.

"I called her Miz Charbonneau. She speaks fair English and a smatterin' of French, too. She lives with them Shoshonis outside the fort."

The days were hot. The midafternoon sun stabbed through the opening in the dense leaf canopy of the cottonwoods. Flies buzzed sleepily in the muggy air under the trees, and locusts sawed endlessly in the summer heat. The camp dogs panted and Sacajawea felt her tunic wet across her back as she carried water from the spring, wishing she'd done this earlier in the day. There had been news in the camp that Bridger was coming in any day, accompanied by Shoshoni hunters. These hunters were led by a man called Nowroyawn.

Sacajawea was like a child, so great was her anticipation. Nothing moved in the camp but the insects as she trudged in with her water jug. Toward Morning had been sewing, but she now was sleeping. Crying Basket and Suzanne were asleep near the tepee flap where a breeze could touch them if one came. Sacajawea gazed across the blue haze of distant hills. She could smell the ancient odor of the far, undisturbed, virgin forest duff, never burned, planted, or grazed. The land of the People existed for only an instant, suspended in a void of long-expired emotions. She was in her father's camp, looking at the sun-spotted trees, hearing the sounds of horses and of women chattering as they worked after a summer hunt. The feeling was so strong that for a moment she could taste the air, rank with blood and fur where the venison hung in the sun drying under a pall of writhing cedar smoke. Sacajawea shook her head. These were memories she thought were long forgotten. And it had been happening more and more lately—the recalling of the old times when she lived with the People. It was curious that these memories should come now, when she was looking forward to the new time when she would talk with her son, who was more white than Shoshoni and whose thoughts might be foreign to her own.

"They are coming! They are nearly here!" called a camp crier. Women were moving about, already putting on their best clothes and paint. Sacajawea laid out the pink calicos for Crying Basket and Suzanne as soon as Toward Morning sleepily explained that it must be Bridger's party that was coming in.

Sacajawea carefully put on her yellow dress with two petticoats, and on impulse opened the leather pouch at her waist and took out the now-tarnished peace medal. Long ago she had planned to give this to Baptiste. It was her gift from Sun Woman. She examined the likeness of the man called Jefferson on one side and the hands clasped in friendship on the obverse. The gold outer edge shone in the sun. She fingered her sky blue stone, then left it in the pouch and hunted among her clothes for a piece of thong to slip through the suspension loop on the medal. She hung the medal around her neck, satisfied that it was the thing to wear, even though long ago Charbonneau had said no woman had a right to wear this.

As the riders came on their horses across the valley, she was certain of the man they called Bridger. He was big—more than six feet tall—with a dark beard and eyebrows. He rode his horse with the ease of his Shoshoni companions, legs dangling straight down, back half-bent, shoulders hunched forward.

Toward Morning, with fresh vermilion on her cheeks, tugged at Sacajawea's arm. "Look, he is the most handsome. And look, there among the women, the one with arms waving. She is his, a Flathead. And there is the child, called by his name for her, Mary Ann."

The Flathead woman was large, mainly because she was expecting another child very soon. Her hips were broad, her legs large, matching her puffy hands and arms. She was dark-skinned, almost swarthy, and her hair black as a moonless night. She was a handsome woman, without being pretty.

Mary Ann was about the age of Suzanne. She had no clothing, but there was a bear-claw necklace about her throat. Her hair was ragged and unkempt. She jumped up and down at the sight of her father. The Shoshoni riders coming in whooped and hollered so that the camp dogs began barking. In front of the Shoshonis rode another big man with an eagle-feather headdress. He looked from side to side and around at the crowd gathered to welcome them. He waved his arms and hollered. He stood up on the back of his gray horse and waved again. The crowd cheered. He drew up to them, making the palms-out sign of peace.

"That one is our great civil chief, Washakie," said Toward Morning, close to Sacajawea's ear, "and behind him comes his subchief, Nowroyawn. And look! There is Nowroyawn's cousin, Shoogan! And here comes Bitter Water and Rock Rabbit! They have all come back!"

It was strange, so nearly miraculous, that Sacajawea was held motionless for a moment. There in front of her was Shoogan, one leg shorter than the other, the smaller foot twisted a little against the flank of his cream bay. Sacajawea thought she'd prepared for every eventuality, every surprise, every strain on her emotions. She knew that what could be dreamed about was capable of happening. She had not dreamed of this. To see the man here before her was such an astounding piece of fortune that it took a moment for her to come to herself.

"*Kiii-yiii!*" called Crying Basket with the crowd. Suzanne was dancing up and down to see the riders better.

The usual feasting and games began immediately after the meat from the hunt had been divided. Sacajawea noticed that Bridger generously gave Toward Morning a hindquarter of a mule doe for her lodge. Toward Morning said something to him about her new neighbor and friend and pointed in the direction of Sacajawea. Bridger then pushed the other hindquarter toward her, smiled broadly, and left quickly for the fort's gate.

Toward Morning tugged at the meat to get it to her lodge, but Sacajawea had not thought of helping. She took a hand of each little girl and moved through the crowd. She had decided to watch carefully to see which lodge Shoogan went into. As if caught in time—a slow-moving dream that etched itself against the brown earth and skin tepees—the brown hulk of the man with the long, sad face moved in and out of the lodges. The man limped exactly as he had when a child, with an easy confidence, sure of his footing and where he was going. Sacajawea knew this was the son of her dead sister. She clearly recalled the day she had first seen Shoogan in the Shoshoni camp when she had been the interpreter for Chief Red Hair. He was a naked child, with a pushed-out stubborn lower lip. His left foot was turned in slightly and smaller than the right, a cursed clubfoot, but he moved without aid, stepping high to clear the stiff, dry grass around the camp. Even then his face resembled that of Sacajawea's brother, Spotted Bear.

Sacajawea knew what she was doing. Shoogan would go into his lodge, speak to his women and relatives, and come out again, waiting to be fed; then he would relax and sit idly, smoking and telling about the hunt.

The greatest problem was the little girls. Whatever she did, she would have to keep them perfectly quiet. If they coughed, giggled, or cried, the man would take his family inside the lodge. Sacajawea made up her mind. She waited until the man had gone inside. She sat the two girls down and told them they must not speak unless she told them, and they must not move. She sat herself down at the side of the tepee with the girls and picked up the bare foot of Crying Basket, pretending the child had a thorn in it that must be pulled out.

And then Shoogan appeared. He sat in front of the tepee with several women and children. He ate soundlessly, smiling once in a while toward his waiting children and women so that his white teeth showed. He lit his cherry-wood pipe and puffed blue-drifting clouds of smoke. The sun made yellow patterns around them, and a small breeze rustled in the cottonwood branches. Shoogan sat, soaking in the calmness of the late afternoon, and Sacajawea sat, squinting into the light and shadow of the trees.

"Tell us now," prompted one of his small boys in Shoshoni. "I want to remember how you came upon that herd of deer." The boy's eyes sparkled as he stretched out on the brown grass. He wore a breechclout and

moccasins too small for him. He turned and grunted
something else in Shoshoni to his small sister.

"Why, we got into some antelope," said Shoogan,
"before we ever found those mule deer all together."
His eyes kindled as he remembered. "I was in the lead,
and we topped a rise and looked into a meadow when
the morning mists were just rising out. They were just
waiting for us to come. We took half a dozen bucks and
a couple of doe and left the rest to breed next spring.
We'll have meat until fall."

As he told it, Sacajawea imagined the place, the summer sun plumbing the water and sparkling in the spring.
She pictured the ancient leaves in patches on the sand
of the bottom, the dense woods rising still and sultry
in the heat, and the jewellike coolness of the meadow
in early morning. She remembered how she had lain
in the cover of brush with her mother and sister while
her father had hunted meadows for deer in the morning
mist.

Then he said, "Nowroyawn and Washakie think we
ought to move to a more sheltered spot in the valley
before the fall rains come."

"Where would we go?" asked a woman, her eyes crinkling. She picked a long piece of stringy meat from the
cooking pot and held it above her mouth, then let it
drop in.

"Could the People go over to the Beaver Head?" asked
Sacajawea impulsively.

Shoogan nodded, sucking reflectively at the pipestem. Then he looked up and seemed to realize that the
voice did not come from his women, but from the one
sitting at the side of his tepee with two sleeping children on her lap.

"Old woman, do not interrupt," he said, curling his
smaller left foot under the right leg and shifting his
weight backward so that he could see the intruder better. "I am talking with only my family."

He was a dry, spare man, not tall, but clean and
quick and furtive in movement. His wide shoulders were
bent forward in that permanent hunch peculiar to those
who have spent their lives perpetually half-crouched,
ready to spring for cover and weapon at the first crack
of a twig or hiss of a war arrow.

"And so—I am talking with my family," said Saca-jawea, closing her eyes in a long, reflective blink.

The coffee-skinned hunter looked at her a long three seconds before deliberately and slowly saying, "Old woman, I am warning you, do not bother us. Go away, now! Vamoose!" He was irritated, more because Saca-jawea had interrupted his talk than because she had claimed to be some relative of his.

Sacajawea looked at him, unable to match his low, clear Shoshoni speech.

"Well, what do you want then?" asked Shoogan with no particular politeness.

"I imagine you are the son of Rain Woman, and then later Spotted Bear and his woman, Cries Alone, raised you."

Shoogan was on his feet.

Sacajawea spoke fast. "One day many white men visited your camp in the mountains when you were a small boy and Black Gun was chief. Can you remember?"

"Old woman, you utter blasphemy when you speak of the dead!" But Shoogan saw it in his mind as Saca-jawea told it: a younger, slimmer woman, with coal-black braids and large warm fawn eyes. She had lifted him into her arms and nuzzled his neck. He could smell the sage scent of her clothing and hear her low voice speaking with his father, Spotted Bear. Shoogan thought, This old woman could be that one. Her voice has the same quality. But that is foolish. It is impos-sible.

Sacajawea gave Shoogan a sidelong glance, as if she had forgotten those she spoke about were now dead. She smiled as if she had forgotten she had other lis-teners and was acknowledging the presence of strangers.

"And so—what happened then?" asked Shoogan.

Sacajawea did not answer immediately. It was as if, in telling, she had put her mind into another time and then found she could not live in both worlds at once. "I found my brother was chief of the Agaidükas, my sister, Rain Woman, dead, and I made a young girl's promise to come back and raise you as my son. I never returned until now," she said finally.

"Old woman, I have told you to go. You are a nui-

sance. I do not know who you are." His answer was
drawled, but it hit Sacajawea across the face like the
haft of a war ax.

Sacajawea hitched her blanket closer about her yellow dress. "Where is Willow Bud?" she said. "She will
remember the day the Minnetarees dragged us from
our families and the chief was killed."

"Many of the People are dead, but the Minnetaree
raid is tribal tradition," said Shoogan, as if that made
any other answer unnecessary.

The women were beginning to chatter among themselves, and the children had run to the back of the tepee
to chase a brown dog. Sacajawea sat quietly, and the
two girls slept on her lap.

"Where is the one called *Tooettecone*, Chief Black
Gun?" she asked.

Now Shoogan's eyes appeared to slit as they fastened
on the vexatious woman. "That name cannot be spoken!
That chief was much loved and is gone on the trail to
the Land of Everfeasting. He was shot down on a raid
by the Crows." Shoogan slowly walked around Sacajawea, looking her over.

"That chief was my brother, and the one called Spotted Bear was my brother. My sister was Rain Woman,
your first mother." Now she waited while the birds sang
and the locust chanted in the heat, like insane crones
who talk to themselves all day and never weary.

The softness of her tone caused Shoogan to step closer.
She held out the Jefferson medal for him to examine.

He turned it over and over, breathing hard. Finally
he let it drop back to her breast. "The chief you call
brother had a medicine piece such as that. It is still on
his breast giving him courage for his last long journey
to the Unknown. And it is true that many times he told
of recognizing his sister who came with many whites
and was a chief woman to them. He said she helped
them understand what the white men had to say. She
had a child. She also had a man that did much complaining and told foolish stories. For many years our
women have had a saying if a child complains or twists
his tongue, 'Beware, you will grow face hair and be left
to do the cooking.'" Shoogan's black eyes sparkled like
chipped obsidian. He was reed-thin, with grease-black-

ened buckskins. The leggings were heavily fringed, and his moccasins quilled and beaded. His lank hair hung shoulder-long and straight against his broad, bare shoulders. His face was angular and flint-keen as a lance blade.

"The man's name was Charbonneau," said Sacajawea. "I was his woman."

Shoogan knew now that the old woman could not be lying. He fingered the gold-rimmed medal again, sucking in his cheeks. Finally he called to his three women, who jumped, startled, "Fix a meal for this old woman and her children. She is one of my mothers." He looked at Sacajawea and decided that her story was not thin as April grass. He liked her and wondered what other events flickered behind her shining black eyes.

In her turn, Sacajawea was sizing up the grown Shoogan. She could see that he had been well brought up to live on the land. He was decent and honest, slow, with caution in both manner and mind. She could see that he read the nature of man or animal quickly and unerringly. She dared ask the one question close to her heart. "Tell me of the man the people call Bap?"

"We have heard of him. We do not see him much. He is a white man and stays at the fort. I think he is mostly white, like Jake Connor in the post store. Once I heard this Bap yell at mules pulling a cart full of supplies. He is like the white men, having little patience. Why do you ask about him?"

Sacajawea was amused, but she did not show it. "First tell me about another, called Tess or Toussaint. About the same age as Bap. They could be brothers."

A shadow passed over Shoogan's face, and he did not smile, but he looked at the woman with curiosity. "He does not come this way. I do not know about this man." His voice flashed with a thin stringer of iron. "Tell now why you want to know these things."

"Porivo! Porivo!" It was the Spanish accent of Louis Vasquez calling. He had to shout to be heard above the din of Shoshoni voices, as each family was celebrating and catching the news of the hunt. "I'm looking for the woman called Porivo," stated Vasquez.

"Who is this woman?" asked Shoogan.

"The woman who can speak many tongues."

"You have need for a translator?" asked Shoogan with his hands.

"Goddammit, no!" stated Vasquez. "Never had need of a translator myself, unless you count that time those Cayuses wandered across the mountains and I had to listen to their palaverin' most of the night."

He took off his straw hat and scratched vigorously at his head, where the black hair lay dank with sweat. He stepped to the side of Shoogan and noticed Sacajawea sitting quietly with the sleeping children in her lap. He spoke to her. "I come on account of Bridger wants to meet the mother of Bap Charbonneau. Says he can hardly believe Bap ever had a mother at all."

Sacajawea looked at Vasquez keenly; then she looked at Shoogan, whose mouth hung open. Her black eyes were guarded and half-shut with the pleasure of anticipation. "I'm coming," she said, stretching herself, "if one of these women will look after my sleeping papooses."

"Oh, I will," said Shoogan's first woman, Dancing Leaf. "I like girls. All I have is a boy."

Sacajawea ambled after Vasquez toward the fort, feeling a mixture of timidity and victory. They reached the edge of the Shoshoni camp, where the leather tepees stopped and the trail wound into the cottonwoods, where grasshoppers whirred in the tall grass.

"We sometimes call Bridger Old Gabe," said Vasquez. "I suppose it is from the angel named likewise, but who knows. Anyway, he'll likely have some stories to tell about your boy. He's rested some and had some whiskey to make his insides alive. Now he wants to talk."

Sacajawea understood half his Spanish words, and smiled—a long, slow smile that held the warmth of friendship.

"Hell, he'll talk through the night," Vasquez said.

It was near sundown when they went inside the fort. "This here is Old Gabe," said Vasquez, facing the big mountain man. "He wants to shake your hand."

She held her hand out. Bridger took it in his big callused one. "So—you are the mama of Bap?" He belched.

"*Ai*," said Sacajawea emphatically, noticing that the

woman stood behind him, her eyes glinting black jealousy. She was even more heavyset than Sacajawea had noticed earlier in the afternoon.

"Oh, this is Emma," said Bridger, nodding toward the big woman. "She is as good as any Christian wife. Reverend Sam Parker christened her Emma, and married us according to his Presbyterian service."

Sacajawea looked at Vasquez to see if he were making hand signs so she could better understand the words of this Bridger. Vasquez was standing very still, watching to see how much Sacajawea understood. He made no motion to help her. So then she remained inside the privacy of her closed eyes as Bridger talked and she drifted mentally to the mountain meadow where her mother and father had camped. She made a comparison. At that time her people were laughing and joyful. Somber were the Agaidükas now. What had driven them from the mountains to live here beside this white man's fort?

Sacajawea opened her eyes slowly and smiled toward Emma. Vasquez had left quietly. Bridger motioned her to sit on the split-log bench near the trading store. He sat beside her. She moved to the end of the log, so as not to sit too close to this handsome stranger. Emma nodded approval and blinked her eyes and sat herself at Bridger's feet, glancing adoringly toward him every now and then. Bridger talked, scratching his bearded chin, telling stories about himself. He was muscular—without an ounce of superfluous flesh. His cheekbones were high, his nose hooked, the expression of his eyes mild and thoughtful, and his face grave, almost to solemnity. From an Indian viewpoint he was very handsome. Sacajawea found that his serious expression could be deceptive, for he was most expert in relating wildly fantastic stories without the slightest change of expression. Sacajawea liked him immediately.

"Injuns ain't never so mean as when they've took a beatin'. They're half-froze to make up for it, don't matter on who," Bridger continued. "And they put an arrow in my back. Buried it deep. Stayed there three years, that Blackfoot iron point. Doc Marcus Whitman came through and stayed to visit a couple days. Said he could take the goldarned arrow point out in a minute." Bridger

wrenched himself around and pointed to a place below
his right shoulder. "I've never laid on such a foofaraw
bed in all my days. That Whitman concocted a bed under this same cottonwood here in the middle of my fort
with liquor kegs and lodgepoles piled with beaver skins.
Then he took the largest scalpel from a leather loop
under the purple-velvet flaps of his instrument roll.
That grapplin' iron looked to be poor doin's." Bridger
glanced at Sacajawea, as if waiting for her to speak.[2]

She could not understand what he was talking so
fast about, and she wanted desperately for him to tell
about Bap. "Was Baptiste in this story?" she asked
slowly.

"Darn tootin'! My good friend Baptiste come up from
the crowd and gave me somethin' from a jug for my
dry, and he hunted in his possibles for a piece of rawhide
for me to bite in. The Doc was pleased with his help.
Then a Medicine Man came from nowhere and writhed
and danced his way to the head of my bed, smeared
with red vermilion on his bronze face. Then the Doc
said, 'Outen my way, Medicine Man, it's gettin' dark.'
Then the Doc felt over my back explorin' with his fingertips until he felt iron in that there flesh. Then he
said, 'Bite, man—here goes,' and he cut deep and clean
until he came to where the shaft had pulled off that
iron arrow point. Blood—wagh—he mopped it out with
a shirt-tail cut in strips. Things went black. Then I
came back as the Doc sliced in deeper still and with his
thumb and finger gave that arrow tip a turn. I could
feel the muscles in my back cordin'. The Medicine Man
leaped into the air with a shriek.

"Bap, he held on to my heels as the Doc cut a little
deeper around the sides of the arrow. The air was still,
and the Doc worked in a greenish darkness; then a
spatter of rain settled on the cottonwood leaves.

"The Medicine Man groveled in the dirt and increased the volume of his incantations as the Doc pulled
hard. His hand skidded on the slippery blood, and he
tried again. Then there in his hand was the iron tip.
For a minute I must have passed out; then I came up
on my knees and slid off the bed onto my feet. I reeled
some, but my voice came steady. Bap came up to move

me to the Doc's tepee. 'By gar!' I said. 'No old coon's goin' to fotch this beaver nowhere.'

"Bap took me under the legs and boosted me to his shoulder and forced me to the Doc's tepee. I protested all the way that he had no call to haul me around, since I warn't no bellerin' squaw. I settled myself on a beer-robe pallet. Some Injun gal spread her white antelope cape over me. The Doc said, 'Gabe, you're more of a man than I knew!' The arrowhead covered his palm. 'Quite a hunk of iron you been carryin' 'round. You ought to of died of gangrene years ago.'

"I tole him meat don't spoil in these mountains, and grabbed for that souvenir arrow and held up the trophy for that Injun gal to admire. She touched that arrow, and there was a warm light in her eyes.

"Bap said, 'I'll stay with you tonight, Gabe. Just to see that everythin's all right.'

"I raised up on one elbow and give it to him straight. 'By gar, Bap, if ye don't git outen here, I'll know sartin sure ye are layin' for my gal.'

"Not more'n a week later, I got my day's tradin' done early and I rode acrosst the river and talked that Flat-head chief 'round to tossin' the blanket over that gal and me."

Emma tittered. It was getting cold, with the sun gone. A little breeze ran along the ground, making Sacajawea draw into herself.

Bridger got out tobacco and stuffed in it his cheek and let it soak. "You know Joe Meek?" he asked.

"Huh?" asked Sacajawea. "I know no Joe."

"Well, sartin sure, ever' white man and Injun and Spaniard and Frenchman and half-breed in the mountains knows old Joe Meek. And old Joe knows Baptiste Charbonneau. Once he tole about beatin' the daylight out of Bap in a two-day game of euchre at the rendevous of thirty-seven, on the Green River. Joe could tell us where Bap's figurin' on hidin' hisself when he's finished with that Stewart adventure." Bridger lit up his pipe, indicating the talking was over.

For the next several days, Emma came to the stream that ran close by the fort to wash her clothing beside Sacajawea. Her jealousy was gone. She told how impressed her man was with Sacajawea's intelligence and attentiveness. "Not once did you fall asleep while he told stories about himself. That is something. You are really a Chief Woman, Porivo."

One morning, Emma did not come to wash. Beside Sacajawea was a woman who shyly said she lived with a redheaded white man. Sacajawea held herself calm. "What is he called?" The only red-haired men she'd seen were William Clark and old Bill Williams.

"He is called Joseph Walker. I call him Mountain Man." The woman's eyes looked big and fluid in her thin face. Over her shoulders was drawn a tatter of blanket, and her legs came from under the white man's calico and ended in a small pair of worn moccasins. She had a papoose, nearly four seasons of life behind him, sitting on the sandy bank. "I hear you look for a son," said the woman slowly, her eyes liquid, as if dark water ran in them. "Mountain Man talks about Baptiste. He says he is the best man on foot in plains and mountains."

Sacajawea forgot to worry about Emma's absence and moved closer to the woman. "Could I speak with your man?"

"Maybe, when he is back. He is catching animals to keep alive in woven baskets for white men to look at," she giggled. Then Sacajawea giggled. It was a very funny concept that white men would want to keep animals alive just to look at. What could cause such a fear in them of being without something in their villages that would drive them to such precautions of saving the animals in a pen so they could look at them? Then Sacajawea remembered that Chief Red Hair had spent considerable time building a container in which a prairie dog could live as it traveled down the Missouri River in a keelboat so that the Great White Father, called Jefferson, could have a look at him. The strangest thing, she thought, was that white men still wanted the forest animals sent to their villages so men could look at them. She wondered if anyone ever built a box for the grizzly bear. She would like to see that box.

"My man went as far as the Salty Lake. I will tell you when he is back."

In her lodge, Sacajawea built up the fire and called Toward Morning in to talk.

"I am going to see a man called Joseph Walker. He is now at the Salty Lake. Do you know anything about him?"

"No," said Toward Morning. "I could go to the fort and ask Bridger, the Blanket Chief, when this man will return. He knows everything."

Sacajawea closed her eyes and considered that suggestion, weighing it with what she already knew of Toward Morning. She was pretty, not beautiful; probably she had seen at least twenty-five summers already, late for a Shoshoni woman not to have a man. She seemed to seek out Bridger at every opportunity. She talked about him, what he said, how he looked, and she even knew he liked buffalo hump broiled slowly over hickory wood with twigs of sassafras added for the smoke flavor.

Toward Morning watched Sacajawea, wondering what her strange friend could be thinking. Now she saw Sacajawea in a different light, and it somehow seemed bold for a woman to make a deliberate effort to hunt down a son who had gone from his mother's care long ago.

Sacajawea was not thinking about boldness. She opened her eyes slowly. "We'll go talk with Bridger," she said.

Toward Morning nodded happily.

"I don't want you making eyes at a man that has a woman like Emma. White men take only one woman. And I think you have a special feeling for that man with the heavy eyebrows."

Toward Morning colored and looked at her moccasins. "I will tell you," she said, twisting the fringes at one side of her tunic. "There is only one man in my heart. But he cannot see me. *Ai*, it is the Blanket Chief and his eyebrows."

"Huh!" snorted Sacajawea. "You make things hard for yourself and the Shoshoni braves who look from the corner of their eyes at you. You know it is time you found a man."

"We'll eat, then go to the fort," said Toward Morning. "I will hold the hand of Crying Basket. You will hold the hand of Suzanne."

In silence the women ate together in Sacajawea's

tepee and waited as the children chattered and ate little. "We are gone," Sacajawea said.

Inside the fort, Jake Connor waved to Sacajawea. "We look for Bridger," she said.

"He's out. I'm here as chief factor. And Vasquez is at his own fort now. But I heard Bridger's lookin' for another woman. Some say he just couldn't stand it around here no longer and went off in the mountains to be by hisself."

"Why would he want another woman?" asked Sacajawea, bewildered by these actions from a white man.

"Wal, didn't you hear yet? He keened and carried on like a squaw when his Emma died birthin' that scrawny papoose a day or so ago."

Sacajawea felt her throat constrict, her knees grow weak, and her head swim with Jake's words. She tried to tell Toward Morning, and her voice became a croak. "Emma never saw her son," went on Jake. "Gabe gave the young'un the name Jake and is doin' his best to care for him. A squaw is here now tryin' to mother them kids of his. That Mary Ann is a cussed 'un, though. Wet-nursin' ain't in Gabe's line. He'd better find another woman fast, I says."[3]

Toward Morning tugged at Sacajawea to explain what Jake was saying. Sacajawea sat on the split-log bench and did her best. Then she waited for Toward Morning to speak.

"He needs a woman that understands," said Toward Morning softly, "how to prepare his meat, clean his papoose, and sing to his little girl." She began to hum a Shoshoni lullaby and smile to herself.

The next day, Joe Walker's woman ran to Sacajawea at the washing place. "My man is home. He has many animals in cages. He tells strange things about the Salty Lake. But he has not seen your son, called Baptiste, for, he says, nearly five summers. It is sad. Maybe your son is dead, his bones white powder."

Sacajawea eyed the woman, then turned away, gathered her soiled clothing, and trudged back to her lodge. She could not wash this day. Her heart was not in it.

CHAPTER

53

The Mormons

Trouble started in 1853 when the Utah Territorial Legislature had granted a charter to a firm to operate the emigrant ferries at Green River, held to be in a part of the Mormon area called Deseret. The mountaineers who had monopolized the business did not recognize the legal claim, and at gunpoint they carried on business as usual. Consequently, the Mormons sued for the amount collected during the summer.

Bridger seems to have no direct connection with the suit, but the Mormons, thwarted at the ferries, turned their attention to him. Had he not boasted at Fort Laramie that he had furnished guns to the Shoshonis? Had he not been connected by marriage with the Utes, who under Walkara, had dealt the Mormon settlers much grief? If the Mormons could not settle their problems with the mountain men at the ferries, they would have the satisfaction of putting a stop to Bridger's interference. Therefore, they decided to clean out Fort Bridger, "lock, stock, and barrel."

Beginning with an affidavit charging him with furnishing the Indians guns to shoot Mormons, the sheriff and his posse of 150 select men went to the fort to arrest him. Finding the place deserted except for Rutta, Bridger's Shoshoni wife, they pitched camp near by. When they finally became tired of waiting for Blanket Chief's

*return, they made a drive upon his stronghold only to
find that Rutta, too, had vanished.*

JAMES S. BROWN, *Life of a Pioneer*. Salt Lake City: George
Q. Cannon and Sons, 1900, p. 324.

During the next couple of summers it was not an unusual sight to see large trains of white-top wagons come down the trail to Fort Bridger. The trains were led by men called Lansford Hastings, James Clyman, Donner, and Bonneville, who came to get supplies and mend their trains at Fort Bridger. The Mormons, under the direction of Brigham Young, moved across the country in search of a new land in which to farm and build their community. "If there is a place on this earth that nobody wants," said the Prophet, Young, "that's the place we are hunting for."

"In that case, I know the exact spot," said Bridger, chuckling deep inside his belly. "The flat, barren plain of the Great Salt Lake Basin that bakes under the white glare of them vast salt beds is a no-man's-land. There are not many freshwater streams, and that land is enclosed by mountains on all sides. It looks like the bottom of a spent coffee cup with some of the sugar still sittin' in the bottom."

Sacajawea did not hear the men talk, but she heard the rumors well enough. Brigham Young asked Jim Bridger about the exact nature of that country in the Great Salt Lake Basin. "Well, you are imprudent if you bring your people to live in that place until you know for sartin what can be grown in that salty soil. In fact, I'll give you one thousand dollars on the barrel head for the first bushel of corn raised in that basin."

Bridger went on, oblivious to the fact that he had offended Young, and generously told him about the Great Salt Lake, the climate, the minerals, the timber, and the Indians. "Be on guard against them treacherous Utes—they are bad people around Utah Lake, and they are mostly armed. But they won't attack large parties. On t'other hand, they might, however, rob, abuse, or even kill anyone caught alone." While Bridger felt that the soil was fertile, he felt the nights were too cold for growing corn. "You ought to take your people and hightail it to the land at the north end of the California mountains where there's good timber and it's known grain and fruit can be grown easy. There's an Indian tribe that is entirely unknown to most men, especially to travelers and geographers, who raise crops of every kind and harvest the cedar berries. Those there berries are something like juniper berries, yellow-colored, about the size of a plum. You can easily gather a hundred bushel off one tree. The Indians grind the fruit and make the best kind of meal. You ought to go there as fast as possible."

Young replied with tight lips, "My Saints will know more about the country after they see it for themselves." Young did not like to be told what he could or could not do, and from then on, there was an antagonism between these two men.

The Mormons had come to found an empire, regardless of Bridger and his warnings or of the Indians who claimed the country. A week later, the Mormons began to take up residence in the Great Salt Lake Basin.

Sacajawea and Toward Morning watched the wagon trains as they stopped at Fort Bridger. The Shoshoni women stared in awe at the wagons carrying large mirrors, pianos, chairs, rolled carpets, parlor stoves, dishes, oil paintings, glass lamps, and other white household foofaraw. Toward Morning snickered and asked how much further the broken-down horses and oxen could be expected to go.

"Maybe some of the goods they will leave outside," suggested Sacajawea. Then she tried to explain the fine home of Judy Clark and the foofaraw that was inside, but gave up. Toward Morning did not believe the words and could not imagine what Sacajawea was talking about. Sacajawea pointed to plows, hand tools, cattle, goats, swine, and flocks of poultry that had been left beside the riverbank. "These animals cannot be expected to go much farther," said Sacajawea. "The white men lighten their loads, and the Shoshoni find easy food for their lodges."

Bridger did his best for these hundreds of homesick people. The Shoshoni women made moccasins to sell at the fort so that the emigrants would have proper covering on their feet. They made white doeskin tunics for the white women, who were not interested in dressing like Shoshoni squaws, but had no other choice for a time.

During these years a sadness hung around Sacajawea's heart. Her limbs and back seemed bone-tired. She felt older than her fifty-odd years. In their respective ways, Suzanne, with good humor, and Crying Basket, with quick wit, chided their mother about moping day after day.

"You are dull as a broken knife," said Suzanne.

"Haven't you been drawn to a flower, then found it the first to fade?" added Crying Basket. "And most new tunics you have made for yourself fall a little short of your expectations."

"Well, now, if you had not expected so much, you would not be disappointed. Pick your heart off the ground before it begins to decay," suggested Suzanne.

"I see my papooses are growing more wise and older than I had thought," sighed Sacajawea.

One late afternoon, the horizon to the north lay piled high with lumpy shoulders of lead gray clouds. Toward Morning came to sit with Sacajawea, hoping to draw her out of her despondency. "Crying Basket, add the *yampa* root to the cooking pot to give strength to your mother," she said. "You are not the only one with a sorrow, Porivo. I have one for the man we call the Blanket Chief. I have heard he has a new woman, a Ute."

"And so—she must be a good woman," sighed Sacajawea.

"Happen you know Utes?" asked Toward Morning, her eyes narrowed to slits. "Well, so—they know how to make a man feel his best most times, and they are known to be the mothering kind. And so—I'm saddened the Blanket Chief did not even consider my goodness, my cooking, or my warm bed first. And so—there is this deep sorrow hung on my heart since this happening."

Sacajawea looked crosswise at Toward Morning and chuckled deep inside her throat. "One day he'll notice you. While you wait, listen."

The winds had dropped to a muttering whisper, and an uneasy quiet lay over Fort Bridger and the Shoshonis' camp.

"Snow is coming. I smell it on the wind, tonight," said Toward Morning. "I heard Washakie wants to winter on the Little Popo Agie as soon as we can move the camp."

Later that same evening Shoogan and his first woman, Dancing Leaf, brought half a length of cleaned bear gut and two skinned rabbits to Sacajawea's lodge.

"You'll need meat, Old Mother. The storm is going to last more than a day." Shoogan nodded toward the dirty color in the sky. "We'll move out as soon as it quiets down and warms."

Dancing Leaf stepped forward. "We came to invite you and Toward Morning to build your lodge closer to ours so that we can keep an eye on you."

"Well, it is more an order than an invitation," said Shoogan. "It is best if we keep our family together. Since you've shown a liking for Toward Morning, rather than leave her alone, she should come as your family."

Sacajawea raised her eyes across the cooking fire to where Shoogan now sat cross-legged. Something in her melted. Her failure to find Baptiste did not seem so large at this moment. Hot tears scalded her cheeks and ran down into her tunic front. Twice she sniffed before controlling herself.

Suzanne laughed, looking at Sacajawea. "I think your days are in the yellow leaf, but your looks are as good as always, and you are easier on your children than some mothers."

Sacajawea laughed and wrinkled up her face toward Shoogan. "Ah, whenever a child tells her mother about looking young, she may be sure that the child thinks the mother is growing old. And so—now age is the worst thing that can happen to me. Other things will heal, but this gets worse."

Now everyone was laughing with her. It pleased Sacajawea that Suzanne knew of the softening that age brings to the trail of life. She looked about her and felt a warm feeling for Suzanne, remembering how she had held her as a little girl and patted her back and how the child had snuggled close and slept in her arms many an evening. It is good to have a family, she thought, it heals the heart.

"With your help we'll move closer to Shoogan tonight," said Sacajawea, looking at Suzanne.

"Aw, maybe I only thought you were easier," Su-

zanne teased, but pulled at Crying Basket to help pack
up the clothing in order to move quickly in the cold
night air.

"We'll make the tepee double thick with the old skins
from my lodge," said Toward Morning, leaving to pack
her belongings and to strike her tepee.

Shortly after the fish-belly twilight, one snug tepee
was up beside the tall, firm tepee of Shoogan and his
family. The snow was already beginning to pile in low-
driving waves against the bottom skirt of the tepee
walls. By morning the snow was calf-deep and the cold
deepening.

Sacajawea went out to find wood to keep the fire red-
hot all day. The instant she stepped out, her nostrils
were driven flat together and sealed shut as though by
the grip of a giant's fingers. To breathe she had to open
her mouth, gasping to get the air in, then, deprived of
any warming progress through the nose passages, the
inhalation struck her lungs, frost-cold. Fifty breaths
and her chest ached so badly she could scarcely draw
the fifty-first. Within ten minutes of leaving shelter,
her hands were feeling less to the wrists, her feet numbed
stumps upon which her best progress could be only a
lurching, blind stumble. In twenty minutes, the frost
had gone to her shoulders and knees, leaving her to
clump along the icy path like an armless stilt-walker.
No one could stand more than half an hour of such
exposure and be left active. She ducked back inside her
tepee and laced the flap tightly when her hands thawed.

To the frozen watchers at the fort, it seemed that the
Good Lord had forgotten Fort Bridger. The men were
numbed by the ferocious cold. In such temperatures a
man could barely hold on to a rifle, let alone operate
one. But there was no joker in this cold deck—Bridger
had foreseen the early winter and counseled his men
to get wood and hay into the fort ahead of all other
tasks. He knew the Shoshoni camp could take care of
itself, as could the Cheyennes' farther down Ham's Fork.
There was nothing to do but wait out the weather.

"Hang it all," he said one evening to his Ute woman,
Belle, "can't we find something to do each night but
make babies? I wish to hell that old woman called Porivo had found Bap Charbonneau. I'd git him to read

to me all day and night and we'd argy about those there
words until another daylight showed."

Two weeks later when the weather broke and
warmed, the Shoshonis broke camp and headed for the
Little Popo Agie.

That winter, Sacajawea had time to study the Agaidüka Shoshonis and to think about the changes that
had taken place. They did not talk of hiding from the
Blackfeet; they could defend themselves with guns and
ammunition traded for moccasins, hides, and trousers
at Fort Bridger. They now had a reputation of not seeking warfare, but they fought if provoked and had a
fearlessness and bravery that the warring tribes had
come to respect. The Shoshonis became friends of the
white traders. Chief Washakie took his subchiefs and
bravest men to attend the fall rendezvous of the fur
traders. There they learned to speak some French and
a smattering of English. Washakie made a vow never
to go to war against the white men.[1]

Sacajawea learned to love Dancing Leaf and her two
children, Lance and Red Dust. Her girls called them
brothers, in the Shoshoni fashion. She liked Shoogan's
younger woman, Devoted.

During the winter, the band was out of direct touch
with the white men. In the spring, they moved camp
back to Fort Bridger, and Sacajawea heard rumors that
Baptiste had been to the traders' rendezvous on the
headwaters of the Platte, on a creek called Bijou.
Fitzpatrick and Bill Williams and Bill Bent had been
there. There were other rumors, too. More white soldiers were coming toward Fort Platte to the north with
their white-top wagons. Then it was said that Washakie
went to Fort Platte to meet the chief of the white soldiers, Colonel Stephen Watts Kearny. Red Cloud, chief
of the Oglala Sioux, and Sitting Bull, chief of the Hunkpapa Sioux, were there.

When Shoogan returned with Washakie, he called
Sacajawea to his tepee. "Old Mother, Porivo, at that
camp of the white soldiers was a Black Robe, a priest,
who smiled each time he saw the Sioux paint their faces
and put on the blue coats of the soldiers with a sword
hanging at their sides. I asked this Black Robe, who

was called Father by all the whites, if he had ever heard of one called Bap Charbonneau."

Sacajawea straightened and looked Shoogan in the face. "So—then, did he?"

"He said this: 'I know he worked trap lines nearly five summers ago with a man called Lilburn Boggs and he has been with Bill Bent. Now where he is I have not heard.'"

"Five summers," she whispered, disappointed. "Our trails are no closer."

The next winter, the Shoshonis remained on the Black Fork near Fort Bridger. Old Joe Meek came to the fort. When the Indian grapevine told news of his arrival, Sacajawea found an excuse to go to the fort. He was thin and worn, his beard gray and scraggly. He brought dreadful news. With tears in his eyes, he told of his half-breed child, Helen Mar, who, with measles, was held captive by Cayuses until her death. Then with sadness deep within his heart, he told how the Cayuses had raped all the women and older girls at Fort Walla Walla, including the spunky daughter of Jim Bridger, Mary Ann. Mary Ann had been sent west to go to the school run by Doc Whitman in Oregon. She died from her ordeal. The Whitmans were brutally slain.

Neither Joe Meek nor Jim Bridger was himself. Neither would talk with the other. Meek had no funny stories to tell. Bridger had no tall tales to report in his usual matter-of-fact voice that made them sound like true facts. Meek sat around the fort and stared at the sky. He ignored Sacajawea, who tried to talk with him more than once. Bridger never seemed to be around. He worked in the blacksmith shop, shoeing with iron the horses of emigrants, branding the several dozen foals he had in his own large herd of horses outside the fort, or helping the mountain men at the narrow crossing on the Green River ferry emigrants or Indians and their goods across to either side of the river.

One morning Belle, Bridger's Ute woman with the small round face and shining brown eyes, came to the tepee of Sacajawea. She came on the suggestion of Louis Vasquez.

"Well then," she said, "tell me what's right—those

men who stare at the sky or the ones who work until they drop when night comes? The heart of my man is lying on the ground beside the broken heart of Joe Meek. Each suffers; one works all day, but the other does nothing. What can I do? What is your answer?"

Sacajawea frowned, then answered with one word: "Time." Her black eyes squinted from under her crow-wing brows, showing she was most pleased to share this trouble with Belle.

"Porivo, I should have thought of that when Vasquez asked me. You know about life as well as a bear cub knows the musky odor of coyote."

"Listen," said Sacajawea, "I am only an old woman lengthened in mind as her step is shortened."

"Louis Vasquez sent me with this message after I had your advice," said Belle. "The man Meek told my man that Bap Charbonneau is guiding some men from New Mexico to a place called California. He said this Bap is great among the whites and Indians alike and you would want to know this."

"*Ai*," said Sacajawea and asked if there was more. But that was all Belle knew.

"Why do you want to know about this Bap?" asked Belle. "Louis does not tell me. He said you'd know who he meant."

"*Ai*, I know who he means, but I am beginning to wonder why I want to know about him, because our trails never cross. He is my firstborn."

Later that same day, Joe Meek disappeared from the fort as mysteriously as he had come.

A week later, when Sacajawea took willow baskets to the fort for trading, Bridger moseyed up to her. "Say, old Joe was here this morning for some grub and supplies before he went out somewhere trapping by hisself. He left a message. He'd heard your gallivantin' son was off on a tour of the south with a Lieutanant Colonel Philip St. George Cooke. Yeee-hah! By grabs!" he shouted, throwing his wrinkled neckerchief over his head. "I knowed it! I said to myself, 'Gabe,' I said, 'you just tell Chief Woman the full name of those her boy is trottin' with, and she'll grin proud as any fresh trapper when hurrying out in a frost-sharp dawn to visit his first beaver traps.' Cooke took your young'un because he can talk with the Mexicans. I wish to heaven I could git that man up here again to read to me. Louis Vasquez comes up and reads, but he prefers to read in French. Wagh, some dude he is." Bridger went on talking to himself about the vicissitudes of overeducation. "And what did it git Mary Ann?" he ended. "None but kilt."

That was the spring Bridger took Belle and her children, Josephine and Felix, and Emma's Jake to his farm in Westport, Missouri. By the following spring, 1850, Bridger could not endure life as a farmer. He placed his children in a Catholic school in Saint Louis and hurried back with Belle to his fort.

Some of the Mormons were pushing into the Utah Lake Territory. The Utes resented them on their land and attacked the settlements. Brigham Young blamed this attack on Jim Bridger because the Indians were all so friendly with Bridger. Belle and Sacajawea often talked together about the strange beliefs and ways of these newcomers, the Mormons.

Sacajawea said, "These Mormons have a reason for everything. They call it religion. With this they can explain away all things. Remember when the Mormon Chief, Brigham Young, explained the death of his woman who just sat and would not eat? He said, 'The Lord intended it.'" Her eyes contained a gleam that hinted at a secret joke. "There was plenty of meat in her lodge."

"I have thought about the land all these white men are abandoning in the east. We could move to it and not feel crowded," said Toward Morning.

In the fall of that year, Vasquez announced to Bridger that he would work at their supply station, which he would set up in—of all places—Salt Lake City. "You stay here among the Indians, and I will stay in the city."

"But how can we be partners in a venture that's so close to the Mormons that I don't dare come see my own operation?" asked Bridger.

"That's where you have to trust me," replied Vasquez.

Bridger paced up and down and shouted at Vasquez all day and most of the night before any kind of an agreement was made. This was enough to upset Belle and trigger early contractions. Before the sun rose she had given birth to a baby girl.

Bridger sent Vasquez for the surgeon in Salt Lake City, but when he arrived it was too late. While waiting for the surgeon, Belle asked for the Ute Medicine Man, but the Utes had moved their camp and were south in a warmer climate. In desperation Bridger went into the Shoshoni camp to hunt some woman who could help with the situation. Sacajawea and Toward Morning both hurried back with him.

Toward Morning took care of the newborn girl, and Sacajawea packed Belle with cattail fluff to stanch her steady flow of blood. She wiped her face and hands with cool water and tried to coax the life to stay. In the last moments, Belle smiled at Bridger and then lay back as though sleeping. She did not breathe. Belle could not survive the hemorrhage. Bridger could not speak the rest of the day. Sacajawea prepared Belle's body for burial and asked Vasquez to bury it in the white man's burial ground behind the fort. Vasquez and the surgeon seemed glad for something to do. The fort had turned as quiet as a tomb. By the next day, Toward Morning had brought in a wet nurse to feed the baby. Vasquez went back to Salt Lake City with the surgeon. The fort remained quiet except for the small cries of the newborn.

Finally Bridger began to notice the baby and let his big hand feel her smooth, fine hair and soft baby hands. "I'm going to call her Virginia," he said to Toward Morning in Shoshoni.

"*Ai*, Belle would like that name because it means her daughter will be raised like a white woman. She wanted that," said Toward Morning, who made dresses and moccasins for the child. She made a cradleboard so she could carry the child as she managed her chores in her room and around the fort. She cooed over the baby and held her as often as she could. In the spring, Bridger told Toward Morning to take the child to her own tepee if it would be more convenient. He said, "I will come to see Ginny often enough so she knows who her papa is."

Suzanne, nearly fourteen, and Crying Basket, thirteen summers, enjoyed having a baby in their tepee to care for. The spring continued into summer and fall. As unalterable days went on into weeks, and Indian summer still lingered, something smiled over the fort. In the Shoshoni encampment the Shoshonis were distinctly aware of it. The weather seemed to pause. Perhaps it was only a feeling—that internal necessity that events should be brought to a climax and resolved by action.

One day Bridger patiently explained to Toward Morning that she must be stricter with his child. "Discipline is a state of tension, and it must either be used or relaxed. If not used, it relaxes itself and the child will be nothing but a brat."

Toward Morning watched him intently and nodded her head as if understanding perfectly. She was exalted into a blithe happiness with Jim Bridger near.

Bridger turned to Sacajawea, who sat beside the fire stirring in a tin can containing water and coffee. "This here man, Captain Howard Stansbury, is looking for a new route between the Green River and Salt Lake. You and I know where that is, but not him. I took him to the high ridge and pointed out the route through the mountains and valleys. He was most amazed when he tried that trail and found that it was what he had looked for. This man brought word that the government, the damn Great White Father, wants to make my fort a garrison with soldiers coming here, and an Indian agency here, and of course Stansbury would be the agent. Then this Stansbury had the guts to ask me to guide an expedition from here to the South Platte. I drew him a pitcher with the end of my pipe in the dirt and told him to copy it before rain washed it out. He did that, and of a sartin it was right."[2]

Sacajawea passed the coffee around, and Bridger continued, "I'm going to check on Louis Vasquez in Salt Lake City real fast because I don't fancy them Saints much; then I'm going out trappin', and after the busy season at this fort, I've decided to go to Independence to exchange pelts for supplies, then to Saint Louis and check on the well-bein' of my Josephine, and Felix, and Jake." Bridger looked grim. He was not thinking about the past. He was trying to rearrange the future, and in certain ways he could see it clearly enough. He was alone now, and realized that life lay in himself and not elsewhere. Something heroic was set free. Time was still going on, and he went with it.

"Ginny?" asked Sacajawea. "What about her? She will need a father if she is to be as disciplined as you wish. A mother and a father."

Bridger looked at Toward Morning holding the child. Toward Morning's heart leaped at the look. "I cain't take a babe with me, and she ain't old enough to go to school."

"You could take the squaw that loves your daughter," said Sacajawea, looking directly at Toward Morning, who was blushing scarlet.

"Chief Woman," spat Bridger, "do you know what you say?"

"*Ai*," chuckled Sacajawea with her hand covering her mouth.

"Would you marry an old codger like me?" asked Bridger.

"No," said Sacajawea, bursting into deep laughter, "but Toward Morning loves even the trees you walk under."

Bridger looked questioningly at Toward Morning. "I've been in this goldurn rut and couldn't see outside it."

"*Ai*," answered Toward Morning softly. "It is my wish to take care of the papoose and you."

"Bring your gear, then," said Bridger brusquely. He put out one of his great hands, and Toward Morning pumped it to seal the bargain. "I'll just call you Rutta from now on." He smiled so his eyes crinkled and looked like pinpoints of light.

In 1853, Brigham Young, governor of the Utah Territory—despite the fact that Congress denied statehood to the Utah Territory—ordered the arrest of Bridger and seizure of all his properties because he sold powder and lead to the Indians. He also sold powder and lead to the Mormons from the supply station in Salt Lake City.

Sacajawea heard of these underhanded goings-on

through the Indian grapevine. "This Young is lining up warriors," she warned Bridger.

While she was talking with Bridger, a Ute runner puffed into the fort and talked with Rutta. "I bring my message from Vasquez that your man's life is in danger if he stays here." He filled his heaving lungs with air and was gone before Rutta could call Bridger.

"I will see that he finds a way to get out," said Rutta to herself.

Darkness moved under the cloud coming southward fast. Its frontlet stretched across the fort like the forehead of night. And before the advancing cloud wall, flashing up in great swooping circles was a flock of darting hawks, torn between their fear of the oncoming storm and darkness and the temptations of the drying meat and plums in the Shoshoni camp below.

So sinister, brooding, and threatening was the slow advance of the great storm with the hawks before it, that something primevally fearful was appealed to in the recess of Rutta's simple soul.

"Go off on the winter buffalo hunt with Washakie and Shoogan," suggested Rutta. "Or make that trip back to Saint Louis."

Far down the river, patches of white appeared here and there, touched by the last long rays of the sunset, and from where the cloud billowed lowest descended streaks of shining sleet.

"Winter comes at last!" explained Bridger, stifling a nervous laugh. He did not wait to see what the storm would do. "Saint Louis is out."

The powers of nature were not the only things loose that evening. The Morman sheriff with a posse of one hundred and fifty armed men was also manifesting its sovereignty in physical and visible form. When they rode in to arrest Bridger, he was safe in the mountains with Chief Washakie and his hunting party.

The men questioned Rutta. She said her man was on a peaceful buffalo hunt with his Shoshoni friends. The men wondered about a buffalo hunt in this weather, with the coming of the winter.[3]

"The fur is much thicker," Rutta assured them in her soft, calm voice.

Apparently convinced that Bridger's woman knew

nothing of her man's whereabouts, the sheriff and posse
started back to Salt Lake. The dark water of Black's
Fork turned to cream under the feet of the posse. Behind
it were black masses of men moving swiftly up the river
road, pouring themselves out unceasingly from under
the darkness of the cloud. The cloud and the hawks
followed the posse. The sheriff started back to retrace
steps and station his men at points overlooking Fort
Bridger. Answering the men's calls across the valley of
the insane darkness came the long, babbled monosyl-
lables of owls and whippoorwill. Then the snow began
to drift past their faces. Young had told them not to
return without Bridger. They camped in the snow and
cold for several weeks watching for Bridger. One morning the sheriff said, "I'm damn glad the wind ain't whistlin' down from the mountings," as he heaved part of
an old stump on the fire. "It's cold and gettin' colder.
Tomorrow you'll see it'll come on to snow in earnest.
We'll wait until spring if need be in order to get that
elusive Blanket Chief."

The log, full of resin, unexpectedly blazed up into a
sudden glare. "Lord!" said the sheriff, "what did it do
that fer? We'll have all the Injuns for miles around
comin' down on us now. We go back if that happens. If
not, we stay here until we find Bridger. And don't throw
no more wood on that there fire!" he shouted to the
nearest man.

Sacajawea and her two girls stayed inside the fort
that winter with Rutta and Ginny, who was getting as
wild as Mary Ann had been.

"We will teach this child to be Shoshoni, quiet, respectful, and knowledgeable in sewing," suggested Sacajawea. The child did not care for sewing. The women
tried to teach Ginny cooking. She liked to eat, but not
to prepare the food. Finally, in desperation, Sacajawea
taught Ginny to make an acceptable bow and neat
feathered arrows.

In the spring, the emigrants began to straggle in
again. The sheriff could delay no longer. He was afraid
Bridger would move into the fort under the guise of an
emigrant. He seized Fort Bridger and stripped it of all
movable property. The inhabitants had fled to Fort Lar-

amie and Fort Hall two days before, after being warned
by Vasquez through the Ute runner once again.

"That man has his ear in the Mormon camp. We must
get out of here in a hurry," said Sacajawea.

Ginny had wanted to stay so that she could try her
skill with her bow and arrows on a moving target, mainly
the pants of the sheriff and some of his Saints. Rutta
hurried the unruly child off to Fort Laramie under the
supervision of Shoogan and his two women and the rest
of the Shoshonis who had been camped around the fort.

The Mormons hurried to the Green River to kill several mountain men, frighten the others, and take over
the ferries, then the several hundred horses, oxen, and
other Bridger properties.

The sheriff reported to Governor Young that the
Mormons were now in the Green River Valley to stay.
He was boastful too soon. Jim Bridger had been at Fort
Laramie trapping, never out of touch with the Shoshoni
and Ute grapevine. Hoofprints in the wet spring snow
left by the homebound Mormon posse had not yet melted
away when he was back at Fort Bridger with his woman
and child. With him came John Hockaday, a U.S. surveyor. That spring, Bridger and Hockaday surveyed
every acre Fort Bridger occupied. Bridger put that survey in his pocket and went trapping beaver again. When
he returned in the fall, he took Rutta and Ginny to his
old farm in Westport, Missouri, and filed with the government in Washington his claim for those acres on
Black's Fork.[4]

Six days after Bridger left with his family, Sacajawea left with Shoogan's family under the guidance of
the Shoshoni chief, Washakie. He moved his tribe to
better hunting grounds near the vicinity of Fort Hall
on the Snake River. The Agaidüka tribe was prepared
for a hundred-and-eighty-mile trek on the well-marked
Oregon Trail and planned seven to eight days for the
trip if they did not hurry. Traveling with them were
several dozen mountain men from the Bridger ferries,
which were now forsaken.

Shortly after leaving, Washakie stopped the band on
a hill and looked back toward Fort Bridger. To his
amazement he saw some ninety well-armed Mormons,
with wagons, cattle, horses, mules, and plows moving

into the deserted fort. "Someone must have told them
we were moving out," grunted Washakie. Suddenly
Shoogan shouted and pointed in the direction of the
Mormons. They were readying an attack on the Shoshoni tribe. Then, just as suddenly, they laid down their
arms. The Mormons had spotted the mountain men,
who looked like desperadoes. They left the vicinity of
Fort Bridger and retreated a few miles north until the
weather became bad. Then the Mormons stopped. They
had not made much headway and were still close to
Bridger's Fort. There they built themselves a temporary shelter from their own wagons and supplies and
gave the place a name, Fort Supply.

The Shoshonis learned that the Mormons grew vegetables in the spring for the emigrants that passed by
in wagon-train loads. Then the Mormons took over the
ferries and Fort Bridger. They added new buildings and
replaced the rickety log stockade with a concrete wall.

Sacajawea was delighted to see her old friend Tom
Fitzpatrick again that spring at Fort Hall. He shook
her hand and sat to smoke while he told her he'd heard
some vague rumors about Baptiste. "While I was packing beaver pelts, some miners came into Fort Laramie
last fall. Those men had run acrost Lieutenant Colonel
Cooke, and sure 'nuf it was Baptiste driving a mule cart
and helping read maps for the lieutenant. These boys
had known Baptiste in Saint Louis and asked him how
come it was he had wandered so far from home. 'I come
to California following the gold rush and ended up at
Sutter's Fort. Cooke hired me from there.' Those miners
said he looked fit and was good-natured. And then last
winter in Saint Louis I heard this. That German, Duke
Paul, has come back and is pushing on to Sutter's Fort
to find Baptiste."

"Come summer, I will travel to this fort and see him
myself," said Sacajawea with enthusiasm, shaking
Fitzpatrick's good hand. "How many days away?"

"Maybe four, five weeks—might be more. I've not
been to Sutter's Fort yet myself."

But that summer Sacajawea did not leave for California. Suzanne was pregnant. The father was one of
the mountain men, Joe Coiner. He was happy enough

to have Suzanne remain with him at Fort Hall to keep his lodge fire going and the stew hot. Sacajawea forever won Suzanne's abiding trust and lasting affection by simply accepting the fact and talking it over with the girl as a bright hope and comfort for the future. Suzanne had no innate sense of bodily guilt. Now there was hope for her, something to comfort her, an event and a future to look forward to—and, best of all, affection.

Crying Basket had known long before, and the fact that she had known something before her mother was something that made her smile. The three of them drew hope and comfort out of the well of nature in the thought of Suzanne's coming baby. To them it was the pledge and hope that the world was going on, that not even the winter's cold could stop it.

Seated by the fire, smoking his pipe and watching the women conferring eagerly about some little problem of sewing an infant's garment, Joe, a trapper, mountain man, and river-ferry operator, smiled and marveled at the similarity between these squaws and his own mother and two sisters, one of whom married young.

Suzanne's son was named Joe, and she was content to live in the trapper's cabin near Fort Hall. Her man shot bear, antelope, and elk. If he did not sell the hides, he papered the walls of his cabin with them. This was something new and quite lovely to Suzanne.

Toward fall, the Shoshoni horses were raided. Some said it was the Crows. The scouts said they had seen a large band of Arapahos heading toward an opening in the hills.

Washakie called a quick powwow. The men decided that they would track the Arapahos. They followed the Snake River north until the going became too rough and they were forced to make camp. At dawn they forded the river and found Arapaho tracks. They moved cautiously toward the Lost River. The terrain was rugged and they made little mileage. About noon, bullets spattered around Nowroyawn and Shoogan. The Shoshonis fired back. They were spread along a steep, broken slope. Minutes later they charged, using mostly bows and war axes—bullets were precious. The Arapahos were unhorsed and soon running, leaving three warriors dead. Then the Shoshonis dug in.

At nightfall, the firing ceased. Two Shoshonis had been wounded. The others collected the dead Arapahos' rifles and rounded up half a dozen horses. All night the Shoshonis kept watch with a chorus of whooping and drum-pounding, hoping to discourage their foe from further attack. The next morning, Washakie was sure the Arapahos had been chased off. They returned to Fort Hall, admitting that they had not seen a sign of their own stolen horses. "And so—the Arapahos are our natural enemies, anyway," said Nannaggai, Washakie's oldest son. "It serves them right to be sent running like the white man's chickens."

In the fall, it was decided to move the whole Shoshoni band, under the guidance of Washakie, closer to the Salmon River country. The land was full of hills and valleys and rocks and deer. It was the latter the Shoshonis wanted for their winter's supply of food. Nowroyawn assured the people the Arapahos had left the country weeks before. Sacajawea and Crying Basket packed their goods and folded the tepee coverings. When all was packed and ready to go, they said their goodbyes to Suzanne and the baby, Joe. Sacajawea promised to come back for a visit as soon as she could, perhaps by the next summer.

The band followed the Snake River to the ford. It took an entire day to get the whole band with all the supplies across the river safely. The air was cool and crisp and bracing as they made the night camp. Getting herself up to make the small morning fire, Sacajawea knew that the first gray of dawn must have come into the sky behind the mountains, though she could see no glint of it yet. She could hear the running hoofbeats of a scout's horse as he rode into camp. Then she thought she saw some stirring around the fire of Washakie, and at the same instant came the insistent whisper, "Get ready! We move out! Over the next two hills is a camp of Arapahos." The whisper went all through the camp, and when it quieted, the fires were black and the people were packing, soothing children with bits of jerky stuffed into their mouths, and then they were moving out to the northwest.

The next few days were uneventful. The men found the deer plentiful. Some wanted to find a suitable place here for a winter camp. Washakie said it was too close to the Arapahos. They should put more days and nights between their two camps. He did not want the Arapahos to recognize the horses he'd raided earlier, so he ordered several young warriors to paint all the horses with patches of brown mud.

On the fifth day out from Fort Hall, the Shoshonis stopped to smoke the meat they had so far. Sacajawea set up drying racks alongside the other women. The country began to seem familiar to her in a remote way. "This must be the same country my feet traveled when I was a small child," she said to Crying Basket. "This is what I remember—rocks and cedars, and white water in the streams. This is the Agaidüka country." When the meat was smoked and dried, it was packed in leather bags and loaded with the other supplies on the travois. The Shoshonis moved on. Grass and water became more plentiful as they neared the Salmon River. Just after sunrise one morning occurred an incident that embittered them against the Arapahos.

Scouts had located a small Arapaho hunting party, and one of the men appeared to be badly cut up, as though mauled by a bear. The party seemed undecided what to do next, because they were one horse short.

"How many of them?" asked Washakie.

"Four, counting the one cut," said a scout.

"We could send them a horse—just let it wander into their camp," suggested Nowroyawn. "One of their own horses. What could it matter?"

"No," said Nannaggai. "Would they do that for us?"

Sacajawea could not hold herself in. "*Ai,*" she said, coming around the circle of men. "They would if we did it for them and they knew we wished to help the wounded one back to his camp."

"How would they know if we let the horse loose and hid ourselves?" asked Nowroyawn's son, Pina Quanah, or Smell of Sugar.

"Use the mud to make the markings of our band on the chosen horse."

"This would be a good joke on them. One of their own horses wandering back with the markings of the

Shoshonis on it," laughed the scout. "Porivo gives the best advice!"

Their compassionate effort was brutally rewarded. The Arapahos spotted the two scouts leading the painted horse and met them with gunfire, even though the Shoshonis made signs of friendship. Soon one scout lay dead. The Arapahos stripped his body and cut off his arms and feet. They took his horse and the one he led. The other scout could hardly tell the rest of the story. They killed the painted horse and roasted some of its flesh before leaving southward. Most of the horsemeat was left to rot.

Now the Shoshoni warriors were enraged. No Arapaho anywhere, it seemed, could ever be trusted. Shoshoni hearts would be set against all Arapahos from this time on.

The band crowded together in a canyon. It was decided that six men should pursue the Arapahos while the rest waited one night for them. The next day, the six men came back panting; they had traveled all night. There were many Arapahos in a place half a day's ride away. The Shoshonis now crowded together. The last thing they wanted was a fight in which they were outnumbered. So the band of Shoshonis now traveled day and night, pressing hard, at times covering up to fifty miles in twenty-four hours. When they came to the place where the Salmon River branched, they stopped for a day's rest. Then they traveled down the river's branch until they were in a warm valley at the base of the mountains. There they could not believe their eyes. The white men had built some wooden houses, log cabins. There were tepees of a band of Bannocks nearby.

"*Ai*," said Washakie, "this is where we will spend the winter. Here we will be safe."

While Washakie and his subchiefs met with the important men of the Bannock tribe, Sacajawea introduced herself to the Bannock women, and asked about the white people who had moved onto this land.

"Oh, these are called the Saints," said one of the women, Black Hair. "They teach us to grow squash and beans and to make bread. You go to them and they give you bread each time." Black Hair's eyes sparkled as she showed Sacajawea a part-eaten loaf of salt-rising bread. She gave Sacajawea a green squash for her kettle.

During that winter, Chief Washakie thought a great deal about the white men who had pushed Bridger out of his fort and the Arapahos who had pushed him up the Salmon River to live beside the Mormom missionaries at their Salmon River Mission. We all seem to be running from enemies and seeking friends, he thought. That is a race that should be stopped. It is best if we are at peace with whites, at least. He thought perhaps if the Shoshonis did some trading with the Mormons they could better understand one another.

In the spring, Nowroyawn and several others tried raising a small garden of beans, squash, and wheat. When the crops were prospering, they were invited by the Mormon missionaries to be baptized into the Mormon faith. Nowroyawn was baptized and named Snag. Nannaggai was given the name of Elijah.

Sacajawea attended all the important festivals and prayer days of the missionaries and each time came back with a fresh loaf of salt-rising bread, and a broad smile on her face.

The Mormon missionaries named the branch of the Salmon River on which they had built their fort the Lemhi, after a neophyte king (Limhi) in the Book of Mormon. They also began calling the Agaidüka Shoshonis the Lemhi Shoshonis because their camp was on the banks of the newly named river. The name of Lemhi Shoshonis is even now used by historians for that band to distinguish them from other Shoshoni bands.

In the fall, the Mormons decided to tighten the ties of the Lemhi band to themselves and asked several of the important people to participate in their Pioneer Day celebration. At this celebration Shoogan made this speech:

"I feel well to see grain growing on the Shoshoni land, for our children can get bread to eat, also milk. Before you came here, our children were often hungry; now they can get bread and vegetables when not fortunate in hunting meat."

Sacajawea noticed that the Mormons received Shoogan's talk well and distributed loaves of bread to the Lemhi families that were there. Secretly she hoped they

SACAJAWEA

would not give out any more cow's milk. It was sick-
eningly sweet to her taste, and she knew Crying Basket
would throw it all out behind the tepee. Sacajawea was
convinced that it was not all bad to learn farming, for
she had seen other nations do this to supplement their
meat supply. And she had noticed over the last several
years a scarcity of buffalo, antelope, and deer. She knew
the Shoshoni men did not really care for the farming,
but maybe she could convince some of the women to
work in the fields in order to put food in the bellies of
their hungry children.

Crying Basket was not interested in field work; she
was making calf eyes at the young braves. Sacajawea
knew that soon she would be alone in her tepee unless
she could talk Crying Basket into following the old way
and bring her man to live with her mother. But the old
way was not so popular. The older ones believed that
those who rode and hunted were stronger than those
who planted corn and beans. The younger ones were
breaking the rules and learning things from the whites.
They learned to carry heavy loads with wheels instead
of the old travois. Even Chief Washakie was learning
new rules. He learned to capture water and spill it
slowly on the dry lands when there were no rains so
that the crops of the Shoshonis would grow tall and
green. He accepted a Book of Mormon from the missionaries during a ceremony at their Salmon River Mission. In accepting the gift graciously, even though he
could not read, he caused the Saints to say that he,
Chief Washakie, and his Lemhi band were noble, hospitable, and honorable.

When Washakie came to the tepee of Shoogan to
show off his black book, Sacajawea could not contain
herself. She shook his hand in the manner of congrat-
ulating on receipt of such a fine thing, then said with
a smile, "This book is of no real value to you. If the
Mormon had nothing better to give, he should have cut
out the paper and thrown it away, then sewn up the
ends and put a leather strap on it. You can see it would
make a fine bag to carry the white man's money in.
But then you have no use for that, for there is no money
in your pocket to put in it."

Dancing Leaf snickered behind her hand.

Chief Washakie pointed to the far side of the tepee, indicating that Sacajawea should sit there for the remainder of his visit. "Porivo has made a little joke about my gift," he said. "But if the white man can make this"—he held up a pocket watch—"a little thing he carries in his pocket so that he can tell where the sun is on a dark day—and when it is night he can tell when it will come daylight—his mind is strong. If we learn enough of the white man's ways, we will be able to make astonishing things. Do not anger the white men. Do not raid their farms and pull plants to put into your own gardens."

Sacajawea hung her head. She was truly sorry she had made fun of such a thing as a gift belonging to the chief. She wished there was some way she could make up for her quick tongue.

"I used to think that a few white men in our land would make no difference at all," Washakie confessed. "But look, I was wrong; it has made so much difference that some of my subchiefs and braves are raising crops instead of hunting for meat. That is not a sign they are weak squaws; it is a sign that they understand the shortage of meat in our mountains better than I."

With the first chill of winter in 1858, the Mormons and U.S. Army troops were engaged in rebellion. There was an uneasiness in the air once again. The winter was hard on the Shoshoni band. The Mormons no longer gave handouts each time one of the Lemhi women went to the missions. In fact, much of the time the mission was closed to all Shoshonis and Bannocks. The Lemhis were weakened by illness, cold weather, and little food. Eventually they wore out with time and the elements, and surrendered to move southward in early spring.

Before the move, Crying Basket brought her man to live in the tepee of Sacajawea. He was Nowroyawn's son, Pina Quanah, or Smell of Sugar. Sacajawea gave her daughter the pearl earrings, which had been a gift from Judy Clark, as a wedding present.

"We will go back to Fort Hall," announced Washakie. "It is better to live near the white man's forts than be raided and shot up by our enemies."

This announcement gladdened the heart of Sacajawea. She would now have time to visit with Suzanne and hold her grandson before he became too old for hugging. She sniffed the air. If it snowed, the horses would slip on the rocks they must travel over. She checked the packs on her horses and thought the damp leather had a good, rich smell. The haze darkened; if it snowed, the men would hunt deer. The women would wait in a temporary camp, their feet near a fire. She saw streams winding dark and unfrozen between white banks, then piñons too closely matted to be penetrated, and open meadows where one could walk freely. She was ready to move out.

The day darkened. Wet scented the earth. The snow fell, but melted. The streams were full. Sacajawea shook her head to get rid of a vague anxiety. She feared no beasts; nor, exactly, did she fear men. But it was true she did not trust the Arapahos. She rode her horse a little to one side of the rest, listening. She laughed to herself, knowing full well that scouts were sent well ahead of the rest of the band. If there were any danger, they would come back to report. She took a bit of brittle jerky from a bag at her waistband and bit into it, then cocked her head, holding the mouthful without chewing.

"Fool!" she said. "There's no one about."

Sacajawea took another bite of dried meat. She chewed this mouthful, but did not swallow. She had not dreamed the harsh sounds—men were talking angrily. Their fast pace showed they must be walking in a trail. They passed, but did not go out of hearing. If they had been Arapahos, she would have announced their presence to the others, but these were Sioux. She dropped back from the others, going more slowly.

The hoarse voices grew louder. A faint glow appeared under the trees beyond a thicket. There, close to the stream, stood several conical tepees. The Sioux were squaws, she thought; they couldn't hunt without a rifle these days. They had forgotten how to use their bows. Nevertheless, it was wise to know what they were up to. She tethered her horse and crept backward. The fire leaped; she could see many Sioux. Meat was cooking; she smelled also the odor of whiskey. Fifty Sioux at least had gathered, and there was one who looked like the headman reeling as he walked and talked.

Dangerous though it was, Sacajawea crept on and lay on her belly, her head in a bush. The Sioux sat in a semicircle near the fire. One spoke whiningly; the chief spoke angrily. Another leaped up shouting. His features were not altogether Sioux features; his face was rounder than that of any Sioux, and his thick black hair was long. His language was that of a white man who had lived with the Indians, who was perhaps part French. He used hand signs. The mannerisms of the man reminded Sacajawea of Charbonneau.

"I am your friend. Didn't I give you plenty of the crazy-water and never asked anything in return? I'll help you get back your land. The white men from the east took your land and made you women; now even the tribes you call friends drive you from that land on which you lived before the recollection of the oldest man. They believe you are women. They'd let any tribe chop you into fine pieces. It's dog against dog." His lips were thick, and his mouth drew downward.

Fierce shouts replied.

"Arm yourselves. First lend me one horse to scout ahead. You can see the horse on which I came to you is played out. He hasn't moved yet. Maybe he'll never stand on his feet again. I give him to you for your stew. I rode him fast to give you this news."

A young Sioux began to leap around the fire. Others followed, lifting their knees high, screaming and whirling tomahawks. Sacajawea slid backward. When the Sioux shouted, she moved; when they were silent, she lay motionless. Protected by a loud outburst, she rose and began to walk slowly and carefully. A little farther and she would catch her horse and hurry on to her people. She would warn them to sit in a bushy hollow and wait for moonrise, then go through the valley to the Snake River and not stop until they saw Fort Hall before them.

That evening, Washakie sent a man out for the scouts. They shook their heads. *Ai*, they had known about the Sioux camp, but they had also known that the stranger who was in the camp had given them crazy-water and so none of the Sioux would move out for a raid or attack—in fact, they couldn't even see well. They had not noticed a whole band of Shoshonis pass. And one of the Shoshoni women had sat close to their fire and listened to them talk. Ha-ha, he-he, that was certainly funny. That Porivo had a lot of courage. The Sioux must be completely blind by now. He-he, ha-ha.

The remainder of the journey was uneventful. At Fort Hall the Lemhi band learned that their good friend the Blanket Chief, Jim Bridger, was in full possession of his fort once again. This caused some shouting and dancing in the evening. Many of the Lemhis wanted to go back to Fort Bridger for the summer.

Sacajawea showed Suzanne a pair of tiny moccasins and a carrying frame, together with a beautifully embroidered band to support the frame from her shoulders.

"Joe is too old for that now!" cried Suzanne, putting her arms around Sacajawea. "See, he walks."

"*Ai*, for the new one," Sacajawea said, smiling. She looked Suzanne up and down. She counted six months on her fingers. "I know this time."

"Girl, maybe," said Suzanne.

"Boy," said Sacajawea.

Before summer barely began, the Lemhi band was back on the old ground at Fort Bridger. And what a reunion that was. Even Bridger and Rutta, dressed in bright calicos, came to the feasting in camp that evening. Bridger was in one of his storytelling moods, and the morning stars were in the sky before he went back into the fort.

It was still early summer when a Lemhi scout rode into the camp, followed by another man on horseback. The other man was tense, looking here and there. His face was dark and round, and his thick black hair long. He wore a red neckcloth and seemed to be a man of middle years who had seen much of life. His mouth was drawn down at the corners, and his lips were thick. His shirt was blue cotton, and his trousers were made like the white man's, from black wool. The scout went directly to Sacajawea's tepee, calling softly, "Porivo, Chief Woman, come on out."

As usual when anyone came into the camp, a crowd gathered. The leading men of the band were nearest; others stayed farther back. The stranger was greeted by Washakie, and noticed in turn by several of the subchiefs. Shoogan looked strangely at the man, as if trying to recognize him from some other place.

"Is this the lodge of my *umbea*, Sacajawea?" the stranger asked.

"There is no woman by that name here," said Shoogan curtly. "Porivo lives here with her daughter and son-in-law."

Sacajawea came out of her tepee and stared at the scout, who seemed to have a hard time explaining that the man he was leading seemed to believe she was his mother. The scout was apologetic and turned to leave.

"Wait," she said, holding up her hand. "What did the man say? Whom did he ask for?"

Shoogan laughed. "Chief Woman, this man asked for some stranger called Sacajawea."

"What?" Sacajawea asked. "Explain yourself. What is his name?"

"He says only that he heard you were looking for your son and that he is your son," the scout said.

She looked hard at the heavyset man. "What is your name?" she asked.

"Baptiste Charbonneau," the stranger said, drawing his eyes down to a fine line, so that only black shone through the slits.

A variety of shouts rose from the nearby men. "What's he say?" "Is he her son?" "It can't be true!" "He's crazy!"

"I was called Sacajawea," she said firmly.

"My *umbea*!" called the man, and dismounted from his spotted horse, whose tail was tied in the Sioux fashion, with wide leather strips. He embraced her.

"It's impossible to believe," Shoogan said.

"She's my mother," the stranger said. He spoke in a low voice, so they found it necessary to be quiet to hear him. "I have searched long for her."

All around in the crowd people were asking, "Is she happy?"

Sacajawea's eyes were filled with tears, so great was her joy. She could not see the face of this man who called her mother. She held his head close to hers, feeling his hair and face, his strong back and neck, the back of his head, under his ears.

"*Umbea*," he said again.

Slowly, numbed, she pulled away and blinked the

tears back. It was like an apparition. This man resembled Toussaint Charbonneau so completely.

Shoogan watched the scene as Sacajawea dried her eyes with the back of her hand. The others were still talking, "See, he wears white man's clothing—a cloth shirt and trousers and a big black hat."

"I thought her son was a tall man," said someone. "This man is short and runty."

"Maybe he is a good warrior and a fine hunter, though," said someone else.

With dry eyes Sacajawea again searched the round face of the man before her. She put her hand on his shoulder, searching for some familiar pattern. She moved her hand slowly behind his left ear, against the hard bone. It was smooth and warm from his ride to the camp. She closed her eyes to better feel any possible ridge or small bit of scar tissue. Nothing.

He grabbed her hands and murmured, "*Umbea*, it has been long since I saw you leave our cabin in Saint Louis. I would know you anywhere. You have not changed. The same snapping eyes and firm mouth, the same beautiful black hair. *Belle*. You are beautiful."

Dancing Leaf, Shoogan's woman, took his horse and hobbled it behind Sacajawea's tepee. Crying Basket brought him a horn of cool water.

"My son," Sacajawea said, louder than she had intended, "you must be tired from riding, and hungry. You will eat; then you will tell of your life." She motioned him toward her tepee. Shoogan's family followed after him—after all, if he was a relative of Sacajawea, he was a relative of theirs as well.

Sitting across from this man, Sacajawea looked intently at his face. It was so familiar—an exact copy of his father's. She was surprised now that she had not recognized him and cried out loud that day she had spied on the Sioux encampment.

He glanced at her, and a shy smile caught at his full lips. "I had a woman down at Bent's Fort a couple of years back. She wanted to visit her relatives. Carson ran into me while I was in her Ute camp. He knew my father was Charbonneau, and he could have knocked me over with a buzzard's feather when he said he knew old man Charbonneau's woman, who was then at Bridg-

er's. I just didn't believe him at first. I thought he was
making fun of me because I had a Shoshoni mother and
was a breed, same as my old man. But not that Carson;
he finally made me believe every word about this
Shoshoni squaw. I headed this way, then heard there
was some trouble here with the Saints, so I waited some
before coming in right away." He rummaged around
inside his shirt and found a metal bottle. He passed it
to Shoogan. Shoogan opened it and found it was not
water and had to spit out his mouthful. The man laughed
and drank a big swallow. Sacajawea could smell rum.
The man went on talking. Everyone watched him carefully.

"That Carson talked a lot about what a fine woman
this squaw was. And he hoped I'd find you. He's a
talker—a big chief white man who thinks he can order
people around and parcel out land like it was his own.
Then I finally got up to this place called Fort Hall—a
measly place where the miners hang out. I'd heard about
this man Broken Hand, but never run across him until
a couple of weeks ago. He sold me a couple of jugs of
watered rum and told me I ought to look up this old
mother—who once lived with my father—if I was actually a Charbonneau. So—I came as soon as I could.
That Broken Hand Fitzpatrick is as bad as Carson about
ordering people around. *Ki-ti* white men I can do without! How about you, Brother Shoogan?"

Shoogan looked startled, but nodded his head. His
face darkened and remained blank. It was coming back
to him where he'd met this man before.

The man passed the bottle of rum to Shoogan again.
Shoogan refused. The man took small drinks until it
was all gone. Then he said, "I will bring my women,
and we will stay in your tepee, *Umbea*."

This time Sacajawea looked startled. "You have no
lodge of your own? Your women cannot put one together?"

"Well—ha—a tent, but this is larger, and you, Old
Mother, can cook much better."

"Can't your women cook?" asked Dancing Leaf
timidly, looking shyly at this new relative.

"Not like this," said the man, reaching for some
stringy bits of bear meat from the kettle.

"Come with me." Sacajawea's voice was stern, almost like one she would use when scolding a child for some small wrongdoing. Her hand motion was serious as she led this man from the lodge. She led him to Shoogan's tepee and told the children inside, "Shoo, shoo, go to my tepee now. Tell your mothers to make a kettle of coffee. One of you find the small bag near the dried *yampa.*"

"Aw, we want to look at the new man," said the oldest boy, Lance.

"*Non!* Vamoose!" she said. The children fled as if she were a woman chief.

She sat on the tepee floor and motioned for the man who called himself Baptiste Charbonneau to do the same.

"Aren't we going to sit on hides?" he asked, dismayed at her lack of hospitality.

"A weasel needs no comforts."

"What? What does that mean?"

"You are old Charbonneau's son. You are so much like your father that my legs turn to water when I hear you speak. But you are not my firstborn. There is no rough scar behind your left ear such as Baptiste carries from a painful sickness long ago when we traveled with Chief Red Hair. You are Otter Woman's son. You are Toussaint. So why? Why do you call yourself by your brother's name?" Her voice was barely audible.

"*Ai*," said Toussaint, his head bowed, his eyes on the ground. He felt in his shirt for the bottle. It was empty, and he threw it across to the far wall of the tepee. "My brother, Baptiste, will not come to live with you!" he shouted. He seemed to search for his words. "He is a chief among the white men. He can talk with them, laugh with them. He knows their ways. He knows the ways of the Indians. He has always been this way. Quick to learn and get ahead. Carson told me fine things and how he could be as tough as a mule driver, yet as gentle as a young squaw with her firstborn. Then that Fitz-patrick told me everyone likes him—Indians, squaws, traders, everyone. These words were enough to make me sick and vomit up everything in my stomach. That damn Bap leaves a trail of goodness wherever he goes. I hate him. I hated him when he went to the gold fields in Montana and staked a decent claim. I couldn't find a thing in those hills, and I got out before I ended up as buzzard bait. I didn't hear anything more about my brother for quite a while. No one is sure where he might be—maybe in California, maybe not—so then I think maybe he is dead. I hope so. So—I will walk on his glory trail now. I will be him."

Sacajawea's shoulders sagged. She wept.

In full control of himself now, Toussaint sneered. "Two suns ago on my way here, I was given food and a new name by those damn men who call themselves Saints. They knew you and called you Porivo. I knew it was you because they said once you had even made a speech for one of their celebrations. You are the only Shoshoni woman I know who would get up and make a speech. I remember you have always spoken out."

She nodded. "That was more than several years ago, before the mission closed," she said. "It is a wonder they recalled such a thing."

"I told them I would like the name of Baptiste instead of my Shoshoni name, Bull Head. They never guessed I had any other name. So now that is my name. They wrote it in a small book and promised it would go in a larger one kept at their headquarters in Salt Lake City. I am your son, Baptiste, then. And so—I will bring my women and we will live with you. Rejoice, old woman, your son is finally home!"

"Ho!" Sacajawea exclaimed, drying her eyes with her fists. "You can never live in my lodge. You can live in this camp, but at the very edge. If you put your tepee close to mine, I will tell my Shoshoni relatives about your forked tongue." Her voice broke, and she put her face in her hands and sobbed.

"We will go back to your tepee," he said. "I will sit around the storytelling fire and tell of my travels to Germany. Bap told enough that I can make them last awhile."

She tried to tell Toussaint to be quiet, but nothing seemed to make him close his mouth. "Bap was with Duke Paul six winters and speaks German better than the instructors in Father Neil's school. He told about the *Wobenamptike*, Wooden Shoe White Man. He hunted and fished and was a big man in Germany, too. I do hate him!"

Sacajawea went outside. She took a deep breath and looked up. The stars were bright in the dark sky. They were the same; they had not changed.

Toussaint had not really changed. He was always short and stocky—a trademark of the Shoshoni—but there was little of the youth she had known and loved in him. He had become bitter, and his tongue was split, and he was scheming. She wondered if she could ever cross the gap of years that lay between them.

She stood straight in the late spring air. "Son," she said.

He stood slouched beside her for many moments, waiting.

"You will talk with Shoogan now. You will tell him that you have decided to pitch your tepee at the far side of the camp where you get the fresh breeze."

They walked toward the tepee.

Inside, Toussaint said, "If she had a good man, he would whip her for crying." He pointed to the reddened eyes of Sacajawea. "She is glad to have me home."

When Shoogan and his family had drunk hot, sugared coffee, by the gallon—because Sacajawea kept filling the kettle and boiling coffee and filling the cups—they left. Crying Basket and her man went outside to see the stars. Sacajawea said, "Tell me about the last time you saw your brother."

"It was five, six, seven summers back. We were at Bent's. He got me a job as hunter for the fort. I was going to help him get meat for those white dudes to eat all winter. That was when I first took my Ute woman. And some jackasses, along with my brother, pounded kettles and sang loud outside the tepee. They fired someone's rifle and had that woman so scared all she'd do was huddle at the far end of the sleeping robe. The next morning, I was still sore, and took a shot at Sam, the black blacksmith who'd sung loudest. St. Vrain came out and ordered me away from the fort. The white man ordering me around again! Bap saw I got two horses, a cart, and supplies; then I went away. I suppose he paid for those things from his own pocket—I never laid out a cent for them." He paused and looked up. His face brightened. "Say, maybe Shoogan and his woman will let me and my family live with them. They seemed impressed with me tonight. They think I am somebody!"

"You will not! You will pitch your own tepee and hunt for your own meat. Shoogan is a chief. He cannot read or write, but he can lead men and he commands respect and love from his people. You can read and write and talk in the white man's tongue, and yet you have not become a man. You even take advantage of the Sioux and ride out of their camp with one of their good war-horses. You are a spoiled child."

Toussaint looked at her from under his eyebrows. His mouth turned down farther, his eyes uncertain. "But, *Umbea!*"

"When your lodge is set up at the edge of this camp, I would like to meet your women. I will never call you by your new name, but I will call you son as long as you stay to yourself."

That fall, the Lemhi Shoshonis under the leadership of Washakie traveled near the headwaters of the Green River on their annual antelope hunt. Toussaint was among the hunters. Sacajawea had seen him leave with the men and wondered if he would bring back enough meat to last his two wives and children most of the winter or whether he would beg Shoogan for more before the winter season was half-over. She'd shook her head watching him ride his horse out, wondering about this man who so resembled his father and called her mother.

On the way back to camp after the successful hunt, the Lemhi men were attacked by a large party of Sioux, who were after the horse they recognized as their own, the one Toussaint had loaded with fresh meat.

The Sioux came across a creek and surprised the Lemhis as they came down a narrow slope leading from a bluff top flanked by a gully-washed ravine in the bottom of a meadow. The crafty Sioux had an instinct for surprise attack as keen as the nose of a wolf for a newborn buffalo calf, and they sensed that the Lemhis would not watch this ravine, since they would assume it could not pass a horse and rider. Also, they knew the Lemhis would have to go around the head of it, up on the bluff, to get to the slope that led down to their camp.

The Sioux were hidden in the rocks at the top of the
ravine just as Washakie started around it with his
hunters. Nearly all the Sioux had rifles besides their
bows and arrows. The fire they put into the Lemhis
starting around the head of the ravine was like the
blade of a four-horse reaper in a field of ripe wheat.
Washakie led his men back to a low spot where they
could hide. They fought all afternoon as long as there
was light.

During the early night a fitful fire was kept up by
both sides, but the Lemhis began to go back to camp
before the middle of the night, certain that the Sioux
were already whipped enough and would make no trouble the next day. Dawn found the Lemhis straggling
home with their wounded. Nannaggai, the oldest son
of Washakie, was dead, and so was one of Washakie's
finest subchiefs, Nowroyawn, or Snag. Shoogan was
wounded in his left knee. He pulled the arrow point out
himself and stanched the blood flow by stuffing part of
his red trade shirt in the wound.

There was still plenty of good light left when they
reached camp. The relatives of the dead men began
their high-pitched keening. Crying Basket went with
Smell of Sugar to comfort the lodge of his dead father,
Nowroyawn. Sacajawea worked with the women tending the wounded. She and Dancing Leaf treated Shoogan as best they could. It was hard for them to handle
him, as his knee was stiff by this time. His woman,
Devoted, would not permit the Medicine Man to put his
herbs and beaver fur on the wound, saying that Porivo
would treat it best, and prayer to the Great Spirit would
heal as fast as anything he might pull out of his bulging
bundle.

As the women worked on the wound, Shoogan groaned
and swore. When his women went for soft leather strips
for wrappings, Shoogan motioned Sacajawea to come
closer. "Old Mother, you and I both know that man is
not your son, Bap. That half-breed is the other one you
asked about, the mean one called Tess. I have seen him
before, but did not want to admit it. He is no good. He
has fought against our band on the side of the Sioux. I
am certain he tried to make some bargain as a spy to
get horses for the Sioux and himself this time. A man

with such a forked tongue cannot be trusted. When the fight was thickest at the ravine, I saw him crouched low with a Sioux behind a pile of downfall. Conquering Bear was with me. I said nothing, but he might have recognized him. Conquering Bear took careful aim and shot the Sioux in the head. This man, Tess, rolled over out of sight, and I did not see him again during the rest of the time. He is not in camp yet. His women wait at the doorway of their lodge for him to come with antelope meat."

Sacajawea bit her lower lip. Her voice would not come out of her throat.

"Do not worry, Old Mother, I will not tell this secret. Perhaps to a mother, finding this son is better than finding no son at all." The bond between Shoogan and Sacajawea grew with this love and trust.

When the evening fires were low and the women's keening subdued, Toussaint rode into camp, staked out his horses, and called to his women to take off the bundles of meat. Washakie had seen him ride into camp. Grieving and angered that this man had not taken part in the deadly skirmish, he walked to Toussaint's lodge and said loudly, "You come like a squaw into camp after the fight is over."

"I was picking up my meat, and I do not like you to tell me what I look like." Toussaint waved the barrel of his rifle toward Washakie.

"I never gave orders to my men in battle or council," Washakie spoke out. "But it is fitting for a chief to give advice when it is necessary."

Indignant that Washakie would speak to him in such a manner, Toussaint stepped over the bundles of meat his women were preparing to open, climbed back on his horse, and rode out of camp. He came back before dawn broke and sulked in his lodge, complaining that the cries of the women mourners kept him awake.

54

The Great
Treaty Council

The Great Treaty Council, officially known as the Fort Bridger Treaty Council of 1868, was highly significant as it was the last treaty council called for the purpose of establishing a reservation. Thereafter, all reservations were created by executive order.

A legend grew out of this council that Porivo [Sacajawea] spoke. The elders present insisted that she was there and that she arose and addressed her remarks to Washakie's subchief, Bazil [Shoogan].

From *The Shoshonis: Sentinels of the Rockies*, by Virginia Cole Trenholm and Maurine Carley. Copyright 1964 by the University of Oklahoma Press, pp. 219–20.

In 1861, a stagecoach route was established along the Oregon Trail. A year later, because of Indian attacks, the mail and passenger coaches were withdrawn and transferred to the Cherokee Trail, which gradually became known as the Overland Trail. It was known that Washakie and his tribe were not involved in the killing of emigrants along either trail.

The white men let Sacajawea know that she could ride the stage to Fort Hall anytime. They seemed to think she was somebody important. She did not know that Bridger had told them she was the squaw who had guided Lewis and Clark to the west. She visited Suzanne and went to Fort Benton, and she followed the Bozeman Trail to Virginia City, where she set up her tepee among the Bannocks. Now she asked no one about Baptiste Charbonneau, but she looked and listened, still hunting her firstborn.

One evening, she was getting on the stage leaving Virginia City. She had decided to go as far west as California, leaving her goods in a pack with a friendly Bannock family. Henry Plummer, the road agent, serving as sheriff in the country around Virginia City, lounged up against the stage.

"I knowed they all let ye ride for nuttin' because ye are something big to the whites and Injuns. Ye har headed southwest. But ye cain't go this one time. Here, take these home to yer kids." He placed three sacks of flour on the ground. Sacajawea looked from the flour to the sheriff. He motioned with his thumb. She climbed off, determined to go another time. That night the stage was shot up and robbed.

A scout for the government came into Virginia City looking for an interpreter. Sacajawea talked to the man, John Renshaw, after the stage pulled out and told him she would work as interpreter for him. He seemed overjoyed to find a squaw who could speak English so well. He slept outside her tepee that night in his bedroll, but before the night was over, he must have felt the cold wind and crept inside the tepee and lay on the robe beside Sacajawea.

"Will ye be my woman?" he muttered quietly.

She grabbed for the nearest weapon, the thighbone of an elk, and brought it down on his head. Renshaw left as soon as he got his bearings.

She struck her tepee and again packed her belongings and took the stage toward home, not even looking back. There will be a better day for going southwest, she thought.

When she arrived at Fort Bridger, she put her packs down by the gate and went inside to see what had been going on since she had been gone. Washakie and several Lemhis stood at the store counter. Jake rummaged around under the counter.

"This here came in a couple of weeks back with a load of provisions from the U.S. Govmint. It's for you. Has your name right here. See? That there stands for your name."

Washakie was perplexed at why the U.S. Government would send something so small to him and not to all the other men in his tribe. He stood where all could see him and slowly opened the package and then beamed with pleasure.

Sacajawea moved closer for a better look, then cried, "Yi-hi! It is something grand!" He was holding up a silver medal bearing the likeness of the Great White Father, Andrew Johnson. Washakie walked through the crowd smiling. When he passed Sacajawea he held out his medal and pointed to the Jefferson peace medal she wore around her neck. Then his smile became broader because her medal was smaller than his. It was a medal for a squaw.

"So, then—you are not the only one called chief in our band who wears a fine neckpiece," he said.

"That must be a gift for your service and friendship to the white men over the years. Especially for staying out of skirmishes with emigrants on the Overland Trail," said Bridger, coming through the Lemhis to shake Washakie's hand.

A few weeks later, Washakie wore his medal on a visit to Salt Lake City, where he let his picture be taken. He was given the picture several days later. He thought his outfit looked so handsome with the medal hanging from his neck that he had the superintendent of Indian affairs at Fort Bridger send the picture, carefully wrapped in soft white doeskin, to President Johnson.

That summer the Lemhis camped on the bank of the Sweetwater. Each day Toussaint raved against the white men who put boundaries on the Shoshoni land. He ranted against the Mormons because of their farming in lands no one wanted but which used to be a place the Shoshonis could wander through at will.

"So—the white men have not yet taken our horses or our guns," said Shoogan, trying to calm him. Shoogan was even more a cripple now in his left leg. Whenever he walked, only the toes of his foot touched the ground, and his knee remained stiff. "Why do you think we can't learn to grow vegetables and live peaceably with the whites if we must?"

Challenged to explain, Toussaint could not, but would only insist that they would all starve in time. "God! I don't want to die like a hungry wolf," moaned Toussaint. "That argument about the Shoshonis being farmers in order to live in peace is as old as shit. We've all seen it before. Instead, we'll be like crazy, starving animals, scratching and biting at each other."

"Take hold of yourself," said Shoogan calmly. "For many years our people lived in the mountains on roots and fish, and seldom had large game. We survived. Our chief, who was brother to the woman you call *umbea*, let no one go more hungry than another. Now Washakie is the same. None of us will go hungry if he does not wish it."

Toussaint looked sideways at Shoogan. There was something in his words that disturbed him. He could not put his finger directly on it.

The next summer the tribe moved back to Fort Bridger. By then it was well known that the white men often killed the buffalo just for sport, taking the tongue, a piece of the choice hump meat, and perhaps a loin from the hindquarter, while the remainder was left to rot. The builders of the transcontinental railroads lived on buffalo meat. Their hunters left the thick hides to decay. Then the eastern market for hides opened, and there was the last systematic slaughter of the remaining buffalo. Countless carcasses were again left on the prairie to rot.

Sacajawea found one such slaughtering ground near Black's Fork while she was out digging sunflower roots one morning. The smell was so sickening she pinched her nostrils together. The screech of the crows was so disagreeable she could not stay. There were enough buffalo left to rot to feed Washakie's band for four, maybe five years. Sacajawea recalled the dead buffalo in the Comanches' land. She came back into camp with a look of disgust and sickness on her face.

Someone asked, "What happened?" Another said, "What did you see out there?" Others asked questions, then said, "Tell us."

Washakie was angry. He sat with Sacajawea for a long time. "They've gone too far! I gave a promise not to raid the white hunter! But they take our hunting ground wherever they please and then insult us by this waste!"

Some of the men wanted to prepare for war immediately. There was little laughter in the camp. Washakie tried to keep his people calm. He spent much time in his lodge making medicine. Once or twice he came out and walked along the paths, frowning. Once Sacajawea spoke to him, but he did not answer. Days passed, and he came out searching for omens in the cries of the night birds, the pattern of rising smoke, or the formation of clouds. He could make no prediction or decision from any of the signs.

He seemed not to notice the other bands of Shoshonis that came to make camp near Bridger's Fort; even the Bannocks moved in. By the second week in May, there were ninety-six lodges of Shoshonis and forty-nine of Bannocks. Rumors of another treaty council began.

Sacajawea spoke often with Crying Basket during this summer about living in the white man's way. She was certain there was no other way open to them but to accept quietly the land, food, housing, and education the white men offered.

"There is an iron horse puffing black smoke through the village of the Cheyennes. Smell of Sugar told me of plans for a trail for this iron horse in the neighborhood of Bridger's Fort," said Crying Basket, combing her long black hair against the sides of her clear face. She resembled her mother; only she was taller and her hands broader.

Sacajawea put her hands to her mouth in disbelief, then wondered aloud when the white tops were coming with more supplies. "It does not take long to use the meat they bring or the flour in biscuits."

"I can tell you something else," said Crying Basket, lifting her small daughter, Berry, off the floor and setting her comfortably on her lap so that she could plait the child's hair. "I hear that one of the women of your son Baptiste boiled the bacon of the white man in water and swore that the meat was not fit to eat. She threw her bacon portions out to the dogs, and she did not know what to do with the flour. I thought this Baptiste knew the ways of the white man and would tell his women what to do with such supplies. I think it would be good, maybe, if you taught them how to cook the bacon on sizzling-hot iron plates, and to save the grease to make flour biscuits."

"That man can tell his women how to cook if he wishes hot biscuits or his bacon crisp. It is not my affair," Sacajawea said sharply.

On July 1, 1868, Sacajawea stood with the other women to watch the supply wagons come in with bacon, flour, sugar, coffee, beads, mirrors, trade cloth, stockings, tobacco, and woolen blankets.

The Shoshonis pushed and shoved to get their share of food and gifts being distributed by the agent, Mann, who sat with a ledger at a small wooden table set out in front of the fort's gates. A steady file went on until the Shoshonis were all given their share of food, stockings, a blanket, and tobacco, and ticketed so that Mann would know which Shoshonis had been through the line already.

Finally, when the goods were distributed and the happy families sat on the grass in relaxed picnic groups, General C. C. Augur came through the fort's gates. Sacajawea looked at him and wondered if he was somebody newly appointed to give out more gifts. She pinched Crying Basket and pointed, saying, "I think the men wearing the best clothes should shake hands with this important stranger."

"Oh, Mother," hissed Crying Basket, rocking gently to and fro on her haunches with Berry, who was nearly asleep, "he is going to tell us who he is. Then the men will know what formality to take."

"Well, he moves slower than I," Sacajawea hissed back.

Augur was perhaps thirty years old, with a ruddy, smooth-shaven face, wide-open blue eyes, and a good, though somewhat plump, figure. On this day he was dressed impeccably in the uniform of the U.S. Army. He had been authorized by the Indian Peace Commission at Fort Laramie to come to Fort Bridger for the sole purpose of negotiating with the Bannocks and Shoshonis.

Washakie stepped forward. Sacajawea nodded her approval. Washakie took the pipe offered him and passed it through the four cardinal points, to the sky, then the earth, then took a long puff and handed it back to Augur. As unobtrusively as possible, another man came to sit cross-legged between Augur and Washakie. He was the interpreter. Crying Basket pinched Sacajawea and pointed. The interpreter was Shoogan. Augur told the Shoshonis and Bannocks to seat themselves in a great semicircle to hear the council of the generous white men. "The Great White Father wishes to give you land into which no white man will be permitted to go."

There was a formidable grunt from Washakie. Some of the Shoshonis seated alongside him let the air out of their mouths in a loud manner. Sacajawea looked expectantly to see what the white man might do next.

General Augur continued speaking, his face not changing expression. He suggested the bands move as soon as possible to this land, where there would be wooden lodges and men to show the right way to plant seeds and harvest vegetables. He said the children would go to school. Augur's voice went on, in a humdrum manner. Shoogan waved his arms and tried to keep the Indians awake as he did his best to translate.

"For each man there will be a coat, hat, trousers,

shirt, woolen socks. For each woman, a skirt of flannel, trade cloth, and woolen socks."

Sacajawea moved her shoulders in the warm sun. She removed the new red blanket and got up. This was too much talk. She was going home. Crying Basket pulled her back as Chief Washakie stood to put an end to this talk.

"We will come here again tomorrow," translated Shoogan. "At the end of all the talk, if it is satisfactory with our chief, he will mark the paper with an X. The paper must say the white hunters will never come on our land."

Sacajawea looked at Chief Washakie. He had dignity and confidence. His people loved and respected him; the whites respected him. She thought of the leaders in the Comanche nation and could think of none so great as Washakie, none who would sit calmly in the hot sun listening to talk of supplies of sickening sweet meat of the cow, and of giving the children the cow's milk with its sick taste. This Washakie fully understood what was happening to his people under the overriding push of the white men in Shoshoni country. He wore his eagle feathers and a fresh breechclout, the wide apron hanging to his knees in front and behind, and new moccasins and leggings to the thighs, and across his arm hung the thin red-wool blanket.

The next afternoon, Augur stood and held up his hand. The People murmured.

Shoogan translated loudly. "This I have to say first. The Bannocks will receive four thousand dollars' worth of goods from the treaty funds and a place in the Shoshoni Reservation land."

Another murmur went through the crowd. The Bannocks were standing, each one moving forward to press the hand of Augur to seal the bargain. Augur held up both hands and made the cut-off sign. He was through talking, and it was time for Washakie to say something. The Bannocks stopped and stumbled back to their places in the semicircle.

"I should get up to walk around myself," sighed Sacajawea. "My legs would feel better then."

"Do not complain, Mother," said Crying Basket. "Most

of us have the patience to sit politely while our chief speaks."

"Humph," muttered Sacajawea, wiping perspiration from her forehead with the red blanket.

Washakie shook General Augur's hand, then took Shoogan's hand and pumped it. Solemnly he pointed his own redstone pipe to the four directions and to heaven and earth. Then he stared into the bright sunlight at the semicircle of Shoshonis and Bannocks. No one stirred. No one was disrespectful. He handed his pipe to the general. After a few moments his deep voice projected to the outer edge of the semicircle.

"I am laughing because I am happy. Because my heart is good. As I said one day ago, I like the country you mentioned, then for us, the Wind River Valley....

"I want for my home the valley of the Wind River and the lands on its tributaries as far east as the Popo Agie, and I want the privilege of going over the mountains to hunt where I please, never to be disturbed by white hunters."

Then Chief Taghee of the Bannocks spoke. He had a straight body and an impassive face with jutting jaw, strong, flat-planed cheeks, and deep-set eyes. He wore denim trousers, a cotton shirt, a broad-brimmed black hat, and moccasins.

"As far away as Virginia City our tribe has roamed. But I want only the Port Neuf Country and Camass Plains. We are friends with the Shoshonis and like to hunt with them, but we want a home for ourselves."

Augur raised his hands to tell the assembly to return to the council tomorrow, when the formal treaty would be read. He unbuttoned the top of his coat, then quickly rebuttoned it, saying, "I am not acquainted with the country to locate a reservation for you, but when someone comes to lay it out, then the Bannocks will be told to move there."

There was much buzzing about this treaty around the evening fires. The Bannocks were still not happy. The Shoshonis made it a time of feasting and merriment.

In the firelight Sacajawea caught sight of Toussaint sitting far on the edge of the camp with his two women, Dirty and Contrary Woman. His children ran about noisily, ragged and unclean. Her heart sank to see these children learning no responsibility to themselves or others. She'd caught two of the boys creeping up to her tepee and peering inside the rolled skirts on warm afternoons. She longed to invite them inside and hold them. But she could not. She had told Toussaint not to come to her lodge, and that meant his family also. One child, Race Horse, looked much like Toussaint—with tousled, thick hair and a round, flat face with shining, large eyes. His mouth seldom smiled, but did not seem sad, only resigned. The other, Squirrel Chaser, was small and built like his mother, Contrary Woman. Yelling Falls, a little girl, was not kept at her lodge, but permitted to toddle everywhere after her two older brothers. She was naked and streaked with dirt and grease. Joy, a girl of about fifteen summers, was oldest. Joy was Dirty's only child. She seemed shy, staying close to her lodge.

Several times Sacajawea knew the boys pilfered small things from her tepee, like a butcher knife, a leather box half-full of tallow, and bits of meat. Toussaint never seemed to challenge where the youngsters found their new items. Neither he nor his women seemed to have an understanding of children. Toussaint possessed a certain amount of natural affection, but he never showed it, and he was erratic in his dealings, so that the boys never knew whether they would be punished severely for some minor offense or ignored when guilty of some far more serious misdeed. The children naturally feared their father, and Toussaint sensed this. They ignored their mothers. But they held Sacajawea in some respectful awe, always hoping that one day they might be permitted to hear the mystical stories she could tell.

To Toussaint, Sacajawea seemed the consistent ally of his children. This gave him a feeling of being defied in his own lodge, which added greatly to his resentment. Yet he never hinted that he wished to move out, nor did he ever speak to Sacajawea about his feelings. She knew he was irritable whenever his children came near her tepee. She never once invited them even to sit with her during a tribal meeting or festival. She watched the four children with pity in her heart.

She often thought, Is this the way all our people will

become? Will they be irresponsible and shiftless when the white men give them land and provide food and clothing? Will the incentive to be a proud, dignified being be lost? Even Toussaint, a man who received the white man's learning, has lapsed into a state of dependence upon the white men for food and clothing.

And the white men—what are they? Some are leaders and learn quickly. There are good and bad among them. The white man will not let himself be dominated by another and also wishes to be free in his own way.

Toussaint sat there at the edge of the camp to remind Sacajawea of old Charbonneau and his sullen ways, to remind her of the good times she had with Otter Woman when Toussaint and her firstborn, Baptiste, were small.

One evening Sacajawea asked Shoogan if one of his children could sleep in her lodge. The child chosen was Little Red Eyes. He was old enough to ride a horse, but not old enough to hunt. He was pensive, but not sad. He sat quietly with Berry around the stew pot until it was his turn to eat. Then he asked, "Grandmother, tell the story of another feast day. The one that honored you where the whites gathered around."

"Oh, that was when the Saints from Salt Lake gathered around and touched the silver medal I wear."

"What did they say?" begged Little Red Eyes.

"Oh, 'Something grand,' they said." Sacajawea took the child's hand and let him sit close to her.

Berry sat in Crying Basket's arms. Berry was small, with piercing black eyes.

"My father has papers the men from Salt Lake gave to you—why?" asked Little Red Eyes, as though it were a secret he should not have told.

"Ai, those are precious papers, signed by the leader of the Saints, their chief, Brigham Young. He said I was a good woman and his God approved of my ways. That was on the paper. He told me to keep it forever. I will not live forever. So—I gave it to your father to keep because he will live longer. He can pass it on to one of his sons—Lance or you—to keep forever. Then you will know, when you are a man, that your grandmother was a friend of the whites and tried to understand and live in peace with them."

"Did you make the design on the leather wallet the papers are in?"

"*Ai*, I learned to sew the wild-rose design from the Mandans, who live to the north."

"Oooo, you have lived everywhere," said Little Red Eyes, yawning sleepily.

"No, not in the east, where the white men come from, and not in the far west, California, where many whites are taking the trail now."

"But that is why our people call you Chief Woman," said Little Red Eyes. "You have been over more land than most any other woman." He patted Sacajawea's knee. "I believe you are Chief Woman."

"That is because I am your grandmother," laughed Sacajawea in a pleased way. "Every child loves a grandmother who has time to tell stories and listen to what is in the bottom of a child's heart. Here, you wear this medal while I tell you a story to make your eyes grow heavy with sleep as Berry's have done." She slipped the Jefferson medal over Little Red Eye's head and watched it settle on his bare neck and chest. It was large for a child, but it did not seem to weigh him down. It is good-looking on a child, she thought. She took it off and slipped it back around her own neck, after telling the story of the great whale on the west coast.

"Something grand," repeated the child. "Only you and Chief Washakie wear such a thing, and yours came first."

Early the next day, the Shoshonis and Bannocks were in their large semicircle before General Augur, Washakie, Taghee, Shoogan, and other important men.

Washakie did not wait for Augur to begin talking. As soon as the pipe-smoking was over, he stood up and asked, "How is the land going to be marked off that the Shoshonis can call it their own?"

Augur looked surprised that a Shoshoni would ask such a thing. He began to explain the meaning of latitude and longitude as determined by the sun and stars. Shoogan began to use hand signs and stuttered in his interpretation. Washakie was respectfully silent. When Augur was finished, Washakie asked, "Would an Indian ever measure the height of a mountain that he could climb? No, never. The legends of his tribe tell him nothing about quadrants and baselines and angles. Someday I hope that I learn more about the sun and stars and how to measure the land from them. For the present I prefer to have the boundaries of my reservation explained in terms of rivers and mountains."

Washakie then looked through the surveyor's transit that had been brought out. "White man's medicine," he murmured.

Augur ran his finger between his neck and collar several times. Then he pointed out that the reservation would be temporarily shared with Chief Taghee and his Bannocks until they could move to Fort Hall the following year. The reservation would begin at the mouth of Owl Creek and run due south to the crest of the Divide, between Sweetwater and Popo Agie; along the crest and the summit of the Wind River Mountains to the North Fork of the Wind River; due north to the mouth of the North Fork and up its channel to a point twenty miles above the mouth; then in a straight line to the headwaters of Owl Creek and along the middle of its channel to the place of the beginning.

Chief Washakie smiled broadly. The boundaries of the Wind River Reservation had been defined in a language he could understand.

The remainder of the treaty had been gone over the day before, and nothing was left but the official signing.

Sacajawea stood up as if to stretch her legs. Crying Basket motioned for her to sit down until the signing was over. But the urge to add something to this important treaty was greater than she could bear, and she found herself standing in front of the semicircle blurting out her words before they could be swallowed.

"The white men are great chiefs. Our chief is great. The Bannocks' chief is great." Her heart was beating so fast she thought everyone could see. She moved slightly so that she could see Shoogan. Her hands shook, but the words could not be held in. "I listen and wonder. Does the white man know that the Bannocks want a place of their own now? If they are going to live near Fort Hall and it is already known where, send them today. They will be happier. You gave the buffalo hunters of our tribe a plow to break up the land. What is a plow? Why would anyone want to break up the land? Seeds can be put in the ground by making small holes with a stick. I can show the hunters that. Maybe I should show the white men before they open up our land, the way you heard the man called Augur explain, with this thing called a plow. It is nothing we want. And these stockings the white man gives to us, we do not need them. But if we did, we need more than one pair. I know these stockings, they do not wear— *whoosht*—gone before one season has passed. Moccasins are better."

Sacajawea looked over the crowd of people, then at the general. Her nervousness came back. Had he understood her words? Shoogan was making hand signs. Was her tongue plain enough, her English words slow enough? Shoogan's head shook as though he approved, and there seemed to be a smile at the corners of his mouth. She breathed deeply and faced him.

"These red blankets are so thin. They will not keep a small child warm in cold weather. We need two of these. Or we need to throw them away and use our buffalo robes. They keep the wind off our backs. But even so—my heart is glad. The white men have given back our land, our woods to walk in. A woods where I can walk for half a day and never come to the edge is one of the finest gifts to give anyone. On this land I can place my feet on some old, grown-over trail of our ancestors and follow it until it ends; then I can make a trail of my own. In this land I can feel the springiness of moss and leaves beneath my feet, hear the crunch of pinecones and the snap of dry sticks. The outcropping boulders covered with lichen will cause me to stop and marvel at their small green twigs, like a painting.

"In spring I will find a patch of bloodroot, dogtooth violets, and wild moccasins. There is peace in those places where trading and squabbling are not known."

She was more calm now, and her voice low and slow. Her words were absorbed by the whole assemblage; no child cried out as she talked, and when she lapsed into Shoshoni, Shoogan, noticeably moved, spoke her words accurately to the white man.

"There will be squirrels and birds to greet me. I may sit on a rotting stump and see the new sprouts of kinnikinnick coming up, telling me that life dies, but life lives on.

"In summer I will see branches overhead, making it cool underneath. I will look through at Father Sun and the blueness of the sky and wonder about the endlessness of our land.

"I will go to the hills in the fall and drink in the tangy smell of the yellow grass, leaving behind the noisy trading post, to walk in quietness.

"In winter the trees with no leaves show the backbone of life. They teach us to face the stark realities of life. I will feel the crystal coldness of wind in my face, and the cold, deep sleep of Mother Earth. The white chiefs have given us back the land that belonged to us for all ages. I am grateful.

"I, then, give this gift to the white man. I let him walk alone in our woods so that he will receive peace with himself."

No one stirred for a few seconds. The quietness spoke as an ovation for something reverent, akin to a prayer.

In later years this speech became something woven into the winter tales and traditions of the Shoshonis. It was to be forever remembered. Those who heard it kept it alive by retelling it to those who had not heard. It is still told on the Wind River Reservation.

With their X's Chief Washakie and his subchiefs, and Chief Taghee and his subchiefs, signed the treaty officially titled the Treaty with the Western Shoshoni and Bannocks, but more generally known as the Great Treaty of July 3, 1868. This signing was actually an anticlimax after Sacajawea's speech. The reservation was almost as large as the state of Connecticut. To have, however, was not to hold. For later, by the cessions of 1872, 1896, and 1904, it was reduced to less than one-fifth the original area.

Despite treaties, atrocities were committed by both whites and red men against one another. During the Shoshoni fall elk hunt, the women put up a temporary hunting camp and went with their men. Sacajawea, Crying Basket, and Dancing Leaf were waiting for Shoogan and Smell of Sugar to bring down the grazing elk ahead. The women were hidden behind some tall

cottonwoods watching the men approach the elk slowly.
Crying Basket moved quickly to the other two women.
"Quick, my man motions that enemies are near. Quietly, now."

Hidden behind some brush was Smell of Sugar, who
motioned for the women to stop and squat down. In the
valley below they saw several braves strutting in ladies'
bonnets. Colored silks were thrown garishly around their
shoulders and waists.

"I think they are Cheyennes," said Shoogan. "The
whites were in that white top. See out on the trail. They
were going west, maybe following a group of white tops
that went by two, three days ago." He breathed deeply.
"I will ride my pony around the other way and warn
the other hunters. It is best if you go quickly back to
camp with the children by going around the other side
of these hills."

He was gone. No sign, no noise was heard in his
direction. Below, they heard the cries of a white woman
and her children as her man was killed and mutilated.
The leader of this small group of Cheyennes grabbed
the younger child and hit his head against a tree. He
dropped the jerking body and brained the second child
in the same manner.

Sacajawea made a low, guttural sound in her throat.
"It is not right. It cannot be," she murmured. Crying
Basket moved around the hill and retched in the bushes.
Berry stood waiting for the older women to lead her.
She was pale and shaking.

That evening, the men came back with only two elk.
They had not seen what the Cheyennes had done.

Around the evening meal, Smell of Sugar told about
the white man called Chivington. "This man was given
a feast in a white village because he killed the Cheyenne chief Left Hand, and the same day he also killed
women and children in another Cheyenne camp. Now
the Cheyennes are avenged with what you saw on the
trail of the white tops."

Shoogan spoke up. "I heard that the half-breed son
of the man known as Bill Bent led his own band of Dog
Soldiers and lives as a Cheyenne constantly raiding the
whites."

Sacajawea's hand went to her mouth. She recalled

the Cheyenne woman of Bill Bent, Owl Woman, and how kind she had been years back. Was this half-breed her son? she wondered.

Smell of Sugar said, "Half-breeds are not the same. Their world is split, and there comes a time when they can no longer straddle it. They will become white or Indian all the way. When they become Indian, they become more wolflike. When they become white, they are dandies, not wanting to do any hard work."

Shoogan said, "If Bill Bent were in charge, he could have all the Indian nations at peace. It is he and Kit Carson who know how to deal with hostile men of any nation. It is said that he wept like a squaw, alone in the woods, when his Owl Woman was scalped by Pawnees."

Sacajawea gasped. The voice of Shoogan went on, "But those whites do not interest me. They are traitors to their own people. They are nothing but Cheyenne-lovers. I think a man ought to work for his own tribe and not mix in the affairs of another, the way the white men do. We ought to stand up to those white men and tell them we will live in the old way, the way we know and love best. They have no business ordering us around on our own land."

All the way back to the main camp, Sacajawea felt the ground was cut from under her feet. To know that Owl Woman was gone caused a penetrating loneliness to pervade her body. The old ways were leaving. Her friends were leaving.

The next several days, little things seemed to go wrong. She could feel her own emotions shaking her usually fine balance. The grandchildren had the power to disturb her as never before.

One day she found herself on her knees, hugging the weeping Berry to her breast in a passion of self-blame. She had just taken a beaded necklace away from the child that was made as a gift for Dancing Leaf. Oh, oh, she thought, why do I take my feelings out on a baby? She should be permitted to look and to feel the necklace. Why didn't I give it to her? I could easily have made another. Why did I grab it away from her childish eyes so fast?

It was that very evening that Toussaint hesitatingly came to her tepee in much embarrassment.

"I want you to leave my boys alone," he said, shamefaced. His head hung toward his moccasins.

It was after the evening meal and Sacajawea was tidying the lodge before the others came back from some visiting. She was alone.

Toussaint looked around the tepee. It was the first time since his arrival that he'd been inside. Now he looked strangely complacent.

She looked at him questioningly, not understanding his request.

"What is the matter, Mother? You want to deny that you let those boys have this?" He took the Jefferson peace medal from his back trouser pocket. He knew full well she had not given the boys the medal—they had seen its shininess and taken it.

But Toussaint knew that Sacajawea would deny it.

"I am sorry," she said. "I did not think to tell them they had no real use for such a thing and it was best left here with me. Perhaps they liked the neck string—see, I have beaded it a little."

"Mother," said Toussaint, "you mean to tell me that you would let them have this and say nothing?"

She shook her head. She was not sure what she would have done if she had found that the medal was missing. Toussaint had jockeyed her into a position of appearing to have condoned the boys' taking anything they wished. She was thinking it over. Angry as it made her, there was nothing much she could do about it. She had long ago decided never to criticize Toussaint and his women, never to offer them advice, never to really notice them if possible.

"This medallion rightfully belongs to me. I am called your son, and so it is mine."

Sacajawea was appalled and stepped back. He was trying to take advantage of her. Her arm darted out, and she pulled back the medal.

"It rightfully belongs to Baptiste. It is mine until I find him or until I see fit to give it to someone," she said.

"You will give it to me, or at your death it will be given to me," he sneered. A secret look of triumph was in Toussaint's eyes. "Years ago, just after my brother came back from Germany acting like some kind of dandy, the two of us were in Saint Louis selling peltries and we met Bill Clark in Chouteau's trading post. Old Bill Clark was so glad to see Bap he hardly noticed me at first. When he asked about you, I was the one who stepped up and told him right out about how you'd run off. Bap still felt so bad about that he went off to look at some tooled saddles while I told Clark the details."

Sacajawea's hands flew to her mouth.

"So I told him that wolves had found you sleeping on the prairie and devoured your flesh to the bone. I said I knew it was you by the little blue stone on the leather thong around your bare neckbones. And I saw the surprise and hurt that came to his face."

Sacajawea stared, stunned.

"I used my head and suggested that Clark not say a word to Bap about your death because it had upset him so. Clark knew how sensitive he was and had seen how he'd left me to tell the facts. So he agreed not to discuss it with Bap."[1]

Sacajawea could think of nothing to say, nor did she really wish to say anything. The perfidiousness—the utter perfidiousness—crushed her. She drew herself down into a knot, staring unbelieving, wounded beyond any power of expression.

Toussaint looked at her, standing away from him. Suddenly there came conviction. He truly had known all along she'd been alive, even though no one could find her. Sacajawea could take care of herself no matter where she went—on the prairie, in the mountains, anywhere. Why had he made up such a story and told it to a man he really respected, Bill Clark—and then half believed it himself for a time?

She had withdrawn to the side of her tepee. Her face was averted now, and she placed a hand on her pallet and guided herself down upon it. Toussaint could not see her, but he knew she was crying—crying deep inside herself, not sobbing or weeping, but breaking far within, her tears being tears of the soul and infinitely more poignant than any tears of the surface.

He said no more. He'd come again and see to it she

gave him the old Jefferson medal. Then the Shoshonis would think he was something—maybe look up to him the way they looked up to old Washakie. Slowly he moseyed on toward his own tepee, grimly, stubbornly silent.

CHAPTER

55

The Jefferson Peace Medal

One of Sacajawea's great-grandsons, named James McAdams, who was the son of Nancy Bazil, daughter of Shoogan, contributed certain interesting information regarding the medal which Sacajawea had. This medal bore Jefferson's head and his name, and had a gold rim about it.[1]

"I have seen it many times. At Salt Lake the people, when they saw this medal, said to Porivo or Chief, 'Something grand!' and they gave Sacajawea and her people who were with her a big feast in honor of her wonderful achievements for the white people when they were on their way to the big waters."

Reprinted by permission of the publishers, The Arthur H. Clark Company, from *Sacajawea, Guide and Interpreter of the Lewis and Clark Expedition*, by Grace Raymond Hebard, 1957, pp. 200–1.

Washakie kept his band close to the Fort Bridger Agency. Often Sacajawea went to visit with Washakie's Crow woman, White Curly Bear. White Curly Bear was always pleasant and always working hard. She was not old, but not very young, either. She had white hairs growing from a small mole on her chin.

One morning the two women were making moccasins together, each sewing on blue-and-white beads they had bought earlier from the sutler's store inside Fort Bridger. Sacajawea was amusing White Curly Bear with stories about the antics of Ben York and the big dog, Scannon. "That black warrior was the envy of all the young native girls," said Sacajawea. "They would trade anything to have a strong black child who resembled him, for strength and protection in their lodge."

White Curly Bear looked up, her eyes big. She put a finger on her chin, then slid it slowly across her lips. "Shhh," she said. "That is like a story of my own from long ago. Now, do not interrupt and I will tell you about a band of Crows that came to visit our tribe one spring. They had a magnificent chief who was dark as a burned log, except on the soles of his feet and the palms of his hands. His hair was curly like the buffalo grass, and he let it grow long and bushy. He had four women to take care of it. They tied it with grasses and put shining black crow feathers in it. He could speak the language of the white man and sometimes entertained travelers and mountain men. He trained one of his camp dogs to stand on its hind feet and bark for meat. He taught the dog to roll over and over. My mother told me he lifted me to his shoulders one time and danced around until I sang with delight. I was a child and remember only what my mother told. She said he went into council with the chief of our tribe and wore a beautiful white shirt with threads pink as the sunset on it. These threads were made into flowers like the wild rose. He was very careful with that shirt and would not let his women fold it. He himself did that, and he kept it in a parfleche high on a lodgepole peg—stop interrupting me."

Sacajawea was waving her hands in the air. She

could hardly keep her mouth shut in her excitement. "His name? What name did he go by?"

"How do I know? I cannot remember if my mother ever told me. He was a grand chief. He stood tall and big and black. He sang loud in a tongue that the Crows could not understand. He could sing up high and down low; he did not chant as the Crows do. My mother said he had once lived with white men."

"The shirt—did he tell where it came from?"

"I do not know about that, except I think my mother said a white woman made it for him."

"Did the shirt have lacing at the neck and wrists?"

"*Ai*, it did, and those beautiful pink flowers on that pure whiteness of the material. It was not like fine doeskin, but white as birchbark and soft and thin. Nothing like the Crow women could sew."

Sacajawea was speechless. She did not know who else it could be but Ben York, wearing the shirt she had so carefully made for him in Saint Louis. She thought awhile. She thought about the people she had known and decided now that they did not die with the years, they came back to her. Her own world was as large as the whole nation of white men to the east, the Comanches and Mexicans to the south, the Mandans to the north, and now the Crows to the west.

"I cannot remember more except that the big black chief made little children laugh when he swung them up in the air and caught them in his powerful arms. He liked children, and he had many in his lodge."

"It is some story," said Sacajawea finally, her eyes fastened on White Curly Bear's face as though she had not heard the end.

"You do not believe it?" asked White Curly Bear.

"Oh, I do, *ai*. It is just something that is gnawing at my thoughts. I think it is the Great Spirit telling us that we can all live together in happiness, no matter where we come from. If we get to know a person, we can like him."

"Chief Woman, your mouth won't stay shut. I feel like pinching it closed," said White Curly Bear. "I tell you a childhood story, and you start telling about people getting along. Even members of families fight, you know. It seems to be the nature of people to be happy for a time, then to make some sadness, like fighting or death. Happiness is never long lasting. Now, why are you making a design of roses on those moccasins instead of the sun with rays?"

"I do not really know. It is just something that was in my mind," answered Sacajawea softly.

"There is something going on that puzzles me," said White Curly Bear. "That man called General Augur sent three men of the Arapahos to talk with my man. He would tell me nothing, except that the Arapahos wish to live with us on the Wind River Reservation. I could not believe it. The Arapahos are our enemies; they cannot be trusted. Why would they suddenly wish to join us now?"

"Perhaps if we knew them, we could be friends," said Sacajawea.

"I hesitated to tell you this. But now it is time. It is the family of the man you call your son. There is a girl in that family who has made a friendship with an Arapaho youth. She meets him on the other side of the fort. It is the girl called Joy. You knew about this affair? That is why you talk about being friends with everyone?"

"No," said Sacajawea, "I did not know." She sat quite still, her head reeling with thoughts.

"And the man you call son has a loose tongue. He boldly told my man, Washakie, he was too old to be chief. He told him he could never win any battles or take a scalp now. He said further that the war blood has ceased to flow through his veins and that he, who was named Baptiste, should now be leader of the Lemhi Shoshoni."

Sacajawea's head reeled with the words. Several times she bit her tongue so that she would not say what came to her mind.

"Washakie has gone off on his horse alone. I do not know when he will return. He and I do not blame you for the ways of that man who calls himself Baptiste. We respect you as a true friend. What we do not understand is how you can have a son like that man."

Sacajawea sat hunched over her sewing for a long time. To have publicly claimed a son that was not truly hers was neither right nor wrong. He was the son of

Otter Woman, her friend, and never would she let the spirit of this old friend find her rude or discourteous to something so valuable as the grown son of a true friend.

But she could not understand Toussaint. Maybe he'd had too much schooling or maybe it was the poor, thin cows of the white men he brought home pretending it was buffalo meat; maybe it was the raw trade whiskey that made him stormy one time and peaceable the next. She could not tell ahead what little things might set him off. She hated him and at the same time loved him.

Late one evening not long afterward, the girl, Joy, came limping to Sacajawea's tepee. Her right leg was stiff. Sacajawea rolled up the legging and saw the two tiny holes with blood in them. By this time they were turning black and the flesh was beginning to swell and puff. Sacajawea pulled the lacing from the legging, and around and around she bound it as tightly as she could, just above the knee, twisting the knot with a piece of stick to stop the flow of blood. The girl fainted as nausea swept over her and the earth swam. At first horror filled Sacajawea; then, as it ebbed away, anxiety for the safety of this young life took hold of her.

"What happened?" she asked when the girl was conscious.

"I was out on the trail beside the water hole on the far side of the fort," explained Joy slowly. "I waited for High Horse, the son of the Arapaho subchief Sorrel Horse. He did not come, and I grew impatient and stepped off the trail only to see the moon better."

Numbness was climbing to her knee, and her leg was swelling terribly. Another great spasm of vertigo overcame the girl. She tried to fight the sickness.

Sacajawea's decisive and authoritative voice cut across her nausea. "I'll get your mother."

"No, please, no. Do not tell them. Not any of them." Then when the great twisting nausea was over, Joy knew she had vomited; her tunic was covered. She then found she was lying down on a bed of robes. She lay half-conscious as Sacajawea worked over her. Her clothes came off. A cotton cloth covered her.

"Be still now," Sacajawea said. "Do not stir up your blood."

The girl obeyed. She was small, light-complexioned,

frail-looking. Her face seemed coarse and vacant. She
seemed to have no volition of her own.

Sacajawea looked up as she heard footsteps. Dirty,
the girl's mother, pushed aside the tepee flap and entered. "The boy, Squirrel Chaser, told me she was hurt
and had come here. I brought whiskey. It's the one cure-
all. Where is she?"

"You're not going to let her drink the whiskey?" asked
Sacajawea.

"*Ai.*" Dirty's fat fingers pressed at the leg's swelling.
"And so she found herself next to a rattler. It looks
bad."

Sacajawea wished she had called Dancing Leaf to
come. Her mind seemed numbed for a moment. Crying
Basket was gone with her man and baby to Fort Hall.
She knew that drinking whiskey was not good for
snakebite. Kicking Horse, the Comanche Medicine Man,
would never use it. But he would use mescal powder to
edge off the pain. And what else did he use? Her mind
reeled and fell into her past.

"Please, do not give the child whiskey to drink. Pour
it over the wound," commanded Sacajawea.

Dirty did not answer. Her breathing was rasping as
air hissed through her clenched teeth. "I can see my
daughter has come where she was forbidden," rasped
Dirty.

"The child came for help. I could not refuse. See how
the foot is swollen so it fills the moccasin? Take this
knife and cut the moccasin off."

Dirty put the whiskey to one side and began severing
whang leather. The moccasin dropped off.

Sacajawea went out to find the yucca spears she remembered growing near the wall of Bridger's Fort.
Yucca spears to stab the swollen flesh. She was remembering what Kicking Horse would have done. Everything was dark near the wall and quiet. She ran holding
out her hands to feel the tall daggers. She found the
huge plant and whacked the long spears off one by one,
trying to see where they fell in the darkness. The clouds
moved across the face of the moon, and she saw clearly.
Finally holding a bundle of sharp leaves, she ran back
to her tepee.

Inside, she stood frozen. Dirty had put the girl's swollen leg over a piece of firewood. "I'm going to cut the poison out."

There was barely an exhalation from the girl.

Dirty then slid her arm back of the girl's shoulders, lifting her. Whiskey went down her throat. The girl's eyes flickered open.

Sacajawea's face was beside the woman, disapproval strong on it. Dirty's face mirrored fear and concern.

"No!" shouted Sacajawea.

Gulp, gulp, gulp—the fire swirled through the girl. It came too fast, and she coughed the sour, wet stuff all over her face. She felt it was all coming up; then the whiskey seemed to numb the sickness.

"She will take more!" scolded Dirty.

"No!" cried Sacajawea. "It is bad! It takes the poison through the blood faster." She pulled the bottle from Dirty's hands; half was gone.

Then Dirty's rump was turned toward Sacajawea, the butcher knife in her hand.

Dirty spoke. "See there—the fang there? It has to be butchered out. Look at all that black blood."

She had cut a sizable piece of flesh from the girl's ankle. The flesh was dark and blood-covered. Sacajawea could see no fang in that mess. She wondered why she had not seen it before if it had really been there.

"Stop that!" shouted Sacajawea. "If you want your daughter to live! Pour some of the whiskey over the wound! Warm that blanket and tear it into thin strips. That hole in her leg has to be covered. Move faster, you butchering fool."

"I think she'll die, anyway," sobbed Dirty. "No one can live with a leg that has such a big hole in it."

Then Toussaint put his head through the tepee flap. He looked ready for a rampage. "Disgusting!" he said in a flat voice. "She's a goner. No use working over her more. This is her reward for sneaking around with a dirty Arapaho. I just found out where's she's been. I ought to cut her nose off!"

It was not fear that answered. Sacajawea was not afraid. It was all the sores coming to one head. "She'll pull through it if you keep your cheap whiskey out of her mouth and take your woman home with you. I'll see to her this night myself."

There was a moment of will against scared will. Toussaint's words broke it. "A rattler's bite means death. She let the Arapaho put his hands on her, and that's same as a rattler's bite to a true Shosoni." He turned and marched out of the tepee, but halted at the flap and turned toward the inside, his face as black as anthracite. "Go to it! But her death will be on your hands!" He went on out.

These words of warning struck Sacajawea deep and added to her anxiety for the girl.

"She's hardly breathing! You have killed my daughter!" Dirty wailed the death keen.

"Stop that! Her mind has only wandered away for a while. She may be all right."

"No, no, she's gone. She was a quiet child. Afraid of her father. She was going to run away with a rotten Arapaho. What would the rest of the tribe say to that? Arapahos are enemies, not some band to go to live with. Maybe you were helping her, you stinking skunk." Dirty held the half-empty whiskey bottle to her own lips. Sacajawea pulled it away and told Dirty to find more firewood. Dirty wiped her hands on the shredded wool blanket and ran from the tepee.

Sacajawea washed the dark blood from the wound, noting that the leg above the knee was turning dark. Suddenly sharp lancets punctured the girl's flesh. Wielding the yucca spears like a handful of daggers, Sacajawea stabbed again and again at the swollen leg, stabbing and striking with all her strength. Black blood ran in oily ooze from many holes at once. The smell of whiskey was in the enclosed air of the tepee, and it burned in the girl's open wounds. Sacajawea poured most of it in the unnecessary hole Dirty had cut. Sacajawea wrapped hot wool strips around the leg.

Joy stirred. Her foot and leg throbbed with each beat of her heart. She tried to move the terrible hurting, but her leg did not stir. It was still night. The center fire glowed weakly. Somebody sat beside the pallet. "Mother?" said the girl through thick lips. "Mother, stop the pain."

"Be still." The voice was Sacajawea's. "Your mother has gone."

She brought the girl bits of mescal button. "Try to swallow without water. Water comes back."

The drug took some of the edge off her pain and seemed to settle her stomach. Again consciousness slipped away.

When she awoke again, Sacajawea removed the binding on the leg and gave Joy more dry mescal bits. Joy felt the prickles of circulation creep down her leg, and the throbbing seemed less severe. She rewrapped the leg.

From outside in the early morning came the thin sound of high keening—the death wail.

"Who has died?" asked the girl feebly.

"No one has died," said Sacajawea abruptly. "That is a coyote's call, nothing more."

The girl lapsed into another period of blackness. The next day, Sacajawea carefully unwrapped the bandages and soaked them in yucca suds; then she wrung them and replaced them on the swollen leg. She propped Joy up and forced some thin broth between her lips. Immediately the broth spurted to the dirt floor.

"Rest," said Sacajawea's compassionate voice. "You have plenty of time to try later." Her cool fingers, with a grateful pressure, were on Joy's forehead. "The one you call High Horse was here early, before dawn today, to see about you," whispered Sacajawea. "He calls me grandmother and seems well mannered. His father is at the agency trying to make plans for a council. He is waiting for Chief Washakie to return. He says one day the Shoshonis and Arapahos will not be enemies. I like him."

How did he know I was here? Joy wondered. Who told him? Did the boy Squirrel Chaser follow me? Her mind was too far away to concern itself. She lay back, and her consciousness again departed.

Long afterward, Sacajawea heard Joy groan, and she saw her eyelids open. The girl was as thin as a lodgepole. Sacajawea placed a cool cloth on her forehead and bent over her.

"How do you feel?"

"My head," she answered thickly. "My head."

"You've been far away, but I hoped you'd come back." There was a catch in Sacajawea's voice.

"You did not believe the others when they said I would die?"

"They had never seen one bitten so by the rattler live. I thought you could fight such an enemy."

Sacajawea lit her pipe, her hands trembling as with palsy. She steadied the bowl and held a lighted stick to it. She studied the dirt floor through the slowly rising smoke. Her voice seemed weary with its burden of dead days remembered. "A storm is coming on. The sun is covered, and the wind comes very strong and cold. I need more wood for the fire."

The girl moved across the pallet. "High Horse says nothing bad about my family. He is not bad, as my father thinks. I can put my foot on the floor. The pain is gone."

"You must not be too quick," Sacajawea objected. "The flesh must fill in your ankle before it is strong enough to stand on."

Sacajawea left to gather an armload of cottonwood chunks Shoogan had piled beside a stump outside the circle of tepees. She met Dancing Leaf, also gathering wood against the oncoming storm.

"How is the girl?"

"She will be all right," answered Sacajawea. "The swelling is about gone. She may limp—that is all."

"I saw her mother going to visit. Her eyes were red and puffed, and she mumbled the Death Song. It is not good for Dirty to carry on so when her daughter is getting better."

Sacajawea's face turned white. "Hmmm," she said high up in her nose and hurried back.

When she raised the flap of the tepee, she stooped in a puff of pleasant warmth and placed the armload of wood chunks beside the fire. Then she noticed Dirty in the shadows against the wall, her hair straggling to her shoulders about her aquiline face, which had been handsome, surely, before her niggardly way of life had squeezed the flesh down to the bone.

Dirty moved forward and threw the robe from Joy. Sacajawea gave a cry that stopped halfway up her throat. The girl seemed a stranger. Her hair was caked with sweat, her eyes were empty, her face was ashen, and her mouth was still open for the words she was saying

when death took her. Blood clotted on her ankle and
on the pallet; she had the smell of sour whiskey.

"What happened?" said Sacajawea accusingly. "She
was well enough when I went for the wood."

"I gave her whiskey to stop the ache in her head and
cut the leg to let the last of the poison out."

"But the swelling of her leg was hardly to be noticed.
She had asked to put the foot down!"

"Porivo, you think you know all! You think you have
some mysterious power, some great medicine, but see—
you could not make my daughter well!"

Dirty flung the empty whiskey bottle on the floor
and staggered to the tepee flap. "She was going to live
with an Arapaho. She would have disgraced me." Her
keening was loud outside the tepee.

Sacajawea wept quietly. Her anger was as strong as
her sorrow. She peered at Joy for a while, still letting
the tears roll over her cheeks. Finally she said to herself, I am old and have learned so many things that I
do not know much anymore. Maybe I was wiser before
my ears were troubled with so many forked words.

She washed the girl and rubbed her body with bear's
oil and sage. Then she unbraided her hair and combed
it. When it was shiny, she braided it very carefully. She
painted a thin red line down the center part and put
red paint inside Joy's ears. "Your black road of trouble
has ended," she said out loud to the girl. "You will go
to a place where the grass is green forever and the sky
is always blue and no one is afraid and no one is old."
She dressed the girl in a soft white tunic with a yoke
of small blue beads. The tunic was too large, and she
cinched the middle with a leather belt, decorated with
porcupine quills.

When she had finished, she walked to the far side of
the village to the tepee of Toussaint. Outside, she called,
"I have prepared the body of my granddaughter for her
long journey."

Contrary Woman poked her head out, followed by
two boys, who recognized Sacajawea immediately. "Dirty
is with you?"

"No, I have not seen her since morning," said Sacajawea.

"She said she was going out to see her dead child.

But we had not heard that she had actually died until this moment."

"Nor I," said Sacajawea.

Contrary Woman helped Sacajawea wrap the body in a buffalo robe and tie it with thongs until it was only a large bundle.

"She was not really a bad child. She was shy and had few friends. She seemed lonely, sad at times. Is it really bad, loving one of the enemy?" said Contrary Woman.

"I do not think so," said Sacajawea. "They have the same feelings as we."

The two women sat with tears shining on their cheeks in the firelight and sang a low song over and over so that this daughter would have courage on her journey to the Spirit World.

After a while, Toussaint came to the tepee and suggested that Sacajawea give away her most prized possessions in honor of the granddaughter who had died there. "I will take the silver medal," he said. "Joy was my daughter, and I ought to have some payment for her death."

Sacajawea looked at him, stunned. "I have nothing but sorrow now," she answered. "When this day goes to the Spirit Land, I will look to see what I wish to give you."

Toussaint placed the bundle on a drag behind his pony and started for the hills. Behind the drag were Contrary Woman and her boys, Squirrel Chaser and Race Horse, and the toddler, Yelling Falls. Sacajawea followed. As they walked, they wept.

In the fading sunlight on the hilltop was a new scaffold that Dirty had had Toussaint build a week before.

Toussaint unhitched the pony and leaned the drag against the scaffold. He climbed up and pulled the bundle to the top and tied it down with thongs. That night the coyotes heard the weeping and moaning and raised their high, sharp song of sorrow. When they stopped, the night was large with the howling wind, and Dirty sat among them, and nothing mattered.

The next day they sat where they were and felt bad, and the young women squabbled between themselves.

The old times were better, thought Sacajawea, wan-

dering alone and mourning and praying. Then it was
like dying with the dear one and coming back all new
again and stronger to live. Now when someone dies we
do not go anywhere, and we quarrel; we have forgotten
how to learn.

After a while, they went back to the village.

Late that afternoon, White Curly Bear called out to
Sacajawea, "I can wait no longer, but must tell you
about Washakie."

Inside the tepee, she seated herself in front of Sacajawea, saying, "This morning my man came into camp
holding seven scalps. The men came out and greeted
him. Shoogan held his horse as he dismounted. Women
and children came and formed a circle around their
chief, and circled him from left to right. 'Let him,' said
Washakie, 'who can do a greater feat than this claim
the chieftainship.' And he held the scalps high above
his head. 'Let him who would take my place count as
many scalps.' Then he told that he had been out on the
warpath single-handed to test his skill, that he had
come across a band of Sioux, and that each scalp was
his own trophy." White Curly Bear had a mock-serious
crinkling about her eyes. "I am glad to find you back
among the living."

Sacajawea smiled broadly at her friend. "*Ai*, it is
good to be here. It is even better to hear the news about
your man."

When Toussaint heard the news of Washakie, he
stayed in his tepee, avoiding the other men of the tribe.
He wished to speak to no one about his foolish talk with
Washakie. He told his women his grief was large and
he could not bear to go out among people.

So—from that time until his death, Washakie was
the unchallenged leader and chief of the Lemhi Shoshonis.

The next day, Washakie rode his horse to the agency
to meet in council with Sorrel Horse, Medicine Man,
Friday, and other important Arapahos.

Many waved to him as he left. He sat high on his
horse, wearing his medallion and shaking his good-luck
token, an old dried buffalo scrotum filled with small
pebbles and sewn back up. When he could no longer be
seen, Sacajawea went about her daily chores, wishing

that Crying Basket had left little Berry for her to look after. Crying Basket and her man had gone by horseback to Fort Hall to trade Joe Coiner some beaver furs for a few bear skins to use on the floor of their lodge. Joe was well known as one of the best skinners. His hides had no slash marks nor splits. Suzanne had learned to tan most any animal skin to perfection.

A dark figure came to her side and pulled her blanket. "Porivo, my *umbea*," said Toussaint, "my heart is heavy. To lighten it I would like to wear the medal you have. I will look distinguished then."

Sacajawea stumbled once, then caught herself, saying, "I think there is something the matter with you. I think you have been drinking too much whiskey."

"Oho!" he said, uttering with explosive force the syllable of emphasis. "Oho! So what about it? I want Washakie to look at me and say, 'He must be a big man to wear such a neckpiece.'"

"You mean you would wear my medal to make you look big? You who would not keep your woman from causing the death of your own daughter?"

He was silent. He blinked, then stared at Sacajawea. He let go of her blanket and stumbled backward. Swearing, he picked himself up. "I will come for the medal when the sun slants across the sky. I will have it then."

Sacajawea sat in her tepee alone, drawing hollow-cheeked upon the stem of her pipe. She smoked awhile and brooded in the little cloud she made. Then she got up and went to see Dancing Leaf.

"But won't you let me tell your son where you are going? They will worry," said Shoogan's woman.

"No, those women will not miss me. They would only say I should act my age and sit in my tepee before the fire all day. I go now to think. I will visit Suzanne myself and see my grandchildren there. I will be back before the moon is full."

Sacajawea walked to the road that ran through Camp Augur, the white soldiers' camp near Fort Bridger, carrying an old leather case that held her calico dress and a clean skin tunic. The stage stopped in front of the headquarters' building. It went on to Fort Hall.

The stage driver recognized her as the old Shoshoni squaw who, some said, guided some white soldiers

through the Rocky Mountains. He had never heard her
tell it personally; in fact, he had not heard her say any
English except, "Hello, Chief," "Thank you, Chief," or
"Goodbye, Chief."

"The soldiers here tell me you ride without fare. So,
get in, Old Grandmother."

"Thank you, Chief," she said.

He squinted in the sun and spit a long brown streak
of tobacco. "I heard a week or so ago President Johnson
was impeached," he called to her as he was rubbing
down the horses. "General Grant might be the next
President."

Sacajawea knew that Jefferson had been the name
of the Great White Father at one time. But she did not
know the name *Johnson* nor *impeached*, and so she tried
not to hear things she did not understand. The driver
came around to put away the baggage and help the
womenfolk into the coach. Sacajawea put a moccasined
foot on the step and was boosted. The stage had an
arched roof and a thin, brass railing around the outside.[2] Under the driver's seat was the treasure box,
which held tools, a water bucket, a dusty buffalo robe,
and mail pouches. On the back was a platform covered
with leather flaps. The driver tossed Sacajawea's case
on that platform along with the other grips and packages.

Sacajawea sat facing forward on one of two benches
inside. The seats had leather cushions and padded backs.
Between the seats was a leather strap fastened crosswise that could be used as an extra seat if necessary.

She nodded and smiled as the other passengers seated
themselves. Fort Hall was a two-day, one-night ride.
Each station was about twelve miles apart. At the swing
station the horses were changed; the home station was
larger and there the drivers were changed and the passengers had an opportunity to eat. No matter what time
of day the meals were about the same: bacon and eggs,
biscuits, tea, coffee, dried peaches, apples, and raisin
pies. Sacajawea carried several silver dollars tucked in
the bottom of the possibles bag that she had tied to her
belt.[3] The price for any meal was a dollar.

There was always the chance that Arapaho or Sioux
might attack a stage in this area, but there was also a

chance that the attack would come from robbers interested in the mail or packages of currency going from one bank to another. The miles of telegraph poles strung with lines, called "talking wires" by the Indians, and the miles of railroad tracks laid for the "iron horse" caused the Indians to hate the whites for intruding on hunting lands. The intruding whites feared the wrath of the local Indians.

Sacajawea closed her eyes. She looked forward to some time spent with her memories. One of the men sitting on the same seat with her said in a hushed tone to his companion in the seat opposite, "It's a wonder they permit Indians to ride on the stage. That squaw could attract Injun raiders."

"Oh no," said the other fellow wearing a tall top hat made of beaver fur. "I've seen her on here before." The man spoke in a normal tone as though they thought Sacajawea were hard of hearing or could not understand a word of English. "She's just some squaw that likes to visit relatives. She may be the wife of some important chief, because I hear she rides free. Her presence means a safe ride. No war party or horse raiders will be after this stage. And you can bet they know. They have a communication system that is uncanny. It's faster than the telegraph." Both men laughed knowingly.

Sacajawea gave no indication that she understood.

At the end of two days everyone was weary and very irritable. Sacajawea was glad to pick up her leather case and head down the road that led into the walled fort. Just outside the fort was a row of log cabins and in front of the cabins was the inevitable line of tepees. She grinned when dogs came out to bark and smell at her heels, but not follow her. The old trick of putting a dab of skunk urine on the back seam of her moccasins had worked. She hoped that Crying Basket and her family were still here. She counted three in from the west to make sure she was headed for the right one. She passed a cabin with a tin roof, home of the Chinese laundryman. The next had a large canvas tent attached to one side; this was the local hotel for itinerant miners who came to the fort. The mercantile or trading post was located inside the fort. She saw Little Joe swing off the porch of the third cabin and run to meet her. He wore leather boots instead of moccasins and he had on a cloth shirt.

"Granma, come in! We gots another baby. He looks terrible."

Sacajawea gave the five-year-old a hug and handed him her leather case. She almost forgot her stiff legs in the rush to get inside. From the open doorway she saw Crying Basket sitting on the floor holding a newborn. Berry, who had grown so pretty, was helping put bear's grease on the red, wrinkled body. The other little boy, also with boots instead of moccasins, stood beside his father, Joe Coiner. Joe had one foot resting on a packing crate, his arm around the boy. Smell of Sugar sat on another wooden crate. Suzanne was asleep on the rope-and-lath bed built into one corner. A red and green cotton comforter was under her chin. Dark circles were under her eyes. White man's pillows of blue strouding, stuffed with goose down, were pushed to one side.

"*Umbea!*" called Crying Basket as soon as she saw Sacajawea in the doorway. "We have a new boy! He arrived not so long ago."

"What is wrong with him?" she asked fearfully.

"Nothing. Come and see, sit down and hold him. I will pack and wrap him so he cannot wet you."

"But—Little Joe said he was terrible," she insisted.

"Mother, Little Joe is feeling left out. Besides, he wanted a brother at least as big as Jack. He does not remember they come little. He had one look and stuck his tongue out in disgust, saying that the baby was shriveled up like an old man with no teeth, weak legs, and no control over wetting and messing itself. He wanted to send it back."

Sacajawea chuckled and examined the papoose. It was well formed and had a head of thick, black hair and seemed far from being an old man. She was about to put the baby over her shoulder when she felt Little Joe nudge her thigh. "Wait till he wails. You'll have to hold your ears. I'm going to pinch his nose so he can't breath if he does it once more."

"You hold him." She pushed Little Joe down to the floor. "Hold him while I tell you about riding the stage and show what I have in my possibles for you." She opened up the little bag and suddenly the other little boy, called Jack, was there standing next to her. She gave Joe a biscuit. The other little boy held out grimy hands.

"Tell me which one of you is Jack and I'll tell you which is Joe," she said. The smaller child pointed toward his chest. "There." She gave him a biscuit also. Then she took the silver dollars out and shook the crumbs and dried fruit from the beaded pouch. She picked up the dried chips of peaches and passed them to Berry. "You are not too old for gifts."

"Grandmother, of course not. Tell us about the stage ride." Now the adults crowded around as she began to tell how it felt to ride on something that lurched back and forth and rumbled like thunder for two days and a night. She used her hands and facial expressions and frequently looked at Little Joe, who rocked his upper body back and forth so that the papoose slept in his care.

Joe Coiner smiled. He was as much at home among this adopted family of Suzanne's as he was with his own family. He was impressed with their easy ways and special concern with each other's feelings. He had seen how this grandmother had made his oldest son feel a part of the family once again, erasing sibling jealousy as if it had never been.

After a supper of boiled potatoes and jerky, Sacajawea took Crying Basket aside and scolded her for giving Suzanne meat. "It is not like the old times when there was no mistaking the rules and they were all kept." She clicked her tongue. "And so, I suppose these men and children were here while Suzanne moaned and bared her teeth and clenched her fists and pushed to pop out the papoose. Oh, my daughter, it is from bad to worse."

Crying Basket tried to explain that Suzanne took the white man's path and did not even go to a special birth lodge. The afterbirth was thrown out with the bloody wash water on the garbage heap and white lime was sprinkled on top to speed decay and hold off the stench.

"Pah, that should be buried or thrown in a creek and the cord wrapped in a soft cloth and hung in a tree or else wrapped and buried in the ground. The life of the new papoose will be short if the old ways are so completely ignored."

"Mother, none of the whites follow those ways and some live a long while."

"Well, there must be something else they do. Do not let Suzanne cut the new one's fingernails with anything metal. You bite them yourself, or I will, so his fingers will grow long and beautiful as his mother's."

Suzanne called to Sacajawea. "I heard what you said. I know we do not do everything alike, but you will always be a mother to me. I will bite his fingernails. I bite my own, see!" Suzanne pulled Sacajawea down laughing and hugged her.

"You also pick your nose," teased Sacajawea.

Suzanne sobered. "I have to tell you before I forget. Little Joe goes to school. One of the miner's women has a school for the little children when she comes in for supplies. Her man has the trading post at Miner's Delight and she gets the supplies from here about once a week. She spends part of the time talking and singing with the children. Little Joe goes each time, but Jack is too little to sit still that long. Before you leave promise me you'll ask Little Joe what he learned. It is something you should hear."

Sacajawea nodded. She would try to remember. Little Joe was curled up on the floor asleep beside the papoose, who was still wrapped as tight as he had been before supper.

Joe fixed her a corncob pipe with real tobacco. "It is better if the tobacco is pounded to shreds and mixed with crushed sumac leaves," she told Joe with a twinkle in her eye. "There was a time when white men smoking the brown-paper cigarettes irritated me. Maybe it was because I can almost remember the time when the People had little tobacco. Then I saw the Comanches trade for it with the Mexicans. They rolled cigarettes in leaves of catbrier vine because the Mexicans kept the paper for themselves. Now I've learned to enjoy a pipe in the evening. I think more things are changing than I would like to believe."

Joe smiled and puffed contentedly on his own pipe, and after a time said, "Buffalo are going. Beaver are about gone—maybe all the coal will be dug out of the earth one day. People have to change. I will bet you that more people ride the iron horse by the time I am your age than ride regular horseback now."

She smiled and took his hand. "And they will all become stiff-legged from not using them. I do not want to live to see that."

Four days and a dozen cups of snowberry tea later it was decided Suzanne could take care of the new papoose and the others all right. Sacajawea dallied over the morning meal and asked Berry to bring in water for the dishwashing. She went out to the trash heap and poked around with a stick. Finally she found what was left of the placenta and cord. She pushed the dried, black mess onto a small square of hide, folded it up, and with the stick she dug a shallow hole in the ground by the northeast corner of the cabin. She put the package in the hole and she scraped the dirt over with her foot, tamping it firm. Just as she finished Little Joe slammed the back door. He was dragging a stiff buffalo hide along the ground and he motioned for Sacajawea to come sit on the crackling hide with him. He lay on his belly and reached out in the dirt to draw a wide ring. "I'm going to show you how to play white man's marbles." His marbles were rounded plum pits.

"What did you bury by the house, Granma?"

"Oh, it wasn't anything. Just something the People did for long life years ago."

"Whose long life?"

"Your new brother's."

"Did you do something for mine?"

"*Ai*—I did. If we go inside Berry will have the hot water ready. Help your old grandmother wash bowls and cups. I'll tell you about a time before you were born."

Joe looked up from his marbles. "Oh, Granma, I gots to tell you something, but I cannot do woman's work." He put the plum pits in his pocket.

"Does your father help your mother, sometimes?"

"*Ai*." He said the word like Sacajawea did.

"Then, you can see it has not hurt him. Come in with me. I want to hear about this woman who tells you stories and has a school inside the fort each week."

"That is what I have to tell." The boy forgot about the marble game and went in behind her, slamming the door again. He waited until there were several bowls, cups, and saucers before he dried them on a clean, threadbare, old, cotton shirt. "You tell your story first," she urged the child.

"Well, there was a girl that went on a long hike with some men toward the setting sun. This girl put her baby on a backboard and took him. She made moccasins for the men and picked berries for their food."

Sacajawea had stopped washing. She watched the child, and when he hesitated, helped him along with his storytelling.

"Did they walk all the time?" she asked.

"No, they went in a canoe and on horseback."

"Was there a dog with them?"

"Granma! Don't make fun. This is a real live story."

"Where did they find horses?"

"The girl asked the chief for some. He was her brother. He was Shoshoni—like you." Little Joe looked at her through squinted eyes and she was half-afraid to hear more.

"The baby was named Pomp. The girl was named Sacajawea." He paused. "Granma, you told me about the big, black man, whose color would not rub off. Remember?"

"*Ai*, and did your teacher tell you what happened to the girl and her papoose?" She tried to express no emotion.

Little Joe looked at the floor where a line of ants had come in to carry away crumbs from under the wash-stand. Now she was afraid he would lose interest and not go on with the story.

"Captains Lewis and Clark were the leaders, the chiefs of that journey." She said her words slow and steady.

"I know that. The girl, she wandered away or went back to her people. The boy, Pomp, grew and went on other trips, even across the ocean and back. When he was older and in a place called Cally Forny he made a school for Indians. Did you know?"

"No." Her eyes were wide open.

"Then one day he and a friend went north to the gold

mines. Pomp really went to find news of his mother.
He got a sick fever in the mountains. He never got to
the Montana gold mines 'cause he died."

Sacajawea felt the tears. She could not hold them
back.

"The ending is sad. He did not find his mother either," whispered Little Joe. "You want to know what
Captain Clark called the baby?"

She nodded and wiped her face on the sleeve of the
dish towel.

"My Dancing Boy! Like you called me! It is your
story, Granma! I told Miss Ginny it was. She said my
tongue would turn black and fall out if I told lies. But
it is not a lie! Is it?"

"No." Sacajawea shook her head as she dried her
hands. She reached with both hands for the leather
string around her neck and pulled it over her head. For
a long time she looked at the silver peace medal swinging on the string. Little Joe stood close to her. She could
hear him breathing through his mouth. She wiped the
medal on the hem of her cotton skirt and held it up to
the light coming through the open back door.

The bucket of dirty dishwater cooled and congealed.

"That is a likeness of the Great White Father years
ago. And see the hands?" She held the medal so that
Little Joe could look. "That is the friendship sign. See,
I hold your hand in friendship." She clasped his right
hand in hers. "Look, there is a peace pipe and a war
ax. They are crossed for peace between the red man and
the white man."

Little Joe put his fingers on the medal. "Oh, Granma,
this is something plenty strong. How valuable is it?"

"Little Joe, here is proof your tongue is not forked
and will not turn black and fall out. Wear this and
people will know you are distinguished." She fingered
the small colored beads she had threaded on the buckskin thong. She tied a knot across a thin place. "Here
is the medal Sacajawea carried on the journey to the
Western Sea and back to her own people." She lowered
the string with the silver medal over Little Joe's head
until it rested on his chest. It looked good right there.
"You must not lose it. If you give it away, you give

away the story at the same time. They go together. Can
you remember?"

"*Ai*." Little Joe's eyes were wide. "I was right. You
are Sacajawea."

"You are right; you are the next generation to bring
peace between your race and mine."

She leaned against the wooden washstand and closed
her eyes. She thought it fitting for her white foster
grandchild to be the bond between herself and the
Shoshonis. He could be a bridge for understanding and
tolerance between the red and white men.

"What is your story, Granma?" The child's voice
brought her back from her visionary notion. She had
actually forgotten she had a story to tell. She threw the
cold dishwater on the scraggly bed of field daisies Suzanne had transplanted by the back steps, giving herself a moment to think.

"My own grandmother was a girl and camped in
Dinwoody canyon one winter. The buffalo and antelope
were gone because the snow was three squaws deep.
The People were starving and wanted others to know
they had lived and suffered. So, they carved a great
picture story on the steep side of a rock wall. The work
gave them something to look forward to each day. They
wanted their story to live after them. All those people
are now gone, but today you and I can read the story
of that bad winter in the canyon." She helped Little Joe
dry the pewter knives and forks and the work brought
a vivid memory of the little girl, Lizette—another story.

By midmorning Sacajawea was riding the packhorse,
with a bundle of well-tanned bear hides behind her.
"I'm glad I came to Fort Hall when I did," she said to
Crying Basket, "but the gait of this old packhorse is
even worse than the shaking and joggling of the stage.
I'll be bound-up four days after this trip."

Toussaint did not mention the Jefferson peace medal
again. He must have noticed she no longer wore it.
Maybe he thought she'd lost it. Maybe he looked through
her things on the sly and found nothing. Once he called
her a muddle-headed old squaw when she could not
remember where she left her little beaded bag with a
few silver dollars inside.

CHAPTER

56

I Could Cry All Night

Ann W. Hafen, Clyde H. Porter, and Irving W. Anderson have done remarkable, historical searches to trace the life of Sacajawea's son, Jean Baptiste Charbonneau. They found that for fifteen years, after returning to America from Germany in 1829, Jean Baptiste spent most of his time as a trapper and fur trader with people who were prominent in the early, western history of this country.

Jean Baptiste worked first for the American Fur Company, and was with the Robidoux Fur Brigade in Idaho and Utah in the fall of 1830. In 1831 he was traveling with Joe Meek, and also in 1831 he was with Jim Bridger, reading Shakespeare and Chaucer to him on long winter nights. He attended the great fur trade rendezvous on the bank of the Green River in 1833 and was a guide for Captain Nathaniel James Wyeth in 1834.[1] Thomas Jefferson Farnham wrote of meeting Jean Baptiste Charbonneau, the infant of the Lewis and Clark Expedition, in 1839 at Fort El Pueblo, five miles from Bent's Fort.[2] By the end of that year Jean Baptiste was trapping furs with a party that included Louis Vasquez and Andrew Sublette. During the winter the party was holed up in a camp near Fort Vasquez and Fort Davy Crockett, close to present-day Platteville, Colorado. Baptiste took a great deal of pride in telling stories he'd either heard from his famous mother, Sacajawea, or his notorious father, Charbonneau, about the Lewis and Clark Expedition. In the spring the party brought out seven

*hundred buffalo robes and four hundred smoked buffalo
tongues in a thirty-six-foot long, eight-foot wide boat,
traveling down the shallow Platte River and eventually
into St. Louis.*³

In 1842 Jean Baptiste was in charge of another party
boating fur down the South Platte. This particular spring
the river was too low for canoe travel, so the party had
to send out several men for packhorses and mule-drawn
carts. The remaining men stayed in camp on an island
not far from the present Fort Morgan, Colorado. John
C. Frémont visited the island camp and wrote about the
good wild mint julep Jean Baptiste made and the tasty
boiled buffalo tongue and coffee with the luxury of sugar
that was served him. He noted that Jean Baptiste was
the baby of the Lewis and Clark Expedition and had
been educated in St. Louis with funds from General
Clark. He wrote that Jean Baptiste called the island "St.
Helena."⁴

A month later Rufus B. Sage stopped at the island
camp and made a note in his journal about Jean Baptiste's extraordinary education, from St. Louis to Europe,
and the ease with which he spoke German, Spanish,
French, English, and several Indian languages. Not long
after that the packhorses and carts arrived, and the party
took the overland trek into St. Louis to sell several
hundred bales of furs.⁵

The records show that Jean Baptiste was next on his
way to the Rockies in the spring of 1843 with the Scots-
man, Sir William Drummond Stewart, and his party of
eighty men, all of whom were well equipped for sport
hunting. William Clark Kennerly, a nephew, and Jefferson Clark, a son of William Clark, were with this
expedition to the Yellowstone country. Jean Baptiste told
stories he'd heard as a child about the Lewis and Clark
Expedition. Jefferson Clark told stories he'd heard from
his celebrated father. The two boys formed a close friendship, bound partially by the fact that they shared the
same nickname, Pomp or Pompey. Jean Baptist was hired
as a cart driver and hunter for the Stewart outfit. The
carts were two-wheeled, the wheels made from one block
of wood. They had red covers and were drawn by two
mules traveling side by side. This sporting expedition

*took no more than four or five months and in August
Jean Baptiste was back in St. Louis.*[6]

A Mr. Francis Pensoneau wrote a promissory note to
Jean Baptiste: "I promise to pay to J. B. Charbonno the
sum of three hundred and twenty dollars as soon as I
dispose of land claimed by him said Charbonno from
the estate of his deceased father, St. Louis, August 14,
1843." On the back of this note Jean Baptiste wrote that
the money was to be paid to Mr. A. Sublette. This last
statement was dated August 17, 1843 and signed by
J. B. Charbonneau. The note is among the Sublette Papers in the archives of the Missouri Historical Society.

By the next year he was at Bent's Fort in the employ-
ment of William Bent and Céran St. Vrain. William M.
Boggs, son of Governor Lillburn W. Boggs of Missouri,
met him at Bent's Fort and wrote in his journal that
Jean Baptiste was the Indian papoose of the "elder Charbenau" that was hired by the Lewis and Clark Expedition when the party went from the Missouri River on
to the Pacific Ocean. He described Jean Baptiste as an
educated half-breed with long hair who was said to be
"the best man on foot in the plains or in the Rocky Mountains."[7]

During the spring of 1844 Jean Baptiste was with
Solomon Sublette and Céran St. Vrain capturing antelope and bighorn sheep alive to take to St. Louis and
ship to Sir William Drummond Stewart in Scotland.[8]

During 1845 Jean Baptiste and Tom Fitzpatrick were
on a War Department exploration with Lieutenant J. W.
Abert of the Topographical Engineers, traveling south
from Bent's Fort down the Canadian River.[9] An English
writer and sportsman hunter from Her Majesty's 89th
Regiment, Lieutenant George F. Ruxton, camped with
Abert's party a few nights. Ruxton was most impressed
with the story that Jean Baptiste had been carried halfway across the continent on his mother's back. He wrote
that he was also impressed that Jean Baptiste "sat with
Bill Gary in camp for twenty hours at a deck of Euker."[10]

In 1846 Jean Baptiste enlisted as a guide for the Mormon Battalion under the command of Colonel Philip St.
George Cook. The Battalion traveled from Santa Fe to
San Diego, breaking new roads for their wagons across
seven hundred miles of mountains and plateaus.

During the last week of November 1846, Colonel Cook moved the battalion of five hundred men through a mountain pass. Jean Baptiste was the one who rode ahead to look for water and game and point out the navigable passes. On November 29, Cooke wrote: "I discovered Charbonneaux near the summit in pursuit of bears. I saw three of them up among the rocks, whilst the bold hunter was gradually nearing them. Soon he fired, and in ten seconds again; then there was confused action, one bear falling down, the others rushing about with loud fierce cries, amid which the hunter's too could be distinguished; the mountain fairly echoed. I much feared he was lost, but soon, in his red shirt, he appeared on a rock; he had cried out, in Spanish, for more balls. The bear was rolled down, and butchered before the wagons passed."[11]

Colonel Cooke, more than a year later, wrote in his journal, on January 11, 1847: "I found here on the high bank above the well, stuck on a pole, a note, 'No water, January 2—Charbonneaux.'"[12]

The Mormon Battalion arrived in San Diego in January, 1847. A few days later General Stephen Watts Kearny, who had Kit Carson as his civilian guide, bivouacked his "Army of the West" beside Colonel Cooke's Battalion. These camps were near the Indian community of the San Luis Rey Mission, north of San Diego.[13]

The U.S. soldiers become acquainted with the Luisena and Digger Indians that had lived at or near the mission since the Spanish occupation in 1795. These Indians were coerced into serving as slaves for the Spanish and built the first adobe buildings of the mission. By 1822 the Franciscans were in charge of the mission. The Padres encouraged the Indian men to continue raising grain, grapes, figs, olives, and oranges, tending thousands of head of cattle, sheep, along with goats, pigs, horses, and mules. All the food and livestock raised belonged to the Franciscans. The Indian women were encouraged to weave the wool, use dyes, and sew for the mission personnel. They were so adept at pottery making that most of their products were used in the kitchens of the mission. The Indians were not abused by the Franciscans as they were under the Spanish, but they still often went hungry and died young of pneumonia and tuberculosis. In exchange for their hard labor, they were closely disciplined into a submissive mode of behavior. The Padres baptized them, married them, and buried them.[14]

Suddenly in 1826 the Indians were proclaimed Mexican citizens. As such, they had no obligations to the Franciscans. They were given title to small plots of land, but they floundered and were not able to live as a group without an authority figure. There were no leaders among the Indians because such assertiveness had been drilled out during all the years of being slaves to the Spanish and subservient to the Padres. The Indians had become lazy and fought among themselves, using their meager Spanish reals to buy whiskey.

The Indians were even more perplexed when the U.S. military took over the mission in 1846. At first the soldiers looked down on these sickly, destitute people. However, they were given medical treatment whenever they asked for it. Gradually the Indian men began working around the army camp—feeding, watering, and caring for the horses and livestock. Then some worked in the fields and orchards. The women worked as housekeepers, cooks, laundresses, and seamstresses. All the Indian workers were paid for their labors in cash or in livestock or other foodstuffs. This was dignified treatment they had never experienced before. The old people appreciated this unusual freedom and security and began to practice traditional customs and hold religious festivities. The young people mixed the old ways with the Christianity they had learned from the Franciscans.

Jean Baptiste understood these people. The poor Digger Indians were related in language and cultural practices with the Shoshoni, so that he could talk with them, and through the Diggers he was able to communicate with the Luisena people. He understood their need for tribal cohesiveness and a sense of identity. He began a school for the children. In November of 1847 Jean Baptiste was given a release from his civilian guide obligation to the military so that he could take an appointment as Alcalde at the San Luis Rey Mission. This meant that he acted as a kind of mayor, justice of the peace, and magistrate for the Indian community. At the same time, a friend of Jean Baptiste's, Captain Hunter, was ap-

*pointed by Kearny to be the Sub-Indian Agent for this
Southern District. Jean Baptiste and Captain Hunter
worked well together on behalf of the Indians.*

Another year went by, and Jean Baptiste was more
than content with the work he was doing in his school
and with the Indian people. He was certain he was bringing about a healthy understanding between the Indians
and the soldiers. Thus, he was taken completely by surprise when he learned that he was implicated with an
Indian rebellion. It was a false accusation. He had no
previous knowledge of unrest at the Mission of San Luis
Rey. Nonetheless, he was forced to resign.[15]

Porter wrote that Baptiste resigned as Alcalde "because of white dissatisfaction arising from his policy of
treating the Indians too kindly."[16]

As the Alcalde, Jean Baptiste wrote an order on April
24th, 1848, which stated that "a fair settlement" for an
account of $51.37½, owed by an Indian to the general
store and dram shop owner, Don Jose Aut. Pico, could
be worked off at the rate of 12½ cents a day.[17]

Anderson pointed out that this also may have been a
reason for Jean Baptiste's resignation. Jean Baptiste was
obligated to sentence these people to slavery if they worked
for only 12½ cents a day to pay a debt, since the debt
became greater all the time if there was a wife and children to support. A man like Jean Baptiste, with integrity,
high principles, and moral convictions, would resign.[18]

On July 24, 1848, the Civil Governor of California,
Richard B. Mason, received a report from Colonel J. D.
Stevenson, who was Commander of the South Military
District. The report stated that Jean Baptiste Charbon-
neau had nothing to do with the planned uprising, but
being "a half-breed Indian of the U.S. is regarded by
the people as favoring the Indians more than he should
do, and hence there is much complaint against him."
Stevenson went on to suggest that the expenses of Jean
Baptiste's office be paid from the Civil Fund because
"Alcaldes are not paid." Jean Baptiste's friend, Captain
Hunter, put in his resignation at this time. He was given
a six months' leave of absence.[19]

Jean Baptiste and Captain Hunter went prospecting
for gold together in the Sacramento Valley. Jim Beckwourth and Tom Buckner found the two on the banks

*of the Middle Fork of the American River, a place known
as Murderer's Bar, panning for gold.*[20]

*The 1860 U.S. Census of Placer County, California,
listed: J. B. Charbonneau, male, age 57, born in Missouri, P.O., Secret Ravine. Secret Ravine was ten miles
from the town of Auburn, California. In 1861 the Di-
rectory of Placer County listed a John B. Charbonneau
as a clerk in the Orleans Hotel, at Auburn.*

*Five years later on the editorial page of the Placer
Herald, Auburn, California, for July 7, 1866 was the
following article:*

*J. B. Charbonneau—Death of a California Pi-
oneer.*—We are informed by Mr. Dana Perkins, that
he has received a letter announcing the death of J. B.
Charbonneau, who left this country some weeks ago,
with two companions, for Montana Territory. The
letter is from one of the party, who says Mr. C. was
taken sick with mountain fever, on the Owyhee, and
died after a short illness.

Mr. Charbonneau was known to most of the pioneer citizens of this region of country, being himself
one of the first adventurers (into the territory now
known as Placer County) upon the discovery of gold;
where he has remained with little intermission until
his recent departure for the new gold field, Montana,
which, strangely enough, was the land of his birth,
whither he was returning in the evening of life, to
spend the few remaining days that he felt was in
store for him.

Mr. Charbonneau was born in the western wilds,
and grew up a hunter, trapper, and pioneer, among
that class of men of which Bridger, Beckwourth, and
other noted trappers of the woods were the representatives. He was born in the country of the Crow
Indians—his father being a Canadian Frenchman,
and his mother a half breed of the Crow tribe. He
had, however, better opportunities than most of the
rough spirits, who followed the calling of trapper, as
when a young man he went to Europe and spent
several years, where he learned to speak, as well as
write several languages. At the breaking out of the

Mexican War he was on the frontiers, and upon the organization of the Mormon Battalion he was engaged as a guide and came with them to California.

Subsequently upon the discovery of gold, he, in company with Jim Beckwourth, came upon the North Fork of the American River, and for a time it is said were mining partners.

Our acquaintance with Charbonneau dates back to '52, when we found him a resident of this county, where he has continued to reside almost continuously since—having given up frontier life. The reported discoveries of gold in Montana, and the rapid peopling of the Territory excited the imagination of the old trapper, and he determined to return to the scenes of his youth. Though strong of purpose, the weight of years was too much for the hardships of the trip undertaken, and he now sleeps alone by the bright waters of the Owyhee.

Our information is very meager of the history of the deceased—a fact we much regret, as he was of a class that for years lived among stirring and eventful scenes.

The old man, on departing for Montana, gave us a call, and said he was going to leave California, probably for good, as he was about returning to familiar scenes. We felt then as if we met him for the last time.

Mr. Charbonneau was of pleasant manners, intelligent, well read in the topics of the day, and was generally esteemed in the community in which he lived, as a good meaning and inoffensive man."

A report of Jean Baptiste's death also appeared in the Butte Record *of Oroville, California, July 14, 1866. The* Owyhee Avalanche *in Ruby City, Idaho, June 2, 1866, stated:*

Died.—We have received a note (don't know who from) dated May 16, '66, requesting the publication of the following:

At Inskip's Ranche, Cow Creek, in Jordan Valley, J. B. Charbonneau aged sixty-three years—of pneumonia. Was born at St. Louis, Mo.; one of the oldest trappers and pioneers; he piloted the Mormon Brigade through the Lower Mexico in '46; came to California in '49, and has resided since that time mostly in Placer County; was en route to Montana."

Reprinted by permission of the publishers, The Arthur H. Clark Company, from *The Mountain Men and the Fur Trade of the Far West*, edited by LeRoy R. Hafen, with "Jean Baptiste Charbonneau," by Ann W. Hafen, Vol. I, 1965, p. 205.

Gertrude Inskeep Ropp of Yakima, Washington, pointed out in 1980 that the Inskeep (Inskip) Stage Station, the old Ruby Ranch and home, is located at the mouth of Cow Creek and Jordan Creek, near Danner, Oregon. Mrs. Ropp's grandfather, Oliver Wilton Inskeep, owned the Stage Station, ranch, and home in Jordan Valley. Even today there are wagon wheel marks where the original toll road ran from Ruby City, Idaho, to Winnemucca, Nevada. Danner, which used to be called Ruby City, is three miles north of U.S. 95 and fifteen miles west of Jordan Valley, Malheur County, Oregon.[21]
In 1966 Chris Moore wrote:

Local legends tell of a half breed, presumably Charbonneau, and two soldiers and two children being buried there, all before the turn of the century. ...Probably Charbonneau's grave is the earliest of the five as the station was established in 1865....It was rescued from complete oblivion several years ago by S. K. Skinner, a Jordan Valley rancher, who stopped a county roadgrader as it was plowing into the west end of the graves. He and his wife have done considerable research locating Charbonneau's grave and hope to see it suitably marked and protected before it is completely obliterated.[22]

The Danner burial ground lies next to the Inskip Station fortification, stagecoach stables, rock corrals, and a rock-enclosed well.[23]
There was a wooden marker, put in place by local schoolchildren, indicating the grave believed to be Jean Baptiste Charbonneau's. It was carved with the words:

"Charbonneau—RIP—Baptiste, Son of Sacajawea 1805–66." Nearby was another large sign erected by the Jordan Valley, Oregon, Commercial Club. This wooden marker read:

Grave of Jean Baptiste Charbonneau, February 11, 1805
Born to Sacajawea and Toussaint Charbonneau
Interpreters for the Lewis and Clark Expedition.
Guide, Trapper, Miner, World Traveler, Scholar, and Politician.
In the Spring of 1866 he set out for the mines of Montana,
contracted pneumonia and died here,
Inskip's Ranch, May 16, 1866.

J. V. Commercial Club[24]

On August 17, 1971, a large wooden board became the Jean Baptiste Charbonneau Monument and Marker. William Clark Adreon of St. Louis, the great, great grandson of William Clark, was the dedication speaker on this Inskip site. The legend on the marker is:

Oregon History
Jean Baptiste Charbonneau
1805–1866

This site marks the final resting place of the youngest member of the Lewis and Clark Expedition. Born to Sacajawea and Toussaint Charbonneau at Fort Mandan (North Dakota) on February 11, 1805. Baptiste and his mother symbolized the peaceful nature of the "Corps of Discovery." Educated by Captain William Clark at St. Louis, Baptiste at age 18, traveled to Europe where he spent six years, becoming fluent in English, German, French and Spanish. Returning to America in 1829. He ranged the far west for nearly four decades, as mountain man, guide, interpreter, magistrate and forty-niner. In 1866, he left the California gold fields for a new strike in Montana, contracted pneumonia enroute, reached "Inskip's Ranche," here, and died on May 16, 1866.[25]

Sacajawea was more than seventy-five winters. Her skin was dark, dry, and wrinkled. She seemed shapeless beneath her smoke-stained leather tunic. She was like the shale behind her tepee, the thinly stratified structure eroded by weather and pushed earthward with slumping. The many snows weighed heavily on her back, and when she walked, she was like a three-legged horse, pushing along first with her burled cedar stick to steady her thin legs, all bone and hide.

She visited from one tepee to another, from one village to another, and inside Fort Bridger. She gossiped with Shoshoni women, Bannock women, once in a while with an Arapaho woman who did not recognize her as an enemy. The women exchanged wit and wisdom. She was known by all. Many a frantic mother came to her tepee flap in the dark of the night begging for some healing herb or ointment for a sick child. Chief Washakie came to smoke silently with her and consult on important matters, such as the white men building roads into the Shoshoni land or what to do with the Shoshoni men who hunted the white men's cattle as if they were buffalo in the valley.

Often she sat in silence on a grassy spot in the red shale behind the village. She mulled over the words spoken by her gray-eyed foster grandchild in Fort Hall. "Pomp really went to find news of his mother. He got a sick fever in the mountains....He died." In the fading evening light she looked at the sixty-some lodges of her people. They were beautiful white cones, some with colorful paintings on the outside, others plain so that the fine stitching could be admired. She tried to recall what her firstborn had looked like. Sometimes tears rolled down her wrinkled cheeks. I could cry all night, but it does not help brighten my faded memory of my Dancing Boy, Pomp, Jean Baptiste, my first son.

What was he during his lifetime? She knew he had traveled and worked for the white men. She knew that the white men respected him as a leader. She was satisfied he had withstood the ebb and flow of the seasons, the sullen hostility of man, the anesthesia of the white

man's religion and wealth—all the passions that warp
the mind, flesh, and spirit of man. She had given him
a good beginning. She no longer sought him with every
passing white-top wagon, and she forgot to ask travelers if they had heard his name.

She seemed to withdraw inside herself a little, and
so to make herself immune from all but the ultimate
destruction of her nonessential outer shell.

Late one afternoon during the annual midwinter thaw
as Sacajawea built up her cook fire, she noticed Toussaint sitting outside her doorway on the damp ground.
When she went out to speak to him she saw that he
had been drinking. He wore government-issue clothing
and appeared half-comical, half-tragic in black, shoddy
pants made for someone weighing at least two hundred
pounds. The seat was cut out, revealing the back flap
of his breechclout and the tail of his red flannel shirt.
The sleeves were cut off his large black coat, converting
it into a vest.

"I came to tell you that Washakie is getting senile,"
said Toussaint. "He wants to move the whole camp back
to the Carter Station and let the white men show us
how to run water in a ditch to irrigate the wheat." He
lurched a couple of steps sideways, then sat down cross-
legged in front of the lodge.

"I have heard some talk about this," she said. "Is
that what you came to say?" She was surprised he would
bring her this old news. She thought everyone was ready
to go.

"Well—you know what happens when water goes
into a ditch and fills up the gopher holes. The gopher
comes out, looks at us, and we die."[26]

"Are you asking me to talk with Washakie about
this?"

"Yes, do it right away. I do not want to plow up land
to grow grain." He hiccoughed. "That is hard work. So,
then I do not want to die."

"You are a disgrace," she said, watching him carefully. "You fortify yourself with the white man's firewater before you have nerve to talk with your mother.
Is that being a man?"

He laughed at her. "It is true I traded a buffalo hide
for a little whiskey. The bottom of the bottle was filled

with hard buffalo tallow and I suspect that white trader diluted the whiskey with water and colored it with tobacco juice. So you see I did not have so much that you could accuse me of being drunk. Ha! Tee-hee! That was no buffalo hide the white son of a bitch got off me. That was a damn cowhide and he didn't know the difference!" He had to hold his sides he laughed so hard.

Some children chasing dogs around heard him and came to see what the joke was. They hung back in the drifted snowbank beside the leafless cottonwood trees.

"If you will not talk to the chief, maybe you will see Jakie Moore at the post store," said Toussaint. "He's white, but he's a friend of mine. You get him to persuade that confused old man that the braves of his band do not want to be farmers. You tell Jakie to tell Chief Weasel Guts Washakie his warriors can race horses or go on a buffalo hunt and do a better job than farming."

"Everyone knows you do not approve of Washakie. Why do you ask me to speak for you? I know there is no buffalo left to hunt. Some in the band are hungry because of that."

"Oh, I am hungry. The white man's firewater makes me hungry. My good mother, do you have something delicious in your kettle?"

"Not for you!" she cried. "I have told you that there is no welcome here for you. Go, or I will break your brittle bones."

Toussaint laughed, "Tee-hee!" He threw his arms around his head and looked foolish. The children by the cottonwood laughed out loud at his antics.

Sacajawea went inside her lodge and built up the fire again. She opened the tepee flap, but did not invite Toussaint inside. She sat close to the fire, her eyes half-closed. After a few moments she called to Toussaint. "Hey! *Ai!* You who calls yourself my son! Listen, I know Jean Baptiste is not living. My true son is dead." She fumbled for her tobacco pouch at her waist, filled and lit her pipe from a stick in the fire, and drew a few deep puffs.

Toussaint roused himself out of his drunkenness. "That is not a certainty. You should not repeat that." He got up and began to stumble around the outside of the lodge, slashing at it with his hunting knife.[27]

She called to him, "Stop that! If you sit I will give you coffee with plenty of sugar." She added another fistful of crushed coffee beans to a blackened lard bucket of day-old coffee already warming beside the fire.

He poked his head in the doorway. "That does smell good, old mother. I'll stay. But if you say or breathe one word about my half-breed stepbrother, I will bury an arrowhead in your back."

She looked at him with sad, soft eyes, turned her back to him and got an empty tin cup. She rummaged around under her bed to find a small bottle of laudanum that had been given to her by Jakie Moore to ease the old, dull ache in her arthritic knees. She upended the bottle in the cup, covered the bottom with sugar from a hard leather box, and poured in coffee. The mixture was stirred with an old, bent spoon.

Toussaint found the cup handle too hot, and he pulled out his red shirt tail to wrap around it. He blew on the coffee to cool it, then tasted carefully and smacked his lips. "You know how to make coffee, with lots of sugar."

She grunted and made herself sit quietly. When she felt it was time, she looked. He was lying on the wet ground, snoring. Sacajawea yelled to the children. "Go home and tell your fathers to come here. You can see this man needs to be taken to his lodge. He is very tired. Go!"

They scampered away. She closed her tepee flap and quietly prepared her supper of thin vegetable stew. In the middle of the meal she heard the men come. At first they tried to waken Toussaint. Someone said, "He will be a red-eye by morning. I smell the bay rum, you know—like in hair tonic." Someone else said, "That lousy stuff makes me cough up my insides. I drink it for the kick it has and get the Devil inside my belly." Another said, "We can drag him to his lodge. It's a pity the son of Chief Woman lets firewater rule him." The first voice agreed, "*Ai*, and the dog drinks anything. He ought to share something good with us for lugging him home so he will not freeze in the night." Finally they were too far away for her to hear them talking.

Sacajawea packed her belongings and struck her tepee. She was ready when the band moved to another camp. Some were afraid to cross the iron road of the Union Pacific Railroad. They thought the horses were also afraid, but one by one they crossed it on the run. They hid when the great iron horse went by, snorting smoke and pulling many big wagons.

She watched her people during this year of scant meat and heard them go out on frosty mornings hunting for game; anything, even a white man's stray cow, would taste good. It all went on outside her as it went on in memory inside, changing but changeless, and so a kind of illusion. What stood out was the common core. It was this reality she pondered.

Wind and snow matted her straggly hair. Sun and frost made leather of her cheeks and hands. Her eyes took on a remoteness. At times her steady gaze seemed turned inward—as if it had gone around the earth and returned.

Sometimes her meditations were interrupted. She had gone long to her people and neighbors; now they came to her.

"Chief Woman," a mother would say, respectfully standing before her. "Forgive this interruption, but many are sick with the fever and there is talk about the spotted sickness. It has come to some of the northern camps."

"Did you see the white medicine man at Augur's camp?"

"Oh, no! Old Puffbelly, our Shaman, came and put dried buffalo dung around the eyes of my children who were ill."

"They are better?"

"*Ai*, but I fear they will get the spotted sickness, for they are weak."

Sacajawea grunted. "And he carried a buffalo skull and danced from left to right, which is the sacred manner, stopping to face the place where the sun comes up?"

"*Ai*."

"Go to the Blanket Chief. He has a new way to keep your children well. If he has no time for talk, see his woman, Rutta. Tell her I sent you."

"Porivo is strange and wise," her own people said of

her. "Even Chief Washakie consults with her on matters his mind is forked on."

She gave advice on all matters whenever consulted.

Jim Bridger came to the village. He rode in a rattletrap wagon pulled by two piebalds across the white, trackless road. The snow was deep and heaped along the creeks. He came with flour and dried beef. He told the Shoshonis and Bannocks to drink much water with the beef and soon the fever would be washed away.

He was the guest of Chief Washakie, who confided in Bridger that he was now anxious for his people to remain on a reservation and farm. The children should learn at the school. He realized game was scarce and his people would have to find another way to have full bellies, and the only way left was to join with the white men. Change was coming. It was better not to fight something that could not be stopped. For he was wise and knew that there were ten or twelve white men for every native, and never could these strangers be wiped out. It was far better to try to live with them and understand their thoughts.

Bridger bent his six-foot frame over the chief and clapped him on the shoulder. Bridger's cheekbones were high and his nose hooked, giving him the facial appearance of a hawk. If he had been shorter, he could easily have passed for one of Washakie's old warriors.

Washakie was taller and lighter complexioned than most Shoshonis. He resembled his Flathead father, Paseego. That morning he wore his government-issue, high crown, puritanical black hat with the wide brim. On the hat he wore a prized possession, a silver casket plate which read, "Our Baby."[28] He also wore another favorite ornament, a translucent pink seashell, as his kerchief holder. On the left side of his large nose was a deep scar left by a penetrating Blackfoot arrow. Two thick, graying braids hung over his bare chest.[29]

"I'm not young now," said Washakie, cocking his head to one side. "It used to be I spent much time and energy trying to get things done that don't really seem so worthwhile now. But this change is something the white men are bringing, and it will defeat us if we spend time and energy fighting it. The Shoshonis would be wiped out. I do not want my people wiped out. I want them to stay and see what is going to happen on the bosom of our Mother Earth. The young ones will learn the new ways easier than you and I. You ancient bastard," he added in English, giving Bridger a crooked grin.

"Yep," said Bridger, "even the Sioux and Cheyennes will give in."

Bridger was shrewd. After he completed his talk with Washakie, the two smoked awhile, then he called for a council—not a council with the important men of the camp, but with the women. He began with his own woman, Rutta, and Sacajawea, taking them with him around the camp as he called out the other women. He spoke to them softly about their recent illness and about their children who still had the fever. He then led them slowly to the idea that the spotted sickness could come to any one of them in an unsuspecting time if they had just been sick or fighting off the pangs of hunger.

Next he bribed the post physician at Camp Augur to give cowpox serum. The man refused, but only at first.

"Well, then," said Bridger, his broad face beaded with perspiration, "you go and explain to a couple hundred savages why they ought to have their arm scratched to prevent scarifying their faces. Smallpox is goin' through Injun camps like dried prunes through the soldiers. Think of the little brown children, not knowin' what ails 'em, or the same with old folks, so they wander alone out in the field grass."

The post physician had no interest in Indians and their general health, but he cared even less to spend a day among them, or to have them spread smallpox to one another and die like bloated cows in a peyote patch so that he and other soldiers had to bury them after the rest had fled trying to outrun the sickness.

Few of the squaws understood what Bridger was talking about, but they knew the dreaded spotted sickness. They could not see how scratching an arm could ward off the disease. Protestations, pleas, tears—nothing availed against the Blanket Chief. With a set, stern face, he sent out Sacajawea to explain to the People.

"*Ai*, it is something good," Sacajawea explained, memory flooding back to the time Chief Red Hair had scratched her leg and even the leg of her baby, Pomp. "See the scar?" She pulled up her tunic hem. "It is like a badge to scare off the sickness. I have been with those who are sick, but I remain well. See, I have no face scars." She bent her face around the circle of women. Some put their hands on her juiceless, wrinkled skin. "When the smoke whirls around inside your tepee, as if afraid to go outside in winter wind, the sickness will pass over you and your children."

The women returned to Bridger and formed a line, pushing their children forward so they could be scratched first. Some were yet weak from the fever, and some coughed or wiped their runny noses on the backs of their hands.

"Ai," the women told Bridger, "Chief Woman is wise. The sickness could come to any of us. The scratch is small, but important. Our men will come for the scratch also."

Rutta showed where she was scratched. Washakie's women and all twelve of his children submitted to the vaccination. Toussaint and his two women stayed behind. They would not admit that the white man's medicines were of any value. Their grandchildren, however, were among the two hundred that Bridger vaccinated that day.

During this time, the white men in Washington, D.C., were busy assigning new names to old posts and establishing new posts in the west. On March 28, 1870, Camp Augur was renamed Camp Brown in honor of Captain Frederick Brown, one of the victims of the Fetterman Fight. That summer, Camp Brown was made independent from Fort Bridger, and remained on the Popo Agie until the next year, when it was moved into the Wind River Reservation and renamed Fort Washakie.

Chief Washakie took his people to Utah, where many were washed or baptized by the Mormons. Lance, the son of Shoogan (earlier given the name Bazil by the Mormons), was given the new name Andrew Bazil. Little Red Eyes was named Eli Bazil. Their young sister, Stay Home, was renamed Nancy Bazil. The daughter of Toussaint and Contrary Woman, Yelling Falls, was renamed Barbara Baptiste, because earlier the Mormons had given her father the name Baptiste. One of Chief Washakie's sons was named Dick, another Charley, another George, and a fourth Bishop Washakie.

This renaming was acceptable. The Shoshonis often were renamed by their family or friends according to some deed or mishap that came their way. Sacajawea sat beside her small fire, nodding in approval, as Andrew Bazil told her all the new names. After all, she had worn out several names herself.

"There is no strength in this meat," she remarked one fall morning, stirring her kettle. "A fat buffalo cow— that is meat, and so tender even I could chew it with these few teeth."

"When spring comes," said Andrew in English, "we will put seeds in the earth and have corn and squash. That might taste good to you. Better than this stringy beef cow."

She was suddenly thoughtful. "Even an old horse would taste better." Andrew smiled, then laughed. He wore a white man's shirt and trousers and hard shoes; his unbraided hair hung to his shoulders.

"Grandmother," said Andrew, sobering, "do you know a man called Brunot, Felix Brunot?"

Sacajawea shrugged.

"I think he came from Saint Louis."

"Oh." Her eyes lit up and she sucked in her cheeks, making hollows. Then a sadness came into her face and she was silent.

"Maybe he comes from Washington," said Andrew. "We could mosey over to the post and see what he talks to our chief about."

She followed behind. The grass was brittle and dry on the red soil. Dozens of yellow-winged grasshoppers flew up in front of them, their wings whirring, their jumping legs popping. Sacajawea had no trouble keeping up. Her cedar stick cane tapped out little dust puffs where the grass was thin. She never shrank from walking, although her bowlegs seemed better for hugging the sides of a horse. She looked short and squat. Andrew's legs were straight and he looked tall. However, he did not like to walk and much preferred traveling by horse.

"Look at this parched grass! I suppose it is green and tender on the other side of the mountain." Sacajawea chuckled.

Felix Brunot, chairman of the Board of Indian Commissioners, was sent to buy the title to the land occupied by Miner's Delight and to clear title to certain land that had been taken up by white settlers prior to the Fort Bridger treaty.

Despite the hot fall morning, Brunot wore a coat over his white shirt. His trousers matched the blue of the coat, and his heavy black shoes wore a thick coat of yellow dust. He stood on the wooden porch of the agent's new house. Some of Washakie's subchiefs stood beside the chief on the steps. Among them was Shoogan, or Bazil, Andrew's father.

There were twenty-four square log houses a story and a half high, built for the Shoshonis by the Great White Father in Washington. Few of the houses were really occupied. The house nearest the agent's was given to Shoogan and his family because he was able to interpret and use fairly good English. Toussaint, generally called Baptiste, lived farther down the street. Several hundred yards away were tepees scattered along a running stream. The older Indians preferred them to the one-room cabins, which were too close together and too much side by side for their liking.

Sacajawea's old patched tepee was down beside the creek. At times when the winter was its bitterest, she stayed in the log house with Shoogan and his children and grandchildren.

Farther down the stream was another square wood house and a plank barn. That was the home of the boss farmer, Finn Burnett. Farther away, beside a crooked rail fence, was the cabin of James Patten, the reservation teacher.

Back beside the agency offices and home of the agent was the Moore store and the church.

It was a fine autumn morning. Brunot cleared his throat and twisted the end of his mustache. He had blue eyes, fair skin, and a sharp tongue, which lurked behind a perpetual smile. He had little regard for the welfare of the Indians, and had maneuvered Washakie into agreeing to give up some of his best land. In trade, land, and argument, Brunot was shrewd.

Sacajawea felt uneasy watching him. Something did not set right with her, as if she had eaten spoiled fish. She thought about this man. He had power. Yet, she thought, all men are like brothers. Each has the same lusts, thirsts, hungers. The desire for land is common to all. The white men have it, and so do I. Man is but his land. It rises to shelter him in life and holds him in death. By eating its game, seeds, and roots, he builds his flesh into walls of his own land. He has its hardness or its softness. So—I know my own land, and I want it, and that is right. Does not a baby cry for his mother's breast? But when this white man desires my land, it is not right. It is bad. For he would not belong to it. So, then—I suspect this man.

Sacajawea listened, sitting in the shade with her grandson beside her, and remained silent but watchful.

Fingering his mustache, Brunot stepped directly in front of Chief Washakie. "President Grant appreciates all the fine deeds Washakie has performed to help the white men and knows he has saved the lives of many innocent women and children in the early days of the Oregon Trail. This Great Father in Washington knows that you have helped to educate the Shoshonis in their farming and by sending your grandchildren to the mission school. Take, then, this saddle, Washakie, as a gift from one of your admirers."

This was a surprise. No word was spoken by the old chief, who stood up straight and tall, arms folded.

"What word shall I take back to your Great White Father?" asked Brunot, placing the saddle in the chief's arm.

"Nothing," said Chief Washakie. "I cannot speak. My heart is so full my tongue will not work."

"Try to say a few words," urged Brunot, "so that President Grant may know how pleased you are."

The chief was thoughtful. No one spoke. Then he held his head high and spoke slowly, "When a favor is shown a white man, he feels it in his head and his tongue speaks. When a kindness is shown to an Indian, he feels it in his heart. The heart has no tongue."[30]

The saddle had bright silver mountings, red, blue,

and yellow ribbons. There was much applauding and
stamping of feet. "Fine thing," the Shoshonis said to
each other. "Fine thing."

The Shoshonis received cattle for the land they had
ceded to the government—601,120 acres, or all of their
reservation south of the North Fork of the Big Popo
Agie.

Cattle have some virtues, no doubt, thought Sacajawea. There are no large buffalo herds left, and the
Shoshoni are not good farmers—their corn crop is small.
Now with a big herd of cattle and the promise of more
government money to buy cattle each year, there will
be no hunger pains or starvation deaths among the
Lemhis. There will be milk for the children. The white
teacher, Mr. Patten, said it makes them grow strong.
But what a taste! A child had to be strong to drink that!

This white man says he is a brother to the Shoshonis,
she thought. He says, "Just put your mark on this paper
to show that you will not forget what we have agreed
upon." And then the white man very quickly takes away
Shoshoni land. *Whoosht!*

Wagh! Can one believe a man who says he loves his
family, when he allows them no room to ride their horse?
Can a man love his land, and then build iron roads
through cornfields?

Sacajawea was no fool. She realized there is no love
of abstract humanity. There is only the love we show
each man as an individual.

So several weeks later, Sacajawea questioned Colonel Lander's intent to benefit the Shoshonis when he
negotiated a treaty with Chief Washakie for a right-of-
way through the country owned by the Shoshonis. The
road would extend westward from the Sweetwater to
Fort Hall. She questioned Lander so much that he finally made certain that the Shoshonis were paid for
this right-of-way in horses, rifles, ammunition, blankets, and some trinkets Washakie wanted.

Winter passed quietly, and spring came to the land.
Sacajawea pulled her red blanket closer around her
shoulders; the spring air still had a winter chill. She
smoked her pipe with Chief Washakie. "Why is it the
white men are always in a hurry?" she asked. "It is not
good." Then for a time she seemed unconscious of Wa-

shakie sitting inside her tepee. She seemed to be studying the ground. "It is bad!" she whispered.

"Chief Woman, what is bad?" asked Washakie.

"Old people have strange dreams. But after I was
stolen from the People as a child, I had plenty of dreams.
More than once I saw bearded men come from the sunrise. The buffalo changed to bones on the prairie and
the People starved. Their bones were beside the buffalo's. Next the face of Mother Earth was scarred and
the bearded men made odd, square houses from many
lodgepoles."

"*Ai*, it is so," sighed Washakie.

"*Ai*, we have seen it. I did not know what it meant
when I was a child. I have not thought of it since. It
was especially my own grandmother who had these
mysterious dreams. I do not like the square wooden
house to live in. Yet, would you believe that long ago
in a white village I lived in one and was happy for a
time? Things change, then come back to their beginnings. Like the circle of the sun and moon, the sky, the
bodies of men and animals, nests of birds, the days and
seasons—all come back in a circle. The young grow old,
and from the old the young begin and grow. It is the
Great Spirit's way," she sighed.

"My adopted son in the gray wooden house is good;
he feeds me of the little meat he has, and my grandsons
bring me wood. I was born an Agaidüka, and so I will
die in a tepee, for I have seen it in a dream. I have seen
another dream where some of our young men will have
their bones scattered on the prairie to show where they
fell in battle. Perhaps it is good—for it is hard to grow
old." For a while her mind turned inward and she was
silent, staring at the ground.

Washakie moved a little and cleared his throat in
preparation for speaking. "While riding alone, I have
been thinking. Two days ago, two men came to see me.
They were sent by Three Stars, General Crook. The
men were Left Hand and Straight Tongue. I have met
them before in councils with the white men. They told
me that the Great White Father told Three Stars to
ask us to help him. They said Three Stars's camp is on
Goose Creek and he has many soldiers and some of our
new friends, such as the Crows from the village at the

mouth of Grapevine Creek. I am inclined to help this man. He has many soldiers, and we will all destroy our old enemies, the Sioux, Cheyennes, and Arapahos. This will be a fight for peace."

Sacajawea took a deep breath, then said, "I do not feel so old. I have many thoughts not yet put into talk. Perhaps it is really not hard to grow old. Maybe this talk of fighting for peace, here on our reservation, is a waste of time. Maybe we are fools." She stopped and relighted her pipe. "Our fights over land with the Sioux and Blackfeet have always been fierce; too much of it has killed us also. Now we have our own land marked out on the white man's paper. The Sioux have their land, but they will not stay on it; they run into the white man's land. Should we fight this white man's battle against our enemies? Do we feel that friendly toward the white man?"

Washakie knocked the dottle from his pipe and laid the empty pipe in his lap. "There is no other way. We cannot join our enemies, and there are more white men than there were buffalo. We have to join them. To help them will make them our friends. We have always fought the Sioux, Cheyennes, and Arapahos, anyway, so why not now?"

Sacajawea puffed deliberately. She knew Washakie's mind was made up—not because he loved the white men who were crowding other tribes into Shoshoni lands, or because he hated the three enemy nations, but because he saw plainly that this course was the only one that might save his land. It was the only way to act.

Chief Washakie collected one hundred and eighty warriors—some Shoshonis, some Crows. Luishaw was his war chief.

It was late spring and the warriors had not come back. The winds howled in the night and the smoke whirled around inside Sacajawea's tepee as though it were afraid to go out. She crawled deep under her blankets on the buffalo robe. The night when the wind went dead, she peeked out through the tepee flap. The stars were big and sharp, and everything was listening. She let her fire die and carried her blankets to the warm square cabin of Shoogan.

In the morning, she watched her grandchildren go to the mission school. Dancing Leaf explained that the boys learned to farm and the girls learned cooking vegetables and pancakes and sewing with cotton goods. They both learned to wear stockings and heavy shoes.

Later there were footsteps on the warped pine steps. It was Sarah Irwin, wife of the agent. Dancing Leaf smiled and beckoned her to come in out of the cold. Sarah, a powerful, heavy woman past fifty now, shrewd, dominating, yet strangely childlike, had studied astronomy and botany in the east before marrying a physician, James Irwin. One day he came home and announced he was going west to a mission that had been an Indian school. He taught Sioux children reading, writing, and arithmetic. School attendance constantly fluctuated. The Sioux did not relish reservation life. Dr. Irwin was then sent to Wind River as the Indian agent. His wife now made grim jokes about those early days. "Hair-raising times," she said. She had taught the Hunkpapa girls to sew and wear sunbonnets and worship the one Father named Lord who was more powerful than the Great Spirit.

Sarah, red-faced from the last stinging snow of spring, came blustering inside the log house. Sacajawea was lifting a cottonwood chunk into the sheet-iron stove.

"I have come to learn Shoshoni," Sarah indicated by hand signs. "I will teach you my tongue in payment." Behind spectacles the eyes of the white woman were soft blue and kind.

Sarah sat down with Dancing Leaf on the floor and began using hand signs, then single English words. Dancing Leaf used hand signs and Shoshoni words. Sacajawea could not contain her tongue, and often she interpreted for one or the other. After almost an hour, Sarah got up and shook Sacajawea's hand, then excused herself. She came back the next morning at the same time for another lesson.

"Would you like to learn to read?" Sarah asked Sacajawea one morning.

"How long to learn?"

"A year, maybe more."

"No," said Sacajawea. "It is better for my grandchildren to learn. It is late for me. My life is coming to

a close. I can look back to times that you cannot remember."

"Would you tell me about those times?" asked Sarah,
leaning toward Sacajawea.

"*Ai*, but it takes time for telling my stories all on
one string."

"How long?"

"A year, maybe."

"Tomorrow we'll start. I'll bring paper and pen and
ink. After the talking lesson, you will tell me something
you can remember from long ago." Sarah pushed her
glasses back on her nose. She was eager. She wanted
to get the whole life story of this old Shoshoni woman,
who it was rumored had crossed the continent with
Lewis and Clark nearly seventy years before.

"*Ai*. Tomorrow I will tell a story that will make me
young again a short time, and you will put it down on
the paper as my tongue says the words. There are strange
things to be remembered, strange ways, and strange
faces. There is a man's face that is black; there is a boy
who cries out in the night for his mother."

Sacajawea lit her pipe, and her lean cheeks hollowed
with a long draw upon the stem. Her brooding face went
dim behind the cloud of smoke. When it emerged, it
was shining, and a light was in her eyes. "Boinaiv! My
grandmother is calling to me. It is what I see clearer
than all the rest. And that is strange for it was the
farthest away in my memory." She thought awhile, a
slow smile spreading until she fell to giggling like a
small girl. Then her face went sober, and fixing her
eyes upon Sarah, she said with great dignity and deliberation, "It is a long way back, and I am weary. You
come tomorrow, and we start."[31]

The weather became warm, and she moved back to
her own tepee. Each morning Sarah knew when Sacajawea was up and waiting for her by the thin stem
of smoke from the tepee fire.

One morning Chief Washakie was sitting outside the
tepee. The summer sun was already hot on Sarah's back
as she walked alongside the stream to write more of
Sacajawea's story. She did not want to stay and interrupt the first guest, but Sacajawea waved her to sit on
the ground outside.

"You must sit quietly, my daughter," Sacajawea said. "Washakie has seen much with the soldiers, and he is telling me. Do not write his words, for they are about your people."

Sarah pushed up her steel-rimmed glasses and opened her mouth to speak.

"Shhh," cautioned Sacajawea again. "Try to be more patient. It is polite to sit and wait a few minutes. You can enjoy the sun on your back."

"It is all a mistake," Washakie began after they had sat silent for a while, listening to the warm wind and the whipping of the leather on the tepee poles. "I have known, forever, it seems, that we cannot drive all the white men from our country. We fought beside them on the Rosebud, and it was a great victory for the Sioux and Arapahos. They moved their whole camp into the valley of the Greasy Grass. The white men claimed the victory on their side because the Cheyennes pulled away from their chase of the mule soldiers of Three Stars. I was a scout for Three Stars, and I heard that Sitting Bull forbade any celebration for that fight. He was preparing Crazy Horse and himself for another. He had a vision of a hundred white soldiers dropping dead in neat rows around his feet.

"The white soldiers laughed at this dream. They sat in their camp on Goose Creek and licked their wounds and lied to themselves about the strength of Sitting Bull's dream and his warriors. I tried to make them understand there would be ten thousand hostiles gathered along the banks of the Greasy Grass." Washakie clutched at his brown, wrinkled face, remembering how the white pony soldiers had prepared for the coming battle.

His husky voice began slowly. "While the white warriors drilled with Straight Tongue, Tom Cosgrove, each morning our warriors hunted and fished. Once I held the peace-waver of the Shoshonis, a standard of eagle feathers attached to a lance staff twelve feet long. My warriors wore a small piece of white cloth in their headdress as a distinguishing mark so that the soldiers would know we were their Shoshoni friends. But the Sioux heard of this and also placed white strips in their hair.

"Then one day a message was brought into our Goose

Creek camp telling about what happened to Son of the Morning Star, Custer, and his soldiers on the Greasy Grass. I believe the white men might have done a better job in their fights with our enemies if they had been more careful and had kept together better. Son of the Morning Star was killed because he did not wait for his friends to help him do a big job. Three Stars was waiting and drilling his pony soldiers, but no word came to him to help on the Greasy Grass, so he just stayed in camp, not knowing about that fight. Son of the Morning Star with two mortal wounds was destroyed, and so were all his white pony soldiers.

"I believe that the Other One, Terry, told Son of the Morning Star to look a little for Three Stars, and that when Son of the Morning Star saw the enemy's trail he forgot, because he wished to fight. The Other One must have known the country between him and Three Stars was full of hostiles—any soldier would have known it. Each morning on Goose Creek I looked over the hillside with the bring-close glasses of Three Stars, and each morning I saw the Arapahos skulking behind every bush and tree.[32] And so—I believe Son of the Morning Star disobeyed his orders and did not wait for more reinforcements, and so all was lost that day.[33]

"I talked one evening to Three Stars and plainly told him that my warriors would not remain any longer with him because his transportation of supplies was too terrible. With those mules nothing could be done. It slowed us all the way. So—then I brought my men back here because they were ready to come home.

"I have finished my story, and I am tired." Washakie folded his arms over his leather shirt and closed his eyes. "I do not believe in fighting any more battles than we are forced into. Sitting Bull has run into Canada." He seemed to forget the two women sitting in front of him.

"Chief Washakie," Sarah said at length, "this is the first I have heard of this fight and the great loss by the whites. Is it truth?"

The old man regarded her for a while with a crinkled look about his mouth. "Granddaughter, you know I do not speak with a forked tongue. If you listen now, you can hear the mourning of the women for the Shoshonis and Crows who did not come home with us. My power is gone. I could cry all night."

Indeed, there was the sound of the piercing wails of women carried into the treetops by the warm winds. Sacajawea sat quite still, her eyes toward the other tepees farther down the stream sympathetic and understanding.

The land in that direction was nearly flat. It was rich, sandy brown, with grass thick and yellow. The broomweeds held tiny flowers and a resinous oil in their leaves that lent a faintly spicy scent to the summer air. Locusts sang in the grass.

Nothing Is Lost

*James I. Patten, who in 1871 became teacher and lay
missionary to the Indians on the Wind River Reservation, wrote a letter to the Commissioner of Indian Affairs
in Washington, April 18, 1878:*

Dear Sir:

*I do not believe that much difficulty will be experi-
enced in settling this tribe, Arapahos, on this reservation. It is known to be the desire of the government to
have this accomplished. The Shoshones, although they
are opposed to it, and look upon it as an encroachment
of their rights, yet will make no great objections to the
settlement of the former tribe upon their land, knowing
that it is the wish of the Great Father to bring several
small tribes of Indians together upon the same reservation. Washakie and the head men, though they dislike
utterly to divide their property with other bands, have
too great hearts to say no.*

*But my sense of right and justice is that if other tribes
are brought upon the Shoshone land, that it should be
with the full consent of the tribe owning the land by
right of their treaty, and that such Indians should receive
reasonable compensation for diminishment of their reservation.*

*I would, therefore, earnestly ask that the Shoshones
be allowed a just sum for the relinquishment of a certain*

*tract of land within the limits of their reservation to the
Northern Arapahos.*

Respectfully yours,
JAMES I. PATTEN

GRACE RAYMOND HEBARD, *Washakie*. Cleveland: The Arthur H. Clark Co., 1930, p. 210. Letter from James I. Patten to E. A. Hayt, Commissioner of Indian Affairs, Washington, D.C., April 8, 1878.

Because Sacajawea had asked several times for one of her great-grandchildren to come help with her chores, Shoogan's family finally persuaded the son of Nancy Bazil to go to her lodge. Speedy Jim had been baptized and named James McAdams by the Mormons at Salt Lake City.

"This boy," Shoogan said, "is good, but a little wild because he has not been taught the old ways properly. He needs counseling. We wish you to take him, Porivo."

"I will take him for the winter, to instruct him," Sacajawea said, smiling, anticipating the companionship of a young person.

He was small, quick as a chipmunk, and more inquisitive. He was impulsive. He was sixteen, maybe seventeen years old. Sacajawea liked him.

Thin, wispy, gray hair hung against Sacajawea's shoulders. Her forehead, cheeks, and chin were crisscrossed with fine, lined indentations. Dark, pigmented blotches spotted her face and beaklike nose, the backs of her bony hands, and her thin arms. Her bright eyes were large for her shrunken face, and her mouth looked pinched together when closed. She wore a government-issue, black woolen skirt and over that a soiled, blue calico dress that fit her like a sack. On her shoulders she held a tattered red blanket. She had cut the feet from her government-issue black stockings and wore them for leggings. When she walked she thrust ahead with her polished cedar stick. She did not walk frequently now, but received visitors when seated in front of her door on warm, pleasant days, or in front of her fire on cool, blustery days. The Lemhis had an interminable respect for this old woman. Everyone knew her and if they gossiped or laughed as they approached her tepee, they suddenly stopped, and resumed only after passing a courteous distance.

During the day Speedy Jim cut wood with a rusty ax and carried water. On allotment days, he carried the flour and bacon to her tepee and helped her store it in old leather boxes.

One day she was at the agency warehouse drawing

her weekly rations herself. Toussaint was there, but he ignored the old woman, who was lying on her back, her shoulders resting on the fifty-pound sack of meat, around which was looped a strap, the ends of which were brought over her shoulders and held in her hands in front. She was just ready to rise with her burden when Shoogan came to her rescue and assisted her to her feet. Shoogan called to Toussaint, "The load is too heavy for our mother to carry. She is staggering. You can see she is quite old and weak."

Toussaint said curtly, "*Ai*, pretty old. I should know; she's my mother. But you have sent your grandson to help her, so she is not my concern." He walked to where the Shoshonis were gathering up their rations, spitting on the ground as though defiling the path his mother took.

From then on, Speedy Jim was seen at the warehouse carrying the beef issue, tin of lard, sacks of salt, sugar, and coffee beans, and the heavy sack of meal loaded on a tired old horse.

At times he helped her strip out the meat and dry it over a slow fire.

At night they crouched together before the fire. Once Speedy Jim asked her age. She answered that she had probably outlived most of her girlhood friends. "I suspect I am older than my good friend Washakie. Some days I believe he is approaching his second childhood, but no need to tell him that."

"But the new ways do not frighten you as they do some of the old ones."

"Grandson," said Sacajawea, "to children, age is something they cannot understand. To ignorance, knowledge is frightening. So that the new ways represent a learning which the old ones let pass by them. This is wrong. But even some of the young people have it. They have book learning and knowledge, and fear the wisdom which they have not yet. So then you learn to be unafraid of anything new or different. Then you will have reached true maturity, which is eternal youth."

The fire faded. Speedy Jim threw on another stick. Sacajawea filled and lighted her pipe, sucking noisily.

"Ho-ho!" exclaimed Speedy Jim, keenly aware of what Sacajawea was about to suggest to him.

"Shhh!" Sacajawea raised an admonishing forefinger and continued slowly, speaking scarcely above a whisper. "I want you to go to the Carlisle School. I want my people to have the best they can of the white man's knowledge and the Shoshoni wisdom."

"But I hear at the Carlisle School one must learn about what has happened many years in the past in countries across the seas. I want to know of the future, not the dead past. I want to go on to the new. I am not afraid." His black eyes glistened, and he brushed the coarse dark hair from his face with a dirty brown hand.

"You are like the coyote on the trail of a rabbit. He has no sense of the past, only a hunger to devour the future. But to follow the rabbit he soon stops and raises his head and sniffs the air. He sees signs and listens to the world around him. He sees the trail behind as well as the one ahead. But still the future is ahead, up toward the red cliff top covered with mist. He angles up and up. *Wagh!* That dreaded and hungered-for future is no more than the present which resembles the past. They are all one. But you must learn this for yourself. Each man must travel his own trail."

And Sacajawea, with shining eyes that saw more, nearsighted with age, than when they had been perfect, reached for her little sack of tobacco. "When I am alone I can hear steps. I look up and see a man in my doorway. He might be the one called Jerk Meat, or a certain white man called Chief Red Hair—both dead these many years. No! It does not surprise me if he is any of these. There are shapes of men less alive than shadows of men. So then even I confuse what has been and will be with what is."

In her wisdom she taught that winter the lessons that must be learned by each alone, and she saw the comprehension in the boy's bright eyes and dreamed of his reading and writing at the Carlisle School.

She thought of the changes. The Indians always hunted twice a year, the white men hunted the year around. The Indians enjoyed the old raiding back and forth, but the whites preached tranquillity. Indian women took pride in a well-tanned hide, sewing, painting, and cooking, but white women had someone else do these things for them. How will a person distinguish himself from every other individual? she thought.[1]

She said to Speedy Jim, "The Story Writer Woman makes believe she understands what is in my heart through my words. But writing will only show my life cold and pale as the paper she marks on, for she can not feel my feelings as if she has been with me all those long-gone years."

"Oh, Grandmother," said Speedy Jim, "certainly there will be those who read your story and will know you are somebody grand in the memories of both the Indians and the whites."

"No, I say what I now feel"—she sat bent over the fire, her thin hand holding the red blanket together— "I shall never see this story on paper all together, and neither will you, nor any other person."

Sometimes she told Speedy Jim stories about herself just before the reservation time. "Once I traded moccasins with Mr. Bocker at the sutler store at Bridger's Fort. I traded them for a dollar and fifty cents and some blue and red beads. Another time I gave him a fine buffalo robe for three dollars, some hard candy, and a small looking glass. The next time I brought him a fine buffalo robe he paid me in 'shin-plasters,' or paper money. 'I do not want this white man's paper,' I told him. 'I want hard money.' You see, I did not know the value of this kind of paper money. But I would know now. The Story Writer Woman and Jakie Moore have taught me how to count carefully, so that I get full value for what I trade."

In the spring, Sacajawea said to the family of Shoogan, "This grandson of mine is not wild and no longer so ignorant of the old ways. He learns quickly. Let him go to Carlisle now and learn the new ways."

To Speedy Jim alone, she said, "You have helped me well, Grandson. You can help your people now by going away. So leave this place. Go to the school."

Speedy Jim was shocked. "To the white man's school? Who will pay? I never thought you really meant I would have to go."

"And so, then, you know." Sacajawea went on quietly, "I have traded much at the stores and have saved.

The money does me no good. It is yours." And Sacajawea
drew back into the loneliness of her tepee.

In the spring, Sacajawea could see the fields of corn
and wheat that the reservation Shoshonis had planted.
Small green shoots coming up from the yellow and reddish brown soil contrasted with the tall alder and aspen
and slender, graceful birch on the upper hills.

Indian Agent Irwin at Fort Washakie planned for
months with Finn Burnett, the Government Agricultural Agent, to have on some particular issue day a
special feast and some horse racing to build a better
feeling between the government employees and their
Indian charges.

It was midmorning, and Shoogan walked with his
family toward the large gathering of people in the open
area north of Jakie's store. Shoogan was old and withered with a face like a sick hawk's. He limped and half
hopped along on his bad leg. He grunted through closed
lips, sending a small quiver through a sprout of turkey
feathers he wore on his head. The others, held up, waited
for him. Only their eyes stirred, looking here and there.
Dancing Leaf walked proudly beside him, older and
heavier, pulling her blanket tightly around her up to
her neck. His other woman, Devoted, shuffled along
behind. Andrew Bazil, squatty, wearing a white man's
hat, came next with his woman and children. The children darted around Nancy Bazil, her braids swinging
as her face turned. She had put a red line down her
center hair part. Her man had ambled off for a cup of
coffee laced heavily with sugar.

Out past Jakie's store a dance had started. They
walked toward the beat of drums and the chants of the
dancers. "This is some new dance," said Dancing Leaf.
"I do not recognize the beat."

Some of the more forward young men had come to
Sacajawea's tepee not more than a week before and
asked her about the Sun Dance of the Sioux. They wondered why the Shoshoni never had such a dance.

"What?" she asked, scraping flesh from a horse hide
she had bought with that week's rations. "You want to
perform the dance of our enemies?" She shouted, after

a look at their faces, "You are certain you could do such a thing?"

One of the young men said, "But, Grandmother, we just want to try it."

"Can you not see I am busy making this hide soft for moccasins?"

"We want to see for ourselves if we like this dance."

"It would not be in good taste for a Shoshoni to adopt a ceremony from his enemy."

"Tell us how it is done."

A broad-faced youth, knife-scarred from eye to jaw, growled words and stepped toward her.

She regarded the young men for a moment with a crinkled look of amusement about her eyes. "Grandsons, you are in a hurry," she said. "Can you not wait for the story?"

Her thoughts came slowly—the remembrances of the Mandan torture rites, from which the Sioux had taken a small part and called it their Sun Dance. Then it had traveled to the Cheyennes and Arapahos, so that now it was well known that the Plains Indians had used the Sun Dance to prove manhood. She clearly remembered the voices of the women who had had men performing the torture ceremony. The sounds of their voices carried their own indisputable meaning; they were proud and frightened. Here in this different place it was true again. These youths with no deep understanding of the older ways were demanding that she tell them about the rites. How could she do that without making certain they understood the whole reasoning behind the rituals, the feelings of the families and friends, the pride and honor the ceremony brought, the anticipation and concern and worry? The voices of the youths were crass and disrespectful.

With fumbling fingers Sacajawea put down her hide scraper and pushed aside the pile of hair and tissue. "Keep your ears uncovered while I talk," she said. "You chop weeds and sell it for grass. You stir up the dirt and grow corn. You build fences and pen up cattle. And so, the men who danced the old time Sun Dance did not do these things." Then she held out her pipe to the broad-faced youth. "Please, fill it. My hands shake. I waste half my good tobacco." Then she told, as best she could, the story of the Mandan Okeepa. After a few moments the boys settled down, their eyes fastened on Sacajawea's expressive old face.

Shoogan's son, Andrew, said the issue day festivities planned by Dr. James Irwin were to persuade the foolish families who lived poorly off the reservation to come and live with the loafers who lived badly on the reservation. "One senseless brave told me he would rather eat dung than be corralled on a reservation," Andrew said to his father.

The fort's soldiers made huge amounts of coffee in five-gallon lard buckets. Most Shoshoni brought their tin cups already prepared with sugar in the bottom.

There was a line of women with their yards of government-issue domestic cotton wrapped around themselves blanket-style. They laughed and chatted as they filed by various clerks who marked their cards and gave them their allotment of cornmeal, sugar, salt, coffee, and soap. The People were most eager for the coffee and sugar, but the cornmeal they fed to their horses.[2]

In front of the agency corral, the men, stripped to the waist, waited on horseback for the beef to be issued on the hoof. The cattle were soon turned loose in the field behind the agency. The men *kiyi*-ed and dug their heels into the horses' sides and pretended they were on an old-time buffalo hunt. They fired pistols to bring down the animals. When all the cattle were killed the women and children ran out to help the men skin and butcher the cows. Several heated arguments took place, as more than one family owned each cow and the choice rump roasts could not always be divided among all the owners. Shoogan passed around pieces of raw liver sprinkled with a few drops of gall. Andrew thought the warm raw liver alone not too bad. It tasted like raw oyster. The women cleaned the cow's entrails. Then they wound them around green willow sticks and let the squealing children hold the meat in the hot ashes of the roasting trench until the wound-up meat was ready for eating.

When it was time for the horse racing, the soldiers barricaded the long, level dirt road between the agency buildings with wooden horses and empty barrels. Along the road they laid out a half-mile track where two horses could race at one time. When one race was finished and all bets were paid, another race took place, as long as there were riders and horses to compete. In the nick of time, several frantic mothers pulled their young children from playing in the street. The galloping horses could have run them down. The freight wagons were detoured around the racers or stopped and detained until the show was over. Some of the losers were left without their horses. Some lost money earned from grass leases or hauling jobs. Some lost all the rations they had collected on this issue day. Shoogan watched the man who lost the last race explain to his wife that he had bet her ration of twelve yards of cotton goods. She was obligated to honor the winner. She and her children would go without the dresses and shirts they needed.

A broad-faced youth ambled toward Shoogan, grinning and pushing his big hat toward the back of his head. "Hi there, Grandfather."

"Hello, Son," said Shoogan, not recognizing the youth.

"How's everything going?"

"Fine."

"I'm sure glad to find you. You see over there?" He pointed toward the circle of young people dancing from left to right in a circle. "Some of us have started a real old-time Sun Dance, and we want you to direct us. To be director—master of ceremonies."

"But—I've never—"

"Oh, we'll tell you what to do. We got all the details from old Porivo."

Bewildered, Shoogan limped between two young men who pushed him along the inside of the circle. "Now sing—anything," instructed one. "Stamp your feet a little and hold your face to the south," said another.

"But—"

"Go ahead," someone said.

Shoogan glimpsed the shine of a hunting knife clasped in the right hand of the speaker.

"Grab hands and dance serpentine until you have circled the flagpole," said Shoogan. "Come on, do as I say if you want a real dance. Where else can you find a straighter pole?" The youth with the knife grabbed his hand. Shoogan bent his head low to the ground and

straightened with his head in the air, bent and straightened with each heel-toe step. The ones behind him did
the same. They circled the flagpole. For a moment Shoogan watched a hawk caught in a high thermal. It flew
above the mountain peaks against the clouds. The clouds
were blown away and the hawk was left in a calm against
the blue sky. Shoogan thought, Hawk, are you still my
helper? He pulled from the circle and stood inside. He
coughed once to attract attention. "Listen, I know a
Shoshoni dance, older than the Sun Dance of the Sioux."
He was not certain what else he was going to say or
do.

"Hey, Grandfather, old Porivo told us about the Mandans' dance. You know that one? We want a genuine
Sun Dance. We will give Porivo credit for telling us
about the Sun Dance first. But you be the leader."[3]

"*Ai*, my dance belongs to our people. Pay attention!"
Shoogan looked at the top of the fort's flagpole, where
the stars and stripes snapped brightly next to the sky.
"On a long, straight, lodgepole pine, your grandfathers
hung their battle scalps. Can you imagine ten, fifteen
scalp locks whipping way up there in the wind? What
a sight! At sunset when the flag is brought down, we
can pretend there are real scalps popping and flapping
up there. The bravest man among you will recite about
the time he actually counted coup on an enemy or a
charging buffalo or moose or grizzly."

"You mean like the time Joe Ptarmigan struck a
marshal in Rock Springs?" called out one of the youths.
The others snickered at the old joke of Joe getting liq-
uored up on vanilla extract and punching the territorial
marshal.

"You know what I mean. This is an old-fashioned,
time-honored dance. Sing about the buffalo, moose, or
grizzly, and dance. I will get my big whip so that it will
all be really authentic. Someone else get a drummer.
Clap and move back and forth until I get back!"

Shoogan slipped from the circle of youths and walked
as fast as he could, limping behind the agency buildings
through the brilliant red paintbrush and orange gail-
lardia to the barren, red dirt path to Sacajawea's tepee.
He wiped perspiration from his face with a faded red
kerchief.

She had heard the clapping of hands and stamping of dancing feet. She could not make out the words of the leader, but knew it was old Shoogan. She sat in front of her door feeling the warmth of the sun on her head. She thought of boys and girls dancing in two circles, the girls on the outside. It was a relic of the past. But even then they enjoyed the flirting. Then she heard Shoogan's uneven footsteps.

"Porivo, I have your rations and will bring them later, but now I feel like I am in a box canyon with no way out. Those piercy-eyed boys want me to lead a Sun Dance. They said you told them about the revered Mandans. I cannot do that dance! They cannot do that! I thought about doing a Shoshoni Round or Scalp Dance with the big whip. I told them I was going to get my whip, but I do not have one."[4]

Sacajawea went into a deep chuckle for a moment, then slowly got to her feet and motioned for Shoogan to follow her into the tepee. Together they rummaged through several old parfleches and leather boxes. They discarded everything until Sacajawea pulled out a big wooden comb with pictures of leaves carved on the back.

"*Ai!*" yelled Shoogan, "that's perfect! See, it is enough like the wooden blade with the serrated edge and the carved scalp symbols on top. Now, how can I put two otter-skin whips on the end of this handle?"

Sacajawea was pulling the binding off a cracked and peeled leather case. Several good beaver skins were inside. "I recall the Comanche also used the big whip to brag about their bravery," she said, shaking out a skin and measuring it against the comb handle. "I can make a couple beaver-skin whips and tie them on here. What do those feisty youths know about the old ways? This will be a shabby fake. We both know that. But it will take you out of the box canyon. The dancers will be satisfied, my son." She cut the strips with her butcher knife and tied them to the end of the big wooden comb.

Shoogan nodded and smiled his thanks and hurried back with a grin on his face.

Sacajawea put the parfleches and boxes in their places, picked up her cane, and left her tepee. She shuffled along the dusty flat to the agency grounds, passing the jack pines, mountain ash, harebells, asters, a chip-

munk, and several ground squirrels. She smiled when
people passed and nodded toward her. She rested on one
of the overturned barrels the soldiers had moved to the
side of the road after the horse races.

The mountains behind the agency had changed from
blue to purple in the sunset. The bugle was blown and
the flag lowered. She stood up and her mouth fell open
when she saw the broad-faced youth hand the flag to
the soldier. The soldier took it quickly before the trailing end touched the ground. She thought he folded that
big bright banner more carefully than a mother would
fold her baby's newest blanket. She moved closer so
that she could hear what Shoogan told the youths moving around the flagpole.

"Anytime during the dance, if I point the big whip
at anybody he must stop and tell of some bravery or
good hunt, as I said before."

The youths nodded in agreement.

"The story ends with the sun curse, which goes like
this: 'Oh Father Sun, shine on me, draw away all my
juices so that I am crisp as a leaf in winter if I speak
with a forked tongue about my brave exploits.'"

The youths nodded again. They understood and for
the first time thought it was an honest Sun Dance if
the dancers called upon the sun to prove their truthfulness. Most felt it was better than the Sun Dance old
Porivo told about. Hers was a violent, grisly affair that
was probably made up to frighten them, they thought.
The Sioux might subject themselves to hanging by thin
thongs from wooden pegs implanted in the chest and
shoulder muscles, but only a crazy would also add heavy
buffalo skulls to his arms and legs.

Shoogan continued, "When I point my big whip at
somebody, he has to come to the center by this tall pole
and tell of a coup. If not I give him a sound lashing."
He swung the whips through the air, stopping suddenly
so they cracked. "If your coup is not as good as the one
I will tell, I can whip you four times." He pointed at
the chest of the young man who had the knife. The man
looked around and gave a stifled laugh. He told about
stealing watermelon in Riverton and being shot with
rock salt in his butt and legs. He pulled up his black
woolen pants and showed scars on his legs. "I ran like

a cougar, doubled back, and picked up another melon
before the night was gone."

Someone said, "Good coup."

Shoogan growled deep into his throat and looked at
the circle of youths. He was amazed to see that a few
young girls had joined in the circle and were holding
hands with the smiling youths. This made him growl
again in disgust. In the old times the females danced
behind the braves. He looked through the circle toward
the crowd sitting on the dry grass watching. He wondered how many of the old people knew the dance was
only a flouting of the real thing, a big sham.

Sacajawea was sitting in the front row with some of
the other grandmothers when the watermelon story was
told. She was afraid to look at the others, so great was
the feeling of sick distaste. Was this what the youths
who had listened to her speak had come away with?
Was this all they honestly believed the Sun Dance was?
No, it could not be. The young braves were doing this
because they could not bring themselves to try a true
Sun Dance. Now there was no need for the real thing.
So, maybe the youths had kept their ears uncovered,
she thought.

"I tell about counting coup on the enemy and getting
one of my legs shorter than the other," said Shoogan.
While he recited, the young men and women circled
around him and the steel flagpole, slowly heel-toeing,
bending, straightening. As soon as he finished he pointed
the big whip to the boy with the knife. "You must stay
in the dance until the end," he said. "Your coup was
weak."

He did not strike the boy four times with the whip,
because he felt it was useless and would only rile him
to some unpleasantness. Not thinking straight, he carelessly pointed the whip toward a young woman. She
had nothing more to recite than how she fought off an
overly passionate brave in the juniper breaks. "You
must dance until I announce the end," he said, feeling
shame for his part in this watery imitation of the old
ways. Another young woman told how she had licked
the whooping cough by regularly eating a little bit of
the gray-green, spineless cactus brought in by some
traders from the south. "I no longer felt worn out, but

instead felt I was a living part of all the tribe. And see, now I do not cough."

One of the young men told about how he wrapped a thong with sinew, softened it in warm water, and pushed it down the throat of a younger brother who was choking from lung congestion. "That cleared his throat better than my finger," he bragged. Shoogan indicated they all must continue dancing by cracking his big whip four times above his head.

When the stars became visible a bonfire flared up in one of the meat-roasting trenches and threw a flickering yellow light in a wide circle on the field behind the agency. The drummer got up and sauntered toward the fire. Then the dancers stopped. One couple followed the drummer, saying they were tired of dancing and wanted some hot coffee with sugar.

"I did not end the dance!" shouted Shoogan.

"It is ended, Grandfather," said the young man with the knife.

Several of the grandmothers Sacajawea was sitting beside got up and shuffled toward the bonfire. "The dance was a fake," whispered one.

"Our young people didn't seem to notice or care," said another.

"The dance is officially over!" announced Shoogan. He knew the momentum was gone and it could not last through the night as the old dances did.

Sacajawea waited until Shoogan came limping from the flagpole area. She shook her pointing finger at him. "I have been thinking. Maybe this white man's peace is nothing. On the other hand, when the red man had war there was death. Can there be only two directions?"

Shoogan ran his kerchief over his face and through his graying hair and grunted. "As I see it, maybe we are all in a box canyon with only game trails marking sides that are steeper than man can climb, and a swift creek running in the narrow gorge that is too treacherous for a canoe and too deep for wading." He searched for his women and children and found them around the crackling bonfire holding tin mugs of coffee.

Sacajawea started toward her path home, then noticed a white man, well dressed in dark trousers and a dark coat. On his head he had a black, wide-brimmed hat with a chin strap. His hair and mustache were gray. She knew who he was, but could not recall seeing him more than once or twice before.

He held up his hand and said, "Ho!" Then he began to make clumsy signs. Sacajawea held out her shaking left hand and said impulsively in English, "Hello, Dr. Irwin. How are Sarah and your two daughters?"

The agent was surprised at the good English. He was pleased and said, "What is your name, Grandmother?"

"I go by many names," she said. "Your woman has come often to my tepee. She calls me Porivo."

"So you are the one she has been writing about."

"I guess so," Sacajawea said. She was thinking, This man does not really care about the People. He does not even know where it is his woman goes each morning.

"May I say good-bye?" He tipped his hat. "This is our last day at Wind River. We are moving to the Pine Ridge Agency."

"The Sioux Reservation?" Surprise showed on her face. The Story Writer Woman had not mentioned this.

"Grandmother, I am a doctor, and my duty is where I am called. I'd like to have you cooperate with the new agent as soon as he comes.[5] Tell the mothers to keep sending their children to Bishop Randall's church and mission school." He again tipped his hat and turned away.

It was not lost on Sacajawea that the man had mentioned Bishop Randall when there were so few that attended his Sunday morning services, but most of the reservation children went to the school. Whether the statement reflected on the agent's ignorance or forgetfulness, she could not guess.

It had been debated at the agency before Dr. Irwin was transferred about bringing the Arapahos in to live on the Shoshoni Reservation a short while, until a reservation of their own could be laid out. It had been discussed for several weeks during issuing of rations, in the camps and degenerating councils. Finally, after many words, Chief Washakie and Chief Black Coal, of the Northern Arapahos, gave their reluctant consent. Chief Black Coal's final speech was, "My people have no land to call their own because the Cheyennes drive them off hunting grounds, the Blackfeet drive our camps away from drinking water. Our women are thin, and our children cry out at night with hunger pains."

"I do not wish to see anyone starve or have little children freeze to death on the cold plains or in the icy mountains," said Washakie with his head bowed.

"Perhaps these people will stay only during the cold winter until another place can be found for them," said Jim Patten, the teacher. He shifted his seat on the ground, finding patience in the thought that their talk did not matter now because they all knew once the Arapahos came in they would stay. He looked off to where dusk was putting a dull shine on the Wind River.

Chief Washakie was also staring at the river, thinking it was good water before the people had begun coming in to spoil it, bringing plows to rip up pastures and cattle to graze ranges, and now the Arapahos with sheep to make affairs worse. This was the new way—too many people, too much stock, too many homestead claims, so that wildlife disappeared and streams ran tame and clouded.

Chief Black Coal spoke. "You won't be sorry." He spoke as if he wanted to say it again so that Washakie could hold tight to that thought and not lose it, an elbow resting on his cocked knee, his upheld hand fixed to his pipe.

The Shoshonis accepted this brief alliance only as a necessity.[6] "The filthy Arapahos can sleep on the prairie with their sheep!" some said. Others said, "Why don't they eat their sheep instead of trying to sell them to the white men? Then they would have full bellies and warm fur robes!" "We don't want them near us!" "They cry like old women in a snowstorm."

Some talked with Sacajawea, who shook her head and grinned at them. "I have no confidence in the Arapahos," she answered. "I have seen them offer large amounts in trade for rifles and ammunition. They cannot be trusted. But someone must listen to them if they wish to live with the Shoshonis on the reservation. Someone must tell them they must live without arms and ammunition except for hunting meat."

"There are more of us than them. One of our men is worth three of theirs," someone said.

Sacajawea believed it was a natural thing that the strong dominated the weak. But she was against any deliberate wrong done by someone in power which advanced the powerful, but was paid for by the weaker underdogs. She believed in individualism, though the progress brought about by individual self-interest was slower than that achieved by one strong leader pushing around the masses. Her way required much patience and much time.

She saw the white man's government temporarily place the Arapahos with the Wind River Shoshonis in 1872, then move the Arapahos back to Pine Ridge with their allies, the Sioux, and now return them to Wind River. The government men seemed at a loss for finding a home for the Arapaho, maybe because they repeatedly attacked miners, settlers, and other Indians in the Sweetwater, Bridger, and Wind River areas.[7] The government men were now demanding that titles for the most productive portion of the Wind River Reservation be cleared for the Arapaho.

Sacajawea saw the shadow on her mind. She and Washakie had talked about the plight of the Arapahos, who had no land of their own and never enough to eat. Both agreed there was plenty of suffering, but it would be an injustice to reward the Arapaho by making them a permanent gift of the Shoshonis' best land. The Arapahos were traditional enemies, the same as the Blackfeet, Sioux, and Cheyenne. Washakie admitted that he was sick and cold, meaning he was troubled. "I will hold a council with them. When I see their faces, I can understand their intentions," he said.[8]

The wind had come up again. It shrieked through the pines, whistled over the rocks, and blew up the dust. Another winter was coming. Sacajawea would need plenty of wood before she would find herself slowly walking the trail to Shoogan's wooden house next to the agent.

Now the Shoshonis did not refer much to the old times and the fights with their enemies. They had stopped referring to the winter tales and legends because they began to question them. But they passed around the story about some suspicious Arapahos who had murdered eight white men and escaped with livestock and horses. "Stinking Arapahos," they said. The settlers from a Sweetwater mining settlement organized and went into the Popo Agie to hunt the Arapahos and met a small band under the leadership of Chief Black Bear. The white men killed Black Bear and ten of his braves. Black Bear's woman and seven children were captured. The word had been, "Serves them right."

One small boy was brought to Fort Washakie by General C. A. Coolidge. This Arapaho boy had hidden from the white men and was wandering dazed when Coolidge, of the Seventh Infantry, found him. He was given the name Sherman Coolidge and dressed in soldier blue. "See the crybaby Arapaho who thinks he is white," some Shoshonis said, pointing a finger at the child.[9]

The morning air was cold when Sacajawea walked behind her cedar stick to Jakie's store. She noticed that a crowd was gathering near the trail to the fort. She recognized Toussaint, by himself. The winter before, both his women had been sick and had died not more than a day apart. He seemed small and withered, brittle as a dead twig. He looks old, she thought. His face was sharp and sallow. She began to follow the crowd; she was mostly curious.

On March 18, 1878, 938 starving Arapahos were brought en masse to the Wind River Shoshoni Reservation under military escort.[10] The Arapahos were taken to the eastern side of the fort where the ground was not strewn with shale, but was covered with fertile soil, so that in summer it was thick with prairie grass, sage, and camass. The grass could be scythed and sold to the soldiers as hay. Now the grass was damp and yellow and lay close to the red soil wherever the fierce winds had blown the snow off the land. The sage looked like upright, gray skeletons.

Most of the Shoshoni and some Bannocks had come to stare at the newcomers. The gaunt Arapaho men staked out their few horses. They beat bare arms across their chests to keep warm, or crossed them on their chests so that they could keep their hands warm in their armpits.

Frail-looking women cleared off the wet grass and put some cooking pots on the frozen ground. Then they sent children for sticks, old cow-pies, or dry grass for a small fire.

Toussaint shuffled near and spoke English to them, and French, and bits of nearly forgotten Mandan. They only stared, not even offering hand signs.

The young man with the broad face yelled, "Are you just a band of old women?"

The Lemhis were surprised because a poorly dressed man stepped over and spoke to them in Shoshoni. "I am their chief, Sorrel Horse, and we wish to thank you for your generosity." Another sad-looking man stepped near, saying, "I am Friday, a subchief. You will not be sorry for this kindness."

Sacajawea watched the man called Sorrel Horse entertain the children and white soldiers. She decided he was an Arapaho medicine man because he performed magic tricks and feats of ventriloquism. His woman stood close behind him as protection from the chilling wind. She had no blanket. The children's lips looked purple in the cold that blew from the snow-covered hills. Sacajawea's fingers picked at her old red blanket. It had seen better days, but it was still warm. She turned to face her own people and said with a loud voice so they could hear past the rush of wind, "I am stunned! You Shoshonis walk around like you have always lived on a high horse! Get down and look at these newcomers and remember how an empty belly pinches and how the wind bites your bones." The people were silent. "These people have no skins nor canvas for tepees." Her body straighted a little and she pointed to a huddled group of shivering children. "I will put my blanket here to start a pile. The rest of you give what you can to give some comfort to these people."

A woman in the crowd yelled, "Old Grandmother, they are Dog-Eaters."[11]

"I am ashamed you said that. Maybe their dogs were the only thing that has kept them alive. Look how skinny they are." Just then a baby cried out with a thin, piercing wail.

"Skinny and ugly and noisy!" some discourteous Bannock yelled.

"I add my moccasins to the blanket," said Sacajawea, kicking her fur-lined winter moccasins next to the blanket. She shivered and looked at her people, whose eyes were downcast, until someone moved forward and dropped his robe on the blanket. One by one they came forward until the pile of warm outer-wear was good-sized. Sacajawea smiled at them, and her large, sunken eyes seemed to emit two points of warm light.

Someone else gave the chief, Sorrel Horse, a blanket. "I have some old skins you can build a shelter with," another called and hurried back down the trail to get them. Someone else brought up their ration of cornmeal and gave it to an Arapaho woman. Toussaint called out in an oily, crude voice, "I have some skins I will trade for hard coins." Then there was much laughing and making of hand signs until the Shoshonis and Bannocks left to go about their own business, each thinking in his own way, The Arapahos aren't so bad. They are in need of many things; they are as hungry as the Shoshonis have been.

In time, Washakie went to the tepee of Sacajawea to tell his feeling about the Arapahos occupying the best farmland of the reservation. "I do not think it is just," he said, his bony finger pointing in the direction of the circle of canvas tepees. "If the government wants the Shoshonis to be happy on this reservation, the Arapahos must go to a reservation of their own. Our people have less meat because they had to divide with their friends the Bannocks, and now they are without flour and must eat cornmeal, which they do not like, because of the Arapahos."

Sacajawea placed an arm about his shoulder and pulled him close. Then, as though she were making an announcement to the universe in general, she said, "You are an old goat! You are like an old grandfather! I would have thought you would look at life more closely than at the things of this day. Days change, but life endures. To have a little less meat is not so bad, but the meat is not the same. It has no strength to it. You and I cannot chew it because most of our teeth are uprooted. What you truly long for is the first young calf you killed when you were a boy. That meat was tender, and you believed it would make you stronger. *Ai?*"

Washakie searched her face with a vaguely grieved,

apprehensive look. "Ho-ho! But then, surely you are right! I am an old goat! Ho-ho!"

When school was over in May, Jim McAdams left Carlisle and went back to Sacajawea's lodge on the Wind River Reservation. The two of them talked about the Shoshonis' land division. They talked about the bitter hatred between Arapahos and Shoshonis. They talked about Washakie withdrawing more and more into his dreams: dreams where the mountain streams were thick with trout, where there were plenty of deer in the meadows, and where the horses never tired; dreams in which his women never scolded, but saw to his every need, and his people lived in comfortable lodges and did not know hunger.

"It was this lack of reality in our chief," said Sacajawea, "and the idea of living so close to the Arapahos that drove off some of the tribe under the leadership of Norkuk, the half-breed. They are living in the Green River area."

"I know Norkuk," said Jim. "Some say his father was a white soldier. He is crafty, but mostly ambitious. He wants to be civil chief, but Washakie is in his way."

"Washakie's heart is still great. He will never push the Arapahos away now. Everyone will have to learn to walk in the new road, even Norkuk."

"I heard Norkuk took his warriors to Utah to get washed," said Jim. "They will come back calling themselves Mormons."

Sacajawea sat silently. She passed her pipe to be filled and lit. She thought about the young people, like her grandson, who were not as stoic in their fear of the white man as the old people were. The young people had discarded their comfortable leather clothing for cowboy boots, blue jeans, and wide-brimmed hats. They earned diplomas from the mission schools and some went on to Carlisle with a cardboard suitcase tied shut with a horsehair rope. The rope was the same braided lasso they had used in calf roping on reservation field days. Jim McAdams transferred his feelings to his great-grandmother, Sacajawea. These were the same feelings other Indian youths throughout the country were beginning to experience—restlessness and discontent.

Together they spoke quietly about human beings and their place on Mother Earth. They did not talk of laws and property so much as the value of a man's life.

In the twilight of midsummer, Jim found his great-grandmother bent to a horizontal from the hips, her thin hair white against the background of the dark earth, her sharp face shining with beads of perspiration, plying an ax among the gnarled remainders of the woodpile.

"Wagh!" she remarked, smiling brightly up at him and panting. "You see, I can get my own wood if you stay overlong with your white friends in the wooden lodges." Yielding the ax to Jim with some reluctance, she shuffled toward the tepee, apparently unaware of the worn moccasins that gave no protection to her heels and toes against the stones and prickly pear.

When the evening cook fire was going merrily, Jim said, "Grandmother, I have brought you a gift."

With something girlish lighting her face, she made a nasal sound, an elevated crescendo of pleasure and surprise as Jim handed her a pair of high, gray kidskin, side-button shoes.

"I traded some used schoolbooks for them," he said.

She held them in her hands and giggled like a schoolgirl, then kicked off the ragged moccasins and pushed her bare feet into the new, hard-soled shoes, pulling and pushing until her feet settled comfortably inside. "Thank you, my grandson," she said, her eyes squinting at him for a few minutes. "I am very old, though sometimes I do not feel so old. But in my heart I know that I have learned so many things that I do not know much anymore." She was quiet for some minutes, and Jim sat patiently waiting for the old woman to emerge from her reveries. Finally, as she gave no indication of emerging, Jim broke the silence. "There is a funny story going around Carlisle. I want to tell it."

"All right." She nodded and was silent again while she filled her pipe carefully and lit it.

"The story is about a legendary dog that was sacred to a tribe up the Missouri River as far as the Knife. The tribe was wiped out by smallpox, but their legend lasts."

A tension tightened the muscles like a little wave

in Sacajawea's face; then she relaxed and said, "You can tell me, my grandson."

"A young girl was taken captive when she was but a baby and she lived with this tribe, which was called the Big Bellies. She was unusually bright, but not friendly with the Big Bellies. She worked in the fields and always wore a covering robe, even on the warmest days. She sang as she planted, and her corn came up out of the earth greener and stronger than her neighbors'. The women began to watch how she worked. Her bright smile seemed to be the sun that warmed Mother Earth beneath her feet, and her flowing hair the cool breeze that kept the land from parching. They asked her advice, and soon the harvests were bountiful. But the girl did not care about the people and their crops; she loved only the beasts she romped with when the moon was bright. She was leader of a pack of wild dogs. And it is said she was the mate of the most powerful dog."

"Why are you telling me this?"

Jim knew he must not say anything foolish, yet he must go on. The words were in his throat, but they stuck. He took a deep breath and wondered what he feared. Would his grandmother be angry? Would she laugh? Would she sit back with tears in her eyes and say the story was false, made up by someone with a forked tongue? He went on without answering Sacajawea's question.

"Once the dog became bold and wanted to come in the lodge with the girl. The owner of the lodge became frightened and killed the dog."

"Who thinks this is funny?" asked Sacajawea, her mouth twitching.

"The girl danced as she wept, keeping her head lowered, and the Big Bellies saw she never opened her eyes. She danced like a being far away, with no part in what surrounded her. 'She is not of us,' the chief of the village said. 'She is with the wild dog even now. We must do away with her.'"

Sacajawea put her two hands over her face.

"During a period of feasting they left all the meat bones under the sacred tree where the dog's remains were tied. At the end of the feasting, the bone pile was so high it covered the lower branches of the tree. At night they heard the spirit howls of the dog. They believed he was crying for his mate."

Sacajawea was rocking in the hard, leather-heeled, kidskin shoes. "There was no feasting and the girl was not mated to any dog, which was more coyote than anything else!"

Jim went straight ahead in the telling. "The Big Bellies shot arrows into the girl, and she was not wrapped or cleansed, but given back to Mother Earth, ragged and dirty and wild, and she was placed on top of the bones. Then their crops began to fall off and shrivel in the summer heat. Some Big Bellies saw the spirit of the girl. She lived with a neighboring tribe. They left more gifts on the bone pile. But they lay down and died like dogs in their lodges. The spotted sickness destroyed them. But their neighbors say it was the spirit or memory of the girl that really destroyed them. The Big Belly land is barren now, as it was in the beginning before any came to live there."

Oddly enough, Jim found it hard to continue with the most important part. His mouth was dry and his hands were sweaty. He was not so sure his grandmother would answer his final question. He wondered if he ought to not ask, but just make a statement and see her reaction. He tried licking his lips. "I heard you once say that you were a small girl among the Big Bellies and that you tamed a wild dog yourself."

Sacajawea was silent now for a long time. Then, drawing hollow-cheeked upon her pipestem, she smoked awhile and brooded.

"In the story going around Carlisle, what did you hear was the girl's name?"

Jim's mouth was so dry he had to prime himself with a drink of water. "They mentioned a name that is neither Comanche nor Shoshoni."

"I was thinking," she admitted with a deep, explosive chuckle, "of making you stop in the middle of the story—but then I wanted to see what the Big Bellies or their neighbors made up next." She rubbed her hands together as if to loosen the tension.

"Can you say the girl's name?" asked Jim, feeling

now as if something had been released inside his stomach.

"*Ai,*" she said.

"Then say it!" he said. "Say it! I can't wait to hear if it is the name used for the woman who traveled to the west with the soldiers."

"Sacajawea," she said as the tears welled in her eyes.

Jim stared at his great-grandmother in awe. After a time he said, "Then it is true, all the stories you have told and what some of the Carlisle boys say? You have traveled and seen more than any other woman alive. You met the white men after you left the Big Bellies, and you came back and lived near the Mandans for a while. You have relatives that call you Wadzewipe, from the south in Indian Territory, going to Carlisle. These boys said their grandmother went to the Great Western Waters with white soldiers. When our teacher told us about two captains appointed by President Jefferson to go west, these relatives of yours asked many questions about a Comanche woman who went with them. Then someone from Dakota Territory told the story of the Big Bellies, because he said he'd been told this girl's spirit followed the white men to the Great Western Waters. I've waited all this time to ask you. But I believe I knew the whole time who they were speaking about. My great-grandmother!"

"See, it is legend now. I belong to my time, and it has passed. Even the old Hidatsa story is turned inside out and put together wrong. People try to blame something they do not understand on something they do. It will always be that way. And when you listened you heard those Comanche boys say that the woman they knew was Comanche—but you knew she was Shoshoni." She dropped her sunken eyes down to her new boots. "Your thoughts come out in a straight line. I think if it were the other times now, you would be in line to be a chief because I can see you standing above yourself. And you are generous with old people." Again she glanced at her new boots. "Bring me the leather pouch that hangs just inside behind the tepee flap."

When Jim returned, she had stretched out on an old torn gray blanket. "This Mary you visit in the wooden houses of the whites—is she pretty?"

Jim colored and mumbled, "Of course she's pretty."

"I have never seen her, but her smell I know well. When you come back from the agency, you bring it on your shirt and in your hair. Oh, do not deny it. You are a man, and it is time you sought out a woman. The spring of life rises in you, and it cannot be denied. Now, I have a gift for you."

She fumbled with the pouch strings. Into her lap fell a blue feather, a small red feather, then a small, smooth polished stone, rusty red, with a white free-form bird embossed on the surface. One clawlike finger darted inside the pouch and dug out a thin leather thong that had the sky blue polished stone threaded in the center. It was an exquisite piece of rare turquoise. "A woman needs pretties," Sacajawea said, passing the sky blue stone on the thin thong slowly to Jim. "She will make a good woman and mother, and her sewing will improve each season."

Jim knelt beside his great-grandmother and whispered near the sallow, wrinkled face, "I shall not forget this day. I think you should know that Mary is half-white. The other half is Shoshoni from Tendoy's band. She is going to Carlisle." He placed the knotted hands of Sacajawea over his heart, signifying love between them.

Sacajawea leaned toward her great-grandson. Her voice seemed caught in her throat. "I am lonely for the people I used to know. The longer one lives, the shorter life seems. At night when the stars are close to the earth I think I can reach out and touch one. I know I never can and I know that I am nothing in the big scheme of the Mother Earth. When I was your age I thought everything I did was important and meant something, but now I see nothing is of much importance. People all go, their bones crumble to dust and finally no one remembers them. Only a few live on in memories. Some that linger in memories are not the ones that were most important." She sat still, as though half-frightened by her own words. Her thin, bony hands shook. "People make heroes from anyone, because they need to believe all life's activity is important. It's important to respect each other. I have known some highly esteemed people—they are gone now and forgotten by most. In an-

other age or two no one will know they were even here."
She began to sing softly to herself.

"Grandmother," interrupted Jim, "everyone is important, because what each of us does is built from what
those before us have done. One bead on a string might
be forgotten if it is lost, but it is missed. With all the
beads in place, one after the other, the string is something good to look at, and to keep adding to. You know
what I mean to say?" He rubbed his hands together and
looked at his grandmother, whose beady eyes seemed
to have a faraway, watery luster.

When summer was over, Jim made a large woodpile
for Sacajawea, and together they dried half a dozen
large boxes of beef strips. On the day Jim left for Carlisle Sacajawea said, "Please, make the sleeping couch
in my tepee comfortable with more pine boughs. Also,
I would like some sweet wild parsnips for my stew, my
grandson."

That winter was mild and she spent no more than
six weeks in the wooden lodge of old Shoogan and his
family. The noise of the great-grandchildren was harsh
in her ears and she was happy to be back in her quiet
tepee. She talked to herself for company. "When I was
getting wood this morning, I could see the snow on the
Wind River Mountains was shrinking. The wind is
warmer and carries moisture. The month of melting
snow is here."

The chinook wind rose by evening, and there was
water running deeper in the streams. The tepee skins
bellied out with the warm gusts of wind and Sacajawea
found more rocks of red sandstone to hold the skirt
firmly to the ground.

When the snow melted or was blown from her path-
way she walked slowly and stiffly with the help of her
cane to pick up her rations. The agency had a new
Episcopalian Minister—the Reverend John Roberts,
who was called White Robe. He was middle-aged and
wore a brown beard on his chin. He was determined
that the Shoshonis and Arapahos have the full benefit
of Sunday school, church, prayer meeting, Bible reading, and grace. There was to be no working on the Sab-
bath, except what could not be avoided. There was to

be no laughter, no card playing, no dancing, no gambling, no horse racing, and positively no drinking. Whenever he passed a group of young men sitting on the ground gambling with hidden plum pits, drinking eighty percent alcohol, fruit-flavored extract from innocuous tin cups, they all rose up and smiled. He bowed and said, "How do you do?"

Sacajawea could not figure him, so she avoided him as much as possible.

Late one night the chinook wind died and the last cold snap of the season fell over the land, making the melted snow hard and slick as glass. Then just as suddenly it was April and the snow was nearly gone, except for the deeper drifts on the north sides of the hills. This was the month when the meadowlark's song brightened the greening meadows. Sacajawea sat, wrapped in a thick blanket, against the cottonwood near her tepee. She dozed in the sunshine while listening to the sounds of spring.

Her grease-stained tunic seemed as old as the ground she sat on. The sun moved down little by little, giving the mountains a rose-colored glow and casting a gold shimmer on the river's water. Then, without warning, a strange radiance lit up the dusky evening. The light seemed to come from the agency. It flickered brilliantly over the tops of the wind-stunted trees, then died and left only a fleeting smell of charred pine resin.

Sacajawea rose unsteadily to her feet, feeling no sense of emergency. She took her time checking the adequate woodpile and stack of brush behind her tepee. She went inside and poked at the small pile of molding parsnips. She looked in her coffee tin and saw there was some left. She opened the cornmeal sack and saw only a few weevils on top, so she knotted the sack closed. She had forgotten to go after her last rations. She had not been hungry and even now did not eat much. But she felt fine and her mind was clear as the mountain air.

She scuffled around with the high, side-button shoes on for a while, then she pulled them off. She rested a few moments before slipping her stockinged feet into the comfortable old frayed moccasins. She turned her head to one side, listening. The sound of footsteps came up the trail and stopped outside her tepee. She got up and shuffled out. She could see a lighted lantern swinging back and forth held by a man in heavy, black wool coat and wool cap. His eyes were watery blue, and his mouth pulled in a tight line above the neatly trimmed brown beard on his chin. It was Reverend Roberts.

"How do you do?" she asked in a low but clear voice.

"I have come to tell you not to be alarmed—there was a fire at the agency, but it is under control now and nothing to worry about. We saved most everything, except a box of old papers and some things left by Dr. Irwin and his wife. He probably won't miss it. Don't worry now. Goodnight." Then, as an afterthought, he turned back. "Could I send someone out Sunday to bring you in to church, Old Grandmother?"

"Thank you," she said in a calm voice, without anxiety. "You are considerate. But by Sunday I shall be gone. Goodnight."

"I don't advise you to go anywhere in this upcoming weather, Old Grandmother," Reverend Roberts said. "It seems mild now, but it will be raining by tomorrow or the next day for sure. Can't you smell the rain coming in that wind? Take care."

She listened to his receding footsteps.

She went back inside and put her side-button shoes on the shelf. She undid the cornmeal sack again and scooped a heaping pie tin full of the meal for her old horse. After feeding it she left the horse unhobbled for the night. Then she scooped out more cornmeal and scattered it on the ground for the birds and chipmunks. When she came back inside to close the cornmeal sack, she left the tepee flap pinned open so that the night spirits could come in or go out as they wished. The night air was chilly, with a feel of frost, so she pulled on her woolen skirt and wrapped the blanket tighter about her shoulders. She was breathing heavily and sat to rest on her pine-bough couch. When her legs stopped shaking and she felt stronger, she got up and pulled down the old, beaded leather pouch. Her bent, clawlike fingers fished out the polished, rusty red stone with the white bird marking. She held it in her fist until it took in her body warmth.

Keeping the red stone in her fist she clumsily folded two thin, but new, woolen blankets given to her by the

government. She put them beside her open tepee flap
along with several of her favorite cooking pots and polished horn dippers and stirrers. She broke the tops off
the limp parsnips, and threw them out the doorway.
She dipped the parsnips in her water bucket and washed
them, then dropped them in the kettle of simmering
stew. She did not build up the smoldering fire. She
swept the dirt floor with a straw broom, so that it looked
as if a fine rake had gone over it. All the while she held
the red stone in her fist. Then she lay down on the
couch to rest. When her breathing steadied, she pulled
a worn buffalo robe over herself.

After a short nap, her scrawny, hooked hand came
out with the red stone. She fumbled with the old, thick
blanket she had wrapped around her shoulders and then
she reached under her tunic and placed the warm stone
between her sagging breasts. This was the only thing
that held many memories for her. She had a long lifetime. She knew nothing was lost, only the forgotten
memories. Nothing was gained, only the addition of
remembered knowledge.

Sometime in the middle of the night, the smoldering
coals turned cold, as did the body warmth of the old
woman on the pine-bough couch. All was dark and still
inside the old tepee. Outside, dark clouds hung low,
ready to rain in teardrop-size splatters over the Wind
River area, making the dust and rock deep red and
shiny. The heads of all the prairie plants bowed with
the wind.

Epilogue

There were several fires at the agency of the Wind River Reservation in the late 1870s and early 1880s. But the United States Government has no documents in its present files stating exactly when those fires took place or whether they were in fact at the agency or the government barracks at Fort Washakie.[1]

Finn. G. Burnett, government farmer on the Wind River Reservation, wrote in 1926:

> I can remember distinctly how interested Mrs. Irwin [her husband, Dr. James Irwin, was Indian agent and surgeon] was in Sacajawea's description of the expedition. Mrs. Irwin was well educated. The paper on which she wrote this history was legal cap, with a red line down the side, and it was more than twenty-five sheets; rolling it up, it made quite a large roll. I cannot definitely state the number of pages. The last time I saw it, it was kept with an autographed letter from President Lincoln to Dr. Irwin, for services rendered by him on the field of the battle of Shiloh. The last time I saw it, it was at the office of the agency, which was burned. I can't remember the date, but it seemed that part of the records were saved. We hunted diligently for the letter from President Lincoln and the manuscript, realizing even then that they were valuable. Some years after, at the request of Mrs. Irwin's daughter, I hunted for the letter and manuscript, but was unable to discover either one.[2]

It seems unusual that the Irwins did not take their personal, valuable papers with them when they were transferred to the Pine Ridge Indian Reservation in 1873. Instead, they apparently left them behind at the agency office on the Wind River Reservation.

Reverend John Roberts, Episcopalian minister on the Wind River Reservation, conducted a Christian burial ceremony over Sacajawea's grave in the cemetery of the *reservation on the day she died. Dr. Hebard stated in her book that Sacajawea had no last illness and was found in her tepee lifeless on the morning of April 9, 1884.*[3]

In the parish records kept by Reverend Roberts appears this record:

DATE   *April 9, 1884*
NAME   *Bazil's mother (Shoshone)*
AGE   *Near one hundred*
RESIDENCE   *Shoshone agency*
CAUSE OF DEATH   *Old age*
PLACE OF BURIAL   *Burial ground, Shoshone agency*
SIGNATURE OF CLERGYMAN   *J. Roberts*[4]

One of Sacajawea's neighbors, Mrs. Lane, wife of an Indian trader, told Dr. Hebard about Sacajawea's death.

One morning word was received that Bazil's mother was dead. Mr. Lane, the Indian trader, said, "I'll go to the tepee." At the door of the tent Bazil arrived with tears running down his face. Speaking to me, he said, "Mrs. Lane, my mother is dead." I saw Bazil's mother taken from the tepee wrapped in skins and sewed up for burial. The body was placed on her favorite horse, the horse being led by Bazil. Probably the body was to be taken to where the coffin was, for she was buried in a coffin according to the statement by Reverend Roberts and others.[5]

The Reverend John Roberts had a remarkable memory to be able to state that the woman called "Bazil's mother" was in fact Sacajawea after he had been on the reservation only a year before this old woman died. The old woman probably did not go far from her lodge; possibly she never went to services in the Episcopalian church, at least while he was there. She was very old and feeble. Dr. Hebard did not question Reverend Roberts overly in this matter.

In 1885, the man called Baptiste died on the reservation. His body was taken by a few Indians and carried into the mountains west of the agency and let down forty feet between two crags. After the body had been lowered by rope, a few rocks were thrown down upon the corpse, one of which struck the skull and crushed it. Later a rock slide completely buried his remains.

Edward N. Wentworth of Chesterton, Indiana, wrote to Clyde Porter, a collector of western relics, on December 2, 1955.

There used to be a big fellow from Lander [Wyoming], Ed Farlow, who was with Buffalo Bill for a while in charge of the Indians who went to Europe and I had many talks with him concerning the reservation and the Indians up there. He finally told me that he thought neither the Indians nor the whites had the slightest idea who was buried there. He was quite certain that the man who they claimed to be Sacajawea's son was not a son of Sacajawea. However, he was a publicity man more than a student and I didn't pay much attention to him then—I wish I had.

"One of the biggest hoaxes in history had its beginning in 1904 at Laramie, Wyoming," according to Blanche Schroer, who lives in Lander, Wyoming, and was a resident of the Wind River Indian Reservation.[6] Schroer does not believe that the Wind River woman called Porivo was Sacajawea at all, but some other Shoshoni woman, who knew little of the Lewis and Clark Expedition, and that the closest she ever came to a large body of water was the Great Salt Lake in Utah.

In 1886, Shoogan, or Bazil, a subchief under Washakie, died. He was wrapped in a sheet and blanket and taken by a few Indians up to a stream called Mill Creek, and placed in a new gulch that was dug into the bank and that caved down and covered the body.

In 1924, Andrew Bazil, son of old Bazil, gave his consent to Dr. Charles Eastman, inspector and investigator for the U.S. Department of the Interior, Office of Indian Affairs, to have his father's grave site dug into. He recalled that his father was buried with the papers that had belonged to Sacajawea and many of them from members of the Lewis and Clark Expedition and Brigham Young of the Mormon Church. The wallet was found lying underneath the skull "in good condition." But the *contents were "ruined by moisture and the passage of time" so that they could not be read. The skeleton was found in poor condition. An old saddle lay across the feet, and beside the skeleton was a handsome pipe of peace. On January 12, 1925, the bones were reinterred beside the bones of Sacajawea in the Shoshoni cemetery. On account of freezing weather, it was impossible to hold a formal ceremony beyond the reading of the prayers for the dead.[7]*

This raises the question of why Dr. Eastman, who was college-educated, did not send the leather wallet with its "moisture-ruined" papers to a museum or some university's anthropology department or the Smithsonian Institution, where people qualified to open and take the papers apart carefully would have been delighted at the chance to "prove" that this man buried in the Shoshoni cemetery was the nephew of Sacajawea and that the papers had, indeed, belonged to Sacajawea. And why was the grave of the old Shoshoni woman, said to be Sacajawea, not opened at the same time? There might have been some identifying thing buried with her.

Finn Burnett, the government farmer on the reservation, never went to school, but taught himself to read and write. He said that all he ever knew of the Lewis and Clark Expedition he learned from the squaw called Porivo, whom he believed to be Sacajawea. He said he had heard her speak English, French, and Shoshoni, and seen her good form of hand language.[8]

James I. Patten, U.S. Government teacher, religious instructor, and Indian Agent to the Shoshonis from 1874 to 1880, said:

I believe most sincerely in the identity of this Shoshone woman. From the very first of my acquaintance with her in 1874, I was sure of this fact. She must have been Sacajawea for how could an old Shoshone squaw have known of Lewis and Clark if she had not seen them and had not been associated with them at least for some time?[9]

Tom Rivington, a western pioneer who lived his last years in Gering, Nebraska, wrote to Dr. Hebard about being with Sacajawea in Virginia City, Montana, in the

years 1860 and 1861, when he was an orphaned boy.[10]
*At that time there was no Virginia City. Gold was not
discovered in Alder Gulch until May 26, 1863, and Virginia City came into existence in June of that year. It is
known that Tom was a tall-story teller, and he probably
wrote some of his tall ones to Dr. Hebard to please her
and to have his name in her famous book.*

Rivington told Dr. Hebard that all U.S. Army officers
at Fort Washakie knew Sacajawea and gave her presents. She traveled constantly through the mountains,
helped by the stage drivers, who never charged for her
rides. Rivington went on to say that Henry Plummer,
the sheriff and onetime road agent, gave her three sacks
of flour to keep her from going on a certain stage. That
night the stage was robbed and the passengers shot.[11]

Rivington also wrote to Dr. Hebard the following,
which shows he had a flair for writing as well as storytelling:

> She never liked to stay or live where she could not
> see the mountains, for them she called home. For the
> unseen spirits dwelt in the hills, and a swift running
> creek could preach a better sermon for her than any
> mortal could have done. Every morning she thanked
> the spirits for a new day. She worshipped the white
> flowers that grew at the snow line on the sides of the
> tall mountains for, as she said, she sometimes be-
> lieved that they were the spirits of little children that
> had gone away, but reappeared every spring to glad-
> den the pathway of those now living.
>
> I was just a boy then, but those words sunk down
> deep in my soul. I believed them, and I believe now,
> that if there is a hereafter, that the good Indian wom-
> an's name will be on the right side of the ledger. Sa-
> ca-ja-we is gone.[12]

Merrill J. Mattes of the National Park Service, U.S.
Department of the Interior, wrote about Tom Rivington's
character:

> It so happens I remember very vividly my conver-
> sations with Tom Rivington of Gering, Nebraska, way
> back in the 1930's and I distinctly remember his tell-

*ing me that he knew Sacajawea and rode in the stage
coach with her, etc. At the time I believed him, because
I didn't have much background in western history.
Now, however, I think this was a fabrication, or else
the woman he claims he knew as Sacajawea was actually someone else with an assumed name.*

*It is a difficult thing to come right out and admit
that the famous grave at Fort Washakie is not that of
Sacajawea after all, but of some other historical nobody.*[13,14]

The people in the state of Wyoming freely admit the
veracity of the journal entries of Judge Brackenridge
and Clerk John Luttig stating that Charbonneau was
on the keelboat going up the Missouri in 1811. But they
believe that the woman with him, who later died at Fort
Manuel, was a Shoshoni, but not Sacajawea. Charbonneau always had several young squaws; Otter Woman
was also a Shoshoni.

Will Robinson, secretary of the South Dakota State
Historical Society, wrote:

*I have not the slightest doubt but that she died at
Fort Manuel [South Dakota]. The Wyoming myth was
a good one before the Luttig Journals were unearthed
in 1912, suggesting she died in 1812. Add the testimony of Brackenridge and others as to her being at
Ft. Manuel and Clark's final statement, and no one
could possibly have known better of her death than
he and you have the final rivet in the coffin of the
Wyoming myth.*[15]

The people in Oklahoma like to quote Edith Connelley
Clift, wife of the late William H. Clift, a Lawton businessman, cotton gin owner, and historian. Edith Clift
was a researcher and writer of historical articles. She
says:

*She left a son among the Comanche and during
recent years, a daughter of that son visited us here
on this reservation. One time when she was on the
reservation she explained to me that she was a granddaughter of Sacajawea. The tradition was very com-*

*mon among this tribe of Indians that Sacajawea had
led a large body of white men to the west to a body
of big waters.*

*The daughter of Sacajawea's son, Ticannaf, above
referred to was Ta-soon-da-hipe or Tah-cu-tine, which
translated means Take Pity On. She resided within
a few miles of Lawton, Oklahoma, on the Reservation
there.*

*And so, Oklahoma may claim contact with the his-
tory of our earlier days as a nation; and an important
link with the famed Lewis and Clark Expedition.*[16]

*And so Montana, Wyoming, and South Dakota claim
to have the burial ground of Sacajawea. Oklahoma takes
much pride in having her grandchildren grow up near
Lawton. Even the city of Cloverport, Kentucky, population about 1,400, celebrates an annual Sacajawea festival in August. The city's inhabitants believe, although
they are incorrect, that Sacajawea was already with
Captain Lewis when he was sent to Louisville to recruit
nine Kentucky woodsmen in 1803 for the expedition.*[17]
*The state of Idaho claims to have Sacajawea's birthplace
near Fort Lemhi. North Dakota, Washington, and Oregon have statues commemorating Sacajawea as the
"guide for the Lewis and Clark Expedition."*

*The cemetery at Wind River Reservation, Fort Wa-
shakie, Wyoming, where it is believed by many that
Sacajawea lies buried, is a forty-acre tract of ground enclosed by a fence of cedar posts and barbed wire, with
an irrigation ditch running along the left side, that once
belonged to Andrew Bazil. Among the grave decorations,
iron bedsteads, neatly painted white, hold the most
prominent place. They are placed around the graves; the
head- and footboard and two sides mark a small fence
to protect the grave. Many wagons are likewise given an
honored place, though the boxes and tongues have been
removed from them.*

*When the woman called Porivo, believed to be Sac-
ajawea, was buried, a small wooden slab was placed
at the head of her grave.*[18] *The spring grass stood high,
brushing the moccasins of the mourners. Groves of yellow-green cottonwood trees sheltered the splashing waters
of the Wind River. Sage covered the ridges and mesas.*

On the lower hills were stands of sycamore, of alder and aspen. Near the water, always, were the slender white trunks of graceful birch rising out of the bloodred soil. Above all loomed the distant high peaks of the Shining Mountains, the magnificent snowclad Wind River Range to the west and the Owl Creek Mountains to the northeast.

Today, however, a substantial gray-granite column placed on a raised concrete slab marks the grave. On the face of this rough stone is a large polished area containing the inscription:[19]

SACAJAWEA
DIED APRIL 9, 1884
A GUIDE WITH THE
LEWIS AND CLARK
EXPEDITION
1805——1806
IDENTIFIED, 1907 BY
REV. J. ROBERTS
WHO OFFICIATED AT
HER BURIAL

Under this inscription is a bronze plaque with the words:

DEDICATED BY
THE WYOMING STATE ORGANIZATION
OF THE WYOMING SOCIETY
OF THE DAUGHTERS
OF THE AMERICAN REVOLUTION
1943

Annually, hundreds of people visit this commemoration of the final resting place of Sacajawea. She was the first woman to travel across half the continent with American soldiers to the Pacific Coast.

Notes

Many facts and stories from a variety of sources came to my attention during the writing of this novel that were interesting sidelights, but did not necessarily further the life story of Sacajawea. Collected here, they give authenticity and perspective to our Indian heroine. In most cases, the citations include: author's name, year of publication if more than one work of the author appears in the Bibliography, and relevant page numbers. More complete information regarding these sources may be found in the Bibliography that follows these Notes. Notes that do not have source references are my own explications. In some cases copyright owners requested that the complete source be included here in the owners' particular format.

—A.L.W.

CHAPTER 1 *Old Grandmother*

1. The Agaidükas, or Salmon Eaters, were the Lemhi Shoshonis first seen by explorers in Montana's Bitterroot Mountains. The Tukadükas, or Sheep Eaters, probably merged with the Agaidükas just prior to discovery by white men. From *The Shoshonis, Sentinels of the Rockies*, by Virginia Trenholm and Maurine Carley, p. 22. Copyright 1964 by the University of Oklahoma Press.

2. Halfway up the mountain toward the large med-

icine circle, there are several huge horseshoe prints, and another close to the top. All are made of stones. Apparently pointing to the large circle from nearly one hundred miles away to the southwest is a fifty-eight-foot-long arrow made of stones. Trenholm and Carley, p. 25.

3. A Shoshoni chief's office was not hereditary. The chief depended on his valor and integrity to acquire and retain the office. Trenholm and Carley, p. 32.

4. Many Native Americans, including the Shoshonis, incorporate a story of a great flood in their myths and legends. Trenholm and Carley, p. 35.

5. A mother bear seldom leaves her cubs very far away, even during the second summer. She will attack anything she thinks is trying to molest the cubs. Scharff, p. 126.

CHAPTER 2 *Captured*

1. The journals of Lewis and Clark give a most complete record of the daily progress of their expedition. The inventive spelling and laconic prose style have endeared both men to generations of readers.

2. Some say that the storytelling period of the Shoshonis is during December, January, and February, and that they refuse to tell their stories any other time. Good storytellers were always in demand, but no one had exclusive right to any particular tale. From *The Shoshonis, Sentinels of the Rockies*, by Virginia Trenholm and Maurine Carley, p. 36. Copyright 1964 by the University of Oklahoma Press.

3. On July 28, 1805, nearly five years later, Captains Lewis and Clark named the eastern fork of the Missouri, which was 2,500 miles from its mouth, Gallatin, after Secretary of the Treasury, Albert Gallatin; the middle fork, the Madison, for Secretary of State, James Madison; and the western fork, the Jefferson, "in honor of that illustrious personage Thomas Jefferson." R. G. Ferris, pp. 149, 152.

CHAPTER 3 *People of the Willows*

1. Flintlock is a term used indiscriminately for any type of gun that has a spring that activates a hammer so that it strikes a piece of flint against a vertical,

pivoted, striking plate to produce sparks that ignite the charge. From the late 1600s to the early 1800s the flint-lock was the dominant firearm in use. From *Encyclopedia of Firearms*, edited by Harold L. Peterson. Copyright © by George Rainbird Ltd., 1964. Reprinted by permission of the publisher, E. P. Dutton, Inc., p. 130.

CHAPTER 4 *Bird Woman*

1. Mandan bull boats were different from any boats made by other tribes. They were surprisingly similar to the Welsh *coracle*. Both were made of rawhide stretched on a frame of willow and shaped round, like a tub. It was light enough for a woman to carry from storage to the water. The Mandan woman stood in the front of her bull boat and dipped the paddle forward, drawing it back to her. She did not paddle at the side. She moved rapidly in her little round boat. Catlin, Vol. II, p. 261.

2. This Shoshoni girl's name is spelled in this fashion only because it is the most common spelling found in the U.S. Most readers are probably aware of the good-natured disagreement the various spellings of her name can inspire. The National Park Service, in 1979, adopted the spelling *Sacagawea*, because despite the varied spelling in the Lewis and Clark Journals, the *g* is generally present. Also, since she was Shoshoni, this is a Shoshoni word (meaning *boat launcher*).

Historian John Bakeless used *Sacagawea* because Clark wrote in his journal on Monday, May 20, 1805, "...this stream we called Sah-ca-gah-we-a or bird woman's River, after our interpreter, the Snake woman."

It was George Shannon who spelled the Shoshoni woman's name *Sacajawea*, with the soft *j* in the middle.

The people in the Dakotas, close to Hidatsa territory, write *Sakakawea*. The famed Mandan and Hidatsa anthropologist, Dr. Alfred Bowers of Moscow, Idaho, told me in May 1979 that she was given her name while living among the Hidatsa, and it means *Bird Woman*.

In 1970 the Lemhi County Historical Society, Salmon, Idaho, published a letter written by a historian, John E. Rees, sometime in the mid-1920s to the Hon. Charles H. Burke, U.S. Commissioner of Indian Affairs. The

1970 reprint of the letter was edited by David G. Ainsworth and titled, "Madame Charbonneau: The Indian Woman Who Accompanied the Lewis and Clark Expedition, 1804–6: How she received her Indian Name and what became of her." Rees points out that both *Sacajawea* and *Sacagawea* are Shoshoni versions and mean "travels with the boats that are being pulled." The Hidatsa language contains no *j* or *g*. *Sakaka* in Hidatsa means "bird" and *wea* means "woman." The Lewis and Clark Journals are clear that her name means *Bird Woman*.

3. Coyotes belong to the same mammalian family as domestic dogs. In summer they hunt and kill small prey, gophers, mice, and squirrels, and in winter they feed on large, dead prey such as carrion of deer, moose, and elk. Coyotes mate once a year and the same pair returns to the same den site each year. Bekoff and Wells, pp. 130–48.

4. Catlin writes about these people's "extraordinary art of manufacturing a very beautiful and lasting kind of blue glass beads." Catlin, Vol. II, pp. 260–1.

It is assumed that by the early 1800s there had been a cultural exchange between the Mandan and Hidatsa (origin, early Crow). They lived close together in the five-village area near the confluence of the Knife and Missouri Rivers, in what is now North Dakota. Thus, their lodges, food, clothing, religious rites, etc. were quite similar.

CHAPTER 5 *The Wild Dog*

1. Besides hunting the buffalo, the Mandan also "gathered" buffalo meat. Every spring when the ice of the Missouri River and its tributaries began to melt and break up, the buffalo which had drowned or been frozen in the ice floated downstream. The Mandans swam or floated out on the river on blocks of ice to gather in these buffalo. This soft, rotten meat was a great delicacy to these people. Spicer, p. 219.

CHAPTER 6 *The Trading Fair*

1. In 1736 a Jesuit missionary told about the Assiniboins' annual spring visit to the Mandan to trade for dried corn. La Verendrye, two years later, experienced

the Mandan trade fair and wrote about the dried corn, tobacco, grain, and squash exchanged for flintlocks, axes, kettles, powder, knives, and awls. A decade later the Arapaho were holding trade fairs on a branch of the Platte River to obtain British steel knives and axes from the Cheyenne, who in turn had traded them from the Mandan. During this heightened trade period, the Crees traded their furs and snowshoes for guns and in a period of a few years turned from a secluded Woodland type people to a typical nomadic Plains people. From *Indians of the Plains*, by Robert H. Lowie, pp. 22, 130, 211, Natural History Press. Copyright 1954 by the American Museum of Natural History.

CHAPTER 7   *Toussaint Charbonneau*

1. Grace Raymond Hebard, *Sacajawea, A Guide and Interpreter of the Lewis and Clark Expedition*. Glendale, CA: The Arthur H. Clark Co., 1957, p. 93.

2. Hebard, 1957, p. 93.

3. Hebard, 1957, p. 94.

4. The big timber was heavy that was used to build this fort near the Mandan villages so the men used what were called hand sticks to carry it. Hand sticks were usually made of ash, about the diameter of a man's wrist, and were pushed under the large log at each end. Four men could then carry the log by having two men on each stick, one at each end.

5. John Bakeless, *Lewis and Clark, Partners in Discovery*. New York: William Morrow and Co., 1947, p. 155.

6. Bakeless, p. 155.

7. Bakeless, p. 155.

8. Bakeless, pp. 155–56; Hebard, 1957, p. 98.

9. Hebard, 1957, pp. 89–90. Charbonneau evidently did not care for the life of a farmer or staying in one place for too long.

10. Bakeless, p. 454; Hebard, 1957, p. 90.

11. Hebard, 1957, p. 99.

12. Hebard, 1957, p. 99.

13. Hebard, 1957, pp. 99–100.

14. Hebard, 1957, p. 100.

Duke Paul visited General Clark at his home on Main and Vine in St. Louis in 1823 to ask questions

about the fertile land in the Midwest. Five years later
Duke Paul was back on the Missouri River. This was
his third trip to look for good areas in which to establish
German agricultural, utopian communities. Marshall
Sprague, *A Gallery of Dudes*. Boston: Little Brown and
Company, 1966–7, pp. 34, 37.

In the fall of 1832, Prince Maximilian of Germany
was in this country and fell ill. He stayed all winter in
New Harmony, Indiana, a town established by Swabian
rebels from Duke Paul's Württemberg. The rebels called
themselves Harmonists. Later, in 1833, Maximilian
visited the town of Economy on the Ohio below Pittsburgh, which was founded by the same Harmony Society. These Harmonists were in disharmony over the
question of being celibate or not. Sprague, pp. 36–7.

15. Sprague, p. 50.

It was said by Captain R. Holmes of the U.S. Army
in 1830 that Charbonneau never carried a gun. He had
only his skinning knife as a weapon. Hebard, 1957, p.
100.

Charbonneau took Prince Maximilian and the artist,
Karl Bodmer, to one of the Mandan villages to arrange
a time for portrait sittings with the village chief and
his subchiefs. Maximilian was most interested in the
mode of dress and behavior of the Mandans until "a
young warrior took hold of my pocket compass which I
wore suspended by a ribbon, and attempted to take it
by force. . . . I refused his request, but the more I insisted
in my refusal, the more importunate he became. He
offered me a handsome horse for my compass, and then
all his handsome clothes and arms into the bargain,
and as I still refused, he became angry, and" it was at
this point that old Charbonneau dissuaded the Mandan
by explaining that the white man would never trade
the compass for any amount of goods. Sprague, p. 48.

At this time Maximilian wrote in his journal of old
Charbonneau's inability to pronounce the Minnetaree
language, even after living among these people for more
than thirty years. "He generally lives at Awaticai [Me-
taharta], the second village of the Manitaries, and ex-
cepting some journeys, has always remained at this
spot; hence, he is well acquainted with the Manitaries
and their language, though as he candidly confessed he

could never learn to pronounce it." Hebard, 1957, p. 103.

While at Fort Clark, Maximilian was given the opportunity to read a document which he later wrote about in his journal. This document was written on long paper in English and Manitari language. Most of the Indian names, which were doubtless given by Charbonneau, were incorrectly written. Hebard, 1957, p. 104.

16. Bakeless, p. 454.

17. Bakeless, p. 454; Hebard, 1957, p. 105.

18. Bakeless, p. 454; Hebard, 1957, p. 105.

19. Bakeless, p. 454.

20. Bakeless, p. 455; Hebard, 1957, p. 105.

21. *Sublette Papers*, Missouri Historical Society, St. Louis.

22. Hebard, 1957, pp. 106–7.

23. Personal letter, 1968.

24. Bakeless, p. 155.

25. R. G. Ferris, p. 115.

26. Personal interview, May 1979. A similar story written by Jo Rainbolt appeared in *The Missourian* and was reprinted in *The Jefferson Republic*, DeSoto, Missouri, Feb. 22, 1979, Sec. 2, p. 1.

27. Bakeless, p. 155.

28. Chief Kakoakis was called *Le Borgne* or *One-Eye* by traders. He was known for his brutality, gigantic stature, huge aquiline nose, and coarse features. He glared savagely out of his good, left eye, while the white, opaque membrane that had destroyed the sight of the other made him most forbidding. "One white acquaintance remarked that if his one eye had only been in the middle of his forehead, he would have made a good Cyclops." Bakeless, p. 146.

29. This Shoshoni girl was *Penzo-bert* or Otter; sometimes she is called Otter Woman.

30. Ecclesiastes III, 1–8.

The Mandan may have had an ancient tradition of Christianity from relationships with the twelfth-century Welsh or other early European travelers. Enough of that early tradition was handed down, age after age, so that the Shaman and singer used familiar Biblical quotations that were altered over the years into a kind of poetry similar in form to that used by old

Welsh bards, who recited or sang about their country-
men and important events. It is a fact that most early
Indian religions were neither propagandistic nor dog-
matic. Thus, the Mandans easily combined Christian
doctrines from early priests and French-Canadian fur
traders with a belief in the reality of spirits who appeared in dreams and the Indian, hunger-induced visions.

31. When Shoshoni children were small, they were
frightened into proper behavior with stories of red-haired
cannibals or the cannibal owls that were able to catch
an arrow flying through the air. The Shoshoni who first
saw white men seemed to equate the men with the owls
and were terrified to see "their big white eyes" staring
from their hairy faces. From *The Shoshonis, Sentinels
of the Rockies*, by Virginia Trenholm and Maurine Carley, pp. 83–4. Copyright 1964 by the University of
Oklahoma Press.

CHAPTER 8　*The Mandans*

1. Deacon, pp. 108–12, 184, 217.

2. Paul Herrmann, *Conquest by Man*, transl. by Michael Bullock. New York: Harper and Bros., 1954. Copyright Hoffman und Campe Verlag, c/o Curtis Brown,
Ltd.

3. Williams, pp. 11–12.

4. The titular head of the Mandans was The Wolf
Chief, *Ha-na-ta-nu-mauk*, who was so haughty and
overbearing that he was more feared than loved by his
people. From *George Catlin and the Old Frontier*, by
Harold McCracken, p. 94. Copyright 1959, Crown Publishers, Inc.

5. *Mah-to-toh-pa*, Four Bears, second chief, was first
in popularity. He was generous, gentlemanly, and
handsome. Catlin thought him a most extraordinary
man. Catlin, Vol. I, p. 92.

6. Pheasants were not introduced into Dakota Territory until at least twenty years after both North and
South Dakota became states in 1889. Presumably, the
fool hens, prairie chickens, and various species of grouse
in the Dakota region at this time were generally called
pheasants.

George Catlin translates the Mandans' name, *See-*

pohs-ka-nu-mah-ka-kee, as *People of the Pheasants.*
Catlin, Vol. I, p. 80.

7. The homosexual male Indian generally remained
in the village to take care of the women and children
when the other men were hunting or at war. The Indians thought that these men had been informed by a
dream or "medicine vision" to dress and act as women.
They had no loss of status. The nineteenth-century
writer referred to gay Indians as *beaus* or *dandies.*
McCracken, pp. 87–8.

CHAPTER 9 *The Okeepa*
1. In Mandan *Okeepa* means *to look alike.* In this
important ceremony the Bull Dancers were the same
height and stature, painted and dressed alike. Alfred
W. Bowers, *Mandan Social and Ceremonial Organization.* Chicago: University of Chicago Press, 1950;
Midway Reprints, 1973, p. 111.

2. The Lone Man collected the knives and sharp-
edged tools and threw them into the Missouri River as
an offering to the Grandfather Snake. A few robes along
with seven corn balls were thrown into the water also.
Bowers, p. 150.

3. Besides the rod the Devil wore as an artificial
penis, he had two small pumpkins representing testi-
cles. His limbs seemed to have holes through them at
the joints, due to the manner of painting a red spot with
a white circle around it. Bowers, p. 145.

4. During the "Going In" ceremony, two skewers were
inserted through the skin on the back or on the breast
by which the candidate was suspended in midair. Other
skewers were inserted through the skin of the legs from
which buffalo skulls were hung. The Mandans believed
that the experience with the supernatural at this time
was intensely spiritual. Bowers, p. 135.

CHAPTER 10 *The Game of Hands*
1. Lowie, pp. 131–34, describes the game of hands
and states that it was played by tribes even beyond the
Plains area. It was played with pairs of small objects,
either bone, stone, sticks, or plum pits. One object was
always marked by carvings or an incised line or string
around the middle. The other object was left plain. The

guesser had to guess the hand holding the unmarked
object. The game was accompanied by singing and the
person hiding the objects swayed his body, arms, and
hands to the rhythm of the music. The movements were
graceful, yet intricate enough to be confusing to the
guesser. Sometimes horses were the main prize, or the
entire contents of a man's lodge, or his wife or wives.

Garcia, pp. 185–86, also gives an excellent description of how skilled the Native Americans were in ma-
nipulating the small, polished, hand-hidden objects of
this game. Also see Lavender, pp. 149–50.

CHAPTER 11   *Lewis and Clark*

1. Blanket points were five-inch lines woven into the
blanket edge behind the front color stripe to denote size,
from one to four points. The wool blankets cost one
beaver pelt per point. The Hudson's Bay Company four-
point today is a double blanket, 144 inches long.

2. The French explorer Pierre Gaultier de Varennes
de la Vérendrye had visited the Mandans as long ago
as 1738. He found nine Mandan villages at that time
near the mouth of the Heart River, about sixty miles
downstream from where Lewis and Clark found them.
A French-Canadian named Ménard, who was engaged
by a British fur company, found the Mandans in the
late 1780s and lived among them for nearly fourteen
years. The nine villages were decimated by smallpox
about 1790, and the number of people gradually decreased until only two villages were found by Lewis
and Clark in 1804. Lewis and Clark also found two
Hidatsa (Minnetaree) villages and one Amahami village in the same general area on the banks of the Missouri in what is now North Dakota.

3. Big White was amiable, fat, weak in character,
and not much respected by his people. Sergeant Gass
thought he was "best looking Indian I ever saw." John
Bakeless, *Lewis and Clark, Partners in Discovery*. New
York: William Morrow and Co., 1947, pp. 145–46.

4. The explorers built their fort none too soon for
safety. On November 5 the Sioux held a powwow, inviting many of their tribes and the Arikaras to join
them in the spring in a fight against the white explorers. The Sioux put off the fight until spring to catch

the white men by surprise and because they saw the fort was equipped with the air gun, the swivel, which was adapted for mounting on stockades, rifles, and blunderbusses. Bakeless, pp. 152–53.

The air gun was bought by Lewis in 1803 in Pennsylvania. The air was compressed about ten times so that the single ball went as far as sixty to seventy yards. This air gun was not a repeater, but it could be fired as fast as one could drop the balls into the muzzle. When Lewis first purchased the gun someone examined it and accidently pulled the trigger. The ball grazed the temple of a woman forty yards away. Bakeless, p. 102.

Lewis wrote on the 7th of August, 1805, "My air gun was out of order and her sights had been removed by some accident. I put her in order and regulated her. She shot again as well as she ever did." From *The Journals of Lewis and Clark*, edited by Bernard DeVoto, pp. 180–81. Copyright 1953 by Houghton Mifflin Co.

This air gun was used in 1806 at the mouth of the Columbia to impress local natives, so it may be assumed that the gun went back to St. Louis with the Expedition. From Carl P. Russell, "The Guns of the Lewis and Clark Expedition," *North Dakota History*, 27-1 (Winter, 1960), p. 29. Copyright, State Historical Society of North Dakota, 1960. Used by permission.

The swivel gun was frequently referred to in the expedition's journals. It was a small cannon that was fired on such occasions as Christmas and New Year's Day and for farewells from various tribes. On June 26, 1805, it was placed in a cache below the Missouri's Great Falls. On the return trip the explorers took it back to the Mandans and gave it as a farewell gift to Chief Kakoakis. Russell, pp. 32–3.

Lewis's 1803 requisition asks for 15 US Model 1803 rifles, along with 15 powder horns and pouches, 15 pairs of bullet molds, 15 pairs of wipers or gun worms, 15 ball screws, 15 gun slings, plus extra parts of locks and tools for repairs, and 500 best flints, 200 pounds of the best rifle powder and 400 pounds of lead. Any broken rifles could easily be repaired. Probably Lewis believed 15 regular Army men were sufficient to make up privates and noncommissioned officers. However, by 1804 there were 31 enlisted men in the permanent party and

seven other soldiers who went as far as Fort Mandan.
The journals do not make it clear if Lewis ordered more
than 15 rifles for the extra men of the expedition. The
ten civilian boatmen, who accompanied the party from
St. Louis to Fort Mandan and back, may have had muskets of the short, light fusee variety. Charbonneau had
such a musket that was lost in the June 29, 1805, cloudburst. Russell 1960, p. 29.

Russell wrote that Clark refers to his "small rifle,"
in addition to his "rifle." From this comparison Russell
suggests that the small rifle is probably a Kentucky
squirrel rifle. He also suggests that because the journals mention gunpowder grades and musket balls, that
the US Flintlock Musket, Model 1795, was among the
expedition's arms. On July 15, Hugh McNeal broke his
musket in two pieces when he clubbed a charging grizzly,
according to Lewis. Russell, pp. 30–1.

The blunderbuss was a short firearm with an expanding bore, flaring out like a bell at the muzzle. It
was developed in Europe in the first half of the sev-
enteenth century. The name may have come from the
German, *Dunder Buchse* (thunder gun). The load for
the early gun was as many pistol balls or as much
buckshot as the chamber could hold. Later the exag-
gerated flares were modified to an almost round bore
and the flare was only a decorative thickening of the
metal on the outside. This decorative bell had no effect
on the spread of the shot, but if the gun were pointed
at anyone, it had a frightening effect. The blunderbuss
was used during the flintlock period and larger versions
of this gun could be mounted on swivels. From *Encyclopedia of Firearms*, edited by Harold L. Peterson.
Copyright © by George Rainbird Ltd., 1964. Reprinted
by permission of the publisher, E. P. Dutton, Inc.,
pp. 57–8.

The two blunderbusses of the Lewis and Clark Expedition were equipped with swivels and could be
mounted on either of the two pirogues as the men went
up the Missouri River. Unfortunately, the guns were
mounted on the keelboat on September 25, 1804, when
the explorers had trouble with the Teton Sioux. DeVoto,
1953, p. 37.

At Fort Mandan the blunderbusses must have been

mounted on the roof of the storeroom for use by the sentry in case of any Indian trouble. Russell, p. 30.

Russell believes that even though little was written in the journals about hand guns, it was a general custom then for U.S. Army officers to carry their own personal pistols. On July 27, 1806, Lewis wrote about using his pistol in the fight with the Piegans. Russell thinks that if Lewis's pistol were not personally owned by him and specially made for him, it had to be the Model 1799 made by Simeon North. Russell, p. 32.

The Indians near the mouth of the Williamette River had been supplied with pistols before the coming of the Lewis and Clark Expedition, according to the journals for November 4, 1805. The explorers saw their first Indian trade gun on October 30, 1805, at the Cascades of the Columbia. From that time on to the west coast the explorers saw Indians with light fusees. The explorers obtained one of the common trade guns on the Columbia and one when Lewis fought the Piegans. Russell, p. 31; see also DeVoto, 1953, pp. 438–39; Barbour has an excellent writeup on the guns used by the expedition in the 1964 *Gun Digest*.

5. On November 11, 1804, Captain Clark was visited by two Indian girls known among the Minnetarees as the "Snake" or Shoshoni women of Charbonneau. On December 25 Sergeant Gass and Private Whitehouse wrote that the only females at their Christmas Dance were "the three wives of our interpreter." Two of these "wives" or girls were not mentioned again in the expedition's journals—the other girl was Sacajawea. Clark and Edmonds, p. 12.

CHAPTER 12   *Birth of Jean Baptiste Charbonneau*

1. Lewis recorded in his journal of February 11, 1805, that Jussome suggested rattlesnake rattles be given in small portions to Sacajawea to hasten the birth of her child. He also wrote, "perhaps this remedy may be worthy of future experiments, but I must confess that I want faith as to its efficacy." Chuinard 1980, p. 270, says that Lewis "demonstrated the attitude of the true scientist: doubt, but willingness to investigate."

Chuinard also points out that none of the explorers mention Sacajawea or the baby having any postpartum complications. From E. G. Chuinard, *Only One Man Died: The Medical Aspects of the Lewis and Clark Expedition.* Glendale, CA: The Arthur H. Clark Co., 1980, pp. 269–70.

CHAPTER 13   *Farewell*

1. Antoine Larocque, Charles McKenzie, and one other man were sent by the Canadian, Charles Chaboillez, from Fort Assiniboine in Canada, to go up the Missouri River to the Rocky Mountains. These three men left two months after the Lewis and Clark Expedition left Fort Mandan. The three men never reached the Rockies in the four and a half months they were gone. They explored what is today Montana and Wyoming. Larocque's maps were so poorly drawn it is impossible to tell where the three men explored. John Bakeless, *Lewis and Clark, Partners in Discovery.* New York: William Morrow and Co., 1947, p. 159.

CHAPTER 14   *A Sudden Squall*

1. Drewyer and Drouillard are the same person. The difference is the American and French spelling of his name.

2. Dr. Antoine Saugrain was a protégé of Benjamin Franklin, who lured him to America from Paris. Dr. Saugrain's work in St. Louis earned him the title of the First Scientist of the Mississippi Valley. He built one of the finest homes in St. Louis, occupying the block bounded by Second and Third Streets, Gratiot and Lombards Streets. The block was surrounded by a seven-foot stone wall to keep Indians from running through his property. Dr. Saugrain had one of the largest libraries in St. Louis at that time. Legend says that he not only provided medicinals, a well-stocked medical kit, friction matches and medical advice to both Lewis and Clark, but that he made the explorers' thermometers by blowing and calibrating glass tubes which he filled with mercury melted from his wife's mirrors. Between the mid 1600s and mid 1800s, mirrors were made from sheets of glass backed with a silver-colored amalgam of tin and mercury. From E. G. Chuinard, *Only One Man Died: The Medical Aspects of the Lewis and*

Clark Expedition. Glendale, CA: The Arthur H. Clark Co., 1980, pp. 195–212.

3. Dr. Chuinard wrote that Dr. Antoine Saugrain perhaps knew of Jenner's smallpox vaccine at the time Lewis and Clark studied with him in St. Louis just before the expedition. Dr. Saugrain had treated smallpox with inoculation when he was at the French community of Gallipolis, Ohio, in the 1790s. Chuinard, pp. 200–6. He was the first doctor in St. Louis to vaccinate. Kennerly, p. 140, quotes an advertisement in the *Missouri Gazette* for June 7, 1809: "having been politely favored by a friend with the genuine Vaccine infection [he] has successfully communicated that inestimable preventive of Small Pox to a number of the inhabitants of St. Louis and its vicinity.... Persons in indigent circumstances, paupers, and Indians, will be attended gratis on application." From *Persimmon Hill*, by William Clark Kennerly. Copyright 1948 by the University of Oklahoma Press.

4. On the 11th of April, 1805, Lewis reported that the white material that makes up the riverbanks and hills "tastes like a mixture of common salt and glauber salts...and had a purgative effect." Coues, Vol. I, p. 266.

CHAPTER 15 *Beaver Bite*

1. Lewis wrote in his journal on May 19, 1805: "one of the party wounded a beaver, and my dog as usual swam out to catch it; the beaver bit him through the hind leg and cut the artery; it was with great difficulty that I could stop the blood; I fear it will yet prove fatal to him." Clark only wrote one sentence about the incident. From *The Journals of Lewis and Clark*, edited by Bernard DeVoto, p. 113. Copyright 1953 by Houghton Mifflin Co.

CHAPTER 16 *Sacajawea's Illness*

1. There was but one way for the men of the expedition to identify the correct course of the Missouri—by finding the legendary Great Falls. Captain Lewis was puzzled that the Mandans had not mentioned these forks where he now stood and that the Wolf Chief had not pictured it in this place on the elk-hide map. The

truth was that the North Fork, Maria's River, and the River-Which-Scolds-At-All-Others had simply been misplaced farther downstream in the memory of the Wolf Chief. They were on the map, but in the wrong place.

CHAPTER 17 *Cloudburst*

1. The men working with the portage were working with their shirts off in the scorching June heat when the hailstorm began. The axle-tree broke. One man was knocked down three times, and the backs of others were bruised and bleeding when the storm stopped. Clark wrote that one of the hailstones "was 7 Inches in circumfrence and waied three ounces." No one had expected the storm to be so violent, nor to last as long as thirty minutes, nor to have hailstones larger then hen's eggs. From *The Journals of Lewis and Clark*, edited by Bernard DeVoto, p. 148. Copyright 1953 by Houghton Mifflin Co.

CHAPTER 18 *Tab-ba-bone*

1. This was the worst thing he could have said. He was probably trying to say the Shoshoni word *tai-va-vone*, which means "stranger" or "outsider." No doubt Lewis learned the word from Sacajawea, and he may not have understood her, or she may not have remembered the name for "white man." Maybe the Shoshonis of that time had no name for "white man." Sacajawea had been only a child when captured and had not seen a white man when she was with her people. Therefore, she never knew she would need to know a word for "white man." The lone Shoshoni scout saw armed men who were outsiders and strangers. Spreading the blanket and yelling that they were strangers was not a reassuring gesture in a land where every stranger was an enemy.

2. Thirty years later, the American traveler R. J. Farnham was told by Shoshonis the story of the scout that Lewis saw. The Indian was so surprised at seeing a pale-faced man who could make both "thunder and lightning," that he could not move for a few moments. Then he hurried to tell the astonishing news to his people. The Shoshoni were skeptical and said that

all people were brown as they were. They called the scout a dreamer, meaning he made up the story of men with skin pale as ashes. They told the scout that he had to show them the pale men or be killed for telling an untruth. Eventually, the scout led the Shoshoni tribesmen to the spot where they met Lewis, and his truthfulness was reestablished. John Bakeless, *Lewis and Clark, Partners in Discovery*. New York: William Morrow and Co., 1947, pp. 236–37; Thwaites, Vol. 28, 1816, 1904–7, pp. 176–79.

3. Captain Lewis was right, he and his men had crossed the Continental Divide that day by way of the Lemhi Pass (due west of Armstead, Montana). But the clear, cold water he drank was from one of the headwater streams of the Lemhi River, a tributary of the Salmon River, a tributary (Snake River) of the Columbia River.

CHAPTER 19 *The People*
1. Captain Lewis was thirty-one years old on August 18, 1805. He wrote philosophically about his age, resolving to live for mankind from that day forward. Four years later on October 10, 1809, he was dead. It was a great loss for mankind, and has remained one of the unsolved mysteries, because no one today knows if his death was murder or suicide.

CHAPTER 20 *Big Moose*
1. John Rees of the Lemhi County Historical Society wrote that the Shoshoni called Ben York, *Too-tivo*. Rees says, in Shoshoni this means *a black white man*. Rees, 1970, p. 23.

CHAPTER 21 *Divided*
1. The Lewis River is now called the Snake River.
2. This branding iron is now displayed at the Oregon Historical Society, 1230 Southwest Park Ave., Portland, Oregon.

CHAPTER 22 *Over the Mountains*
1. These Indians were Ootlashoots and lived in the valley known today as Ross's Hole. They were later identified as Selish Flathead. But these people never

practiced flattening the skull, which was popular among some Pacific coast Indians.

2. Pheasants were not established in the Willamette Valley, Oregon, until the late nineteenth century. However, Clark wrote in his journal on Sept. 13, 1805: "One Deer and Some Pheasants killed this morning. I shot 4 Pheasants of the Common Kind except the tale was black." Lewis wrote in his journal of Sept. 18, 1805: "...there is nothing upon earth except ourselves and a few small pheasants, small gray squirrels, and a blue bird of the vulture kind..." John Bakeless, p. 262, wrote about the expedition's food while going through the Rocky Mountains: "For a time they had nothing to eat but a diet of wolf and crayfish, ameliorated by three pheasants and a duck." In all these instances the men were probably describing the ruffed grouse or sage hens which were often called pheasants at that time. John Bakeless, *Lewis and Clark, Partners in Discovery*. New York: William Morrow and Co., 1947.

3. The soup was made by Francois Baillet in Philadelphia for the expedition. On May 30, 1803, he presented a bill for $289.50 for 193 pounds of Portable Soup. Lewis had the soup stored in canisters because it was not dry, but more of a paste or gluelike consistency. Before it was consumed it was to be mixed with water. From E. G. Chuinard, *Only One Man Died: The Medical Aspects of the Lewis and Clark Expedition*, Glendale, CA: The Arthur H. Clark Co., 1980, pp. 161–62.

4. Now called White Sand Creek.

5. "The trouble was dysentery, in Clark's words a universal 'Lax and heaviness at the stomack.'" This might have been from spoiled salmon, but the Nez Percé were not ill. From *The Journals of Lewis and Clark*, edited by Bernard DeVoto, p. 241. Copyright 1953 by Houghton Mifflin Co.

The men were weak and depressed. There was not much to eat but some bear grease and twenty pounds of candles. Bakeless, p. 262.

CHAPTER 23 *Dog Meat*

1. A Nez Percé chief, Lawyer, enjoyed recalling to his white friends the story of how his people were ter-

rified when they first saw a redheaded pale face, who
was accompanied by a gigantic black man and a squaw
with a papoose on her back. These three were leading
other pale faces and a string of packhorses on a direct
path toward his village near the present Kamiah, Idaho.
The entire village took to the brush for hiding. At that
time Lawyer was himself a papoose in a cradleboard
hanging from a tree. His mother was so frightened she
forgot to pick him up and take him into the brush with
her. Lawyer's father finally crept back to the deserted
village after sundown and to his surprise he found the
strangers peaceful and friendly. He picked up his child
and then ran to get his woman. The entire village followed him back to greet these strangers. From p. 266
in *Lewis and Clark: Partners in Discovery* by John
Bakeless. Copyright 1947 by John Bakeless. By permission of William Morrow and Company, N.Y.

2. The first horses of the Nez Percés came from the
Shoshonis and were descendants of horses brought into
Mexico by the early Spanish explorers. The piebald rump
was a characteristic, perhaps inherited from the Mo-
roccan "barb," an Arabian strain that the Moors brought
into Spain. The Nez Percés improved the quality of their
herds, and one of the best-known strains developed by
them is the Appaloosa. Mathieson, p. 16.

3. Chinook jargon was the name for the old Hudson's
Bay Company trade lingo, the universal conversational
vehicle for all Indians along the Northwest coast.

4. After seventeen arduous months the expedition
entered what is now the State of Washington on October
11, 1805. They canoed down the swift and hazardous
Snake River, making as much as forty miles a day.

CHAPTER 24   *The Columbia*

1. Twisted Hair used a piece of charcoal to draw on
a white elkskin. He drew the course of the main river,
which was two sleeps to some large forks, five sleeps
to a great falls. John Bakeless, *Lewis and Clark, Partners in Discovery*. New York: William Morrow and Co.,
1947, p. 269.

2. On October 16th the expedition finally reached
the Columbia River.

3. Bakeless writes that the successful experiment

by Private Collins was the high point of the journey.
Collins was a resourceful fellow who became thirsty
and made some beer, which was excellent to the uncritical explorers. "...the expedition quaffed it gratefully." Bakeless, p. 275.

4. On Monday, October 21, 1805, Clark wrote: "One
of our party J. Collins presented us with verry good
beer made of the Pa-shi-co-quar-mash (probably camass, belonging to the lily family, with a bulbous root)
bread, which bread is the remains of what was laid in
as a part of our Stores of Provisions, at the first flat
heads or Chopunnish Nation at the head of the Koss-
koske river (Clearwater) which by being frequently wet
molded and sowered." (The Chopunnish are actually
the Nez Percé, not the Flatheads. It is remarkable that
the captains didn't confuse more names of the various
tribes than they did, as the names were all new to them
and the spelling entirely their own.)

5. Clark and two men explored up the Columbia in
a light canoe, visiting along the way with Indians who
were busy splitting and drying salmon. After reaching
the mouth of the Tapteal (Yakima) River, Clark and
his party turned back to rejoin the others and continued
the journey down the Columbia.

CHAPTER 25   *The Pacific*

1. The Great Shoot is now known as the Cascades
of the Columbia.

2. On October 22, 1805, the expedition portaged a
distance of 1,200 yards around the Great Falls of the
Columbia (Celilo Falls). This was a favorite salmon
fishing area of the Nez Percé prior to inundation by
backwater of the Dalles Dam. Salmon were trapped in
weirs, harpooned from rocky outthrusts at narrows, or
dipped up with long-handled, woven rush nets from the
pools at the bottom of rapids and falls where they circled
around attempting to leap over the rapids. At the Dalles
the Indians built scaffoldings or fragile wooden platforms extending over the swift waters. Choice sites were
where the water was strongest or where salmon passed
close to rocks to avoid the strong current. A good Nez
Percé fisherman would bring in 500 salmon a day. An
adaptation of page 17 from *Empire of the Columbia: A*

History of the Pacific Northwest by Dorothy O. Johansen and Charles M. Gates. Copyright 1957 by Harper and Row, Publishers, Inc. Reprinted by permission of the publisher.

3. On November 2, 1805, the explorers passed Beacon Rock on their journey down the Columbia River. They called it a "remarkable high detached rock." Their journals indicate it was here that the effect of tidewater was first noticed. Clark wrote: "The ebb tide rose here about 9 inches, the flood tide must rise here much higher." Coues, Vol. II, pp. 688–89.

4. These Pacific Coast peoples were great artisans of sea canoes. Some of the flat-bottom dugouts were forty to fifty feet long and could carry fifty warriors or a crew of five and a ton and a half of dead weight, such as salmon. Usually a great cedar log was split so that more than half its thickness was left for shaping, which was done by chipping and burning to get the rough form. The final job took patience, with small chipping strokes and expert use of hot coals. The thin walls were made pliable with water and hot rocks, then stretched out with thwarts. When the canoe dried, the thwarts could be fastened in place without cracking fragile sides. It was painted inside and out and decorated with high end pieces carved in animal or human figures. Clark said, "butifull...neeter made than any I have ever seen and calculated to ride the waves and carry emence burthens." Thwaites, Vol. III, 1904–5, 1969, p. 151.

Men, women, and children could navigate the roughest waters. If the canoe capsized, the occupants stayed in the water until the craft was righted and emptied, then they climbed back in. The Chinooks at the mouth of the Columbia traveled north to Vancouver Island and south to California in these low, fragile craft, powered by matting sail and paddles. Johansen and Gates, p. 12.

5. The wapato was the root of the Columbia. Round and white like a small potato, it was baked into a crisp bread by the Chinooks.

6. One of the most often quoted sayings of the expedition is their repetition of "we proceeded on." In fact, the official publication of the Lewis and Clark Trail Heritage Foundation is titled *We Proceeded On.* Pos-

sibly the next most quoted saying of the Expedition was Clark's "Ocian in view! O! the joy." He wrote that in his field notebook on November 7, 1805. However, he was mistaken this day because they were camped near Pillar Rock on the Columbia, but the actual ocean could not be seen yet. From *The Journals of Lewis and Clark*, edited by Bernard DeVoto, p. 279. Copyright 1953 by Houghton Mifflin Co.

7. Point Distress is now called Point Ellice.

8. Haley's Bay is the present site of Fort Columbia.

9. On this night of November 14, 1805, Clark wrote, "The rain and which has continued without a longer intermition than 2 hours at a time for ten days past has destroyed the robes and rotted nearly one half of the fiew clothes the party has, particularly the leather clothes...Squar displeased with me for not..." DeVoto, p. 284.

The last sentence is not finished. But it is evident that Sacajawea has enough self-confidence to speak up now when something is not done to her liking.

CHAPTER 26   *The Blue Coat*

1. Many of the Chinook Indians were in poor health. On November 18, 1805, Clark wrote, "I saw 4 womin and Some children one of the women in a desperate Situation, covered with sores scabs and ulsers no doubt the effects of venereal disorders which several of this nation which I have Seen appears to have...."

On November 21, 1805, Clark wrote, "...Several Indians and squars came this evening I beleave for the purpose of gratifying the passions of our men, Those people appear to view sensuality as a necessary evill, and do not appear to abhore this as crime in the unmarried females. The young women sport openly with our men, and appear to receve the approbation of theer friends and relations for so doing maney of the women have handsom faces...large legs and thighs which are generally Swelled from a Stopage of the circulation in the feet (which are Small) by maney Strands of Beeds or curious Strings which are drawn tight around the leg above the ankle, their legs are also picked tattooed with defferent figures...." From *The Journals of Lewis and Clark*, edited by Bernard DeVoto, pp. 289–90. Copyright 1953 by Houghton Mifflin Co.

2. The November 24, 1805, journal entry by Clark is actually the first time that he uses the name "Janey" for Sacajawea in his writing. Clark and Edmonds, p. 51.

CHAPTER 27 *Weasel Tails*

1. The remainder of the tobacco was saved for trading purposes on the return trip. Ordway's journal sadly states, "we have no ardent Spirits." From *The Journals of Lewis and Clark*, edited by Bernard DeVoto, p. 294. Copyright 1953 by Houghton Mifflin Co.

Bakeless notes that in March all the tobacco gave out. Thirty of the party habitually smoked or chewed. The men tried smoking the bark of red willow and the bark of crab apple trees for chewing. John Bakeless, *Lewis and Clark, Partners in Discovery*. New York: William Morrow and Co., 1947, pp. 297–98.

2. Point William is now called Tongue Point.

3. These "vultures" are among the rarest birds in America today. They were the California condor. No one alive today has seen a condor as far north as the Columbia River.

4. The original Meriwether Bay is now called Young's Bay.

5. The river called Netual by the Chinooks is now the Lewis and Clark River.

6. The Coast Range blacktail deer never get over a hundred and fifty-odd pounds; a buck is well grown that dresses out at a hundred and twenty.

7. This table survived until 1860. Visitors at the fort today can see how the table looked, but it is not the original tree trunk.

8. Fort Clatsop National Memorial about six miles southwest of Astoria, Oregon, was built in 1955 by the Oregon Historical Society, which donated the site to the U.S. Government in 1958. Then Fort Clatsop became part of the National Park Service. In constructing the replica, the floor plan dimensions drawn by Clark on the elkhide cover of his fieldbook were faithfully followed. From the middle of June through Labor Day a living history program is presented by buckskin-clad

rangers depicting various members of the expedition,
including Sacajawea. Firing of flintlock rifles, hollowing out of a pirogue, bead and quillwork, and activities
that show life at Fort Clatsop during the winter of 1805–
6 are demonstrated. Within 25 miles of this site is the
salt cairn at Seaside, the trail over Tillamook Head to
Cannon Beach, and in the State of Washington, the
camp and trail sites at McGowan, Cape Disappointment, and Long Beach.

9. It was not until the captains were back in the
States that they learned Jack Ramsay was a deserter
from a British trading vessel who had lived for years
among the Clatsops. When his son was born, he forbade
his squaw to flatten the child's skull between boards
after the local custom. He tattooed his name on his son's
arm, so that thereafter he was also called Jack Ramsay
by those who could read. Bakeless, pp. 296–97.

CHAPTER 28   *The Whale*

1. The journal that Sergeant Pryor kept that winter
was never found, nor the ones kept by Privates Frazier
and Shannon, nor any of the many Indian vocabularies
the captains, especially Lewis, so painfully compiled
while at Fort Clatsop.

2. The traders had probably come from the southwest, since whalers and seal hunters usually sailed home
by way of Hawaii and China. In China they sold seal-
skins and beaver fur. These merchants made three prof-
its: first on the goods they exchanged with the Pacific
Coast natives for furs; then on the furs they exchanged
for Oriental wares, such as silks, china, and wallpaper,
which they sold for cash on their return home. John
Bakeless, *Lewis and Clark, Partners in Discovery*. New
York: William Morrow and Co., 1947, p. 293.

3. Spuck is the name given to baby otter.

4. Captain Youens and the others did not come in
their trading vessels that year. The following year none
of these names could be identified by any mariner's list,
but then no complete record was ever kept of ships
sailing around the Horn and up the Pacific Ocean between 1780 and 1820. Bakeless, p. 292.

CHAPTER 29 *Ahn-cutty*

1. Chief Comowool made Fort Clatsop his winter home during the remainder of his life, until 1825. Years passed, and the stockade fell and young trees grew up through the cabins, but the spring is still there, cool and clear.

A small clearing in the woods now marks the original site of Fort Clatsop. On the high bank of the river is a replica of the fort. Old Chief Comowool's three daughters grew used to white men's cabins, and they all married white men. Comowool's grandson, Silas B. Smith, was educated in New Hampshire and became a member of the Oregon bar. John Bakeless, *Lewis and Clark, Partners in Discovery*. New York: William Morrow and Co., 1947, pp. 304–5.

2. The "Indian Commissions" were paper and perishable. Thus it is remarkable that one of these papers, presented on the return trip to Warchapa, a Teton Sioux, is in the Huntington Library, San Merino, California. It bears the name of the chief and signatures of Lewis as "Captain, First Infantry" and Clark as "Captain on an Expedition for North Western Discovery."

3. A description of this paper which was nailed inside the Fort Clatsop officers' quarters is found in Elliott Coues, ed., *The History of the Lewis and Clark Expedition*, Vol. III, 1965, p. 903.

Captain Samuel Hill, commander of the brig, Lydia, found a paper inside a leather shirt worn by a Clatsop. Captain Hill took the paper with him to Canton, where he let an American copy it and send the copy to Boston. The copy contained this message:

Captain Hill, while on the coast, met some Indian natives near the mouth of the Columbia river, who delivered to him a paper, of which I enclose you a copy. It had been committed to their charge by captains Clarke and Lewis, who had penetrated to the Pacific ocean. The original is a rough draft with a pen of their outward route, and that which they intended returning by. Just below the junction of Madison's river, they found an immense fall of three hundred and sixty two feet perpendicular. This, I believe, exceeds in magnitude any other known. From the natives Captain Hill learned that they were all in good health and spirites; had met many difficulties on their progress, from various tribes of Indians, but had found them about the sources of the Missouri very friendly, as were those on Columbia river and the coast. [Bakeless, pp. 292–93, 302; R. G. Ferris, pp. 202, 373; Coues, Vol. III, pp. 903–4.]

4. Somehow the expedition missed, by only a fortnight, the *Lydia.* This ship was anchored about ten miles up the Columbia River.

5. This flat, green prairie was the future site of Vancouver, Washington.

6. The Shahala village near which the expedition camped was next to the base of Mount Hood at the Sandy River.

7. The artillery fuse was a paper case filled with slow-burning material. It was often called a port fire-match.

8. They were on what is today the Willamette River, where the peaks of Mount Rainier, Hood, St. Helens, Adams, and Jefferson can be seen. The Yakima Indians call these mountains, "the five sisters who scold each other."

9. Clark tried to measure the bottom of the river, but his instruments could not measure its great depth. Today, international trade ships glide along the deep estuary to the wharves of Portland, Oregon.

10. The Chinooks and other nearby coastal Indians had learned *damned rascal, sun of a pitch,* and some reputable English such as *heave the lead, knife, file, musket, powder,* and *shot.* They knew no other European language according to Lewis and Clark. They didn't seem to know where traders came from, but they knew they sailed away to the southwest, where both whalers and traders of the day went by way of Hawaii and China. Bakeless, p. 293.

11. When a horse is hobbled his hind legs are tied or one fore and one hind leg are tied together with a short rope. The horse can graze but cannot move around far, so can be easily found.

In later years some men used bells on their horses so they could easily be found. This became dangerous because the Indians could steal the horse, ring the bell, and scalp the owner when he arrived.

CHAPTER 30 *The Sick Papoose*

1. "Imposthume" is an old word for any kind of abscess.

2. The Kooskooskee is the Clearwater River.

3. This sword is probably the same one found between two Walla Walla graves at Cathlamet, Oregon, in 1904, which had the name "Clark" engraved on the scabbard.

4. The Kogohue tribe was probably a part of the Comanche Nation by this time.

5. The villages in the south where horses were raided by the Comanches were Spanish or Mexican.

6. This village kept a breeding stallion enclosed by a high fence built of thick brush. Inside, the sire would have from twenty-five to forty mares per season. The Nez Percés knew that if horses run wild and breed as nature prompts, they will degenerate in size and shape. They knew that the inbred horses were heavy and slow. The Nez Percés bred Appaloosas, which were solid black or brown with a white patch over the hips. Sometimes the patch was interspersed with small round spots of the same color as the body. These crossbred horses were sleek and fast, with more stamina than the inbred variety. Clark noted that the Nez Percés liked horses of a basic solid color with white dots over the entire body, or all white with colored dots. The name of the Palouse River in Idaho and Washington State came from these Appaloosas of the early Nez Percés. R. G. Ferris, pp. 208–9; Mathieson, p. 16; personal communication with Charles Bennett, Phoenix, Ariz., Oct. 2, 1982.

7. Commearp Creek is called Lawyer's Canyon Creek today.

CHAPTER 31 *Retreat*

1. Sergeant Charles Floyd was the only casualty of the expedition. He died on August 20, 1804, near the southern edge of what today is Sioux City, Iowa, probably from an infected appendix that was perforated or ruptured.

In 1980 Chuinard wrote "that appendicitis is not a

diagnosis that would have entered the minds of either Lewis or Clark. Not long after the Expedition, appendicitis was recognized, but it was years after, that it was treated successfully." Chuinard goes on to say that "Sergeant Floyd was the first American soldier to be buried west of the Mississippi River." From E. G. Chuinard, *Only One Man Died: The Medical Apsects of the Lewis and Clark Expedition.* Glendale, CA: The Arthur H. Clark Co., 1980, pp. 238–39.

The men of the Lewis and Clark party placed a cedar cross over the grave. In 1811 Henry Brackenridge passed the grave and wrote in his journal, "The grave occupies a beautiful rising ground, now covered with grass and wild flowers. The pretty little river, which bears his name, is neatly fringed with willow and shrubbery....No one has disturbed the cross;...even Indians who pass, venerate the place, and often leave a present as offering near it." Thwaites, Vol. VI, 1816, 1904, p. 85.

Sometime later a Sioux chief camping nearby the grave site lost a son and had him buried in the same grave with Floyd, because of a belief that the white men had a better hereafter. However, when Floyd's body was moved in 1857 because the Missouri River had cut into the bank of Floyd's Bluff some of the bones were already lost, so that the story of the young son of the Sioux chief cannot be verified. On August 20, 1895, the few bones that had been found and placed in urns were reburied and a concrete slab marker was put over the grave. The Sioux City Museum has a plaster model of Floyd's skull and a piece of his first coffin. Chuinard, pp. 240–42.

2. Garcia, pp. 132–33, tells how a young woman makes a whistling sound that is carried some distance by cupping her hands to her mouth. She uses this to call her lover. He somehow knows the special sound of her whistle and finds a way to meet her out in the night.

Lowie writes that the Plains Indians used a flutelike stick that was usually carved of wood, hollowed out, with as many as seven holes in it and a whistle type mouthpiece. The males used these flutelike whistles for courting. "A young Assiniboin...a hundred yards" away "could send messages to his girl while she was inside her tipi without her family's catching on." He could whistle such messages as "I am waiting for you," "Meet me tomorrow," "I'll come again," or "I am watched," and "Remain." From *Indians of the Plains*, by Robert H. Lowie, pp. 132–33. Natural History Press. Copyright 1954 by the American Museum of Natural History; Mathieson, p. 16; *Bent's Fort* by David Lavender, pp. 174–75. Copyright 1954 by Doubleday and Co., Inc.

3. The camass or quamash was in bloom in the moist valleys. When the horses walked through a bed of these beautiful blue flowers their legs became yellow from the knee down from the thick pollen. The root or bulb is usually dug in early summer. It can be boiled as a potato, made into a thin, crisp bread or a thick biscuit, or eaten raw. It can be stored like potatoes and will keep all winter long in a cool place, if not frozen. Personal communication with Ann Samsell, *Somethings Productions*, Monmouth, Oregon, during fall 1981, 175th Anniversary Lewis and Clark Expedition Re-enactment.

CHAPTER 32 *Pompeys Pillar*

1. This northeast slope of the Rockies that the explorers descended was in what is now the State of Montana, beyond Glade Creek.

2. Their old camp, Traveler's Rest, was not far from today's Missoula, Montana.

3. The first white settlers of Montana came into the Bitterroot Valley. From the Hellgate Pass of the Rockies, above the present site of Missoula, Montana, the bloodthirsty Blackfeet came again and again to attack those first settlers. Old trappers and fur traders said, "It is as safe to enter the gates of hell as to enter that Hellgate Pass." John Bakeless, *Lewis and Clark, Partners in Discovery*. New York: William Morrow and Co., 1947, p. 332.

4. The pass from the Jefferson River across the Continental Divide is now known as Gibbon's Pass. This pass leads down into the Big Hole Valley.

5. Willard Creek is where the first paying gold was to be discovered in Montana.

6. This small timbered area would be the future city limits of Bozeman, Montana.

7. At one time in the nineteenth century, the river

moved far enough from its bed to lap against this tall,
wide rock pillar. Almost every explorer passing this
way paused at Pompey's Tower. The ancient carvings
are nearly gone through weathering. Clark carved his
name about two-thirds of the way up the side. Today
the signature of Clark is somewhat weathered, but it
is clearly legible through the glass in the frame that
protects it from vandalism and further weathering.
Clark commented about the multitudes of mosquitoes
in this place. Even today the area is plagued with hordes
of mosquitoes.

CHAPTER 33   *Big White*

1. Joseph Dickson, or Dixon, and Forest Hancock
were fur traders. The captains settled accounts with
John Colter on August 16, 1806. He stayed in the wilderness for four more years, during which time he discovered the present Yellowstone National Park.

2. Big White and his family were among the first
Indians to be received by the President of the United
States. Henry M. Brackenridge, an early historian of
the West, wrote that Big White rather inclined to cor-
pulency and was a little talkative, which were regarded
among the Indians as defects. From *Persimmon Hill*,
by William Clark Kennerly, pp. 18–19. Copyright 1948
by the University of Oklahoma Press.

CHAPTER 34   *Good-Byes*

1. A year before the expedition left for the west coast,
President Jefferson and Captain Lewis, who was the
President's private secretary, worked out a special cipher
for coded correspondence, if that kind of communication
became necessary. The key word was "artichokes." There
is no evidence that this was used, either in the letters
sent back by the keelboat from Fort Mandan, nor in
the journals that were brought back to St. Louis by the
expedition. Jackson, Vol. I, pp. 9–10; Abrams, 1979,
p. 16.

By the summer of 1806, no one in the United States
thought that the explorers were still safe and alive, soon
to be returning home. The Lewis and Clark Expedition
had been given up for lost. There had been no word of
them since Corporal Warfington and his men had re-

turned from Fort Mandan in the keelboat nearly two years before.

2. The expedition would no longer need the swivel gun, so on Friday, August 16, 1806, with much ceremony, just before leaving to go downriver, Clark gave it to Kakoakis, the one-eyed chief. Clark told Kakoakis, "When you fire this gun remember the words of your greatfather" to keep peace among the Indians. "The gun was fired and the chief appeared to be much pleased and conveyed it immediately to his village." From *The Journals of Lewis and Clark*, edited by Bernard DeVoto, pp. 456–57. Copyright 1953 by Houghton Mifflin Co.

CHAPTER 35 *Saint Louis*

1. The nearest relatives buried the bones of their deceased after the scaffolding, where the body first rested, decayed and fell to the ground. The skull was bleached white by weathering. It was carefully placed on a bed of wild sage, in the circumference of a circle of skulls on the prairie grass, about ten inches from other skulls on either side. All the skull faces looked inward or at one another. These circles of skulls, just outside the village, were religiously protected and kept in that exact position year after year. Each wife knew the skull of her husband, child, or other relative and visited it every day. She took food out to the prairie and placed it beside the skull, replaced the bed of sage, and talked to the skull. From *George Catlin and the Old Frontier*, by Harold McCracken, p. 99. Copyright 1959, Crown Publishers, Inc.

2. A. J. Forsyth, a Scottish clergyman, is given credit for discovering the percussion compound that explodes when struck a sharp blow. The compound is mainly potassium chlorate. The chief difference between ordinary powder and fulminate is the amount of percussion needed to produce an explosion and the rapidity of the explosion. Black gunpowder can be ignited by detonation between steel or metal faces, but the explosion is no more violent than if produced by burning splint. A fulminate exploded by percussion exerts a much greater force in less time.

There was always a danger of accidental discharge

when loading the old muzzle loading gun. The ramming down of a charge carrying dampness gave irregular results. The ramrod broke often. The nipple became rusty and fouled by previous shots and caused misfires. After 1785 a roller bearing was fit to the steel-spring, which reduced friction so that the steel flew back faster and gave more sparks. At this time a swivel linked the mainspring to the tumbler to help reduce friction. Some were fitted with waterproof pans. These consisted of a raised rim over which the pan cover fit and a curved fence behind the pan to protect the shooter's eye. The pan was punctured with a tiny drainhole.

Even before Forsyth was credited with inventing the percussion system of forearms ignition (but not the percussion cap) there were others at the end of the eighteenth century who had discovered the same principle. Forsyth began his experiments in the Tower of London in 1806. The early experimenters found that sparks would not set off the fulminate in an open pan, that there had to be a lock that could confine the salt and direct its explosion through a touchhole. By 1805 there were successful locks being sold for use. Greener, pp. 111–12, 119–20, 228.

Forsyth patented his invention in 1807. It was called the "scent-bottle" lock because it had a magazine of fulminate shaped like a perfume bottle, which replaced the old priming pan. By an ingenious action a small amount of compound was detonated by a hammer. The validity of his patent application was disputed because so many others had already been using the same principle. From Encyclopedia of Firearms, edited by Harold L. Peterson. Copyright © by George Rainbird Ltd., 1964. Reprinted by permission of the publisher, E. P. Dutton, Inc., p. 138.

3. After using gunpowder the Indians learned to make a fire easily by putting a rag around the point of friction and sprinkling on gunpowder. Hoebel and Wallace say that sometimes the Indians would shoot a gun against a tree where a rag was stuck that had been generously sprinkled with gunpowder. The rag would light and could easily start a fire, especially in wet weather. From *The Comanches, Lords of the South*

Plains, by Ernest Wallace and E. Adamson Hoebel, p. 90. Copyright 1952 by the University of Oklahoma Press.

4. An incision was made in the young boy's back where the arrowhead lay and sucking was done through a small horn placed over the cut. The Shaman spit out what he sucked from the wound. Sometimes the patient might be shown stones or arrowheads that the Shaman had put in his mouth and pretended to suck out with the help of his medicine power. A good medicine man or Shaman was good with the use of sleight of hand or illusions. Wallace and Hoebel, p. 171.

5. A dozen wapiti, with an average weight of about seven hundred pounds, divided among forty lodges in that village would give each lodge four hundred and twenty pounds of meat, bone, and hide to make into jerky, pemmican, scrapers, spoons, moccasins, and robes. These elk or large American deer have nearly 30 percent of their total weight in meat that was edible by the Indians' standards.

6. A copy of Clark's August 20, 1806, letter to Charbonneau was discovered in the possession of Mrs. Julia Clark Vorhees and Miss Ellen Vorhees. It was published first in the *Century Magazine*, in October, 1904. Then it was published in Thwaites, Vol. III, 1904–5, 1969, p. 247.

7. When Earth-Woman was seventeen, in 1821, she married a white fur trader from the Columbia Fur Company, Captain James Kipp. Many times during her life she retold the stories she had heard from Sacajawea about the expedition to the West. Kipp's son and grandson lived for some time near Browning, Montana.

8. Captains Lewis and Clark stopped at the grave of Sergeant Floyd on the homeward journey to show their respect to the memory of a brave man, who was a cousin of Sergeant Pryor and distant relative of Clark. Today on Floyd's Bluff at Sioux City, Iowa, is a 100-foot obelisk monument dedicated to Floyd.

CHAPTER 36 *Judy Clark*

1. Today the Lewis River is called the Snake River.
2. Kennerly, p. 29, describes early St. Louis streets as "narrow, thirty to thirty-five feet from house to house, barely accommodating the heavily freighted wagons."

Six or eight oxen or horses were necessary for a team to pull the wagons along the muddy roads beyond the city. When St. Louis was three years old in 1767 there were two billiard parlors, and as the city grew there were more and more. From *Persimmon Hill,* by William Clark Kennerly. Copyright 1948 by the University of Oklahoma Press. Lavender, p. 22, wrote a good description of early St. Louis.

3. Dr. Bernard Gaines Farrar was an important early St. Louis physician. In his account book for 1811 and 1812 he records the cost of one bloodletting as fifty cents. From E. G. Chuinard, *Only One Man Died: The Medical Aspects of the Lewis and Clark Expedition.* Glendale, CA: The Arthur H. Clark Co., 1980, p. 75.

When Julia Clark's health failed Dr. Farrar was called to diagnose and care for her illness. He died of cholera during the terrible epidemic of 1849. Kennerly, pp. 52, 64, 224.

CHAPTER 37 *Lewis's Death*

1. In 1832, the trapper Zenas Leonard found a huge black chief among the Crow Indians. This black man spoke the Crow language fluently. He also spoke English and a little French. He had distinguished himself as a warrior and boasted of his wealth by showing off four of his Crow women. This black man told Leonard that he first saw the Crow country when he came as the manservant to William Clark on the now-famous Lewis and Clark Expedition. The black chief explained that he had been married to a tiny black girl, but he did not like the life of getting up each morning to work at a job, so he told his wife he was sick, very sick, and then he just left her. "I come back to this here Crow country with a trader, Mackinney, and now I plan to stay here the rest of my days," the black chief told Leonard. John Bakeless, *Lewis and Clark, Partners in Discovery.* New York: William Morrow and Co., 1947, pp. 442–43.

In 1971 at a Western History Symposium at Southern Illinois University, Edwardsville, John C. Ewers, Planning Officer for the Museum of History and Technology at the Smithsonian Institution, Washington, D.C., said he did not believe this black man was Ben

York. He believed the man was the mulatto, Edward Rose, who went up the Missouri with Manuel Lisa in 1807 and remained among the Crows to become a leader of some influence. These facts are hard to verify. At this time Ben York may have been in St. Louis with Clark, but again, this cannot be proven. Ewers, pp. 51–2, 139.

Many men, both white and black, went to live with Indians in comparative luxury as chiefs when they found they could not take the civilized life of the river towns. So perhaps it is just possible that Ben York did enjoy freedom more than Cindy Lou believed and found that the best way to enjoy it was to disappear. Would it not be more desirable to be a chief and warrior of high position, with four women, among the Crows, than a jeered-at, depressed freedman, who could not support one woman with his impoverished freight business?

2. Nicholas Biddle, then a young lawyer living in Philadelphia, edited Clark's journals. Several times Clark went to Philadelphia to help Biddle. The editing occupied Biddle from March 25, 1810, until July 8, 1811. He rewrote the journals in narrative form because he felt this made the story more interesting and readable. Actually Biddle lost the flavor of Lewis's and Clark's own words and unique spelling.

Several times Clark sent George Shannon to help with the editing process between his studies for the law. Once Clark wrote to Shannon (April 20, 1811), "Dear George, write me all about my Book." Bakeless, p. 430.

Clark chose the Philadelphia botanist, Dr. Benjamin Smith Barton, to rewrite the scientific notes of his journal. But Dr. Barton died and the scientific notes never appeared.

Toward the end of Biddle's editing, he ran for and was elected to the legislature. Biddle then turned over the final editing work to another Philadelphia man, Paul Allen. Allen's name appears on the title page of the completed works. Allen could not find a publisher for the two small volumes he finally put together until 1814. A printing of two thousand was made of these two volumes, but 583 were lost or defective. The publishers went bankrupt and sales were nil. Two years later Clark tried to locate a printed copy of his own journals and could not. Neither Clark, Biddle, nor Shannon received any part of the $154.10 profit Paul Allen made on the two volumes. Bakeless, pp. 430–1; R. G. Ferris, pp. 239, 247–49; Kennerly, p. 28.

3. George Shannon was studying to be a lawyer at Transylvania University, Lexington, Kentucky.

CHAPTER 38   *Otter Woman's Sickness*
1. Charbonneau sold his land to Clark for $100 and the transaction is recorded in the St. Louis court for March 26, 1811.

2. Father François Neil's school, which young Toussaint, called Tess, attended, grew and finally became what is now St. Louis University in St. Louis, Missouri. This same school, then an academy for boys, was attended by General Clark's son, Bill.

3. The Baptist minister, Mr. J. E. Welch, specifically boarded Indians and half-breed boys. Jean Baptiste Charbonneau, or Pomp, was enrolled in this school in the fall of 1811, when he was six years old. Several years later, Clark sent his youngest son, Jefferson, who was nicknamed Pomp after Sacajawea's son, Jean Baptiste, to college at The Barrens, which was on the Missouri side of the river, but across from the Illinois French town of Kaskaskia. Clark firmly believed in education to teach his boys responsibility for the obligations they incurred in their future frontier life. From *Persimmon Hill*, by William Clark Kennerly, p. 83. Copyright 1948 by the University of Oklahoma Press.

CHAPTER 39   *New Madrid Earthquake*
1. Clark's Spanish style home in St. Louis had once been the home of Benito Vasquez, father of Pierre Louis Vasquez, who with his mountain-man partner, Jim Bridger, opened Fort Bridger on the Oregon Trail. Franzwa, p. 284.

Kennerly, p. 25, wrote that General Clark rented the house of Benito Vasquez, on the corner of Pine and Main streets. Clark brought a piano from New York for his wife, Judy. It was a great event, as she was the only lady in the area who could play it. From *Persimmon Hill*, by William Clark Kennerly. Copyright 1948 by the University of Oklahoma Press.

2. The 1811 New Madrid earthquake was one of the heaviest on record. Aftershocks went on for more than a year. This is an earthquake hotspot, 150 miles from St. Louis. The New Madrid fault seems to be a 1,700 mile rift around the intersection of the Missouri Gravity Low and the Reelfoot Rift. Underwood, Sec. E, pp. 1, 3; also, Penick, pp. 1–181.

Book Five   LIFE AND DEATH

1. Henry M. Brackenridge, "Journal of a Voyage up the River Missouri," in Thwaites, Vol. VI, 1816, 1904, pp. 32–3.

2. The Missouri Fur Company was organized in 1807 by Manuel Lisa, with William Clark as one of the principal stockholders.

3. From John C. Luttig, *Journal of a Fur-Trading Expedition on the Upper Missouri, 1812–1813*, edited by Stella M. Drumm, 1920.

Frazier says, "The infant Lizette is never mentioned again. This may be due to the unimportance of girl babies in the minds of chroniclers, or she may die soon." Neta Lohnes Frazier, *Sacajawea, The Girl Nobody Knows*. New York: David McKay Co., Inc., 1967, p. 147.

4. This cash accounts book is in the Graff Collection at the Newberry Library, Chicago. It has sixty-eight leaves, 22.2 x 14 cm., bound in original gray boards, with sheep backstrip and corners. The binding has been repaired. It is in a black, half-morocco case. Former owners: William Clark, George Rogers Hancock Clark, Mrs. Julia Clark Voorhis. Sold at auction by G. A. Baker and Co., 1941.

5. American State Papers, Abstract of Expenditures by Captain W. Clark as Superintendent of Indian Affairs, 1822; Washington, D.C., 1834.

6. Will Robinson, secretary of the South Dakota State Historical Society, wrote to A.L.W. in 1968 that he was certain Sacajawea had died when she was about twenty-five years old, at Fort Manuel.

7. From *Persimmon Hill*, by William Clark Kennerly, p. 351. Copyright 1948 by the University of Oklahoma Press; Grace Raymond Hebard, *Sacajawea, A Guide and Interpreter of the Lewis and Clark Expedi-*

tion. Glendale, CA: The Arthur H. Clark Co., 1957, p. 116.

8. Published in Portland, Oregon, by Binfords and Mort, 1936.

9. Hugh Monroe, a Canadian fur trader, told a story about his being caught in a blizzard and attacked by Assiniboins on the upper Missouri River. When he arrived at one of the Mandan villages he was taken in by old Toussaint Charbonneau. Monroe was given food and a place in the lodge to sleep by one of the women of Charbonneau, Sacajawea. During Monroe's stay, old Charbonneau grumbled because he had lost his horse in a game of chance and now could do no trading until he could buy another horse. Monroe gave him one of the horses from his string to show his appreciation for the food and lodging. The eleven-year-old Jean Baptiste was happy the family had another horse and told Monroe how he felt. However, in a couple of days old Charbonneau lost this new horse. Jean Baptiste became so angry with his father that he cried. This story took place in 1816. Thus, if it is true, Sacajawea was alive in 1816, and did not die in 1812. Schultz, pp. 37–62.

10. Hebard, 1957, p. 115.

11. Hebard, 1957, pp. 118, 121, 123–4, 127.

12. Hebard, 1957, p. 174.

13. Eastman, *Report to the Commissioner of Indian Affairs,* 1925.

14. Hafen, Ann W., 1950, p. 39–66.

15. After about 1821, when Toussaint, son of old Charbonneau and Otter Woman, finished his schooling at Clark's expense, nothing is found about him in the early writings of the hunters, explorers, and traders until William Boggs discovered him at Bent's Fort on the Arkansas River in 1844. Jean Baptiste is at Bent's Fort at the same time.

"Another half-breed at the Fort was 'Tessou.' His father was French and his mother an Indian, but the writer was not informed of what tribe. 'Tessou' was in some way related to Charbenau (Jean Baptiste). Both of them were very high strung but Tessou was quick and passionate. He fired a rifle across the court of the Fort at the head of a large negro blacksmith,

*only missing his skull about a quarter of an inch,
because the negro had been in a party that chivaried
Tessou the evening before (maybe Tessou was just
married) and being a dangerous man, Captain Vrain
gave him an outfit and sent him away from the Fort."*
[Boggs, pp. 66–7.]

This son of Charbonneau is not mentioned in any
early western writing again, as far as has been determined to date. However, Frazier builds a case for Tess
arriving on the Shoshoni Wind River Reservation,
keeping his true identity hidden and passing himself
off as his famous half brother, Jean Baptiste. Frazier,
pp. 163–66.

16. Hebard was the first to try to show that the old
woman who died on the Wind River Reservation in 1884
was Sacajawea. Since then there have been others, no-
tably Frazier, pp. 140–74; Clark and Edmonds, pp. 109–
45. Harold Howard has written a fine biography titled
Sacajawea, published in 1971 by the University of
Oklahoma Press, which surmises that Sacajawea died
at Fort Manuel Lisa in 1812. Schroer wrote an article
for *In Wyoming* in 1978 supporting Sacajawea's early
death.

CHAPTER 40   *Lizette*

1. Between December 16, 1811, and March 15, 1812,
Jared Brooks of Louisville, Kentucky, recorded 1,874
shocks. He classified eight as "violent," 10 as "severe,"
35 as "moderate," 65 as "generally perceptible," 89 as
"fifth-rate," and 1,667 as "indistinctly felt." Most people
claimed that the three earthquakes occurring on December 16, 1811, January 23, 1812, and February 7,
1812, were the largest. Some thought the last was the
most severe, with the earth in "a nearly constant motion" for several days. Aftershocks occurred for more
than a year. James Audubon, like many people, seemed
to adapt. He said, "Strange to say, I for one became
accustomed to the feeling." Underwood, Sec. E, pp. 1, 3.

2. James Schultz says Charbonneau had two Snake
wives and it was Otter Woman who died shortly after

the expedition returned. Clark and Edmonds, p. 107.

CHAPTER 41   *School*

1. Charles Lucas was twenty-five years old, United States Attorney for the Territory of Missouri. "Had he lived, he doubtless would have attained eminence at the Missouri bar." Kennerly says that this duel was one of the most regrettable ones ever fought in St. Louis. From *Persimmon Hill*, by William Clark Kennerly, pp. 77–9. Copyright 1948 by the University of Oklahoma Press; see also, Lavender, p. 23.

2. This coin was presented to Clark by Chief Strawberry on the day both General Lafayette and the Duke of Saxe-Weimar visited this famous museum. The museum was a wing attached to the south end of the Clarks' newly built residence, a two-story brick, set on a lot going half a block south on Main and east down to the river. The museum was a great hall, one hundred feet long and thirty-five feet wide. Kennerly, p. 41.

CHAPTER 42   *Duke Paul*

1. The Kaw River is the present Kansas River.

2. About half a mile up the right bank of the Missouri River from where the Kansas flows into the Missouri, within the present Kansas City, Kansas, was a settlement of fur traders and two large buildings owned by Cyrus Curtis and Andrew Woods. The latter worked for the Chouteau fur enterprises. Mrs. Woods was a Creole and daughter of the eighty-three-year-old Canadian, Jacques Chauvin, who lived near St. Charles, Missouri. Others in that small settlement were mainly Creoles and half-breeds who farmed, hunted, and traded with the Kansas Indians. From *Travels in North America, 1822–1824*, by Paul Wilhelm, Duke of Württemberg, transl. by W. Robert Nitske and edited by Savoie Lottinville, p. 270. Copyright 1973 by the University of Oklahoma Press.

3. Louis Caillou was a Creole boatman. Grand Louis was a hunter and trapper from Cahokia and later from St. Charles. Duke Paul wrote: "This true son of the wilderness, reared in the dense forest and in the communion of Indian tribes and company of hunters and boatmen, whose inclination to drink and immorality

often exceeded the bounds of all human dignity, had under his leather jacket a heart sensitive to better feelings." From *Travels in North America, 1822–1824*, by Paul Wilhelm, Duke of Württemberg, translated by W. Robert Nitske and edited by Savoie Lottinville, p. 268. Copyright 1973 by the University of Oklahoma Press.

Old Roudeau may have been Joseph Robidoux, who had a trading post close to present-day St. Joseph, Missouri.

4. On May 5, 1823, Paul Wilhelm requested General Clark in St. Louis to furnish him a passport to travel up the Missouri River. He explained that the object of this trip was for his own instruction. The request was granted on June 10, 1823, by the secretary of war. Grace Raymond Hebard, *Sacajawea, A Guide and Interpreter of the Lewis and Clark Expedition*. Glendale, CA: The Arthur H. Clark Co., 1957, p. 118.

5. In a personal letter, June 2, 1967, Dr. Lissberger, head of the Library Board, Württembergische Landesbibliothek, in Stuttgart, Germany, wrote, "Duke Paul's journals have been handed over to the Stuttgart National Library. However, they had been destroyed here in 1944 by war operations, despite the protection of a concrete cover. Solely, three small notebooks, with records about the fourth trip, and encompassing the time from December 11, 1852, until May 30, 1853, have remained preserved, by chance."

Dr. Karin v. Maur, director of Staatsgalerie, Stuttgart, Germany, in a letter to A.L.W. dated December 27, 1966, stated that: "An old painting of Duke Paul and his Indian Boy hung in one of the school buildings in Stuttgart, but must have been destroyed during the war, or it was a watercolor by Mollhausen which has a more ethnographic rather than artistic value, and may be kept in the National Museum in Washington."

The National Museum in Washington, D.C., has no record and cannot find such a picture, oil or watercolor.

Linda Virga, a student at the University of Hamburg, 1968, forwarded these references on the life of Duke Paul: *Allgemeinen Deutschen Biographie*, Vol. 25, 1887, p. 243; *Bibliographie der Württembergischen Geschichte*, by Wilhelm Heyd, Vol. 2, 1896, p. 701. No mention is made of Jean Baptiste Charbonneau in either reference.

On January 10, 1967, Dr. Schuz, Museumsdirektor Staatliches Museum für Naturkunde in Stuttgart, wrote that he read in an old copy of the *Franconian Chronical Mergenthein*, November 11, 1926: "Duke Paul brought a young Sioux chief to Germany at the end of his 1850 trip to the United States. The Sioux's name was Haucmonc. He was so unhappy that he was soon back to New York and then on to his native village."

CHAPTER 43 *Kitten*

1. On November 3, 1823, Duke Paul Wilhelm of Württemberg and Jean Baptiste Charbonneau traveled by boat from St. Louis downriver. They reached New Orleans on December 19. There they booked passage with Captain Packard, who worked for Vincente Nolte and Company, on the brig, *Smyrna*. The *Smyrna* was loaded on Sunday, December 21, but drifted around on the Mississippi River until the wind was favorable and it could sail. On January 10 the people on the brig sighted Cuba and by the last of that month the outside temperature was measured at fourteen degrees below zero off the banks of Newfoundland. The *Smyrna* sailed into Havre de Grace on February 14, 1824. For the next six years Jean Baptiste was with Duke Paul, who lived in the Württemberg castle about thirty miles from Stuttgart. Together they traveled through France, England, Germany, and North Africa. In 1829 they returned to America. Wilhelm, trans. by Bek, pp. 459–62; and Butscher, pp. 181–92.

CHAPTER 44 *Jerk Meat*

1. The grooves may have been made to permit the blood to escape and weaken the victim. The grooves symbolized lightning, which was believed would make the arrows fatal. Wallace and Hoebel, pp. 102–3, also state that it seems possible the grooves were made to prevent the arrow shaft from warping. The arrow feathers were of owl, buzzard, or wild turkey, because these feathers were not ruined by blood as were hawk or eagle feathers. Wing feathers were split at the stems, dipped in glue or blood and bound in the grooves on either side

of the shaft with sinew and blood, then sun dried. A notch was made for the arrowhead to be fastened in the same way. The Shoshoni and their relatives placed the blade of the hunting arrow in the same plane with the notch for the string, so that it would be more likely to pass between the ribs of the animal, which are up and down. From *The Comanches, Lords of the South Plains*, by Ernest Wallace and E. Adamson Hoebel. Copyright 1952 by the University of Oklahoma Press.

2. Comanches also think of themselves as *The People*, as do the Shoshonis and most other western plains tribes. In the Ute language the word *Comanche* means, "Anyone who wants to fight me all the time." Wallace and Hoebel, p. 4.

3. Wallace and Hoebel write that the language and culture of the Comanches point to a Shoshonean origin. When the first recorded studies were made by whites, the Comanches were so similar to the Shoshonis that it was impossible to distinguish between the two groups. Crow tradition says they were once in the Snake River region. Omaha tradition says the Comanches were on the Middle Loup River until the start of the nineteenth century. According to Comanche tradition they came from the Shoshonis in the Rocky Mountain country. Today it is not known why the Comanches and Shoshonis separated. There are several legendary accounts, which include disputes over distribution of bear meat, hard feelings over an accidental death of a chief's son, a split caused by the aggressive northern tribes equipped with guns, or the desire for more horses from the southwest. Probably a combination of all these factors contributed to the split of the two groups. Wallace and Hoebel, pp. 8–11.

4. Sacajawea was usually called *Wadzewipe*, meaning *Lost Woman*, while she was among the Comanches, according to Clark and Edmonds, p. 117, and Grace Raymond Hebard, *Sacajawea, A Guide and Interpreter of the Lewis and Clark Expedition*. Glendale, CA: The Arthur H. Clark Co., 1957, p. 265. *Penat* meant *honey* in Comanche.

5. There were many Comanche tribes. The largest was the *Penataka*, or Honey Eaters. There were *Nokoni*, Wandering People; *Tanima*, Liver Eaters; *Yamparika*,

Yap Eaters; *Kutsueka*, Buffalo Eaters; *Tenawa*, Down Stream People; *Parkeenaum*, Water People; and a dozen other tribes. Sacajawea went to the *Quohada*, Antelope People. Personal letter to A.W.L. from H. D. Corwin, March 7, 1967.

Logic tells us that if Sacajawea were to leave the area around St. Louis, she would follow a more northerly route, following the Missouri River, a trail she already knew, to the Mandan villages, where she had friends. Or she would continue along the Missouri River route until she located her own people, the Shoshonis. However, the legends of her leaving St. Louis always take her into the southwest and to the Comanche country, an area that was totally new to her.

6. No tepee stood straight, but tilted slightly backward into the prevailing winds. Most tepees faced east as winds come from the west or southwest. The smoke hole, above the entrance near the top, was made by folding back two ends of skins and attaching these flaps, which were really pockets, like pointed ears, to outside poles. The "ears" could be adjusted by moving the outside poles so that the hole was closed, open, or something in between. This opening controlled the amount of wind that was allowed to enter, and helped create a draft to carry off smoke.

In warm weather the covering could be rolled several inches off the ground to provide more ventilation. In cold weather the cover could be drawn tightly to the ground. To maintain a continual draft to carry away smoke, an inner lining, or doubling, of buffalo hide was secured to the poles inside to a height of about six feet above the ground. The lining was tucked under the edge of beds and leather boxes stored about the inner edge of the tepee. Without the lining, wind could blow in from the bottom or rain water could run down poles to drip over everything inside. With this lining, any air that got in under the outer cover was sent upward and never felt by the people inside the tepee. Rain that got in through the smoke hole ran down the poles between the outer cover and lining into a narrow trench at the base of the tepee and was drained away, leaving the floor dry. This air space between the two skins gave good insulation and kept the tepee warm or cool, de-

pending on the weather outside. Wallace and Hoebel,
pp. 86–91. For excellent material on the making of
lodges see Reginald and Gladys Laubin, *The Indian
Tipi, Its History, Construction, and Use*. Norman: University of Oklahoma Press, 1957.

7. The Comanches did not spank their children, but
taught by object lessons. They knew that parental control caused resentment and so, like most Native Americans, when discipline was needed they called on a close
relative, such as an aunt or uncle, grandmother or
grandfather. From *Indians of the Plains*, by Robert H.
Lowie, p. 83. Natural History Press. Copyright 1954 by
the American Museum of Natural History.

8. Wallace and Hoebel, p. 68, say that the medicine
hunt was not used often, but the Comanches were pos-
itive that the magic charms worked. Maybe the circle
of shouting, rushing hunters who crowded and tired the
animals made it work.

9. The most courageous thing a man could do was
to count coup on a live enemy. Coup was striking the
enemy at close range rather than shooting him from a
distance. Wallace and Hoebel, p. 246.

10. To avoid the risk of incest, brothers and sisters
were kept apart as much as possible. Custom demanded
that a male who was touched or even approached by
his sexually developed sister should kill the girl. Otherwise, there were few sex taboos among the Comanche.
Nonincestuous exploration and experimentation were
not frowned upon, and sex was not considered a moral
issue. Older, unmarried girls often initiated younger
boys in sex games. There was little rape within bands.
Husbands permitted unmarried brothers to use their
women in expectation of later reciprocity. This practice
tended to make close family groups. T. R. Fehrenbach,
Comanches: The Destruction of a People. New York:
Alfred A. Knopf, Inc., 1979, pp. 41–2.

CHAPTER 45 *Comanche Marriage*
1. According to Wallace and Hoebel, p. 48, Comanche rescues were most often made by two men working
together. "Rushing neck by neck on either side of the
prostrate person, both riders stooped at the same instant and swung the body in front of one of the riders."

This trick was practiced day after day on all kinds of ground until the men and ponies did it perfectly. From *The Comanches, Lords of the South Plains*, by Ernest Wallace and E. Adamson Hoebel. Copyright 1952 by the University of Oklahoma Press.

2. A Comanche medicine man watched for flocks of small birds rhythmically swooping down and up, because they followed herds of buffalo to eat the insects off their infested hides. These swooping birds told him buffalo were close by.

3. The Mandan women and some of the Plains tribes women did all the work of skinning and butchering as soon as their men shot the buffalo. However, Comanche men did their own skinning and the first phase of butchering. The slicing, fileting, stripping for drying, and hide curing were left for the women. Wallace and Hoebel, pp. 58–61.

4. A Comanche butchering or feast would sicken the sensibilities of most civilized men, but because they ate and used most of the animal, they got the nutrients needed to survive. If they had eaten only lean meat, they would have sickened and died. However, hunger and constant exposure did take terrible tolls, as many Comanches and other early Native Americans died from pneumonia and suffered from rheumatism and intestinal disorders. T. R. Fehrenbach, *Comanches: The Destruction of a People*. New York: Alfred A. Knopf, Inc., 1979, pp. 35–6.

5. The pipes were straight tubes from the shank bone of a deer or antelope, cut off at either end, the marrow pushed out, and the mouth end smoothed. The pipe was wrapped with the ligament from the back of a buffalo bull's neck to reinforce the bone and make the pipe last long. The straight pipes were easy to carry, so were taken on raids and hunting expeditions. Wallace and Hoebel, p. 98.

6. The metal arrowheads became important as trade items for the Plains Indians beginning about 1820. The eastern traders made the points and put them in packages of a dozen. The cost to the trader was about six cents a package and he traded the package for one buffalo robe. One kind of metal arrowhead had no barb and was easily extracted from game. The war points

had one barb. When it was shot into a body and the shaft pulled, it caught and the point turned crosswise so that it was impossible to pull out without tearing or cutting. Wallace and Hoebel, p. 104.

7. Herrmann believes, pp. 179–80, that most all Native Americans were familiar with the wheel. They used wheels on their children's toys. Before the time of Columbus they did not use the wheel because they did not have large domesticated animals suitable for pulling heavy loads, and the terrain was rocky and uneven in many places. After the arrival of horses, it was the lack of knowledge in road construction that kept the people from using carts on wheels. Paul Herrmann, *Conquest by Man*, transl. by Michael Bullock, N.Y., Harper and Bros., 1954. Copyright Hoffman und Campe Verlag, c/o Curtis Brown, Ltd.

8. The Comanches venerated the rare, pure white horse. They also liked and bred spotted ponies. Most of their stallions were gelded, a trick they learned from the Spanish. Fehrenbach, p. 98.

9. Bride gifts were never delivered directly, for that was considered bad manners. They were just left. Sometimes a relative of the suitor was used as a mediator, to take horses or goods to the lodge of the girl's parents and talk politely with them. If the gift was refused, it was left untouched and nothing was said. But if the family took the gifts the meaning was clear that the family approved of the match and the prospective bride was willing to live with the suitor. Fehrenbach, p. 100; also Wallace and Hoebel, p. 135.

10. Later when the Comanches had guns, they captured mustangs even more easily with the trick called "creasing." Creasing took excellent marksmanship. The horse was shot through the muscular part of the neck, above the backbone. The trick was to not fracture the spine, so that the horse dropped paralyzed for two or three minutes. Then the man had time to rope and tie the horse before it knew what had happened. The horse recovered and when the crease healed it never seemed to bother the horse. Wallace and Hoebel, pp. 41–2.

11. Sometimes after the gift of horses had been delivered and accepted, the bridegroom killed one of the least valuable, removed the heart, and hung it at the

door of his betrothed. The bride roasted it, divided it in half, and the couple ate it. Fehrenbach, p. 136.

CHAPTER 46   *Joy and Sorrow*

1. Many of the Plains tribes had a Foolish Society. The men sometimes acted like clowns or did deeds generally thought foolish by most people. These men believed they obeyed instructions given them by some spirit person. From *Indians of the Plains*, by Robert H. Lowie, p. 188. Natural History Press. Copyright 1954 by the American Museum of Natural History.

2. If the umbilical cord was undisturbed before it rotted, it was believed that the child would have a long, fortunate life. A woman assisting with the birth threw the afterbirth in a creek or running stream because moving water was a purifier and wiped out any evil. If running water was not available, the afterbirth was buried in the ground. From *The Comanches, Lords of the South Plains*, by Ernest Wallace and E. Adamson Hoebel, p. 144. Copyright 1952 by the University of Oklahoma Press.

3. If the band was moving, the unfit baby was left behind, near the location of the last camp. Wallace and Hoebel, p. 120.

4. Another type of cradleboard was the buckskin sheath, laced in the front and fastened to a back board. Undoing the cradleboard and unwrapping the baby each time it was soiled would have been a bother. The baby boy's penis was placed in a small hole in the lacings, and for the baby girl a leather drain tube was placed between the legs and fitted to a hole in the lacings. Dry moss or cattail down was used to catch the soiled excretion. Wallace and Hoebel, p. 120.

5. The space was usually packed with feathers or hair and in some cases paper to stop the force of arrows or bullets or blows from spear points. The Comanches' interest in books was usually for the purpose of using the paper to pack their shields. Wallace and Hoebel, pp. 106–7.

CHAPTER 47   *Gray Bone*

1. This living bark turns white when exposed to sunlight. The bark of the year before does not grow any

more and thus it does not expand enough to fit around the growing trunk, and so it is forced off in patches. The sycamore is one of the earth's first hardwood trees, and has survived millions of years. Platt, pp. 44–5.

2. When the ruffle or movement of the feathers was constant, as when the shield was shaken, it served to disturb the aim of the enemy. From *The Comanches, Lords of the South Plains,* by Ernest Wallace and E. Adamson Hoebel, p. 107. Copyright 1952 by the University of Oklahoma Press.

CHAPTER 48 *Shooting Stars*

1. Usually no woman gave advice or became proficient in the use of medicinals until she had passed the menopause. The menstruation was believed to cancel all medicine or magic. This curse reinforced the social inferiority of women. If the woman lived long enough the menses disappeared with menopause and she could then make medicine on her own or act in the capacity of a chief. T. R. Fehrenbach, *Comanches: The Destruction of a People.* New York: Alfred A. Knopf, Inc., 1979, p. 43. Also from *The Comanches, Lords of the South Plains,* by Ernest Wallace and E. Adamson Hoebel, p. 166. Copyright 1952 by the University of Oklahoma Press.

2. The first vision quest was made before the adolescent male had been on the warpath. The vision was usually caused by hallucinations from going without food.

3. Lavender, pp. 140–4, wrote that on November 12, 1833, the stars seemed to tumble from the skies. The warriors of various Indian tribes who saw this spectacular meteor shower dressed in clothes for battle and put on war paints. This was something they could not fight, but they could die as brave warriors, mounted on their horses, riding single file around their village. The women and children cried and the dogs barked and wolves howled. Next morning everything was normal. From that time on the night the stars fell became a part of legendary history. Many tribes marked future events from "the night the stars fell." From *Bent's Fort*

by David Lavender. Copyright 1954 by Doubleday and Co., Inc.

CHAPTER 49   *The Raid*

1. While the abduction of children angered the Mexicans more than rapes, murders, and robberies, the republic had no money for an intelligent ransom policy. Once adopted, the captive had the rights and recognition of a born Comanche. A child forgot its native language and old associations and strove to be accepted. For example, the girls looked forward to becoming the wife of a great warrior. A captive, adjusted to Comanche life, was almost never able to readjust again to civilization. T. R. Fehrenbach, *Comanches: The Destuction of a People*. New York: Alfred A. Knopf, Inc., 1979, pp. 256–57.

2. In Lawton, Oklahoma, on February 15, 1925, a Comanche woman, sixty-six years old, named Tahcutine, told Dr. Charles Eastman that she was the daughter of Ticannaf, who was the son of Wadziwipe, the supposed Sacajawea. Tahcutine told about a young Mexican girl her father captured. The Mexican girl's name was Choway and she lived with Wadziwipe until the woman took her youngest child and left the band. Several other Comanche women who knew the wife of Jerk Meat or the tradition of her disappearance told Dr. Eastman about the young Mexican captive, Choway, who lived with Wadziwipe. Eastman, *Report to the Commissioner of Indian Affairs*, 1925, which includes Eastman's statements from Lawton and the Comanche Reservation, Fort Sill, Oklahoma.

CHAPTER 50   *Bent's Fort to Lupton's Fort*

1. To see a *glory* close up, you must view a cloud of uniform water droplets in such a way that your shadow is projected on that cloud. You will then also see the shadow of your head surrounded by a series of colored haloes. These haloes are caused by the scatter of sunlight by droplets of water of uniform size. Bryant and Jarmie, pp. 60–71.

2. Owl Woman was the daughter of Gray Thunder. She became William Bent's woman when he was twenty-

eight years old. Bill Bent named their first child Mary. From *Bent's Fort* by David Lavender, pp. 174–76. Copyright 1954 by Doubleday and Co., Inc.

3. Céran St. Vrain helped the Bents build their fort. Its front wall facing east was 137 feet long, 14 feet high and 3 or more feet thick. The northern and southern walls were 178 feet long. Inside were 25 rooms built along the walls, with their doors facing an inner court or *placita*. The main entrance was a kind of tunnel between the walls of the storerooms. There was a second story with another row of apartments and a watchtower with windows on four sides. On top of the watchtower was a bell that called the men to meals and on top of the belfrey was the flagpole which carried Old Glory. Lavender, pp. 135–40, 385–87.

CHAPTER 51 *St. Vrain's Fort*

1. Some historians feel this was the site of a second fort built by Jim Bridger. Jackson and Penal, 1970, pp. 468–69.

2. These were primitive carts constructed of two pieces of timber ten or twelve feet long, framed together by two or more crosspieces, upon one end of which the wickerwork body was placed. The front ends were rounded to serve as the shaft, and the whole arrangement was set on the crosspieces connecting opposite wheels. These were used to carry baggage, clothing, food, and supplies.

3. This route runs parallel with the present-day line of the Union Pacific Railroad.

CHAPTER 52 *Bridger's Fort*

1. The fort was built by James Bridger and Louis Vasquez on the trail that led to Oregon and California. Bridger had no saloon nor gambling at this fort. At first there were only a few log houses inside a log wall, eight feet high. Gray, pp. 80–1, quotes one of the early travelers who stopped there:

> It was built of poles and daubed with mud; it is a shabby concern. Here are about twenty-five lodges of Indians, or rather white trappers' lodges occupied by their Indian wives. They have a good supply of deer, elk, and antelope skins, coats, pants, moccasins, and

other Indian fixens, which they trade low for flour,
pork, powder, lead, blankets, butcher-knives, spirits,
hats, ready-made clothes, coffee, sugar, etc. They ask
for a horse from twenty-five to fifty dollars in trade.
Their wives are mostly Pyentes and Snake Indians.
They have a herd of cattle, twenty-five to thirty goats,
and some sheep. They generally abandon this fort
during the winter months. At this place the bottoms
are wide and covered with good grass. Cotton wood
timber is plenty. The streams abound with trout.

Arthur Amos Gray, *Men Who Built the West.* Caldwell,
Idaho: Caxton Printers Ltd., 1945.

Ten years after the fort was built, Bridger found the
Mormons wanted it for a supply station. They put a
stone wall around the fort, and paid Bridger eight thousand dollars for the buildings plus a tenth of his thirty-
mile-square tract of land. Vera Kelsy, *Young Men So*
Daring: Fur Traders Who Carried the Frontier West.
New York: The Bobbs-Merrill Co., Inc., 1956, pp. 254–
55, 266.

2. In the spring of 1832 Jim Bridger and Tom Fitzpatrick had a skirmish with the Blackfeet in the area
of the Missouri's Three Forks. Bridger was shot in the
back with two iron-headed arrows. Fitzpatrick pulled
one out, but the shaft of the other broke, so that even
probing with a knife, he could not get the three-inch-
long piece of iron out of Bridger's back. For three years
the arrowhead caused Bridger great pain. Kelsey, pp.
202–3.; *Across the Wide Missouri*, by Bernard DeVoto,
p. 90. Copyright 1947 by Houghton Mifflin Co.

Dr. Marcus Whitman removed the arrowhead in 1835.
Afterwards Bridger had Reverend Samuel Parker perform his Presbyterian wedding ceremony. Bridger married the daughter of a Flathead chief, whom Parker
christened Emma. Kelsey, pp. 205–7; DeVoto, 1947, pp.
230–31.

3. Bridger's first child was a girl, named Mary Ann
after his sister. Mary Ann was sent to the Whitman's
in Oregon after the death of Emma. Bridger then married a Ute woman, whom he called Belle. They had
three children. Two years later, in 1846, Mary Ann was
dead. DeVoto, 1947, p. 372.

Bridger was heartbroken and took his family to his farm on the outskirts of Westport, Missouri. Next to Bridger's farm was the Bent farm and Vasquez farm. The Vasquez children were white, the Bridger and Bent children were half-breeds, and they were all friends and playmates. From *Bent's Fort* by David Lavender, p. 325. Copyright 1954 by Doubleday and Co., Inc.

Finally, Bridger tired of farming and put his children in a St. Louis Catholic school and brought his wife, Belle, back to his Wyoming fort in 1850. Belle died, leaving a baby girl called Virginia. Bridger found himself a Shoshoni wife to care for the baby. Kelsey, pp. 250–51. Grace Raymond Hebard, *Sacajawea, A Guide and Interpreter of the Lewis and Clark Expedition.* Glendale, CA: The Arthur H. Clark Co., 1957, pp. 187, 241.

CHAPTER 53   *The Mormons*

1. Washakie's name is interpreted as Rawhide Rattle, Shoots Straight, Shoots-on-the-Fly, Sure Shot, or Gambler's Gourd. The Shoshoni story of how he acquired this name states that when he killed his first buffalo, he skinned the head, scraped the hair off, puckered it up, and tied it around a stick with a hole in it, so that it could be blown up like a bladder. He put stones in it and dried it so that it would rattle. When he went to war against the Sioux he rode among them, shook the rattle, and scared their horses. They called him *The Rattle* or *Wash-a-ki*. From *The Shoshonis, Sentinels of the Rockies*, by Virginia Trenholm and Maurine Carley, p. 98. Copyright 1964 by the University of Oklahoma Press.

When young he lived with his father's band of Flatheads. When his father was killed by Blackfeet, his mother and her five small children found a band of her people, the Shoshonis, on the banks of the Salmon River. As he grew older, Washakie was distinguished for his friendship to the white man. Trenholm and Carley, p. 99.

2. That map was so exact and practical that it became the route of the Overland Stage, the Pony Express, and later the Union Pacific Railroad.

3. The Mormon sheriff seemed convinced Bridger's

wife did not know where he was, but stationed men at several points to watch the fort and for the return of Bridger. In the spring of 1854, Governor Brigham Young of the Utah Territory ordered Mormon forces to take over Fort Bridger. The Mormons added several new buildings and replaced the logs of the stockade with fireproof concrete. Vera Kelsey, *Young Men So Daring: Fur Traders Who Carried the Frontier West*. New York: The Bobbs-Merrill Co., Inc., 1956, pp. 251–55.

4. Jim Bridger filed this claim on March 9, 1854.

CHAPTER 54   *The Great Treaty Council*

1. This is a reference to the cash accounts book kept by William Clark from 1825 to 1828. The book's front cover contains the record Clark kept of most of the people on the expedition. After Sacajawea's name he wrote: *Dead.* The book is now at the Newberry Library, Chicago. See page 821.

CHAPTER 55   *The Jefferson Peace Medal*

1. Personal letter to A.W.L. from Dr. Kenneth O. Leonard, Garrison Clinic, Garrison, North Dakota, February 18, 1968: "...as to the Medal (the one Sacajawea supposedly wore at Wind River Reservation) it obviously wouldn't have been one Lewis and Clark handed out as they were silver. It could have been an early English one with a copper rim as many did come down from Canada. It was also highly unlikely that a woman would have been wearing a peace medal. Lewis and Clark didn't give any to women as far as I can remember—and they were highly selective in which chief they did give them to." Another letter from Dr. Leonard on February 29, 1968, states, "...it could have been a religious medal which the missionaries handed out by the car loads. These seemed to be very common and all descriptions from crosses to medals."

2. The stagecoach most generally used was the Concord, which was made in New Hampshire. Blacksmith and repair shops were at the western division points. These points were also the main replacement places for the drivers and horses. Dick, pp. 234–36.

3. A possibles bag was a small purse made from leather or cloth, carried by women. The name came

from the white women, who carried all possible necessities, such as comb, handkerchief, coins, hair pins, etc. in the small, decorated bag.

CHAPTER 56 *I Could Cry All Night*

1. Young, Vol. I, Parts 3 to 6, p. 207.
2. Thwaites, Vol. 28, 1816, 1904–7, pp. 176–79.
3. Rufus B. Sage, *Rufus B. Sage, His Letters and Papers*, ed. by LeRoy R. Hafen and Ann W. Hafen, Glendale, CA: The Arthur H. Clark Co., Vol. II, 1956, pp. 155–56, 192–93.
4. Frémont, pp. 30–1.
5. Sage, pp. 52–4.
6. From *Persimmon Hill*, by William Clark Kennerly, pp. 144, 158, 187, 258. Copyright 1948 by the University of Oklahoma Press; Porter and Davenport, 1963, Chap. 23.
7. L. R. Hafen, 1930, pp. 66–7.
8. *Sublette Papers and Letters* by Solomon Sublette, May 5 and June 6, 1844, in the Missouri Historical Society, St. Louis.
9. Abert, Sen. ex. doc. 438, 29 Cong. 1 Sess.
10. Ruxton, p. 713.
11. Cooke, 1878, pp. 131–34.
12. Sen. doc., no. 2, 31 Cong. Special Session, p. 69.
13. Bancroft, p. 568.
14. *San Luis Rey, California's Mission.*
15. *Bandini Documents*, San Diego Archives and Bancroft Library, University of California, Berkeley, pp. 328–33.
16. C. H. Porter, 1961, p. 8.
17. Anderson, pp. 260–61.
18. Anderson, p. 261.
19. *Bandini Documents*, p. 333.
20. Angel and Fairchild, p. 71; Bonner, pp. 353–64.

According to T. D. Bonner, who wrote the story of Jim Beckwourth in 1856, the "wife of a Canadian named Chapineau, who acted as interpreter and guide to Lewis and Clarke during their explorations of the Rocky Mountains...gave birth to a son." The "Redheaded Chief (Clarke) adopted..." him, and "on his return to St. Louis took the infant with him, and baptized it John Baptiste Clarke Chapineau. After a careful culture of his mind,

the boy was sent to Europe to complete his education."
Bonner, p. 528.

21. A personal letter to A.L.W. from Merle W. Wells,
historian and archivist, the Idaho Historical Society,
Boise, Idaho, September 18, 1967, says that the prob-
able grave of Jean Baptiste Charbonneau is at the edge
of a road not far from the old stage station, near Danner,
Oregon, which no longer exists as a town.

22. Moore, sec. 2.

23. Anderson, p. 264.

24. Anderson, p. 246.

25. Schroer, p. 26.

26. Rocky Mountain spotted fever is caused by a
rickettsia microorganism found in certain wood ticks
(*Dermacentor*). The tick is sometimes found on gophers.
Therefore the Shoshonis believed that the gopher caused
the disease of fever, muscular pains and skin eruptions,
rather than the tick. From *The Shoshonis, Sentinels of
the Rockies*, by Virginia Trenholm and Maurine Carley,
p. 282. Copyright 1964 by the University of Oklahoma
Press. Also see Chuinard, p. 221.

27. Quantan Quay, a Shoshoni living on the Wind
River Reservation in 1929, remembered Shoogan
(named Bazil by the Mormons) as a man of fine character, physically splendid, gentle in speech and never
loud or boisterous. He also remembered Toussaint (who,
he said, was called Baptiste by the Mormons and others)
as "a treacherous man, because he liked his firewater
and used it often." Grace Raymond Hebard, *Sacajawea,
A Guide and Interpreter of the Lewis and Clark Expedition.* Glendale, CA: The Arthur H. Clark Co., 1957,
p. 178.

28. Washakie purchased the casket plate from the
son of a furniture dealer for the price of a bow and
arrow. Grace Raymond Hebard, *Washakie*. Cleveland:
The Arthur H. Clark Co., 1930, pp. 233–34.

29. Washakie was said to have a "'fine open countenance' which became so animated and expressive when
he spoke that it was a real pleasure to look at him."
He had great dignity and pride in his simple possessions. On the walls of his reservation cabin were pictures of his warring exploits, drawn by himself and his
son Charlie. Trenholm and Carley, pp. 285–86.

30. This was Chief Washakie's most famous statement. After Washakie's death in 1900, his son Dick presented the saddle to Jakie Moore (J. K. Moore, at the Fort Washakie store), who was a great friend. Jakie's son, J. K. Moore, Jr., of Lander, Wyoming, recalls seeing the saddle, but has no knowledge of its whereabouts now.

31. "Mrs. Irwin wrote, from Sacajawea's description, a history of the Lewis and Clark Expedition and the part that Sacajawea had taken in the expedition." Hebard, 1957, p. 232.

32. These field glasses were later given to Washakie by General Crook.

33. This was the Battle of the Little Big Horn, in Montana, June 25, 1876. Linderman, 1930, pp. 154–77; Kuhlman, 1951; U.S. Govt. Printing Office, *Custer Battlefield*. Custer Battlefield Historical and Museum Assoc., *Entrenchment Trail*.

CHAPTER 57 *Nothing Is Lost*

1. An important personality problem for the males was finding a suitable substitute for the ancient goals. With the buffalo gone and warfare a thing of the past, they found it very hard to discover any objectives that made life worth living. "Some strongly expressed sentiment that they preferred the old existence with all its hazards, but with the chance for glory, to the pedestrian career of a farmer or mechanic." From *Indians of the Plains*, by Robert H. Lowie, pp. 221–22. Natural History Press. Copyright 1954 by the American Museum of Natural History.

2. Some ration days—which took place once a week, every two weeks, or once a month—they were given bacon or salt pork, dried beans, flour, rice, or hominy. Each family was given a card with their family name and number of persons in the family. The card was punched when rations were issued by a military officer who was required to be present. From *The Comanches, Lords of the South Plains*, by Ernest Wallace and E. Adamson Hoebel, pp. 330, 338. Copyright 1952 by the University of Oklahoma Press.

3. Andrew Bazil, Shoogan's son, said that Sacajawea introduced the Sun Dance among the Lemhi Shoshonis

and that his father was leader of the dance. Grace Raymond Hebard, *Sacajawea, A Guide and Interpreter of the Lewis and Clark Expedition.* Glendale, CA: The Arthur H. Clark Co., 1957, pp. 259-60, 275.

4. In the old days, in each tribe there was at least one whip holder. The whip was a wooden, serrated blade with carved scalp symbols of the owner's victims. Tied at one end were two short otter-skin lashes. The owners of the whip were always the bravest men of the tribe. The man that owned a whip could stop any dance and recite one of his coups. In the end he was required to bring the sun curse upon himself if he stated any untruth. He could dance up to any lounging spectator, point his whip, and that person was obligated to jump right in and dance, or be whipped. No brave could be excused from the dance for any reason, if the whip were pointed at him. The man had to recite his strongest deed and then the whip holder countered with his strongest deed. If the whip holder's deed was as good as the brave's, the brave had to dance the rest of the time. If it was not, then the brave was excused from dancing and the whip owner had to dance. Wallace and Hoebel 1952, p. 271.

5. Dr. James Irwin studied and practiced naturopathy, a method of treating diseases with natural agencies.

6. In 1870 the government urged and invited the Northern Arapahos to make a treaty with the Shoshonis and locate permanently with them. Chief Washakie was angered by these demands and refused to allow them to settle on his reservation, and "he also accused them of all of the murders that had taken place in the Wind River Valley and at the mining camps the summer before." He said the Arapahos were storing ammunition and planned to act with the Sioux to make war against his camp. Eight years later Washakie allowed the Arapahos to be placed temporarily on his reservation. Some believe he was away hunting at the time and actually had no say in the matter, and other historians say that he did not object because he himself did not want to be moved from his "beloved Wind River Mountains, home of Tamapah, the Sun-Father." From *The Shoshonis, Sentinels of the Rockies*, by Virginia

Trenholm and Maurine Carley, pp. 276–8. Copyright 1964 by the University of Oklahoma Press.

7. The Arapahos were broken people even before they were given a permanent place on the Wind River Reservation. Colonel John M. Chivington killed many of their warriors, women, and children when he attacked a camp of Cheyennes and Arapahos on Sand Creek, near Fort Lupton, Colorado, on November 29, 1864. Then they suffered a loss of hunting territories and food supply, broken treaties by the whites, first free access to liquor, prostitution, disease, and a general harassing that led to placement on the Pine Ridge Reservation. By then the Arapahos had nothing left but their dreams. The Peyote Cult was accepted by the Arapahos at Wind River a decade before it found its way into the Shoshoni tribe. Trenholm and Carley, pp. 277, 281–82.

8. Friday, the adopted Arapaho son of Thomas Fitzpatrick, who was Washakie's friend, may have talked him into holding a council with the Arapahos. Trenholm and Carley, p. 276.

9. Later this boy became an Episcopal minister at Fort Washakie and then a canon of a cathedral in Denver, Colorado.

10. When the Arapahos came to the reservation they were "in such indigent circumstances as to be wholly unable, without generous assistance from the government to speedily emerge from their present state of mendicity." The once proud tribe was reduced to 198 warriors, the rest women, children, and old men. Trenholm and Carley, p. 279.

11. Even today the Shoshoni young people are embarrassed when one of their elders spitefully calls an Arapaho "Dog-Eater" to his face. Trenholm and Carley, p. 281.

EPILOGUE

1. Personal letters to A.L.W. from the Commission of Indian Affairs, December 14, 1968, January 18, 1969, and March 5, 1969.

2. Grace Raymond Hebard, *Sacajawea, A Guide and Intrepreter of the Lewis and Clark Expidition.* Glendale, CA: The Arthur H. Clark Co., 1957, pp. 232–33.

3. Hebard, 1957, pp. 205–17.

4. Wind River Reservation Church Register of Burials, no. 114.

5. Hebard, 1957, p. 208.

6. Schroer, p. 21.

7. Hebard, 1957, p. 213.

8. Robert Beebe David, *Finn Burnett, Frontiersman*, Glendale, CA: The Arthur H. Clark Co., 1937.

9. Hebard, 1957, p. 151.

10. Hebard, 1957, p. 188.

Personal letter to A.L.W. from P. D. Riley, Nebraska State Historical Society, February 9, 1968, says, "I would hesitate to use his [Rivington's] information—he was a tall-tale spinner of the first class."

A personal letter from Warren C. Wood, editor, *Gering Courier*, February 19, 1968: "I sincerely regret that Tom Rivington, who had a lot of people fooled for a time, when he lived here, was pretty much of a fake. He had just enough semi-factual data to fool a casual historian. I liked old Tom, but he wasn't a pioneer and doubt he ever lived with the Indians, let alone the Bird Woman."

Personal letter to A.L.W. from Merrill J. Mattes, U.S. Department of the Interior, National Park Service, San Francisco, March 6, 1968: "...the woman he claims he [Rivington] knew as Sacajawea was actually someone else with an assumed name." The Rivington letters to Dr. Hebard and typed interviews of 1929 are in a collection called "The Hebard Papers" at the University of California, Berkeley, where they were once in the possession of Dr. C. L. Camp in the Department of Paleontology.

11. Hebard, 1957, *Sacajawea*, pp. 188, 191, 240–42.

12. Hebard, 1957, p. 191; see also, Frazier, pp. 171–74; and Clark and Edmonds, pp. 118–20, 145.

13. A personal letter to A.L.W. from Merrill J. Mattes of the National Park Service, U.S. Department of the Interior, March 6, 1968.

14. On December 8 and 21, 1967, Mary K. Dempsey, Librarian of the Montana Historical Society, wrote that "Montanans are inclined to believe that she [Sacajawea] died at Fort Union, December 20, 1812." Actually Fort Union was not built until 1829 and this whole

area is now under the waters impounded by the Garrison Reservoir.

Mary Dempsey also wrote: "There is a queer story told by the Minnetaree warrior, Bull's Eye, in open council, where other Indians could hear and correct his story. He claimed to be the grandson of Sacajawea, wife of 'Sharbonish,' with whom she went 'far away somewhere, and she was killed,' said Bull's Eye, 'by hostile Indians near Glasgow, Montana, when I was four years old, in 1869.'"

15. A personal letter to A.L.W. from Will Robinson, secretary of the South Dakota State Historical Society, January 18, 1968.

16. Clift, p. 194.

17. Hall, August 15, 1971..

18. From *Sacajawea*, by Harold P. Howard. Copyright 1971 by the University of Oklahoma Press.

At a later time large boulders were set at the head and foot of the grave. A stone marker was erected at the grave in 1909 by H. E. Wadsworth, the Shoshoni agent. This marker was a gift from Timothy F. Burke, of Cheyenne, Wyoming. On the inclined face of the marker was a bronze tablet describing Sacajawea as a guide with the Lewis and Clark Expedition. The tablet also carried the words: "Identified 1908 by Rev. J. Roberts."

19. This new marker carries the date 1907 when Reverend J. Roberts identified the grave of Sacajawea.

Bibliography

ABERT, J. W. "Journal of Lieutenant J. W. Abert from Bent's Fort to St. Louis, 1845," Senate, ex-doc. 438, 29 Congress, 1st Session.

ABRAMS, ROCHONNE. "Meriwether Lewis: The Logistical Imagination," *The Bulletin* (Missouri Historical Society, St. Louis) 36 (July 1980).

ABRAMS, ROCHONNE. "Meriwether Lewis: Two Years with Jefferson, the Mentor," *The Bulletin* (Missouri Historical Society, St. Louis) 36 (October 1979.)

ADAMSON, EDWARD. *The Political Organization and Law-Ways of the Comanche Indians.* Memoirs of the American Anthropological Association, no. 54. Menasha, Wis.: American Anthropological Association, 1940.

ADREON, WILLIAM CLARK. *William Clark of the Village of St. Louis, Missouri Territory.* St. Louis: Lewis and Clark Heritage Federation, 1970.

ALLARD, WILLIAM ALBERT. "Chief Joseph," *National Geographic* 151 (March 1977).

ALLEN, JOHN L. "Lewis and Clark on the Upper Missouri: Decision at the Marias," *Montana, Magazine of Western History* 21 (Summer 1971).

ALLEN, PAUL, ed. *History of the Expedition under the Command of Captains Lewis and Clark——Performed during the Years 1804–5–6,* 2 vols. Philadelphia: Bradford and Inskeep, 1814. Reprinted by University Microfilms, Inc., Ann Arbor, Mich., 1966.

Allgemeinen Deutschen Biographie 25 (1887).

ALTER, J. CECIL. *James Bridger, Trapper, Frontiersman, Scout, and Guide: A Historical Narrative.* Salt Lake City: Shepard Book Co., 1925.

ALTHOFF, SHIRLEY. "Earthquakes," *St. Louis Globe-Democrat Sunday Magazine,* April 11, 1971.

American Heritage Book of Indians. New York: Simon and Schuster, 1961.

ANDERSON, IRVING W. "J. B. Charboneau, Son of Sacajawea," *Oregon Historical Society Quarterly 71 (September 1970).*

ANDRIST, RALPH K. *To the Pacific with Lewis and Clark.* New York: Harper, 1967.

ANGEL, MYRON, and M. D. FAIRCHILD. *History of Placer County.* Oakland, Calif.: Thompson and West, 1882.

APPLEMAN, ROY E. "Lewis and Clark: The Route 160 Years After," *Pacific Northwest Quarterly* 57 (January 1966).

ATHEARN, ROBERT G. *Forts of the Upper Missouri.* Englewood Cliffs, N.J.: Prentice-Hall, Inc., 1967.

BAKELESS, JOHN. *Lewis and Clark, Partners in Discovery,* New York: William Morrow and Co., 1947.

BANCROFT, H. H. *History of California, Vol. V.* San Francisco: 1925.

Bandini Documents and Unbound Documents. San Diego Archives, pp. 328-33. (Also, in the Bancroft Library, University of California, Berkeley.)

BARBOUR, WILLIAM R. "The Guns of Lewis and Clark," *Gun Digest,* 18th ed., 1964.

BEK, WILLIAM, ed. and transl. "First Journey to North America in the Years 1822 to 1824," by Wilhelm, Paul Friedrich, Duke of Württemberg. *South Dakota Historical Collections,* Vol. XIX, 1938.

BEKOFF, MARC, and MICHAEL C. WELLS. "The Social Ecology of Coyotes," *Scientific American,* 242, no. 4 (1980).

BENNETT, CHARLES M. Phoenix, Arizona. Personal communication, October 1-2, 1982.

BERRY, DON. *A Majority of Scoundrels, An Informal History of the Rocky Mountain Fur Company.* New York: Harper and Bros., 1961.

BIDDLE, NICHOLAS, ed. *History of the Expedition Under the Command of Captains Lewis and Clarke,* 2 vols. Philadelphia, Branford and Inskeep, 1814.

BLEVINS, WINFRED. *Charbonneau.* New York: Avon, 1976.

BODMER, KARL, and PRINCE MAXIMILIAN. "A Great Painter, A Royal Naturalist on Wild Missouri," *Smithsonian* 7 (October 1976).

BOGGS, WILLIAM. *Colorado Magazine* 7 (March 1930).

BONNER, T. D. *The Life and Adventures of James P. Beckwourth.* New York: Harper and Brothers, 1856. (Reprinted 1931.)

BORDWELL, CONSTANCE. *March of the Volunteers: Soldiering with Lewis and Clark.* Portland, Ore.: Beaver Books, 1960.

BOWERS, ALFRED W. *Mandan Social and Ceremonial Organization*. Chicago: University of Chicago Press, 1950.

BRACKENRIDGE, HENRY. *Journal of a Voyage up the Missouri (1811)*. Edited by Reuben Gold Thwaites. Cleveland: The Arthur H. Clark Co., 1904.

BRINDLEY, W. E. "Sacajawea, Tardy Honor for a Neglected Heroine," *Contributions* (Historical Society of Montana) 7 (1910).

BROOKS, NOAH. *First across the Continent: The Story of the Exploring Expedition of Lewis and Clark in 1803–4–5*. New York: Charles Scribner's Sons, 1901.

BROWN, JAMES S. *Life of a Pioneer*. Salt Lake City: George Q. Cannon and Sons, 1900.

BRUNER, EDWARD M. "Mandan," edited by Edward H. Spicer in *Perspectives in American Indian Culture Change*. Chicago: The University of Chicago Press, 1961.

BRYANT, HOWARD C., and NELSON JARMIE. "The Glory," *Scientific American* 231, no. 1, (July 1974).

BUDDE, G. EDWARD (GUS). "Historic Sites and Landmarks Along the Lewis and Clark Trail," *Lewis and Clark Trail Newsletter* 6, no. 1 (October 1978).

BUDDE, G. EDWARD (GUS). "Lewis and Clark Expedition," *Lewis and Clark Trail Newsletter* 6, no. 3 (April 1979).

BUDDE, G. EDWARD (GUS). "Missouri," "Lewis and Clark Trail Important to History," *Lewis and Clark Trail Newsletter* 6, no. 2 (January 1979).

BURGET, BETTYLOU. *The Legend of Sacajawea*. A poem based on the Lewis and Clark Journals. Astoria, Oregon, 1979.

BURROUGHS, RAYMOND DARWIN. *Exploration Unlimited: The Story of the Lewis and Clark Expedition*. Detroit: Wayne University Press, 1953.

BURROUGHS, RAYMOND DARWIN. *The Natural History of the Lewis and Clark Expedition*. East Lansing: Michigan State University Press, 1961.

BURROUGHS, RAYMOND D. *The Natural History of the Lewis and Clark Expedition*. Ann Arbor: University of Michigan Press, 1961.

BUTSCHER, LOUIS C. "A Brief Biography of Prince Paul Wilhelm of Württemberg (1797–1860)," *New Mexico Historical Review* 17 (July 1942).

Butte Record (Oroville, Calif.), July 14, 1866.

California's Mission San Luis Rey. San Luis Rey, Calif. Franciscan Padres, Old Mission, Calif.

CANTLON, CLEO. "McLean County Historical Society, Fort Mandan," *The Minot Daily News*, Minot, N.D., June 24, 1972.

CARSON, CHRISTOPHER. *Kit Carson's Own Story of His Life.* Edited by Blanche C. Grant. Taos, N.M. 1926.

CATLIN, GEORGE. *Letters and Notes on the Manners, Customs, and Conditions of North American Indians,* Vol. I and II. Piccadilly: Egyptian Hall, 1842; Reprint. New York: Dover Publications, Inc., 1973.

CHADWICK, DOUGLAS H. "The Flathead," *National Geographic* 152 (July 1977).

"Charbonneau, J. B.—Death of a California Pioneer," *Placer Herald,* Auburn, Calif., July 7, 1866.

"Charbonneau, Jean Baptist, February 11, 1805–May 16, 1866," Idaho Historical Society, Boise, Ida., Reference Series, no. 428.

"Charbonneau's, J. B., Obituary," *Owyhee Avalanche,* Ruby City, Ida., June 2, 1866.

CHATTERS, ROY M. "The Not-So-Enigmatic Lewis and Clark Airgun," *We Proceeded On,* 3, no. 2.

CHAVEZ, RAY. "Heritage," *Yakima Herald-Republic,* June 3, 1980.

CHIDSEY, DONALD BARR. *Lewis and Clark.* New York: Crown Publishers, Inc., 1970.

CHITTENDEN, HIRAM MARTIN. *The American Fur Trade of the Far West.* New York: F. P. Harper, 1902.

CHUINARD, E. G. *Only One Man Died: The Medical Aspects of the Lewis and Clark Expedition.* Glendale, CA: The Arthur H. Clark Co., 1980.

CHURCHILL, CLAIRE WARNER. *South of the Sunset—An Interpretation of Sacajawea.* New York: Rufus Rockwell Wilson, Inc., 1936.

CHURCHILL, SAM. "Sam's Valley, 'Farewell at Celilo,'" *Yakima Herald-Republic,* March 10, 1970.

CLARK, ELLA E. and MARGOT EDMONDS. *Sacagawea of the Lewis and Clark Expedition.* Berkeley: University of California Press, 1979.

CLARK, GENERAL WILLIAM. *Abstract of Expenditures as Superintendent of Indian Affairs, 1822.* Washington, D.C.: American State Papers, 1934. (Class II, Vol II, No 5., p. 289.)

CLARK, WILLIAM. *The Century Magazine,* October 1904.

CLARKE, CHARLES G. *The Men of the Lewis and Clark Expedition.* Glendale, CA: The Arthur H. Clark Co., 1970.

CLARKE, CHARLES G. "The Roster of the Lewis and Clark Expedition," *Oregon Historical Quarterly* 45 (December 1944).

CLIFT, EDITH CONNELLY. "Sacajawea, Guide to the Lewis and Clark Expedition," *'Neath August Sun—1901.* Lawton, Okla., 1933. Also published in *Prairie Lore* Southwestern Oklahoma Historical Society, Lawton, Okla. 3 (April 1967).

COHEN, VICTOR H. "James Bridger's Claims," *Annals of Wyoming* 12 (July 1940).

COLBY, C. B. *Animal Signs.* New York: Franklin Watts, Inc., 1966.

Commission of Indian Affairs, Washington, D.C.. Personal Letters, December 14, 1968, January 18 and March 5, 1969.

COOKE, PHILIP ST. GEORGE. *Conquest of New Mexico and California.* New York, 1878.

COOKE, PHILIP ST. GEORGE. *Scenes and Adventures in the Army: or Romance of Military Life.* Philadelphia: Lindsay and Blakiston, 1857.

CORWIN, HUGH D. Editor of *Prairie Lore*, Southwestern Oklahoma Historical Society. Personal letter, March 7, 1967.

COUES, ELLIOTT, ed. *History of the Expedition under the Command of Lewis and Clark*, 4 vols. New York: F. P. Harper, 1893. Reprint, New York: Dover Publishing Co., 1965.

CRAWFORD, HELEN. "Sakakawea," *North Dakota Historical Quarterly* 1 (April 1927).

CRISWELL, ELIJAH HARRY. *Lewis and Clark, Linguistic Pioneers.* University of Missouri Studies, Vol. 15, No. 2. Columbia, Mo.: University of Missouri, 1940.

CUSHMAN, DAN. *The Great North Trail.* New York: McGraw-Hill Book Co., 1966.

Custer Battlefield National Monument. U.S. Govt. Printing Office, 1959.

CUTRIGHT, PAUL RUSSELL. *A History of the Lewis and Clark Journals.* Norman: University of Oklahoma Press, 1976.

CUTRIGHT, PAUL RUSSELL. "Lewis and Clark Begin a Journey," *The Bulletin* (Missouri Historical Society, Saint Louis) 24 (October 1967).

CUTRIGHT, PAUL RUSSELL. "Lewis and Clark Indian Peace Medals," *The Bulletin* (Missouri Historical Society, Saint Louis) 24 (January 1968).

CUTRIGHT, PAUL RUSSELL. *Lewis and Clark: Pioneering Naturalists.* Urbana: University of Illinois Press, 1969.

CUTRIGHT, PAUL RUSSELL. "Meriwether Lewis on the Marias," *Montana, Magazine of Western History* 18 (July 1968).

CUTRIGHT, PAUL R., and MICHAEL J. BRODHEAD. "Dr. Elliott Coues and Sergeant Charles Floyd," *We Proceeded On* 4, no. 3 (July 1978).

DARY, DAVID A. *The Buffalo Book.* New York: Avon, 1974.

DAVID, ROBERT BEEBE. *Finn Burnett, Frontiersman.* Glendale, CA: The Arthur H. Clark Co., 1937.

DEACON, RICHARD. *Madoc and the Discovery of America: Some New Light on an Old Controversy.* New York: George Braziller, 1966.

DEDERS, DON. "A Dawning on the Prairie," *Exxon USA* (1st Quarter, 1979).

DEMPSEY, MARY K., Librarian of the Montana Historical Society, Helena. Personal letters, December 8 and 21, 1967.

DESMET, PIERRE-JEAN. *Life, Letters and Travels of Father Pierre-Jean DeSmet*. Edited by Hiram M. Chittenden and Alfred T. Richardson. New York: F. P. Harper, 3, 1905.

DEVOTO, BERNARD. *Across the Wide Missouri*. Boston: Houghton Mifflin Co., 1947.

DEVOTO, BERNARD. *The Course of Empire*. Boston: Houghton Mifflin Co., 1952.

DEVOTO, BERNARD, ed. *The Journals of Lewis and Clark*. Boston: Houghton Mifflin Co., 1953.

DICK, EVERETT. *Tales of the Frontier*. Lincoln: University of Neb. Press, 1963.

DILLON, RICHARD. *Meriwether Lewis: A Biography*. New York: Coward-McCann, Inc., 1956.

DOUGHERTY, JAMES HENRY. *Of Courage Undaunted: Across the Continent with Lewis and Clark*. New York: Viking Press, 1951.

DRUMM, STELLA M., ed. *Upper Missouri, 1812–1813*. St. Louis: Missouri Historical Society, 1920.

DRURY, CLIFFORD M. "Sacajawea's Death—1812 or 1884?" *Oregon Historical Quarterly* 5 (1955).

DYE, EVA EMERY. *The Conquest*. Portland, Ore.: Binfords and Mort, 1936.

EASTMAN, CHARLES A. *Report to Commissioner of Indian Affairs*. Washington D.C.: Department of the Interior, 1925.

EDDY, JOHN A. "Astronomical Alignment of the Big Horn Medicine Wheel," *Science* 184 (June 1974).

EDDY, JOHN A. "Probing the Mystery of the Medicine Wheels," *National Geographic* 151 (January 1977).

EIDE, INGVARD HENRY, ed. *American Odyssey: The Journey of Lewis and Clark*. New York: Rand McNally and Co., 1969.

ENGELHARDT, FR. ZEPHYRIN. *San Luis Rey Mission*. Missions and Missionaries Series. San Francisco: James H. Berry Co., 1921.

Entrenchment Trail. Custer Battlefield National Monument, Crow Agency, Montana. Custer Battlefield Historical and Museum Association, 1961.

EVERHART, WILLIAM C. "So Long St. Louis, We're Heading West." *National Geographic* 128 (November 1965).

EWERS, JOHN C., ed. *Adventures of Zenas Leonard Fur Trader*. Norman: University of Oklahoma Press, 1959.

FAHERTY, WILLIAM BARNABY. "St. Louis College: First Community School," *The Bulletin* (Missouri Historical Society, St. Louis) 24, no. 2 (1968).

Famous Indians, A Collection of Short Biographies. U.S. Department of the Interior, Bureau of Indian Affairs. Washington, D.C.. U.S. Printing Office.

FARNSWORTH, FRANCES JOYCE. *Winged Moccasins.* New York: Messner, 1954.

FAULK, ODIE B. *Arizona—A Short History.* Norman: University of Oklahoma Press, 1980.

FAVOUR, ALPHEUS H. *Old Bill Williams, Mountain Man.* Chapel Hill: University of North Carolina Press, 1936.

FEHRENBACH, T.R. *Comanches: The Destruction of a People.* New York: Alfred A. Knopf, 1979.

FERRIS, ROBERT G., ed. Prepared by Roy E. Appleman. *Lewis and Clark.* Washington, D.C.: U.S. Department of Interior, National Park Service, 1975.

FERRIS, W. A. *Life in the Rocky Mountains.* Denver: Alan Swallow, 1940.

FISHER, VARDIS. *Suicide or Murder? The Strange Death of Governor Meriwether Lewis.* Denver: Alan Swallow, 1962.

FLANDRAU, GRACE. "The Verendrye Overland Quest of the Pacific," *The Quarterly of the Oregon Historical Society* 26, (June 1925).

FOGARTY, WILLIAM C. "Promotes Lewis-Clark Trail Marking," *St. Louis Post-Dispatch,* Feb. 16, 1968.

FRANZWA, GREGORY M. *The Oregon Trail Revisited.* St. Louis, Missouri: Patrice Press, 1972.

FRAZIER, NETA LOHNES. *Sacajawea, The Girl Nobody Knows.* New York: David McKay Co., Inc., 1967.

FRÉMONT, JOHN CHARLES. *Report of the Exploring Expedition on the Rocky Mountains in the Year 1842, and to Oregon and North California in the Years 1843–44* (28th Cong., 2d Sess., Sen. Doc. No. 174). Washington, D.C.: Gales and Seaton, Printers, 1845.

FULLER, MYRON L. *The New Madrid Earthquake.* Washington, D.C.: U.S. Geological Survey, 1912. Bulletin 494.

GARCIA, ANDREW. *Tough Trip through Paradise 1878–1879.* Edited by Bennett H. Stein. Boston: Houghton Mifflin Co., 1967.

GASS, PATRICK. *Journal of the Lewis and Clark Expedition.* Chicago: A. C. McClurg and Co., 1904.

GASS, PATRICK A. *Journal of the Voyages and Travels of a Corps of Discovery,* David McKeehan, ed. Minneapolis: Ross and Haines, Inc. 1958.

GILL, LARRY. "The Great Portage," *Great Falls Tribune* (Great Falls, Mont.), Aug. 15, 1965.

GRAY, ARTHUR AMOS. *Men Who Built the West.* Caldwell, Idaho: The Caxton Printers, Ltd., 1945.

GREENER, W. W., ed. *The Gun and Its Development.* 9th ed. New York: Bonanza Books, 1910.

GRINNELL, G. B. "Bent's Fort and Its Builders," *Collections,* Kansas Historical Society, 1919.

HAFEN, ANN W. "Baptiste Charbonneau, Son of Bird Woman," *The Westerners' Brand Book.* Denver: 1950.

HAFEN, LEROY R., ed. *The Mountain Men and the Fur Trade of the Far West.* "Jean Baptiste Charbonneau," by Ann W. Hafen. Glendale, CA: The Arthur H. Clark Co., Vol. I, 1965.

HAFEN, LEROY R., and ANN W. HAFEN, eds. *Scenes in the Rocky Mountains, 1820–1875.* "Rufus B. Sage, His Letters and Papers." Glendale, CA: The Arthur H. Clark Co., Vol. II, 1956.

HAFEN, LEROY R., and ANN W. HAFEN. *To the Rockies and Oregon: 1839–1842.* Glendale, CA: The Arthur H. Clark Co., 1935.

HAFEN, LEROY R., ed. "The W. M. Boggs Manuscript about Bent's Fort," *Colorado Magazine* 7 (1930).

HAFEN, LEROY, and W. J. GHENT. *Broken Hand.* Denver: Alan Swallow, 1931.

HAGAN, HARRY M. *This Is Our Saint Louis.* Saint Louis: Knight Publishing Co., 1970.

HALL, BOB. "Sacajawea Festival in Cloverport," *Sunday Courier and Press* (Evansville, Ind.,) Aug. 15, 1971.

HARPER, FRANK B. *Fort Union and Its Neighbors on the Upper Missouri, A Chronological Record of Events.* St. Paul, Minn.: Great Northern Railway, 1925.

HARRIS, BURTON. *John Colter, His Years in the Rockies.* New York: Scribner, 1952.

HAWGOOD, JOHN A. *America's Western Frontiers: The Exploration and Settlement of the Trans-Mississippi West.* New York: Alfred A. Knopf, 1967.

HAWTHORNE, HILDEGARDE. *Westward the Course: A Story of the Lewis and Clark Expedition.* New York: Longmans, Green and Co., 1946.

HEBARD, GRACE RAYMOND. *Sacajawea, A Guide and Interpreter of the Lewis and Clark Expedition.* Glendale, CA: The Arthur H. Clark Co., 1957.

HEBARD, GRACE RAYMOND. *Washakie.* Cleveland: The Arthur H. Clark Co., 1930.

Hebard Papers, The. "The Rivington Letters and Interviews, 1929," Berkeley: The University of California.

HENRY, WILL. *The Gates of the Mountains.* New York: Random House, 1963.

HERNON, PETER. "Ancient Crack Discovered across Missouri's Heart-Land," *St. Louis Globe-Democrat,* Dec. 16, 1981.

HERRMANN, PAUL. *Conquest by Man.* New York: Harper and Bros., 1954.

HEYD, WILHELM. *Bibliographie der Württembergischen Geschichte.* Vol 2, 1896.

HITCHCOCK, RIPLEY. *The Lewis and Clark Expedition.* Boston: Ginn and Co., 1905.

HODGE, F. W. *Handbook of American Indians North of Mexico,* 2 vols. Washington, D.C.: Bureau of American Ethnology, 1907.

HOEBEL, E. ADAMSON, and E. WALLACE. *Comanches, Lords of the Southern Plains.* Norman: University of Oklahoma Press, 1964.

HOLLOWAY, DAVID. *Lewis and Clark and the Crossing of North America.* New York: Saturday Review Press, 1974.

HOSMER, CHARLES K., ed. *History of the Expedition of Captains Lewis and Clark,* 2 vols. Chicago: A. C. McClurg and Co., 1924.

HOTCHKISS, BILL. *The Medicine Calf.* New York: W. W. Norton and Co., 1981.

HOWARD, HAROLD P. *Sacajawea.* Norman: University of Oklahoma Press, 1971.

HOWARD, HELEN ADDISON. "The Mystery of Sacagawea's Death," *Pacific Northwest Quarterly* 58 (January 1967).

HOWARD, HELEN ADDISON. *Frontier, Frontiersmen, American Frontier Tales.* Missoula, Montana: Gateway Printing, 1982.

HUESTON, ETHEL. *Star of the West: The Romance of the Lewis and Clark Expedition.* New York: Bobbs-Merrill Co., 1935.

HUFFMAN, MARIAN. *Sacajawea.* Havre, Montana: Griggs Printing and Publishing, 1980.

IRBY, R. E. *Beneath Stilled Waters.* 28 min. 16 mm color documentary on Pacific Northwest Indians at Celilo Falls before inundation by the Dalles Dam. Tualatin, Oregon: Geopub Media Service.

JACKSON, DONALD, ed. *Letters of the Lewis and Clark Expedition, With Related Documents 1783–1854.* 2 vols. Urbana: University of Illinois Press, 1962.

JACKSON, DONALD. "On Reading Lewis and Clark: A Bibliographical Essay," *Montana, the Magazine of Western History* 18 (July 1968).

JACKSON, DONALD. "Some Advice for the Next Editor of Lewis

and Clark," *The Bulletin* (Missouri Historical Society, St. Louis) 24 (October 1967).

JACKSON, DONALD, and MARY LEE PENAL, eds. *The Expedition of John Charles Fremont, Travels from 1838 to 1844,* Vol. I, Urbana: University of Illinois Press, 1970.

JAEGER, ELLSWORTH. *Tracks and Trailcraft.* New York: Macmillan Co., 1948.

JOHANSEN, DOROTHY O., and CHARLES M. GATES. *Empire of the Columbia.* New York: Harper and Brothers, 1957.

KELSEY, VERA. *Young Men So Daring—Fur Traders Who Carried the Frontier West.* New York: The Bobbs-Merrill Co., Inc., 1956.

KENNEDY, MICHAEL S. *The Red Man's West.* New York: Hastings House, 1965.

KENNERLY, WILLIAM CLARK, as told to Elizabeth Russell, *Persimmon Hill.* Norman: University of Oklahoma Press, 1948.

KIMBROUGH, MARY. "Following in the Footsteps of Lewis and Clark," *St. Louis Globe-Democrat Sunday Magazine,* Sept. 23, 1979.

KING, LINDA. "This Museum Is Alive," "The Dreamer," "The Treaty," "Chief Owhi," "Braveheart," *Yakima Herald-Republic,* June 3, 1980.

KINGSTON, C. S. "Sacajawea as Guide," *Pacific Northwest Quarterly* 35 (January 1944).

KIRSCHTEN, ERNEST. *Catfish and Crystal.* Garden City, N.Y.: Doubleday, 1965.

KUHLMAN, CHARLES. *Legend into History, The Custer Mystery.* Harrisburg, Pa.: The Stackpole Co., 1951.

LANGE, ROBERT E. "The Expedition's Brothers: Joseph and Reuben Field," *We Proceeded On* 4, no. 3 (July 1978).

LARGE, ARLEN J. "Lewis and Clarkers Keep an Adventure Alive," *The Wall Street Journal,* Aug. 29, 1978.

LAROCQUE, FRANCOIS ANTOINE. "Journal," translated by Ruth Hazlitt, *Frontier and Midland* 14–15 (1934).

LAROCQUE, FRANCOIS ANTOINE. *Journal from the Assiniboine to the Yellowstone, 1805.* Ottawa: Government Printing Bureau, 1911.

LARSELL, OLOF. "Medical Aspects of the Lewis and Clark Expedition," *Surgery, Gynecology and Obstetrics* 85 (November 1947).

LAUBIN, REGINALD, and GLADYS LAUBIN. *The Indian Tipi, Its History, Construction, and Use.* Norman: University of

Oklahoma Press, 1957. Reprint. New York: Ballantine Books, 1971.

LAVENDER, DAVID. *Bent's Fort*. New York: Doubleday and Co., Inc., 1954.

LEE, NELSON. *Three Years among the Comanches*. Norman: University of Oklahoma Press, 1957.

LEONARD, KENNETH O. Garrison Clinic, Garrison, North Dakota, personal letter, February 18, 1968.

Lewis and Clark in Washington State. Lewis and Clark Trail Advisory Committee and Washington State Parks and Recreation Commission. February, 1968.

LEWIS, MERIWETHER. *The Lewis and Clark Expedition*. Edited by Nicholas Biddle. 3 vols. New York: J. B. Lippincott Co., 1961.

LIBERTY, MARGOT. *Fights with the Shoshone 1855–1870*. Missoula: Montana State University Press, 1961.

LIGHTON, WILLIAM R. *Lewis and Clark*. Boston: Houghton Mifflin Co., 1901.

LINDERMAN, FRANK B. *American*. New York: John Day Co., 1930.

LINDERMAN, FRANK B. *Pretty Shield*. Lincoln: University of Nebraska Press, 1972 (*Red Mother*, 1932).

LINK, LOUIS W. *Lewis and Clark Expedition 1804–1806*. Cardwell, Mont., 1964.

LISA, MANUEL. Papers. Envelope I, June 7, 1809 (license to trade on the Upper Missouri given by Meriwether Lewis). Missouri Historical Society Library, Saint Louis, Mo.

LISSBERGER, DR., Head of the Library Board, Württembergische Landesbibliothek, Stuttgart, Germany. Personal letter, June 2, 1967.

LONG, JACK. "A Special Kind of Justice," *The Lamp* (Exxon Corp.) Summer 1980.

LOTTINVILLE, SAVOIE, ed. *Paul Wilhelm, Duke of Württemberg, Travels in North America 1822–1824*. Trans. W. Robert Nitske. Norman: University of Oklahoma Press, 1973.

LOWIE, ROBERT H. *Indians of the Plains*. New York: Natural History Press, the American Museum of Natural History, 1954.

LUTTIG, JOHN C. *Journal of a Fur-Trading Expedition of the Upper Missouri, 1812–1813*. Edited by Stella M. Drumm. Saint Louis: Missouri Historical Society, 1920.

MAGUIRE, AMY JANE. *The Indian Girl Who Led Them*. Portland, Oregon: The J. K. Gill Co., 1905.

MALONE, HENRY THOMPSON. *The White Comanche*. New York: Comet Press Books, 1957.

MASSON, J. *Les Bourgeois de la Compagnie du Nord-Ouest*, 2

vols. New York, 1950. (Charles MacKenzie, "The Missouri Indians," in Vol I; "Missouri Journal of François Antoine Larocque.")

MATHIESON, THEODORE. *The Nez Perce Indian War*. Derby, Connecticut: Monarch Books, Inc., 1964.

MATTES, MERRILL J., U.S. Department of the Interior, National Park Service, San Francisco. Personal letter, March 6, 1968.

MAUR, DR. KARIN V., Director of Staatsgalerie, Stuttgart, Germany. Personal letter, December 27, 1966.

MAXIMILIAN, PRINCE OF WIED. *Travels in Interior of North America 1833*. Translated by H. E. Lloyd, edited by R. G. Thwaites. 3 vols. Cleveland: The Arthur H. Clark Co., 1904.

MCCRACKEN, HAROLD. *George Catlin and the Old Frontier*. New York: Crown Publishers, Inc., 1959.

MCDERMOTT, JOHN FRANCIS. "Museums in Early Saint Louis," *The Bulletin* (Missouri Historical Society, Saint Louis) 4 (April 1948).

MCDERMOTT, JOHN FRANCIS. "William Clark's Museum Once More," *The Bulletin* (Missouri Historical Society, Saint Louis 16 (January 1960).

McLean County Historical Society. *Fort Mandan*, printed material.

MILLER, DAVID HUMPHREYS. "Echoes of the Little Bighorn," *American Heritage* 22 (1971).

MITCHELL, JOHN G. "Our Wily White-Tailed Deer: Elegant But Perplexing Neighbors," *Smithsonian* 13, no. 8 (November 1982).

MOMADAY, N. SCOTT. "A First American Views His Land," *National Geographic* 150 (July 1976).

Monsanto Magazine 45 (October 1965): 24. A picture of Lewis and Clark and Sacajawea in a pirogue on the Missouri River.

Montana, A State Guide Book. Compiled and written by the Federal Writers' Project of the Work Projects Administration for the State of Montana. New York: The Viking Press, 1939.

MOORE, CHRIS. *Argus Observer* (Ontario, Oregon), Feb. 10, 1966, Sec. 2.

MORROW, LYNN. "New Madrid and Its Hinterland: 1783–1826," *The Bulletin* (Missouri Historical Society), 36, no. 4 (July 1980).

MURPHY, DAN. *Lewis and Clark, Voyage of Discovery*. Las Vegas, Nev.: KC Publications, 1977.

MURPHY, ROBERT FRANCIS, and YOLANDA MURPHY. *Shoshone-*

Bannock Subsistence and Society. Berkeley: University of California Press, 1960.

National Park Service, U.S. Department of the Interior. *Fort Clatsop National Memorial*, printed material.

National Park Service, U.S. Department of the Interior. *Pompeys Pillar*, printed material.

NEIL, WILFRED T. "Bird Woman's Real Story," *The West, True Stories of the Old West* 9 (July and August 1968).

NEUBERGER, RICHARD. "Was Sacajawea Really the Guide of Lewis and Clark?" *Inland Empire Magazine, Spokesman Review* (Spokane, Wash.), July 6, 1952.

OSGOOD, ERNEST STAPLES, ed. *The Field Notes of Captain William Clark, 1803–1805*. New Haven: Yale University Press, 1964.

OSGOOD, ERNEST STAPLES. "The Return Journey in 1806: William Clark on the Yellowstone," *Montana, Magazine of Western History* 18 (July 1968).

PATTEN, JAMES I. *Original Letters and Manuscripts from the G. R. Hebard Papers*. Glendale, CA: The Arthur H. Clark Co.

PENICK, JAMES, JR. *The New Madrid Earthquakes of 1811–1812*. Columbia: University of Missouri Press, 1976.

PETERSON, HAROLD L., ed. *Encyclopedia of Firearms*. New York: E. P. Dutton and Co., Inc., 1964.

Phillips Petroleum Company, *Pasture and Range Plants*. Bartlesville, Okla.: 1963.

PLATT, RUTHERFORD. *A Pocket Guide to the Trees*. New York: Pocket Books, 1953.

POOLE, EDWIN A. "Charbono's Squar," *All Posse-Corral Brand Book of the Westerners. Denver Posse*, 19th Annual ed., 1963; 184. *The Pacific Northwesterner* 8 (1963).

PORTER, CLYDE H. "Jean Baptiste Charbonneau," *Idaho Yesterdays* 5 (Fall 1961).

PORTER, MAE REED, and ODESSA DAVENPORT. *Scotsman in Buckskin*. New York: Hastings House, 1963.

PREUSS, CHARLES. *Exploring with Frémont: The Private Diaries of Charles Preuss, Cartographer for John C. Frémont on His First, Second, and Fourth Expeditions to the Far West*. Edited and translated by Erwin G. Gudde and Elizabeth K. Gudde. Norman: University of Oklahoma Press, 1966.

QUAIFE, MILO M., ed. *The Journals of Captain Meriwether Lewis and Sergeant John Ordway, Kept on the Expedition of West-*

ern Exploration, 1803–1806. Madison: State Historical Society of Wisconsin, 1916.

RAINBOLT, JO. "Lewis and Clark Expedition, Part of Her Family History," *The Jefferson Republic* (DeSoto, Missouri), Feb. 22, 1979, Sec. 2.

RAMSEY, JAROLD, ed. *Coyote Was Going There—Indian Literature of the Oregon Country.* Seattle: University of Washington Press, 1977.

RAY, VERNE F. "Lower Chinook Ethnographic Notes," University of Washington, *Publications in Anthropology* 7 (May 1938).

REES, JOHN E. *Madame Charbonneau, The Indian Woman Who Accompanied the Lewis and Clark Expedition, 1804–6: How She Received Her Indian Name and What Became of Her.* Edited by David G. Ainsworth. Salmon, Ida.: The Lemhi County Historical Society, 1970.

REES, JOHN E. "The Shoshoni Contribution to Lewis and Clark," *Idaho Yesterdays* 2 (Summer 1958).

REID, RUSSELL. "Sakakawea The Bird Woman," *North Dakota History* 30 (1963).

RICE, JACK. "Louisville Says That Lewis and Clark Started There," *St. Louis Post-Dispatch*, May 19, 1968. (Tells about the great-great-grandson of William Clark, William Clark Adreon, who lives in St. Louis.)

RICKOVER, VICE ADMIRAL HYMAN. Letter to Charles E. Pierson, executive editor of *The Globe-Democrat*, "Rickover Pays Tribute to Lewis and Clark," *St. Louis Globe-Democrat*, Nov. 20–21, 1965.

RILEY, P. D., Nebraska State Historical Society. Personal letter, February 9, 1968.

RIVINGTON, TOM. "Picturesque as Pioneer Is Dead," *Gering Courier* (Gering, Nebr.), June 2, 1939, p. 1, c.1.

ROBINSON, DOANE. "Sacajawea vs. Sakakawea," paper presented before the Academy of Science and Letters, Sioux City, Iowa, Jan. 24, 1924.

ROBINSON, WILL, Secretary of the South Dakota State Historical Society. Personal letter, January 18, 1968.

ROBINSON, WILL. G. "Sakakawea-Sacajawea: When and Where Did Sakakawea the Indian Bird Woman Die and Where Was She Buried?" *The Wi-iyohi* (South Dakota Historical Society, Pierre, S.D.) 10 (Sept. 1, 1956).

ROE, JOANN. "Harvest of the Northwest: Indian-style Salmon," *American West* 18, no. 5 (Sept.–Oct. 1981).

ROSEN, KENNETH, ed. *The Man to Send Rain Clouds.* New York: Vintage Books, 1975.

RUSSELL, CARL P. "The Guns of the Lewis and Clark Expe-
    dition," *North Dakota History* 27 (Winter 1960).
RUXTON, G. F. "Life in the 'Far West,'" *Blackwood's Edin-
    burgh Magazine*, June 1848.

"Sacajawea: A Symposium," *Annals of Wyoming* 13 (July
    1941).
"Sac-a-jawe vs. Sa-kaka-wea: The Name of the Bird Woman:
    The Putrid Fever of 1812: Fort Manuel," Department of
    History Collections, South Dakota State Historical Society,
    Pierre, S.D., 1938.
SAGE, RUFUS B. *Scenes in the Rocky Mountains by a New
    Englander*. Philadelphia, 1846, Vol. V.
SAINDON, ROBERT. "The Abduction of Sacagawea," *We Pro-
    ceeded On* 2, no. 2.
SAINDON, ROBERT. "The Assiniboines—Some Notes on the As-
    siniboine Indians Before Lewis and Clark: 1600–1800," *A
    Squawl of Wind* (Valley County Lewis and Clark Trail
    Society, Glasgow, Montana) 2, no. 4 (1978).
SALISBURY, ALBERT, and JANE SALISBURY. *Two Captains West:
    An Historical Tour of the Lewis and Clark Trail*. Seattle:
    Superior Publishing Co., 1950.
SAMSELL, ANN. *175th Anniversary Lewis and Clark Expedition
    Re-enactment*. Monmouth, Oregon: Somethings Produc-
    tions. Personal communication, Fall 1981.
SANDOZ, MARIA. *The Beaver Men*. New York: Hastings House,
    1964.
SANDOZ, MARIA. *The Buffalo Men*. New York: Hastings House,
    1954.
San Luis Rey, California's Mission. See *California's Mission*.
San Luis Rey Mission, National Monument, printed material,
    pamphlet.
SATTERFIELD, ARCHIE. *The Lewis and Clark Trail*. Harrisburg,
    Pa.: Stackpole Books, 1978.
SCHARFF, ROBERT, ed. *Glacier National Park and Waterton
    Lakes National Park*. New York: David McKay Co., Inc.,
    1967.
SCHROER, BLANCHE. "Sacajawea: The Legend and the Truth,"
    In Wyoming, Dec.–Jan. 1978.
SCHULTZ, JAMES WILLARD. *Bird Woman (Sacajawea): The Guide
    of Lewis and Clark*. Boston: Houghton Mifflin Co., 1918.
SCHUZ, DR., Museumsdirektor Staatliches Museum für Na-
    turkunde, Stuttgart, Germany. Personal letter, January
    10, 1967.
SCOTT, LAURA TOLMAN. *Sacajawea*. Montana Federation of
    Women's Club, 1915.
SCOTT, LAURA TOLMAN. "Sacajawea, The Unsung Heroine of

Montana 1805–6," program from the Lewis and Clark Sesquicentennial Celebration Pageant, Dillon, Mont., July 31, 1955.

SEA, DAVID S. *Animal Tracks.* Washington, D.C.: National Park Service, 1969. Bulletin 11.

SEIBERT, JERRY. *Sacajawea, Guide to Lewis and Clark.* Boston: Houghton Mifflin Co., 1960.

SELSAM, M. E. *Plants That Heal.* New York: William Morrow and Co., 1959.

Senate Documents, Serial 547, no. 2, 31 Congress, Special Session, March 19, 1849, p. 69.

SETZER, HENRY H. "Zoological Contribution of the Lewis and Clark Expedition," *Washington Academy of Sciences Journal* 44 (November 1954).

SKARSTEN, M. O. *George Drouillard.* Glendale, CA: The Arthur H. Clark Co., 1964.

SKINNER, OLIVIA. "Keelboat on the Missouri," *St. Louis Post-Dispatch, Sunday Pictures,* Aug. 14, 1966.

SMITH, FREDRIKA SHUMAY. *Frémont: Soldier, Explorer, Statesman.* New York: Rand McNally and Co., 1966.

SNYDER, GERALD S. *In the Footsteps of Lewis and Clark.* Washington, D.C.: National Geographic Society, 1970.

SPENCER, ROBERT, F., JESSE D. JENNINGS, et al. *The Native Americans.* New York: Harper & Row, 1965.

SPICER, EDWARD H., ed. *Perspectives in American Indian Culture Change.* Chicago: University of Chicago Press, 1969.

SPRAGUE, MARSHALL. *A Gallery of Dudes.* Boston: Little Brown and Co., 1966, 1967.

STEVENS, ALDEN. "Fort Clatsop, Oregon, The End of Lewis' and Clark's Trail," *The American Legion Magazine,* April 1965.

STIRLING, MATTHEW W. "Arikara Glassworking," *Washington Academy of Sciences Journal* 37 (August 1947).

STYLES, SHOWELL. *What to See in Beddgelert and How to See It.* Caernarvonshire, Wales: William H. Eastwood, 1973.

Sublette Papers and Letters. Missouri Historical Society, St. Louis. Promissory note to Jean Baptiste Charbonneau for $320 for sale of land belonging to Toussaint Charbonneau, Aug. 17, 1843.

TATUM, LAWRIE. *Our Red Brothers and the Peace Policy of President Ulysses S. Grant.* Philadelphia: Winston and Co., 1899.

THWAITES, REUBEN GOLD, ed. *Early Western Travelers 1804–1807.* "Journal of a Voyage Up the River Missouri," by Henry M. Brackenridge. Baltimore: Coale and Maxwell,

Vol. VI, 1816. Cleveland: The Arthur H. Clark Co., Vol. VI, 1904.

THWAITES, REUBEN GOLD, ed. *Early Western Travelers 1804–1807*. "Farnham's Travels," by T. J. Farnham. Baltimore: Coale and Maxwell (32 vols.) Vol. XXIIX, 1816. Cleveland: The Arthur H. Clark Co., Vol. XXIIX, 1816. Cleveland: The Arthur H. Clark Co., Vol. XXIIX, 1904–7.

THWAITES, REUBEN GOLD, ed. *The Original Journals of the Lewis and Clark Expedition 1804–1806*, 8 vols. New York: Dodd, Mead and Co., 1904–5. Reprinted by Arno Press, N.Y.: 1969.

TILGHMAN, ZOE AGNES. *Quanah, The Eagle of the Comanches*. Oklahoma: Harrow Publishing Corp., 1938.

TOMKINS, CALVIN. "The Lewis and Clark Case," *The New Yorker*, Oct. 29, 1966.

Trappers and Mountain Men. Edited by *American Heritage*. New York: American Heritage Publishing Co., Inc., 1961.

TRENHOLM, VIRGINIA, and MAURINE CARLEY. *The Shoshonis, Sentinels of the Rockies*. Norman: University of Oklahoma Press, 1964.

TREXLER, H. A. "Sacajawea — Just a Squaw," *The Daily Missoulian*, Missoula, Montana, June 25, 1916.

TUNIS, EDWIN. *Indians*. New York: The World Publishing Co., 1959.

UNDERWOOD, LARRY. "The Time the Earth Shook and the River Ran Backward," *St. Louis Globe-Democrat*, Dec. 16, 1981.

Utah, A Guide to the State. Compiled by Workers of the Writers' Program of the Work Projects Administration of the State of Utah. New York: Hastings House, 1941.

VAN DOREN, MARK, and GARIBALDI M. LAPOLLA, eds. *The World's Best Poems*. New York: The World Publishing Co., 1946.

VÉRENDRYE, PIERRE GAULTIER DE VARENNES DE LA. "Journals of La Vérendrye Trips to the Mandan Villages on the Missouri River in 1738–39 and to the Foothills of the Rocky Mountains in 1742–43," *The Quarterly of the Oregon Historical Society* 26 (June 1925). Trans. Douglas Brymner. Ed. Anne H. Blegen.

VÉRENDRYE, PIERRE GAULTIER DE VARENNES DE LA. "Journal of the Voyage Made by Chevalier de La Vérendrye with One of His Brothers in Search of the Western Sea, Addressed to the Marquis de Beauharnois," *The Quarterly of the Oregon Historical Society* 26 (June 1925). Trans. Margry Papers. Ed. Anne H. Blegen.

VÉRENDRYE, PIERRE GAULTIER DE VARENNES DE LA. *Journals*

and Letters of La Vérendrye and His Sons. Edited by Lawrence J. Burpee. Champlain Society Publication, 16. Toronto, 1927.

VESTAL, STANLEY. *The Missouri*. New York: Ferrar and Rinehart, Inc., 1945.

VIRGA, LINDA, University of Hamburg. Personal letter, February 29, 1968.

VOIGHT, VIRGINIA FRANCES. *Sacajawea*. New York: G. P. Putnam's Sons, 1967.

WALLACE, ERNEST, and E. ADAMSON HOEBEL. *The Comanches, Lords of the South Plains*. Norman: University of Oklahoma Press, 1952.

Washington State Parks and Recreation Commission, Sacajawea Interpretive Center, Sacajawea State Park, Pasco, Washington. *Dedication Program*, April 16, 1978.

WELLS, MERLE W., Historian and Archivist, The Idaho Historical Society, Boise, Idaho. Personal letter, September 18, 1967.

WHEELER, OLIN D. *The Trail of Lewis and Clark*, 2 vols. New York: G. Putnam's Sons, 1904.

WHEELER, WILLIAM F. "Sacajawea," *Contributions* (Historical Society of Montana) 7 (1910).

WHITNEY, FREDERICK C. "Custer's Nemesis at Little Big Horn," *St. Louis Globe-Democrat*, Aug. 9, 1967.

WILHELM, PAUL FRIEDRICH, HERZOG VON WÜRTTEMBERG. *Erste Reise nach dem nördlichen Amerika in den Jahren 1822 bis 1824*, 2 Vols., Stuttgart: J. G. Cotta, 1835. Microfilm copy obtained from the Henry E. Huntington Library.

WILL, DRAKE W. "The Medical and Surgical Practices of the Lewis and Clark Expedition," *Journal of the History of Medicine* 14 (July 1959).

WILLIAMS, GWYN A. *Madoc, The Making of a Myth*. London: Eyre Methuen, Ltd., 1979.

WILSON, CHARLES MORROW. *Meriwether Lewis of Lewis and Clark*. New York: Thomas Y. Crowell Co., 1934.

Wind River Shoshoni Reservation Church Register of Burials, no. 114.

WISSLER, CLARK. *Indians of the United States*. Garden City, N.Y.: Doubleday and Co., Inc., 1966.

WOOD, WARREN C., editor, *Gering Courier*, Gering, Neb. Personal letter, February 19, 1968.

Wyoming, A Guide to Its History, Highways, and People. Compiled by Workers of the Writers' Program of the Work Projects Administration in the State of Wyoming. New York: Oxford University Press, 1941.

Wyoming State Archives and Historical Department and Wyoming Recreation Commission. *Fort Bridger*, printed material.

YOUNG, E. G., ed. "Captain N. J. Wyeth, Correspondence and Journals, 1831–1836," *Sources of the History of Oregon* (Oregon Historical Society), Vol. I, Parts 3 to 6.